Joseph Conrad

*

Selected Novels and Stories

JOSEPH CONRAD

Selected novels and stories

HAMLYN

Cover illustrations: background seascape, Greece, by John Waters. *Seaphot*. Portrait of Joseph Conrad by Walter Tittle. *National Portrait Gallery, London*.

First published 1986 by
Hamlyn Publishing
Bridge House, London Road
Twickenham, Middlesex

ISBN 0 600 50106 X

Typeset, printed and bound in Great Britain by
Hazell Watson & Viney Limited
Member of the BPCC Group
Aylesbury, Bucks

Contents

The Nigger of the 'Narcissus'

To Edward Garnett
this tale about my friends of the sea

Preface to
The Nigger of the 'Narcissus'

A WORK THAT ASPIRES, however humbly, to the condition of art should carry its justification in every line. And art itself may be defined as a single-minded attempt to render the highest kind of justice to the visible universe, by bringing to light the truth, manifold and one, underlying its every aspect. It is an attempt to find in its forms, in its colours, in its light, in its shadows, in the aspects of matter, and in the facts of life what of each is fundamental, what is enduring and essential – their one illuminating and convincing quality – the very truth of their existence. The artist, then, like the thinker or the scientist, seeks the truth and makes his appeal. Impressed by the aspect of the world the thinker plunges into ideas, the scientists into facts – whence, presently, emerging they make their appeal to those qualities of our being that fit us best for that hazardous enterprise of living. They speak authoritatively to our common sense, to our intelligence, to our desire of peace, or to our desire of unrest; not seldom to our prejudices, sometimes to our fears, often to our egoism – but always to our credulity. And their words are heard with reverence, for their concern is with weighty matters: with the cultivation of our minds and the proper care of our bodies, with the attainment of our ambitions, with the perfection of the means and the glorification of our precious aims.

It is otherwise with the artist.

Confronted by the same enigmatical spectacle the artist descends within himself, and in that lonely region of stress and strife, if he be deserving and fortunate, he finds the terms of his appeal. His appeal is made to our less obvious capacities: to that part of our nature which, because of the warlike conditions of existence, is necessarily kept out of sight within the more resisting and hard qualities – like the vulnerable body within a steel armour. His appeal is less loud, more profound, less distinct, more stirring – and sooner forgotten. Yet its effect endures for ever. The changing wisdom of successive generations discards ideas, questions facts, demolishes theories. But the artist appeals to that part of our being which is not dependent on wisdom; to that in us which is a gift and not an acquisition – and, therefore, more permanently enduring. He speaks to our capacity for delight and wonder, to the sense of mystery surrounding our lives; to our sense of pity, and beauty, and pain; to the latent feeling of fellowship with all creation – and to the subtle but invincible conviction of solidarity that knits together the loneliness of innumerable hearts, to the solidarity in dreams, in joy, in sorrow, in aspirations, in illusions, in hope, in fear, which binds men to each other, which binds together all humanity – the dead to the living and the living to the unborn.

It is only some such train of thought, or rather of feeling, that can in a measure explain the aim of the attempt, made in the tale which follows, to present an unrestful episode in the obscure lives of a few individuals out of all the disregarded multitude of the bewildered, the simple, and the voiceless. For, if any part of truth dwells in the belief confessed above, it becomes evident that there is not a place of splendour or a dark corner of the earth that does not deserve, if only a passing glance of wonder and pity. The motive then, may be held to justify the matter of the work; but this preface; which is simply an avowal of endeavour, cannot end here – for the avowal is not yet complete.

Fiction – if it at all aspires to be art – appeals to temperament. And in truth it must be, like painting, like music, like all art, the appeal of one temperament to all the other innumerable temperaments whose subtle and resistless power endows passing events with their true meaning, and creates the moral, the emotional atmosphere of the place and time. Such an appeal to be effective must be an impression conveyed through the senses; and, in fact, it cannot be made in any other way, because temperament, whether individual or collective, is not amenable to persuasion. All art, therefore, appeals primarily to the senses, and the artistic aim when expressing itself in written words must also make its appeal through the senses, if its high desire is to reach the secret spring of responsive emotions. It must strenuously aspire to the plasticity of sculpture, to the colour of painting, and to the magic suggestiveness of music – which is the art of arts. And it is only through complete, unswerving devotion to the perfect blending of form and substance; it is only through an unremitting never-discouraged care for the shape and ring of sentences that an approach can be made to plasticity, to colour, and that the light of magic suggestiveness may be brought to play for an evanescent instant over the commonplace surface of words: of the old, old words, worn thin, defaced by ages of careless usage.

The sincere endeavour to accomplish that creative task, to go as far on that road as his strength will carry him, to go undeterred by faltering, weariness, or reproach, is the only valid justification for the worker in prose. And if his conscience is clear, his answer to those who in the fulness of a wisdom which looks for immediate profit, demand specifically to be edified, consoled, amused; who demand to be promptly improved, or encouraged, or frightened, or shocked, or charmed, must run thus: My task which I am trying to achieve is, by the power of the written word to make you hear, to make you feel – it is, before all, to make you *see*. That – and no more, and it is everything. If I succeed, you shall find there according to your deserts: encouragement, consolation, fear, charm – all you demand – and, perhaps, also that glimpse of truth for which you have forgotten to ask.

To snatch in a moment of courage, from the remorseless rush of time, a passing phase of life, is only the beginning of the task. The task approached in tenderness and faith is to hold up unquestioningly, without choice and without fear, the rescued fragment before all eyes in the light of a sincere mood. It is to show its vibration, its colour, its form; and through its movement, its form, and its colour, reveal the substance of its truth – disclose its inspiring secret: the stress and passion within the core of each convincing moment. In a single-minded attempt of that kind, if one be deserving and fortunate, one may perchance attain to such clearness of sincerity that at last the presented vision of regret or pity, of terror or mirth, shall awaken in the hearts of the beholders that feeling of unavoidable solidarity; of the solidarity in mysterious origin, in toil, in joy, in hope, in uncertain fate, which binds men to each other and all mankind to the visible world.

It is evident that he who, rightly or wrongly, holds by the convictions expressed above cannot be faithful to any one of the temporary formulas of his craft. The enduring part of them – the truth which each only imperfectly veils – should abide with him as the most precious of his possessions, but they all: Realism, Romanticism, Naturalism, even the unofficial sentimentalism (which like the poor, is exceedingly difficult to get rid of), all these gods must, after a short period of fellowship, abandon him – even on the very threshold of the temple – to the stammerings of his conscience and to the outspoken consciousness of the difficulties of his work. In that uneasy solitude the supreme cry of Art for Art itself loses the exciting ring of its apparent immorality. It sounds far off. It has ceased to be a cry, and is heard only as a whisper, often incomprehensible, but at times faintly encouraging.

Sometimes, stretched at ease in the shade of a roadside tree, we watch the motions of a labourer in a distant field, and after a time, begin to wonder languidly as to what the fellow may be at. We watch the movements of his body, the waving of his arms, we see him bend down, stand up, hesitate, begin again. It may add to the charm of an idle hour to be told the purpose of his exertions. If we know he is trying to lift a stone, to dig a ditch, to uproot a stump, we look with a more real interest at his efforts; we are disposed to condone the jar of his agitation upon the restfulness of the landscape; and even, if in a brotherly frame of mind, we may bring ourselves to forgive his failure. We understood his object, and, after all, the fellow has tried, and perhaps he had not the strength – and perhaps he had not the knowledge. We forgive, go on our way – and forget.

And so it is with the workman of art. Art is long and life is short, and success is very far off. And thus, doubtful of strength to travel so far, we talk a little about the aim – the aim of art, which, like life itself, is inspiring, difficult – obscured by mists. It is not in the clear logic of a triumphant conclusion; it is not in the unveiling of one of those heartless secrets which are called the Laws of Nature. It is not less great, but only more difficult.

To arrest, for the space of a breath, the hands busy about the work of the earth, and compel men entranced by the sight of distant goals to glance for a moment at the surrounding vision of form and colour, of sunshine and shadows; to make them pause for a look, for a sigh, for a smile – such is the aim, difficult and evanescent, and reserved only for a very few to achieve. But sometimes, by the deserving and the fortunate, even that task is accomplished. And when it is accomplished – behold! – all the truth of life is there: a moment of vision, a sigh, a smile – and the return to an eternal rest.

1897 J.C.

CHAPTER I

MR BAKER, chief mate of the ship *Narcissus*, stepped in one stride out of his lighted cabin into the darkness of the quarterdeck. Above his head, on the break of the poop, the night-watchman rang a double stroke. It was nine o'clock. Mr Baker, speaking up to the man above him, asked: 'Are all the hands aboard, Knowles?'

The man limped down the ladder, than said reflectively:

'I think so, sir. All our old chaps are there, and a lot of new men has come. . . . They must be all there.'

'Tell the boatswain to send all hands aft,' went on Mr Baker; 'and tell one of the youngsters to bring a good lamp here. I want to muster our crowd.'

The main deck was dark aft, but half-way from forward, through the open doors of the forecastle, two streaks of brilliant light cut the shadow of the quiet night that lay upon the ship. A hum of voices was heard there, while port and starboard, in the illuminated doorways, silhouettes of moving men appeared for a moment, very black, without relief, like figures cut out of sheet tin. The ship was ready for sea. The carpenter had driven in the last wedge of the main-hatch battens, and, throwing down his maul, had wiped his face with great deliberation, just on the stroke of five. The decks had been swept, the windlass oiled and made ready to heave up the anchor; the big tow-rope lay in long bights along one side of the main deck, with one end carried up and hung over the bows, in readiness for the tug that would come paddling and hissing noisily, hot and smoky, in the limpid, cool quietness of the early morning. The captain was ashore, where he had been engaging some new hands to make up his full crew; and, the work of the day over, the ship's officers had kept out of the way, glad of a little breathing-time. Soon after dark the few liberty-men and the new hands began to arrive in shore-boats rowed by white-clad Asiatics, who clamoured fiercely for payment before coming alongside the gangway-ladder. The feverish and shrill babble of Eastern language struggled against the masterful tones of tipsy seamen, who argued against brazen claims and dishonest hopes by profane shouts. The resplendent and bestarred peace of the East was torn into squalid tatters by howls of rage and shrieks of lament raised over sums ranging from five annas to half a rupee; and every soul afloat in Bombay Harbour became aware that the new hands were joining the *Narcissus*.

Gradually the distracting noise had subsided. The boats came no longer in splashing clusters of three or four together, but dropped alongside singly, in a subdued buzz of expostulation cut short by a 'Not a pice more! You go to the devil!' from some man staggering up the accommodation-ladder – a dark figure, with a long bag poised on the shoulder. In the forecastle the newcomers, upright and swaying amongst corded boxes and bundles of bedding, made friends with the old hands, who sat one above another in the two tiers of bunks, gazing at their future shipmates with glances critical but friendly. The two forecastle lamps were turned up high, and shed an intense hard glare; shore-going round hats were pushed far on the backs of heads, or rolled about on the deck amongst the chain-cables; white collars, undone, stuck out on each side of red faces; big arms in white sleeves gesticulated; the growling voices hummed steady amongst bursts of laughter and hoarse calls. 'Here, sonny take that bunk!' – 'Don't you do it!' – 'What's your last ship?' – 'I know her' – 'Three years ago, in Puget Sound' – 'This berth leaks, I tell you!' – 'Come on; give us a chance to swing that chest!' – 'Did you bring a bottle, any of you shore toffs?' – 'Give us a bit of baccy' – 'I know her; her skipper drank himself to death' – 'He was a dandy boy!' – 'Liked his lotion inside, he did!' – 'No!' – 'Hold your row, you chaps!' – 'I tell you, you came on board a hooker, where they get their money's worth out of poor Jack, by –!'

A little fellow, called Craik and nicknamed Belfast, abused the ship violently, romancing on principle, just to give the new hands something to think over. Archie, sitting aslant on his sea-chest, kept his knees out of the way, and pushed the needle steadily through a white patch in a pair of blue trousers. Men in black jackets and stand-up collars, mixed with men bare-footed, bare-armed, with coloured shirts open on hairy chests, pushed against one another in the middle of the forecastle. The group swayed, reeled, turning upon itself with the motion of a scrimmage, in a haze of tobacco smoke. All were speaking together, swearing at every second word. A Russian Finn, wearing a yellow shirt with pink stripes, stared upwards, dreamy-eyed, from under a mop of tumbled hair. Two young giants with smooth, baby faces – two Scandinavians – helped each other to spread their bedding, silent, and smiling placidly at the tempest of good-humoured and meaningless curses. Old Singleton, the oldest able seaman in the ship, sat apart on the deck right under the lamps, stripped to the waist, tattooed like a cannibal chief all over his powerful chest and enormous biceps. Between the blue and red patterns his white skin gleamed like satin; his bare back was propped against the heel of the bowsprit, and he held a book at arm's length before his big, sunburnt face. With his spectacles and a venerable white beard, he resembled a learned and savage patriarch, the incarnation of barbarian wisdom serene in the blasphemous turmoil of the world. He was intensely absorbed, and as he turned the pages an expression of grave surprise would pass over his rugged features. He was reading *Pelham*. The popularity of Bulwer Lytton in the forcastles of southern-going ships is a wonderful and bizarre phenomenon. What ideas do his polished and so curiously insincere sentences awaken in the simple minds of the big children who people those dark and wandering places of the earth? What meaning their rough, inexperienced souls can find in the elegant verbiage of his pages? What excitement? – what forgetfulness? – what appeasement? Mystery! Is it the fascination of the incomprehensible? – is it the charm of the impossible? Or are those beings who exist beyond the pale of life stirred by his tales as by an enigmatical disclosure of a resplendent world that exists within the frontier of infamy and filth, within that border of dirt and hunger, of misery and dissipation, that comes down on all sides to the water's edge of the incorruptible ocean, and is the only thing they know of life, the only thing they see of surrounding land – those life-long prisoners of the sea? Mystery!

Singleton, who had sailed to the southward since the age of twelve, who in the last forty-five years had lived (as we had calculated from his papers) no more than forty months ashore – old Singleton, who boasted, with the mild composure of long years well spent, that generally from the day he was paid off from one ship till the day he shipped in another he seldom was in a condition to distinguish daylight – old Singleton sat unmoved in the clash of voices and cries, spelling through *Pelham* with slow labour, and lost in an absorption profound enough to resemble a trance. He breathed regularly. Every time he turned the book in his enormous and blackened hands the muscles of his big white arms rolled slightly under the smooth skin. Hidden by the white moustache, his lips, stained with tobacco-juice that trickled down the long beard, moved in inward whisper. His bleared eyes gazed fixedly from behind the glitter of black-rimmed glasses. Opposite to him, and on a level with his face, the ship's cat sat on the barrel of the windlass in the pose of a crouching chimera, blinking its green eyes at its old friend. It seemed to meditate a leap on to the old man's lap over the bent back of the ordinary seaman who sat at Singleton's feet. Young Charley was lean and long-necked. The ridge of his backbone made a chain of small hills under the old shirt. His face of a street-boy – a face precocious, sagacious, and ironic, with deep downward folds on each side of the thin, wide mouth – hung low over his bony knees. He was learning to make a lanyard knot with a bit of an old rope. Small drops of perspiration stood out on his bulging forehead; he sniffed strongly from time to time, glancing out of the corners of his restless eyes at the old seaman, who took no notice of the puzzled youngster muttering at his work.

The noise increased. Little Belfast seemed, in the heavy heat of the forecastle, to boil with facetious fury. His eyes danced; in the crimson of his face, comical as a mask, the mouth yawned black with strange grimaces. Facing him, a half-undressed man held his sides, and, throwing his head back, laughed with wet eyelashes. Others stared with amazed eyes. Men sitting doubled up in the upper bunks smoked short pipes, swinging bare brown feet above the heads of those who, sprawling below on sea-chests, listened, smiling stupidly or scornfully. Over the white rims of berths stuck out heads with blinking eyes; but the bodies were lost in the gloom of those places, that resembled narrow niches for coffins in a white-washed and lighted mortuary. Voices buzzed louder. Archie, with compressed lips, drew himself in, seemed to shrink into a smaller space, and sewed steadily, industrious and dumb. Belfast shrieked like an inspired Dervish: '. . . So I seez to him, boys seez I, "Beggin' yer pardon, sorr," seez I to that second mate of that steamer – "beggin' your-r-r pardon, sorr, the Board of Trade must 'ave been drunk when they granted you your certificate!" "What do you say, you—!" seez he, comin' at me like a mad bull . . . all in his white clothes; and I up with my tar-pot and capsizes it all over his blamed lovely face and his lovely jacket . . . "Take that!" seez I. "I am a sailor, anyow, you nosing, skipper-licking, useless, sooperfloos bridge-stanchion you!" "That's the kind of man I am!" shouts I . . . You should have seed him skip, boys! Drowned, blind with tar, he was! So . . .'

'Don't 'ee believe him! He never upset no tar; I was there!' shouted somebody. The two Norwegians sat on a chest side by side, alike and placid, resembling a pair of love-birds on a perch, and with round eyes stared innocently; but the Russian Finn, in the racket of explosive shouts and rolling laughter, remained motionless, limp, and dull, like a deaf man without a backbone. Near him Archie smiled at his needle. A broad-chested, slow-eyed newcomer spoke deliberately to Belfast during an exhausted lull in the noise: 'I wonder any of the mates here are alive yet with such a chap as you on board! I concloode they ain't that bad now, if you had the taming of them, sonny.'

'Not bad! Not bad!' screamed Belfast. 'If it wasn't for us sticking together . . . Not bad! They ain't never bad when they ain't got a chawnce, blast their black 'arts . . .' He foamed, whirling his arms, then suddenly grinned and, taking a tablet of black tobacco out of his pocket, but a piece off with a funny show of ferocity. Another new hand – a man with shifty eyes and yellow hatchet face, who had been listening open-mouthed in the shadow of the midship locker – observed in a squeaky voice: 'Well, it's a 'omeward trip, anyhow. Bad or good, I can do it on my 'ed – s'long as I get 'ome. And I can look after my rights! I will show 'em!' All the heads turned towards him. Only the ordinary seaman and the cat took no notice. He stood with arms akimbo, a little fellow with white eyelashes. He looked as if he had known all the degradations and all the furies. He looked as if he had been cuffed, kicked, rolled in the mud; he looked as if he had been scratched, spat upon, pelted with unmentionable filth . . . and he smiled with a sense of security at the faces around. His ears were bending down under the weight of his battered felt hat. The torn tails of his black coat flapped in fringes about the calves of his legs. He unbuttoned the only two buttons that remained and everyone saw that he had no shirt under it. It was his deserved misfortune that those rags which nobody could possibly be supposed to own looked on him as if they had been stolen. His neck was long and thin; his eyelids were red; rare hairs hung about his jaws; his shoulders were peaked and drooped like the broken wings of a bird; all his left side was caked with mud which showed that he had lately slept in a wet ditch. He had saved his inefficient carcass from violent destruction by running away from an American ship where, in a moment of forgetful folly, he had dared to engage himself; and he had knocked about for a fortnight ashore in the native quarter, cadging for drinks, starving, sleeping on rubbish-heaps, wandering in sunshine: a startling visitor from a world of nightmares. He stood repulsive and smiling in the sudden silence. This clean white forecastle was his refuge; the place where he could be lazy; where he could wallow, and lie and eat – and curse the food he ate; where he could display his talents for shirking work, for cheating, for cadging; where he could find surely someone to wheedle and someone to bully – and where he would be paid for doing all this. They all knew him. Is there a spot on earth where such a man is unknown, an ominous survival testifying to the eternal fitness of lies and impudence? A taciturn long-armed shellback, with hooked fingers, who had been lying on his back smoking, turned in his bed to examine him dispassionately, then, over his head, sent a long jet of clear saliva towards the door. They all knew him! He was the man that cannot steer, that cannot splice, that dodges the work on dark nights; that, aloft, holds on frantically with both arms and legs, and swears at the wind, the sleet, the darkness; the man who curses the sea while others work. The man who is the last out and the first in when all hands are called. The man who can't do most things and won't do the rest. The pet of philanthropists and self-seeking landlubbers. The sympathetic and deserving creature that knows all about his rights, but knows nothing of courage, of endurance, and of the unexpressed faith, of the unspoken loyalty that knits together a ship's company. The independent offspring of the ignoble freedom of the slums full of disdain and hate for the austere servitude of the sea.

Someone cried at him: 'What's your name?' 'Donkin,' he said, looking round with cheerful effrontery. 'What are you?' asked another voice. 'Why, a sailor like you, old man,' he replied, in a tone that meant to be hearty but was impudent. 'Blamme if you don't look a blamed sight worse than a broken-down fireman,' was the comment in a convinced mutter. Charley lifted his head and piped in a cheeky voice: 'He is a man and a sailor' – then wiping his nose with the back of his hand, bent down industriously over his bit of rope. A few laughed. Others stared doubtfully. The ragged newcomer was indignant – 'That's a fine way to welcome a chap into a fo'c'sle,' he snarled. 'Are you men or a lot of'artless cannybals?' 'Don't take your shirt off for a word, shipmate,' called out Belfast, jumping up in front, fiery, menacing, and friendly at the same time. 'Is that 'ere bloke blind?' asked the indomitable scarecrow, looking right and left with affected surprise. 'Can't 'ee see I 'aven't got no shirt?'

He held both his arms out crosswise and shook the rags that hung over his bones with dramatic effect.

''Cos why?' he continued very loud. 'The bloody Yankees been tryin' to jump my guts out 'cos I stood up for my rights like a good'un. I am an Englishman, I am. They set upon me an' I 'ad to run. That's why. A'n't yer never seed a man 'ard up? Yah! What kind of blamed ship is this? I'm dead broke. I 'aven't got nothink. No bag, no bed, no blanket, no shirt – not a bloomin' rag but what I stand in. But I 'ad the 'art to stand up agin' them Yankees. 'As any of you 'art enough to spare a pair of old pants for a chum?'

He knew how to conquer the naïve instincts of that crowd. In a moment they gave him their compassion, jocularly, contemptuously, or surlily; and at first it took the shape of a blanket thrown at him as he stood there with the white skin of his limbs showing his human kinship through the black fantasy of his rags. Then a pair of old shoes fell at his muddy feet. With a cry: 'From under,' a rolled-up pair of canvas trousers, heavy with tar stains, struck him on the shoulder. The gust of their benevolence sent a wave of sentimental pity through their doubting hearts. They were touched by their own readiness to alleviate a shipmate's misery. Voices cried: 'We will fit you out, old man.' Murmurs: 'Never seen seech a hard case' – 'Poor beggar' – 'I've got an old singlet' – 'Will that be of any use to you?' – 'Take it, matey.' Those friendly murmurs filled the forecastle. He pawed around with his naked foot, gathering the things in a heap, and looked about for more. Unemotional Archie perfunctorily contributed to the pile an old cloth cap with the peak torn off. Old Singleton, lost in the serene regions of fiction, read on unheeding. Charley, pitiless with the wisdom of youth, squeaked: 'If you want brass buttons for your new unyforms I've got two for you.' The filthy object of universal charity shook his fist at the youngster. 'I'll make you keep this 'ere fo'c'sle clean, young feller,' he snarled viciously. 'Never you fear. I will learn you to be civil to an able seaman, you ignerant ass.' He glared harmfully, but saw Singleton shut his book, and his little beady eyes began to roam from berth to berth. 'Take that bunk by the door there – it's pretty fair,' suggested Belfast. So advised, he gathered the gifts at his feet, pressed them in a bundle against his breast, then looked cautiously at the Russian Finn, who stood on one side with an unconscious gaze, contemplating, perhaps, one of those weird visions that haunt the men of his race. 'Get out of my road, Dutchy,' said the victim of Yankee brutality. The Finn did not move – did not hear. 'Get out, blast ye,' shouted the other, shoving him aside with his elbow. 'Get out, you blanked deaf and dumb fool. Get out.' The man staggered, recovered himself, and gazed at the speaker in silence. 'Those damned furriners should be kept under,' opined the amiable Donkin to the forecastle. 'If you don't teach 'em their place they put on you like anythink.' He flung all his worldly possessions into the empty bed-place, gauged with another shrewd look the risks of the proceeding, then leaped up to the Finn, who stood pensive and dull. 'I'll teach you to swell around,' he yelled. 'I'll plug your eyes for you, you blooming square-head.' Most of the men were now in their bunks and the two had the forecastle clear to themselves. The development of the destitute Donkin aroused interest. He danced all in tatters before the amazed Finn, squaring from a distance at the heavy, unmoved face. One or two men cried encouragingly: 'Go it, Whitechapel!' settling themselves luxuriously in their beds to survey the fight. Others shouted: 'Shut yer row! . . . Go an' put yer'ed in a bag! . . .' The hubbub was recommencing. Suddenly many heavy blows struck with a handspike on the deck above boomed like discharges of small cannon through the forecastle. Then the boatswain's voice rose outside the door with an authoritative note in its drawl: 'D'ye hear, below there? Lay aft! Lay aft to muster all hands!'

There was a moment of surprised stillness. Then the forecastle floor disappeared under men whose bare feet flopped on the planks as they sprang clear out of their berths. Caps were rooted for amongst tumbled blankets. Some, yawning, buttoned waistbands. Half-smoked pipes were knocked hurriedly against woodwork and stuffed under pillows. Voices growled: 'What's up? . . . Is there no rest for us?' Donkin yelped: 'If that's the way of this ship, we'll 'ave to change all that. . . . You leave me alone. . . . I will soon. . . .' None of the crowd noticed him. They were lurching in twos and threes through the doors, after the manner of merchant Jacks who cannot go out of a door fairly, like mere landsmen. The votary of change followed them. Singleton, struggling into his jacket, came last, tall and fatherly, bearing high his head of a weatherbeaten sage on the body of an old athlete. Only Charley remained alone in the white glare of the empty place, sitting between the two rows of iron links that stretched into the narrow gloom forward. He pulled hard at the strands in a hurried endeavour to finish his knot. Suddenly he started up, flung the rope at the cat, and skipped after the black tom which went off leaping sedately over chain compressors, with its tail carried stiff and upright, like a small flagpole.

Outside the glare of the steaming forecastle the serene purity of the night enveloped the seamen with its soothing breath, with its tepid breath flowing under the stars that hung countless above the mastheads in a thin cloud of luminous dust. On the town side the blackness of the water was streaked with trails of light which undulated gently on slight ripples, similar to filaments that float rooted to the shore. Rows of other lights stood away in straight lines as if drawn up on parade between towering buildings; but on the the other side of the harbour sombre hills arched high their black spines, on which, here and there, the point of a star resembled a spark fallen from the sky. Far off, Byculla way, the electric lamps at the dock gates shone on the end of lofty standards with a glow blinding and frigid like captive ghosts of some evil moons. Scattered all over the dark polish of the roadstead, the ships at anchor floated in perfect stillness under the feeble gleam of their riding-lights, looming up, opaque and bulky, like strange and monumental structures abandoned by men to an everlasting repose.

Before the cabin door Mr Baker was mustering the crew. As they stumbled and lurched along past the mainmast, they could see aft his round, broad face with a white paper before it, and beside his shoulder the sleepy head, with dropped eyelids, of the boy, who held, suspended at the end of his raised arm, the luminous globe of a lamp. Even before the shuffle of naked soles had ceased along the decks, the mate began to call over the names. He called distinctly in a serious tone befitting this roll-call to unquiet loneliness, to inglorious and obscure struggle, or to the more trying endurance of small privations and wearisome duties. As the chief mate read out a name, one of the men would answer: 'Yes, sir!' or 'Here!' and, detaching himself from the shadowy mob of heads visible above the blackness of starboard bulwarks, would step barefooted into the circle of light, and in two noiseless strides pass into the shadows on the port side of the quarter-deck. They answered in divers tones: in thick mutters, in clear, ringing voices; and some, as if the whole thing had been an outrage on their feelings, used an injured intonation: for discipline is not ceremonious in merchant ships, where the sense of hierarchy is weak, and where all feel themselves equal before the unconcerned immensity of the sea and the exacting appeal of the work.

Mr Baker read on steadily: 'Hansen – Campbell – Smith – Wamibo. Now, then, Wamibo. Why don't you answer? Always got to call your name twice.' The Finn emitted at last an uncouth grunt, and, stepping out, passed through the patch of light, weird and gaudy, with the face of a man marching through a dream. The mate went on faster: 'Craik – Singleton – Donkin . . . O Lord!' he involuntarily ejaculated as the incredibly dilapidated figure appeared in the light. It stopped; it uncovered pale gums and long, upper teeth in malevolent grin. 'Is there anything wrong with me, Mister Mate?' it asked, with a flavour of insolence in the forced simplicity of its tone. On both sides of the deck subdued titters were heard. 'That'll do. Go over,' growled Mr Baker, fixing the new hand with steady blue eyes. And Donkin vanished suddenly out of the light into the dark group of mustered men, to be slapped on the back and to hear flattering whispers: 'He ain't afeard, he'll give sport to 'em, see if he don't' – 'Reg'lar Punch and Judy show' – 'Did ye see the mate start at him?' – 'Well! Damme, if I ever!'

The last man had gone over, and there was a moment of silence while the mate peered at his list. 'Sixteen, seventeen,' he muttered. 'I am one hand short, bo'sun,' he said aloud. The big west-countryman at his elbow, swarthy and bearded like a gigantic Spaniard, said in a rumbling bass: 'There's not one left forward, sir. I had a look around. He ain't aboard, but he may turn up before daylight.' 'Ay. He may or he may not,' commented the mate, 'can't make out that last name. It's all a smudge . . . That will do, men. Go below.'

The distinct and motionless group stirred, broke up, began to move forward.

'Wait!' cried a deep, ringing voice.

All stood still. Mr Baker, who had turned away yawning, spun round open-mouthed. At last, furious, he blurted out: 'What's this? Who said "Wait"? What . . .'

But he saw a tall figure standing on the rail. It came down and pushed through the crowd, marching with a heavy tread towards the light on the quarter-deck. Then again the sonorous voice said with insistence: 'Wait!' The lamplight lit up the man's body. He was tall. His head was away up in the shadows of lifeboats that stood on skids above the deck. The whites of his eyes and his teeth gleamed distinctly, but the face was indistinguishable. His hands were big and seemed gloved.

Mr Baker advanced intrepidly. 'Who are you? How dare you . . .?' he began.

The boy, amazed like the rest, raised the light to the man's face. It was black. A surprised hum – a faint hum that sounded like the suppressed mutter of the word 'Nigger' – ran along the deck and escaped out into the night. The nigger seemed not to hear. He balanced himself where he stood in a swagger that marked time. After a moment he said calmly: 'My name is Wait – James Wait.'

'Oh! said Mr Baker. Then, after a few seconds of smouldering silence, his temper blazed out. 'Ah! Your name is Wait. What of that? What do you want? What do you mean, coming shouting here?'

The nigger was calm, cool, towering, superb. The men had approached and stood behind him in a body. He overtopped the tallest by half a head. He said: 'I belong to the ship.' He enunciated distinctly, with soft precision. The deep, rolling tones of his voice filled the deck without effort. He was naturally scornful, unaffectedly condescending, as if from his height of six foot three he had surveyed all the vastness of human folly and had made up his mind not to be too hard on it. He went on: 'The captain shipped me this morning. I couldn't get aboard sooner. I saw you all aft as I came up the ladder, and could see directly you were mustering the crew. Naturally I called out my name. I thought you had it on your list, and would understand. You misapprehended.' He stopped short. The folly around him was confounded. He was right as ever, and as ever ready to forgive. The disdainful tones had ceased, and breathing heavily, he stood still, surrounded by all these white men. He held his head up in the glare of the lamp – a head vigorously modelled into deep shadows and shining lights – a head powerful and misshapen with a tormented and flattened face – a face pathetic and brutal: the tragic, the mysterious, the repulsive mask of a nigger's soul.

Mr Baker, recovering his composure, looked at the paper close. 'Oh, yes; that's so. All right. Wait. Take your gear forward,' he said.

Suddenly the nigger's eyes rolled wildly, became all white. He put his hand to his side and coughed twice, a cough metallic, hollow, and tremendously loud; it resounded like two explosions in a vault; the dome of the sky rang to it, and the iron plates of the ship's bulwarks seemed to vibrate in unison, then he marched off forward with the others. The officers lingering by the cabin door could hear him say: 'Won't some of you chaps lend a hand with my dunnage?

I've got a chest and a bag.' The words, spoken sonorously, with an even intonation, were heard all over the ship, and the question was put in a manner that made refusal impossible. The short, quick shuffle of men carrying something heavy went away forward, but the tall figure of the nigger lingered by the main hatch in knot of smaller shapes. Again he was heard asking: 'Is your cook a coloured gentleman?' Then a disappointed and disapproving 'Ah! h'm?' was his comment upon the information that the cook happened to be a mere white man. Yet, as they went all together towards the forecastle, he condescended to put his head through the galley door and boom out inside a magnificent 'Good evening, doctor!' that made all the saucepans ring. In the dim light the cook dozed on the coal locker in front of the captain's supper. He jumped up as if he had been cut with a whip, and dashed wildly on deck to see the backs of several men going away laughing. Afterwards, when talking about the voyage, he used to say: 'The poor fellow had scared me. I thought I had seen the devil.' The cook had been seven years in the ship with the same captain. He was a serious-minded man with a wife and three children, whose society he enjoyed on an average one month out of twelve. When on shore he took his family to church twice every Sunday. At sea he went to sleep every evening with his lamp turned up full, a pipe in his mouth, and an open Bible in his hand. Some one had always to go during the night to put out the light, take the book from his hand, and the pipe from between his teeth. 'For' – Belfast used to say, irritated and complaining – 'some night, you stupid cookie, you'll swallow your ould clay, and we will have no cook.' 'Ah! sonny, I am ready for my Maker's call . . . wish you all were,' the other would answer with a benign serenity that was altogether imbecile and touching. Belfast outside the galley door danced with vexation. 'You holy fool! I don't want you to die,' he howled, looking up with furious, quivering face and tender eyes. 'What's the hurry? You blessed wooden-headed ould heretic, the divvle will have you soon enough. Think of Us . . . of Us . . . of Us!' And he would go away, stamping, spitting aside, disgusted, and worried; while the other, stepping out, saucepan in hand, hot, begrimed, and placid, watched with a superior, cock-sure smile the back of his 'queer little man' reeling in a rage. They were great friends.

Mr Baker, lounging over the after-hatch, sniffed the humid night in the company of the second mate. 'Those West India niggers run fine and large – some of them . . . Ough! . . . Don't they? A fine, big man that, Mr Creighton. Feel him on a rope. Hey? Ough! I will take him into my watch, I think.' The second mate, a fair, gentlemanly young fellow, with a resolute face and splendid physique, observed quietly that it was just about what he expected. There could be felt in his tone some slight bitterness which Mr Baker very kindly set himself to argue away. 'Come, come, young man,' he said, grunting between the words. 'Come! Don't be too greedy. You had that big Finn in your watch all the voyage. I will do what's fair. You may have those two young Scandinavians and I . . . Ough! . . . I get the nigger, and will take that . . . Ough! that cheeky costermonger chap in a black frock-coat. I'll make him . . . Ough! . . . make him toe the mark, or my . . . Ough! . . . name isn't Baker. Ough! Ough! Ough!'

He grunted thrice – furiously. He had that trick of grunting so between his words and at the end of sentences. It was a fine, effective grunt that went well with his menacing utterance, with his heavy, bullnecked frame, his jerky, rolling gait; with his big, seamed face, his steady eyes, and sardonic mouth. But its effect had been long ago discounted by the men. They liked him; Belfast – who was a favourite, and knew it – mimicked him, not quite behind his back. Charley – but with greater caution – imitated his rolling gait. Some of his sayings became established, daily quotations in the forecastle. Popularity can go no farther! Besides, all hands were ready to admit that on a fitting occasion the mate could 'jump down a fellow's throat a reg'lar Western Ocean style'.

Now he was giving his last orders. 'Ough! . . . You, Knowles! Call all hands at four. I want . . . Ough! . . . to heave short before the tug comes. Look out for the captain. I am going to lie down in my clothes . . . Ough! . . . Call me when you see the boat coming. Ough! Ough! . . . The old man is sure to have something to say when he gets aboard,' he remarked to Creighton. 'Well, good night . . . Ough! A long day before us tomorrow . . . Ough! . . . Better turn in now. Ough! Ough!'

Upon the dark deck a band of light flashed, then a door slammed, and Mr Baker was gone into his neat cabin. Young Creighton stood leaning over the rail, and looked dreamily into the night of the East. And he saw in it a long country lane, a lane of waving leaves and dancing sunshine. He saw stirring boughs of old trees outspread, and framing in their arch the tender, the caressing blueness of an English sky. And through the arch a girl in a light dress, smiling under a sunshade, seemed to be stepping out of the tender sky.

At the other end of the ship the forecastle, with only one lamp burning now, was going to sleep in a dim emptiness traversed by loud breathings, by sudden short sighs. The double row of berths yawned black, like graves tenanted by uneasy corpses. Here and there a curtain of gaudy chintz, half drawn, marked the resting-place of sybarite. A leg hung over the edge very white and lifeless. An arm stuck straight out with a dark palm turned up, and thick fingers half closed. Two light snores, that did not synchronize, quarrelled in funny dialogue. Singleton stripped again – the old man suffered much from prickly heat – stood cooling his back in the doorway, with his arms crossed on his bare and adorned chest. His head touched the beam of the deck above. The nigger, half undressed, was busy casting adrift the lashing of his box, and spreading his bedding in an upper berth. He moved about in his socks, tall and noiseless, with a pair of braces beating about his calves. Amongst the shadows of stanchions and bowsprit, Donkin munched a piece of hard ship's bread, sitting on the deck with upturned feet and restless eyes; he held the biscuit up before his mouth in the whole fist and snapped his jaws at it with a raging face. Crumbs fell between his outspread legs. Then he got up.

'Where's our water-cask?' he asked in a contained voice.

Singleton, without a word, pointed with a big hand that held a short smouldering pipe. Donkin bent over the cask, drank out of the tin, splashing the water, turned round, and noticed the nigger looking at him over the shoulder with calm loftiness. He moved up sideways.

'There's a blooming supper for a man,' he whispered bitterly. 'My dorg at'ome wouldn't 'ave it. It's fit enouf for you an' me. 'Ere's a big ship's fo'c'sle! . . . Not a blooming scrap of meat in the kids. I've looked in all the lockers . . .'

The nigger stared like a man addressed unexpectedly in a foreign language. Donkin changed his tone: 'Giv' us a bit of baccy, mate,' he breathed out confidentially, 'I 'aven't 'ad smoke or chew for the last month. I am rampin' mad for it. Come on, old man!'

'Don't be familiar,' said the nigger. Donkin started and sat down on a chest near by, out of sheer surprise. 'We haven't kept pigs together,' continued James Wait in a deep undertone. 'Here's your tobacco.' Then, after a pause, he inquired: 'What ship?' '*Golden State*,' muttered Donkin indistinctly, biting the tobacco. The nigger whistled low. 'Ran?' he said curtly. Donkin nodded: one of his cheeks bulged out. 'In course I ran,' he mumbled. 'They booted the life hout of one Dago chap on the passage 'ere, then started on me. I cleared hout 'ere.' 'Left your dunnage behind?' 'Yes, dunnage and money,' answered Donkin, raising his voice a little: 'I got nothink. No clothes, no bed. A bandy-legged little Hirish chap 'ere 'as give me a blanket . . . Think I'll go an' sleep in the fore topmast staysail tonight.'

He went on deck trailing behind his back a corner of the blanket. Singleton, without a glance, moved slightly aside to let him pass. The nigger put away his shore togs and sat in clean working clothes on his box, one arm stretched over his knees. After staring at Singleton for some time he asked without emphasis: 'What kind of ship is this? Pretty fair? Eh?'

Singleton didn't stir. A long while after he said, with unmoved face: 'Ship! . . . Ships are all right. It is the men in them!'

He went on smoking in the prfound silence. The wisdom of half a century spent in listening to the thunder of the waves had spoken unconsciously through his old lips. The cat purred on the windlass. Then James Wait had a fit of roaring, rattling cough, that shook him, tossed him like a hurricane, and flung him panting with staring eyes headlong on his sea-chest. Several men woke up. One said sleepily out of his bunk: ' 'Struth! what a blamed row!' 'I have a cold on my chest,' gasped Wait. 'Cold! you call it,' grumbled the man; 'should think 'twas something more . . .' 'Oh! you think so,' said the nigger upright and loftily scornful again. He climbed into his berth and began coughing persistently while he put his head out to glare all round the forecastle. There was no further protest. He fell back on the pillow, and could be heard there wheezing regularly like a man oppressed in his sleep.

Singleton stood at the door with his face to the light and his back to the darkness. And alone in the dim emptiness of the sleeping forecastle he appeared bigger, colossal, very old; old as Father Time himself, who should have come there into this place as quiet at a sepulchre to contemplate with patient eyes the short victory of sleep, the consoler. Yet he was only a child of time, a lonely relic of a devoured and forgotten generation. He stood, still strong, as ever unthinking; a ready man with a vast empty past and with no future, with his childlike impulses and his man's passions already dead within his tattooed breast. The men who could understand his silence were gone – those men who knew how to exist beyond the pale of life and within sight of eternity. They had been strong, as those are strong who know neither doubts nor hopes. They had been impatient and enduring, turbulent and devoted, unruly and faithful. Well-meaning people had tried to represent those men as whining over every mouthful of their food; as going about their work in fear of their lives. But in truth they had been men who knew toil, privation, violence, debauchery – but knew not fear, and had no desire of spite in their hearts. Men hard to manage, but easy to inspire; voiceless men – but men enough to scorn in their hearts the sentimental voices that bewailed the hardness of their fate. It was a fate unique and their own; the capacity to bear it appeared to them the privilege of the chosen! Their generation lived inarticulate and indispensable, without knowing the sweetness of affections or the refuge of a home – and died free from the dark menace of a narrow grave. They were the everlasting children of the mysterious sea. Their successors are the grown-up children of a discontented earth. They are less naughty, but less innocent; less profane, but perhaps also less believing; and if they had learned how to speak they have also learned how to whine. But the others were strong and mute; they were effaced, bowed, and enduring, like stone caryatids that hold up in the night the lighted halls of a resplendent and glorious edifice. They are gone now – and it does not matter. The sea and the earth are unfaithful to their children: a truth, a faith, a generation of men goes – and is forgotten, and it does not matter! Except, perhaps, to the few of those who believed the truth, confessed the faith – or loved the men.

A breeze was coming. The ship that had been lying tide-rode swung to a heavier puff; and suddenly the slack of the chain cable between the windlass and the hawse-pipe clinked, slipped forward an inch, and rose gently off the deck with a startling suggestion as of unsuspected life that had been lurking stealthily in the iron. In the hawse-pipe the grinding links sent through the ship a sound like a low groan of a man sighing under a burden. The strain came on the windlass, the chain tautened like a string, vibrated – and the handle of the screwbrake moved in slight jerks. Singleton stepped forward.

Till then he had been standing meditative and unthinking, reposeful and hopeless, with a face grim and blank – a sixty-year-old child of the mysterious sea. The thoughts of all his lifetime could have been expressed in six words, but the stir of those things that were as much part of his existence as his beating heart called up a gleam of alert understanding upon the sternness of his aged face. The flame of the lamp swayed, and the old man, with knitted and bushy eyebrows, stood over the brake, watchful and motionless in the wild saraband of dancing shadows. Then the ship, obedient to the call of her anchor, forged ahead slightly and eased the strain. The cable relieved, hung down, and after swaying imperceptibly to and fro dropped with a loud tap on the hard wood planks. Singleton seized the high lever, and, by a violent throw forward of his body, wrung out another half-turn from the brake. He recovered himself, breathed largely, and remained for a while glaring down at the powerful and compact engine that squatted on the deck at his feet like some quiet monster – a creature amazing and tame.

'You . . . hold!' he growled at it masterfully, in the incult tangle of his white beard.

Chapter II

Next morning, at daylight, the *Narcissus* went to sea.

A slight haze blurred the horizon. Outside the harbour the measureless expanse of smooth water lay sparkling like a floor of jewels, and as empty as the sky. The short black tug gave a pluck to windward, in the usual way, then let go the rope, and hovered for a moment on the quarter with her engines stopped; while the slim, long hull of the ship moved ahead slowly under lower topsails. The loose upper canvas blew out in the breeze with soft round contours, resembling small white clouds snared in the maze of ropes. Then the sheets were hauled home, the yards hoisted, and the ship became a high and lonely pyramid, gliding, all shining and white, through the sunlit mist. The tug turned short round and went away away towards the land. Twenty-six pairs of eyes watched her low broad stern crawling languidly over the smooth swell between the two paddle-wheels that turned fast, beating the water with fierce hurry. She resembled an enormous and aquatic black beetle, surprised by the light, overwhelmed by the sunshine, trying to escape with ineffectual effort into the distant gloom of the land. She left a lingering smudge of smoke on the sky, and two vanishing trails of foam on the water. On the place where she had stopped a round black patch of soot remained, undulating on the swell – an unclean mark of the creature's rest.

The *Narcissus* left alone, heading south, seemed to stand resplendent and still upon the restless sea, under the moving sun. Flakes of foam swept past her sides; the water struck her with flashing blows; the land glided away slowly fading; a few birds screamed on motionless wings over the swaying mastheads. But soon the land disappeared, the birds went away; and to the west the pointed sail of an Arab dhow running for Bombay, rose triangular and upright above the sharp edge of the horizon, lingered and vanished like an illusion. Then the ship's wake, long and straight, stretched itself out through a day of immense solitude. The setting sun, burning on the level of the water, flamed crimson below the blackness of heavy rain clouds. The sunset squall, coming up from behind, dissolved itself into the short deluge of a hissing shower. It left the ship glistening from trucks to waterline, and with darkened sails. She ran easily before a fair monsoon, with her decks cleared for the night, and, moving along with her, was heard the sustained and monotonous swishing of the waves, mingled with the low whispers of men mustered aft for the setting of watches; the short plaint of some block aloft; or, now and then, a loud sigh of wind.

Mr Baker, coming out of his cabin, called out the first name sharply before closing the door behind him. He was going to take charge of the deck. On the homeward trip, according to an old custom of the sea, the chief officer takes the first nightwatch – from eight till midnight. So Mr Baker, after he had heard the last 'Yes, sir!' said moodily, 'Relieve the wheel and look-out'; and climbed with heavy feet the poop ladder to windward. Soon after Mr Creighton came down, whistling softly, and went into the cabin. On the doorstep the steward lounged, in slippers, meditative, and with his shirt-sleeves rolled up to the armpits. On the main deck the cook, locking up the galley doors, had an altercation with young Charley about a pair of socks. He could be heard saying impressively, in the darkness amidships: 'You don't deserve a kindness. I've been drying them for you, and now you complain about the holes – and you swear, too! Right in front of me! If I hadn't been a Christian – which you ain't, you young ruffian – I would give you a clout on the head. . . . Go away!' Men in couples or threes stood pensive or moved silently along the bulwarks in the waist. The first busy day of a homeward passage was sinking into the dull peace of resumed routine. Aft, on the high poop, Mr Baker walked shuffling and grunted to himself in the pauses of his thoughts. Forward, the look-out man, erect between the flukes of the two anchors, hummed an endless tune, keeping his eyes fixed dutifully ahead in a vacant stare. A multitude of stars coming out into the clear night peopled the emptiness of the sky. They glittered, as if alive above the sea; they surrounded the running ship on all sides; more intense than the eyes of a staring crowd, and as inscrutable as the souls of men.

The passage had begun, and the ship, a fragment detached from the earth, went on lonely and swift like a small planet. Round her the abysses of sky and sea met in an unattainable frontier. A great circular solitude moved with her, ever changing and ever the same, always monotonous and always imposing. Now and then another wandering white speck, burdened with life, appeared far off – disappeared; intent on its own destiny. The sun looked upon her all day, and every morning rose with a burning, round stare of undying curiosity. She had her own future; she was alive with the lives of those beings who trod her decks; like that earth which had given her up to the sea, she had an intolerable load of regrets and hopes. On her lived timid truth and audacious lies; and, like the earth, she was unconscious, fair to see – and condemned by men to an ignoble fate. The august loneliness of her path lent dignity to the sordid inspiration of her pilgrimage. She drove foaming to the southward, as if guided by the courage of a high endeavour. The smiling greatness of the sea dwarfed the extent of time. The days raced after one another, brilliant and quick like the flashes of a lighthouse, and the nights, eventful and short, resembled fleeting dreams.

The men had shaken into their places, and the half-hourly voice of the bells ruled their life of unceasing care. Night and day the head and shoulders of a seaman could be seen aft by the wheel, outlined high against sunshine or starlight, very steady above the stir of revolving spokes. The faces changed, passing in rotation. Youthful faces, bearded faces, dark faces: faces serene, or faces moody, but all akin with the brotherhood of the sea; all with the same attentive expression of eyes, carefully watching the compass or the sails. Captain Allistoun, serious, and with an old red muffler round his throat, all day long pervaded the poop. At night, many times he rose out of the darkness of the companion, such as a phantom above a grave, and stood watchful and mute under the stars, his night-shirt fluttering like a flag – then, without a sound, sank down again. He was born on the shores of the Pentland Firth. In his youth he attained the rank of harpooner in Peterhead whalers. When he spoke of that time his restless grey eyes became still and cold, like the loom of ice. Afterwards he went into the East Indian trade for the sake of change. He had commanded the *Narcissus* since she was built. He loved his ship, and drove her unmercifully; for his secret ambition was to make her accomplish some day a brilliantly quick passage which would be mentioned in nautical papers. He pronounced his owner's name with a sardonic smile, spoke but seldom to his officers, and reproved errors in a gentle voice, with words that cut to the quick. His hair was iron-grey, his face hard and of the colour of pump-leather. He shaved every morning of his life – at six – but once (being caught in a fierce hurricane eighty miles south-west of Mauritius) he had missed three consecutive days. He feared naught but an unforgiving God, and wished to end his days in a little house, with a plot of ground attached – far in the country – out of sight of the sea.

He, the ruler of that minute world, seldom descended from the Olympian heights of his poop. Below him – at his feet, so to speak – common mortals led their busy and insignificant lives. Along the main deck, Mr Baker grunted in a manner bloodthirsty and innocuous; and kept all our noses to the grindstone, being – as he once remarked – paid for doing that very thing. The men working about the deck were healthy and contented – as most seamen are, when once well out to sea. The true peace of God begins at any spot a thousand miles from the nearest land; and when He sends there the messengers of His might it is not in terrible wrath against crime, presumption, and folly, but paternally, to chasten simple hearts – ignorant hearts that know nothing of life, and beat undisturbed by envy or greed.

In the evening the cleared decks had a reposeful aspect, resembling the autumn of the earth. The sun was sinking to rest, wrapped in a mantle of warm clouds. Forward, on the end of the spare spars, the boatswain and the carpenter sat together with crossed arms; two men friendly, powerful, and deep-chested. Beside them the short, dumpy, sailmaker – who had been in the Navy – related, between the whiffs of his pipe, impossible stories about Admirals. Couples tramped backwards and forwards, keeping step and balance without effort, in a confined space. Pigs grunted in the big pigsty. Belfast, leaning thoughtfully on his elbow, above the bars, communed with them through the silence of his meditation. Fellows with shirts open wide on sunburnt breasts sat upon the mooring bits, and all up the steps of the forecastle ladders. By the foremast a few discussed in a circle the characteristics of a gentleman. One said: 'It's money as does it.' Another maintained: 'No, it's the way they speak.' Lame Knowles stumped up with an unwashed face (he had the distinction of being the dirty man of the forecastle), and showing a few yellow fangs in a shrewd smile, explained craftily that he 'had seen some of their pants'. The backsides of them – he had observed – were thinner than paper from constant sitting down in offices, yet otherwise they looked first-rate and would last for years. It was all appearance. 'It was,' he said, 'bloomin' easy to be a gentleman when you had a clean job for life.' They disputed endlessly, obstinate and childish; they repeated in shouts and with inflamed faces their amazing arguments; while the soft breeze, eddying down the enormous cavity of the foresail, distended above their bare heads, stirred the tumbled hair with a touch passing and light like an indulgent caress.

They were forgetting their toil, they were forgetting themselves. The cock approached to hear, and stood by, beaming with the inward consciousness of his faith, like a conceited saint unable to forget his glorious reward; Donkin, solitary and brooding over his wrongs on the forecastle-head, moved closer to catch the drift of the discussion below him; he turned his sallow face to the sea, and his thin nostrils moved, sniffing the breeze, as he lounged negligently by the rail. In the glow of sunset faces shone with interest, teeth flashed, eyes sparkled. The walking couples stood still suddenly, with broad grins; a man, bending over a washtub, sat up, entranced, with the soapsuds flecking his wet arms. Even the three petty officers listened leaning back, comfortably propped, and with superior smiles. Belfast left off scratching the ear of his favourite pig, and, open mouthed, tried with eager eyes to have his say. He lifted his arms, grimacing and baffled. From a distance Charley screamed at the ring: 'I know about gentlemen morn'n any of you. I've been intermit with 'em. . . . I've blacked their boots.' The cook, craning his neck to hear better, was scandalized. 'Keep your mouth shut when your elders speak, you impudent young heathen – you.' 'All right, old Hallelujah, I'm done,' answered Charley, soothingly. At some opinion of dirty Knowles, delivered with an air of supernatural cunning, a ripple of laughter ran along, rose like a wave, burst with a startling roar. They stamped with both feet; they turned their shouting faces to the sky; many, spluttering, slapped their thighs; while one or two, bent double, gasped, hugging themselves with both arms like men in pain. The carpenter and the boatswain, without changing their attitude, shook with laughter where they sat; the sailmaker, charged with an anecdote about a Commodore, looked sulky; the cook was wiping his eyes with a greasy rag; and lame Knowles, astonished at his own success, stood in their midst showing a slow smile.

Suddenly the face of Donkin leaning high-shouldered over the after-rail became grave. Something like a weak rattle was heard through the forecastle door. It became a murmur; it ended in a sighing groan. The washerman plunged both his arms into the tub abruptly; the cook became more crestfallen than an exposed backslider; the boatswain moved his shoulders uneasily; the carpenter got up with a spring and walked away – while the sailmaker seemed mentally to give his story up, and began to puff at his pipe with sombre determination. In the blackness of the doorway a pair of eyes glimmered white, and big, and staring. Then James Wait's head protruding, became visible, as if suspended between the two hands that grasped a doorpost on each side of the face. The tassel of his blue woollen nightcap, cocked forward, danced gaily over his left eyelid. He stepped out in a tottering stride. He looked powerful as ever, but showed a strange and affected unsteadiness in his gait; his face was perhaps a trifle thinner, and his eyes appeared rather startlingly prominent. He seemed to hasten the retreat of departing light by his very presence; the setting sun dipped sharply, as though fleeing before our nigger; a black mist emanated from him; a subtle and dismal influence; a something cold and gloomy that floated out and settled on all the faces like a mourning veil. The circle broke up. The joy of laugher died on stiffened lips. There was not a smile left among all the ship's company. Not a word was spoken. Many turned their backs, trying to look unconcerned; others, with averted heads, sent half-reluctant glances out of the corners of their eyes. They resembled criminals conscious of misdeeds more than honest men distracted by doubt; only two or three stared frankly, but stupidly, with lips slightly open. All expected James Wait to say something, and, at the same time, had the air of knowing beforehand what he would say. He leaned his back against the doorpost, and with heavy eyes swept over them a glance domineering and pained, like a sick tyrant overawing a crowd of abject but untrustworthy slaves.

No one went away. They waited in fascinated dread. He said ironically, with gasps between the words:

'Thank you . . . chaps. You . . . are nice . . . and . . . quiet . . . you are! Yelling so . . . before . . . the door. . . .'

He made a longer pause, during which he worked his ribs in an exaggerated labour of breathing. It was intolerable. Feet were shuffled. Belfast let out a groan; but Donkin above blinked his red eyelids with invisible eyelashes, and smiled bitterly over the nigger's head.

The nigger went on again with surprising ease. He gasped no more, and his voice rang, hollow and loud, as though he had been talking in an empty cavern. He was comptemptuously angry.

'I tried to get a wink of sleep. You know I can't sleep o' nights. And you come jabbering near the door here like a blooming lot of old women. . . . You think yourselves good shipmates. Do you? . . . Much you care for a dying man!'

Belfast spun away from the pigsty. 'Jimmy,' he cried tremulously, 'if you hadn't been sick I would –'

He stopped. The nigger waited awhile, then said, in a gloomy tone: 'You would . . . What? Go an' fight another such one as yourself. Leave me alone. It won't be for long. I'll soon die. . . . It's coming right enough!'

Men stood around very still and with exasperated eyes. It was just what they had expected, and hated to hear, that idea of a stalking death, thrust at them many times a day like a boast and like a menace by this obnoxious nigger. He seemed to take a pride in that death which, so far, had attended only upon the ease of his life; he was overbearing about it, as if no one else in the world had ever been intimate with such a companion; he paraded it unceasingly before us with an affectionate persistence that made its presence indubitable, and at the same time incredible. No man could be suspected of such monstrous friendship! Was he a reality – or was he a sham – this ever-expected visitor of Jimmy's? We hesitated between pity and mistrust, while, on the slightest provocation, he shook before our eyes the bones of his bothersome and infamous skeleton. He was for ever trotting him out. He would talk of that coming death as though it had been already there, as if it had been walking the deck outside, as if it would presently come in to sleep in the only empty bunk; as if it had sat by his side at every meal. It interfered daily with our occupations, with our leisure, with our amusements. We had no songs and no music in the evening, because Jimmy (we all lovingly called him Jimmy, to conceal our hate of his accomplice) had managed, with that prospective decease of his, to disturb even Archie's mental balance. Archie was the owner of the concertina; but after a couple of stinging lectures from Jimmy he refused to play any more. He said: 'Yon's an uncanny joker. I dinna ken what's wrang wi' him, but there's something verra wrang, verra wrang. It's nae manner of use asking me. I won't play.' Our singers became mute because Jimmy was a dying man. For the same reason no chap – as Knowles remarked

– could 'drive in a nail to hang his few poor rags upon', without being made aware of the enormity he committed in disturbing Jimmy's interminable last moments. At night, instead of the cheerful yell, 'One bell! Turn out! Do you hear there? Hey! hey! hey! Show leg!' the watches were called man by man, in whispers, so as not to interfere with Jimmy's, possibly, last slumber on earth. True, he was always awake, and managed, as we sneaked out on deck, to plant in our backs some cutting remark that, for the moment, made us feel as if we had been brutes, and afterwards made us suspect ourselves of being fools. We spoke in low tones within that fo'c'sle as though it had been a church. We ate our meals in silence and dread, for Jimmy was capricious with his food, and railed bitterly at the salt meat, at the biscuits, at the tea, as at articles unfit for human consumption – 'let alone for a dying man!' He would say: 'Can't you find a better slice of meat for a sick man who's trying to get home to be cured – or buried? But there! If I had a chance, you fellows would do away with it. You would poison me. Look at what you have given me!' We served him in his bed with rage and humility, as though we had been the base courtiers of a hated prince; and he rewarded us by his unconciliating criticism. He had found the secret of keeping for ever on the run the fundamental imbecility of mankind; he had the secret of life, that confounded dying man, and he made himself master of every moment of our existence. We grew desperate, and remained submissive. Emotional little Belfast was for ever on the verge of assault or on the verge of tears. One evening he confided to Archie: 'For a ha'penny I would knock his ugly black head off – the skulking dodger!' And the straightforward Archie pretended to be shocked! Such was the infernal spell which that casual St Kitt's nigger had cast upon our guileless manhood! But the same night Belfast stole from the galley the officers' Sunday fruit pie, to tempt the fastidious appetite of Jimmy. He endangered not only his long friendship with the cook but also – as it appeared – his eternal welfare. The cook was overwhelmed with grief; he did not know the culprit but he knew that wickedness flourished; he knew that Satan was abroad amongst those men, whom he looked upon as in some way under his spiritual care. Whenever he saw three or four of us standing together he would leave his stove, to run out and preach. We fled from him; and only Charley (who knew the thief) affronted the cook with a candid gaze which irritated the good man. 'It's you, I believe,' he groaned, sorrowful and with a patch of soot on his chin. 'It's you. You are a brand for the burning! No more of YOUR socks in my galley.' Soon, unofficially, the information was spread about that, should there be another case of stealing, our marmalade (an extra allowance: half a pound per man) would be stopped. Mr Baker ceased to heap jocular abuse upon his favourites, and grunted suspiciously at all. The captain's cold eyes, high up on the poop, glittered mistrustful, as he surveyed us trooping in a small mob from halyards to braces for the usual evening pull at all the ropes. Such stealing in a merchant ship is difficult to check, and may be taken as a declaration by men of their dislike for their officers. It is a bad sympton. It may end in God knows what trouble. The *Narcissus* was still a peaceful ship, but mutual confidence was shaken. Donkin did not conceal his delight. We were dismayed.

Then illogical Belfast reproached our nigger with great fury. James Wait, with his elbow on the pillow, choked, gasped out: 'Did I ask you to bone the dratted thing? Blow your blamed pie. It has made me worse – you little Irish lunatic, you!' Belfast, with scarlet face and trembling lips, made a dash at him. Every man in the forecastle rose with a shout. There was a moment of wild tumult. Someone shrieked piercingly: 'Easy, Belfast! Easy! . . .' We expected Belfast to strangle Wait without more ado. Dust flew. We heard through it the nigger's cough, metallic and explosive like a gong. Next moment we saw Belfast hanging over him. He was saying plaintively: 'Don't! Don't, Jimmy! Don't be like that. An angel couldn't put up with ye – sick as ye are.' He looked round at us from Jimmy's bedside, his comical mouth twitching, and through tearful eyes; then he tried to put straight the disarranged blankets. The unceasing whisper of the sea filled the forecastle. Was James Wait frightened, or touched, or repentant? He lay on his back with a hand to his side, and as motionless as if his expected visitor had come at last. Belfast fumbled about his feet, repeating with emotion: 'Yes. We know. Ye are bad, but . . . Just say what ye want done, and . . . We all know ye are bad – very bad. . . .' No! Decidedly James Wait was not touched or repentant. Truth to say, he seemed rather startled. He sat up with incredible suddenness and ease. 'Ah! You think I am bad, do you!' he said gloomily, in his clearest baritone voice (to hear him speak sometimes you would never think there was anything wrong with that man). 'Do you? . . . Well, act according! Some of you haven't sense enough to put a blanket shipshape over a sick man. There! Leave it alone! I can die anyhow!' Belfast turned away limply with a gesture of discouragement. In the silence of the forecastle, full of interested men, Donkin pronounced distinctly: 'Well, I'm blowed!' and sniggered. Wait looked at him. He looked at him in a quite friendly manner. Nobody could tell what would please our incomprehensible invalid: but for us the scorn of that snigger was hard to bear.

Donkin's position in the forecastle was distinguished but unsafe. He stood on the bad eminence of a general dislike. He was left alone; and in his isolation he could do nothing but think of the gales of the Cape of Good Hope and envy us the possession of warm clothing and waterproofs. Our sea-boots, our oilskin coats, our well-filled sea-chests, were to him so many causes for bitter meditation: he had none of those things, and he felt instinctively that no man, when the need arose, would offer to share them with him. He was impudently cringing to us and systematically insolent to the officers. He anticipated the best results, for himself, from such a line of conduct – and was mistaken. Such natures forget that under extreme provocation men will be just – whether they want to be so or not. Donkin's insolence to long-suffering Mr Baker became at last intolerable to us, and we rejoiced when the mate, one dark night, tamed him for good. It was done neatly, with great decency and decorum, and with little noise. We had been called – just before midnight – to trim the yards, and Donkin – as usual – made insulting remarks. We stood sleepily in a row with the forebrace in our hands waiting for the next order, and heard in the darkness a scuffly trampling of feet, an exclamation of surprise, sounds of cuffs and slaps, suppressed, hissing whispers: 'Ah! Will you!' – 'Don't! . . . Don't!' – 'Then behave' – 'Oh! Oh! . . .' Afterwards there were soft thuds mixed with the rattle of iron things as if a man's body had been tumbling helplessly amongst the main-pump rods. Before we could realize the situation, Mr Baker's voice was heard very near and a little impatient: 'Haul away, men! Lay back on that rope!' And we did lay back on the rope with great alacrity. As if nothing had happened, the chief mate went on trimming the yards with his usual and exasperating fastidiousness. We didn't at the time see anything of Donkin, and did not care. Had the chief officer thrown him overboard, no man would have said as much as 'Hallo! he's gone!' But, in truth, no great harm was done – even if Donkin did lose one of his front teeth. We perceived this in the morning, and preserved a ceremonious silence: the etiquette of the forecastle commanded us to be blind and dumb in such a case, and we cherished the decencies of our life more than ordinary landsmen respect theirs. Charley, with unpardonable want of *savoir vivre*, yelled out: ' 'Ave you been to your dentyst? . . . Hurt ye, didn't it?' He got a box on the ear from one of his best friends. The boy was surprised, and remained plunged in grief for at least three hours. We were sorry for him, but youth requires even more discipline than age. Donkin grinned venomously. From that day he became pitiless; told Jimmy that he was a 'black fraud'; hinted to us that we were an imbecile lot, daily taken in by a vulgar nigger. And Jimmy seemed to like the fellow!

Singleton lived untouched by human emotions. Taciturn and unsmiling, he breathed amongst us – in that alone resembling the rest of the crowd. We were trying to be decent chaps, and found it jolly difficult; we oscillated between the desire of virtue and the fear of ridicule; we wished to save ourselves from the pain of remorse, but did not want to be made the contemptible dupes of our sentiment. Jimmy's hateful accomplice seemed to have blown with his impure breath undreamt-of subtleties into our hearts. We were disturbed and cowardly. That we knew. Singleton seemed to know nothing, understand nothing. We had thought him till then as wise as he looked, but now we dared, at times, suspect him of being stupid – from old age. One day, however, at dinner, as we sat on our boxes round a tin dish that stood on the deck within the circle of our feet, Jimmy expressed his general disgust with men and things in words that were particularly disgusting. Singleton lifted his head. We became mute. The old man, addressing Jimmy, asked: 'Are you dying?' Thus interrogated, James Wait appeared horribly startled and confused. We all were startled. Mouths remained open; hearts thumped, eyes blinked; a dropped tin fork rattled in the dish; a man rose as if to go out, and stood still. In less than a minute Jimmy pulled himself together: 'Why? Can't you see I am?' he answered shakily. Singleton lifted a piece of soaked biscuit ('his teeth' – he declared – 'had no edge on them now') to his lips. 'Well, get on with your dying,' he said with venerable mildness; 'don't raise a blamed fuss with us over that job. We can't help you.' Jimmy fell back in his bunk, and for a long time lay very still wiping the perspiration off his chin. The dinner-tins were put away quickly. On deck we discussed the incident in whispers. Some showed a chuckling exultation. Many looked grave. Wamibo, after long periods of staring dreaminess, attempted abortive smiles; and one of the young Scandinavians, much tormented by doubt, ventured in the second dog-watch to approach Singleton (the old man did not encourage us much to speak to him) and ask sheepishly: 'You think he will die?' Singleton looked up. 'Why, of course he will die,' he said deliberately. This seemed decisive. It was promptly imparted to everyone by him who had consulted the oracle. Shy and eager, he would step up and with averted gaze recite his formula: 'Old Singleton says he will die.' It was a relief! At last we knew that our compassions would not be misplaced, and we could again smile without misgivings – but we reckoned without Donkin. Donkin 'didn't want to 'ave no truck with 'em dirty furriners'. When Nilsen came to him with the news: 'Singleton says he will die,' he answered him by a spiteful 'And so will you – you fat-headed Dutchman. Wish you Dutchmen were all dead – 'stead comin' takin' our money inter your starvin' country.' We were appalled. We perceived that after all Singleton's answer meant nothing. We began to hate him for making fun of us. All our certitudes were going; we were on doubtful terms with our officers; the cook had given us up for lost; we had overheard the boatswain's opinion that 'we were a crowd of softies'. We suspected Jimmy, one another, and even our very selves. We did not know what to do. At every insignificant turn of our humble life we met Jimmy overbearing and blocking the way, arm-in-arm with his awful and veiled familiar. It was a weird servitude.

It began a week after leaving Bombay and came on us stealthily like any other great misfortune. Everyone had remarked that Jimmy from the first was very slack at his work; but we thought it simply the outcome of his philosophy of life. Donkin said: 'You put no more weight on a rope than a bloody sparrer.' He disdained him. Belfast, ready for a fight, exclaimed provokingly: 'You don't kill yourself, old man!' 'Would YOU?' He retorted with extreme scorn – and Belfast retired. One morning, as we were washing decks, Mr Baker called to him: 'Bring your broom over here, Wait.' He strolled languidly. 'Move yourself! Ough!' grunted Mr Baker: 'what's the matter with your hind legs?' He stopped dead short. He gazed slowly with eyes that bulged out with an expression audacious and sad. 'It isn't my legs,' he said, 'it's my lungs.' Everybody listened. 'What's . . . Ough! . . . What's wrong with them?' inquired Mr Baker. All the watch stood around on the wet deck, grinning, and with brooms or buckets in their hands. He said mournfully: 'Going – or gone. Can't you see I'm a dying man? I know it!' Mr Baker was disgusted. 'Then why the devil did you ship aboard here?' 'I must live till I die – mustn't I?' he replied. The grins became audible. 'Go off the deck – get out of my sight,' said Mr Baker. He was nonplussed. It was an unique experience. James Wait, obedient, dropped his broom, and walked slowly forward. A burst of laughter followed him. it was too funny. All hands laughed. . . . They laughed! . . . Alas!

He became the tormentor of all our moments; he was worse than a nightmare. You couldn't see that there was anything wrong with him: on a nigger it does not show. He was not very fat – certainly – but then he was no leaner than other niggers we had known. He coughed often, but the most prejudiced person could perceive that, mostly, he coughed when it suited his purpose. He wouldn't, or couldn't, do his work – and he wouldn't lie-up. One day he would skip aloft with the best of them, and next time we would be obliged to risk our lives to get his limp body down. He was reported, he was examined; he was remonstrated with, threatened, cajoled, lectured. He was called into the cabin to interview the captain. There were wild rumours. It was said he had cheeked the old man; it was said he had frightened him. Charley maintained that the 'skipper, weepin', 'as giv' 'im 'is blessin' an' a pot of jam'. Knowles had it from the steward that the unspeakable Jimmy had been reeling against the cabin furniture; that he had groaned; that he had complained of general brutality and disbelief; and had ended by coughing all over the old man's meteorological journals which were then spread on the table. At any rate, Wait returned forward supported by the steward, who, in a pained and shocked voice, entreated us: 'Here! Catch hold of him, one of you. He is to lie-up.' Jimmy drank a tin mugful of coffee, and, after bullying first one and then another, went to bed. He remained there most of the time, but when it suited him would come on deck and appear amongst us. He was scornful and brooding; he looked ahead upon the sea, and no one could tell what was the meaning of that black man sitting apart in meditative attitude and as motionless as a carving.

He refused steadily all medicine; he threw sago and cornflour overboard till the steward got tired of bringing it to him. He asked for paregoric. They sent him a big bottle; enough to poison a wilderness of babies. He kept it between his mattress and the deal lining of the ship's side; and nobody ever saw him take a dose. Donkin abused him to his face, jeered at him while he gasped; and the same day Wait would lend him a warm jersey. Once Donkin reviled him for half an hour; reproached him with the extra work his malingering gave to the watch; and ended by calling him 'a black-faced swine'. Under the spell of our accursed perversity we were horror-struck. But Jimmy positively seemed to revel in that abuse. It made him look cheerful – and Donkin had a pair of old sea boots thrown at him. 'Here, you East End trash,' boomed Wait, 'you may have that.'

At last Mr Baker had to tell the captain that James Wait was disturbing the peace of the ship. 'Knock discipline on the head – he will, Ough,' grunted Mr Baker. As a matter of fact, the starboard watch came as near as possible to refusing duty, when ordered one morning by the boastwain to wash out their forecastle. It appears Jimmy objected to a wet floor – and that morning we were in a compassionate mood. We thought the boatswain a brute, and, practically, told him so. Only Mr Baker's delicate tact prevented an all-fired row: he refused to take us seriously. He came bustling forward, and called us many unpolite names but in such a hearty and seamanlike manner that we began to feel ashamed of ourselves. In truth, we thought him much too good a sailor to annoy him willingly: and after all Jimmy might have been a fraud – probably was! The forecastle got a clean up that morning; but in the afternoon a sick-bay was fitted up in the deck-house. It was a nice little cabin opening on deck, and with two berths. Jimmy's belongings were transported there, and then – notwithstanding his protests – Jimmy himself. He said he couldn't walk. Four men carried him on a blanket. He complained that he would have to die there alone, like a dog. We grieved for him, and were delighted to have him removed from the forecastle. We attended him as before. The galley was next door, and the cook looked in many times a day. Wait became a little more cheerful. Knowles affirmed having heard him laugh to himself in peals one day. Others had seen him walking about on deck at night. His little place, with the door ajar on a long hook, was always full of tobacco smoke. We spoke through the crack cheerfully, sometimes abusively, as we passed by, intent on our work. He fascinated us. He would never let doubt die. He overshadowed the ship. Invulnerable in his promise of speedy corruption he trampled on our self-respect, he demonstrated to us daily our want of moral courage; he tainted our lives. Had we been a miserable gang of wretched immortals, unhallowed alike by hope and fear, he could not have lorded it over us with a more pitiless assertion of his sublime privilege.

Chapter III

Meantime the *Narcissus*, with square yards, ran out of the fair monsoon. She drifted slowly, swinging round and round the compass, through a few days of baffling light airs. Under the patter of short warm showers, grumbling men whirled the heavy yards from side to side; they caught hold of the soaked ropes with groans and sighs, while their officers, sulky and dripping with rain water, unceasingly ordered them about in wearied voices. During the short respites they looked with disgust into the smarting palms of their stiff hands, and asked one another bitterly: 'Who would be a sailor if he could be a farmer?' All the tempers were spoilt, and no man cared what he said. One black night, when the watch, panting in the heat and half-drowned with the rain, had been through four mortal hours hunted from brace to brace, Belfast declared that he would 'chuck the sea for ever and go in a steamer'. This was excessive, no doubt. Captain Allistoun, with great self-control, would mutter sadly to Mr Baker: 'It is not so bad – not so bad,' when he had managed to shove, and dodge, and manoeuvre his smart ship through sixty miles in twenty-four hours. From the doorstep of the little cabin, Jimmy, chin in hand, watched our distasteful labours with insolent and melancholy eyes. We spoke to him gently – and out of his sight exchanged sour smiles.

Then, again, with a fair wind and under a clear sky, the ship went on piling up the South Latitude. She passed outside Madagascar and Mauritius without a glimpse of the land. Extra lashings were put on the spare spars. Hatches were looked to. The steward in his leisure moments and with a worried air tried to fit washboards to the cabin doors. Stout canvas was bent with care. Anxious eyes looked to the westward, towards the cape of storms. The ship began to dip into a south-west swell, and the softly luminous sky of low latitudes took on a harder sheen from day to day above our heads: it arched high above the ship, vibrating and pale, like an immense dome of steel, resonant with the deep voice of freshening gales. The sunshine gleamed cold on the white curls of black waves. Before the strong breath of westerly squalls the ship, with reduced sail, lay slowly over, obstinate and yielding. She drove to and fro in the unceasing endeavour to fight her way through the invisible violence of the winds: she pitched headlong into dark smooth hollows; she struggled upwards over the snowy ridges of great running seas; she rolled, restless, from side to side, like a thing in pain. Enduring and valiant, she answered to the call of men; and her slim spars waving for ever in abrupt semicircles, seemed to beckon in vain for help towards the stormy sky.

It was a bad winter off the Cape that year. The relieved helmsmen came off flapping their arms, or ran stamping hard and blowing into swollen, red fingers. The watch on deck dodged the sting of cold sprays, or, crouching in sheltered corners, watched dismally the high and merciless seas boarding the ship time after time in unappeasable fury. Water tumbled in cataracts over the forecastle doors. You had to dash through a waterfall to get into your damp bed. The men turned in wet and turned out stiff to face the redeeming and ruthless exactions of their glorious and obscure fate. Far aft, and peering watchfully to windward, the officers could be seen through the mist of squalls. They stood by the weather-rail, holding on grimly, straight and glistening in their long coats; and in the disordered plunges of the hard-driven ship, they appeared high up, attentive, tossing violently above the grey line of a clouded horizon in motionless attitudes.

They watched the weather and the ship as men on shore watch the momentous chances of fortune. Captain Allistoun never left the deck, as though he had been part of the ship's fittings. Now and then the steward, shivering, but always in shirt sleeves, would struggle towards him with some hot coffee, half of which the gale blew out of the cup before it reached the master's lips. He drank what was left gravely in one long gulp, while heavy sprays pattered loudly on his oilskin coat, the seas swishing broke about his high boots; and he never took his eyes off the ship. He kept his gaze riveted upon her as a loving man watches the unselfish toil of a delicate woman upon the slender thread of whose existence is hung the whole meaning and joy of the world. We all watched her. She was beautiful and had a weakness. We loved her no less for that. We admired her qualities aloud, we boasted of them to one another, as though they had been our own, and the consciousness of her only fault we kept buried in the silence of our profound affection. She was born in the thundering peal of hammers beating upon iron, in black eddies of smoke, under a grey sky, on the banks of the Clyde. The clamorous and sombre steam gives birth to things of beauty that float away into the sunshine of the world to be loved by men. The *Narcissus* was one of the perfect brood. Less perfect than many perhaps, but she was ours, and, consequently, incomparable. We were proud of her. In Bombay, ignorant landlubbers alluded to her as that 'pretty grey ship'. Pretty! A scurvy meed of commendation! We knew she was the most magnificent sea-boat ever launched. We tried to forget that, like many good sea-boats, she was at times rather crank. She was exacting. She wanted care in loading and handling, and no one knew exactly how much care would be enough. Such are the imperfections of mere men! The ship knew, and sometimes would correct the presumptuous human ignorance by the wholesome discipline of fear. We had heard ominous stories about past voyages. The cook (technically a seaman, but in reality no sailor) – the cook, when unstrung by some misfortune, such as the rolling over of a saucepan, would mutter gloomily while he wiped the floor: 'There! Look at what she has done! Some voy'ge she will drown all hands! You'll see if she won't.' To which the steward, snatching in the galley a moment to draw breath in the hurry of his worried life, would remark philosophically: 'Those that see won't tell, anyhow. I don't want to see it.' We derided those fears. Our hearts went out to the old man when he pressed her hard so as to make her hold her own, hold to every inch gained to windward; when he made her, under reefed sails, leap obliquely at enormous waves. The men, knitted together aft into a ready group by the first sharp order of an officer coming to take charge of the deck in bad weather: 'Keep handy the watch,' stood admiring her valiance. Their eyes blinked in the wind; their dark faces were wet with drops of water more salt and bitter than human tears; beards and moustaches, soaked, hung straight and dripping like fine seaweed. They were fantastically misshapen; in high boots, in hats like helmets, and swaying clumsily, stiff and bulky in glistening oilskins, they resembled men strangely equipped for some fabulous adventure. Whenever she rose easily to a towering green sea, elbows dug ribs, faces brightened, lips murmured: 'Didn't she do it cleverly,' and all the heads turning like one watched with sardonic grins the foiled wave go roaring to leeward, white with the foam of a monstrous rage. But when she had not been quick enough and, struck heavily, lay over trembling under the blow, we clutched at ropes, and looking up at the narrow bands of drenched and strained sails waving desperately aloft, we thought in our hearts: 'No wonder. Poor thing!'

The thirty-second day out of Bombay began inauspiciously. In the morning a sea smashed one of the galley doors. We dashed in through lots of steam and found the cook very wet and indignant with the ship: 'She's getting worse every day. She's trying to drown me in front of my own stove!' He was very angry. We pacified him, and the carpenter, though washed away twice from there, managed to repair the door. Through that accident our dinner was not ready till late, but it didn't matter in the end because Knowles, who went to fetch it, got knocked down by a sea and the dinner went over the side. Captain Allistoun, looking more hard and thin-lipped than ever, hung on to full topsails and foresail, and would not notice that the ship, asked to do too much, appeared to lose heart altogether for the first time since we knew her. She refused to rise, and bored her way sullenly through the seas. Twice running, as though she had been blind or weary of life, she put her nose deliberately into a big wave and swept the decks from end to end. As the boatswain observed with marked annoyance, while we were splashing about in a body to try and save a worthless wash-tub: 'Every blooming thing in the ship is going overboard this afternoon.' Venerable Singleton broke his habitual silence and said with a glance aloft: 'The old man's in a temper with the weather, but it's no good bein' angry with the winds of heaven.' Jimmy had shut his door, of course. We knew he was dry and comfortable within his little cabin, and in our absurd way were pleased one moment, exasperated the next, by that certitude. Donkin skulked shameless, uneasy and miserable. He grumbled: 'I'm perishin' with cold outside in bloomin' wet rags, an' that 'ere black sojer sits dry on a blamed chest full of bloomin' clothes; blank his black soul!' We took no notice of him; we hardly gave a thought to Jimmy and his bosom friend. There was no leisure for idle probing of hearts. Sails blew adrift. Things broke loose. Cold and wet, we were washed about the deck while trying to repair damages. The ship tossed about, shaken furiously, like a toy in the hand of a lunatic. Just at sunset there was a rush to shorten sail before the menace of a sombre hail cloud. The hard gust of wind came brutal like the blow of a fist. The ship relieved of her canvas in time received it pluckily: she yielded reluctantly to the violent onset; then, coming up with a stately and irresistible motion, brought her spars to windward in the teeth of the screeching squall. Out of the abysmal darkness of the black cloud overhead white hail streamed on her, rattled on the rigging, leaped in handfuls off the yards, rebounded on the deck – round and gleaming in the murky turmoil like a shower of pearls. It passed away. For a moment a livid sun shot horizontally the last rays of sinister light between the hills of steep, rolling waves. Then a wild night rushed in – stamped out in a great howl that dismal remnant of a stormy day.

There was no sleep on board that night. Most seamen remember in their life one or two such nights of a culminating gale. Nothing seems left of the whole universe but darkness, clamour, fury – and the ship. And like the last vestige of a shattered creation she drifts, bearing an anguished remnant of sinful mankind, through the distress, tumult, and pain of an avenging terror. No one slept in the forecastle. The tin oil-lamp suspended on a long strong, smoking, described wide circles; wet clothing made dark heaps on the glistening floor; a thin layer of water rushed to and fro. In the bed-places men lay booted, resting on elbows and with open eyes. Hung-up suits of oilskin swung out and in, lively and disquieting like reckless ghosts of decapitated seamen dancing in a tempest. No one spoke and all listened. Outside the night moaned and sobbed to the accompaniment of a continuous loud tremor as of innumerable drums beating far off. Shrieks passed through the air. Tremendous dull blows made the ship tremble while she rolled under the weight of the seas toppling on her deck. At times she soared up swiftly as if to leave this earth for ever, then during interminable moments fell through a void with all the hearts on board of her standing still, till a frightful shock, expected and sudden, started them off again with a big thump. After every dislocating jerk of the ship, Wamibo, stretched full length, his face on the pillow, groaned slightly with the pain of his tormented universe. Now and then, for the fraction of an intolerable second, the ship, in the fiercer burst of a terrible uproar, remained on her side, vibrating and still, with a stillness more appalling than the wildest motion. Then upon all those prone bodies a stir would pass, a shiver of suspense. A man would protrude his anxious head and a pair of eyes glistened in the sway of light glaring wildly. Some moved their legs a little as if making ready to jump out. But several, motionless on their backs and with one hand gripping hard the edge of the bunk, smoked nervously with quick puffs, staring upwards; immobilized in a great craving for peace.

At midnight, orders were given to furl the fore and mizen topsails. With immense efforts men crawled aloft through a merciless buffeting, saved the canvas and crawled down almost exhausted, to bear in panting silence the cruel battering of the seas. Perhaps for the first time in the history of the merchant service the watch, told to go below, did not leave the deck, as if compelled to remain there by the fascination of a venomous violence. At every heavy gust men, huddled together, whispered to one another: 'It can blow no harder' – and presently the gale would give them the lie with a piercing shriek, and drive their breath back into their throats. A fierce squall seemed to burst asunder the thick mass of sooty vapours; and above the wrack of torn clouds glimpses could be caught of the high moon rushing backwards with frightful speed over the sky, right into the wind's eye. Many hung their heads, muttering that it 'turned their inwards out' to look at it. Soon the clouds closed up and the world again became a raging, blind darkness that howled, flinging at the lonely ship salt sprays and sleet.

About half past seven the pitchy obscurity round us turned a ghastly grey, and we knew that the sun had risen. This unnatural and threatening daylight, in which we could see one another's wild eyes and drawn faces, was only an added tax on our endurance. The horizon seemed to have come on all sides within arm's length of the ship. Into that narrowed circle furious seas leaped in, struck, and leaped out. A rain of salt, heavy drops flew aslant like mist. The main-topsail had to be goose-winged, and with stolid resignation every one prepared to go aloft once more; but the officers yelled, pushed back, and at last we understood that no more men would be allowed to go on the yard than were absolutely necessary for the work. As at any moment the masts were likely to be jumped out or blown overboard, we concluded that the captain didn't want to see all his crowd go over the side at once. That was reasonable. The watch then on duty, led by Mr Creighton, began to struggle up the rigging. The wind flattened them against the ratlines; then, easing a little, would let them ascend a couple of steps; and again, with a sudden gust, pin all up the shrouds the whole crawling line in attitudes of crucifixion. The other watch plunged down on the main deck to haul up the sail. Men's heads bobbed up as the water flung them irresistibly from side to side. Mr Baker grunted encouragingly in our midst, spluttering and blowing amongst the tangled ropes like an energetic porpoise. Favoured by an ominous and untrustworthy lull, the work was done without anyone being lost either off the deck or from the yard. For the moment the gale seemed to take off, and the ship, as if grateful for our efforts, plucked up heart and made better weather of it.

At eight the men off duty, watching their chance, ran forward over the flooded deck to get some rest. The other half of the crew remained aft for their turn of 'seeing her through her trouble', as they expressed it. The two mates urged the master to go below. Mr Baker grunted in his ear: 'Ough! surely now . . . Ough! . . . confidence in us . . . nothing more to do . . . she must lay it out or go. Ough! Ough!' Tall young Mr Creighton smiled down at him cheerfully: '. . . She's as right as a trivet! Take a spell, sir.' He looked at them stonily with bloodshot, sleepless eyes. The rims of his eyelids were scarlet, and he moved his jaw unceasingly with a slow effort, as though he had been masticating a lump of india-rubber. He shook his head. He repeated: 'Never mind me. I must see it out – I must see it out,' but he consented to sit down for a moment on the skylight, with his hard face turned unflinchingly to windward. The sea spat at it – and stoical, it streamed with water as though he had been weeping. On the weather side of the poop the watch, hanging on to the mizen rigging and to one another, tried to exchange encouraging words. Singleton, at the wheel, yelled out: 'Look out for yourselves!' His voice reached them in a warning whisper. They were startled.

A big, foaming sea came out of the mist; it made for the ship, roaring wildly, and in its rush it looked as mischievous and discomposing as a madman with an axe. One or two, shouting, scrambled up the rigging; most, with a convulsive catch of the breath, held on where they stood. Singleton dug his knees under the wheel-box, and carefully eased the helm to the headlong pitch of ship, but without taking his eyes off the coming wave. It towered close-to and high, like a wall of green glass topped with snow. The ship rose to it as though she had soared on wings, and for a moment rested poised upon the foaming crest as if she had been a great sea-bird. Before we could draw breath a heavy gust struck her, another roller took her unfairly under the weather bow, she gave a toppling lurch, and filled her decks. Captain Allistoun leaped up, and fell; Archie rolled over him, screaming: 'She will rise!' She gave another lurch to leeward; the lower deadeyes dipped heavily; the men's feet flew from under them, and they hung kicking above the slanting poop. They could see the ship putting her side in the water, and shouted all together: 'She's going!' Forward the forecastle doors flew open, and the watch below were seen leaping out one after another, throwing their arms up; and, falling on hands and knees, scrambled aft on all fours along the high side of the deck, sloping more than the roof of a house. From leeward the seas rose, pursuing them; they looked wretched in a hopeless struggle, like vermin fleeing before a flood; they fought up the weather ladder of the poop one after another, half naked and staring wildly; and as soon as they got up they shot to leeward in clusters, with closed eyes, till they brought up heavily with their ribs against the iron stanchions of the rail; then, groaning, they rolled in a confused mass. The immense volume of water thrown forward by the last scend of the ship had burst the lee door of the forecastle. They could see their chests, pillows, blankets, clothing, come out floating upon the sea. While they struggled back to windward they looked in dismay. The straw beds swam high, the blankets, spread out, undulated; while the chests, waterlogged and with a heavy list, pitched heavily like dismasted hulks, before they sank; Archie's big coat passed with outspread arms, resembling a drowned seaman floating with his head under water. Men were slipping down while trying to dig their fingers into the planks; others, jammed in corners, rolled enormous eyes. They all yelled unceasingly: 'The masts! Cut! Cut! . . .' A black squall howled low over the ship, that lay on her side with the weather yard-arms pointing to the clouds; while the tall masts, inclined nearly to the horizon, seemed to be of an immeasurable length. The carpenter let go his hold, rolled against the skylight, and began to crawl to the cabin entrance, where a big axe was kept ready for just such an emergency. At that moment the topsail sheet parted, the end of the heavy chain racketed aloft, and sparks of red fire streamed down through the flying sprays. The sail flapped once with a jerk that seemed to tear our hearts out through our teeth, and instantly changed into a bunch of fluttering narrow ribbons that tied themselves into knots and became quiet along the yard. Captain Allistoun struggled, managed to stand up with his face near the deck, upon which men swung on the ends of ropes, like nest robbers upon a cliff. One of his feet was on somebody's chest; his face was purple; his lips moved. He yelled also; he yelled, bending down: 'No! No!' Mr Baker, one leg over the binnacle-stand, roared out: 'Did you say no? Not cut?' He shook his head madly. 'No! No!' Between his legs the crawling carpenter heard, collapsed at once, and lay full length in the angle of the skylight. Voices took up the shout – 'No! No!' Then all became still. They waited for the ship to turn over altogether, and shake them out into the sea; and upon the terrific noise of wind and sea not a murmur of remonstrance came out from those men, who each would have given ever so many years of life to see 'then damned sticks go overboard!' They all believed it their only chance; but a little hard-faced man shook his grey head and shouted 'No!' without giving them as much as a glance. They were silent, and gasped. They gripped rails, they had wound ropes'-ends under their arms; they clutched ringbolts, they crawled in heaps where there was foothold; they held on with both arms, hooked themselves to anything to windward with elbows, with chins, almost with their teeth: and some, unable to crawl away from where they had been flung, felt the sea leap up, striking against their backs as they struggled upwards. Singleton had stuck to the wheel. His hair flew out in the wind; the gale seemed to take its life-long adversary by the beard and shake his old head. He wouldn't let go, and, with his knees forced between the spokes, flew up and down like a man on a bough. As Death appeared unready, they began to look about. Donkin, caught by one foot in a loop of some rope, hung, head down, below us, and yelled, with his face to the deck: 'Cut! Cut!' Two men lowered themselves cautiously to him; others hauled on the rope. They caught him up, shoved him into a safer place, held him. He shouted curses at the master, shook his fist at him with horrible blasphemies, called upon us in filthy words to 'Cut! Don't mind that murdering fool! Cut, some of you!' One of his rescuers struck him a back-handed blow over the mouth; his head banged on the deck, and he became suddenly very quiet, with a white face, breathing hard, and with a few drops of blood trickling from his cut lip. On the lee side another man could be seen stretched out as if stunned; only the washboard prevented him from going over the side. It was the steward. We had to sling him up like a bale for he was paralysed with fright. He had rushed up out of the pantry when he felt the ship go over, and had rolled down helplessly, clutching a china mug. It was not broken. With difficulty we tore it away from him, and when he saw it in our hands he was amazed. 'Where did you get that thing?' he kept on asking us in a trembling voice. His shirt was blown to shreds; the ripped sleeves flapped like wings. Two men made him fast, and, doubled over the rope that held him, he resembled a bundle of wet rags. Mr Baker crawled along the line of men, asking: 'Are you all there?' and looking them over. Some blinked vacantly, others shook convulsively; Wamibo's head hung over his breast; and in painful attitudes, cut by lashings, exhausted with clutching, screwed up in corners, they breathed heavily. Their lips twitched, and at every sickening heave of the overturned ship they opened them wide as if to shout. The cook, embracing a wooden stanchion, unconsciously repeated a prayer. In every short interval of the fiendish noises around he could be heard there, without cap or slippers, imploring in that storm that Master of our lives not to lead him into temptation. Soon he also became silent. In all that crowd of cold and hungry men, waiting wearily for a violent death, not a voice was heard; they were mute, and in sombre thoughtfulness listened to the horrible imprecations of the gale.

Hours passed. They were sheltered by the heavy inclination of the ship from the wind that rushed in one long unbroken moan above their heads, but cold rain showers fell at times into the uneasy calm of their refuge. Under the torment of that new infliction a pair of shoulders would writhe a little. Teeth chattered. The sky was clearing, and bright sunshine gleamed over the ship. After every burst of battering seas, vivid and fleeting rainbows arched over the drifting hull in the flick of sprays. The gale was ending in a clear blow, which gleamed and cut like a knife. Between two bearded shellbacks Charley, fastened with somebody's long muffler to a deck ring-bolt, wept quietly, with rare tears wrung out by bewilderment, cold, hunger, and general misery. One of his neighbours punched him in the ribs asking roughly: 'What's the matter with your cheek? In fine weather there's no holding you, youngster.' Turning about with prudence he worked himself out of his coat and threw it over the boy. The other man closed up, muttering: ' 'Twill make a bloomin' man of you, sonny.' They flung their arms over and pressed against him. Charley drew his feet up and his eyelids dropped. Sighs were heard, as men, perceiving that they were not to be 'drowned in a hurry,' tried easier positions. Mr Creighton, who had hurt his leg, lay amongst us with compressed lips. Some fellows belonging to his watch set about securing him better. Without a word or a glance he lifted his arms one after another to facilitate the operation, and not a muscle moved in his stern, young face. They asked him with solicitude: 'Easier now, sir?' He answered with a curt: 'That'll do.' He was a hard young officer, but many of his watch used to say they liked him well enough because he had 'such a gentlemanly way of damning us up and down the deck'. Others unable to discern such fine shades of refinement, respected him for his smartness. For the first time since the ship had gone on her beam ends Captain Allistoun gave a short glance down at his men. He was almost upright – one foot against the side of the skylight, one knee on the deck; and with the end of the vang round his waist swung back and forth with his gaze fixed ahead, watchful, like a man looking out for a sign. Before his eyes the ship, with half her deck below water, rose and fell on heavy seas that rushed from under her flashing in the cold sunshine. We began to think she was wonderfully buoyant – considering. Confident voices were heard shouting: 'She'll do, boys!' Belfast exclaimed with fervour: 'I would giv' a month's pay for a draw at a pipe!' One or two, passing dry tongues on their salt lips, muttered something about a 'drink of water'. The cook, as if inspired, scrambled up with his breast against the poop water-cask and looked in. There was a little at the bottom. He yelled, waving his arms, and two men began to crawl backwards and forwards with the mug. We had a good mouthful all round. The master shook his head impatiently, refusing. When it came to Charley one of his neighbours shouted: 'That bloomin' boy's asleep.' He slept as though he had been dosed with narcotics. They let him be. Singleton held to the wheel with one hand while he drank, bending down to shelter his lips from the wind. Wamibo had to be poked and yelled at before he saw the mug held before his eyes. Knowles said sagaciously: 'It's better'n a tot o' rum.' Mr Baker grunted: 'Thank ye.' Mr Creighton drank and nodded. Donkin gulped greedily, glaring over the rim. Belfast made us laugh when with grimacing mouth he shouted: 'Pass it this way. We're all taytottlers here.' The master, presented with the mug again by a crouching man, who screamed up at him: 'We all had a drink, captain,' groped for it without ceasing to look ahead, and handed it back stiffly as though he could not spare half a glance away from the ship. Faces brightened. We shouted to the cook: 'Well done, doctor!' He sat to leeward, propped by the water-cask and yelled back abundantly, but the seas were breaking in thunder just then, and we only caught snatches that sounded like: 'Providence' and 'born again'. He was at his old game of preaching. We made friendly but derisive gestures at him, and from below he lifted one arm, holding on with the other, moved his lips; he beamed up to us, straining his voice – earnest, and ducking his head before the sprays.

Suddenly someone cried: 'Where's Jimmy?' and we were appalled once more. On the end of the row the boatswain shouted hoarsely: 'Has anyone seed him come out?' Voices exclaimed dismally: 'Drowned – is he? . . . No! In his cabin! . . . Good Lord! . . . Caught like a bloomin' rat in a trap. . . . Couldn't open his door . . . Aye! She went over too quick and the water jammed it . . . Poor beggar! . . . No help fo r 'im. . . . Let's go and see . . .' 'Damn him, who could go?' screamed Donkin. 'Nobody expects you to,' growled the man next to him: 'you're only a thing.' 'Is there half a chance to get at 'im?' inquired two or three men together. Belfast untied himself with blind impetuosity, and all at once shot down to leeward quicker than a flash of lightning. We shouted all together with dismay; but with his legs overboard he held and yelled for a rope. In our extremity nothing could be terrible; so we judged him funny kicking there, and with his scared face. Someone began to laugh, and, as if hysterically infected with screaming merriment, all those haggard men went off laughing, wild-eyed, like a lot of maniacs tied up on a wall. Mr Baker swung off the binnacle-stand and tendered him one leg. He scrambled up rather scared, and consigning us with abominable words to the 'divvle'. 'You are. . . . Ough! You're a foul-mouthed beggar, Craik,' grunted Mr Baker. He answered, stuttering with indignation: 'Look at 'em, sorr. The bloomin' dirty images! Laughing at a chum going overboard. Call themselves men, too.' But from the break of the poop the boatswain called out: 'Come along,' and Belfast crawled away in a hurry to join him. The five men, poised and gazing over the edge of the poop, looked for the best way to get forward. They seemed to hesitate. The others, twisting in their lashings, turning painfully, stared with open lips. Captain Allistoun saw nothing; he seemed with his eyes to hold the ship up in a superhuman concentration of effort. The wind screamed loud in sunshine; columns of spray rose straight up; and in the glitter of rainbows bursting over the trembling hull the men went over cautiously, disappearing from sight with deliberate movements. They went swinging from belaying pin to cleat above the seas that beat the half-submerged deck. Their toes scraped the planks. Lumps of green cold water toppled over the bulwark and on their heads. They hung for a moment on strained arms, with the breath knocked out of them, and with closed eyes – then, letting go with one hand, balanced with lolling heads, trying to grab some rope or stanchion further forward. The long-armed and athletic boatswain swung quickly, gripping things with a fist hard as iron, and remembering suddenly snatches of the last letter from his 'old woman'. Little Belfast scrambled in a rage spluttering 'cursed nigger'. Wamibo's tongue hung out with excitement; and Archie, intrepid and calm, watched his chance to move with intelligent coolness.

When above the side of the house, they let go one after another, and falling heavily, sprawled, pressing their palms to the smooth teak wood. Round them the backwash of waves seethed white and hissing. All the doors had become trapdoors, of course. The first was the galley door. The galley extended from side to side, and they could hear the sea splashing with hollow noises in there. The next door was that of the carpenter's shop. They lifted it, and looked down. The room seemed to have been devastated by an earthquake. Everything in it had tumbled on the bulkhead facing the door, and on the other side of that bulkhead there was Jimmy, dead or alive. The bench, a half-finished meat-safe, saws, chisels, wire rods, axes, crowbars, lay in a heap besprinkled with loose nails. A sharp adze stuck up with a shining edge that gleamed dangerously down there like a wicked smile. The men clung to one another peering. A sickening, sly lurch of the ship nearly sent them overboard in a body. Belfast howled 'Here goes!' and leaped down. Archie followed cannily, catching at shelves that gave way with him, and eased himself in a great crash of ripped wood. There was hardly room for three men to move. And in the sunshiny blue square of the door, the boatswain's face, bearded and dark, Wamibo's face, wild and pale, hung over – watching.

Together they shouted: 'Jimmy! Jim!' From above the boatswain contributed a deep growl: 'You . . . Wait!' In a pause, Belfast entreated: 'Jimmy, darlin', are ye aloive?' The boatswain said: 'Again! All together, boys!' All yelled excitedly. Wamibo made noises resembling loud barks. Belfast drummed on the side of the bulkhead with a piece of iron. All ceased suddenly. The sound of screaming and hammering went on thin and distinct – like a solo after a chorus. He was alive. He was screaming and knocking below us with the hurry of a man prematurely shut up in a coffin. We went to work. We attacked with desperation the abominable heap of things heavy, of things sharp, of things clumsy to handle. The boatswain crawled away to find somewhere a flying end of a rope; and Wamibo, held back by shouts: 'Don't jump! . . . Don't come in here, muddle-head!' – remained glaring above us – all shining eyes, gleaming fangs, tumbled hair; resembling an amazed and half-witted fiend gloating over the extraordinary agitation of the damned. The boatswain adjured us to 'bear a hand', and a rope descended. We made things fast to it and they went up spinning, never to be seen by man again. A rage to fling things overboard possessed us. We worked fiercely, cutting our hands and speaking brutally to one another. Jimmy kept up a distracting row; he screamed piercingly, without drawing breath, like a tortured woman; he banged with hands and feet. The agony of his fear wrung our hearts so terribly that we longed to abandon him, to get out of that place deep as a well and swaying like a tree, to get out of his hearing, back on the poop where we could wait passively for death in incomparable repose. We shouted to him to 'shut up, for God's sake'. He redoubled his cries. He must have fancied we could not hear him. Probably he heard his own clamour but faintly. We could picture him crouching on the edge of the upper berth, letting out with both fists at the wood, in the dark, and with his mouth wide open for that unceasing cry. Those were loathsome moments. A cloud driving across the sun would darken the doorway menacingly. Every movement of the ship was pain. We scrambled about with no room to breathe, and felt frightfully sick. The boatswain yelled down at us: 'Bear a hand! Bear a hand! We two will be washed away from here directly if you ain't quick!' Three times a sea leaped over the high side and flung bucketfuls of water on our heads. Then Jimmy, startled by the shock, would stop his noise for a moment – waiting for the ship to sink, perhaps – and began again, distressingly loud, as if invigorated by the gust of fear. At the bottom the nails lay in a layer several inches thick. It was ghastly. Every nail in the world, not driven in firmly somewhere, seemed to have found its way into that carpenter's shop. There they were, of all kinds, the remnants of stores from seven voyages. Tin-tacks, copper tacks (sharp as needles), pump nails, with big heads, like tiny iron mushrooms; nails without any heads (horrible); French nails polished and slim. They lay in a solid mass more inabordable than a hedgehog. We hesitated, yearning for a shovel, while Jimmy below us yelled as though he had been flayed. Groaning, we dug our fingers in, and very much hurt, shook our hands, scattering nails and drops of blood. We passed up our hats full of assorted nails to the boatswain, who, as if performing a mysterious and appeasing rite, cast them wide upon a raging sea.

We got to the bulkhead at last. Those were stout planks. She was a ship, well finished in every detail – the *Narcissus* was. They were the stoutest planks every put into a ship's bulkhead – we thought – and then we perceived that, in our hurry, we had sent all the tools overboard. Absurd little Belfast wanted to break it down with his own weight, and with both feet leaped straight up like a springbok, cursing the Clyde shipwrights for not scamping their work. Incidentally he reviled all North Britain, the rest of the earth, the sea – and all his companions. He swore, as he alighted heavily on his heels, that he would never, never any more associate with any fool that 'hadn't saveee enough to know his knee from his elbow'. He managed by his thumping to scare the last remnant of wits out of Jimmy. We could hear the object of our exasperated solicitude darting to and fro under the planks. He had cracked his voice at last, and could only squeak miserably. His back or else his head rubbed the planks, now here, now there, in a puzzling manner. He squeaked as he dodged the invisible blows. It was more heartrending even than his yells. Suddenly Archie produced a crowbar. He had kept it back; also a small hatchet. We howled with satisfaction. He struck a mighty blow and small chips flew at our eyes. The boatswain above shouted: 'Look out! Look out there. Don't kill the man. Easy does it!' Wamibo, maddened with excitement, hung head down and insanely urged us: 'Hoo! Strook 'im! Hoo! Hoo!' We were afraid he would fall in and kill one of us and, hurriedly, we entreated the boatswain to 'shove the blamed Finn overboard'. Then, all together, we yelled down at the planks: 'Stand from under! Get forward,' and listened. We only heard the deep hum and moan of the wind above us, the mingled roar and hiss of the seas. The ship, as if overcome with despair, wallowed lifelessly, and our heads swam with that unnatural motion. Belfast clamoured: 'For the love of God, Jimmy, where are ye? . . . Knock! Jimmy darlint! . . . Knock! You bloody black beast! Knock!' He was as quiet as a dead man inside a grave; and, like men standing above a grace, we were on the verge of tears – but with vexation, the strain, the fatigue; with the great longing to be done with it, to get away, and lay down to rest somewhere where we could see our danger and breathe. Archie shouted: 'Gi'e me room!' We crouched behind him, guarding our heads, and he struck time after time in the joint of planks. They cracked. Suddenly the crowbar went half-way in through a splintered oblong hole. It must have missed Jimmy's head by less than an inch. Archie withdrew it quickly, and that infamous nigger rushed at the hole, put his lips to it, and whispered 'Help' in an almost extinct voice; he pressed his head to it, trying madly to get out through that opening one inch wide and three inches long. In our disturbed state we were absolutely paralysed by his incredible action. It seemed impossible to drive him away. Even Archie at last lost his composure. 'If ye don't clear oot I'll drive the crowbar thro' your head,' he shouted in a determined voice. He meant what he said, and his earnestness seemed to make an impression on Jimmy. He disappeared suddenly, and we set to prising and tearing at the planks with the eagerness of men trying to get at a mortal enemy, and spurred by the desire to tear him limb from limb. The wood split, cracked, gave way. Belfast plunged in head and shoulders and groped viciously. 'I've got 'im! Got 'im,' he shouted. 'Oh! There! . . . He's gone; I've got 'im! . . . Pull at my legs! . . . Pull!' Wamibo hooted unceasingly. The boatswain shouted directions: 'Catch hold of his hair, Belfast; pull straight up, you two! . . . Pull fair!' We pulled fair. We pulled Belfast out with a jerk, and dropped him with disgust. In a sitting posture, purple-faced, he sobbed despairingly: 'How can I hold on to 'is blooming short wool?' Suddenly Jimmy's head and shoulders appeared. He stuck half-way, and with rolling eyes foamed at our feet. We flew at him with brutal impatience, we tore the shirt off his back, we tugged at his ears, we panted over him; and all at once he came away in our hands as though somebody had let go his legs. With the same movement, without a pause we swung him up. His breath whistled, he kicked our upturned faces, he grasped two pairs of arms above his head, and he squirmed up with such precipitation that he seemed positively to escape from our hands like a bladder full of gas. Streaming with perspiration, we swarmed up the rope, and, coming into the blast of cold wind, gasped like men plunged into icy water. With burning faces we shivered to the very marrow of our bones. Never before had the gale seemed to us more furious, the sea more mad, the sunshine more merciless and mocking, and the position of the ship more hopeless and appalling. Every movement of her was ominous of the end of her agony and of the beginning of ours. We staggered away from the door, and, alarmed by a sudden roll, fell down in a bunch. It appeared to us that the side of the house was more smooth than glass and more slippery than ice. There was nothing to hang on to but a long brass hook used sometimes to keep back an open door. Wamibo held on to it and we held on to Wamibo, clutching our Jimmy. He had completely collapsed now. He did not seem to have the strength to close his hand. We stuck to him blindly in our fear. We were not afraid of Wamibo letting go (we remembered that the brute was stronger than any three men in the ship), but we were afraid of the hook giving way, and we also believed that the ship had made up her mind to turn over at last. But she didn't. A sea swept over us. The boatswain spluttered: 'Up and away. There's a lull. Away aft with you, or we will all go to the devil here.' We stood up surrounding Jimmy. We begged him to hold up, to hold on, at least. He glared with his bulging eyes, mute as a fish, and with all the stiffening knocked out of him. He wouldn't stand; he wouldn't even as much as clutch at our necks; he was only a cold black skin loosely stuffed with soft cotton wool; his arms and legs swung jointless and pliable; his head rolled about; the lower lip hung down, enormous and heavy. We pressed round him, bothered and dismayed; sheltering him we swung here and there in a body; and on the very brink of eternity we tottered all together with concealing and absurd gestures, like a lot of drunken men embarrassed with a stolen corpse.

Something had to be done. We had to get him aft. A rope was tied slack under his armpits, and, reaching up at the risk of our lives, we hung him on the foresheet cleet. He emitted no sound; he looked as ridiculously lamentable as a doll that had lost half its sawdust, and we started on our perilous journey over the main deck, dragging along with care that pitiful, that limp, that hateful burden. He was not very heavy, but had he weighed a ton he could not have been more awkward to handle. We literally passed him from hand to hand. Now and then we had to hang him up on a handy belaying-pin, to draw a breath and re-form the line. Had the pin broken he would have irretrievably gone into the Southern Ocean, but he had to take his chance of that; and after a little while, becoming apparently aware of it, he groaned slightly, and with a great effort whispered a few words. We listened eagerly. He was reproaching us with our carelessness in letting him run such risks: 'Now, after I got myself out from there,' he breathed out weakly. 'There' was his cabin. And he got himself out. We had nothing to do with it apparently! . . . No matter. . . . We went on and let him take his chances, simply because we could not help it; for though at that time we hated him more than ever – more than anything under heaven – we did not want to lose him. We had so far saved him; and it had become a personal matter between us and the sea. We meant to stick to him. Had we (by an incredible hypothesis) undergone similar toil and trouble for an empty cask, that cask would have become as precious to us as Jimmy was. More precious, in fact, because we would have had no reason to hate the cask. And we hated James Wait. We could not get rid of the monstrous suspicion that this astounding black-man was shamming sick, had been malingering heartlessly in the face of our toil, of our scorn, of our patience – and now was malingering in the face of our devotion – in the face of death. Our vague and imperfect morality rose with disgust at his unmanly lie. But he stuck to it manfully – amazingly. No! It couldn't be. He was at all extremity. His cantankerous temper was only the result of the provoking invincibleness of that death he felt by his side. Any man may be angry with such a masterful chum. But, then, what kind of men were we – with our thoughts! Indignation and doubt grappled within us in a scuffle that trampled upon the finest of our feelings. And we hated him because of the suspicion; we detested him because of the doubt. We could not scorn him safely – neither could we pity him without risk to our dignity. So we hated him, and passed him carefully from hand to hand. We cried, 'Got him?' 'Yes. All right. let go.' And he swung from one enemy to another, showing about as much of life as an old bolster would do. His eyes made two narrow white slits in the black face. The air escaped through his lips with a noise like the sound of bellows. We reached the poop ladder at last, and it being a comparatively safe place, we lay for a moment in an exhausted heap to rest a little. He began to mutter. We were always incurably anxious to hear what he had to say. This time he mumbled peevishly, 'It took you some time to come. I began to think the whole smart lot of you had been washed overboard. What kept you back? Hey? Funk?' We said nothing. With sighs we started again to drag him up. The secret and ardent desire of our hearts was the desire to beat him viciously with our fists about the head; and we handled him as tenderly as though he had been made of glass. . . .

The return on the poop was like the return of wanderers after many years amongst people marked by the desolation of time. Eyes were turned slowly in their sockets glancing at us. Faint murmurs were heard, 'Have you got 'im after all?' The well-known faces looked strange and familiar; they seemed faded and grimy; they had a mingled expression of fatigue and eagerness. They seemed to have become much thinner during our absence, as if all these men had been starving for a long time in their abandoned attitudes. The captain, with a round turn of a rope on his wrist, and kneeling on one knee, swung with a face cold and stiff; but with living eyes he was still holding the ship up, heeding no one, as if lost in the unearthly effort of that endeavour. We fastened up James Wait in a safe place. Mr Baker scrambled along to lend a hand. Mr Creighton, on his back, and very pale, muttered, 'Well done,' and gave us, Jimmy, and the sky, a scornful glance, then closed his eyes slowly. Here and there a man stirred a little, but most of them remained apathetic, in cramped positions, muttering between shivers. The sun was setting. A sun enormous, unclouded and red, declining low as if bending down to look into their faces. The wind whistled across long sunbeams that, resplendent and cold, struck full on the dilated pupils of staring eyes without making them wink. The wisps of hair and the tangled beards were grey with the salt of the sea. The faces were earthy, and the dark patches under the eyes extended to the ears, smudged into the hollows of sunken cheeks. The lips were livid and thin, and when they moved it was with difficulty, as though they had been glued to the teeth. Some grinned sadly in the sunlight, shaking with cold. Others were sad and still. Charley, subdued by the sudden disclosure of the insignificance of his youth, darted fearful glances. The two smooth-faced Norwegians resembled decrepit children, staring stupidly. To leeward, on the edge of the horizon, black seas leaped up towards the glowing sun. It sank slowly, round and blazing, and the crests of waves splashed on the edge of the luminous circle. One of the Norwegians appeared to catch sight of it, and, after giving a violent start, began to speak. His voice, startling the others, made them stir. They moved their heads stiffly, or turning with difficulty, looked at him with surprise, with fear, or in grave silence. He chattered at the setting sun, nodding his head, while the big seas began to roll across the crimson disc; and over miles of turbulent waters the shadows of high waves swept with a running darkness the faces of men. A crested roller broke with a loud hissing roar, and the sun, as if put out, disappeared. The chattering voice faltered, went out together with the light. There were sighs. in the sudden lull that follows the crash of a broken sea a man said wearily, 'Here's that blooming Dutchman gone off his chump.' A seaman, lashed by the middle, tapped the deck with his open hand with unceasing quick flaps. In the gathering greyness of twilight a bulky form was seen rising aft, and began marching on all fours with the movements of some big cautious beast. It was Mr Baker passing along the line of men. He grunted encouragingly over every one, felt their fastenings. Some, with half-open eyes, puffed like men oppressed by heat; others mechanically and in dreamy voices answered him, 'Aye! aye! sir!' He went from one to another grunting, 'Ough! . . . See her through it yet'; and unexpectedly, with loud angry outbursts, blew up Knowles for cutting off a long piece from the fall of the relieving tackle. 'Ough! . . . Ashamed of yourself . . . Relieving tackle . . . Don't you know better! . . . Ough! . . . Able seaman! Ough!' The lame man was crushed. He muttered, 'Get som'think for a lashing for myself, sir.' 'Ough! Lashing . . . yourself. Are you a tinker or a sailor . . . What? Ough! . . . May want that tackle directly. . . . Ough! . . . More use to the ship than your lame carcass. Ough! . . . Keep it! . . . Keep it, now you've done it.' He crawled away slowly, muttering to himself about some men being 'worse than children'. It had been a comforting row. Low exclamations were heard: 'Hallo . . . Hallo.' . . . Those who had been painfully dozing asked with convulsive starts, 'What's up? . . . What is it?' The answers came with unexpected cheerfulness: 'The mate is going bald-headed for lame Jack about something or other' – 'No!' – 'What 'as he done?' Someone even chuckled. It was like a whiff of hope, like a reminder of safe days. Donkin, who had been stupefied with fear, revived suddenly and began to shout: ' 'Ear 'im; that's the way they tawlk to us. Vy donch 'ee 'it 'im – one ov yer? 'It 'im. 'It 'im! Comin' the mate over us. We are as good men as 'ee! We're all goin' to 'ell now. We 'ave been starved in this rotten ship, an' now we're goin' to be drowned for them black 'earted bullies! 'It 'im!' He shrieked in the deepening gloom, he blubbered and sobbed, screaming: ' 'It 'im! 'It 'im!' The rage and fear of his disregarded right to live tried the steadfastness of hearts more than the menacing shadows of the night that advanced through the unceasing clamour of the gale. From aft Mr Baker was heard: 'Is one of you men going to stop him – must I come along?' 'Shut up!' . . . 'Keep quiet!' cried various voices, exasperated, trembling with cold. 'You'll get one across the mug from me directly,' said an invisible seaman, in a weary tone. 'I won't let the mate have the trouble.' He ceased and lay still with the silence of despair. On the black sky the stars, coming out, gleamed over an inky sea that, speckled with foam, flashed back at them the evanescent and pale light of a dazzling whiteness born from the black turmoil of the waves. Remote in the eternal calm they glittered hard and cold above the uproar of the earth; they surrounded the vanquished and tormented ship on all sides; more pitiless than the eyes of a triumphant mob, and as unapproachable as the hearts of men.

The icy south wind howled exultingly under the sombre splendour of the sky. The cold shook the men with a resistless violence as though it had tried to shake them to pieces. Short moans were swept unheard off the stiff lips. Some complained in mutters of 'not feeling themselves below the waist'; while those who had closed their eyes, imagined they had a block of ice on their chests. Others, alarmed at not feeling any pain in their fingers, beat the deck feebly with their hands – obstinate and exhausted. Wamibo stared vacant and dreamy. The Scandinavians kept on a meaningless mutter through chattering teeth. The spare Scotchmen, with determined efforts, kept their lower jaws still. The West-country men lay big and stolid in an invulnerable surliness. A man yawned and swore in turns. Another breathed with a rattle in his throat. Two elderly hardweather shellbacks, fast side by side, whispered dismally to one another about the landlady of a boarding-house in Sunderland, whom they both knew. They extolled her motherliness and her liberality; they tried to talk about the joint of beef and the big fire in the downstairs kitchen. The words dying faintly on their lips, ended in light sighs. A sudden voice cried into the cold night, 'Oh Lord!' No one changed his position or took any notice of the cry. One or two passed, with a repeated and vague gesture, their hand over their faces, but most of them kept very still. In the benumbed immobility of their bodies they were excessively wearied by their thoughts, which rushed with the rapidity and vividness of dreams. Now and then, by an abrupt and startling exclamation, they answered the weird hail of some illusion; then, again, in silence contemplated the vision of known faces and familiar things. They recalled the aspect of forgotten shipmates and heard the voice of dead and gone skippers. They remembered the noise of gaslit streets, the steamy heat of tap-rooms or the scorching sunshine of calm days at sea.

Mr Baker left his insecure place, and crawled, with stoppages, along the poop. In the dark and on all fours he resembled some carnivorous animal prowling amongst corpses. At the break, propped to windward of a stachion, he looked down on the main deck. It seemed to him that the ship had a tendency to stand up a little more. The wind had eased a little, he thought, but the sea ran as high as ever. The waves foamed viciously, and the lee side of the deck disappeared under a hissing whiteness as of boiling milk, while the rigging sang steadily with a deep vibrating note, and, at every upward swing of the ship, the wind rushed with a long-drawn clamour amongst the spars. Mr Baker watched very still. A man near him began to make a blabbing noise with his lips, all at once and very loud, as though the cold had broken brutally through him. He went on: 'Ba – ba – ba – brrr – brr – ba – ba.' 'Stop that!' cried Mr Baker, groping in the dark. 'Stop it!' He went on shaking the leg he found under his hand. 'What is it, sir?' called out Belfast, in the tone of a man awakened suddenly; 'we are looking after that 'ere Jimmy.' 'Are you? Ough! Don't make that row then. Who's that near you?' 'It's me – the boatswain, sir,' growled the West-country man; 'we are trying to keep life in that poor devil.' Aye, aye!' said Mr Baker. 'Do it quietly, can't you.' 'He wants us to hold him up above the rail,' went on the boatswain, with irritation, 'says he can't breathe here under our jackets.' 'If we lift 'im, we drop 'im overboard,' said another voice, 'we can't feel our hands with cold.' 'I don't care. I am choking!' exclaimed James Wait in a clear tone. 'Oh, no, my son,' said the boatswain, desperately, 'you don't go till we all go on this fine night.' 'You will see yet many a worse,' said Mr Baker, cheerfully. 'It's no child's play, sir!' answered the boatswain. 'Some of us further aft, here, are in a pretty bad way.' 'If the blamed sticks had been cut out of her she would be running along on her bottom now like any decent ship, an' giv' us all a chance,' said someone, with a sigh. 'The old man wouldn't have it . . . much he cares for us,' whispered another. 'Care for you!' exclaimed Mr Baker, angrily. 'Why should he care for you? Are you a lot of women passengers to be taken care of? We are here to take care of the ship – and some of you ain't up to that. Ough! . . . What have you done so very smart to be taken care of? Ough! . . . Some of you can't stand a bit of a breeze without crying over it.' 'Come, sorr. We ain't so bad,' protested Belfast, in a voice shaken by shivers; 'we ain't . . . brrr . . .' 'Again,' shouted the mate, grabbing at the shadowy form; 'again! . . . Why, you're in your shirt! What have you done?' 'I've put my oilskin and jacket over that half-dead nayggur – and he says he chokes,' said Belfast, complainingly. 'You wouldn't call me nigger if I wasn't half dead, you Irish beggar!' boomed James Wait, vigorously. 'You . . . brrr . . . You wouldn't be white if you were ever so well . . . I will fight you . . . brrrr . . . in fine weather . . . brrr . . . with one hand tied behind my back . . . brrrrrr . . .' 'I don't want your rags – I want air,' gasped out the other faintly, as if suddenly exhausted.

The sprays swept over whistling and pattering. Men disturbed in their peaceful torpor by the pain of quarrelsome shouts, moaned, muttering curses.

Mr Baker crawled off a little way to leeward where a watercask loomed up big, with something white against it. 'Is it you, Podmore?' asked Mr Baker. He had to repeat the question twice before the cook turned, coughing feebly. 'Yes, sir. I've been praying in my mind for a quick deliverance; for I am prepared for any call. . . . I—' 'Look here, cook,' interrupted Mr Baker, 'the men are perishing with cold.' 'Cold!' said the cook, mournfully; 'they will be warm enough before long.' 'What?' asked Mr Baker, looking along the deck into the faint sheen of frothing water. 'They are a wicked lot,' continued the cook solemnly, but in an unsteady voice, 'about as wicked as any ship's company in this sinful world! Now, I' – he trembled so that he could hardly speak; his was an exposed place, and in a cotton shirt, a thin pair of trousers, and with his knees under his nose, he received, quaking, the flicks of stinging, salt drops; his voice sounded exhausted – 'now, I – any time . . . My eldest youngster, Mr Baker . . . a clever boy . . . last Sunday on shore before this voyage he wouldn't go to church, sir. Says I, "You go and clean yourself, or I'll know the reason why!" What does he do? . . . Pond Mr Baker – fell into the pond in his best rig, sir! . . . Accident? . . . "Nothing will save you, fine scholar though you are!" says I. . . . Accident! . . . I whopped him, sir, till I couldn't lift my arm. . . .' His voice faltered. 'I whopped 'im!' he repeated, rattling his teeth; then, after a while, let out a mournful sound that was half a groan, half a snore. Mr Baker shook him by the shoulders. 'Hey! Cook! Hold up, Podmore! Tell me – is there any fresh water in the galley tank? The ship is lying along less, I think; I would try to get forward. A little water would do them good. Hallo! Look out! Look out!' The cook struggled. 'Not you, sir – not you!' He began to scramble to windward. 'Galley! . . . my business!' he shouted. 'Cook's going crazy now,' said several voices. He yelled: 'Crazy, am I? I am more ready to die than any of you, officers incloosive – there! As long as she swims I will cook! I will get you coffee.' 'Cook, ye are a gentleman!' cried Belfast. But the cook was already going over the weather-ladder. He stopped for a moment to shout back on the poop: 'As long as she swims I will cook!' and disappeared as though he had gone overboard. The men who had heard sent after him a cheer that sounded like a wail of sick children. An hour or more afterwards some one said distinctly: 'He's gone for good.' 'Very likely,' assented the boatswain; 'even in fine weather he was as smart about the deck as a milch-cow on her first voyage. We ought to go and see.' Nobody moved. As the hours dragged slowly through the darkness Mr Baker crawled back and forth along the poop several times. Some men fancied they had heard him exchange murmurs with the master, but at that time the memories were incomparably more vivid than anything actual, and they were not certain whether the murmurs were heard now or many years ago. They did not try to find out. A mutter more or less did not matter. It was too cold for curiosity, and almost for hope. They could not spare a moment or a thought from the great mental occupation of wishing to live. And the desire of life kept them alive, apathetic and enduring, under the cruel persistence of wind and cold; while the bestarred black dome of the sky revolved slowly above the ship, that drifted, bearing their patience and their suffering, through the stormy solitude of the sea.

Huddled close to one another, they fancied themselves utterly alone. They heard sustained loud noises, and again bore the pain of existence through long hours of profound silence. In the night they saw sunshine, felt warmth, and suddenly, with a start, thought that the sun would never rise upon a freezing world. Some heard laughter, listened to songs; others, near the end of the poop, could hear loud human shrieks, and opening their eyes, were surprised to hear them still, though very faint, and far away. The boatswain said: 'Why, it's the cook, hailing from forward, I think.' He hardly believed his own words or recognized his own voice. It was a long time before the man next to him gave a sign of life. He punched hard his other neighbour and said: 'The cook's shouting!' Many did not understand, others did not care; the majority further aft did not believe. But the boatswain and another man had the pluck to crawl away forward to see. They seemed to have been gone for hours, and were very soon forgotten. Then suddenly men who had been plunged in a hopeless resignation became as if possessed with a desire to hurt. They belaboured one another with fists. In the darkness they struck persistently anything soft they could feel near, and, with a greater effort than for a shout, whispered excitedly: 'They've got some hot coffee. . . . Bos'n got it. . . .' 'No! . . . Where?' – 'It's coming! Cook made it.' James Wait moaned. Donkin scrambled viciously, caring not where he kicked, and anxious that the officers should have none of it. It came in a pot, and they drank in turns. It was hot, and while it blistered the greedy palates, it seemed incredible. The men sighed out, parting with the mug: 'How 'as he done it?' Some cried weakly: 'Bully for you, doctor!'

He had done it somehow. Afterwards Archie declared that the thing was 'meeraculous'. For many days we wondered, and it was the one ever-interesting subject of conversation to the end of the voyage. We asked the cook, in fine weather, how he felt when he saw his stove 'reared up on end'. We inquired, in the north-east trade and on serene evenings, whether he had to stand on his head to put things right somewhat. We suggested he had used his bread-board for a raft, and from there comfortably had stoked his grate; and we did our best to conceal our admiration under the wit of fine irony. He affirmed not to know anything about it, rebuked our levity, declared himself, with solemn animation, to have been the object of a special mercy for the saving of our unholy lives. Fundamentally he was right, no doubt; but he need not have been so offensively positive about it – he need not have hinted so often that it would have gone hard with us had he not been there, meritorious and pure, to receive the inspiration and the strength for the work of grace. Had we been saved by his recklessness or his agility, we could have at length become reconciled to the fact; but to admit our obligation to anybody's virtue and holiness alone was as difficult for us as for any other handful of mankind. Like many benefactors of humanity, the cook took himself too seriously, and reaped the reward of irreverence. We were not ungrateful, however. He remained heroic. His saying – *the* saying of his life – became proverbial in the mouths of men as are the sayings of conquerors or stages. Later, whenever one of us was puzzled by a task and advised to relinquish it, he would express his determination to persevere and to succeed by the words: 'As long as she swims I will cook!'

The hot drink helped us through the bleak hours that precede the dawn. The sky low by the horizon took on the delicate tints of pink and yellow like the inside of a rare shell. And higher, where it glowed with a pearly sheen, a small black cloud appeared, like a forgotten fragment of the night set in a border of dazzling gold. The beams of light skipped on the crests of waves. The eyes of men turned to the eastward. The sunlight flooded their weary faces. They were giving themselves up to fatigue as though they had done for ever with their work. On Singleton's black oilskin coat the dried salt glistened like hoar frost. He hung on by the wheel, with open and lifeless eyes. Captain Allistoun, unblinking, faced the rising sun. His lips stirred, opened for the first time in twenty-four hours, and with a fresh firm voice he cried, 'Wear ship!'

The commanding sharp tones made all these torpid men start like a sudden flick of a whip. Then again, motionless where they lay, the force of habit made some of them repeat the order in hardly audible murmurs. Captain Allistoun glanced down at his crew, and several, with fumbling fingers and hopeless movements, tried to cast themselves adrift. He repeated impatiently, 'Wear ship. Now then, Mr Baker, get the men along. What's the matter with them?' 'Wear ship. Do you hear there? – Wear ship!' thundered out the boatswain suddenly. His voice seemed to break through a deadly spell. Men began to stir and crawl. 'I want the fore-topmast staysail run up smartly,' said the master, very loudly; 'if you can't manage it standing up you must do it lying down – that's all. Bear a hand!' 'Come along! Let's give the old girl a chance,' urged the boatswain. 'Aye! aye! Wear ship!' exclaimed quavering voices. The forecastle men, with reluctant faces, prepared to go forward. Mr Baker pushed ahead grunting on all fours to show the way, and they followed him over the break. The others lay still with a vile hope in their hearts of not being required to move till they got saved or drowned in peace.

After some time they could be seen forward appearing on the forecastle head, one by one in unsafe attitudes; hanging on to the rails, clambering over the anchors; embracing the cross-head of the windlass or hugging the fore-capstan. They were restless with strange exertions, waved their arms, knelt, lay flat down, staggered up, seemed to strive their hardest to go overboard. Suddenly a small white piece of canvas fluttered amongst them, grew larger, beating. Its narrow head rose in jerks – and at last it stood distended and triangular in the sunshine. 'They have done it!' cried the voices aft. Captain Allistoun let go the rope he had round his wrist and rolled to leeward headlong. He could be seen casting the lee main braces off the pins while the backwash of waves splashed over him. 'Square the main yard!' he shouted up to us – who stared at him in wonder. We hesitated to stir. 'The main brace, men. Haul! haul anyhow! Lay on your backs and haul!' he screeched, half drowned down there. We did not believe we could move the main yard, but the strongest and the less discouraged tried to execute the order. Others assisted half-heartedly. Singleton's eyes blazed suddenly as he took a fresh grip of the spokes. Captain Allistoun fought his way up to windward. 'Haul men! Try to move it! Haul, and help the ship.' His hard face worked suffused and furious. 'Is she going off, Singleton?' he cried. 'Not a move yet, sir,' croaked the old seaman in a horribly hoarse voice. 'Watch the helm, Singleton,' spluttered the master. 'Haul men! Have you no more strength than rats? Haul, and earn your salt.' Mr Creighton, on his back, with a swollen leg and a face as white as a piece of paper, blinked his eyes; his bluish lips twitched. In the wild scramble men grabbed at him, crawled over his hurt leg, knelt on his chest. He kept perfectly still, setting his teeth without a moan, without a sigh. The master's ardour, the cries of that silent man inspired us. We hauled and hung in bunches on the rope. We heard him say with violence to Donkin, who sprawled abjectly on his stomach: 'I will brain you with this belaying pin if you don't catch hold of the brace,' and that victim of men's injustice, cowardly and cheeky, whimpered: 'Are you goin' to murder us now?' while with sudden desperation he gripped the rope. Men sighed, shouted, hissed meaningless words, groaned. The yards moved, came slowly square against the wind, that hummed loudly on the yard-arms. 'Going off, sir,' shouted Singleton, 'she's just started.' 'Catch a turn with that brace. Catch a turn!' clamoured the master. Mr Creighton, nearly suffocated and unable to move, made a mighty effort, and with his left hand managed to nip the rope. 'All fast!' cried someone. He closed his eyes as if going off into a swoon, while huddled together about the brace we watched with scared looks what the ship would do now.

She went off slowly as though she had been weary and disheartened like the men she carried. She paid off very gradually, making us hold our breath till we choked, and as soon as she had brought the wind abaft the beam she started to move, and fluttered our hearts. It was awful to see her, nearly overturned, begin to gather way and drag her submerged side through the water. The dead-eyes of the rigging churned the breaking seas. The lower half of the deck was full of mad whirlpools and eddies; and the long line of the lee rail could be seen showing black now and then in the swirls of a field of foam as dazzling and white as a field of snow. The wind sang shrilly amongst the spars; and at every slight lurch we expected her to slip to the bottom sideways from under our backs. When dead before it she made the first distinct attempt to stand up, and we encouraged her with a feeble and discordant howl. A great sea came running up aft and hung for a moment over us with a curling top; then crashed down under the counter and spread out on both sides into a great sheet of bursting froth. Above its fierce hiss we heard Singleton's croak: 'She is steering!' He had both his feet now planted firmly on the grating, and the wheel spun fast as he eased the helm. 'Bring the wind on the port quarter and steady her!' called out the master, staggering to his feet, the first man up from amongst our prostrate heap. One or two screamed with excitement: 'She rises!' Far away forward, Mr Baker and three others were seen erect and black on the clear sky, lifting their arms, and with open mouths as though they had been shouting all together. The ship trembled, trying to lift her side, lurched back, seemed to give up with a nerveless dip, and suddenly with an unexpected jerk swung violently to windward, as though she had torn herself out from a deadly grasp. The whole immense volume of water, lifted by her deck, was thrown bodily across to starboard. Loud cracks were heard. Iron ports breaking open thundered with ringing blows. The water topped over the starboard rail with the rush of a river falling over a dam. the sea on deck, and the seas on every side of her, mingled together in a deafening roar. She rolled violently. We got up and were helplessly run or flung about from side to side. Men, rolling over and over, yelled: 'The house will go!' – 'She clears herself!' Lifted by a towering sea she ran along with it for a moment, spouting thick streams of water through every opening of her wounded sides. The lee braces having been carried away or washed off the pins, all the ponderous yards on the fore swung from side to side and with appalling rapidity at every roll. The men forward were seen crouching here and there with fearful glances upwards at the enormous spars that whirled about over their heads. The torn canvas and the ends of broken gear streamed in the wind like wisps of hair. Through the clear sunshine, over the flashing turmoil and uproar of the seas, the ship ran blindly, dishevelled and headlong, as if fleeing for her life; and on the poop we spun, we tottered about, distracted and noisy. We all spoke at once in a thin babble; we had the aspect of invalids and the gestures of maniacs. Eyes shone, large and haggard, in smiling, meagre faces that seemed to have been dusted over with powdered chalk. We stamped, clapped our hands, feeling ready to jump and do anything; but in reality hardly able to keep on our feet. Captain Allistoun, hard and slim, gesticulated madly from the poop at Mr Baker: 'Steady these fore-yards! Steady them the best you can!' On the main deck, men excited by his cries, splashed, dashing aimlessly here and there with the foam swirling up to their waists. Apart, far aft, and alone by the helm, old Singleton had deliberately tucked his white beard under the top button of his glistening coat. Swaying upon the din and tumult of the seas, with the whole battered length of the ship launched forward on a rolling rush before his steady old eyes, he stood rigidly still, forgotten by all, and with an attentive face. In front of his erect figure only two arms moved crosswise with a swift and sudden readiness, to check or urge again the rapid stir of circling spokes. He steered with care.

Chapter IV

On men reprieved by its disdainful mercy, the immortal sea confers in its justice the full privilege of desired unrest. Through the perfect wisdom of its grace they are not permitted to meditate at ease upon the complicated and acrid savour of existence. They must without pause justify their life to the eternal pity that commands toil to be hard and unceasing, from sunrise to sunset, from sunset to sunrise; till the weary succession of nights and days tainted by the obstinate clamour of sages, demanding bliss and an empty heaven, is redeemed at last by the vast silence of pain and labour, by the dumb fear and the dumb courage of men obscure, forgetful, and enduring.

The master and Mr Baker coming face to face stared for a moment, with the intense and amazed looks of men meeting unexpectedly after years of trouble. Their voices were gone, and they whispered desperately at one another. 'Anyone missing?' asked Captain Allistoun. 'No. All there.' 'Anybody hurt?' 'Only the second mate.' 'I will look after him directly. We're lucky.' 'Very,' articulated Mr Baker, faintly. He gripped the rail and rolled bloodshot eyes. The little grey man made an effort to raise his voice above a dull mutter, and fixed his chief mate with a cold gaze, piercing like a dart. 'Get sail on the ship,' he said, speaking authoritatively and with an inflexible snap of his thin lips. 'Get sail on her as soon as you can. This is a fair wind. At once, sir – Don't give the men time to feel themselves. They will get done up and stiff, and we will never . . . We must get her along now . . .' He reeled to a long heavy roll; the rail dipped into the glancing, hissing water. He caught a shroud, swung helplessly against the mate . . . 'now we have a fair wind at last. . . . Make . . . sail.' His head rolled from shoulder to shoulder. His eyelids began to beat rapidly. 'And the pumps . . . pumps, Mr Baker.' He peered as though the face within a foot of his eyes had been half a mile off. 'Keep the men on the move to . . . to get her 'long,' he mumbled in a drowsy tone, like a man going off into a doze. He pulled himself together suddenly. 'Mustn't stand. Won't do,' he said with a painful attempt at a smile. He let go his hold, and, propelled by the dip of the ship, ran aft unwillingly, with small steps, till he brought up against the binnacle stand. Hanging on there he looked up in an objectless manner at Singleton, who, unheeding him, watched anxiously the end of the jib-boom. 'Steering gear works all right?' he asked. There was a noise in the old seaman's throat, as though the words had been rattling together before they could come out. 'Steers . . . like a little boat,' he said, at last, with hoarse tenderness, without giving the master as much as half a glance – then, watchfully, spun the wheel down, steadied, flung it back again. Captain Allistoun tore himself away from the delight of leaning against the binnacle, and began to walk the poop, swaying and reeling to preserve his balance. . . .

The pump-rods, clanking, stamped in short jumps while the fly-wheels turned smoothly, with great speed, at the foot of the mainmast, flinging back and forth with a regular impetuosity two limp clusters of men clinging to the handles. They abandoned themselves, swaying from the hip with twitching faces and stony eyes. The carpenter, sounding from time to time, exclaimed mechanically: 'Shake her up! Keep her going!' Mr Baker could not speak, but found his voice to shout; and under the goad of his objurgations, men looked to the lashings, dragged out new sails; and thinking themselves unable to move, carried heavy blocks aloft – overhauled the gear. They went up the rigging with faltering and desperate efforts. Their heads swam as they shifted their hold, stepped blindly on the yards like men in the dark; or trusted themselves to the first rope at hand with the negligence of exhausted strength. The narrow escapes from falls did not disturb the languid beat of their hearts; the roar of the seas seething far below them sounded continuous and faint like an indistinct noise from another world: the wind filled their eyes with tears, and with heavy gusts tried to push them off from where they swayed in insecure positions. With streaming faces and blowing hair they flew up and down between sky and water, bestriding the ends of yard-arms, crouching on footropes, embracing lifts to have their hands free, or standing up against chain ties. Their thoughts floated vaguely between the desire of rest and the desire of life, while their stiffened fingers cast off head-earrings, fumbled for knives, or held with tenacious grip against the violent shocks of beating canvas. They glared savagely at one another, made frantic signs with one hand while they held their life in the other, looked down on the narrow strip of flooded deck, shouted along to leeward: 'Light-to!'. . . 'Haul out!' . . . 'Make fast!' Their lips moved, their eyes started, furious and eager with the desire to be understood, but the wind tossed their words unheard upon the disturbed sea. In an unendurable and unending strain they worked like men driven by a merciless dream to toil in an atmosphere of ice or flame. They burnt and shivered in turns. Their eyeballs smarted as if in the smoke of a conflagration; their heads were ready to burst with every shout. Hard fingers seemed to grip their throats. At every roll they thought: Now I must let go. It will shake us all off – and thrown about aloft they cried wildly: 'Look out there – catch the end.' . . . 'Reeve clear' . . . 'Turn this block. . . .' They nodded desperately, shook infuriated faces, 'No! No! From down up.' They seemed to hate one another with a deadly hate. The longing to be done with it all gnawed their breasts, and the wish to do things well was a burning pain. They cursed their fate, contemned their life, and wasted their breath in deadly imprecations upon one another. The sailmaker, with his bald head bared, worked feverishly, forgetting his intimacy with so many admirals. The boatswain, climbing up with marlinspikes and bunches of spunyarn rovings, or kneeling on the yard and ready to take a turn with the midship-stop, had acute and fleeting visions of his old woman and the youngsters in a moorland village. Mr Baker, feeling very weak, tottered here and there, grunting and inflexible, like a man of iron. He waylaid those who, coming from aloft, stood gasping for breath. He ordered, encouraged, scolded. 'Now then – to the main topsail now! Tally on to that gantline. Don't stand about there!' 'Is there no rest for us?' muttered voices. He spun round fiercely, with a sinking heart. 'No! No rest till the work is done. Work till you drop. That's what you're here for.' A bowed seaman at his elbow gave a short laugh. 'Do or die,' he croaked bitterly, then spat into his broad palms, swung up his long arms, and grasping the rope high above his head sent out a mournful, wailing cry for a pull all together. A sea boarded the quarter-deck and sent the whole lot sprawling to leeward. Caps, handspikes floated. Clenched hands, kicking legs, with here and there a spluttering face, stuck out of the white hiss of foaming water. Mr Baker, knocked down with the rest, screamed: 'Don't let go that rope! Hold on to it! Hold!' And sorely bruised by the brutal fling, they held on to it, as though it had been the fortune of their life. The ship ran, rolling heavily, and the topping crests glanced past port and starboard flashing their white heads. Pumps were freed. Braces were rove. The three topsails and foresail were set. She spurted faster over the water, outpacing the swift rush of waves. The menacing thunder of distanced seas rose behind her – filled the air with the tremendous vibrations of its voice. And devastated, battered, and wounded she drove foaming to the northward, as though inspired by the courage of a high endeavour. . . .

The forecastle was a place of damp desolation. They looked at their dwelling with dismay. It was slimy, dripping; it hummed hollow with the wind, and was strewn with shapeless wreckage like a half-tide cavern in a rocky and exposed coast. Many had lost all they had in the world, but most of the starboard watch had preserved their chests; thin streams of water trickled out of them, however. The beds were soaked; the blankets spread out and saved by some nail squashed under foot. They dragged wet rags from evil-smelling corners, and wringing the water out, recognized their property. Some smiled stiffly. Others looked round blank and mute. There were cries of joy over old waistcoats, and groans of sorrow over shapeless things found among the splinters of smashed bed boards. One lamp was discovered jammed under the bowsprit. Charley whimpered a little. Knowles stumped here and there, sniffing, examining dark places for salvage. He poured dirty water out of a boot, and was concerned to find the owner. Those who, overwhelmed by their losses, sat on the forepeak hatch, remained elbows on knees, and, with a fist against each cheek, disdained to look up. He pushed it under their noses. 'Here's a good boot. Yours?' They snarled, 'No – get out.' One snapped at him, 'Take it to hell out of this.' He seemed surprised. 'Why? It's a good boot,' but remembering suddenly that he had lost every stitch of his clothing, he dropped his find and began to swear. In the dim light cursing voices clashed. A man came in and, dropping his arms, stood still, repeating from the doorstep, 'Here's a bloomin' old go! Here's a bloomin' old go!' A few rooted anxiously in flooded chests for tobacco. They breathed hard, clamoured with heads down. 'Look at that Jack!' . . . 'Here! Sam! Here's my shore-going rig spoilt for ever.' One blasphemed tearfully holding up a pair of dripping trousers. No one looked at him. The cat came out from somewhere. He had an ovation. They snatched him from hand to hand, caressed him in a murmur of pet names. They wondered where he had 'weathered it out'; disputed about it. A squabbling argument began. Two men brought in a bucket of fresh water, and all crowded round it; but Tom, lean and mewing, came up with every hair astir and had the first drink. A couple of hands went aft for oil and biscuits.

Then in the yellow light and in the intervals of mopping the deck they crunched hard bread, arranging to 'worry through somehow'. Men chummed as to beds. Turns were settled for wearing boots and having the use of oilskin coats. They called one another 'old man' and 'sonny' in cheery voices. Friendly slaps resounded. Jokes were shouted. One or two stretched on the wet deck, slept with heads pillowed on their bent arms, and several, sitting on the hatch, smoked. Their weary faces appeared through a thin blue haze, pacified and with sparkling eyes. The boatswain put his head through the door. 'Relieve the wheel, one of you' – he shouted inside – 'it's six. Blamme if that old Singleton hasn't been there more'n thirty hours. You are a fine lot.' He slammed the door again. 'Mate's watch on deck,' said someone. 'Hey, Donkin, it's your relief!' shouted three or four together. He had crawled into an empty bunk and on wet planks lay still. 'Donkin, your wheel.' He made no sound. 'Donkin's dead,' guffawed someone. 'Sell 'is bloomin' clothes,' shouted another. 'Donkin, if ye don't go to the bloomin' wheel they will sell your clothes – d'ye hear?' jeered a third. He groaned from his dark hole. He complained about pains in all his bones, he whimpered pitifully. 'He won't go,' exclaimed a contemptuous voice, 'your turn, Davis.' The young seaman rose painfully squaring his shoulders. Donkin stuck his head out, and it appeared in the yellow light, fragile and ghastly. 'I will giv' yer a pound of tobaccer,' he whined in a conciliating voice, 'so soon as I draw it from aft. I will – s'elp me. . . .' Davis swung his arm backhanded and the head vanished. 'I'll go,' he said, 'but you will pay for it.' He walked unsteady but resolute to the door. 'So I will,' yelped Donkin, popping out behind him. 'So I will – s'elp me . . . a pound . . . three bob they chawrge.' Davis flung the door open. 'You will pay my price . . . in fine weather,' he shouted over his shoulder. One of the men unbuttoned his wet coat rapidly, threw it at his head. 'Here, Taffy – take that, you thief!' 'Thank you!' he cried from the darkness above the swish of rolling water. He could be heard splashing; a sea came on board with a thump. 'He's got his bath already,' remarked a grim shellback. 'Aye, aye!' grunted others. Then, after a long silence, Wamibo made strange noises. 'Hallo, what's up with you?' said someone grumpily. 'He says he would have gone for

Davy,' explained Archie, who was the Finn's interpreter generally. 'I believe him!' cried voices. . . . 'Never mind, Dutchy' . . . 'You'll do, muddle-head.' . . . 'Your turn will come soon enough.' . . . 'You don't know when ye're well off.' They ceased, and all together turned their faces to the door. Singleton stepped in, made two paces, and stood swaying slightly. The sea hissed, flowed roaring past the bows, and the forecastle trembled, full of deep murmurs; the lamp flared, swinging like a pendulum. He looked with a dreamy and puzzled stare, as though he could not distinguish the still men from their restless shadows. There were awestruck exclamations: 'Hallo, hallo' . . . 'How does it look outside now, Singleton?' Those who sat on the hatch lifted their eyes in silence, and the next oldest seaman in the ship (those two understood one another, though they hardly exchanged three words in a day) gazed up at his friend attentively for a moment, then taking a short clay pipe out of his mouth, offered it without a word. Singleton put out his arm towards it, missed, staggered, and suddenly fell forward, crashing down, stiff and headlong like an uprooted tree. There was a swift rush. Men pushing, crying: 'He's done!' . . . 'Turn him over!' . . . 'Stand clear there!' Under a crowd of startled faces bending over him he lay on his back, staring upwards in a continuous and intolerable manner. In the breathless silence of a general consternation, he said in a grating murmur: 'I am all right,' and clutched with his hands. They helped him up. He mumbled despondently: 'I am getting old . . . old.' 'Not you,' cried Belfast, with ready tact. Supported on all sides, he hung his head. 'Are you better?' they asked. He glared at them from under his eyebrows with large black eyes, spreading over his chest the bushy whiteness of a beard long and thick. 'Old! old!' he repeated sternly. Helped along, he reached his bunk. There was in it a slimy soft heap of something that smelt, as does at dead low water a muddy foreshore. It was his soaked straw bed. With a convulsive effort he pitched himself on it, and in the darkness of the narrow place could be heard growling angrily, like an irritated and savage animal uneasy in its den: 'Bit of breeze . . . small thing . . . can't stand up . . . old!' He slept at last, high-booted, sou'wester on head, and his oilskin clothes rustled, when with a deep sighing groan he turned over. Men conversed about him in quiet, concerned whispers. 'This will break 'im up' . . . 'Strong as a horse' . . . 'Aye. But he ain't what he used to be.' . . . In sad murmurs they gave him up. Yet at midnight he turned out to duty as if nothing had been the matter, and answered to his name with a mournful 'Here!' He brooded alone more than ever, in an impenetrable silence and with a saddened face. For many years he had heard himself called 'Old Singleton', and had serenely accepted the qualification, taking it as a tribute of respect due to a man who through half a century had measured his strength against the favours and the rages of the sea. He had never given a thought to his mortal self. He lived unscathed, as though he had been indestructible, surrendering to all the temptations, weathering many gales. He had panted in sunshine, shivered in the cold; suffered hunger, thirst, debauch; passed through many trials – known all the furies. Old! It seemed to him he was broken at last. And like a man bound treacherously while he sleeps, he woke up fettered by the long chain of disregarded years. He had to take up at once the burden of all his existence, and found it almost too heavy for his strength. Old! He moved his arms, shook his head, felt his limbs. Getting old . . . and then? He looked upon the immortal sea with the awakened and groping perception of its heartless might; he saw it unchanged, black and foaming under the eternal scrutiny of the stars; he heard its impatient voice calling for him out of a pitiless vastness full of unrest, of turmoil, and of terror. He looked afar upon it, and he saw an immensity tormented and blind, moaning and furious, that claimed all the days of his tenacious life, and, when life was over, would claim the worn-out body of its slave. . . .

This was the last of the breeze. It veered quickly, changed to a black south-easter, and blew itself out, giving the ship a famous shove to the northward into the joyous sunshine of the trade. Rapid and white she ran homewards in a straight path, under a blue sky and upon the plain of a blue sea. She carried Singleton's completed wisdom, Donkin's delicate suceptibilities, and the conceited folly of us all. The hours of ineffective turmoil were forgotten; the fear and anguish of these dark moments were never mentioned in the glowing peace of fine days. Yet from that time our life seemed to start afresh as though we had died and had been resuscitated. All the first part of the voyage, the Indian Ocean on the other side of the Cape, all that was lost in a haze, like an ineradicable suspicion of some previous existence. It had ended – then there were blank hours: a livid blurr – and again we lived! Singleton was possessed of sinister truth; Mr Creighton of a damaged leg; the cook of fame – and shamefully abused the opportunities of his distinction. Donkin had an added grievance. He went about repeating with insistence: ''E said 'e would brain me – did yer 'ear? They are goin' to murder us now for the least little thing.' We began at last to think it was rather awful. And we were conceited! We boasted of our pluck, of our capacity for work, of our energy. We remembered honourable episodes: our devotion, our indomitable perseverance – and were proud of them as though they had been the outcome of our unaided impulses. We remembered our danger, our toil – and conveniently forgot our horrible scare. We decried our officers – who had done nothing – and listened to the fascinating Donkin. His care for our rights, his disinterested concern for our dignity, were not discouraged by the invariable contumely of our words, by the disdain of our looks. Our contempt for him was unbounded – and we could not but listen with interest to that consummate artist. He told us we were good men – a 'bloomin' condemned lot of good men'. Who thanked us? Who took any notice of our wrongs? Didn't we lead a 'dorg's loife for two poun' ten a month?' Did we think that miserable pay enough to compensate us for the risk to our lives and for the loss of our clothes? 'We've lost every rag!' he cried. He made us forget that he, at any rate, had lost nothing of his own. The younger men listened, thinking – this 'ere Donkin's a long-headed chap, though no kind of man, anyhow. The Scandinavians were frightened at his audacities; Wamibo did not understand; and the older seamen thoughtfully nodded their heads making the thin gold earrings glitter in the fleshy lobes of hairy ears. Severe, sunburnt faces were propped meditatively on tattooed forearms. Veined, brown fists held in their knotted grip the dirty white clay of smouldering pipes. They listened, impenetrable, broad-backed, with bent shoulders, and in grim silence. He talked with ardour, despised and irrefutable. His picturesque and filthy loquacity flowed like a troubled stream from a poisoned source. His beady little eyes danced, glancing right and left, ever on the watch for the approach of an officer. Sometimes Mr Baker going forward to take a look at the head sheets would roll with his uncouth gait through the sudden stillness of the men; or Mr Creighton limped along, smooth-faced, youthful, and more stern than ever, piercing our short silence with a keen glance of his clear eyes. Behind his back Donkin would begin again darting stealthy, sidelong looks. ''Ere's one of 'em. Some of yer 'as made 'im fast that day. Much thanks yer got for it. Ain't 'ee a-drivin' yer wusse'n ever? . . . Let 'im slip overboard. . . . Vy not? It would 'ave been less trouble. Vy not?' He advanced confidentially, backed away with great effect; he whispered, he screamed, waved his miserable arms no thicker than pipestems – stretched his lean neck – spluttered – squinted. In the pauses of his impassioned orations the wind sighed quietly aloft, the calm sea unheeded murmured in a warning whisper along the ship's side. We abominated the creature and could not deny the luminous truth of his contentions. It was all so obvious. We were indubitably good men; our deserts were great and our pay small. Through our exertions we had saved the ship and the skipper would get the credit of it. What had he done? we wanted to know. Donkin asked: 'What'ee could do without hus?' and we could not answer. We were oppressed by the injustice of the world, surprised to perceive how long we had lived under its burden without realizing our unfortunate state, annoyed by the uneasy suspicion of our undiscerning stupidity. Donkin assured us it was all our 'good 'eartedness', but we would not be consoled by such shallow sophistry. We were men enough to courageously admit to ourselves our intellectual shortcomings; though from that time we refrained from kicking him, tweaking his nose, or from accidentally knocking him about, which last, after we had weathered the Cape, had been rather a popular amusement. Davis ceased to talk at him provokingly about black eyes and flattened noses. Charley, much subdued since the gale, did not jeer at him. Knowles deferentially and with a crafty air propounded questions such as: 'Could we all have the same grub as the mates? Could we all stop ashore till we got it? What would be the next thing to try for if we got that?' He answered readily with contemptuous certitude; he strutted with assurance in clothes that were much too big for him as though he had tried to disguise himself. These were Jimmy's clothes mostly – though he would accept anything from anybody; but nobody, except Jimmy, had anything to spare. His devotion to Jimmy was unbounded. He was for ever dodging in the little cabin, ministering to Jimmy's wants, humouring his whims, submitting to his exacting peevishness, often laughing with him. Nothing could keep him away from the pious work of visiting the sick, especially when there was some heavy hauling to be done on deck. Mr Baker had on two occasions jerked him out from there by the scruff of the neck to our inexpressible scandal. Was a sick chap to be left without attendance? Were we to be ill-used for attending a shipmate? 'What?' growled Mr Baker, turning menacingly at the mutter, and the whole half-circle like one man stepped back a pace. 'Set the topmast stunsail. Away aloft, Donkin, overhaul the gear,' ordered the mate inflexibly. 'Fetch the sail along; bend the down-haul clear. Bear a hand.' Then, the sail set, he would go slowly aft and stand looking at the compass for a long time, careworn, pensive, and breathing hard as if stifled by the taint of unaccountable ill-will that pervaded the ship. 'What's up amongst them?' he thought. 'Can't make out this hanging back and growling. A good crowd, too, as they go nowadays.' On deck the men exchanged bitter words, suggested by a silly exasperation against something unjust and irremediable that would not be denied, and would whisper into their ears long after Donkin had ceased speaking. Our little world went on its curved and unswerving path carrying a discontented and aspiring population. They found comfort of a gloomy kind in an interminable and conscientious analysis of their unappreciated worth; and inspired by Donkin's hopeful doctrines they dreamed enthusiastically of the time when every lonely ship would travel over a serene sea, manned by a wealthy and well-fed crew of satisfied skippers.

It looked as if it would be a long passage. The south-east trades, light and unsteady, were left behind; and then, on the equator and under a low grey sky, the ship, in close heat, floated upon a smooth sea that resembled a sheet of ground glass. Thunder squalls hung on the horizon, circled round the ship, far off and growling angrily, like a troop of wild beasts afraid to charge home. The invisible sun, sweeping above the upright masts, made on the clouds a blurred stain of rayless light, and a similar patch of faded radiance kept pace with it from east to west over the unglittering level of the waters. At night, through the impenetrable darkness of earth and heaven, broad sheets of flame waved noiselessly; and for half a second the becalmed craft stood out with its masts and rigging, with every sail and every rope distinct and black in the centre of a fiery outburst, like a charred ship enclosed in a globe of fire. And, again, for long hours she remained lost in a vast universe of night and silence where gentle sighs wandering here and there like forlorn souls, made the still sails flutter as in sudden fear, and the ripple of a beshrouded ocean whisper its compassion afar – in a voice mournful, immense, and faint. . . .

When the lamp was put out, and through the door thrown wide open, Jimmy, turning on his pillow, could see vanishing beyond the straight line of top-gallant rail, the quick, repeated visions of a fabulous world made up of leaping fire and sleeping water. The lightning gleamed in his big sad eyes that seemed in a red flicker to burn themselves out in his black face, and then he would lie blinded and invisible in the midst of an intense darkness. He could hear on the quiet deck soft footfalls, the breaking of some man lounging on the doorstep; the low creak of swaying masts; or the calm voice of the watch-officer reverberating aloft, hard and loud, amongst the unstirring sails. He listened with avidity, taking a rest in the attentive perception of the slightest sound from the fatiguing wanderings of his sleeplessness. He was cheered by the rattling of blocks, reassured by the stir and murmur of the watch, soothed by the slow yawn of some sleepy and weary seaman settling himself deliberately for a snooze on the planks. Life seemed an indestructible thing. It went on in darkness, in sunshine, in sleep; tireless, it hovered affectionately round the imposture of his ready death. It was bright, like the twisted flare of lightning, and more full of surprises than the dark night. It made him safe, and the calm of its overpowering darkness was as precious as its restless and dangerous light.

But in the evening, in the dog-watches, and even far into the first night-watch, a knot of men could always be seen congregated before Jimmy's cabin.

They leaned on each side of the door peacefully interested and with crossed legs; they stood astride the doorstep discoursing, or sat in silent couples on his sea-chest; while against the bulwark along the spare topmast, three or four in a row stared meditatively; with their simple faces lit up by the projected glare of Jimmy's lamp. The little place, repainted white, had, in the night, the brilliance of a silver shrine where a black idol, reclining stiffly under a blanket, blinked its weary eyes and received our homage. Donkin officiated. He had the air of a demonstrator showing a phenomenon, a manifestation bizarre, simple, and meritorious that, to the beholders, should be a profound and an everlasting lesson. 'Just look at 'im, 'ee knows what's what – never fear!' he exclaimed now and then, flourishing a hand hard and fleshless like the claw of a snipe. Jimmy, on his back, smiled with reserve and without moving a limb. He affected the languor of extreme weakness, so as to make it manifest to us that our delay in hauling him out from his horrible confinement, and then that night spent on the poop among our selfish neglect of his needs, had 'done for him'. He rather liked to talk about it, and of course we were always interested. He spoke spasmodically, in fast rushes with long pauses between, as a tipsy man walks. . . . 'Cook had just given me a pannikin of hot coffee. . . . Slapped it down there, on my chest – banged the door to. . . . I felt a heavy roll coming; tried to save my coffee, burnt my fingers . . . and fell out of my bunk. . . . She went over so quick. . . . Water came in through the ventilator. . . . I couldn't move the door . . . dark as a grave . . . tried to scramble up into the upper berth. . . . Rats . . . a rat bit my finger as I got up. . . . I could hear him swimming below me. . . . I thought you would never come. . . . I thought you were all gone overboard . . . of course . . . Could hear nothing but the wind. . . . Then you came . . . to look for the corpse, I suppose. A little more and . . .'

'Man! But ye made a rare lot of noise in here,' observed Archie, thoughtfully.

'You chaps kicked up such a confounded row above. . . . Enough to scare anyone . . . I didn't know what you were up to. . . . Bash in the blamed planks . . . my head. . . . Just what a silly, scary gang of fools would do. . . . Not much good to me anyhow. . . . Just as well . . . drown. . . . Pah.'

He groaned, snapped his big white teeth, and gazed with scorn. Belfast lifted a pair of dolorous eyes, with a brokenhearted smile, clenched his fists stealthily; blue-eyed Archie caressed his red whiskers with a hesitating hand; the boatswain at the door stared a moment, and brusquely went away with a loud guffaw. Wamibo dreamed. . . . Donkin felt all over his sterile chin for the few rare hairs, and said, triumphantly, with a sidelong glance at Jimmy: 'Look at 'im! Wish I was 'arf has 'ealthy as 'ee is – I do.' He jerked a short thumb over his shoulder towards the after end of the ship. 'That's the blooming way to do 'em!' he yelped, with forced heartiness. Jimmy said: 'Don't be a damn fool,' in a pleasant voice. Knowles, rubbing his shoulder against the doorpost, remarked shrewdly: 'We can't all go an' be took sick – it would be mutiny.' 'Mutiny – gawn!' jeered Donkin, 'there's no bloomin' law against bein' sick.' 'There's six weeks' hard for refoosing dooty,' argued Knowles. 'I mind I once seed in Cardiff the crew of an overloaded ship – leastways she weren't overloaded, only a fatherly old gentleman with a white beard and an umbreller came along the quay and talked to the hands. Said as how it was crool hard to be drownded in winter just for the sake of a few pounds more for the owner – he said. Nearly cried over them – he did; and he had a square mainsail coat, and a gaff-topsail hat too – all proper. So they chaps they said they wouldn't go to be drownded in winter – depending upon that 'ere Plimsoll man to see 'em through the court. They thought to have a bloomin' lark and two or three days' spree. And the beak giv' 'em six weeks – coss the ship warn't overloaded. Anyways they made it out in court that she wasn't. There wasn't one overloaded ship in Penarth Dock at all. 'Pears that old coon he was only on pay and allowance from some kind people, under orders to look for overloaded ships, and he couldn't see no further than the length of his umbreller. Some of us in the boarding-house, where I live when I'm looking for a ship in Cardiff, stood by to duck that old weeping spunger in the dock. We kept a good look-out, too – but he topped his boom directly he was outside the court. . . . Yes. They got six weeks' hard. . . .'

They listened, full of curiosity, nodding in the pauses their rough pensive faces. Donkin opened his mouth once or twice, but restrained himself. Jimmy lay still with open eyes and not at all interested. A seaman emitted the opinion that after a verdict of atrocious partiality 'the bloomin' beaks go an' drink at the skipper's expense'. Others assented. It was clear, of course. Donkin said: 'Well, six weeks ain't much trouble. You sleep all night in, reg'lar, in hokey. Do it on my 'ead.' 'You are used to it ainch'ee, Donkin?' asked somebody. Jimmy condescended to laugh. It cheered up everyone wonderfully. Knowles, with surprising mental agility, shifted his ground. 'If we all went sick what would become of the ship? eh?' He posed the problem and grinned all round. 'Let 'er go to 'ell,' sneered Donkin. 'Damn 'er. She ain't yourn.' 'What? Just let her drift?' insisted Knowles in a tone of unbelief. 'Aye! Drift, an' be blowed,' affirmed Donkin with fine recklessness. The other did not see it – meditated. 'The stores would run out,' he muttered, 'and . . . never get anywhere . . . and what about pay-day?' he added with greater assurance. 'Jack likes a good pay-day, exclaimed a listener on the doorstep. 'Aye, because then the girls put one arm round his neck an' t'other in his pocket, and call him ducky. Don't they, Jack?' – 'Jack, you're a terror with the gals' – 'He takes three of 'em in tow to once, like one of 'em Watkinses two-funnel tugs waddling away with three schooners behind' – 'Jack, you're a lame scamp' – 'Jack tell us about that one with a blue eye and a black eye. Do' – 'There's plenty of girls with one black eye along the Highway by . . .' – 'No, that's a speshul one – come Jack.' Donkin looked severe and disgusted; Jimmy very bored; a grey-haired sea-dog shook his head slightly, smiling at the bowl of his pipe, discreetly amused. Knowles turned about bewildered; stammered first at one, then at another. 'No! . . . I never! . . . can't talk sensible sense midst you. . . . Always on the kid.' He retired bashfully – muttering and pleased. They laughed hooting in the crude light, around Jimmy's bed, where on a white pillow his hollowed black face moved to and fro restlessly. A puff of wind came, made the flame of the lamp leap, and outside, high up, the sails fluttered, while near by the block of the foresheet struck a ringing blow on the iron bulwark. A voice far off cried, 'Helm up!' another, more faint, answered, 'Hard-up, sir!' They became silent – waited expectantly. The grey-haired seaman knocked his pipe on the doorstep and stood up. The ship leaned over gently and the sea seemed to wake up, murmuring drowsily.

'Here's a little wind comin',' said someone very low. Jimmy turned over slowly to face the breeze. The voice in the night cried loud and commanding: 'Haul the spanker out.' The group before the door vanished out of the light. They could be heard tramping aft while they repeated with varied intonations: 'Spanker out!' . . . 'Out spanker, sir!' Donkin remained alone with Jimmy. There was a silence. Jimmy opened and shut his lips several times as if swallowing draughts of fresher air; Donkin moved the toes of his bare feet and looked at them thoughtfully.

'Ain't you going to give them a hand with the sail?' asked Jimmy.

'No. If six ov 'em ain't 'nough beef to set that blamed, rotten spanker, they ain't fit to live,' answered Donkin in a bored, far-away voice, as though he had been talking from the bottom of a hole. Jimmy considered the conical, fowl-like profile with a queer kind of interest; he was leaning out of his bunk with the calculating, uncertain expression of a man who reflects how best to lay hold of some strange creature that looks as though it could sting or bite. But he said only: 'The mate will miss you – and there will be ructions.'

Donkin got up to go. 'I will do for 'im some dark night; see if I don't,' he said over his shoulder.

Jimmy went on quickly: 'You're like a poll-parrot, like a screechin' poll-parrot.' Donkin stopped and cocked his head attentively on one side. His big ears stood out, transparent and veined, resembling the thin wings of a bat.

'Yuss?' he said, with his back towards Jimmy.

'Yes! Chatter out all you know – like . . . like a dirty white cockatoo.'

Donkin waited. He could hear the other's breathing, long and slow; the breathing of a man with a hundredweight or so on the breastbone. Then he asked calmly: 'What do I know?'

'What? . . . What I tell you . . . not much. What do you want . . . to talk about my health so. . . .'

'It's a blooming imposyshun. A bloomin', stinkin', first-class imposyshun – but it don't tyke me in. Not it.'

Jimmy kept still. Donkin put his hands in his pockets, and in one slouching stride came up to the bunk.

'I talk – what's the odds. They ain't men 'ere – sheep they are. A driven lot of sheep. I 'old you up . . . Vy not? You're well orf.'

'I am . . . I don't say anything about that. . . .'

'Well. Let 'em see it. Let 'em larn what a man can do. I am a man, I know all about yer. . . .' Jimmy threw himself further away on the pillow; the other stretched out his skinny neck, jerked his bird face down at him as though pecking at the eyes. 'I am a man. I've seen the inside of every chokey in the Colonies rather'n give up my rights. . . .'

'You are a jail-prop,' said Jimmy, weakly.

'I am . . . an' proud of it, too. You! You 'aven't the bloomin' nerve – so you inventyd this 'ere dodge. . . .' He paused; then with marked afterthought accentuated slowly: 'Yer ain't sick – are yer?'

'No,' said Jimmy, firmly. 'Been out of sorts now and again this year,' he mumbled with a sudden drop in his voice.

Donkin closed one eye, amicable and confidential. He whispered: 'Ye 'ave done this afore 'aven'tchee?' Jimmy smiled – then as if unable to hold back he let himself go: 'Last ship – yes. I was out of sorts on the passsge. See? It was easy. They paid me off in Calcutta, and the skipper made no bones about it either. . . . I got my money all right. Laid up fifty-eight days! The fools! O Lord! The fools! Paid right off.' He laughed spasmodically. Donkin chimed in giggling. Then Jimmy coughed violently. 'I am as well as ever,' he said, as soon as he could draw breath.

Donkin made a derisive gesture. 'In course,' he said, profoundly, 'anyone can see that.' 'They don't,' said Jimmy, gasping like a fish. 'They would swallow any yarn,' affirmed Donkin. 'Don't you let on too much,' admonished Jimmy in an exhausted voice. 'You're little gyme? Eh?' commented Donkin, jovially. Then with sudden disgust: 'Yer all for yerself, s'long as ye're right. . . .'

So charged with egoism James Wait pulled the blanket up to his chin and lay still for awhile. His heavy lips protruded in an everlasting black pout. 'Why are you so hot on making trouble?' he asked without much interest.

' 'Cos it's a bloomin' shayme. We are put upon. . . bad food, bad pay . . . I want us to kick up a bloomin' row; a blamed 'owling row that would make 'em remember! Knocking people about . . . brains us . . . indeed! Ain't we men?' His altruistic indignation blazed. Then he said calmly: 'I've been airing yer clothes.' 'All right,' said Jimmy, languidly, 'bring them in.' 'Giv' us the key of your chest, I'll put 'em away for yer,' said Donkin with friendly eagerness. 'Bring 'em in, I will put them away myself,' answered James Wait with severity. Donkin looked down muttering. . . . . 'What d'you say? What d'you say?' inquired Wait anxiously. 'Nothink. The night's dry, let'em'ang out till the morning,' said Donkin, in a strangely trembling voice, as though restraining laughter or rage. Jimmy seemed satisfied. 'Give me a little water for the night in my mug – there,' he said. Donkin took a stride over the doorstep. 'Git it yerself,' he replied in a surly tone. 'You can do it, unless you *are* sick.' 'Of course I can do it,' said Wait, 'only . . .' 'Well, then, do it,' said Donkin, viciously, 'if yer can look after yer clothes, yer can look after yerself.' He went on deck without a look back.

Jimmy reached out for the mug. Not a drop. He put it back gently with a faint sigh – and closed his eyes. He thought: That lunatic Belfast will bring me some water if I ask. Fool. I am very thirsty. . . . It was very hot in the cabin, and it seemed to turn slowly round, detach itself from the ship, and swing out smoothly into a luminous, arid space where a black sun shone, spinning very fast. A place without any water! No water! A policeman with the face of Donkin drank a glass of beer by the side of an empty well, and flew away flapping vigorously. A ship whose mastheads protruded through the sky and could not be seen, was discharging grain, and the wind whirled the dry husks in spirals along the quay of a dock with no water in it, He whirled along with the husks – very tired and light. All his inside was gone. He felt lighter than the husks – and more dry. He expanded his hollow chest. The air streamed in carrying away in its rush a lot of strange things that resembled houses, trees, people, lamp-posts. . . . No more! There was no more air – and he had not finished drawing his long breath. But he was in jail! They were locking him up. A door slammed. They turned the key twice, flung a bucket of water over him – Phoo! What for?

He opened his eyes, thinking the fall had been very heavy for an empty man

– empty – empty. He was in his cabin. Ah! All right! His face was streaming with perspiration, his arms heavier than lead. He saw the cook standing in the doorway, a brass key in one hand and a bright tin hook-pot in the other.

'I have locked up the galley for the night,' said the cook, beaming benevolently. 'Eight bells just gone. I brought you a pot of cold tea for your night's drinking, Jimmy. I sweetened it with some white cabin sugar, too. Well – it won't break the ship.'

He came in, hung the pot on the edge of the bunk, asked perfunctorily, 'How goes it?' and sat down on the box. 'H'm,' grunted Wait, inhospitably. The cook wiped his face with a dirty cotton rag, which, afterwards, he tied round his neck. 'That's how them firemen do in steamboats,' he said, serenely, and much pleased with himself. 'My work is as heavy as theirs – I'm thinking – and longer hours. Did you ever see them down the stokehold? Like fiends they look – firing – firing – firing – down there.'

He pointed his forefinger at the deck. Some gloomy thought darkened his shining face, fleeting, like the shadow of a travelling cloud over the light of a peaceful sea. The relieved watch tramped noisily forward, passing in a body across the sheen of the doorway. Someone cried, 'Good night!' Belfast stopped for a moment and looked at Jimmy, quivering and speechless with repressed emotion. He gave the cook a glance charged with dismal foreboding, and vanished. The cook cleared his throat. Jimmy stared upwards and kept as still as a man in hiding.

The night was clear, with a gentle breeze. Above the mastheads the resplendent curve of the Milky Way spanned the sky like a triumphal arch of eternal light, thrown over the dark pathway of the earth. On the forecastle head a man whistled with loud precision a lively jig, while another could be heard faintly, shuffling and stamping in time. There came from forward a confused murmur of voices, laughter – snatches of song. The cook shook his head, glanced obliquely at Jimmy, and began to mutter. 'Aye. Dance and sing. That's all they think of. I am surprised that Providence don't get tired. . . . They forget the day that's sure to come . . . but you. . . .'

Jimmy drank a gulp of tea, hurriedly, as though he had stolen it, and shrank under his blanket, edging away towards the bulkhead. The cook got up, closed the door, then sat down again and said distinctly:

'Whenever I poke my galley fire I think of you chaps – swearing, stealing, lying, and worse – as if there was no such thing as another world. . . . . Not bad fellows, either, in a way,' he conceded, slowly; then, after a pause of regretful musing, we went on in a resigned tone: 'Well, well. They will have a hot time of it. Hot! Did I say? The furnaces of one of them White Star boats ain't nothing to it.'

He kept very quiet for a while. There was a great stir in his brain; an addled vision of bright outlines; an exciting row of rousing songs and groans of pain. He suffered, enjoyed, admired, approved. he was delighted, frightened, exalted – as on that evening (the only time in his life – twenty-seven years ago; he loved to recall the number of years) when as a young man he had – through keeping bad company – became intoxicated in an East End music-hall. A tide of sudden feeling swept him clean out of his body. He soared. He contemplated the secret of the hereafter. It commended itself to him. It was excellent; he loved it, himself, all hands, and Jimmy. His heart overflowed with tenderness, with comprehension, with the desire to meddle, with anxiety for the soul of that black man, with the pride of possessed eternity, with the feeling of might. Snatch him up in his arms and pitch him right into the middle of salvation. . . . The black soul – blacker – body – rot – devil. No! Talk – strength – Samson. . . . There was a great din as of cymbals in his ears; he flashed through an ecstatic jumble of shining faces, lilies, prayer-books, unearthly joy, white shirts, gold harps, black coats, wings. He saw flowing garments, clean-shaved faces, a sea of light – a lake of pitch. There were sweet scents, a smell of sulphur – red tongues of flame licking a white mist. An awesome voice thundered! . . . It lasted three seconds.

'Jimmy!' he cried in an inspired tone. Then he hesitated. A spark of human pity glimmered yet through the infernal fog of his supreme conceit.

'What?' said James Wait, unwillingly. There was a silence. He turned his head just the least bit, and stole a cautious glance. The cook's lips moved without a sound; his face was rapt, his eyes turned up. He seemed to be mentally imploring deck beams, the brass hook of the lamp, two cockroaches.

'Look here,' said Wait, 'I want to go to sleep. I think I could.'

'This is no time for sleep!' exclaimed the cook, very loud. He had prayerfully divested himself of the last vestige of his humanity. He was a voice – a fleshless and sublime thing, as on that memorable night – the night when he went walking over the sea to make coffee for perishing sinners. 'This is no time for sleeping,' he repeated with exaltation. '*I* can't sleep.'

'Don't care damn,' said Wait, with factitious energy. 'I can. Go an' turn in.'

'Swear . . . in the very jaws! . . . In the very jaws! Don't you see the everlasting fire . . . don't you feel it? Blind, chock-full of sin! Repent, repent! I can't bear to think of you. I hear the call to save you. Night and day. Jimmy, let me save you!' The words of entreaty and menace broke out of him in a roaring torrent. The cockroaches ran away. Jimmy perspired, wriggling stealthily under his blanket. The cook yelled. . . . 'Your days are numbered! . . .' 'Get out of this,' boomed Wait, courageously. 'Pray with me! . . .' 'I won't! . . .' The little cabin was as hot as an oven. It contained an immensity of fear and pain; an atmosphere of shrieks and moans; prayers vociferated like blasphemies and whispered curses. Outside, the men called by Charley, who informed them in tones of delight that there was a holy row going on in Jimmy's place, crowded before the closed door, too startled to open it. All hands were there. The watch below had jumped out on deck in their shirts, as after a collision. Men running up, asked: 'What is it?' Others said: 'Listen!' The muffled screaming went on: 'On your knees! On your knees!' – 'Shut up!' – 'Never! You are delivered into my hands. . . . Your life has been saved. . . . Purpose. . . . Mercy. . . . Repent.' 'You are a crazy fool! . . .' 'Account of you . . . you . . . Never sleep in this world, if I . . .' 'Leave off.' 'No! . . . stokehold . . . only think! . . .' Then an impassioned screeching babble where words pattered like hail. 'No!' shouted Wait. 'Yes. You are! . . . No help. . . . Everybody says so.' 'You lie!' 'I see you dying this minyt . . . before my eyes . . . as good as dead already.' 'Help!' shouted Jimmy, piercingly. 'Not in this valley. . . . look upwards,' howled the other. 'Go away! Murder! Help!' clamoured Jimmy. His voice broke. There were moanings, low mutters, a few sobs.

'What's the matter now?' said a seldom-heard voice. 'Fall back, men! Fall back, there!' repeated Mr Creighton, sternly, pushing through. 'Here's the old man,' whispered some. 'The cook's in there, sir,' exclaimed several, backing away. The door clattered open; a broad stream of light darted out on wondering faces; a warm whiff of vitiated air passed. The two mates towered head and shoulders above the spare, grey-haired man who stood revealed between them, in shabby clothes, stiff and angular, like a small carved figure, and with a thin, composed face. The cook got up from his knees. Jimmy sat high in the bunk, clasping his drawn-up legs. The tassel of the blue night-cap almost imperceptibly trembled over his knees. They gazed astonished at his long, curved back, while the white corner of one eye gleamed blindly at them. He was afraid to turn his head, he shrank within himself; and there was an aspect astounding and animal-like in the perfection of his expectant immobility. A thing of instinct – the unthinking stillness of a scared brute.

'What are you doing here?' asked Mr Baker, sharply. 'My duty,' said the cook, with ardour. 'Your . . . what?' began the mate. Captain Allistoun touched his arm lightly. 'I know his caper,' he said, in a low voice. 'Come out of that, Podmore,' he ordered, aloud.

The cook wrung his hands, shook his fists above his head, and his arms dropped as if too heavy. For a moment he stood distracted and speechless. 'Never,' he stammered, 'I . . . he . . . I.' 'What – do – you – say?' pronounced Captain Allistoun. 'Come out at once – or . . .' 'I am going,' said the cook, with a hasty and sombre resignation. He strode over the doorstep firmly – hesitated – made a few steps. They looked at him in silence. 'I make you responsible!' he cried, desperately, turning half round. 'That man is dying. I make you . . .' 'You there yet?' called the master in a threatening tone. 'No, sir,' he exclaimed, hurriedly, in a startled voice. The boastwain led him away by the arm; someone laughed; Jimmy lifted his head for a stealthy glance, and in one unexpected leap sprang out of his bunk; Mr Baker made a clever catch and felt him very limp in his arms; the group at the door grunted with surprise. 'He lies,' gasped Wait, 'he talked about black devils – he is a devil – a white devil – I am all right.' He stiffened himself, and Mr Baker, experimentally, let him go. He staggered a pace or two; Captain Allistoun watched him with a quiet and penetrating gaze; Belfast ran to his support. He did not appear to be aware of anyone near him; he stood silent for a moment, battling single-handed with a legion of nameless terrors, amidst the eager looks of excited men who watched him far off, utterly alone in the impenetrable solitude of his fear. The sea gurgled through the scuppers as the ship heeled over to a short puff of wind.

'Keep him away from me,' said James Wait at last in his fine baritone voice, and leaning with all his weight on Belfast's neck. 'I've been better this last week . . . I am well . . . I was going back to duty . . . tomorrow – now if you like – Captain.' Belfast hitched his shoulders to keep him upright.

'No,' said the master, looking at him, fixedly.

Under Jimmy's armpit Belfast's red face moved uneasily. A row of eyes gleaming stared on the edge of light. They pushed one another with elbows, turned their heads, whispered. Wait let his chin fall on his breast and, with lowered eyelids, looked round in a suspicious manner.

'Why not?' cried a voice from the shadows, 'the man's all right, sir.'

'I am all right,' said Wait, with eagerness. 'Been sick . . . better . . . turn-to-now.' He sighed. 'Howly Mother!' exclaimed Belfast with a heave of the shoulders, 'stand up, Jimmy.' 'Keep away from me then,' said Wait, giving Belfast a petulant push, and reeling fetched against the doorpost. His cheekbones glistened as though they had been varnished. He snatched off his night-cap, wiped his perspiring face with it, flung it on the deck. 'I am coming out,' he declared without stirring.

'No. You don't,' said the master, curtly. Bare feet shuffled, disapproving voices murmured all round; he went on as if he had not heard: 'You have been skulking nearly all the passage and now you want to come out. You think you are near enough to the pay-table now. Smell the shore, hey?'

'I've been sick . . . now – better,' mumbled Wait, glaring in the light. 'You have been shamming sick,' retorted Captain Allistoun with severity; 'Why . . .' he hesitated for less than half a second. 'Why, anybody can see that. There's nothing the matter with you, but you choose to lie-up to please yourself – and now you shall lie-up to please me. Mr Baker, my orders are that this man is not to be allowed on deck to the end of the passage.'

There were exclamations of surprise, triumph, indignation. The dark group of men swung across the light. 'What for?' – 'Told you so . . .' – 'Bloomin' shame. . . .' 'We've got to say somethink about that,' screeched Donkin from the rear. 'Never mind, Jim – we will see you righted,' cried several together. An elderly seaman stepped to the front. 'D'ye mean to say, sir,' he asked, ominously, 'that a sick chap ain't allowed to get well in this 'ere hooker?' Behind him Donkin whispered excitedly amongst a staring crowd where no one spared him a glance, but Captain Allistoun shook a forefinger at the angry bronzed face of the speaker. 'You – you hold your tongue,' he said, warningly. 'This isn't the way,' clamoured two or three younger men. 'Are we bloomin' masheens?' inquired Donkin in piercing tone, and dived under the elbows of the front rank. 'Soon show 'im we ain't boys . . .' – 'The man's a man if he is black' – 'We ain't goin' to work this bloomin' ship shorthanded if Snowball's all right . . .' – 'He says he is' – 'Well then, strike, boys, strike!' – 'That's the bloomin' ticket.' Captain Allistoun said sharply to the second mate: 'Keep quiet, Mr Creighton,' and stood composed in the tumult, listening with profound attention to mixed growls and screeches, to every exclamation and every curse of the sudden outbreak. Somebody slammed the cabin door to with a kick; the darkness full of menacing mutters leaped with a short clatter over the streak of light, and the men became gesticulating shadows that growled, hissed, laughed excitedly. Mr Baker whispered: 'Get away from them, sir.' The big shape of Mr Creighton hovered silently about the slight figure of the master. 'We have been hymposed upon all this voyage,' said a gruff voice, 'but this 'ere fancy takes the cake.' 'That man is a shipmate' – 'Are we bloomin' kids?' – 'The port watch will refuse duty.' Charley carried away by his feeling whistled shrilly, then yelped: 'Giv' us our Jimmy!' This seemed to cause a variation in the disturbance. There was a fresh burst of squabbling uproar. A lot of quarrels were set going at once. 'Yes' – 'No' – 'Never been sick' – 'Go for them for once – 'Shut yer mouth, youngster – this is men's work.' 'Is it?' muttered Captain Allistoun, bitterly. Mr Baker grunted: 'Ough!

They're gone silly. They've been simmering for the last month.' 'I did notice,' said the master. 'They have started a row amongst themselves now,' said Mr Creighton with disdain, 'better get aft, sir. We will soothe them.' 'Keep your temper, Creighton,' said the master. And the three men began to move slowly towards the cabin door.

In the shadows of the fore rigging a dark mass stamped, eddied, advanced, retreated. There were words of reproach, encouragement, unbelief, execration. The elder seamen, bewildered and angry, growled their determination to go through with something or other; but the younger school of advanced thought exposed their and Jimmy's wrongs with confused shouts, arguing amongst themselves. They clustered round that moribund carcass, the fit emblem of their aspirations, and encouraging one another they swayed, they tramped on one spot, shouting that they would not be 'put upon'. Inside the cabin, Belfast, helping Jimmy into his bunk, twitched all over in his desire not to miss all the row, and with difficulty restrained the tears of his facile emotion. James Wait, flat on his back under the blanket, gasped complaints. 'We will back you up, never fear,' assured Belfast, busy about his feet. 'I'll come out tomorrow morning . . . take my chance . . . you fellows must . . .' mumbled Wait, 'I come out tomorrow . . . skipper or no skipper.' He lifted one arm with great difficulty, passed the hand over his face; 'Don't you let that cook . . .' he breathed out. 'No, no,' said Belfast, turning his back on the bunk, 'I will put a head on him if he comes near you.' 'I will smash his mug!' exclaimed Wait faintly, enraged and weak; 'I don't want to kill a man, but . . .' He panted fast like a dog after a run in sunshine. Someone just outside the door shouted, 'He's as fit as any ov us!' Belfast put his hand on the doorhandle. 'Here!' called James Wait, hurriedly and in such a clear voice that the other spun round with a start. James Wait, stretched out black and deathlike in the dazzling light, turned his head on the pillow. His eyes stared at Belfast, appealing and impudent. 'I am rather weak from lying-up so long,' he said, distinctly. Belfast nodded. 'Getting quite well now,' insisted Wait. 'Yes. I noticed you getting better this . . . last month,' said Belfast, looking down. 'Hallo! What's this?' he shouted and ran out.

He was flattened directly against the side of the house by two men who lurched against him. A lot of disputes seemed to be going on all round. He got clear and saw three indistinct figures standing alone in the fainter darkness under the arched foot of the mainsail, that rose above their head like a convex wall of a high edifice. Donkin hissed: 'Go for them . . . it's dark!' The crowd took a short run aft in a body – then there was a check. Donkin, agile and thin, flitted past with his right arm going like a windmill – and then stood still suddenly with his arm pointing rigidly above his head. The hurtling flight of some heavy object was heard; it passed between the heads of the two mates, bounded heavily along the deck, struck the after hatch with a ponderous and deadened blow. The bulky shape of Mr Baker grew distinct. 'Come to your sense, men!' he cried, advancing at the arrested crowd. 'Come back, Mr Baker!' called the master's quiet voice. He obeyed unwillingly. There was a minute of silence, then a deafening hubbub arose. Above it Archie was heard energetically: 'If ye do oot ageen I wull tell!' There were shouts. 'Don't! – 'Drop it!' – 'We ain't that kind!' The black cluster of human forms reeled against the bulwark, back again towards the house.

Ringbolts rang under stumbling feet. 'Drop it!' – 'Let me!' – 'No!' – 'Curse you . . . hah!' Then sounds as of someone's face being slapped; a piece of iron fell on the deck; a short scuffle, and someone's shadowy body scuttled rapidly across the main hatch before the shadow of a kick. A raging voice sobbed out a torrent of filthy language. . . . 'Throwing things – good God!' grunted Mr Baker in dismay. 'That was meant for me,' said the master, quietly; 'I felt the wind of that thing; what was it – an iron belaying-pin?' 'By Jove!' muttered Mr Creighton. The confused voices of men talking amidships mingled with the wash of the sea, ascended between the silent and distended sails – seemed to flow away into the night, further than the horizon, higher than the sky. The stars burned steadily over the inclined mastheads. Trails of light lay on the water, broke before the advancing hull, and, after she had passed, trembled for a long time as if in awe of the murmuring sea.

Meantime the helmsman, anxious to know what the row was about, had let go the wheel, and, bent double, ran with long, stealthy footsteps to the break of the poop. The *Narcissus*, left to herself, came up gently to the wind without anyone being aware of it. She gave a slight roll, and the sleeping sails woke suddenly, coming all together with a mighty flap against the masts, then filled again one after another in a quick succession of loud reports that ran down the lofty spars, till the collapsed mainsail flew out last with a violent jerk. The ship trembled from trucks to keel; the sails kept on rattling like a discharge of musketry; the chain sheets and loose shackles jingled aloft in a thin peal; the gin blocks groaned. It was as if an invisible land had given the ship an angry shake to recall the men that peopled her decks to the sense of reality, vigilance, and duty. 'Helm up!' cried the master, sharply. 'Run aft, Mr Creighton, and see what that fool there is up to.' 'Flatten in the head sheets. Stand by the weather fore-braces,' growled Mr Baker. Startled men ran swiftly repeating the orders. The watch below, abandoned all at once by the watch on deck, drifted towards the forecastle in twos and threes, arguing noisily as they went: 'We shall see tomorrow!' cried a loud voice, as if to cover with a menacing hint an inglorious retreat. And then only orders were heard, the falling of heavy coils of rope, the rattling of blocks. Singleton's white head flitted here and there in the night, high above the deck, like the ghost of a bird. 'Going off, sir!' shouted Mr Creighton from aft. 'Full again' – 'All right. . . .' 'Ease off the head sheets. That will do the braces. Coil the ropes up,' grunted Mr Baker, bustling about.

Gradually the tramping noises, the confused sound of voices, died out, and the officers, coming together on the poop, discussed the events. Mr Baker was bewildered and grunted; Mr Creighton was calmly furious; but Captain Allistoun was composed and thoughtful. He listened to Mr Baker's growling argumentation, to Creighton's interjected and severe remarks, while looking down on the deck he weighed in his hand the iron belaying-pin – that a moment ago had just missed his head – as if it had been the only tangible fact of the whole transaction. He was one of those commanders who speak little, seem to hear nothing, look at no one – and know everything, hear every whisper, see every fleeting shadow of their ship's life. His two big officers towered above his lean, short figure; they talked over his head; they were dismayed, surprised, and angry, while between them the little quiet man seemed to have found his taciturn serenity in the profound depths of a larger experience. Lights were burning in the forecastle; now and then a loud gust of babbling chatter came from forward, swept over the decks, and became faint, as if the unconscious ship, gliding gently through the great peace of the sea, had left behind and for ever the foolish noise of turbulent mankind. But it was renewed again and again. Gesticulating arms, profiles of heads with open mouths appeared for a moment in the illuminated squares of doorways; black fists darted – withdrew . . . 'Yes. It was most damnable to have such an unprovoked row sprung on one,' assented the master. . . . A tumult of yells rose in the light, abruptly ceased. . . . He didn't think there would be any further trouble just then. . . . A bell was struck aft, another, forward, answered in a deeper tone, and the clamour of ringing metal spread round the ship in a circle of wide vibrations that ebbed away into the immeasurable night of empty sea. . . . Didn't he know them! Didn't he! In past years. Better men, too. Real men to stand by one in a tight place. Worse than devils too sometimes – downright, horned devils. Pah! This – nothing. A miss as good as a mile. . . . The wheel was being relieved in the usual way. 'Full and by,' said, very loud, the man going off. 'Full and by,' repeated the other, catching hold of the spokes. 'This head wind is my trouble,' exclaimed the master, stamping his foot in sudden anger; 'head wind! all the rest is nothing.' He was calm again in a moment. 'Keep them on the move tonight, gentlemen; just to let them feel we've got hold all the time – quietly, you know. Mind you keep your hands off them, Creighton. Tomorrow I will talk to them like a Dutch Uncle. A crazy crowd of tinkers! Yes, tinkers! I could count the real sailors amongst them on the fingers of one hand. Nothing will do but a row – if – you – please.' He paused. 'Did you think I had gone wrong there, Mr Baker?' He tapped his forehead, laughed short. 'When I saw him standing there, three parts dead and so scared – black amongst that gaping lot – no grit to face what's coming to us all – the notion came to me all at once, before I could think. Sorry for him – like you would be for a sick brute. If ever creature was in a mortal funk to die! . . . I thought I would let him go out in his own way. Kind of impulse. It never came into my head, those fools. . . . H'm! Stand to it now – of course.' He stuck the belaying-pin in his pocket, seemed ashamed of himself, then sharply: 'If you see Podmore at his tricks again tell him I will have him put under the pump. Had to do it once before. The fellow breaks out like that now and then. Good cook tho'.' He walked away quickly, came back to the companion. The two mates followed him through the starlight with amazed eyes. He went down three steps, and changing his tone, spoke with his head near the deck: 'I shan't turn in tonight, in case of anything; just call out if . . . Did you see the eyes of that sick nigger, Mr Baker? I fancied he begged me for something. What? Past all help. One lone black beggar amongst the lot of us, and he seemed to look through me into the very hell. Fancy, this wretched Podmore! Well, let him die in peace. I am master here after all. Let him be. He might have been half a man once. . . . Keep a good look-out.' He disappeared down below, leaving his mates facing one another, and more impressed than if they had seen a stone image shed a miraculous tear of compassion over the incertitudes of life and death. . . .

In the blue mist spreading from twisted threads that stood upright in the bowls of pipes, the forecastle appeared as vast as a hall. Between the beams a heavy cloud stagnated; and the lamps surrounded by halos burned each at the core of a purple glow in two lifeless flames without rays. Wreaths drifted in denser wisps. Men sprawled about on the deck, sat in negligent poses, or, bending a knee, drooped with one shoulder against a bulkhead. Lips moved, eyes flashed, waving arms made sudden eddies in the smoke. The murmur of voices seemed to pile itself higher and higher as if unable to run out quick enough through the narrow doors. The watch below in their shirts, and striding on long white legs, resembled raving somnambulists; while now and then one of the watch on deck would rush in, looking strangely over-dressed, listen a moment, fling a rapid sentence into the noise, and run out again; but a few remained near the door, fascinated, and with one ear turned to the deck. 'Stick together, boys,' roared Davis. Belfast tried to make himself heard. Knowles grinned in a slow, dazed way. A short fellow with a thick clipped beard kept on yelling periodically: 'Who's afeard? Who's afeard?' Another one jumped up, excited, with glazing eyes, sent out a string of unattached curses and sat down quietly. Two men discussed familiarly, striking one another's breast in turn, to clinch arguments. Three others, with their heads in a bunch, spoke all together with a confidential air, and at the top of their voices. It was a stormy chaos of speech where intelligible fragments, tossing, struck the ear. One could hear: 'In the last ship' – 'Who cares? Try it on any one of us if –' – 'Knock under' – 'Not a hand's turn' – 'He says he is all right' – 'I always thought' – 'Never mind. . . .' Donkin, crouching all in a heap against the bowsprit, hunched his shoulderblades as high as his ears, and hanging a peaked nose, resembled a sick vulture with ruffled plumes. Belfast, straddling his legs, had a face red with yelling, and with arms thrown up, figured a Maltese cross. The two Scandinavians, in a corner, had the dumbfounded and distracted aspect of men gazing at a cataclysm. And, beyond the light, Singleton stood in the smoke, monumental, indistinct, with his head touching the beam; like a statue of heroic size in the gloom of a crypt.

He stepped forward, impassive and big. The noise subsided like a broken wave: but Belfast cried once more with uplifted arms: 'The man is dying I tell ye!' then sat down suddenly on the hatch and took his head between his hands. All looked at Singleton, gazing upwards from the deck, staring out of dark corners, or turning their heads with curious glances. They were expectant and appeased as if that old man, who looked at no one, had possessed the secret of their uneasy indignations and desires, a sharper vision, a clearer knowledge. And indeed standing there amongst them, he had the uninterested appearance of one who had seen multitudes of ships, had listened many times to voices such as theirs, had already seen all that could happen on the wide seas. They heard his voice rumble in his broad chest as though the words had been rolling towards them out of a rugged past. 'What do you want to do?' He asked. No one answered. Only Knowles muttered – 'Aye, aye,' and somebody said low: 'It's a bloomin' shame.' He waited, made a contemptuous gesture. 'I have seen rows aboard ship before some of you were born,' he said, slowly, 'for something or nothing; but never for such a thing.' 'The man is dying, I tell ye,' repeated Belfast, woefully, sitting at Singleton's feet. 'And a black fellow, too,' went on the old seaman, 'I have seen them die like flies.' He stopped, thoughtful, as if trying to recollect gruesome things, details, of horrors, hecatombs of niggers.

They looked at him fascinated. He was old enough to remember slavers, bloody mutinies, pirates perhaps; who could tell through what violences and terrors he had lived! What would he say? He said: 'You can't help him; die he must.' He made another pause. His moustache and beard stirred. He chewed words, mumbled behind tangled white hairs; incomprehensible and exciting, like an oracle behind a veil. . . . 'Stop ashore . . . sick. . . . Instead . . . bringing all this head wind. Afraid. The sea will have her own. . . . Die in sight of land. Always so. They know it . . . long passage . . . more days, more dollars. . . . You keep quiet. . . . What do you want? Can't help him.' He seemed to wake up from a dream. 'You can't help yourselves,' he said, austerely. 'Skipper's no fool. He has something in his mind. Look out – I say! I know 'em!' With eyes fixed in front he turned his head from right to left, from left to right, as if inspecting a long row of asture skippers. ' 'Ee said 'ee would brain me!' cried Donkin in a heartrending tone. Singleton peered downwards with puzzled attention, as though he couldn't find him. 'Damn you!' he said, vaguely, giving it up. He radiated unspeakable wisdom, hard unconcern, the chilling air of resignation. Round him all the listeners felt themselves somehow completely enlightened by their disappointment, and mute, they lolled about with the careless ease of men who can discern perfectly the irremediable aspect of their existence. He, profound and unconscious, waved his arm once, and strode out on deck without another word.

Belfast was lost in a round-eyed meditation. One or two vaulted heavily into upper berths, and, once there, sighed; others dived head first inside lower bunks – swift, and turning round instantly upon themselves, like animals going into lairs. The grating of a knife scraping burnt clay was heard. Knowles grinned no more. Davies said, in a tone of ardent conviction: 'Then our skipper's looney.' Archie muttered: 'My faith! we haven't heard the last of it yet!' Four bells were struck. 'Half our watch below gone!' cried Knowles in alarm, then reflected. 'Well, two hours' sleep is something towards a rest,' he observed, consolingly. Some already pretended to slumber; and Charley, sound asleep, suddenly said a few slurred words in an arbitrary, blank voice. 'This blamed boy has worrums!' commented Knowles from under a blanket, in a learned manner. Belfast got up and approached Archie's berth. 'We pulled him out,' he whispered, sadly. 'What?' said the other, with sleepy discontent. 'And now we will have to chuck him overboard,' went on Belfast, whose lower lip trembled. 'Chuck what? asked Archie. 'Poor Jimmy,' breathed out Belfast. 'He be blowed!' said Archie with untruthful brutality, and sat up in his bunk; 'It's all through him. If it hadn't been for me, there would have been murder on board this ship!' ' 'Tain't his fault, is it?' argued Belfast, in a murmur; 'I've put him to bed . . . an' he ain't no heavier than an empty beef-cask,' he added, with tears in his eyes. Archie looked at him steadily, then turned his nose to the ship's side with determination. Belfast wandered about as though he had lost his way in the dim forecastle, and nearly fell over Donkin. He contemplated him from on high for a while. 'Ain't ye going to turn in?' he asked. Donkin looked up hopelessly. 'That black 'earted Scotch son of a thief kicked me!' he whispered from the floor, in a tone of utter desolation. 'And a good job, too!' said Belfast, still very depressed; 'You were as near hanging as damn-it tonight, sonny. Don't you play any of your murthering games around my Jimmy! You haven't pulled him out. You just mind! 'Cos if I start to kick you' – he brightened up a bit – 'if I start to kick you, it will be Yankee fashion – to break something!' He tapped lightly with his knuckles the top of the bowed head. 'You moind that, my bhoy!' he concluded, cheerily. Donkin let it pass. 'Will they split on me?' he asked, with pained anxiety. 'Who – split?' hissed Belfast, coming back a step. 'I would split your nose this minyt if I hadn't Jimmy to look after! Who d'ye think we are?' Donkin rose and watched Belfast's back lurch through the doorway. On all sides invisible men slept, breathng calmly. He seemed to draw courage and fury from the peace around him. Venomous and thin-faced, he glared from the ample misfit of borrowed clothes as if looking for something he could smash. His heart leaped wildly in his narrow chest. They slept! He wanted to wring necks, gouge eyes, spit on faces. He shook a dirty pair of meagre fists at the smoking lights. 'Ye're no men!' he cried, in a deadened tone. No one moved. 'Yer 'aven't the pluck of a mouse!' His voice rose to a husky screech. Wamibo darted out a dishevelled head, and looked at him wildly. 'Ye're sweepings ov ships! I 'ope you will all rot before you die!' Wamibo blinked, uncomprehending but interested. Donkin sat down heavily; he blew with force through quivering nostrils, he ground and snapped his teeth, and, with the chin pressed hard against the breast, he seemed busy gnawing his way through it, as if to get at the heart within. . . .

In the morning the ship, beginning another day of her wandering life, had an aspect of sumptuous freshness, like the spring-time of the earth. The washed decks glistened in a long clear stretch; the oblique sunlight struck the yellow brasses in dazzling splashes, darted over the polished rods in lines of gold, and the single drops of salt water forgotten here and there along the rail were as limpid as drops of dew, and sparkled more than scattered diamonds. The sails slept, hushed by a gentle breeze. The sun, rising lonely and splendid in the blue sky, saw a solitary ship gliding close-hauled on the blue sea.

The men pressed three deep abreast of the mainmast and opposite the cabin-door. They shuffled, pushed, had an irresolute mien and stolid faces. At every slight movement Knowles lurched heavily on his short leg. Donkin glided behind backs, restless and anxious, like a man looking for an ambush. Captain Allistoun came out on the quarter-deck suddenly. He walked to and fro before the front. He was grey, slight, alert, shabby in the sunshine, and as hard as adamant. He had his right hand in the side-pocket of his jacket, and also something heavy in there that made folds all down that side. One of the seamen cleared his throat ominously. 'I haven't till now found fault with you men,' said the master, stopping short. He faced them with his worn, steely gaze, that by an universal illusion looked straight into every individual pair of the twenty pairs of eyes before his face. At his back Mr Baker, gloomy, and bull-necked, grunted low; Mr Creighton, fresh as paint, had rosy cheeks and a ready, resolute bearing. 'And I don't now,' continued the master; 'but I am here to drive this ship and keep every man-jack aboard of her up to the mark. If you knew your work as well as I do mine, there would be no trouble. You've been braying in the dark about "See tomorrow morning!" Well, you see me now. What do you want?' He waited, stepping quickly to and fro, giving them searching glances. What did they want? They shifted from foot to foot, they balanced their bodies; some, pushing back their caps, scratched their heads. What did they want? Jimmy was forgotten; no one thought of him, alone forward in his cabin, fighting great shadows, clinging to brazen lies, chuckling painfully over his transparent deceptions. No, not Jimmy; he was more forgotten than if he had been dead. They wanted great things. And suddenly all the simple words they knew seemed to be lost for ever in the immensity of their vague and burning desire. They knew what they wanted, but they could not find anything worth saying. They stirred on one spit, swinging, at the end of muscular arms, big tarry hands with crooked fingers. A murmur died out. 'What is it – food?' asked the master, 'you know the stores have been spoiled off the Cape.' 'We know that, sir,' said a bearded shell-back in the front rank. 'Work too hard – eh? Too much for your strength?' he asked again. There was an offended silence. 'We don't want to go shorthanded, sir,' began at last Davies in a wavering voice, 'and this 'ere black . . .' 'Enough!' cried the master. He stood scanning them for a moment, then walking a few steps this way and that began to storm at them coldly, in gusts violent and cutting like the gales of those icy seas that had known his youth. 'Tell you what's the matter? Too big for your boots. Think yourselves damn good men. Know half your work. Do half your duty. Think it too much. If you did ten times as much it wouldn't be enough.' 'We did our best by her, sir,' cried someone with shaky exasperation. 'Your best,' stormed on the master: 'You hear a lot on shore, don't you? They don't tell you there your best isn't much to boast of. I tell you – your best is no better than bad. You can do no more? No, I know, and say nothing. But you stop your caper or I will stop it for you. I am ready for you! Stop it!' He shook a finger at the crowd. 'As to that man,' he raised his voice very much; 'as to that man, if he puts his nose out on deck without my leave I will clap him in irons. There!' The cook heard him forward, ran out of the galley lifting his arms, horrified, unbelieving, amazed, and ran in again. There was a moment of profound silence during which a bow-legged seaman, stepping aside, expectorated decorously into the scupper. 'There is another thing,' said the master, calmly. He made a quick stride and with a swing took an iron belaying-pin out of his pocket. 'This!' His movement was so unexpected and sudden that the crowd stepped back. He gazed fixedly at their faces, and some at once put on a surprised air as though they had never seen a belaying-pin before. He held it up. 'This is my affair. I don't ask you any questions, but you all know it; it has got to go where it came from.' His eyes became angry. The crowd stirred uneasily. They looked away from the piece of iron, they appeared shy, they were embarrassed and shocked as though it had been something horrid, scandalous or indelicate, that in common decency should not have been flourished like this in broad daylight. The master watched them attentively. 'Donkin,' he called out in a short, sharp tone.

Donkin dodged behind one, then behind another, but they looked over their shoulders and moved aside. The ranks kept on opening before him, closing behind, till at last he appeared alone before the master as though he had come up through the deck. Captain Allistoun moved close to him. They were much of a size, and at short range the master exchanged a deadly glance with the beady eyes. They wavered. 'You know this,' asked the master. 'No, I don't,' answered the other with cheeky trepidation. 'You are a cur. Take it,' ordered the master.

Donkin's arms seemed glued to his thighs; he stood, eyes front, as if drawn on parade. 'Take it,' repeated the master, and stepped closer; they breathed on one another. 'Take it,' said Captain Allistoun again, making a menacing gesture. Donkin tore away one arm from his side. 'Vy are yer down on me?' he mumbled with effort and as if his mouth had been full of dough. 'If you don't . . .' began the master. Donkin snatched at the pin as though his intention had been to run away with it, and remained stock still holding it like a candle. 'Put it back where you took it from,' said Captain Allistoun, looking at him fiercely. Donkin stepped back opening wide eyes. 'Go, you blackguard, or I will make you,' cried the master, driving him slowly backwards by a menacing advance. He dodged, and with the dangerous iron tried to guard his head from a threatening fist. Mr Baker ceased grunting for a moment. 'Good! By Jove,' Mr Creighton murmured appreciatively in the tone of a connoisseur. 'Don't tech me,' snarled Donkin, backing away. 'Then go. Go faster.' 'Don't yer 'it me. . . . I will pull yer up afore the magistryt. . . . I'll show yer up.' Captain Allistoun made a long stride, and Donkin, turning his back fairly, ran off a little, then stopped and over his shoulder showed yellow teeth. 'Further on, fore-rigging,' urged the master, pointing with his arm. 'Are yer goin' to stand by and see me bullied,' screamed Donkin at the silent crowd that watched him. Captain Allistoun walked at him smartly. He started off again with a leap, dashed at the fore-rigging, rammed the pin into its hole violently. 'I'll be even with yer yet,' he screamed at the ship at large and vanished beyond the foremast. Captain Allistoun spun round and walked back aft with a composed face, as though he had already forgotten the scene. Men moved out of his way. He looked at no one. 'That will do, Mr Baker. Send the watch below,' he said, quietly. 'And you men try to walk straight for the future,' he added in a calm voice. He looked pensively for a while at the backs of the impressed and retreating crowd. 'Breakfast, steward,' he called in a tone of relief through the cabin door. 'I didn't like to see you – Ough! – give that pin to that chap, sir,' observed Mr Baker; 'he could have bust – Ough! – bust your head like an eggshell with it.' 'O! he!' muttered the master absently. 'Queer lot,' he went on in a low voice. 'I suppose it's all right now. Can never tell tho', nowadays, with such a . . . Years ago; I was a young master then – one China voyage I had a mutiny; real mutiny, Baker. Different men tho'. I knew what they wanted: they wanted to broach the cargo and get at the liquor. Very simple. . . . We knocked them about for two days, and when they had enough – gentle as lambs. Good crew. And a smart trip I made.' He glanced aloft at the yards braced sharp up. 'Head wind day after day,' he exclaimed, bitterly. 'Shall we never get a decent slant this passage?' 'Ready, sir,' said the steward, appearing before them as if by magic and with a stained napkin in his hand. 'Ah! All right. Come along, Mr Baker – it's late – with all this nonsense.'

Chapter V

A heavy atmosphere of oppressive quietude pervaded the ship. In the afternoon men went about washing clothes and hanging them out to dry in the unprosperous breeze with the meditative languor of disenchanted philosophers. Very little was said. The problem of life seemed too voluminous for the narrow limits of human speech, and by common consent it was abandoned to the great sea that had from the beginning enfolded it in its immense grip; to the sea that knew all, and would in time infallibly unveil to each the wisdom hidden in all the errors, the certitude that lurks in doubts, the realm of safety and peace beyond the frontiers of sorrow and fear. And in the confused current of impotent thoughts that set unceasingly this way and that through bodies of men, Jimmy bobbed up upon the surface, compelling attention, like a black buoy chained to the bottom of a muddy stream. Falsehood triumphed. It triumphed through doubt, through stupidity, through pity, through sentimentalism. We set ourselves to bolster it up, from compassion, from recklessness, from a sense of fun. Jimmy's steadfastness to his untruthful attitude in the face of the inevitable truth had the proportions of a colossal enigma – of a manifestation grand and incomprehensible that at times inspired a wondering awe; and there was also, to many, something exquisitely droll in fooling him thus to the top of his bent. The latent egoism of tenderness to suffering appeared in the developing anxiety not to see him die. His obstinate non-recognition of the only certitude whose approach we could watch from day to day was as disquieting as the failure of some law of nature. He was so utterly wrong about himself that one could not but suspect him of having access to some source of supernatural knowledge. He was absurd to the point of inspiration. He was unique, and as fascinating as only something inhuman could be; he seemed to shout his denials already from beyond the awful border. He was becoming immaterial like an apparition; his cheekbones rose, the forehead slanted more; the face was all hollows, patches of shade; and the fleshless head resembled a disinterred black skull, fitted with two restless globes of silver in the sockets of eyes. He was demoralizing. Through him we were becoming highly humanized, tender, complex, excessively decadent: we understood the subtlety of his fear, sympathized with all his repulsions, shrinkings, evasions, delusions – as though we had been over-civilized, and rotten, and without any knowledge of the meaning of life. We had the air of being initiated in some infamous mysteries; we had the profound grimaces of conspirators, exchanged meaning glances, significant short words. We were inexpressibly vile and very much pleased with ourselves. We lied to him with gravity, with emotion, with unction, as if performing some moral trick with a view to an eternal reward. We made a chorus of affirmation to his wildest assertions, as though he had been a millionaire, a politician, or a reformer – and we a crowd of ambitious lubbers. When we ventured to question his statements we did it after the manner of obsequious sycophants, to the end that his glory should be augmented by the flattery of our dissent. He influenced the moral tone of our world as though he had it in his power to distribute honours, treasures, or pain; and he could give us nothing but his contempt. It was immense; it seemed to grow gradually larger, as his body day by day shrank a little more, while we looked. It was the only thing about him – of him – that gave the impression of durability and vigour. It lived within him with an unquenchable life. It spoke through the eternal pout of his black lips; it looked at us through the impertinent mournfulness of his languid and enormous stare. We watched him intently. He seemed unwilling to move, as if distrustful of his own solidity. The slightest gesture must have disclosed to him (it could not surely be otherwise) his bodily weakness, and caused a pang of mental suffering. He was chary of movements. He lay stretched out, chin on blanket, in a kind of sly, cautious immobility. Only his eyes roamed over faces: his eyes disdainful, penetrating, and sad.

It was at that time that Belfast's devotion – and also his pugnacity – secured universal respect. He spent ever moment of his spare time in Jimmy's cabin. He tended him, talked to him; was as gentle as a woman, as tenderly gay as an old philanthropist, as sentimentally careful of his nigger as a model slave-owner. But outside he was irritable, explosive as gunpowder, sombre, suspicious, and never more brutal than when most sorrowful. With him it was a tear and a blow: a tear for Jimmy, a blow for anyone who did not seem to take a scrupulously orthodox view of Jimmy's case. We talked about nothing else. The two Scandinavians, even, discussed the situation – but it was impossible to know in what spirit, because they quarrelled in their own language. Belfast suspected one of them of irreverence, and in this incertitude thought that there was no option but to fight them both. They became very much terrified by his truculence, and henceforth lived amongst us, dejected, like a pair of mutes. Wamibo never spoke intelligibly, but he was as smileless as an amimal – seemed to know much less about it all than the cat – and consequently was safe. Moreover, he had belonged to the chosen band of Jimmy's rescuers, and was above suspicion. Archie was silent generally, but often spent an hour or so talking to Jimmy quietly with an air of proprietorship. At any time of the day and often through the night some man could be seen sitting on Jimmy's box. In the evening, between six and eight, the cabin was crowded, and there was an interested group at the door. Everyone stared at the nigger.

He basked in the warmth of our interest. His eyes gleamed ironically, and in a weak voice he reproached us with our cowardice. He would say, 'If you fellows had stuck out for me I would be now on deck.' We hung our heads. 'Yes, but if you think I am going to let them put me in irons just to show you sport. . . . Well, no. . . . It ruins my health, this lying-up, it does. You don't care.' We were as abashed as if it had been true. His superb impudence carried all before it. We would not have dared to revolt. We didn't want to, really. We wanted to keep him alive till home – to the end of the voyage.

Singleton as usual held aloof, appearing to scorn the insignificant events of an ended life. Once only he came along, and unexpectedly stopped in the doorway. He peered at Jimmy in profound silence, as if desirous to add that black image to the crowd of Shades that peopled his old memory. We kept very quiet, and for a long time Singleton stood there as though he had come by appointment to call for someone, or to see some important event. James Wait lay perfectly still, and apparently not aware of the gaze scrutinizing him with a steadiness full of expectation. There was a sense of a contest in the air. We felt the inward strain of men watching a wrestling bout. At last Jimmy with perceptible apprehension turned his head on the pillow. 'Good evening,' he said in a conciliating tone. 'H'm,' answered the old seaman grumpily. For a moment longer he looked at Jimmy with severe fixity, then suddenly went away. It was a long time before anyone spoke in the little cabin, though we all breathed more freely as men do after an escape from some dangerous situation. We all knew the old man's ideas about Jimmy, and nobody dared to combat them. They were unsettling, they caused pain; and, what was worse, they might have been true for all we knew. Only once did he condescend to explain them fully, but the impression was lasting. He said that Jimmy was the cause of head winds. Mortally sick men – he maintained – linger till the first sight of land, and then die; and Jimmy knew that the very first land would draw his life from him. It is so in every ship. Didn't we know it? He asked us with austere contempt: what did we know? What would we doubt next? Jimmy's desire encouraged by us and aided by Wamibo's (he was a Finn – wasn't he? Very well!) by Wamibo's spells delayed the ship in the open sea. Only lubberly fools couldn't see it. Whoever heard of such a run of calms and head winds? It wasn't natural. . . . We could not deny that it was strange. We felt uneasy. The common saying, 'More days, more dollars', did not give the usual comfort because the stores were running short. Much had been spoiled off the Cape, and we were on half allowance of biscuit. Peas, sugar and tea had been finished long ago. Salt meat was giving out. We had plenty of coffee but very little water to make it with. We took up another hole in our belts and went on scraping, polishing, painting the ship from morning to night. And soon she looked as though she had come out of a band-box; but hunger lived on board of her. Not dead starvation, but steady, living hunger that stalked about the decks, slept in the forecastle; the tormentor of waking moments, the disturber of dreams. We looked to windward for signs of change. Every few hours of night and day we put her round with the hope that she would come up on that tack at last! She didn't. She seemed to have forgotten the way home; she rushed to and fro, heading north-west, heading east; she ran backwards and forwards, distracted like a timid creature at the foot of a wall. Sometimes, as if tired to death, she would wallow languidly for a day in the smooth swell of an unruffled sea. All up the swinging masts the sails thrashed furiously through the hot stillness of the calm. We were weary, hungry, thirsty; we commenced to believe Singleton, but with unshaken fidelity dissembled to Jimmy. We spoke to him with jocose allusiveness, like cheerful accomplices in a clever plot; but we looked to the westward over the rail with longing eyes for a sign of hope, for a sign of fair wind; even if its first breath should bring death to our reluctant Jimmy. In vain! The universe conspired with James Wait. Light airs from the northward sprang up again; the sky remained clear; and round our weariness the glittering sea, touched by the breeze, basked voluptuously in the great sunshine, as though it had forgotten our life and trouble.

Donkin looked out for a fair wind along with the rest. No one knew the venom of his thoughts now. He was silent, and appeared thinner, as if consumed slowly by an inward rage at the injustice of men and of fate. He was ignored by all and spoke to no one, but his hate for every man dwelt in his furtive eyes. He talked with the cook only, having somehow persuaded the good man that he – Donkin – was a much calumniated and persecuted person. Together they bewailed the immorality of the ship's company. There could be no greater criminals than we, who by our lies conspired to send the unprepared soul of a poor ignorant black man to everlasting perdition. Podmore cooked what there was to cook, remorsefully, and felt all the time that by preparing the food of such sinners he imperilled his own salvation. As to the Captain – he had sailed with him for seven years, now, he said, and would not have believed it possible that such a man . . . 'Well. Well . . . There it was. . . . Can't get out of it. Judgement capsized all in a minute. . . . Struck in all his pride. . . . More like a sudden visitation than anything else.' Donkin, perched sullenly on the coal-locker, swung his legs and concurred. He paid in the coin of spurious assent for the privilege to sit in the galley; he was disheartened and scandalized; he agreed with the cook; could find no words severe enough to criticize our conduct; and when in the heat of reprobation he swore at us, Podmore, who would have liked to swear also if it hadn't been for his principles, pretended not to hear. So Donkin, unrebuked, cursed enough for two, cadged for matches, borrowed tobacco, loafed for hours and very much at home before the stove. From there he could hear us on the other side of the bulkhead, talking to Jimmy. The cook knocked the saucepans about, slammed the oven door, muttered prophesies of damnation for all the ship's company; and Donkin, who did not admit of any hereafter (except for purposes of blasphemy, listened, concentrated and angry, gloating fiercely over a called-up image of infinite torment – as men gloat over the accursed images of cruelty and revenge, of greed and of power. . . .

On clear evenings the silent ship, under the cold sheen of the dead moon, took on a false aspect of passionless repose resembling the winter of the earth. Under her a long band of gold barred the black disc of the sea. Footsteps echoed on her quiet decks. The moonlight clung to her like a frosted mist, and the white sails stood out in dazzling cones as of stainless snow. In the magnificence of the phantom rays the ship appeared pure like a vision of ideal beauty, illusive like a tender dream of serene peace. And nothing in her was real, nothing was distinct and solid but the heavy shadows that filled her decks with their unceasing and noiseless stir: the shadows darker than the night and more restless than the thoughts of men.

Donkin prowled spiteful and alone amongst the shadows, thinking that Jimmy too long delayed to die. That evening land had been reported from aloft, and the master, while adjusting the tubes of the long glass, had observed with quiet bitterness to Mr Baker that, after fighting our way inch by inch to the Western Islands, there was nothing to expect now but a spell of calm. The sky was clear and the barometer high. The light breeze dropped with the sun, and an enormous stillness, forerunner of a night without wind, descended upon the heated waters of the ocean. As long as daylight lasted, the hands collected on the forecastle-head watched on the eastern sky the island of Flores, that rose above the level expanse of the sea with irregular and broken outlines like a sombre ruin upon a vast and deserted plain. It was the first land seen for nearly four months. Charley was excited, and in the midst of general indulgence took liberties with his betters.

Men strangely elated without knowing why, talked in groups, and pointed with bared arms. For the first time that voyage Jimmy's sham existence seemed for a moment forgotten in the face of a solid reality. We had got so far anyhow. Belfast dicoursed, quoting imaginary examples of short homeward runs from the Islands. 'Them smart fruit schooners do it in five days,' he affirmed. 'What do you want? – only a good little breeze.' Archie maintained that seven days was the record passage, and they disputed amicably with insulting words. Knowles declared he could already smell home from there, and with a heavy list on his short leg laughed fit to split his sides. A group of grizzled sea-dogs looked out for a time in silence and with grim absorbed faces. One said suddenly: ' 'Tain't far to London now.' 'My first night ashore, blamme if I haven't steak and onions for supper . . . and a pint of bitter,' said another. 'A barrel ye mean,' shouted someone. 'Ham an' eggs three times a day. That's the way I live!' cried an excited voice. There was a stir, appreciative murmurs; eyes began to shine; jaws champed; short, nervous laughs were heard. Archie smiled with reserve all to himself. Singleton came up, gave a careless glance, and went down again without saying a word, indifferent, like a man who had seen Flores an incalculable number of times. The night travelling from the East blotted out of the limpid sky the purple stain of the high land. 'Dead calm,' said somebody quietly. The murmur of lively talk suddenly wavered, died out; the clusters broke up; men began to drift away one by one, descending the ladders slowly and with serious faces as if sobered by that reminder of their dependence upon the invisible. And when the big yellow moon ascended gently above the sharp rim of the clear horizon it found the ship wrapped up in a breathless silence; a fearless ship that seemed to sleep profoundly, dreamlessly on the bosom of the sleeping and terrible sea.

Donkin chafed at the peace – at the ship – at the sea that stretching away on all sides merged into the illimitable silence of all creation. He felt himself pulled up sharp by unrecognized grievances. He had been physically cowed, but his injured dignity remained indomitable, and nothing could heal his lacerated feelings. Here was land already – home very soon – a bad pay-day – no clothes – more hard work. How offensive all this was. Land. The land that draws away life from sick sailors. That nigger there had money – clothes – easy times, and would not die. Land draws life away. . . . He felt tempted to go and see whether it did. Perhaps already . . . It would be a bit of luck. There was money in the beggar's chest. He stepped briskly out of the shadows into the moonlight, and, instantly, his craving, hungry face from sallow became livid. He opened the door of the cabin and had a shock. Sure enough, Jimmy was dead! He moved no more than a recumbent figure with clasped hands, carved on the lid of a stone coffin. Donkin glared with avidity. Then Jimmy, without stirring, blinked his eyelids, and Donkin had another shock. Those eyes were rather startling. He shut the door behind his back with gentle care, looking intently the while at James Wait as though he had come in there at a great risk to tell some secret of startling importance. Jimmy did not move but glanced languidly out of the corners of his eyes. 'Calm?' he asked. 'Yuss,' said Donkin, very disappointed, and sat down on the box.

Jimmy was used to such visits at all times of night or day. Men succeeded one another. They spoke in clear voices, pronounced cheerful words, repeated old jokes, listened to him; and each, going out, seemed to leave behind a little of his own vitality, surrender some of his own strength, renew the assurance of life – the indestructible thing! He did not like to be alone in his cabin, because, when he was alone, it seemed to him as if he hadn't been there at all. There was nothing. No pain. Not now. Perfectly right – but he couldn't enjoy his healthful repose unless someone was by to see it. This man would do as well as anybody. Donkin watched him stealthily. 'Soon home now,' observed Wait. 'Vy d'yer whisper?' asked Donkin with interest, 'can't yer speak up?' Jimmy looked annoyed and said nothing for a while; then in a lifeless, unringing voice: 'Why should I shout? You ain't deaf that I know.' 'Oh! I can 'ear right enough,' answered Donkin in a low tone, and looked down. He was thinking sadly of going out when Jimmy spoke again. 'Time we did get home . . . to get something decent to eat. . . . I am always hungry.' Donkin felt angry all of a sudden. 'What about me,' he hissed, 'I am 'ungry too an' got ter work. You, 'ungry!' 'Your work won't kill you,' commented Wait, feebly; 'there's a couple of biscuits in the lower bunk there – you may have one. I can't eat them.' Donkin dived in, groped in the corner and when he came up again his mouth was full. He munched with ardour. Jimmy seemed to doze with open eyes. Donkin finished his hard bread and got up. 'You're not going?' asked Jimmy, staring at the ceiling. 'No,' said Donkin, impulsively, and instead of going out leaned his back against the closed door. He looked at James Wait, and saw him long, lean, dried up, as though all his flesh had shrivelled on his bones in the heat of a white furnace; the meagre fingers of one hand moved lightly upon the edge of the bunk playing an endless tune. To look at him was irritating and fatiguing; he could last like this for days; he was outrageous – belonging wholly neither to death nor life, and perfectly invulnerable in his apparent ignorance of both. Donkin felt tempted to enlighten him. 'What are yer thinkin' of?' he asked, surlily. James Wait had a grimacing smile that passed over the death-like impassiveness of his bony face, incredible and frightful as would, in a dream, have been the sudden smile of a corpse.

'There is a girl,' whispered Wait. . . . 'Canton Street girl. . . . She chucked a third engineer of a Rennie boat . . . for me. Cooks oysters just I like. . . . She says . . . she would chuck . . . any toff . . . for a coloured gentleman. . . . That's me. I am kind to wimmen,' he added, a shade louder.

Donkin could hardly believe his ears. He was scandalized – 'Would she? Yer wouldn't be any good to'er,' he said with unrestrained disgust. Wait was not there to hear him. He was swaggering up the East India Dock Road; saying kindly, 'Come along for a treat,' pushing glass swing-doors, posing with superb assurance in the gaslight above a mahogany counter. 'D'yer think yer will ever get ashore?' asked Donkin angrily. Wait came back with a start. 'Ten days,' he said, promptly, and returned at once to the regions of memory that know nothing of time. He felt untired, calm, and safely withdrawn within himself beyond the reach of every grave incertitude. There was something of the immutable quality of eternity in the slow moments of his complete restfulness. He was very quiet and easy amongst his vivid reminiscences which he mistook joyfully for images of an undoubted future. He cared for no one. Donkin felt this vaguely like a blind man feeling in his darkness the fatal antagonism of all the surrounding existences, that to him shall for ever remain irrealizable, unseen and enviable. He had a desire to assert his importance, to break, to crush; to be even with everybody for everything; to tear the veil, unmask, expose, leave no refuge – a perfidious desire of truthfulness! He laughed in a mocking splutter and said:

'Ten days. Strike me blind if I ever! . . . You will be dead by this time tomorrow p'r'aps. Ten days!' He waited for a while. 'D'ye 'ear me? Blamme if yer don't look dead already.'

Wait must have been collecting his strength for he said almost aloud: 'You're a stinking, cadging liar. Everyone knows you.' And sitting up, against all probability, startled his visitor horribly. But very soon Donkin recovered himself. He blustered:

'What? What? Who's a liar? You are – the crowd are – the skipper – everybody. I ain't! Putting on airs! Who's yer?' He nearly choked himself with indignation. 'Who's yer to put on airs,' he repeated, trembling. ''Ave one – 'ave one, says 'ee – an' cawn't eat 'em 'isself. Now I'll 'ave both. By Gawd – I will! Yer nobody!'

He plunged into the lower bunk, rooted in there, and brought to light another dusty biscuit. He held it up before Jimmy – then took a bite defiantly.

'What now?' he asked with feverish impudence. 'Yer may take one – says yer. Why not giv' me both? No. I'm a mangy dorg. One fur a mangy dorg I'll tyke both. Can yer stop me? Try. Come on. Try.'

Jimmy was clasping his legs and hiding his face on the knees. His shirt clung to him. Every rib was visible. His emaciated back was shaken in repeated jerks by the panting catches of his breath.

'Yer won't? Yer can't! What did I say?' went on Donkin, fiercely. He swallowed another dry mouthful with a hasty effort. The other's silent helplessness, his weakness, his shrinking attitude exasperated him. 'Ye're done!' he cried. 'Who's yer to be lied to; to be waited on 'and an' foot like a bloomin' ymperor. Yer nobody. Yer no one at all!' he spluttered with such a strength of unerring conviction that it shook him from head to foot in coming out, and left him vibrating like a released string.

James Wait rallied again. He lifted his head and turned bravely at Donkin, who saw a strange face, an unknown face, a fantastic and grimacing mask of despair and fury. Its lips moved rapidly; and hollow, moaning, whistling sounds filled the cabin with a vague mutter full of menace, complaint, and desolation, like the far-off murmur of a rising wind. Wait shook his head; rolled his eyes; he denied, cursed, threatened – and not a word had the strength to pass beyond the sorrowful pout of those black lips. It was incomprehensible and disturbing; a gibberish of emotions, a frantic dumb show of speech pleading for impossible things, promising a shadowy vengeance. It sobered Donkin into a scrutinizing watchfulness.

'Yer can't oller. See? What did I tell yer?' he said, slowly, after a moment of attentive examination. The other kept on headlong and unheard, nodding passionately, grinning with grotesque and appalling flashes of big white teeth. Donkin, as if fascinated by the dumb eloquence and anger of that black phantom, approached, stretching his neck out with distrustful curiosity; and it seemed to him suddenly that he was looking only at the shadow of a man crouching high in the bunk on the level with his eyes. 'What? What?' he said. He seemed to catch the shape of some words in the continuous panting hiss. 'Yer will tell Belfast! Will yer? Are yer a bloomin' kid?' He trembled with alarm and rage, 'Tell yer gran'mother! Yer afeard! Who's yer ter be afeard more'n anyone?' His passionate sense of his own importance ran away with a last remnant of caution. 'Tell an' be damned! Tell, if yer can!' he cried. 'I've been treated worser'n a dorg by your blooming back-lickers. They 'as set me on, only to turn aginst me. I am the only man 'ere. They clouted me, kicked me – an' yer laffed – yer black, rotten incumbrance, you! You will pay fur it. They giv' yer their grub, their water – yer will pay fur it to me, by Gawd! Who axed me ter 'ave a drink of water? They put their bloomin' rags on yer that night, an' what did they giv' ter me – a clout on the bloomin' mouth – blast their . . . S'elp me! . . . Yer will pay fur it with yer money. I'm going' ter ave it in a minyt; as soon has ye're dead, yer bloomin' useless fraud. That's the man I am. An' ye're a thing – a bloody thing. Yah – you corpse!'

He flung at Jimmy's head the biscuit he had been all the time clutching hard, but it only grazed, and striking with a loud crack the bulkhead beyond burst like a hand-grenade into flying pieces. James Wait, as if wounded mortally, fell back on the pillow. His lips ceased to move and the rolling eyes became quiet and stared upwards with an intense and steady persistence. Donkin was surprised; he sat suddenly on the chest, and looked down, exhausted and gloomy. After a moment, he began to mutter to himself, 'Die, you beggar – die. Somebody'll come in. . . . I wish I was drunk. . . . Ten days . . . oysters . . .' He looked up and spoke louder. 'No . . . No more for yer . . . no more bloomin' gals that cook oysters. . . . Who's yer? It's my turn now. . . . I wish I was drunk; I would soon giv' you a leg up. That's where yer bound to go. Feet fust, through a port. . . . Splash! Never see yer any more. Overboard! Good 'nuff fur yer.'

Jimmy's head moved slightly and he turned his eyes to Donkin's face; a gaze unbelieving, desolated, and appealing, of a child frightened by the menace of being shut up alone in the dark. Donkin observed him from the chest with hopeful eyes; then, without rising, tried the lid. Locked. 'I wish I was drunk,' he muttered and getting up listened anxiously to the distant sound of footsteps on the deck. They approached – ceased. Someone yawned interminably just outside the door, and the footsteps went away shuffling lazily. Donkin's fluttering heart eased its pace, and when he looked towards the bunk again Jimmy was staring as before at the white beam. ''Ow d'yer feel now?' he asked. 'Bad,' breathed out Jimmy.

Donkin sat down patient and purposeful. Every half-hour the bells spoke to one another ringing along the whole length of the ship. Jimmy's respiration was so rapid that it couldn't be counted, so faint that it couldn't be heard. His eyes were terrified as though he had been looking at unspeakable horrors; and by his face one could see that he was thinking of abominable things. Suddenly with an incredibly strong and heart-breaking voice he sobbed out:

'Overboard! . . . I! . . . My God!'

Donkin writhed a little on the box. He looked unwillingly. James Wait was mute. His two long bony hands smoothed the blanket upwards, as though he had wished to gather it all up under his chin. A tear, a big solitary tear, escaped from the corner of his eye and, without touching the hollow cheek, fell on the pillow. His throat rattled faintly.

And Donkin, watching the end of that hateful nigger, felt the anguishing grasp of a great sorrow on his heart at the thought that he himself, some day, would have to go through it all – just like this – perhaps! His eyes became moist. 'Poor beggar,' he murmured. The night seemed to go by in a flash; it seemed to him he could hear the irremediable rush of precious minutes. How long would this blooming affair last? Too long surely. No luck. He could not restrain himself. He got up and approached the bunk. Wait did not stir. Only his eyes appeared alive and his hands continued their smoothing movement with a horrible and tireless industry. Donkin bent over.

'Jimmy,' he called low. There was no answer, but the rattle stopped. 'D'yer see me?' he asked, trembling. Jimmy's chest heaved. Donkin, looking away, bent his ear to Jimmy's lips, and heard a sound like the rustle of a single dry leaf driven along the smooth sand of a beach. It shaped itself.

'Light . . . the lamp . . . and . . . go,' breathed out Wait.

Donkin, instinctively, glanced over his shoulder at the brilliant flame; then, still looking away, felt under the pillow for a key. He got it at once and for the next few minutes remained on his knees shakily but swiftly busy inside the box. When he got up, his face – for the first time in his life – had a pink flush – perhaps of triumph.

He slipped the key under the pillow again, avoiding to glance at Jimmy, who had not moved. He turned his back squarely from the bunk, and started to the door as though he were going to walk a mile. At his second stride he had his nose against it. He clutched the handle cautiously, but at that moment he received the irresistible impression of something happening behind his back. He spun round as though he had been tapped on the shoulder. He was just in time to see Wait's eyes blaze up and go out at once, like two lamps overturned together by a sweeping blow. Something resembling a scarlet thread hung down his chin out of the corner of his lips – and he had ceased to breathe.

Donkin closed the door behind him gently but firmly. Sleeping men, huddled under jackets, made on the lighted deck shapeless dark mounds that had the appearance of neglected graves. Nothing had been done all through the night and he hadn't been missed. He stood motionless and perfectly astounded to find the world outside as he had left it; there was the sea, the ship – sleeping men; and he wondered absurdly at it, as though he had expected to find the men dead, familiar things gone for ever: as though, like a wanderer returning after many years, he had expected to see bewildering changes. He shuddered a little in the penetrating freshness of the air, and hugged himself forlornly. The declining moon drooped sadly in the western board as if withered by the cold touch of a pale dawn. The ship slept. And the immortal sea stretched away, immense and hazy, like the image of life, with a glittering surface and lightless depths. Donkin gave it a defiant glance and slunk off noiselessly as if judged and cast out by the august silence of its might.

Jimmy's death, after all, came as a tremendous surprise. We did not know till then how much faith we had put in his delusions. We had taken his chances of life so much at his own valuation that his death, like the death of an old belief, shook the foundations of our society. A common bond was gone; the strong, effective, and respectable bond of a sentimental lie. All that day we mooned at our work, with suspicious looks and a disabused air. In our hearts we thought that in the matter of his departure Jimmy had acted in a perverse and unfriendly manner. He didn't back us up, as a shipmate should. In going he took away with himself the gloomy and solemn shadow in which our folly had posed, with humane satisfaction, as a tender arbiter of fate. And now we saw it was no such thing. It was just common foolishness; a silly and ineffectual meddling with issues of majestic import – that is, if Podmore was right. Perhaps he was? Doubt survived Jimmy; and, like a community of banded criminals disintegrated by a touch of grace, we were profoundly scandalized with each other. Men spoke unkindly to their best chums. Others refused to speak at all. Singleton only was not surprised. 'Dead – is he? Of course,' he said, pointing at the island right abeam; for the calm still held the ship spell-bound within sight of Flores. Dead – of course. *He* wasn't surprised. Here was the land, and there, on the fore-hatch and waiting for the sailmaker – there was that corpse. Cause and effect. And for the first time that voyage, the old seaman became quite cheery and garrulous, explaining and illustrating from the stores of experience how, in sickness, the sight of an island (even a very small one) is generally more fatal than the view of a continent. But he couldn't explain why.

Jimmy was to be buried at five, and it was a long day till then – a day of mental disquiet and even of physical disturbance. We took no interest in our work and, very properly, were rebuked for it. This, in our constant state of hungry irritation, was exasperating. Donkin worked with his brow bound in a dirty rag, and looked so ghastly that Mr Baker was touched with compassion at the sight of this plucky suffering. 'Ough! You, Donkin! Put down your work and go lay-up this watch. You look ill.' 'I am bad, sir – in my 'ead,' he said in a subdued voice, and vanished speedily. This annoyed many, and they thought the mate 'bloomin soft today'. Captain Allistoun could be seen on the poop watching the sky to the south-west, and it soon got to be known about the decks that the barometer had begun to fall in the night, and that a breeze might be expected before long. This, by a subtle association of ideas, led to violent quarrelling as to the exact moment of Jimmy's death. Was it before or after 'that 'ere glass started down'? It was impossible to know, and it caused much contemptuous growling at one another. All of a sudden there was a great tumult forward. Pacific Knowles and good-tempered Davies had come to blows over it. The watch below interfered with spirit, and for ten minutes there was a noisy scrimmage round the hatch, where, in the balancing shade of the sails, Jimmy's body wrapped up in a white blanket, was watched over by the sorrowful Belfast, who, in his desolation, disdained the fray. When the noise had ceased, and the passions had calmed into surly silence, he stood up at the head of the swathed body, lifting both arms on high, cried with pained indignation: 'You ought to be ashamed of yourselves! . . .' We were.

Belfast took his bereavement very hard. He gave proofs of unextinguishable devotion. It was he, and no other man, who would help the sailmaker to prepare what was left of Jimmy for a solemn surrender to the insatiable sea. He arranged the weights carefully at the feet: two holystones, an old anchor-shackle without its pin, some broken links of a worn-out stream cable. He arranged them this way, then that. 'Bless my soul! you aren't afraid he will chafe his heel?' said the sailmaker, who hated the job. He pushed the needle, puffing furiously, with his head in a cloud of tobacco smoke; he turned the flaps over, pulled at the stitches, stretched at the canvas. 'Lift his shoulders. . . . Pull to you a bit. . . . So – o – o. Steady.' Belfast obeyed, pulled, lifted, overcome with sorrow, dropping tears on the tarred twine. 'Don't you drag the canvas too taut over his poor face, Sails,' he entreated tearfully. 'What are you fashing yourself for? He will be comfortable enough,' assured the sailmaker, cutting the thread after the last stitch, which came about the middle of Jimmy's forehead. He rolled up the remaining canvas, put away the needles. 'What makes you take on so?' he asked. Belfast looked down at the long package of grey sailcloth. 'I pulled him out,' he whispered, 'and he did not want to go. If I had sat up with him last night he would have kept alive for me . . . but something made me tired.' The sailmaker took vigorous draws at his pipe and mumbled: 'When I . . . West India Station . . . In the *Blanche* frigate . . . Yellow Jack . . . sewed in twenty men a week . . . Portsmouth-Devonport men – townies – knew their fathers, mothers, sisters – the whole boiling of 'em. Thought nothing of it. And these niggers like this one – you don't know where it comes from. Got nobody. No use to nobody. Who will miss him?' 'I do – I pulled him out,' mourned Belfast dismally.

On two planks nailed together and apparently resigned and still under the folds of the Union Jack with a white border, James Wait, carried aft by four men, was deposited slowly, with his feet pointing at an open port. A swell had set in from the westward, and following on the roll of the ship, the red ensign, at half-mast, darted out and collapsed again on the grey sky, like a tongue of flickering fire; Charley tolled the bell; and at every swing to starboard the whole vast semi-circle of steely waters visible on that side seemed to come up with a rush to the edge of the port, as if impatient to get at our Jimmy. Everyone was there but Donkin, who was too ill to come; the Captain and Mr Creighton stood bareheaded on the break of the poop; Mr Baker, directed by the master, who had said to him gravely: 'You know more about the prayer book than I do,' came out of the cabin door quickly and a little embarrassed. All the caps went off. He began to read in a low tone, and with his usual harmlessly menacing utterance, as though he had been for the last time reproving confidentially that dead seaman at his feet. The men listened in scattered groups; they leaned on the fife rail, gazing on the deck; they held their chins in their hands thoughtfully, or, with crossed arms and one knee slightly bent, hung their heads in an attitude of upright meditation. Wamibo dreamed. Mr Baker read on, grunting reverently at the turn of every page. The words, missing the unsteady hearts of men, rolled out to wander without a home upon the heartless sea; and James Wait, silenced for ever, lay uncritical and passive under the hoarse murmur of despair and hopes.

Two men made ready and waited for those words that send so many of our brothers to their last plunge. Mr Baker began the passage. 'Stand by,' muttered the boatswain. Mr Baker read out: 'To the deep,' and paused. The men lifted the inboard end of the planks, the boatswain snatched off the Union Jack, and James

Wait did not move. 'Higher,' muttered the boatswain angrily. All the heads were raised; every man stirred uneasily, but James Wait gave no sign of going. In death and swathed up for all eternity, he yet seemed to cling to the ship with the grip of an undying fear. 'Higher! Lift!' whispered the boatswain, fiercely. 'He won't go,' stammered one of the men, shakily, and both appeared ready to drop everything. Mr Baker waited, burying his face in the book, and shuffling his feet nervously. All the men looked profoundly disturbed; from their midst a faint humming noise spread out – growing louder. . . . 'Jimmy!' cried Belfast in a wailing tone, and there was a second of shuddering dismay.

'Jimmy, be a man!' he shrieked, passionately. Every mouth was wide open, not an eyelid winked. He stared wildly, twitching all over; he bent his body forward like a man peering at a horror. 'Go!' he shouted, and sprang out of the crowd with his arm extended. 'Go, Jimmy! – Jimmy, go! Go!' His fingers touched the head of the body, and the grey package started reluctantly to whizz off the lifted planks all at once, with the suddenness of a flash of lightning. The crowd stepped forward like one man; a deep Ah – h – h! came out vibrating from the broad chests. The ship rolled as if relieved of an unfair burden; the sails flapped. Belfast, supported by Archie, gasped hysterically; and Charley, who anxious to see Jimmy's last drive, leaped headlong on the rail, was too late to see anything but the faint circle of a vanishing ripple.

Mr Baker, perspiring abundantly, read out the last prayer in a deep rumour of excited men and fluttering sails. 'Amen!' he said in an unsteady growl, and closed the book.

'Square the yards!' thundered a voice above his head. All hands gave a jump; one or two dropped their caps; Mr Baker looked up surprised. The master, standing on the break of the poop, pointed to the westward. 'Breeze coming,' he said. 'Man the weather braces.' Mr Baker crammed the book hurriedly into his pocket. 'Forward, there – let go the foretack!' he hailed joyfully, bareheaded and brisk; 'Square the foreyard, you port watch!' 'Fair wind – fair wind,' muttered the men going to the braces. 'What did I tell you?' mumbled old Singleton, flinging down coil after coil with hasty energy; 'I knowed it – he's gone and here it comes.'

It came with the sound of a lofty and powerful sigh. The sails filled, the ship gathered way, and the waking sea began to murmur sleepily of home to the ears of men.

That night, while the ship rushed foaming to the northward before a freshening gale, the boatswain unbosomed himself to the petty officers' berth: 'The chap was nothing but trouble,' he said, 'from the moment he came aboard – d'ye remember – that night in Bombay? Been bullying all that softy crowd – cheeked the old man – we had to go fooling all over a half-drowned ship to save him. Dam' nigh a mutiny all for him – and now the mate abused me like a pickpocket for forgetting to dab a lump of grease on them planks. So I did, but you ought to have known better, too, than to leave a nail sticking up – hey, Chips?'

'And you ought to have known better than to chuck all my tools overboard for 'im, like a skeary greenhorn,' retorted the morose carpenter. 'Well – he's gone after 'em now,' he added in an unforgiving tone. 'On the China Station, I remember once, the Admiral he says to me . . .' began the sailmaker.

A week afterwards the *Narcissus* entered the chops of of the Channel.

Under white wings she skimmed low over the blue sea like a great tired bird speeding to its nest. The clouds raced with her mastheads; they rose astern enormous and white, soared to the zenith, flew past, and, falling down the wide curve of the sky, seemed to dash headlong into the sea – the clouds swifter than the ship, more free, but without a home. The coast to welcome her stepped out of space into the sunshine. The lofty headlands trod masterfully into the sea; the wide bays smiled in the light; the shadows of homeless clouds ran along the sunny plains, leaped over valleys, without a check darted up the hills, rolled down the slopes; and the sunshine pursued them with patches of running brightness. On the brows of dark cliffs white lighthouses shone in pillars of light. The Channel glittered like a blue mantle shot with gold and starred by the silver of the capping seas. The *Narcissus* rushed past the headlands and the bays. Outward-bound vessels crossed her track, lying over, and with their masts stripped for a slogging fight with the hard sou'-wester. And, inshore, a string of smoking steamboats waddled, hugging the coast, like migrating and amphibious monsters, distrustful of the restless waves.

At night the headlands retreated, the bays advanced into one unbroken line of gloom. The lights of the earth mingled with the lights of heaven; and above the tossing lanterns of a trawling fleet a great lighthouse shone steadily, like an enormous riding light burning above a vessel of fabulous dimensions. Below its steady glow, the coast, stretching away straight and black, resembled the high side of an indestructible craft riding motionless upon the immortal and unresting sea. The dark land lay alone in the midst of waters, like a mighty ship bestarred with vigilant lights – a ship carrying the burden of millions of lives – a ship freighted with dross and with jewels, with gold and with steel. She towered up immense and strong, guarding priceless traditions and untold suffering, sheltering glorious memories and base forgetfulness, ignoble virtues and splendid transgressions. A great ship! For ages had the ocean battered in vain her enduring sides; she was there when the world was vaster and darker, when the sea was great and mysterious, and ready to surrender the prize of fame to audacious men. A ship mother of fleets and nations! The great flagship of the race; stronger than the storms! and anchored in the open sea.

The *Narcissus*, heeling over to off-shore gusts, rounded the South Foreland, passed through the Downs, and, in tow, entered the river. Sworn of the glory of her white wings, she wound obediently after the tug through the maze of invisible channels. As she passed them the red-painted light-vessels, swung at their moorings, seemed for an instant to sail with great speed in the rush of tide, and the next moment were left hopelessly behind. The big buoys on the tails of banks slipped past her sides very low, and, dropping in her wake, tugged at their chains like fierce watch-dogs. The reach narrowed; from both sides, the land approached the ship. She went steadily up the river. On the riverside slopes the houses appeared in groups – seemed to stream down the declivities at a run to see her pass, and, checked by the mud of the foreshore, crowded on the banks.

Farther on, the tall factory chimneys appeared in insolent bands and watched her go by, like a straggling crowd of slim giants, swaggering and upright under the black plummets of smoke, cavalierly aslant. She swept round the bends; an impure breeze shrieked a welcome between her stripped spars; and the land, closing in, stepped between the ship and the sea.

A low cloud hung before her – a great opalescent and tremulous cloud, that seemed to rise from the steaming brows of millions of men. Long drifts of smoky vapours soiled it with livid trails; it throbbed to the beat of millions of hearts, and from it came an immense and lamentable murmur – the murmur of millions of lips praying, cursing, sighing, jeering – the undying murmur of folly, regret, and hope exhaled by the crowds of the anxious earth. The *Narcissus* entered the cloud; the shadows deepened; on all sides there was the clang of iron, the sound of mighty blows, shrieks, yells. Black barges drifted stealthily on the murky stream. A mad jumble of begrimed walls loomed up vaguely in the smoke, bewildering and mournful, like a vision of disaster. The tugs backed and filled in the stream, to hold the ship steady at the dock-gates; from her bows two lines went through the air whistling, and struck at the land viciously, like a pair of snakes. A bridge broke in two before her, as if by enchantment; big hydraulic capstans began to turn all by themselves, as though animated by a mysterious and unholy spell. She moved through a narrow lane of water between two low walls of granite, and men with check-ropes in their hands kept pace with her, walking on the broad flag-stones. A group waited impatiently on each side of the vanished bridge: rough heavy men in caps; sallow-faced men in high hats; two bareheaded women; ragged children, fascinated, and with wide eyes. A cart coming at a jerky trot pulled up sharply. One of the women screamed at the silent ship: 'Hallo, Jack!' without looking at anyone in particular, and all hands looked at her from the forecastle head. 'Stand clear! Stand clear of that rope!' cried the dockmen, bending over the stone posts. The crowd murmured, stamped where they stood. 'Let go your quarter-checks! Let go!' sang out a ruddy-faced old man on the quay. The ropes splashed heavily falling in the water, and the *Narcissus* entered the dock.

The stony shores ran away right and left in straight lines, enclosing a sombre and rectangular pool. Brick walls rose high above the water – soulless walls, staring through hundreds of windows as troubled and dull as the eyes of over-fed brutes. At their base monstrous iron cranes crouched, with chains hanging from their long necks, balancing cruel-looking hooks over the decks of lifeless ships. A noise of wheels rolling over stones, the thump of heavy things falling, the racket of feverish winches, the grinding of strained chains, floated on the air. Between high buildings the dust of all the continents soared in short flights; and a penetrating smell of perfumes and dirt, of spices and hides, of things costly and of things filthy, pervaded the space, made for it an atmosphere precious and disgusting. The *Narcissus* came gently into her berth; the shadows of soulless walls fell upon her, the dust of all the continents leaped upon her deck, and a swarm of strange men, clambering up her sides, took possession of her in the name of the sordid earth. She had ceased to live.

A toff in a black coat and high hat scrambled with agility, came up to the second mate, shook hands, and said: 'Hallo Herbert.' It was his brother. A lady appeared suddenly. A real lady, in a black dress and with a parasol. She looked extremely elegant in the midst of us, and as strange as if she had fallen there from the sky. Mr Baker touched his cap to her. It was the master's wife. And very soon the Captain, dressed very smartly and in a white shirt, went with her over the side. We didn't recognize him at all till, turning on the quay, he called to Mr Baker: 'Don't forget to wind up the chronometers tomorrow morning.' An underhand lot of seedy-looking chaps with shifty eyes wandered in and out of the forecastle looking for a job – they said. 'More likely for something to steal,' commented Knowles, cheerfully. Poor beggars. Who cared? Weren't we home! But Mr Baker went for one of them who had given him some cheek, and we were delighted. Everything was delightful. 'I've finished aft, sir,' called out Mr Creighton. 'No water in the well, sir,' reported for the last time the carpenter, sounding-rod in hand. Mr Baker glanced along the decks at the expectant group of sailors, glanced aloft at the yards. 'Ough! That will do, men,' he grunted. The group broke up. The voyage was ended.

Rolled-up beds went flying over the rail; lashed chests went sliding down the gangway – mighty few of both at that. 'The rest is having a cruise off the Cape,' explained Knowles enigmatically to a dock-loafer with whom he had struck a sudden friendship, Men ran, calling to one another, hailing utter strangers to 'lend a hand with the dunnage', then with sudden decorum approached the mate to shake hands before going ashore. 'Good-bye, sir,' they repeated in various tones. Mr Baker grasped hard palms, grunted in a friendly manner at everyone, his eyes twinkled. 'Take care of your money, Knowles. Ough! Soon get a nice wife if you do.' The lame man was delighted. 'Good-bye, sir,' said Belfast, with emotion, wringing the mate's hand, and looked up with swimming eyes. 'I thought I would take 'im ashore with me,' he went on, plaintively. Mr Baker did not understand, but said kindly: 'Take care of yourself, Craik,' and the bereaved Belfast went over the rail mourning and alone.

Mr Baker, in the sudden peace of the ship, moved about solitary and grunting, trying door-handles, peering into dark places, never done – a model chief mate! No one waited for him ashore. Mother dead; father and two brothers, Yarmouth fishermen, drowned together on the Dogger Bank; sister married and unfriendly. Quite a lady. Married to the leading tailor of a little town, and its leading politician, who did not think his sailor brother-in-law quite respectable enough for him. Quite a lady, quite a lady, he thought, sitting down for a moment's rest on the quarter-hatch. Time enough to go ashore and get a bite and sup, and a bed somewhere. He didn't like to part with a ship. No one to think about then. The darkness of a misty evening fell, cold and damp, upon the deserted deck; and Mr Baker sat smoking, thinking of all the successive ships to whom through many long years he had given the best of a seaman's care. And never a command in sight. Not once! 'I haven't somehow the cut of a skipper about me,' he meditated, placidly, while the shipkeeper (who had taken possession of the galley), a wizened old man with bleared eyes, cursed him in whispers for 'hanging about so'. 'Now, Creighton,' he pursued the unenvious train of thought, 'quite a gentleman . . . swell friends . . . will get on. Fine young fellow . . . a little more experience.' He got up and shook himself. 'I'll be back first thing tomorrow morning for the hatches. Don't you let them touch anything before I come, shipkeeper,' he called out. Then, at last, he also went ashore – a model chief mate!

The men scattered by the dissolving contact of the land came together once more in the shipping office. 'The *Narcissus* pays off,' shouted outside a glazed door a brass-bound old fellow with a crown and the capitals B. T. on his cap. A lot trooped in at once but many were late. The room was large, whitewashed, and bare; a counter surmounted by a brass-wire grating fenced off a third of the dusty space, and behind the grating a pasty-faced clerk with his hair parted in the middle, had the quick, glittering eyes and the vivacious, jerky movements of a caged bird. Poor Captain Allistoun also in there, and sitting before a little table with piles of gold and notes on it, appeared subdued by his captivity. Another Board of Trade bird was perching on a high stool near the door: an old bird that did not mind the chaff of elated sailors. The crew of the *Narcissus*, broken up into knots, pushed in the corners. They had new shore togs, smart jackets that looked as if they had been shaped with an axe, glossy trousers that seemed made of crumpled sheet-iron, collarless flannel shirts, shiny new boots. They tapped on shoulders, button-holed one another, asked: 'Where did you sleep last night?' whispered gaily, slapped their thighs with bursts of subdued laughter. Most had clean, radiant faces; only one or two turned up dishevelled and sad; the two young Norwegians looked tidy, meek, and altogether of a promising material for the kind ladies who patronize the Scandinavian Home. Wamibo, still in his working clothes, dreamed, upright and burly in the middle of the room, and, when Archie came in, woke up for a smile. But the wide-awake clerk called out a name, and the paying-off business began.

One by one they came up to the pay-table to get the wages of their glorious and obscure toil. They swept the money with care into broad palms, rammed it trustfully into trousers' pockets, or, turning their backs on the table, reckoned with difficulty in the hollow of their stiff hands. 'Money right? Sign the release. There – there,' repeated the clerk, impatiently. 'How stupid those sailors are!' he thought. Singleton came up, venerable – and uncertain as to daylight; brown drops of tobacco juice hung in his white beard; his hands, that never hesitated in the great light of the open sea, could hardly find the small pile of gold in the profound darkness of the shore. 'Can't write?' said the clerk, shocked. 'Make a mark, then.' Singleton painfully sketched in a heavy cross, blotted the page. 'What a disgusting old brute,' muttered the clerk. Somebody opened the door for him, and the patriarchal seaman passed through unsteadily, without as much as a glance at any of us.

Archie displayed a pocket-book. He was chaffed. Belfast, who looked wild, as though he had already luffed up through a public-house or two, gave signs of emotion and wanted to speak to the Captain privately. The master was surprised. They spoke through the wires, and we could hear the Captain saying: 'I've given it up to the Board of Trade.' 'I should've liked to get something of his,' mumbled Belfast. 'But you can't, my man. It's given up, locked and sealed, to the Marine Office,' expostulated the master; and Belfast stood back, with drooping mouth and troubled eyes. In a pause of the business we heard the master and the clerk talking. We caught: 'James Wait – deceased – found no papers of any kind – no relations – no trace – the Office must hold his wages then.' Donkin entered. He seemed out of breath, was grave, full of business. He went straight to the desk, talked with animation to the clerk, who thought him an intelligent man. They discussed the account, dropping h's against one another as if for a wager – very friendly. Captain Allistoun paid. 'I give you a bad discharge,' he said, quietly. Donkin raised his voice: 'I don't want your bloomin' discharge – keep it. I'm goin' ter 'ave a job ashore.' He turned to us. 'No more bloomin' sea fur me,' he said, aloud. All looked at him. He had better clothes, had an easy air, appeared more at home than any of us; he stared with assurance, enjoying the effect of his declaration. 'Yuss. I 'ave friends well off. That's more'n you got. But I am a man. Yer shipmates for all that. Who's comin' fur a drink?'

No one moved. There was a silence; a silence of blank faces and stony looks. He waited a moment, smiled bitterly, and went to the door. There he faced round once more. 'You won't? You bloomin' lot of yrpocrits. No? What 'ave I done to yer? Did I bully yer? Did I 'urt yer? Did I? . . . You won't drink? . . . No! . . . Then may ye die of thirst, every mother's son of yer! Not one of yer 'as the sperrit of a bug. Ye're the scum of the world. Work and starve!'

He went out, and slammed the door with such violence that the old Board of Trade bird nearly fell off his perch.

'He's mad,' declared Archie. 'No! No! He's drunk,' insisted Belfast, lurching about, and in a maudlin tone. Captain Allistoun sat smiling thoughtfully at the cleared pay-table.

Outside, on Tower Hill, they blinked, hesitated clumsily, as if blinded by the strange quality of the hazy light, as if discomposed by the view of so many men; and they who could hear one another in the howl of gales seemed deafened and distracted by the dull roar of the busy earth. 'To the Black Horse! To the Black Horse!' cried some. 'Let us have a drink together before we part.' They crossed the road, clinging to one another. Only Charley and Belfast wandered off alone. As I came up I saw a red-faced, blowsy woman, in a grey shawl, and with dusty, fluffy hair, fall on Charley's neck. It was his mother. She slobbered over him: 'O, my boy! My boy!' 'Leggo of me,' said Charley. 'Leggo, mother!' I was passing him at the time, and over the untidy head of the blubbering woman he gave me a humorous smile and a glance ironic, courageous, and profound, that seemed to put all my knowledge of life to shame. I nodded and passed on, but heard him say again, good-naturedly: 'If you leggo of me this minyt – ye shall 'ave a bob for a drink out of my pay.' In the next few steps I came upon Belfast. He caught my arm with tremulous enthusiasm. 'I couldn't go wi' 'em,' he stammered, indicating by a nod our noisy crowd, that drifted slowly along the other sidewalk. 'When I think of Jimmy . . . Poor Jim! When I think of him I have no heart for drink. You were his chum, too . . . but I pulled him out . . . didn't I? Short wool he had. . . . Yes. And I stole the blooming pie. . . . He wouldn't go. . . . He wouldn't go for nobody.' He burst into tears. 'I never touched him – never – never!' he sobbed. 'He went for me like . . . like . . . a lamb.'

I disengaged myself gently. Belfast's crying fits generally ended in a fight with someone, and I wasn't anxious to stand the brunt of his inconsolable sorrow. Moreover, two bulky policemen stood near by, looking at us with a disapproving and incorruptible gaze. 'So long!' I said, and went on my way.

But at the corner I stopped to take my last look at the crew of the *Narcissus*. They were swaying irresolute and noisy on the broad flagstones before the Mint. They were bound for the Black Horse, where men in fur caps, with brutal faces and in shirt sleeves, dispense out of varnished barrels the illusions of strength, mirth, happiness; the illusion of splendour and poetry of life, to the paid-off crews of southern-going ships. From afar I saw them discoursing, with jovial eyes and clumsy gestures, while the sea of life thundered into their ears ceaseless and unheeded. And swaying about there on the white stones, surrounded by the hurry and clamour of men, they appeared to be creatures of another kind – lost, alone, forgetful, and doomed; they were like castaways, like reckless and joyous castaways, like mad castaways making merry in the storm and upon an insecure ledge of a treacherous rock. The roar of the town resembled the roar of topping breakers, merciless and strong, with a loud voice and cruel purpose; but overhead the clouds broke; a flood of sunshine streamed down the walls of grimy houses. The dark knot of seamen drifted in sunshine. To the left of them the trees in Tower Gardens sighed. The stones of the Tower gleaming, seemed to stir in the play of light, as if remembering suddenly all the great joys and sorrows of the past, the fighting prototypes of these men; press-gangs; mutinous cries; the wailing of women by the riverside, and the shouts of men welcoming victories. The sunshine of heaven fell like a gift of grace on the mud of the earth, on the remembering and mute stones, on greed, selfishness; on the anxious faces of forgetful men. And to the right of the dark group the stained front of the Mint, cleansed by the flood of light, stood out for a moment dazzling and white like a marble palace in a fairy tale. The crew of the *Narcissus* drifted out of sight.

I never saw them again. The sea took some, the steamers took others, the graveyards of the earth will account for the rest. Singleton has no doubt taken with him the long record of his faithful work into the peaceful depths of a hospitable sea. And Donkin, who never did a decent day's work in his life, no doubt earns his living by discoursing with filthy eloquence upon the right of labour to live. So be it! Let the earth and the sea each have its own.

A gone shipmate, like any other man, is gone for ever; and I never met one of them again. But at times the spring-flood of memory sets with force up the dark River of the Nine Bends. Then on the waters of the forlorn stream drifts a ship – a shadowy ship manned by a crew of Shades. They pass and make a sign, in a shadowy hail. Haven't we, together and upon the immortal sea, wrung out a meaning from our sinful lives? Good-bye, brothers! You were a good crowd. As good a crowd as ever fisted with wild cries the beating canvas of a heavy foresail; or tossing aloft, invisible in the night, gave back yell for yell to a westerly gale.

Heart of Darkness

CHAPTER I

THE *Nellie*, a crusing yawl, swung to her anchor without a flutter of the sails, and was at rest. The flood had made, the wind was nearly calm, and being bound down the river, the only thing for it was to come to and wait for the turn of the tide.

The sea-reach of the Thames stretched before us like the beginning of an interminable waterway. In the offing the sea and the sky were welded together without a joint, and in the luminous space the tanned sails of the barges drifting up with the tide seemed to stand still in red clusters of canvas sharply peaked, with gleams of varnished sprits. A haze rested on the low shores that ran out to sea in vanishing flatness. The air was dark above Gravesend, and farther back still seemed condensed into a mournful gloom, brooding motionless over the biggest, and the greatest, town on earth.

The Director of Companies was our captain and our host. We four affectionately watched his back as he stood in the bows looking to seaward. On the whole river there was nothing that looked half so nautical. He resembled a pilot, which to a seaman is trustworthiness personified. It was difficult to realize his work was not out there in the luminous estuary, but behind him, within the brooding gloom.

Between us there was, as I have already said somewhere, the bond of the sea. Besides holding our hearts together through long periods of separation, it had the effect of making us tolerant of each other's yarns – and even convictions. The Lawyer – the best of old fellows – had, because of his many years and many virtues, the only cushion on deck, and was lying on the only rug. The Accountant had brought out already a box of dominoes, and was toying architecturally with the bones. Marlow sat cross-legged right aft, leaning against the mizzen-mast. He had sunken cheeks, a yellow complexion, a straight back, an ascetic aspect, and, with his arms dropped, the palms of hands outwards, resembled an idol. The Director satisfied the anchor had good hold, made his way aft and sat down amongst us. We exchanged a few words lazily. Afterwards there was silence on board the yacht. For some reason or other we did not begin that game of dominoes. We felt meditative, and fit for nothing but placid staring. The day was ending in a serenity of still and exquisite brilliance. The water shone pacifically; the sky, without a speck, was a benign immensity of unstained light; the very mist on the Essex marshes was like a gauzy and radiant fabric, hung from the wooded rises inland, and draping the low shores in diaphanous folds. Only the gloom to the west, brooding over the upper reaches, became more sombre every minute, as if angered by the approach of the sun.

And at last, in its curved and imperceptible fall, the sun sank low, and from glowing white changed to a dull red without rays and without heat, as if about to go out suddenly, stricken to death by the touch of that gloom brooding over a crowd of men.

Forthwith a change came over the waters, and the serenity became less brilliant but more profound. The old river in its broad reach rested unruffled at the decline of day, after ages of good service done to the race that peopled its banks, spread out in the tranquil dignity of a waterway leading to the uttermost ends of the earth. We looked at the venerable stream not in the vivid flush of a short day that comes and departs for ever, but in the august light of abiding memories. And indeed nothing is easier for a man who has, as the phrase goes, 'followed the sea' with reverence and affection, than to evoke the great spirit of the past upon the lower reaches of the Thames. The tidal current runs to and fro in its unceasing service, crowded with memories of men and ships it had borne to the rest of home or to the battles of the sea. It had known and served all the men of whom the nation is proud, from Sir Francis Drake to Sir John Franklin, knights all, titled and untitled – the great knights-errant of the sea. It had borne all the ships whose names are like jewels flashing in the night of time, from the *Golden Hind* returning with her round flanks full of treasure, to be visited by the Queen's Highness and thus pass out of the gigantic tale, to the *Erebus* and *Terror*, bound on other conquests – and that never returned. It had known the ships and the men. They had sailed from Deptford, from Greenwich, from Erith – the adventurers and the settlers; kings' ships and the ships of men on 'Change; captains, admirals, the dark 'interlopers' of the Eastern trade, and the commissioned 'generals' of East India fleets. Hunters for gold or pursuers of fame, they all had gone out on that stream, bearing the sword, and often the torch, messengers of the might within the land, bearers of a spark from the sacred fire. What greatness had not floated on the ebb of that river into the mystery of an unknown earth! . . . The dreams of men, the seed of commonwealths, the germs of empires.

The sun set; the dusk fell on the stream, and lights began to appear along the shore. The Chapman lighthouse, a three-legged thing erect on a mud-flat, shone strongly. Lights of ships moved in the fairway – a great stir of lights going up and going down. And farther west on the upper reaches the place of the monstrous town was still marked ominously on the sky, a brooding gloom in sunshine, a lurid glare under the stars.

'And this also,' said Marlow suddenly, 'has been one of the dark places of the earth.'

He was the only man of us who still 'followed the sea'. The worst that could be said of him was that he did not represent his class. He was a seaman, but he was a wanderer, too, while most seamen lead, if one may so express it, a sedentary life. Their minds are of the stay-at-home order, and their home is always with them – the ship; and so is their country – the sea. One ship is very much like another, and the sea is always the same. In the immutability of their surroundings the foreign shores, the foreign faces, the changing immensity of life, glide past, veiled not by a sense of mystery but by a slightly disdainful ignorance; for there is nothing mysterious to a seaman unless it be the sea itself, which is the mistress of his existence and as inscrutable as Destiny. For the rest, after his hours of work, a casual stroll or a casual spree on shore suffices to unfold for him the secret of a whole continent, and generally he finds the secret not worth knowing. The yarns of seamen have a direct simplicity, the whole meaning of which lies within the shell of a cracked nut. But Marlow was not typical (if his propensity to spin yarns be excepted), and to him the meaning of an episode was not inside like a kernel but outside, enveloping the tale which brought it out only as a glow brings out a haze, in the likeness of one of these misty halos that sometimes are made visible by the spectral illumination of moonshine.

His remark did not seem at all surprising. It was just like Marlow. It was accepted in silence. No one took the trouble to grunt even; and presently he said, very slow –

'I was thinking of very old times, when the Romans first came here, nineteen hundred years ago – the other day . . . Light came out of this river since – you say Knights? Yes; but it is like a running blaze on a plain, like a flash of lightning in the clouds. We live in the flicker – may it last as long as the old earth keeps rolling! But darkness was here yesterday. Imagine the feelings of a commander of a fine – what d'ye call 'em? – trireme in the Mediterranean, ordered suddenly to the north; run overland across the Gauls in a hurry; put in charge of one of these craft the legionaries – a wonderful lot of handy men they must have been, too – used to build, apparently by the hundred, in a month or two, if we may believe what we read. Imagine him here – the very end of the world, a sea the colour of lead, a sky the colour of smoke, a kind of ship about as rigid as a concertina – and going up this river with stores, or orders, or what you like. Sand-banks, marshes, forests, savages, – precious little to eat fit for a civilized man, nothing but Thames water to drink. No Falernian wine here, no going ashore. Here and there a military camp lost in a wilderness, like a needle in a bundle of hay – cold, fog, tempests, disease, exile, and death – death skulking in the air, in the water, in the bush. They must have been dying like flies here. Oh, yes – he did it. Did it very well, too, no doubt, and without thinking much about it either, except afterwards to brag of what he had done through his time, perhaps. They were men enough to face the darkness. And perhaps he was cheered by keeping his eye on a chance of promotion to the fleet at Ravenna by-and-by, if he had good friends in Rome and survived the awful climate. Or think of a decent young citizen in a toga – perhaps too much dice, you know – coming out here in the train of some prefect, or tax-gatherer, or trader even, to mend his fortunes. Land in a swamp, march through the woods, and in some inland post feel the savagery, the utter savagery, had closed round him, – all that mysterious life of the wilderness that stirs in the forest, in the jungles, in the hearts of wild men. There's no initiation either into such mysteries. He has to live in the midst of the incomprehensible, which is also detestable. And it has a fascination, too, that goes to work upon him. The fascination of the abomination – you know, imagine the growing regrets, the longing to escape, the powerless disgust, the surrender, the hate.'

He paused.

'Mind,' he began again, lifting one arm from the elbow, the palm of the hand outwards, so that, with his legs folded before him, he had the pose of a Buddha preaching in European clothes and without a lotus-flower – 'Mind, none of us would feel exactly like this. What saves us is efficiency – the devotion to efficiency. But these chaps were not much account, really. They were not colonists; their administration was merely a squeeze, and nothing more, I suspect. They were conquerors, and for that you want only brute force – nothing to boast of, when you have it, since your strength is just an accident arising from the weakness of others. They grabbed what they could get for the sake of what was to be got. It was just robbery with violence, aggravated murder on a great scale, and men going at it blind – as is very proper for those who tackle a darkness. The conquest of the earth, which mostly means the taking it away from those who have a different complexion or slightly flatter noses than ourselves, is not a pretty thing when you look into it too much. What redeems it is the idea only. An idea at the back of it; not a sentimental pretence but an idea; and an unselfish belief in the idea – something you can set up, and bow down before, and offer a sacrifice to . . .'

He broke off. Flames glided in the river, small green flames, red flames, white flames pursuing, overtaking, joining, crossing each other – then separating slowly or hastily. The traffic of the great city went on in the deepening night upon the sleepless river. We looked on, waiting patiently – there was nothing else to do till the end of the flood; but it was only after a long silence, when he said, in a hesitating voice. 'I suppose you fellows remember I did once turn fresh-water sailor for a bit,' that we knew we were fated, before the ebb began to run, to hear about one of Marlow's inconclusive experiences.

'I don't want to bother you much with what happened to me personally,' he began, showing in this remark the weakness of many tellers of tales who seem so often unaware of what their audience would best like to hear; 'yet to understand the effect of it on me you ought to know how I got out there, what I saw, how I went up that river to the place where I first met the poor chap. It was the farthest point of navigation and the culminating point of my experience. It seemed somehow to throw a kind of light on everything about me – and into my thoughts. It was sombre enough, too – and pitiful – not extraordinary in any way – not very clear either. No, not very clear. And yet it seemed to throw a kind of light.

'I had then, as you remember, just returned to London after a lot of Indian Ocean, Pacific, China Seas – a regular dose of the East – six years or so, and I was loafing about, hindering you fellows in your work and invading your homes, just as though I had got a heavenly mission to civilize you. It was very fine for a time, but after a bit I did get tired of resting. Then I began to look for a ship – I should think the hardest work on earth. But the ships wouldn't even look at me. And I got tired of that game, too.

'Now when I was a little chap I had a passion for maps. I would look for hours at South America, or Africa, or Australia, and lose myself in all the glories of exploration. At that time there were many blank spaces on the earth, and when I saw one that looked particularly inviting on a map (but they all look that) I would put my finger on it and say, When I grow up I will go there. The North Pole was one of these places, I remember. Well, I haven't been there yet, and shall not try now. The glamour's off. Other places were scattered about the Equator, and in every sort of latitude all over the two hemispheres. I have been in some of them, and . . . well, we won't talk about that. But there was one yet – the biggest, the most blank, so to speak – that I had a hankering after.

'True, by this time it was not a blank space any more. It had got filled since my boyhood with rivers and lakes and names. It had ceased to be a blank space of delightful mystery – a white patch for a boy to dream gloriously over. It had become a place of darkness. But there was in it one river especially, a mighty big river, that you could see on the map, resembling an immense snake uncoiled, with its head in the sea, its body at rest curving afar over a vast country, and its tail lost in the depths of the land. And as I looked at the map of it in a shop-window, it fascinated me as a snake would a bird – a silly little bird. Then I remembered there was a big concern, a Company for trade on that river. Dash it all! I thought to myself, they can't trade without using some kind of craft on that lot of fresh water – steamboats! Why shouldn't I try to get charge of one? I went on along Fleet Street, but could not shake off the idea. The snake had charmed me.

'You understand it was a Continental concern, that Trading society; but I have a lot of relations living on the Continent, because it's cheap and not so nasty as it looks, they say.

'I am sorry to own I began to worry them. This was already a fresh departure for me. I was not used to get things that way, you know. I always went my own road and on my own legs where I had a mind to go. I wouldn't have believed it of myself; but, then – you see – I felt somehow I just get there by hook or by crook. So I worried them. The men said "My dear fellow," and did nothing. Then – would you believe it? – I tried the women. I, Charlie Marlow, set the women to work – to get a job. Heavens! Well, you see, the notion drove me. I had an aunt, a dear enthusiastic soul. She wrote: "It will be delightful. I am ready to do anything, anything for you. It is a glorious idea. I know the wife of a very high personage in the Administration, and also a man who has lots of influence with," etc., etc. She was determined to make no end of fuss to get me appointed skipper of a river steamboat, if such was my fancy.

'I got my appointment – of course; and I got it very quick. It appears the Company had received news that one of their captains had been killed in a scuffle with the natives. This was my chance, and it made me the more anxious to go. It was only months and months afterwards, when I made the attempt to recover what was left of the body, that I heard the original quarrel arose from a misunderstanding about some hens. Yes, two black hens. Fresleven – that was the fellow's name, a Dane – thought himself wronged somehow in the bargain, so he went ashore and started to hammer the chief of the village with a stick Oh, it didn't surprise me in the least to hear this, and at the same time to be told that Fresleven was the gentlest, quietest creature that ever walked on two legs. No doubt he was; but he had been a couple of years already out there engaged in the noble cause, you know, and he probably felt the need at last of asserting his self-respect in some way. Therefore he whacked the old nigger mercilessly, while a big crowd of his people watched him, thunderstruck, till some man – I was told the chief's son – in desperation at hearing the old chap yell, made a tentative jab with a spear at the white man – and of course it went quite easy between the shoulder-blades. Then the whole population cleared into the forest, expecting all kinds of calamities to happen, while, on the other hand, the steamer Fresleven commanded left also in a bad panic, in charge of the engineer, I believe.

Afterwards nobody seemed to trouble much about Fresleven's remains, till I got out and stepped into his shoes. I couldn't let it rest, though; but when an opportunity offered at last to meet my predecessor, the grass growing through his ribs was tall enough to hide his bones. They were all there. The supernatural being had not been touched after he fell. And the village was deserted, the huts gaped black, rotting, all askew within the fallen enclosures. A calamity had come to it, sure enough. The people had vanished. Mad terror had scattered them, men, women, and children, through the bush, and they had never returned. What became of the hens I don't know either. I should think the cause of progress got them, anyhow. However, through this glorious affair I got my appointment, before I had fairly begun to hope for it.

'I flew around like mad to get ready, and before forty-eight hours I was crossing the Channel to show myself to my employers, and sign the contract. In a very few hours I arrived in a city that always makes me think of a white sepulchre. Prejudice no doubt. I had no difficulty in finding the Company's offices. It was the biggest thing in the town, and everybody I met was full of it. They were going to run an over-sea empire, and make no end of coin by trade.

'A narrow and deserted street in deep shadow, high houses, innumerable windows with venetian blinds, a dead silence, grass sprouting between the stones, imposing carriage archways right and left, immense double doors standing ponderously ajar. I slipped through one of these cracks, went up a swept and ungarnished staircase, as arid as a desert, and opened the first door I came to. Two women, one fat and the other slim, sat on straw-bottomed chairs, knitting black wool. The slim one got up and walked straight at me – still knitting with downcast eyes – and only just as I began to think of getting out of her way, as you would for a somnambulist, stood still, and looked up. Her dress was as plain as an umbrella-cover, and she turned round without a word and preceded me into a waiting-room. I gave my name, and looked about. Deal table in the middle, plain chairs all round the walls, on one end a large shining map, marked with all the colours of a rainbow. There was a vast amount of red – good to see at any time, because one knows that some real work is done in there, a deuce of a lot of blue, a little green, smears of orange, and, on the East Coast, a purple patch, to show where the jolly pioneers of progress drink the jolly lager-beer. However, I wasn't going into any of these. I was going into the yellow. Dead in the centre. And the river was there – fascinating – deadly – like a snake. Ough! A door opened, a white-haired secretarial head, but wearing a compassionate expression, appeared, and a skinny forefinger beckoned me into the sanctuary. Its light was dim, and a heavy writing-desk squatted in the middle. From behind that structure came out an impression of pale plumpness in a frock-coat. The great man himself. He was five feet six, I should judge, and had his grip on the handle-end of ever so many millions. He shook hands, I fancy, murmured vaguely, was satisfied with my French. *Bon voyage*.

'In about forty-five seconds I found myself again in the waiting-room with the compassionate secretary, who, full of desolation and sympathy, made me sign some document. I believe I undertook amongst other things not to disclose any trade secrets. Well, I am not going to.

'I began to feel slightly uneasy. You know I am not used to such ceremonies, and there was something ominous in the atmosphere. It was just as though I had been let into some conspiracy – I don't know – something not quite right; and I was glad to get out. In the outer room the two women knitted black wool feverishly. People were arriving, and the younger one was walking back and forth introducing them. The old one sat on her chair. Her flat cloth slippers were propped up on a foot-warmer, and a cat reposed on her lap. She wore a starched white affair on her head, had a wart on one cheek, and silver-rimmed spectacles hung on the tip of her nose. She glanced at me above the glasses. The swift and indifferent placidity of that look troubled me. Two youths with foolish and cheery countenances were being piloted over, and she threw at them the same quick glance of unconcerned wisdom. She seemed to know all about them and about me, too. An eerie feeling came over me. She seemed uncanny and fateful. Often far away there I thought of these two, guarding the door of Darkness, knitting black wool as for a warm pall, one introducing, introducing continuously to the unknown, the other scrutinizing the cheery and foolish faces with unconcerned old eyes. *Ave!* Old knitter of black wool. *Morituri te salutant.* Not many of those she looked at ever saw her again – not half, by a long way.

'There was yet a visit to the doctor. "A simple formality," assured me the secretary, with an air of taking an immense part in all my sorrows. Accordingly a young chap wearing his hat over the left eyebrow, some clerk I suppose – there must have been clerks in the business, though the house was as still as a house in a city of the dead – came from somewhere upstairs, and led me forth. He was shabby and careless, with ink-stains on the sleeves of his jacket, and his cravat was large and billowy, under a chin shaped like the toe of an old boot. It was a little too early for the doctor, so I proposed a drink, and thereupon he developed a vein of joviality. As we sat over our vermouths he glorified the Company's business, and by-and-by I expressed casually my surprise at him not going out there. He became very cool and collected all at once. "I am not such a fool as I look, quoth Plato to his disciples," he said sententiously, emptied his glass with great resolution, and we rose.

'The old doctor felt my pulse, evidently thinking of something else the while. "Good, good for there," he mumbled, and then with a certain eagerness asked me whether I would let him measure my head. Rather surprised, I said Yes, when he produced a thing like calipers and got the dimensions back and front and every way, taking notes carefully. He was an unshaven little man in a threadbare coat like a gaberdine, with his feet in slippers, and I thought him a harmless fool. "I always ask leave, in the interests of science, to measure the crania of those going out there," he said. "And when they come back, too?" I asked. "Oh, I never see them," he remarked; "and, moreover, the changes take place inside, you know." He smiled, as if at some quiet joke. "So you are going out there. Famous. Interesting, too." He gave me a searching glance, and made another note. "Ever any madness in your family?" he asked, in a matter-of-fact tone. I felt very annoyed. "Is that question in the interests of science, too?" "It would be," he said, without taking notice of my irritation, "interesting for science to watch the mental changes of individuals, on the spot, but . . ." "Are you an alienist?" I interrupted. "Every doctor should be – a little," answered that original, imperturbably. "I have a little theory which you Messieurs who go out there must help me to prove. This is my share in the advantages my country shall reap from the possession of such a magnificent dependency. The mere wealth I leave to others. Pardon my questions, but you are the first Englishman coming under my observation . . ." I hastened to assure him I was not in the least typical. "If I were," said I, "I wouldn't be talking like this with you." "What you say is rather profound, and probably erroneous," he said, with a laugh. "Avoid irritation more than exposure to the sun. Adieu. How do you English say, eh? Good-bye. Ah! Good-bye. Adieu. In the tropics one must before everything keep calm." . . . He lifted a warning forefinger . . . "*Du calme, du calme. Adieu.*"

'One thing more remained to do – say good-bye to my excellent aunt. I found her triumphant. I had a cup of tea – the last decent cup of tea for many days – and in a room that most soothingly looked just as you would expect a lady's drawing-room to look, we had a long quiet chat by the fireside. In the course of these confidences it became quite plain to me I had been represented to the wife of the high dignitary, and goodness knows to how many more people besides, as an exceptional and gifted creature – a piece of good fortune for the Company – a man you don't get hold of every day. Good heavens! and I was going to take charge of a two-penny-half-penny river steamboat with a penny whistle attached! It appeared, however. I was also one of the Workers, with a capital – you know. Something like an emissary of light, something like a lower sort of apostle. There had been a lot of such rot let loose in print and talk just about that time, and the excellent woman, living right in the rush of all that humbug, got carried off her feet. She talked about "weaning those ignorant millions from their horrid ways", till, upon my word, she made me quite uncomfortable. I ventured to hint that the Company was run for profit.

' "You forget, dear Charlie, that the labourer is worthy of his hire," she said, brightly. It's queer how out of touch with truth women are. They live in a world of their own, and there had never been anything like it, and never can be. It is too beautiful altogether, and if they were to set it up it would go to pieces before the first sunset. Some confounded fact we men have been living contentedly with ever since the day of creation would start up and knock the whole thing over.

'After this I got embraced, told to wear flannel, be sure to write often, and so on – and I left. In the street – I don't know why – a queer feeling came to me that I was an impostor. Odd thing that I, who used to clear out for any part of the world at twenty-four hours' notice, with less thought than most men give to the crossing of a street, had a moment – I won't say of hesitation, but of startled pause, before this commonplace affair. The best way I can explain it to you is by saying that, for a second or two, I felt as though, instead of going to the centre of a continent, I were about to set off for the centre of the earth.

'I left in a French steamer, and she called in every blamed port they have out there, for, as far as I could see, the sole purpose of landing soldiers and custom-house officers. I watched the coast. Watching a coast as it slips by the ship is like thinking about an enigma. There it is before you – smiling, frowning, inviting, grand, mean, insipid, or savage, and always mute with an air of whispering, Come and find out. This one was almost featureless, as if still in the making, with an aspect of monotonous grimness. The edge of a colossal jungle, so dark-green as to be almost black, fringed with white surf, ran straight, like a ruled line, far, far away along a blue sea whose glitter was blurred by a creeping mist. The sun was fierce, the land seemed to glisten and drip with steam. Here and there greyish-whitish specks showed up clustered inside the white surf, with a flag flying above them perhaps. Settlements some centuries old, and still no bigger than pinheads on the untouched expanse of their background. We pounded along, stopped, landed soldiers; went on, landed custom-house clerks to levy toll in what looked like a God-forsaken wilderness, with a tin shed and a flag-pole lost in it; landed more soldiers – to take care of the custom-house clerks, presumably. Some, I heard, got drowned in the surf; but whether they did or not, nobody seemed particularly to care. They were just flung out there, and on we went. Every day the coast looked the same, as though we had not moved; but we passed various places – trading places – with names like Gran' Bassam, Little Popo; names that seemed to belong to some sordid farce acted in front of a sinister back-cloth. The idleness of a passenger, my isolation amongst all these men with whom I had no point of contact, the oily and languid sea, the uniform sombreness of the coast, seemed to keep me away from the truth of things, within the toil of a mournful and senseless delusion. The voice of the surf now and then was a positive pleasure, like the speech of a brother. It was something natural, that had its reason, that had a meaning. Now and then a boat from the shore gave one a momentary contact with reality. It was paddled by black fellows. You could see from afar the white of their eyeballs glistening. They shouted, sang; their bodies streamed with perspiration; they had faces like grotesque masks – these chaps; but they had bone, muscle, a wild vitality, an intense energy of movement, that was as natural and true as the surf along their coast. They wanted no excuse for being there. They were a great comfort to look at. For a time I would feel I belonged still to a world of straightforward facts; but the feeling would not last long. Something would turn up to scare it away. Once, I remember, we came upon a man-of-war anchored off the coast. There wasn't even a shed there, and she was shelling the bush. It appears the French had one of their wars going on thereabouts. Her ensign dropped limp like a rag; the muzzles of the long six-inch guns stuck out all over the low hull; the greasy, slimy swell swung her up lazily and let her down, swaying her thin masts. In the empty immensity of earth, sky, and water, there she was, incomprehensible, firing into a continent. Pop, would go one of the six-inch guns; a small flame would dart and vanish, a little white smoke would disappear, a tiny projectile would give a feeble screech – and nothing happened. Nothing could happen. There was a touch of insanity in the proceeding, a sense of lugubrious drollery in the sight; and it was not dissipated by somebody on board assuring me earnestly there was a camp of natives – he called them enemies! – hidden out of sight somewhere.

'We gave her her letters (I heard the men in that lonely ship were dying of fever at the rate of three a day) and went on. We called at some more places with farcical names, where the merry dance of death and trade goes on in a still and earthy atmosphere as of an overheated catacomb; all long the formless coast bordered by dangerous surf, as if Nature herself had tried to ward off intruders;

in and out of rivers, streams of death in life, whose banks were rotting into mud, whose waters, thickened into slime, invaded the contorted mangroves, that seemed to writhe at us in the extremity of an impotent despair. Nowhere did we stop long enough to get a particularized impression, but the general sense of vague and oppressive wonder grew upon me. It was like a weary pilgrimage amongst hints for nightmares.

'It was upward of thirty days before I saw the mouth of the big river. We anchored off the seat of the government. But my work would not begin till some two hundred miles farther on. So as soon as I could I made a start for a place thirty miles higher up.

'I had my passage on a little sea-going steamer. Her captain was a Swede, and knowing me for a seaman, invited me on the bridge. He was a young man, lean, fair, and morose, with lanky hair and a shuffling gait. As we left the miserable little wharf, he tossed his head contemptuously at the shore. "Been living there?" he asked. I said, "Yes." "Fine lot these government chaps – are they not?" he went on, speaking English with great precision and considerable bitterness. "It is funny what some people will do for a few francs a month. I wonder what becomes of that kind when it goes up country?" I said to him I expected to see that soon. "So-o-o!" he exclaimed. He shuffled athwart, keeping one eye ahead vigilantly. "Don't be too sure," he continued. "The other day I took up a man who hanged himself on the road. He was a Swede, too." "Hanged himself! Why, in God's name?" I cried. He kept on looking out watchfully. "Who knows? The sun too much for him, or the country perhaps."

'At last we opened a reach. A rocky cliff appeared, mounds of turned-up earth by the shore, houses on a hill, others with iron roofs, amongst a waste of excavations or hanging to the declivity. A continuous noise of the rapids above hovered over this scene of inhabited devastation. A lot of people, mostly black and naked, moved about like ants. A jetty projected into the river. A blinding sunlight drowned all this at times in a sudden recrudescence of glare. "There's your Company's station," said the Swede, pointing to three wooden barrack-like structures on the rocky slope. "I will send your things up. Four boxes did you say? So. Farewell."

'I came upon a boiler wallowing in the grass, then found a path leading up the hill. It turned aside for the boulders, and also for an undersized railway-truck lying there on its back with its wheels in the air. One was off. The thing looked as dead as the carcass of some animals. I came upon more pieces of decaying machinery, a stack of rusty rails. To the left a clump of trees made a shady spot, where dark things seemed to stir feebly. I blinked, the path was steep. A horn tooted to the right, and I saw the black people run. A heavy and dull detonation shook the ground, a puff of smoke came out of the cliff, and that was all. No change appeared on the face of the rock. They were building a railway. The cliff was not in the way or anything; but this objectless blasting was all the work going on.

'A slight clinking behind me made me turn my head. Six black men advanced in a file, toiling up the path. They walked erect and slow, balancing small baskets full of earth on their heads, and the clink kept time with their footsteps. Black rags were wound round their loins, and the short ends behind waggled to and fro like tails. I could see every rib, the joints of their limbs were like knots in a rope; each had an iron collar on his neck, and all were connected together with a chain whose bights swung between them, rhythmically clinking. Another report from the cliff made me think suddenly of that ship of war I had seen firing into a continent. It was the same kind of ominous voice; but these men could by no stretch of imagination be called enemies. They were called criminals, and the outraged law, like the bursting shells, had come to them, an insoluble mystery from the sea. All their meagre breasts panted together, the violently dilated nostrils quivered, the eyes stared stonily uphill. They passed me within six inches, without a glance, with that complete, deathlike indifference of unhappy savages. Behind this raw matter one of the reclaimed, the product of the new forces at work, strolled despondently, carrying a rifle by its middle. He had a uniform jacket with one button off, and seeing a white man on the path, hoisted his weapon to his shoulder with alacrity. This was simple prudence, white men being so much alike at a distance that he could not tell who I might be. He was speedily reassured, and with a large, white, rascally grin, and a glance at his charge, seemed to take me into partnership in his exalted trust. After all, I also was a part of the great cause of these high and just proceedings.

'Instead of going up, I turned and descended to the left. My idea was to let that chain-gang get out of sight before I climbed the hill. You know I am not particularly tender; I've had to strike and to fend off. I've had to resist and to attack sometimes – that's only one way of resisting – without counting the exact cost, according to the demands of such sort of life as I had blundered into. I've seen the devil of violence, and the devil of greed, and the devil of hot desire; but, by all the stars! these were strong, lusty, red-eyed devils, that swayed and drove men – men, I tell you. But as I stood on this hillside, I foresaw that in the blinding sunshine of that land I would become acquainted with a flabby, pretending, weak-eyed devil of a rapacious and pitiless folly. How insidious he could be, too, I was only to find out several months later and a thousand miles farther. For a moment I stood appalled, as though by a warning. Finally I descended the hill, obliquely, towards the trees I had seen.

'I avoided a vast artificial hole somebody had been digging on the slope, the purpose of which I found it impossible to divine. It wasn't a quarry or a sandpit, anyhow. It was just a hole. It might have been connected with the philanthropic desire of giving the criminals something to do. I don't know. Then I nearly fell into a very narrow ravine, almost no more than a scar in the hillside. I discovered that a lot of imported drainage-pipes for the settlement had been tumbled in there. There wasn't one that was not broken. It was a wanton smash-up. At last I got under the trees. My purpose was to stroll into the shade for a moment; but no sooner within than it seemed to me I had stepped into the gloomy circle of some Inferno. The rapids were near, and an uninterrupted, uniform, headlong, rushing noise filled the mournful stillness of the grove, where not a breath stirred, not a leaf moved, with a mysterious sound – as though the tearing pace of the launched earth had suddenly become audible.

'Black shapes crouched, lay, sat between the trees leaning against the trunks, clinging to the earth, half coming out, half effaced within the dim light, in all the attitudes of pain, abandonment, and despair. Another mine on the cliff went off, followed by a slight shudder of the soil under my feet. The work was going on. The work! And this was the place where some of the helpers had withdrawn to die.

'They were dying slowly – it was very clear. They were not enemies, they were not criminals, they were nothing earthly now – nothing but black shadows of disease and starvation, lying confusedly in the greenish gloom. Brought from all the recesses of the coast in all the legality of time contracts, lost in uncongenial surroundings, fed on unfamiliar food, they sickened, became inefficient, and were then allowed to crawl away and rest. These moribund shapes were free as air – and nearly as thin. I began to distinguish the gleam of the eyes under the trees. Then, glancing down, I saw a face near my hand. The black bones reclined at full length with one shoulder against the tree, and slowly the eyelids rose and the sunken eyes looked up at me, enormous and vacant, a kind of blind, white flicker in the depths of the orbs, which died out slowly. The man seemed young – almost a boy – but you know with them it's hard to tell. I found nothing else to do but to offer him one of my good Swede's ship's biscuits I had in my pocket. The fingers closed slowly on it and held – there was no other movement and no other glance. He had tied a bit of white worsted round his neck – Why? Where did he get it? Was it a badge – an ornament – a charm – a propitiatory act? Was there any idea at all connected with it? It looked startling round his black neck, this bit of white thread from beyond the seas.

'Near the same tree two more bundles of acute angles sat with their legs drawn up. One, with his chin propped on his knees, stared at nothing, in an intolerable and appalling manner: his brother phantom rested its forehead, as if overcome with a great weariness; and all about others were scattered in every pose of contorted collapse, as in some picture of a massacre or a pestilence. While I stood horror-struck, one of these creatures rose to his hands and knees, and went off on all-fours towards the river to drink. He lapped out of his hand, then sat up in the sunlight, crossing his shins in front of him, and after a time let his woolly head fall on his breastbone.

'I didn't want any more loitering in the shade, and I made haste towards the station. When near the buildings I met a white man, in such an unexpected elegance of get-up that in the first moment I took him for a sort of vision. I saw a high starched collar, white cuffs, a light alpaca jacket, snowy trousers, a clear necktie, and varnished boots. No hat. Hair parted, brushed, oiled, under a green-lined parasol held in a big white hand. He was amazing, and had a penholder behind his ear.

'I shook hands with this miracle, and I learned he was the Company's chief accountant, and that all the book-keeping was done at this station. He had come out for a moment, he said, "to get a breath of fresh air". The expression sounded wonderfully odd, with its suggestion of sedentary desk-life. I wouldn't have mentioned the fellow to you at all, only it was from his lips that I first heard the name of the man who is so indissolubly connected with the memories of that time. Moreover, I respected the fellow. Yes; I respected his collars, his vast cuffs, his brushed hair. His appearance was certainly that of a hairdresser's dummy;

but in the great demoralization of the land he kept up his appearance. That's backbone. His starched collars and got-up shirt-fronts were achievements of character. He had been out nearly three years; and later, I could not help asking him how he managed to sport such linen. He had just the faintest blush, and said modestly, "I've been teaching one of the native women about the station. It was difficult. She had a distaste for the work." Thus this man had verily accomplished something. And he was devoted to his books, which were in apple-pie order.

'Everything else in the station was in a muddle – heads, things, buildings. Strings of dusty niggers with splay feet arrived and departed; a stream of manufactured goods, rubbishy cottons, beads, and brass wire sent into the depths of darkness, and in return came a precious trickle of ivory.

'I had to wait in the station for ten days – an eternity. I lived in a hut in the yard, but to be out of the chaos I would sometimes get into the accountant's office. It was built of horizontal planks, and so badly put together that, as he bent over his high desk, he was barred from neck to heels with narrow strips of sunlight. There was no need to open the big shutters to see. It was hot there, too; big flies buzzed fiendishly, and did not sting, but stabbed. I sat generally on the floor, while, of faultless appearance (and even slightly scented), perching on a high stool, he wrote. Sometimes he stood up for exercise. When a truckle-bed with a sick man (some invalid agent from up-country) was put in there, he exhibited a gentle annoyance. "The groans of this sick person," he said, "distract my attention. And without that it is extremely difficult to guard against clerical errors in this climate."

'One day he remarked, without lifting his head, "In the interior you will no doubt meet Mr Kurtz." On my asking who Mr Kurtz was, he said he was a first-class agent; and seeing my disappointment at this information, he added slowly, laying down his pen. "He is a very remarkable person." Further questions elicited from him that Mr Kurtz was at present in charge of a trading post, a very important one, in the true ivory-country, at "the very bottom of there. Sends in as much ivory as all the others put together . . ." He began to write again. The sick man was too ill to groan. The flies buzzed in a great peace.

'Suddenly there was a growing murmur of voices and a great tramping of feet. A caravan had come in, A violent babble of uncouth sounds burst out on the other side of the planks. All the carriers were speaking together, and in the midst of the uproar the lamentable voice of the chief agent was heard "giving it up" tearfully for the twentieth time that day . . . He rose slowly. "What a frightful row," he said. He crossed the room gently to look at the sick man, and returning, said to me, "He does not hear." "What! Dead?" I asked, startled. "No, not yet," he answered, with great composure. Then, alluding with a toss of the head to the tumult in the station yard, "When one has got to make correct entries, one comes to hate those savages – hate them to the death." He remained thoughtful for a moment. "When you see Mr Kurtz," he went on, "tell him from me that everything here" – he glanced at the desk – "is very satisfactory. I don't like to write to him – with those messengers of ours you never know who may get hold of your letter – at that Central Station." He stared at me for a moment with his mild, bulging eyes. "Oh, he will go far, very far," he began again. "He will be a somebody in the Administration before long. They, above – the Council in Europe, you know – mean him to be.'

'He turned to his work. The noise outside had ceased, and presently in going out I stopped at the door. In the steady buzz of flies the homeward-bound agent was lying flushed and insensible; the other, bent over his books, was making correct entries of perfectly correct transactions; and fifty feet below the doorstep I could see the still tree-tops of the grove of death.

'Next day I left that station at last, with a caravan of sixty men, for a two-hundred-mile tramp.

'No use telling you much about that. Paths, paths, everywhere; a stamped-in network of paths spreading over the empty land, through long grass, through burnt grass, through thickets, down and up chilly ravines, up and down stony hills ablaze with heat; and a solitude, a solitude, nobody, not a hut. The population had cleared out a long time ago. Well, if a lot of mysterious niggers armed with all kinds of fearful weapons suddenly took to travelling on the road between Deal and Gravesend, catching the yokels right and left to carry heavy loads for them, I fancy every farm and cottage thereabouts would get empty very soon. Only here the dwellings were gone, too. Still I passed through several abandoned villages. There's something pathetically childish in the ruins of grass walls. Day after day, with the stamp and shuffle of sixty pair of bare feet behind me, each pair under a 60-lb. load. Camp, cook, sleep, strike camp, march. Now and then a carrier dead in harness, at rest in the long grass near the path, with an empty water-gourd and his long staff lying by his side. A great silence around and above. Perhaps on some quiet night the tremor of far-off drums, sinking, swelling, a tremor vast, faint; a sound weird, appealing, suggestive, and wild – and perhaps with as profound a meaning as the sound of bells in a Christian country. Once a white man in an unbuttoned uniform, camping on the path with an armed escort of lank Zanzibaris, very hospitable and festive – not to say drunk. Was looking after the upkeep of the road, he declared. Can't say I saw any road or any upkeep, unless the body of a middle-aged negro, with a bullet-hole in the forehead, upon which I absolutely stumbled three miles farther on, may be considered as a permanent improvement. I had a white companion, too, not a bad chap, but rather too fleshy and with the exasperating habit of fainting on the hot hillsides, miles away from the least bit of shade and water. Annoying, you know, to hold your own coat like a parasol over a man's head while he is coming-to. I couldn't help asking him once what he meant by coming there at all. "To make money, of course. What do you think?" he said, scornfully. Then he got fever, and had to be carried in a hammock slung under a pole. As he weighed sixteen stone I had no end of rows with the carriers. They jibbed, ran away, sneaked off with their loads in the night – quite a mutiny. So, one evening, I made a speech in English with gestures, not one of which was lost to the sixty pairs of eyes before me, and the next morning I started the hammock off in front all right. An hour afterwards I came upon the whole concern wrecked in a bush – man, hammock, groans, blankets, horrors. The heavy pole had skinned his poor nose. He was very anxious for me to kill somebody, but there wasn't the shadow of a carrier near. I remembered the old doctor, – "It would be interesting for science to watch the mental changes of individuals, on the spot." I felt I was becoming scientifically interesting. However, all that is to no purpose. On the fifteenth day I came in sight of the big river again, and hobbled into the Central Station. It was on a backwater surrounded by scrub and forest, with a pretty border of smelly mud on one side, and on the three others enclosed by a crazy fence of rushes. A neglected gap was all the gate it had, and the first glance at the place was enough to let you see the flabby devil was running that show. White men with long staves in their hands appeared languidly from amongst the buildings, strolling up to take a look at me, and then retired out of sight somewhere. One of them, a stout, excitable chap with black moustaches, informed me with great volubility and many digressions, as soon as I told him who I was, that my steamer was at the bottom of the river. I was thunder-struck. What, how, why? Oh, it was "all right". The "manager himself" was there. All quite correct. "Everybody had behaved splendidly! splendidly!" – "You must," he said in agitation, "go and see the general manager at once. He is waiting!"

'I did not see the real significance of that wreck at once. I fancy I see it now, but I am not sure – not at all. Certainly the affair was too stupid – when I think of it – to be altogether natural. Still . . . But at the moment it presented itself simply as a confounded nuisance. The steamer was sunk. They had started two days before in a sudden hurry up the river with the manager on board, in charge of some volunteer skipper, and before they had been out three hours they tore the bottom out of her on stones, and she sank near the south bank. I asked myself what I was to do there, now my boat was lost. As a matter of fact, I had plenty to do in fishing my command out of the river. I had to set about it the very next day. That, and the repairs when I brought the pieces to the station, took some months.

'My first interview with the manager was curious. He did not ask me to sit down after my twenty-mile walk that morning. He was commonplace in complexion, in feature, in manners, and in voice. He was of middle size and of ordinary build. His eyes, of the usual blue, were perhaps remarkably cold, and he certainly could make his glance fall on one as trenchant and heavy as an axe. But even at these times the rest of his person seemed to disclaim the intention. Otherwise there was only an indefinable, faint expression of his lips, something stealthy – a smile – not a smile – I remember it, but I can't explain. It was unconscious, this smile was, though just after he had said something it got intensified for an instant. It came at the end of his speeches like a seal applied on the words to make the meaning of the commonest phrase appear absolutely inscrutable. He was a common trader, from his youth up employed in these parts – nothing more. He was obeyed, yet he inspired neither love nor fear, nor even respect. He inspired uneasiness. That was it! Uneasiness. Not a definite mistrust – just uneasiness – nothing more. You have no idea how effective such a . . . a . . . faculty can be. He had no genius for organizing, for initiative, or for order even. That was evident in such things as the deplorable state of the station. He had no learning, and no intelligence. His position had come to him – why? Perhaps because he was never ill . . . He had served three terms of three years out there . . . Because triumphant health in the general rout of constitutions is a kind of power in itself. When he went home on leave he rioted on a large scale

– pompously. Jack ashore – with a difference – in externals only. This one could gather from his casual talk. He originated nothing, he could keep the routine going – that's all. But he was great. He was great by this little thing that it was impossible to tell what could control such a man. He never gave that secret away. Perhaps there was nothing within him. Such a suspicion made one pause – for out there there were no external checks. Once when various tropical diseases had laid low almost every "agent" in the station, he was heard to say, "Men who come out here should have no entrails." He sealed the utterance with that smile of his, as though it had been a door opening into a darkness he had in his keeping. You fancied you had seen things – but the seal was on. When annoyed at meal-times by the constant quarrels of the white men about precedence, he ordered an immense round table to be made, for which a special house had to be built. This was the station's mess-room. Where he sat was the first place – the rest were nowhere. One felt this to be his unalterable conviction. He was neither civil nor uncivil. He was quiet. He allowed his "boy" – an overfed young Negro from the coast – to treat the white men, under his very eyes, with provoking insolence.

'He began to speak as soon as he saw me. I had been very long on the road. He could not wait. Had to start without me. The upriver stations had to be relieved. There had been so many delays already that he did not know who was dead and who was alive, and how they got on – and so on, and so on. He paid no attention to my explanations, and, playing with a stick of sealing-wax, repeated several times that the situation was "very grave, very grave". There were rumours that a very important station was in jeopardy, and its chief, Mr Kurtz, was ill. Hoped it was not true. Mr Kurtz was . . . I felt weary and irritable. Hang Kurtz, I thought. I interrupted him by saying I had heard of Mr Kurtz on the coast. "Ah! So they talk of him down there," he murmured to himself. Then he began again, assuring me Mr Kurtz was the best agent he had, an exceptional man, of the greatest importance to the Company: therefore I could understand his anxiety. He was, he said, "very, very uneasy". Certainly he fidgeted on his chair a good deal, exclaimed, "Ah, Mr Kurtz!", broke the stick of sealing-wax and seemed dumbfounded by the accident. Next thing he wanted to know "how long it would take to" . . . I interrupted him again. Being hungry, you know, and kept on my feet, too, I was getting savage. "How could I tell?" I said. "I hadn't even seen the wreck yet – some months, no doubt." All this talk seemed to me so futile. "Some months," he said. "Well, let us say three months before we can make a start. Yes. That ought to do the affair." I flung out of his hut (he lived all alone in a clay hut with a sort of verandah) muttering to myself my opinion of him. He was a chattering idiot. Afterwards I took it back when it was borne in upon me startlingly with what extreme nicety he had estimated the time requisite for the "affair".

'I went to work the next day, turning, so to speak, my back on that station. In that way only it seemed to me I could keep my hold on the redeeming facts of life. Still, one must look about sometimes; and then I saw this station, these men strolling aimlessly about in the sunshine of the yard. I asked myself sometimes what it all meant. They wandered here and there with their absurd long staves in their hands, like a lot of faithless pilgrims bewitched inside a rotten fence. The word "ivory" rang in the air, was whispered, was sighed. You would think they were praying to it. A taint of imbecile rapacity blew through it all, like a whiff from some corpse. By Jove! I've never seen anything so unreal in my life. And outside, the silent wilderness surrounding this cleared speck on the earth struck me as something great and invincible, like evil or truth, waiting patiently for the passing away of this fantastic invasion.

'Oh, these months! Well, never mind. Various things happened. One evening a grass shed full of calico, cotton print, beads, and I don't know what else, burst into a blaze so suddenly that you would have thought the earth had opened to let an avenging fire consume all that trash. I was smoking my pipe quietly by my dismantled steamer, and saw them all cutting capers in the light, with their arms lifted high, when the stout man with moustaches came tearing down to the river, a tin pail in his hand, assured me that everybody was "behaving splendidly, splendidly", dipped about a quart of water and tore back again. I noticed there was a hole in the bottom of his pail.

'I strolled up. There was no hurry. You see the thing had gone off like a box of matches. It had been hopeless from the very first. The flame had leaped high, driven everybody back, lighted up everything – and collapsed. The shed was already a heap of embers glowing fiercely. A nigger was being beaten near by. They said he had caused the fire in some way; be that as it may, he was screeching most horribly. I saw him, later, for several days, sitting in a bit of shade looking very sick and trying to recover himself: afterwards he arose and went out – and the wilderness without a sound took him into its bosom again. As I approached the glow from the dark I found myself at the back of two men, talking. I heard the name of Kurtz pronounced, then the words, "take advantage of this unfortunate accident". One of the men was the manager. I wished him a good evening. "Did you ever see anything like it – eh? it is incredible," he said, and walked off. The other man remained. He was a first-class agent, young, gentlemanly, a bit reserved, with a forked little beard and a hooked nose. He was stand-offish with the other agents, and they on their side said he was the manager's spy upon them. As to me, I had hardly ever spoken to him before. We got into talk, and by-and-by we strolled away from the hissing ruins. Then he asked me to his room, which was in the main building of the station. He struck a match, and I perceived that this young aristocrat had not only a silver-mounted dressing-case but also a whole candle all to himself. Just at that time the manager was the only man supposed to have any right to candles. Native mats covered the clay walls: a collection of spears, assegais, shields, knives was hung up in trophies. The business entrusted to this fellow was the making of bricks – so I had been informed; but there wasn't a fragment of a brick anywhere in the station, and he had been there more than a year – waiting. It seems he could not make bricks without something, I don't know what – straw maybe. Anyways, it could not be found there, and as it was not likely to be sent from Europe, it did not appear clear to me what he was waiting for. An act of special creation perhaps. However, they were all waiting – all the sixteen or twenty pilgrims of them – for something; and upon my word it did not seem an uncongenial occupation, from the way they took it, though the only thing that ever came to them was disease – as far as I could see. They beguiled the time by backbiting and intriguing against each other in a foolish kind of way. There was an air of plotting about that station, but nothing came of it, of course. It was as unreal as everything else – as the philanthropic pretence of the whole concern, as their talk, as their government, as their show of work. The only real feeling was a desire to get appointed to a trading post where ivory was to be had, so that they could earn percentages. They intrigued and slandered and hated each other only on that account – but as to effectually lifting a little finger – oh, no. By heavens! there is something after all in the world allowing one man to steal a horse while another must not look at a halter. Steal a horse straight out. Very well. He has done it. Perhaps he can ride. But there is a way of looking at a halter that would provoke the most charitable of saints into a kick.

'I had no idea why he wanted to be sociable, but as we chatted in there it suddenly occurred to me the fellow was trying to get at something – in fact, pumping me. He alluded constantly to Europe, to the people I was supposed to know there – putting leading questions as to my acquaintances in the sepulchral city, and so on. His little eyes glittered like mica discs – with curiosity – though he tried to keep up a bit of superciliousness. At first I was astonished, but very soon I became awfully curious to see what he would find out from me. I couldn't possibly imagine what I had in me to make it worth his while. It was very pretty to see how he baffled himself, for in truth my body was full only of chills, and my head had nothing in it but that wretched steamboat business. It was evident he took me for a perfectly shameless prevaricator. At last he got angry, and to conceal a movement of furious annoyance, he yawned. I rose. Then I noticed a small sketch in oils, on a panel, representing a woman, draped and blindfolded, carrying a lighted torch. The background was sombre – almost black. The movement of the woman was stately, and the effect of the torch-light on the face was sinister.

'It arrested me, and he stood by civilly, holding an empty half-pint champagne bottle (medical comforts) with the candle stuck in it. To my question he said Mr Kurtz had painted this – in this very station more than a year ago – while waiting for means to go to his trading post. "Tell me, pray," said I, "who is this Mr Kurtz?"

' "The chief of the Inner Station," he answered in a short tone, looking away. "Much obliged," I said, laughing. "And you are the brickmaker of the Central Station. Everyone knows that." He was silent for a while. "He is a prodigy," he said at last. "He is an emissary of pity, and science, and progress, and devil knows what else. We want," he began to declaim suddenly, "for the guidance of the cause entrusted to us by Europe, so to speak, higher intelligence, wide sympathies, a singleness of purpose." "Who says that?" I asked. "Lots of them," he replied. "Some even write that; and so *he* comes here, a special being, as you ought to know." "Why ought I to know?" I interrupted, really surprised. He paid no attention. "Yes. Today he is chief of the best station, next year he will be assistant-manager, two years more and . . . but I daresay you know what he will be in two years' time. You are of the new gang – the gang of virtue. The same people who sent him specially also recommended you. Oh, don't say no. I've my own eyes to trust." Light dawned upon me. My dear aunt's influential acquaintances were producing an unexpected effect upon that young man.

I nearly burst into a laugh. "Do you read the Company's confidential correspondence?" I asked. He hadn't a word to say. It was great fun. "When Mr Kurtz," I continued, severely, "is General Manager, you won't have the opportunity."

'He blew the candle out suddenly, and we went outside. The moon had risen. Black figures strolled about listlessly, pouring water on the glow, whence proceeded a sound of hissing; steam ascended in the moonlight, the beaten nigger groaned somewhere. "What a row the brute makes!" said the indefatigable man with the moustaches, appearing near us. "Serve him right. Transgression – punishment – bang! Pitiless, pitiless. That's the only way. This will prevent all conflagrations for the future. I was just telling the manager . . ." He noticed my companion, and became crestfallen all at once. "Not in bed yet," he said, with a kind of servile heartiness; "it's so natural. Ha! Danger – agitation." He vanished. I went on to the river-side, and the other followed me. I heard a scathing murmur at my ear, "Heap of muffs – go to." The pilgrims could be seen in knots gesticulating, discussing. Several had still their staves in their hands. I verily believe they took these sticks to bed with them. Beyond the fence the forest stood up spectrally in the moonlight, and through the dim stir, through the faint sounds of that lamentable courtyard, the silence of the land went home to one's very heart – its mystery, its greatness, the amazing reality of its concealed life. The hurt nigger moaned feebly somewhere near by, and then fetched a deep sigh that made me mend my pace away from there. I felt a hand introducing itself under my arm. "My dear sir," said the fellow, "I don't want to be misunderstood, and especially by you, who will see Mr Kurtz long before I can have that pleasure. I wouldn't like him to get a false idea of my disposition . . ."

'I let him run on, this papier-mâché Mephistopheles, and it seemed to me that if I tried I could poke my forefinger through him, and would find nothing inside but a little loose dirt, maybe. He, don't you see, had been planning to be assistant-manager by-and-by under the present man, and I could see that the coming of that Kurtz had upset them both not a little. He talked precipitately, and I did not try to stop him. I had my shoulders against the wreck of my steamer, hauled up on the slope like a carcass of some big river animal. The smell of mud, of primeval mud, by Jove! was in my nostrils, the high stillness of primeval forest was before my eyes; there were shiny patches on the black creek. The moon had spread over everything a thin layer of silver – over the rank grass, over the mud, upon the wall of matted vegetation standing higher than the wall of a temple, over the great river I could see through a sombre gap glittering, glittering, as it flowed broadly by without a murmur. All this was great, expectant, mute, while the man jabbered about himself. I wondered whether the stillness on the face of the immensity looking at us two were meant as an appeal or as a menace. What were we who had strayed in here? Could we handle that dumb thing, or would it handle us? I felt how big, how confoundedly big, was that thing that couldn't talk, and perhaps was deaf as well. What was in there? I could see a little ivory coming out from there, and I had heard Mr Kurtz was in there. I had heard enough about it, too – God knows! Yet somehow it didn't bring any image with it – no more than if I had been told an angel or a fiend was in there. I believed it in the same way one of you might believe there are inhabitants in the planet Mars. I knew once a Scotch sailmaker who was certain, dead sure, there were people in Mars. If you asked him for some idea how they looked and behaved, he would get shy and mutter something about "walking on all fours". If you as much as smiled, he would – though a man of sixty – offer to fight you. I would not have gone so far as to fight for Kurtz, but I went for him near enough to a lie. You know I hate, detest, and can't bear a lie, not because I am straighter than the rest of us, but simply because it appals me. There is a taint of death, a flavour of mortality in lies – which is exactly what I hate and detest in the world – what I want to forget. It makes me miserable and sick, like biting something rotten would do. Temperament, I suppose. Well, I went near enough to it by letting the young fool there believe anything he liked to imagine as to my influence in Europe. I became in an instant as much of a pretence as the rest of the bewitched pilgrims. This simply because I had a notion it somehow would be of help to that Kurtz whom at the time I did not see – you understand. He was just a word for me. I did not see the man in the name any more than you do. Do you see him? Do you see the story? Do you see anything? It seems to me I am trying to tell you a dream – making a vain attempt, because no relation of a dream can convey the dream-sensation, that commingling of absurdity, surprise, and bewilderment in a tremor of struggling revolt, that notion of being captured by the incredible which is of the very essence of dreams . . .'

He was silent for a while.

'. . . No, it is impossible; it is impossible to convey the life-sensation of any given epoch of one's existence – that which makes its truth, its meaning – its subtle and penetrating essence. It is impossible. We live, as we dream – alone . . .'

He paused again as if reflecting, then added –

'Of course in this you fellows see more than I could then. You see me, whom you know . . .'

It had become so pitch dark that we listeners could hardly see one another. For a long time already he, sitting apart, had been no more to us than a voice. There was not a word from anybody. The others might have been asleep, but I was awake. I listened, I listened on the watch for the sentence, for the word, that would give me the clue to the faint uneasiness inspired by this narrative that seemed to shape itself without human lips in the heavy night-air of the river.

'. . . Yes – I let him run on,' Marlow began again, 'and think what he pleased about the powers that were behind me. I did! And there was nothing behind me! There was nothing but that wretched, old, mangled steamboat I was leaning against, while he talked fluently about "the necessity for every man to get on". "And when one comes out here, you conceive, it is not to gaze at the moon." Mr Kurtz was a "universal genius", but even a genius would find it easier to work with "adequate tools – intelligent men". He did not make bricks – why, there was a physical impossibility in the way – as I was well aware; and if he did secretarial work for the manager, it was because "no sensible man rejects wantonly the confidence of his superiors". Did I see it? I saw it. What more did I want? What I really wanted was rivets, by heaven! Rivets. To get on with the work – to stop the hole. Rivets I wanted. There were cases of them down at the coast – cases – piled up – burst – split! You kicked a loose rivet at every second step in that station yard on the hillside. Rivets had rolled into the grove of death. You could fill your pockets with rivets for the trouble of stooping down – and there wasn't one rivet to be found where it was wanted. We had plates that would do, but nothing to fasten them with. And every week the messenger, a lone negro, letter-bag on shoulder and staff in hand, left our station for the coast. And several times a week a coast caravan came in with trade goods – ghastly glazed calico that made you shudder only to look at it, glass beads value about a penny a quart, confounded spotted cotton handkerchiefs. And no rivets. Three carriers could have brought all that was wanted to set that steamboat afloat.

'He was becoming confidential now, but I fancy my unresponsive attitude must have exasperated him at last, for he judged it necessary to inform me he feared neither God nor devil, let alone any mere man. I said I could see that very well, but what I wanted was a certain quantity of rivets – and rivets were what really Mr Kurtz wanted, if he had only known it. Now letters went to the coast every week . . . "My dear sir," he cried, "I write from dictation." I demanded rivets. There was a way – for an intelligent man. He changed his manner; became very cold, and suddenly began to talk about a hippopotamus; wondered whether sleeping on board the steamer (I stuck to my salvage night and day) I wasn't disturbed. There was an old hippo that had the bad habit of getting out on the bank and roaming at night over the station grounds. The pilgrims used to turn out in a body and empty every rifle they could lay hands on at him. Some even had sat up o' nights for him. All this energy was wasted, though. "That animal has a charmed life," he said; "but you can say this only of brutes in this country. No man – you apprehend me? – no man here bears a charmed life." He stood there for a moment in the moonlight with his delicate hooked nose set a little askew, and his mica eyes glittering without a wink, then, with a curt Good-night, he strode off. I could see he was disturbed and considerably puzzled, which made me feel more hopeful than I had been for days. It was a great comfort to turn from that chap to my influential friend, the battered, twisted, ruined, tin-pot steamboat. I clambered on board. She rang under my feet like an empty Huntley & Palmers biscuit-tin kicked along a gutter; she was nothing so solid in make, and rather less pretty in shape, but I had expended enough hard work on her to make me love her. No influential friend would have served me better She had given me a chance to come out a bit – to find out what I could do. No, I don't like work. I had rather laze about and think of all the fine things that can be done. I don't like work, – no man does – but I like what is in the work – the chance to find yourself. Your own reality – for yourself, not for others – what no other man can ever know. They can only see the mere show, and never can tell what it really means.

'I was not surprised to see somebody sitting aft, on the deck, with his legs dangling over the mud. You see I rather chummed with the few mechanics there were in that station, whom the other pilgrims naturally despised – on account of their imperfect manners, I suppose. This was the foreman – a boiler-maker by trade – a good worker. He was a lank, bony, yellow-faced man, with big intense eyes. His aspect was worried, and his head was as bald as the palm of my hand; but his hair in falling seemed to have stuck to his chin, and had prospered in the new locality, for his beard hung down to his waist. He was a widower with six young children (he had left them in charge of a sister of his to come out there), and the passion of his life was pigeon-flying. He was an enthusiast and a connoisseur. He would rave about pigeons. After work hours he used sometimes to come over from his hut for a talk about his children and his pigeons; at work, when he had to crawl in the mud under the bottom of the steamboat, he would tie up that beard of his in a kind of white serviette he brought for the purpose. It had loops to go over his ears. In the evening he could be seen squatted on the bank rinsing that wrapper in the creek with great care, then spreading it solemnly on a bush to dry.

'I slapped him on the back and shouted "We shall have rivets!" He scrambled to his feet exclaiming "No! Rivets!" as though he couldn't believe his ears. Then in a low voice, "You . . . eh?" I don't know why we behaved like lunatics. I put my finger to the side of my nose and nodded mysteriously. "Good for you!" he cried, snapped his fingers above his head, lifting one foot. I tried a jig. We capered on the iron deck. A frightful clatter came out of that hulk, and the virgin forest on the other bank of the creek sent it back in a thundering roll upon the sleeping station. It must have made some of the pilgrims sit up in their hovels. A dark figure obscured the lighted doorway of the manager's hut, vanished, then, a second or so after, the doorway itself vanished, too. We stopped, and the silence driven away by the stamping of our feet flowed back again from the recesses of the land. The great wall of vegetation, an exuberant and entangled mass of trunks, branches, leaves, boughs, festoons, motionless in the moonlight, was like a rioting invasion of soundless life, a rolling wave of plants, piled up, crested, ready to topple over the creek, to sweep every little man of us out of his little existence. And it moved not. A deadened burst of mighty splashes and snorts reached us from afar, as though an ichthyosaurus had been taking a bath of glitter in the great river. "After all," said the boiler-maker in a reasonable tone, "why shouldn't we get the rivets?" Why not, indeed! I did not know of any reason why we shouldn't. "They'll come in three weeks," I said, confidently.

'But they didn't. Instead of rivets there came an invasion, an infliction, a visitation. It came in sections during the next three weeks, each section headed by a donkey carrying a white man in new clothes and tan shoes, bowing from that elevation right and left to the impressed pilgrims. A quarrelsome band of footsore sulky niggers trod on the heels of the donkey; a lot of tents, campstools, tin boxes, white cases, brown bales would be shot down in the courtyard, and the air of mystery would deepen a little over the muddle of the station. Five such instalments came, with their absurd air of disorderly flight with the loot of innumerable outfit shops and provision stores, that, one would think, they were lugging, after a raid, into the wilderness for equitable division. It was an inextricable mess of things decent in themselves but that human folly made look like spoils of thieving.

'This devoted band called itself the Eldorado Exploring Expedition, and I believe they were sworn to secrecy. Their talk, however, was the talk of sordid buccaneers: it was reckless without hardihood, greedy without audacity, and cruel without courage; there was not an atom of foresight or of serious intention in the whole batch of them, and they did not seem aware these things are wanted for the work of the world. To tear treasure out of the bowels of the land was their desire, with no more moral purpose at the back of it than there is in burglars breaking into a safe. Who paid the expenses of the noble enterprise I don't know; but the uncle of our manager was leader of that lot.

'In exterior he resembled a butcher in a poor neighbourhood, and his eyes had a look of sleepy cunning. He carried his fat paunch with ostentation on his short legs, and during the time his gang infested the station spoke to no one but his nephew. You could see these two roaming about all day long with their heads close together in an everlasting confab.

'I had given up worrying myself about the rivets. One's capacity for that kind of folly is more limited than you would suppose. I said Hang! – and let things slide. I had plenty of time for meditation, and now and then I would give some thought to Kurtz. I wasn't very interested in him. No. Still, I was curious to see whether this man, who had come out equipped with moral ideas of some sort, would climb to the top after all and how he would set about his work when there.'

CHAPTER II

'ONE EVENING as I was lying flat on the deck of my steamboat, I heard voices approaching – and there were the nephew and the uncle strolling along the bank. I laid my head on my arm again, and had nearly lost myself in a doze, when somebody said in my ear, as it were: "I am as harmless as a little child, but I don't like to be dictated to. Am I the manager – or am I not? I was ordered to send him there. It's incredible." . . . I became aware that the two were standing on the shore alongside the forepart of the steamboat, just below my head. I did not move; it did not occur to me to move: I was sleepy. "It *is* unpleasant," grunted the uncle. "He has asked the Administration to be sent there," said the other, "with the idea of showing what he could do; and I was instructed accordingly. Look at the influence that man must have. Is it not frightful?" They both agreed it was frightful, then made several bizarre remarks: "Make rain and fine weather – one man – the Council – by the nose" – bits of absurd sentences that got the better of my drowsiness, so that I had pretty near the whole of my wits about me when the uncle said, "The climate may do away with this difficulty for you. Is he alone there?" "Yes," answered the manager; "he sent his assistant down the river with a note to me in these terms: 'Clear this poor devil out of the country, and don't bother sending more of that sort. I had rather be alone than have the kind of men you can dispose of with me.' It was more than a year ago. Can you imagine such impudence!" "Anything since then?" asked the other, hoarsely. "Ivory," jerked the nephew; "lots of it – prime sort – lots – most annoying, from him." "And with that?" questioned the heavy rumble. "Invoice," was the reply fired out, so to speak. Then silence. they had been talking about Kurtz.

'I was broad awake by this time, but, lying perfectly at ease, remained still, having no inducement to change my position. "How did that ivory come all this way?" growled the elder man, who seemed very vexed. The other explained that it had come with a fleet of canoes in charge of an English half-caste clerk Kurtz had with him; that Kurtz had apparently intended to return himself, the station being by that time bare of goods and stores, but after coming three hundred miles, had suddenly decided to go back, which he started to do alone in a small dugout with four paddlers, leaving the half-caste to continue down the river with the ivory. The two fellows there seemed astounded at anybody attempting such a thing. They were at a loss for an adequate motive. As to me, I seemed to see Kurtz for the first time. It was a distinct glimpse: the dugout, four paddling savages, and the lone white man turning his back suddenly on the headquarters, on relief, on thoughts of home – perhaps; setting his face towards the depths of the wilderness, towards his empty and desolate station. I did not know the motive. Perhaps he was just simply a fine fellow who stuck to his work for its own sake. His name, you understand, had not been pronounced once. He was "that man". The half-caste, who, as far as I could see, had conducted a difficult trip with great prudence and pluck, was invariably alluded to as "that scoundrel". The "scoundrel" had reported that the "man" had been very ill – had recovered imperfectly . . . The two below me moved away then a few paces, and strolled back and forth at some little distance. I heard: "Military post – doctor – two hundred miles – quite alone now – unavoidable delays – nine months – no news – strange rumours." They approached again, just as the manager was saying, "No one, as far as I know, unless a species of wandering trader – a pestilential fellow, snapping ivory from the natives." Who was it they were talking about now? I gathered in snatches that this was some man supposed to be in Kurtz's district, and of whom the manager did not approve. "We will not be free from unfair competition till one of these fellows is hanged for an example," he said. "Certainly," grunted the other; "get him hanged! Why not! Anything – anything can be done in this country. That's what I say; nobody here, you understand, *here*, can endanger your position. And why? You stand the climate – you outlast them all. The danger is in Europe; but there before I left I took care to –" They moved off and whispered, then their voices rose again. "The extraordinary series of delays is not my fault. I did my best." The fat man sighed. "Very sad." "And the pestiferous absurdity of his talk," continued the other; "he bothered me enough when he was here. 'Each station should be like a beacon on the road towards better things, a centre for trade of course, but also for humanizing, improving, instructing.' Conceive you – that ass! And he wants to be manager! No, it's –" Here he got choked by excessive indignation, and I lifted my head the least bit. I was surprised to see how near they were – right under me. I could have spat upon their hats. They were looking on the ground, absorbed in thought. The manager was switching his leg with a slender twig: his sagacious relative lifted his head. "You have been well since you came out this time?" he asked. The other gave a start. "Who? I? Oh! Like a charm – like a charm. But the rest – oh, my goodness! All sick. They die so quick, too, that I haven't the time to send them out of the country – it's incredible!" "H'm. Just so," grunted the uncle. "Ah! my boy, trust to this – I say, trust to this." I saw him extend his short flipper of an arm for a gesture that took in the forest, the creek, the mud, the river – seemed to beckon with a dishonouring flourish before the sunlit face of the land a treacherous appeal to the lurking death, to the hidden evil, to the profound darkness of its heart. It was so startling that I leaped to my feet and looked back at the edge of the forest, as though I had expected an answer of some sort fo that black display of confidence. You know the foolish notions that come to one sometimes. The high stillness confronted these two figures with its ominous patience, waiting for the passing away of a fantastic invasion.

'They swore aloud together – out of sheer fright, I believe – then pretending not to know anything of my existence, turned back to the station. The sun was low; and leaving forward side by side, they seemed to be tugging painfully uphill their two ridiculous shadows of unequal length, that trailed behind them slowly over the tall grass without bending a single blade.

'In a few days the Eldorado Expedition went into the patient wilderness, that closed upon it as the sea closes over a diver. Long afterwards the news came that all the donkeys were dead. I know nothing as to the fate of the less valuable animals. They, no doubt, like the rest of us, found what they deserved. I did not inquire. I was then rather excited at the prospect of meeting Kurtz very soon. When I say very soon I mean it comparatively. It was just two months from the day we left the creek when we came to the bank below Kurtz's station.

'Going up that river was like travelling back to the earliest beginnings of the world, when vegetation rioted on the earth and the big trees were kings. An empty stream, a great silence, an impenetrable forest. The air was warm, thick, heavy, sluggish. There was no joy in the brilliance of sunshine. The long stretches of the the waterway ran on, deserted, into the gloom of overshadowed distances. On silver sandbanks hippos and alligators sunned themselves side by side. The broadening waters flowed through a mob of wooded islands; you lost your way on that river as you would in a desert, and butted all day long against shoals, trying to find the channel, till you thought yourself bewitched and cut off for ever from everything you had known once – somewhere – far away – in another existence perhaps. There were moments when one's past came back to one, as it will sometimes when you have not a moment to spare to yourself; but it came in the shape of an unrestful and noisy dream, remembered with wonder amongst the overwhelming realities of this strange world of plants, and water, and silence. And this stillness of life did not in the least resemble a peace. It was the stillness of an implacable force brooding over an inscrutable intention. It looked at you with a vengeful aspect. I got used to it afterwards; I did not see it any more; I had no time. I had to keep guessing at the channel; I had to discern, mostly by inspiration, the signs of hidden banks; I watched for sunken stones; I was learning to clap my teeth smartly before my heart flew out, when I shaved by a fluke some infernal sly old snag that would have ripped the life out of the tin-pot steamboat and drowned all the pilgrims; I had to keep a look-out for the signs of dead wood we could cut up in the night for next day's steaming. When you have to attend to things of that sort, to the mere incidents of the surface, the reality – the reality, I tell you – fades. The inner truth is hidden – luckily, luckily. But I felt it all the same; I felt often its mysterious stillness watching me at my monkey tricks, just as it watches you fellows performing on your respective tight-ropes for – what is it? half-a-crown a tumble –'

'Try to be civil, Marlow,' growled a voice, and I knew there was at least one listener awake besides myself.

'I beg your pardon. I forgot the heartache which makes up the rest of the price. And indeed what does the price matter, if the trick be well done? You do your tricks very well. And I didn't do badly either, since I managed not to sink that steamboat on my first trip. It's a wonder to me yet. Imagine a blindfolded man set to drive a van over a bad road. I sweated and shivered over that business considerably, I can tell you. After all, for a seaman, to scrape the bottom of the thing that's supposed to float all the time under his care is the unpardonable sin. No one may know of it, but you never forget the thump – eh? A blow on the very heart. You remember it, you dream of it, you wake up at night and think of it – years after – and go hot and cold all over. I don't pretend to say that steamboat floated all the time. More than once she had to wade for a bit, with twenty cannibals splashing around and pushing. We had enlisted some of these chaps on the way for a crew. Fine fellows – cannibals – in their place. They were men one could work with, and I am grateful to them. And, after all, they did not eat each other before my face: they had brought along a provision of hippo-meat which went rotten, and made the mystery of the wilderness stink in my nostrils. Phoo! I can sniff it now. I had the manager on board and three or four pilgrims with their staves – all complete. Sometimes we came upon a station close by the bank, clinging to the skirts of the unknown, and the white men rushing out of a tumbledown hovel, with great gestures of joy and surprise and welcome, seemed very strange – had the appearance of being held there captive by a spell. The word ivory would ring in the air for a while – and on we went again into the silence, along empty reaches, round the still bends, between the high walls of our winding way, reverberating in hollow claps the ponderous beat of the stern-wheel. Trees, trees, millions of trees, massive, immense, running up high; and at their foot, hugging the bank against the stream, crept the little begrimed steamboat, like a sluggish beetle crawling on the floor of a lofty portico. It made you feel very small, very lost, and yet it was not altogether depressing, that feeling. After all, if you were small, the grimy beetle crawled on – which was just what you wanted it to do. Where the pilgrims imagined it crawled to I don't know. To some place where they expected to get something, I bet! For me it crawled towards Kurtz – exclusively; but when the steam-pipes started leaking we crawled very slow. The reaches opened before us and closed behind, as if the forest had stepped leisurely across the water to bar the way for our return. We penetrated deeper and deeper into the heart of darkness. It was very quiet there. At night sometimes the roll of drums behind the curtain of trees would run up the river and remain sustained faintly, as if hovering in the air high over our heads, till the first break of day. Whether it meant war, peace, or prayer we could not tell. The dawns were heralded by the descent of a chill stillness; the wood-cutters slept, their fires burned low; the snapping of a twig would make you start. We were wanderers on prehistoric earth, on an earth that wore the aspect of an unknown planet. We could have fancied ourselves the first of men taking possession of an accursed inheritance, to be subdued at the cost of profound anguish and of excessive toil. But suddenly, as we struggled round a bend, there would be a glimpse of rush walls, of peaked grass-roofs, a burst of yells, a whirl of black limbs, a mass of hands clapping, of feet stamping, of bodies swaying, of eyes rolling, under the droop of heavy and motionless foliage. The steamer toiled along slowly on the edge of a black and incomprehensible frenzy. The prehistoric man was cursing us, praying to us, welcoming us – who could tell? We were cut off from the comprehension of our surroundings; we glided past like phantoms, wondering and secretly appalled, as sane men would be before an enthusiastic outbreak in a madhouse. We could not understand because we were too far and could not remember, because we were travelling in the night of first ages, of those ages that are gone, leaving hardly a sign – and no memories.

'The earth seemed unearthly. We are accustomed to look upon the shackled form of a conquered monster, but there – there you could look at a thing monstrous and free. It was unearthly, and the men were – No, they were not inhuman. Well, you know, that was the worst of it – this suspicion of their not being inhuman. It would come slowly to one. They howled and leaped, and spun, and made horrid faces; but what thrilled you was just the thought of their humanity – like yours – the thought of your remote kinship with this wild and passionate uproar. Ugly. Yes, it was ugly enough; but if you were man enough you would admit to yourself that there was in you just the faintest trace of a response to the terrible frankness of that noise, a dim suspicion of there being a meaning in it which you – you so remote from the night of first ages – could comprehend. And why not? The mind of man is capable of anything – because everything is in it, all the past as well as all the future. What was there after all? Joy, fear, sorrow, devotion, valour, rage – who can tell? – but truth – truth stripped of its cloak of time. Let the fool gape and shudder – the man knows, and can look on without a wink. But he must at least be as much of a man as these on the shore. He must meet that truth with his own true stuff – with his own inborn strength. Principles won't do. Acquisitions, clothes, pretty rags – rags that would fly off at the first good shake. No; you want a deliberate belief. An appeal to me in this fiendish row – is there? Very well; I hear; I admit, but I have a voice, too, and for good or evil mine is the speech that cannot be silenced. Of course, a fool, what with sheer fright and find sentiments, is always safe. Who's that grunting? You wonder I didn't go ashore for a howl and a dance? Well, no – I didn't. Fine sentiments, you say? Fine sentiments, be hanged! I had no time. I had to mess about with white-lead and strips of woollen blanket helping to put bandages on those leaky steampipes – I tell you. I had to watch the steering, and circumvent those snags, and get the tin-pot along by hook or by crook. There was surface-truth enough in these things to save a wiser man. And between whiles I had to look after the savage who was fireman. He was an improved specimen; he could fire up a vertical boiler. He was there below me, and, upon my word, to look at him was as edifying as seeing a dog in a parody of breeches and a feather hat, walking on his hind-legs. A few months of training had done for that really fine chap. He squinted at the steam-gauge and at the water-gauge with an evident effort of intrepidity – and he had filed teeth, too, the poor devil, and the wool of his pate shaved into queer patterns, and three ornamental scars on each of his cheeks. He ought to have been clapping his hands and stamping his feet on the bank, instead of which he was hard at work, a thrall to strange witchcraft, full of improving knowledge. He was useful because he had been instructed; and what he knew was this – that should the water in that transparent thing disappear, the evil spirit inside the boiler would get angry through the greatness of his thirst, and take a terrible vengeance. So he sweated and fired up and watched the glass fearfully (with an impromptu charm, made of rags, tied to his arm, and a piece of polished bone, as big as a watch, stuck flatways through his lower lip), while the wooded banks slipped past us slowly, the short noise was left behind, the interminable miles of silence – and we crept on, towards Kurtz. But the snags were thick, the water was treacherous and shallow, the boiler seemed indeed to have a sulky devil in it, and thus neither that fireman nor I had any time to peer into our creepy thoughts.

'Some fifty miles below the Inner Station we came upon a hut of reeds, an inclined and melancholy pole, with the unrecognizable tatters of what had been a flag of some sort flying from it, and a neatly stacked wood-pile. This was unexpected. We came to the bank, and on the stack of firewood found a flat piece of board with some faded pencil-writing on it. When deciphered it said: "Wood for you. Hurry up. Approach cautiously." There was a signature, but it was illegible – not Kurtz – a much longer word. Hurry up. Where? Up the river? "Approach cautiously." We had not done so. But the warning could not have been meant for the place where it could be only found after approach. Something was wrong above. But what – and how much? That was the question. We commented adversely upon the imbecility of that telegraphic style. The bush around said nothing, and would not let us look very far, either. A torn curtain of red twill hung in the doorway of the hut, and flapped sadly in our faces. The dwelling was dismantled; but we could see a white man had lived there not very long ago. There remained a rude table – a plank on two posts; a heap of rubbish reposed in a dark corner, and by the door I picked up a book. It had lost its covers, and the pages had been thumbed into a state of extremely dirty softness; but the back had been lovingly stitched afresh with white cotton thread, which looked clean yet. It was an extraordinary find. Its title was, *An Inquiry into some Points of Seamanship*, by a man, Tower, Towson – some such name – Master in His Majesty's Navy. The matter looked dreary reading enough, with illustrative diagrams and repulsive tables of figures, and the copy was sixty years old. I handled this amazing antiquity with the greatest possible tenderness, lest it should dissolve in my hands. Within, Towson or Towser was inquiring earnestly into the breaking strain of ships' chains and tackle, and other such matters. Not a very enthralling book; but at the first glance you could see there a singleness of intention, an honest concern for the right way of going to work, which made these humble pages, thought out so many years ago, luminous with another than a professional light. The simple old sailor, with his talk of chains and purchases, made me forget the jungle and the pilgrims in a delicious sensation of having come upon something unmistakably real. Such a book being there was wonderful enough; but still more astounding were the notes pencilled in the margin, and plainly referring to the text. I couldn't believe my eyes! They were in cipher! Yes, it looked like cipher. Fancy a man lugging with him a book of that description into this nowhere and studying it – and making notes – in cipher at that! It was an extravagant mystery.

'I had been dimly aware for some time of a worrying noise, and when I lifted my eyes I saw the wood-pile was gone, and the manager, aided by all the pilgrims, was shouting at me from the river-side. I slipped the book into my pocket. I assure you to leave off reading was like tearing myself away from the shelter of an old and solid friendship.

'I started the lame engine ahead. "It must be this miserable trader – this intruder," exclaimed the manager, looking back malevolently at the place we had left. "He must be English," I said. "It will not save him from getting into trouble if he is not careful," muttered the manager darkly. I observed with assumed innocence that no man was safe from trouble in this world.

'The current was more rapid now, the steamer seemed at her last gasp, the stern-wheel flopped languidly, and I caught myself listening on tiptoe for the next beat of the boat, for in sober truth I expected the wretched thing to give up every moment. It was like watching the last flickers of a life. But still we crawled. Sometimes I would pick out a tree a little way ahead to measure our progress towards Kurtz by, but I lost it invariably before we got abreast. To keep the eyes so long on one thing was too much for human patience. The manager displayed a beautiful resignation. I fretted and fumed and took to arguing with myself whether or no I would talk openly with Kurtz; but before I could come to any conclusion it occurred to me that my speech or my silence, indeed any action of mine, would be a mere futility. What did it matter what anyone knew or ignored? What did it matter who was manager? One gets sometimes such a flash of insight. The essentials of this affair lay deep under the surface, beyond my reach, and beyond my power of meddling.

'Towards the evening of the second day we judged ourselves about eight miles from Kurtz's station. I wanted to push on; but the manager looked grave, and told me the navigation up there was so dangerous that it would be advisable, the sun being very low already, to wait where we were till next morning. Moreover, he pointed out that if the warning to approach cautiously were to be followed, we must approach in daylight – not at dusk, or in the dark. This was sensible enough. Eight miles meant nearly three hours' steaming for us, and I could also see suspicious ripples at the upper end of the reach. Nevertheless, I was annoyed beyond expression at the delay, and most unreasonably, too, since one night more could not matter much after so many months. As we had plenty of wood, and caution was the word, I brought up in the middle of the stream. The reach was narrow, straight, with high sides like a railway cutting. The dusk came gliding into it long before the sun had set. The current ran smooth and swift, but a dumb immobility sat on the banks. The living trees, lashed together by the creepers and every living bush of the undergrowth, might have been changed into stone, even to the slenderest twig, to the lightest leaf. It was not sleep – it seemed unnatural, like a state of trance. Not the faintest sound of any kind could be heard. You looked on amazed, and began to suspect yourself of being deaf – then the night came suddenly, and struck you blind as well. About three in the morning some large fish leaped, and the loud splash made me jump as though a gun had been fired. When the sun rose there was a white fog, very warm and clammy, and more blinding than the night. It did not shift or drive; it was just there, standing all round you like something solid. At eight or nine, perhaps, it lifted as a shutter lifts. We had a glimpse of the towering multitude of trees, of the immense matted jungle, with the blazing little ball of the sun hanging over it – all perfectly still – and then the white shutter came down again, smoothly, as if sliding in greased grooves. I ordered the chain, which we had begun to heave in, to be paid out again. Before it stopped running with a muffled rattle, a cry, a very loud cry, as of infinite desolation, soared slowly in the opaque air. It ceased. A complaining clamour, modulated in savage discords, filled our ears. The sheer unexpectedness of it made my hair stir under my cap. I don't know how it struck the others: to me it seemed as though the mist itself had screamed, so suddenly, and apparently from all sides at once, did this tumultuous and mournful uproar arise. It culminated in a hurried outbreak of almost intolerably excessive shrieking, which stopped short, leaving us stiffened in a variety of silly attitudes, and obstinately listening to the nearly as appalling and excessive silence. "Good God! What is the meaning – " stammered at my elbow one of the pilgrims, – a little fat man, with sandy hair and red whiskers, who wore side-spring boots, and pink pyjamas tucked into his socks. Two others remained open-mouthed a whole minute, then dashed into the little cabin, to rush out incontinently and stand darting scared glances, with Winchesters at "ready" in their hands. What we could see was just the steamer we were on, her outlines blurred as though she had been on the point of dissolving, and a misty strip of water, perhaps two feet broad, around her – and that was all. The rest of the world was nowhere, as far as our eyes and ears were concerned. Just nowhere. Gone, disappeared; swept off without leaving a whisper or a shadow behind.

'I went forward, and ordered the chain to be hauled in short, so as to be ready to trip the anchor and move the steamboat at once if necessary. "Will they attack?" whispered an awed voice. "We will all be butchered in this fog," murmured another. The faces twitched with the strain, the hands trembled slightly, the eyes forgot to wink. It was very curious to see the contrast of expressions of the white men and of the black fellows of our crew, who were as much strangers to that part of the river as we, though their homes were only eight hundred miles away. The whites, of course greatly discomposed, had besides a curious look of being painfully shocked by such an outrageous row. The others had an alert, naturally interested expression; but their faces were essentially quiet, even those of the one or two who grinned as they hauled at the chain. Several exchanged short, grunting phrases, which seemed to settle the matter to their satisfaction. Their headman, a young, broad-chested black, severely draped in dark-blue fringed cloths, with fierce nostrils and his hair all done up artfully in oily ringlets, stood near me. "Aha!" I said, just for good fellowship's sake. "Catch 'im," he snapped, with a bloodshot widening of his eyes and a flash of sharp teeth – "catch 'im. Give 'im to us." "To you, eh?" I asked; "what would you do with them?" "Eat 'im!" he said, curtly, and, leaning his elbow on the rail, looked out into the fog in a dignified and profoundly pensive attitude. I would no doubt have been properly horrified, had it not occurred to me that he and his chaps must be very hungry: that they must have been growing increasingly hungry for at least this month past. They had been engaged for six months (I don't think a single one of them had any clear idea of time, as we at the end of countless ages have. They still belonged to the beginnings of time – had no inherited experience to teach them, as it were), and, of course, as long as there was a piece of paper written over in accordance with some farcical law or other made down the river, it didn't enter anybody's head to trouble how they would live. Certainly they had brought with them some rotten hippo-meat, which couldn't have lasted very long, anyway, even if the pilgrims hadn't, in the midst of a shocking hullabaloo, thrown a considerable quantity of it overboard. It looked like a high-handed proceeding; but it was really a case of legitimate self-defence. You can't breathe dead hippo waking, sleeping, and eating, and at the same time keep your precarious grip on existence. Besides that, they had given them every week three pieces of brass wire, each about nine inches long; and the theory was they were to buy their provisions with that currency in river-side villages. You can see how *that* worked. There were either no villages, or the people were hostile, or the director, who like the rest of us fed out of tins, with an occasional old he-goat thrown in, didn't want to stop the steamer for some more or less recondite reason. So, unless they swallowed the wire itself, or made loops of it to snare the fishes with, I don't see what good their extravagant salary could be to them. I must say it was paid with a regularity worthy of a large and honourable trading company. For the rest, the only thing to eat – though it didn't look eatable in the least – I saw in their possession was a few lumps of some stuff like half-cooked dough, of a dirty lavender colour, they kept wrapped in leaves, and now and then swallowed a piece of, but so small that it seemed done more for the looks of the thing than for any serious purpose of sustenance. Why in the name of all the gnawing devils of hunger they didn't go for us – they were thirty to five – and have a good tuck in for once, amazes me now when I think of it. They were big powerful men, with not much capacity to weigh the consequences, with courage, with strength, even yet, though their skins were no longer glossy and their muscles no longer hard. And I saw that something restraining, one of those human secrets that baffle probability, had come into play there. I looked at them with a swift quickening of interest – not because it occurred to me I might be eaten by them before very long, though I own to you that just then I perceived – in a new light, as it were – how unwholesome the pilgrims looked, and I hoped, yes, I positively hoped, that my aspect was not so – what shall I say? – so – unappetizing: a touch of fantastic vanity which fitted well with the dream-sensation that pervaded all my days at that time. perhaps I had a little fever, too. One can't live with one's finger everlastingly on one's pulse. I had often "a little fever", or a little touch of other things – the playful paw-strokes of the wilderness, the preliminary trifling before the more serious onslaught which came in due course. Yes; I looked at them as you would on any human being, with a curiosity of their impulses, motives, capacities, weaknesses, when brought to the test of an inexorable physical necessity. Restraint! What possible restraint? Was it superstition, disgust, patience, fear – or some kind of primitive honour? No fear can stand up to hunger, no patience can wear it out, disgust simply does not exist where hunger is; and as to superstition, beliefs, and what you may call principles, they are less than chaff in a breeze. Don't you know the devilry of lingering starvation, its exasperating torment, its black thoughts, its sombre and brooding ferocity? Well, I do. It takes a man all his inborn strength to fight hunger properly. It's really easier to face bereavement, dishonour, and the perdition of one's soul – than this kind of prolonged hunger. Sad, but true. And these chaps, too, had no earthly reason for any kind of scruple. Restraint! I would just as soon have expected restraint from a hyena prowling amongst the corpses of a battlefield. But there was the fact facing me – the fact dazzling, to be seen, like the foam on the depths of the sea, like a ripple on an unfathomable enigma, a mystery greater – when I thought of it – than the curious inexplicable note of desperate grief in this savage clamour that had swept by us on the river-bank, behind the blind whiteness of the fog.

'Two pilgrims were quarrelling in hurried whispers as to which bank. "Left." "No, no; how can you? Right, right, of course." "It is very serious," said the manager's voice behind me; "I would be desolated if anything should happen to Mr Kurtz before we came up." I looked at him, and had not the slightest doubt he was sincere. He was just the kind of man who would wish to preserve appearances. That was his restraint. But when he muttered something about going on at once, I did not even take the trouble to answer him. I knew, and he knew, that it was impossible. Were we to let go our hold of the bottom, we would be absolutely in the air – in space. We wouldn't be able to tell where we were going to – whether up or down stream, or across – till we fetched against one bank or the other – and then we wouldn't know at first which it was. Of course I made no move. I had no mind for a smash-up. You couldn't imagine a more deadly place for a shipwreck. Whether drowned at once or not, we were sure to perish speedily in one way or another. "I authorize you to take all the risks,' he said, after a short silence. "I refuse to take any," I said, shortly; which was just the answer he expected, though its tone might have surprised him. "Well, I must defer to your judgement. You are captain," he said, with marked civility. I turned my shoulder to him in sign of my appreciation, and looked into the fog. How long would it last? It was the most hopeless look-out. The approach to this Kurtz grubbing for ivory in the wretched bush was beset by as many dangers as though he had been an enchanted princess sleeping in a fabulous castle. "Will they attack, do you think?" asked the manager, in a confidential tone.

'I did not think they would attack, for several obvious reasons. The thick fog was one. If they left the bank in their canoes they would get lost in it, as we would be if we attempted to move. Still, I had also judged the jungle of both banks quite impenetrable – and yet eyes were in it, eyes that had seen us. The river-side bushes were certainly very thick; but the undergrowth behind was evidently penetrable. However, during the short lift I had seen no canoes anywhere in the reach – certainly not abreast of the steamer. But what made the idea of attack inconceivable to me was the nature of the noise – of the cries we had heard. They had not the fierce character boding of immediate hostile intention. Unexpected, wild, and violent as they had been, they had given me an irresistible impression of sorrow. The glimpse of the steamboat had for some reason filled those savages with unrestrained grief. The danger, if any, I expounded, was from our proximity to a great human passion let loose. Even extreme grief may ultimately vent itself in violence – but more generally takes the form of apathy . . .

'You should have seen the pilgrims stare! They had no heart to grin, or even to revile me: but I believe they thought me gone mad – with fright, maybe. I delivered a regular lecture. My dear boys, it was no good bothering. Keep a look-out? Well, you may guess I watched the fog for the signs of lifting as a cat watches a mouse; but for anything else our eyes were of no more use to us than if we had been buried miles deep in a heap of cotton-wool. It felt like it, too – choking, warm, stifling. Besides, all I said, though it sounded extravagant, was absolutely true to fact. What we afterwards alluded to as an attack was really an attempt at repulse. The action was very far from being aggressive – it was not even defensive, in the usual sense: it was undertaken under the stress of desperation, and in its essence was purely protective.

'It developed itself, I should say, two hours after the fog lifted, and its commencement was at a spot, roughly speaking, about a mile and a half below Kurtz's station. We had just floundered and flopped round a bend, when I saw an islet, a mere grassy hummock of bright green, in the middle of the stream. it was the only thing of the kind; but as we opened the reach more, I perceived it was the head of a long sandbank, or rather of a chain of shallow patches stretching down the middle of the river. They were discoloured, just awash, and the whole lot was seen just under the water, exactly as a man's backbone is seen running down the middle of his back under the skin. Now, as far as I did see, I could go to the right or to the left of this. I didn't know either channel, of course. The banks looked pretty well alike, the depth appeared the same; but as I had been informed the station was on the west side, I naturally headed for the western passage.

'No sooner had we fairly entered it than I became aware it was much narrower than I had supposed. To the left of us there was the long uninterrupted shoal, and to the right a high, steep bank heavily overgrown with bushes. Above the bush the trees stood in serried ranks. The twigs overhung the current thickly, and from distance to distance a large limb of some tree projected rigidly over the stream. It was then well on in the afternoon, the face of the forest was gloomy, and a broad strip of shadow had already fallen on the water. In this shadow we steamed up – very slowly, as you may imagine. I steered her well inshore – the water being deepest near the bank, as the sounding-pole informed me.

'One of my hungry and forbearing friends was sounding in the bows just below me. This steamboat was exactly like a decked scow. On the deck, there were two little teak-wood houses, with doors and windows. The boiler was in the fore-end, and the machinery right astern. Over the whole there was a light roof, supported on stanchions. The funnel projected through that roof, and in front of the funnel a small cabin built of light planks served for a pilot-house. It contained a couch, two camp-stools, a loaded Martini-Henry leaning in one corner, a tiny table, and the steering-wheel. It had a wide door in front and a broad shutter at each side. All these were always thrown open, of course. I spent my days perched up there on the extreme fore-end of that roof, before the door. At night I slept, or tried to, on the couch. An athletic black belonging to some coast tribe, and educated by my poor predecessor, was the helmsman. He sported a pair of brass earrings, wore a blue cloth wrapper from the waist to the ankles, and thought all the world of himself. He was the most unstable kind of fool I had ever seen. He steered with no end of a swagger while you were by; but if he lost sight of you, he became instantly the prey of an abject funk, and would let that cripple of a steamboat get the upper hand of him in a minute.

'I was looking down at the sounding-pole, and feeling much annoyed to see at each try a little more of it stick out of that river, when I saw my poleman give up the business suddenly, and stretch himself flat on the deck, without even taking the trouble to haul his pole in. He kept hold on it though, and it trailed in the water. At the same time the fireman, whom I could also see below me, sat down abruptly before his furnace and ducked his head. I was amazed. Then I had to look at the river mighty quick, because there was a snag in the fairway. Sticks, little sticks, were flying about – thick: they were whizzing before my nose, dropping below me, striking behind me against my pilot-house. All this time the river, the shore, the woods, were very quiet – perfectly quiet. I could only hear the heavy splashing thump of the stern-wheel and the patter of these things. We cleared the snag clumsily. Arrows, by Jove! We were being shot at! I stepped in quickly to close the shutter on the land-side. That fool-helmsman, his hands on the spokes, was lifting his knees high, stamping his feet, champing his mouth, like a reined-in horse. Confound him! And we were staggering within ten feet of the bank. I had to lean right out to swing the heavy shutter, and I saw a face amongst the leaves on the level with my own, looking at me very fierce and steady and then suddenly, as though a veil had been removed from my eyes, I made out, deep in the tangled gloom, naked breasts, arms, legs, glaring eyes, – the bush was swarming with human limbs in movement, glistening, of bronze colour. The twigs shook, swayed, and rustled, the arrows flew out of them, and then the shutter came to. "Steer her straight," I said to the helmsman. He held his head rigid, face forward; but his eyes rolled, he kept on, lifting and setting down his feet gently, his mouth foamed a little. "Keep quiet!" I said in a fury. I might just as well have ordered a tree not to sway in the wind. I darted out. Below me there was a great scuffle of feet on the iron deck; confused exclamations; a voice screamed, "Can you turn back?" I caught sight of a V-shaped ripple on the water ahead. What? Another snag! A fusillade burst out under my feet. The pilgrims had opened with their Winchesters, and were simply squirting lead into that bush. A deuce of a lot of smoke came up and drove slowly forward. I swore at it. Now I couldn't see the ripple or the snag either. I stood in the doorway, peering, and the arrows came in swarms. They might have been poisoned, but they looked as though they wouldn't kill a cat. The bush began to howl. Our wood-cutters raised a warlike whoop; the report of a rifle just at my back deafened me. I glanced over my shoulder, and the pilot-house was yet full of noise and smoke when I made a dash at the wheel. The fool-nigger had dropped everything, to throw the shutter open and let off that Martini-Henry. He stood before the wide opening, glaring, and I yelled at him to come back, while I straightened the sudden twist out of that steamboat. There was no room to turn even if I had wanted to, the snag was somewhere very near ahead in that confounded smoke, there was no time to lose, so I just crowded her into the bank – right into the bank, where I knew the water was deep.

'We tore slowly along the overhanging bushes in a whirl of broken twigs and flying leaves. The fusillade below stopped short, as I had foreseen it would when the squirts got empty. I threw my head back to a glinting whizz that traversed the pilot-house, in at one shutterhole and out at the other. Looking past that mad helmsman, who was shaking the empty rifle and yelling at the shore, I saw vague forms of men running bent double, leaping, gliding, indistinct, incomplete, evanescent. Something big appeared in the air before the shutter, the rifle went overboard, and the man stepped back swiftly, looked at me over his shoulder in an extraordinary, profound, familiar manner, and fell upon my feet. The side of his head hit the wheel twice, and the end of what appeared to be a long cane clattered round and knocked over a little camp-stool. It looked us though after wrenching that thing from somebody ashore he had lost his balance in the effort. The thin smoke had blown away, we were clear of the snag, and looking ahead I could see that in another hundred yards or so I would be free to sheer off, away from the bank; but my feet felt so very warm and wet that I had to look down. The man had rolled on his back and stared straight up at me; both his hands clutched that cane. It was the shaft of a spear that, either thrown or lunged through the opening, had caught him in the side just below the ribs; the blade had gone in out of sight, after making a frightful gash; my shoes were full; a pool of blood lay very still, gleaming dark-red under the wheel; his eyes shone with an amazing lustre. The fusillade burst out again. He looked at me anxiously, gripping the spear like something precious, with an air of being afraid I would try to take it away from him. I had to make an effort to free my eyes from his gaze and attend to the steering. With one hand I felt above my head for the line of the steam-whistle, and jerked out screech after screech hurriedly. The tumult of angry and warlike yells was checked instantly, and then from the depths of the woods went out such a tremulous and prolonged wail of mournful fear and utter despair as may be imagined to follow the flight of the last hope from the earth. There was a great commotion in the bush; the shower of arrows stopped, a few dropping shots rang out sharply – then silence, in which the languid beat of the stern-wheel came plainly to my ears. I put the helm hard a-starboard at the moment when the pilgrim in pink pyjamas, very hot and agitated, appeared in the doorway. "The manager sends me –" he began in an official tone, and stopped short. "Good God!" he said, glaring at the wounded man.

'We two whites stood over him, and his lustrous and inquiring glance envoloped us both. I declare it looked as though he would presently put to us some question in an understandable language; but he died without uttering a sound, without moving a limb, without twitching a muscle. Only in the very last moment, as though in response to some sign we could not see, to some whisper we could not hear, he frowned heavily, and that frown gave to his black death-mask an inconceivably sombre, brooding, and menacing expression. The lustre of the inquiring glance faded swiftly into vacant glassiness. "Can you steer?" I asked the agent eagerly. He looked very dubious; but I made a grab at his arm, and he undertood at once I meant him to steer whether or no. To tell you the truth, I was morbidly anxious to change my shoes and socks. "He is dead," murmured the fellow, immensely impressed. "No doubt about it," said I, tugging like mad at the shoe-laces. "And by the way, I suppose Mr Kurtz is dead as well by this time."

'For the moment that was the dominant thought. There was a sense of extreme disappointment, as though I had found out I had been striving after something altogether without a substance. I couldn't have been more disgusted if I had travelled all this way for the sole purpose of talking with Mr Kurtz. Talking with . . . I flung one shoe overboard, and became aware that that was exactly what I had been looking forward to – a talk with Kurtz. I made the strange discovery that I had never imagined him as doing, you know, but as discoursing. I didn't say to myself, "Now I will never see him," or "Now I will never shake him by the hand," but, "Now I will never hear him." The man presented himself as a voice. Not of course that I did not connect him with some sort of action. Hadn't I been told in all the tones of jealousy and admiration that he had collected, bartered, swindled, or stolen more ivory than all the other agents together? That was not the point. The point was in his being a gifted creature, and that of all his gifts the one that stood out pre-eminently, that carried with it a sense of real presence, was his ability, to talk, his words – the gift of expression, the bewildering, the illuminating, the most exalted and the most contemptible, the pulsating stream of light, or the deceitful flow from the heart of an impenetrable darkness.

'The other shoe went flying unto the devil-god of that river. I thought, By Jove! it's all over. We are too late; he has vanished – the gift has vanished, by means of some spear, arrow, or club. I will never hear that chap speak after all, – and my sorrow had a startling extravagance of emotion, even such as I had noticed in the howling sorrow of these savages in the bush. I couldn't have felt more of lonely desolation somehow, had I been robbed of a belief or had missed my destiny in life . . . Why do you sigh in this beastly way, somebody? Absurd! Well, absurd. Good Lord! mustn't a man ever – Here, give me some tobacco.'. . .

There was a pause of profound stillness, then a match flared, and Marlow's lean face appeared, worn, hollow, with downward folds and dropped eyelids, with an aspect of concentrated attention; and as he took vigorous draws at his pipe, it seemed to retreat and advance out of the night in the regular flicker of the tiny flame. The match went out.

'Absurd!' he cried. 'This is the worst of trying to tell . . . Here you all are, each moored with two good addresses, like a hulk with two anchors, a butcher round one corner, a policeman round another, excellent appetites, and temperature normal – you hear – normal from year's end to year's end. And you say. Absurd! Absurd be – exploded! Absurd! My dear boys, what can you expect from a man who out of sheer nervousness had just flung overboard a pair of new shoes! Now I think of it, it is amazing I did not shed tears. I am, upon the whole, proud of my fortitude. I was cut to the quick at the idea of having lost the inestimable privilege of listening to the gifted Kurtz. Of course I was wrong. The privilege was waiting for me. Oh, yes, I heard more than enough. And I was right too. A voice. He was very little more than a voice. And I heard – him – it – this voice – other voices – all of them were so little more than voices – and the memory of that time itself lingers around me, impalpable, like a dying vibration of one immense jabber, silly, atrocious, sordid, savage, or simply mean, without any kind of sense. Voices, voices – even the girl herself – now –'

He was silent for a long time.

'I laid the ghost of his gifts at last with a lie,' he began suddenly. 'Girl! What? Did I mention a girl? Oh, she is out of it – completely. They – the women I mean

– are out of it – should be out of it. We must help them to stay in that beautiful world of their own, lest ours gets worse. Oh, she had to be out of it. You should have heard the disinterred body of Mr Kurtz saying, "My Intended." You would have perceived directly then how completely she was out of it. And the lofty frontal bone of Mr Kurtz! They say the hair goes on growing sometimes, but this – ah – specimen, was impressively bald. The wilderness had patted him on the head, and, behold, it was like a ball – an ivory ball; it had caressed him, and – lo! – he had withered; it had taken him, loved him, embraced him, got into his veins, consumed his flesh, and sealed his soul to its own by the inconceivable ceremonies of some devilish initiation. He was its spoiled and pampered favourite. Ivory? I should think so. Heaps of it, stacks of it. The old mud shanty was bursting with it. You would think there was not a single tusk left either above or below the ground in the whole country. "Mostly fossil," the manager had remarked, disparagingly. It was no more fossil than I am; but they call it fossil when it is dug up. It appears these niggers do bury the tusks sometimes – but evidently they couldn't bury this parcel deep enough to save the gifted Mr Kurtz from his fate. We filled the steamboat with it, and had to pile a lot on the deck. Thus he could see and enjoy as long as he could see, because the appreciation of this favour had remained with him to the last. You should have heard him say, "My ivory." Oh yes, I heard him. "My Intended, my ivory, my station, my river, my –" everything belonged to him. It made me hold my breath in expectation of hearing the wilderness burst into a prodigious peal of laughter that would shake the fixed stars in their places. Everything belonged to him – but that was a trifle. The thing was to know what he belonged to, how many powers of darkness claimed him for their own. That was the reflection that made you creepy all over. It was impossible – it was not good for one either – trying to imagine. He had taken a high seat amongst the devils of the land – I mean literally. You can't understand. How could you? – with solid pavement under your feet, surrounded by kind neighbours ready to cheer you or to fall on you, stepping delicately between the butcher and the policeman, in the holy terror of scandal and gallows and lunatic asylums – how can you imagine what particular region of the first ages a man's untrammelled feet may take him into by the way of solitude – utter solitude without a policeman – by the way of silence – utter silence, where no warning voice of a kind neighbour can be heard whispering of public opinion? These little things make all the great difference. When they are gone you must fall back upon your own innate strength, upon your own capacity for faithfulness. Of course you may be too much of a fool to go wrong – too dull even to know you are being assaulted by the powers of darkness. I take it, no fool ever made a bargain for his soul with the devil: the fool is too much of a fool, or the devil too much of a devil – I don't know which. Or you may be such a thunderingly exalted creature as to be altogether deaf and blind to anything but heavenly sights and sounds. Then the earth for you is only a standing place – and whether to be like this is your loss or your gain I won't pretend to say. But most of us are neither one nor the other. The earth for us is a place to live in, where we must put up with sights, with sounds, with smells, too, by Jove! – breathe dead hippo, so to speak, and not be contaminated. And there, don't you see? your strength comes in, the faith in your ability for the digging of unostentatious holes to bury the stuff in – your power of devotion, not to yourself, but to an obscure, back-breaking business. And that's difficult enough. Mind, I am not trying to excuse or even explain – I am trying to account to myself for – for – Mr Kurtz – for the shade of Mr Kurtz. This initiated wraith from the back of Nowhere honoured me with its amazing confidence before it vanished altogether. This was because it could speak English to me. The original Kurtz had been educated partly in England, and – as he was good enough to say himself – his sympathies were in the right place. His mother was half-English, his father was half-French. All Europe contributed to the making of Kurtz; and by-and-by I learned that, most appropriately, the International Society for the Suppression of Savage Customs had entrusted him with the making of a report, for its future guidance. And he had written it, too. I've seen it. I've read it. It was eloquent, vibrating with eloquence, but too high-strung, I think. Seventeen pages of close writing he had found time for! But this must have been before his – let us say – nerves, went wrong, and caused him to preside at certain midnight dances ending with unspeakable rites, which – as far as I reluctantly gathered from what I heard at various times – were offered up to him – do you understand? – to Mr Kurtz himself. But it was a beautiful piece of writing. The opening paragraph, however, in the light of later information, strikes me now as ominous. He began with the argument that we whites, from the point of development we had arrived at, "must necessarily appear to them [savages] in the nature of supernatural beings – we approach them with the might as of a deity," and so on, and so on. "By the simple exercise of our will we can exert a power for good practically unbounded," etc., etc. From that point he soared and took me with him. The peroration was magnificent, though difficult to remember, you know. It gave me the notion of an exotic Immensity ruled by an august Benevolence. It made me tingle with enthusiasm. This was the unbounded power of eloquence – of words – of burning noble words. There were no practical hints to interrupt the magic current of phrases, unless a kind of note at the foot of the last page, scrawled evidently much later, in an unsteady hand, may be regarded as the exposition of a method. It was very simple, and at the end of that moving appeal to every altruistic sentiment it blazed at you, luminous and terrifying, like a flash of lightning in a serene sky: "Exterminate all the brutes!" The curious part was that he had apparently forgotten all about that valuable postscriptum, because, later on, when he in a sense came to himself, he repeatedly entreated me to take good care of "my pamphlet" (he called it), as it was sure to have in the future a good influence upon his career. I had full information about all these things, and, besides, as it turned out, I was to have the care of his memory. I've done enough for it to give me the indisputable right to lay it, if I choose, for an everlasting rest in the dust-bin of progress, amongst all the sweepings and, figuratively speaking, all the dead cats of civilization. But then, you see, I can't choose. He won't be forgotten. Whatever he was, he was not common. He had the power to charm or frighten rudimentary souls into an aggravated witch-dance in his honour; he could also fill the small souls of the pilgrims with bitter misgivings: he had one devoted friend at least, and he had conquered one soul in the world that was neither rudimentary nor tainted with self-seeking. No; I can't forget him, though I am not prepared to affirm the fellow was exactly worth the life we lost in getting to him. I missed my late helmsman awfully, – I missed him even while his body was still lying in the pilot-house. Perhaps you will think it passing strange, this regret for a savage who was of no more account than a grain of sand in a black Sahara. Well, don't you see, he had done something, he had steered; for months I had him at my back – a help – an instrument. It was a kind of partnership. He steered for me – I had to look after him, I worried about his deficiencies, and thus a subtle bond had been created, of which I only became aware when it was suddenly broken. And the intimate profundity of that look he gave me when he received his hurt remains to this day in my memory – like a claim of distant kinship affirmed in a supreme moment.

'Poor fool! If he had only left that shutter alone. He had no restraint, no restraint – just like Kurtz – a tree swayed by the wind. As soon as I had put on a dry pair of slippers, I dragged him out, after first jerking the spear out of his side, which operation I confess I performed with my eyes shut tight. His heels leaped together over the little doorstep; his shoulders were pressed to my breast; I hugged him from behind desperately. Oh! he was heavy, heavy; heavier than any man on earth, I should imagine. Then without more ado I tipped him overboard. The current snatched him as though he had been a wisp of grass, and I saw the body roll over twice before I lost sight of it for ever. All the pilgrims and the manager were then congregated on the awning-deck about the pilot-house, chattering at each other like a flock of excited magpies, and there was a scandalized murmur at my heartless promptitude. What they wanted to keep that body hanging about for I can't guess. Embalm it, maybe. But I had also heard another, and a very ominous, murmur on the deck below. My friends the wood-cutters were likewise scandalized, and with a better show of reason – though I admit that the reason itself was quite inadmissable. Oh, quite! I had made up my mind that if my late helmsman was to be eaten, the fishes alone should have him. He had been a very second-rate helmsman while alive, but now he was dead he might have become a first-class temptation, and possibly cause some startling trouble. Besides, I was anxious to take the wheel, the man in pink pyjamas showing himself a hopeless duffer at the business.

'This I did directly the simple funeral was over. We were going half-speed, keeping right in the middle of the stream, and I listened to the talk about me. They had given up Kurtz, they had given up the station; Kurtz was dead, and the station had been burnt – and so on – and so on. The red-haired pilgrim was beside himself with the thought that at least this poor Kurtz had been properly avenged. "Say! We must have made a glorious slaughter of them in the bush. Eh? What do you think? Say?" He positively danced, the bloodthirsty little gingery beggar. And he had nearly fainted when he saw the wounded man! I could not help saying, "You made a glorious lot of smoke, anyhow." I had seen, from the way the tops of the bushes rustled and flew, that almost all the shots had gone too high. You can't hit anything unless you take aim and fire from the shoulder; but these chaps fired from the hip with their eyes shut. The retreat, I maintained – and I was right – was caused by the screeching of the steam-whistle. Upon this they forgot Kurtz, and began to howl at me with indignant protests.

'The manager stood by the wheel murmuring confidentially about the necessity of getting well away down the river before dark at all events, when I saw in the distance a clearing on the river-side and the outlines of some sort of building. "What's this?" I asked. He clapped his hands in wonder. "The station!" he cried. I edged in at once, still going half-speed.

'Through my glasses I saw the slope of a hill interspersed with rare trees and perfectly free from undergrowth. A long decaying building on the summit was half buried in the high grass; the large holes in the peaked roof gaped black from afar; the jungle and the woods made a background. There was no enclosure or fence of any kind; but there had been one apparently, for near the house half-a-dozen slim posts remained in a row, roughly trimmed, and with their upper ends ornamented with round carved balls. The rails, or whatever there had been between, had disappeared. Of course the forest surrounded all that. The river-bank was clear, and on the water-side I saw a white man under a hat like a cartwheel beckoning persistently with his whole arm. Examining the edge of the forest above and below, I was almost certain I could see movements – human forms gliding here and there. I steamed past prudently, then stopped the engines and let her drift down. The man on the shore began to shout, urging us to land. "We have been attacked," screamed the manager. "I know – I know. It's all right,' yelled back the other, as cheerful as you please. "Come along. It's all right. I am glad."

'His aspect reminded me of something I had seen – something funny I had seen somewhere. As I manoeuvred to get alongside, I was asking myself, "What does this fellow look like?" Suddenly I got it. He looked like a harlequin. His clothes had been made of some stuff that was brown holland probably, but it was covered with patches all over, with bright patches, blue, red, and yellow, – patches on the back, patches on the front, patches on elbows, on knees; coloured binding around his jacket, scarlet edging at the bottom of his trousers; and the sunshine made him look extremely gay and wonderfully neat withal, because you could see how beautifully all this patching had been done. A beardless, boyish face, very fair, no feature to speak of, nose peeling, little blue eyes, smiles and frowns chasing each other over that open countenance like sunshine and shadow on a wind-swept plain. "Look out, captain!" he cried; "there's a snag lodged in here last night." What! Another snag? I confess I swore shamefully. I had nearly holed my cripple, to finish off that charming trip. The harlequin on the bank turned his little pug-nose up to me. "You English?" he asked, all smiles. "Are you?" I shouted from the wheel. The smiles vanished, and he shook his head as if sorry for my disappointment. Then he brightened up. "Never mind!" he cried, encouragingly. "Are we in time?" I asked. "He is up there," he replied, with a toss of the head up the hill, and becoming gloomy all of a sudden. His face was like the autumn sky, overcast one moment and bright the next.

'When the manager, escorted by the pilgrims, all of them armed to the teeth, had gone to the house this chap came on board. "I say. I don't like this. These natives are in the bush," I said. He assured me earnestly it was all right. "They are simple people," he added; "well, I am glad you came. It took me all my time to keep them off." "But you said it was all right," I cried. "Oh, they meant no harm," he said; and as I stared he corrected himself, "Not exactly." Then vivaciously, "My faith, your pilot-house wants a clean-up!" In the next breath he advised me to keep enough steam on the boiler to blow the whistle in case of any trouble. "One good screech will do more for you than all your rifles. They are simple people," he repeated. He rattled away at such a rate he quite overwhelmed me. He seemed to be trying to make up for lots of silence, and actually hinted, laughing, that such was the case. "Don't you talk with Mr Kurtz?" I said. "You don't talk with that man – you listen to him," he exclaimed with severe exaltation. "But now –" He waved his arm, and in the twinkling of an eye was in the uttermost depths of despondency. In a moment he came up again with a jump, possessed himself of both hands, shook them continuously, while he gabbled: "Brother sailor . . . honour . . . pleasure . . . delight . . . introduce myself . . . Russian . . . son of an arch-priest . . . Government of Tambov . . . What? Tobacco! English tobacco; the excellent English tobacco! Now, that's brotherly. Smoke? Where's a sailor that does not smoke?"

'The pipe soothed him, and gradually I made out he had run away from school, had gone to sea in a Russian ship; ran away again; served some time in English ships; was now reconciled with the arch-priest. He made a point of that. "But when one is young one must see things, gather experience, ideas; enlarge the mind." "Here!" I interrupted. "You can never tell! Here I met Mr Kurtz," he said, youthfully solemn and reproachful. I held my tongue after that. It appears he had persuaded a Dutch trading-house on the coast to fit him out with stores and goods, and had started for the interior with a light heart, and no more idea of what would happen to him than a baby. He had been wandering about that river for nearly two years alone, cut off from everybody and everything. "I am not so young as I look. I am twenty-five," he said. "At first old Van Shuyten would tell me to go to the devil," he narrated with keen enjoyment; "but I stuck to him, and talked and talked, till at last he got afraid I would talk the hind-leg off his favourite dog, so he gave me some cheap things and a few guns, and told me he hoped he would never see my face again. Good old Dutchman, Van Shuyten. I've sent him one small lot of ivory a year ago, so that he can't call me a little thief when I get back. I hope he got it. And for the rest I don't care. I had some wood stacked for you. That was my old house. Did you see?"

'I gave him Towson's book. He made as though he would kiss me, but restrained himself. "The only book I had left, and I thought I had lost it," he said, looking at it ecstatically. "So many accidents happen to a man going about alone, you know. Canoes get upset sometimes – and sometimes you've got to clear out so quickly when the people get angry." He thumbed the pages. "You made notes in Russian?" I asked. He nodded. "I thought they were written in cipher," I said. He laughed, then became serious. "I had lots of trouble to keep these people off," he said. "Did they want to kill you?" I asked. "Oh, no!" he cried, and checked himself. "Why did they attack us?" I pursued. He hesitated, then said shamefacedly, "They don't want him to go." "Don't they?" I said, curiously. He nodded a nod full of mystery and wisdom. "I tell you," he cried, "this man has enlarged my mind." He opened his arms wide, staring at me with his little blue eyes that were perfectly round.'

CHAPTER III

'I LOOKED AT HIM, lost in astonishment. There he was before me, in motley, as though he had absconded from a troupe of mimes, enthusiastic, fabulous. His very existence was improbable, inexplicable, and altogether bewildering. He was an insoluble problem. It was inconceivable how he had existed, how he had succeeded in getting so far, how he had managed to remain – why he did not instantly disappear. "I went a little farther," he said, "then still a little farther – till I had gone so far that I don't know how I'll ever get back. Never mind. Plenty time. I can manage. You take Kurtz away quick – quick – I tell you." The glamour of youth enveloped his parti-coloured rags, his destitution, his loneliness, the essential desolation of his futile wanderings. For months – for years – his life hadn't been worth a day's purchase; and there he was gallantly, thoughtlessly alive, to all appearance indestructible solely by the virtue of his few years and of his unreflecting audacity. I was seduced into something like admiration – like envy. Glamour urged him on, glamour kept him unscathed. He surely wanted nothing from the wilderness but space to breathe in and to push on through. His need was to exist, and to move onwards at the greatest possible risk, and with a maximum of privation. If the absolutely pure, uncalculating, unpractical spirit of adventure had ever ruled a human being, it ruled this be-patched youth. I almost envied him the possession of this modest and clear flame. It seemed to have consumed all thought of self so completely, that even while he was talking to you, you forgot that it was he – the man before your eyes – who had gone through these things. I did not envy him his devotion to Kurtz, though. He had not meditated over it. It came to him, and he accepted it with a sort of eager fatalism. I must say that to me it appeared about the most dangerous thing in every way he had come upon so far.

"They had come together unavoidably, like two ships becalmed near each other, and lay rubbing sides at last. I suppose Kurtz wanted an audience, because on a certain occasion, when encamped in the forest, they had talked all night, or more probably Kurtz had talked. "We talked of everything," he said, quite transported at the recollection. "I forgot there was such a thing as sleep. The night did not seem to last an hour. Everything! Everything! . . . Of love, too." "Ah, he talked to you of love!" I said, much amused. "It isn't what you think," he cried, almost passionately. "It was in general. He made me see things – things."

'He threw his arms up. We were on deck at the time, and the headman of my wood-cutters, lounging near by, turned upon him his heavy and glittering eyes. I looked around, and I don't know why, but I assure you that never, never before, did this land, this river, this jungle, the very arch of this blazing sky, appear to me so hopeless and so dark, so impenetrable to human thought, so pitiless to human weakness. "And, ever since, you have been with him, of course?" I said.

'On the contrary. It appears their intercourse had been very much broken by various causes. He had, as he informed me proudly, managed to nurse Kurtz through two illnesses (he alluded to it as you would to some risky feat), but as a rule Kurtz wandered alone, far in the depths of the forest. "Very often coming to this station, I had to wait days and days before he would turn up," he said. "Ah, it was worth waiting for! – sometimes." "What was he doing? exploring or what?" I asked. "Oh, yes, of course"; he had discovered lots of villages, a lake, too – he did not know exactly in what direction; it was dangerous to inquire too much – but mostly his expeditions had been for ivory. "But he had no goods to trade with by that time," I objected. "There's a good lot of cartridges left even yet," he answered, looking away. "To speak plainly, he raided the country," I said. He nodded. "Not alone, surely!" He muttered something about the villages round that lake. "Kurtz got the tribe to follow him, did he?" I suggested. He fidgeted a little. "They adored him," he said. The tone of these words was so extraordinary that I looked at him searchingly. It was curious to see his mingled eagerness and reluctance to speak of Kurtz. The man filled his life, occupied his thoughts, swayed his emotions. "What can you expect?" he burst out; "he came to them with thunder and lightning, you know – and they had never seen anything like it – and very terrible. He could be very terrible. You can't judge Mr Kurtz as you would an ordinary man. No, no, no! Now – just to give you an idea – I don't mind telling you, he wanted to shoot me, too, one day – but I don't judge him." "Shoot you!" I cried. "What for?" "Well, I had a small lot of ivory the chief of that village near my house gave me. You see I used to shoot game for them. Well, he wanted it, and wouldn't hear reason. He declared he would shoot me unless I gave him the ivory and then cleared out of the country, because he could do so, and had a fancy for it, and there was nothing on earth to prevent him killing whom he jolly well pleased. And it was true, too. I gave him the ivory. What did I care! But I didn't clear out. No, no. I couldn't leave him. I had to be careful, of course, till we got friendly again for a time. He had his second illness then. Afterwards I had to keep out of the way; but I didn't mind. He was living for the most part in those villages on the lake. When he came down to the river, sometimes he would take to me, and sometimes it was better for me to be careful. This man suffered too much. He hated all this, and somehow he couldn't get away. When I had a chance I begged him to try and leave while there was time; I offered to go back with him. And he would say yes, and then he would remain; go off on another ivory hunt; disappear for weeks; forget himself amongst these people – forget himself – you know." "Why! he's mad," I said. He protested indignantly. Mr Kurtz couldn't be mad. If I had heard him talk, only two days ago, I wouldn't dare hint at such a thing . . . I had taken up my binoculars while we talked, and was looking at the shore, sweeping the limit of the forest at each side and at the back of the house. The consciousness of there being people in that bush, so silent, so quite – as silent and quite as the ruined house on the hill – made me uneasy. There was no sign on the face of nature of this amazing tale that was not so much told as suggested to me in desolate exclamations, completed by shrugs, in interrupted phrases, in hints ending in deep sighs. The woods were unmoved, like a mask – heavy, like the closed door of a prison – they looked with their air of hidden knowledge, of patient expectation, of unapproachable silence. The Russian was explaining to me that it was only lately that Mr Kurtz had come down to the river, bringing along with him all the fighting men of that lake tribe. He had been absent for several months – getting himself adored, I suppose – and had come down unexpectedly, with the intention to all appearance of making a raid either across the river or down stream. Evidently the appetite for more ivory had got the better of the – what shall I say? – less material aspirations. However he had got much worse suddenly. "I heard he was lying helpless, and so I came up – took my chance," said the Russian. "Oh, he is bad, very bad." I directed my glass to the house. There were no signs of life, but there was the ruined roof, the long mud wall peeping above the grass, with three little square window-holes, no two the same size: all this brought within reach of my hand, as it were. And then I made a brusque movement, and one of the remaining posts of that vanished fence leaped up in the field of my glass. You remember I told you I had been struck at the distance by certain attempts at ornamentation, rather remarkable in the ruinous aspect of the place. Now I had suddenly a nearer view, and its first result was to make me throw my head back as if before a blow. Then I went carefully from post to post with my glass, and I saw my mistake. These round knobs were not ornamental but symbolic; they were expressive and puzzling, striking and disturbing – food for thought and also for the vultures if there had been any looking down from the sky; but at all events for such ants as were industrious enough to ascend the pole. They would have been even more impressive, those heads on the stakes, if their faces had not been turned to the house. Only one, the first I had made out, was facing my way. I was not so shocked as you may think. The start back I had given was really nothing but a movement of surprise. I had expected to see a knob of wood there, you know. I returned deliberately to the first I had seen – and there it was, black, dried, sunken, with closed eyelids – a head that seemed to sleep at the top of that pole, and, with the shrunken dry lips showing a narrow white line of teeth, was smiling, too, smiling continuously at some endless and jocose dream of that eternal slumber.

'I am not disclosing any trade secrets. In fact, the manager said afterwards that Mr Kurtz's methods had ruined the district. I have no opinion on that point, but I want you clearly to understand that there was nothing exactly profitable in these heads being there. They only showed that Mr Kurtz lacked restraint in the gratification of his various lusts, that there was something wanting in him – some small matter which, when the pressing need arose, could not be found under his magnificent eloquence. Whether he knew of this deficiency himself I can't say. I think the knowledge came to him at last – only at the very last. But the wilderness had found him out early, and had taken on him a terrible vengeance for the fantastic invasion. I think it had whispered to him things about himself which he did not know, things of which he had no conception till he took counsel with this great solitude – and the whisper had proved irresistibly fascinating. It echoed loudly within him because he was hollow at the core . . . I put down the glass, and the head that had appeared near enough to be spoken to seemed at once to have leaped away from me into inaccessible distance.

'The admirer of Mr Kurtz was a bit crestfallen. In a hurried, indistinct voice he began to assure me he had not dared to take these – say, symbols – down. He was not afraid of the natives; they would not stir till Mr Kurtz gave the word. His ascendancy was extraordinary. The camps of these people surrounded the place, and the chiefs came every day to see him. They would crawl . . . "I don't want to know anything of the ceremonies used when approaching Mr Kurtz," I shouted. Curious, this feeling that came over me that such details would be more intolerable than those heads drying on the stakes under Mr Kurtz's windows. After all, that was only a savage sight, while I seemed at one bound to have been transported into some lightless region of subtle horrors, where pure, uncomplicated savagery was a positive relief, being something that had a right to exist – obviously – in the sunshine. The young man looked at me with surprise. I suppose it did not occur to him that Mr Kurtz was no idol of mine. He forgot I hadn't heard any of these splendid monologues on, what was it? on love, justice, conduct of life – or what not. If it had come to crawling before Mr Kurtz, he crawled as much as the veriest savage of them all. I had no idea of the conditions, he said: these heads were the heads of rebels. I shocked him excessively by laughing. Rebels! What would be the next definition I was to hear? There had been enemies, criminals, workers – and these were rebels. Those rebellious heads looked very subdued to me on their sticks. "You don't know how such a life tries a man like Kurtz," cried Kurtz's last disciple. "Well, and you?" I said. "I! I! I am a simple man. I have no great thoughts. I want nothing from anybody. How can you compare me to? . . ." His feelings were too much for speech, and suddenly he broke down. "I don't understand," he groaned. "I've been doing my best to keep him alive, and that's enough. I had no hand in all this. I had no abilities. There hasn't been a drop of medicine or a mouthful of invalid food for months here. He was shamefully abandoned. A man like this, with such ideas. Shamefully! Shamefully! I – I – haven't slept for the last ten nights . . ."

'His voice lost itself in the calm of the evening. The long shadows of the forest had slipped down hill while we talked, had gone far beyond the ruined hovel, beyond the symbolic row of stakes. All this was in the gloom, while we down there were yet in the sunshine, and the stretch of the river abreast of the clearing glittered in a still and dazzling splendour, with a murky and overshadowed bend above and below. Not a living soul was seen on the shore. The bushes did not rustle.

'Suddenly round the corner of the house a group of men appeared, as though they had come up from the ground. They waded waist-deep in the grass, in a compact body, bearing an improvised stretcher in their midst. Instantly, in the emptiness of the landscape, a cry arose whose shrillness pierced the still air like a sharp arrow flying straight to the very heart of the land; and, as if by enchantment, streams of human beings – of naked human beings – with spears in their hands, with bows, with shields, with wild glances and savage movements, were poured into the clearing by the darkfaced and pensive forest. The bushes shook, the grass swayed for a time, and then everything stood still in attentive immobility.

' "Now, if he does not say the right thing to them we are all done for," said the Russian at my elbow. The knot of men with the stretcher had stopped, too, halfway to the steamer, as if petrified. I saw the man on the stretcher sit up, lank and with an unlifted arm, above the shoulders of the bearers. "Let us hope that the man who can talk so well of love in general will find some particular reason to spare us this time," I said. I resented bitterly the absurd danger of our situation, as if to be at the mercy of that atrocious phantom had been a dishonouring necessity. I could not hear a sound, but through my glasses I saw the thin arm extended commandingly, the lower jaw moving, the eyes of that apparition shining darkly far in its bony head that nodded with grotesque jerks. Kurtz – Kurtz – that means short in German – don't it? Well, the name was as true as everything else in his life – and death. He looked at least seven feet long. His covering had fallen off, and his body emerged from it pitiful and appalling as from a winding-sheet. I could see the cage of his ribs all astir, the bones of his arm waving. It was as though an animated image of death carved out of old ivory had been shaking its hand with menaces at a motionless crowd of men made of dark and glittering bronze. I saw him open his mouth wide – it gave him a weirdly voracious aspect, as though he had wanted to swallow all the air, all the earth, all the men before him. A deep voice reached me faintly. He must have been shouting. He fell back suddenly. The stretcher shook as the bearers staggered forward again, and almost at the same time I noticed that the crowd of savages was vanishing without any perceptible movement of retreat, as if the forest that had ejected these beings so suddenly had drawn them in again as the breath is drawn in a long aspiration.

'Some of the pilgrims behind the stretcher carried his arms – two shot-guns, a heavy rifle, and a light revolver-carbine – the thunderbolts of that pitiful Jupiter. The manager bent over him murmuring as he walked beside his head. They laid him down in one of the little cabins – just a room for a bedplace and a campstool or two, you know. We had brought his belated correspondence, and a lot of torn envelopes and open letters littered his bed. His hand roamed feebly amongst these papers. I was struck by the fire of his eyes and the composed languor of his expression. It was not so much the exhaustion of disease. He did not seem in pain. This shadow looked satiated and calm, as though for the moment it had had its fill of all the emotions.

'He rustled one of the letters, and looking straight in my face said, "I am glad." Somebody had been writing to him about me. These special recommendations were turning up again. The volume of tone he emitted without effort, almost without the trouble of moving lips, amazed me. A voice! a voice! It was grave, profound, vibrating, while the man did not seem capable of a whisper. However, he had enough strength in him – factitious no doubt – to very nearly make an end of us, as you shall hear directly.

'The manager appeared silently in the doorway; I stepped out at once and he drew the curtain after me. The Russian, eyed curiously by the pilgrims, was staring at the shore. I followed the direction of his glance.

'Dark human shapes could be made out in the distance, flitting indistinctly against the gloomy border of the forest, and near the river two bronze figures, leaning on tall spears, stood in the sunlight under fantastic head-dresses of spotted skins, warlike and still in statuesque repose. And from right to left along the lighted shore moved a wild and gorgeous apparition of a woman.

'She walked with measured steps, draped in striped and fringed cloths, treading the earth proudly, with a slight jingle and flash of barbarous ornaments. She carried her head high; her hair was done in the shape of a helmet; she had brass leggings to the knees, brass wire gauntlets to the elbow, a crimson spot on her tawny cheek, innumerable necklaces of glass beads on her neck; bizarre things, charms, gifts of witch-men, that hung about her, glittered and trembled at every step. She must have had the value of several elephant tusks upon her. She was savage and superb, wild-eyed and magnificent; there was something ominous and stately in her deliberate progress. And in the hush that had fallen suddenly upon the whole sorrowful land, the immense wilderness, the colossal body of the fecund and mysterious life seemed to look at her, pensive, as though it had been looking at the image of its own tenebrous and passionate soul.

'She came abreast of the steamer, stood still, and faced us. Her long shadow fell to the water's edge. Her face had a tragic and fierce aspect of wild sorrow and of dumb pain mingled with the fear of some struggling, half-shaped resolve. She stood looking at us without a stir, and like the wilderness itself, with an air of brooding over an inscrutable purpose. A whole minute passed, and then she made a step forward. There was a low jingle, a glint of yellow metal, a sway of fringed draperies, and she stopped as if her heart had failed her. The young fellow by my side growled. The pilgrims murmured at my back. She looked at us all as if her life had depended upon the unswerving steadiness of her glance. Suddenly she opened her bared arms and threw them up rigid above her head, as though in an uncontrollable desire to touch the sky, and at the same time the swift shadows darted out on the earth, swept around on the river, gathering the steamer into a shadowy embrace. A formidable silence hung over the scene.

'She turned away slowly, walked on, following the bank, and passed into the bushes to the left. Once only her eyes gleamed back at us in the dusk of the thickets before she disappeared.

' "If she had offered to come aboard I really think I would have tried to shoot her," said the man of patches, nervously. "I had been risking my life every day for the last fortnight to keep her out of the house. She got in one day and kicked up a row about those miserable rags I picked up in the storeroom to mend my clothes with. I wasn't decent. At least it must have been that, for she talked like a fury to Kurtz for an hour, pointing at me now and then. I don't understand the dialect of this tribe. Luckily for me, I fancy Kurtz felt too ill that day to care, or there would have been mischief. I don't understand . . . No – it's too much for me. Ah, well, it's all over now."

'At this moment I heard Kurtz's deep voice behind the curtain: "Save me! – save the ivory, you mean. Don't tell me. Save *me*! Why, I've had to save you. You are interrupting my plans now. Sick! Sick! Not so sick as you would like to believe. Never mind. I'll carry my ideas out yet – I will return. I'll show you what can be done. You with your little peddling notions – you are interfering with me. I will return. I . . ."

"The manager came out. He did me the honour to take me under the arm and lead me aside. "He is very low, very low," he said. He considered it necessary to sigh, but neglected to be consistently sorrowful. "We have done all we could for him – haven't we? But there is no disguising the fact, Mr Kurtz has done more harm than good to the Company. He did not see the time was not ripe for vigorous action. Cautiously, cautiously – that's my principle. We must be cautious yet. The district is closed to us for a time. Deplorable! Upon the whole, the trade will suffer. I don't deny there is a remarkable quantity of ivory – mostly fossil. We must save it, at all events – but look how precarious the position is – and why? Because the method is unsound." "Do you," said I, looking at the shore, "call it 'unsound method'?" "Without doubt," he exclaimed, hotly. "Don't you?" . . .

' "No method at all,' I murmured after a while. "Exactly," he exulted. "I anticipated this. Shows a complete want of judgement. It is my duty to point it out in the proper quarter." "Oh," said I, "that fellow – what's his name? – the brickmaker, will make a readable report for you." He appeared confounded for a moment. It seemed to me I had never breathed an atmosphere so vile, and I turned mentally to Kurtz for relief – positively for relief. "Nevertheless I think Mr Kurtz is a remarkable man," I said with emphasis. He started, dropped on me a cold heavy glance, said very quietly, "He *was*," and turned his back on me. My hour of favour was over; I found myself lumped along with Kurtz as a partisan of methods for which the time was not ripe: I was unsound! Ah! but it was something to have at least a choice of nightmares.

'I had turned to the wilderness really, not to Mr Kurtz, who, I was ready to admit, was as good as buried. And for a moment it seemed to me as if I also were buried in a vast grave full of unspeakable secrets. I felt an intolerable weight oppressing my breast, the smell of the damp earth, the unseen presence of victorious corruption, the darkness of an impenetrable night . . The Russian tapped me on the shoulder. I heard him mumbling and stammering something about "brother seaman – couldn't conceal – knowledge of matters that would affect Mr Kurtz's reputation." I waited. For him evidently Mr Kurtz was not in his grave; I suspect that for him Mr Kurtz was one of the immortals. "Well!" said I at last, "speak out. As it happens, I am Mr Kurtz's friend – in a way."

'He stated with a good deal of formality that had we not been "of the same profession", he would have kept the matter to himself without regard to consequences. "He suspected there was an active ill will towards him on the part of these white men that –" "You are right," I said, remembering a certain conversation I had overheard. "The manager thinks you ought to be hanged." He showed a concern at this intelligence which amused me at first. "I had better get out of the way quietly," he said, earnestly. "I can do no more for Kurtz now, and they would soon find some excuse. What's to stop them? There's a military post three hundred miles from here." "Well, upon my word," said I, "perhaps you had better go if you have any friends amongst the savages near by." "Plenty," he said. "They are simple people – and I want nothing, you know." He stood biting his lip, then: "I don't want any harm to happen to these whites here, but of course I was thinking of Mr Kurtz's reputation – but you are a brother seaman and –" "All right," said I, after a time. "Mr Kurtz's reputation is safe with me." I did not know how truly I spoke.

'He informed me, lowering his voice, that it was Kurtz who had ordered the attack to be made on the steamer. "He hated sometimes the idea of being taken away – and then again . . . But I don't understand these matters. I am a simple man. He thought it would scare you away – that you would give it up, thinking him dead. I could not stop him. Oh, I had an awful time of it this last month," "Very well," I said. "He is all right now." "Ye-e-es," he muttered, not very convinced apparently. "Thanks," said I; "I shall keep my eyes open." But quiet – eh?" he urged, anxiously. "It would be awful for his reputation if anybody here –" I promised a complete discretion with great gravity. "I have a canoe and three black fellows waiting not very far. I am off. Could you give me a few Martini-Henry cartridges?" I could, and did, with proper secrecy. He helped himself, with a wink at me, to a handful of my tobacco. "Between sailors – you know – good English tobacco." At the door of the pilot-house he turned round – "I say, haven't you a pair of shoes you could spare?" He raised one leg. "Look." The soles were tied with knotted strings sandal-wise under his bare feet. I rooted out an old pair, at which he looked with admiration before tucking them under his left arm. One of his pockets (bright red) was bulging with cartridges, from the other (dark blue) peeped "Towson's Inquiry", etc., etc. He seemed to think himself excellently well equipped for a renewed encounter with the wilderness. "Ah! I'll never, never meet such a man again. You ought to have heard him recite poetry – his own, too, it was, he told me. Poetry!" He rolled his eyes at the recollection of these delights. "Oh, he enlarged my mind!" "Good-bye," said I. He shook hands and vanished in the night. Sometimes I ask myself whether I had ever really seen him – whether it was possible to meet such a phenomenon! . . .

'When I woke up shortly after midnight his warning came to my mind with its hint of danger that seemed, in the starred darkness, real enough to make me get up for the purpose of having a look round. On the hill a big fire burned, illuminating fitfully a crooked corner of the station-house. One of the agents with a picket of a few of our blacks, armed for the purpose, was keeping guard over the ivory; but deep within the forest, red gleams that wavered, that seemed to sink and rise from the ground amongst confused columnar shapes of intense blackness, showed the exact position of the camp where Mr Kurtz's adorers were keeping their uneasy vigil. The monotonous beating of a big drum filled the air with muffled shocks and a lingering vibration. A steady droning sound of many men chanting each to himself some weird incantation came out from the black, flat wall of the woods as the humming of bees comes out of a hive, and had a strange narcotic effect upon my half-awake senses. I believe I dozed off leaning over the rail, till an abrupt burst of yells, an overwhelming outbreak of a pent-up and mysterious frenzy, woke me up in a bewildered wonder. It was cut short all at once, and the low droning went on with an effect of audible and soothing silence. I glanced casually into the little cabin. A light was burning within, but Mr Kurtz was not there.

'I think I would have raised an outcry if I had believed my eyes. But I didn't believe them at first – the thing seemed so impossible. The fact is I was completely unnerved by a sheer blank fright, pure abstract terror, unconnected with any distinct shape of physical danger. What made this emotion so overpowering was – how shall I define it? – the moral shock I received, as if something altogether monstrous, intolerable to thought and odious to the soul, had been thrust upon me unexpectedly. This lasted of course the merest fraction of a second, and then the usual sense of commonplace, deadly danger, the possibility of a sudden onslaught and massacre, or something of the kind, which I saw impending, was positively welcome and composing. It pacified me, in fact, so much, that I did not raise an alarm.

'There was an agent buttoned up inside an ulster and sleeping on a chair on deck within three feet of me. The yells had not awakened him; he snored very slightly; I left him to his slumbers and leaped ashore. I did not betray Mr Kurtz – it was ordered I should never betray him – it was written I should be loyal to the nightmare of my choice. I was anxious to deal with this shadow by myself alone, – and to this day I don't know why I was so jealous of sharing with anyone the peculiar backness of that experience.

'As soon as I got on the bank I saw a trail – a broad trail through the grass. I remember the exultation with which I said to myself, "He can't walk – he is crawling on all-fours – I've got him." The grass was wet with dew. I strode rapidly with clenched fists. I fancy I had some vague notion of falling upon him and giving him a drubbing. I don't know. I had some imbecile thoughts. The knitting old woman with the cat obtruded herself upon my memory as a most improper person to be sitting at the other end of such an affair. I saw a row of pilgrims squirting lead in the air out of Winchesters held to the hip. I thought I would never get back to the steamer, and imagined myself living alone and unarmed in the woods to an advanced age. Such silly things – you know. And I remember I confounded the beat of the drum with the beating of my heart, and was pleased at its calm regularity.

'I kept to the track though – then stopped to listen. The night was very clear; a dark blue space, sparkling with dew and starlight, in which black things stood very still. I thought I could see a kind of motion ahead of me. I was strangely cocksure of everything that night. I actually left the track and ran in a wide semicircle (I verily believe chuckling to myself) so as to get in front of that stir, of that motion I had seen – if indeed I had seen anything. I was circumventing Kurtz as though it had been a boyish game.

'I came upon him, and, if he had not heard me coming, I would have fallen over him, too, but he got up in time. He rose, unsteady, long, pale, indistinct, like a vapour exhaled by the earth, and swayed slightly, misty and silent before me; while at my back the fires loomed between the trees, and the murmur of many voices issued from the forest. I had cut him off cleverly; but when actually confronting him I seemed to come to my senses, I saw the danger in its right proportion. It was by no means over yet. Suppose he began to shout? Though he could hardly stand, there was still plenty of vigour in his voice. "Go away – hide yourself," he said, in that profound tone. It was very awful. I glanced back. We were within thirty yards from the nearest fire. A black figure stood up, strode on long black legs, waving long black arms, across the glow. It had horns – antelope horns, I think – on its head. Some sorcerer, some witch-man, no doubt: it looked fiend-like enough. "Do you know what you are doing?" I whispered. "Perfectly," he answered, raising his voice for that single word: it sounded to me far off and yet loud, like a hail through a speaking-trumpet. If he makes a row we are lost, I thought to myself. This clearly was not a case for fisticuffs, even apart from the very natural aversion I had to beat that Shadow – this wandering and tormented thing. "You will be lost," I said – "utterly lost." One gets sometimes such a flash of inspiration, you know. I did say the right thing, though indeed he could not have been more irretrievably lost than he was at this very moment, when the foundations of our intimacy were being laid – to endure – to endure – even to the end – even beyond.

' "I had immense plans," he muttered irresolutely. "Yes," said I; "but if you try to shout I'll smash your head with –" There was not a stick or a stone near. "I will throttle you for good," I corrected myself. "I was on the threshold of great things," he pleaded, in a voice of longing, with a wistfulness of tone that made my blood run cold. "And now for this stupid scoundrel –" "Your success in Europe is assured in any case," I affirmed, steadily. I did not want to have the throttling of him, you understand – and indeed it would have been very little use for any practical purpose. I tried to break the spell – the heavy, mute spell of the wilderness – that seemed to draw him to its pitiless breast by the awakening of forgotten and brutal instincts, by the memory of gratified and monstrous passions. This alone, I was convinced, had driven him out to the edge of the forest, to the bush, towards the gleam of fires, the throb of drums, the drone of weird incantations; this alone had beguiled his unlawful soul beyond the bounds of permitted aspirations. And, don't you see, the terror of the position was not in being knocked on the head – though I had a very lively sense of that danger, too – but in this, that I had to deal with a being to whom I could not appeal in the name of anything high or low. I had, even like the niggers, to invoke him – himself – his own exalted and incredible degradation. There was nothing either above or below him, and I knew it. He had kicked himself loose of the earth. Confound the man! he had kicked the very earth to pieces. He was alone, and I before him did not know whether I stood on the ground or floated in the air. I've been telling you what we said – repeating the phrases we pronounced – but what's the good? They were common everyday words – the familiar, vague sounds exchanged on every waking day of life. But what of that? They had behind them, to my mind, the terrific suggestiveness of words heard in dreams, of phrases spoken in nightmares. Soul! If anybody had ever struggled with a soul, I am the man. And I wasn't arguing with a lunatic either. Believe me or not, his intelligence was perfect clear – concentrated, it is true, upon himself with horrible intensity, yet clear; and therein was my only chance – barring, of course, the killing him there and then, which wasn't so good, on account of unavoidable noise. But his soul was mad. Being alone in the wilderness, it had looked within itself, and, by heavens! I tell you, it had gone mad. I had – for my sins, I suppose – to go through the ordeal of looking into it myself. No eloquence could have been so withering to one's belief in mankind as his final burst of sincerity. He struggled with himself, too. I saw it, I heard it. I saw the inconceivable mystery of a soul that knew no restraint, no faith, and no fear, yet struggling blindly with itself. I kept my head pretty well; but when I had him at last stretched on the couch, I wiped my forehead, while my legs shook under me as though I had carried half a ton on my back down that hill. And yet I had only supported him, his bony arm clasped round my neck – and he was not much heavier than a child.

'When next day we left at noon, the crowd, of whose presence behind the curtain of trees I had been acutely conscious all the time, flowed out of the woods again, filled the clearing, covered the slope with a mass of naked, breathing, quivering, bronze bodies. I steamed up a bit, then swung downstream, and two thousand eyes followed the evolutions of the splashing, thumping, fierce river-demon beating the water with its terrible tail and breathing black smoke into the air. In front of the first rank, along the river, three men, plastered with bright red earth from head to foot, strutted to and fro restlessly. When we came abreast again, they faced the river, stamped their feet, nodded their horned heads, swayed their scarlet bodies; they shook towards the fierce river-demon a bunch of black feathers, a mangy skin with a pendent tail – something that looked like a dried gourd; they shouted periodically together strings of amazing words that resembled no sounds of human language; and the deep murmurs of the crowd, interrupted suddenly, were like the responses of some satanic litany.

'We had carried Kurtz into the pilot-house; there was more air there. Lying on the couch, he stared through the open shutter. There was an eddy in the mass of human bodies, and the woman with helmeted head and tawny cheeks rushed out to the very brink of the stream. She put out her hands, shouted something, and all that wild mob took up the shout in a roaring chorus of articulated, rapid, breathless utterance.

' "Do you understand this?" I asked.

'He kept on looking out past me with fiery, longing eyes, with a mingled expression of wistfulness and hate. He made no answer. but I saw a smile, a smile of indefinable meaning, appear on his colourless lips that a moment after twitched convulsively. "Do I not?" he said slowly, gasping, as if the words had been torn out of him by a supernatural power.

'I pulled the string of the whistle, and I did this because I saw the pilgrims on deck getting out their rifles with an air of anticipating a jolly lark. At the sudden screech there was a movement of abject terror through that wedged mass of bodies. "Don't! don't you frighten them away," cried someone on deck disconsolately. I pulled the string time after time. They broke and ran, they leaped, they crouched, they swerved, they dodged the flying terror of the sound. The three red chaps had fallen flat, face down on the shore, as though they had been shot dead. Only the barbarous and superb woman did not so much as flinch and stretched tragically her bare arms after us over the sombre and glittering river.

'And then that imbecile crowd down on the deck started their little fun, and I could see nothing more for smoke.

'The brown current ran swiftly out of the heart of darkness, bearing us down towards the sea with twice the speed of our upward progress; and Kurtz's life was running swiftly, too, ebbing, ebbing out of his heart into the sea of inexorable time. The manager was very placid, he had no vital anxieties now, he took us both in with a comprehensive and satisfied glance: the "affair" had come off as well as could be wished. I saw the time approaching when I would be left alone of the party of "unsound method". The pilgrims looked upon me with disfavour. I was, so to speak, numbered with the dead. It is strange how I accepted this unforeseen partnership, this choice of nightmares forced upon me in the tenebrous land invaded by these mean and greedy phantoms.

'Kurtz discoursed. A voice! a voice! It rang deep to the very last. It survived his strength to hide in the magnificent folds of eloquence the barren darkness of his heart. Oh, he struggled! he struggled! The wastes of his weary brain were haunted by shadowy images now – images of wealth and fame revolving obsequiously round his unextinguishable gift of noble and lofty expression. My Intended, my station, my career, my ideas – these were the subjects for the occasional utterances of elevated sentiments. The shade of the original Kurtz frequented the bedside of the hollow sham, whose fate it was to be buried presently in the mould of primeval earth. But both the diabolic love and the unearthly hate of the mysteries it had penetrated fought for the possession of that soul satiated with primitive emotions, avid of lying fame, of sham distinction, of all the appearances of success and power.

'Sometimes he was contemptibly childish. He desired to have kings meet him at railway-stations on his return from some ghastly Nowhere, where he intended to accomplish great things. "You show them you have in you something that is really profitable, and then there will be no limits to the recognition of your ability," he would say. "Of course you must take care of the motives – right motives – always." The long reaches that were like one and the same reach, monotonous bends that were exactly alike, slipped past the steamer with their multitude of secular trees looking patiently after this grimy fragment of another world, the forerunner of change, of conquest, of trade, of massacres, of blessings. I looked ahead – piloting. "Close the shutter," said Kurtz suddenly one day; "I can't bear to look at this." I did so. There was a silence. "Oh, but I will wring your heart yet!" he cried at the invisible wilderness.

'We broke down – as I had expected – and had to lie up for repairs at the head of an island. This delay was the first thing that shook Kurtz's confidence. One morning he gave me a packet of papers and a photograph – the lot tied together with a shoe-string. "Keep this for me," he said. "This noxious fool" (meaning the manager) "is capable of prying into my boxes when I am not looking." In the afternoon I saw him. He was lying on his back with closed eyes, and I withdrew quietly, but I heard him mutter, "Live rightly, die, die . . ." I listened. There was nothing more. Was he rehearsing some speech in his sleep, or was it a fragment of a phrase from some newspaper article? He had been writing for the papers and meant to do so again, "for the furthering of my ideas. It's a duty."

'His was an impenetrable darkness. I looked at him as you peer down at a man who is lying at the bottom of a precipice where the sun never shines. But I had not much time to give him, because I was helping the engine-driver to take to pieces the leaky cylinders, to straighten a bent connecting-rod, and in other such matters. I lived in an infernal mess of rust, filings, nuts, bolts, spanners, hammers, ratchet-drills – things I abominate, because I don't get on with them. I tended the little forge we fortunately had aboard; I toiled wearily in a wretched scrap-heap – unless I had the shakes too bad to stand.

'One evening coming in with a candle I was startled to hear him say a little tremulously, "I am lying here in the dark waiting for death." The light was within a foot of his eyes. I forced myself to murmur, "Oh, nonsense!" and stood over him as if transfixed.

'Anything approaching the change that came over his features I have never seen before, and hope never to see again. Oh, I wasn't touched. I was fascinated. It was as though a veil had been rent. I saw on that ivory face the expression of sombre pride, of ruthless power, of craven terror – of an intense and hopeless despair. Did he live his life again in every detail of desire, temptation, and surrender during that supreme moment of complete knowledge? He cried in a whisper at some image, at some vision – he cried out twice, a cry that was no more than a breath –

' "The horror! The horror!"

'I blew the candle out and left the cabin. The pilgrims were dining in the mess-room, and I took my place opposite the manager, who lifted his eyes to give me a questioning glance, which I successfully ignored. He leaned back, serene, with that peculiar smile of his sealing the unexpressed depths of his meanness. A continuous shower of small flies streamed upon the lamp, upon the cloth, upon our hands and faces. Suddenly the manager's boy put his insolent black head in the doorway, and said in a tone of scathing contempt –

' "Mistah Kurtz – he dead."

'All the pilgrims rushed out to see. I remained, and went on with my dinner. I believe I was considered brutally callous. However, I did not eat much. There was a lamp in there – light, don't you know – and outside it was so beastly, beastly dark. I went no more near the remarkable man who had pronounced a judgement upon the adventures of his soul on this earth. The voice was gone. What else had been there? But I am of course aware that next day the pilgrims buried something in a muddy hole.

'And then they very nearly buried me.

'However, as you see, I did not go to join Kurtz there and then. I did not. I remained to dream the nightmare out to the end, and to show my loyalty to Kurtz once more. Destiny. My Destiny! Droll thing life is – that mysterious arrangement of merciless logic for a futile purpose. The most you can hope from it is some knowledge of yourself – that comes too late – a crop of unextinguishable regrets. I have wrestled with death. It is the most unexciting contest you can imagine. It takes place in an impalpable greyness, with nothing underfoot, with nothing around, without spectators, without clamour, without glory, without the great desire of victory, without the great fear of defeat, in a sickly atmosphere of tepid scepticism, without much belief in your own right, and still less in that of your adversary. If such is the form of ultimate wisdom, then life is a greater riddle than some of us think it to be. I was within a hair's-breadth of the last opportunity for pronouncement, and I found with humiliation that probably I would have nothing to say. This is the reason why I affirm that Kurtz was a remarkable man. He had something to say. He said it. Since I had peeped over the edge myself, I understand better the meaning of his stare, that could not see the flame of the candle, but was wide enough to embrace the whole universe, piercing enough to penetrate all the hearts that beat in the darkness. He had summed up – he had judged. "The horror!" He was a remarkable man. After all, this was the expression of some sort of belief; it had candour, it had conviction, it had a vibrating note of revolt in its whisper, it had the appalling face of a glimpsed truth – the strange commingling of desire and hate. And it is not my own extremity I remember best – a vision of greyness without form filled with physical pain, and a careless contempt for the evanescence of all things – even of this pain itself. No! It is his extremity that I seem to have lived through. True, he had made that last stride, he had stepped over the edge, while I had been permitted to draw back my hesitating foot. And perhaps in this is the whole difference; perhaps all the wisdom, and all truth, and all sincerity, are just compressed into that inappreciable moment of time in which we step over the threshold of the invisible. Perhaps! I like to think my summing-up would not have been a word of careless contempt. Better his cry – much better. It was an affirmation, a moral victory, paid for by innumerable defeats, by abominable terrors, by abominable satisfactions. But it was a victory! That is why I have remained loyal to Kurtz to the last, and even beyond, when a long time after I heard once more, not his own voice, but the echo of his magnificent eloquence thrown to me from a soul as translucently pure as a cliff of crystal.

'No, they did not bury me, though there is a period of time which I remember mistily, with a shuddering wonder, like a passage through some inconceivable world that had no hope in it and no desire. I found myself back in the sepulchral city resenting the sight of people hurrying through the streets to filch a little money from each other, to devour their infamous cookery, to gulp their unwholesome beer, to dream their insignificant and silly dreams. They trespassed upon my thoughts. They were intruders whose knowledge of life was to me an irritating pretence, because I felt so sure they could not possibly know the things I knew. Their bearing, which was simply the bearing of commonplace individuals going about their business in the assurance of perfect safety, was offensive to me like the outrageous flauntings of folly in the face of a danger it is unable to comprehend. I had no particular desire to enlighten them, but I had some difficulty in restraining myself from laughing in their faces, so full of stupid importance. I daresay I was not very well at that time. I tottered about the streets – there were various affairs to settle – grinning bitterly at perfectly respectable persons. I admit my behaviour was inexcusable, but then my temperature was seldom normal in these days. My dear aunt's endeavours to "nurse up my strength" seemed altogether beside the mark. It was not my strength that wanted nursing, it was my imagination that wanted soothing. I kept the bundle of papers given me by Kurtz, not knowing exactly what to do with it. His mother had died lately, watched over, as I was told, by his Intended. A clean-shaved man, with an official manner and wearing gold-rimmed spectacles, called on me one day and made inquiries, at first circuitous, afterwards suavely pressing, about what he was pleased to denominate certain "documents". I was not surprised, because I had had two rows with the manager on the subject out there. I had refused to give up the smallest scrap out of that package, and I took the same attitude with the spectacled man. He became darkly menacing at last, and with much heat argued that the Company had the right to every bit of information about its "territories". And said he, "Mr Kurtz's knowledge of unexplored regions must have been necessarily extensive and peculiar – owing to his great abilities and to the deplorable circumstances in which he had been placed: therefore –" I assured him Mr Kurtz's knowledge, however extensive, did not bear upon the problems of commerce or administration. He invoked then the name of science. "It would be an incalculable loss if," etc., etc. I offered him the report on the "Suppression of Savage Customs", with the postscriptum torn off. He took it up eagerly, but ended by sniffing at it with an air of contempt. "This is not what we had a right to expect," he remarked. "Expect nothing else," I said. "There are only private letters." He withdrew upon some threat of legal proceedings, and I saw him no more; but another fellow, calling himself Kurtz's cousin, appeared two days later, and was anxious to hear all the details about his dear relative's last moments. Incidentally he gave me to understand that Kurtz had been essentially a great musician. "There was the making of an immense success," said the man, who was an organist, I believe, with lank grey hair flowing over a greasy coat-collar. I had no reason to doubt his statement; and to this day I am unable to say what was Kurtz's profession, whether he ever had any – which was the greatest of his talents. I had taken him for a painter who wrote for the papers, or else for a journalist who could paint – but even the cousin (who took snuff during the interview) could not tell me what he had been – exactly. He was a universal genius – on that point I agreed with the old chap, who thereupon blew his nose noisily into a large cotton handkerchief and withdrew in senile agitation, bearing off some family letters and memoranda without importance. Ultimately a journalist anxious to know something of the fate of his "dear colleague" turned up. This visitor informed me Kurtz's proper sphere ought to have been politics "on the popular side". He had furry straight eyebrows, bristly hair cropped short, an eye-glass on a broad ribbon, and, becoming expansive, confessed his opinion that Kurtz really couldn't write a bit – "but heavens! how that man could talk. He electrified large meetings. He had faith – don't you see? – he had the faith. He could get himself to believe anything – anything. He would have been a splendid leader of an extreme party." "What party?" I asked. "Any party," answered the other. "He was an – an – extremist." Did I not think so? I assented. Did I know, he asked, with a sudden flash of curiosity, "what it was that had induced him to go out there?" "Yes," said I, and forthwith handed him the famous Report for publication, if he thought fit. He glanced through it hurriedly, mumbling all the time, judged "it would do", and took himself off with this plunder.

'Thus I was left at last with a slim packet of letters and the girl's portrait. She struck me as beautiful – I mean she had a beautiful expression. I know that the sunlight can be made to lie, too, yet one felt that no manipulation of light and pose could have conveyed the delicate shade of truthfulness upon those features. She seemed ready to listen without mental reservation, without suspicion, without a thought for herself. I concluded I would go and give her back her portrait and those letters myself. Curiosity? Yes; and also some other feelings perhaps. All that had been Kurtz's had passed out of my hands: his soul, his body, his station, his plans, his ivory, his career. There remained only his memory and his Intended – and I wanted to give that up, too, to the past, in a way – to surrender personally all that remained of him with me to that oblivion which is the last word of our common fate. I don't defend myself. I had no clear perception of what it was I really wanted. Perhaps it was an impulse of unconscious loyalty, or the fulfilment of one of these ironic necessities that lurk in the facts of human existence. I don't know. I can't tell. But I went.

'I thought his memory was like the other memories of the dead that accumulate in every man's life – a vague impress on the brain of shadows that had fallen on it in their swift and final passage; but before the high and ponderous door, between the tall houses of a street as still and decorous as a well-kept alley in a cemetery, I had a vision of him on the stretcher, opening his mouth voraciously, as if to devour all the earth with all its mankind. He lived then before me; he lived as much as he had ever lived – a shadow insatiable of splendid appearances, of frightful realities; a shadow darker than the shadow of the night, and draped nobly in the folds of a gorgeous eloquence. The vision seemed to enter the house with me – the stretcher, the phantom-bearers, the wild crowd of obedient worshippers, the gloom of the forests, the glitter of the reach between the murky bends, the beat of the drum, regular and muffled like the beating of a heart – the heart of a conquering darkness. It was a moment of triumph for the wilderness, an invading and vengeful rush which, it seemed to me, I would have to keep back alone for the salvation of another soul. And the memory of what I had heard him say afar there, with the horned shapes stirring at my back, in the glow of fires, within the patient woods, those broken phrases came back to me, were heard again in their ominous and terrifying simplicity. I remembered his abject pleading, his abject threats, the colossal scale of his vile desires, the meanness, the torment, the tempestuous anguish of his soul. And later on I seemed to see his collected languid manner, when he said one day, "This lot of ivory now is really mine. The Company did not pay for it. I collected it myself at a very great personal risk. I am afraid they will try to claim it as theirs though. H'm. It is a difficult case. What do you think I ought to do – resist? Eh? I want no more than justice." . . . He wanted no more than justice – no more than justice. I rang the bell before a mahogany door on the first floor, and while I waited he seemed to stare at me out of the glassy panel – stare with that wide and immense stare embracing, condemning, loathing all the universe. I seemed to hear the whispered cry, "The horror! The horror!"

'The dusk was falling. I had to wait in a lofty drawing-room with three long windows from floor to ceiling that were like three luminous and bedraped columns. The bent gilt legs and backs of the furniture shone in indistinct curves The tall marble fireplace had a cold and monumental whiteness. A grand piano stood massively in a corner; with dark gleams on the flat surfaces like a sombre and polished sarcophagus. A high door opened – closed. I rose.

'She came forward, all in black, with a pale head, floating towards me in the dusk. She was in mourning. It was more than a year since his death, more than a year since the news came; she seemed as though she would remember and mourn for ever. She took both my hands in hers and murmured, "I had heard you were coming." I noticed she was not very young – I mean not girlish. She had a mature capacity for fidelity, for belief, for suffering. The room seemed to have grown darker, as if all the sad light of the cloudy evening had taken refuge on her forehead. This fair hair, this pale visage, this pure brow, seemed surrounded by an ashy halo from which the dark eyes looked out at me. Their glance was guileless, profound, confident, and trustful. She carried her sorrowful head as though she were proud of that sorrow, as though she would say, I – I alone know how to mourn for him as he deserves. But while we were still shaking hands, such a look of awful desolation came upon her face that I perceived she was one of those creatures that are not the playthings of Time. For her he had died only yesterday. And, by Jove! the impression was so powerful that for me, too, he seemed to have died only yesterday – nay, this very minute, I saw her and him in the same instant of time – his death and her sorrow – I saw her sorrow in the very moment of his death. Do you understand? I saw them together – I heard them together. She had said, with a deep catch of the breath, "I have survived" while my strained ears seemed to hear distinctly, mingled with her tone of despairing regret, the summing-up whisper of his eternal condemnation. I asked myself what I was doing there, with a sensation of panic in my heart as though I had blundered into a place of cruel and absurd mysteries not fit for a human being to behold. She motioned me to a chair. We sat down. I laid the packet gently on the little table, and she put her hand over it . . . "You knew him well," she murmured, after a moment of mourning silence.

' "Intimacy grows quickly out there," I said. "I knew him as well as it is possible for one man to know another."

' "And you admired him," she said. "It was impossible to know him and not to admire him. Was it?"

' "He was a remarkable man," I said, unsteadily. Then before the appealing fixity of her gaze, that seemed to watch for more words on my lips, I went on. "It was impossible not to –"

' "Love him," she finished eagerly, silencing me into an appalled dumbness. "How true! how true! But when you think that no one knew him so well as I! I had all his noble confidence. I knew him best."

' "You knew him best," I repeated. And perhaps she did. But with every work spoken the room was growing darker, and only her forehead, smooth and white, remained illumined by the unextinguishable light of belief and love.

' "You were his friend," she went on. "His friend," she repeated, a little louder. "You must have been, if he had given you this, and sent you to me. I feel I can speak to you – and oh! I must speak. I want you – you who have heard his last words – to know I have been worthy of him . . . It is not pride . . . Yes! I am proud to know I understood him better than anyone on earth – he told me so himself. And since his mother died I have had no one – no one – to – to –"

'I listened. The darkness deepened. I was not even sure whether he had given me the right bundle. I rather suspect he wanted me to take care of another batch of his papers which, after his death, I saw the manager examining under the lamp. And the girl talked, easing her pain in the certitude of my sympathy; she talked as thirsty men drink. I had heard that her engagement with Kurtz had been disapproved by her people. He wasn't rich enough or something. And indeed I don't know whether he had not been a pauper all his life. He had given me some reason to infer that it was his impatience of comparative poverty that drove him out there.

' ". . . Who was not his friend who had heard him speak once?" she was saying. "He drew men towards him by what was best in them." She looked at me with intensity. "It is the gift of the great," she went on, and the sound of her low voice seemed to have the accompaniment of all the other sounds, full of mystery, desolation, and sorrow, I had ever heard – the ripple of the river, the soughing of the trees swayed by the wind, the murmurs of the crowds, the faint ring of incomprehensible words cried from afar, the whisper of a voice speaking from beyond the threshold of an eternal darkness. "But you have heard him! You know!" she cried.

' "Yes, I know," I said with something like despair in my heart, but bowing my head before the faith that was in her, before that great and saving illusion that shone with an unearthly glow in the darkness, in the triumphant darkness from which I could not have defended her – from which I could not even defend myself.

' "What a loss to me – to us!" – she corrected herself with beautiful generosity; then added in a murmur, "To the world." By the last gleams of twilight I could see the glitter of her eyes, full of tears – of tears that would not fall.

' "I have been very happy – very fortunate – very proud," she went on. "Too fortunate. Too happy for a little while. And now I am unhappy for – for life."

'She stood up; her fair hair seemed to catch all the remaining light in a glimmer of gold. I rose, too.

' "And of all this," she went on, mournfully, "of all his promise, and of all his greatness, of his generous mind, of his noble heart, nothing remains – nothing but a memory. You and I –"

' "We shall always remember him," I said, hastily.

' "No!" she cried. "It is impossible that all this should be lost – that such a life should be sacrificed to leave nothing – but sorrow. You know what vast plans he had. I knew of them, too – I could not perhaps understand – but others knew of them. Something must remain. His words, at least, have not died."

' "His words will remain," I said.

' "And his example," she whispered to herself. "Men looked up to him – his goodness shone in every act. His example –"

' "True," I said; "his example, too. Yes, his example. I forgot that."

' "But I do not. I cannot – I cannot believe – not yet. I cannot believe that I shall never see him again, that nobody will see him again, never, never, never."

'She put out her arms as if after a retreating figure, stretching them black and with clasped pale hands across the fading and narrow sheen on the window. Never see him! I saw him clearly enough then. I shall see this eloquent phantom as long as I live, and I shall see her, too, a tragic and familiar Shade, resembling in this gesture another one, tragic also, and bedecked with powerless charms, stretching bare brown arms over the glitter of the infernal stream, the stream of darkness. She said suddenly very low, "He died as he lived."

' "His end," said I, with dull anger stirring in me, "was in every way worthy of his life."

' "And I was not with him," she murmured. My anger subsided before a feeling of infinite pity.

' "Everything that could be done –" I mumbled.

' "Ah, but I believed in him more than anyone on earth – more than his own mother, more than – himself. He needed me! Me! I would have treasured every sigh, every word, every sign, every glance."

'I felt like a chill grip on my chest. "Don't," I said, in a muffled voice.

' "Forgive me. I – I – have mourned so long in silence – in silence . . . You were with him – to the last? I think of his loneliness. Nobody near to understand him as I would have understood. Perhaps no one to hear . . ."

' "To the very end," I said, shakily. "I heard his very last words . . ." I stopped in a fright.

' "Repeat them," she murmured in a heart-broken tone. "I want – I want – something – something – to – to live with."

'I was on the point of crying at her, "Don't you hear them?" The dusk was repeating them in a persistent whisper all around us, in a whisper that seemed to swell menacingly like the first whisper of a rising wind. "The horror! The horror!"

' "His last word – to live with," she insisted. "Don't you understand I loved him – I loved him – I loved him!"

'I pulled myself together and spoke slowly.

' "The last word he pronounced was – your name."

'I heard a light sigh and then my heart stood still, stopped dead short by an exulting and terrible cry, by the cry of inconceivable triumph and of unspeakable pain. "I knew it – I was sure!" . . . She knew. She was sure. I heard her weeping; she had hidden her face in her hands. It seemed to me that the house would collapse before I could escape, that the heavens would fall upon my head. But nothing happened. The heavens do not fall for such a trifle. Would they have fallen, I wonder, if I had rendered Kurtz that justice which was his due? Hadn't he said he wanted only justice? But I couldn't. I could not tell her. It would have been too dark – too dark altogether . . .'

Marlow ceased, and sat apart, indistinct and silent, in the pose of a meditating Buddha. Nobody moved for a time. 'We have lost the first of the ebb', said the Director, suddenly. I raised my head. The offing was barred by a black bank of clouds, and the tranquil waterway leading to the uttermost ends of the earth flowed sombre under an overcast sky – seemed to lead into the heart of an immense darkness.

NOSTROMO

A Tale of the Seaboard

'so foul a sky clears not
without a storm'
Shakespeare

To John Galsworthy

Contents

Author's Note

Nostromo is the most anxiously meditated of the longer novels which belong to the period following upon the publication of the *Typhoon* volume of short stories.

I don't mean to say that I became then conscious of any impending change in my mentality and in my attitude towards the tasks of my writing life. And perhaps there was never any change, except in that mysterious, extraneous thing which has nothing to do with the theories of art; a subtle change in the nature of the inspiration; a phenomenon for which I can not in any way be held responsible. What, however, did cause me some concern was that after finishing the last story of the *Typhoon* volume it seemed somehow that there was nothing more in the world to write about.

This so strangely negative but disturbing mood lasted some little time; and then, as with many of my longer stories, the first hint for *Nostromo* came to me in the shape of a vagrant anecdote completely destitute of valuable details.

As a matter of fact in 1875 or '76, when very young, in the West Indies or rather in the Gulf of Mexico, for my contacts with land were short, few, and fleeting, I heard the story of some man who was supposed to have stolen single-handed a whole lighterful of silver, somewhere on the Tierra Firme seaboard during the troubles of a revolution.

On the face of it this was something of a feat. But I heard no details, and having no particular interest in crime *qua* crime I was not likely to keep that one in mind. And I forgot it till twenty-six or -seven years afterwards I came upon the very thing in a shabby volume picked up outside a second-hand bookshop. It was the life story of an American seaman written by himself with the assistance of a journalist. In the course of his wanderings that American sailor worked for some months on board a schooner, the master and owner of which was the thief of whom I had heard in my very young days. I have no doubt of that because there could hardly have been two exploits of that peculiar kind in the same part of the world and both connected with a South American revolution.

The fellow had actually managed to steal a lighter with silver, and this, it seems, only because he was implicitly trusted by his employers, who must have been singularly poor judges of character. In the sailor's story he is represented as an unmitigated rascal, a small cheat, stupidly ferocious, morose, of mean appearance, and altogether unworthy of the greatness this opportunity had thrust upon him. What was interesting was that he would boast of it openly.

He used to say: 'People think I make a lot of money in this schooner of mine. But that is nothing. I don't care for that. Now and then I go away quietly and lift a bar of silver. I must get rich slowly – you understand.'

There was also another curious point about the man. Once in the course of some quarrel the sailor threatened him: 'What's to prevent me reporting ashore what you have told me about that silver?'

The cynical ruffian was not alarmed in the least. He actually laughed. 'You fool, if you dare talk like that on shore about me you will get a knife stuck in your back. Every man, woman, and child in that port is my friend. And who's to prove the lighter wasn't sunk? I didn't show you where the silver is hidden. Did I? So you know nothing. And suppose I lied? Eh?'

Ultimately the sailor, disgusted with the sordid meanness of that impenitent thief, deserted from the schooner. The whole episode takes about three pages of his autobiography. Nothing to speak of; but as I looked them over, the curious confirmation of the few casual words heard in my early youth evoked the memories of that distant time when everything was so fresh, so surprising, so venturesome, so interesting; bits of strange coasts under the stars, shadows of hills in the sunshine, men's passions in the dusk, gossip half-forgotten, faces grown dim . . . Perhaps, there still was in the world something to write about. Yet I did not see anything at first in the mere story. A rascal steals a large parcel of a valuable commodity – so people say. It's either true or untrue; and in any case it has no value in itself. To invent a circumstantial account of the robbery did not appeal to me, because my talents not running that way I did not think that the game was worth the candle. It was only when it dawned upon me that the purloiner of the treasure need not necessarily be a confirmed rogue, that he could be even a man of character, an actor, and possibly a victim in the changing scenes of a revolution, it was only then that I had the first vision of a twilight country which was to become the province of Sulaco, with its high shadowy Sierra and its misty Campo for mute witnesses of events flowing from the passions of men short-sighted in good and evil.

Such are in very truth the obscure origins of *Nostromo* – the book. From the moment, I suppose, it had to be. Yet even then I hesitated, as if warned by the instinct of self-preservation from venturing on a distant and toilsome journey into a land full of intrigues and revolutions. But it had to be done.

It took the best part of the years 1903–4 to do; with many intervals of revewed hesitation, lest I should lose myself in the ever-enlarging vistas opening before me as I progressed deeper in my knowledge of the country. Often, also, when I had thought myself to a standstill over the tangled-up affairs of the Republic, I would, figuratively speaking, pack my bag, rush away from Sulaco for a change of air, and write a few pages of *The Mirror of the Sea*. But generally, as I've said before, my sojourn on the continent of Latin America, famed for its hospitality, lasted for about two years. On my return I found (speaking somewhat in the style of Captain Gulliver) my family all well, my wife heartily glad to learn that the fuss was all over, and our small boy considerably grown during my absence.

My principal authority for the history of Costaguana is, of course, my venerated friend, the late Don José Avellanos, Minister to the Courts of England and Spain, etc., etc., in his impartial and eloquent *History of Fifty Years of Misrule*. That work was never published – the reader will discover why – and I am in fact the only person in the world possessed of its contents. I have mastered them in not a few hours of earnest meditation, and I hope that my accuracy will be trusted. In justice to myself, and to allay the fears of prospective readers, I beg to point out that the few historical allusions are never dragged in for the sake of parading my unique erudition, but that each of them is closely related to actuality; either throwing a light on the nature of current events or affecting directly the fortunes of the people of whom I speak.

As to their own histories I have tried to set them down. Aristocracy and People, men and women, Latin and Anglo-Saxon, bandit and politician, with as cool a hand as was possible in the heat and clash of my own conflicting emotions. And after all this is also the story of their conflicts. It is for the reader to say how far they are deserving of interest in their actions and in the secret purposes of their hearts revealed in the bitter necessities of the time. I confess that, for me, that time is the time of firm friendships and unforgotten hospitalities. And in my gratitude I must mention here Mrs Gould, 'the first lady of Sulaco', whom we may safely leave to the secret devotion of Dr Monygham, and Charles Gould, the Idealist-creator of Material Interests whom we must leave to his Mine – from which there is no escape in this world.

About Nostromo, the second of the two racially and socially contrasted men, both captured by the silver of the San Tomé Mine, I feel bound to say something more.

I did not hesitate to make that central figure an Italian. First of all the thing is perfectly credible: Italians were swarming into the Occidental Province at the time, as anybody who will read further can see; and secondly, there was no one who could stand so well by the side of Giorgio Viola, the Garibaldino, the Idealist of the old, humanitarian revolutions. For myself I needed there a man of the People as free as possible from his class-conventions and all settled modes of thinking. This is not a side-snarl at conventions. My reasons were not moral but artistic. Had he been an Anglo-Saxon he would have tried to get into local politics. But Nostromo does not aspire to be a leader in a personal game. He does not want to raise himself above the mass. He is content to feel himself a power – within the People.

But mainly Nostromo is what he is because I received the inspiration for him in my early days from a Mediterranean sailor. Those who have read certain pages of mine will see at once what I mean when I say that Dominic, the *padrone* of the *Tremolino*, might under given circumstances have been a Nostromo. At any rate Dominic would have understood the younger man perfectly – if scornfully. He and I were engaged together in a rather absurd adventure, but the absurdity does not matter. It is a real satisfaction to think that in my very young days there must, after all, have been something in me worthy to command that man's half-bitter fidelity, his half-ironic devotion. Many of Nostromo's speeches I have heard first in Dominic's voice. His hand on the tiller and his fearless eyes roaming the horizon from within the monkish hood shadowing his face, he would utter the usual exordium of his remorseless wisdom: '*Vous autres gentilhommes!*' in a caustic tone that hangs on my ear yet. Like Nostromo! 'You *hombres finos*!' Very much like Nostromo. But Dominic the Corsican nursed a certain pride of ancestry from which my Nostromo is free; for Nostromo's lineage had to be more ancient still. He is a man with the weight of countless generations behind him and no parentage to boast of . . . Like the People.

In his firm grip on the earth he inherits, in his improvidence and generosity, in his lavishness with his gifts, in his manly vanity, in the obscure sense of his greatness, and in his faithful devotion with something despairing as well as desperate in its impulses, he is a Man of the People, their very own unenvious force, disdaining to lead but ruling from within. Years afterwards, grown older as the famous Captain Fidanza, with a stake in the country, going about his many affairs followed by respectful glances in the modernized streets of Sulaco, calling on the widow of the *cargador*, attending the Lodge, listening in unmoved silence to anarchist speeches at the meeting, the enigmatical patron of the new revolutionary agitation, the trusted, the wealthy comrade Fidanza with the knowledge of his moral ruin locked up in his breast, he remains essentially a Man of the People. In his mingled love and scorn of life and in the bewildered conviction of having been betrayed, of dying betrayed he hardly knows by what or by whom, he is still of the People, their undoubted Great Man – with a private history of his own.

One more figure of those stirring times I would like to mention: and that is Antonia Avelanos – the 'beautiful Antonia'. Whether she is a possible variation of Latin-American girlhood I wouldn't dare to affirm. But, for me, she *is*. Always a little in the background by the side of her father (my venerated friend) I hope she was yet relief enough to make intelligible what I am going to say. Of all the people who had seen with me the birth of the Occidental Republic, she is the only one who has kept in my memory the aspect of continued life. Antonia the Aristocrat and Nostromo the Man of the People are the artisans of the New Era, the true creators of the New State; he by his legendary and daring feat, she, like a woman, simply by the force of what she is: the only being capable of inspiring a sincere passion in the heart of a trifler.

If anything could induce me to revisit Sulaco (I should hate to see all these changes) it would be Antonia. And the true reason for that – why not be frank about it? – the true reason is that I have modelled her on my first love. How we, a band of tallish schoolboys, the chums of her two brothers, how we used to look up to that girl just out of the schoolroom herself, as the standard-bearer of a faith to which we all were born but which she alone knew how to hold aloft with an unflinching hope! She had perhaps more glow and less serenity in her soul than Antonia, but she was an uncompromising Puritan of patriotism with no taint of the slightest worldliness in her thoughts. I was not the only one in love with her; but it was I who had to hear oftenest her scathing criticism of my levities – very much like poor Decoud – or stand the brunt of her austere, unanswerable invective. She did not quite understand – but never mind. That afternoon when I came in, a shrinking yet defiant sinner, to say the final good-bye I received a hand-squeeze that made my heart leap and saw a tear that took my breath away. She was softened at the last as though she had suddenly perceived (we were such children still!) that I was really going away for good, going very far away – even as far as Sulaco, lying unknown, hidden from our eyes in the darkness of the Placid Gulf.

That's why I long sometimes for another glimpse of the 'beautiful Antonia' (or can it be the Other?) moving in the dimness of the great cathedral, saying a short prayer at the tomb of the first and last Cardinal-Archbishop of Sulaco, standing absorbed in filial devotion before the monument of Don José Avellanos, and, with a lingering, tender, faithful glance at the medallion-memorial to Martin Decoud, going out serenely into the sunshine of the Plaza with her upright carriage and her white head; a relic of the past disregarded by men awaiting impatiently the Dawns of other New Eras, the coming of more Revolutions.

But this is the idlest of dreams; for I did understand perfectly well at the time that the moment the breath left the body of the Magnificent Capataz, the Man of the People, freed at last from the toils of love and wealth, there was nothing more for me to do in Sulaco.

October 1917 J.C.

Part One

The Silver of the Mine

Chapter I

In the time of Spanish rule, and for many years afterwards, the town of Sulaco – the luxuriant beauty of the orange gardens bears witness to its antiquity – had never been commercially anything more important than a coasting port with a fairly large local trade in ox-hides and indigo. The clumsy deep-sea galleons of the conquerors that, needing a brisk gale to move at all, would lie becalmed, where your modern ship built on clipper lines forges ahead by the mere flapping of her sails, had been barred out of Sulaco by the prevailing calms of its vast gulf. Some harbours of the earth are made difficult of access by the treachery of sunken rocks and the tempests of their shores. Sulaco had found an inviolable sanctuary from the temptations of a trading world in the solemn hush of the deep Golfo Placido as if within an enormous semi-circular and unroofed temple open to the ocean, with its walls of lofty mountains hung with the mourning draperies of cloud.

On one side of this broad curve in the straight seaboard of the Republic of Costaguana, the last spur of the coast range forms an insignificant cape whose name is Punta Mala. From the middle of the gulf the point of the land itself is not visible at all; but the shoulder of a steep hill at the back can be made out faintly like a shadow on the sky.

On the other side, what seems to be an isolated patch of blue mist floats lightly on the glare of the horizon. This is the peninsula of Azuera, a wild chaos of sharp rocks and stony levels cut about by vertical ravines. It lies far out to sea like a rough head of stone stretched from a green-clad coast at the end of a slender neck of sand covered with thickets of thorny scrub. Utterly waterless, for the rainfall runs off at once on all sides into the sea, it has not soil enough – it is said – to grow a single blade of grass, as if it were blighted by a curse. The poor, associating by an obscure instinct of consolation the ideas of evil and wealth, will tell you that it is deadly because of its forbidden treasures. The common folk of the neighbourhood, peons of the *estancias, vaqueros* of the seaboard plains, tame Indians coming miles to market with a bundle of sugar-cane or a basket of maize worth about threepence, are well aware that heaps of shining gold lie in the gloom of the deep precipices cleaving the stony levels of Azuera. Tradition has it that many adventurers of olden time had perished in the search. The story goes also that within men's memory two wandering sailors – *Americanos*, perhaps, but *gringos* of some sort for certain – talked over a gambling, good-for-nothing *mozo*, and the three stole a donkey to carry for them a bundle of dry sticks, a water-skin, and provisions enough to last a few days. Thus accompanied, and with revolvers at their belts, they had started to chop their way with machetes through the thorny scrub on the neck of the peninsula.

On the second evening an upright spiral of smoke (it could only have been from their camp-fire) was seen for the first time within memory of man standing up faintly upon the sky above a razor-backed ridge on the stony head. The crew of a coasting schooner, lying becalmed three miles off the shore, stared at it with amazement till dark. A Negro fisherman, living in a lonely hut in a little bay near by, had seen the start and was on the lookout for some sign? He called to his wife just as the sun was about to set. They had watched the strange portent with envy, incredulity, and awe.

The impious adventurers gave no other sign. The sailors, the Indian, and the stolen *burro* were never seen again. As to the *mozo*, a Sulaco man – his wife paid for some Masses, and the poor four-footed beast, being without sin, had been probably permitted to die; but the two *gringos*, spectral and alive, are believed to be dwelling to this day amongst the rocks, under the fatal spell of their success. Their souls cannot tear themselves away from their bodies mounting guard over the discovered treasure. They are now rich and hungry and thirsty – a strange theory of tenacious *gringo* ghosts suffering in their starved and parched flesh of defiant heretics, where a Christian would have renounced and been released.

These, then, are the legendary inhabitants of Azuera guarding its forbidden wealth; and the shadow on the sky on one side, with the round patch of blue haze blurring the bright skirt of the horizon on the other, mark the two outermost points of the bend which bears the name of Golfo Placido, because never a strong wind had been known to blow upon its waters.

On crossing the imaginary line drawn from Punta Mala to Azuera the ships from Europe bound to Sulaco lose at once the strong breezes of the ocean. They become the prey of capricious airs that play with them for thirty hours at a stretch sometimes. Before them the head of the calm gulf is filled on most days of the year by a great body of motionless and opaque clouds. On the rare clear mornings another shadow is cast upon the sweep of the gulf. The dawn breaks high behind the towering and serrated wall of the Cordillera, a clear-cut vision of dark peaks rearing their steep slopes on a lofty pedestal of forest rising from the very edge of the shore. Amongst them the white head of Higuerota rises majestically upon the blue. Bare clusters of enormous rocks sprinkle with tiny black dots the smooth dome of snow.

Then, as the midday sun withdraws from the gulf the shadow of the mountains, the clouds begin to roll out of the lower valleys. They swathe in sombre tatters the naked crags of precipices above the wooded slopes, hide the peaks, smoke in stormy trails across the snows of Higuerota. The Cordillera is gone from you as if it had dissolved itself into great piles of grey and black vapours that travel out slowly to seaward and vanish into thin air all along the front before the blazing heat of the day. The wasting edge of the cloud-bank always strives for, but seldom wins, the middle of the gulf. The sun – as the sailors say – is eating it up. Unless perchance a sombre thunder-head breaks away from the main body to career all over the gulf till it escapes into the offing beyond Azuera, where it bursts suddenly into flame and crashes like a sinister pirate-ship of the air, hove-to above the horizon, engaging the sea.

At night the body of clouds advancing higher up the sky smothers the whole quiet gulf below with an impenetrable darkness, in which the sound of the falling showers can be heard beginning and ceasing abruptly – now here, now there.

Indeed, these cloudy nights are proverbial with the seamen along the whole west coast of a great continent. Sky, land, and sea disappear together out of the world when the Placido – as the saying is – goes to sleep under its black poncho. The few stars left below the seaward frown of the vault shine feebly as into the mouth of a black cavern. In its vastness your ship floats unseen under your feet, her sails flutter invisible above your head. The eye of God Himself – they add with grim profanity – could not find out what work a man's hand is doing in there; and you would be free to call the devil to your aid with impunity if even his malice were not defeated by such a blind darkness.

The shores on the gulf are steep-to all round; three uninhabited islets basking in the sunshine just outside the cloud veil, and opposite the entrance to the harbour of Sulaco, bear the name of 'The Isabels'.

There is the Great Isabel; the Little Isabel, which is round; and Hermosa, which is the smallest.

That last is no more than a foot high, and about seven paces across, a mere flat top of a grey rock which smokes like a hot cinder after a shower, and where no man would care to venture a naked sole before sunset. On the Little Isabel an old ragged palm with a thick bulging trunk rough with spines, a very witch amongst palm trees, rustles a dismal bunch of dead leaves above the coarse sand. The Great Isabel has a spring of fresh water issuing from the overgrown side of a ravine. Resembling an emerald green wedge of land a mile long, and laid flat upon the sea, it bears two forest trees standing close together, with a wide spread of shade at the foot of their smooth trunks. A ravine extending the whole length of the island is full of bushes; and presenting a deep tangled cleft on the high side spreads itself out on the other into a shallow depression abutting on a small strip of sandy shore.

From that low end of the Great Isabel the eye plunges through an opening two miles away, as abrupt as if chopped with an axe out of the regular sweep of the coast, right into the harbour of Sulaco. It is an oblong, lake-like piece of water. On one side the short wooded spurs and valleys of the Cordillera come down at right angles to the very strand; on the other the open view of the great Sulaco plain passes into the opal mystery of great distances overhung by dry haze. The town of Sulaco itself – tops of walls, a great cupola, gleams of white miradors in a vast grove of orange trees – lies between the mountains and the plain, at some little distance from its harbour and out of the direct line of sight from the sea.

Chapter II

The only sign of commercial activity within the harbour, visible from the beach of the Great Isabel, is the square blunt end of the wooden jetty which the Oceanic Steam Navigation Company (the O.S.N. of familiar speech) had thrown over the shallow part of the bay soon after they had resolved to make of Sulaco one of their ports of call for the Republic of Costaguana. The State possesses several harbours on its long seaboard, but except Cayta, an important place, all are either small and inconvenient inlets in an iron-bound coast – like Esmeralda, for instance, sixty miles to the south – or else mere open roadsteads exposed to the winds and fretted by the surf.

Perhaps the very atmospheric conditions which had kept away the merchant fleets of bygone ages induced the O.S.N. Company to violate the sanctuary of peace sheltering the calm existence of Sulaco. The variable airs sporting lightly with the vast semi-circle of waters within the head of Azuera could not baffle the steam power of their excellent fleet. Year after year the black hulls of their ships had gone up and down the coast, in and out, past Azuera, past the Isabels, past Punta Mala – disregarding everything but the tyranny of time. Their names, the names of all mythology, became the household words of a coast that had never been ruled by the gods of Olympus. The *Juno* was known only for her comfortable cabins amidships, the *Saturn* for the geniality of her captain and the painted and gilt luxuriousness of her saloon, whereas the *Ganymede* was fitted out mainly for cattle transport, and to be avoided by coastwise passengers. The humblest Indian in the osbscurest village on the coast was familiar with the *Cerberus*, a little black puffer without charm or living accommodation to speak of, whose mission was to creep inshore along the wooded beaches close to mighty ugly rocks, stopping obligingly before every cluster of huts to collect produce, down to three-pound parcels of indiarubber bound in a wrapper of dry grass.

And as they seldom failed to account for the smallest package, rarely lost a bullock, and had never drowned a single passenger, the name of the O.S.N. stood very high for trustworthiness. People declared that under the Company's care their lives and property were safer on the water than in their own houses on shore.

The O.S.N.'s superintendent in Sulaco for the whole Costaguana section of the service was very proud of his Company's standing. He resumed it in a saying which was very often on his lips, 'We never make mistakes.' To the Company's officers it took the form of a severe injunction. 'We must make no mistakes. I'll have no mistakes here, no matter what Smith may do at his end.'

Smith, on whom he had never set eyes in his life, was the other superintendent of the service, quartered some fifteen hundred miles away from Sulaco. 'Don't talk to me of your Smith.'

Then, calming down suddenly, he would dismiss the subject with studied negligence.

'Smith knows no more of this continent than a baby.'

'Our excellent Señor Mitchell' for the business and official world of Sulaco; 'Fussy Joe' for the commanders of the Company's ships, Captain Joseph Mitchell prided himself on his profound knowledge of men and things in the country – *cosas de Costaguana*. Amongst these last he accounted as most unfavourable to the orderly working of his Company the frequent changes of government brought about by revolutions of the military type.

The political atmosphere of the Republic was generally stormy in these days. The fugitive patriots of the defeated party had the knack of turning up again on the coast with half a steamer's load of small arms and ammunition. Such resourcefulness Captain Mitchell considered as perfectly wonderful in view of their utter destitution at the time of the flight. He had observed that 'they never seemed to have enough change about them to pay for their passage ticket out of the country'. And he could speak with knowledge; for on a memorable occasion he had been called upon to save the life of a dictator, together with the lives of a few Sulaco officials – the political chief, the director of the customs, and the head of police – belonging to an overturned government. Poor Señor Ribiera (such was the dictator's name) had come pelting eighty miles over mountain tracks after the lost battle of Socorro, in the hope of out-distancing the fatal news – which, of course, he could not manage to do on a lame mule. The animal, moreover, expired under him at the end of the Alameda, where the military band plays sometimes in the evenings between the revolutions. 'Sir,' Captain Mitchell would pursue with portentous gravity, 'the ill-timed end of that mule attracted attention to the unfortunate rider. His features were recognized by several deserters from the Dictatorial army amongst the rascally mob already engaged in smashing the windows of the Intendencia.'

Early on the morning of that day the local authorities of Sulaco had fled for refuge to the O.S.N. Company's offices, a strong building near the shore end of the jetty, leaving the town to the mercies of a revolutionary rabble; and as the Dictator was execrated by the populace on account of the severe recruitment law his necessities had compelled him to enforce during the struggle, he stood a good chance of being torn to pieces. Providentially, Nostromo – invaluable fellow – with some Italian workmen, imported to work upon the National Central Railway, was at hand, and managed to snatch him away – for the time at least. Ultimately, Captain Mitchell succeeded in taking everybody off in his own gig to one of the Company's steamers – it was the *Minerva* – just then, as luck would have it, entering the harbour.

He had to lower these gentlemen at the end of a rope out of a hole in the wall at the back, while the mob which, pouring out of the town, had spread itself all along the shore, howled and foamed at the foot of the building in front. He had to hurry them then the whole length of the jetty; it had been a desperate dash, neck or nothing – and again it was Nostromo, a fellow in a thousand, who, at the head, this time, of the Company's body of lightermen, held the jetty against the rushes of the rabble, thus giving the fugitives time to reach the gig lying ready for them at the other end with the Company's flag at the stern. Sticks, stones, shots flew; knives, too, were thrown. Captain Mitchell exhibited willingly the long cicatrice of a cut over his left ear and temple, made by a razor-blade fastened to a stick – a weapon, he explained, very much in favour with the 'worst kind of nigger out here'.

Captain Mitchell was a thick, elderly man, wearing high, pointed collars and short side-whiskers, partial to white waistcoats, and really very communicative under his air of pompous reserve.

'These gentlemen,' he would say, staring with great solemnity, 'had to run like rabbits, sir. I ran like a rabbit myself. Certain forms of death are – er – distasteful to a – a – er respectable man. They would have pounded me to death, too. A crazy mob, sir, does not discriminate. Under providence we owed our preservation to my Capataz de Cargadores, as they called him in the town, a man who, when I discovered his value, sir, was just the bos'n of an Italian ship, a big Genoese ship, one of the few European ships that ever came to Sulaco with a general cargo before the building of the National Central. He left her on account of some very respectable friends he made here, his own countrymen, but also, I suppose, to better himself. Sir, I am a pretty good judge of character. I engaged him to be the foreman of our lightermen, and caretaker of our jetty. Thats all that he was. But without him Señor Ribiera would have been a dead man. This Nostromo, sir, a man absolutely above reproach, became the terror of all the thieves in the town. We were infested, overrun, sir, here at that time by *ladrones* and *matreros*, thieves and murderers from the whole province. On this occasion they had been flocking into Sulaco for a week past. They had scented the end, sir. Fifty per cent of that murdering mob were professional bandits from the Campo, sir, but there wasn't one that hadn't heard of Nostromo. As to the town *leperos*, sir, the sight of his black whiskers and white teeth was enough for them. They quailed before him, sir. That's what the force of character will do for you.'

It could very well be said that it was Nostromo alone who saved the lives of these gentlemen. Captain Mitchell, on his part, never left them till he had seen them collapse, panting, terrified, and exasperated, but safe, on the luxuriant velvet sofas in the first-class saloon of the *Minerva*. To the very last he had been careful to address the ex-Dictator as 'Your Excellency'.

'Sir, I could do no other. The man was down – ghastly, livid, one mass of scratches.'

The *Minerva* never let go her anchor that call. The superintendent ordered her out of the harbour at once. No cargo could be landed, of course, and the passengers for Sulaco naturally refused to go ashore. They could hear the firing and see plainly the fight going on at the edge of the water. The repulsed mob devoted its energies to an attack upon the Custom House, a dreary, unfinished-looking structure with many windows two hundred yards away from the O.S.N. Offices, and the only other building near the harbour. Captain Mitchell, after directing the commander of the *Minerva* to land 'these gentlemen' in the first port of call outside Costaguana, went back in his gig to see what could be done for the protection of the Company's property. That and the property of the railway were preserved by the European residents; that is, by Captain Mitchell himself and the staff of engineers building the road, aided by the Italian and Basque workmen who rallied faithfully round their English chiefs. The Company's lightermen, too, natives of the Republic, behaved very well under their Capataz. An outcast lot of very mixed blood, mainly Negroes, everlastingly at feud with the other customers of low grog shops in the town, they embraced with delight this opportunity to settle their personal scores under such favourable auspices. There was not one of them that had not, at some time or other, looked with terror at Nostromo's revolver poked very close at his face, or been otherwise daunted by Nostromo's resolution. He was 'much of a man', their Capataz was, they said, too scornful in his temper ever to utter abuse, a tireless taskmaster, and the more to be feared because of his aloofness. And behold! there he was that day, at their head, condescending to make jocular remarks to this man or the other.

Such leadership was inspiriting, and in truth all the harm the mob managed to achieve was to set fire to one – only one – stack of railway-sleepers, which, being creosoted, burned well. The main attack on the railway yards, on the O.S.N. Offices, and especially on the Custom House, whose strong-room, it was well known, contained a large treasure in silver ingots, failed completely. Even the little hotel kept by old Giorgio, standing alone half-way between the harbour and the town, escaped looting and destruction, not by a miracle, but because with the safes in view they had neglected it at first, and afterwards found no leisure to stop. Nostromo, with his *cargadores*, was pressing them too hard then.

Chapter III

It might have been said that there he was only protecting his own. From the first he had been admitted to live in the intimacy of the family of the hotel-keeper who was a countryman of his. Old Giorgio Viola, a Genoese with a shaggy white leonine head – often called simply 'the Garibaldino' (as Mohammedans are called after their prophet) – was, to use Captain Mitchell's own words, the 'respectable married friend' by whose advice Nostromo had left his ship to try for a run of shore luck in Costaguana.

The old man, full of scorn for the populace, as your austere republican so often is, had disregarded the preliminary sounds of trouble. He went on that day as usual pottering about the *casa* in his slippers, muttering angrily to himself his contempt of the non-political nature of the riot, and shrugging his shoulders. In the end he was taken unawares by the out-rush of the rabble. It was too late then to remove his family, and, indeed, where could he have run to with the portly Signora Teresa and two little girls on that great plain? So, barricading every opening, the old man sat down sternly in the middle of the darkened café with an old shot-gun on his knees. His wife sat on another chair by his side, muttering pious invocations to all the saints of the calendar.

The old republican did not believe in saints, or in prayers, or in what he called 'priests' religion'. Liberty and Garibaldi were his divinities; but he tolerated 'superstition' in women, preserving in these matters a lofty and silent attitude.

His two girls, the eldest fourteen, and the other two years younger, crouched on the sanded floor, on each side of the Signora Teresa, with their heads on their mother's lap, both scared, but each in her own way, the dark-haired Linda indignant and angry, the fair Giselle, the younger, bewildered and resigned. The Padrona removed her arms, which embraced her daughters, for a moment to cross herself and wring her hands hurriedly. She moaned a little louder.

'Oh! Gian' Battista, why art thou not here? Oh! why art thou not here?'

She was not then invoking the saint himself, but calling upon Nostromo, whose patron he was. And Giorgio, motionless on the chair by her side, would be provoked by these reproachful and distracted appeals.

'Peace, woman! Where's the sense of it? There's his duty,' he mumured in the dark; and she would retort, panting:

'Eh! I have no patience. Duty! What of the woman who has been like a mother to him? I bent my knee to him this morning; don't you go out, Gian'

Battista – stop in the house, Battistino – look at those two little innocent children!'

Mrs Viola was an Italian, too, a native of Spezzia, and though considerably younger than her husband, already middle-aged. She had a handsome face, whose complexion had turned yellow because the climate of Sulaco did not suit her at all. Her voice was a rich contralto. When, with her arms folded tight under her ample bosom, she scolded the squat, thick-legged China girls handling linen, plucking fowls, pounding corn in wooden mortars amongst the mud outbuildings at the back of the house, she could bring out such an impassioned, vibrating, sepulchral note that the chained watch-dog bolted into his kennel with a great rattle. Luis, a cinnamon-coloured mulatto with a sprouting moustache and thick, dark lips, would stop sweeping the café with a broom of palm-leaves to let a gentle shudder run down his spine. His languishing almond eyes would remain closed for a long time.

This was the staff of the Casa Viola, but all these people had fled early that morning at the first sounds of the riot, preferring to hide on the plain rather than trust themselves in the house; a preference for which they were in no way to blame, since, whether true or not, it was generally believed in the town that the Garibaldino had some money buried under the clay floor of the kitchen. The dog, an irritable, shaggy brute, barked violently and whined plaintively in turns at the back, running in and out of his kennels as rage or fear prompted him.

Bursts of great shouting rose and died away, like wild gusts of wind on the plain round the barricaded house; the fitful popping of shots grew louder above the yelling. Sometimes there were intervals of unaccountable stillness outside, and nothing could have been more gaily peaceful than the narrow bright lines of sunlight from the cracks in the shutters, ruled straight across the café over the disarranged chairs and tables to the wall opposite. Old Giorgio had chosen that bare, whitewashed room for a retreat. It had only one window, and its only door swung out upon the track of thick dust fenced by aloe hedges between the harbour and the town, where clumsy carts used to creak along behind slow yokes of oxen guided by boys on horseback.

In a pause of stillness Giorgio cocked his gun. The ominous sound wrung a low moan from the rigid figure of the woman sitting by his side. A sudden outbreak of defiant yelling quite near the house sank all at once to a confused murmur of growls. Somebody ran along; the loud catching of his breath was heard for an instant passing the door; there were hoarse mutters and footsteps near the wall; a shoulder rubbed against the shutter, effacing the bright lines of sunshine pencilled across the whole breadth of the room. Signora Teresa's arms thrown about the kneeling forms of her daughters embraced them closer with a convulsive pressure.

The mob, driven away from the Custom House, had broken up into several bands, retreating across the plain in the direction of the town. The subdued crash of irregular volleys fired in the distance was answered by faint yells far away. In the intervals the single shots rang feebly, and the low, long, white building blinded in every window seemed to be the centre of a turmoil widening in a great circle about its closed-up silence. But the cautious movements and whispers of a routed party seeking a momentary shelter behind the wall made the darkness of the room, striped by threads of quiet sunlight, alight with evil, stealthy sounds. The Violas had them in their ears as though invisible ghosts hovering about their chairs had consulted in mutters as to the advisability of setting fire to this foreigner's *casa*.

It was trying to the nerves. Old Viola had risen slowly, gun in hand, irresolute, for he did not see how he could prevent them. Already voices could be heard talking at the back. Signora Teresa was beside herself with terror.

'Ah! the traitor!' she mumbled, almost inaudibly. 'Now we are going to be burnt; and I bent my knee to him. No! he must run at the heels of his English.'

She seemed to think that Nostromo's mere presence in the house would have made it perfectly safe. So far, she, too, was under the spell of that reputation the Capataz de Cargadores had made for himself by the waterside, along the railway line, with the English, and with the populace of Sulaco. To his face, and even against her husband, she invariably affected to laugh it to scorn, sometimes good-naturedly, more often with a curious bitterness. But then women are unreasonable in their opinions, as Giorgio used to remark calmly on fitting occasions. On this occasion, with his gun held at ready before him, he stooped down to his wife's head, and, keeping his eyes steadfastly on the barricaded door, he breathed out into her ear that Nostromo would have been powerless to help. What could two men shut up in a house do against twenty or more bent upon setting fire to the roof? Gian' Battista was thinking of the *casa* all the time, he was sure.

'He think of the *casa*! He!' gasped Signora Viola, crazily. She struck her breast with her open hands. 'I know him. He thinks of nobody but himself.'

A discharge of firearms nearby made her throw her head back and close her eyes. Old Giorgio set his teeth hard under his white moustache, and his eyes began to roll fiercely. Several bullets struck the end of the wall together; pieces of plaster could be heard falling outside; a voice screamed 'Here they come!' and after a moment of uneasy silence there was a rush of running feet along the front.

Then the tension of old Giorgio's attitude relaxed, and a smile of contemptuous relief came upon his lips of an old fighter with a leonine face. These were not a people striving for justice, but thieves. Even to defend his life against them was a sort of degradation for a man who had been one of Garibaldi's immortal thousand in the conquest of Sicily. He had an immense scorn for this outbreak of scoundrels and *leperos*, who did not know the meaning of the word 'liberty'.

He grounded his old gun, and, turning his head, glanced at the coloured lithograph of Garibaldi in a black frame on the white wall; a thread of strong sunshine cut it perpendicularly. His eyes, accustomed to the luminous twilight, made out the high colouring of the face, the red of the shirt, the outlines of the square shoulders, the black patch of the Bersagliere hat with cock's feathers curling over the crown. An immortal hero! This was your liberty; it gave you not only life, but immortality as well!

For that one man his fanaticism had suffered no diminution. In the moment of relief from the apprehension of the greatest danger, perhaps, his family had been exposed to in all their wanderings, he had turned to the picture of his old chief, first and only, then laid his hand on his wife's shoulder.

The children kneeling on the floor had not moved. Signora Teresa opened her eyes a little, as though he had awakened her from a very deep and dreamless slumber. Before he had time in his deliberate way to say a reassuring word she jumped up, with the children clinging to her, one on each side, gasped for breath, and let out a hoarse shriek.

It was simultaneous with the bang of a violent blow struck on the outside of the shutter. They could hear suddenly the snorting of a horse, the restive tramping of hoofs on the narrow, hard path in front of the house; the toe of a boot struck at the shutter again; a spur jingled at every blow, and an excited voice shouted, 'Hola! hola, in there!'

Chapter IV

ALL THE morning Nostromo had kept his eye from afar on the Casa Viola, even in the thick of the hottest scrimmage near the Custom House. 'If I see smoke rising over there,' he thought to himself, 'they are lost.' Directly the mob had broken he pressed with a small band of Italian workmen in that direction, which, indeed, was the shortest line towards the town. That part of the rabble he was pursuing seemed to think of making a stand under the house; a volley fired by his followers from behind an aloe hedge made the rascals fly. In a gap chopped out for the rails of the harbour branch-line Nostromo appeared, mounted on his silver-grey mare. He shouted, sent after them one shot from his revolver, and galloped up to the café window. He had an idea that old Giorgio would choose that part of the house for a refuge.

His voice had penetrated to them, sounding breathlessly hurried: '*Hola! vecchio! O, vecchio*! Is it all well with you in there?'

'You see –' murmured old Viola to his wife.

Signora Teresa was silent now. Outside Nostromo laughed.

'I can hear the *padrona* is not dead.'

'You have done your best to kill me with fear,' cried Signora Teresa. She wanted to say something more, but her voice failed her.

Linda raised her eyes to her face for a moment, but old Giorgio shouted apologetically:

'She is a little upset.'

Outside Nostromo shouted back with another laugh:

'She cannot upset me.'

Signora Teresa found her voice.

'It is what I say. You have no heart – and you have no conscience, Gian' Battista –'

They heard him wheel his horse away from the shutters. The party he led were babbling excitedly in Italian and Spanish, inciting each other to the pursuit. He put himself at their head, crying, '*Avanti!*'

'He has not stopped very long with us. There is no praise from strangers to be got here,' Signora Teresa said, tragically. '*Avanti!* Yes! That is all he cares for. To be first somewhere – somehow – to be first with these English. They will be showing him to everybody. "This is our Nostromo!" ' She laughed ominously. 'What a name! What is that? Nostromo? He would take a name that is properly no word from them.'

Meantime Giorgio, with tranquil movements, had been unfastening the door; the flood of light fell on Signora Teresa, with her two girls gathered to her side, a picturesque woman in a pose of maternal exaltation. Behind her the wall was dazzlingly white, and the crude colours of the Garibaldi lithograph paled in the sunshine.

Old Viola, at the door, moved his arm upwards as if referring all his quick, fleeting thoughts to the picture of his old chief on the wall. Even when he was cooking for the '*signori inglesi*' – the engineers (he was a famous cook, though the kitchen was a dark place) – he was, as it were, under the eye of the great man who had led him in a glorious struggle where, under the walls of Gaeta, tyranny would have expired for ever had it not been for that accursed Piedmontese race of kings and ministers. When sometimes a frying-pan caught fire during a delicate operation with some shredded onions, and the old man was seen backing out of the doorway, swearing and coughing violently in an acrid cloud of smoke, the name of Cavour – the arch intriguer sold to kings and tyrants – could be heard involved in imprecations against the China girls, cooking in general, and the brute of a country where he was reduced to live for the love of liberty that traitor had strangled.

Then Signora Teresa, all in black, issuing from another door, advanced, portly and anxious, inclining her fine, black-browed head, opening her arms and crying in a profound tone –

'Giorgio! thou passionate man! *Misericordia divina*! In the sun like this! He will make himself ill.'

At her feet the hens made off in all directions, with immense strides; if there were any engineers from up the line staying in Sulaco, a young English face or two would appear at the billiard-room occupying one end of the house; but at the other end, in the café, Luis, the mulatto, took good care not to show himself. The Indian girls, with hair like flowing black manes, and dressed only in a shift and short petticoat, stared dully from under the square-cut fringes on their foreheads; the noisy frizzling of fat had stopped, the fumes floated upwards in sunshine, a strong smell of burnt onions hung in the drowsy heat, enveloping the house; and the eye lost itself in a vast flat expanse of grass to the west, as if the plain between the Sierra overtopping Sulaco and the coast range away there towards Esmeralda had been as big as half the world.

Signora Teresa, after an impressive pause, remonstrated:

'Eh, Giorgio! Leave Cavour alone and take care of yourself now we are lost in this country all alone with the two children, because you cannot live under a king.'

And while she looked at him she would sometimes put her hand hastily to her side with a short twitch of her fine lips and a knitting of her black, straight eyebrows like a flicker of angry pain or an angry thought on her handsome, regular features.

It was pain; she suppressed the twinge. It had come to her first a few years after they had left Italy to emigrate to America and settle at last in Sulaco after wandering from town to town, trying shopkeeping in a small way here and there; and once an organized enterprise of fishing – in Maldonado – for Giorgio, like the great Garibaldi, had been a sailor in his time.

Sometimes she had no patience with pain. For years its gnawing had been part of the landscape embracing the glitter of the harbour under the wooded spurs of the range; and the sunshine itself was heavy and dull – heavy with pain – not like the sunshine of her girlhood, in which middle-aged Giorgio had wooed her gravely and passionately on the shores of the gulf of Spezzia.

'You go in at once, Giorgio,' she directed. 'One would think you do not wish to have any pity on me – with four Signori Inglesi staying in the house.'

'Va bene, va bene,' Giorgio would mutter.

He obeyed. The Signori Inglesi would require their midday meal presently. He had been one of the immortal and invincible band of liberators who had made the mercenaries of tyranny fly like chaff before a hurricane, '*un uragano terribile*'. But that was before he was married and had children; and before tyranny had reared its head again amongst the traitors who had imprisoned Garibaldi, his hero.

There were three doors in the front of the house, and each afternoon the Garibaldino could be seen at one or another of them with his big bush of white hair, his arms folded, his legs crossed, leaning back his leonine head against the lintel, and looking up the wooded slopes of the foothills at the snowy dome of Higuerota. The front of his house threw off a black long rectangle of shade, broadening slowly over the soft ox-cart track. Through the gaps, chopped out in the oleander hedges, the harbour branch railway, laid out temporarily on the level of the plain, curved away its shining parallel ribbons on a belt of scorched and withered grass within sixty yards of the end of the house. In the evening the empty material trains of flat cars circled round the dark green grove of Sulaco, and ran, undulating slightly with white jets of steam, over the plain towards the Casa Viola, on their way to the railway yards by the harbour. The Italian drivers saluted him from the footplate with raised hand, while the Negro brakesmen sat carelessly on the brakes, looking straight forward, with the rims of their big hats flapping in the wind. In return Giorgio would give a slight sideways jerk of the head, without unfolding his arms.

On this memorable day of the riot his arms were not folded on his chest. His hand grasped the barrel of the gun grounded on the threshold; he did not look up once at the white dome of Higuerota, whose cool purity seemed to hold itself aloof from a hot earth. His eyes examined the plain curiously. Tall trails of dust subsided here and there. In a speckless sky the sun hung clear and blinding. Knots of men ran headlong; others made a stand; and the irregular rattle of firearms came rippling to his ears in the fiery, still air. Single figures on foot raced desperately. Horsemen galloped towards each other, wheeled round together, separated at speed. Giorgio saw one fall, rider and horse disappearing as if they had galloped into a chasm, and the movements of the animated scene were like the passages of a violent game played upon the plain by dwarfs mounted and on foot, yelling with tiny throats, under the mountain that seemed a colossal embodiment of silence. Never before had Giorgio seen this bit of plain so full of active life; his gaze could not take in all its details at once; he shaded his eyes with his hand, till suddenly the thundering of many hoofs near by startled him.

A troop of horses had broken out of the fenced paddock of the Railway Company. They came on like a whirlwind, and dashed over the line snorting, kicking, squealing in a compact, piebald, tossing mob of bay, brown, grey backs, eyes staring, necks extended, nostrils red, long tails streaming. As soon as they had leaped upon the road the thick dust flew upwards from under their hoofs, and within six yards of Giorgio only a brown cloud with vague forms of necks and cruppers rolled by, making the soil tremble on its passage.

Viola coughed, turning his face away from the dust, and shaking his head slightly.

'There will be some horse-catching to be done before tonight,' he muttered.

In the square of sunlight falling through the door Signora Teresa, kneeling before the chair, had bowed her head, heavy with a twisted mass of ebony hair streaked with silver, into the palm of her hands. The black lace shawl she used to drape about her face dropped to the ground by her side. The two girls had got up, hand-in-hand, in short skirts, their loose hair falling in disorder. The younger had thrown her arm across her eyes, as if afraid to face the light. Linda, with her hand on the other's shoulder, stared fearlessly. Viola looked at his children.

The sun brought out the deep lines on his face, and, energetic in expression, it had the immobility of a carving. It was impossible to discover what he thought. Bushy grey eyebrows shaded his dark glance.

'Well! And do you not pray like your mother?'

Linda pouted, advancing her red lips, which were almost too red; but she had admirable eyes, brown, with a sparkle of gold in the irises, full of intelligence and meaning, and so clear that they seemed to throw a glow upon her thin, colourless face. There were bronze glints in the sombre clusters of her hair, and the eyelashes, long and coal black, made her complexion appear still more pale.

'Mother is going to offer up a lot of candles in the church. She always does when Nostromo has been away fighting. I shall have some to carry up to the Chapel of the Madonna in the Cathedral.'

She said all this quickly, with great assurance, in an animated, penetrating voice. Then, giving her sister's shoulder a slight shake, she added:

'And she will be made to carry one, too!'

'Why made?' inquired Giorgio, gravely. 'Does she not want to?'

'She is timid,' said Linda, with a little burst of laughter. 'People notice her fair hair as she goes along with us. They call out after her, "Look at the *rubia*! Look at the *rubiacita*!" They call out in the streets. She is timid.'

'And you? You are not timid – eh?' the father pronounced, slowly.

She tossed back all her dark hair.

'Nobody calls out after me.'

Old Giorgio contemplated his children thoughtfully. There was two years difference between them. They had been born to him late, years after the boy had died. Had he lived he would have been nearly as old as Gian' Battista – he whom the English called Nostromo; but as to his daughters, the severity of his temper, his advancing age, his absorption in his memories, had prevented his taking much notice of them. He loved his children, but girls belong more to the mother, and much of his affection had been expended in the worship and service of liberty.

When quite a youth he had deserted from a ship trading to La Plata, to enlist in the navy of Montevideo, then under the command of Garibaldi. Afterwards, in the Italian legion of the Republic struggling against the encroaching tyranny of Rosas, he had taken part, on great plains, on the banks of immense rivers, in the fiercest fighting perhaps the world had ever known. He had lived amongst men who had declaimed about liberty, suffered for liberty, died for liberty, with a desperate exaltation, and with their eyes turned towards an oppressed Italy. His own enthusiasm had been fed on scenes of carnage, on the examples of lofty devotion, on the din of armed struggle, on the inflamed language of proclamations. He had never parted from the chief of his choice – the fiery apostle of independence – keeping by his side in America and in Italy till after the fatal day of Aspromonte, when the treachery of kings, emperors, and ministers had been revealed to the world in the wounding and imprisonment of his hero – a catastrophe that had instilled into him a gloomy doubt of ever being able to understand the ways of divine justice.

He did not deny it, however. It required patience, he would say. Though he disliked priests, and would not put his foot inside a church for anything, he believed in God. Were not the proclamations against tyrants addressed to the peoples in the name of God and liberty? 'God for men – religions for women,' he muttered sometimes. In Sicily, an Englishman who had turned up in Palermo after its evacuation by the army of the king, had given him a Bible in Italian – the publication of the British and Foreign Bible Society, bound in a dark leather cover. In periods of political adversity, in the pauses of silence when the revolutionists issued no proclamations, Giorgio earned his living with the first work that came to hand – as sailor, as dock labourer on the quays of Genoa, once as a hand on a farm in the hills above Spezzia – and in his spare time he studied the thick volume. He carried it with him into battles. Now it was his only reading, and in order not to be deprived of it (the print was small) he had consented to accept the present of a pair of silver-mounted spectacles from Señora Emilia Gould, the wife of the Englishman who managed the silver mine in the mountain three leagues from the town. She was the only Englishwoman in Sulaco.

Giorgio Viola had a great consideration for the English. This feeling, born on the battlefields of Uruguay, was forty years old at the very least. Several of them had poured their blood for the cause of freedom in America, and the first he had ever known he remembered by the name of Samuel; he commanded a Negro company under Garibaldi, during the famous siege of Montevideo, and died heroically with his Negroes at the fording of the Boyana. He, Giorgio, had reached the rank of ensign – *alferez* – and cooked for the general. Later, in Italy, he, with the rank of lieutenant, rode with the staff and still cooked for the general. He had cooked for him in Lombardy through the whole campaign; on the march to Rome he had lassoed his beef in the Campagna after the American manner; he had been wounded in the defence of the Roman Republic; he was one of the four fugitives who, with the general, carried out of the woods the inanimate body of the general's wife into the farmhouse where she died, exhausted by the hardships of that terrible retreat. He had survived that disastrous time to attend his general in Palermo when the Neapolitan shells from the castle crashed upon the town. He had cooked for him on the field of Volturno after fighting all day. And everywhere he had seen Englishmen in the front rank of the army of freedom. He respected their nation because they loved Garibaldi. Their very countesses and princesses had kissed the general's hands in London, it was said. He could well believe it; for the nation was noble, and the man was a saint. It was enough to look once at his face to see the divine force of faith in him and his great pity for all that was poor suffering, and oppressed in this world.

The spirit of self-forgetfulness, the simple devotion to a vast humanitarian idea which inspired the thought and stress of that revolutionary time, had left its mark upon Giorgio in a sort of austere contempt for all personal advantage. This man, whom the lowest class in Sulaco suspected of having a buried hoard in his kitchen, had all his life despised money. The leaders of his youth had lived poor, had died poor. It had been a habit of his mind to disregard tomorrow. It was engendered partly by an existence of excitement, adventure, and wild warfare. But mostly it was a matter of principle. It did not resemble the carelessness of a *Condottiere*, it was a puritanism of religion.

This stern devotion to a cause had cast a gloom upon Giorgio's old age. It cast a gloom because the cause seemed lost. Too many kings and emperors flourished yet in the world which God had meant for the people. He was sad because of his simplicity. Though always ready to help his countrymen, and greatly respected by the Italian emigrants wherever he lived (in his exile he called it), he could not conceal from himself that they cared nothing for the wrongs of down-trodden nations. They listened to his tales of war readily, but seemed to ask themselves what he had got out of it after all. There was nothing that they could see. 'We wanted nothing, we suffered for the love of all humanity!' he cried out furiously sometimes, and the powerful voice, the blazing eyes, the shaking of the white mane, the brown, sinewy hand pointing upwards as if to call heaven to witness, impressed his hearers. After the old man had broken off abruptly with a jerk of the head and a movement of the arm, meaning clearly, 'But what's the good of talking to you?' they nudged each other. There was in old Giorgio an energy of feeling, a personal quality of conviction, something they called '*terribilità*' – 'an old lion', they used to say of him. Some slight incident, a chance word, would set him off talking on the beach to the Italian fishermen of Maldonado; in the little shop he kept afterwards (in Valparaiso) to his countrymen customers; of an evening, suddenly, in the café at one end of the Casa Viola (the other was reserved for the English engineers) to the select clientele of engine-driver and foremen of the railway shops.

With their handsome, bronzed, lean faces, shiny black ringlets, glistening eyes, broad-chested, bearded, sometimes a tiny gold ring in the lobe of the ear, the aristocracy of the railway works listened to him, turning away from the cards or dominoes. Here and there a fair-haired Basque studied his hand meantime, waiting without protest. No native of Costaguana intruded there. This was the Italian stronghold. Even the Sulaco policemen on a night patrol let their horses pace softly by, bending low in the saddle to glance through the window at the heads in a fog of smoke; and the drone of old Giorgio's declamatory narrative seemed to sink behind them into the plain. Only now and then the assistant of the chief of police, some broad-faced, brown little gentleman, with a great deal of Indian in him, would put in an appearance. Leaving his man outside with the horses he advanced with a confident, sly smile, and without a word up to the long trestle table. He pointed to one of the bottles on the shelf; Giorgio, thrusting his pipe into his mouth abruptly, served him in person. Nothing would be heard but the slight jingle of the spurs. His glass emptied, he would take a leisurely, scrutinizing look all round the room, go out, and ride away slowly, circling towards the town.

Chapter V

In this way only was the power of the local authorities vindicated amongst the great body of strong-limbed foreigners who dug the earth, blasted the rocks, drove the engines for the 'progressive and patriotic undertaking'. In these very words eighteen months before the Excellentissimo Señor don Vincente Ribiera, the Dictator of Costaguana, had described the National Central Railways in his great speech at the turning of the first sod.

He had come on purpose to Sulaco, and there was a one-o'clock dinner-party, a *convité* offered by the O.S.N. Company on board the *Juno* after the function on shore. Captain Mitchell had himself steered the cargo lighter, all draped with flags, which, in tow of the *Juno*'s steam launch, took the Excellentissimo from the jetty to the ship. Everybody of note in Sulaco had been invited – the one or two foreign merchants, all the representatives of the old Spanish families then in town, the great owners of estates on the plain, grave, courteous, simple men, *caballeros* of pure descent, with small hands and feet, conservative, hospitable, and kind. The Occidental Province was their stronghold; their Blanco party had triumphed now; it was their President-Dictator, a Blanco of the Blancos, who sat smiling urbanely between the representatives of two friendly foreign powers. They had come with him from Sta Marta to countenance by their presence the enterprise in which the capital of their countries was engaged.

The only lady of that company was Mrs Gould, the wife of Don Carlos, the administrator of the San Tomé silver mine. The ladies of Sulaco were not advanced enough to take part in the public life to that extent. They had come out strongly at the great ball at the Intendencia the evening before, but Mrs Gould alone had appeared, a bright spot in the group of black coats behind the President-Dictator, on the crimson cloth-covered stage erected under a shady tree on the shore of the harbour, where the ceremony of turning the first sod had taken place. She had come off in the cargo lighter, full of notabilities, sitting under the flutter of gay flags, in the place of honour by the side of Captain Mitchell, who steered, and her clear dress gave the only truly festive note to the sombre gathering in the long, gorgeous saloon of the *Juno*.

The head of the chairman of the railway board (from London), handsome and pale in a silvery mist of white hair and clipped beard, hovered near her shoulder attentive, smiling, and fatigued. The journey from London to Sta Marta in mail boats and the special carriages of the Sta Marta coast-line (the only railway so far) had been tolerable – even pleasant – quite tolerable. But the trip over the mountains to Sulaco was another sort of experience, in an old *diligencia* over impassable roads skirting awful precipices.

'We have been upset twice in one day on the brink of very deep ravines,' he was telling Mrs Gould in an undertone. 'And when we arrived here at last I don't know what we should have done without your hospitality. What an out-of-the-way place Sulaco is! – and for a harbour, too! Astonishing!'

'Ah, but we are very proud of it. It used to be historically important. The highest ecclesiastical court, for two viceroyalties, sat here in the olden time,' she instructed him with animation.

'I am impressed. I didn't mean to be disparaging. You seem very patriotic.'

'The place is lovable, if only by its situation. Perhaps you don't know what an old resident I am.'

'How old, I wonder,' he murmured, looking at her with a slight smile. Mrs Gould's appearance was made youthful by the mobile intelligence of her face. 'We can't give you your ecclesiastical court back again; but you shall have more steamers, a railway, a telegraph-cable – a future in the great world which is worth infinitely more than any amount of ecclesiastical past. You shall be brought in touch with something greater than two viceroyalties. But I had no notion that a place on a sea-coast could remain so isolated from the world. If it had been a thousand miles inland now – most remarkable! Has anything ever happened here for a hundred years before today?'

While he talked in a slow, humorous tone, she kept her little smile. Agreeing ironically, she assured him that certainly not – nothing ever happened in Sulaco. Even the revolutions, of which there had been two in her time, had respected the repose of the place. Their course ran in the more populous southern parts of the Republic, and in the great valley of Sta Marta, which was like one great battlefield of the parties, with the possession of the capital for a prize and an outlet to another ocean. They were more advanced over there. Here in Sulaco they heard only the echoes of these great questions, and, of course, their official world changed each time, coming to them over their rampart of mountains which he himself had traversed in an old *diligencia*, with such a risk to life and limb.

The chairman of the railway had been enjoying her hospitality for several days, and he was really grateful for it. It was only since he had left Sta Marta that he had utterly lost touch with the feeling of European life on the background of his exotic surroundings. In the capital he had been the guest of the Legation, and had been kept busy negotiating with the members of Don Vincente's Government – cultured men, men to whom the conditions of civilized business were not unknown.

What concerned him most at the time was the acquisition of land for the railway. In the Sta Marta Valley, where there was already one line in existence, the people were tractable, and it was only a matter of price. A commission had been nominated to fix the values, and the difficulty resolved itself into the judicious influencing of the Commissioners. But in Sulaco – the Occidental Province for whose very development the railway was intended – there had been trouble. It had been lying for ages ensconced behind its natural barriers, repelling modern enterprise by the precipices of its mountain range, by its shallow harbour opening into the everlasting calms of a gulf full of clouds, by the benighted state of mind of the owners of its fertile territory – all these aristocratic old Spanish families, all these Don Ambrosios this and Don Fernandos that, who seemed actually to dislike and distrust the coming of the railway over their lands. It had happened that some of the surveying parties scattered all over the province had been warned off with threats of violence. In other cases outrageous pretensions as to price had been raised. But the man of railways prided himself on being equal to every emergency. Since he was met by the inimical sentiment of blind conservatism in Sulaco he would meet it by sentiment, too, before taking his stand on his right alone. The Government was bound to carry out its part of the contract with the board of the new railway company, even if it had to use force for the purpose. But he desired nothing less than an armed disturbance in the smooth working of his plans. They were much too vast and far reaching, and too promising to leave a stone unturned; and so he imagined to get the President-Dictator over there on a tour of ceremonies and speeches, culminating in a great function at the turning of the first sod by the harbour shore. After all he was their own creature – that Don Vincente. He was the embodied triumph of the best elements in the State. These were facts, and, unless facts meant nothing, Sir John argued to himself, such a man's influence must be real, and his personal action would produce the conciliatory effect he required. He had succeeded in arranging the trip with the help of a very clever advocate, who was known in Sta Marta as the agent of the Gould silver mine, the biggest thing in Sulaco, and even in the whole Republic. It was indeed a fabulously rich mine. Its so-called agent, evidently a man of culture and ability, seemed, without official position, to possess an extraordinary influence in the highest Government spheres. He was able to assure Sir John that the President-Dictator would make the journey. He regretted, however, in the course of the same conversation, that General Montero insisted upon going, too.

General Montero, whom the beginning of the struggle had found an obscure army captain employed on the wild eastern frontier of the State, had thrown in his lot with the Ribiera party at a moment when special circumstances had given that small adhesion a fortuitous importance. The fortunes of war served him marvellously, and the victory of Río Seco (after a day of desperate fighting) put a seal to his success. At the end he emerged General, Minister of War, and the military head of the Blanco party, although there was nothing aristocratic in his descent. Indeed, it was said that he and his brother, orphans, had been brought up by the munificence of a famous European traveller, in whose service their father had lost his life. Another story was that their father had been nothing but a charcoal burner in the woods, and their mother a baptized Indian woman from the far interior.

However that might be, the Costaguana Press was in the habit of styling Montero's forest march from his commandancia to join the Blanco forces at the beginning of the troubles, the 'most heroic military exploit of modern times'. About the same time, too, his brother had turned up from Europe, where he had gone apparently as secretary to a consul. Having, however, collected a small band of outlaws, he showed some talent as guerrilla chief and had been rewarded at the pacification by the post of Military Commandant of the capital.

The Minister of War, then, accompanied the Dictator. The board of the O.S.N. Company, working hand-in-hand with the railway people for the good of the Republic, had on this important occasion instructed Captain Mitchell to put the mailboat *Juno* at the disposal of the distinguished party. Don Vincente, journeying south from Sta Marta, had embarked at Cayta, the principal port of Costaguana, and came to Sulaco by sea. But the chairman of the railway company had courageously crossed the mountains in a ramshackle *diligencia*, mainly for the purpose of meeting his engineer-in-chief engaged in the final survey of the road.

For all the indifference of a man of affairs to nature, whose hostility can always be overcome by the resources of finance, he could not help being impressed by his surroundings during his halt at the surveying camp established at the highest point his railway was to reach. He spent the night there, arriving just too late to see the last dying glow of sunlight upon the snowy flank of Higuerota. Pillared masses of black basalt framed like an open portal a portion of the white field lying aslant against the west. In the transparent air of the high altitudes everything seemed very near, steeped in a clear stillness as in an imponderable liquid; and with his ear ready to catch the first sound of the expected *diligencia* the engineer-in-chief, at the door of a hut of rough stones, had contemplated the changing hues on the enormous side of the mountain, thinking that in this sight, as in a piece of inspired music, there could be found together the utmost delicacy of shaded expression and a stupendous magnificence of effect.

Sir John arrived too late to hear the magnificent and inaudible strain sung by the sunset amongst the high peaks of the Sierra. It had sung itself out into the breathless pause of deep dusk before, climbing down the fore wheel of the *diligencia* with stiff limbs, he shook hands with the engineer.

They gave him his dinner in a stone hut like a cubical boulder, with no door or windows in its two openings; a bright fire of sticks (brought on muleback from the first valley below) burning outside sent in a wavering glare; and two candles in tin candlesticks lighted, it was explained to him, in his honour – stood on a sort of rough camp table, at which he sat on the right hand of the chief. He knew how to be amiable; and the young men of the engineering staff, for whom the surveying of the railway track had the glamour of the first steps on the path of life, sat there, too, listening modestly, with their smooth faces tanned by the weather, and very pleased to witness so much affability in so great a man.

Afterwards, late at night, pacing to and fro outside, he had a long talk with his chief engineer. He knew him well of old. This was not the first undertaking in which their gifts, as elementally different as fire and water, had worked in conjunction. From the contact of these two personalities, who had not the same vision of the world, there was generated a power for the world's service – a subtle force that could set in motion mighty machines, men's muscles, and awaken also in human breasts an unbounded devotion to the task. Of the young fellows at the table, to whom the survey of the track was like the tracing of the path of life, more than one would be called to meet death before the work was done. But the work would be done: the force would be almost as strong as a faith. Not quite, however. In the silence of the sleeping camp upon the moonlit plateau forming the top of the pass like the floor of a vast arena surrounded by the basalt walls of precipices, two strolling figures in thick ulsters stood still, and the voice of the engineer pronounced distinctly the words:

'We can't move mountains!'

Sir John, raising his head to follow the pointing gesture, felt the full force of the words. The white Higuerota soared out of the shadows of rock and earth like a frozen bubble under the moon. All was still, till near by, behind the wall of a corral for the camp animals, built roughly of loose stones in the form of a circle, a pack mule stamped his forefoot and blew heavily twice.

The engineer-in-chief had used the phrase in answer to the chairman's tentative suggestion that the tracing of the line could, perhaps, be altered in deference to the prejudices of the Sulaco landowners. The chief engineer believed that the obstinacy of men was the lesser obstacle. Moreover, to combat that they had the great influence of Charles Gould, whereas tunnelling under Higuerota would have been a colossal undertaking.

'Ah, yes! Gould. What sort of a man is he?'

Sir John had heard much of Charles Gould in Sta Marta, and wanted to know more. The engineer-in-chief assured him that the administrator of the San Tomé silver mine had an immense influence over all these Spanish Dons. He had also one of the best houses in Sulaco, and the Gould hospitality was beyond all praise.

'They received me as if they had known me for years,' he said. 'The little lady is kindness personified. I stayed with them for a month. He helped me to organize the surveying parties. His practical ownership of the San Tomé silver mine gives him a special position. He seems to have the ear of every provincial authority apparently, and, as I said, he can wind all the *hidalgos* of the province round his little finger. If you follow his advice the difficulties will fall away, because he wants the railway. Of course, you must be careful in what you say. He's English, and besides he must be immensely wealthy. The Holroyd house is in with him in that mine, so you may imagine –'

He interrupted himself as, from before one of the little fires burning outside the low wall of the corral, arose the figure of a man wrapped in a poncho up to the neck. The saddle which he had been using for a pillow made a dark patch on the ground against the red glow of embers.

'I shall see Holroyd himself on my way back through the States,' said Sir John. 'I've ascertained that he, too, wants the railway.'

The man who, perhaps disturbed by the proximity of the voices, had arisen from the ground, struck a match to light a cigarette. The flame showed a bronzed, black-whiskered face, a pair of eyes gazing straight; then, rearranging his wrappings, he sank full length and laid his head again on the saddle.

'That's our camp-master, whom I must send back to Sulaco now we are going to carry our survey into the Sta Marta Valley,' said the engineer. 'A most useful fellow, lent me by Captain Mitchell of the O.S.N. Company. It was very good of Mitchell. Charles Gould told me I couldn't do better than take advantage of the offer. He seems to know how to rule all these muleteers and peons. We had not the slightest trouble with our people. He shall escort your *diligencia* right into Sulaco with some of our railway peons. The road is bad. To have him at hand may save you an upset or two. He promised me to take care of your person all the way down as if you were his father.'

This camp-master was the Italian sailor whom all the Europeans in Sulaco, following Captain Mitchell's mispronunciation, were in the habit of calling Nostromo. And indeed, taciturn and ready, he did take excellent care of his charge at the bad parts of the road, as Sir John himself acknowledged to Mrs Gould afterwards.

Chapter VI

At that time Nostromo had been already long enough in the country to raise to the highest pitch Captain Mitchell's opinion of the extraordinary value of his discovery. Clearly he was one of those invaluable subordinates whom to possess is a legitimate cause of boasting. Captain Mitchell plumed himself upon his eye for men – but he was not selfish – and in the innocence of his pride was already developing that mania for 'lending you my Capataz de Cargadores' which was to bring Nostromo into personal contact, sooner or later, with every European in Sulaco, as a sort of universal factotum – a prodigy of efficiency in his own sphere of life.

'The fellow is devoted to me, body and soul!' Captain Mitchell was given to affirm; and though nobody, perhaps, could have explained why it should be so, it was impossible on a survey of their relation to throw doubt on that statement, unless, indeed, one were a bitter, eccentric character like Dr Monygham – for instance – whose short, hopeless laugh expressed somehow an immense mistrust of mankind. Not that Dr Monygham was a prodigal either of laughter or of words. He was bitterly taciturn when at his best. At his worst people feared the open scornfulness of his tongue. Only Mrs Gould could keep his unbelief in men's motives within due bounds; but even to her (on an occasion not connected with Nostromo, and in a tone which for him was gentle), even to her, he had said once, 'Really, it is most unreasonable to demand that a man should think of other people so much better than he is able to think of himself.'

And Mrs Gould had hastened to drop the subject. There were strange rumours of the English doctor. Years ago, in the time of Guzman Bento, he had been mixed up, it was whispered, in a conspiracy which was betrayed and, as people expressed it, drowned in blood. His hair had turned grey, his hairless, seamed face was of a brick-dust colour; the large check pattern of his flannel shirt and his old stained Panama hat were an established defiance to the conventionalities of Sulaco. Had it not been for the immaculate cleanliness of his apparel he might have been taken for one of those shiftless Europeans that are a moral eyesore to the respectability of a foreign colony in almost every exotic part of the world. The young ladies of Sulaco, adorning with clusters of pretty faces the balconies along the Street of the Constitution, when they saw him pass, with his limping gait and bowed head, a short linen jacket drawn on carelessly over the flannel check shirt, would remark to each other, 'Here is the Señor Doctor going to call on Doña Emilia. He has got his little coat on.' The inference was true. Its deeper meaning was hidden from their simple intelligence. Moreover, they expended no store of thought on the doctor. He was old, ugly, learned – and a little *loco* – mad, if not a bit of a sorcerer, as the common people suspected him of being. The little white jacket was in reality a concession to Mrs Gould's humanizing influence. The doctor, with his habit of sceptical, bitter speech, had no other means of showing his profound respect for the character of the woman who was known in the country as the English Señora. He presented this tribute very seriously indeed; it was no trifle for a man of his habits. Mrs Gould felt that, too, perfectly. She would never have thought of imposing upon him this marked show of deference.

She kept her old Spanish house (one of the finest specimens in Sulaco) open for the dispensation of the small graces of existence. She dispensed them with simplicity and charm because she was guided by an alert perception of values. She was highly gifted in the art of human intercourse which consists in delicate shades of self-forgetfulness and in the suggestion of universal comprehension. Charles Gould (the Gould family, established in Costaguana for three generations, always went to England for their education and for their wives) imagined that he had fallen in love with a girl's sound common sense like any other man, but these were not exactly the reasons why, for instance, the whole surveying camp, from the youngest of the young men to their mature chief, should have found occasion to allude to Mrs Gould's house so frequently amongst the high peaks of the Sierra. She would have protested that she had done nothing for them, with a low laugh and a surprised widening of her grey eyes, had anybody told her how convincingly she was remembered on the edge of the snow-line above Sulaco. But directly, with a little capable air of setting her wits to work, she would have found an explanation. 'Of course, it was such a surprise for these boys to find any sort of welcome here. And I suppose they are homesick. I suppose everybody must be always just a little homesick.'

She was always sorry for homesick people.

Born in the country, as his father before him, spare and tall, with a flaming moustache, a neat chin, clear blue eyes, auburn hair, and a thin, fresh, red face, Charles Gould looked like a new arrival from over the sea. His grandfather had fought in the cause of independence under Bolívar, in that famous English legion which on the battlefield of Carabobo had been saluted by the great Liberator as Saviours of his country. One of Charles Gould's uncles had been the elected President of that very province of Sulaco (then called a State) in the days of Federation, and afterwards had been put up against the wall of a church and shot by the order of the barbarous Unionist general, Guzman Bento. It was the same Guzman Bento who, becoming later Perpetual President, famed for his ruthless and cruel tyranny, reached his apotheosis in the popular legend of a sanguinary land-haunting spectre whose body had been carried off by the devil in person from the brick mausoleum in the nave of the Church of Assumption in Sta Marta. Thus, at least, the priests explained its disappearance to the barefooted multitude that streamed in, awestruck, to gaze at the hole in the side of the ugly box of bricks before the great altar.

Guzman Bento of cruel memory had put to death great numbers of people besides Charles Gould's uncle; but with a relative martyred in the cause of aristocracy, the Sulaco Oligarchs (this was the phraseology of Guzman Bento's time; now they were called Blancos, and had given up the federal idea), which meant the families of pure Spanish descent, considered Charles as one of themselves. With such a family record, no one could be more of a Costaguanero than Don Carlos Gould; but his aspect was so characteristic that in the talk of common people he was just the Inglés – the Englishman of Sulaco. He looked more English than a casual tourist, a sort of heretic pilgrim, however, quite unknown in Sulaco. He looked more English than the last arrived batch of young railway engineers, than anybody out of the hunting-field pictures in the numbers of *Punch* reaching his wife's drawing-room two months or so after date. It astonished you to hear him talk Spanish (Castillan, as the natives say) or the Indian dialect of the country-people so naturally. His accent had never been English; but there was something so indelible in all these ancestral Goulds – liberators, explorers, coffee planters, merchants, revolutionists – of Costaguana, that he, the only representative of the third generation in a continent possessing its own style of horsemanship, went on looking thoroughly English even on horseback. This is not said of him in the mocking spirit of the *llaneros* – men of the great plains – who think that no one in the world knows how to sit a horse but themselves. Charles Gould, to use the suitably lofty phrase, rode like a centaur. Riding for him was not a special form of exercise; it was a natural faculty, as walking straight is to all men sound of mind and limb; but, all the same, when cantering beside the rutty ox-cart track to the mine he looked in his English clothes and with his imported saddlery as though he had come this moment to Costaguana at his easy swift *pasotrote*, straight out of some green meadow at the other side of the world.

His way would lie along the old Spanish road – the Camino Real of popular speech – the only remaining vestige of a fact and name left by that royalty old Giorgio Viola hated, and whose very shadow had departed from the land; for the big equestrian statue of Charles IV at the entrance of the alameda, towering white against the trees, was only known to the folk from the country and to the beggars of the town that slept on the steps around the pedestal, as the Horse of Stone. The other Carlos, turning off to the left with a rapid clatter of hoofs on the disjointed pavement – Don Carlos Gould, in his English clothes, looked as incongruous, but much more at home than the kingly cavalier reining in his steed on the pedestal above the sleeping *leperos*, with his marble arm raised towards the marble rim of a plumed hat.

The weather-stained effigy of the mounted king, with its vague suggestion of a saluting gesture, seemed to present an inscrutable breast to the political changes which had robbed it of its very name; but neither did the other horseman, well known to the people, keen and alive on his well-shaped, slate-coloured beast with a white eye, wear his heart on the sleeve of his English coat. His mind preserved its steady poise as if sheltered in the passionless stability of private and public decencies at home in Europe. He accepted with a like calm the shocking manner in which the Sulaco ladies smothered their faces with pearl powder till they looked like white plaster casts with beautiful living eyes, the peculiar gossip of the town, and the continuous political changes, the constant 'saving of the country', which to his wife seemed a puerile and bloodthirsty game of murder and rapine played with terrible earnestness by depraved children. In the early days of her Costaguan life, the little lady used to clench her hands with exasperation at not being able to take the public affairs of the country as seriously as the incidental atrocity of methods deserved. She saw in them a comedy of naïve pretences, but hardly anything genuine except her own appalled indignation. Charles, very quiet and twisting his long moustaches, would decline to discuss them at all. Once, however, he observed to her gently:

'My dear, you seem to forget that I was born here.'

These few words made her pause as if they had been a sudden revelation. Perhaps the mere fact of being born in the country did make a difference. She had a great confidence in her husband; it had always been very great. He had struck her imagination from the first by his unsentimentalism, by that very quietude of mind which she had erected in her thought for a sign of perfect competency in the business of living. Don José Avellanos, their neighbour across the street, a statesman, a poet, a man of culture, who had represented his country at several European Courts (and had suffered untold indignities as a state prisoner in the time of the tyrant Guzman Bento), used to declare in Doña Emilia's drawing-room that Carlos had all the English qualities of character with a truly patriotic heart.

Mrs Gould, raising her eyes to her husband's thin, red and tan face, could not detect the slightest quiver of a feature at what he must have heard said of his patriotism. Perhaps he had just dismounted on his return from the mine; he was English enough to disregard the hottest hours of the day. Basilio, in a livery of white linen and a red sash, had squatted for a moment behind his heels to unstrap the heavy, blunt spurs in the patio; and then the Señor Administrator would go up the staircase into the gallery. Rows of plants in pots, ranged on the balustrade between the pilasters of the arches, screened the *corredor* with their leaves and flowers from the quadrangle below, whose paved space is the true hearthstone of a South American house, where the quiet hours of domestic life are marked by the shifting of light and shadow on the flagstones.

Señor Avellanos was in the habit of crossing the patio at five o'clock almost every day. Don José chose to come over at teatime because the English rite at Doña Emilia's house reminded him of the time when he lived in London as Minister Plenipotentiary to the Court of St James. He did not like tea; and, usually, rocking his American chair, his neat little shiny boots crossed on the footrest, he would talk on and on with a sort of complacent virtuosity wonderful in a man of his age, while he held the cup in his hands for a long time. His close-cropped head was perfectly white; his eyes coal-black.

On seeing Charles Gould step into the *sala* he would nod provisionally and go on to the end of the oratorial period. Only then he would say:

'Carlos, my friend, you have ridden from San Tomé in the heat of the day. Always the true English activity. No? What?'

He drank up all the tea at once in one draught. This performance was invariably followed by a slight shudder and a low, involuntary 'br-r-r-r', which was not covered by the hasty exclamation, 'Excellent!'

Then giving up the empty cup into his young friend's hand, extended with a smile, he continued to expatiate upon the patriotic nature of the San Tomé mine for the simple pleasure of talking fluently, it seemed, while his reclining body jerked backwards and forwards in a rocking-chair of the sort exported from the United States. The ceiling of the largest drawing-room of the Casa Gould extended its white level far above his head. The loftiness dwarfed the mixture of heavy, straight-backed Spanish chairs of brown wood with leathern seats, and European furniture, low, and cushioned all over, like squat little monsters gorged to bursting with steel springs and horsehair. There were knick-knacks on little tables, mirrors let into the wall above marble consoles, square spaces of carpet under the two groups of armchairs, each presided over by a deep sofa; smaller rugs scattered all over the floor of red tiles; three windows from ceiling down to the ground, opening on a balcony, and flanked by the perpendicular folds of the dark hangings. The stateliness of ancient days lingered between the four high, smooth walls, tinted a delicate primrose-colour; and Mrs Gould, with her little head and shining coils of hair, sitting in a cloud of muslin and lace before a slender mahogany table, resembled a fairy posed lightly before dainty philtres dispensed out of vessels of silver and porcelain.

Mrs Gould knew the history of the San Tomé mine. Worked in the early days mostly by means of lashes on the backs of slaves, its yield had been paid for in its own weight of human bones. Whole tribes of Indians had perished in the exploitation; and then the mine was abandoned, since with this primitive method it had ceased to make a profitable return, no matter how many corpses were thrown into its maw. Then it became forgotten. It was rediscovered after the War of Independence. An English company obtained the right to work it, and found so rich a vein that neither the exactions of successive governments, nor the periodical raids of recruiting officers upon the population of paid miners they had created, could discourage their perseverance. But in the end, during the long turmoil of *pronunciamientos* that followed the death of the famous Guzman Bento, the native miners, incited to revolt by the emissaries sent out from the capital, had risen upon their English chiefs and murdered them to a man. The decree of confiscation which appeared immediately afterwards in the *Diario Oficial*, published in Sta Marta, began with the words:

> Justly incensed at the grinding oppression of foreigners, actuated by sordid motives of gain rather than by love for a country where they come impoverished to seek their fortunes, the mining population of San Tomé, etc . . .

and ended with the declaration:

> The chief of the State has resolved to exercise to the full his power of clemency. The mine, which by every law, international, human, and divine, reverts now to the Government as national property, shall remain closed till the sword drawn for the sacred defence of liberal principles has accomplished its mission of securing the happiness of our beloved country.

And for many years this was the last of the San Tomé mine. What advantage that Government had expected from the spoliation, it is impossible to tell now.

Costaguana was made with difficulty to pay a beggarly money compensation to the families of the victims, and then the matter dropped out of diplomatic dispatches. But afterwards another Government bethought itself of that valuable asset. It was an ordinary Costaguana Government – the fourth in six years – but it judged of its opportunities sanely. It remembered the San Tomé mine with a secret conviction of its worthlessness in their own hands, but with an ingenious insight into the various uses a silver mine can be put to, apart from the sordid process of extracting the metal from under the ground. The father of Charles Gould, for a long time one of the most wealthy merchants of Costaguana, had already lost a considerable part of his fortune in forced loans to the successive Governments. He was a man of calm judgement, who never dreamed of pressing his claims; and when, suddenly, the perpetual concession of the San Tomé mine was offered to him in full settlement, his alarm became extreme. He was versed in the ways of Governments. Indeed, the intention of this affair, though no doubt deeply meditated in the closet, lay open on the surface of the document presented urgently for his signature. The third and most important clause stipulated that the concession-holder should pay at once to the Government five years' royalties on the estimated output of the mine.

Mr Gould, senior, defended himself from this fatal favour with many arguments and entreaties, but without success. He knew nothing of mining; he had no means to put his concession on the European market; the mine as a working concern did not exist. The buildings had been burst down, the mining plant had been destroyed, the mining population had disappeared from the neighbourhood years and years ago; the very road had vanished under a flood of tropical vegetation as effectually as if swallowed by the sea; and the main gallery had fallen in within a hundred yards from the entrance. It was no longer an abandoned mine; it was a wild, inaccessible, and rocky gorge of the Sierra, where vestiges of charred timber, some heaps of smashed bricks, and a few shapeless pieces of rusty iron could have been found under the matted mass of thorny creepers covering the ground. Mr Gould, senior, did not desire the perpetual possession of that desolate locality; in fact, the mere vision of it arising before his mind in the still watches of the night had the power to exasperate him into hours of hot and agitated insomnia.

It so happened, however, that the Finance Minister of the time was a man to whom, in years gone by, Mr Gould had, unfortunately, declined to grant some small pecuniary assistance, basing his refusal on the ground that the applicant was a notorious gambler and cheat, besides being more than half suspected of a robbery with violence on a wealthy *ranchero* in a remote country district, where he was actually exercising the function of a judge. Now, after reaching his exalted position, that politician had proclaimed his intention to repay evil with good to Señor Gould – the poor man. He affirmed and reaffirmed this resolution in the drawing-rooms of Sta Marta, in soft and implacable voice, and with such malicious glances that Mr Gould's best friends advised him earnestly to attempt no bribery to get the matter dropped. It would have been useless. Indeed, it would not have been a very safe proceeding. Such was also the opinion of a stout, loud-voiced lady of French extraction, the daughter, she said, of an officer of high rank (*officier supérieur de l'armée*), who was accommodated with lodgings within the walls of a secularized convent next door to the Ministry of Finance. That florid person, when approached on behalf of Mr Gould in a proper manner, and with a suitable present, shook her head despondently. She was good-natured, and her despondency was genuine. She imagined she could not take money in consideration of something she could not accomplish. The friend of Mr Gould, charged with the delicate mission, used to say afterwards that she was the only honest person closely or remotely connected with the Government he had ever met. 'No go,' she had said with a cavalier, husky intonation which was natural to her, and using turns of expression more suitable to a child of parents unknown than to the orphaned daughter of a general officer. 'No; it's no go. *Pas moyen, mon garçon. C'est dommage, tout de même. Ah! zut! Je ne vole pas mon monde. Je ne suis pas ministre – moi! Vous pouvez emporter votre petit sac*'.

For a moment, biting her carmine lip, she deplored inwardly the tyranny of the rigid principles governing the sale of her influence in high places. Then, significantly, and with a touch of impatience, '*Allez,*' she added, '*et dites bien à votre bonhomme – entendez-vous? – qu'il faut avaler la pilule.*'

After such a warning there was nothing for it but to sign and pay. Mr Gould had swallowed the pill, and it was as though it had been compounded of some subtle poison that acted directly on his brain. He became at once mine-ridden, and as he was well read in light literature it took to his mind the form of the Old Man of the Sea fastened upon his shoulders. He also began to dream of vampires. Mr Gould exaggerated to himself the disadvantages of his new position, because he viewed it emotionally. His position in Costaguana was no worse than before. But man is a desperately conservative creature, and the extravagant novelty of this outrage upon his purse distressed his sensibilities. Everybody around him was being robbed by the grotesque and murderous bands that played their game of governments and revolutions after the death of Guzman Bento. His experience had taught him that, however short the plunder might fall of their legitimate expectations, no gang in possession of the Presidential Palace would be so incompetent as to suffer itself to be baffled by the want of a pretext. The first casual colonel of the barefooted army of scarecrows that came along was able to expose with force and precision to any mere civilian his titles to a sum of ten thousand dollars; the while his hope would be immutably fixed upon a gratuity, at any rate, of no less than a thousand. Mr Gould knew that very well, and, armed with resignation, had waited for better times. But to be robbed under the forms of legality and business was intolerable to his imagination. Mr Gould, the father, had one fault in his sagacious and honourable character: he attached too much importance to form. It is a failing common to mankind, whose views are tinged by prejudices. There was for him in that affair a malignancy of perverted justice which, by means of a moral shock, attacked his vigorous physique. 'It will end by killing me,' he used to affirm many times a day. And, in fact, since that time he began to suffer from fever, from liver pains, and mostly from a worrying inability to think of anything else. The Finance Minister could have formed no conception of the profound subtlety of his revenge. Even Mr Gould's letters to his fourteen-year-old boy Charles, then away in England for his education, came at last to talk of practically nothing but the mine. He groaned over the injustice, the persecution, the outrage of that mine; he occupied whole pages in the exposition of the fatal consequences attaching to the possession of that mine from every point of view, with every dismal inference, with words of horror at the apparently eternal character of that curse. For the Concession had been granted to him and his descendants for ever. He implored his son never to return to Costaguana, never to claim any part of his inheritance there, because it was tainted by the infamous Concession; never to touch it, never to approach it, to forget that America existed, and pursue a mercantile career in Europe. And each letter ended with bitter self-reproaches for having stayed too long in that cavern of thieves, intriguers, and brigands.

To be told repeatedly that one's future is blighted because of the possession of a silver mine is not, at the age of fourteen, a matter of prime importance as to its main statement; but in its form it is calculated to excite a certain amount of wonder and attention. In course of time the boy, at first only puzzled by the angry jeremiads, but rather sorry for his dad, began to turn the matter over in his mind in such moments as he could spare from play and study. In about a year he had evolved from the lecture of the letters a definite conviction that there was a silver mine in the Sulaco province of the Republic of Costaguana, where poor Uncle Harry had been shot by soldiers a great many years before. There was also connected closely with that mine a thing called the 'iniquitous Gould Concession', apparently written on a paper which his father desired ardently to 'tear and fling into the faces' of presidents, members of judicature, and ministers of State. And this desire persisted, though the names of these people, be noticed, seldom remained the same for a whole year together. This desire (since the thing was iniquitous) seemed quite natural to the boy, though why the affair was iniquitous he did not know. Afterwards, with advancing wisdom, he managed to clear the plain truth of the business from the fantastic intrusions of the Old Man of the Sea, vampires, and ghouls, which had lent to his father's correspondence the flavour of a gruesome Arabian Nights tale. In the end, the growing youth attained to as close an intimacy with the San Tomé mine as the old man who wrote these plaintive and enraged letters on the other side of the sea. He had been made several times already to pay heavy fines for neglecting to work the mine, he reported, besides other sums extracted from him on account of future royalties, on the ground that a man with such a valuable concession in his pocket could not refuse his financial assistance to the Government of the Republic. The last of his fortune was passing away from him against worthless receipts, he wrote, in a rage, whilst he was being pointed out as an individual who had known how to secure enormous advantages from the necessities of his country. And the young man in Europe grew more and more interested in that thing which could provoke such a tumult of words and passion.

He thought of it every day; but he thought of it without bitterness. It might have been an unfortunate affair for his poor dad, and the whole story threw a queer light upon the social and political life of Costaguana. The view he took of it was sympathetic to his father, yet calm and reflective. His personal feelings had not been outraged, and it is difficult to resent with proper and durable indignation the physical or mental anguish of another organism, even if that other organism is one's own father. By the time he was twenty Charles Gould had, in his turn, fallen under the spell of the San Tomé mine. But it was another form of enchantment, more suitable to his youth, into whose magic formula there entered hope, vigour, and self-confidence, instead of weary indignation and despair. Left after he was twenty to his own guidance (except for the severe injunction not to return to Costaguana), he had pursued his studies in Belgium and France with the idea of qualifying for a mining engineer. But this scientific aspect of his labours remained vague and imperfect in his mind. Mines had acquired for him a dramatic interest. He studied their peculiarities from a personal point of view, too, as one would study the varied characters of men. He visited them as one goes with curiosity to call upon remarkable persons. He visited mines in Germany, in Spain, in Cornwall. Abandoned workings had for him strong fascination. Their desolation appealed to him like the sight of human misery, whose causes are varied and profound. They might have been worthless, but also they might have been misunderstood. His future wife was the first, and perhaps the only person to detect this secret mood which governed the profoundly sensible, almost voiceless attitude of this man towards the world of material things. And at once her delight in him, lingering with half-open wings like those birds that cannot rise easily from a flat level, found a pinnacle from which to soar up into the skies.

They had become acquainted in Italy, where the future Mrs Gould was staying with an old and pale aunt who, years before, had married a middle-aged, impoverished Italian marquis. She now mourned that man, who had known how to give up his life to the independence and unity of his country, who had known how to be as enthusiastic in his generosity as the youngest of those who fell for that very cause of which old Giorgio Viola was a drifting relic, as a broken spar is suffered to float away disregarded after a naval victory. The Marchesa led a still, whispering existence, nun-like in her black robes and a white band over the forehead, in a corner of the first floor of an ancient and ruinous palace, whose big, empty halls downstairs sheltered under their painted ceilings the harvests, the fowls, and even the cattle, together with the whole family of the tenant farmer.

The two young people had met in Lucca. After that meeting Charles Gould visited no mines, though they went together in a carriage, once, to see some marble quarries, where the work resembled mining in so far that it also was the tearing of the raw material of treasure from the earth. Charles Gould did not open his heart to her in any set speeches. He simply went on acting and thinking in her sight. This is the true method of sincerity. One of his frequent remarks was, 'I think sometimes that poor father takes a wrong view of that San Tomé business.' And they discussed that opinion long and earnestly, as if they could influence a mind across half the globe; but in reality they discussed it because the sentiment of love can enter into any subject and live ardently in remote phrases. For this natural reason these discussions were precious to Mrs Gould in her engaged state. Charles feared that Mr Gould, senior, was wasting his strength and making himself ill by his efforts to get rid of the Concession. 'I fancy that this is not the kind of handling it requires,' he mused aloud, as if to himself. And when she wondered frankly that a man of character should devote his energies to plotting and intrigues, Charles would remark, with a gentle concern that understood her wonder, 'You must not forget that he was born there.'

She would set her quick mind to work upon that, and then make the inconsequent retort, which he accepted as perfectly sagacious, because, in fact, it was so –

'Well, and you? You were born there, too.'

He knew his answer.

'That's different. I've been away ten years. Dad never had such a long spell; and it was more than thirty years ago.'

She was the first person to whom he opened his lips after receiving the news of his father's death.

'It has killed him!' he said.

He had walked straight out of town with the news, straight out before him in the noonday sun on the white road, and his feet had brought him face to face with her in the hall of the ruined *palazzo*, a room magnificent and naked, with here and there a long strip of damask, black with damp and age, hanging down on a bare panel of the wall. It was furnished with exactly one gilt armchair, with a broken back, and an octagon columnar stand bearing a heavy marble vase ornamented with sculptured masks and garlands of flowers, and cracked from top to bottom. Charles Gould was dusty with the white dust of the road lying on his boots, on his shoulders, on his cap with two peaks. Water dripped from under it all over his face, and he grasped a thick oaken cudgel in his bare right hand.

She went very pale under the roses of her big straw hat, gloved, swinging a clear sunshade, caught just as she was going out to meet him at the bottom of the hill, where three poplars stand near the wall of a vineyard.

'It has killed him!' he repeated. 'He ought to have had many years yet. We are a long-lived family.'

She was too startled to say anything; he was contemplating with a penetrating and motionless stare the cracked marble urn as though he had resolved to fix its shape for ever in his memory. It was only when, turning suddenly to her, he blurted out twice, 'I've come to you – I've come straight to you –,' without being able to finish his phrase, that the great pitifulness of that lonely and tormented death in Costaguana came to her with the full force of its misery. He caught hold of her hand, raised it to his lips, and at that she dropped her parasol to pat him on the cheek, murmured 'Poor boy', and began to dry her eyes under the downward curve of her hat-brim, very small in her simple, white frock, almost like a lost child crying in the degraded grandeur of the noble hall, while he stood by her, again perfectly motionless in the contemplation of the marble urn.

Afterwards they went out for a long walk, which was silent till he exclaimed suddenly:

'Yes. But if he had only grappled with it in a proper way!'

And then they stopped. Everywhere there were long shadows lying on the hills, on the roads, on the enclosed fields of olive trees; the shadows of poplars, of wide chestnuts, of farm buildings, of stone walls; and in mid-air the sound of a bell, thin and alert, was like the throbbing pulse of the sunset glow. Her lips were slightly parted as though in surprise that he should not be looking at her with his usual expression. His usual expression was unconditionally approving and attentive. He was in his talks with her the most anxious and deferential of dictators, an attitude that pleased her immensely. It affirmed her power without detracting from his dignity. That slight girl, with her little feet, little hands, little face attractively overweighted by great coils of hair; with a rather large mouth, whose mere parting seemed to breathe upon you the fragrance of frankness and generosity, had the fastidious soul of an experienced woman. She was, before all things and all flatteries, careful of her pride in the object of her choice. But now he was actually not looking at her at all; and his expression was tense and irrational, as is natural in a man who elects to stare at nothing past a young girl's head.

'Well, yes. It was iniquitous. They corrupted him thoroughly, the poor old boy. Oh! why wouldn't he let me go back to him? But now I shall know how to grapple with this.'

After pronouncing these words with immense assurance, he glanced down at her, and at once fell a prey to distress, incertitude, and fear.

The only thing he wanted to know now, he said, was whether she did love him enough – whether she would have the courage to go with him so far away? He put these questions to her in a voice that trembled with anxiety – for he was a determined man.

She did. She would. And immediately the future hostess of all the Europeans in Sulaco had the physical experience of the earth falling away from under her. It vanished completely, even to the very sound of the bell. When her feet touched the ground again, the bell was still ringing in the valley; she put her hands up to her hair, breathing quickly, and glanced up and down the stony lane. It was reassuringly empty. Meantime, Charles, stepping with one foot into a dry and dusty ditch, picked up the open parasol, which had bounded away from them with a martial sound of drum taps. He handed it to her soberly, a little crestfallen.

They turned back, and after she had slipped her hand on his arm, the first words he pronounced were:

'It's lucky that we shall be able to settle in a coast town. You've heard its name. It is Sulaco. I am so glad poor Father did get that house. He bought a big house there years ago, in order that there should always be a Casa Gould in the principal town of what used to be called the Occidental Province. I lived there once, as a small boy, with my dear mother, for a whole year, while poor Father was away in the United States on business. You shall be the new mistress of the Casa Gould.'

And later, in the inhabited corner of the *palazzo* above the vineyards, the marble hills, the pines and olives of Lucca, he also said:

'The name of Gould has been always highly respected in Sulaco. My uncle Harry was chief of the State for some time, and has left a great name amongst the first families. By this I mean the pure Creole families, who take no part in the miserable farce of governments. Uncle Harry was no adventurer. In Costaguana we Goulds are no adventurers. He was of the country, and he loved it, but he remained essentially an Englishman in his ideas. He made use of the political cry of his time. It was Federation. But he was no politician. He simply stood up for social order out of pure love for rational liberty and from his hate of oppression. There was no nonsense about him. He went to work in his own way because it seemed right, just as I feel I must lay hold of that mine.'

In such words he talked to her because his memory was very full of the country of his childhood, his heart of his life with that girl, and his mind of the San Tomé Concession. He added that he would have to leave her for a few days to find an American, a man from San Francisco, who was still somewhere in Europe. A few months before he had made his acquaintance in an old historic German town, situated in a mining district. The American had his womankind with him, but seemed lonely while they were sketching all day long the old doorways and the turreted corners of the medieval houses. Charles Gould had with him the inseparable companionship of the mine. The other man was interested in mining enterprises, knew something of Costaguana, and was no stranger to the name of Gould. They had talked together with some intimacy which was made possible by the difference of their ages. Charles wanted now to find that capitalist of shrewd mind and accessible character. His father's fortune in Costaguana, which he had supposed to be still considerable, seemed to have melted in the rascally crucible of revolutions. Apart from some ten thousand pounds deposited in England, there appeared to be nothing left except the house in Sulaco, a vague right of forest exploitation in a remote and savage district, and the San Tomé Concession, which had attended his poor father to the very brink of the grave.

He explained those things. It was late when they parted. She had never before given him such a fascinating vision of herself. All the eagerness of youth for a strange life, for great distances, for a future in which there was an air of adventure, of combat – a subtle thought of redress and conquest – had filled her with an intense excitement, which she returned to the giver with a more open and exquisite display of tenderness.

He left her to walk down the hill, and directly he found himself alone he became sober. That irreparable change a death makes in the course of our daily thoughts can be felt in a vague and poignant discomfort of mind. It hurt Charles Gould to feel that never more, by no effort of will, would he be able to think of his father in the same way he used to think of him when the poor man was alive. His breathing image was no longer in his power. This consideration, closely affecting his own identity, filled his breast with a mournful and angry desire for action. In this his instinct was unerring. Action is consolatory. It is the enemy of thought and the friend of flattering illusions. Only in the conduct of our action can we find the sense of mastery over the Fates. For his action, the mine was obviously the only field. It was imperative sometimes to know how to disobey the solemn wishes of the dead. He resolved firmly to make his disobedience as thorough (by way of atonement) as it well could be. The mine had been the cause of an absurd moral disaster; its working must be made a serious and moral success. He owed it to the dead man's memory. Such were the – properly speaking – emotions of Charles Gould. His thoughts ran upon the means of raising a large amount of capital in San Francisco or elsewhere; and incidentally there occurred to him also the general reflection that the counsel of the departed must be an unsound guide. Not one of them could be aware beforehand what enormous changes the death of any given individual may produce in the very aspect of the world.

The latest phase in the history of the mine Mrs Gould knew from personal experience. It was in essence the history of her married life. The mantle of the

Goulds' hereditary position in Sulaco had descended amply upon her little person; but she would not allow the peculiarities of the strange garment to weigh down the vivacity of her character, which was the sign of no mere mechanical sprightliness, but of an eager intelligence. It must not be supposed that Mrs Gould's mind was masculine. A woman with a masculine mind is not a being of superior efficiency; she is simply a phenomenon of imperfect differentiation – interestingly barren and without importance. Doña Emilia's intelligence being feminine led her to achieve the conquest of Sulaco, simply by lighting the way for her unselfishness and sympathy. She could converse charmingly, but she was not talkative. The wisdom of the heart having no concern with the erection or demolition of theories any more than with the defence of prejudices, has no random words at its command. The words it pronounces have the value of acts of integrity, tolerance, and compassion. A woman's true tenderness, like the true virility of man, is expressed in action of a conquering kind. The ladies of Sulaco adored Mrs Gould. 'They still look upon me as something of a monster,' Mrs Gould had said pleasantly to one of the three gentlemen from San Francisco she had to entertain in her new Sulaco house just about a year after her marriage.

They were her first visitors from abroad, and they had come to look at the San Tomé mine. She jested most agreeably, they thought; and Charles Gould, besides knowing thoroughly what he was about, had shown himself a real hustler. These facts caused them to be well disposed towards his wife. An unmistakable enthusiasm, pointed by a slight flavour of irony, made her talk of the mine absolutely fascinating to her visitors, and provoked them to grave and indulgent smiles in which there was a good deal of deference. Perhaps had they known how much she was inspired by an idealistic view of success they would have been amazed at the state of her mind as the Spanish–American ladies had been amazed at the tireless activity of her body. She would – in her own words – have been for them 'something of a monster'. However, the Goulds were in essentials a reticent couple, and their guests departed without the suspicion of any other purpose but simple profit in the working of a silver mine. Mrs Gould had out her own carriage, with two white mules, to drive them down to the harbour, whence the *Ceres* was to carry them off into the Olympus of plutocrats. Captain Mitchell had snatched at the occasion of leave-taking to remark to Mrs Gould, in a low, confidential mutter, 'This marks an epoch.'

Mrs Gould loved the patio of her Spanish house. A broad flight of stone steps was overlooked silently from a niche in the wall by a Madonna in blue robes with the crowned child sitting on her arm. Subdued voices ascended in the early mornings from the paved well of the quadrangle, with the stamping of horses and mules led out in pairs to drink at the cistern. A tangle of slender bamboo stems drooped its narrow, blade-like leaves over the square pool of water, and the fat coachman sat muffled up on the edge, holding lazily the ends of halters in his hand. Barefooted servants passed to and fro, issuing from dark, low doorways below; two laundry girls with baskets of washed linen; the baker with the tray of bread made for the day; Leonarda – her own *camerista* – bearing high up, swung from her hand raised above her raven black head, a bunch of starched underskirts dazzlingly white in the slant of sunshine. Then the old porter would hobble in, sweeping the flagstones, and the house was ready for the day. All the lofty rooms on three sides of the quadrangle opened into each other and into the *corredor*, with its wrought-iron railings and a border of flowers, whence, like the lady of the medieval castle, she could witness from above all the departures and arrivals of the Casa, to which the sonorous arched gateway lent an air of stately importance.

She had watched her carriage roll away with the three guests from the north. She smiled. Their three arms went up simultaneously to their three hats. Captain Mitchell, the fourth, in attendance, had already begun a pompous discourse. Then she lingered. She lingered, approaching her face to the clusters of flowers here and there as if to give time to her thoughts to catch up with her slow footsteps along the straight vista of the corridor.

A fringed Indian hammock from Aroa, gay with coloured featherwork, had been swung judiciously in a corner that caught the early sun; for the mornings are cool in Sulaco. The cluster of *flor de noche buena* blazed in great masses before the open glass doors of the reception-rooms. A big green parrot, brilliant like an emerald in a cage that flashed like gold, screamed out ferociously, '*Viva Costaguana*!' then called twice mellifluously, '*Leonarda! Leonarda*!' in imitation of Mrs Gould's voice, and suddenly took refuge in immobility and silence. Mrs Gould reached the end of the gallery and put her head through the door of her husband's room.

Charles Gould, with one foot on a low wooden stool, was already strapping his spurs. He wanted to hurry back to the mine. Mrs Gould, without coming in, glanced about the room. One tall, broad bookcase, with glass doors, was full of books; but in the other, without shelves, and lined with red baize, were arranged firearms: Winchester carbines, revolvers, a couple of shot-guns, and even two pairs of double-barrelled holster pistols. Between them, by itself, upon a strip of scarlet velvet, hung an old cavalry sabre, once the property of Don Enrique Gould, the hero of the Occidental Province, presented by Don José Avellanos, the hereditary friend of the family.

Otherwise, the plastered white walls were completely bare, except for a water-colour sketch of the San Tomé mountain – the work of Doña Emilia herself. In the middle of the red-tiled floor stood two long tables littered with plans and papers, a few chairs, and a glass show-case containing specimens of ore from the mine. Mrs Gould, looking at all these things in turn, wondered aloud why the talk of these wealthy and enterprising men discussing the prospects, the working, and the safety of the mine rendered her so impatient and uneasy, whereas she could talk of the mine by the hour with her husband with unwearied interest and satisfaction.

And dropping her eyelids expressively, she added:

'What do *you* feel about it, Charley?'

Then, surprised at her husband's silence, she raised her eyes, opened wide, as pretty as pale flowers. He had done with the spurs, and, twisting his moustache with both hands, horizontally, he contemplated her from the height of his long legs with a visible appreciation of her appearance. The consciousness of being thus contemplated pleased Mrs Gould.

'They are considerable men,' he said.

'I know. But have you listened to their conversation? They don't seem to have understood anything they have seen here.'

'They have seen the mine. They have understood that to some purpose,' Charles Gould interjected, in defence of the visitors; and then his wife mentioned the name of the most considerable of three. He was considerable in finance and in industry. His name was familiar to many millions of people. He was so considerable that he would never have travelled so far away from the centre of his activity if the doctors had not insisted, with veiled menaces, on his taking a long holiday.

'Mr Holroyd's sense of religion,' Mrs Gould pursued, 'was shocked and disgusted at the tawdriness of the dressed-up saints in the cathedral – the worship, he called it, of wood and tinsel. But it seemed to me that he looked upon his own God as a sort of influential partner, who gets his share of profits in the endowment of churches. That's a sort of idolatry. He told me he endowed churches every year, Charley.'

'No end of them,' said Mr Gould, marvelling inwardly at the mobility of her physiognomy. 'All over the country. He's famous for that sort of munificence.'

'Oh, he didn't boast,' Mrs Gould declared, scrupulously. 'I believe he's really a good man, but so stupid! A poor Cholo who offers a little silver arm or leg to thank his god for a cure is as rational and more touching.'

'He's at the head of immense silver and iron interests,' Charles Gould observed.

'Ah, yes! The religion of silver and iron. He's a very civil man, though he looked awfully solemn when he first saw the Madonna on the staircase, who's only wood and paint; but he said nothing to me. My dear Charley, I heard those men talk among themselves. Can it be that they really wish to become, for an immense consideration, drawers of water and hewers of wood to all the countries and nations of the earth?'

'A man must work to some end,' Charles Gould said, vaguely.

Mrs Gould, frowning, surveyed him from head to foot. With his riding-breeches, leather leggings (an article of apparel never before seen in Costaguana), a Norfolk coat of grey flannel, and those great flaming moustaches, he suggested an officer of cavalry turned gentleman farmer. This combination was gratifying to Mrs Gould's tastes. 'How thin the poor boy is!' she thought. 'He overworks himself.' But there was no denying that his fine-drawn, keen red face, and his whole, long-limbed, lank person had an air of breeding and distinction. And Mrs Gould relented.

'I only wondered what you felt,' she murmured, gently.

During the last few days, as it happened, Charles Gould had been kept too busy thinking twice before he spoke to have paid much attention to the state of his feelings. But theirs was a successful match, and he had no difficulty in finding his answer.

'The best of my feelings are in your keeping, my dear,' he said lightly; and there was so much truth in that obscure phrase that he experienced towards her at the moment a great increase of gratitude and tenderness.

Mrs Gould, however, did not seem to find this answer in the least obscure. She brightened up delicately; already he had changed his tone.

'But there are facts. The worth of the mine – as a mine – is beyond doubt. It shall make us very wealthy. The mere working of it is a matter of technical knowledge, which I have – which ten thousand other men in the world have. But its safety, its continued existence as an enterprise, giving a return to men – to strangers, comparative strangers – who invest money in it, is left altogether in my hands. I have inspired confidence in a man of wealth and position. You seem to think this perfectly natural – do you? Well, I don't know. I don't know why I have; but it is a fact. This fact makes everything possible, because without it I would never have thought of disregarding my father's wishes. I would never have disposed of the Concession as a speculator disposes of a valuable right to a company – for cash and shares, to grow rich eventually if possible, but at any rate to put some money at once in his pocket. No. Even if it had been feasible – which I doubt – I would not have done so. Poor Father did not understand. He was afraid I would hang on to the ruinous thing, waiting for just some such chance, and waste my life miserably. That was the true sense of his prohibition, which we have deliberately set aside.'

They were walking up and down the corridor. Her head just reached to his shoulder. His arm, extended downwards, was about her waist. His spurs jingled slightly.

'He had not seen me for ten years. He did not know me. He parted from me for my sake, and he would never let me come back. He was always talking in his letters of leaving Costaguana, of abandoning everything and making his escape. But he was too valuable a prey. They would have thrown him into one of their prisons at the first suspicion.'

His spurred feet clinked slowly. He was bending over his wife as they walked. The big parrot, turning its head askew, followed their pacing figures with a round, unblinking eye.

'He was a lonely man. Ever since I was ten years old he used to talk to me as if I had been grown up. When I was in Europe he wrote to me every month. Ten, twelve pages every month of my life for ten years. And, after all, he did not know me! Just think of it – ten whole years away; the years I was growing up into a man. He could not know me. Do you think he could?'

Mrs Gould shook her head negatively; which was just what her husband had expected from the strength of the argument. But she shook her head negatively only because she thought that no one could know her Charles – really know him for what he was but herself. The thing was obvious. It could be felt. It required no argument. And poor Mr Gould, senior, who had died too soon to ever hear of their engagement, remained too shadowy a figure for her to be credited with knowledge of any sort whatever.

'No, he did not understand. In my view this mine could never have been a thing to sell. Never! After all his misery I simply could not have touched it for money alone,' Charles Gould pursued: and she pressed her head to his shoulder approvingly.

These two young people remembered the life which had ended wretchedly just when their own lives had come together in that splendour of hopeful love, which to the most sensible minds appears like a triumph of good over all the evils of the earth. A vague idea of rehabilitation had entered the plan of their life. That it was so vague as to elude the support of argument made it only the stronger. It had presented itself to them at the instant when the woman's instinct of devotion and the man's instinct of activity receive from the strongest of illusions their most powerful impulse. The very prohibition imposed the necessity of success. It was as if they had been morally bound to make good their vigorous view of life against the unnatural error of weariness and despair. If the idea of wealth was present to them it was only so far as it was bound with that other success. Mrs Gould, an orphan from early childhood and without fortune, brought up in an atmosphere of intellectual interests, had never considered the aspects of great wealth. They were too remote, and she had not learned that they were desirable. On the other hand, she had not known anything of absolute want. Even the very poverty of her aunt, the Marchesa, had nothing intolerable to a refined mind; it seemed in accord with a great grief; it had the austerity of a sacrifice offered to a noble ideal. Thus even the most legitimate touch of materialism was wanting in Mrs Gould's character. The dead man of whom she thought with tenderness (because he was Charley's father), and with some impatience (because he had been weak), must be put completely in the wrong. Nothing else would do to keep their prosperity without a stain on its only real, on its immaterial side!

Charles Gould, on his part, had been obliged to keep the idea of wealth well to the fore; but he brought it forward as a means, not as an end. Unless the mine was good business it could not be touched. He had to insist on that aspect of the enterprise. It was his lever to move men who had capital. And Charles Gould believed in the mine. He knew everything that could be known of it. His faith in the mine was contagious, though it was not served by a great eloquence; but businessmen are frequently as sanguine and imaginative as lovers. They are affected by a personality much oftener than people would suppose; and Charles Gould, in his unshaken assurance, was absolutely convicing. Besides, it was a matter of common knowledge to the men to whom he addressed himself that mining in Costaguana was a game that could be made considerably more than worth the candle. The men of affairs knew that very well. The real difficulty in touching it was elsewhere. Against that there was an implication of calm and implacable resolution in Charles Gould's very voice. Men of affairs venture sometimes on acts that the common judgement of the world would pronounce absurd; they make their decisions on apparently impulsive and human grounds. 'Very well,' had said the considerable personage to whom Charles Gould on his way out through San Francisco had lucidly exposed his point of view. 'Let us suppose that the mining affairs of Sulaco are taken in hand. There would then be in it: first, the house of Holroyd, which is all right; then, Mr Charles Gould, a citizen of Costaguana, who is also all right; and, lastly, the Government of the Republic. So far this resembles the first start of the Atacama nitrate fields, where there was a financing house, a gentleman of the name of Edwards, and – a Government; or, rather, two Governments – two South American Governments. And you know what came of it. War came of it; devastating and prolonged war came of it, Mr Gould. However, here we possess the advantage of having only one South American Government hanging around for plunder out of the deal.

It is an advantage; but then there are degrees of badness, and that Government is the Costaguana Government.'

Thus spoke the considerable personage, the millionaire endower of churches on a scale befitting the greatness of his native land – the same to whom the doctors used the language of horrid and veiled menaces. He was a big-limbed, deliberate man, whose quiet burliness lent to an ample silk-faced frock-coat a superfine dignity. His hair was iron grey, his eyebrows were still black, and his massive profile was the profile of a Caesar's head on an old Roman coin. But his parentage was German and Scotch and English, with remote strains of Danish and French blood, giving him the temperament of a Puritan and an insatiable imagination of conquest. He was completely unbending to his visitor, because of the warm introduction the visitor had brought from Europe, and because of an irrational liking for earnestness and determination wherever met, to whatever end directed.

'The Costaguana Government shall play its hand for all it's worth – and don't you forget it, Mr Gould. Now, what is Costaguana? It is the bottomless pit of ten-per-cent loans and other fool investments. European capital has been flung into it with both hands for years. Not ours, though. We in this country know just about enough to keep indoors when it rains. We can sit and watch. Of course, some day we shall step in. We are bound to. But there's no hurry. Time itself has got to wait on the greatest country in the whole of God's Universe. We shall be giving the word for everything: industry, trade, law, journalism, art, politics, and religion, from Cape Horn clear over to Smith's Sound, and beyond, too, if anything worth taking hold of turns up at the North Pole. And then we shall have the leisure to take in hand the outlying islands and continents of the earth. We shall run the world's business whether the world likes it or not. The world can't help it – and neither can we, I guess.'

By this he meant to express his faith in destiny in words suitable to his intelligence, which was unskilled in the presentation of general ideas. His intelligence was nourished on facts; and Charles Gould, whose imagination had been permanently affected by the one great fact of a silver mine, had no objection to this theory of the world's future. If it had seemed distasteful for a moment it was because the sudden statement of such vast eventualities dwarfed almost to nothingness the actual matter in hand. He and his plans and all the mineral wealth of the Occidental Province appeared suddenly robbed of every vestige of magnitude. The sensation was disagreeable; but Charles Gould was not dull. Already he felt that he was producing a favourable impression; the consciousness of that flattering fact helped him to a vague smile, which his big interlocutor took for a smile of discreet and admiring assent. He smiled quietly, too; and immediately Charles Gould, with that mental agility mankind will display in defence of a cherished hope, reflected that the very apparent insignificance of his aim would help him to success. His personality and his mine would be taken up because it was a matter of no great consequence, one way or another, to a man who referred his action to such a prodigious destiny. And Charles Gould was not humiliated by this consideration, because the thing remained as big as ever for him. Nobody else's vast conceptions of destiny could diminish the aspect of his desire for the redemption of the San Tomé mine. In comparison to the correctness of his aim, definite in space and absolutely attainable within a limited time, the other man appeared for an instant as a dreamy idealist of no importance.

The great man, massive and benignant, had been looking at him thoughtfully; when he broke the short silence it was to remark that concessions flew about thick in the air of Costaguana. Any simple soul that just yearned to be taken in could bring down a concession at the first shot.

'Our consuls get their mouths stopped with them,' he continued, with a twinkle of genial scorn in his eyes. But in a moment he became grave. 'A conscientious, upright man, that cares nothing for boodle, and keeps clear of their intrigues, conspiracies, and factions, soon gets his passports. See that, Mr Gould? *Persona non grata*. That's the reason our Government is never properly informed. On the other hand, Europe must be kept out of this continent, and for proper interference on our part the time is not yet ripe, I dare say. But we here – we are not this country's Government, neither are we simple souls. Your affair is all right. The main question for us is whether the second partner, and that's you, is the sort to hold his own against the third and unwelcome partner, which is one or another of the high and mighty robber gangs that run the Costaguana Government. What do you think, Mr Gould, eh?'

He bent forward to look steadily into the unflinching eyes of Charles Gould, who, remembering the large box full of his father's letters, put the accumulated scorn and bitterness of many years into the tone of his answer:

'As far as the knowledge of these men and their methods and their politics is concerned, I can answer for myself. I have been fed on that sort of knowledge since I was a boy. I am not likely to fall into mistakes from excess of optimism.'

'Not likely, eh? That's all right. Tact and a stiff upper lip is what you'll want; and you could bluff a little on the strength of your backing. Not too much, though. We will go with you as long as the thing runs straight. But we won't be drawn into any large trouble. This is the experiment which I am willing to make. There is some risk, and we will take it; but if you can't keep up your end, we will stand our loss, of course, and then – we'll let the thing go. This mine can wait; it has been shut up before, you know. You must understand that under no circumstances will we consent to throw good money after bad.'

Thus the great personage had spoken then, in his own private office, in a great city where other men (very considerable in the eyes of a vain populace) waited with alacrity upon a wave of his hand. And rather more than a year later, during his unexpected appearance in Sulaco, he had emphasized his uncompromising attitude with a freedom of sincerity permitted to his wealth and influence. He did this with the less reserve, perhaps, because the inspection of what had been done, and more still the way in which successive steps had been taken, had impressed him with the conviction that Charles Gould was perfectly capable of keeping up his end.

'This young fellow,' he thought to himself, 'may yet become a power in the land.'

This thought flattered him, for hitherto the only account of this young man he could give to his intimates was:

'My brother-in-law met him in one of these one-horse old German towns, near some mines, and sent him on to me with a letter. He's one of the Costaguana Goulds, pure-bred Englishmen, but all born in the country. His uncle went into politics, was the last Provincial President of Sulaco, and got shot after a battle. His father was a prominent businessman in Sta Marta, tried to keep clear of their politics, and died ruined after a lot of revolutions. And that's your Costaguana in a nutshell.'

Of course, he was too great a man to be questioned as to his motives, even by his intimates. The outside world was at liberty to wonder respectfully at the hidden meaning of his actions. He was so great a man that his lavish patronage of the 'purer forms of Christianity' (which in its naïve form of church-building amused Mrs Gould) was looked upon by his fellow-citizens as the manifestation of a pious and humble spirit. But in his own circles of the financial world the taking up of such a thing as the San Tomé mine was regarded not with respect, indeed, but rather as a subject for discreet jocularity. It was a great man's caprice. In the great Holroyd building (an enormous pile of iron, glass, and blocks of stone at the corner of two streets, cobwebbed aloft by the radiation of telegraph wires) the heads of principal departments exchanged humorous glances, which meant that they were not let into the secrets of the San Tomé business. The Costaguana mail (it was never large – one fairly heavy envelope) was taken unopened straight into the great man's room, and no instructions dealing with it had ever been issued thence. The office whispered that he answered personally – and not by dictation either, but actually writing in his own hand, with pen and ink, and, it was to be supposed, taking a copy in his own private press copybook, inaccessible to profane eyes. Some scornful young men, insignificant pieces of minor machinery in that eleven-storey-high workshop of great affairs, expressed frankly their private opinion that the great chief had done at last something silly, and was ashamed of his folly; others, elderly and insignificant, but full of romantic reverence for the business that had devoured their best years, used to mutter darkly and knowingly that this was a portentous sign; that the Holroyd connection meant by-and-by to get hold of the whole Republic of Costaguana, lock, stock, and barrel. But, in fact, the hobby theory was the right one. It interested the great man to attend personally to the San Tomé mine; it interested him so much that he allowed this hobby to give a direction to the first complete holiday he had taken for quite a startling number of years. He was not running a great enterprise there; no mere railway board or individual corporation. He was running a man! A success would have pleased him very much on refreshingly novel grounds; but, on the other side of the same feeling, it was incumbent upon him to cast it off utterly at the first sign of failure. A man may be thrown off. The papers had unfortunately trumpeted all over the land his journey to Costaguana. If he was pleased at the way Charles Gould was going on, he infused an added grimness into his assurances of support. Even at the very last interview, half an hour or so before he rolled out of the patio, hat in hand, behind Mrs Gould's white mules, he had said in Charles's room:

'You go ahead in your own way, and I shall know how to help you as long as you hold your own. But you may rest assured that in a given case we shall know how to drop you in time.'

To this Charles Gould's only answer had been: 'You may begin sending out the machinery as soon as you like.'

And the great man had liked this imperturbable assurance. The secret of it was that to Charles Gould's mind these uncompromising terms were agreeable. Like this the mine preserved its identity, with which he had endowed it as a boy; and it remained dependent on himself alone. It was a serious affair, and he, too, took it grimly.

'Of course,' he said to his wife, alluding to this last conversation with the departed guest, while they walked slowly up and down the corridor, followed by the irritated eye of the parrot – 'of course, a man of that sort can take up a thing or drop it when he likes. He will suffer from no sense of defeat. He may have to give in, or he may have to die tomorrow, but the great silver and iron interests shall survive, and some day shall get hold of Costaguana along with the rest of the world.'

They had stopped near the cage. The parrot, catching the sound of a word belonging to his vocabulary, was moved to interfere. Parrots are very human.

'*Viva Costaguana!*' he shrieked, with intense self-assertion, and, instantly ruffling up his feathers, assumed an air of puffed-up somnolence behind the glittering wires.

'And do you believe that, Charley?' Mrs Gould asked. 'This seems to me most awful materialism, and –'

'My dear, it's nothing to me,' interrupted her husband, in a reasonable tone. 'I make use of what I see. What's it to me whether his talk is the voice of destiny or simply a bit of clap-trap eloquence? There's a good deal of eloquence of one sort or another produced in both Americas. The air of the New World seems favourable to the art of declamation. Have you forgotten how dear Avellanos can hold forth for hours here –?'

'Oh, but that's different,' protested Mrs Gould, almost shocked. The allusion was not to the point. Don José was a dear good man, who talked very well, and was enthusiastic about the greatness of the San Tomé mine. 'How can you compare them, Charles?' she exlaimed, reproachfully. 'He has suffered – and yet he hopes.'

The working competence of men – which she never questioned – was very surprising to Mrs Gould, because upon so many obvious issues they showed themselves strangely muddle-headed.

Charles Gould, with a careworn calmness which secured for him at once his wife's anxious sympathy, assured her that he was not comparing. He was an American himself, after all, and perhaps he could understand both kinds of eloquence – 'if it were worth while to try,' he added, grimly. But he had breathed the air of England longer than any of his people had done for three generations, and really he begged to be excused. His poor father could be eloquent, too. And he asked his wife whether she remembered a passage in one of his father's last letters where Mr Gould had expressed the conviction that 'God looked wrathfully at these countries, or else He would let some ray of hope fall through a rift in the appalling darkness of intrigue, bloodshed, and crime that hung over the Queen of Continents'.

Mrs Gould had not forgotten. 'You read it to me, Charley,' she murmured.

'It was a striking pronouncement. How deeply your father must have felt its terrible sadness!'

'He did not like to be robbed. It exasperated him,' said Charles Gould. 'But the image will serve well enough. What is wanted here is law, good faith, order, security. Anyone can declaim about these things, but I pin my faith to material interests. Only let the material interests once get a firm footing, and they are bound to impose the conditions on which alone they can continue to exist. That's how your money-making is justified here in the face of lawlessness and disorder. It is justified because the security which it demands must be shared with an oppressed people. A better justice will come afterwards. That's your ray of hope.' His arm pressed her slight form closer to his side for a moment. 'And who knows whether in that sense even the San Tomé mine may not become that little rift in the darkness which poor Father despaired of ever seeing?'

She glanced up at him with admiration. He was competent; he had given a vast shape to the vagueness of her unselfish ambitions.

'Charley,' she said, 'you are splendidly disobedient.'

He left her suddenly in the *corredor* to go and get his hat, a soft, grey sombrero, an article of national costume which combined unexpectedly well with his English get-up. He came back, a riding-whip under his arm, buttoning up a dogskin glove; his face reflected the resolute nature of his thoughts. His wife had waited for him at the head of the stairs, and before he gave her the parting kiss he finished the conversation:

'What should be perfectly clear to us,' he said, 'is the fact that there is no going back. Where could we begin life afresh? We are in now for all that there is in us.'

He bent over her upturned face very tenderly and a little remorsefully. Charles Gould was competent because he had no illusions. The Gould Concession had to fight for life with such weapons as could be found at once in the mire of corruption that was so universal as to almost lose its significance. He was prepared to stoop for his weapons. For a moment he felt as if the silver mine, which had killed his father, had decoyed him further than he meant to go; and with the roundabout logic of emotions, he felt that the worthiness of his life was bound up with success. There was no going back.

Chapter VII

Mrs Gould was too intelligently sympathetic not to share that feeling. It made life exciting, and she was too much of a woman not to like excitement. But it frightened her, too, a little; and when Don José Avellanos, rocking in the American chair, would go so far as to say, 'Even, my dear Carlos, if you had failed; even if some untoward event were yet to destroy your work – which God forbid! – you would have deserved well of your country,' Mrs Gould would look up from the tea-table profoundly at her unmoved husband stirring the spoon in the cup as though he had not heard a word.

Not that Don José anticipated anything of the sort. He could not praise enough dear Carlos's tact and courage. His English, rock-like quality of character was his best safeguard, Don José affirmed; and, turning to Mrs Gould, 'As to you, Emilia, my soul' – he would address her with the familiarity of his age and old friendship – 'you are as true a patriot as though you had been born in our midst.'

This might have been less or more than the truth. Mrs Gould, accompanying her husband all over the province in the search for labour, had seen the land with a deeper glance than a trueborn Costaguanero could have done. In her travel-worn riding habit, her face powdered white like a plaster cast, with a further protection of a small silk mask during the heat of the day, she rode on a well-shaped, light-footed pony in the centre of a little cavalcade. Two *mozos de campo*, picturesque in great hats, with spurred bare heels, in white embroidered *calzoneras*, leather jackets, and striped ponchos, rode ahead with carbines across their shoulders, swaying in unison to the pace of the horses. A *tropilla* of pack mules brought up the rear in charge of a thin brown muleteer, sitting his long-eared beast very near the tail, legs thrust far forward, the wide brim of his hat set far back, making a sort of halo for his head. An old Costaguana officer, a retired senior major of humble origins, but patronized by the first families on account of his Blanco opinions, had been recommended by Don José for commissary and organizer of that expedition. The points of his grey moustache hung far below his chin, and, riding on Mrs Gould's left hand, he looked about with kindly eyes, pointing out the features of the country, telling the names of the little *pueblos* and of the estates, of the smooth-walled *haciendas* like long fortresses crowning the knolls above the level of the Sulaco Valley. It unrolled itself, with green young crops, plains, woodland, and gleams of water, park-like, from the blue vapour of the distant sierra to an immense quivering horizon of grass and sky, where big white clouds seemed to fall slowly into the darkness of their own shadows.

Men ploughed with wooden ploughs and yoked oxen, small on a boundless expanse, as if attacking immensity itself. The mounted figures of *vaqueros* galloped in the distance, and the great herds fed with all their horned heads one way, in one single wavering line as far as eye could reach across the broad *potreros*. A spreading cotton-wool tree shaded a thatched *rancho* by the road; the trudging files of burdened Indians, taking off their hats, would lift sad, mute eyes to the cavalcade raising the dust of the crumbling *camino real* made by the hands of their enslaved forefathers. And Mrs Gould, with each day's journey, seemed to come nearer to the soul of the land in the tremendous disclosure of this interior unaffected by the slight European veneer of the coast towns, a great land of plain and mountain and people, suffering and mute, waiting for the future in a pathetic immobility of patience.

She knew its sights and its hospitality, dispensed with a sort of slumbrous dignity in those great houses presenting long, blind walls and heavy portals to the windswept pastures. She was given the head of the tables, where masters and dependants sat in a simple and patriarchal state. The ladies of the house would talk softly in the moonlight under the orange trees of the courtyards, impressing upon her the sweetness of their voices and the something mysterious in the quietude of their lives. In the morning the gentlemen, well mounted in braided sombreros and embroidered riding-suits, with much silver on the trappings of their horses, would ride forth to escort the departing guests before committing them, with grave good-byes, to the care of God at the boundary pillars of their estates. In all these households she could hear stories of political outrage; friends, relatives, ruined, imprisoned, killed in the battles of senseless civil wars, barbarously executed in ferocious proscriptions, as though the government of the country had been a struggle of lust between bands of absurd devils let loose upon the land with sabres and uniforms and grandiloquent phrases. And on all the lips she found a weary desire for peace, the dread of officialdom with its nightmarish parody of administration without law, without security, and without justice.

She bore a whole two months of wandering very well; she had that power of resistance to fatigue which one discovers here and there in some quite frail-looking women with surprise – like a state of possession by a remarkably stubborn spirit. Don Pepe – the old Costaguana major – after much display of solicitude for the delicate lady, had ended by conferring upon her the name of the 'Never-tired Señora'. Mrs Gould was indeed becoming a Costaguanera. Having acquired in southern Europe a knowledge of true peasantry, she was able to appreciate the great worth of the people. She saw the man under the silent, sad-eyed beast of burden. She saw them on the road carrying loads, lonely figures upon the plain, toiling under great straw hats, with their white clothing flapping about their limbs in the wind; she remembered the villages by some group of Indian women at the fountain impressed upon her memory, by the face of some young Indian girl with a melancholy and sensual profile, raising an earthenware vessel of cool water at the door of a dark hut with a wooden porch cumbered with great brown jars. The solid wooden wheels of an ox-cart, halted with its shafts in the dust, showed the strokes of the axe; and a party of charcoal carriers, with each man's load resting above his head on the top of the low mud wall, slept stretched in a row within the strip of shade.

The heavy stonework of bridges and churches left by the conquerors proclaimed the disregard of human labour, the tribute-labour of vanished nations. The power of king and church was gone, but at the sight of some heavy ruinous pile overtopping from a knoll the low mud walls of a village, Don Pepe would interrupt the tale of his campaigns to exclaim:

'Poor Costaguana! Before, it was everything for the padres, nothing for the people; and now it is everything for these great *políticos* in Sta Marta, for Negroes and thieves.'

Charles talked with the *alcades*, with the *fiscales*, with the principal people in towns, and with the *caballeros* on the estates. The *commandantes* of the districts offered him escorts – for he could show an authorization from the Sulaco political chief of the day. How much the document had cost him in gold twenty-dollar pieces was a secret between himself, a great man in the United States (who condescended to answer the Sulaco mail with his own hand), and a great man of another sort, with a dark olive complexion and shifty eyes, inhabiting then the Palace of the Intendencia in Sulaco, and who piqued himself on his culture and Europeanism generally in a rather French style because he had lived in Europe for some years – in exile, he said. However, it was pretty well known that just before this exile he had incautiously gambled away all the cash in the Custom House of a small port where a friend in power had procured for him the post of sub-collector. That youthful indiscretion had, amongst other inconveniences, obliged him to earn his living for a time as a café waiter in Madrid; but his talents must have been great, after all, since they had enabled him to retrieve his political fortunes so splendidly. Charles Gould, exposing his business with an imperturbable steadiness, called him Excellency.

The provincial Excellency assumed a weary superiority, tilting his chair far back near an open window in the true Costaguana manner. The military band happened to be braying operatic selections on the *plaza* just then, and twice he raised his hand imperatively for silence in order to listen to a favourite passage.

'Exquisite, delicious!' he murmured; while Charles Gould waited, standing by with inscrutable patience. 'Lucia, Lucia di Lammermoor! I am passionate for music. It transports me. Ha! the divine – ha! – Mozart. *Si!* divine . . . What is it you were saying?'

Of course, rumours had reached him already of the newcomer's intentions. Besides, he had received an official warning from Sta Marta. His manner was intended simply to conceal his curiosity and impress his visitor. But after he had locked up something valuable in the drawer of a large writing-desk in a distant part of the room, he became very affable, and walked back to his chair smartly.

'If you intend to build villages and assemble a population near the mine, you shall require a decree of the Minister of the Interior for that,' he suggested in a businesslike manner.

'I have already sent a memorial,' said Charles Gould, steadily, 'and I reckon now confidently upon your Excellency's favourable conclusions.'

The Excellency was a man of many moods. With the receipt of the money a great mellowness had descended upon his simple soul. Unexpectedly he fetched a deep sigh.

'Ah, Don Carlos! What we want is advanced men like you in the province. The lethargy – the lethargy of these aristocrats! The want of public spirit! The absence of all enterprise! I, with my profound studies in Europe, you understand –'

With one hand thrust into his swelling bosom, he rose and fell on his toes, and for ten minutes, almost without drawing breath, went on hurling himself intellectually to the assault of Charles Gould's polite silence; and when, stopping abruptly, he fell back into his chair, it was as though he had been beaten off from a fortress. To save his dignity he hastened to dismiss this silent man with a solemn inclination of the head and the words, prounced with moody, fatigued condescension:

'You may depend upon my enlightened goodwill as long as your conduct as a good citizen deserves it.'

He took up a paper fan and began to cool himself with a consequential air, while Charles Gould bowed and withdrew. Then he dropped the fan at once, and stared with an appearance of wonder and perplexity at the closed door for quite a long time. At last he shrugged his shoulders as if to assure himself of his disdain. Cold, dull. No intellectuality. Red hair. A true Englishman. He despised him.

His face darkened. What meant this unimpressed and frigid behaviour? He was the first of the successive politicians sent out from the capital to rule the Occidental Province whom the manner of Charles Gould in official intercourse was to strike as offensively independent.

Charles Gould assumed that if the appearance of listening to deplorable balderdash must form part of the price he had to pay for being left unmolested, the obligation of uttering balderdash personally was by no means included in the bargain. He drew the line there. To these provincial autocrats, before whom the peaceable population of all classes had been accustomed to tremble, the reserve of that English-looking engineer caused an uneasiness which swung to and fro between cringing and truculence. Gradually all of them discovered that, no matter what party was in power, that man remained in most effective touch with the higher authorities in Sta Marta.

This was a fact, and it accounted perfectly for the Goulds being by no means so wealthy as the engineer-in-chief on the new railway could legitimately suppose. Following the advice of Don José Avellanos, who was a man of good counsel (though rendered timid by his horrible experiences of Guzman Bento's time), Charles Gould had kept clear of the capital; but in the current gossip of the foreign residents there he was known (with a good deal of seriousness underlying the irony) by the nickname of 'King of Sulaco'. An advocate of the Costaguana Bar, a man of reputed ability and good character, member of the distinguished Moraga family possessing extensive estates in the Sulaco Valley, was pointed out to strangers, with a shade of mystery and respect, as the agent of the San Tomé mine – 'political, you know'. He was tall, black-whiskered, and discreet. It was known that he had easy access to ministers, and that the numerous Costaguana generals were always anxious to dine at his house. Presidents granted him audience with facility. He corresponded actively with his maternal uncle, Don José Avellanos; but his letters – unless those expressing formally his dutiful affection – were seldom entrusted to the Costaguana post office. There the envelopes are opened, indiscriminately, with the frankness of a brazen and childish impudence characteristic of some Spanish–American Governments. But it must be noted that at about the time of the reopening of the San Tomé mine the muleteer who had been employed by Charles Gould in his preliminary travels on the Campo added his small train of animals to the thin stream of traffic carried over the mountain passes between the Sta Marta upland and the Valley of Sulaco. There are no travellers by that arduous and unsafe route unless under very exceptional circumstances, and the state of inland trade did not visibly require additional transport facilities; but the man seemed to find his account in it. A few packages were always found for him whenever he took the road. Very brown and wooden, in goatskin breeches with the hair outside, he sat near the tail of his own smart mule, his great hat turned against the sun, an expression of blissful vacancy on his long face, humming day after day a love-song in a plaintive key, or, without a change of expression, letting out a yell at his small *tropilla* in front. A round little guitar hung high up on his back; and there was a place scooped out artistically in the wood of one of his pack-saddles where a tightly rolled piece of paper could be slipped in, the wooden plug replaced, and the coarse canvas nailed on again. When in Sulaco it was his practice to smoke and doze all day long (as though he had no care in the world) on a stone bench outside the doorway of the Casa Gould and facing the windows of the Avellanos house. Years and years ago his mother had been chief laundry-woman in that family – very accomplished in the matter of clear-starching. He himself had been born on one of their *haciendas*. His name was Bonifacio, and Don José, crossing the street about five o'clock to call on Doña Emilia, always acknowledged his humble salute by some movement of hand or head. The porters of both houses conversed lazily with him in tones of grave intimacy. His evenings he devoted to gambling and to calls in a spirit of generous festivity upon the *peyne d'oro* girls in the more remote side-streets of the town. But he, too, was a discreet man.

Chapter VIII

Those of us whom business or curiosity took to Sulaco in these years before the first advent of the railway can remember the steadying effect of the San Tomé mine upon the life of that remote province. The outward appearances had not changed then as they have changed since, as I am told, with cable cars running along the streets of the Constitution, and carriage roads far into the country, to Rincón and other villages, where the foreign merchants and the *ricos* generally have their modern villas, and a vast railway goods-yard by the harbour, which has a quay-side, a long range of warehouses, and quite serious, organized labour troubles of its own.

Nobody had ever heard of labour troubles then. The Cargadores of the port formed, indeed, an unruly brotherhood of all sorts of scum, with a patron saint of their own. They went on strike regularly (every bullfight day), a form of trouble that even Nostromo at the height of his prestige could never cope with efficiently; but the morning after each fiesta, before the Indian market-women had opened their mat parasols on the *plaza*, when the snows of Higuerota gleamed pale over the town on a yet black sky, the appearance of a phantom-like horseman mounted on a silver-grey mare solved the problem of labour without fail. His steed paced the lanes of the slums and the weed-grown enclosures within the old ramparts, between the black, lightless cluster of huts, like cow-byres, like dog-kennels. The horseman hammered with the butt of a heavy revolver at the doors of low *pulperías*, of obscene lean-to-sheds sloping against the tumble-down piece of a noble wall, at the wooden sides of dwellings so flimsy that the sound of snores and sleepy mutters within could be heard in the pauses of the thundering clatter of his blows. He called out men's names menacingly from the saddle, once, twice. The drowsy answers – grumpy, conciliating, savage, jocular, or deprecating – came out into the silent darkness in which the horseman sat still, and presently a dark figure would flit out coughing in the still air. Sometimes a low-toned woman cried through the window-hole softly, 'He's coming directly, *señor*,' and the horseman waited silent on a motionless horse. But if perchance he had to dismount, then, after a while, from the door of that hovel or of that *pulpería*, with a ferocious scuffle and stifled imprecations, a *cargador* would fly out head first and hands abroad, to sprawl under the forelegs of the silver-grey mare, who only pricked forward her sharp little ears. She was used to that work; and the man, picking himself up, would walk away hastily from Nostromo's revolver, reeling a little along the street and snarling low curses. At sunrise Captain Mitchell, coming out anxiously in his night attire on to the wooden balcony running the whole length of the O.S.N. Company's lonely building by the shore, would see the lighters already under way, figures moving busily about the cargo cranes, perhaps hear the invaluable Nostromo, now dismounted and in the checked shirt and red sash of a Mediterranean sailor, bawling orders from the end of the jetty in a stentorian voice. A fellow in a thousand!

The material apparatus of perfected civilization which obliterates the individuality of old towns under the stereotyped conveniences of modern life had not intruded as yet; but over the worn-out antiquity of Sulaco, so characteristic with its stuccoed houses and barred windows, with the great yellowy-white walls of abandoned convents behind the rows of sombre green cypresses, that fact – very modern in its spirit – the San Tomé mine had already thrown its subtle influence. It had altered, too, the outward character of the crowds on feast days on the *plaza* before the open portal of the cathedral, by the number of white ponchos with a green stripe affected as holiday wear by the San Tomé miners. They had also adopted white hats with green cord and braid – articles of good quality, which could be obtained in the storehouse of the administration for very little money. A peaceable *cholo* wearing these colours (unusual in Costaguana) was somehow very seldom beaten to within an inch of his life on a charge of disrespect to the town police; neither ran he much risk of being suddenly lassoed on the road by a recruiting party of *lanceros* – a method of voluntary enlistment looked upon as almost legal in the Republic. Whole villages were known to have volunteered for the army in that way; but, as Don Pepe would say with a hopeless shrug to Mrs Gould, 'What would you! Poor people! *Pobrecitos! Pobrecitos*! But the State must have its soldiers.'

Thus professionally spoke Don Pepe, the fighter, with pendent moustaches, a nut-brown, lean face, and a clean run of a cast-iron jaw, suggesting the type of a cattle-herd horseman from the great Llanos of the South. 'If you will listen to an old officer of Paez, *señores*,' was the exordium of all his speeches in the Aristocratic Club of Sulaco, where he was admitted on account of his past services to the extinct cause of Federation. The club, dating from the days of the proclamation of Costaguana's independence, boasted many names of liberators amongst its first founders. Suppressed arbitrarily innumerable times by various Governments, with memories of proscriptions and of at least one wholesale massacre of its members, sadly assembled for a banquet by the order of a zealous military *comandante* (their bodies were afterwards stripped naked and flung into the *plaza* out of the windows by the lowest scum of the populace), it was again flourishing, at that period, peacefully. It extended to strangers the large hospitality of the cool, big rooms of its historic quarters in the front part of a house, once the residence of a high official of the Holy Office. The two wings, shut up, crumbled behind the nailed doors, and what may be described as a grove of young orange trees grown in the unpaved *patio* concealed the utter ruin of the back part facing the gate. You turned in from the street, as if entering a secluded orchard, where you came upon the foot of a disjointed staircase, guarded by a moss-stained effigy of some saintly bishop, mitred and staffed, and bearing the indignity of a broken nose meekly, with his fine stone hands crossed on his breast. The chocolate-coloured faces of servants with mops of black hair peeped at you from above; the click of billiard balls came to your ears, and ascending the steps, you would perhaps see in the first *sala*, very stiff upon a straight-backed chair, in a good light, Don Pepe moving his long moustaches as he spelt his way, at arm's length, through an old Sta Marta newspaper. His horse – a stony-hearted but persevering black brute with a hammer head – you would have seen in the street dozing motionless under an immense saddle, with its nose almost touching the kerbstone of the sidewalk.

Don Pepe, when 'down from the mountain', as the phrase, often heard in Sulaco, went, could also be seen in the drawing-room of the Casa Gould. He sat with modest assurance at some distance from the tea-table. With his knees close together, and a kindly twinkle of drollery in his deep-set eyes, he would throw his small and ironic pleasantries into the current of conversation. There was in that man a sort of sane, humorous shrewdness, and a vein of genuine humanity so often found in simple old soldiers of proved courage who have seen much desperate service. Of course he knew nothing whatever of mining, but his employment was of a special kind. He was in charge of the whole population in the territory of the mine, which extended from the head of the gorge to where the cart-track from the foot of the mountain enters the plain, crossing a stream over a little wooden bridge painted green – green, the colour of hope, being also the colour of the mine.

It was reported in Sulaco that up there 'at the mountain' Don Pepe walked about precipitous paths, girt with a great sword and in a shabby uniform with tarnished bullion epaulettes of a senior major. Most miners being Indians, with big wild eyes, addressed him as 'Taita' (father), as these barefooted people of Costaguana will address anybody who wears shoes; but it was Basilio, Mr Gould's own *mozo* and the head servant of the Casa, who, in all good faith and from a sense of propriety, announced him once in the solemn words, 'El Señor Gobernador has arrived.'

Don José Avellanos, then in the drawing-room, was delighted beyond measure at the aptness of the title, with which he greeted the old major banteringly as soon as the latter's soldierly figure appeared in the doorway. Don Pepe only smiled in his long moustaches, as much as to say, 'You might have found a worse name for an old soldier.'

And 'El Señor Gobernador' he had remained, with his small jokes upon his function and upon his domain, where he affirmed with humorous exaggeration to Mrs Gould:

'No two stones could come together anywhere without the Gobernador hearing the click, *señora*.'

And he would tap his ear with the tip of his forefinger knowingly. Even when the number of the miners alone rose to over six hundred he seemed to know each of them individually, all the innumerable Josés, Manuels, Ignacios, from the villages *primero – segundo –* or *tercero* (there were three mining villages) under his government. He could distinguish them not only by their flat, joyless faces, which to Mrs Gould looked all alike, as if run into the same ancestral mould of suffering and patience, but apparently also by the infinitely graduated shades of reddish-brown, of blackish-brown, of coppery-brown backs, as the two shifts, stripped to linen drawers and leather skull-caps, mingled together with a confusion of naked limbs, of shouldered picks, swinging lamps, in a great shuffle of sandalled feet on the open plateau before the entrance of the main tunnel. It was a time of pause. The Indian boys leaned idly against the long line of little cradle wagons standing empty; the screeners and ore-breakers squatted on their heels smoking long cigars; the great wooden shoots slanting over the edge of the tunnel plateau were silent; and only the ceaseless, violent rush of water in the open flumes could be heard, murmuring, fiercely, with the splash and rumble of revolving turbine-wheels, and the thudding march of the stamps pounding to powder the treasure rock on the plateau below. The heads of gangs, distinguished by brass medals hanging on their bare breasts, marshalled their squads; and at last the mountain would swallow one half of the silent crowd, while the other half would move off in long files down the zigzag paths leading to the bottom of the gorge. It was deep; and, far below, a thread of vegetation winding between the blazing rock faces resembled a slender green cord, in which three lumpy knots of banana patches, palm-leaf roots, and shady trees marked the Village One, Village Two, Village Three, housing the miners of the Gould Concession.

Whole families had been moving from the first towards the spot in the Higuerota range, whence the rumour of work and safety had spread over the pastoral Campo, forcing its way also, even as the waters of a high flood, into the nooks and crannies of the distant blue walls of the Sierras. Father first, in a pointed straw hat, then the mother with the bigger children, generally also a diminutive donkey, all under burdens, except the leader himself, or perhaps some grown girl, the pride of the family, stepping barefooted and straight as an arrow, with braids of raven hair, a thick, haughty profile, and no load to carry but the small guitar of the country and a pair of soft leather sandals tied together on her back. At the sight of such parties strung out on the cross trails between the pastures, or camped by the side of the royal road, travellers on horseback would remark to each other:

'More people going to the San Tomé mine. We shall see others tomorrow.'

And spurring on in the dusk they would discuss the great news of the province, the news of San Tomé mine. A rich Englishman was going to work it – and perhaps not an Englishman, *Quién sabe*! A foreigner with much money. Oh, yes, it had begun. A party of men who had been to Sulaco with a herd of black bulls for the next *corrida* had reported that from the porch of the *posada* in Rincón, only a short league from the town, the lights on the mountain were visible, twinkling above the trees. And there was a woman seen riding a horse sideways, not in the chair seat, but upon a sort of saddle, and a man's hat on her head. She walked about, too, on foot up the mountain paths. A woman engineer, it seemed she was.

'What an absurdity! Impossible, *señor*!'

'*Sí! Sí! Una americana del Norte*.'

'Ah, well! if your worship is informed. *Una Americana*; it need be something of that sort.'

And they would laugh a little with astonishment and scorn, keeping a wary eye on the shadows of the road, for one is liable to meet bad men when travelling late on the Campo.

And it was not only the men that Don Pepe knew so well, but he seemed able, with one attentive, thoughtful glance, to classify each woman, girl, or growing youth of his domain. It was only the small fry that puzzled him sometimes. He and the padre could be seen frequently side by side, meditative and gazing across the street of a village at a lot of sedate brown children, trying to sort them out, as it were, in low, consulting tones, or else they would together put searching questions as to the parentage of some small, staid urchin met wandering, naked and grave, along the road with a cigar in his baby mouth, and perhaps his mother's rosary, purloined for purposes of ornamentation, hanging in a loop of beads low down on his rotund little stomach. The spiritual and temporal pastors of the mine flock were very good friends. With Dr Monygham, the medical pastor, who had accepted the charge from Mrs Gould, and lived in the hospital building, they were on not so intimate terms. But no one could be on intimate terms with El Señor Doctor, who, with his twisted shoulders, drooping head, sardonic mouth, and side-long bitter glance, was mysterious and uncanny. The other two authorities worked in harmony. Father Román, dried-up, small, alert, wrinkled, with big round eyes, a sharp chin, and a great snuff-taker, was an old campaigner, too; he had shriven many simple souls on the battlefields of the Republic, kneeling by the dying on hillsides, in the long grass, in the gloom of the forests, to hear the last confession with the smell of gunpowder smoke in his nostrils, the rattle of muskets, the hum and spatter of bullets in his ears. And where was the harm if, at the presbytery, they had a game with a pack of greasy cards in the early evening, before Don Pepe went his last rounds to see that all the watchmen of the mine – a body organized by himself – were at their posts? For that last duty before he slept Don Pepe did actually gird his old sword on the veranda of an unmistakable American white frame-house, which Father Román called the presbytery. Near by, a long, low, dark building, steeple-roofed, like a vast barn with a wooden cross over the gable, was the miners' chapel. There Father Román said Mass every day before a sombre altarpiece representing the Resurrection, the grey slab of the tombstone balanced on one corner, a figure soaring upwards, long-limbed and vivid, in an oval of pallid light, and a helmeted brown legionary smitted down, right across the bituminous foreground. 'This picture, my children, *muy linda e maravillosa*,' Father Román would say to some of his flock, 'which you behold here through the munificence of the wife of our Señor Administrator, has been painted in Europe, a country of saints and miracles, and much greater than our Costaguana.' And he would take a pinch of snuff with unction. But when once an inquisitive spirit desired to know in what direction this Europe was situated, whether up or down the coast, Father Román, to conceal his perplexity, became very reserved and severe. 'No doubt it is extremely far away. But ignorant sinners like you of the San Tomé mine should think earnestly of everlasting punishment instead of inquiring into the magnitude of the earth, with its countries and populations altogether beyond your understanding.'

With a 'Good night, Padre'; 'Good night, Don Pepe,' the Gobernador would go off, holding up his sabre against his side, his body bent forward, with a long, plodding stride in the dark. The jocularity proper to an innocent card game for a few cigars or a bundle of yerba was replaced at once by the stern duty mood of an officer setting out to visit the outposts of an encamped army. One loud blast of the whistle that hung from his neck provoked instantly a great shrilling of responding whistles, mingled with the barking of dogs, that would calm down slowly at last, away up at the head of the gorge; and in the stillness two *serenos*, on guard by the bridge, would appear walking noiselessly towards him. On one side of the road a long frame-building – the store – would be closed and barricaded from end to end; facing it another white frame-house, still longer, and with a veranda – the hospital – would have lights in the two windows of Dr Monygham's quarters. Even the delicate foliage of a clump of pepper trees did not stir, so breathless would be the darkness warmed by the radiation of the overheated rocks. Don Pepe would stand still for a moment with the two motionless *serenos* before him, and, abruptly, high up on the sheer face of the mountain, dotted with single torches, like drops of fire fallen from the two great blazing clusters of lights above, the ore shoots would begin to rattle. The great clattering, shuffling noise, gathering speed and weight, would be caught up by the walls of the gorge, and sent upon the plain in a growl of thunder. The *posadero* in Rincón swore that on calm nights, by listening intently, he could catch the sound in his doorway as of a storm in the mountains.

To Charles Gould's fancy it seemed that the sound must reach the uttermost limits of the province. Riding at night towards the mine, it would meet him at the edge of a little wood just beyond Rincón. There was no mistaking the growling mutter of the mountain pouring its stream of treasure under the stamps; and it came to his heart with the peculiar force of a proclamation thundered forth over the land and the marvellousness of an accomplished fact fulfilling an audacious desire. He had heard this desire. He had heard this very sound in his imagination on that far-off evening when his wife and himself, after a tortuous ride through a strip of forest, had reined in their horses near the stream, and had gazed for the first time upon the jungle-grown solitude of the gorge. The head of a palm rose here and there. In a high ravine round the corner of the San Tomé mountain (which is square like a blockhouse) the thread of a slender waterfall flashed bright and glassy through the dark green of the heavy fronds of tree-ferns. Don Pepe, in attendance, rode up, and, stretching his arm up the gorge, had declared with mock solemnity, 'Behold the very paradise of snakes, *señora*.'

And then they had wheeled their horses and ridden back to sleep that night at Rincón. The *alcalde* – an old, skinny Moreno, a sergeant of Guzman Bento's time – had cleared respectfully out of his house with his three pretty daughters, to make room for the foreign *señora* and their worships the *caballeros*. All he asked Charles Gould (whom he took for a mysterious and official person) to do for him was to remind the supreme Government – *el Gobierno supremo* – of a pension (amounting to about a dollar a month) to which he believed himself entitled. It had been promised to him, he affirmed, straightening his bent back martially, 'many years ago, for my valour in the wars with the wild *indios* when a young man, *señor*'.

The waterfall existed no longer. The tree-ferns that had luxuriated in its spray had dried around the dried-up pool, and the high ravine was only a big trench half filled up with the refuse of excavations and tailings. The torrent, dammed up above, sent its water rushing along the open flumes of scooped tree trunks striding on trestle-legs to the turbines working the stamps on the lower plateau – the *mesa grande* of the San Tomé mountain. Only the memory of the waterfall, with its amazing fernery, like a hanging garden above the rocks of the gorge, was preserved in Mrs Gould's water-colour sketch; she had made it hastily one day from a cleared patch in the bushes, sitting in the shade of a roof of straw erected for her on three rough poles under Don Pepe's direction.

Mrs Gould had seen it all from the beginning: the clearing of the wilderness, the making of the road, the cutting of new paths up the cliff face of San Tomé. For weeks together she had lived on the spot with her husband; and she was so little in Sulaco during that year that the appearance of the Gould carriage on the Alameda would cause social excitement. From the heavy family coaches full of stately *señoras* and black-eyed *señoritas* rolling solemnly in the shaded alley white hands were waved towards her with animation in a flutter of greetings. Doña Emilia was 'down from the mountain'.

But not for long. Doña Emilia would be gone 'up to the mountain' in a day or two, and her sleek carriage mules would have an easy time of it for another spell. She had watched the erection of the first frame-house put up on the lower *mesa* for an office and Don Pepe's quarters; she heard with a thrill of thankful emotion the first wagon-load of ore rattle down the then only shoot; she had stood by her husband's side perfectly silent, and gone cold all over with excitement at the instant when the first battery of only fifteen stamps was put in motion for the first time. On the occasion when the fires under the first set of retorts in their shed had glowed far into the night she did not retire to rest on the rough cadre set up for her in the as yet bare frame-house till she had seen the first spongy lump of silver yielded to the hazards of the world by the dark depths of the Gould Concession; she had laid her unmercenary hands, with an eagerness that made them tremble, upon the first silver ingot turned out still warm from the mould; and by her imaginative estimate of its power she endowed that lump of metal with a justificative conception, as though it were not a mere fact, but something far-reaching and impalpable, like the true expression of an emotion or the emergence of a principle.

Don Pepe, extremely interested, too, looked over her shoulder with a smile that, making longitudinal folds on his face, caused it to resemble a leathern mask with a benignantly diabolic expression.

'Would not the *muchachos* of Hernandez like to get hold of this insignificant object, that looks, *por Dios*, very much like a piece of tin?' he remarked, jocularly.

Hernandez, the robber, had been an inoffensive, small *ranchero*, kidnapped in circumstances of peculiar atrocity from his home during one of the civil wars, and forced to serve in the army. There his conduct as soldier was exemplary, till, watching his chance, he killed his colonel, and managed to get clear away. With a band of deserters, who chose him for their chief, he had taken refuge beyond the wild and waterless Bolson de Tonoro. The *haciendas* paid him blackmail in cattle and horses; extraordinary stories were told of his powers and of his wonderful escapes from capture. He used to ride, single-handed, into the villages and the little towns on the Campo, driving a pack mule before him, with two revolvers in his belt, go straight to the shop or store, select what he wanted, and ride away unopposed because of the terror his exploits and his audacity inspired. Poor country people he usually left alone; the upper class were often stopped on the roads and robbed; but any unlucky official that fell into his hands was sure to get a severe flogging. The army officers did not like his name to be mentioned in their presence. His followers, mounted on stolen horses, laughed at the pursuit of the regular cavalry sent to hunt them down, and whom they took pleasure to ambush most scientifically in the broken ground of their own fastness. Expeditions had been fitted out; a price had been put upon his head; even attempts had been made, treacherously of course, to open negotiations with him, without in the slightest way affecting the even tenor of his career. At last, in true Costaguana fashion, the Fiscal of Tonoro, who was ambitious of the glory of having reduced the famous Hernandez, offered him a sum of money and a safe conduct out of the country for the betrayal of his band. But Hernandez evidently was not of the stuff of which the distinguished military politicians and conspirators of Costaguana are made. This clever but common device (which frequently works like a charm in putting down revolutions) failed with the chief of vulgar Salteadores. It promised well for the Fiscal at first, but ended very badly for the squadron of *lanceros* posted (by the Fiscal's directions) in a fold of the ground into which Hernandez had promised to lead his unsuspecting followers. They came, indeed, at the appointed time, but creeping on their hands and knees through the bush, and only let their presence be known by a general discharge of firearms, which emptied many saddles. The troopers who escaped came riding very hard into Tonoro. It is said that their commanding officer (who, being better mounted, rode far ahead of the rest) afterwards got into a state of despairing intoxication and beat the ambitious Fiscal severely with the flat of his sabre in the presence of his wife and daughters, for bringing this disgrace upon the National Army. The highest civil official of Tonoro, falling to the ground in a swoon, was further kicked all over the body and rowelled with sharp spurs about the neck and face because of the great sensitiveness of his military colleague. This gossip of the inland Campo, so characteristic of the rulers of the country and its story of oppression, inefficiency, fatuous methods, treachery, and savage brutality, was perfectly known to Mrs Gould. That it should be accepted with no indignant comment by people of intelligence, refinement, and character as something inherent in the nature of things was one of the symptoms of degradation that had the power to exasperate her almost to the verge of despair. Still looking at the ingot of silver, she shook her head at Don Pepe's remark:

'If it had not been for the lawless tyranny of your Government, Don Pepe, many an outlaw now with Hernandez would be living peaceably and happy by the honest work of his hands.'

'*Señora*,' cried Don Pepe, with enthusiasm, 'it is true! It is as if God had given you the power to look into the very breasts of people. You have seen them working round you, Doña Emilia – meek as lambs, patient like their own *burros*, brave like lions. I have led them to the very muzzles of guns – I, who stand here before you, *señora* – in the time of Paez, who was full of generosity, and in courage only approached by the uncle of Don Carlos here, as far as I know. No wonder there are bandits in the Campo when there are none but thieves, swindlers, and sanguinary *macaques* to rule us in Sta Marta. However, all the same, a bandit is a bandit, and we shall have a dozen good straight Winchesters to ride with the silver down to Sulaco.'

Mrs Gould's ride with the first silver escort to Sulaco was the closing episode of what she called 'my camp life' before she had settled in her town-house permanently, as was proper and even necessary for the wife of the administrator of such an important institution as the San Tomé mine. For the San Tomé mine was to become an institution, a rallying-point for everything in the province that needed order and stability to live. Security seemed to flow upon this land from the mountain-gorge. The authorities of Sulaco had learned that the San Tomé mine could make it worth their while to leave things and people alone. This was the nearest approach to the rule of common sense and justice Charles Gould felt it possible to secure at first. In fact, the mine, with its organization, its population growing fiercely attached to their position of privileged safety, with its armoury, with its Don Pepe, with its armed body of *serenos* (where, it was said, many an outlaw and deserter – and even some members of Hernandez's band – had found a place), the mine was a power in the land. As a certain prominent man in Sta Marta had exclaimed with a hollow laugh, once, when discussing the line of action taken by the Sulaco authorities at a time of political crisis:

'You call these men Government officials? They? Never! They are officials of the mine – officials of the Concession – I tell you.'

The prominent man (who was then a person in power, with a lemon-coloured face and a very short and curly, not to say woolly, head of hair) went so far in his temporary discontent as to shake his yellow fist under the nose of his interlocutor, and shriek:

'Yes! All! Silence! All! I tell you! The political *jefe*, the chief of the police, the chief of the customs, the general, all, all are the officials of that Gould.'

Thereupon an intrepid but low and argumentative murmur would flow on for a space in the ministerial cabinet, and the prominent man's passion would end in a cynical shrug of the shoulders. After all, he seemed to say, what did it matter as long as the minister himself was not forgotten during his brief day of authority? But all the same, the unofficial agent of the San Tomé mine, working for a good cause, had his moments of anxiety, which were reflected in his letters to Don José Avellanos, his maternal uncle.

'No sanguinary *macaque* from Sta Marta shall set foot on that part of Costaguana which lies beyond the San Tomé bridge,' Don Pepe used to assure Mrs Gould. 'Except, of course, as an honoured guest – for our Señor Administrador is a deep *político*.' But to Charles Gould, in his own room, the old Major would remark with a grim and soldierly cheeriness, 'We are all playing our heads at this game.'

Don José Avellanos would mutter '*Imperium in imperio*, Emilia, my soul,' with an air of profound self-satisfaction which, somehow, in a curious way, seemed to contain a queer admixture of bodily discomfort. But that, perhaps, could only be visible to the initiated.

And for the initiated it was a wonderful place, this drawing-room of the Casa Gould, with its momentary glimpses of the master – El Señor Administrador – older, harder, mysteriously silent, with the lines deepened on his English, ruddy, out-of-doors complexion; flitting on his thin cavalryman's legs across the doorways, either just 'back from the mountain' or with jingling spurs and riding-whip under his arm, on the point of starting 'for the mountain'. Then Don Pepe, modestly martial in his chair, the *llanero* who seemed somehow to have found his martial jocularity, his knowledge of the world, and his manner perfect for his station, in the midst of savage armed contests with his kind; Avellanos, polished and familiar, the diplomatist with his loquacity covering much caution and wisdom in delicate advice, with his manuscript of a historical work on Costaguana, entitled *Fifty Years of Misrule*, which, at present, he thought it was not prudent (even if it were possible) 'to give to the world'; these three, and also Doña Emilia amongst them, gracious, small, and fairy-like, before the glittering tea-set, with one common master-thought in their heads, with one common feeling of a tense situation, with one ever-present aim to preserve the inviolable character of the mine at every cost. And there was also to be seen Captain Mitchell, a little apart, near one of the long windows, with an air of old-fashioned neat old bachelorhood about him, slightly pompous, in a white waistcoat, a little disregarded and unconscious of it; utterly in the dark, and imagining himself to be in the thick of things. The good man, having spent a clear thirty years of his life on the high seas before getting what he called a 'shore billet', was astonished at the importance of transactions (other than relating to shipping) which take place on dry land. Almost every event out of the usual daily course 'marked an epoch' for him or else was 'history'; unless with his pomposity struggling with a discomfited droop of his rubicund, rather handsome face, set off by snow-white close hair and short whiskers, he would mutter:

'Ah, that! That, sir, was a mistake.'

The reception of the first consignment of San Tomé silver for shipment to San Francisco in one of O.S.N. Company's mailboats had, of course, 'marked an epoch' for Captain Mitchell. The ingots packed in boxes of stiff ox-hide with plaited handles, small enough to be carried easily by two men, were brought down by the *serenos* of the mine walking in careful couples down the half mile or so of steep, zigzag paths to the foot of the mountain. There they would be loaded into a string of two-wheeled carts, resembling roomy coffers with a door at the back, and harnessed tandem with two mules each, waiting under the guard of armed and mounted *serenos*. Don Pepe padlocked each door in succession, and at the signal of his whistle the string of carts would move off, closely surrounded by the clank of spur and carbine, with jolts and cracking of whips, with a sudden deep rumble over the boundary bridge ('into the land of thieves and sanguinary *macaques*', Don Pepe defined that crossing); hats bobbing in the first light of the dawn, on the heads of cloaked figures; Winchesters on hip; bridle hands protruding lean and brown from under the falling folds of the ponchos. The convoy, skirting a little wood, along the mine trail, between the mud huts and low walls of Rincón, increased its pace on the *camino real*, mules urged to speed, escort galloping, Don Carlos riding alone ahead of a dust storm affording a vague vision of long ears of mules, of fluttering little green and white flags stuck upon each cart; of raised arms in a mob of sombreros with the white gleam of ranging eyes; and Don Pepe, hardly visible in the rear of that rattling dust trail, with a stiff seat and impassive face, rising and falling rhythmically on a ewe-necked silver-bitted black brute with a hammer head.

The sleepy people in the little clusters of huts, in the small *ranchos* near the road, recognized by the headlong sound the charge of the San Tomé silver escort towards the crumbling wall of the city on the Campo side. They came to the doors to see it dash by over ruts and stones, with a clatter and clank and cracking of whips, with the reckless rush and precise driving of a field battery hurrying into action, and the solitary English figure of the Señor Administrador riding far ahead in the lead.

In the fenced roadside paddocks loose horses galloped wildly for a while; the heavy cattle stood up breast deep in the grass, lowing mutteringly at the flying noise; a meek Indian villager would glance back once and hasten to shove his loaded little donkey bodily against a wall, out of the way of the San Tomé silver escort going to the sea; a small knot of chilly *leperos* under the Stone Horse of the Alameda would mutter: '*Caramba*!' on seeing it take a wide curve at a gallop and dart into the empty street of the Constitution; for it was considered the correct thing, the only proper style by the mule-drivers of the San Tomé mine to go through the waking town from end to end without a check in the speed as if chased by a devil.

The early sunshine glowed on the delicate primrose, pale pink, pale blue fronts of the big houses with all their gates shut yet, and no face behind the iron bars of the windows. In the whole sunlit range of empty balconies along the street only one white figure would be visible high up above the clear pavement – the wife of the Señor Administrador – leaning over to see the escort go by to the harbour, a mass of heavy, fair hair twisted up negligently on her little head, and a lot of lace about the neck of her muslin wrapper. With a smile to her husband's single, quick, upward glance, she would watch the whole thing stream past below her feet with an orderly uproar, till she answered by a friendly sign the salute of the galloping Don Pepe, the stiff, deferential inclination with a sweep of the hat below the knee.

The string of padlocked carts lengthened, the size of the escort grew bigger as the years went on. Every three months an increasing stream of treasure swept through the streets of Sulaco on its way to the strong room in the O.S.N. Company's building by the harbour, there to await shipment for the north. Increasing in volume, and of immense value also; for, as Charles Gould told his wife once with some exultation, there had never been seen anything in the world to approach the vein of the Gould Concession. For them both, each passing of the escort under the balconies of the Casa Gould was like another victory gained in the conquest of peace for Sulaco.

No doubt the initial action of Charles Gould had been helped at the beginning by a period of comparative peace which occurred just about that time; and also by the general softening of manners as compared with the epoch of civil wars whence had emerged the iron tyranny of Guzman Bento of fearful memory. In the contests that broke out at the end of his rule (which had kept peace in the country for a whole fifteen years) there was more fatuous imbecility, plenty of cruelty and suffering still, but much less of the old-time fierce and blindly ferocious political fanaticism. It was all more vile, more base, more contemptible, and infinitely more manageable in the very outspoken cynicism of motives. It was more clearly a brazen-faced scramble for a constantly diminishing quantity of booty; since all enterprise had been stupidly killed in the land. Thus it came to pass that the province of Sulaco, once the field of cruel party vengeances, had become in a way one of the considerable prizes of political career. The great of the earth (in Sta Marta) reserved the posts in the old Occidental State to those nearest and dearest to them; nephews, brothers, husbands of favourite sisters, bosom friends, trusty supporters – or prominent supporters of whom perhaps they were afraid. It was the blessed province of great opportunities and of largest salaries; for the San Tomé mine had its own unofficial pay list, whose items and amounts, fixed in consultation by Charles Gould and Señor Avellanos, were known to a prominent businessman in the United States, who for twenty minutes or so in every month gave his undivided attention to Sulaco affairs. At the same time the material interests of all sorts, backed up by the influence of the San Tomé mine, were quietly gathering substance in that part of the Republic. If, for instance, the Sulaco Collectorship was generally understood, in the political world of the capital, to open the way to the Ministry of Finance, and so on for every official post, then, on the other hand, the despondent business circles of the Republic had come to consider the Occidental Province as the promised land of safety, especially if a man managed to get on good terms with the administration of the mine. 'Charles Gould; excellent fellow! Absolutely necessary to make sure of him before taking a single step. Get an introduction to him from Moraga if you can – the agent of the King of Sulaco, don't you know.'

No wonder, then, that Sir John, coming from Europe to smooth the path for his railway, had been meeting the name (and even the nickname) of Charles Gould at every turn in Costaguana. The agent of San Tomé Administration in Sta Marta (a polished, well-informed gentleman, Sir John thought him) had certainly helped so greatly in bringing about the presidential tour that he began to think that there was something in the faint whispers hinting at the immense occult influence of the Gould Concession. What was currently whispered was this – that the San Tomé Administration had, in part, at least, financed the last revolution, which had brought into a five-year dictatorship Don Vincente Ribiera, a man of culture and of unblemished character, invested with a mandate of reform by the best elements of the State. Serious, well-informed men seemed to believe the fact, to hope for better things, for the establishment of legality, of good faith and order in public life. So much the better, then, thought Sir John. He worked always on a great scale; there was a loan to the State, and a project for systematic colonization of the Occidental Province, involved in one vast scheme with the construction of the National Central Railway. Good faith, order, honesty, peace, were badly wanted for this great development of material interests. Anybody on the side of these things, and especially if able to help, had an importance in Sir John's eyes. He had not been disappointed in the 'King of

Sulaco'. The local difficulties had fallen away, as the engineer-in-chief had foretold they would, before Charles Gould's mediation. Sir John had been extremely fêted in Sulaco, next to the President-Dictator, a fact which might have accounted for the evident ill-humour General Montero displayed at lunch given on board the *Juno* just before she was to sail, taking away from Sulaco the President-Dictator and the distinguished foreign guests in his train.

The Excellentissimo ('the hope of honest men', as Don José had addressed him in a public speech delivered in the name of the Provincial Assembly of Sulaco) sat at the head of the long table; Captain Mitchell, positively stony-eyed and purple in the face with the solemnity of this 'historical event', occupied the foot as the representative of the O.S.N. Company in Sulaco, the hosts of that informal function, with the captain of the ship and some minor officials from the shore around him. Those cheery, swarthy little gentlemen cast jovial side-glances at the bottles of champagne beginning to pop behind the guests' backs in the hands of the ship's stewards. The amber wine creamed up to the rims of the glasses.

Charles Gould had his place next to a foreign envoy, who, in a listless undertone, had been talking to him fitfully of hunting and shooting. The well-nourished, pale face, with an eye-glass and drooping yellow moustache, made the Señor Administrador appear by contrast twice as sunbaked, more flaming red, a hundred times more intensely and silently alive. Don José Avellanos touched elbows with the other foreign diplomat, a dark man with a quiet, watchful, self-confident demeanour, and a touch of reserve. All etiquette being laid aside on the occasion, General Montero was the only one there in full uniform, so stiff with embroideries in front that his braod chest seemed protected by a cuirass of gold. Sir John at the beginning had got away from high places for the sake of sitting near Mrs Gould.

The great financier was trying to express to her his grateful sense of her hospitality and of his obligation to her husband's 'enormous influence in this part of the country', when she interrupted him by a low 'Hush!' The President was going to make an informal pronouncement.

The Excellentissimo was on his legs. He said only a few words, evidently deeply felt, and meant perhaps mostly for Avellanos – his old friend – as to the necessity of unremitting effort to secure the lasting welfare of the country emerging after this last struggle, he hoped, into a period of peace and material prosperity.

Mrs Gould, listening to the mellow, slightly mournful voice, looking at this rotund, dark, spectacled face, at the short body, obese to the point of infirmity, thought that this man of delicate and melancholy mind, physically almost a cripple, coming out of his retirement into a dangerous strife at the call of his fellows, had the right to speak with the authority of his self-sacrifice. And yet she was made uneasy. He was more pathetic than promising, this first civilian Chief of the State Costaguana had ever known, pronouncing, glass in hand, his simple watchwords of honesty, peace, respect for law, political good faith abroad and at home – the safeguards of national honour.

He sat down. During the respectful, appreciative buzz of voices that followed the speech, General Montero raised a pair of heavy, drooping eyelids and rolled his eyes with a sort of uneasy dullness from face to face. The military backwoods hero of the party, though secretly impressed by the sudden novelties and splendours of his position (he had never been on board a ship before, and had hardly ever seen the sea except from a distance), understood by a sort of instinct the advantage his surly, unpolished attitude of a savage fighter gave him amongst all these refined Blanco aristocrats. But why was it that nobody was looking at him? he wondered to himself angrily. He was able to spell out the print of newspapers, and knew that he had performed the 'greatest military exploit of modern times'.

'My husband wanted the railway,' Mrs Gould said to Sir John in the general murmur of resumed conversations. 'All this brings nearer the sort of future we desire for the country, which has waited for it in sorrow long enough, God knows. But I will confess that the other day, during my afternoon drive when I suddenly saw an Indian boy ride out of a wood with the red flag of a surveying party in his hand, I felt something of a shock. The future means change – an utter change. And yet even here there are simple and picturesque things that one would like to preserve.'

Sir John listened, smiling. But it was his turn now to hush Mrs Gould.

'General Montero is going to speak,' he whispered, and almost immediately added, in comic alarm, 'Heavens! he's going to propose my own health, I believe.'

General Montero had risen with a jingle of steel scabbard and a ripple of glitter on his gold-embroidered breast; a heavy swordhilt appeared at his side above the edge of the table. In this gorgeous uniform, with his bull neck, his hooked nose flattened on the tip upon a blue-black, dyed moustache, he looked like a disguised and sinister *vaquero*. The drone of his voice had a strangely rasping, soulless ring. He floundered, lowering, through a few vague sentences; then suddenly raising his big head and his voice together, burst out harshly:

'The honour of the country is in the hands of the army. I assure you I shall be faithful to it.' He hesitated till his roaming eyes met Sir John's face, upon which he fixed a lurid, sleepy glance; and the figure of the lately negotiated loan came into his mind. He lifted his glass. 'I drink to the health of the man who brings us a million and a half of pounds.'

He tossed off his champagne, and sat down heavily with a half-surprised, half-bullying look all round the faces in the profound, as if appalled, silence which succeeded the felicitous toast. Sir John did not move.

'I don't think I am called upon to rise,' he murmured to Mrs Gould. 'That sort of thing speaks for itself.' But Don José Avellanos came to the rescue with a short oration, in which he alluded pointedly to England's goodwill towards Costaguana – 'a goodwill,' he continued significantly, 'of which I, having been in my time accredited to the Court of St James, am able to speak with some knowledge.'

Only then Sir John thought fit to respond, which he did gracefully in bad French, punctuated by bursts of applause and the 'Hear! Hears!' of Captain Mitchell, who was able to understand a word now and then. Directly he had done, the financier of railways turned to Mrs Gould:

'You were good enough to say that you intended to ask me for something,' he reminded her, gallantly. 'What is it? Be assured that any request from you would be considered in the light of a favour to myself.'

She thanked him by a gracious smile. Everybody was rising from the table.

'Let us go on deck,' she proposed, 'where I'll be able to point out to you the very object of my request.'

An enormous national flag of Costaguana, diagonal red and yellow, with two green palm trees in the middle, floated lazily at the mainmast head of the *Juno*. A multitude of fireworks being let off in their thousands at the water's edge in honour of the President kept up a mysterious crepitating noise half round the harbour. Now and then a lot of rockets, swishing upwards invisibly, detonated overhead with only a puff of smoke in the bright sky. Crowds of people could be seen between the town gate and the harbour, under the bunches of multicoloured flags fluttering on tall poles. Faint bursts of military music would be heard suddenly, and the remote sound of shouting. A knot of ragged Negroes at the end of the wharf kept on loading and firing a small iron cannon time after time. A greyish haze of dust hung thin and motionless against the sun.

Don Vincente Ribiera made a few steps under the deck-awning, leaning on the arm of Señor Avellanos; a wide circle was formed round him, where the mirthless smile of his dark lips and the sightless glitter of his spectacles could be seen turning amiably from side to side. The informal function arranged on purpose on board the *Juno* to give the President-Dictator an opportunity to meet intimately some of his most notable adherents in Sulaco was drawing to an end. On one side, General Montero, his bald head covered now by a plumed cocked hat, remained motionless on a skylight seat, a pair of big gauntleted hands folded on the hilt of the sabre standing upright between his legs. The white plume, the coppery tint of his broad face, the blue-black of the moustaches under the curved beak, the mass of gold on sleeves and breast, the high shining boots with enormous spurs, the working nostrils, the imbecile and domineering stare of the glorious victor of Río Seco had in them something ominous and incredible; the exaggeration of a cruel caricature, the fatuity of solemn masquerading, the atrocious grotesqueness of some military idol of Aztec conception and European bedecking, awaiting the homage of worshippers. Don José approached diplomatically this weird and inscrutable portent, and Mrs Gould turned her fascinated eyes away at last.

Charles, coming up to take leave of Sir John, heard him say, as he bent over his wife's hand, 'Certainly. Of course, my dear Mrs Gould, for a protégé of yours! Not the slightest difficulty. Consider it done.'

Going ashore in the same boat with the Goulds, Don José Avellanos was very silent. Even in the Gould carriage he did not open his lips for a long time. The mules trotted slowly away from the wharf between the extended hands of the beggars, who for that day seemed to have abandoned in a body the portals of churches. Charles Gould sat on the back seat and looked away upon the plain. A multitude of booths made of green boughs, of rushes, of odd pieces of plank eked out with bits of canvas had been erected all over it for the sale of cana, of dulces, of fruit, of cigars. Over little heaps of glowing charcoal Indian women, squatting on mats, cooked food in black earthen pots, and boiled the water for the maté gourds, which they offered in soft, caressing voices to the country people. A racecourse had been staked out for the *vaqueros*; and away to the left, from where the crowd was massed thickly about a huge temporary erection, like a circus tent of wood with a conical grass roof, came the resonant twanging of harp strings, the sharp ping of guitars, with the grave drumming throb of an Indian gombo pulsating steadily through the shrill choruses of the dancers.

Charles Gould said presently:

'All this piece of land belongs now to the Railway Company. There will be no more popular feasts held here.'

Mrs Gould was rather sorry to think so. She took this opportunity to mention how she had just obtained from Sir John the promise that the house occupied by Giorgio Viola should not be interfered with. She declared she could never understand why the survey engineers ever talked of demolishing that old building. It was not in the way of the projected harbour branch of the line in the least.

She stopped the carriage before the door to reassure at once the old Genoese, who came out bare-headed and stood by the carriage step. She talked to him in Italian, of course, and he thanked her with calm dignity. An old Garibaldino was grateful to her from the bottom of his heart for keeping the roof over the heads of his wife and children. He was too old to wander any more.

'And is it for ever, *signora*?' he asked.

'For as long as you like.'

'*Bene*. Then the place must be named. It was not worth while before.'

He smiled ruggedly, with a running together of wrinkles at the corners of his eyes. 'I shall set about the painting of the name tomorrow.'

'And what is it going to be, Giorgio?'

'Albergo d'Italia Una,' said the old Garibaldino, looking away for a moment. 'More in memory of those who have died,' he added, 'than for the country stolen from us soldiers of liberty by the craft of that accursed Piedomontese race of kings and ministers.'

Mrs Gould smiled slightly, and, bending over a little, began to inquire about his wife and children. He had sent them into town on that day. The *padrona* was better in health; many thanks to the *signora* for inquiring.

People were passing in twos and threes, in whole parties of men and women attended by trotting children. A horseman mounted on a silver-grey mare drew rein quietly in the shade of the house after taking off his hat to the party in the carriage, who returned smiles and familiar nods. Old Viola, evidently very pleased with the news he had just heard, interrupted himself for a moment to tell him rapidly that the house was secured, by the kindness of the English *signora*, for as long as he liked to keep it. The other listened attentively, but made no response.

When the carriage moved on he took off his hat again, a grey sombrero with a silver cord and tassels. The bright colours of a Mexican serape twisted on the cantle, the enormous silver buttons on the embroidered leather jacket, the row of tiny silver buttons down the seam of the trousers, the snowy linen, a silk sash with embroidered ends, the silver plates on headstall and saddle, proclaimed the unapproachable style of the famous Capataz de Cargadores – a Mediterranean sailor – got up with more finished splendour than any well-to-do young *ranchero* of the Campo had ever displayed on a high holiday.

'It is a great thing for me,' murmured old Giorgio, still thinking of the house, for now he had grown weary of change. 'The *signora* just said a word to the Englishman.'

'The old Englishman who has enough money to pay for a railway? He is going off in an hour,' remarked Nostromo, carelessly. '*Buon viaggio*, then. I've guarded his bones all the way from the Entrada pass down to the plain and into Sulaco, as though he had been my own father.'

Old Giorgio only moved his head sideways absently. Nostromo pointed after the Goulds' carriage, nearing the grass-grown gate in the old town wall that was like a wall of matted jungle.

'And I have sat alone at night with my revolver in the Company's warehouse time and again by the side of that other Englishman's heap of silver, guarding it as though it had been my own.'

Viola seemed lost in thought. 'It is a great thing for me,' he repeated again, as if to himself.

'It is,' agreed the magnificent Capataz de Cargadores, calmly. 'Listen, *vecchio* – go in and bring me out a cigar, but don't look for it in my room. There's nothing there.'

Viola stepped into the café and came out directly, still absorbed in this idea, and tendered him a cigar, mumbling thoughtfully in his moustache. 'Children growing up – and girls, too! Girls!' He sighed and fell silent.

'What, only one?' remarked Nostromo, looking down with a sort of comic inquisitiveness at the unconscious old man. 'No matter,' he added, with lofty negligence; 'one is enough till another is wanted.'

He lit and let the match drop from his passive fingers. Giorgio Viola looked up, and said abruptly:

'My son would have been just such a fine young man as you, Gian' Battista, if he had lived.'

'What? Your son? But you are right, *padrone*. If he had been like me he would have been a man.'

He turned his horse slowly, and paced on between the booths, checking the mare almost to a standstill now and then for children, for the groups of people from the distant Campo, who stared after him with admiration. The Company's lightermen saluted him from afar; and the greatly envied Capataz de Cargadores advanced, amongst murmurs of recognition and obsequious greetings, towards the huge circus-like erection. The throng thickened; the guitars tinkled louder; other horsemen sat motionless, smoking calmly above the heads of the crowd; it eddied and pushed before the doors of the high-roofed building, whence issued a shuffle and thumping of feet in time to the dance music vibrating and shrieking with a racking rhythm, overhung by the tremendous, sustained, hollow roar of the gombo. The barbarous and imposing noise of the big drum, that can madden a crowd, and that even Europeans cannot hear without a strange emotion, seemed to draw Nostromo on to its source, while a man, wrapped up in a faded, torn poncho, walked by his stirrup, and, buffeted right and left, begged 'his worship' insistently for employment on the wharf. He whined, offering the Señor Capataz half his daily pay for the privilege of being admitted to the swaggering fraternity of *cargadores*; the other half would be enough for him, he protested.

But Captain Mitchell's right-hand man – 'invaluable for our work – perfectly incorruptible fellow' – after looking down critically at the ragged *mozo*, shook his head without a word in the uproar going on around.

The man fell back; and a little farther on Nostromo had to pull up. From the doors of the dance-hall men and women emerged tottering, streaming with sweat, trembling in every limb, to lean, panting, with staring eyes and parted lips, against the wall of the structure, where the harps and guitars played on with mad speed in an incessant roll of thunder. Hundreds of hands clapped in there; voices shrieked, and then all at once would sink low, chanting in unison the refrain of a love song, with a dying fall. A red flower, flung with a good aim from somewhere in the crowd, struck the resplendent Capataz on the cheek.

He caught it as it fell, neatly, but for some time did not turn his head. When at last he condescended to look round, the throng near him had parted to make way for a pretty Morenita, her hair held up by a small golden comb, who was walking towards him in the open space.

Her arms and neck emerged plump and bare from a snowy chemisette; the blue woollen skirt, with all the fullness gathered in front, scanty on the hips and tight across the back, disclosed the provoking action of her walk. She came straight on and laid her hand on the mare's neck with a timid, coquettish look upwards out of the corner of her eyes.

'*Querido*,' she murmured, caressingly, 'why do you pretend not to see me when I pass?'

'Because I don't love thee any more,' said Nostromo, deliberately, after a moment of reflective silence.

The hand on the mare's neck trembled suddenly. She dropped her head before all the eyes in the wide circle formed round the generous, the terrible, the inconstant Capataz de Cargadores, and his Morenita.

Nostromo, looking down, saw tears beginning to fall down her face.

'Has it come true, then, ever beloved of my heart?' she whispered. 'Is it true?'

'No,' said Nostromo, looking away carelessly. 'It was a lie. I love thee as much as ever.'

'Is that true?' she cooed, joyously, her cheeks still wet with tears.

'It is true.'

'True on the life?'

'As true as that; but thou must not ask me to swear it on the Madonna that stands in thy room.' And the Capataz laughed a little in response to the grins of the crowd.

She pouted – very pretty – a little uneasy.

'No, I will not ask for that. I can see love in your eyes.' She laid her hand on his knee. 'Why are you trembling like this? From love?' she continued, while the cavernous thundering of the gombo went on without a pause. 'But if you love her as much as that, you must give your Paquita a gold-mounted rosary of beads for the neck of her Madonna.'

'No,' said Nostromo, looking into her uplifted, begging eyes, which suddenly turned stony with surprise.

'No? Then what else will your worship give me on the day of the fiesta?' she asked, angrily: 'so as not to shame me before all these people.'

'There is no shame for thee in getting nothing from thy lover for once.'

'True! The shame is your worship's – my poor lover's,' she flared up, sarcastically.

Laughs were heard at her anger, at her retort. What an audacious spitfire she was! The people aware of this scene were calling out urgently to others in the crowd. The circle round the silver-grey mare narrowed slowly.

The girl went off a pace or two, confronting the mocking curiosity of the eyes, then flung back to the stirrup, tiptoeing, her enraged face turned up to Nostromo with a pair of blazing eyes. He bent low to her in the saddle.

'Juan,' she hissed, 'I could stab thee to the heart!'

The dreaded Capataz de Cargadores, magnificent and carelessly public in his amours, flung his arm round her neck and kissed her spluttering lips. A murmur went round.

'A knife!' he demanded at large, holding her firmly by the shoulder.

Twenty blades flashed out together in the circle. A young man in holiday attire, bounding in, thrust one in Nostromo's hand and bounded back into the ranks, very proud of himself. Nostromo had not even looked at him.

'Stand on my foot,' he commanded the girl, who, suddenly subdued, rose lightly, and when he had her up, encircling her waist, her face near to his, he pressed the knife into her little hand.

'No, Morenita! You shall not put me to shame,' he said. 'You shall have your present; and so that everyone should know who is your lover today, you may cut all the silver buttons off my coat.'

There were shouts of laughter and applause at this witty freak, while the girl passed the keen blade, and the impassive rider jingled in his palm the increasing hoard of silver buttons. He eased her to the ground with both her hands full. After whispering for a while with a very strenuous face, she walked away, staring haughtily, and vanished into the crowd.

The circle had broken up, and the lordly Capataz de Cargadores, the indispensable man, the tried and trusty Nostromo, the Mediterranean sailor come ashore casually to try his luck in Costaguana, rode slowly towards the harbour. The *Juno* was just then swinging round; and even as Nostromo reined up again to look on, a flag ran up on the improvised flagstaff erected in an ancient and dismantled little fort at the harbour entrance. Half a battery of field guns had been hurried over there from the Sulaco barracks for the purpose of firing the regulation salutes for the President-Dictator and the War Minister. As the mail-boat headed through the pass, the badly timed reports announced the end of Don Vincente Ribiera's first official visit to Sulaco, and for Captain Mitchell the end of another 'historic occasion'. Next time when the 'Hope of honest men' was to come that way, a year and a half later, it was unofficially, over the mountain tracks, fleeing after a defeat on a lame mule, to be only just saved by Nostromo from an ignominious death at the hands of a mob. It was a very different event, of which Captain Mitchell used to say:

'It was history – history, sir! And that fellow of mine, Nostromo, you know, was right in it. Absolutely making history, sir.'

But this event, creditable to Nostromo, was to lead immediately to another, which could not be classed either as 'history' or as 'a mistake' in Captain Mitchell's phraseology. He had another word for it.

'Sir,' he used to say afterwards, 'that was no mistake. It was a fatality. A misfortune, pure and simple, sir. And that poor fellow of mine was right in it – right in the middle of it! A fatality, if ever there was one – and to my mind he has never been the same man since.'

Part Two

The Isabels

Chapter I

Through good and evil report in the varying fortune of that struggle which Don José had characterized in the phrase, 'the fate of national honesty trembles in the balance', the Gould Concession, '*Imperium in Imperio*', had gone on working; the square mountain had gone on pouring its treasure down the wooden shoots to the unresting batteries of stamps; the lights of San Tomé had twinkled night after night upon the great, limitless shadow of the Campo; every three months the silver escort had gone down to the sea as if neither the war nor its consequences could ever affect the ancient Occidental State secluded beyond its high barrier of the Cordillera. All the fighting took place on the other side of that mighty wall of serrated peaks lorded over by the white dome of Higuerota and as yet breached by the railway, of which only the first part, the easy Campo part from Sulaco to the Ivie Valley at the foot of the pass, had been laid. Neither did the telegraph line cross the mountains yet; its poles, like slender beacons on the plain, penetrated into the forest fringe of the foothills cut by the deep avenue of the track; and its wire ended abruptly in the construction camp at a white deal table supporting a Morse apparatus, in a long hut of planks with a corrugated-iron roof overshadowed by gigantic cedar trees – the quarters of the engineer in charge of the advance section.

The harbour was busy too, with the traffic in railway material, and with the movements of troops along the coast. The O.S.N. Company had found much occupation for its fleet. Costaguana had no navy, and, apart from a few coastguard cutters, there were no national ships except a couple of old merchant steamers used as transports.

Captain Mitchell, feeling more and more in the thick of history, found time for an hour or so during an afternoon in the drawing-room of the Casa Gould, where, with a strange ignorance of the real forces at work around him, he professed himself delighted to get away from the strain of affairs. He did not know what he would have done without his invaluable Nostromo, he declared. Those confounded Costaguana politics gave him more work – he confided to Mrs Gould – than he had bargained for.

Don José Avellanos had displayed in the service of the endangered Ribiera Government an organizing activity and an eloquence of which the echoes reached even Europe. For, after the new loan to the Ribiera Government, Europe had become interested in Costaguana. The Sala of the Provincial Assembly (in the Municipal Buildings of Sulaco), with its portraits of the Liberators on the walls and an old flag of Cortés preserved in a glass case above the President's chair, had heard all these speeches – the early one containing the impassioned declaration 'Militarism is the enemy', the famous one of the 'trembling balance' delivered on the occasion of the vote for the raising of a second Sulaco regiment in the defence of the reforming Government; and when the provinces again displayed their old flags (proscribed in Guzman Bento's time) there was another of those great orations, when Don José greeted these old emblems of the war of Independence, brought out again in the name of new Ideals. The old idea of Federalism had disappeared. For his part he did not wish to revive old political doctrines. They were perishable. They died. But the doctrine of political rectitude was immortal. The second Sulaco regiment, to whom he was presenting this flag, was going to show its valour in a contest for order, peace, progress; for the establishment of national self-respect without which – he declared with energy – 'we are a reproach and a byword amongst the powers of the world'.

Don José Avellanos loved his country. He had served it lavishly with his fortune during his diplomatic career, and the later story of his captivity and barbarous ill-usage under Guzman Bento was well known to his listeners. It was a wonder that he had not been a victim of the ferocious and summary executions which marked the course of that tyranny; for Guzman had ruled the country with the sombre imbecility of political fanaticism. The power of Supreme Government had become in his dull mind an object of strange worship, as if it were some sort of cruel deity. It was incarnated in himself, and his adversaries, the Federalists, were the supreme sinners, objects of hate, abhorrence, and fear, as heretics would be to a convinced Inquisitor. For years he had carried about at the tail of the Army of Pacification, all over the country, a captive band of such atrocious criminals, who considered themselves most unfortunate at not having been summarily executed. It was a diminishing company of nearly naked skeletons, loaded with irons, covered with dirt, with vermin, with raw wounds, all men of positions, of education, of wealth, who had learned to fight amongst themselves for scraps of rotten beef thrown to them by soldiers, or to beg a Negro cook for a drink of muddy water in pitiful accents. Don José Avellanos, clanking his chains amongst the others, seemed only to exist in order to prove how much hunger, pain, degradation, and cruel torture a human body can stand without parting with the last spark of life. Sometimes interrogatories, backed by some primitive method of torture, were administered to them by a commission of officers hastily assembled in a hut of sticks and branches, and made pitiless by the fear for their own lives. A lucky one or two of that spectral company of prisoners would perhaps be led tottering behind a bush to be shot by a file of soldiers. Always an army chaplain – some unshaven, dirty man, girt with a sword and with a tiny cross embroidered in white cotton on the left breast of a lieutenant's uniform – would follow, cigarette in the corner of the mouth, wooden stool in hand, to hear the confession and give absolution; for the Citizen Saviour of the Country (Guzman Bento was called thus officially in petitions) was not averse from the exercise of rational clemency. The irregular report of the firing squad would be heard, followed sometimes by a single finishing shot; a little bluish cloud of smoke would float up above the green bushes, and the Army of Pacification would move on over the savannas, through the forests, crossing rivers, invading rural *pueblos*, devastating the *haciendas* of the horrid aristocrats, occupying the inlaid towns in the fulfilment of its patriotic mission, and leaving behind a united land wherein the evil taint of Federalism could no longer be detected in the smoke of burning houses and the smell of spilt blood.

Don José Avellanos had survived that time.

Perhaps, when contemptuously signifying to him his release, the Citizen Saviour of the Country might have thought this benighted aristocrat too broken in health and spirit and fortune to be any longer dangerous. Or, perhaps, it may have been a simple caprice. Guzman Bento, usually full of fanciful fears and brooding suspicions, had sudden accesses of unreasonable self-confidence when he perceived himself elevated on a pinnacle of power and safety beyond the reach of mere mortal plotters. At such times he would impulsively command the celebration of a solemn Mass of thanksgiving which would be sung in great pomp in the cathedral of Sta Marta by the trembling, subservient Archbishop of his creation. He heard it sitting in a gilt armchair placed before the high altar, surrounded by the civil and military heads of his Government. The unofficial world of Sta Marta would crowd into the cathedral, for it was not quite safe for anybody of mark to stay away from these manifestations of presidential piety. Having thus acknowledged the only power he was at all disposed to recognize as above himself, he would scatter acts of political grace in a sardonic wantonness of clemency. There was no other way left now to enjoy his power but by seeing his crushed adversaries crawl impotently into the light of day out of the dark, noisome cells of the Collegio. Their harmlessness fed his insatiable vanity, and they could always be got hold of again. It was the rule for all the women of their families to present thanks afterwards in a special audience. The incarnation of that strange god, El Gobierno Supremo, received them standing, cocked hat on head, and exhorted them in a menacing mutter to show their gratitude by bringing up their children in fidelity to the democratic form of government, 'which I have established for the happiness of our country'. His front teeth having been knocked out in some accident of his former herdsman's life, his utterance was spluttering and indistinct. He had been working for Costaguana alone in the midst of treachery and opposition. Let it cease now lest he should become weary of forgiving!

Don José Avellanos had known this forgiveness.

He was broken in health and fortune deplorably enough to present a truly gratifying spectacle to the supreme chief of democratic institutions. He retired to Sulaco. His wife had an estate in that province, and she nursed him back to life out of the house of death and captivity. When she died, their daughter, an only child, was old enough to devote herself to 'poor papa'.

Miss Avellanos, born in Europe and educated partly in England, was a tall, grave girl, with a self-possessed manner, a wide, white forehead, a wealth of rich brown hair, and blue eyes.

The other young ladies of Sulaco stood in awe of her character and accomplishments. She was reputed to be terribly learned and serious. As to pride, it was well known that all the Corbeláns were proud, and her mother was a Corbelán. Don José Avellanos depended very much upon the devotion of his beloved Antonia. He accepted it in the benighted way of men, who, though made in God's image, are like stone idols without sense before the smoke of certain burnt offerings. He was ruined in every way, but a man possessed of passion is not bankrupt in life. Don José Avellanos desired passionately for his country: peace, prosperity, and (as the end of the preface to *Fifty Years of Misrule* has it) 'an honourable place in the comity of civilized nations'. In this last phrase the Minister Plenipotentiary, cruelly humiliated by the bad faith of his Government towards the foreign bondholders, stands disclosed in the patriot.

The fatuous turmoil of greedy factions succeeding the tyranny of Guzman Bento seemed to bring his desire to the very door of opportunity. He was too old to descend personally into the centre of the arena at Sta Marta. But the men who acted there sought his advice at every step. He himself thought that he could be most useful at a distance, in Sulaco. His name, his connections, his former position, his experience commanded the respect of his class. The discovery that this man, living in dignified poverty in the Corbelán town residence (opposite the Casa Gould), could dispose of material means towards the support of the cause increased his influence. It was his open letter of appeal that decided the candidature of Don Vincente Ribiera for the Presidency. Another of these informal State papers drawn up by Don José (this time in the shape of an address from the Province) induced that scrupulous constitutionalist to accept the extraordinary powers conferred upon him for five years by an overwhelming vote of congress in Sta Marta. It was a specific mandate to establish the prosperity of the people on the basis of firm peace at home, and to redeem the national credit by the satisfaction of all just claims abroad.

In the afternoon the news of that vote had reached Sulaco by the usual roundabout postal way through Cayta, and up the coast by steamer. Don José, who had been waiting for the mail in the Gould's drawing-room, got out of the rocking-chair, letting his hat fall off his knees. He rubbed his silvery, short hair with both hands, speechless with the excess of joy.

'Emilia, my soul,' he had burst out, 'let me embrace you! Let me –'

Captain Mitchell, had he been there, would no doubt have made an apt remark about the dawn of a new era; but if Don José thought something of the kind, his eloquence failed him on this occasion. The inspirer of that revival of the Blanco party tottered where he stood. Mrs Gould moved forward quickly and, as she offered her cheek with a smile to her old friend, managed very cleverly to give him the support of her arm he really needed.

Don José had recovered himself at once, but for a time he could do no more than murmur. 'Oh, you two patriots! Oh, you two patriots!' – looking from one to the other. Vague plans of another historical work, wherein all the devotions to the regeneration of the country he loved would be enshrined for the reverent worship of posterity, flitted through his mind. The historian who had enough elevation of soul to write of Guzman Bento: 'Yet this monster, imbrued in the blood of his countrymen, must not be held unreservedly to the execration of future years. It appears to be true that he, too, loved his country. He had given it twelve years of peace; and, absolute master of lives and fortunes as he was, he died poor. His worst fault, perhaps, was not his ferocity, but his ignorance'; the man who could write thus of a cruel persecutor (the passage occurs in his *History of Misrule*) felt at the foreshadowing of success an almost boundless affection for his two helpers, for these two young people from over the sea.

Just as years ago, calmly, from the conviction of practical necessity, stronger than any abstract political doctrine, Henry Gould had drawn the sword, so now, the times being changed, Charles Gould had flung the silver of the San Tomé into the fray. The Inglés of Sulaco, the 'Costaguana Englishman' of the third generation, was as far from being a political intriguer as his uncle from a revolutionary swashbuckler. Springing from the instinctive uprightness of their natures their action was reasoned. They saw an opportunity and used the weapon to hand.

Charles Gould's position – a commanding position in the background of that attempt to retrieve the peace and the credit of the Republic – was very clear. At the beginning he had had to accommodate himself to existing circumstances of corruption so naïvely brazen as to disarm the hatred of a man courageous enough not to be afraid of its irresponsible potency to ruin everything it touched. It seemed to him too contemptible for hot anger even. He made use of it with a cold, fearless scorn, manifested rather than concealed by the forms of stony courtesy which did away with much of the ignominy of the situation. At bottom, perhaps, he suffered from it, for he was not a man of cowardly illusions, but he refused to discuss the ethical view with his wife. He trusted that, though a little disenchanted, she would be intelligent enough to understand that his character safeguarded the enterprise of their lives as much as or more than his policy. The extraordinary development of the mine had put a great power into his hands. To feel that prosperity always at the mercy of unintelligent greed had grown irksome to him. To Mrs Gould it was humiliating. At any rate, it was dangerous. In the confidential communications passing between Charles Gould, the King of Sulaco, and the head of the silver and steel interests far away in California, the conviction was growing that any attempt made by men of education and integrity ought to discreetly supported. 'You may tell your friend Avellanos that I think so,' Mr Holroyd had written at the proper moment from his inviolable sanctuary within the eleven-storey-high factory of great affairs. And shortly afterwards, with a credit opened by the Third Southern Bank (located next door but one to the Holroyd Building), the Ribierist party in Costaguana took a practical shape under the eye of the administrator of the San Tomé mine. And Don José, the hereditary friend of the Gould family, could say: 'Perhaps, my dear Carlos, I shall not have believed in vain.'

CHAPTER II

AFTER ANOTHER armed struggle, decided by Montero's victory of Río Seco, had been added to the tale of civil wars, the 'honest men', as Don José called them, could breathe freely for the first time in half a century. The Five-Year-Mandate law became the basis of that regeneration, the passionate desire and hope for which had been like the elixir of everlasting youth for Don José Avellanos.

And when it was suddenly – and not quite unexpectedly – endangered by that 'brute Montero', it was a passionate indignation that gave him a new lease of life, as it were. Already, at the time of the President-Dictator's visit to Sulaco, Moraga had sounded a note of warning from Sta Marta about the War Minister.

Montero and his brother made the subject of an earnest talk between the Dictator-President and the Nestor-inspirer of the party. But Don Vincente, a doctor of philosophy from the Cordova University, seemed to have an exaggerated respect for military ability, whose mysteriousness – since it appeared to be altogether independent of intellect – imposed upon his imagination. The Victor of Río Seco was a popular hero. His services were so recent that the President-Dictator quailed before the obvious charge of political ingratitude. Great regenerating transactions were being initiated – the fresh loan, a new railway line, a vast colonization scheme. Anything that could unsettle the public opinion in the capital was to be avoided. Don José bowed to these arguments and tried to dismiss from his mind the gold-laced portent in boots, and with a sabre, made meaningless now at last, he hoped, in the new order of things.

Less than six months after the President-Dictator's visit, Sulaco learned with stupefaction of the military revolt in the name of national honour. The Minister of War, in a barrack-square allocution to the officers of the artillery regiment he had been inspecting, had declared the national honour sold to foreigners. The Dictator, by his weak compliance with the demands of the European powers – for the settlement of long outstanding money claims – had showed himself unfit to rule. A letter from Moraga explained afterwards that the initiative, and even the very test, of the incendiary allocution came, in reality, from the other Montero, the ex-*guerrillero*, the Commandante de Plaza. The energetic treatment of Dr Monygham, sent for in haste 'to the mountain', who came galloping three leagues in the dark, saved Don José from a dangerous attack of jaundice.

After getting over the shock, Don José refused to let himself be prostrated. Indeed, better news succeeded at first. The revolt in the capital had been suppressed after a night of fighting in the streets. Unfortunately, both the Monteros had been able to make their escape south, to their native province of Entre-Montes. The hero of the forest march, the victor of Río Seco, had been received with frenzied acclamations in Nicoya, the provincial capital. The troops in garrison there had gone to him in a body. The brothers were organizing an army, gathering malcontents, sending emissaries primed with patriotic lies to the people, and with promises of plunder to the wild *llaneros*. Even a Monterist press had come into existence, speaking oracularly of the secret promises of support given by 'our great sister Republic of the North' against the sinister land-grabbing designs of European powers, cursing in every issue the 'miserable Ribiera', who had plotted to deliver his country, bound hand and foot, for a prey to foreign speculators.

Sulaco, pastoral and sleepy, with its opulent Campo and the rich silver mine, heard the din of arms fitfully in its fortunate isolation. It was nevertheless in the very forefront of the defence with men and money; but the very rumours reached it circuitously – from abroad even, so much was it cut off from the rest of the Republic, not only by natural obstacles, but also by the vicissitudes of the war. The Monteristos were besieging Cayta, an important postal link. The overland couriers ceased to come across the mountains, and no muleteer would consent to risk the journey at last; even Bonifacio on one occasion failed to return from Sta Marta, either not daring the start, or perhaps captured by the parties of the enemy raiding the country between the Cordillera and the capital. Monterist publications, however, found their way into the province, mysteriously enough; and also Monterist emissaries preaching death to aristocrats in the villages and towns of the Campo. Very early, at the beginning of the trouble, Hernandez, the bandit, had proposed (through the agency of an old priest of a village in the wilds) to deliver two of them to the Ribierist authorities in Tonoro. They had come to offer him a free pardon and the rank of colonel from General Montero in consideration of joining the rebel army with his mounted band. No notice was taken at the time of the proposal. It was joined, as an evidence of good faith, to a petition praying the Sulaco Assembly for permission to enlist, with all his followers, in the forces being then raised in Sulaco for the defence of the Five-Year-Mandate of its regeneration. The petition, like everything else, had found its way into Don José's hands. He had showed to Mrs Gould these pages of dirty-greyish rough paper (perhaps looted in some village store), covered with the crabbed, illiterate handwriting of the old padre, carried off from his hut by the side of a mud-walled church to be the secretary of the dreaded *Saiteador*. They had both bent in the lamplight of the Gould drawing-room over the document containing the fierce and yet humble appeal of the man against the blind and stupid barbarity turning an honest *ranchero* into a bandit. A postscript of the priest stated that, but for being deprived of his liberty for ten days, he had been treated with humanity and the respect due to his sacred calling. He had been, it appears, confessing and absolving the chief and most of the band, and he guaranteed the sincerity of their good disposition. He had distributed heavy penances, no doubt in the way of litanies and fasts; but he argued shrewdly that it would be difficult for them to make their peace with God durably till they made peace with men.

Never before, perhaps, had Hernandez's head been in less jeopardy than when he petitioned humbly for permission to buy a pardon for himself and his gang of deserters by armed service. He could range afar from the waste lands protecting his fastness, unchecked, because there were no troops left in the whole province. The usual garrison of Sulaco had gone south to the war, with its brass band playing the 'Bolívar March' on the bridge of one of the O.S.N. Company's steamers. The great family coaches drawn up along the shore of the harbour were made to rock on the high leathern springs by the enthusiasm of the *señoras* and the *señoritas* standing up to wave their lace handkerchiefs, as lighter after lighter packed full of troops left the end of the jetty.

Nostromo directed the embarkation, under the superintendence of Captain Mitchell, red-faced in the sun, conspicuous in a white waistcoat, representing the allied and anxious goodwill of all the material interest of civilization. General Barrios, who commanded the troops, assured Don José on parting that in three weeks he would have Montero in a wooden cage drawn by three pair of oxen ready for a tour through all the towns of the Republic.

'And then, *señora*,' he continued, baring his curly iron-grey head to Mrs Gould in her landau – 'and then, *señora*, we shall convert our swords into ploughshares and grow rich. Even I, myself, as soon as this little business is settled, shall open a *fundación* on some land I have on the *llanos* and try to make a little money in peace and quietness. *Señora*, you know, all Costaguana knows

– what do I say? – this whole South American continent knows, that Pablo Barrios has had his fill of military glory.'

Charles Gould was not present at the anxious and patriotic send-off. It was not his part to see the soldiers embark. It was neither his part, nor his inclination, nor his policy. His part, his inclination, and his policy were united in one endeavour to keep unchecked the flow of treasure he had started single-handed from the re-opened scar in the flank of the mountain. As the mine developed he had trained for himself some native help. There were foremen, artificers, and clerks, with Don Pepe for the *gobernador* of the mining population. For the rest his shoulders alone sustained the whole weight of the '*Imperium in Imperio*', the great Gould Concession whose mere shadow had been enough to crush the life out of his father.

Mrs Gould had no silver mine to look after. In the general life of the Gould Concession she was represented by her two lieutenants, the doctor and the priest, but she fed her woman's love for excitement on events whose significance was purified to her by the fire of her imaginative purpose. On that day she had brought the Avellanos, father and daughter, down to the harbour with her.

Amongst his other activities of that stirring time, Don José had become the chairman of a Patriotic Committee which had armed a great proportion of troops in the Sulaco command with an improved model of a military rifle. It had been just discarded for something still more deadly by one of the great European powers. How much of the market-price for second-hand weapons was covered by the voluntary contributions of the principal familes, and how much came from those funds Don José was understood to command abroad, remained a secret which he alone could have disclosed; but the *ricos*, as the populace called them, had contributed under the pressure of their Nestor's eloquence. Some of the more enthusiastic ladies had been moved to bring offerings of jewels into the hands of the man who was the life and soul of the party.

There were moments when both his life and his soul seemed overtaxed by so many years of undiscouraged belief in regeneration. He appeared almost inanimate, sitting rigidly by the side of Mrs Gould in the landau, with his fine, old, clean-shaven face of a uniform tint as if modelled in yellow wax, shaded by a soft felt hat, the dark eyes looking out fixedly. Antonia, the beautiful Antonia, as Miss Avellanos was called in Sulaco, leaned back, facing them; and her full figure, the grave oval of her face with full red lips, made her look more mature than Mrs Gould, with her mobile expression and small, erect person under a slightly swaying sunshade.

Whenever possible Antonia attended her father; her recognized devotion weakened the shocking effect of her scorn for the rigid conventions, regulating the life of Spanish–American girlhood. And, in truth, she was no longer girlish. It was said that she often wrote State papers from her father's dictation, and was allowed to read all the books in his library. At the receptions – where the situation was saved by the presence of a very decrepit old lady (a relation of the Corbeláns), quite deaf and motionless in an armchair – Antonia could hold her own in a discussion with two or three men at a time. Obviously she was not the girl to be content with peeping through a barred window at a cloaked figure of a lover ensconced in a doorway opposite – which is the correct form of

Costaguana courtship. It was generally believed that with her foreign upbringing and foreign ideas the learned and proud Antonia would never marry – unless, indeed, she married a foreigner from Europe or North America, now that Sulaco seemed on the point of being invaded by all the world.

Chapter III

When General Barrios stopped to address Mrs Gould, Antonia raised negligently her hand holding an open fan, as if to shade from the sun her head, wrapped in a light lace shawl. The clear gleam of her blue eyes gliding behind the black fringe of eyelashes paused for a moment upon her father, then travelled farther to the figure of a young man of thirty at most, of medium height, rather thick-set, wearing a light overcoat. Bearing down with the open palm of his hand upon the knob of a flexible cane, he had been looking on from a distance; but directly he saw himself noticed, he approached quietly and put his elbow over the door of the landau.

The shirt collar, cut low in the neck, the big bow of his cravat, the style of his clothing, from the round hat to the varnished shoes, suggested an idea of French elegance; but otherwise he was the very type of a fair Spanish creole. The fluffy moustache and the short, surly, golden beard did not conceal his lips, rosy, fresh, almost pouting in expression. His full, round face was of that warm, healthy creole white which is never tanned by its native sunshine. Martin Decoud was seldom exposed to the Costaguana sun under which he was born. His people had been long settled in Paris, where he had studied law, had dabbled in literature, had hoped now and then in moments of exaltation to become a poet like that other foreigner of Spanish blood, José Maria Heredia. In other moments he had, to pass the time, condescended to write articles on European affairs for the *Semenario*, the principal newspaper in Sta Marta, which printed them under the heading 'From our special correspondent', though the authorship was an open secret. Everybody in Costaguana, where the tale of compatriots in Europe is jealously kept, knew that it was 'the son Decoud', a talented young man, supposed to be moving in the higher spheres of Society. As a matter of fact, he was an idle boulevardier, in touch with some smart journalists, made free of a few newspaper offices, and welcomed in the pleasure-haunts of pressmen. This life, whose dreary superficiality is covered by the glitter of universal *blague*, like the stupid clowning of a harlequin by the spangles of a motley costume, induced in him a Frenchified – but most un-French – cosmopolitanism, in reality a mere barren indifferentism posing as intellectual superiority. Of his own country he used to say to his French associates: 'Imagine an atmosphere of *opéra bouffe* in which all the comic business of stage statesmen, brigands, etc., etc., all their farcical stealing, intriguing, and stabbing is done in dead earnest. It is screamingly funny, the blood flows all the time, and the actors believe themselves to be influencing the fate of the universe. Of course, government in general, any government anywhere, is a thing of exquisite comicality to a discerning mind; but really we Spanish–Americans do overstep the bounds. No man of ordinary intelligence can take part in the intrigues of *une farce macabre*. However, these Ribierists, of whom we hear so much just now, are really trying in their own comical way to make the country habitable, and even to pay some of its debts. My friends, you had better write up Señor Ribiera all you can in kindness to your own bondholders. Really, if what I am told in my letters is true, there is some chance for them at last.'

And he would explain with railing verve what Don Vincente Ribiera stood for – a mournful little man oppressed by his own good intentions, the significance of battles won, who Montero was (*un grotesque vaniteux et féroce*), and the manner of the new loan connected with railway development, and the colonization of vast tracts of land in one great financial scheme.

And his French friends would remark that evidently this little fellow Decoud *connaissait la question à fond*. An important Parisian review asked him for an article on the situation. It was composed in a serious tone and in a spirit of levity. Afterwards he asked one of his intimates:

'Have you read my thing about the regeneration of Costaguana – *une bonne blague, hein?*'

He imagined himself Parisian to the tips of his fingers. But far from being that he was in danger of remaining a sort of nondescript dilettante all his life. He had pushed the habit of universal raillery to a point where it blinded him to the genuine impulses of his own nature. To be suddenly selected for the executive member of the patriotic small-arms committee of Sulaco seemed to him the height of the unexpected, one of those fantastic moves of which only his 'dear countrymen' were capable.

'It's like a tile falling on my head. I – I – executive member! It's the first I hear of it! What do I know of military rifles? *C'est funambulesque!*' he had exclaimed to his favourite sister; for the Decoud family – except the old father and mother – used the French language amongst themselves. 'And you should see the explanatory and confidential letter! Eight pages of it – no less!'

This letter, in Antonia's handwriting, was signed by Don José, who appealed to the 'young and gifted Costaguanero' on public grounds, and privately opened his heart to his talented godson, a man of wealth and leisure, with wide relations, and by his parentage and bringing-up worthy of all confidence.

'Which means,' Martin commented, cynically, to his sister, 'that I am not likely to misappropriate the funds, or go blabbing to our Chargé d'Affaires here.'

The whole thing was being carried out behind the back of the War Minister, Montero, a mistrusted member of the Ribiera Government, but difficult to get rid of at once. He was not to know anything of it till the troops under Barrio's command had the new rifle in their hands. The President-Dictator, whose position was very difficult, was alone in the secret.

'How funny!' commented Martin's sister and confidant; to which the brother, with an air of best Parisian *blague*, had retorted:

'It's immense! The idea of that Chief of the State engaged, with the help of private citizens, in digging a mine under his own indispensable War Minister. No! We are unapproachable!' And he laughed immoderately.

Afterwards his sister was surprised at the earnestness and ability he displayed in carrying out his mission, which circumstances made delicate, and his want of special knowledge rendered difficult. She had never seen Martin take so much trouble about anything in his whole life.

'It amuses me,' he had explained, briefly. 'I am beset by a lot of swindlers trying to sell all sorts of gaspipe weapons. They are charming; they invite me to expensive luncheons; I keep up their hopes; it's extremely entertaining. Meanwhile, the real affair is being carried through in quite another quarter.'

When the business was concluded he declared suddenly his intention of seeing the precious consignment delivered safely in Sulaco. The whole burlesque business, he thought, was worth following up to the end. He mumbled his excuses, tugging at his golden beard, before the acute young lady who (after the first wide stare of astonishment) looked at him with narrowed eyes, and pronounced slowly:

'I believe you want to see Antonia.'

'What Antonia?' asked the Costaguana boulevardier, in a vexed and disdainful tone. He shrugged his shoulders, and spun round on his heel. His sister called out after him joyously:

'The Antonia you used to know when she wore her hair in two plaits down her back.'

He had known her some eight years since, shortly before the Avellanos had left Europe for good, as a tall girl of sixteen, youthfully austere, and of a character already so formed that she ventured to treat slightingly his pose of disabused wisdom. On one occasion, as though she had lost all patience, she flew out at him about the aimlessness of his life, and the levity of his opinions. He was twenty then, an only son, spoiled by his adoring family. This attack disconcerted him so greatly that he had faltered in his affection of amused superiority before that insignificant chit of a school-girl. But the impression left was so strong that ever since all the girl friends of his sisters recalled to him Antonia Avellanos by some faint resemblance, or by the great force of contrast. It was, he told himself, like a ridiculous fatality. And, of course, in the news the Decouds received regularly from Costaguana, the name of their friends, the Avellanos, cropped up frequently – the arrest and the abominable treatment of the ex-Minister, the dangers and hardships endured by the family, its withdrawal in poverty to Sulaco, the death of the mother.

The Monterist *pronunciamiento* had taken place before Martin Decoud reached Costaguana. He came out in a roundabout way, through Magellan's Straits by the main line and the West Coast Service of the O.S.N. Company. His precious consignment arrived just in time to convert the first feelings of consternation into a mood of hope and resolution. Publicly he was made much of by the *familias principales*. Privately Don José, still shaken and weak, embraced him with tears in his eyes.

'You have come out yourself! No less could be expected from a Decoud. Alas! our worst fears have been realized,' he moaned, affectionately. And again he hugged his godson. This was indeed the time for men of intellect and conscience to rally round the endangered cause.

It was then that Martin Decoud, the adopted child of Western Europe, felt the absolute change of atmosphere. He submitted to being embraced and talked to without a word. He was moved in spite of himself by that note of passion and sorrow unknown on the more refined stage of European politics. But when the tall Antonia, advancing with her light step in the dimness of the big bare *sala* of the Avellanos house, offered him her hand (in her emancipated way), and murmured, 'I am glad to see you here, Don Martin,' he felt how impossible it would be to tell these two people that he had intended to go away by the next month's packet. Don José, meantime, continued his praises. Every accession added to public confidence, and, besides, what an example to the young men at home from the brilliant defender of the country's regeneration, the worthy expounder of the party's political faith before the world! Everybody had read the magnificent article in the famous *Parisian Review*. The world was now informed: and the author's appearance at this moment was like a public act of faith. Young Decoud felt overcome by a feeling of impatient confusion. His plan had been to return by way of the United States through California, visit Yellowstone Park, see Chicago, Niagara, have a look at Canada, perhaps make a short stay in New York, a longer one in Newport, use his letters of introduction. The pressure of Antonia's hand was so frank, the tone of her voice was so unexpectedly unchanged in its approving warmth, that all he found to say after his low bow was:

'I am inexpressibly grateful for your welcome; but why need a man be thanked for returning to his native country? I am sure Doña Antonia does not think so.'

'Certainly not, *señor*,' she said, with that perfectly calm openness of manner which characterized all her utterances. 'But when he returns, as you return, one may be glad – for the sake of both.'

Martin Decoud said nothing of his plans. He not only never breathed a word of them to anyone, but only a fortnight later asked the mistress of the Casa Gould (where he had of course obtained admission at once), leaning forward in his chair with an air of well-bred familiarity, whether she could not detect in him that day a marked change – an air, he explained, of more excellent gravity. At this Mrs Gould turned her face full towards him with the silent inquiry of slightly widened eyes and the merest ghost of a smile, a habitual movement with her, which was very fascinating to men by something subtly devoted, finely self-forgetful in its lively readiness of attention. Because, Decoud continued imperturbably, he felt no longer an idle cumberer of the earth. She was, he assured her, actually beholding at that moment the Journalist of Sulaco. At once Mrs Gould glanced towards Antonia, posed upright in the corner of a high, straight-backed Spanish sofa, a large black fan waving slowly against the curves of her fine figure, the tips of crossed feet peeping from under the hem of the black skirt. Decoud's eyes also remained fixed there, while in an undertone he added that Avellanos was quite aware of his new and unexpected vocation, which in Costaguana was generally the speciality of half-educated Negroes and wholly penniless lawyers. Then, confronting with a sort of urbane effrontery Mrs Gould's gaze, not turned sympathetically upon himself, he breathed out the words, '*Pro patria!*'

What had happened was that he had all at once yielded to Don José's pressing entreaties to take the direction of a newspaper that would 'voice the aspirations of the province'. It had been Don José's old and cherished idea. The necessary plant (on a modest scale) and a large consignment of paper had been received from America some time before; the right man alone was wanted. Even Señor Moraga in Sta Marta had not been able to find one, and the matter was now becoming pressing; some organ was absolutely needed to counteract the effect of the lies disseminated by the Monterist Press: the atrocious calumnies, the appeals of the people calling upon them to rise with their knives in their hands and put an end once for all to the Blancos, to these Gothic remnants, to these sinister mummies, these impotent *paralíticos*, who plotted with foreigners for the surrender of the lands and the slavery of the people.

The clamour of this 'Negro Liberalism' frightened Señor Avellanos. A newspaper was the only remedy. And now that the right man had been found in Decoud, great black letters appeared painted between the windows above the arcaded ground floor of a house on the Plaza. It was next to Anzani's great emporium of boots, silks, ironware, muslins, wooden toys, tiny silver arms, legs, heads, hearts (for ex-voto offerings), rosaries, champagne, women's hats, patent medicines, even a few dusty books in paper covers and mostly in the French language. The big black letters formed the words, 'Offices of the *Porvenir*'. From these offices a single folded sheet of Martin's journalism issued three times a week; and the sleek yellow Anzani prowling in a suit of ample black and carpet slippers, before the many doors of his establishment, greeted by a deep, sidelong inclination of his body the Journalist of Sulaco going to and fro on the business of his august calling.

Chapter IV

Perhaps it was in the exercise of his calling that he had come to see the troops depart. The *Porvenir* of the day after next would no doubt relate the event, but its editor, leaning his side against the landau, seemed to look at nothing. The front rank of the company of infantry drawn up three deep across the shore-end of the jetty when pressed too close would bring their bayonets to the charge ferociously, with an awful rattle; and then the crowd of spectators swayed back bodily, even under the noses of the big white mules. Notwithstanding the great multitude there was only a low, muttering noise; the dust hung in a brown haze, in which the horsemen, wedged in the throng here and there, towered from the hips upwards, gazing all one way over the heads. Almost every one of them had mounted a friend, who steadied himself with both hands grasping his shoulders from behind; and the rims of their hats touching, made like one disc sustaining the cones of two pointed crowns with a double face underneath. A hoarse *mozo* would bawl out something to an acquaintance in the ranks, or a woman would shriek suddenly the word *Adiós!* followed by the Christian name of a man.

General Barrios, in a shabby blue tunic and white peg-top trousers falling upon strange red boots, kept his head uncovered and stooped slightly, propping himself up with a thick stick. No! He had earned enough military glory to satiate any man, he insisted to Mrs Gould, trying at the same time to put an air of gallantry into his attitude. A few jetty hairs hung sparsely from his upper lip, he had a salient nose, a thin, long jaw, and a black silk patch over one eye. His other eye, small and deep-set, twinkled erratically in all directions, aimlessly affable. The few European spectators, all men, who had naturally drifted into the neighbourhood of the Gould carriage, betrayed by the solemnity of their faces their impression that the general must have had too much punch (Swedish punch, imported in bottles by Anzani) at the Amarilla Club before he had started with his Staff on a furious ride to the harbour. But Mrs Gould bent forward, self-possessed, and declared her conviction that still more glory awaited the general in the near future.

'*Señora*!' he remonstrated, with great feeling, 'in the name of God, reflect! How can there be any glory for a man like me in overcoming that bald-headed *embustero* with the dyed moustaches?'

Pablo Ignacio Barrios, son of a village *alcalde*, general of division, commanding in chief the Occidental Military district, did not frequent the higher society of the town. He preferred the unceremonious gatherings of men where he could tell jaguar-hunt stories, boast of his powers with the lasso, with which he could perform extremely difficult feats of the sort 'no married man should attempt', as the saying goes amongst the *llaneros*; relate tales of extraordinary night rides, encounters with wild bulls, struggles with crocodiles, adventures in the great forests, crossings of swollen rivers. And it was not mere boastfulness that prompted the general's reminiscences, but a genuine love of that wild life which he had led in his young days before he turned his back for ever on the thatched roof of the parental *tolderia* in the woods. Wandering away as far as Mexico he had fought against the French by the side (as he said) of Juarez, and was the only military man of Costaguana who had ever encountered European troops in the field. That fact shed a great lustre upon his name till it became eclipsed by the rising star of Montero. All his life he had been an inveterate gambler. He alluded himself quite openly to the current story how once, during some campaign (when in command of a brigade), he had gambled away his horses, pistols, and accoutrements, to the very epaulettes, playing *monte* with his colonels the night before the battle. Finally, he had sent under escort his sword (a presentation sword, with a gold hilt) to the town in the rear of his position to be immediately pledged for five hundred pesetas with a sleepy and frightened shopkeeper. By daybreak he had lost the last of that money, too, when his only remark, as he rose calmly, was, 'Now let us go and fight to the death.' From that time he had become aware that a general could lead his troops into battle very well with a simple stick in his hand. 'It has been my custom ever since,' he would say.

He was always overwhelmed with debts; even during the periods of splendour in his varied fortunes of a Costaguana general, when he held high military commands, his gold-laced uniforms were almost always in pawn with some tradesman. And at last, to avoid the incessant difficulties of costume caused by the anxious lenders, he had assumed a disdain of military trappings, an eccentric fashion of shabby old tunics, which had become like a second nature. But the faction Barrios joined needed to fear no political betrayal. He was too much of a real soldier for the ignoble traffic of buying and selling victories. A member of the foreign diplomatic body in Sta Marta had once passed a judgement upon him: 'Barrios is a man of perfect honesty and even of some talent for war, *mais il manque de tenue*.' After the triumph of the Ribierists he had obtained the reputedly lucrative Occidental command, mainly through the exertions of his creditors (the Sta Marta shopkeepers, all great politicians), who moved heaven and earth in his interest publicly, and privately besieged Señor Moraga, the influential agent of the San Tomé mine, with the exaggerated lamentations that if the general were passed over, 'we shall all be ruined'. An incidental but favourable mention of his name in Mr Gould senior's long correspondence with his son had something to do with his appointment, too; but most of all undoubtedly his established political honesty. No one questioned the personal bravery of the Tiger-killer, as the populace called him. He was, however, said to be unlucky in the field – but this was to be the beginning of an era of peace. The soldiers liked him for his humane temper, which was like a strange and precious flower unexpectedly blooming on the hotbed of corrupt revolutions; and when he rode slowly through the streets during some military display, the contemptuous good humour of his solitary eye roaming over the crowds extorted the acclamations of the populace. The women of that class especially seemed positively fascinated by the long drooping nose, the peaked chin, the heavy lower lip, the black silk eye-patch and band slanting rakishly over the forehead. His high rank always procured an audience of *caballeros* for his sporting stories, which he detailed very well with a simple, grave enjoyment. As to the society of ladies, it was irksome by the restraints it imposed without any equivalent, as far as he could see. He had not, perhaps, spoken three times on the whole to Mrs Gould since he had taken up his high command; but he had observed her frequently riding with the Señor Administrador, and had pronounced that there was more sense in her little bridle-hand than in all the female heads in Sulaco. His impulse had been to be very civil on parting to a woman who did not wobble in the saddle, and happened to be the wife of a personality very important to a man always short of money. He even pushed his attentions so far as to desire the aide-de-camp at his side (a thick-set, short captain with a Tartar physiognomy) to bring along a corporal with a file of men in front of the carriage, lest the crowd in its backward surges would 'incommode the mules of the *señora*'. Then, turning to the small knot of silent Europeans looking on within earshot, he raised his voice protectingly:

'*Señores*, have no apprehension. Go on quietly making your Ferro Carril – your railways, your telegraphs. Your – There's enough wealth in Costaguana to pay for everything – or else you would not be here. Ha! ha! Don't mind this little *picardía* of my friend Montero. In a little while you shall behold his dyed moustaches through the bars of a strong wooden cage. *Sí, señores*! Fear nothing, develop the country, work, work!'

The little group of engineers received this exhortation without a word, and after waving his hand at them loftily, he addressed himself again to Mrs Gould:

'That is what Don José says we must do. Be enterprising! Work! Grow rich! To put Montero in a cage is my work; and when that insignificant piece of business is done, then, as Don José wishes us, we shall grow rich, one and all, like so many Englishmen, because it is money that saves a country, and –'

But a young officer in a very new uniform, hurrying up from the direction of the jetty, interrupted his interpretation of Señor Avellanos's ideals. The general made a movement of impatience; the other went on talking to him insistently, with an air of respect. The horses of the Staff had been embarked, the steamer's gig was awaiting the general at the boat steps; and Barrios, after a fierce stare of his one eye, began to take leave. Don José roused himself for an appropriate phrase pronounced mechanically. The terrible strain of hope and fear was telling on him, and he seemed to husband the last sparks of his fire for those oratorical efforts of which even the distant Europe was to hear. Antonia, her red lips firmly closed, averted her head behind the raised fan; and young Decoud, though he felt the girl's eyes upon him, gazed away persistently, hooked on his elbow, with a scornful and complete detachment. Mrs Gould heroically concealed her dismay at the appearance of men and events so remote from her racial conventions, dismay too deep to be uttered in words even to her husband. She understood his voiceless reserve better now. Their confidential intercourse fell, not in moments of privacy, but precisely in public, when the quick meeting of their glances would comment upon some fresh turn of events. She had gone to his school of uncompromising silence, the only one possible, since so much that seemed shocking, weird, and grotesque in the working out of their purposes had to be accepted as normal in this country. Decidedly, the stately Antonia looked more mature and infinitely calm; but she would never have known how to reconcile the sudden sinkings of her heart with an amiable mobility of expression.

Mrs Gould smiled a good-bye at Barrios, nodded round to the Europeans (who raised their hats simultaneously) with an engaging invitation, 'I hope to see you all presently, at home'; then said nervously to Decoud, 'Get in, Don Martin,' and heard him mutter to himself in French, as he opened the carriage door, '*Le sort en est jeté*. She heard him with a sort of exasperation. Nobody ought to have known better than himself that the first cast of dice had been already thrown long ago in a most desperate game. Distant acclamations, words of command yelled out, and a roll of drums on the jetty greeted the departing general. Something like a slight faintness came over her, and she looked blankly at Antonia's face, wondering what would happen to Charley if that absurd man failed. '*A la casa, Ignacio*,' she cried at the motionless broad back of the coachman, who gathered the reins without haste, mumbling to himself under his breath, '*Sí, la casa. Sí, sí, niña*.'

The carriage rolled noiselessly on the soft track, the shadows fell long on the dusty little plain interspersed with dark bushes, mounds of turned-up earth, low wooden buildings with iron roofs of the Railway Company; the sparse row of telegraph poles strode obliquely clear of the town, bearing a single, almost invisible wire far into the great *campo* – like a slender, vibrating feeler of that progress waiting outside for a moment of peace to enter and twine itself about the weary heart of the land.

The café window of the Albergo d'Italia Una was full of sunburnt, whiskered faces of railway men. But at the other end of the house, the end of the Signori Inglesi, old Giorgio, at the door with one of his girls on each side, bared his bushy head, as white as the snows of Higuerota. Mrs Gould stopped the carriage. She seldom failed to speak to the protégé; moreover, the excitement, the heat, and the dust had made her thirsty. She asked for a glass of water. Giorgio sent the children indoors for it, and approached with pleasure expressed in his whole rugged countenance. It was not often that he had occasion to see his benefactress, who was also an Englishwoman – another title to his regard. He offered some excuses for his wife. It was a bad day with her; her oppressions – he tapped his own broad chest. She could not move from her chair that day.

Decoud, ensconced in the corner of his seat, observed gloomily Mrs Gould's old revolutionist, then, offhand:

'Well, and what do you think of it all, Garibaldino?'

Old Giorgio, looking at him with some curiosity, said civilly that the troops had marched very well. One-eyed Barrios and his officers had done wonders with the recruits in a short time. Those *Indios*, only caught the other day, had gone swinging past in double-quick time, like *bersaglieri*; they looked well fed, too, and had whole uniforms. 'Uniforms!' he repeated with a half-smile of pity. A look of grim retrospect stole over his piercing, steady eyes. It had been otherwise in his time when men fought against tyranny, in the forests of Brazil, or on the plains of Uruguay, starving on half-raw beef without salt, half naked, with often only a knife tied to a stick for a weapon. 'And yet we used to prevail against the oppressor,' he concluded, proudly.

His animation fell; the slight gesture of his hand expressed discouragement; but he added that he had asked one of the sergeants to show him the new rifle. There was no such weapon in his fighting days; and if Barrios could not –

'Yes, yes,' broke in Don José, almost trembling with eagerness. 'We are safe. The good Señor Viola is a man of experience. Extremely deadly – is it not so? You have accomplished your mission admirably, my dear Martin.'

Decoud, lolling back moodily, contemplated old Viola.

'Ah! Yes. A man of experience. But who are you for, really, in your heart?'

Mrs Gould leaned over to the children. Linda had brought out a glass of water on a tray, with extreme care; Giselle presented her with a bunch of flowers gathered hastily.

'For the people,' declared old Viola, sternly.

'We are all for the people – in the end.'

'Yes,' muttered old Viola, savagely. 'And meantime they fight for you. Blind. *Esclavos*!'

At that moment young Scarfe of the railway staff emerged from the door of the part reserved for the Signori Inglesi. He had come down to headquarters from somewhere up the line on a light engine, and had had just time to get a bath and change his clothes. He was a nice boy, and Mrs Gould welcomed him.

'It's a delightful surprise to see you, Mrs Gould. I've just come down. Usual luck. Missed everything, of course. This show is just over, and I hear there has been a great dance at Don Juste Lopez's last night. Is it true?'

'The young patricians,' Decoud began suddenly in his precise English, 'have indeed been dancing before they started off to the war with the Great Pompey.'

Young Scarfe stared, astounded. 'You haven't met before,' Mrs Gould intervened. 'Mr Decoud – Mr Scarfe.'

'Ah! But we are not going to Pharsalia,' protested Don José, with nervous haste, also in English. 'You should not jest like this, Martin.'

Antonia's breast rose and fell with a deeper breath. The young engineer was utterly in the dark. 'Great what?' he muttered, vaguely.

'Luckily, Montero is not a Caesar,' Decoud continued. 'Not the two Monteros put together would make a decent parody of a Caesar.' He crossed his arms on his breast, looking at Señor Avellanos, who had returned to his immobility. 'It is only you, Don José, who are a genuine old Roman – *vir Romanus* – eloquent and inflexible.'

Since he had heard the name of Montero pronounced, young Scarfe had been eager to express his simple feelings. In a loud and youthful tone he hoped that this Montero was going to be licked once for all and done with. There was no saying what would happen to the railway if the revolution got the upper hand. Perhaps it would have to be abandoned. It would not be the first railway gone to pot in Costaguana. 'You know, it's one of their so-called national things,' he ran on, wrinkling up his nose as if the world had a suspicious flavour to his profound experience of South American affairs. And, of course, he chatted with animation, it had been such an immense piece of luck for him at his age to get appointed on the staff 'of a big thing like that – don't you know'. It would give him the pull over a lot of chaps all through life, he asserted. 'Therefore – down with Montero! Mrs Gould.' His artless grin disappeared slowly before the unanimous gravity of the faces turned upon him from the carriage; only that 'old chap', Don José, presenting a motionless, waxy profile, stared straight on as if deaf. Scarfe did not know the Avellanos very well. They did not give balls, and Antonia never appeared at a ground-floor window, as some other young ladies used to do attended by elder women, to chat with the *caballeros* on horseback in the *calle*. The stares of these creoles did not matter much; but what on earth had come to Mrs Gould? She said, 'Go on, Ignacio,' and gave him a slow inclination of the head. He heard a short laugh from that round-faced, Frenchified fellow. He coloured up to the eyes, and stared at Giorgio Viola, who had fallen back with the children, hat in hand.

'I shall want a horse presently,' he said with some asperity to the old man.

'*Sí, señor*. There are plenty of horses,' murmured the Garibaldino, smoothing absently, with his brown hands, the two heads, one dark with bronze glints, the other fair with a coppery ripple, of the two girls by his side. The returning stream of sightseers raised a great dust on the road. Horsemen noticed the group. 'Go to your mother,' he said. 'They are growing up as I am growing older, and there is nobody –'

He looked at the young engineer and stopped, as if awakened from a dream; then, folding his arms on his breast, took up his usual position, leaning back in the doorway with an upward glance fastened on the white shoulder of Higuerota far away.

In the carriage Martin Decoud, shifting his position as though he could not make himself comfortable, muttered as he swayed towards Antonia, 'I suppose you hate me.' Then in a loud voice he began to congratulate Don José upon all the engineers being convinced Ribierists. The interest of all those foreigners was gratifying. 'You have heard this one. He is an enlightened well-wisher. It is pleasant to think that the prosperity of Costaguana is of some use to the world.'

'He is very young,' Mrs Gould remarked, quietly.

'And so very wise for his age,' retorted Decoud. 'But here we have the naked truth from the mouth of that child. You are right, Don José. The natural treasures of Costaguana are of importance to the progressive Europe represented by this youth, just as three hundred years ago the wealth of our Spanish fathers was a serious object to the rest of Europe – as represented by the bold buccaneers. There is a curse of futility upon our character: Don Quixote and Sancho Panza, chivalry and materialism, high-sounding sentiments and a supine morality, violent efforts for an idea and a sullen acquiescence in every form of corruption. We convulsed a continent for our independence only to become the passive prey of a democratic parody, the helpless victims of scoundrels and cut-throats, our institutions a mockery, our laws a farce – a Guzman Bento our master! And we have sunk so low that when a man like you has awakened our conscience, a stupid barbarian of a Montero – Great Heavens! a Montero! – becomes a deadly danger, and an ignorant, boastful *indio*, like Barrios, is our defender.'

But Don José, disregarding the general indictment as though he had not heard a word of it, took up the defence of Barrios. The man was competent enough for his special task in the plan of campaign. It consisted in an offensive movement, with Cayta as base, upon the flank of the revolutionist forces advancing from the south against Sta Marta, which was covered by another army with the President-Dictator in its midst. Don José became quite animated with a great flow of speech, bending forward anxiously under the steady eyes of his daughter. Decoud, as if silenced by so much ardour, did not make a sound. The bells of the city were striking the hour of *Oración* when the carriage rolled under the old gateway facing the harbour like a shapeless monument of leaves and stones. The rumble of wheels under the sonorous arch was traversed by a strange, piercing shriek, and Decoud, from his back seat, had a view of the people behind the carriage trudging along the road outside, all turning their heads, in sombreros and rebozos, to look at a locomotive which rolled quickly out of sight behind Giorgio Viola's house, under a white trail of steam that seemed to vanish in the breathless, hysterically prolonged scream of warlike triumph. And it was all like a fleeting vision, the shrieking ghost of a railway engine fleeing across the frame of the archway, behind the startled movement of the people streaming back from a military spectacle with silent footsteps on the dust of the road. It was a material train returning from the Campo to the palisaded yards. The empty cars rolled lightly on the single track; there was no rumble of wheels, no tremor on the ground. The engine-driver, running past the Casa Viola with the salute of an uplifted arm, checked his speed smartly before entering the yard; and when the ear-splitting screech of the steam-whistle for the brakes had stopped, a series of hard, battering shocks, mingled with the clanking of chain-couplings, made a tumult of blows and shaken fetters under the vault of the gate.

CHAPTER V

THE GOULD carriage was the first to return from the harbour to the empty town. On the ancient pavement, laid out in patterns, sunk into ruts and holes, the portly Ignacio, mindful of the springs of the Parisian-built landau, had pulled up to a walk, and Decoud in his corner contemplated moodily the inner aspect of the gate. The squat turreted sides held up between them a mass of masonry with bunches of grass growing at the top, and a grey, heavily scrolled armorial shield of stone above the apex of the arch with the arms of Spain nearly smoothed out as if in readiness from some new device typical of the impending progress.

The explosive noise of the railway trucks seemed to augment Decoud's irritation. He muttered something to himself, then began to talk aloud in curt, angry phrases thrown at the silence of the two women. They did not look at him at all; while Don José, with his semi-translucent, waxy complexion, overshadowed by the soft grey hat, swayed a little to the jolts of the carriage by the side of Mrs Gould.

'This sound puts a new edge on a very old truth.'

Decoud spoke in French, perhaps because of Ignacio on the box above him; the old coachman, with his broad back filling a short, silver-braided jacket, had a big pair of ears, whose thick rims stood well away from his cropped head.

'Yes, the noise outside the city wall is new, but the principle is old.'

He ruminated his discontent for a while, then began afresh with a sidelong glance at Antonia:

'No, but just imagine our forefathers in morions and corselets drawn up outside this gate, and a band of adventurers just landed from their ships in the harbour there. Thieves, of course. Speculators, too. Their expeditions, each one, were the speculations of grave and reverend persons in England. That is history, as that absurd sailor Mitchell is always saying.'

'Mitchell's arrangements for the embarkation of the troops were excellent!' exclaimed Don José.

'That! – that! oh, that's really the work of that Genoese seaman! But to return to my noises; there used to be in the old days the sound of trumpets outside that gate. War trumpets! I'm sure they were trumpets. I have read somewhere that Drake, who was the greatest of these men, used to dine alone in his cabin on board ship to the sound of trumpets. In those days this town was full of wealth. Those men came to take it. Now the whole land is like a treasure-house, and all these people are breaking into it, whilst we are cutting each other's throats. The only thing that keeps them out is mutual jealousy. But they'll come to an agreement some day – and by the time we've settled our quarrels and become decent and honourable, there'll be nothing left for us. It has always been the same. We are wonderful people, but it has always been our fate to be' – he did not say 'robbed', but added, after a pause – 'exploited!'

Mrs Gould said, 'Oh, this is unjust!' And Antonia interjected, 'Don't answer him, Emilia. He is attacking me.'

'You surely do not think I was attacking Don Carlos!' Decoud answered.

And then the carriage stopped before the door of the Casa Gould. The young man offered his hand to the ladies. They went in first together; Don José walked by the side of Decoud, and the gouty old porter tottered after them with some light wraps on his arm.

Don José slipped his hand under the arm of the journalist of Sulaco.

'The *Porvenir* must have a long and confident article upon Barrios and the irresistibleness of his army of Cayta! The moral effect should be kept up in the country. We must cable encouraging extracts to Europe and the United States to maintain a favourable impression abroad.'

Decoud muttered, 'Oh, yes, we must comfort our friends, the speculators.'

The long open gallery was in shadow, with its screen of plants in vases along the balustrade, holding out motionless blossoms, and all the glass doors of the reception-rooms thrown open. A jingle of spurs died out at the farther end.

Basilio, standing aside against the wall, said in a soft tone to the passing ladies, 'The Señor Administrador is just back from the mountain.'

In the great *sala*, with its groups of ancient Spanish and modern European furniture making as if different centres under the high white spread of the ceiling, the silver and porcelain of the tea-service gleamed among a cluster of dwarf chairs, like a bit of a lady's boudoir, putting in a note of feminine and intimate delicacy.

Don José in his rocking-chair placed his hat on his lap, and Decoud walked up and down the whole length of the room, passing between tables loaded with knick-knacks and almost disappearing behind the high backs of leathern sofas. He was thinking of the angry face of Antonia; he was confident that he would make his peace with her. He had not stayed in Sulaco to quarrel with Antonia.

Martin Decoud was angry with himself. All he saw and heard going on around him exasperated the preconceived views of his European civilization. To contemplate revolutions from the distance of the Parisian Boulevards was quite another matter. Here on the spot it was not possible to dismiss their tragic comedy with the expression, '*Quelle farce!*'

The reality of the political action, such as it was, seemed closer, and acquired poignancy by Antonia's belief in the cause. Its crudeness hurt his feelings. He was surprised at his own sensitiveness.

'I suppose I am more of a Costaguanero than I would have believed possible,' he thought to himself.

His disdain grew like a reaction of his scepticism against the action into which he was forced by his infatuation for Antonia. He soothed himself by saying he was not a patriot, but a lover.

The ladies came in bareheaded, and Mrs Gould sank low before the little tea-table. Antonia took up her usual place at the reception hour – the corner of a leathern couch, with a rigid grace in her pose and a fan in her hand. Decoud, swerving from the straight line of his march, came to lean over the high back of her seat.

For a long time he talked into her ear from behind, softly, with a half smile and an air of apologetic familiarity. Her fan lay half grasped on her knees. She never looked at him. His rapid utterance grew more and more insistent and caressing. At last he ventured a slight laugh.

'No, really. You must forgive me. One must be serious sometimes.' He paused. She turned her head a little; her blue eyes glided slowly towards him, slightly upwards, mollified and questioning.

'You can't think I am serious when I call Montero a *gran' bestia* every second day in the *Porvenir*? That is not a serious occupation. No occupation is serious, not even when a bullet through the heart is the penalty of failure!'

Her hand closed firmly on her fan.

'Some reason, you understand, I mean some sense, may creep into thinking; some glimpse of truth. I mean some effective truth, for which there is no room in politics or journalism. I happen to have said what I thought. And you are angry! If you do me the kindness to think a little you will see that I spoke like a patriot.'

She opened her red lips for the first time, not unkindly.

'Yes, but you never see the aim. Men must be used as they are. I suppose nobody is really disinterested, unless, perhaps, you, Don Martin.'

'God forbid! It's the last thing I should like you to believe of me.' He spoke lightly, and paused.

She began to fan herself with a slow movement without raising her hand. After a time he whispered passionately:

'Antonia!'

She smiled, and extended her hand after the English manner towards Charles Gould, who was bowing before her; while Decoud, with his elbows spread on the back of the sofa, dropped his eyes and murmured, '*Bonjour.*'

The Señor Administrador of the San Tomé mine bent over his wife for a moment. They exchanged a few words, of which only the phrase, 'The greatest enthusiasm,' pronounced by Mrs Gould, could be heard.

'Yes,' Decoud began in a murmur. 'Even he!'

'This is sheer calumny,' said Antonia, not very severely.

'You just ask him to throw his mine into the melting-pot for the great cause,' Decoud whispered.

Don José had raised his voice. He rubbed his hands cheerily. The excellent aspect of the troops and the great quantity of new deadly rifles on the shoulders of those brave men seemed to fill him with an ecstatic confidence.

Charles Gould, very tall and thin before his chair, listened, but nothing could be discovered in his face except a kind and deferential attention.

Meantime, Antonia had risen, and, crossing the room, stood looking out of one of the three long windows giving on the street. Decoud followed her. The window was thrown open, and he leaned against the thickness of the wall. The long folds of the damask curtain, falling straight from the broad brass cornice, hid him partly from the room. He folded his arms on his breast, and looked steadily at Antonia's profile.

The people returning from the harbour filled the pavements; the shuffle of sandals and a low murmur of voices ascended to the window. Now and then a coach rolled slowly along the disjointed roadway of the Calle de la Constitución. There were not many private carriages in Sulaco; at the most crowded hour on the Alameda they could be counted with one glance of the eye. The great family arks swayed on high leathern springs, full of pretty powdered faces in which the eyes looked intensely alive and black. And first Don Juste Lopez, the President of the Provincial Assembly, passed with his three lovely daughters, solemn in a black frock-coat and stiff white tie, as when directing a debate from a high tribune. Though they all raised their eyes, Antonia did not make the usual greeting gesture of a fluttered hand, and they affected not to see the two young people, Costaguaneros with European manners, whose eccentricities were discussed behind the barred windows of the first families in Sulaco. And then the widowed Señora Gavilaso de Valdes rolled by, handsome and dignified, in a great machine in which she used to travel to and from her country house, surrounded by an armed retinue in leather suits and big sombreros, with carbines at the bows of their saddles. She was a woman of most distinguished family, proud, rich, and kind-hearted. Her second son, Jaime, had just gone off on the Staff of Barrios. The eldest, a worthless fellow of a moody disposition, filled Sulaco with the noise of his dissipations, and gambled heavily at the club. The two youngest boys, with yellow Ribierist cockades in their caps, sat on the front seat. She, too, affected not to see the Señor Decoud talking publicly with Antonia in defiance of every convention. And he not even her *novio* as far as the world knew! Though, even in that case, it would have been scandal enough. But the dignified old lady, respected and admired by the first families, would have been still more shocked if she could have heard the words they were exchanging.

'Did you say I lost sight of the aim? I have only one aim in the world.'

She made an almost imperceptible negative movement of her head, still staring across the street at the Avellanos's house, grey, marked with decay, and with iron bars like a prison.

'And it would be so easy of attainment,' he continued, 'this aim which, whether knowingly or not, I have always had in my heart – ever since the day when you snubbed me so horribly once in Paris, you remember.'

A slight smile seemed to move the corner of the lip that was on his side.

'You know you were a very terrible person, a sort of Charlotte Corday in a schoolgirl's dress; a ferocious patriot. I suppose you would have stuck a knife into Guzman Bento?'

She interrupted him. 'You do me too much honour.'

'At any rate,' he said, changing suddenly to a tone of bitter levity, 'you would have sent me to stab him without compunction.'

'Ah, *par exemple*!' she murmured in a shocked tone.

'Well,' he argued, mockingly, 'you do keep me here writing deadly nonsense. Deadly to me! It has already killed my self-respect. And you may imagine,' he continued, his tone passing into light banter, 'that Montero, should he be successful, would get even with me in the only way such a brute can get even with a man of intelligence who condescends to call him a *gran' bestia* three times a week. It's a sort of intellectual death; but there is the other one in the background for a journalist of my ability.'

'If he is successful!' said Antonia, thoughtfully.

'You seem satisfied to see my life hang on a thread,' Decoud replied, with a broad smile. 'And the other Montero, the "my trusted brother" of the proclamations, the *guerrillero* – haven't I written that he was taking the guests' overcoats and changing plates in Paris at our Legation in the intervals of spying on our refugees there, in the time of Rojas? He will wash out that sacred truth in blood. In my blood! Why do you look annoyed? This is simply a bit of the biography of one of our great men. What do you think he will do to me? There is a certain convent wall round the corner of the Plaza, opposite the door of the Bull Ring. You know? Opposite the door with the inscription, "Intrada de la Sombra". Appropriate, perhaps! That's where the uncle of our host gave up his Anglo-South-American soul. And, note, he might have run away. A man who has fought with weapons may run away. You might have let me go with Barrios if you had cared for me. I would have carried one of those rifles, in which Don José believes, with the greatest satisfaction, in the ranks of poor peons and *indios*, that know nothing either of reason or politics. The most forlorn hope in the most forlorn army on earth would have been safer than that for which you made me stay here. When you make war you may retreat, but not when you spend your time in inciting poor ignorant fools to kill and to die.'

His tone remained light, and as if unaware of his presence she stood motionless, her hands clasped lightly, the fan hanging down from her interlaced fingers. He waited for a while, and then:

'I shall go to the wall,' he said, with a sort of jocular desperation.

Even that declaration did not make her look at him. Her head remained still, her eyes fixed upon the house of the Avellanos, whose chipped pilasters, broken cornices, the whole degradation of dignity was hidden now by the gathering dusk of the street. In her whole figure her lips alone moved, forming the words:

'Martin, you will make me cry.'

He remained silent for a minute, startled, as if overwhelmed by a sort of awed happiness, with the lines of the mocking smile still stiffened about his mouth, and incredulous surprise in his eyes. The value of a sentence is in the personality which utters it, for nothing new can be said by man or woman; and those were the last words, it seemed to him, that could ever have been spoken by Antonia. He had never made it up with her so completely in all their intercourse of small encounters; but even before she had time to turn towards him, which she did slowly with a rigid grace, he had begun to plead:

'My sister is only waiting to embrace you. My father is transported with joy. I won't say anything of my mother! Our mothers were like sisters. There is the mail-boat for the south next week – let us go. That Morago is a fool! A man like Montero is bribed. It's the practice of the country. It's tradition – it's politics. Read *Fifty Years of Misrule*.'

'Leave poor papa alone, Don Martin. He believes –'

'I have the greatest tenderness for your father,' he began, hurriedly. 'But I love you, Antonia! And Moraga has miserably mismanaged this business. Perhaps your father did, too; I don't know. Montero was bribable. Why, I suppose he only wanted his share of this famous loan for national development. Why didn't the stupid Sta Marta people give him a mission to Europe, or something? He would have taken five years' salary in advance, and gone on loafing in Paris, this stupid, ferocious *indio*!'

'This man,' she said, thoughtfully, and very calm before this outburst, 'was intoxicated with vanity. We had all the information, not from Morago only; from others, too. There was his brother intriguing, too.'

'Oh yes!' he said. 'Of course you know. You know everything. You read all the correspondence, you write all the papers – all those State papers that are inspired here, in this room, in blind deference to a theory of political purity. Hadn't you Charles Gould before your eyes? "Rey de Sulaco!" He and his mine are the practical demonstration of what could have been done. Do you think he succeeded by his fidelity to a theory of virtue? And all those railway people, with their honest work! Of course, their work is honest! But what if you cannot work honestly till the thieves are satisfied? Could he not, a gentleman, have told this Sir John what's-his-name that Montero had to be bought off – he and all his Negro liberals hanging on to his gold-laced sleeve? He ought to have been bought off with his own stupid weight of gold – his weight of gold, I tell you, boots, sabre, spurs, cocked hat, and all.'

She shook her head slightly. 'It was impossible,' she murmured.

'He wanted the whole lot? What?'

She was facing him now in the deep recess of the window, very close and motionless. Her lips moved rapidly. Decoud, leaning his back against the wall, listened with crossed arms and lowered eyelids. He drank the tones of her even voice, and watched the agitated life of her throat, as if waves of emotion had run from her heart to pass out into the air in her reasonable words. He also had his aspirations, he aspired to carry her away out of these deadly futilities of *pronunciamientos* and reforms. All this was wrong – utterly wrong; but she fascinated him, and sometimes the sheer sagacity of a phrase would break the charm, replace the fascination by a sudden unwilling thrill of interest. Some women hovered, as it were, on the threshold of genius, he reflected. They did not want to know, or think, or understand. Passion stood for all that, and he was ready to believe that some startlingly profound remark, some appreciation of character, or a judgement upon an event, bordered on the miraculous. In the mature Antonia he could see with an extraordinary vividness the austere schoolgirl of the earlier days. She seduced his attention; sometimes he could not restrain a murmur of assent; now and then he advanced an objection quite seriously. Gradually they began to argue; the curtain half hid them from the people in the *sala*.

Outside it had grown dark. From the deep trench of shadow between the houses, lit up vaguely by the glimmer of street lamps, ascended the evening silence of Sulaco; the silence of a town with a few carriages, of unshod horses, and a softly sandalled population. The windows of the Casa Gould flung their shining parallelograms upon the house of Avellanos. Now and then a shuffle of feet passed below with the pulsating red glow of a cigarette at the foot of the walls; and the night air, as if cooled by the snows of Higuerota, refreshed their faces.

'We Occidentals,' said Martin Decoud, using the usual term the provincials of Sulaco applied to themselves, 'have been always distinct and separated. As long as we hold Cayta nothing can reach us. In all our troubles no army has marched over these mountains. A revolution in the central provinces isolates us at once. Look how complete it is now! The news of Barrios's movement will be cabled to the United States, and only in that way will it reach Sta Marta by the cable from the other seaboard. We have the greatest riches, the greatest fertility, the purest blood in our great families, the most laborious population. The Occidental Province should stand alone. The early Federalism was not bad for us. Then came this union which Don Henrique Gould resisted. It opened the road to tyranny; and, ever since, the rest of Costaguana hangs like a millstone round our necks. The Occidental territory is large enough to make any man's country. Look at the mountains! Nature itself seems to cry to us "Separate!" '

She made an energetic gesture of negation. A silence fell.

'Oh, yes, I know it's contrary to the doctrine laid down in the *History of Fifty Years' Misrule*. I am only trying to be sensible. But my sense seems always to give you cause for offence. Have I startled you very much with this perfectly reasonable aspiration?'

She shook her head. No, she was not startled, but the idea shocked her early convictions. Her patriotism was larger. She had never considered that possibility.

'It may yet be the means of saving some of your convictions,' he said, prophetically.

She did not answer. She seemed tired. They leaned side by side on the rail of the little balcony, very friendly, having exhausted politics, giving themselves up to the silent feeling of their nearness, in one of those profound pauses that fall upon the rhythm of passion. Towards the *plaza* end of the street the glowing coals in the *brazeros* of the market women cooking their evening meal gleamed red along the edge of the pavement. A man appeared without a sound in the light of a street lamp, showing the coloured inverted triangle of his bordered poncho, square on his shoulders, hanging to a point below his knees. From the harbour end of the *calle* a horseman walked his soft-stepping mount, gleaming silver-grey abreast each lamp under the dark shape of the rider.

'Behold the illustrious Capataz de Cargadores,' said Decoud, gently, 'coming in all his splendour after his work is done. The next great man of Sulaco after Don Carlos Gould. But he is good-natured, and let me make friends with him.'

'Ah, indeed!' said Antonia. 'How did you make friends?'

'A journalist ought to have his finger on the popular pulse, and this man is one of the leaders of the populace. A journalist ought to know remarkable men – and this man is remarkable in his way.'

'Ah, yes!' said Antonia, thoughtfully. 'It is known that this Italian has a great influence.'

The horseman has passed below them, with a gleam of dim light on the shining broad quarters of the grey mare, on a bright heavy stirrup, on a long silver spur; but the short flick of yellowish flame in the dusk was powerless against the muffled-up mysteriousness of the dark figure with an invisible face concealed by a great sombrero.

Decoud and Antonia remained leaning over the balcony, side by side, touching elbows, with their heads overhanging the darkness of the street, and the brilliantly lighted *sala* at their backs. This was a *tête-à-tête* of extreme impropriety; something of which in the whole extent of the Republic only the extraordinary Antonia could be capable – the poor, motherless girl, never accompanied, with a careless father, who had thought only of making her learned. Even Decoud himself seemed to feel that this was as much as he could expect of having her to himself till – till the revolution was over and he could carry her off to Europe, away from the endlessness of civil strife, whose folly seemed even harder to bear than its ignominy. After one Montero there would be another, the lawlessness of a populace of all colours and races, barbarism, irremediable tyranny. As the great Liberator Bolívar had said in the bitterness of his spirit, 'America is ungovernable. Those who worked for her independence have ploughed the sea.' He did not care, he declared boldly; he seized every opportunity to tell her that though she had managed to make a Blanco journalist of him, he was no patriot. First of all, the word had no sense for cultured minds, to whom the narrowness of every belief is odious; and secondly, in connection with the everlasting troubles of this unhappy country it was hopelessly besmirched; it had been the cry of dark barbarism, the cloak of lawlessness, of crimes, of rapacity, of simple thieving.

He was surprised at the warmth of his own utterance. He had no need to drop his voice; it had been low all the time, a mere murmur in the silence of dark houses with their shutters closed early against the night air, as is the custom of Sulaco. Only the *sala* of the Casa Gould flung out defiantly the blaze of its four windows, the bright appeal of light in the whole dumb obscurity of the street. And the murmur on the little balcony went on after a short pause.

'But we are labouring to change all that,' Antonia protested. 'It is exactly what we desire. It is our object. It is the great cause. And the word you despise has stood also for sacrifice, for courage, for constancy, for suffering. Papa, who –'

'Ploughing the sea,' interrupted Decoud, looking down.

There was below the sound of hasty and ponderous footsteps.

'Your uncle, the Grand Vicar of the cathedral, has just turned under the gate,' observed Decoud. 'He said Mass for the troops in the Plaza this morning. They had built for him an altar of drums, you know. And they brought outside all the painted blocks to take the air. All the wooden saints stood militarily in a row at the top of the great flight of steps. They looked like a gorgeous escort attending the Vicar-General. I saw the great function from the windows of the *Porvenir*. He is amazing, your uncle, the last of the Corbeláns. He glittered exceedingly in his vestments with a great crimson velvet cross down his back. And all the time our saviour Barrios sat in the Amarilla Club drinking punch at an open window. *Espirit fort* – our Barrios. I expected every moment your uncle to launch an ex-communication there and then at the black eye-patch in the window across the Plaza. But not at all. Ultimately the troops marched off. Later Barrios came down with some of the officers, and stood with his uniform all unbuttoned, discoursing at the edge of the pavement. Suddenly your uncle appeared, no longer glittering, but all black, at the cathedral door with that threatening aspect he has – you know, like a sort of avenging spirit. He gives one look, strides over straight at the group of uniforms, and leads away the general by the elbow. He walked him for a quarter of an hour in the shade of a wall. Never let go his elbow for a moment, talking all the time with exaltation, and gesticulating with a long black arm. It was a curious scene. The officers seemed struck with astonishment. Remarkable man, your missionary uncle. He hates an infidel much less than a heretic, and prefers a heathen many times to an infidel. He condescends graciously to call me a heathen, sometimes, you know.'

Antonia listened with her hands over the balustrade, opening and shutting the fan gently; and Decoud talked a little nervously, as if afraid that she would leave him at the first pause. Their comparative isolation, the precious sense of intimacy, the slight contact of their arms, affected him softly; for now and then a tender inflection crept into the flow of his ironic murmurs.

'Any slight sign of favour from a relative of yours is welcome, Antonia. And perhaps he understands me, after all! But I know him, too, our Padre Corbelán. The idea of political honour, justice, and honesty for him consists in the restitution of the confiscated Church property. Nothing else could have drawn that fierce converter of savage Indians out of the wilds to work for the Ribierist cause! Nothing else but that wild hope! He would make a *pronunciamiento* himself for such an object against any Government if he could only get followers! What does Don Carlos Gould think of that? But, of course, with his English impenetrability, nobody can tell what he thinks. Probably he thinks of nothing apart from his mine; of his "*Imperium in Imperio*". As to Mrs Gould, she thinks of her schools, of her hospitals, of the mothers with the young babies, of every sick old man in the three villages. If you were to turn your head now you would see her extracting a report from that sinister doctor in a check shirt – what's his name? Monygham – or else catechizing Don Pepe or perhaps listening to Padre Román. They are all down here today – all her ministers of state. Well, she is a sensible woman, and perhaps Don Carlos is a sensible man. It's a part of solid English sense not to think too much; to see only what may be of practical use at the moment. These people are not like ourselves. We have no political reason; we have political passions – sometimes. What is a conviction? A particular view of our personal advantage either practical or emotional. No one is a patriot for nothing. The word serves us well. But I am clear-sighted, and I shall not use that word to you, Antonia! I have no patriotic illusions. I have only the supreme illusion of a lover.'

He paused, then muttered almost inaudibly, 'That can lead one very far, though.'

Behind their backs the political tide that once in every twenty-four hours set with a strong flood through the Gould drawing-room could be heard, rising higher in a hum of voices. Men had been dropping in singly, or in twos and threes: the higher officials of the province, engineers of the railway, sunburnt and in tweeds, with the frosted head of their chief smiling with slow, humorous indulgence amongst the young eager faces. Scarfe, the lover of fandangos, had already slipped out in search of some dance, no matter where, on the outskirts of the town. Don Juste Lopez, after taking his daughters home, had entered solemnly, in a black creased coat buttoned up under his spreading brown beard. The few members of the Provincial Assembly present clustered at once around their President to discuss the news of the war and the last proclamation of the rebel Montero, the miserable Montero, calling in the name of 'a justly incensed democracy' upon all the Provincial Assemblies of the Republic to suspend their sittings till his sword had made peace and the will of the people could be consulted. It was practically an invitation to dissolve: an unheard-of audacity of that evil madman.

The indignation ran high in the knot of deputies behind José Avellanos. Don

José, lifting up his voice, cried out to them over the high back of his chair, 'Sulaco has answered by sending today an army upon his flank. If all the other provinces show only half as much patriotism as we, Occidentals –'

A great outburst of acclamations covered the vibrating treble of the life and soul of the party. Yes! Yes! This was true! A great truth! Sulaco was in the forefront as ever! It was a boastful tumult, the hopefulness inspired by the event of the day breaking out amongst those *caballeros* of the Campo thinking of their herds, of their lands, of the safety of their families. Everything was at stake . . . No! It was impossible that Montero should succeed! This criminal, this shameless *indio*! The clamour continued for some time, everybody else in the room looking towards the group where Don Juste had put on his air of impartial solemnity as if presiding at a sitting of the Provincial Assembly. Decoud had turned round at the noise, and, leaning his back on the balustrade, shouted into the room with all the strength of his lungs, '*Gran' bestia!*'

This unexpected cry had the effect of stilling the noise. All the eyes were directed to the window with an approving expectation; but Decoud had already turned his back upon the room, and was again leaning out over the quiet street.

'This is the quintessence of my journalism; this is the supreme argument,' he said to Antonia. 'I have invented this definition, this last word on a great question. But I am no patriot. I am no more of a patriot than the Capataz of the Sulaco Cargadores, this Genoese who has done such great things for this harbour – this active usher-in of the material implements for our progress. You have heard Captain Mitchell confess over and over again that till he got this man he could never tell how long it would take to unload a ship. That is bad for progress. You have seen him pass by after his labours on his famous horse to dazzle the girls in some ballroom with an earthen floor. He is a fortunate fellow! His work is an exercise of personal powers; his leisure is spent in receiving the marks of extraordinary adulation. And he likes it, too. Can anybody be more fortunate? To be feared and admired is –'

'And are these your highest aspirations, Don Martin?' interrupted Antonia.

'I was speaking of a man of that sort,' said Decoud, curtly. 'The heroes of the world have been feared and admired. What more could he want?'

Decoud had often felt his familiar habit of ironic thought fall shattered against Antonia's gravity. She irritated him as if she, too, had suffered from that inexplicable feminine obtuseness which stands so often between a man and a woman of the more ordinary sort. But he overcame his vexation at once. He was very far from thinking Antonia ordinary, whatever verdict his scepticism might have pronounced upon himself. With a touch of penetrating tenderness in his voice he assured her that his only aspiration was to a felicity so high that it seemed almost unrealizable on this earth.

She coloured invisibly, with a warmth against which the breeze from the sierra seemed to have lost its cooling power in the sudden melting of the snows. His whisper could not have carried so far, though there was enough ardour in his tone to melt a heart of ice. Antonia turned away abruptly, as if to carry his whispered assurance into the room behind, full of light, noisy with voices.

The tide of political speculation was beating high within the four walls of the great *sala*, as if driven beyond the marks by a great gust of hope. Don Juste's fan-shaped beard was still the centre of loud and animated discussions. There was a self-confident ring in all the voices. Even the few Europeans around Charles Gould – a Dane, a couple of Frenchmen, a discreet fat German, smiling, with down-cast eyes, the representatives of those material interests that had got a footing in Sulaco under the protecting might of the San Tomé mine – had infused a lot of good humour into their deference. Charles Gould, to whom they were paying their court, was the visible sign of the stability that could be achieved on the shifting ground of revolutions. They felt hopeful about their various undertakings. One of the two Frenchmen, small, black, with flittering eyes lost in an immense growth of bushy beard, waved his tiny brown hands and delicate wrists. He had been travelling in the interior of the province for a syndicate of European capitalists. His forcible '*Monsieur l'Administrateur*' returning every minute shrilled above the steady hum of conversations. He was relating his discoveries. He was ecstatic. Charles Gould glanced down at him courteously.

At a given moment of these necessary receptions it was Mrs Gould's habit to withdraw quietly into a little drawing-room, especially her own, next to the great *sala*. She had risen, and, waiting for Antonia, listened with a slightly worried graciousness to the engineer-in-chief of the railway, who stooped over her, relating slowly, without the slightest gesture, something apparently amusing, for his eyes had a humorous twinkle. Antonia, before she advanced into the room to join Mrs Gould, turned her head over her shoulder towards Decoud, only for a moment.

'Why should any one of us think his aspirations unrealizable?' she said, rapidly.

'I am going to cling to mine to the end, Antonia,' he answered, through clenched teeth, then bowed very low, a little distantly.

The engineer-in-chief had not finished telling his amusing story. The humours of railway building in South America appealed to his keen appreciation of the absurd, and he told his instances of ignorant prejudice and ignorant cunning very well. Now, Mrs Gould gave him all her attention as he walked by her side escorting the ladies out of the room. Finally all three passed unnoticed through the glass doors in the gallery. Only a tall priest stalking silently in the noise of the *sala* checked himself to look after them. Father Corbelán, whom Decoud had seen from the balcony turning into the gateway of the Casa Gould, had addressed no one since coming in. The long, skimpy soutane accentuated the tallness of his stature; he carried his powerful torso thrown forward; and the straight, black bar of his joined eyebrows, the pugnacious outline of the bony face, the white spot of a scar on the bluish shaven cheeks (a testimonial to his apostolic zeal from a party of unconverted Indians), suggested something unlawful behind his priesthood, the idea of a chaplain of bandits.

He separated his bony knotted hands clasped behind his back, to shake his finger at Martin.

Decoud had stepped into the room after Antonia. But he did not go far. He had remained just within, against the curtain, with an expression of not quite genuine gravity, like a grown-up person taking part in a game of children. He gazed quietly at the threatening finger.

'I have watched your reverence converting General Barrios by a special sermon on the Plaza,' he said, without making the slightest movement.

'What miserable nonsense!' Father Corbelán's deep voice resounded all over the room, making all the heads turn on the shoulders. 'The man is a drunkard. *Señores*, the God of your General is a bottle!'

His contemptuous arbitrary voice caused an uneasy suspension of every sound, as if the self-confidence of the gathering had been staggered by a blow. But nobody took up Father Corbelán's declaration.

It was known that Father Corbelán had come out of the wilds to advocate the sacred rights of the Church with the same fanatical fearlessness with which he had gone preaching to blood-thirsty savages, devoid of human compassion or worship of any kind. Rumours of legendary proportions told of his successes as a missionary beyond the eye of Christian men. He had baptized whole nations of Indians, living with them like a savage himself. It was related that the padre used to ride with his Indians for days, half naked, carrying a bullock-hide shield, and, no doubt, a long lance, too – who knows? That he had wandered clothed in skins, seeking for proselytes somewhere near the snow line of the Cordillera. Of these exploits Padre Corbelán himself was never known to talk. But he made no secret of his opinion that the politicians of Sta Marta had harder hearts and more corrupt minds than the heathen to whom he had carried the word of God. His injudicious zeal for the temporal welfare of the Church was damaging the Ribierist cause. It was common knowledge that he had refused to be made titular bishop of the Occidental diocese till justice was done to a despoiled Church. The political *jefe* of Sulaco (the same dignitary whom Captain Mitchell saved from the mob afterwards) hinted with naïve cynicism that doubtless their Excellencies the Ministers sent the padre over the mountains to Sulaco in the worst season of the year in the hope that he would be frozen to death by the icy blasts of the high *páramos*. Every year a few hardy muleteers – men inured to exposure – were known to perish in that way. But what would you have? Their Excellencies possibly had not realized what a tough priest he was. Meantime, the ignorant were beginning to murmur that the Ribierist reforms meant simply the taking away of the land from the people. Some of it was to be given to foreigners who made the railway; the greater part was to go to the padres.

These were the results of the Grand Vicar's zeal. Even from the short allocution to the troops on the Plaza (which only the first ranks could have heard) he had not been able to keep out his fixed idea of an outraged Church waiting for reparation from a penitent country. The political *jefe* had been exasperated. But he could not very well throw the brother-in-law of Don José into the prison of the Cabildo. The chief magistrate, an easy-going and popular official, visited the Casa Gould, walking over after sunset from the Intendencia, unattended, acknowledging with dignified courtesy the salutations of high and low alike. That evening he had walked up straight to Charles Gould and had hissed out to him that he would have liked to deport the Grand Vicar out of Sulaco, anywhere, to some desert island, to the Isabels, for instance. 'The one without water preferably – eh, Don Carlos?' he had added in a tone between jest and earnest. This uncontrollable priest, who had rejected his offer of the episcopal palace for a residence and preferred to hang his shabby hammock amongst the rubble and spiders of the sequestrated Dominican Convent, had taken into his head to advocate an unconditional pardon for Hernandez the Robber! And this was not enough; he seemed to have entered into communication with the most audacious criminal the country had known for years. The Sulaco police knew, of course, what was going on. Padre Corbelán had got hold of that reckless Italian, the Capataz de Cargadores, the only man fit for such an errand, and had sent a message through him. Father Corbelán had studied in Rome, and could speak Italian. The Capataz was known to visit the old Dominican Convent at night. An old woman who served the Grand Vicar had heard the name of Hernandez pronounced; and only last Saturday afternoon the Capataz had been observed galloping out of town. He did not return for two days. The police would have laid the Italian by the heels if it had not been for fear of the *cargadores*, a turbulent body of men, quite apt to raise a tumult. Nowadays it was not so easy to govern Sulaco. Bad characters flocked into it, attracted by the money in the pockets of the railway workmen. The populace was made restless by Father Corbelán's discourses. And the first magistrate explained to Charles Gould that now the province was stripped of troops any outbreak of lawlessness would find the authorities with their boots off, as it were.

Then he went away moodily to sit in an armchair, smoking a long, thin cigar, not very far from Don José, with whom, bending over sideways, he exchanged a few words from time to time. He ignored the entrance of the priest, and whenever Father Corbelán's voice was raised behind him, he shrugged his shoulders impatiently.

Father Corbelán had remained quite motionless for a time with that something vengeful in his immobility which seemed to characterize all his attitudes. A lurid glow of strong convictions gave its peculiar aspect to the black figure. But its fierceness became softened as the padre, fixing his eyes upon Decoud, raised his long, black arm slowly, impressively:

'And you – you are a perfect heathen,' he said, in a subdued, deep voice.

He made a step nearer, pointing a forefinger at the young man's breast. Decoud, very calm, felt the wall behind the curtain with the back of his head. Then, with his chin tilted well up, he smiled.

'Very well,' he agreed with the slightly weary nonchalance of a man well used to these passages. 'But is it perhaps that you have not discovered yet what is the God of my worship? It was an easier task with our Barrios.'

The priest suppressed a gesture of discouragement. 'You believe neither in stick nor stone,' he said.

'Nor bottle,' added Decoud without stirring. 'Neither does the other of your reverence's confidants. I mean the Capataz of the Cargadores. He does not drink. Your reading of my character does honour to your perspicacity. But why call me a heathen?'

'True,' retorted the priest. 'You are ten times worse. A miracle could not convert you.'

'I certainly do not believe in miracles,' said Decoud, quietly. Father Corbelán shrugged his high, broad shoulders doubtfully.

'A sort of Frenchman – godless – a materialist,' he pronounced slowly, as if weighing the terms of a careful analysis. 'Neither the son of his own country nor of any other,' he continued thoughtfully.

'Scarcely human, in fact,' Decoud commented under his breath, his head at rest against the wall, his eyes gazing up at the ceiling.

'The victim of his faithless age,' Father Corbelán resumed in a deep but subdued voice.

'But of some use as a journalist.' Decoud changed his pose and spoke in a more animated tone. 'Has your worship neglected to read the last number of the *Porvenir*? I assure you it is just like the others. On the general policy it continues to call Montero a *gran' bestia*, and stigmatize his brother, the *guerrillero*, for a combination of lacquey and spy. What could be more effective? In local affairs it urges the Provincial Government to enlist bodily into the national army the band of Hernandez the Robber – who is apparently the protégé of the Church – or at least of the Great Vicar. Nothing could be more sound.'

The priest nodded and turned on the heels of his square-toed shoes with big steel buckles. Again, with his hands clasped behind his back, he paced to and fro, planting his feet firmly. When he swung about, the skirt of his soutane was inflated slightly by the brusqueness of his movements.

The great *sala* had been emptying itself slowly. When the Jefe Politico rose to go, most of those still remaining stood up suddenly in sign of respect, and Don José Avellanos stopped the rocking of the chair. But the good-natured First Official made a deprecatory gesture, waved his hand to Charles Gould, and went out discreetly.

In the comparative peace of the room the screaming '*Monsieur l'Administrateur*' of the frail, hairy Frenchman seemed to acquire a preternatural shrillness. The explorer of the Capitalist syndicate was still enthusiastic. 'Ten million dollars' worth of copper practically in sight, *Monsieur l'Administrateur*. Ten millions in sight! And a railway coming – a railway! They will never believe my report. *C'est trop beau*.' He fell a prey to a screaming ecstasy, in the midst of sagely nodding heads, before Charles Gould's imperturbable calm.

And only the priest continued his pacing, flinging round the skirt of his soutane at each end of his beat. Decoud murmured to him ironically: 'Those gentlemen talk about their gods.'

Father Corbelán stopped short, looked at the journalist of Sulaco fixedly for a moment, shrugged his shoulders slightly, and resumed his plodding walk of an obstinate traveller.

And now the Europeans were dropping off from the group around Charles Gould till the Administrator of the Great Silver Mine could be seen in his whole lank length, from head to foot, left stranded by the ebbing tide of his guests on the great square of carpet, as it were a multi-coloured shoal of flowers and arabesques under his brown boots. Father Corbelán approached the rocking-chair of Don José Avellanos.

'Come, brother,' he said, with kindly brusqueness and a touch of relieved impatience a man may feel at the end of a perfectly useless ceremony. '*A la Casa! A la Casa*! This has been all talk. Let us now go and think and pray for guidance from Heaven.'

He rolled his black eyes upwards. By the side of the frail diplomatist – the life and soul of the party – he seemed gigantic, with a gleam of fanaticism in the glance. But the voice of the party, or, rather, its mouthpiece, the 'son Decoud' from Paris, turned journalist for the sake of Antonia's eyes, knew very well that it was not so, that he was only a strenuous priest with one idea, feared by the women and execrated by the men of the people. Martin Decoud, the dilettante in life, imagined himself to derive an artistic pleasure from watching the picturesque extreme of wrong-headedness into which an honest, almost sacred, conviction may drive a man. 'It is like madness. It must be – because it's self-destructive,' Decoud had said to himself often. It seemed to him that every conviction, as soon as it became effective, turned into that form of dementia the gods send upon those they wish to destroy. But he enjoyed the bitter flavour of that example with the zest of a connoisseur in the art of his choice. Those two men got on well together, as if each had felt respectively that a masterful conviction, as well as utter scepticism, may lead a man very far on the by-paths of political action.

Don José obeyed the touch of the big hairy hand. Decoud followed out the brothers-in-law. And there remained only one visitor in the vast empty *sala*, bluishly hazy with tobacco smoke, a heavy-eyed, round-cheeked man, with a drooping moustache, a hide merchant from Esmeralda, who had come overland to Sulaco, riding with a few peons across the coast range. He was very full of his journey, undertaken mostly for the purpose of seeing the Señor Administrador of San Tomé in relation to some assistance he required in his hide-exporting business. He hoped to enlarge it greatly now that the country was going to be settled. It was going to be settled, he repeated several times, degrading by a strange, anxious whine the sonority of the Spanish language, which he pattered rapidly, like some sort of cringing jargon. A plain man could carry on his little business now in the country, and even think of enlarging it – with safety. Was it not so? He seemed to beg Charles Gould for a confirmatory word, a grunt of assent, a simple nod even.

He could get nothing. His alarm increased, and in the pauses he would dart his eyes here and there; then, loth to give up, he would branch off into feeling allusion to the dangers of his journey. The audacious Hernandez, leaving his usual haunts, had crossed the Campo of Sulaco, and was known to be lurking in the ravines of the coast range. Yesterday, when distant only a few hours from Sulaco, the hide merchant and his servants had seen three men on the road arrested suspiciously, with their horses' heads together. Two of these rode off at once and disappeared in a shallow *quebrada* to the left. 'We stopped,' continued the man from Esmeralda, 'and I tried to hide behind a small bush. But none of my *mozos* would go forward to find out what it meant, and the third horseman seemed to be waiting for us to come up. It was no use. We had been seen. So we rode slowly on, trembling. He let us pass – a man on a grey horse with his hat down on his eyes – without a word of greeting; but by-and-by we heard him galloping after us. We faced about, but that did not seem to intimidate him. He rode up at speed, and touching my foot with the toe of his boot, asked me for a cigar, with a blood-curdling laugh. He did not seem armed, but when he put his hand back to reach for the matches I saw an enormous revolver strapped to his waist. I shuddered. He had very fierce whiskers, Don Carlos, and as he did not offer to go on we dared not move. At last, blowing the smoke of my cigar into the air through his nostrils, he said, "*Señor*, it would be perhaps better for you if I rode behind your party. You are not very far from Sulaco now. Go you with God." What would you? We went on. There was no resisting him. He might have been Hernandez himself; though my servant, who has been many times to Sulaco by sea, assured me that he had recognized him very well for the Capataz of the Steamship Company's *cargadores*. Later, that same evening, I saw that very man at the corner of the Plaza talking to a girl, a Morenita, who stood by the stirrup with her hand on the grey horse's mane.'

'I assure you, Señor Hirsch,' murmured Charles Gould, 'that you ran no risk on this occasion.'

'That may be, *señor*, though I tremble yet. A most fierce man – to look at. And what does it mean? A person employed by the Steamship Company talking with *salteadores* – no less, *señor*; the other horsemen were *salteadores* – in a lonely place, and behaving like a robber himself! A cigar is nothing, but what was there to prevent him asking me for my purse?'

'No, no, Señor Hirsch,' Charles Gould murmured, letting his glance stray away a little vacantly from the round face, with its hooked beak upturned towards him in an almost childlike appeal. 'If it was the Capataz de Cargadores you met – and there is no doubt, is there? – you were perfectly safe.'

'Thank you. You are very good. A very fierce-looking man, Don Carlos. He asked me for a cigar in a most familiar manner. What would have happened if I had not had a cigar? I shudder yet. What business had he to be talking with robbers in a lonely place?'

But Charles Gould, openly preoccupied now, gave not a sign, made no sound. The impenetrability of the embodied Gould Concession had its surface shades. To be dumb is merely a fatal affliction; but the King of Sulaco had words enough to give him all the mysterious weight of a taciturn force. His silences, backed by the power of speech, had as many shades of significance as uttered words in the way of assent, of doubt, of negation – even of simple comment. Some seemed to say plainly, 'Think it over'; others meant clearly 'Go ahead', a simple, low 'I see', with an affirmative nod, at the end of a patient listening half-hour was the equivalent of a verbal contract, which men had learned to trust implicitly, since behind it all there was the great San Tomé mine, the head and front of the material interests, so strong that it depended on no man's goodwill in the whole length and breadth of the Occidental Province – that is, on no goodwill which it could not buy ten times over. But to the little hook-nosed man from Esmeralda, anxious about the export of hides, the silence of Charles Gould portended a failure. Evidently this was no time for extending a modest man's business. He enveloped in a swift mental malediction the whole country, with all its inhabitants, partisans of Ribiera and Montero alike; and there were incipient tears in his mute anger at the thought of the innumerable ox-hides going to waste upon the dreamy expanse of the Campo, with its single palms rising like ships at sea within the perfect circle of horizon, its clumps of heavy timber motionless like solid islands of leaves above the running waves of grass. There were hides there, rotting, with no profit to anybody – rotting where they had been dropped by men called away to attend the urgent necessities of political revolutions. The practical, mercantile soul of Señor Hirsch rebelled against all that foolishness, while he was taking a respectful but disconcerted leave of the might and majesty of the San Tomé mine in the person of Charles Gould. He could not restrain a heart-broken murmur, wrung out of his very aching heart, as it were.

'It is a great, great foolishness, Don Carlos, all this. The price of hides in Hamburg is gone way up – up. Of course the Ribierist Government will do away with all that – when it gets established firmly. Meantime –'

He sighed.

'Yes, meantime,' repeated Charles Gould, inscrutably.

The other shrugged his shoulders. But he was not ready to go yet. There was a little matter he would like to mention very much if permitted. It appeared he had some good friends in Hamburg (he murmured the name of the firm) who were very anxious to do business, in dynamite, he explained. A contract for dynamite with the San Tomé mine, and then, perhaps, later on, other mines, which were sure to – The little man from Esmeralda was ready to enlarge, but Charles interrupted him. It seemed as though the patience of the Señor Administrador was giving way at last.

'Señor Hirsch,' he said, 'I have enough dynamite stored up at the mountain to send it down crashing into the valley' – his voice rose a little – 'to send half Sulaco into the air if I liked.'

Charles Gould smiled at the round, startled eyes of the dealer in hides, who was murmuring hastily, 'Just so. Just so.' And now he was going. It was impossible to do business in explosives with an Administrador so well provided and so discouraging. He had suffered agonies in the saddle and had exposed himself to the atrocities of the bandit Hernandez for nothing at all. Neither hides nor dynamite – and the very shoulders of the enterprising Israelite expressed dejection. At the door he bowed low to the engineer-in-chief. But at the bottom of the stairs in the patio he stopped short, with his podgy hand over his lips in attitude of meditative astonishment.

'What does he want to keep so much dynamite for?' he muttered. 'And why does he talk like this to me?'

The engineer-in-chief, looking in at the door of the empty *sala*, whence the political tide had ebbed out to the last insignificant drop, nodded familiarly to the master of the house, standing motionless like a tall beacon amongst the deserted shoals of furniture.

'Good night, I am going. Got my bike downstairs. The railway will know where to go for dynamite should we get short at any time. We have done cutting and chopping for a while now. We shall begin soon to blast our way through.'

'Don't come to me,' said Charles Gould, with perfect serenity. 'I shan't have an ounce to spare for anybody. Not an ounce. Not for my own brother, if I had a brother, and he were the engineer-in-chief of the most promising railway in the world.'

'What's that?' asked the engineer-in-chief, with equanimity. 'Unkindness?'

'No,' said Charles Gould, stolidly. 'Policy.'

'Radical, I should think,' the engineer-in-chief observed from the doorway.

'Is that the right name?' Charles Gould said, from the middle of the room.

'I mean, going to the roots, you know,' the engineer explained, with an air of enjoyment.

'Why, yes,' Charles pronounced, slowly. 'The Gould Concession has struck such deep roots in this country, in this province, in that gorge of the mountains, that nothing but dynamite shall be allowed to dislodge it from there. It's my choice. It's my last card to play.'

The engineer-in-chief whistled low. 'A pretty game,' he said, with a shade of discretion. 'And have you told Holroyd of that extraordinary trump card you hold in your hand?'

'Card only when it's played; when it falls at the end of the game. Till then you may call it a – a –'

'Weapon,' suggested the railway man.

'No. You may call it rather an argument,' corrected Charles Gould, gently. 'And that's how I've presented it to Mr Holroyd.'

'And what did he say to it?' asked the engineer, with undisguised interest.

'He' – Charles Gould spoke after a slight pause – 'he said something about holding on like grim death and putting our trust in God. I should imagine he must have been rather startled. But then' – pursued the Administrador of the San Tomé mine – 'but then, he is very far away, you know, and, as they say in this country, God is very high above.'

The engineer's appreciative laugh died away down the stairs, where the Madonna with the Child on her arm seemed to look after his shaking broad back from her shallow niche.

Chapter VI

A profound stillness reigned in the Casa Gould. The master of the house, walking along the corridor, opened the door of his room, and saw his wife sitting in a big armchair – his own smoking armchair – thoughtful, contemplating her little shoes. And she did not raise her eyes when he walked in.

'Tired?' asked Charles Gould.

'A little,' said Mrs Gould. Still without looking up, she added with feeling. 'There is an awful sense of unreality about all this.'

Charles Gould, before the long table strewn with papers, on which lay a hunting crop and a pair of spurs, stood looking at his wife: 'The heat and dust must have been awful this afternoon by the waterside,' he murmured, sympathetically. 'The glare on the water must have been simply terrible.'

'One could close one's eyes to the glare,' said Mrs Gould. 'But, my dear Charley, it is impossible for me to close my eyes to our position; to this awful . . .'

She raised her eyes and looked at her husband's face, from which all sign of sympathy or any other feeling had disappeared. 'Why don't you tell me something?' she almost wailed.

'I thought you had understood me perfectly from the first,' Charles Gould said, slowly. 'I thought we had said all there was to say a long time ago. There is nothing to say now. There were things to be done. We have done them; we have gone on doing them. There is no going back now. I don't suppose that, even from the first, there was really any possible way back. And, what's more, we can't even afford to stand still.'

'Ah, if one only knew how far you mean to go,' said his wife, inwardly trembling, but in an almost playful tone.

'Any distance, any length, of course,' was the answer, in a matter-of-fact tone, which caused Mrs Gould to make another effort to repress a shudder.

She stood up, smiling graciously, and her little figure seemed to be diminished still more by the heavy mass of her hair and the long train of her gown.

'But always to success,' she said, persuasively.

Charles Gould, enveloping her in the steely blue glance of his attentive eyes, answered without hesitation:

'Oh, there is no alternative.'

He put an immense assurance into his tone. As to the words, this was all that his conscience would allow him to say.

Mrs Gould's smile remained a shade too long upon her lips. She murmured:

'I will leave you; I've a slight headache. The heat, the dust, were indeed – I suppose you are going back to the mine before the morning?'

'At midnight,' said Charles Gould. 'We are bringing down the silver tomorrow. Then I shall take three whole days off in town with you.'

'Ah, you are going to meet the escort. I shall be on the balcony at five o'clock to see you pass. Till then, good-bye.'

Charles Gould walked rapidly round the table, and, seizing her hands, bent down, pressing them both to his lips. Before he straightened himself up again to his full height she had disengaged one to smooth his cheek with a light touch, as if he were a little boy.

'Try to get some rest for a couple of hours,' she murmured, with a glance at a hammock stretched in a distant part of the room. Her long train swished softly after her on the red tiles. At the door she looked back.

Two big lamps with unpolished glass globes bathed in a soft and abundant light the four white walls of the room, with a glass case of arms, the brass hilt of Henry Gould's cavalry sabre on its square of velvet, and the water-colour sketch of the San Tomé gorge. And Mrs Gould, gazing at the last in its black wooden frame, sighed out:

'Ah, if we had left it alone, Charley!'

'No,' Charles Gould said, moodily; 'it was impossible to leave it alone.'

'Perhaps it was impossible,' Mrs Gould admitted, slowly. Her lips quivered a little, but she smiled with an air of dainty bravado. 'We have disturbed a good many snakes in that Paradise, Charley, haven't we?'

'Yes, I remember,' said Charles Gould, 'it was Don Pepe who called the gorge the Paradise of snakes. No doubt we have disturbed a great many. But remember, my dear, that it is not now as it was when you made that sketch.' He waved his hand towards the small water-colour hanging alone upon the great bare wall. 'It is no longer a Paradise of snakes. We have brought mankind into it, and we cannot turn our backs upon them to go and begin a new life elsewhere.'

He confronted his wife with a firm, concentrated gaze, which Mrs Gould returned with a brave assumption of fearlessness before she went out, closing the door gently after her.

In contrast with the white glaring room the dimly lit corridor had the restful mysteriousness of a forest glade, suggested by the stems and the leaves of the plants ranged along the balustrade of the open side. In the streaks of light falling through the open doors of the reception-rooms, the blossoms, white and red and pale lilac, came out vivid with the brilliance of flowers in a stream of sunshine; and Mrs Gould, passing on, had the vividness of a figure seen in the clear patches of sun that chequer the gloom of open glades in the woods. The stones in the rings upon her hand pressed to her forehead glittered in the lamplight abreast of the door of the *sala*.

'Who's there?' she asked, in a startled voice. 'Is that you, Basilio?' She looked in, and saw Martin Decoud walking about, with an air of having lost something, amongst the chairs and tables.

'Antonia has forgotten her fan in here,' said Decoud, with a strange air of distraction; 'so I entered to see.'

But, even as he said this, he had obviously given up his search, and walked straight towards Mrs Gould, who looked at him with doubtful surprise.

'*Señora,*' he began, in a low voice.

'What is it, Don Martin?' asked Mrs Gould, And then she added, with a slight laugh, 'I am so nervous today,' as if to explain the eagerness of the question.

'Nothing immediately dangerous,' said Decoud, who now could not conceal his agitation. 'Pray don't distress yourself. No, really, you must not distress yourself.'

Mrs Gould, with her candid eyes very wide open, her lips composed into a smile, was steadying herself in the doorway with a little bejewelled hand.

'Perhaps you don't know how alarming you are, appearing like this unexpectedly –'

'I! Alarming!' he protested, sincerely vexed and surprised. 'I assure you that I am not in the least alarmed myself. A fan is lost; well, it will be found again. But I don't think it is here. It is a fan I am looking for. I cannot understand how Antonia could – Well! Have you found it, *amigo*?'

'No, *señor*,' said behind Mrs Gould the soft voice of Basilio, the head servant of the Casa. 'I don't think the *señorita* could have left it in this house at all.'

'Go and look for it in the patio again. Go now, my friend; look for it on the steps, under the gate; examine every flagstone; search for it till I come down again . . . That fellow' – he addressed himself in English to Mrs Gould – 'is always stealing up behind one's back on his bare feet. I set him to look for that fan directly I came into justify my reappearance, my sudden return.'

He paused and Mrs Gould said, amiably, 'You are always welcome.' She paused for a second, too. 'But I am waiting to learn the cause of your return.'

Decoud affected suddenly the utmost nonchalance.

'I can't bear to be spied upon. Oh, the cause? Yes, there is a cause; there is something else that is lost besides Antonia's favourite fan. As I was walking home after seeing Don José and Antonia to their house, the Capataz de Cargadores, riding down the street, spoke to me.'

'Has anything happened to the Violas?' inquired Mrs Gould.

'The Violas? You mean the old Garibaldino who keeps the hotel where the engineers live? Nothing happened there. The Capataz said nothing of them; he only told me that the telegraphist of the Cable Company was walking on the Plaza, bareheaded, looking out for me. This is news from the interior, Mrs Gould. I should rather say rumours of news.'

'Good news?' said Mrs Gould in a low voice.

'Worthless, I should think. But if I must define them. I would say bad. They are to the effect that a two days' battle has been fought near Sta Marta, and that the Ribierists are defeated. It must have happened a few days ago – perhaps a week. The rumour has just reached Cayta, and the man in charge of the cable station there has telegraphed the news to his colleague here. We might just as well have kept Barrios in Sulaco.'

'What's to be done now?' murmured Mrs Gould.

'Nothing. He's at sea with the troops. He will get to Cayta in a couple of days' time and learn the news there. What he will do then, who can say? Hold Cayta? Offer his submission to Montero? Disband his army – this last most likely, and go himself in one of the O.S.N. Company's steamers, north or south – to Valparaiso or to San Francisco, no matter where. Our Barrios has a great practice in exiles and repatriations, which mark the points in the political game.'

Decoud, exchanging a steady stare with Mrs Gould, added, tentatively, as it were, 'And yet, if we had Barrios with his 2,000 improved rifles here, something could have been done.'

'Montero victorious, completely victorious!' Mrs Gould breathed out in a tone of unbelief.

'A canard, probably. That sort of a bird is hatched in great numbers in such times as these. And even if it were true? Well, let us put things at their worst, let us say it is true.'

'Then everything is lost,' said Mrs Gould, with the calmness of despair.

Suddenly she seemed to divine, she seemed to see Decoud's tremendous excitement under its cloak of studied carelessness. It was, indeed, becoming visible in his audacious and watchful stare, in the curve, half-reckless, half-contemptuous, of his lips. And a French phrase came upon them as if, for this Costaguanero of the Boulevard, that had been the only forcible language:

'*Non, Madame. Rien n'est perdu.*'

It electrified Mrs Gould out of her benumbed attitude, and she said, vivaciously:

'What would you think of doing?'

But already there was something of mockery in Decoud's suppressed excitement.

'What would you expect a true Costaguanero to do? Another revolution, of course. On my word of honour, Mrs Gould, I believe I am a true *hijo del pais*, a true son of the country, whatever Father Corbelán may say. And I'm not so much of an unbeliever as not to have faith in my own ideas, in my own remedies, in my own desires.'

'Yes,' said Mrs Gould, doubtfully.

'You don't seem convinced,' Decoud went on again in French. 'Say, then, in my passions.'

Mrs Gould received this addition unflinchingly. To understand it thoroughly she did not require to hear his muttered assurance:

'There is nothing I would not do for the sake of Antonia. There is nothing I am not prepared to undertake. There is no risk I am not ready to run.'

Decoud seemed to find a fresh audacity in this voicing of his thoughts. 'You would not believe me if I were to say that it is the love of the country which –'

She made a sort of discouraged protest with her arm, as if to express that she had given up expecting that motive from anyone.

'A Sulaco revolution,' Decoud pursued in a forcible undertone. 'The Great Cause may be served here, on the very spot of its inception, in the place of its birth, Mrs Gould.'

Frowning, and biting her lower lip thoughtfully, she made a step away from the door.

'You are not going to speak to your husband?' Decoud arrested her anxiously.

'But you will need his help?'

'No doubt,' Decoud admitted without hesitation. 'Everything turns upon the San Tomé mine, but I would rather he didn't know anything as yet of my – my hopes.'

A puzzled look came upon Mrs Gould's face, and Decoud, approaching, explained confidentially:

'Don't you see, he's such an idealist.'

Mrs Gould flushed pink, and her eyes grew darker at the same time.

'Charley an idealist!' she said, as if to herself, wonderingly. 'What on earth do you mean?'

'Yes,' conceded Decoud, 'it's a wonderful thing to say with the sight of the San Tomé mine, the greatest fact in the whole of South America, perhaps, before our very eyes. But look even at that, he has idealized this fact to a point –' He paused. 'Mrs Gould, are you aware to what point he has idealized the existence, the worth, the meaning of the San Tomé mine? Are you aware of it?'

He must have known what he was talking about.

The effect he expected was produced. Mrs Gould, ready to take fire, gave it up suddenly with a low little sound that resembled a moan.

'What do you know?' she asked in a feeble voice.

'Nothing,' answered Decoud, firmly. 'But, then, don't you see, he's an Englishman?'

'Well, what of that?' asked Mrs Gould.

'Simply that he cannot act or exist without idealizing every simple feeling, desire, or achievement. He could not believe his own motives if he did not make them first a part of some fairy tale. The earth is not quite good enough for him, I fear. Do you excuse my frankness? Besides, whether you excuse it or not, it is part of the truth of things which hurts the – what do you call them? – the Anglo-Saxon's susceptibilities, and at the present moment I don't feel as if I could treat seriously either his conception of things or – if you allow me to say so – or yet yours.'

Mrs Gould gave no sign of being offended. 'I suppose Antonia understands you thoroughly?'

'Understands? Well, yes. But I am not sure that she approves. That, however, makes no difference. I am honest enough to tell you that, Mrs Gould.'

'Your idea, of course, is separation,' she said.

'Separation, of course,' declared Martin. 'Yes; separation of the whole Occidental Province from the rest of the unquiet body. But my true idea, the only one I care for, is not to be separated from Antonia.'

'And that is all?' asked Mrs Gould, without severity.

'Absolutely. I am not deceiving myself about my motives. She won't leave Sulaco for my sake, therefore Sulaco must leave the rest of the Republic to its fate. Nothing could be clearer than that. I like a clearly defined situation. I cannot part with Antonia, therefore the one and indivisible Republic of Costaguana must be made to part with its western province. Fortunately it happens to be also a sound policy. The richest, the most fertile part of this land may be saved from anarchy. Personally, I care little, very little; but it's a fact that the establishment of Montero in power would mean death to me. In all the proclamations of general pardon which I have seen, my name, with a few others, is specially excepted. The brothers hate me, as you know very well, Mrs Gould; and behold, here is the rumour of them having won a battle. You say that supposing it is true, I have plenty of time to run away.'

The slight, protesting murmur on the part of Mrs Gould made him pause for a moment, while he looked at her with a sombre and resolute glance.

'Oh, but I would, Mrs Gould. I would run away if it served that which at present is my only desire. I am courageous enough to say that, and to do it, too. But women, even our women, are idealists. It is Antonia that won't run away. A novel sort of vanity.'

'You call it vanity,' said Mrs Gould, in a shocked voice.

'Say pride, then, which, Father Corbelán would tell you, is a mortal sin. But I am not proud. I am simply too much in love to run away. At the same time I want to live. There is no love for a dead man. Therefore it is necessary that Sulaco should not recognize the victorious Montero.'

'And you think my husband will give you his support?'

'I think he can be drawn into it, like all idealists, when he once sees a sentimental basis for his action. But I wouldn't talk to him. Mere clear facts won't appeal to his sentiment. It is much better for him to convince himself in his own way. And, frankly, I could not, perhaps, just now pay sufficient respect to either his motives or even, perhaps, to yours, Mrs Gould.'

It was evident that Mrs Gould was very determined not to be offended. She smiled vaguely, while she seemed to think the matter over. As far as she could judge from the girl's half-confidences, Antonia understood that young man. Obviously there was promise of safety in his plan, or rather in his idea. Moreover, right or wrong, the idea could do no harm. And it was quite possible, also, that the rumour was false.

'You have some sort of a plan,' she said.

'Simplicity itself. Barrios has started, let him go on then; he will hold Cayta, which is the door of the sea route to Sulaco. They cannot send a sufficient force over the mountains. No; not even to cope with the band of Hernandez. Meantime we shall organize our resistance here. And for that, this very Hernandez will be useful. He has defeated troops as a bandit; he will no doubt accomplish the same thing if he is made a colonel or even a general. You know the country well enough not to be shocked by what I say, Mrs Gould. I have heard you assert that this poor bandit was the living, breathing example of cruelty, injustice, stupidity, and oppression, that ruin men's souls as well as their fortunes in this country. Well, there would be some poetical retribution in that man arising to crush the evils which had driven an honest *ranchero* into a life of crime. A fine idea of retribution in that, isn't there?'

Decoud had dropped easily into English, which he spoke with precision, very correctly, but with too many *z* sounds.

'Think also of your hospitals, of your schools, of your ailing mothers and feeble old men, of all that population which you and your husband have brought into the rocky gorge of San Tomé. Are you not responsible to your conscience for all these people? Is it not worth while to make another effort, which is not at all so desperate as it looks, rather than –'

Decoud finished his thought with an upward toss of the arm, suggesting annihilation; and Mrs Gould turned away her head with a look of horror.

'Why don't you say all this to my husband?' she asked, without looking at Decoud, who stood watching the effect of his words.

'Ah! But Don Carlos is so English,' he began. Mrs Gould interrupted:

'Leave that alone, Don Martin. He's as much a Costaguanero – No! He's more of a Costaguanero than yourself.'

'Sentimentalist, sentimentalist,' Decoud almost cooed, in a tone of gentle and soothing deference. 'Sentimentalist, after the amazing manner of your people. I have been watching El Rey de Sulaco since I came here on a fool's errand, and perhaps impelled by some treason of fate lurking behind the unaccountable turns of a man's life. But I don't matter, I am not a sentimentalist, I cannot endow my personal desires with a shining robe of silk and jewels. Life is not for me a moral romance derived from the tradition of a pretty fairy tale. No, Mrs Gould; I am practical. I am not afraid of my motives. But, pardon me, I have been rather carried away. What I wish to say is that I have been observing. I won't tell you what I have discovered –'

'No. That is unnecessary,' whispered Mrs Gould, once more averting her head.

'It is. Except one little fact, that your husband does not like me. It's a small matter, which, in the circumstances, seems to acquire a perfectly ridiculous importance. Ridiculous and immense; for, clearly, money is required for my plan,' he reflected; then added, meaningly, 'and we have two sentimentalists to deal with.'

'I don't know that I understand you, Don Martin,' said Mrs Gould, coldly, preserving the low key of their conversation. 'But, speaking as if I did, who is the other?'

'The great Holroyd in San Francisco, of course,' Decoud whispered, lightly. 'I think you understand me very well. Women are idealists; but then they are so perspicacious.'

But whatever was the reason of that remark, disparaging and complimentary at the same time, Mrs Gould seemed not to pay attention to it. The name of Holroyd had given a new tone to her anxiety.

'The silver escort is coming down to the harbour tomorrow; a whole six months' working, Don Martin!' she cried in dismay.

'Let it come down, then,' breathed out Decoud, earnestly, almost into her ear.

'But if the rumour should get about, and especially if it turned out true, troubles might break out in the town,' objected Mrs Gould.

Decoud admitted that it was possible. He knew well the town children of the Sulaco Campo: sullen, thievish, vindictive, and bloodthirsty, whatever great qualities their brothers of the plain might have had. But then there was that other sentimentalist, who attached a strangely idealistic meaning to concrete facts. This stream of silver must be kept flowing north to return in the form of financial backing from the great house of Holroyd. Up at the mountain in the strong-room of the mine the silver bars were worth less for his purpose than so much lead, from which at least bullets may be run. Let it come down to the harbour, ready for shipment.

The next north-going steamer would carry it off for the very salvation of the San Tomé mine, which has produced so much treasure. And, moreover, the rumour was probably false, he remarked, with much conviction in his hurried tone.

'Besides, *señora*,' concluded Decoud, 'we may suppress it for many days. I have been talking with the telegraphist in the middle of the Plaza Mayor; thus I am certain that we could not have been overheard. There was not even a bird in the air near us. And also let me tell you something more. I have been making friends with this man called Nostromo, the Capataz. We had a conversation this very evening, I walking by the side of his horse as he rode slowly out of the town just now. He promised me that if a riot took place for any reason – even for the most political of reasons, you understand – his *cargadores*, an important part of the populace, you will admit, should be found on the side of the Europeans.'

'He has promised you that?' Mrs Gould inquired, with interest. 'What made him make that promise to you?'

'Upon my word, I don't know,' declared Decoud, in a slightly surprised tone. 'He certainly promised me that, but now you ask me why I certainly could not tell you his reasons. He talked with his usual carelessness, which, if he had been anything else but a common sailor, I would call a pose or an affectation.'

Decoud, interrupting himself, looked at Mrs Gould curiously.

'Upon the whole,' he continued, 'I suppose he expects something to his advantage from it. You mustn't forget that he does not exercise his extraordinary power over the lower classes without a certain amount of personal risk and without a great profusion in spending his money. One must pay in some way or other for such a solid thing as individual prestige. He told me after we made friends at a dance, in a *posada* kept by a Mexican just outside the walls, that he had come here to make his fortune. I suppose he looks upon his prestige as a sort of investment.'

'Perhaps he prizes it for its own sake,' Mrs Gould said in a tone as if she were repelling an undeserved aspersion. 'Viola, the Garibaldino, with whom he has lived for some years, calls him the Incorruptible.'

'Ah! he belongs to the group of your protégés out there towards the harbour, Mrs Gould. *Muy bien*. And Captain Mitchell calls him wonderful. I have heard no end of tales of his strength, his audacity, his fidelity. No end of fine things. H'm! incorruptible! It is indeed a name of honour for the Capataz of the Cargadores of Sulaco. Incorruptible! Fine, but vague. However, I suppose he's sensible, too. And I talked to him upon that sane and practical assumption.'

'I prefer to think him disinterested, and therefore trustworthy,' Mrs Gould said, with the nearest approach to curtness it was in her nature to assume.

'Well, if so, then the silver will be still more safe. Let it come down, *señora*. Let it come down, so that it may go north and return to us in the shape of credit.'

Mrs Gould glanced along the corridor towards the door of her husband's room. Decoud, watching her as if she had his fate in her hands, detected an almost imperceptible nod of assent. He bowed with a smile, and, putting his hand into the breast pocket of his coat, pulled out a fan of light feathers set upon painted leaves of sandal-wood. 'I had it in my pocket,' he murmured, triumphantly, 'for a plausible pretext.' He bowed again. 'Good night, *señora*.'

Mrs Gould continued along the corridor away from her husband's room. The fate of the San Tomé mine was lying heavy upon her heart. It was a long time now since she had begun to fear it. It had been an idea. She had watched it with misgivings turning into a fetish, and now the fetish had grown into a monstrous and crushing weight. It was as if the inspiration of their early years had left her heart to turn into a wall of silver-bricks, erected by the silent work of evil spirits, between her and her husband. He seemed to dwell alone within a circumvallation of precious metal, leaving her outside with her school, her hospital, the sick mothers, and the feeble old men, mere insignificant vestiges of the initial inspiration. 'Those poor people!' she murmured to herself.

Below she heard the voice of Martin Decoud in the patio speaking loudly: 'I have found Doña Antonia's fan, Basilio. Look, here it is!'

Chapter VII

It was part of what Decoud would have called his sane materialism that he did not believe in the possibility of friendship between man and woman.

The one exception he allowed confirmed, he maintained, that absolute rule. Friendship was possible between brother and sister, meaning by friendship the frank unreserve, as before another human being, of thoughts and sensations; all the objectless and necessary sincerity of one's innermost life trying to react upon the profound sympathies of another existence.

His favourite sister, the handsome, slightly arbitrary, and resolute angel, ruling the father and mother Decoud in the first-floor apartments of a very fine Parisian house, was the recipient of Martin Decoud's confidences as to his thoughts, actions, purposes, doubts, and even failures . . .

Prepare our little circle in Paris for the birth of another South American Republic. One more or less, what does it matter? They may come into the world like evil flowers on a hotbed of rotten institutions; but the seed of this one has germinated in your brother's brain, and that will be enough for your devoted assent. I am writing this to you by the light of a single candle, in a sort of inn, near the harbour, kept by an Italian called Viola, a protégé of Mrs Gould. The whole building, which, for all I know, may have been contrived by a Conquistador farmer of the pearl fishery three hundred years ago, is perfectly silent. So is the plain between the town and the harbour; silent, but not so dark as the house, because the pickets of Italian workmen guarding the railway have lighted little fires all along the line. It was not so quiet around here yesterday. We had an awful riot – a sudden outbreak of the populace, which was not suppressed till late today. Its object, no doubt, was loot, and that was defeated, as you must have learned already from the cablegram sent via San Francisco and New York last night, when the cables were still open. You have read already there that the energetic action of the Europeans of the railway has saved the town from destruction, and you may believe that. I wrote out the cable myself. We have no Reuter's agency man here. I have also fired at the mob from the windows of the club, in company with some other young men of position. Our object was to keep the Calle de la Constitución clear for the exodus of the ladies and children, who have taken refuge on board a couple of cargo ships now in the harbour here. That was yesterday. You should also have learned from the cable that the missing President, Ribiera, who had disappeared after the battle of Sta Marta, has turned up here in Sulaco by one of those strange coincidences that are almost incredible, riding on a lame mule into the very midst of the street fighting. It appears that he had fled, in company with a muleteer called Bonifacio, across the mountains from the threats of Montero into the arms of an enraged mob.

The Capataz of Cargadores, that Italian sailor of whom I have written to you before, has saved him from an ignoble death. That man seems to have a particular talent for being on the spot whenever there is something picturesque to be done.

He was with me at four o'clock in the morning at the offices of the *Porvenir*, where he had turned up so early in order to warn me of the coming trouble, and also to assure me that he would keep his *cargadores* on the side of order. When the full daylight came we were looking together at the crowd on foot and on horseback, demonstrating on the Plaza and shying stones at the windows of the Intendencia. Nostromo (that is the name they call him by here) was pointing out to me his *cargadores* interspersed in the mob.

The sun shines late upon Sulaco, for it has first to climb above the mountains. In that clear morning light, brighter than twilight, Nostromo saw right across the vast Plaza, at the end of the street beyond the cathedral, a mounted man apparently in difficulties with a yelling knot of *leperos*. At once he said to me. 'That's a stranger. What is it they are doing to him?' Then he took out the silver whistle he is in the habit of using on the wharf (this man seems to disdain the use of any metal less precious than silver) and blew into it twice, evidently a preconcerted signal for his *cargadores*. He ran out immediately, and they rallied round him. I ran out, too, but was too late to follow them and help in the rescue of the stranger, whose animal had fallen. I was set upon at once as a hated aristocrat, and was only too glad to get to the club, where Don Jaime Berges (you may remember him visiting at our house in Paris some three years ago) thrust a sporting gun into my hands. They were already firing from the windows. There were little heaps of cartridges lying about on the open card-tables. I remember a couple of overturned chairs, some bottles rolling on the floor amongst the packs of cards scattered suddenly as the *caballeros* rose from their game to open fire upon the mob. Most of the young men had spent the night at the club in the expectation of some such disturbance. In two of the candelabra, on the consoles, the candles were burning down in their sockets. A large iron nut, probably stolen from the railway workshops, flew in from the street as I entered, and broke one of the large mirrors set in the wall. I noticed also one of the club servants tied up hand and foot with the cords of the curtain and flung in a corner. I have a vague recollection of Don Jaime assuring me hastily that the fellow had been detected putting poison into the dishes at supper. But I remember distinctly he was shrieking for mercy, without stopping at all, continuously, and so absolutely disregarded that nobody even took the trouble to gag him. The noise he made was so disagreeable that I had half a mind to do it myself. But there was no time to waste on such trifles. I took my place at one of the windows and began firing.

I didn't learn till later in the afternoon whom it was that Nostromo, with his *cargadores* and some Italian workmen as well, had managed to save from those drunken rascals. That man has a peculiar talent when anything striking to the imagination has to be done. I made that remark to him afterwards when we met after some sort of order had been restored in the town, and the answer he made rather surprised me. He said quite moodily, 'And how much do I get of that, *señor*?' Then it dawned upon me that perhaps this man's vanity has been satiated by the adulation of the common people and the confidences of his superiors!

Decoud paused to light a cigarette, then, with his head still over his writing, he blew a cloud of smoke, which seemed to rebound from the paper. He took up the pencil again.

That was yesterday evening on the Plaza, while he sat on the steps of the cathedral, his hands between his knees, holding the bridle of his famous silver-grey mare. He had led his body of *cargadores* splendidly all day long. He looked fatigued. I don't know how I looked. Very dirty. I suppose. But I suppose I also looked pleased. From the time the fugitive President had been got off to the s.s. *Minerva*, the tide of success had turned against the mob. They had been driven off the harbour, and out of the better streets of the town, into their own maze of ruins and *tolderías*. You must understand that this riot, whose primary object was undoubtedly the getting hold of the San Tomé silver stored in the lower rooms of the Custom House (besides the general looting of the *ricos*), had acquired a political colouring from the fact of two Deputies to the Provincial Assembly, Señores Gamacho and Fuentes, both from Bolson, putting themselves at the head of it – late in the afternoon, it is true, when the mob, disappointed in their hopes of loot, made a stand in the narrow streets to the cries of '*Viva la libertad!* Down with Feudalism!' (I wonder what they imagine feudalism to be?) 'Down with the Goths and Paralytics.' I suppose the Señores Gamacho and Fuentes knew what they were doing. They were prudent gentlemen. In the Assembly they called themselves Moderates, and opposed every energetic measure with philantropic pensiveness. At the first rumours of Montero's victory, they began to shop a subtle change of the pensive temper, and began to defy poor Don Juste Lopez in his Presidential tribune with an effrontery to which the poor man could only respond by a dazed smoothing of his beard and ringing of the Presidential bell. Then, when the downfall of the Ribierist cause became confirmed beyond the shadow of a doubt, they have blossomed into convinced Liberals, acting together as if they were Siamese twins, and ultimately taking charge, as it were, of the riot in the name of Monterist principles.

Their last move of eight o'clock last night was to organize themselves into a Monterist Committee which sits, as far as I know, in a *posada* kept by a retired Mexican bull-fighter, a great politician, too, whose name I have forgotten. Thence they have issued a communication to us, the Goths and Paralytics of the Amarilla Club (who have our own committee), inviting us to come to some provisional understanding for a truce, in order, they have the impudence to say, that the noble cause of Liberty 'should not be stained by the criminal excesses of Conservative selfishness'! As I came out to sit with Nostromo on the cathedral steps the club was

> busy considering a proper reply in the principal room, littered with exploded cartridges, with a lot of broken glass, blood smears, candlesticks, and all sorts of wreckage on the floor. But all this is nonsense. Nobody in the town has any real power except the railway engineers, whose men occupy the dismantled houses acquired by the Company for their town station on one side of the Plaza, and Nostromo, whose *cargadores* were sleeping under the arcades along the front of Anzani's shops. A fire of broken furniture out of the Intendencia saloons, mostly gilt, was burning on the Plaza, in a high flame swaying right upon the statue of Charles IV. The dead body of a man was lying on the steps of the pedestal, his arms thrown wide open, and his sombrero covering his face – the attention of some friend, perhaps. The light of the flame touched the foliage of the first trees on the Alameda, and played on the end of the side-street near by, blocked up by a jumble of ox-carts and dead bullocks. Sitting on one of the carcases, a *lepero*, muffled up, smoked a cigarette. It was a truce, you understand. The only other living being on the Plaza besides ourselves was a *cargador* walking to and fro, with a long, bare knife in his hand, like a sentry before the Arcades, where his friends were sleeping. And the only other spot of light in the dark town were the lighted windows of the club, at the corner of the Calle.

After having written so far, Don Martin Decoud, the exotic dandy of the Parisian boulevard, got up and walked across the sanded floor of the café at one end of the Albergo of United Italy, kept by Giorgio Viola, the old companion of Garibaldi. The highly coloured lithograph of the Faithful Hero seemed to look dimly, in the light of one candle, at the man with no faith in anything except the truth of his own sensations. Looking out of the window, Decoud was met by a darkness so impenetrable that he could see neither the mountains nor the town, nor yet the buildings near the harbour; and there was not a sound, as if the tremendous obscurity of the Placid Gulf, spreading from the waters over the land, had made it dumb as well as blind. Presently Decoud felt a light tremor of the floor and a distant clank of iron. A bright white light appeared, deep in the darkness, growing bigger with a thundering noise. The rolling stock usually kept on the sidings in Rincón was being run back to the yards for safe keeping. Like a mysterious stirring of the darkness behind the headlight of the engine, the train passed in a gust of hollow uproar, by the end of the house, which seemed to vibrate all over in response. And nothing was clearly visible but, on the end of the last car a Negro, in white trousers and naked to the waist, swinging a blazing torch basket incessantly with a circular movement of his bare arm. Decoud did not stir.

Behind him, on the back of the chair from which he had risen, hung his elegant Parisian overcoat, with a pearl-grey silk lining. But when he turned back to come to the table the candlelight fell upon a face that was grimy and scratched. His rosy lips were blackened with heat, the smoke of gun-powder. Dirt and rust tarnished the lustre of his short beard. His shirt collar and cuffs were crumpled; the blue silken tie hung down his breast like a rag; a greasy smudge crossed his white brow. He had not taken off his clothing nor used water, except to snatch a hasty drink greedily, for some forty hours. An awful restlessness had made him its own, had marked him with all the signs of desperate strife, and put a dry, sleepless stare into his eyes. He mumured to himself in a hoarse voice, 'I wonder if there's any bread here,' looked vaguely about him, then dropped into the chair and took the pencil up again. He became aware he had not eaten anything for many hours.

It occured to him that no one could understand him so well as his sister. In the most sceptical heart there lurks at such moments, when the chances of existence are involved, a desire to leave a correct impression of the feelings, like a light by which the action may be seen when personality is gone, gone where no light of investigation can ever reach the truth which every death takes out of the world. Therefore, instead of looking for something to eat, or trying to snatch an hour or so of sleep, Decoud was filling the pages of a large pocket-book with a letter to his sister.

In the intimacy of that intercourse he could not keep out his weariness, his great fatigue, the close touch of his bodily sensations. He began again as if he were talking to her. With almost an illusion of her presence, he wrote the phrase, 'I am very hungry.'

> I have the feeling of a great solitude around me [he continued]. Is it, perhaps, because I am the only man with a definite idea in his head, in the complete collapse of every resolve, intention, and hope about me? But the solitude is also very real. All the engineers are out, and have been for two days, looking after the property of the National Central Railway, of that great Costaguana undertaking which is to put money into the pockets of Englishmen, Frenchmen, Americans, Germans, and God knows who else. The silence about me is ominous. There is above the middle part of this house a sort of first floor, with narrow openings like loopholes for windows, probably used in old times for the better defence against the savages, when the persistent barbarism of our native continent did not wear the black coats of politicians, but went about yelling, half-naked, with bows and arrows in its hands. The woman of the house is dying up there, I believe, all along with her old husband. There is a narrow staircase, the sort of staircase one man could easily defend against a mob, leading up there, and I have just heard, through the thickness of the wall, the old fellow going down into their kitchen for something or other. It was a sort of noise a mouse might make behind the plaster of a wall. All the servants they had ran away yesterday and have not returned yet, if ever they do. For the rest, there are only two children here, two girls. The father has sent them downstairs, and they have crept into this café, perhaps because I am here. They huddle together in a corner, in each other's arms; I just noticed them a few minutes ago, and I feel more lonely than ever.

Decoud turned half round in his chair, and asked, 'Is there any bread here?'

Linda's dark head was shaken negatively in response, above the hair head of her sister nestling on her breast.

'You couldn't get me some bread?' insisted Decoud. The child did not move; he saw her large eyes stare at him very dark from the corner. 'You're not afraid of me?' he said.

'No,' said Linda,' 'we are not afraid of you. You came here with Gian' Battista.'

'You mean Nostromo?' said Decoud.

'The English call him so, but that is no name either for man or beast,' said the girl, passing her hand gently over her sister's hair.

'But he lets people call him so,' remarked Decoud.

'Not in this house,' retorted the child.

'Ah! well, I shall call him the Capataz then.'

Decoud gave up the point, and after writing steadily for a while turned round again.

'When do you expect him back?' he asked.

'After he brought you here he rode off to fetch the Señor Doctor from the town for mother. He will be back soon.'

'He stands a good chance of getting shot somewhere on the road,' Decoud murmured to himself audibly; and Linda declared in her high-pitched voice:

'Nobody would dare to fire a shot at Gian' Battista.'

'You believe that,' asked Decoud, 'do you?'

'I know it,' said the child, with conviction. 'There is no one in this place brave enough to attack Gian' Battista.'

'It doesn't require much bravery to pull a trigger behind a bush,' muttered Decoud to himself. 'Fortunately, the night is dark, or there would be but little chance of saving the silver of the mine.'

He turned again to his pocket-book, glanced back through the pages, and again started his pencil.

That was the position yesterday, after the *Minerva* with the fugitive President had gone out of harbour, and the rioters had been driven back into the side-lanes of the town. I sat on the steps of the cathedral with Nostromo, after sending out the cable message for the information of a more or less attentive world. Strangely enough, though the offices of the Cable Company are in the same building as the *Porvenir*, the mob, which has thrown my presses out of the window and scattered the type all over the Plaza, has been kept from interfering with the instruments on the other side of the courtyard. As I sat talking with Nostromo, Bernhardt, the telegraphist, came out from under the Arcades with a piece of paper in his hand. The little man had tied himself up to an enormous sword and was hung all over with revolvers. He is ridiculous, but the bravest German of his size that ever tapped the key of a Morse transmitter. He had received the message from Cayta reporting the transports with Barrios's army just entering the port, and ending with the words, 'The greatest enthusiasm prevails.' I walked off to drink some water at the fountain, and I was shot at from the Alameda by somebody hiding behind a tree. But I drank, and didn't care; with Barrios in Cayta and the great Cordillera between us and Montero's victorious army I seemed, notwithstanding Messrs Gamacho and Fuentes, to hold my new State in the hollow of my hand. I was ready to sleep, but when I got as far as the Casa Gould I found the patio full of wounded laid out on straw. Lights were burning, and in that enclosed courtyard on that hot night a faint odour of chloroform and blood hung about. At one end Dr Monygham, the doctor of the mine, was dressing the wounds; at the other, near the stairs, Father Corbelán, kneeling, listened to the confession of a dying *cargador*. Mrs Gould was walking about through these shambles with a large bottle in one hand and a lot of cotton wool in the other. She just looked at me and never even winked. Her *camerista* was following her, also holding a bottle, and sobbing gently to herself.

I busied myself for some time in fetching water from the cistern for the wounded. Afterwards I wandered upstairs, meeting some of the first ladies of Sulaco, paler than I had ever seen them before, with bandages over their arms. Not all of them had fled to the ships. A good man had taken refuge for the day in the Casa Gould. On the landing a girl, with her hair half down, was kneeling against the wall under the niche where stands a Madonna in blue robes and a gilt crown on her head. I think it was the eldest Miss Lopez; I couldn't see her face, but I remember looking at the high French heel of her little shoe. She did not make a sound, she did not stir, she was not sobbing; she remained there, perfectly still, all black against the white wall, a silent figure of passionate piety. I am sure she was no more frightened then the other white-faced ladies I met carrying bandages. One was sitting on the top step tearing a piece of linen hastily into strips – the young wife of an elderly man of fortune here. She interrupted herself to wave her hand to my bow, as though she were in her carriage on the Alameda. The women of our country are worth looking at during a revolution. The rouge and pearl powder fall off, together with that passive attitude towards the outer world which education, tradition, custom impose upon them from the earliest infancy. I though of your face, which from your infancy had the stamp of intelligence instead of that patient and resigned cast which appears when some political commotion tears down the veil of cosmetics and usage.

In the great *sala* upstairs a sort of Junta of Notables was sitting, the remnant of the vanished Provincial Assembly. Don Juste Lopez had had half his beard singed off at the muzzle of a *trabuco* loaded with slugs, of which every one missed him, providentially. And as he turned his head from side to side it was exactly as if there had been two men inside his frock-coat, one nobly whiskered and solemn, the other untidy and scared.

They raised a cry of 'Decoud! Don Martin!' at my entrance. I asked them, 'What are you deliberating upon, gentlemen?' There did not seem to be any president, thought Don José Avellanos sat at the head of the table. They all answered together, 'On the preservation of life and property.' 'Till the new officials arrive,' Don Juste explained to me, with the solemn side of his face offered to my view. It was as if a steam of water had been poured upon my glowing idea of a new State. There was a hissing sound in my ears, and the room grew dim, as if suddenly filled with vapour.

I walked up to the table blindly, as though I had been drunk. 'You are deliberating upon surrender,' I said. They all sat still, with their noses over the sheet of paper each had before him, God only knows why. Only Don José hid his face in his hands, muttering, 'Never, never!' But as I looked at him, it seemed to me that I could have blown him away with my breath, he looked so frail, so weak, so worn out. Whatever happens, he will not survive. The deception is too great for a man of his age; and hasn't he seen the sheets of *Fifty Years of Misrule*, which we have begun printing on the presses of the *Porvenir*, littering the Plaza, floating in the gutters, fired out as wads for *trabucos* loaded with handfuls of type, blown in the wind, trampled in the mud? I have seen pages floating upon the very waters of the harbour. It would be unreasonable to expect him to survive. It would be cruel.

'Do you know,' I cried, 'what surrender means to you, to your women, to your children, to your property?'

I declaimed for five minutes without drawing breath, it seems to me, harping on our best chances, on the ferocity of Montero, whom I made out to be as great a beast as I have no doubt he would like to be if he had intelligence enough to conceive a systematic reign of terror. And then for another five minutes or more I poured out an impassioned appeal to their courage and manliness, with all the passion of my love for Antonia. For if ever man spoke well, it would be from a personal feeling, denouncing an enemy, defending himself, or pleading for what really may be dearer than life. My dear girl, I absolutely thundered at them. It seemed as if my voice would burst the walls asunder, and when I stopped I saw all their scared eyes looking at me dubiously. And that was all the effect I had produced! Only Don José's head had sunk lower and lower on his breast. I bent my ear to his withered lips, and made out his whisper, something like, 'In God's name, then, Martin, my son!' I don't know exactly. There was the name of God in it, I am certain. It seems to me I have caught his last breath – the breath of his departing soul on his lips.

He lives yet, it is true. I have seen him since; but it was only a senile body, lying on its back, covered to the chin, with open eyes, and so still that you might have said it was breathing no longer. I left him thus, with Antonia kneeling by the side of the bed, just before I came to this Italian's *posada*, where the ubiquitous death is also waiting. But I know that Don José has really died there, in the Casa Gould, with that whisper urging me to attempt what no doubt his soul, wrapped up in the sanctity of diplomatic treaties and solemn declarations, must have abhorred. I had exclaimed very loud, 'There is never any God in a country where men will not help themselves.'

Meanwhile, Don Juste had begun a pondered oration whose solemn effect was spoiled by the ridiculous disaster to his beard. I did not wait to make it out. He seemed to argue that Montero's (he called him The General) intentions were probably not evil, though, he went on, 'that distinguished man' (only a week ago we used to call him a *gran' bestia*) 'was perhaps mistaken as to the true means'. As you may imagine, I didn't stay to hear the rest. I know the intentions of Montero's brother, Pedrito, the *guerrillero*, whom I exposed in Paris, some years ago, in a café frequented by South American students, where he tried to pass himself off for a Secretary of Legation. He used to come in and talk for hours, twisting his felt hat in his hairy paws, and his ambition seemed to be to become a sort of Duc de Morny to a sort of Napoleon. Already, then, he used to talk of his brother in inflated terms. He seemed fairly safe from being found out, because the students, all of the Blanco families, did not, as you may imagine, frequent the Legation. It was only Decoud, a man without faith and principles, as they used to say, that went in there sometimes for the sake of the fun, as it were to an assembly of trained monkeys. I know his intentions. I have seen him change the plates at table. Whoever is allowed to live on in terror, I must die the death.

No, I didn't stay to the end to hear Don Juste Lopez trying to persaude himself in a grave oration of the clemency and justice, and honesty, and purity of the brothers Montero. I went out abruptly to seek Antonia. I saw her in the gallery. As I opened the door, she extended to me her clasped hands.

'What are they doing in there?' she asked.

'Talking,' I said, with my eyes looking into hers.

'Yes, yes, but—'

'Empty speeches,' I interrupted her. 'Hiding their fears behind imbecile hopes. They are all great Parliamentarians there – on the English model, as you know.' I was so furious that I could hardly speak. She made a gesture of despair.

Through the door I held a little ajar behind me, we heard Don Juste's measured mouthing monotone go on from phrase to phrase, like a sort of awful and solemn madness.

'After all, the Democratic aspirations have, perhaps, their legitimacy. The ways of human progress are inscrutable, and if the fate of the country is in the hand of Montero, we ought—'

I crashed the door to on that; it was enough; it was too much. There was never a beautiful face expressing more horror and despair than the face of Antonia. I couldn't bear it; I seized her wrists.

'Have they killed my father in there?' she asked.

Her eyes blazed with indignation, but as I looked on, fascinated, the light in them went out.

'It is a surrender,' I said. And I remember I was shaking her wrists I held apart in my hands. 'But it's more than talk. Your father told me to go on in God's name.'

My dear girl, there is that in Antonia which would make me believe in the feasibility of anything. One look at her face is enough to set my brain on fire. And yet I love her as any other man would – with the heart, and with that alone. She is more to me than his Church to Father Corbelán (the Grand Vicar disappeared last night from the town; perhaps gone to join the band of Hernandez). She is more to me than his precious mine to that sentimental Englishman. I won't speak of his wife. She may have been sentimental once. The San Tomé mine stands now between those two people. 'Your father himself, Antonia,' I repeated; 'your father, do you understand? has told me to go on.'

She averted her face, and in a pained voice—

'He has?' she cried. 'Then, indeed, I fear he will never speak again.'

She freed her wrists from my clutch and began to cry in her handkerchief. I disregarded her sorrow; I would rather see her miserable then not see her at all, never any more; for whether I escaped or stayed to die, there was for us no coming together, no future. And that being so, I had no pity to waste upon the passing moments of her sorrow. I sent her off in tears to fetch Doña Emilia and Don Carlos, too. Their sentiment was necessary to the very life of my plan; the sentimentalism of the people that will never do anything for the sake of their passionate desire, unless it comes to them clothed in the fair robes of an idea.

Late at night we formed a small junta of four – the two women, Don Carlos, and myself – in Mrs Gould's blue-and-white boudoir.

El Rey de Sulaco thinks himself, no doubt, a very honest man. And so he is, if one could look behind his taciturnity. Perhaps he thinks that this alone makes his honesty unstained. Those Englishmen live on illusions which somehow or other help them to get a firm hold of the substance. When he speaks it is by a rare 'yes' or 'no' that seems as impersonal as the words of an oracle. But he could not impose on me by his dumb reserve. I knew what he had in his head; he has his mine in his head; and his wife had nothing in her head but his precious person, which he has bound up with the Gould Concession and tied to that little woman's neck. No matter. The thing was to make him present the affair to Holroyd (the Steel and Silver King) in such a manner as to secure his financial support. At that time last night, just twenty-four hours ago, we thought the silver of the mine safe in the Custom House vaults till the northbound steamer came to take it away. And as long as the treasure flowed north, without a break, that utter sentimentalist, Holroyd, would not drop his idea of introducing, not only justice, industry, peace, to the benighted continents, but also that pet dream of his of a purer form of Christianity. Later on, the principal European really in Sulaco, the engineer-in-chief of the railway, came riding up the *calle*, from the harbour, and was admitted to our conclave. Meantime, the Junta of the Notables in the great *sala* was still deliberating; only, one of them had run out in the corridor to ask the servant whether something to eat couldn't be sent in. The first words the engineer-in-chief said as he came into the boudoir were, 'What is your house, dear Mrs Gould? A war hospital below, and apparently a restaurant above. I saw them carrying trays full of good things into the *sala*.'

'And here, in this boudoir,' I said, 'you behold the inner cabinet of the Occidental Republic that is to be.'

He was so preoccupied that he didn't smile at that, he didn't even look surprised.

He told us that he was attending to the general dispositions for the defence of the railway property at the railway yards when he was sent for to go into the railway telegraph office. The engineer of the railhead, at the foot of the mountains, wanted to talk to him from his end of the wire. There was nobody in the office but himself and the operator of the railway telegraph, who read off the clicks aloud as the tape coiled its length upon the floor. And the purport of that talk, clicked nervously from a wooden shed in the depths of the forests, had informed the chief that President Ribiera had been, or was being, pursued. This was news, indeed, to all of us in Sulaco. Ribiera himself, when rescued, revived, and soothed by us, had been inclined to think that he had not been pursued.

Ribiera had yielded to the urgent solicitations of his friends, and had left the headquarters of his discomfited army alone, under the guidance of Bonifacio, the muleteer, who had been willing to take the responsibility with the risk. He had departed at daybreak of the third day. His remaining forces had melted away during the night. Bonifacio and he rode hard on horses towards the Cordillera; then they obtained mules, entered the passes, and crossed the Paramo of Ivie just before a freezing blast swept over that stony plateau, burying in a drift of snow the little shelter-hut of stones in which they had spent the night. Afterwards poor Ribiera had many adventures, got separated from his guide, lost his mount, struggled down to the Campo on foot, and if he had not thrown himself on the mercy of a *ranchero* would have perished a long way from Sulaco. That man, who, as a matter of fact, recognized him at once, let him have a fresh mule, which the fugitive, heavy and unskilful, had ridden to death. And it was true he had been pursued by a party commanded by no less a person than Pedro Montero, the brother of the general. The cold wind of the Paramo luckily caught the pursuers on the top of the pass. Some few men, and all the animals, perished in the icy blast. The stragglers died, but the main body kept on. They found poor Bonifacio lying half-dead at the foot of a snow slope, and bayoneted him promptly in the true Civil War style. They would have had Ribiera, too, if they had not, for some reason or other, turned off the track of the old *camino real*, only to lose their way in the forests at the foot of the lower slopes. And there they were at last, having stumbled in unexpectedly upon the construction camp. The engineer at the railhead told his chief by wire that he had Pedro Montero absolutely there, in the very office, listening to the clicks. He was going to take possession of Sulaco in the name of the Democracy. He was very overbearing. His men slaughtered some of the Railway Company's cattle without asking leave, and went to work broiling the meat on the embers. Pedrito made many pointed inquiries as to the silver mine, and what had become of the product of the last six months' working. He had said peremptorily, 'Ask your chief up there by wire, he ought to know; tell him that Don Pedro Montero, Chief of the Campo and Minister of the Interior of the new Government, desires to be correctly informed.'

He had his feet wrapped up in blood-stained rags, a lean, haggard face, ragged beard and hair, and had walked in limping, with a crooked branch of a tree for a staff. His followers were, perhaps, in a worse plight, but apparently they had not thrown away their arms, and, at any rate, not all their ammunition. Their lean faces filled the door and the windows of the telegraph hut. As it was at the same time the bedroom of the engineer-in-charge there, Montero had thrown himself on his clean blankets and lay there shivering and dictating requisitions to be transmitted by wire to Sulaco. He demanded a train of cars to be sent down at once to transport his men up.

'To this I answered from my end,' the engineer-in-chief related to us, 'that I dared not risk the rolling-stock in the interior, as there had been attempts to wreck trains all along the line several times. I did that for your sake, Gould,' said the chief engineer. 'The answer to this was, in the words of my subordinate, "The filthy brute on my bed said, 'Suppose I were to have you shot?' " To which my subordinate, who, it appears, was himself operating, remarked that it would not bring the cars up. Upon that, the other, yawning, said, "Never mind, there is no lack of horses on the Campo." And, turning over, went to sleep on Harris's bed.'

This is why, my dear girl, I am a fugitive tonight. The last wire from the railhead says that Pedro Montero and his men left at daybreak, after feeding on *asado* beef all night. They took all the horses; they will find more on the road; they'll be here in less than thirty hours, and thus Sulaco is no place either for me or the great store of silver belonging to the Gould Concession.

But that is not the worst. The garrison of Esmeralda has gone over to the victorious party. We have heard this by means of the telegraphist of the Cable Company, who came to the Casa Gould in the early morning with the news. In fact, it was so early that the day had not yet quite broken over Sulaco. His colleague in Esmeralda had called him up to say that the Garrison, after shooting some of their officers, had taken possession of a Government steamer laid up in the harbour. It is really a heavy blow for me. I thought I could depend on every man in this province. It was a mistake. It was a Monterist Revolution in Esmeralda, just such as was attempted in Sulaco, only that *that* one came off. The telegraphist was signalling to

Bernhardt all the time, and his last transmitted words were. 'They were bursting in the door, and taking possession of the cable office. You are cut off. Can do no more.'

But, as a matter of fact, he managed somehow to escape the vigilance of his captors, who had tried to stop the communication with the outer world. He did manage it. How it was done I don't know, but a few hours afterwards he called up Sulaco again, and what he said was, 'The insurgent army has taken possession of the Government transport in the bay and are filling her with troops, with the intention of going round the coast to Sulaco. Therefore look out for yourselves. They will be ready to start in a few hours, and may be upon you before daybreak.'

This is all he could say. They drove him away from his instrument this time for good, because Bernhardt has been calling up Esmeralda ever since without getting an answer.

After setting these words down in the pocket-book which he was filling up for the benefit of his sister, Decoud lifted his head to listen. But there were no sounds, neither in the room nor in the house, except the drip of the water from the filter into the vast earthenware jar under the wooden stand. And outside the house there was a great silence. Decoud lowered his head again over the pocket-book.

I am not running away, you understand [he wrote on]. I am simply going away with that great treasure of silver which must be saved at all costs. Pedro Montero from the Campo and the revolted garrison of Esmeralda from the sea are converging upon it. That it is there lying ready for them is only an accident. The real objective is the San Tomé mine itself, as you may well imagine; otherwise the Occidental Province would have been, no doubt, left alone for many weeks, to be gathered at leisure into the arms of the victorious party. Don Carlos Gould will have enough to do to save his mine, with its organization and its people; this '*Imperium in Imperio*', this wealth-producing thing, to which his sentimentalism attaches a strange idea of justice. He holds to it as some men hold to the idea of love or revenge. Unless I am much mistaken in the man, it must remain inviolate or perish by an act of his will alone. A passion has crept into his cold and idealistic life. A passion which I can only comprehend intellectually. A passion that is not like the passions we know, we men of another blood. But it is as dangerous as any of ours.

His wife has understoof it, too. That is why she is such a good ally of mine. She seizes upon all my suggestions with a sure instinct that in the end they make for the safety of the Gould Concession. And he defers to her because he trusts her perhaps, but I fancy more rather as if he wished to make up for some subtle wrong, for that sentimental unfaithfulness which surrenders her happiness, her life, to the seduction of an idea. The little woman has discovered that he lives for the mine rather than for her. But let them be. To each his fate, shaped by passion or sentiment. The principal thing is that she has backed up my advice to get the silver out of the town, out of the country, at once, at any cost, at any risk. Don Carlos's mission is to preserve unstained the fair name of his mine; Mrs Gould's mission is to save him from the effects of that cold and overmastering passion, which she dreads more than if it were an infatuation for another woman. Nostromo's mission is to save the silver. The plan is to load it into the largest of the Company's lighters, and send it across the gulf to a small port out of Costaguana territory just on the other side of the Azuera, where the first northbound steamer will get orders to pick it up. The waters here are calm. We shall slip away into the darkness of the gulf before the Esmeralda rebels arrive; and by the time the day breaks over the ocean we shall be out of sight, invisible, hidden by Azuera, which itself looks from the Sulaco shore like a faint blue cloud on the horizon.

The incorruptible Capataz de Cargadores is the man for that work; and I, the man with a passion, but without a mission, I go with him to return – to play my part in the farce to the end, and, if successful, to receive my reward, which no one but Antonia can give me.

I shall not see her again now before I depart. I left her, as I have said, by Don José's bedside. The street was dark, the houses shut up, and I walked out of the town in the night. Not a single street-lamp had been lit for two days, and the archway of the gate was only a mass of darkness in the vague form of a tower, in which I heard low, dismal groans that seemed to answer the murmurs of a man's voice.

I recognized something impassive and careless in the tone, characteristic of that Genoese sailor who, like me, has come casually here to be drawn into the events for which his scepticism as well as mine seems to entertain a sort of passive contempt. The only thing he seems to care for, as far as I have been able to discover, is to be well spoken of. An ambition fit for noble souls, but also a profitable one for an exceptionally intelligent scoundrel. Yes. His very words, 'To be well spoken of. *Sí, señor*.' He does not seem to make any difference between speaking and thinking. Is it sheer naïveness or the practical point of view, I wonder? Exceptional individualities interest me, because they are true to the general formula expressing the moral state of humanity.

He joined me on the harbour road after I had passed them under the dark archway without stopping. It was a woman in trouble he had been talking to. Through discretion I kept silent while he walked by my side. After a time he began to talk himself. It was not what I expected. It was only an old woman, an old lace-maker, in search of her son, one of the street-sweepers employed by the municipality. Friends had come the day before at daybreak to the door of their hovel calling him out. He had gone with them, and she had not seen him since; so she had left the food she had been preparing half-cooked on the extinct embers and had crawled out as far as the harbour, where she had heard that some town *mozos* had been killed on the morning of the riot. One of the *cargadores* guarding the Custom House had brought out a lantern, and had helped her to look at the few dead left lying about there. Now she was creeping back, having failed in her search. So she sat down on the stone seat under the arch, moaning, because she was very tired. The Capataz had questioned her, and after hearing her broken and groaning tale had advised her to go and look amongst the wounded in the patio of the Casa Gould. He had also given her a quarter dollar, he mentioned carelessly.

'Why did you do that?' I asked. 'Do you know her?'

'No, *señor*. I don't suppose I have ever seen her before. How should I? She has not probably been out in the streets for years. She is one of those old women that you find in this country at the back of huts, crouching over fireplaces, with a stick on the ground by their side, and almost too feeble to drive away the stray dogs from their cooking-pots. *Caramba!* I could tell by her voice that death had forgotten her. But, old or young, they like money, and will speak well of the man who gives it to them.' He laughed a little '*Señor*, you should have felt the clutch of her paw as I put the piece in her palm.' He paused. 'My last, too,' he added.

I made no comment. He's known for his liberality, and his bad luck at the game of *monte*, which keeps him as poor as when he first came here.

'I suppose, Don Martin,' he began, in a thoughtful, speculative tone, 'that the Señor Administrador of San Tomé will reward me some day if I save his silver?'

I said that it could not be otherwise, surely. He walked on, muttering to himself. '*Sí, sí*, without doubt, without doubt; and, look you, *Señor* Martin, what it is to be well spoken of! There is not another man that could have been even thought of for such a thing. I shall get something great for it some day. And let it come soon,' he mumbled. 'Time passes in this country as quick as anywhere else.'

This, *sœur chérie*, is my companion in the great escape for the sake of the great cause. He is more naïve than shrewd, more masterful then crafty, more generous with his personality than the people who make use of him are with their money. At least, that is what he thinks himself with more pride than sentiment. I am glad I have made friends with him. As a companion he acquires more importance than he ever had as a sort of minor genius in his way – as an original Italian sailor whom I allowed to come in in the small hours and talk familiarly to the editor of the *Porvenir* while the paper was going through the press. And it is curious to have met a man for whom the value of life seems to consist in personal prestige.

I am waiting for him here now. On arriving at the *posada* kept by Viola we found the children alone down below, and the old Genoese shouted to his countryman to go and fetch the doctor. Otherwise we would have gone on to the wharf, where it appears Captain Mitchell with some volunteer Europeans and a few picked *cargadores* are loading the lighter with the silver that must be saved from Montero's clutches in order to be used for Montero's defeat. Nostromo galloped furiously back towards the town. He has been long gone already. This delay gives me time to talk to you. By the time this pocket-book reaches your hands much will have happened. But now it is a pause under the hovering wing of death in that silent house buried in the black night, with this dying woman, the two children crouching without a sound, and that old man whom I can hear through the thickness of the wall passing up and down with a light rubbing noise no louder than a mouse. And I, the only other with them, don't really know whether to count myself with the living or with the dead. '*Quién sabe?*' as the people here are prone to say in answer to every question. But no! feeling for you is certainly not dead, and the whole thing, the house, the dark night, the silent children in this dim room, my very presence here – all this is life, must be life, since it is so much like a dream.

With the writing of the last line there came upon Decoud a moment of sudden and complete oblivion. He swayed over the table as if struck by a bullet. The next moment he sat up, confused, with the idea that he had heard his pencil roll on the floor. The low door of the café, wide open, was filled with the glare of a torch in which was visible half of a horse, switching its tail against the leg of a rider with a long iron spur strapped to the naked heel. The two girls were gone, and Nostromo, standing in the middle of the room, looked at him from under the round brim of the sombrero low down over his brow.

'I have brought that sour-faced English doctor in Señora Gould's carriage,' said Nostromo. 'I doubt if, with all his wisdom, he can save the Padrona this time. They have sent for the children. A bad sign that.'

He sat down on the end of a bench. 'She wants to give them her blessing, I suppose.'

Dazedly Decoud observed that he must have fallen sound asleep, and Nostromo said, with a vague smile, that he had looked in at the window and had seen him lying still across the table with his head on his arms. The English *señora* had also come in the carriage, and went upstairs at once with the doctor. She had told him not to wake up Don Martin yet; but when they sent for the children he had come into the café.

The half of the horse with its half of the rider swung round outside the door; the torch of tow and resin in her iron basket which was carried on a stick at the saddle-bow flared right into the room for a moment, and Mrs Gould entered hastily with a very white, tired face. The hood of her dark, blue cloak had fallen back. Both men rose.

'Teresa wants to see you, Nostromo,' she said.

The Capataz did not move. Decoud, with his back to the table, began to button up his coat.

'The silver, Mrs Gould, the silver,' he murmured in English. 'Don't forget that the Esmeralda garrison have got a steamer. They may appear at any moment at the harbour entrance.'

'The doctor says there is no hope,' Mrs Gould spoke rapidly, also in English. 'I shall take you down to the wharf in my carriage and then come back to fetch away the girls.' She changed swiftly into Spanish to address Nostromo. 'Why are you wasting time? Old Giorgio's wife wishes to see you.'

'I am going to her, *señora*,' muttered the Capataz.

Dr Monygham now showed himself, bringing back the children. To Mrs Gould's inquiring glance he only shook his head and went outside at once, followed by Nostromo.

The horse of the torch-bearer, motionless, hung his head low, and the rider had dropped the reins to light a cigarette. The glare of the torch played on the front of the house crossed by the big black letters of his inscription in which only the word ITALIA was lighted fully. The patch of wavering glare reached as far as Mrs Gould's carriage waiting on the road, with the yellow-faced, portly Ignacio apparently dozing on the box. By his side Basilio, dark and skinny, held a Winchester carbine in front of him, with both hands, and peered fearfully into the darkness. Nostromo touched lightly the doctor's shoulder.

'Is she really dying, Señor Doctor?'

'Yes,' said the doctor, with a strange twitch of his scarred cheek. 'And why she wants to see you I cannot imagine.'

'She has been like that before,' suggested Nostromo, looking away.

'Well, Capataz, I can assure you she will never be like that again,' snarled Dr Monygham. 'You may go to her or stay away. There is very little to be got from talking to the dying. But she told Doña Emilia in my hearing that she has been like a mother to you ever since you first set foot ashore here.'

'*Sí!* And she never had a good word to say for me to anybody. It is more as if she could not forgive me for being alive, and such a man, too, as she would have liked her son to be.'

'Maybe!' exclaimed a mournful deep voice near them. 'Women have their own ways of tormenting themselves.' Giorgio Viola had come out of the house. He threw a heavy black shadow in the torchlight, and the glare fell on his big face, on the great bushy head of white hair. He motioned the Capataz indoors with his extended arm.

Dr Monygham, after busying himself with a little medicament box of polished wood on the seat of the landau, turned to old Giorgio and thrust into his big, trembling hand one of the glass-stoppered bottles out of the case.

'Give her a spoonful of this now and then, in water,' he said. 'It will make her easier.'

'And there is nothing more for her?' asked the old man patiently.

'No. Not on earth,' said the doctor, with his back to him, clicking the lock of the medicine case.

Nostromo slowly crossed the large kitchen, all dark but for the glow of a heap of charcoal under the heavy mantel of the cooking-range, where water was boiling in an iron pot with a loud bubbling sound. Between the two walls of a narrow staircase a bright light steamed from the sick-room above; and the magnificent Capataz de Cargadores stepping noiselessly in soft leather sandals, bushy whiskered, his muscular neck and bronzed chest bare in the open check shirt, resembled a Mediterranean sailor just come ashore from some wine-or fruit-laden felucca. At the top he paused, broad shouldered, narrow hipped, and supple, looking at the large bed, like a white couch of state, with a profusion of snowy linen, amongst which the Padrona sat unpropped and bowed, her handsome, black-browed face bent over her chest. A mass of raven hair with only a few white threads in it covered her shoulders; one thick strand fallen forward half veiled her cheek. Perfectly motionless in that pose, expressing physical anxiety and unrest, she turned her eyes alone towards Nostromo.

The Capataz had a red sash wound many times round his waist, and a heavy silver ring on the forefinger of the hand he raised to give a twist to his moustache.

'Their revolutions, their revolutions,' gasped Señora Teresa. 'Look, Gian' Battista, it has killed me at last!'

Nostromo said nothing, and the sick woman with an upward glance insisted. 'Look, this one has killed me, while you were away fighting for what did not concern you, foolish man.'

'Why talk like this?' mumbled the Capataz between his teeth. 'Will you never believe in my good sense? It concerns me to keep on being what I am: every day alike.'

'You never change, indeed,' she said, bitterly. 'Always thinking of yourself and taking your pay out in fine words from those who care nothing for you.'

There was between them an intimacy of antagonism as close in its way as the intimacy of accord and affection. He had not walked along the way of Teresa's expectations. It was she who had encouraged him to leave his ship, in the hope of securing a friend and defender for the girls. The wife of old Giorgio was aware of her precarious health, and was haunted by the fear of her aged husband's loneliness and the unprotected state of the children. She had wanted to annex that apparently quiet and steady young man, affectionate and pliable, an orphan from his tenderest age, as he had told her, with no ties in Italy except an uncle, owner and master of a felucca, from whose ill-usage he had run away before he was fourteen. He had seemed to her courageous, a hard worker, determined to make his way in the world. From gratitude and the ties of habit he would become like a son to herself and Giorgio; and then, who knows, when Linda had grown up . . . Ten years' difference between husband and wife was not so much. Her own great man was nearly twenty-years older than herself. Gian' Battista was an attractive young fellow, besides; attractive to men, women, and children, just by that profound quietness of personality which, like a serene twilight, rendered more seductive the promise of his vigorous form and the resolution of his conduct.

Old Giorgio, in profound ignorance of his wife's views and hopes, had a great regard for his young countryman. 'A man ought not to be tame,' he used to tell her, quoting the Spanish proverb in defence of the splendid Capataz. She was growing jealous of his success. He was escaping from her, she feared. She was practical, and he seemed to her to be an absurd spendthrift of these qualities which made him so valuable. He got too little for them. He scattered them with both hands amongst too many people, she thought. He laid no money by. She railed at his poverty, his exploits, his adventures, his lives, and his reputation; but in her heart she had never given him up, as though, indeed, he had been her son.

Even now, ill as she was, ill enough to feel the chill, black breath of the approaching end, she had wished to see him. It was like putting out her benumbed hand to regain her hold. But she had presumed too much on her strength. She could not command her thoughts; they had become dim, like her vision. The words faltered on her lips, and only the paramount anxiety and desire of her life seemed to be too strong for death.

The Capataz said, 'I have heard these things many times. You are unjust, but it does not hurt me. Only now you do not seem to have much strength to talk, and I have but little time to listen. I am engaged in a work of very great moment.'

She made an effort to ask him whether it was true that he had found time to go and fetch a doctor for her. Nostromo nodded affirmatively.

She was pleased: it relieved her sufferings to know that the man had condescended to do so much for those who really wanted his help. It was a proof of his friendship. Her voice became stronger.

'I want a priest more than a doctor,' she said, pathetically. She did not move her head; only her eyes ran into the corners to watch the Capataz standing by the side of her bed. 'Would you go to fetch a priest for me now? Think! A dying woman asks you!'

Nostromo shook his head resolutely. He did not believe in priests in their sacerdotal character. A doctor was an efficacious person; but a priest, as priest, was nothing, incapable of doing either good or harm. Nostromo did not even dislike the sight of them as old Giorgio did. The utter uselessness of the errand was what struck him most.

'Padrona,' he said, 'you have been like this before, and got better after a few days. I have given you already the very last moments I can spare. Ask Señora Gould to send you one.'

He was feeling uneasy at the impiety of this refusal. The Padrona believed in priests, and confessed herself to them. But all women did that. It could not be of much consequence. And yet his heart felt oppressed for a moment – at the thought of what absolution would mean to her if she believed in it only ever so little. No matter. It was quite true that he had given her already the very last moment he could spare.

'You refuse to go?' she gasped. 'Ah! you are always yourself, indeed.'

'Listen to reason, Padrona,' he said. 'I am needed to save the silver of the mine. Do you hear? A greater treasure than the one which they say is guarded by ghosts and devils in Azuera. It is strue. I am resolved to make this the most desperate affair I was ever engaged on in my whole life.'

She felt a despairing indignation. The supreme test had failed. Standing above her, Nostromo did not see the distorted features of her face, distorted by a paroxysm of pain and anger. Only she began to tremble all over. Her bowed head shook. The broad shoulders quivered.

'Then God, perhaps, will have some mercy upon me! But do you look to it, man, that you get something for yourself out of it, besides the remorse that shall overtake you some day.'

She laughed feebly. 'Get riches at least for once, you indispensable, admired Gian' Battista, to whom the peace of a dying woman is less than the praise of people who have given you a silly name – and nothing besides – in exchange for your soul and body.'

The Captain de Cargadores swore to himself under his breath.

'Leave my soul alone, Padrona, and I shall know how to take care of my body. Where is the harm of people having need of me? What are you envying me that I have robbed you and the children of? Those very people you are throwing in my teeth have done more for old Giorgio than they ever thought of doing for me.'

He struck his breast with his open palm; his voice had remained low though he had spoken in a forcible tone. He twisted his moustaches one after another, and his eyes wandered a little about the room.

'Is it my fault that I am the only man for their purposes? What angry nonsense are you talking, mother? Would you rather have me timid and foolish, selling water-melons on the market-place or rowing a boat for passengers along the harbour, like a soft Neapolitan without courage or reputation? Would you have a young man live like a monk? I do not believe it. Would you want a monk for your eldest girl? Let her grow. What are you afraid of? You have been angry with me for everything I did for years; ever since you first spoke to me, in secret from old Giorgio, about your Linda. Husband to one and brother to the other, did you say? Well, why not! I like the little ones, and a man must marry some time. But ever since that time you have been making little of me to everyone. Why? Did you think you could put a collar and chain on me as if I were one of the watchdogs they keep over there in the railway yards? Look here, Padrona, I am the same man who came ashore one evening and sat down in the thatched *rancho* you lived in at that time on the other side of the town and told you all about himself. You were not unjust to me then. What has happened since? I am no longer an insignificant youth. A good name, Giorgio says, is a treasure, Padrona.'

'They have turned your head with their praises,' gasped the sick woman. 'They have been paying you with words. Your folly shall betray you into poverty, misery, starvation. The very *leperos* shall laugh at you – the great Capataz.'

Nostromo stood for a time as if struck dumb. She never looked at him. A self-confident, mirthless smile passed quickly from his lips, and then he backed away. His disregarded figure sank down beyond the doorway. He descended the stairs backwards, with the usual sense of having been somehow baffled by this woman's disparagement of this reputation he had obtained and desired to keep.

Downstairs in the big kitchen a candle was burning, surrounded by the shadows of the walls, of the ceiling, but no ruddy glare filled the open square of the outer door. The carriage with Mrs Gould and Don Martin, preceded by the horseman bearing the torch, had gone on to the jetty. Dr Monygham, who had remained, sat on the corner of a hard wood table near the candlestick, his seamed, shaved face inclined sideways, his arms crossed on his breast, his lips pursed up, and his prominent eyes glaring stonily upon the floor of black earth.

Near the overhanging mantel of the fireplace, where the pot of water was still boiling violently, old Giorgio held his chin in his hand, one foot advanced, as if arrested by a sudden thought.

'*Adios, viejo*,' said Nostromo, feeling the handle of his revolver in the belt and loosening his knife in its sheath. He picked up a blue poncho lined with red from the table, and put it over his head. '*Adios*, look after my things in my sleeping-room, and if you hear from me no more, give up the box to Paquita. There is not much of value there, except my new serape from Mexico, and a few silver buttons on my best jacket. No matter! The things will look well enough on the next lover she gets, and the man need not be afraid I shall linger on earth after I am dead, like those *gringos* that haunt the Azuera.'

Dr Monygham twisted his lips into a bitter smile. After old Giorgio, with an almost imperceptible nod and without a word, had gone up the narrow stairs, he said:

'Why, Capataz! I thought you could never fail in anything.'

Nostromo, glancing contemptuously at the doctor, lingered in the doorway rolling a cigarette, then struck a match, and, after lighting it, held the burning piece of wood above his head till the flame nearly touched his fingers.

'No wind!' he muttered to himself. 'Look here, *señor* – do you know the nature of my undertaking?'

Dr Monygham nodded sourly.

'It is as if I were taking up a curse upon me, Señor Doctor. A man with a treasure on this coast will have every knife raised against him in every place upon the shore. You see that, Señor Doctor? I shall float along with a spell upon my life till I meet somewhere the north-bound steamer of the Company, and then indeed they will talk about the Capataz of the Sulaco Cargadores from one end of America to another.'

Dr Monygham laughed his short, throaty laugh. Nostromo turned round in the doorway.

'But if your worship can find any other man ready and fit for such business I will stand back. I am not exactly tired of my life, though I am so poor that I can carry all I have with myself on my horse's back.'

'You gamble too much, and never say "no" to a pretty face, Capataz,' said Dr Monygham, with sly simplicity. 'That's not the way to make a fortune. But nobody that I know ever suspected you of being poor. I hope you have made a good bargain in case you come back safe from this adventure.'

'What bargain would your worship have made?' asked Nostromo, blowing the smoke out of his lips through the doorway.

Dr Monygham listened up the staircase for a moment before he answered, with another of his short, abrupt laughs:

'Illustrious Capataz, for taking the curse of death upon my back, as you call it, nothing else but the whole treasure would do.'

Nostromo vanished out of the doorway with a grunt of discontent at his jeering answer. Dr Monygham heard him gallop away. Nostromo rode furiously in the dark. There were lights in the buildings of the O.S.N. Company near the wharf, but before he got there he met the Gould carriage. The horseman preceded it with the torch, whose light showed the white mules trotting, the portly Ignacio driving, and Basilio with the carbine on the box. From the dark body of the landau Mrs Gould's voice cried, 'They are waiting for you, Capataz!' She was returning, chilly and excited, with Decoud's pocket-book still held in her hand. He had confided it to her to send to his sister. 'Perhaps my last words to her,' he had said, pressing Mrs Gould's hand.

The Capataz never checked his speed. At the head of the wharf vague figures with rifles leapt to the head of his horse; others closed upon him – *cargadores* of the company posted by Captain Mitchell on the watch. At a word from him they fell back with subservient murmurs, recognizing his voice. At the other end of the jetty, near a cargo crane, in a dark group with glowing cigars, his name was pronounced in a tone of relief. Most of the Europeans in Sulaco were there, rallied round Charles Gould, as if the silver of the mine had been the emblem of a common cause, the symbol of the supreme importance of material interests. They had loaded it into the lighter with their own hands. Nostromo recognized Don Carlos Gould, a thin, tall shape, standing a little apart and silent, to whom another tall shape, the engineer-in-chief, said aloud, 'If it must be lost, it is a million times better that it should go to the bottom of the sea.'

Martin Decoud called out from the lighter, '*Au revoir, messieurs*, till we clasp hands again over the new-born Occidental Republic.' Only a subdued murmur responded to his clear ringing tones; and then it seemed to him that the wharf was floating away into the night; but it was Nostromo, who was already pushing against a pile with one of the heavy sweeps. Decoud did not move; the effect was that of being launched into space. After a splash or two there was not a sound but the thud of Nostromo's feet leaping about the boat. He hoisted the big sail; a breath of wind fanned Decoud's cheek. Everything had vanished but the light of the lantern Captain Mitchell had hoisted upon the post at the end of the jetty to guide Nostromo out of the harbour.

The two men, unable to see each other, kept silent till the lighter, slipping before the fitful breeze, passed out between almost invisible headlands into the still deeper darkness of the gulf. For a time the lantern on the jetty shone after them. The wind failed, then fanned up again, but so faintly that the big, half-decked boat slipped along with no more noise than if she had been suspended in the air.

'We are out in the gulf now,' said the calm voice of Nostromo. A moment after he added, 'Señor Mitchell has lowered the light.'

'Yes,' said Decoud; 'nobody can find us now.'

A great recrudescence of obscurity embraced the boat. The sea in the gulf was as black as the clouds above. Nostromo, after striking a couple of matches to get a glimpse of the boat-compass he had with him in the lighter, steered by the feel of the wind on his cheek.

It was a new experience for Decoud, this mysteriousness of the great waters spread out strangely smooth, as if their restlessness had been crushed by the weight of that dense night. The Placido was sleeping profoundly under its black poncho.

The main thing now for success was to get away from the coast and gain the middle of the gulf before day broke. The Isabels were somewhere at hand. 'On your left as you look forward, *señor*,' said Nostromo, suddenly. When his voice ceased, the enormous stillness, without light or sound, seemed to affect Decoud's senses like a powerful drug. He didn't even know at times whether he were sleep or awake. Like a man most in slumber, he heard nothing, he saw nothing. Even his hand held before his face did not exist for his eyes. The change from the agitation, the passions and the dangers, from the sights and sounds of the shore, was so complete that it would have resembled death had it not been for the survival of his thoughts. In this foretaste of eternal peace they floated vivid and light, like unearthly clear dreams of earthly things that may haunt the souls freed by death from the misty atmosphere of regrets and hopes. Decoud shook himself, shuddered a bit, though the air that drifted past him was warm. He had the strangest sensation of his soul having just returned into his body from the circumambient darkness in which land, sea, sky, the mountains, and the rocks were as if they had not been.

Nostromo's voice was speaking, though he, at the tiller, was also as if he were not. 'Have you been asleep, Don Martin? *Caramba!* If it were possible I would think that I, too, have dozed off. I have a strange notion somehow of having dreamt that there was a sound of blubbering, a sound a sorrowing man could make, somewhere near this boat. Something between a sigh and a sob.'

'Strange!' muttered Decoud, stretched upon the pile of treasure boxes covered by many tarpaulins. 'Could it be that there is another boat near us in the gulf? We could not see it, you know.'

Nostromo laughed a little at the absurdity of the idea. They dismissed it from their minds. The solitude could almost be felt. And when the breeze ceased, the blackness seemed to weigh upon Decoud like a stone.

'This is overpowering,' he muttered. 'Do we move at all, Capataz?'

'Not so fast as a crawling beetle tangled in the grass,' answered Nostromo, and his voice seemed deadened by the thick veil of obscurity that felt warm and hopeless all about them. There were long periods when he made no sound, invisible and inaudible as if he had mysteriously stepped out of the lighter.

In the featureless night Nostromo was not even certain which way the lighter headed after the wind had completely died out. He peered for the islands. There was not a hint of them to be seen, as if they had sunk to the bottom of the gulf. He threw himself down by the side of Decoud at last, and whispered into his ear that if daylight caught them near the Sulaco shore through want of wind, it would be possible to sweep the lighter behind the cliff at the high end of the Great Isabel, where she would lie concealed. Decoud was surprised at the grimness of his anxiety. To him the removal of the treasure was a political move. It was necessary for several reasons that it should not fall into the hands of Montero, but here was a man who took another view of this enterprise. The *caballeros* over there did not seem to have the slightest idea of what they had given him to do. Nostromo, as if affected by the gloom around, seemed nervously resentful. Decoud was surprised. The Capataz, indifferent to those dangers that seemed obvious to his companion, allowed himself to become scornfully exasperated by the deadly nature of the trust put, as a matter of course, into his hands. It was more dangerous, Nostromo said, with a laugh and a curse, than sending a man to get the treasure that people said was guarded by devils and ghosts in the deep ravines of Azuera. '*Señor*,' he said, 'we must catch the steamer at sea. We must keep out in the open looking for her till we have eaten and drunk all that has been put on board here. And if we miss her by some mischance, we must keep away from the land till we grow weak, and perhaps mad, and die, and drift dead, until one or another of the steamers of the Compania comes upon the boat with the two dead men who have saved the treasure. That, *señor*, is the only way to save it; for, don't you see? for us to come to the land anywhere in a hundred miles along this coast with this silver in our possession is to run the naked breast against the point of a knife. This thing has been given to me like a deadly disease. If men discover it I am dead, and you, too, *señor*, since you would come with me. There is enough silver to make a whole province rich, let alone a seaboard *pueblo* inhabited by thieves and vagabonds. *Señor*, they would think that heaven itself sent these riches into their hands, and would cut our throats without hesitation. I would trust no fair words from the best man around the shores of this gulf. Reflect that, even by giving up the treasure at the first demand, we would not be able to save our lives. Do you understand this, or must I explain?'

'No, you needn't explain,' said Decoud, a little listlessly. 'I can see it well enough myself, that the possession of this treasure is very much like a deadly disease for men situated as we are. But it had to removed from Sulaco, and you were the man for the task.'

'I was; but I cannot believe,' said Nostromo, 'that its loss would have impoverished Don Carlos Gould very much. There is more wealth in the mountain. I have heard it rolling down the shoots on quiet nights when I used to ride to Rincón to see a certain girl, after my work at the harbour was done. For years the rich rocks have been puring down with a noise like thunder, and the miners say that there is enough at the heart of the mountain to thunder on for years and years to come. And yet, since the day before yesterday, we have been fighting to save it from the mob, and tonight I am sent out with it into this darkness, where there is no wind to get away with; as if it were the last lot of silver on earth to get bread for the hungry with. Ha! ha! Well, I am going to make it the most famous and desperate affair of my life – wind or no wind. It shall be talked about when the little children are grown up and the grown men are old. Aha! The Monterists must not get hold of it, I am told, whatever happens to Nostromo the Capataz; and they shall not have it, I tell you, since it has been tied for safety round Nostromo's neck.'

'I see it,' murmured Decoud. He saw, indeed, that his companion had his own peculiar view of this enterprise.

Nostromo interrupted his reflections upon the way men's qualities are made use of, without any fundamental knowledge of their nature, by the proposal that they should slip the long oars out and sweep the lighter in the direction of the Isabels. It wouldn't do for daylight to reveal the treasure floating within a mile or so of the harbour entrance. The denser the darkness generally, the smarter were the puffs of wind on which he had reckoned to make his way; but tonight the gulf, under its poncho of clouds, remained breathless, as if dead rather than asleep.

Don Martin's soft hands suffered cruelly, tugging at the thick handle of the enormous oar. He stuck to it manfully, setting his teeth. He, too, was in the toils of an imaginative existence, and that strange work of pulling a lighter seemed to belong naturally to the inception of a new state, and acquired an ideal meaning from his love for Antonia. For all their efforts, the heavily laden lighter hardly moved. Nostromo could he heard swearing to himself between the regular splashes of the sweeps. 'We are making a crooked path,' he muttered to himself. 'I wish I could see the islands.'

In his unskilfulness Don Martin over-exerted himself. Now and then a sort of muscular faintness would run from the tips of his aching fingers through every fibre of his body, and pass off in a flush of heat. He had fought, talked, suffered mentally and physically, exerting his mind and body for the last forty-eight hours without intermission. He had had no rest, very little food, no pause in the stress of his thoughts and his feelings. Even his love for Antonia, whence he drew his strength and his inspiration, had reached the point of tragic tension during their hurried interview by Don José's bedside. And now, suddenly, he was thrown out of all this into a dark gulf, whose very gloom, silence, and breathless peace added a torment to the necessity for physical exertion. He imagined the lighter sinking to the bottom with an extraordinary shudder of delight. 'I am on the verge of delirium,' he thought. He mastered the trembling of all his limbs, of his breast, the inward trembling of all his body exhausted of its nervous force.

'Shall we rest, Capataz?' he proposed in a careless tone. 'There are many hours of night yet before us.'

'True. It is but a mile or so, I suppose. Rest your arms, *señor*, if that is what you mean. You will find no other sort of rest, I can promise you, since you let yourself be bound to this treasure whose loss would make no poor man poorer. No, *señor*; there is no rest till we find a northbound steamer, or else some ship finds us drifting about stretched out dead upon the Englishman's silver. Or rather – no; *por Dios!* I shall cut down the gunwale with the axe right to the water's edge before thirst and hunger rob me of my strength. By all the saints and devils I shall let the sea have the treasure rather than give it up to any stranger. Since it was the good pleasure of the *caballeros* to send me off on such an errand, they shall learn I am just the man they take me for.'

Decoud lay on the silver boxes panting. All his active sensations and feelings from as far back as he could remember seemed to him the maddest of dreams. Even his passionate devotion to Antonia into which he had worked himself up out of the depths of his scepticism had lost all appearance of reality. For a moment he was the prey of an extremely languid but not unpleasant indifference.

'I am sure they didn't mean you to take such a desperate view of this affair,' he said.

'What was it, then? A joke?' snarled the man, who on the paysheets of the O.S.N. Company's establishment in Sulaco was described as 'Foreman of the wharf' against the figure of his wages. 'Was it for a joke they woke me up from my sleep after two days of street fighting to make me stake my life upon a bad card? Everybody knows, too, that I am not a lucky gambler.'

'Yes, everybody knows of your good luck with women, Capataz,' Decoud propitiated his companion in a weary drawl.

'Look here, *señor*,' Nostromo went on. 'I never even remonstrated about this affair. Directly I heard what was wanted I saw what a desperate affair it must be, and I made up my mind to see it out. Every minute was of importance. I had to wait for you first. Then, when we arrived at the Italia Una, old Giorgio shouted to me to go for the English doctor. Later on, that poor dying woman wanted to see me, as you know. *Señor*, I was reluctant to go. I felt already this cursed silver growing heavy upon my back, and I was afraid that, knowing herself to be dying, she would ask me to ride off again for a priest. Father Corbelán, who is fearless, would have come at a word; but Father Corbelán is far away, safe with the band of Hernandez, and the populace, that would have liked to tear him to pieces, are much incensed against the priests. Not a single fat padre would have consented to put his head out of his hiding-place tonight to save a Christian soul, except, perhaps, under my protection. That was in her mind. I pretended I did not believe she was going to die. *Señor*, I refused to fetch a priest for a dying woman . . .'

Decoud was heard to stir.

'You did, Capataz!' he exclaimed. His tone changed. 'Well, you know – it was rather fine.'

'You do not believe in priests, Don Martin? Neither do I. What was the use of wasting time? But she – she believes in them. The thing sticks in my throat. She may be dead already, and here we are floating helpless with no wind at all. Curse on all superstition. She died thinking I deprived her of Paradise, I suppose. It shall be the most desperate affair of my life.'

Decoud remained lost in reflection. He tried to analyse the sensations awakened by what he had been told. The voice of the Capataz was heard again:

'Now, Don Martin, let us take up the sweeps and try to find the Isabels. It is either that or sinking the lighter if the day overtakes us. We must not forget that the steamer from Esmeralda with the soldiers may be coming along. We will pull straight on now. I have discovered a bit of a candle here, and we must take the risk of a small light to make a course by the boat compass. There is not enough wind to blow it out – may the curse of Heaven fall upon this blind gulf!'

A small flame appeared burning quite straight. It showed fragmentarily the stout ribs and planking in the hollow, empty part of the lighter. Decoud could see Nostromo standing up to pull. He saw him as high as the red sash on his waist, with a gleam of white-handled revolver and the wooden haft of a long knife protruding on his left side. Decoud nerved himself for the effort of rowing. Certainly there was not enough wind to blow the candle out, but its flame swayed a little to the slow movement of the heavy boat. It was so big that with their utmost efforts they could not move it quicker then about a mile an hour. This was sufficient, however, to sweep them amongst the Isabels long before daylight came. There was a good six hours of darkness before them, and the distance from the harbour to the Great Isabel did not exceed two miles. Decoud put this heavy toil to the account of the Capataz's impatience. Sometimes they paused, and then strained their ears to hear the boat from Esmeralda. In this perfect quietness a steamer moving would have been heard from far off. As to seeing anything it was out of the question. They could not see each other. Even the lighter's sail, which remained set, was invisible. Very often they rested.

'*Caramba!*' said Nostromo, suddenly, during one of those intervals when they lolled idly against the heavy handles of the sweeps. 'What is is? Are you distressed, Don Martin?'

Decoud assured him that he was not distressed in the least. Nostromo for a time kept perfectly still, and then in a whisper invited Martin to come aft.

With lips touching Decoud's ear he declared his belief that there was somebody else besides themselves upon the lighter. Twice now he had heard the sound of stifled sobbing.

'*Señor*,' he whispered with awed wonder, 'I am certain that there is somebody weeping in this lighter.'

Decoud had heard nothing. He expressed his incredulity. However, it was easy to ascertain the truth of the matter.

'It is most amazing,' muttered Nostromo. 'Could anybody have concealed himself on board while the lighter was lying alongside the wharf?'

'And you say it was like sobbing?' asked Decoud, lowering his voice, too. 'If he is weeping, whoever he is he cannot be very dangerous.'

Clambering over the precious pile in the middle, they crouched low on the foreside of the mast and groped under the half-deck. Right forward, in the narrowest part, their hands came upon the limbs of a man, who remained as silent as death. Too startled themselves to make a sound, they dragged him aft by one arm and the collar of his coat. He was limp – lifeless.

The light of the bit of candle fell upon a round, hook-nosed face with black moustaches and little side-whiskers. He was extremely dirty. A greasy growth of beard was sprouting on the shaven parts of the cheeks. The thick lips were slightly parted, but the eyes remained closed. Decoud, to his immense astonishment, recognized Señor Hirsch, the hide merchant from Esmeralda. Nostromo, too, had recognized him. And they gazed at each other across the body, lying with its naked feet higher than its head, in an absurd pretence of sleep, faintness, or death.

Chapter VIII

For a moment, before this extraordinary find, they forgot their own concerns and sensations. Señor Hirsch's sensations as he lay there must have been those of extreme terror. For a long time he refused to give a sign of life, till at last Decoud's objurgations, and, perhaps more, Nostromo's impatient suggestion that he should be thrown overboard, as he seemed to be dead, induced him to raise one eyelid first, and then the other.

It appeared that he had never found a safe opportunity to leave Sulaco. He lodged with Anzani, the universal storekeeper, on the Plaza Mayor. But when the riot broke out he had made his escape from his host's house before daylight, and in such a hurry that he had forgotten to put on his shoes. He had run out impulsively in his socks, and with his hat in his hand, into the garden of Anzani's house. Fear gave him the necessary agility to climb over several low walls, and afterwards he blundered into the overgrown cloisters of the ruined Franciscan convent in one of the by-streets. He forced himself into the midst of matted bushes with the recklessness of desperation, and this accounted for his scratched body and his torn clothing. He lay hidden there all day, his tongue cleaving to the roof of his mouth with all the intensity of thirst engendered by heat and fear. Three times different bands of men invaded the place with shouts and imprecations, looking for Father Corbelán; but towards the evening, still lying on his face in the bushes, he thought he would die from the fear of silence. He was not very clear as to what had induced him to leave the place, but evidently he had got out and slunk successfully out of town along the deserted back lanes. He wandered in the darkness near the railway, so maddened by apprehension that he dared not even approach the fires of the pickets of Italian workmen guarding the line. He had a vague idea evidently of finding refuge in the railway yards, but the dogs rushed upon him, barking; men began to shout; a shot was fired at random. He fled away from the gates. By the merest accident, as it happened, he took the direction of the O.S.N. Company's offices. Twice he stumbled upon the bodies of men killed during the day. But everything living frightened him much more. He crouched, crept, crawled, made dashes, guided by a sort of animal instinct, keeping away from every light and from every sound of voices. His idea was to throw himself at the feet of Captain Mitchell and beg for shelter in the Company's offices. It was all dark there as he approached on his hands and knees, but suddenly someone on guard challenged loudly, '*Quién vive?*' There were more dead men lying about, and he flattened himself down at once by the side of a cold corpse. He heard a voice saying, 'Here is one of those wounded rascals crawling about. Shall I go and finish him?' And another voice objected that it was not safe to go out without a lantern upon such an errand; perhaps it was only some Negro liberal looking for a chance to stick a knife into the stomach of an honest man. Hirsch didn't stay to hear any more, but crawling away to the end of the wharf, hid himself amongst a lot of empty casks. After a while some people came along, talking, and with glowing cigarettes. He did not stop to ask himself whether they would be likely to do him any harm, but bolted incontinently along the jetty, saw a lighter lying moored at the end, and threw himself into it. In his desire to find cover he crept right forward under the half-deck, and he had remained there more dead than alive, suffering agonies of hunger and thirst, and almost fainting with terror, when he heard numerous footsteps and the voices of the Europeans who came in a body escorting the wagon-load of treasure, pushed along the rails by a squad of *cargadores*. He understood perfectly what was being done from the talk, but did not disclose his presence from the fear that he would not be allowed to remain. His only idea at the time, overpowering and masterful, was to get away from this terrible Sulaco. And now he regretted it very much. He had heard Nostromo talk to Decoud, and wished himself back on shore. He did not desire to be involved in any desperate affair – in a situation where one could not run away. The involuntary groans of his anguished spirit had betrayed him to the sharp ears of the Capataz.

They had propped him up in a sitting posture against the side of the lighter, and he went on with the moaning account of his adventures till his voice broke, and his head fell forward. 'Water,' he whispered, with difficulty. Decoud held one of the cans to his lips. He revived after an extraordinarily short time, and scrambled up to his feet wildly. Nostromo, in an angry and threatening voice, ordered him forward. Hirsch was one of those men whom fear lashed like a whip, and he must have had an appalling idea of the Capataz's ferocity. He displayed an extraordinary agility in disappearing forward into the darkness. They heard him getting over the tarpaulin; then there was the sound of a heavy fall, followed by a weary sigh. Afterwards all was still in the fore-part of the lighter, as though he had killed himself in his headlong tumble. Nostromo shouted in a menacing voice:

'Lie still there! Do not move a limb. If I hear as much as a loud breath from you I shall come over there and put a bullet through your head.'

The mere presence of a coward, however passive, brings an element of treachery into a dangerous situation. Nostromo's nervous impatience passed into gloomy thoughtfulness. Decoud, in an undertone, as if speaking to himself, remarked that, after all, this bizarre event made no great difference. He could not conceive what harm the man could do. At most he would be in the way, like an inanimate and useless object – like a block of wood, for instance.

'I would think twice before getting rid of a piece of wood,' said Nostromo, calmly. 'Something may happen unexpectedly where you could make use of it. But in an affair like ours a man like this ought to be thrown overboard. Even if he were as brave as a lion we would not want him here. We are not running away for our lives. *Señor*, there is no harm in a brave man trying to save himself with ingenuity and courage; but you have heard his tale, Don Martin. His being here is a miracle of fear –' Nostromo paused. 'There is no room for fear in this lighter,' he added through his teeth.

Decoud had no answer to make. It was not a position for argument, for a display of scruples or feelings. There were a thousand ways in which a panic-stricken man could make himself dangerous. It was evident that Hirsch could not be spoken to, reasoned with, or persuaded into a rational line of conduct. The story of his own escape demonstrated that clearly enough. Decoud thought that it was a thousand pities the wretch had not died of fright. Nature, who had made him what he was, seemed to have calculated cruelly how much he could bear in the way of atrocious anguish without actually expiring. Some compassion was due to so much terror. Decoud, though imaginative enough for sympathy, resolved not to interfere with any action that Nostromo would take. But Nostromo did nothing. And the fate of Señor Hirsch remained suspended in the darkness of the gulf at the mercy of events which could not be foreseen.

The Capataz, extending his hand, put out the candle suddenly. It was to Decoud as if his companion had destroyed, by a single touch, the world of affairs, of loves, of revolution, where his complacent superiority analysed fearlessly all motives and all passions, including his own.

He gasped a little. Decoud was affected by the novelty of his position. Intellectually self-confident, he suffered from being deprived of the only weapon he could use with effect. No intelligence could penetrate the darkness of the placid Gulf. There remained only one thing he was certain of, and that was the overweening vanity of his companion. It was direct, uncomplicated, naïve, and effectual. Decoud, who had been making use of him, had tried to understand his man thoroughly. He had discovered a complete singleness of motive behind the varied manifestations of a consistent character. This was why the man remained so astonishingly simple in the jealous greatness of his conceit. And now there was a complication. It was evident that he resented having been given a task in which there were so many chances of failure. 'I wonder,' thought Decoud, 'how he would behave if I were not here.'

He heard Nostromo mutter again, 'No! there is no room for fear on this lighter. Courage itself does not seem good enough. I have a good eye and a steady hand; no man can say he ever saw me tired or uncertain what to do; but *por Dios*, Don Martin, I have been sent out into this black calm on a business where neither a good eye, nor a steady hand, nor judgement are any use . . .' He swore a string of oaths in Spanish and Italian under his breath. 'Nothing but sheer desperation will do for this affair.'

These words were in strange contrast to the prevailing peace – to this almost stolid stillness of the gulf. A shower fell with an abrupt whispering sound all round the boat, and Decoud took off his hat, and, letting his head get wet, felt greatly refreshed. Presently a steady little draught of air caressed his cheek. The lighter began to move, but the shower distanced it. The drops ceased to fall upon his head and hands, the whispering died out in the distance. Nostromo emitted a grunt of satisfaction, and grasping the tiller, chirruped softly, as sailors do, to encourage the wind. Never for the last three days had Decoud felt less the need for what the Capataz would call desperation.

'I fancy I hear another shower on the water,' he observed in a tone of quiet content. 'I hope it will catch us up.'

Nostromo ceased chirruping at once. 'You hear another shower?' he said, doubtfully. A sort of thinning of the darkness seemed to have taken place, and Decoud could see now the outline of his companion's figure, and even the sail came out of the night like a square block of dense snow.

The sound which Decoud had detected came along the water harshly. Nostromo recognized that noise partaking of a hiss and a rustle which spreads out on all sides of a steamer making her way through a smooth water on a quiet night. It could be nothing else but the captured transport with troops from Esmeralda. She carried no lights. The noise of her steaming, growing louder every minute, would stop at times altogether, and then begin again abruptly, and sound startlingly nearer, as if that invisible vessel, whose position could not be precisely guessed, were making straight for the lighter. Meantime, that last kept on sailing slowly and noiselessly before a breeze so faint that it was only by leaning over the side and feeling the water slip through his fingers that Decoud convinced himself they were moving at all. His drowsy feeling had departed. He was glad to know that the lighter was moving. After so much stillness the noise of the steamer seemed uproarious and distracting. There was a weirdness in not being able to see her. Suddenly all was still. She had stopped, but so close to them that the steam, blowing off, sent its rumbling vibration right over their heads.

'They are trying to make out where they are,' said Decoud in a whisper. Again he leaned over and put his fingers into the water. 'We are moving quite smartly,' he informed Nostromo.

'We seem to be crossing her bows,' said the Capataz in a cautious tone. 'But this is a blind game with death. Moving on is of no use. We mustn't be seen or heard.'

His whisper was hoarse with excitement. Of all his face there was nothing visible but a gleam of white eyeballs. His fingers gripped Decoud's shoulder. 'That is the only way to save this treasure from this steamer full of soldiers. Any other would have carried lights. But you observe there is not a gleam to show us where she is.'

Decoud stood as if paralysed; only his thoughts were wildly active. In the space of a second he remembered the desolate glance of Antonia as he left her at the bedside of her father in the gloomy house of Avellanos with shuttered windows, but all the doors standing open, and deserted by all the servants except an old Negro at the gate. He remembered the Casa Gould on his last visit, the arguments, the tones of his voice, the impenetrable attitude of Charles, Mrs Gould's face so blanched with anxiety and fatigue that her eyes seemed to have changed colour, appearing nearly black by contrast. Even whole sentences of the proclamation which he meant to make Barrios issue from his headquarters at Cayta as soon as he got there passed through his mind; the very germ of the new State, the Separationist proclamation which he had tried before he left to read hurriedly to Don José, stretched out on his bed under the fixed gaze of his daughter. God knows whether the old statesman had understood it; he was unable to speak, but he had certainly lifted his arm off the coverlet; his hand had moved as if to make the sign of the cross in the air, a gesture of blessing, of consent. Decoud had that very draft in his pocket, written in pencil on several loose sheets of paper, with the heavily printed heading. 'Administration of the San Tomé Silver Mine. Sulaco. Republic of Costaguana.' He had written it furiously, snatching page after page on Charles Gould's table. Mrs Gould had looked several times over his shoulder as he wrote; but the Señor Administrador standing straddle-legged, would not even glance at it when it was finished. He had waved it away firmly. It must have been scorn, and not caution, since he never made a remark about the use of the Administration's paper for such a compromising document. And that showed his disdain, the true English disdain of common prudence, as if everything outside the range of their own thoughts and feelings were unworthy of serious recognition. Decoud had the time in a second or two to become furiously angry with Charles Gould, and even resentful against Mrs Gould, in whose care, tacitly it is true, he had left the safety of Antonia. Better perish a thousand times than owe your preservation to such people, he exclaimed mentally. The grip of Nostromo's fingers never removed from his shoulder, tightening fiercely, recalled him to himself.

'The darkness is our friend,' the Capataz murmured into his ear. 'I am going to lower the sail, and trust our escape to this black gulf. No eyes could make us out lying silent with a naked mast. I will do it now, before this steamer closes still more upon us. The faint creak of a block would betray us and the San Tomé treasure into the hands of those thieves.'

He moved about as warily as a cat. Decoud heard no sound; and it was only by the disappearance of the square blotch of darkness that he knew the yard had come down, lowered as carefully as if it had been made of glass. Next moment he heard Nostromo's quiet breathing by his side.

'You had better not move at all from where you are. Don Martin,' advised the Capataz, earnestly. 'You might stumble or displace something which would make a noise. The sweeps and the punting poles are lying about. Move not for your life. *Por Dios*, Don Martin,' he went on in a keen but friendly whisper, 'I am so desperate that if I didn't know your worship to be a man of courage, capable of standing stock still whatever happens, I would drive my knife into your heart.'

A deathlike stillness surrounded the lighter. It was difficult to believe that there was near a steamer full of men with many pairs of eyes peering from her bridge for some hint of land in the night. Her steam had ceased blowing off, and she remained stopped too far off apparently for any other sound to reach the lighter.

'Perhaps you would, Capataz,' Decoud began in a whisper. 'However, you need not trouble. There are other things than the fear of your knife to keep my heart steady. It shall not betray you. Only, have you forgotten –'

'I spoke to you openly as to a man as desperate as myself,' explained the Capataz. 'The silver must be saved from the Monterists. I told Captain Mitchell three times that I preferred to go alone. I told Don Carlos Gould, too. It was in the Casa Gould. They had sent for me. The ladies were there; and when I tried to explain why I did not wish to have you with me, they promised me, both of them, great rewards for your safety. A strange way to talk to a man you are sending out to an almost certain death. Those gentlefolk do not seem to have sense enough to understand what they are giving one to do. I told them I could do nothing for you. You would have been safer with the bandit Hernandez. It would have been possible to ride out of the town with no greater risk than a chance shot sent after you in the dark. But it was as if they had been deaf. I had to promise I would wait for you under the harbour gate. I did wait. And now because you are a brave man you are as safe as the silver. Neither more nor less.'

At that moment, as if by way of comment upon Nostromo's words, the invisible steamer went ahead at half speed only, as could be judged by the leisurely beat of her propeller. The sound shifted its place markedly, but without coming nearer. It even grew a little more distant right abeam of the lighter, and then ceased again.

'They are trying for a sight of the Isabels,' muttered Nostromo, 'in order to make for the harbour in a straight line and seize the Custom House with the treasure in it. Have you ever seen the Commandant of Esmeralda, Sotillo? A handsome fellow, with a soft voice. When I first came here I used to see him in the Calle talking to the *señoritas* at the windows of the houses, and showing his white teeth all the time. But one of my *cargadores*, who had been a soldier, told me that he had once ordered a man to be flayed alive in the remote Campo, where he was sent recruiting amongst the people of the *estancias*. It has never entered his head that the *compañía* had a man capable of baffling his game.'

The murmuring loquacity of the Capataz disturbed Decoud like a hint of weakness. And yet, talkative resolution may be as genuine as grim silence.

'Sotillo is not baffled so far,' he said. 'Have you forgotten that crazy man forward?'

Nostromo had not forgotten Señor Hirsch. He reproached himself bitterly for not having visited the lighter carefully before leaving the wharf. He reproached himself for not having stabbed and flung Hirsch overboard at the very moment of discovery without even looking at his face. That would have been consistent with the desperate character of the affair. Whatever happened, Sotillo *was* already baffled. Even if that wretch, now as silent as death, did anything to betray the nearness of the lighter. Sotillo – if Sotillo it was in command of the troops on board – would be still baffled of his plunder.

'I have an axe in my hand,' Nostromo whispered, wrathfully, 'that in three strokes would cut through the side down to the water's edge. Moreoever, each lighter has a plug in the stern, and I know exactly where it is. I feel it under the sole of my foot.'

Decoud recognized the ring of genuine determination in the nervous murmurs, the vindictive excitement of the famous Capataz. Before the steamer, guided by a shriek or two (for there could be no more than that, Nostromo said, gnashing his teeth audibly), could find the lighter there would be plenty of time to sink this treasure tied up round his neck.

The last words he hissed into Decoud's ear. Decoud said nothing. He was perfectly convinced. The usual characteristic quietness of the man was gone. It was not equal to the situation as he conceived it. Something deeper, something unsuspected by everyone, had come to the surface. Decoud, with careful movements, slipped off his overcoat and divested himself of his boots; he did not consider himself in honour to sink with the treasure. His object was to get down to Barrios, in Cayta, as the Capataz knew very well; and he, too, meant, in his own way, to put into that attempt all the desperation of which he was capable. Nostromo muttered, 'True, true! You are a politician, *señor*. Rejoin the army, and start another revolution.' He pointed out, however, that there was a little boat belonging to every lighter fit to carry two men, if not more. Theirs was towing behind.

Of that Decoud had not been aware. Of course, it was too dark to see, and it was only when Nostromo put his hand upon its painter fastened to a cleat in the stern that he experienced a full measure of relief. The prospect of finding himself in the water and swimming, overwhelmed by ignorance and darkness, probably in a circle, till he sank from exhaustion, was revolting. The barren and cruel futility of such an end intimidated his affectation of careless pessimism. In comparison to it, the chance of being left floating in a boat, exposed to thirst, hunger, discovery, imprisonment, execution, presented itself with an aspect of amenity worth securing even at the cost of some set self-contempt. He did not accept Nostromo's proposal that he should get into the boat at once. 'Something sudden may overwhelm us, *señor*,' the Capataz remarked promising faithfully, at the same time, to let go the painter at the moment when the necessity became manifest.

But Decoud assured him lightly that he did not mean to take to the boat till the very last moment, and that then he meant the Capataz to come along, too. The darkness of the gulf was no longer for him the end of all things. It was part of a living world since, pervading it, failure and death could be felt at your elbow. And at the same time it was a shelter. He exulted in its impenetrable obscurity. 'Like a wall, like a wall,' he muttered to himself.

The only thing which checked his confidence was the thought of Señor Hirsch. Not to have bound and gagged him seemed to Decoud now the height of improvident folly. As long as the miserable creature had the power to raise a yell he was a constant danger. His abject terror was mute now, but there was no saying from what cause it might suddenly find vent in shrieks.

This very madness of fear which both Decoud and Nostromo had seen in the wild and irrational glances, and in the continuous twitchings of his mouth, protected Señor Hirsch from the cruel necessities of this desperate affair. The moment of silencing him for ever had passed. As Nostromo remarked, in answer to Decoud's regrets, it was too late! It could not be done without noise, especially in the ignorance of the man's exact position. Wherever he had elected to crouch and tremble, it was too hazardous to go near him. He would begin probably to yell for mercy. It was much better to leave him quite alone since he was keeping so still. But to trust to his silence became every moment a greater strain upon Decoud's composure.

'I wish, Capataz, you had not let the right moment pass,' he murmured.

'What! To silence him for ever! I thought it good to hear first how he came to be here. It was too strange. Who could imagine that it was all an accident? Afterwards, *señor*, when I saw you giving him water to drink, I would not do it. Not after I had seen you holding up the can to his lips as though he were your brother. *Señor*, that sort of necessity must not be thought of too long. And yet it would have been no cruelty to take away from him his wretched life. It is nothing but fear. Your compassion saved him then, Don Martin, and now it is too late. It couldn't be done without noise.'

In the steamer they were keeping a perfect silence, and the stillness was so profound that Decoud felt as if the slightest sound conceivable must travel unchecked and audible to the end of the world. What if Hirsch coughed or sneezed? To feel himself at the mercy of such an idiotic contingency was too exasperating to be looked upon with irony. Nostromo, too, seemed to be getting restless. Was it possible, he asked himself, that the steamer, finding the night too dark altogether, intended to remain stopped where she was till daylight? He began to think that this, after all, was the real danger. He was afraid that the darkness, which was his protection, would, in the end, cause his undoing.

Sotillo, as Nostromo had surmised, was in command on board the transport. The events of the last forty-eight hours in Sulaco were not known to him; neither was he aware that the telegraphist in Esmeralda had managed to warn his colleague in Sulaco. Like a good many officers of the troops garrisoning the province, Sotillo had been influenced in his adoption of the Ribierist cause by the belief that it had the enormous wealth of the Gould Concession on its side. He had been one of the frequenters of the Casa Gould, where he had aired his Blanco convictions and his ardour for reform before Don José Avellanos, casting frank, honest glances towards Mrs Gould and Antonia the while. He was known to belong to a good family persecuted and impoverished during the tyranny of Guzman Bento. The opinions he expressed appeared eminently natural and proper in a man of his parentage and antecedents. And he was not a deceiver; it was perfectly natural for him to express elevated sentiments while his whole faculties were taken up with what seemed then a solid and practical notion – the notion that the husband of Antonia Avellanos would be, naturally, the intimate friend of the Gould Concession. He even pointed this out to Anzani once, when negotiating the sixth or seventh small loan in the gloomy, damp apartment with enormous iron bars, behind the principal shop in the whole row under the Arcades. He hinted to the universal shopkeeper at the excellent terms he was on with the emancipated *señorita*, who was like a sister to the Englishwoman. He would advance one leg and put his arms akimbo, posing for Anzani's inspection, and fixing him with haughty stare.

'Look, miserable shopkeeper! How can a man like me fail with any woman, let alone an emancipated girl living in scandalous freedom?' he seemed to say.

His manner in the Casa Gould was, of course, very different – devoid of all truculence, and even slightly mournful. Like most of his countrymen, he was carried away by the sound of fine words, especially if uttered by himself. He had no convictions of any sort upon anything except as to the irresistible power of his personal advantages. But that was so firm that even Decoud's appearance in Sulaco, and his intimacy with the Goulds and the Avellanos, did not disquiet him. On the contrary, he tried to make friends with that rich Costaguanero from Europe in the hope of borrowing a large sum by-and-by. The only guiding motive of his life was to get money for the satisfaction of his expensive tastes, which he indulged recklessly, having no self-control. He imagined himself a master of intrigue, but his corruption was as simple as an animal instinct. At times, in solitude, he had his moments of ferocity, and also on such occasions as, for instance, when alone in a room with Anzani trying to get a loan.

He had talked himself into the command of the Esmeralda garrison. That small seaport had its importance as the station of the main submarine cable connecting the Occidental Provinces with the outer world, and the junction with it of the Sulaco branch. Don José Avellanos proposed him, and Barrios, with a rude and jeering guffaw, had said, 'Oh, let Sotillo go. He is a very good man to keep guard over the cable, and the ladies of Esmeralda ought to have their turn.' Barrios, an indubitably brave man, had no great opinion of Sotillo.

It was through the Esmeralda cable alone that the San Tomé mine could be kept in constant touch with the great financier, whose tacit approval made the strength of the Ribierist movement. This movement had its adversaries even there. Sotillo governed Esmeralda with repressive severity till the adverse course of events upon the distant theatre of civil war forced upon him the reflection that, after all, the great silver mine was fated to become the spoil of the victors. But caution was necessary. He began by assuming a dark and mysterious attitude towards the faithful Ribierist municipality of Esmeralda. Later on, the information that the commandant was holding assemblies of officers in the dead of night (which had leaked out somehow) caused those gentlemen to neglect their civil duties altogether, and remain shut up in their houses. Suddenly one day all the letters from Sulaco by the overland courier were carried off by a file of soldiers from the post office to the Comandancia, without disguise, concealment, or apology. Sotillo had heard through Cayta of the final defeat of Ribiera.

This was the first open sign of the change in his convictions. Presently notorious democrats, who had been living till then in constant fear of arrest, leg irons, and even floggings, could be observed going in and out at the great door of the Comandancia, where the horses of the orderlies doze under their heavy saddles, while the men, in ragged uniforms and pointed straw hats, lounge on a bench, with their naked feet stuck out beyond the strip of shade; and a sentry, in a red baize coat with holes at the elbows, stands at the top of the steps glaring haughtily at the common people, who uncover their heads to him as they pass.

Sotillo's ideas did not soar above the care for his personal safety and the chance of plundering the town in his charge, but he feared that such a late adhesion would earn but scant gratitude from the victors. He had believed just a little too long in the power of the San Tomé mine. The seized correspondence had confirmed his previous information of a large amount of silver ingots lying in the Sulaco Custom House. To gain possession of it would be a clear Monterist move; a sort of service that would have to be rewarded. With the silver in his hands he could make terms for himself and his soldiers. He was aware neither of the riots, nor of the President's escape to Sulaco and the close pursuit led by Montero's brother, the *guerrillero*. The game seemed in his own hands. The initial moves were the seizure of the cable telegraph office and the securing of the Government steamer lying in the narrow creek which is the harbour of Esmeralda. The last was effected without difficulty by a company of soldiers swarming with a rush over the gangways as she lay alongside the quay; but the lieutenant charged with the duty of arresting the telegraphist halted on the way before the only café in Esmeralda, where he distributed some brandy to his men, and refreshed himself at the expense of the owner, a known Ribierist. The whole party became intoxicated, and proceeded on their mission up the street yelling and firing random shots at the windows. This little festivity, which might have turned out dangerous to the telegraphist's life, enabled him in the end to send his warning to Sulaco. The lieutenant, staggering upstairs with a drawn sabre, was before long kissing him on both cheeks in one of those swift changes of mood peculiar to a state of drunkenness. He clasped the telegraphist close round the neck, assuring him that all the officers of the Esmeralda garrison were going to be made colonels, while tears of happiness streamed down his sodden face. Thus it came about that the town major, coming along later, found the whole party sleeping on the stairs and in passages, and the telegraphist (who scorned this chance of escape) very busy clicking the key of the transmitter. The major led him away bareheaded, with his hands tied behind his back, but concealed the truth from Sotillo, who remained in ignorance of the warning dispatched to Sulaco.

The colonel was not the man to let any sort of darkness stand in the way of the planned surprise. It appeared to him a dead certainty; his heart was set upon his object with an ungovernable, childlike impatience. Ever since the steamer had rounded Punta Mala, to enter the deeper shadow of the gulf, he had remained on the bridge in a group of officers as excited as himself. Distracted between the coaxings and menaces of Sotillo and his Staff, the miserable commander of the steamer kept her moving with as much prudence as they would let him exercise. Some of them had been drinking heavily, no doubt; but the prospect of laying hands on so much wealth made them absurdly foolhardy, and, at the same time, extremely anxious. The old major of the battalion, a stupid, suspicious man, who had never been afloat in his life, distinguished himself by putting out suddenly the binnacle light, the only one allowed on board for the necessities of navigation. He could not understand of what use it could be for finding the way. To the vehement protestations of the ship's captain, he stamped his foot and tapped the handle of his sword. 'Aha! I have unmasked you,' he cried, triumphantly. 'You are tearing your hair from despair at my acuteness. Am I a child to believe that a light in that brass box can show you where the harbour is? I am an old soldier, I am. I can smell a traitor a league off. You wanted the gleam to betray our approach to your friend the Englishman. A thing like that show you the way! What a miserable lie! *Que picardía!* You Sulaco people are all in the pay of those foreigners. You deserve to be run through the body with my sword.' Other officers, crowding round, tried to calm his indignation, repeating persuasively, 'No, no! This is an appliance of the mariners, major. This is no treachery.' The captain of the transport flung himself face downwards on the bridge, and refused to rise. 'Put an end to me at once,' he repeated in a stifled voice. Sotillo had to interfere.

The uproar and confusion on the bridge became so great that the helmsman fled from the wheel. He took refuge in the engine-room, and alarmed the engineers, who, disregarding the threats of the soldiers set on guard over them, stopped the engines, protesting that they would rather be shot than run the risk of being drowned down below.

This was the first time Nostromo and Decoud heard the steamer stop. After order had been restored, and the binnacle lamp relighted, she went head again, passing wide of the lighter in her search for the Isabels. The group could not be made out, and, at the pitiful entreaties of the captain, Sotillo allowed the engines to be stopped again to wait for one of those periodical lightenings of darkness caused by the shifting of the cloud canopy spread above the waters of the gulf.

Sotillo, on the bridge, muttered from time to time angrily to the captain. The other, in an apologetic and cringing tone, begged *su merced* the colonel to take into consideration the limitations put upon human faculties by the darkness of the night. Sotillo swelled with rage and impatience. It was the chance of a lifetime.

'If your eyes are of no more use to you than this, I shall have them put out,' he burst out.

The captain of the steamer made no answer, for just then the mass of the Great Isabel loomed up darkly after a passing shower, then vanished, as if swept away by a wave of greater obscurity preceding another downpour. This was enough for him. In the voice of a man come back to life again, he informed Sotillo that in an hour he would be alongside the Sulaco wharf. The ship was put then full speed on the course, and a great bustle of preparation for landing arose among the soldiers on her deck.

It was heard distinctly by Decoud and Nostromo. The Capataz understood its meaning. They had made out the Isabels, and were going on now in a straight line for Sulaco. He judged that they would pass close; but believed that lying still like this, with the sail lowered, the lighter could not be seen. 'No, not even if they rubbed sides with us,' he muttered.

The rain began to fall again; first like a wet mist, then with a heavier touch, thickening into a smart, perpendicular downpour; and the hiss and thump of the approaching steamer was coming extremely near. Decoud, with his eyes full of water, and lowered head, asked himself how long it would be before she drew past, when unexpectedly he felt a lurch. An inrush of foam broke swishing over the stern, simultaneously with a crack of timbers and a staggering shock. He had the impression of an angry hand laying hold of the lighter and dragging it along to destruction. The shock, of course, had knocked him down, and he found himself rolling in a lot of water at the bottom of the lighter. A violent churning went on alongside; a strange and amazed voice cried out something about him in the night. He heard a piercing shriek for help from Señor Hirsch. He kept his teeth hard set all the time. It was a collision!

The steamer had struck the lighter obliquely, heeling her over till she was half swamped, starting some of her timbers, and swinging her head parallel to her own course with the force of the blow. The shock of it on board of her was hardly perceptible. All the violence of that collision was, as usual, felt only on board the smaller craft. Even Nostromo himself thought that this was perhaps the end of his desperate adventure. He, too, had been flung away from the long tiller, which took charge of the lurch. Next moment the steamer would have passed on, leaving the lighter to sink or swim after having shouldered her thus out of her way, and without ever getting a glimpse of her form, had it not been that, being deeply laden with stores and the great number of people on board, her anchor was low enough to hook itself into one of the wire shrouds of the lighter's mast. For the space of two or three gasping breaths that new rope held against the sudden strain. It was this that gave Decoud the sensation of the snatching pull, dragging the lighter away to destruction. The cause of it, of course, was inexplicable to him. The whole thing was so sudden that he had no time to think. But all his sensations were perfectly clear; he had kept complete possession of himself; in fact, he was even pleasantly aware of that calmness at the very moment of being pitched head first over the transom, to struggle on his back in a lot of water. Señor Hirsch's shriek he had heard and recognized while he was regaining his feet, always with that mysterious sensation of being dragged headlong through the darkness. Not a word, not a cry escaped him; he had no time to see anything; and following upon the despairing screams for help, the dragging motion ceased so suddenly that he staggered forward with open arms and fell against the pile of the treasure boxes. He clung to them instinctively, in the vague apprehension of being flung about again; and immediately he heard another lot of shrieks for help, prolonged and despairing, not near him at all, but unaccountably in the distance, away from the lighter altogether, as if some spirit in the night were mocking at Señor Hirsch's terror and despair.

Then all was still – as still as when you wake up in your bed in a dark room from a bizarre and agitated dream. The lighter rocked slightly; the rain was still falling. Two groping hands took hold of his bruised sides from behind, and the Capataz's voice whispered, in his ear, 'Silence, for your life! Silence! The steamer has stopped.'

Decoud listened. The gulf was dumb. He felt the water nearly up to his knees. 'Are we sinking?' he asked in a faint breath.

'I don't know,' Nostromo breathed back to him. '*Señor*, make not the slightest sound.'

Hirsch, when ordered forward by Nostromo, had not returned into his first hiding-place. He had fallen near the mast, and had no strength to rise; moreover, he feared to move. He had given himself up for dead, but not on any rational grounds. It was simply a cruel and terrifying feeling. Whenever he tried to think what would become of him his teeth would start chattering violently. He was too absorbed in the utter misery of his fear to take notice of anything.

Though he was stifling under the lighter's sail which Nostromo had unwittingly lowered on top of him, he did not even dare to put out his head till the very moment of the steamer striking. Then, indeed, he leaped right out, spurred on to new miracles of bodily vigour by this new shape of danger. The inrush of water when the lighter heeled over unsealed his lips. His shriek, 'Save me!' was the first distinct warning of the collision for the people on board the steamer. Next moment the wire shroud parted, and the released anchor swept over the lighter's forecastle. It came against the breast of Señor Hirsch, who simply seized hold of it, without in the least knowing what it was, but curling his arms and legs upon the part above the fluke with an invincible, unreasonable tenacity. The lighter yawed off wide, and the steamer, moving on, carried him away, clinging hard, and shouting for help. It was some time, however, after the steamer had stopped that his position was discovered. His sustained yelping for help seemed to come from somebody swimming in the water. At last a couple of men went over the bows and hauled him on board. He was carried straight off to Sotillo on the bridge. His examination confirmed the impression that some craft had been run over and sunk, but it was impracticable on such a dark night to look for the positive proof of floating wreckage. Sotillo was more anxious than ever now to enter the harbour without loss of time; the idea that he had destroyed the principal object of his expedition was too intolerable to be accepted. This feeling made the story he had heard appear the more incredible. Señor Hirsch, after being beaten a little for telling lies, was thrust into the chartroom. But he was beaten only a little. His tale had taken the heart out of Sotillo's Staff, though they all repeated round their chief, 'Impossible! impossible!' with the exception of the old major, who triumphed gloomily.

'I told you; I told you,' he mumbled. 'I could smell some treachery, some *diablería* a league off.'

Meantime, the steamer had kept on her way towards Sulaco, where only the truth of that matter could be ascertained. Decoud and Nostromo heard the loud churning of her propeller diminish and die out; and then, with no useless words, busied themselves in making for the Isabels. The last shower had brought with it a gentle but steady breeze. The danger was not over yet, and there was no time for talk. The lighter was leaking like a sieve. They splashed in the water at every step. The Capataz put into Decoud's hands the handle of the pump which was fitted at the side aft, and at once, without question or remark, Decoud began to pump in utter forgetfulness of every desire but that of keeping the treasure afloat. Nostromo hoisted the sail, flew back to the tiller, pulled at the sheet like mad. The short flare of a match (they had been kept dry in a tight tin box, though the man himself was completely wet), the vivid flare of a match, disclosed to the toiling Decoud the eagerness of his face, bent low over the box of the compass, and the attentive stare of his eyes. He knew now where he was, and he hoped to run the sinking lighter ashore in the shallow cove where the high, cliff-like end of the Great Isabel is divided in two equal parts by a deep and overgrown ravine.

Decoud pumped without intermission. Nostromo steered without relaxing for a second the intense, peering effort of his stare. Each of them was as if utterly alone with his task. It did not occur to them to speak. There was nothing in common between them but the knowledge that the damaged lighter must be slowly but surely sinking. In that knowledge, which was like the crucial test of their desires, they seemed to have become completely estranged, as if they had discovered in the very shock of the collision that the loss of the lighter would not mean the same thing to them both. This common danger brought their differences in aim, in view, in character, and in position, into absolute prominence in the private vision of each. There was no bond of conviction, of common idea; they were merely two adventurers pursuing each his own adventure, involved in the same imminence of deadly peril. Therefore they had nothing to say to each other. But this peril, this only incontrovertible truth in which they shared, seemed to act as an inspiration to their mental and bodily powers.

There was certainly something almost miraculous in the way the Capataz made the cove with nothing but the shadowy hint of the island's shape and the vague gleam of a small sandy strip for a guide. Where the ravine opens between the cliffs, and a slender, shallow rivulet meanders out of the bushes to lose itself in the sea, the lighter was run ashore; and the two men, with a taciturn, undaunted energy, began to discharge her precious freight, carrying each ox-hide box up the bed of the rivulet beyond the bushes to a hollow place which the caving in of the soil had made below the roots of a large tree. Its big smooth trunk leaned like a falling column far over the trickle of water running amongst the loose stones.

A couple of years before Nostromo had spent a whole Sunday, all alone, exploring the island. He explained this to Decoud after their task was done, and they sat, weary in every limb, with their legs hanging down the low bank and their backs against the tree, like a pair of blind men aware of each other and their surroundings by some indefinable sixth sense.

'Yes,' Nostromo repeated, 'I never forget a place I have carefully looked at once.' He spoke slowly, almost lazily, as if there had been a whole leisurely life before him, instead of the scanty two hours before daylight. The existence of the treasure, barely concealed in this improbable spot, laid a burden of secrecy upon every contemplated step, upon every intention and plan of future conduct. He felt the partial failure of this desperate affair entrusted to the great reputation he had known how to make for himself. However, it was also a partial success. His vanity was half appeased. His nervous irritation had subsided.

'You never know what may be of use,' he pursued with his usual quietness of tone and manner. 'I spent a whole miserable Sunday in exploring this crumb of land.'

'A misanthropic sort of occupation,' muttered Decoud, viciously. 'You had no money, I suppose, to gamble with, and to fling about amongst the girls in your usual haunts, Capataz.'

'*È vero!*' exclaimed the Capataz, surprised into the use of his native tongue by so much perspicacity. 'I had not! Therefore I did not want to go amongst those beggarly people accustomed to my generosity. It is looked for from the Capataz of the Cargadores, who are the rich men, and, as it were, the *caballeros* amongst the common people. I don't care for cards but as a pastime; and as to those girls that boast of having opened their doors to my knock, you know I wouldn't look at any one of them twice except for what the people would say. They are queer, the good people of Sulaco, and I have got much useful information simply by listening patiently to the talk of the women that everybody believed I was in love with. Poor Teresa could never understand that. On that particular Sunday, *señor*, she scolded so that I went out of the house swearing that I would never darken their door again unless to fetch away my hammock and my chest of clothes. *Señor*, there is nothing more exasperating than to hear a woman you respect rail against your good reputation when you have not a single brass coin in your pocket. I untied one of the small boats and pulled myself out of the harbour with nothing but three cigars in my pocket to help me spend the day on this island. But the water of this rivulet you hear under your feet is cool and sweet and good, *señor*, both before and after a smoke.' He was silent for a while, then added reflectively, 'That was the first Sunday after I brought the white-whiskered English *rico* all the way down the mountains from the Paramo on the top of the Entrada Pass – and in the coach, too! No coach had gone up or down that mountain road within the memory of man, *señor*, till I brought this one down in charge of fifty peons working like one man with ropes, pick-axes, and poles under my direction. That was the rich Englishman who, as people say, pays for the making of this railway. He was very pleased with me. But my wages were not due till the end of the month.'

He slid down the bank suddenly. Decoud heard the splash of his feet in the brook and followed his footsteps down the ravine. His form was lost among the bushes till he had reached the strip of sand unler the cliff. As often happens in the gulf when the showers during the first part of the night had been frequent and heavy, the darkness had thinned considerably towards the morning though there were no signs of daylight as yet.

The cargo-lighter, relieved of its precious burden, rocked feebly, half-afloat, with her fore-foot on the sand. A long rope stretched away like a black cotton thread across the strip of white beach to the grapnel Nostromo had carried ashore and hooked to the stem of a tree-like shrub in the very opening of the ravine.

There was nothing for Decoud but to remain on the island. He received from Nostromo's hands whatever food the foresight of Captain Mitchell had put on board the lighter and deposited it temporarily in the little dinghy which on their arrival they had hauled up out of sight amongst the bushes. It was to be left with him. The island was to be a hiding-place, not a prison; he could pull out to a passing ship. The O.S.N. Company's mail boats passed close to the islands when going into Sulaco from the north. But the *Minerva*, carrying off the ex-president, had taken the news up north of the disturbances in Sulaco. It was possible that the next steamer down would get instructions to miss the port altogether since the town, as far as the *Minerva*'s officers knew, was for the time being in the hands of the rabble. This would mean that there would be no steamer for a month, as far as the mail service went; but Decoud had to take his chance of that. The island was his only shelter from the proscription hanging over his head. The Capataz was, of course, going back. The unloaded lighter leaked much less, and he thought that she would keep afloat as far as the harbour.

He passed to Decoud, standing knee-deep alongside, one of the two spades which belonged to the equipment of each lighter for use when ballasting ships. By working with it carefully as soon as there was daylight enough to see, Decoud could loosen a mass of earth and stones overhanging the cavity in which they had deposited the treasure, so that it would look as if it had fallen naturally. It would cover up not only the cavity, but even all traces of their work, the footsteps, the displaced stones, and even the broken bushes.

'Besides, who would think of looking either for you or the treasure here?' Nostromo continued, as if he could not tear himself away from the spot. 'Nobody is ever likely to come here. What could any man want with this piece of earth as long as there is room for his feet on the mainland! The people in this country are not curious. There are even no fishermen here to intrude upon your worship. All the fishing that is done in the gulf goes on near Zapiga, over there. *Señor*, if you are forced to leave this island before anything can be arranged for you, do not try to make for Zapiga. It is a settlement of thieves and *matreros*, where they would cut your throat promptly for the sake of your gold watch and chain. And, *señor*, think twice before confiding in anyone whatever; even in the officers of the Company's steamers, if you ever get on board one. Honesty alone is not enough for security. You must look to discretion and prudence in a man. And always remember, *señor*, before you open your lips for a confidence, that this treasure may be left safely here for hundreds of years. Time is on its side, *señor*. And silver is an incorruptible metal that can be trusted to keep its value for ever. . . . An incorruptible metal,' he repeated, as if the idea had given him a profound pleasure.

'As some men are said to be,' Decoud pronounced, inscrutably, while the Capataz, who busied himself in baling out the lighter with a wooden bucket, went on throwing the water over the side with a regular splash. Decoud, incorrigible in his scepticism, reflected, not cynically, but with general satisfaction, that this man was made incorruptible by his enormous vanity, that finest form of egoism which can take on the aspect of every virtue.

Nostromo ceased baling, and, as if struck with a sudden thought, dropped the bucket with a clatter into the lighter.

'Have you any message?' he asked in a lowered voice. 'Remember, I shall be asked questions.'

'You must find the hopeful words that ought to be spoken to the people in town. I trust for that your intelligence and your experience, Capataz. You understand?'

'*Sí, señor* . . . For the ladies.'

'Yes, yes,' said Decoud, hastily. 'Your wonderful reputation will make them attach great value to your words; therefore be careful what you say. I am looking forward,' he continued, feeling the fatal touch of contempt for himself to which his complex nature was subject. 'I am looking forward to a glorious and successful ending to my mission. Do you hear, Capataz? Use the words glorious and successful when you speak to the *señorita*. Your own mission is accomplished gloriously and successfully. You have indubitably saved the silver of the mine. Not only this silver, but probably all the silver that shall ever come out of it.'

Nostromo detected the ironic tone. 'I dare say, Señor Don Martin,' he said, moodily. 'There are very few things that I am not equal to. Ask the foreign *signori*. I, a man of the people, who cannot always understand what you mean. But as to his lot which I must leave here, let me tell you that I would believe it in greater safety if you had not been with me at all.'

An exclamation escaped Decoud, and a short pause followed. 'Shall I go back with you to Sulaco?' he asked in an angry tone.

'Shall I strike you dead with my knife where you stand?' retorted Nostromo, contemptuously. 'It would be the same thing as taking you to Sulaco. Come, *señor*. Your reputation is in your politics, and mine is bound up with the fate of this silver. Do you wonder I wish there had been no other man to share my knowledge? I wanted no one with me, *señor*.'

'You could not have kept the lighter afloat without me,' Decoud almost shouted. 'You would have gone to the bottom with her.'

'Yes,' uttered Nostromo, slowly; 'alone.'

Here was a man, Decoud reflected, that seemed as though he would have preferred to die rather than deface the perfect form of his egoism. Such a man was safe. In silence he helped the Capataz to get the grapnel on board. Nostromo cleared the shelving shore with one push of the heavy oar, and Decoud found himself solitary on the beach like a man in a dream. A sudden desire to hear a human voice once more seized upon his heart. The lighter was hardly distinguishable from the black water upon which she floated.

'What do you think has become of Hirsch?' he shouted.

'Knocked overboard and drowned,' cried Nostromo's voice confidently out of the black wastes of sky and sea around the islet. 'Keep close in the ravine, *señor*. I shall try to come out to you in a night or two.'

A slight swishing rustle showed that Nostromo was setting the sail. It filled all at once with a sound as of a single loud drum-tap. Decoud went back to the ravine. Nostromo, at the tiller, looked back from time to time at the vanishing mass of the Great Isabel, which, little by little, merged into the uniform texture of the night. At last, when he turned his head again, he saw nothing but a smooth darkness, like a solid wall.

Then he, too, experienced that feeling of solitude which had weighed heavily on Decoud after the lighter had slipped off the shore. But while the man on the island was oppressed by a bizarre sense of unreality affecting the very ground upon which he walked, the mind of the Capataz of the Cargadores turned alertly to the problem of future conduct. Nostromo's faculties, working on parallel lines, enabled him to steer straight, to keep a look-out for Hermosa, near which he had to pass, and to try to imagine what would happen tomorrow in Sulaco. Tomorrow, or, as a matter of fact, today, since the dawn was not very far, Sotillo would find out in what way the treasure had gone. A gang of *cargadores* had been employed in loading it into a railway truck from the Custom House storerooms, and running the truck on to the wharf. There would be arrests made, and certainly before noon Sotillo would know in what manner the silver had left Sulaco, and who it was that took it out.

Nostromo's intention had been to sail right into the harbour; but at this thought by a sudden touch of the tiller he threw the lighter into the wind and checked her rapid way. His reappearance with the very boat would raise suspicions, would cause surmises, would absolutely put Sotillo on the track. He himself would be arrested; and once in the *calabozo* there was no saying what they would do to him to make him speak. He trusted himself, but he stood up to look round. Near by, Hermosa showed low its white surface as flat as a table, with the slight run of the sea raised by the breeze washing over its edges noisily. The lighter must be sunk at once.

He allowed her to drift with her sail aback. There was already a good deal of water in her. He allowed her to drift towards the harbour entrance, and, letting the tiller swing about, squatted down and busied himself in loosening the plug. With that out she would fill very quickly, and every lighter carried a little iron ballast – enough to make her go down when full of water. When he stood up again the noisy wash about the Hermosa sounded far away, almost inaudible; and already he could make out the shape of land about the harbour entrance. This was a desperate affair, and he was a good swimmer. A mile was nothing to him, and he knew of an easy place for landing just below the earthworks of the old abandoned fort. It occurred to him with a peculiar fascination that this fort was a good place in which to sleep the day through after so many sleepless nights.

With one blow of the tiller he unshipped for the purpose, he knocked the plug out, but did not take the trouble to lower the sail. He felt the water welling up heavily about his legs before he leaped on to the taffrail. There, upright and motionless, in his shirt and trousers only, he stood waiting. When he had felt her settle he sprang far away with a mighty splash.

At once he turned his head. The gloomy, clouded dawn from behind the mountains showed him on the smooth waters the upper corner of the sail, a dark wet triangle of canvas waving slightly to and fro. He saw it vanish, as if jerked under, and then struck out for the shore.

Part Three

The Lighthouse

Chapter I

Directly the cargo boat had slipped away from the wharf and got lost in the darkness of the harbour the Europeans of Sulaco separated, to prepare for the coming of the Monterist régime, which was approaching Sulaco from the mountains, as well as from the sea.

This bit of manual work in loading the silver was their last concerted action. It ended the three days of danger, during which, according to the newspaper press of Europe, their energy had preserved the town from the calamities of popular disorder. At the shore end of the jetty, Captain Mitchell said good night and turned back. His intention was to walk the planks of the wharf till the steamer from Esmeralda turned up. The engineers of the railway staff, collecting their Basque and Italian workmen, marched them away to the railway yards, leaving the Custom House, so well defended on the first day of the riot, standing open to the four winds of heaven. Their men had conducted themselves bravely and faithfully during the famous 'three days' of Sulaco. In a great part this faithfulness and that courage had been exercised in self-defence rather than in the cause of those material interests to which Charles Gould had pinned his faith. Amongst the cries of the mob not the least loud had been the cry of death to foreigners. It was, indeed, a lucky circumstance for Sulaco that the relations of those imported workmen with the people of the country had been uniformly bad from the first.

Dr Monygham, going to the door of Viola's kitchen, observed this retreat marking the end of the foreign interference, this withdrawal of the army of material progress from the field of Costaguana revolutions.

Algarroba torches carried on the outskirts of the moving body sent their penetrating aroma into his nostrils. Their light, sweeping along the front of the house, made the letters of the inscription, 'Albergo d'Italia Una', leap out black from end to end of the long wall. His eyes blinked in the clear blaze. Several young men, mostly fair and tall, shepherding this mob of dark bronzed heads, surmounted by the glint of slanting rifle barrels, nodded to him familiarly as they went by. The doctor was a well-known character. Some of them wondered what he was doing there. Then, on the flank of their workmen they tramped on, following the line of rails.

'Withdrawing your people from the harbour?' said the doctor, addressing himself to the chief engineer of the railway, who had accompanied Charles Gould so far on his way to the town, walking by the side of the horse, with his hand on the saddlebow. They had stopped just outside the open door to let the workmen cross the road.

'As quick as I can. We are not a political faction,' answered the engineer, meaningly. 'And we are not going to give our new rulers a handle against the railway. You approve me, Gould?'

'Absolutely,' said Charles Gould's impassive voice, high up and outside the dim parallelogram of light falling on the road through the open door.

With Sotillo expected from one side, and Pedro Montero from the other, the engineer-in-chief's only anxiety now was to avoid a collision with either. Sulaco, for him, was a railway station, a terminus, workshops, a great accumulation of stores. As against the mob the railway defended its property, but politically the railway was neutral. He was a brave man; and in that spirit of neutrality he had carried proposals of truce to the self-appointed chiefs of the popular party, the deputies Fuentes and Gamacho. Bullets were still flying about when he had crossed the Plaza on that mission, waving above his head a white napkin belonging to the table linen of the Amarilla Club.

He was rather proud of this exploit; and reflecting that the doctor, busy all day with the wounded in the *patio* of the Casa Gould, had not had time to hear the news, he began a succinct narrative. He had communicated to them the intelligence from the Construction Camp as to Pedro Montero. The brother of the victorious general, he had assured them, could be expected at Sulaco at any time now. This news (as he anticipated), when shouted out of the window by Señor Gamacho, induced a rush of the mob along the Campo Road towards Rincón. The two deputies also, after shaking hands with him effusively, mounted and galloped off to meet the great man. 'I have misled them a little as to the time,' the chief engineer confessed. 'However hard he rides, he can scarcely get here before the morning. But my object is attained. I've secured several hours' peace for the losing party. But I did not tell them anything about Sotillo, for fear they would take it into their heads to try to get hold of the harbour again, either to oppose him or welcome him – there's no saying which. There was Gould's silver, on which rests the remnant of our hopes. Decoud's retreat had to be thought of, too. I think the railway had done pretty well by its friends without compromising itself hopelessly. Now the parties must be left to themselves.'

'Costaguana for the Costaguaneros,' interjected the doctor, sardonically. 'It is a fine country, and they have raised a fine crop of hates, vengeance, murder, and rapine – those sons of the country.'

'Well, I am one of them,' Charles Gould's voice sounded, calmly, 'and I must be going to see to my own crop of trouble. My wife has driven straight on, doctor?'

'Yes. All was quiet on this side. Mrs Gould has taken the two girls with her.'

Charles Gould rode on, and the engineer-in-chief followed the doctor indoors.

'That man is calmness personified,' he said, appreciatively, dropping on a bench, and stretching his well-shaped legs in cycling stockings nearly across the doorway. 'He must be extremely sure of himself.'

'If that's all he is sure of, then he is sure of nothing,' said the doctor. He had perched himself again on the end of the table. He nursed his cheek in the palm of one hand, while the other sustained the elbow. 'It is the last thing a man ought to be sure of.' The candle, half-consumed and burning dimly with a long wick, lighted up from below his inclined fact, whose expression, affected by the drawn-in cicatrices in the cheeks, had something vaguely unnatural, an exaggerated remorseful bitterness. As he sat there he had the air of meditating upon sinister things. The engineer-in-chief gazed at him for a time before he protested.

'I really don't see that. For me there seems to be nothing else. However –'

He was a wise man, but he could not quite conceal his contempt for that sort of paradox; in fact, Dr Monygham was not liked by the Europeans of Sulaco. His outward aspect of an outcast, which he preserved even in Mrs Gould's drawing-room, provoked unfavourable criticism. There could be no doubt of his intelligence; and as he had lived for over twenty years in the country, the pessimism of his outlook could not be altogether ignored. But instinctively, in self-defence of their activities and hopes, his hearers put it to the account of some hidden imperfection in the man's character. It was known that many years before, when quite young, he had been made by Guzman Bento chief medical officer of the army. Not one of the Europeans then in the service of Costaguana had been so much liked and trusted by the fierce old Dictator.

Afterwards his story was not so clear. It lost itself amongst the innumerable tales of conspiracies and plots against the tyrant as a stream is lost in an arid belt of sandy country before it emerges, diminished and troubled, perhaps, on the other side. The doctor made no secret of it that he had lived for years in the wildest parts of the Republic, wandering with almost unknown Indian tribes in the great forests of the far interior where the great rivers have their sources. But it was mere aimless wandering; he had written nothing, collected nothing, brought nothing for science out of the twilight of the forests, which seemed to cling to his battered personality limping about Sulaco, where it had drifted in casually, only to get stranded on the shores of the sea.

It was also known that he had lived in a state of destitution till the arrival of the Goulds from Europe. Don Carlos and Doña Emilia had taken up the mad English doctor, when it became apparent that for all his savage independence he could be tamed by kindness. Perhaps it was only hunger that had tamed him. In years gone by he had certainly been acquainted with Charles Gould's father in Sta Marta; and now, no matter what were the dark passages of his history, as the medical officer of the San Tomé mine he became a recognized personality. He was recognized, but not unreservedly accepted. So much defiant eccentricity and such an outspoken scorn for mankind seemed to point to mere recklessness of judgement, the bravado of guilt. Besides, since he had become again of some account, vague whispers had been heard that years ago, when fallen into disgrace and thrown into prison by Guzman Bento at the time of the so-called Great Conspiracy, he had betrayed some of his best friends amongst the conspirators. Nobody pretended to believe that whisper; the whole story of the Great Conspiracy was hopelessly involved and obscure; it is admitted in Costaguana that there never had been a conspiracy except in the diseased imagination of the Tyrant; and, therefore, nothing and no one to betray; though the most distinguished Costaguaneros had been imprisoned and executed upon that accusation. The procedure had dragged on for years, decimating the better class like a pestilence. The mere expression of sorrow for the fate of executed kinsmen had been punished with death. Don José Avellanos was perhaps the only one living who knew the whole story of those unspeakable cruelties. He had suffered from them himself, and he, with a shrug of the shoulders and a nervous, jerky gesture of the arm, was wont to put away from him, as it were, every allusion to it. But whatever the reason, Dr Monygham, a personage in the administration of the Gould Concession, treated with reverent awe by the miners, and indulged in his peculiarities by Mrs Gould, remained somehow outside the pale.

It was not from any liking for the doctor that the engineer-in-chief had lingered in the inn upon the plain. He liked old Viola much better. He had come to look upon the Albergo d'Italia Una as a dependence of the railway. Many of his subordinates had their quarters there. Mrs Gould's interest in the family conferred upon it a sort of distinction. The engineer-in-chief, with an army of workers under his orders, appreciated the moral influence of the old Garibaldino upon his countrymen. His austere, old-world Republicanism had a severe, soldier-like standard of faithfulness and duty, as if the world were a battlefield where men had to fight for the sake of universal love and brotherhood, instead of a more or less large share of booty.

'Poor old chap!' he said, after he had heard the doctor's account of Teresa. 'He'll never be able to keep the place going by himself. I shall be sorry,'

'He's quite alone up there,' grunted Dr Monygham, with a toss of heavy head towards the narrow staircase. 'Every living soul has cleared out, and Mrs Gould took the girls away just now. It might not be over-safe for them out here before very long. Of course, as a doctor, I can do nothing more here; but she has asked me to stay with old Viola, and as I have no horse to get back to the mine, where I ought to be, I made no difficulty to stay. They can do without me in the town.'

'I have a good mind to remain with you, doctor, till we see whether anything happens tonight at the harbour,' declared the engineer-in-chief. 'He must not be molested by Sotillo's soldiery, who may push on as far as this at once. Sotillo used to be very cordial to me at the Goulds' and at the club. How that man'll ever dare to look any of his friends in the face I can't imagine.'

'He'll no doubt begin by shooting some of them to get over the first awkwardness,' said the doctor. 'Nothing in this country serves better your military man who has changed sides than a few summary executions.' He spoke with a gloomy positiveness that left no room for protest. The engineer-in-chief did not attempt any. He simply nodded several times regretfully, then said:

'I think we shall be able to mount you in the morning, doctor. Our peons have recovered some of our stampeded horses. By riding hard and taking a wide circuit by Los Hatos and along the edge of the forest, clear of Rincón altogether, you may hope to reach the San Tomé bridge without being interfered with. The mine is just now, to my mind, the safest place for anybody at all compromised. I only wish the railway was as difficult to touch.'

'Am I compromised?' Dr Monygham brought out slowly after a short silence.

'The whole Gould Concession is compromised. I could not have remained for ever outside the political life of the country – if those convulsions may be called life. The thing is – can it be touched? The moment was bound to come when neutrality would become impossible, and Charles Gould understood this well. I believe he is prepared for every extremity. A man of his sort has never contemplated remaining indefinitely at the mercy of ignorance and corruption. It was like being a prisoner in a cavern of *banditti* with the price of your ransom in your pocket, and buying your life from day to day. Your mere safety, not your liberty, mind, doctor. I know what I am talking about. The image at which you shrug your shoulders is perfectly correct, especially if you conceive such a prisoner endowed with the power of replenishing his pocket by means as remote from the faculties of his captors as if they were magic. You must have understood that as well as I do, doctor. He was in the position of the goose with the golden eggs. I broached this matter to him as far back as Sir John's visit here. The prisoner of stupid and greedy *banditti* is always at the mercy of the first imbecile ruffian, who may blow out his brains in a fit of temper or for some prospect of an immediate big haul. The tale of killing the goose with the golden eggs has not been evolved for nothing out of the wisdom of mankind. It is a story that will never grow old. That is why Charles Gould in his deep, dumb way has countenanced the Ribierist Mandate, the first public act that promised him safety on other than venal grounds. Ribierism has failed, as everything merely rational fails in this country. But Gould remains logical in wishing to save this big lot of silver. Decoud's plan of a counter-revolution may be practicable or not, it may have a chance, or it may not have a chance. With all my experience of this revolutionary continent, I can hardly yet look at their methods seriously. Decoud has been reading to us his draft of a proclamation, and talking very well for two hours about his plan of action. He had arguments which should have appeared solid enough if we, members of old, stable political and national organizations, were not startled by the mere idea of a new State evolved like this out of the head of a scoffing young man fleeing for his life, with a proclamation in his pocket, to a rough, jeering, half-bred swash-buckler, who in this part of the world is called a general. It sounds like a comic fairy tale – and behold, it may come off; because it is true to the very spirit of the country.'

'Is the silver gone off, then?' asked the doctor, moodily.

The chief engineer pulled out his watch. 'By Captain Mitchell's reckoning – and he ought to know – it has been gone long enough now to be some three or four miles outside the harbour; and, as Mitchell says, Nostromo is the sort of seaman to make the best of his opportunities.' Here the doctor grunted so heavily that the other changed his tone.

'You have a poor opinion of that move, doctor? But why? Charles Gould has got to play his game out, though he is not the man to formulate his conduct even to himself, perhaps, let alone to others. It may be that the game has been partly suggested to him by Holroyd; but it accords with his character, too; and that is why it has been so successful. Haven't they come to calling him "El Rey de Sulaco" in Sta Marta? A nickname may be the best record of a success. That's what I call putting the face of a joke upon the body of a truth. My dear sir, when I first arrived in Sta Marta I was struck by the way all those journalists, demagogues, members of Congress, and all those generals and judges cringed before a sleepy-eyed advocate without practice simply because he was the plenipotentiary of the Gould Concession. Sir John when he came out was impressed too.'

'A new State, with that plump dandy, Decoud, for the first President,' mused Dr Monygham, nursing his cheek and swinging his legs all the time.

'Upon my word, and why not?' the chief engineer retorted in an unexpectedly earnest and confidential voice. It was as if something subtle in the air of Costaguana had inoculated him with the local faith in *pronunciamientos*. All at once he began to talk, like an expert revolutionist, of the instrument ready to hand in the intact army at Cayta, which could be brought back in a few days to Sulaco if only Decoud managed to make his way at once down the coast. For the military chief there was Barrios, who had nothing but a bullet to expect from Montero, his former professional rival and bitter enemy. Barrios's concurrence was assured. As to his army, it had nothing to expect from Montero either; not even a month's pay. From that point of view the existence of the treasure was of enormous importance. The mere knowledge that it had been saved from the Monterists would be a strong inducement for the Cayta troops to embrace the cause of the New State.

The doctor turned round and contemplated his companion for some time.

'This Decoud, I see, is a persuasive young beggar,' he remarked at last. 'And pray is it for this, then, that Charles Gould has let the whole lot of ingots go out to sea in charge of that Nostromo?'

'Charles Gould,' said the engineer-in-chief, 'has said no more about his motive than usual. You know, he doesn't talk. But we all here know his motive, and he has only one – the safety of the San Tomé mine with the preservation of the Gould Concession in the spirit of his compact with Holroyd. Holroyd is another uncommon man. They understand each other's imaginative side. One is thirty, the other nearly sixty, and they have been made for each other. To be a millionaire, and such a millionaire as Holroyd, is like being eternally young. The audacity of youth reckons upon what it fancies an unlimited time at its disposal; but a millionaire has unlimited means in his hand – which is better. One's time on earth is an uncertain quantity, but about the long reach of millions there is no doubt. The introduction of a pure form of Christianity into this continent is a dream for a youthful enthusiast, and I have been trying to explain to you why Holroyd at fifty-eight is like a man on the threshold of life, and better, too. He's not a missionary, but the San Tomé mine holds just that for him. I assure you, in sober truth, that he could not manage to keep this out of a strictly business conference upon the finances of Costaguana he had with Sir John a couple of years ago. Sir John mentioned it with amazement in a letter he wrote to me here, from San Francisco, when on his way home. Upon my word, doctor, things seem to be worth nothing by what they are in themselves. I begin to believe that the only solid thing about them is the spiritual value which everyone discovers in his own form of activity –'

'Bah!' interrupted the doctor, without stopping for an instant the idle swinging movement of his legs. 'Self-flattery. Food for that vanity which makes the world go round. Meantime, what do you think is going to happen to the treasure floating about the gulf with the great Capataz and the great politician?'

'Why are you uneasy about it, doctor?'

'I uneasy! And what the devil is it to me? I put no spiritual value into my desires, or my opinions, or my actions. They have not enough vastness to give me room for self-flattery. Look, for instance, I should certainly have liked to ease the last moments of that poor woman. And I can't. It's impossible. Have you met the impossible face to face – or have you, the Napoleon of railways, no such word in your dictionary?'

'Is she bound to have a very bad time of it?' asked the chief engineer, with humane concern.

Slow, heavy footsteps moved across the planks above the heavy hard wood beams of the kitchen. Then down the narrow opening of the staircase made in the thickness of the wall, and narrow enough to be defended by one man against twenty enemies, came the murmur of two voices, one faint and broken, the other deep and gentle answering it, and in its graver tone covering the weaker sound.

The two men remained still and silent till the murmurs ceased, then the doctor shrugged his shoulders and muttered:

'Yes, she's bound to. And I could do nothing if I went up now.'

A long period of silence above and below ensued.

'I fancy,' began the engineer, in a subdued voice, 'that you mistrust Captain Mitchell's Capataz.'

'Mistrust him!' muttered the doctor through his teeth. 'I believe him capable of anything – even of the most absurd fidelity. I am the last person he spoke to before he left the wharf, you know. The poor woman up there wanted to see him, and I let him go up to her. The dying must not be contradicted, you know. She seemed then fairly calm and resigned, but the scoundrel in those ten minutes or so has done or said something which seems to have driven her into despair. You know,' went on the doctor, hesitatingly, 'women are so very unaccountable in every position, and at all times of life, that I thought sometimes she was in a way, don't you see? in love with him – the Capataz. The rascal has his own charm indubitably, or he would not have made the conquest of all the populace of the town. No, no, I am not absurd. I may have given a wrong name to some strong sentiment for him on her part, to an unreasonable and simple attitude a woman is apt to take up emotionally towards a man. She used to abuse him to me frequently, which, of course, is not inconsistent with my idea. Not at all. It looked to me as if she were always thinking of him. He was something important in her life. You know, I have seen a lot of those people. Whenever I came down from the mine Mrs Gould used to ask me to keep my eye on them. She likes Italians; she has lived a long time in Italy, I believe, and she took a special fancy to that old Garibaldino. A remarkable chap enough. A rugged and dreamy character, living in the republicanism of his young days as if in a cloud. He has encouraged much of the Capataz's confounded nonsense – the high-strung, exalted old beggar!'

'What sort of nonsense?' wondered the chief engineer. 'I found the Capataz always a very shrewd and sensible fellow, absolutely fearless, and remarkably useful. A perfect handyman. Sir John was greatly impressed by his resourcefulness and attention when he made that overland journey from Sta Marta. Later on, as you might have heard, he rendered us a service by disclosing to the then chief of police the presence in the town of some professional thieves, who came from a distance to wreck and rob our monthly pay train. He has certainly organized the lighterage service of the harbour for the O.S.N. Company with great ability. He knows how to make himself obeyed, foreigner though he is. It is true that the *cargadores* are strangers here, too, for the most part – immigrants, *isleños*.'

'His prestige is his fortune,' muttered the doctor, sourly.

'The man has proved his trustworthiness up to the hilt on innumerable occasions and in all sorts of ways,' argued the engineer. 'When this question of the silver arose, Captain Mitchell naturally was very warmly of the opinion that his Capataz was the only man fit for the trust. As a sailor, of course, I suppose so. But as a man, don't you know, Gould, Decoud, and myself judged that it didn't matter in the least who went. Any boatman would have done just as well. Pray, what could a thief do with such a lot of ingots? If he ran off with them he would have in the end to land somewhere, and how could he conceal his cargo from the knowledge of the people ashore? We dismissed that consideration from our minds. Moreover, Decoud was going. There have been occasions when the Capataz has been more implicitly trusted.'

'He took a slightly different view,' the doctor said. 'I heard him declare in this very room that it would be the most desperate affair of his life. He made a sort of verbal will here in my hearing, appointing old Viola his executor; and, by Jove! do you know, he – he's not grown rich by his fidelity to you good people of the railway and the harbour. I suppose he obtains some – how do you say that? – some spiritual value for his labours, or else I don't know why the devil he should be faithful to you, Gould, Mitchell, or anybody else. He knows this country well. He knows, for instance, that Gamacho, the Deputy from Javira, has been nothing else but a *tramposo* of the commonest sort, a petty pedlar of the Campo, till he managed to get enough goods on credit from Anzani to open a little store in the wilds, and got himself elected by the drunken *mozos* that hang about the *estancias* and the poorest sort of *rancheros* who were in his debt. And Gamacho, who tomorrow will be probably one of our high officials, is a stranger, too – an *isleño*. He might have been a *cargador* on the O.S.N. wharf had he not (the *posadero* of Rincón is ready to swear it) murdered a pedlar in the woods and stolen his pack to begin life on. And do you think that Gamacho, then, would have ever become a hero with the democracy of this place, like our Capataz? Of course not. He isn't half the man. No; decidedly, I think that Nostromo is a fool.'

The doctor's talk was distasteful to the builder of railways. 'It is impossible to argue that point,' he said, philosophically. 'Each man has his gifts. You should have heard Gamacho haranguing his friends in the street. He has a howling voice, and he shouted like mad, lifting his clenched fist right above his head, and throwing his body half out of the window. At every pause the rabble below yelled, "Down with the Oligarchs! *Viva la libertad!*" Fuentes inside looked extremely miserable. You know, he is the brother of Jorge Fuentes, who has been Minister of the Interior for six months or so, some few years back. Of course, he has no conscience; but he is a man of birth and education – at one time the director of the Customs of Cayta. That idiot-brute Gamacho fastened himself upon him with his following of the lowest rabble. His sickly fear of that ruffian was the most rejoicing sight imaginable.'

He got up and went to the door to look out towards the harbour. 'All quiet,' he said; 'I wonder if Sotillo really means to turn up here?'

CHAPTER II

CAPTAIN MITCHELL, pacing the wharf, was asking himself the same question. There was always the doubt whether the warning of the Esmeralda telegraphist – a fragmentary and interrupted message – had been properly understood. However, the good man had made up his mind not to go to bed till daylight, if even then. He imagined himself to have rendered an enormous service to Charles Gould. When he thought of the saved silver he rubbed his hands together with satisfaction. In his simple way he was proud at being a party to this extremely clever expedient. It was he who had given it a practical shape by suggesting the possibility of intercepting at sea the northbound steamer. And it was advantageous to his Company, too, which would have lost a valuable freight if the treasure had been left ashore to be confiscated. The pleasure of disappointing the Monterists was also very great. Authoritative by temperament and the long habit of command, Captain Mitchell was no democrat. He even went so far as to profess a contempt for parliamentarism itself. 'His Excellency Don Vincente Ribiera,' he used to say, 'whom I and that fellow of mine, Nostromo, had the honour, sir, and the pleasure of saving from a cruel death, deferred too much to his Congress. It was a mistake – a distinct mistake, sir.'

The guileless old seaman superintending the O.S.N. service imagined that the last three days had exhausted every startling surprise the political life of Costaguana could offer. He used to confess afterwards that the events which followed surpassed his imagination. To begin with, Sulaco (because of the seizure of the cables and the disorganization of the steam service) remained for a whole fortnight cut off from the rest of the world like a besieged city.

'One would not have believed it possible; but so it was, sir. A full fortnight.'

The account of the extraordinary things that happened during that time, and the powerful emotions he experienced, acquired a comic impressiveness from the pompous manner of his personal narrative. He opened it always by assuring his hearer that he was 'in the thick of things from first to last'. Then he would begin by describing the getting away of the silver, and his natural anxiety lest 'his fellow' in charge of the lighter should make some mistake. Apart from the loss of so much precious metal, the life of Señor Martin Decoud, an agreeable, wealthy, and well-informed young gentleman, would have been jeopardized through his falling into the hands of his political enemies. Captain Mitchell also admitted that in his solitary vigil on the wharf he had felt a certain measure of concern for the future of the whole country.

'A feeling, sir,' he exclaimed, 'perfectly comprehensible in a man properly grateful for the many kindnesses received from the best families of merchants and other native gentlemen of independent means, who, barely saved by us from the excesses of the mob, seemed, to my mind's eye, destined to become the prey in person and fortune of the native soldiery, which, as is well known, behave with regrettable barbarity to the inhabitants during their civil commotions. And then, sir, there were the Goulds, for both of whom, man and wife, I could not but entertain the warmest feelings deserved by their hospitality and kindness. I felt, too, the dangers of the gentlemen of the Amarilla Club, who had made me honorary member, and had treated me with uniform regard and civility, both in my capacity of Consular Agent and as Superintendent of an important Steam Service. Miss Antonia Avellanos, the most beautiful and accomplished young lady whom it had ever been my privilege to speak to, was not a little in my mind, I confess. How the interests of my Company would be affected by the impending change of officials claimed a large share of my attention, too. In short, sir, I was extremely anxious and very tired, as you may suppose, by the exciting and memorable events in which I had taken my little part. The Company's building containing my residence was within five minutes' walk, with the attraction of some supper and of my hammock (I always take my nightly rest in a hammock, as the most suitable to the climate); but somehow, sir, though evidently I could do nothing for anyone by remaining about, I could not tear myself away from that wharf, where the fatigue made me stumble painfully at times. The night was excessively dark – the darkest I remember in my life; so that I began to think that the arrival of the transport from Esmeralda could not possibly take place before daylight, owing to the difficulty of navigating the gulf. The mosquitoes bit like fury. We have been infested here with mosquitoes before the late improvements; a peculiar harbour brand, sir, renowned for its ferocity. They were like a cloud about my head, and I shouldn't wonder that but for their attacks I would have dozed off as I walked up and down, and got a heavy fall. I kept on smoking cigar after cigar, more to protect myself from being eaten up alive than from any real relish for the weed. Then, sir, when perhaps for the twentieth time I was approaching my watch to the lighted end in order to see the time, and observing with surprise that it wanted yet ten minutes to midnight, I heard the splash of a ship's propeller – an unmistakable sound to a sailor's ear on such a calm night. It was faint indeed, because they were advancing with precaution and dead slow, both on account of the darkness and from their desire of not revealing too soon their presence: a very unnecessary care, because, I verily believe, in all the enormous extent of this harbour I was the only living soul about. Even the usual staff of watchmen and others had been absent from their posts for several nights owing to the disturbances. I stood still, after dropping and stamping out my cigar – a circumstance highly agreeable, I should think, to the mosquitoes, if I may judge from the state of my face next morning. But that was a trifling inconvenience in comparison with the brutal proceedings I became victim of on the part of Sotillo. Something utterly inconceivable, sir; more like the proceedings of a maniac than the action of a sane man, however lost to all sense of honour and decency. But Sotillo was furious at the failure of his thievish scheme.'

In this Captain Mitchell was right. Sotillo was indeed infuriated. Captain Mitchell, however, had not been arrested at once; a vivid curiosity induced him to remain on the wharf (which is nearly four hundred feet long) to see, or rather hear, the whole process of disembarkation. Concealed by the railway truck used for the silver, which had been run back afterwards to the shore end of the jetty, Captain Mitchell saw the small detachment thrown forward, pass by, taking different directions upon the plain. Meantime, the troops were being landed and formed into a column, whose head crept up gradually so close to him that he made it out, barring nearly the whole width of the wharf, only a very few yards from him. Then the low, shuffling, murmuring, clinking sounds ceased, and the whole mass remained for about an hour motionless and silent, awaiting the return of the scouts. On land nothing was to be heard except the deep baying of the mastiffs at the railway yards, answered by the faint barking of the curs infesting the outer limits of the town. A detached knot of dark shapes stood in front of the head of the column.

Presently the picket at the end of the wharf began to challenge in undertones single figures approaching from the plain. Those messengers sent back from the scouting parties flung to their comrades brief sentences and passed on rapidly, becoming lost in the great motionless mass, to make their report to the Staff. It occurred to Captain Mitchell that his position could become disagreeable and perhaps dangerous, when suddenly, at the head of the jetty, there was a shout of command, a bugle call, followed by a stir and a rattling of arms, and a murmuring noise that ran right up the column. Near by a loud voice directed hurriedly, 'Push that railway car out of the way!' At the rush of bare feet to execute the order Captain Mitchell skipped back a pace or two; the car, suddenly impelled by many hands, flew away from him along the rails, and before he knew what had happened he found himself surrounded and seized by his arms and the collar of his coat.

'We have caught a man hiding here, *mi teniente*!' cried one of his captors.

'Hold him on one side till the rearguard comes along,' answered the voice. The whole column streamed past Captain Mitchell at a run, the thundering noise of their feet dying away suddenly on the shore. His captors held him tightly, disregarding his declaration that he was an Englishman and his loud demands to be taken at once before their commanding officer. Finally he lapsed into dignified silence. With a hollow rumble of wheels on the planks a couple of field guns, dragged by hand, rolled by. Then, after a small body of men had marched past escorting four or five figures which walked in advance, with a jingle of steel scabbards, he felt a tug at his arms, and was ordered to come along. During the passage from the wharf to the Custom House it is to be feared that Captain Mitchell was subjected to certain indignities at the hands of the soldiers – such as jerks, thumps on the neck, forcible application of the butt of a rifle to the small of his back. Their ideas of speed were not in accord with his notion of his dignity. He became flustered, flushed, and helpless. It was as if the world were coming to an end.

The long building was surrounded by troops, which were already piling arms by companies and preparing to pass the night lying on the ground in their ponchos with their sacks under their heads. Corporals moved with swinging lanterns posting sentries all round the walls wherever there was a door or an opening. Sotillo was taking his measures to protect his conquest as if it had indeed contained the treasure. His desire to make his fortune at one audacious stroke of genius had overmastered his reasoning faculties. He would not believe in the possibility of failure; the mere hint of such a thing made his brain reel with rage. Every circumstance pointing to it appeared incredible. The statement of Hirsch, which was so absolutely fatal to his hopes, could by no means be admitted. It is true, too, that Hirsch's story had been told so incoherently, with such excessive signs of distraction, that it really looked improbable. It was extremely difficult, as the saying is, to make head or tail of it. On the bridge of the steamer, directly after his rescue, Sotillo and his officers, in their impatience and excitement, would not give the wretched man time to collect such few wits as remained to him. He ought to have been quieted, soothed, and reassured, whereas he had been roughly handled, cuffed, shaken, and addressed in menacing tones. His struggles, his wriggles, his attempts to get down on his knees, followed by the most violent efforts to break away, as if he meant incontinently to jump overboard, his shrieks and shrinkings and cowering wild glances had filled them first with amazement, then with a doubt of his genuineness, as men are wont to suspect the sincerity of every great passion. His Spanish, too, became so mixed up with German that the better half of his statements remained incomprehensible. He tried to propitiate them by calling them *hochwohlgeborene Herren*, which in itself sounded suspicious. When admonished sternly not to trifle he repeated his entreaties and protestations of loyalty and innocence again in German, obstinately, because he was not aware in what language he was speaking. His identity, of course, was perfectly known as an inhabitant of Esmeralda, but this made the matter no clearer. As he kept on forgetting Decoud's name, mixing him up with several other people he had seen in the Casa Gould, it looked as if they all had been in the lighter together; and for a moment Sotillo thought that he had drowned every prominent Ribierist of Sulaco. The improbability of such a thing threw a doubt upon the whole statement. Hirsch was either mad or playing a part – pretending fear and distraction on the spur of the moment to cover the truth. Sotillo's rapacity, excited to the highest pitch by the prospect of an immense booty, could believe in nothing adverse. This Jew might have been very much frightened by the accident, but he knew where the silver was concealed, and had invented this story, with his Jewish cunning, to put him entirely off the track as to what had been done.

Sotillo had taken up his quarters on the upper floor in a vast apartment with heavy black beams. But there was no ceiling, and the eye lost itself in the darkness under the high pitch of the roof. The thick shutters stood open. On a long table could be seen a large inkstand, some stumpy, inky quill pens, and two square wooden boxes, each holding half a hundredweight of sand. Sheets of grey coarse official paper bestrewed the floor. It must have been a room occupied by some higher official of the Customs, because of a large leathern armchair stood behind the table, with other high-backed chairs scattered about. A net hammock was swung under one of the beams – for the official's afternoon siesta, no doubt. A couple of candles stuck into tall iron candlesticks gave a dim reddish light. The colonel's hat, sword, and revolver lay between them, and a couple of his more trusty officers lounged gloomily against the table. The colonel threw himself into the armchair, and a big Negro with a sergeant's stripes on his ragged sleeve, kneeling down, pulled off his boots. Sotillo's moustache contrasted violently with the livid colouring of his cheeks. His eyes were sombre and as if sunk very far into his head. He seemed exhausted by his perplexities, languid with disappointment; but when the sentry on the landing thrust his head in to announce the arrival of a prisoner, he revived at once.

'Let him be brought in,' he shouted, fiercely.

The door flew open, and Captain Mitchell, bareheaded, his waistcoat open, the bow of his tie under his ear, was hustled into the room.

Sotillo recognized him at once. He could not have hoped for a more precious capture; here was a man who could tell him, if he chose, everything he wished to know – and directly the problem of how to make him talk to the point presented itself to his mind. The resentment of a foreign nation had no terrors for Sotillo. The might of the whole armed Europe would not have protected Captain Mitchell from insults and ill-usage, so well as the quick reflection of Sotillo that this was an Englishman who would most likely turn obstinate under bad treatment, and become quite unmanageable. At all events, the colonel smoothed the scowl on his brow.

'What! The excellent Señor Mitchell!' he cried, in affected dismay. The pretended anger of his swift advance and of his shout, 'Release the *caballero* at once,' was so effective that the astounded soldiers positively sprang away from their prisoner. Thus suddenly deprived of forcible support, Captain Mitchell reeled as though about to fall. Sotillo took him familiarly under the arm, led him to a chair, waved his hand at the room. 'Go out, all of you,' he commanded.

When they had been left alone he stood looking down, irresolute and silent, watching till Captain Mitchell had recovered his power of speech.

Here in his very grasp was one of the men concerned in the removal of the silver. Sotillo's temperament was of that sort that he experienced an ardent desire to beat him; just as formerly when negotiating with difficulty a loan from the cautious Anzani, his fingers always itched to take the shopkeeper by the throat. As to Captain Mitchell, the suddenness, unexpectedness, and general inconceivableness of this experience had confused his thoughts. Moreover, he was physically out of breath.

'I've been knocked down three times between this and the wharf,' he gasped out at last. 'Somebody shall be made to pay for this.' He had certainly stumbled more than once, and had been dragged along for some distance before he could regain his stride. With his recovered breath his indignation seemed to madden him. He jumped up, crimson, all his white hair bristling, his eyes glaring vengefully, and shook violently the flaps of his ruined waistcoat before the disconcerted Sotillo. 'Look! Those uniformed thieves of yours downstairs have robbed me of my watch.'

The old sailor's aspect was very threatening. Sotillo saw himself cut off from the table on which his sabre and revolver were lying.

'I demand restitution and apologies,' Mitchell thundered at him, quite beside himself. 'From you! Yes, from you!'

For the space of a second or so the colonel stood with a perfectly stony expression of face; then, as Captain Mitchell flung out an arm towards the table as if to snatch up the revolver, Sotillo, with a yell of alarm, bounded to the door and was gone in a flash, slamming it after him. Surprise calmed Captain Mitchell's fury. Behind the closed door Sotillo shouted on the landing, and there was a great tumult of feet on the wooden staircase.

'Disarm him! Bind him!' the colonel could be heard vociferating.

Captain Mitchell had just the time to glance once at the windows, with three perpendicular bars of iron each and some twenty feet from the ground, as he well knew, before the door flew open and the rush upon him took place. In an incredibly short time he found himself bound with many turns of a hide rope to a high-backed chair, so that his head alone remained free. Not till then did Sotillo, who had been leaning in the doorway trembling visibly, venture again within. The soldiers, picking up from the floor the rifles they had dropped to grapple with the prisoner, filed out of the room. The officers remained leaning on their swords and looking on.

'The watch! the watch!' raved the colonel, pacing to and fro like a tiger in a cage. 'Give me that man's watch.'

It was true, that when searched for arms in the hall downstairs, before being taken into Sotillo's presence, Captain Mitchell had been relieved of his watch and chain; but at the colonel's clamour it was produced quickly enough, a corporal bringing it up, carried carefully in the palms of his joined hands. Sotillo snatched it, and pushed the clenched fist from which it dangled close to Captain Mitchell's face.

'Now then! You arrogant Englishman! You dare to call the soldiers of the army thieves! Behold your watch.'

He flourished his fist as if aiming blows at the prisoner's nose. Captain Mitchell, helpless as a swathed infant, looked anxiously at the sixty-guinea gold half-chronometer, presented to him years ago by a Committee of Underwriters for saving a ship from total loss by fire. Sotillo, too, seemed to perceive its valuable appearance. He became silent suddenly, stepped aside to the table, and began a careful examination in the light of the candles. He had never seen anything so fine. His officers closed in and craned their necks behind his back.

He became so interested that for an instant he forgot his precious prisoner. There is always something childish in the rapacity of the passionate, clear-minded, Southern races, wanting in the misty idealism of the Northerners, who at the smallest encouragement dream of nothing less than the conquest of the earth. Sotillo was fond of jewels, gold trinkets, of personal adornment. After a moment he turned about, and with a commanding gesture made all his officers fall back. He laid down the watch on the table, then, negligently, pushed his hat over it.

'Ha!' he began, going up very close to the chair. 'You dare call my valiant soldiers of the Esmeralda regiment, thieves. You dare! What impudence! You foreigners come here to rob our country of its wealth. You never have enough! Your audacity knows no bounds.'

He looked towards the officers, among whom there was an approving murmur. The older major was moved to declare:

'*Sí, mi coronel*. They are all traitors.'

'I shall say nothing,' continued Sotillo, fixing the motionless and powerless Mitchell with an angry but uneasy stare. 'I shall say nothing of your treacherous attempt to get possession of my revolver to shoot me while I was trying to treat you with consideration you did not deserve. You have forfeited your life. Your only hope is in my clemency.'

He watched for the effect of his words, but there was no obvious sign of fear on Captain Mitchell's face. His white hair was full of dust, which covered also the rest of his helpless person. As if he had heard nothing, he twitched an eyebrow to get rid of a bit of straw which hung amongst the hairs.

Sotillo advanced one leg and put his arms akimbo. 'It is you, Mitchell,' he said, emphatically, 'who are the thief, not my soldiers!' He pointed at his prisoner a forefinger with a long, almond-shaped nail. 'Where is the silver of the San Tomé mine? I ask you, Mitchell, where is the silver that was deposited in this Custom House? Answer me that! You stole it. You were a party to stealing it. It was stolen from the Government. Aha! you think I do not know what I say; but I am up to your foreign tricks. It is gone, the silver! No? Gone in one of your *lanchas*, you miserable man! How dared you?'

This time he produced his effect. 'How on earth could Sotillo know that?' thought Mitchell. His head, the only part of his body that could move, betrayed his surprise by a sudden jerk.

'Ha! you tremble,' Sotillo shouted, suddenly. 'It is a conspiracy. It is a crime against the State. Did you not know that the silver belongs to the Republic till the Government claims are satisfied? Where is it? Where have you hidden it, you miserable thief?'

At this question Captain Mitchell's sinking spirits revived. In whatever incomprehensible manner Sotillo had already got his information about the lighter, he had not captured it. That was clear. In his outraged heart, Captain Mitchell had resolved that nothing would induce him to say a word while he remained so disgracefully bound, but his desire to help the escape of the silver made him depart from this resolution. His wits were very much at work. He detected in Sotillo a certain air of doubt, of irresolution.

'That man,' he said to himself, 'is not certain of what he advances.' For all his pomposity in social intercourse, Captain Mitchell could meet the realities of life in a resolute and ready spirit. Now he had got over the first shock of the abominable treatment he was cool and collected enough. The immense contempt he felt for Sotillo steadied him, and he said oracularly, 'No doubt it is well concealed by this time.'

Sotillo, too, had had time to cool down. '*Muy bien*, Mitchell,' he said in a cold and threatening manner. 'But can you produce the Government receipt for the royalty and the Custom House permit of embarkation, hey? Can you? No. Then the silver has been removed illegally, and the guilty shall be made to suffer, unless it is produced within five days from this.' He gave orders for the prisoner to be unbound and locked up in one of the smaller rooms downstairs. He walked about the room, moody and silent, till Captain Mitchell, with each of his arms held by a couple of men, stood up, shook himself, and stamped his feet.

'How did you like to be tied up, Mitchell?' he asked, derisively.

'It is the most incredible, abominable use of power!' Captain Mitchell declared in a loud voice. 'And whatever your purpose, you shall gain nothing from it, I can promise you.'

The tall colonel, livid, with his coal-black ringlets and moustache, crouched, as it were, to look into the eyes of the short, thick-set, red-faced prisoner with rumpled white hair.

'That we shall see. You shall know my power a little better when I tie you up to a *potalón* outside in the sun for a whole day.' He drew himself up haughtily, and made a sign for Captain Mitchell to be led away.

'What about my watch?' cried Captain Mitchell, hanging back from the efforts of the men pulling him towards the door.

Sotillo turned to his officers. 'No! But only listen to this *pícaro, caballeros*,' he pronounced with affected scorn, and was answered by a chorus of derisive laughter. 'He demands his watch! . . . He ran up again to Captain Mitchell, for the desire to relieve his feelings by inflicting blows and pain upon this Englishman was very strong within him. 'Your watch! You are a prisoner in war time, Mitchell! In war time! You have no rights and no property! *Caramba*! The very breath in your body belongs to me. Remember that.'

'Bosh!' said Captain Mitchell, concealing a disagreeable impression.

Down below, in a great hall, with the earthen floor and with a tall mound thrown up by white ants in a corner, the soldiers had kindled a small fire with broken chairs and tables near the arched gateway, through which the faint murmur of the harbour waters on the beach could be heard. While Captain Mitchell was being led down the staircase, an officer passed him, running up to report to Sotillo the capture of more prisoners. A lot of smoke hung about in the vast gloomy place, the fire crackled, and, as if through a haze, Captain Mitchell made out, surrounded by short soldiers with fixed bayonets, the heads of three tall prisoners – the doctor, the engineer-in-chief, and the white leonine mane of old Viola, who stood half-turned away from the others with his chin on his breast and his arms crossed. Mitchell's astonishment knew no bounds. He cried out; the other two exclaimed also. But he hurried, on, diagonally, across the big cavern-like hall. Lots of thoughts, surmises, hints of caution, and so on, crowded his head to distraction.

'Is he actually keeping you?' shouted the chief engineer, whose single eyeglass glittered in the firelight.

An officer from the top of the stairs was shouting urgently. 'Bring them all up – all three.'

In the clamour of voices and the rattle of arms, Captain Mitchell made himself heard imperfectly: 'By heavens! the fellow has stolen my watch.'

The engineer-in-chief on the staircase resisted the pressure long enough to shout, 'What? What did you say?'

'My chronometer!' Captain Mitchell yelled violently at the very moment of being thrust head foremost through a small door into a sort of cell, perfectly black, and so narrow that he fetched up against the opposite wall. The door had been instantly slammed. He knew where they had put him. This was the strongroom of the Custom House, whence the silver had been removed only a few hours earlier. It was almost as narrow as a corridor, with a small square aperture, barred by a heavy grating, at the distant end. Captain Mitchell staggered for a few steps, then sat down on the earthen floor with his back to the wall. Nothing, not even a gleam of light from anywhere, interfered with Captain Mitchell's meditation. He did some hard but not very extensive thinking. It was not of a gloomy case. The old sailor, with all his small weaknesses and absurdities, was constitutionally incapable of entertaining for any length of time a fear of his personal safety. It was not so much firmness of soul as the lack of a certain kind of imagination – the kind whose undue development caused intense suffering to Señor Hirsch; that sort of imagination which adds the blind terror of bodily suffering and of death, envisaged as an accident to the body alone, strictly – to all the other apprehensions on which the sense of one's existence is based. Unfortunately, Captain Mitchell had not much penetration of any kind; characteristic, illuminating trifles of expression, action, or movement, escaped him completely. He was too pompously and innocently aware of his own existence to observe that of others. For instance, he could not believe that Sotillo had been really afraid of him, and this simply because it would never have entered into his head to shoot anyone except in the most pressing case of self-defence. Anybody could see he was not a murdering kind of man, he reflected quite gravely. Then why this preposterous and insulting charge? he asked himself. But his thoughts mainly clung around the astounding and unanswerable question: How the devil had the fellow got to know that the silver had gone off in the lighter? It was obvious that he had not captured it. And, obviously, he could not have captured it! In this last conclusion Captain Mitchell was misled by the assumption drawn from his observation of the weather during his long vigil on the wharf. He thought that there had been much more wind than usual that night in the gulf; whereas, as a matter of fact, the reverse was the case.

'How in the name of all that's marvellous did that confounded fellow get wind of the affair?' was the first question he asked directly after the bang, clatter, and flash of the open door (which was closed again almost before he could lift his dropped head) informed him that he had a companion of captivity. Dr Monygham's voice stopped muttering curses in English and Spanish.

'Is that you, Mitchell?' he made answer, surlily. 'I struck my forehead against this confounded wall with enough force to fell an ox. Where are you?'

Captain Mitchell, accustomed to the darkness, could make out the doctor stretching out his hands blindly.

'I am sitting here on the floor. Don't fall over my legs,' Captain Mitchell's voice announced with great dignity of tone. The doctor, entreated not to walk about in the dark, sank down to the ground, too. The two prisoners of Sotillo, with their heads nearly touching, began to exchange confidences.

'Yes,' the doctor related in a low tone to Captain Mitchell's vehement curiosity, 'we have been nabbed in old Viola's place. It seems that one of their pickets, commanded by an officer, pushed as far as the town gate. They had orders not to enter, but to bring along every soul they could find on the plain. We had been talking in there with the door open, and no doubt they saw the glimmer of our light. They must have been making their approaches for some time. The engineer laid himself on a bench in a recess by the fireplace, and I went upstairs to have a look. I hadn't heard any sound from there for a long time. Old Viola, as soon as he saw me come up, lifted his arm for silence. I stole in on tiptoe. By Jove, his wife was lying down and had gone to sleep. The woman had actually dropped off to sleep! "Señor Doctor," Viola whispers to me, "it looks as if her oppression was going to get better." "Yes," I said, very much surprised; "your wife is a wonderful woman, Giorgio." Just then a shot was fired in the kitchen, which made us jump and cower as if at a thunder-clap. It seems that the party of soldiers had stolen quite close up, and one of them had crept up to the door. He looked in, thought there was no one there, and, holding his rifle ready, entered quietly. The chief told me that he had just closed his eyes for a moment. When he opened them, he saw the man already in the middle of the room peering into the dark corners. The chief was so startled that, without thinking, he made one leap from the recess right out in front of the fireplace. The soldier, no less startled, ups with his rifle and pulls the trigger, deafening and singeing the engineer, but in his flurry missing him completely. But, look what happens! At the noise of the report the sleeping woman sat up, as if moved by a spring, with a shriek, "The children, Gian' Battista! Save the children!" I have it in my ears now. It was the truest cry of distress I ever heard. I stood as if paralysed, but the old husband ran across to the bedside, stretching out his hands. She clung to them! I could see her eyes go glazed; the old fellow lowered her down on the pillows and then looked round at me. She was dead! All this took less than five minutes, and then I ran down to see what was the matter. It was no use thinking of any resistance. Nothing we two could say availed with the officer, so I volunteered to go up with a couple of soldiers and fetch down old Viola. He was sitting at the foot of the bed, looking at his wife's face, and did not seem to hear what I said; but after I had pulled the sheet over her head, he got up and followed us downstairs quietly, in a sort of thoughtful way. They marched us off along the road, leaving the door open and the candle burning. The chief engineer strode on without a word, but I looked back once or twice at the feeble gleam. After we had gone some considerable distance, the Garibaldino, who was walking by my side, suddenly said, "I have buried many men on battlefields on this continent. The priests talk of consecrated ground! Bah! All the earth made by God is holy; but the sea, which knows nothing of kings and priests and tyrants, is the holiest of all. Doctor! I should like to bury her in the sea. No mummeries, candles, incense, no holy water mumbled over by priests. The spirit of liberty is upon the waters." . . . Amazing old man. He was saying all this in an undertone as if talking to himself.'

'Yes, yes,' interrupted Captain Mitchell, impatiently. 'Poor old chap! But have you any idea how that ruffian Sotillo obtained his information? He did not get hold of any of our *cargadores* who helped with the truck, did he? But no, it is impossible! These were picked men we've had in our boats for these five years, and I paid them myself specially for the job, with instructions to keep out of the way for twenty-four hours at least. I saw them with my own eyes march on with the Italians to the railway yards. The chief promised to give them rations as long as they wanted to remain there.'

'Well,' said the doctor, slowly, 'I can tell you that you may say good-bye for ever to your best lighter, and to the Capataz of Cargadores.'

At this, Captain Mitchell scrambled up to his feet in the excess of his excitement. The doctor, without giving him time to exclaim, stated briefly the part played by Hirsch during the night.

Captain Mitchell was overcome. 'Drowned!' he muttered, in a bewildered and appalled whisper. 'Drowned!' Afterwards he kept still, apparently listening, but too absorbed in the news of the catastrophe to follow the doctor's narrative with attention.

The doctor had taken up an attitude of perfect ignorance, till at last Sotillo was induced to have Hirsch brought in to repeat the whole story, which was got out of him again with the greatest difficulty, because every moment he would break out into lamentations. At last, Hirsch was led away, looking more dead than alive, and shut up in one of the upstairs rooms to be close at hand. Then the doctor, keeping up his character of a man not admitted to the inner councils of the San Tomé Administration, remarked that the story sounded incredible. Of course, he said, he couldn't tell what had been the action of the Europeans, as he had been exclusively occupied with his own work in looking after the wounded, and also in attending Don José Avellanos. He had succeeded in assuming so well a tone of impartial indifference that Sotillo seemed to be completely deceived. Till then a show of regular inquiry had been kept up; one of the officers sitting at the table wrote down the questions and the answers, the others, lounging about the room, listened attentively, puffing at their long cigars and keeping their eyes on the doctor. But at that point Sotillo ordered everybody out.

Chapter III

Directly they were alone, the colonel's severe official manner changed. He rose and approached the doctor. His eyes shone with rapacity and hope; he became confidential. 'The silver might have been indeed put on board the lighter, but it was not conceivable that it should have been taken out to sea.' The doctor, watching every word, nodded slightly, smoking with apparent relish the cigar which Sotillo had offered him as a sign of his friendly intentions. The doctor's manner of cold detachment from the rest of the Europeans led Sotillo on, till, from conjecture to conjecture, he arrived at hinting that in his opinion this was a put-up job on the part of Charles Gould, in order to get hold of that immense treasure all to himself. The doctor, observant and self-possessed, muttered, 'He is very capable of that.'

Here Captain Mitchell exclaimed with amazement, amusement, and indignation, 'You said that of Charles Gould!' Disgust, and even some suspicion, crept into his tone, for to him, too, as to other Europeans, there appeared to be something dubious about the doctor's personality.

'What on earth made you say that to this watch-stealing scoundrel?' he asked. 'What's the object of an infernal lie of that sort? That confounded pickpocket was quite capable of believing you.'

He snorted. For a time the doctor remained silent in the dark.

'Yes, that is exactly what I did say,' he uttered at last, in a tone which would have made it clear enough to a third party that the pause was not of a reluctant but of a reflective character. Captain Mitchell thought that he had never heard anything so brazenly impudent in his life.

'Well, well!' he muttered to himself, but he had not the heart to voice his thoughts. They were swept away by others full of astonishment and regret. A heavy sense of discomfiture crushed him: the loss of the silver, the death of Nostromo, which was really quite a blow to his sensibilities, because he had become attached to his Capataz as people get attached to their inferiors from love of ease and almost unconscious gratitude. And when he thought of Decoud being drowned, too, his sensibility was almost overcome by this miserable end. What a heavy blow for that poor young woman! Captain Mitchell did not belong to the species of crabbed old bachelors; on the contrary, he liked to see young men paying attentions to young women. It seemed to him a natural and proper thing. Proper especially. As to sailors, it was different; it was not their place to marry, he maintained, but it was on moral grounds as a matter of self-denial, for, he explained, life on board ship is not fit for a woman even at best, and if you leave her on shore, first of all it is not fair, and next she either suffers from it or doesn't care a bit, which, in both cases, is bad. He couldn't have told what upset him most – Charles Gould's immense material loss, the death of Nostromo, which was a heavy loss to himself, or the idea of that beautiful and accomplished young woman being plunged into mourning.

'Yes,' the doctor, who had been apparently reflecting some more, began again, 'he believed me right enough. I thought he would have hugged me "*Sí, sí*," he said, "he will write to that partner of his, the rich *americano* in San Francisco, that it is all lost. Why not? There is enough to share with many people." '

'But this is perfectly imbecile!' cried Captain Mitchell.

The doctor remarked that Sotillo *was* imbecile, and that his imbecility was ingenious enough to lead him completely astray. He had helped him only but a little way.

'I mentioned,' the doctor said, 'in a sort of casual way, that treasure is generally buried in the earth rather than being set afloat upon the sea. At this my Sotillo slapped his forehead. "*Por Dios*, yes," he said; "they must have buried it on the shores of this harbour somewhere before they sailed out." '

'Heavens and earth!' muttered Captain Mitchell, 'I should not have believed that anybody could be ass enough –' He paused, then went on mournfully: 'But what's the good of all this? It would have been a clever enough lie if the lighter had been still afloat. It would have kept that inconceivable idiot perhaps from sending out the steamer to cruise in the gulf. That was the danger that worried me no end.' Captain Mitchell sighed profoundly.

'I had an object,' the doctor pronounced, slowly.

'Had you?' muttered Captain Mitchell. 'Well, that's lucky, or else I would have thought that you went on fooling him for the fun of the thing. And perhaps that was your object. Well, I must say I personally wouldn't condescend to that sort of thing. It is not to my taste. No, no. Blackening a friend's character is not my idea of fun, if it were to fool the greatest blackguard on earth.'

Had it not been for Captain Mitchell's depression, caused by the fatal news, his disgust of Dr Monygham would have taken a more outspoken shape; but he thought to himself that now it really did not matter what that man, whom he had never liked, would say and do.

'I wonder,' he grumbled, 'why they have shut us up together, or why Sotillo should have shut you up at all, since it seems to me you have been fairly chummy up there?'

'Yes, I wonder?' said the doctor, grimly.

Captain Mitchell's heart was so heavy that he would have preferred for the time being a complete solitude to the best of company. But any company would have been preferable to the doctor's, at whom he had always looked askance as a sort of beachcomber of superior intelligence partly reclaimed from his abased state. That feeling led him to ask:

'What has that ruffian done with the other two?'

'The chief engineer he wouldn't have let go in any case,' said the doctor. 'He would not like to have a quarrel with the railway upon his hands. Not just yet, at any rate. I don't think, Captain Mitchell, that you understand exactly what Sotillo's position is –'

'I don't see why I should bother my head about it,' snarled Captain Mitchell.

'No,' assented the doctor, with the same grim composure. 'I don't see why you should. It wouldn't help a single human being in the world if you thought ever so hard upon any subject whatever.'

'No,' said Captain Mitchell, simply, and with evident depression. 'A man locked up in a confounded dark hole is not much use to anybody.'

'As to old Viola,' the doctor continued, as though he had not heard, 'Sotillo released him for the same reason he is presently going to release you.'

'Eh? What?' exclaimed Captain Mitchell, staring like an owl in the darkness. 'What is there in common between me and old Viola? More likely because the old chap has no watch and chain for the pickpocket to steal. And I tell you what, Dr Monygham,' he went on with rising choler, 'he will find it more difficult than he thinks to get rid of me. He will burn his fingers over that job yet, I can tell you. To begin with, I won't go without my watch, and as to the rest – we shall see. I dare say it is no great matter for you to be locked up. But Joe Mitchell is a different kind of man, sir. I don't mean to submit tamely to insult and robbery. I am a public character, sir.'

And then Captain Mitchell became aware that the bars of the opening had become visible, a black grating upon a square of grey. The coming of the day silenced Captain Mitchell as if by the reflection that now in all the future days he would be deprived of the invaluable services of his Capataz. He leaned against the wall with his arms folded on his breast, and the doctor walked up and down the whole length of the place with his peculiar hobbling gait, as if slinking about on damaged feet. At the end farthest from the grating he would be lost altogether in the darkness. Only the slight limping shuffle could be heard. There was an air of moody detachment in that painful prowl kept up without a pause. When the door of the prison was suddenly flung open and his name shouted out he showed no surprise. He swerved sharply in his walk, and passed out at once, as though much depended upon his speed; but Captain Mitchell remained for some time with his shoulders against the wall, quite undecided in the bitterness of his spirit whether it wouldn't be better to refuse to stir a limb in the way of protest. He had half a mind to get himself carried out, but after the officer at the door had shouted three or four times in tones of remonstrance and surprise he condescended to walk out.

Sotillo's manner had changed. The colonel's offhand civility was slightly irresolute, as though he were in doubt if civility were the proper course in this case. He observed Captain Mitchell attentively before he spoke from the big armchair behind the table in a condescending voice:

'I have concluded not to detain you, Señor Mitchell. I am of a forgiving disposition. I make allowances. Let this be a lesson to you, however.'

The peculiar dawn of Sulaco, which seems to break far away to the westward and creep back into the shade of the mountains, mingled with the reddish light of the candles. Captain Mitchell, in sign of contempt and indifference, let his eyes roam all over the room, and he gave a hard stare to the doctor, perched already on the casement of one of the windows, with his eyelids lowered, careless and thoughtful – or perhaps ashamed.

Sotillo, ensconced in the vast armchair, remarked, 'I should have thought that the feelings of a *caballero* would have dictated to you an appropriate reply.'

He waited for it, but Captain Mitchell remaining mute, more from extreme resentment than from reasoned intention. Sotillo hesitated, glanced towards the doctor, who looked up and nodded, then went on with a slight effort:

'Here, Señor Mitchell, is your watch. Learn how hasty and unjust has been your judgement of my patriotic soldiers.'

Lying back in his seat, he extended his arm over the table and pushed the watch away slightly. Captain Mitchell walked up with undisguised eagerness, put it to his ear, then slipped it into his pocket coolly.

Sotillo seemed to overcome an immense reluctance. Again he looked aside at the doctor, who stared at him unwinkingly.

But as Captain Mitchell was turning away, without as much as a nod or a glance, he hastened to say:

'You may go and wait downstairs for the Señor Doctor, whom I am going to liberate, too. You foreigners are insignificant, to my mind.'

He forced a slight, discordant laugh out of himself, while Captain Mitchell, for the first time, looked at him with some interest.

'The law shall take note later on of your transgressions,' Sotillo hurried on. 'But as for me, you can live free, unguarded, unobserved. Do you hear, Señor Mitchell? You may depart to your affairs. You are beneath my notice. My attention is claimed by matters of the very highest importance.'

Captain Mitchell was very nearly provoked to an answer. It displeased him to be liberated insultingly; but want of sleep, prolonged anxieties, a profound disappointment with the fatal ending of the silver-saving business weighed upon his spirits. It was as much as he could do to conceal his uneasiness, not about himself perhaps, but about things in general. It occurred to him distinctly that something underhand was going on. As he went out he ignored the doctor pointedly.

'A brute!' said Sotillo, as the door shut.

Dr Monygham slipped off the window-sill, and, thrusting his hands into the pockets of the long, grey dust coat he was wearing, made a few steps into the room.

Sotillo got up, too, and, putting himself in the way, examined him from head to foot.

'So your countrymen do not confide in you very much, Señor Doctor. They do not love you, eh? Why is that, I wonder?'

The doctor, lifting his head, answered by a long, lifeless stare and the words, 'Perhaps because I have lived too long in Costaguana.'

Sotillo had a gleam of white teeth under the black moustache.

'Aha! But you love yourself,' he said, encouragingly.

'If you leave them alone,' the doctor said, looking with the same lifeless stare at Sotillo's handsome face, 'they will betray themselves very soon. Meantime, may I try to make Don Carlos speak?'

'Ah, Señor Doctor,' said Sotillo, wagging his head, 'you are a man of quick intelligence. We were made to understand each other.' He turned away. He could bear no longer that expressionless and motionless stare, which seemed to have a sort of impenetrable emptiness like the black depth of an abyss.

Even in a man utterly devoid of moral sense there remains an appreciation of rascality which, being conventional, is perfectly clear. Sotillo thought that Dr Monygham, so different from all Europeans, was ready to sell his countrymen and Charles Gould, his employer, for some share of the San Tomé silver. Sotillo did not despise him for that. The colonel's want of moral sense was of a profound and innocent character. It bordered upon stupidity, moral stupidity. Nothing that served his ends could appear to him really reprehensible. Nevertheless, he despised Dr Monygham. He had for him an immense and satisfactory contempt. He despised him with all his heart because he did not mean to let the doctor have any reward at all. He despised him, not as a man without faith and honour, but as a fool. Dr Monygham's insight into his character had deceived Sotillo completely. Therefore he thought the doctor a fool.

Since his arrival in Sulaco the colonel's ideas had undergone some modification.

He no longer wished for a political career in Montero's administration. He had always doubted the safety of that course. Since he had learned from the chief engineer that at daylight most likely he would be confronted by Pedro Montero his misgivings on that point had considerably increased. The *guerrillero* brother of the general – the Pedrito of popular speech – had a reputation of his own. He wasn't safe to deal with. Sotillo had vaguely planned seizing not only the treasure but the town itself, and then negotiating at leisure. But in the face of facts learned from the chief engineer (who had frankly disclosed to him the whole situation) his audacity, never of a very dashing kind, had been replaced by a most cautious hesitation.

'An army – an army has crossed the mountains under Pedrito already,' he had repeated, unable to hide his consternation. 'If it had not been that I am given the news by a man of your position I would never have believed it. Astonishing!'

'An armed force,' corrected the engineer, suavely.

His aim was attained. It was to keep Sulaco clear of any armed occupation for a few hours longer, to let those whom fear impelled leave the town. In the general dismay there were families hopeful enough to fly upon the road towards Los Hatos, which was left open by the withdrawal of the armed rabble under Señores Fuentes and Gamacho, to Rincón, with their enthusiastic welcome for Pedro Montero. It was a hasty and risky exodus, and it was said that Hernandez, occupying with his band the woods about Los Hatos, was receiving the fugitives.

That a good many people he knew were contemplating such a flight had been well known to the chief engineer.

Father Corbelán's efforts in the cause of that most pious robber had not been altogether fruitless. The political chief of Sulaco had yielded at the last moment to the urgent entreaties of the priest, had signed a provisional nomination appointing Hernandez a general, and calling upon him officially in this new capacity to preserve order in the town. The fact is that the political chief, seeing the situation desperate, did not care what he signed. It was the last official document he signed before he left the palace of the Intendencia for the refuge of the O.S.N. Company's office. But even had he meant his act to be effective it was already too late. The riot which he feared and expected broke out in less than an hour after Father Corbelán had left him. Indeed, Father Corbelán, who had appointed a meeting with Nostromo in the Dominican Convent, where he had his residence in one of the cells, never managed to reach the place. From the Intendencia he had gone straight on to the Avellanos's house to tell his brother-in-law, and though he stayed there no more than half an hour he had found himself cut off from his ascetic abode. Nostromo, after waiting there for some time, watching uneasily the increasing uproar in the street, had made his way to the offices of the *Porvenir*, and stayed there till daylight, as Decoud had mentioned in the letter to his sister. Thus the Capataz, instead of riding towards the Los Hatos woods as bearer of Hernandez's nomination, had remained in town to save the life of the President-Dictator, to assist in repressing the outbreak of the mob, and at last to sail out with the silver of the mine.

But Father Corbelán, escaping to Hernandez, had the document in his pocket, a piece of official writing turning a bandit into a general in a memorable last official act of the Ribierist party, whose watchwords were honesty, peace, and progress. Probably neither the priest nor the bandit saw the irony of it. Father Corbelán must have found messengers to send into the town, for early on the second day of the disturbances there were rumours of Hernandez being on the road to Los Hatos ready to receive those who would put themselves under his protection. A strange-looking horseman, elderly and audacious, had appeared in the town, riding slowly while his eyes examined the front of the houses, as though he had never seen such high buildings before. Before the cathedral he had dismounted, and, kneeling in the middle of the Plaza, his bridle over his arm and his hat lying in front of him on the ground, had bowed his head, crossing himself and beating his breast for some little time. Remounting his horse, with a fearless but not unfriendly look round the little gathering formed about his public devotions, he had asked for the Casa Avellanos. A score of hands were extended in answer, with fingers pointing up the Calle de la Constitución.

The horseman had gone on with only a glance of casual curiosity upwards to the windows of the Amarilla Club at the corner. His stentorian voice shouted periodically in the empty street, 'Which is the Casa Avellanos?' till an answer came from the scared porter, and he disappeared under the gate. The letter he was bringing, written by Father Corbelán with a pencil by the camp-fire of Hernandez, was addressed to Don José, of whose critical state the priest was not aware. Antonia read it, and, after consulting Charles Gould, sent it on for the information of the gentlemen garrisoning the Amarilla Club. For herself, her mind was made up; she would rejoin her uncle; she would entrust the last day – the last hour perhaps – of her father's life to the keeping of the bandit, whose existence was a protest against the irresponsible tyranny of all parties alike, against the moral darkness of the land. The gloom of Los Hatos woods was preferable; a life of hardships in the train of a robber band less debasing. Antonia embraced with all her soul her uncle's obstinate defiance of misfortune. It was grounded in the belief in the man whom she loved.

In his message the Vicar-General answered upon his head for Hernandez's fidelity. As to his power, he pointed out that he had remained unsubdued for so many years. In that letter Decoud's idea of the new Occidental State (whose flourishing and stable condition is a matter of common knowledge now) was for the first time made public and used as an argument. Hernandez, ex-bandit and the last general of Ribierist creation, was confident of being able to hold the tract of country between the woods of Los Hatos and the coast range till that devoted patriot, Don Martin Decoud, could bring General Barrios back to Sulaco for the reconquest of the town.

'Heaven itself wills it. Providence is on our side,' wrote Father Corbelán; there was no time to reflect upon or to controvert his statement; and if the discussion started upon the reading of that letter in the Amarilla Club was violent, it was also short-lived. In the general bewilderment of the collapse some jumped at the idea with joyful astonishment as upon the amazing discovery of a new hope. Others became fascinated by the prospect of immediate personal safety for their women and children. The majority caught at it as a drowning man catches at a straw. Father Corbelán was unexpectedly offering them a refuge from Pedrito Montero with his *llaneros* allied to Señores Fuentes and Gamacho with their armed rabble.

All the latter part of the afternoon an animated discussion went on in the big rooms of the Amarilla Club. Even those members posted at the windows with rifles and carbines to guard the end of the street in case of an offensive return of the populace shouted their opinions and arguments over their shoulders. As dusk fell Don Juste Lopez, inviting those *caballeros* who were of his way of thinking to follow him, withdrew into the corridor, where at a little table in the light of two candles he busied himself in composing an address, or rather a solemn declaration to be presented to Pedrito Montero by a deputation of such members of Assembly as had elected to remain in town. His idea was to propitiate him in order to save the form at least of parliamentary institutions. Seated before a blank sheet of paper, a goose-quill in his hand, and surged upon from all sides, he turned to the right and to the left, repeating with solemn insistence:

'*Caballeros*, a moment of silence! A moment of silence! We ought to make it clear that we bow in all good faith to the accomplished facts.'

The utterance of that phrase seemed to give him a melancholy satisfaction. The hubbub of voices round him was growing strained and hoarse. In the sudden pauses the excited grimacing of the faces would sink all at once into the stillness of profound dejection.

Meantime, the exodus had begun. Carretas full of ladies and children rolled swaying across the Plaza, with men walking or riding by their side; mounted parties followed on mules and horses; the poorest were setting out on foot, men and women carrying bundles, clasping babies in their arms, leading old people, dragging along the bigger children. When Charles Gould, after leaving the doctor and the engineer at the Casa Viola, entered the town by the harbour gate, all those that had meant to go were gone, and the others had barricaded themselves in their houses. In the whole dark street there was only one spot of flickering lights and moving figures, where the Señor Administrador recognized his wife's carriage waiting at the door of the Avellanos's house. He rode up, almost unnoticed, and looked on without a word while some of his own servants came out of the gate carrying Don José Avellanos, who, with closed eyes and motionless features, appeared perfectly lifeless. His wife and Antonia walked on each side of the improvised stretcher, which was put at once into the carriage. The two women embraced; while from the other side of the landau Father Corbelán's emissary, with his ragged beard all streaked with grey, and high, bronzed cheek-bones, stared, sitting upright in the saddle. Then Antonia, dry-eyed, got in by the side of the stretcher, and, after making the sign of the cross rapidly, lowered a thick veil upon her face. The servants and the three or four neighbours who had come to assist, stood back, uncovering their heads. On the box, Ignacio, resigned now to driving all night (and to having perhaps his throat cut before daylight) looked back surlily over his shoulder.

'Drive carefully,' cried Mrs Gould in a tremulous voice.

'*Sí*, carefully, *sí niña*,' he mumbled, chewing his lips, his round leathery cheeks quivering. And the landau rolled slowly out of the light.

'I will see them as far as the ford,' said Charles Gould to his wife. She stood on the edge of the sidewalk with her hands clasped lightly, and nodded to him as he followed after the carriage. And now the windows of the Amarilla Club were dark. The last spark of resistance had died out. Turning his head at the corner, Charles Gould saw his wife crossing over to their own gate in the lighted patch of the street. One of their neighbours, a well-known merchant and landowner of the province, followed at her elbow, talking with great gestures. As she passed in all the lights went out in the street, which remained dark and empty from end to end.

The houses of the vast Plaza were lost in the night. High up, like a star, there was a small gleam in one of the towers of the cathedral; and the equestrian statue gleamed pale against the black tress of the Alameda, like a ghost of royalty haunting the scenes of revolution. The rare prowlers they met ranged themselves against the wall. Beyond the last houses the carriage rolled noiselessly on the soft cushion of dust, and with a great obscurity a feeling of freshness seemed to fall from the foliage of the trees bordering the country road. The emissary from Hernandez's camp pushed his horse close to Charles Gould.

'*Caballero*,' he said in an interested voice, 'you are he whom they call the King of Sulaco, the master of the mine? Is it not so?'

'Yes, I am the master of the mine,' answered Charles Gould.

The man cantered for a time in silence, then said, 'I have a brother, a *sereno* in your service in the San Tomé valley. You have proved yourself a just man. There had been no wrong done to anyone since you called upon the people to work in the mountains. My brother says that no official of the Government, no oppressor of the Campo, has been seen on your side of the stream. Your own officials do not oppress the people in the gorge. Doubtless they are afraid of your severity. You are a just man and a powerful one,' he added.

He spoke in an abrupt, independent tone, but evidently he was communicative with a purpose. He told Charles Gould that he had been a *ranchero* in one of the lower valleys, far south, a neighbour of Hernandez in the old days, and godfather to his eldest boy; one of those who joined him in his resistance to the recruiting raid which was the beginning of all their misfortunes. It was he that, when his *compadre* had been carried off, had buried his wife and children, murdered by the soldiers.

'*Sí, señor*,' he muttered, hoarsely, 'I and two or three others, the lucky ones left at liberty, buried them all in one grave near the ashes of their ranch, under the tree that had shaded its roof.'

It was to him, too, that Hernandez came after he had deserted, three years afterwards. He had still his uniform on with the sergeant's stripes on the sleeve, and the blood of his colonel upon his hands and breast. Three troopers followed him, of those who had started in pursuit but had ridden on for liberty. And he told Charles Gould how he and a few friends, seeing those soldiers, lay in ambush behind some rocks ready to pull the trigger on them, when he recognized his *compadre* and jumped up from cover, shouting his name, because he knew that Hernandez could not have been coming back on an errand of injustice and oppression. Those three soldiers, together with the party who lay behind the rocks, had formed the nucleus of the famous band and he, the narrator, had been the favourite lieutenant of Hernandez for many, many years. He mentioned proudly that the officials had put a price upon his head, too; but it did not prevent it getting sprinkled with grey upon his shoulders. And now he had lived long enough to see his *compadre* made a general.

He had a burst of muffled laughter. 'And now from robbers we have become soldiers. But look, *caballero*, all those who made us soldiers and him a general! Look at these people!'

Ignacio shouted. The light of the carriage lamps, running along the nopal hedges that crowned the bank on each side, flashed upon the scared faces of people standing aside in the road, sunk deep, like an English country lane, into the soft soil of the Campo. They cowered; their eyes glistened very big for a second; and then the light, running on, fell upon the half-denuded roots of a big tree, on another stretch of nopal hedge, caught up another bunch of faces glaring back apprehensively. Three women – of whom one was carrying a child – and a couple of men in civilian dress – one armed with a sabre and another with a gun – were grouped about a donkey carrying two bundles tied up in blankets. Farther on Ignacio shouted again to pass a carreta, a long wooden box on two high wheels, with the door at the back swinging open. Some ladies in it must have recognized the white mules, because they screamed out, 'Is it you, Doña Emilia?'

At the turn of the road the glare of a big fire filled the short stretch vaulted over by the branches meeting overhead. Near the ford of a shallow stream a roadside *rancho* of woven rushes and a roof of grass had been set on fire by accident, and the flames, roaring viciously, lit up an open space blocked with horses, mules, and a distracted, shouting crowd of people. When Ignacio pulled up, several ladies on foot assailed the carriage, begging Antonia for a seat. To their clamour she answered by pointing silently to her father.

'I must leave you here,' said Charles Gould, in the uproar. The flames leaped up sky-high, and in the recoil from the scorching heat across the road the stream of fugitives pressed against the carriage. A middle-aged lady dressed in black silk, but with a coarse manta over her head and a rough branch for a stick in her hand, staggered against the front wheel. Two young girls, frightened and silent, were clinging to her arms. Charles Gould knew her very well.

'*Misericordia!* We are getting terribly bruised in this crowd!' she exclaimed, smiling up courageously to him. 'We have started on foot. All our servants ran away yesterday to join the democrats. We are going to put ourselves under the protection of Father Corbelán, of your sainted uncle. Antonia. He has wrought a miracle in the heart of a most merciless robber. A miracle!'

She raised her voice gradually up to a scream as she was borne along by the pressure of people getting out of the way of some carts coming up out of the ford at a gallop, with loud yells and cracking of whips. Great masses of sparks mingled with black smoke flew over the road; the bamboos of the walls detonated in the fire with the sound of an irregular fusillade. And then the bright blaze sank suddenly, leaving only a red dusk crowded with aimless dark shadows drifting in contrary directions; the noise of voices seemed to die away with the flame; and the tumult of heads, arms, quarrelling, and imprecations passed on fleeing into the darkness.

'I must leave you now,' repeated Charles Gould to Antonia. She turned her head slowly and uncovered her face. The emissary and *compadre* of Hernandez spurred his horse close up.

'Has not the master of the mine any message to send to Hernandez, the master of the Campo?'

The truth of the comparison struck Charles Gould heavily. In his determined purpose he held the mine, and the indomitable bandit held the Campo by the same precarious tenure. They were equals before the lawlessness of the land. It was impossible to disentangle one's activity from its debasing contacts. A close-meshed net of crime and corruption lay upon the whole country. An immense and weary discouragement sealed his lips for a time.

'You are a just man,' urged the emissary of Hernandez. 'Look at those people who made my *compadre* a general and have turned us all into soldiers. Look at those oligarchs fleeing for life, with only the clothes on their backs. My *compadre* does not think of that, but our followers may be wondering greatly, and I would speak for them to you. Listen, *señor*! For many months now the Campo has been our own. We need ask no man for anything; but soldiers must have their pay to live honestly when the wars are over. It is believed that your soul is so just that a prayer from you would cure the sickness of every beast, like the orison of the upright judge. Let me have some words from your lips that would act like a charm upon the doubts of our *partida*, where all are men.'

'Do you hear what he says?' Charles Gould said in English to Antonia.

'Forgive us our misery!' she exclaimed, hurriedly. 'It is your character that is the inexhaustible treasure which may save us all yet; your character, Carlos, not your wealth. I entreat you to give this man your word that you will accept any arrangement my uncle may make with their chief. One word. He will want no more.'

On the site of the roadside hut there remained nothing but an enormous heap of embers, throwing afar a darkening red glow, in which Antonia's face appeared deeply flushed with excitement. Charles Gould, with only a short hesitation, pronounced the required pledge. He was like a man who had ventured on a precipitous path with no room to turn, where the only chance of safety is to press forward. At that moment he understood it thoroughly as he looked down at Don José stretched out, hardly breathing, by the side of the erect Antonia, vanquished in a life-long struggle with the powers of moral darkness, whose stagnant depths breed monstrous crimes and monstrous illusions. In a few words the emissary from Hernandez expressed his complete satisfaction. Stoically Antonia lowered her veil, resting the longing to inquire about Decoud's escape. But Ignacio leered morosely over his shoulder.

'Take a good look at the mules, *mi amo*,' he grumbled. 'You shall never see them again!'

Chapter IV

Charles Gould turned towards the town. Before him jagged peaks of the Sierra came out all black in the clear dawn. Here and there a muffled *lepero* whisked round the corner of a grassgrown street before the ringing hoofs of his horse. Dogs barked behind the walls of the gardens; and with the colourless light the chill of the snows seemed to fall from the mountains upon the disjointed pavements and the shuttered houses with broken cornices and the plaster peeling in patches between the flat pilasters of the fronts. The daybreak struggled with the gloom under the arcades on the Plaza, with no signs of country people disposing their goods for the day's market, piles of fruit, bundles of vegetables ornamented with flowers, on low benches under enormous mat umbrellas; with no cheery early-morning bustle of villagers, women, children, and loaded donkeys. Only a few scattered knots of revolutionists stood in the vast space, looking all one way from under their slouched hats for some sign of news from Rincón. The largest of those groups turned about like one man as Charles Gould passed, and shouted, '*Viva la libertad!*' after him in a menacing tone.

Charles Gould rode on, and turned into the archway of his house. In the patio littered with straw, a *practicante*, one of Dr Monygham's native assistants, sat on the ground with his back against the rim of the fountain, fingering a guitar discreetly, while two girls of the lower class, standing up before him, shuffled their feet a little and waved their arms, humming a popular dance tune. Most of the wounded during the two days of rioting had been taken away already by their friends and relations, but several figures could be seen sitting up balancing their bandaged heads in time to the music. Charles Gould dismounted. A sleepy *mozo* coming out of the bakery door took hold of the horse's bridle; the *practicante* endeavoured to conceal his guitar hastily; the girls, unabashed, stepped back smiling; and Charles Gould, on his way to the staircase, glanced into a dark corner of the patio at another group, a mortally wounded *cargador* with a woman kneeling by his side; she mumbled prayers rapidly, trying at the same time to force a piece of orange between the stiffening lips of the dying man.

The cruel futility of things stood unveiled in the levity and sufferings of that incorrigible people; the cruel futility of lives and of deaths thrown away in the vain endeavour to attain an enduring solution of the problem. Unlike Decoud, Charles Gould could not play lightly a part in a tragic farce. It was tragic enough for him in all conscience, but he could see no farcical element. He suffered too much under a conviction of irremediable folly. He was too severely practical and too idealistic to look upon its terrible humours with amusement, as Martin Decoud, the imaginative materialist, was able to do in the dry light of his scepticism. To him, as to all of us, the compromises with his conscience appeared uglier than ever in the light of failure. His taciturnity, assumed with a purpose, had prevented him from tampering openly with his thoughts; but the Gould Concession had insidiously corrupted his judgement. He might have known, he said to himself, leaning over the balustrade of the corridor, that Ribierism could never come to anything. The mine had corrupted his judgement by making him sick of bribing and intriguing merely to have his work left alone from day to day. Like his father, he did not like to be robbed. It exasperated him. He had persuaded himself that, apart from higher considerations, the backing up of Don José's hopes of reform was good business. He had gone forth into the senseless fray as his poor uncle, whose sword hung on the wall of his study, had gone forth – in the defence of the commonest decencies of organized society. Only his weapon was the wealth of the mine, more far-reaching and subtle than an honest blade of steel fitted into a simple brass guard.

More dangerous to the wielder, too, this weapon of wealth, double-edged with the cupidity and misery of mankind, steeped in all the vices of self-indulgence as in a concoction of poisonous roots, tainting the very cause for which it is drawn, always ready to turn awkwardly in the hand. There was nothing for it now but to go on using it. But he promised himself to see it shattered into small bits before he let it be wrenched from his grasp.

After all, with his English parentage and English upbringing, he perceived that he was an adventurer in Costaguana, the descendant of adventurers enlisted in a foreign legion, of men who had sought fortune in a revolutionary war, who had planned revolutions, who had believed in revolutions. For all the uprightness of his character, he had something of an adventurer's easy morality which takes count of personal risk in the ethical appraising of his action. He was prepared, if need be, to blow up the whole San Tomé mountain sky high out of the territory of the Republic. This resolution expressed the tenacity of his character, the remorse of that subtle conjugal infidelity through which his wife was no longer the sole mistress of his thoughts, something of his father's imaginative weakness, and something, too, of the spirit of a buccaneer throwing a lighted match into the magazine rather than surrender his ship.

Down below in the patio the wounded *cargador* had breathed his last. The woman cried out once, and her cry, unexpected and shrill, made all the wounded sit up. The *practicante* scrambled up to his feet, and guitar in hand, gazed steadily in her direction with elevated eyebrows. The two girls – sitting now one on each side of their wounded relative, with their knees drawn up and long cigars between their lips – nodded at each other significantly.

Charles Gould, looking down over the balustrade, saw three men dressed ceremoniously in black frock-coats with white shirts, and wearing European round hats, enter the patio from the street. One of them, head and shoulders taller than the two others, advanced with marked gravity, leading the way. This was Don Juste Lopez, accompanied by two of his friends, members of Assembly, coming to call upon the Administrador of the San Tomé mine at this early hour. They saw him, too, waved their hands to him urgently, walking up the stairs as if in procession.

Don Juste, astonishingly changed by having shaved off altogether his damaged beard, had lost with it nine-tenths of his outward dignity. Even at that time of serious preoccupation Charles Gould could not help noting the revealed ineptitude in the aspect of the man. His companions looked crestfallen and sleepy. One kept on passing the tip of his tongue over his parched lips; the other's eyes strayed dully over the tiled floor of the corridor, while Don Juste, standing a little in advance, harangued the Señor Administrador of the San Tomé mine. It was his firm opinion that forms had to be observed. A new governor is always visited by deputations from the Cabildo, which is the Municipal Council, from the Consulado, the Commercial Board, and it was proper that the Provincial Assembly should send a deputation too, if only to assert the existence of parliamentary institutions. Don Juste proposed that Don Carlos Gould, as the most prominent citizen of the province, should join the Assembly's deputation. His position was exceptional, his personality known through the length and breadth of the whole Republic. Official courtesies must not be neglected, if they are gone through with a bleeding heart. The acceptance of accomplished facts may save yet the precious vestiges of parliamentary institutions. Don Juste's eyes glowed dully; he believed in parliamentary institutions – and the convinced drone of his voice lost itself in the stillness of the house like the deep buzzing of some ponderous insect.

Charles Gould had turned round to listen patiently, leaning his elbow on the balustrade. He shook his head a little, refusing, almost touched by the anxious gaze of the President of the Provincial Assembly. It was not Charles Gould's policy to make the San Tomé mine a party to any formal proceedings.

'My advice, *señores*, is that you should wait for your fate in your houses. There is no necessity for you to give yourselves up formally into Montero's hands. Submission to the inevitable, as Don Juste calls it, is all very well, but when the inevitable is called Pedrito Montero there is no need to exhibit pointedly the whole extent of your surrender. The fault of this country is the want of measure in political life. Flat acquiescence in illegality, followed by sanguinary reaction – that, *señores*, is not the way to a stable and prosperous future.'

Charles Gould stopped before the sad bewilderment of the faces, the wondering, anxious glances of the eyes. The feeling of pity for those men, putting all their trust into words of some sort, while murder and rapine stalked over the land, had betrayed him into what seemed empty loquacity. Don Juste murmured:

'You are abandoning us, Don Carlos . . . And yet, parliamentary institutions –'

He could not finish from grief. For a moment he put his hand over his eyes. Charles Gould, in his fear of empty loquacity, made no answer to the charge. He returned in silence their ceremonious bows. His taciturnity was his refuge. He understood that what they sought was to get the influence of the San Tomé mine on their side. They wanted to go on a conciliating errand to the victor under the wing of the Gould Concession. Other public bodies – the Cabildo, the Consulado – would be coming, too, presently, seeking the support of the most stable, the most effective force they had ever known to exist in their province.

The doctor, arriving with his sharp, jerky walk, found that the master had retired into his own room with orders not to be disturbed on any account. But Dr Monygham was not anxious to see Charles Gould at once. He spent some time in a rapid examination of his wounded. He gazed down upon each in turn, rubbing his chin between his thumb and forefinger; his steady stare met without expression their silently inquisitive look. All these cases were doing well; but when he came to the dead *cargador* he stopped a little longer, surveying not the man who had ceased to suffer, but the woman kneeling in silent contemplation of the rigid face, with its pinched nostrils and a white gleam in the imperfectly closed eyes. She lifted her head slowly, and said in a dull voice:

'It is not long since he had become a *cargador* – only a few weeks. His worship the Capataz had accepted him after many entreaties.'

'I am not responsible for the great Capataz,' muttered the doctor, moving off.

Directing his course upstairs towards the door of Charles Gould's room, the doctor at the last moment hesitated; then, turning away from the handle with a shrug of his uneven shoulders, slunk off hastily along the corridor in search of Mrs Gould's *camerista*.

Leonarda told him that the *señora* had not risen yet. The *señora* had given into her charge the girls belonging to that Italian *posadero*. She, Leonarda, had put them to bed in her own room. The fair girl had cried herself to sleep, but the dark one – the bigger – had not closed her eyes yet. She sat up in bed clutching the sheets right up under her chin and staring before her like a little witch. Leonarda did not approve of the Viola children being admitted to the house. She made this feeling clear by the indifferent tone in which she inquired whether their mother was dead yet. As to the *señora*, she must be asleep. Ever since she had gone into her room after seeing the departure of Doña Antonia with her dying father, there had been no sound behind her door.

The doctor, rousing himself out of profound reflection, told her abruptly to call her mistress at once. He hobbled off to wait for Mrs Gould in the *sala*. He was very tired, but too excited to sit down. In this great drawing-room, now empty, in which his withered soul had been refreshed after many arid years and his outcast spirit had accepted silently the toleration of many side-glances, he wandered haphazardly amongst the chairs and tables till Mrs Gould, enveloped in a morning wrapper, came in rapidly.

'You know that I never approved of the silver being sent away,' the doctor began at once, as a preliminary to the narrative of his night's adventures in association with Captain Mitchell, the engineer-in-chief, and old Viola, at

Sotillo's headquarters. To the doctor, with his special conception of this political crisis, the removal of the silver had seemed an irrational and ill-omened measure. It was as if a general were sending the best part of his troops away on the eve of battle upon some recondite pretext. The whole lot of ingots might have been concealed somewhere where they could have been got at for the purpose of staving off the dangers which were menacing the security of the Gould Concession. The Administrador had acted as if the immense and powerful prosperity of the mine had been founded on methods of probity, on the sense of usefulness. And it was nothing of the kind. The method followed had been the only one possible. The Gould Concession had ransomed its way through all those years. It was a nauseous process. He quite understood that Charles Gould had got sick of it and had left the old path to back up that hopeless attempt at reform. The doctor did not believe in the reform of Costaguana. And now the mine was back again in its old path, with the disadvantage that henceforth it had to deal not only with the greed provoked by its wealth, but with the resentment awakened by the attempt to free itself from its bondage to moral corruption. That was the penalty of failure. What made him uneasy was that Charles Gould seemed to him to have weakened at the decisive moment when a frank return to the old methods was the only chance. Listening to Decoud's wild scheme had been a weakness.

The doctor flung up his arms, exclaiming, 'Decoud! Decoud!' He hobbled about the room with slight, angry laughs. Many years ago both his ankles had been seriously damaged in the course of a certain investigation conducted in the castle of Sta Marta by a commission composed of military men. Their nomination had been signified to them unexpectedly at the dead of night, with scowling brow, flashing eyes, and in a tempestuous voice, by Guzman Bento. The old tyrant, maddened by one of his sudden accesses of suspicion, mingled spluttering appeals to their fidelity with imprecations and horrible menaces. The cells and casements of the castle on the hill had been already filled with prisoners. The commission was charged now with the task of discovering the iniquitous conspiracy against the Citizen-Saviour of his country.

The dread of the raving tyrant translated itself into a hasty ferocity of procedure. The Citizen-Saviour was not accustomed to wait. A conspiracy had to be discovered. The courtyards of the castle resounded with the clanking of leg-irons, sounds of blows, yells of pain; and the commission of high officers laboured feverishly, concealing their distress and apprehensions from each other, and especially from their secretary, Father Berón, an army chaplain, at that time very much in the confidence of the Citizen-Saviour. That priest was a big round-shouldered man, with an unclean-looking, overgrown tonsure on the top of his flat head, of a dingy, yellow complexion, softly fat, with greasy stains all down the front of his lieutenant's uniform, and a small cross embroidered in white cotton on his left breast. He had a heavy nose and a pendant lip. Dr Monygham remembered him still. He remembered him against all the force of his will striving its utmost to forget. Father Berón had been adjoined to the commission by Guzman Bento expressly for the purpose that his enlightened zeal should assist them in their labours. Dr Monygham could by no manner of means forget the zeal of Father Berón, or his face, or the pitiless monotonous voice in which he pronounced the words, 'Will you confess now?'

The memory did not make him shudder, but it had made of him what he was in the eyes of respectable people, a man careless of common decencies, something between a clever vagabond and a disreputable doctor. But not all respectable people would have had the necessary delicacy of sentiment to understand with what trouble of mind and accuracy of vision Dr Monygham, medical officer of the San Tomé mine, remembered Father Berón, army chaplain, and once a secretary of a military commission. After all these years Dr Monygham, in his rooms at the end of the hospital building in the San Tomé gorge, remembered Father Berón as distinctly as ever. He remembered that priest at night, sometimes, in his sleep. On such nights the doctor waited for daylight with a candle lighted, and walked the whole length of his rooms to and fro, staring down at his bare feet, his arms hugging his sides tightly. He would dream of Father Berón sitting at the end of a long black table, behind which, in a row, appeared the heads, shoulders, and epaulettes of the military members, nibbling the feather of a quill pen, and listening with weary and impatient scorn to the protestations of some prisoner calling heaven to witness of his innocence, till he burst out, 'What's the use of wasting time over that miserable nonsense! Let me take him outside for a while.' And Father Berón would go outside after the clanking prisoner, led away between two soldiers. Such interludes happened on many days, many times, with many prisoners. When the prisoner returned he was ready to make a full confession, Father Berón would declare, leaning forward with that dull, surfeited look which can be seen in the eyes of gluttonous persons after a heavy meal.

The priest's inquisitorial instincts suffered but little from the want of classical aparatus of the Inquisition. At no time of the world's history have men been at a loss how to inflict mental and bodily anguish upon their fellow-creatures. This aptitude came to them in the growing complexity of their passions and the early refinement of their ingenuity. But it may safely be said that primeval man did not go to the trouble of inventing tortures. He was indolent and pure of heart. He brained his neighbour ferociously with a stone axe from necessity and without malice. The stupidest mind may invent a rankling phrase or brand the innocent with a cruel aspersion. A piece of string and a ramrod; a few muskets in combination with a length of hide rope; or even a simple mallet of heavy, hard wood applied with a swing to human fingers or to the joints of a human body is enough for the infliction of the most exquisite torture. The doctor had been a very stubborn prisoner, and, as a natural consequence of that 'bad disposition' (so Father Berón called it), his subjugation had been very crushing and very complete. That is why the limp in his walk, the twist of his shoulders, the scars on his cheeks were so pronounced. His confessions, when they came at last, were very complete, too. Sometimes on the nights when he walked the floor, he wondered, grinding his teeth with shame and rage, at the fertility of his imagination when stimulated by a sort of pain which makes truth, honour, self-respect, and life itself matters of little moment.

And he could not forget Father Berón with his monotonous phrase, 'Will you confess now?' reaching him in an awful iteration and lucidity of meaning through the delirious incoherence of unbearable pain. He could not forget. But that was not the worst. Had he met Father Berón in the street after all these years Dr Monygham was sure he would have quailed before him. This contingency was not to be feared now. Father Berón was dead; but the sickening certitude prevented Dr Monygham from looking anybody in the face.

Dr Monygham had become, in a manner, the slave of a ghost. It was obviously impossible to take his knowledge of Father Berón home to Europe. When making his extorted confessions to the Military Board, Dr Monygham was not seeking to avoid death. He longed for it. Sitting half-naked for hours on the wet earth of his prison, and so motionless that the spiders, his companions, attached their webs to his matted hair, he consoled the misery of his soul with acute reasonings that he had confessed to crimes enough for a sentence of death – that they had gone too far with him to let him live to tell the tale.

But, as if by a refinement of cruelty, Dr Monygham was left for months to decay slowly in the darkness of his grave-like prison. It was no doubt hoped that it would finish him off without the trouble of an execution; but Dr Monygham had an iron constitution. It was Guzman Bento who died, not by the knife thrust of a conspirator, but from a stroke of apoplexy, and Dr Monygham was liberated hastily. His fetters were struck off by the light of a candle, which, after months of gloom, hurt his eyes so much that he had to cover his face with his hands. He was raised up. His heart was beating violently with the fear of this liberty. When he tried to walk the extraordinary lightness of his feet made him giddy, and he fell down. Two sticks were thrust into his hands, and he was pushed out of the passage. It was dusk; candles glimmered already in the windows of the officers' quarters round the courtyard; but the twilight sky dazed him by its enormous and overwhelming brilliance. A thin poncho hung over his naked, bony shoulders; the rags of his trousers came down no lower than his knees; an eighteen months' growth of hair fell in dirty grey locks on each side of his sharp cheek-bones. As he dragged himself past the guard-room door, one of the soldiers, lolling outside, moved by some obscure impulse, leaped forward with a strange laugh and rammed a broken old straw hat on his head. And Dr Monygham, after having tottered, continued on his way. He advanced one stick, then one maimed foot, then the other stick; the other foot followed only a very short distance along the ground, toilfully, as though it were almost too heavy to be moved at all; and yet his legs under the hanging angles of the poncho appeared no thicker than the two sticks in his hands. A ceaseless trembling agitated his bent body, all his wasted limbs, his bony head, the conical ragged crown of the sombrero, whose ample flat rim rested on his shoulders.

In such conditions of manner and attire did Dr Monygham go forth to take possession of his liberty. And these conditions seemed to bind him indissolubly to the land of Costaguana like an awful procedure of naturalization, involving him deep in the national life, far deeper than any amount of success and honour could have done. They did away with his Europeanism; for Dr Monygham had made himself an ideal conception of his disgrace. It was a conception eminently fit and proper for an officer and a gentleman. Dr Monygham, before he went out to Costaguana, had been surgeon in one of Her Majesty's regiments of foot. It was a conception which took no account of physiological facts or reasonable arguments; but it was not stupid for all that. It was simple. A rule of conduct resting mainly on severe rejections is necessarily simple. Dr Monygham's view of what it behoved him to do was severe; it was an ideal view, in so much that it was the imaginative exaggeration of a correct feeling. It was also, in its force, influence, and persistency, the view of an eminently loyal nature.

There was a great fund of loyalty in Dr Monygham's nature. He had settled it all on Mrs Gould's head. He believed her worthy of every devotion. At the bottom of his heart he felt an angry uneasiness before the prosperity of the San Tomé mine, because its growth was robbing her of all peace of mind. Costaguana was no place for a woman of that kind. What could Charles Gould have been thinking of when he brought her out there! It was outrageous! And the doctor had watched the course of events with a grim and distant reserve which, he imagined, his lamentable history imposed upon him.

Loyalty to Mrs Gould could not, however, leave out of account the safety of her husband. The doctor had contrived to be in town at the critical time because he mistrusted Charles Gould. He considered him hopelessly infected with the madness of revolutions. That is why he hobbled in distress in the drawing-room of the Casa Gould on that morning, exclaiming, 'Decoud, Decoud!' in a tone of mournful irritation.

Mrs Gould, her colour heightened, and with glistening eyes, looked straight before her at the sudden enormity of that disaster. The finger-tips on one hand rested lightly on a low little table by her side, and the arm trembled right up to the shoulder. The sun, which looks late upon Sulaco, issuing in all the fullness of its power high up on the sky from behind the dazzling snow-edge of Higuerota, had precipitated the delicate, smooth, pearly greyness of light, in which the town lies steeped during the early hours, into sharp-cut masses of black shade and spaces of hot, blinding glare. Three long rectangles of sunshine fell through the windows of the *sala*; while just across the street the front of the Avellanos's house appeared very sombre in its own shadow seen through the flood of light.

A voice said at the door, 'What of Decoud?'

It was Charles Gould. They had not heard him coming along the corridor. His glance just glided over his wife and struck full at the doctor.

'You have brought some news, doctor?'

Dr Monygham blurted it all at once, in the rough. For some time after he had done, the Administrador of the San Tomé mine remained looking at him without a word. Mrs Gould sank into a low chair with her hands lying on her lap. A silence reigned between those three motionless persons. Then Charles Gould spoke:

'You must want some breakfast.'

He stood aside to let his wife pass first. She caught up her husband's hand and pressed it as she went out, raising the handkerchief to her eyes. The sight of her husband had brought Antonia's position to her mind, and she could not contain her tears at the thought of the poor girl. When she rejoined the two men in the dining-room after having bathed her face, Charles Gould was saying to the doctor across the table:

'No, there does not seem any room for doubt.'

And the doctor assented.

'No, I don't see myself how we could question that wretched Hirsch's tale. It's only too true, I fear.'

She sat down desolately at the head of the table and looked from one to the other. The two men, without absolutely turning their heads away, tried to avoid her glance. The doctor even made a show of being hungry; he seized his knife and fork, and began to eat with emphasis, as if on the stage. Charles Gould made no pretence of the sort; with his elbows raised squarely, he twisted both ends of his flaming moustaches – they were so long that his hands were quite away from his face.

'I am not surprised,' he muttered, abandoning his moustaches and throwing one arm over the back of his chair. His face was calm with that immobility of expression which betrays the intensity of a mental struggle. He felt that this accident had brought to a point all the consequences involved in his line of conduct, with its conscious and subconscious intentions. There must be an end now of this silent reserve, of that air of impenetrability behind which he had been safeguarding his dignity. It was the least ignoble form of dissembling forced upon him by that parody of civilized institutions which offended his intelligence, his uprightness, and his sense of right. He was like his father. He had no ironic eye. He was not amused at the absurdities that prevail in this world. They hurt him in his innate gravity. He felt that the miserable death of that poor Decoud took from him his inaccessible position of a force in the background. It committed him openly unless he wished to throw up the game – and that was impossible. The material interests required from him the sacrifice of his aloofness – perhaps his own safety too. And he reflected that Decoud's separationist plan had not gone to the bottom with the lost silver.

The only thing that was not changed was his position towards Mr Holroyd. The head of silver and steel interests had entered into Costaguana affairs with a sort of passion. Costaguana had become necessary to his existence; in the San Tomé he had found the imaginative satisfaction which other minds would get from drama, from art, or from a risky and fascinating sport. It was a special form of the great man's extravagance, sanctioned by a moral intention, big enough to flatter his vanity. Even in this aberration of his genius he served the progress of the world. Charles Gould felt sure of being understood with precision and judged with the indulgence of their common passion. Nothing now could surprise or startle this great man. And Charles Gould imagined himself writing a letter to San Francisco in some such words: '. . . The men at the head of the movement are dead or have fled; the civil organization of the province is at an end for the present; the Blanco party in Sulaco has collapsed inexcusably, but in the characteristic manner of this country. But Barrios, untouched in Cayta, remains still available. I am forced to take up openly the plan of a provincial revolution as the only way of placing the enormous material interests involved in the prosperity and peace of Sulaco in a position of permanent safety . . .' That was clear. He saw these words as if written in letters of fire upon that wall at which he was gazing abstractedly.

Mrs Gould watched his abstraction with dread. It was a domestic and frightful phenomenon that darkened and chilled the house for her like a thunder-cloud passing over the sun. Charles Gould's fits of abstraction depicted the energetic concentration of a will haunted by a fixed idea. A man haunted by a fixed idea is insane. He is dangerous even if that idea is an idea of justice; for may he not bring the heaven down pitilessly upon a loved head? The eyes of Mrs Gould, watching her husband's profile, filled with tears again. And again she seemed to see the despair of the unfortunate Antonia.

'What would I have done if Charley had been drowned while we were engaged?' she exclaimed, mentally, with horror. Her heart turned to ice, while her cheeks flamed up as if scorched by the blaze of a funeral pyre consuming all her earthly affections. The tears burst out of her eyes.

'Antonia will kill herself!' she cried out.

This cry fell into the silence of the room with strangely little effect. Only the doctor, crumbling up a piece of bread, with his head inclined on one side, raised his face, and the few long hairs sticking out of his shaggy eyebrows stirred in a slight frown. Dr Monygham thought quite sincerely that Decoud was a singularly unworthy object for any woman's affection. Then he lowered his head again, with a curl of his lip, and his heart full of tender admiration for Mrs Gould.

'She thinks of that girl,' he said to himself; 'she thinks of the Viola children; she thinks of me; of the wounded; of the miners; she always thinks of everybody who is poor and miserable! But what will she do if Charles gets the worst of it in this infernal scrimmage those confounded Avellanos have drawn him into? No one seems to be thinking of her.'

Charles Gould, staring at the wall, pursued his reflections subtly.

'I shall write to Holroyd that the San Tomé mine is big enough to take in hand the making of a new State. It'll please him. It'll reconcile him to the risk.'

But was Barrios really available? Perhaps. But he was inaccessible. To send off a boat to Cayta was no longer possible, since Sotillo was master of the harbour, and had a steamer at his disposal. And now, with all the democrats in the province up, and every Campo township in a state of disturbance, where could he find a man who would make his way successfully overland to Cayta with a message, a ten days' ride at least; a man of courage and resolution, who would avoid arrest or murder, and if arrested would faithfully eat the paper? The Capataz de Cargadores would have been just such a man. But the Capataz of the Cargadores was no more.

And Charles Gould, withdrawing his eyes from the wall, said gently. 'That Hirsch! What an extraordinary thing! Saved himself by clinging to the anchor, did he? I had no idea that he was still in Sulaco. I thought he had gone back overland to Esmeralda more than a week ago. He came here once to talk to me about his hide business and some other things. I made it clear to him that nothing could be done.'

'He was afraid to start back on account of Hernandez being about,' remarked the doctor.

'And but for him we might not have known anything of what has happened,' marvelled Charles Gould.

Mrs Gould cried out:

'Antonia must not know! She must not be told. Not now.'

'Nobody's likely to carry the news,' remarked the doctor. 'It's no one's interest. Moreover, the people here are afraid of Hernandez as if he were the devil.' He turned to Charles Gould. 'It's even awkward, because if you wanted to communicate with the refugees you could find no messenger. When Hernandez was ranging hundreds of miles away from here the Sulaco populace used to shudder at the tales of him roasting his prisoners alive.'

'Yes,' murmured Charles Gould; 'Captain Mitchell's Capataz was the only man in the town who had seen Hernandez eye to eye. Father Corbelán employed him. He opened the communications first. It is a pity that –'

His voice was covered by the booming of the great bell of the cathedral. Three single strokes, one after another, burst out explosively, dying away in deep and mellow vibrations. And then all the bells in the tower of every church, convent, or chapel in town, even those that had remained shut up for years, pealed out together with a crash. In this furious flood of metallic uproar there was a power of suggesting images of strife and violence which blanched Mrs Gould's cheek. Basilio, who had been waiting at table, shrinking within himself, clung to the sideboard with chattering teeth. It was impossible to hear yourself speak.

'Shut these windows!' Charles Gould yelled at him, angrily. All the other servants, terrified at what they took for the signal of a general massacre, had rushed upstairs, tumbling over each other, men and women, the obscure and generally invisible population of the ground floor on the four sides of the patio. The women, screaming '*Misericordia!*' ran right into the room, and, falling on their knees against the walls, began to cross themselves convulsively. The staring heads of men blocked the doorway in an instant – *mozos* from the stable, gardeners, nondescript helpers living on the crumbs of the munificent house – and Charles Gould beheld all the extent of his domestic establishment, even to the gatekeeper. This was a half-paralysed old man, whose long white locks fell down to his shoulders: an heirloom taken up by Charles Gould's familial piety. He could remember Henry Gould, an Englishman and a Costaguanero of the second generation, chief of the Sulaco province; he had been his personal *mozo* years and years ago in peace and war; had been allowed to attend his master in prison; had, on the fatal morning, followed the firing-squad; and, peeping from behind one of the cypresses growing along the wall of the Franciscan Convent, had seen, with his eyes starting out of his head, Don Enrique throw up his hands and fall with his face in the dust. Charles Gould noted particularly the big patriarchal head of that witness in the rear of the other servants. But he was surprised to see a shrivelled old hag or two, of whose existence within the walls of his house he had not been aware. They must have been the mothers, or even the grandmothers, of some of his people. There were a few children, too, more or less naked, crying and clinging to the legs of their elders. He had never before noticed any sign of a child in his patio. Even Leonarda, the *camerista*, came in a fright, pushing through, with her spoiled, pouting face of a favourite maid, leading the Viola girls by the hand. The crockery rattled on table and sideboard, and the whole house seemed to sway in the deafening wave of sound.

Chapter V

During the night the expectant populace had taken possession of all the belfries in the town in order to welcome Pedrito Montero, who was making his entry after having slept the night in Rincón. And first came straggling in through the land gate the armed mob of all colours, complexions, types, and states of raggedness, calling themselves the Sulaco National Guard, and commanded by Señor Gamacho. Through the middle of the street streamed, like a torrent of rubbish, a mass of straw hats, ponchos, gun-barrels, with an enormous green and yellow flag flapping in their midst, in a cloud of dust, to the furious beating of drums. The spectators recoiled against the walls of the houses shouting their '*Vivas!*' Behind the rabble could be seen the lances of the cavalry, the 'army' of Pedro Montero. He advanced between Señores Fuentes and Gamacho at the head of his *llaneros*, who had accomplished the feat of crossing the *páramos* of the Higuerota in a snow-storm. They rode four abreast, mounted on confiscated Campo horses, clad in the heterogeneous stock of roadside stores they had looted hurriedly in their rapid ride through the northern part of the province; for Pedro Montero had been in a great hurry to occupy Sulaco. The handkerchiefs knotted loosely around their bare throats were glaringly new, and all the right sleeves of their cotton shirts had been cut off close to the shoulder for greater freedom in throwing the *lazo*. Emaciated grey-beards rode by the side of lean dark youths, marked by all the hardships of campaigning, with strips of raw beef twined round the crowns of their hats, and huge iron spurs fastened to their naked heels. Those that in the passes of the mountain had lost their lances had provided themselves with the goads used by the Campo cattlemen: slender shafts of palm fully ten feet long, with a lot of loose rings jingling under the ironshod point. They were armed with knives and revolvers. A haggard fearlessness characterized the expression of all these sun-blacked countenances; they glared down haughtily with their scorched eyes at the crowd, or, blinking upwards insolently, pointed out to each other some particular head amongst the women at the windows. When they had ridden into the Plaza and caught sight of the equestrian statue of the King dazzlingly white in the sunshine, towering enormous and motionless above the surges of the crowd, with its eternal gesture of saluting, a murmur of surprise ran through their ranks. 'What is that saint in the big hat?' they asked each other.

They were a good sample of the cavalry of the plains with which Pedro Montero had helped so much the victorious career of his brother the general. The influence which that man, brought up in coast towns, acquired in a short time over the plainsmen of the Republic can be ascribed only to a genius for treachery of so effective a kind that it must have appeared to those violent men but little removed from a state of utter savagery, as the perfection of sagacity and virtue. The popular lore of all nations testified that duplicity and cunning, together with bodily strength, were looked upon, even more than courage, as heroic virtues by primitive mankind. To overcome your adversary was the great affair of life. Courage was taken for granted. But the use of intelligence awakened wonder and respect. Stratagems, providing they did not fail, were honourable; the easy massacre of an unsuspecting enemy evoked no feelings but those of gladness, pride, and admiration. Not perhaps that primitive men were more faithless than their descendants of today, but that they went straighter to their aim, and were more artless in their recognition of success as the only standard of morality.

We have changed since. The use of intelligence awakens little wonder and less respect. But the ignorant and barbarous plainsmen engaging in civil strife followed willingly a leader who often managed to deliver their enemies bound, as it were, into their hands. Pedro Montero had a talent for lulling his adversaries into a sense of security. And as men learn wisdom with extreme slowness, and are always ready to believe promises that flatter their secret hopes, Pedro Montero was successful time after time. Whether only a servant or some inferior official in the Costaguana Legation in Paris, he had rushed back to his country directly he heard that his brother had emerged from the obscurity of his frontier *comandancia*. He had managed to deceive by his gift of plausibility the chiefs of the Ribierist movement in his capital, and even the acute agent of the San Tomé mine had failed to understand him thoroughly. At once he had obtained an enormous influence over his brother. They were very much alike in appearance, both bald, with bunches of crisp hair above their ears, arguing the presence of some Negro blood. Only Pedro was smaller than the general, more delicate altogether, with an ape-like faculty for imitating all the outward signs of refinement and distinction, and with a parrot-like talent for languages. Both brothers had received some elementary instruction by the munificence of a great European traveller, to whom their father had been a body-servant during his journeys in the interior of the country. In General Montero's case it enabled him to rise from the ranks. Pedrito, the younger, incorrigibly lazy and slovenly, had drifted aimlessly from one coast town to another, hanging about counting-houses, attaching himself to strangers as a sort of *valet de place*, picking up an easy and disreputable living. His ability to read did nothing for him but fill his head with absurd visions. His actions were usually determined by motives so improbable in themselves as to escape the penetration of a rational person.

Thus at first sight the agent of the Gould Concession in Sta Marta had credited him with the possession of sane views, and even with a restraining power over the general's everlastingly discontented vanity. It could never have entered his head that Pedrito Montero, lackey or inferior scribe, lodged in the garrets of the various Parisian hotels where the Costaguana Legation used to shelter its diplomatic dignity, had been devouring the lighter sort of historical works in the French language, such, for instance, as the books of Imbert de Saint Amand upon the Second Empire. But Pedrito had been struck by the splendour of a brilliant court, and had conceived the idea of an existence for himself where, like the Duc de Morny, he would associate the command of every pleasure with the conduct of political affairs and enjoy power supremely in every way. Nobody could have guessed that. And yet this was one of the immediate causes of the Monterist Revolution. This will appear less incredible by the reflection that the fundamental causes were the same as ever, rooted in the political immaturity of the people, in the indolence of the upper classes and the mental darkness of the lower.

Pedrito Montero saw in the elevation of his brother the road wide open to his wildest imaginings. This was what made the Monterist *pronunciamiento* so unpreventable. The general himself probably could have been bought off, pacified with flatteries, dispatched on a diplomatic mission to Europe. It was his brother who had egged him on from first to last. He wanted to become the most brilliant statesman of South America. He did not desire supreme power. He would have been afraid of its labour and risk, in fact. Before all, Pedrito Montero, taught by his European experience, meant to acquire a serious fortune for himself. With this object in view he obtained from his brother, on the very morrow of the successful battle, the permission to push on over the mountains and take possession of Sulaco. Sulaco was the land of future prosperity, the chosen land of material progress, the only province in the Republic of interest to European capitalists. Pedrito Montero, following the example of the Duc de Morny, meant to have his share of this prosperity. This is what he meant literally. Now his brother was master of the country, whether as president, dictator, or even as Emperor – why not as an Emperor? – he meant to demand a share in every enterprise – in railways, in mines, in sugar estates, in cotton mills, in land companies, in each and every undertaking – as the price of his protection. The desire to be on the spot early was the real cause of the celebrated ride over the mountains with some two hundred *llaneros*, an enterprise of which the dangers had not appeared at first clearly to his impatience. Coming from a series of victories, it seemed to him that a Montero had only to appear to be master of the situation. This illusion had betrayed him into a rashness of which he was becoming aware. As he rode at the head of his *llaneros* he regretted that there were so few of them. The enthusiasm of the populace reassured him. They yelled '*Viva Montero! Viva Pedrito*!' In order to make them still more enthusiastic, and from the natural pleasure he had in dissembling, he dropped the reins on his horse's neck, and with a tremendous effect of familiarity and confidence slipped his hands under the arms of Señores Fuentes and Gamacho. In that posture, with a ragged town *mozo* holding his horse by the bridle, he rode triumphantly across the Plaza to the door of the Intendencia. Its old gloomy walls seemed to shake in the acclamations that rent the air and covered the crashing peals of the cathedral bells.

Pedro Montero, the brother of the general, dismounted into a shouting and perspiring throng of enthusiasts whom the ragged Nationals were pushing back fiercely. Ascending a few steps he surveyed the large crowd gaping at him and the bullet-speckled walls of the houses opposite lightly veiled by a sunny haze of dust. The word 'PORVENIR' in immense black capitals, alternating with broken windows, stared at him across the vast space; and he thought with delight of the hour of vengeance, because he was very sure of laying his hands upon Decoud. On his left hand, Gamacho, big and hot, wiping his hairy wet face, uncovered a set of yellow fangs in a grin of stupid hilarity. On his right, Señor Fuentes, small and lean, looked on with compressed lips. The crowd stared literally open-mouthed, lost in eager stillness, as though they had expected the great *guerrillero*, the famous Pedrito, to begin scattering at once some sort of visible largesse.

What he began was a speech. He began it with the shouted word 'Citizens!' which reached even those in the middle of the Plaza. Afterwards the greater part of the citizens remained fascinated by the orator's action alone, his tip-toeing, the arms flung above his head with the fists clenched, a hand laid flat upon the heart, the silver gleam of rolling eyes, the sweeping, pointing, embracing gestures, a hand laid familiarly on Gamacho's shoulder; a hand waved formally towards the little black-coated person of Señor Fuentes, advocate and politician and a true friend of the people. The '*Vivas*!' of those nearest to the orator bursting out suddenly propagated themselves irregularly to the confines of the crowd, like flames running over dry grass, and expired in the opening of the streets. In the intervals, over the swarming Plaza brooded a heavy silence, in which the mouth of the orator went on opening and shutting, and detached phrases – 'The happiness of the people', 'Sons of the country', 'The entire world, *el mundo entiero*' – reached even the packed steps of the cathedral with a feeble clear ring, thin as the buzzing of a mosquito. But the orator struck his breast; he seemed to prance between his two supporters. It was the supreme effort of his peroration. Then the two smaller figures disappeared from the public gaze and the enormous Gamacho, left alone, advanced, raising his hat high above his head. Then he covered himself proudly and yelled out, '*Ciudadanos*!' A dull roar greeted Señor Gamacho, ex-pedlar of the Campo, Comandante of the National Guard.

Upstairs Pedrito Montero walked about rapidly from one wrecked room of the Intendencia to another, snarling incessantly:

'What stupidity! What destruction!'

Señor Fuentes, following, would relax his taciturn disposition to murmur:

'It is all the work of Gamacho and his Nationals'; and then, inclining his head on his left shoulder, would press together his lips so firmly that a little hollow would appear at each corner. He had his nomination for Political Chief of the town in his pocket, and was all impatience to enter upon his functions.

In the long audience-room, with its tall mirrors all starred by stones, the hangings torn down, and the canopy over the platform at the upper end pulled to pieces, the vast, deep muttering of the crowd and the howling voice of Gamacho speaking just below reached them through the shutters as they stood idly in dimness and desolation.

'The brute!' observed his Excellency Don Pedro Montero through clenched teeth. 'We must contrive as quickly as possible to send him and his Nationals out there to fight Hernandez.'

The new Jefe Político only jerked his head sideways, and took a puff at his cigarette in sign of his agreement with this method for ridding the town of Gamacho and his inconvenient rabble.

Pedrito Montero looked with disgust at the absolutely bare floor, and at the belt of heavy gilt picture-frames running round the room, out of which the remnants of torn and slashed canvases fluttered like dingy rags.

'We are not barbarians,' he said.

This was what his Excellency said, the popular Pedrito, the *guerrillero* skilled in the art of laying ambushes, charged by his brother at his own demand with the organization of Sulaco on democratic principles. The night before, during the consultation with his partisans, who had come out to meet him in Rincón, he had opened his intentions to Señor Fuentes:

'We shall organize a popular vote, by yes or no, confiding the destinies of our beloved country to the wisdom and valiance of my heroic brother, the invincible general. A plebiscite. Do you understand?'

And Señor Fuentes, puffing out his leathery cheeks, had inclined his head slightly to the left, letting a thin, bluish jet of smoke escape through his pursed lips. He had understood.

His Excellency was exasperated at the devastation. Not a single chair, table, sofa, *étagère*, or console had been left in the state rooms of the Intendencia. His Excellency, though twitching all over with rage, was restrained from bursting into violence by a sense of his remoteness and isolation. His heroic brother was very far away. Meantime, how was he going to take his siesta? He had expected to find comfort and luxury in the Intendencia after a year of hard camp life, ending with the hardships and privations of the daring dash upon Sulaco – upon the province which was worth more in wealth and influence than all the rest of the Republic's territory. He would get even with Gamacho by-and-by. And Señor Gamacho's oration, delectable to popular ears, went on in the heat and glare of the Plaza like the uncouth howlings of an inferior sort of devil cast into a white-hot furnace. Every moment he had to wipe his streaming face with his bare forearm; he had flung off his coat, and had turned up the sleeves of his shirt high above the elbows; but he kept on his head the large cocked hat with white plumes. His ingenuousness cherished this sign of his rank as Comandante of the National Guard. Approving and grave murmurs greeted his periods. His opinion was that war should be declared at once against France, England, Germany, and the United States, who, by introducing railways, mining enterprises, colonization, and under such other shallow pretences, aimed at robbing poor people of their lands, and with the help of these Goths and paralytics, the aristocrats would convert them into toiling and miserable slaves. And the *leperos*, flinging about the corners of their dirty white mantas, yelled their approbation. General Montero, Gamacho howled with conviction, was the only man equal to the patriotic task. They assented to that, too.

The morning was wearing on; there were already signs of disruption, currents and eddies in the crowd. Some were seeking the shade of the walls and under the trees of the Alameda. Horsemen spurred through, shouting; groups of sombreros set level on heads against the vertical sun were drifting away into the streets, where the open doors of *pulperías* revealed an enticing gloom resounding with the gentle tinkling of guitars. The National Guards were thinking of siesta, and the eloquence of Gamacho, their chief, was exhausted. Later on, when, in the cooler hours of the afternoon, they tried to assemble again for further consideration of public affairs, detachments of Montero's cavalry camped on the Alameda charged them without parley, at speed, with long lances levelled at their flying backs as far as the ends of the streets. The National Guards of Sulaco were surprised by this proceeding. But they were not indignant. No Costaguanero had ever learned to question the eccentricities of a military force. They were part of the natural order of things. This must be, they concluded, some kind of administrative measure, no doubt. But the motive of it escaped their unaided intelligence, and their chief and orator, Gamacho, Comandante of the National Guard, was lying drunk and asleep in the bosom of his family. His bare feet were upturned in the shadows repulsively, in the manner of a corpse. His eloquent mouth had dropped open. His youngest daughter, scratching her head with one hand, with the other waved a green bough over his scorched and peeling face.

Chapter VI

The declining sun had shifted the shadows from west to east amongst the houses of the town. It had shifted them upon the whole extent of the immense Campo, with the white walls of its *haciendas* on the knolls dominating the green distances; with its grass-thatched *ranchos* crouching in the folds of ground by the banks of streams; with the dark islands of clustered trees on a clear sea of grass, and the precipitous range of the Cordillera, immense and motionless, emerging from the billows of the lower forests like the barren coast of a land of giants. The sunset rays striking the snow-slope of Higuerota from afar gave it an air of rosy youth, while the serrated mass of distant peaks remained black, as if calcined in the fiery radiance. The undulating surface of the forests seemed powdered with pale gold dust; and away there, beyond Rincón, hidden from the town by two wooded spurs, the rocks of the San Tomé gorge, with the flat wall of the mountain itself crowned by gigantic ferns, took on warm tones of brown and yellow, with red rusty streaks, and the dark green clumps of bushes rooted in crevices. From the plain the stamp sheds and the houses of the mine appeared dark and small, high up, like the nests of birds clustered on the ledges of a cliff. The zigzag paths resembled faint tracings scratched on the wall of a cyclopean blockhouse. To the two *serenos* of the mine on patrol duty, strolling, carbine in hand, and watchful eyes, in the shade of the trees lining the stream near the bridge, Don Pepe, descending the path from the upper plateau, appeared no bigger than a large beetle.

With his air of aimless, insect-like going to and fro upon the face of the rock, Don Pepe's figure kept on descending steadily, and, when near the bottom, sank at last behind the roofs of storehouses, forges, and workshops. For a time the pair of *serenos* strolled back and forth before the bridge, on which they had stopped a horseman holding a large white envelope in his hand. Then Don Pepe, emerging in the village street from amongst the houses, not a stone's throw from the frontier bridge, approached, striding in wide dark trousers tucked into boots, a white linen jacket, sabre at his side, and revolver at his belt. In this disturbed time nothing could find the Señor Gobernador with his boots off, as the saying is.

At a slight nod from one of the *serenos*, the man, a messenger from the town, dismounted, and crossed the bridge, leading his horse by the bridle.

Don Pepe received the letter from his other hand, slapped his left side and his hips in succession, feeling for his spectacle case. After settling the heavy silver-mounted affair astride his nose, and adjusting it carefully behind his ears, he opened the envelope, holding it up at about a foot in front of his eyes. The paper he pulled out contained some three lines of writing. He looked at them for a long time. His grey moustache moved slightly up and down, and the wrinkles, radiating at the corners of his eyes, ran together. He nodded serenely. '*Bueno*,' he said. 'There is no answer.'

Then, in his quiet, kindly way, he engaged in a cautious conversation with the man, who was willing to talk cheerily, as if something lucky had happened to him recently. He had seen from a distance Sotillo's infantry camped along the shore of the harbour on each side of the Custom House. They had done no damage to the buildings. The foreigners of the railway remained shut up within the yards. They were no longer anxious to shoot poor people. He cursed the foreigners; then he reported Montero's entry and the rumours of the town. The poor were going to be made rich now. That was very good. More he did not know, and, breaking into propitiatory smiles, he intimated that he was hungry and thirsty. The old major directed him to go to the *alcalde* of the first village. The man rode off, and Don Pepe, striding slowly in the direction of a little wooden belfry, looked over a hedge into a little garden, and saw Father Román sitting in a white hammock slung between two orange trees in front of the presbytery.

An enormous tamarind shaded with its dark foliage the whole white frame-house. A young Indian girl with long hair, big eyes, and small hands and feet, carried out a wooden chair, while a thin old woman, crabbed and vigilant, watched her all the time from the veranda.

Don Pepe sat down in the chair and lighted a cigar; the priest drew in an immense quantity of snuff out of the hollow of his palm. On his reddish-brown face, worn, hollowed as if crumbled, the eyes, fresh and candid, sparkled like two black diamonds.

Don Pepe informed Father Román in a mild and humorous voice that Pedrito Montero, by the hand of Señor Fuentes, had asked him on what terms he would surrender the mine in proper working order to a legally constituted commission of patriotic citizens, escorted by a small military force. The priest cast his eyes up to heaven. However, Don Pepe continued, the *mozo* who brought the letter said that Don Carlos Gould was alive, and so far unmolested.

Father Román expressed in a few words his thankfulness at hearing of the Señor Administrador's safety.

The hour of oration had gone by in silvery ringing of a bell in the little belfry. The belt of forest closing the entrance of the valley stood like a screen between the low sun and the street of the village. At the other end of the rocky gorge, between the walls of basalt and granite, a forest-clad mountain, hiding all the range from the San Tomé dwellers, rose steeply, lighted up and leafy to the very top. Three small rosy clouds hung motionless overhead in the great depth of blue. Knots of people sat in the street between the wattled huts. Before the *casa* of the *alcalde*, the foremen of the night-shift, already assembled to lead their men, squatted on the ground in a circle of leather skull-caps, and, bowing their bronze backs, were passing round the gourd of maté. The *mozo* from the town, having fastened his horse to a wooden post before the door, was telling them the news of Sulaco as the blackened gourd of the decoction passed from hand to hand. The grave *alcalde* himself, in a white waist-cloth and a flowered chintz gown with sleeves, open wide upon his naked stout person with an effect of a gaudy bathing robe, stood by, wearing a rough beaver hat at the back of his head, and grasping a tall staff with a silver knob in his hand. These insignia of his dignity had been conferred upon him by the Administration of the mine, the fountain of honour, of prosperity, and peace. He had been one of the first immigrants into this valley; his sons and sons-in-law worked within the mountain which seemed with its treasures to pour down the thundering ore shoots of the upper *mesa*, the gifts of well-being, security, and justice upon the toilers. He listened to the news from the town with curiosity and indifference, as if concerning a world other than his own. And it was true that they appeared to him so. In a very few years the sense of belonging to a powerful organization had been developed in these harassed, half-wild Indians. They were proud of, and attached to, the mine. It had secured their confidence and belief. They invested it with a protecting and invincible virtue as though it were a fetish made by their own hands, for they were ignorant, and in other respects did not differ appreciably from the rest of mankind which puts infinite trust in its own creations. It never entered the *alcalde*'s head that the mine could fail in its protection and force. Politics were good enough for the people of the town and the Campo. His yellow, round face, with wide nostrils, and motionless in expression, resembled a fierce full moon. He listened to the excited vapourings of the *mozo* without misgivings, without surprise, without any active sentiment whatever.

Padre Román sat dejectedly balancing himself, his feet just touching the ground, his hands gripping the edge of the hammock. With less confidence, but as ignorant as his flock, he asked the major what he thought was going to happen now.

Don Pepe, bolt upright in the chair, folded his hands peacefully on the hilt of his sword, standing perpendicular between his thighs, and answered that he did not know. The mine could be defended against any force likely to be sent to take possession. On the other hand, from the arid character of the valley, when the regular supplies from the Campo had been cut off, the population of the three villages could be starved into submission. Don Pepe exposed these contingencies with serenity to Father Román, who, as an old campaigner, was able to understand the reasoning of a military man. They talked with simplicity and directness. Father Román was saddened at the idea of his flock being scattered or else enslaved. He had no illusions as to their fate, not from penetration, but from long experience of political atrocities, which seemed to him fatal and unavoidable in the life of a State. The working of the usual public institutions presented itself to him most distinctly as a series of calamities overtaking private individuals and flowing logically from each other through hate, revenge, folly, and rapacity, as though they had been part of a divine dispensation. Father Román's clearsightedness was served by an uninformed intelligence; but his heart, preserving its tenderness amongst scenes of carnage, spoliation, and violence, abhorred these calamities the more as his association with the victims was closer. He entertained towards the Indians of the valley feelings of paternal scorn. He had been marrying, baptizing, confessing, absolving, and burying the workers of the San Tomé mine with dignity and unction for five years or more; and he believed in the sacredness of these ministrations, which made them his own in a spiritual sense. They were dear to his sacerdotal supremacy. Mrs Gould's earnest interest in the concerns of these people enhanced their importance in the priest's eyes, because it really augmented his own. When talking over with her the innumerable Marias and Brigidas of the villages, he felt his own humanity expand. Padre Román was incapable of fanaticism to an almost reprehensible degree. The English *señora* was evidently a heretic; but at the same time she seemed to him wonderful and angelic. Whenever that confused state of his feelings occurred to him, while strolling, for instance, his breviary under his arm, in the wide shade of the tamarind, he would stop short to inhale with a strong snuffling noise a large quantity of snuff, and shake his head profoundly. At the thought of what might befall the illustrious *señora* presently, he became gradually overcome with dismay. He voiced it in an agitated murmur. Even Don Pepe lost his serenity for a moment. He leaned forward stiffly.

'Listen, Padre. The very fact that those thieving *macaques* in Sulaco are trying to find out the price of my honour proves that Señor Don Carlos and all in the Casa Gould are safe. As to my honour, that also is safe, as every man, woman, and child knows. But the Negro liberals who have snatched the town by surprise do not know that. *Bueno*. Let them sit and wait. While they wait they can do no harm.'

And he regained his composure. He regained it easily, because whatever happened his honour of an old officer of Paez was safe. He had promised Charles Gould that at the approach of an armed force he would defend the gorge just long enough to give himself time to destroy scientifically the whole plant, buildings, and workshops of the mine with heavy charges of dynamite; block with ruins the main tunnel, break down the pathways, blow up the dam of the water-power, shatter the famous Gould Concession into fragments, flying sky-high out of a horrified world. The mine had got hold of Charles Gould with a grip as deadly as ever it had laid upon his father. But this extreme resolution had seemed to Don Pepe the most natural thing in the world. His measures had been taken with judgement. Everything was prepared with a careful completeness. And Don Pepe folded his hands pacifically on his sword hilt, and nodded at the priest. In his excitement, Father Román had flung snuff in handfuls at his face, and, all besmeared with tobacco, round-eyed, and beside himself, had got out of the hammock to walk about, uttering exclamations.

Don Pepe stroked his grey and pendant moustache, whose fine ends hung far below the clean-cut line of his jaw, and spoke with conscious pride in his reputation.

'So, Padre, I don't know what will happen. But I know that as long as I am here Don Carlos can speak to that *macaque*, Pedrito Montero, and threaten the destruction of the mine with perfect assurance that he will be taken seriously. For people know me.'

He began to turn the cigar in his lips a little nervously, and went on:

'But that is talk – good for the *políticos*. I am a military man. I do not know what may happen. But I know what ought to be done – the mine should march upon the town with guns, axes, knives tied up to sticks – *por Dios*. That is what should be done. Only –'

His folded hands twitched on the hilt. The cigar turned faster in the corner of his lips.

'And who should lead but I? Unfortunately – observe – I have given my word of honour to Don Carlos not to let the mine fall into the hands of these thieves. In war – you know this, Padre – the fate of battles is uncertain, and whom could I leave here to act for me in case of defeat? The explosives are ready. But it would require a man of high honour, of intelligence, of judgement, of courage, to carry out the prepared destruction. Somebody I can trust with my honour as I can trust myself. Another officer of Paez, for instance. Or – or – perhaps one of Paez's old chaplains would do.'

He got up, long, lank, upright, hard, with his martial moustache and the bony structure of his face, from which the glance of the sunken eyes seemed to transfix the priest, who stood still, an empty wooden snuff-box held upside down in his hand, and glared back, speechless, at the governor of the mine.

Chapter VII

At about that time, in the Intendencia of Sulaco, Charles Gould was assuring Pedrito Montero, who had sent a request for his presence there, that he would never let the mine pass out of his hands for the profit of a Government who had robbed him of it. The Gould Concession could not be resumed. His father had not desired it. The son would never surrender it. He would never surrender it alive. And once dead, where was the power capable of resuscitating such an enterprise in all its vigour and wealth out of the ashes and ruin of destruction? There was no such power in the country. And where was the skill and capital abroad that would condescend to touch such an ill-omened corpse? Charles Gould talked in the impassive tone which had for many years served to conceal his anger and contempt. He suffered. He was disgusted with what he had to say. It was too much like heroics. In him the strictly practical instinct was in profound discord with the almost mystic view he took of his right. The Gould Concession was symbolic of abstract justice. Let the heavens fall. But since the San Tomé mine had developed its world-wide fame his threat had enough force and effectiveness to reach the rudimentary intelligence of Pedro Montero, wrapped up as it was in the futilities of historical anecdotes. The Gould Concession was a serious asset in the country's finance, and, what was more, in the private budgets of many officials as well. It was traditional. It was known. It was said. It was credible. Every Minister of Interior drew a salary from the San Tomé mine. It was natural. And Pedrito intended to be Minister of the Interior and President of the Council in his brother's Government. The Duc de Morny had occupied those high posts during the Second French Empire with conspicuous advantage to himself.

A table, a chair, a wooden bedstead had been procured for His Excellency, who, after a short siesta, rendered absolutely necessary by the labours and the pomps of his entry into Sulaco, had been getting hold of the administrative machine by making appointments, giving orders, and signing proclamations.

Alone with Charles Gould in the audience room, His Excellency managed with his well-known skill to conceal his annoyance and consternation. He had begun at first to talk loftily of confiscation, but the want of all proper feeling and mobility in the Señor Administrador's features ended by affecting adversely his power of masterful expression. Charles Gould had repeated: 'The Government can certainly bring about the destruction of the San Tomé mine if it likes; but without me it can do nothing else.' It was an alarming pronouncement, and well calculated to hurt the sensibilities of a politician whose mind is bent upon the spoils of victory. And Charles Gould said also that the destruction of the San Tomé mine would cause the ruin of other undertakings, the withdrawal of European capital, the withholding, most probably, of the last instalment of the foreign loan. That stony fiend of a man said all these things (which were accessible to His Excellency's intelligence) in a cold-blooded manner which made one shudder.

A long course of reading historical works, light and gossipy in tone, carried out in garrets of Parisian hotels, sprawling on an untidy bed, to the neglect of his duties, menial or otherwise, had affected the manners of Pedro Montero. Had he seen around him the splendour of the old Intendencia, the magnificent hangings, the gilt furniture ranged along the walls; had he stood upon a daïs on a noble square of red carpet, he would probably have been very dangerous from a sense of success and elevation. But in this sacked and devastated residence, with the three pieces of common furniture huddled up in the middle of the vast apartment, Pedrito's imagination was subdued by a feeling of insecurity and impermanence. That feeling and the firm attitude of Charles Gould who had not once, so far, pronounced the word 'Excellency', diminished him in his own eyes. He assumed the tone of an enlightened man of the world, and begged Charles Gould to dismiss from his mind every cause for alarm. He was now conversing, he reminded him, with the brother of the master of the country, charged with a reorganizing mission. The trusted brother of the master of the country, he repeated. Nothing was farther from the thoughts of that wise and patriotic hero than ideas of destruction. 'I entreat you, Don Carlos, not to give way to your anti-democratic prejudices,' he cried, in a burst of condescending effusion.

Pedrito Montero surprised one at first sight by the vast development of his bald forehead, a shiny yellow expanse between the crinkly coal-black tufts of hair without any lustre, the engaging form of his mouth, and an unexpectedly cultivated voice. But his eyes, very glistening as if freshly painted on each side of his hooked nose, had a round, hopeless, birdlike stare when opened fully. Now, however, he narrowed them agreeably, throwing his square chin up and speaking with closed teeth slightly through the nose, with what he imagined to be the manner of a *grand seigneur*.

In that attitude, he declared suddenly that the highest expression of democracy was Caesarism: the imperial rule based upon the direct popular vote. Caesarism was conservative. It was strong. It recognized the legitimate needs of democracy which requires orders, titles, and distinctions. They would be showered upon deserving men. Caesarism was peace. It was progressive. It secured the prosperity of a country. Pedrito Montero was carried away. Look at what the Second Empire had done in France. It was a régime which delighted to honour men of Don Carlos's stamp. The Second Empire fell, but that was because its chief was devoid of that military genius which had raised General Montero to the pinnacle of fame and glory. Pedrito elevated his hand jerkily to help the idea of pinnacle, of fame. 'We shall have many talks yet. We shall understand each other thoroughly, Don Carlos!' he cried in a tone of fellowship. Republicanism had done its work. Imperial democracy was the power of the future. Pedrito, the *guerrillero*, showing his hand, lowered his voice forcibly. A man singled out by his fellow-citizens for the honourable nickname of El Rey de Sulaco could not but receive a full recognition from an imperial democracy as a great captain of industry and a person of weighty counsel, whose popular designation would be soon replaced by a more solid title. 'Eh, Don Carlos? No! What do you say? Conde de Sulaco – Eh? – or marquis . . .'

He ceased. The air was cool on the Plaza, where a patrol of cavalry rode round and round without penetrating into the streets, which resounded with shouts and the strumming of guitars issuing from the open doors of *pulperías*. The orders were not to interfere with the enjoyments of the people. And above the roofs, next to the perpendicular lines of the cathedral towers, the snowy curve of Higuerota blocked a large space of darkening blue sky before the windows of the Intendencia. After a time Pedrito Montero, thrusting his hand in the bosom of his coat, bowed his head with slow dignity. The audience was over.

Charles Gould on going out passed his hand over his forehead as if to disperse the mists of an oppressive dream, whose grotesque extravagance leaves behind a subtle sense of bodily danger and intellectual decay. In the passages and on the staircases of the old palace Montero's troopers lounged about insolently, smoking and making way for no one; the clanking of sabres and spurs resounded all over the building. Three silent groups of civilians in severe black waited in the main gallery, formal and helpless, a little huddled up, each keeping apart from the others, as if in the exercise of a public duty they had been overcome by a desire to shun the notice of every eye. These were the deputations waiting for their audience. The one from the Provincial Assembly, more restless and uneasy in its corporate expression, was overtopped by the big face of Don Juste Lopez, soft and white, with prominent eyelids and wreathed in impenetrable solemnity as if in a dense cloud. The President of the Provincial Assembly, coming bravely to save the last shred of parliamentary institutions (on the English model), averted his eyes from the Administrador of the San Tomé mine as a dignified rebuke of his little faith in that only saving principle.

The mournful severity of that reproof did not affect Charles Gould, but he was sensible to the glances of the others directed upon him without reproach, as if only to read their own fate upon his face. All of them had talked, shouted, and declaimed in the great *sala* of the Casa Gould. The feeling of compassion for those men, struck with a strange impotence in the toils of moral degradation, did not induce him to make a sign. He suffered from his fellowship in evil with them too much. He crossed the Plaza unmolested. The Amarilla Club was full of festive ragamuffins. Their frowsy heads protruded from every window, and from within came drunken shouts, the thumping of feet, and the twanging of harps.

Broken bottles strewed the pavement below. Charles Gould found the doctor still in his house.

Dr Monygham came away from the crack in the shutter through which he had been watching the street.

'Ah! You are back at last!' he said in a tone of relief. 'I have been telling Mrs Gould that you were perfectly safe, but I was not by any means certain that the fellow would have let you go.'

'Neither was I,' confessed Charles Gould, laying his hat on the table.

'You will have to take action.'

The silence of Charles Gould seemed to admit that this was the only course. This was as far as Charles Gould was accustomed to go towards expressing his intentions.

'I hope you did not warn Montero of what you mean to do,' the doctor said, anxiously.

'I tried to make him see that the existence of the mine was bound up with my personal safety,' continued Charles Gould, looking away from the doctor, and fixing his eyes upon the water-colour sketch upon the wall.

'He believed you?' the doctor asked, eagerly.

'God knows!' said Charles Gould. 'I owed it to my wife to say that much. He is well enough informed. He knows that I have Don Pepe there. Fuentes must have told him. They know that the old major is perfectly capable of blowing up the San Tomé mine without hesitation or compunction. Had it not been for that I don't think I'd have left the Intendencia a free man. He would blow everything up from loyalty and from hate – from hate of these Liberals, as they call themselves. Liberals! The words one knows so well have a nightmarish meaning in this country. Liberty, democracy, patriotism, government – all of them have a flavour of folly and murder. Haven't they, doctor? . . . I alone can restrain Don Pepe. If they were to – to do away with me, nothing could prevent him.'

'They will try to tamper with him,' the doctor suggested, thoughtfully.

'It is very possible,' Charles Gould said very low, as if speaking to himself, and still gazing at the sketch of the San Tomé gorge upon the wall. 'Yes, I expect they will try that.' Charles Gould looked for the first time at the doctor. 'It would give me time,' he added.

'Exactly,' said Dr Monygham, suppressing his excitement. 'Especially if Don Pepe behaves diplomatically. Why shouldn't he give them some hope of success? Eh? Otherwise you wouldn't gain so much time. Couldn't he be instructed to –'

Charles Gould, looking at the doctor steadily, shook his head, but the doctor continued with a certain amount of fire:

'Yes, to enter into negotiations for the surrender of the mine. It is a good notion. You would mature your plan. Of course, I don't ask what it is. I don't want to know. I would refuse to listen to you if you tried to tell me. I am not fit for confidences.'

'What nonsense!' muttered Charles Gould, with displeasure.

He disapproved of the doctor's sensitiveness about that far-off episode of his life. So much memory shocked Charles Gould. It was like morbidness. And again he shook his head. He refused to tamper with the open rectitude of Don Pepe's conduct, both from taste and from policy. Instructions would have to be either verbal or in writing. In either case they ran the risk of being intercepted. It was by no means certain that a messenger could reach the mine; and, besides, there was no one to send. It was on the tip of Charles's tongue to say that only the late Capataz de Cargadores could have been employed with some chance of success and the certitude of discretion. But he did not say that. He pointed out to the doctor that it would have been bad policy. Directly Don Pepe let it be supposed that he could be bought over, the Administrador's personal safety and the safety of his friends would become endangered. For there would be then no reason for moderation. The incorruptibility of Don Pepe was the essential and restraining fact. The doctor hung his head and admitted that in a way it was so.

He couldn't deny to himself that the reasoning was sound enough. Don Pepe's usefulness consisted in his unstained character. As to his own usefulness, he reflected bitterly, it was also his own character. He declared to Charles Gould that he had the means of keeping Sotillo from joining his forces with Montero, at least for the present.

'If you had had all this silver here,' the doctor said, 'or even if it had been known to be at the mine, you could have bribed Sotillo to throw off his recent Monterism. You could have induced him either to go away in his steamer or even to join you.'

'Certainly not that last,' Charles Gould declared, firmly. 'What could one do with a man like that, afterwards – tell me, doctor? The silver is gone, and I am glad of it. It would have been an immediate and strong temptation. The scramble for that visible plunder would have precipitated a disastrous ending. I would have had to defend it, too. I am glad we've removed it – even if it is lost. It would have been a danger and a curse.'

'Perhaps he is right,' the doctor, an hour later, said hurriedly to Mrs Gould, whom he met in the corridor. 'The thing is done, and the shadow of the treasure may do just as well as the substance. Let me try to serve you to the whole extent of my evil reputation. I am off now to play my game of betrayal with Sotillo, and keep him off the town.'

She put out both her hands impulsively. 'Dr Monygham, you are running a terrible risk,' she whispered, averting from his face her eyes, full of tears, for a short glance at the door of her husband's room. She pressed both his hands, and the doctor stood as if rooted to the spot, looking down at her, and trying to twist his lips into a smile.

'Oh, I know you will defend my memory,' he uttered at last, and ran tottering down the stairs across the patio, and out of the house. In the street he kept up a great pace with his smart hobbling walk, a case of instruments under his arm. He was known for being *loco*. Nobody interfered with him. From under the seaward gate, across the dusty, arid plain, interspersed with low bushes, he saw, more than a mile away, the ugly enormity of the Custom House, and the two or three other buildings which at that time constituted the seaport of Sulaco. Far away to the south groves of palm trees edged the curve of the harbour shore. The distant peaks of the Cordillera had lost their identity of clear-cut shapes in the steadily deepening blue of the eastern sky. The doctor walked briskly. A darkling shadow seemed to fall upon him from the zenith. The sun had set. For a time the snows of Higuerota continued to glow with the reflected glory of the west. The doctor, holding a straight course for the Custom House, appeared lonely, hopping amongst the dark bushes like a tall bird with a broken wing.

Tints of purple, gold, and crimson were mirrored in the clear water of the harbour. A long tongue of land, straight as a wall, with the grass-grown ruins of the fort making a sort of rounded green mound, plainly visible from the inner shore, closed its circuit; while beyond the Placid Gulf repeated those splendours of colouring on a greater scale and with a more sombre magnificence. The great mass of cloud filling the head of the gulf had long red smears amongst its convoluted folds of grey and black, as of a floating mantle stained with blood. The three Isabels, overshadowed and clear cut in a great smoothness confounding the sea and sky, appeared suspended, purple-black, in the air. The little wavelets seemed to be tossing tiny red sparks upon the sandy beaches. The glassy bands of water along the horizon gave out a fiery red glow, as if fire and water had been mingled together in the vast bed of the ocean.

At last the conflagration of sea and sky, lying embraced and still in a flaming contact upon the edge of the world, went out. The red sparks in the water vanished together with the stains of blood in the black mantle draping the sombre head of the Placid Gulf; a sudden breeze sprang up and died out after rustling heavily the growth of bushes on the ruined earthwork of the fort. Nostromo woke up from a fourteen hours' sleep, and arose full length from his lair in the long grass. He stood knee deep amongst the whispering undulations of the green blades with the lost air of a man just born into the world. Handsome, robust, and supple, he threw back his head, flung his arms open, and stretched himself with a slow twist of the waist and a leisurely growling yawn of white teeth, as natural and free from evil in the moment of waking as a magnificent and unconscious wild beast. Then, in the suddenly steadied glance fixed upon nothing from under a thoughtful frown, the man appeared.

Chapter VIII

After landing from his swim Nostromo had scrambled up, all dripping, into the main quadrangle of the old fort; and there, amongst ruined bits of walls and rotting remnants of roofs and sheds, he had slept the day through. He had slept in the shadow of the mountains, in the white blaze of noon, in the stillness and solitude of that overgrown piece of land between the oval of the harbour and the spacious semi-circle of the gulf. He lay as if dead. A *rey zamuro*, appearing like a tiny black speck in the blue, stooped, circling prudently with a stealthiness of flight startling in a bird of that great size. The shadow of his pearly-white body, of his black-tipped wings, fell on the grass no more silently than he alighted himself on a hillock of rubbish within three yards of that man, lying as still as a corpse. The bird stretched his bare neck, craned his bald head, loathsome in the brilliance of varied colouring, with an air of voracious anxiety towards the promising stillness of that prostrate body. Then, sinking his head deeply into his soft plumage, he settled himself to wait. The first thing upon which Nostromo's eyes fell on waking was this patient watcher for the signs of death and corruption.

When the man got up the vulture hopped away in great, side-long, fluttering jumps. He lingered for a while, morose and reluctant, before he rose, circling noiselessly with a sinister droop of beak and claws.

Long after he had vanished, Nostromo, lifting his eyes up to the sky, muttered, 'I am not dead yet.'

The Capataz of the Sulaco Cargadores had lived in splendour and publicity up to the very moment, as it were, when he took charge of the lighter containing the treasure of silver ingots.

The last act he had performed in Sulaco was in complete harmony with his vanity, and as such perfectly genuine. He had given his last dollar to an old woman moaning with the grief and fatigue of a dismal search under the arch of the ancient gate. Performed in obscurity and without witnesses, it had still the characteristics of splendour and publicity, and was in strict keeping with his reputation. But this awakening in solitude, except for the watchful vulture, amongst the ruins of the fort, had no such characteristics. His first confused feeling was exactly this – that it was not in keeping. It was more like the end of things. The necessity of living concealed somehow, for God knows how long, which assailed him on his return to consciousness, made everything that had gone before for years appear vain and foolish, like a flattering dream come suddenly to an end.

He climbed the crumbling slope of the rampart, and, putting aside the bushes, looked upon the harbour. He saw a couple of ships at anchor upon the sheet of water reflecting the last gleams of light, and Sotillo's steamer moored to the jetty. And behind the pale long front of the Custom House, there appeared the extent of the town like a grove of thick timber on the plain with a gateway in front, and the cupolas, towers, and miradors rising above the trees, all dark, as if surrendered already to the night. The thought that it was no longer open to him to ride through the streets, recognized by everyone, great and little, as he used to do every evening on his way to play *monte* in the *posada* of the Mexican Domingo; or to sit in the place of honour, listening to songs and looking at dances, made it appear to him as a town that had no existence.

For a long time he gazed on, then let the parted bushes spring back, and, crossing over to the other side of the fort, surveyed the vaster emptiness of the great gulf. The Isabels stood out heavily upon the narrowing long band of red in the west, which gleamed low between their black shapes, and the Capataz thought of Decoud along there with the treasure. That man was the only one who cared whether he fell into the hands of the Monterists or not, the Capataz reflected bitterly. And that merely would be an anxiety for his own sake. As to the rest, they neither knew nor cared. What he had heard Giorgio Viola say once was very true. Kings, ministers, aristocrats, the rich in general, kept the people in poverty and subjection; they kept them as they kept dogs, to fight and hunt for their service.

The darkness of the sky had descended to the line of the horizon, enveloping the whole gulf, the islets, and the lover of Antonia alone with the treasure on the Great Isabel. The Capataz, turning his back on these things invisible and existing, sat down and took his face between his fists. He felt the pinch of poverty for the first time in his life. To find himself without money after a run of bad luck at *monte* in the low, smoky room of Domingo's *posada*, where the fraternity of *cargadores* gambled, sang, and danced of an evening; to remain with empty pockets after a burst of public generosity to some *peyne d'oro* girl or other (for whom he did not care), had none of the humiliation of destitution. He remained rich in glory and reputation. But since it was no longer possible for him to parade the streets of the town, and be hailed with respect in the usual haunts of his leisure, this sailor felt himself destitute indeed.

His mouth was dry. It was dry with heavy sleep and extremely anxious thinking, as it had never been dry before. It may be said that Nostromo tasted the dust and ashes of the fruit of life into which he had bitten deeply in his hunger for praise. Without removing his head from between his fists, he tried to spit before him – 'Tfui' – and muttered a curse upon the selfishness of all the rich people.

Since everything seemed lost in Sulaco (and that was the feeling of his waking), the idea of leaving the country altogether had presented itself to Nostromo. At that thought he had seen, like the beginning of another dream, a vision of steep and tideless shores, with dark pines on the heights and white houses low down near a very blue sky. He saw the quays of a big port, where the coasting feluccas, with their lateen sails outspread like motionless wings, enter gliding silently between the end of long moles of squared blocks that project angularly towards each other, hugging a cluster of shipping to the superb bosom of a hill covered with palaces. He remembered these sights not without some filial emotion, though he had been habitually and severely beaten as a boy on one of these feluccas by a short-necked, shaven Genoese, with a deliberate and distrustful manner, who (he firmly believed) had cheated him out of his orphan's inheritance. But it is mercifully decreed that the evils of the past should appear but faintly in retrospect. Under the sense of loneliness, abandonment, and failure, the idea of return to these things appeared tolerable. But, what? Return? With bare feet and head, with one check shirt and a pair of cotton *calzoneros* for all worldly possessions?

The renowned Capataz, his elbows on his knees and a fist dug into each cheek, laughed with self-derision, as he had spat with disgust, straight out before him into the night. The confused and intimate impressions of universal dissolution which beset a subjective nature at any strong check to its ruling passion had a bitterness approaching that of death itself. He was simple. He was as ready to become the prey of any belief, superstition, or desire as a child.

The facts of his situation he could appreciate like a man with a distinct experience of the country. He saw them clearly. He was as if sobered after a long bout of intoxication. His fidelity had been taken advantage of. He had persuaded the body of *cargadores* to side with the Blancos against the rest of the people; he had had interviews with Don José; he had been made use of by Father Corbelán for negotiating with Hernandez; it was known that Don Martin Decoud had admitted him to a sort of intimacy, so that he had been free of the offices of the *Porvenir*. All these things had flattered him in the usual way. What did he care about their politics? Nothing at all. And at the end of it all – Nostromo here and Nostromo there – where is Nostromo? Nostromo can do this and that – work all day and ride all night – behold! he found himself a marked Ribierist for any sort of vengeance Gamacho, for instance, would choose to take, now the Montero party had, after all, mastered the town. The Europeans had given up; the *caballeros* had given up. Don Martin had indeed explained it was only temporary – that he was going to bring Barrios to the rescue. Where was that now – with Don Martin (whose ironic manner of talk had always made the Capataz feel vaguely uneasy) stranded on the Great Isabel? Everybody had given up. Even Don Carlos had given up. The hurried removal of the treasure out to sea meant nothing else than that. The Capataz de Cargadores, on a revulsion of subjectiveness, exasperated almost to insanity, beheld all his world without faith and courage. He had been betrayed!

With the boundless shadows of the sea behind him, out of his silence and immobility, facing the lofty shapes of the lower peaks crowded around the white, misty sheen of Higuerota, Nostromo laughed aloud again, sprang abruptly to his feet, and stood still. He must go. But where?

'There is no mistake. They keep us and encourage us as if we were dogs born to fight and hunt for them. The *vecchio* is right,' he said, slowly and scathingly. He remembered old Giorgio taking his pipe out of his mouth to throw these words over his shoulder at the café, full of engine-drivers and fitters from the railway workshops. This image fixed his wavering purpose. He would try to find old Giorgio if he could. God knows what might have happened to him! He made a few steps, then stopped again and shook his head. To the left and right, in front and behind him, the scrubby bush rustled mysteriously in the darkness.

'Teresa was right, too,' he added in a low tone touched with awe. He wondered whether she was dead in her anger with him or still alive. As if in answer to this thought, half of remorse and half of hope, with a soft flutter and oblique flight, a big owl, whose appalling cry: 'Ya-acabo! Ya-acabo! – it is finished; it is finished' – announces calamity and death in the popular belief, drifted vaguely like a large dark ball across his path. In the downfall of all the realities that made his force, he was affected by the superstition, and shuddered slightly. Signora Teresa must have died, then. It could mean nothing else. The cry of the ill-omened bird, the first sound he was to hear on his return, was a fitting welcome for his betrayed individuality. The unseen powers which he had offended by refusing to bring a priest to a dying woman were lifting up their voice against him. She was dead. With admirable and human consistency he referred everything to himself. She had been a woman of good counsel always. And the bereaved old Giorgio remained stunned by his loss just as he was likely to require the advice of his sagacity. The blow would render the dreamy old man quite stupid for a time.

As to Captain Mitchell, Nostromo, after the manner of trusted subordinates, considered him as a person fitted by education perhaps to sign papers in an office and to give orders, but otherwise of no use whatever, and something of a fool. The necessity of winding round his little finger, almost daily, the pompous and testy self-importance of the old seaman had grown irksome with use to Nostromo. At first it had given him an inward satisfaction. But the necessity of overcoming small obstacles becomes wearisome to a self-confident personality as much by the certitude of success as by the monotony of effort. He mistrusted his superior's proneness to fussy action. That old Englishman had no judgement, he said to himself. It was useless to suppose that, acquainted with the true state of the case, he would keep it to himself. He would talk of doing impracticable things. Nostromo feared him as one would fear saddling one's self with some persistent worry. He had no discretion. He would betray the treasure. And Nostromo had made up his mind that the treasure should not be betrayed.

The word had fixed itself tenaciously in his intelligence. His imagination had seized upon the clear and simple notion of betrayal to account for the dazed feeling of enlightenment as to being done for, of having inadvertently gone out of his existence on an issue in which his personality had not been taken into account. A man betrayed is a man destroyed. Signora Teresa (may God have her soul!) had been right. He had never been taken into account. Destroyed! Her white form sitting up bowed in bed, the falling black hair, the wide-browed suffering face raised to him, the anger of her denunciations appeared to him now majestic with the awfulness of inspiration and of death. For it was not for nothing that the evil bird had uttered its lamentable shriek over his head. She was dead – may God have her soul!

Sharing in the anti-priestly freethought of the masses, his mind used the pious formula from the superficial force of habit, but with a deep-seated sincerity. The popular mind is incapable of scepticism; and that incapacity delivers their helpless strength to the wiles of swindlers and to the pitiless enthusiasms of leaders inspired by visions of a high destiny. She was dead. But would God consent to receive her soul? She had died without confession or absolution, because he had not been willing to spare her another moment of his time. His scorn of priests as priests remained; but after all, it was impossible to know whether what they affirmed was not true. Power, punishment, pardon are simple and credible notions. The magnificent Capataz de Cargadores, deprived of certain simple realities, such as the admiration of women, the adulation of men, the admired publicity of his life, was ready to feel the burden of sacrilegious guilt descend upon his shoulders.

Bareheaded, in a thin shirt and drawers, he felt the lingering warmth of the fine sand under the soles of his feet. The narrow strand gleamed far ahead in a long curve, defining the outline of this wild side of the harbour. He flitted along the shore like a pursued shadow between the sombre palm-groves and the sheet of water lying as still as death on his right hand. He strode with headlong haste in the silence and solitude as though he had forgotten all prudence and caution. But he knew that on this side of the water he ran no risk of discovery. The only inhabitant was a lonely, silent, apathetic Indian in charge of the *palmarías*, who brought sometimes a load of coconuts to the town for sale. He lived without a woman in an open shed, with a perpetual fire of dry sticks smouldering near an old canoe lying bottom up on the beach. He could be easily avoided.

The barking of the dogs about that man's *ranche* was the first thing that checked his speed. He had forgotten the dogs. He swerved sharply, and plunged into the palm-grove, as into a wilderness of columns in an immense hall, whose dense obscurity seemed to whisper and rustle faintly high above his head. He traversed it, entered a ravine, and climbed to the top of a steep ridge free of trees and bushes.

From there, open and vague in the starlight, he saw the plain between the town and the harbour. In the woods above some night-bird made a strange drumming noise. Below beyond the *palamaría* on the beach, the Indian's dogs continued to bark uproariously. He wondered what had upset them so much, and, peering down from his elevation, was surprised to detect accountable movements of the ground below, as if several oblong pieces of the plain had been in motion. Those dark, shifting patches, alternately catching and eluding the eye, altered their place always away from the harbour, with a suggestion of consecutive order and purpose. A light dawned upon him. It was a column of infantry on a night march towards the higher broken country at the foot of the hills. But he was too much in the dark about everything for wonder and speculation.

The plain had resumed its shadowy immobility. He descended the ridge and found himself in the open solitude, between the harbour and the town. Its spaciousness, extended indefinitely by an effect of obscurity, rendered more sensible his profound isolation. His pace became slower. No one waited for him; no one thought of him; no one expected or wished his return. 'Betrayed! Betrayed!' he muttered to himself. No one cared. He might have been drowned by this time. No one would have cared – unless, perhaps, the children, he thought to himself. But they were with the English *signora*, and not thinking of him at all.

He wavered in his purpose of making straight for the Casa Viola. To what end? What could he expect there? His life seemed to fail him in all its details, even to the scornful reproaches of Teresa. He was aware painfully of his reluctance. Was it that remorse which she had prophesied with, what he saw now, was her last breath?

Meantime, he had deviated from the straight course, inclining by a sort of instinct to the left, towards the jetty and the harbour, the scene of his daily labours. The great length of the Custom House loomed up all at once like the wall of a factory. Not a soul challenged his approach, and his curiosity became excited as he passed cautiously towards the front by the unexpected sight of two lighted windows.

They had the fascination of a lonely vigil kept by some mysterious watcher up there, those two windows shining dimly upon the harbour in the whole vast extent of the abandoned building. The solitude could almost be felt. A strong smell of wood smoke hung about in a thin haze, which was faintly perceptible to his raised eyes against the glitter of the stars. As he advanced in the profound silence, the shrilling of innumerable cicadas in the dry grass seemed positively deafening to his strained ears. Slowly, step by step, he found himself in the great hall, sombre and full of acrid smoke.

A fire built against the staircase had burnt down impotently to a low heap of embers. The hard wood had failed to catch; only a few steps at the bottom smouldered, with a creeping glow of sparks defining their charred edges. At the top he saw a streak of light from an open door. It fell upon the vast landing, all foggy with a slow drift of smoke. That was the room. He climbed the stairs, then checked himself, because he had seen within the shadow of a man cast upon one of the walls. It was a shapeless, high-shouldered shadow of somebody standing still, with lowered head, out of his line of sight. The Capataz, remembering that he was totally unarmed, stepped aside, and, effacing himself upright in a dark corner, waited with his eyes fixed on the door.

The whole enormous ruined barrack of a place, unfinished, without ceilings under its lofty roof, was pervaded by the smoke swaying to and fro in the faint cross-draughts playing in the obscurity of many lofty rooms and barnlike passages. Once one of the swinging shutters came against the wall with a single sharp crack, as if pushed by an impatient hand. A piece of paper scurried out from somewhere, rustling along the landing. The man, whoever he was, did not darken the lighted doorway. Twice the Capataz, advancing a couple of steps out of his corner, craned his neck in the hope of catching sight of what he could be at, so quietly, in there. But every time he saw only the distorted shadow of broad shoulders and bowed head. He was doing apparently nothing, and stirred not from the spot, as though he were meditating – or, perhaps, reading a paper. And not a sound issued from the room.

Once more the Capataz stepped back. He wondered who it was – some Monterist? But he dreaded to show himself. To discover his presence on shore, unless after many days, would, he believed, endanger the treasure. With his own knowledge possessing his whole soul, it seemed impossible that anybody in Sulaco should fail to jump at the right surmise. After a couple of weeks or so it would be different. Who could tell he had not returned overland from some port beyond the limits of the Republic? The existence of the treasure confused his thoughts with a peculiar sort of anxiety, as though his life had become bound up with it. It rendered him timorous for a moment before that enigmatic, lighted door. Devil take the fellow! He did not want to see him. There would be nothing to learn from his face, known or unknown. He was a fool to waste his time there in waiting.

Less than five minutes after entering the place the Capataz began his retreat. He got away down the stairs with perfect success, gave one upward look over his shoulder at the light on the landing, and ran stealthily across the hall. But at the very moment he was turning out of the great door, with his mind fixed upon escaping the notice of the man upstairs, somebody he had not heard coming briskly along the front ran full into him. Both muttered a stifled exclamation of surprise, and leaped back and stood still, each indistinct to the other. Nostromo was silent. The other man spoke first, in an amazed and deadened tone.

'Who are you?'

Already Nostromo had seemed to recognize Dr Monygham. He had no doubt now. He hesitated the space of a second. The idea of bolting without a word presented itself to his mind. No use! An inexplicable repugnance to pronounce the name by which he was known kept him silent a little longer. At last he said in a low voice:

'A *cargador*.'

He walked up to the other. Dr Monygham had received a shock. He flung his arms up and cried out his wonder aloud, forgetting himself before the marvel of this meeting. Nostromo angrily warned him to moderate his voice. The Custom House was not so deserted as it looked. There was somebody in the lighted room above.

There is no more evanescent quality in an accomplished fact than its wonderfulness. Solicited incessantly by the considerations affecting its fears and desires, the human mind turns naturally away from the marvellous side of events. And it was in the most natural way possible that the doctor asked this man whom only two minutes before he believed to have been drowned in the gulf:

'You have seen somebody up there? Have you?'

'No, I have not seen him.'

'Then how do you know?'

'I was running away from his shadow when we met.'

'His shadow?'

'Yes. His shadow in the lighted room,' said Nostromo, in a contemptuous tone. Leaning back with folded arms at the foot of the immense building, he dropped his head, biting his lips slightly, and not looking at the doctor. 'Now,' he thought to himself, 'he will began asking me about the treasure.'

But the doctor's thoughts were concerned with an event not as marvellous as Nostromo's appearance, but in itself much less clear. Why had Sotillo taken himself off with his whole command with this suddenness and secrecy? What did this move portend? However, it dawned upon the doctor that the man upstairs was one of the officers left behind by the disappointed colonel to communicate with him.

'I believe he is waiting for me,' he said.

'It is possible.'

'I must see. Do not go away yet, Capataz.'

'Go away where?' muttered Nostromo.

Already the doctor had left him. He remained leaning against the wall, staring at the dark water of the harbour; the shrilling of cicadas filled his ears. An invincible vagueness coming over his thoughts took from them all power to determine his will.

'Capataz! Capataz!' the doctor's voice called urgently from above.

The sense of betrayal and ruin floated upon his sombre indifference as upon a sluggish sea of pitch. But he stepped out from under the wall, and, looking up, saw Dr Monygham leaning out of a lighted window.

'Come up and see what Sotillo has done. You need not fear the man up here.'

He answered by a slight, bitter laugh. Fear a man! The Capataz of the Sulaco Cargadores fear a man! It angered him that anybody should suggest such a thing. It angered him to be disarmed and skulking and in danger because of the accursed treasure, which was of so little account to the people who had tied it round his neck. He could not shake off the worry of it. To Nostromo the doctor represented all these people . . . And he had never even asked after it. Not a word of inquiry about the most desperate undertaking of his life.

Thinking these thoughts, Nostromo passed again through the cavernous hall, where the smoke was considerably thinned, and went up the stairs, not so warm to his feet now, towards the streak of light at the top. The doctor appeared in it for a moment, agitated and impatient.

'Come up! Come up!'

At the moment of crossing the doorway the Capataz experienced a shock of surprise. The man had not moved. He saw his shadow in the same place. He started, then stepped in with a feeling of being about to solve a mystery.

It was very simple. For an infinitesimal fraction of a second, against the light of two flaring and guttering candles, through a blue, pungent, thin haze which made his eyes smart, he saw the man standing, as he had imagined him, with his back to the door, casting an enormous and distorted shadow upon the wall. Swifter than a flash of lightning followed the impression of his constrained, toppling attitude – the shoulders projecting forward, the head sunk low upon the breast. Then he distinguished the arms behind his back, and wrenched so terribly that the two clenched fists, lashed together, had been forced up higher than the shoulder-blades. From there his eyes traced in one instantaneous glance the hide rope going upwards from the tied wrists over a heavy beam and down to a staple in the wall. He did not want to look at the rigid legs, at the feet hanging down nervelessly, with their bare toes some six inches above the floor, to know that the man had been given the estrapade till he had swooned. His first impulse was to dash forward and sever the rope at one blow. He felt for his knife. He had no knife – not even a knife. He stood quivering, and the doctor, perched on the edge of the table, facing thoughtfully the cruel and lamentable sight, his chin in his hand, uttered, without stirring:

'Tortured – and shot dead through the breast – getting cold.'

This information calmed the Capataz. One of the candles flickering in the socket went out. 'Who did this?' he asked.

'Sotillo, I tell you. Who else? Tortured – of course. But why shot?' the doctor looked fixedly at Nostromo, who shrugged his shoulders slightly. 'And mark, shot suddenly, on impulse. It is evident. I wish I had his secret.'

Nostromo had advanced, and stooped slightly to look. 'I seem to have seen that face somewhere,' he muttered. 'Who is he?'

The doctor turned his eyes upon him again. 'I may yet come to envying his fate. What do you think of that, Capataz, eh?'

But Nostromo did not even hear these words. Seizing the remaining light, he thrust it under the drooping head. The doctor sat oblivious, with a lost gaze. Then the heavy iron candlestick, as if struck out of Nostromo's hand, clattered on the floor.

'Hullo!' exclaimed the doctor, looking up with a start. He could hear the Capataz stagger against the table and gasp. In the sudden extinction of the light within, the dead blackness sealing the window-frames became alive with stars to his sight.

'Of course, of course,' the doctor muttered to himself in English. 'Enough to make him jump out of his skin.'

Nostromo's heart seemed to force itself into his throat. His head swam. Hirsch! The man was Hirsch! He held on tight to the edge of the table.

'But he was hiding in the lighter,' he almost shouted. His voice fell. 'In the lighter, and – and—'

'And Sotillo brought him in,' said the doctor. 'He is no more startling to you than you were to me. What I want to know is how he induced some compassionate soul to shoot him.'

'So Sotillo knows—' began Nostromo, in a more equable voice.

'Everything!' interrupted the doctor.

The Capataz was heard striking the table with his fist. 'Everything? What are you saying, there? Everything? Know everything? It is impossible! Everything?'

'Of course. What do you mean by impossible? I tell you I have heard this Hirsch questioned last night, here, in this very room. He knew your name, Decoud's name, and all about the loading of the silver . . . The lighter was cut in two. He was grovelling in abject terror before Sotillo, but he remembered that much. What do you want more? He knew least about himself. They found him clinging to their anchor. He must have caught at it just as the lighter went to the bottom.'

'Went to the bottom?' repeated Nostromo, slowly. 'Sotillo believes that? *Bueno*!'

The doctor, a little impatiently, was unable to imagine what else anybody could believe. Yes, Sotillo believed that the lighter was sunk, and the Capataz de Cargadores, together with Martin Decoud and perhaps one or two other political fugitives, had been drowned.

'I told you well, Señor Doctor,' remarked Nostromo at that point, 'that Sotillo did not know everything.'

'Eh? What do you mean?'

'He did not know I was not dead.'

'Neither did we.'

'And you did not care – none of you *caballeros* on the wharf – once you got off a man of flesh and blood like yourselves on a fool's business that could not end well.'

'You forget, Capataz, I was not on the wharf. And I did not think well of the business. So you need not taunt me. I tell you what, man, we had but little leisure to think of the dead. Death stands near behind us all. You were gone.'

'I went, indeed!' broke in Nostromo. 'And for the sake of what – tell me?'

'Ah! that is your own affair,' the doctor said, roughly. 'Do not ask me.'

Their flowing murmurs paused in the dark. Perched on the edge of the table with slightly averted faces, they felt their shoulders touch, and their eyes remained directed towards an upright shape nearly lost in the oscurity of the inner part of the room, that with projecting head and shoulders, in ghastly immobility, seemed intent on catching every word.

'*Muy bien!*' Nostromo muttered at last. 'So be it. Teresa was right. It is my own affair.'

'Teresa is dead,' remarked the doctor, absently, while his mind followed a new line of thought suggested by what might have been called Nostromo's return to life. 'She died, the poor woman.'

'Without a priest?' the Capataz asked, anxiously.

'What a question! Who could have got a priest for her last night?'

'May God keep her soul!' ejaculated Nostromo, with a gloomy and hopeless fervour which had no time to surprise Dr Monygham, before, reverting to the previous conversation, he continued in a sinister tone, '*Sí*, Señor Doctor. As you were saying, it is my own affair. A very desperate affair.'

'There are no two men in this part of the world that could have saved themselves by swimming as you have done,' the doctor said, admiringly.

And again there was silence between those two men. They were both reflecting, and the diversity of their natures made their thoughts born from their meeting swing afar from each other. The doctor, impelled to risky action by his loyalty to the Goulds, wondered with thankfulness at the chain of accident which had brought that man back where he would be of the greatest use in the work of saving the San Tomé mine. The doctor was loyal to the mine. It presented itself to his fifty-years-old eyes in the shape of a little woman in a soft dress with a long train, with a head attractively overweighted by a great mass of fair hair and the delicate preciousness of her inner worth, partaking of a gem and a flower, revealed in every attitude of her person. As the dangers thickened round the San Tomé mine this illusion acquired force, permanency, and authority. It claimed him at last! This claim, exalted by a spiritual detachment from the usual sanctions of hope and reward, made Dr Monygham's thinking, acting, individuality, extremely dangerous to himself and to others, all his scruples vanishing in the proud feeling that his devotion was the only thing that stood between an admirable woman and a frightful disaster.

It was a sort of intoxication which made him utterly indifferent to Decoud's fate, but left his wits perfectly clear for the appreciation of Decoud's political idea. It was a good idea – and Barrios was the only instrument of its realization. The doctor's soul, withered and shrunk by the shame of moral disgrace, became implacable in the expansion of its tenderness. Nostromo's return was providential. He did not think of him humanely, as of a fellow-creature just escaped from the jaws of death. The Capataz for him was the only possible messenger to Cayta. The very man. The doctor's misanthropic mistrust of mankind (the bitterer because based on personal failure) did not lift him sufficiently above common weaknesses. He was under the spell of an established reputation. Trumpeted by Captain Mitchell, grown in repetition, and fixed in general assent, Nostromo's faithfulness had never been questioned by Dr Monygham as a fact. It was not likely to be questioned now he stood in desperate need of it himself. Dr Monygham was human; he accepted the popular conception of the Capataz's incorruptibility simply because no word or fact had ever contradicted a mere affirmation. It seemed to be a part of the man, like his whiskers or his teeth. It was impossible to conceive him otherwise. The question was whether he would consent to go on such a dangerous and desperate errand. The doctor was observant enough to have become aware from the first of something peculiar in the man's temper. He was no doubt sore about the loss of the silver.

'It will be necessary to take him into my fullest confidence,' he said to himself, with a certain acuteness of insight into the nature he had to deal with.

On Nostromo's side the silence had been full of black irresolution, anger, and mistrust. He was the first to break it, however.

'The swimming was no great matter,' he said. 'It is what went before – and what comes after that—'

He did not quite finish what he meant to say, breaking off short, as though his thought had butted against a solid obstacle. The doctor's mind pursued its own schemes with Machiavellian subtlety. He said as sympathetically as he was able:

'It is unfortunate, Capataz. But no one would think of blaming you. Very unfortunate. To begin with, the treasure ought never to have left the mountain. But it was Decoud who – however, he is dead. There is no need to talk of him.'

'No,' assented Nostromo, as the doctor paused, 'there is no need to talk of dead men. But I am not dead yet.'

'You are all right. Only a man of your intrepidity could have saved himself.'

In this Dr Monygham was sincere. He esteemed highly the intrepidity of that man, whom he valued but little, being disillusioned as to mankind in general, because of the particular instance in which his own manhood had failed. Having had to encounter single-handed during his period of eclipse many physical dangers, he was well aware of the most dangerous element common to them all: of the crushing, paralysing sense of human littleness, which is what really defeats a man struggling with natural forces, alone, far from the eyes of his fellows. He was eminently fit to appreciate the mental image he made for himself of the Capataz, after hours of tension and anxiety, precipitated suddenly into an abyss of waters and darkness, without earth or sky, and confronting it not only with an undismayed mind, but with sensible success. Of course, the man was an incomparable swimmer, that was known, but the doctor judged that this instance testified to a still greater intrepidity of spirit. It was pleasing to him; he augured well from it for the success of the arduous mission with which he meant to entrust the Capataz so marvellously restored to usefulness. And in a tone vaguely gratified, he observed:

'It must have been terribly dark!'

'It was the worst darkness of the Golfo,' the Capataz assented, briefly. He was mollified by what seemed a sign of some faint interest in such doings as had befallen him, and dropped a few descriptive phrases with an affected and curt nonchalance. At that moment he felt communicative. He expected the continuance of that interest which, whether accepted or rejected, would have restored to him his personality – the only thing lost in that desperate affair. But the doctor, engrossed by a desperate adventure of his own, was terrible in the pursuit of his idea. He let an exclamation of regret escape him.

'I could almost wish you had shouted and shown a light.'

This unexpected utterance astounded the Capataz by its character of cold-blooded atrocity. It was as much as to say, 'I wish you had shown yourself a coward; I wish you had had your throat cut for your pains.' Naturally he referred it to himself, whereas it related only to the silver, being uttered simply and with many mental reservations. Surprise and rage rendered him speechless, and the doctor pursued, practically unheard by Nostromo, whose stirred blood was beating violently in his ears.

'For I am convinced Sotillo in possession of the silver would have turned short round and made for some small port abroad. Economically it would have been wasteful, but still less wasteful than having it sunk. It was the next best thing to having it at hand in some safe place, and using part of it to buy up Sotillo. But I doubt whether Don Carlos would have ever made up his mind to it. He is not fit for Costaguana, and that is a fact, Capataz.'

The Capataz had mastered the fury that was like a tempest in his ears in time to hear the name of Don Carlos. He seemed to have come out of it a changed man – a man who spoke thoughtfully in a soft and even voice.

'And would Don Carlos have been content if I had surrendered this treasure?'

'I should not wonder if they were all of that way of thinking now,' the doctor said, grimly. 'I was never consulted. Decoud had it his own way. Their eyes are opened by this time, I should think. I for one know that if that silver turned up this moment miraculously ashore I would give it to Sotillo. And, as things stand, I would be approved.'

'Turned up miraculously,' repeated the Capataz very low; then raised his voice. 'That, *señor*,' would be a greater miracle than any saint could perform.'

'I believe you, Capataz,' said the doctor, drily.

He went on to develop his view of Sotillo's dangerous influence upon the situation. And the Capataz, listening as if in a dream, felt himself of as little account as the indistinct, motionless shape of the dead man whom he saw upright under the beam, with his air of listening also, disregarded, forgotten, like a terrible example of neglect.

'Is it for an unconsidered and foolish whim that they came to me, then?' he interrupted, suddenly. 'Had I not done enough for them to be of some account, *por Dios*? Is it that the *hombres finos* – the gentlemen – need not think as long as there is a man of the people ready to risk his body and soul? Or, perhaps, we have no souls – like dogs?'

'There was Decoud, too, with his plan,' the doctor reminded him again.

'*Sí!* And the rich man in San Francisco who had something to do with that treasure, too – what do I know? No! I have heard too many things. It seems to me that everything is permitted to the rich.'

'I understand, Capataz,' the doctor began.

'What Capataz?' broke in Nostromo, in a forcible but even voice. 'The Capataz is undone, destroyed. There is no Capataz. Oh, no! You will find the Capataz no more.'

'Come, this is childish!' remonstrated the doctor; and the other calmed down suddenly.

'I have been indeed like a little child,' he muttered.

And as his eyes met again the shape of the murdered man suspended in his awful immobility, which seemed the uncomplaining immobility of attention, he asked, wondering gently:

'Why did Sotillo give the estrapade to this pitiful wretch? Do you know? No torture could have been worse than his fear. Killing I can understand. His anguish was intolerable to behold. But why should he torment him like this? He could tell no more.'

'No; he could tell nothing more. Any sane man would have seen that. He had told him everything. But I tell you what it is, Capataz. Sotillo would not believe what he was told. Not everything.'

'What is it he would not believe? I cannot understand.'

'I can, because I have seen the man. He refuses to believe that the treasure is lost.'

'What?' the Capataz cried out in a discomposed tone.

'That startles you – eh?'

'Am I to understand, *señor*,' Nostromo went on in a deliberate and, as it were, watchful tone, 'that Sotillo thinks the treasure has been saved by some means?'

'No! no! That would be impossible,' said the doctor, with conviction; and Nostromo emitted a grunt in the dark. 'That would be impossible. He thinks that the silver was no longer in the lighter when she was sunk. He has convinced himself that the whole show of getting it away to sea is a mere sham got up to deceive Gamacho and his Nationals, Pedrito Montero, Señor Fuentes, our new Jefe Político, and himself, too. Only, he says, he is no such fool.'

'But he is devoid of sense. He is the greatest imbecile that ever called himself a colonel in this country of evil,' growled Nostromo.

'He is no more unreasonable than many sensible men,' said the doctor. 'He has convinced himself that the treasure can be found because he desires passionately to possess himself of it. And he is also afraid of his officers turning upon him and going over to Pedrito, whom he has not the courage either to fight or trust. Do you see that, Capataz? He need fear no desertion as long as some hope remains of that enormous plunder turning up. I have made it my business to keep this very hope up.'

'You have!' the Capataz de Cargadores repeated cautiously. 'Well, that is wonderful. And how long do you think you are going to keep it up?'

'As long as I can.'

'What does that mean?'

'I can tell you exactly. As long as I live,' the doctor retorted in a stubborn voice. Then, in a few words, he described the story of his arrest and the circumstances of his release. 'I was going back to that silly scoundrel when we met,' he concluded.

Nostromo had listened with profound attention. 'You have made up your mind, then, to a speedy death,' he muttered through his clenched teeth.

'Perhaps, my illustrious Capataz,' the doctor said, testily. 'You are not the only one here who can look an ugly death in the face.'

'No doubt,' mumbled Nostromo, loud enough to be overheard. 'There may be even more than two fools in this place. Who knows?'

'And that is my affair,' said the doctor, curtly.

'As taking the accursed silver out to sea was my affair,' retorted Nostromo. 'I see. *Bueno*. Each of us has his reasons. But you were the last man I conversed with before I started, and you talked to me as if I were a fool.'

Nostromo had a great distaste for the doctor's sardonic treatment of his great reputation. Decoud's faintly ironic recognition used to make him uneasy; but the familiarity of a man like Don Martin was flattering, whereas the doctor was a nobody. He could remember him a penniless outcast, slinking about the streets of Sulaco, without a single friend or acquaintance, till Don Carlos Gould took him into the service of the mine.

'You may be very wise,' he went on, thoughtfully, staring into the obscurity of the room, pervaded by the gruesome enigma of the tortured and murdered Hirsch. 'But I am not such a fool as when I started. I have learned one thing since, and that is that you are a dangerous man.'

Dr Monygham was too startled to do more than exclaim:

'What is it you say?'

'If he could speak he would say the same thing,' pursued Nostromo, with a nod of his shadowy head silhouetted against the starlit window.

'I do not understand you,' said Dr Monygham faintly.

'No?' perhaps, if you had not confirmed Sotillo in his madness, he would have been in no haste to give the estrapade to that miserable Hirsch.'

The doctor started at the suggestion. But his devotion, absorbing all his sensibilities, had left his heart steeled against remorse and pity. Still, for complete relief, he felt the necessity of repelling it loudly and contemptuously.

'Bah! You dare to tell me that, with a man like Sotillo. I confess I did not give a thought to Hirsch. If I had it would have been useless. Anybody can see that the luckless wretch was doomed from the moment he caught hold of the anchor. He was doomed, I tell you! Just as I myself am doomed – most probably.'

This is what Dr Monygham said in answer to Nostromo's remark, which was plausible enough to prick his conscience. He was not a callous man. But the necessity, the magnitude, the importance of the task he had taken upon himself dwarfed all merely humane considerations. He had undertaken it in a fanatical spirit. He did not like it. To lie, to deceive, to circumvent even the basest of mankind was odious to him. It was odious to him by training, instinct, and tradition. To do these things in the character of a traitor was abhorrent to his nature and terrible to his feelings. He had made that sacrifice in a spirit of abasement. He had said to himself bitterly, 'I am the only one fit for that dirty work.' And he believed this. He was not subtle. His simplicity was such that, though he had no sort of heroic idea of seeking death, the risk, deadly enough, to which he exposed himself, had a sustaining and comforting effect. To that spiritual state the fate of Hirsch presented itself as part of the general atrocity of things. He considered that episode practically. What did it mean? Was it a sign of some dangerous change in Sotillo's delusion? That the man should have been killed like this was what the doctor could not understand.

'Yes. But why shot?' he murmured to himself.

Nostromo kept very still.

Chapter IX

Distracted between doubts and hopes, dismayed by the sound of bells pealing out the arrival of Pedrito Montero, Sotillo had spent the morning in battling with his thoughts, a contest to which he was unequal, from the vacuity of his mind and the violence of his passions. Disappointment, greed, anger, and fear made a tumult in the colonel's breast louder than the din of bells in the town. Nothing he had planned had come to pass. Neither Sulaco nor the silver of the mine had fallen into his hands. He had performed no military exploit to secure his position, and had obtained no enormous booty to make off with. Pedrito Montero, either as friend or foe, filled him with dread. The sound of bells maddened him.

Imagining at first that he might be attacked at once, he had made his battalion stand to arms on the shore. He walked to and fro all the length of the room, stopping sometimes to gnaw the finger-tips of his right hand with a lurid sideways glare fixed on the floor; then, with a sullen, repelling glance all round, he would resume his tramping in savage aloofness. His hat, horsewhip, sword, and revolver were lying on the table. His officers, crowding the window giving the view of the town gate, disputed amongst themselves the use of his field-glass bought last year on long credit from Anzani. It passed from hand to hand, and the possessor for the time being was besieged by anxious inquiries.

'There is nothing; there is nothing to see!' he would repeat, impatiently.

There was nothing. And when the picket in the bushes near the Casa Viola had been ordered to fall back upon the main body, no stir of life appeared on the stretch of dusty and arid land between the town and the waters of the port. But late in the afternoon a horseman issuing from the gate was made out riding up fearlessly. It was an emissary from Señor Fuentes. Being all alone he was allowed to come on. Dismounting at the great door he greeted the silent bystanders with cheery impudence, and begged to be taken up at once to the '*muy valiente*' colonel.

Señor Fuentes, on entering upon his functions of Jefe Político, had turned his diplomatic abilities to getting hold of the harbour as well as of the mine. The man he pitched upon to negotiate with Sotillo was a Notary Public, whom the revolution had found languishing in the common jail on a charge of forging documents. Liberated by the mob along with the other 'victims of Blanco tyranny', he had hastened to offer his services to the new Government.

He set out determined to display much zeal and eloquence in trying to induce Sotillo to come into town alone for a conference with Pedrito Montero. Nothing was farther from the colonel's intentions. The mere fleeting idea of trusting himself into the famous Pedrito's hands had made him feel unwell several times. It was out of the question – it was madness. And to put himself in open hostility was madness, too. It would render impossible a systematic search for that treasure, for that wealth of silver which he seemed to feel somewhere about, to scent somewhere near.

But where? Where? Heavens! Where! Oh! why had he allowed that doctor to go! Imbecile that he was. But no! It was the only right course, he reflected distractedly, while the messenger waited downstairs chatting agreeably to the officers. It was in that scoundrelly doctor's true interest to return with positive information. But what if anything stopped him? A general prohibition to leave the town, for instance! There would be patrols!

The colonel, seizing his head in his hands, turned in his tracks as if struck with vertigo. A flash of craven inspiration suggested to him an expedient not unknown to European statesmen when they wish to delay a difficult negotiation. Booted and spurred, he scrambled into the hammock with undignified haste. His handsome face had turned yellow with the strain of weighty cares. The ridge of his shapely nose had grown sharp; the audacious nostrils appeared mean and pinched. The velvety, caressing glance of his fine eyes seemed dead and even decomposed; for these almond-shaped, languishing orbs had become inappropriately bloodshot with much sinister sleeplessness. He addressed the surprised envoy of Señor Fuentes in a deadened, exhausted voice. It came pathetically feeble from under a pile of ponchos, which buried his elegant person right up to the black moustaches, uncurled, pendant, in sign of bodily prostration and mental incapacity. Fever, fever – a heavy fever had overtaken the '*muy valiente*' colonel. A wavering wildness of expression, caused by the passing spasms of a slight colic which had declared itself suddenly, and the rattling teeth of repressed panic, had a genuineness which impressed the envoy. It was a cold fit. The colonel explained that he was unable to think, to listen, to speak. With an appearance of superhuman effort the colonel gasped out that he was not in a state to return a suitable reply or to execute any of his Excellency's orders. But tomorrow! Tomorrow! Ah! tomorrow! Let his Excellency Don Pedro be without uneasiness. The brave Esmeralda Regiment held the harbour, held – And closing his eyes, he rolled his aching head like a half-delirious invalid under the inquisitive stare of the envoy, who was obliged to bend down over the hammock in order to catch the painful and broken accents. Meantime, Colonel Sotillo trusted that his Excellency's humanity would permit the doctor, the English doctor, to come out of town with his case of foreign remedies to attend upon him. He begged anxiously his worship the *caballero* now present for the grace of looking in as he passed the Casa Gould, and informing the English doctor, who was probably there, that his services were immediately required by Colonel Sotillo, lying ill of fever in the Custom House. Immediately. Most urgently required. Awaited with extreme impatience. A thousand thanks. He closed his eyes wearily and would not open them again, lying perfectly still, deaf, dumb, insensible, overcome, vanquished, crushed, annihilated by the fell disease.

But as soon as the other had shut after him the door of the landing, the colonel leaped out with a fling of both feet in an avalanche of woollen coverings. His spurs having become entangled in a perfect welter of ponchos he nearly pitched on his head, and did not recover his balance till the middle of the room. Concealed behind the half-closed jalousies he listened to what went on below.

The envoy had already mounted, and turning to the morose officers occupying the great doorway, took off his hat formally.

'*Caballeros*,' he said, in a very loud tone, 'allow me to recommend you to take great care of your colonel. It has done me much honour and gratification to have seen you all, a fine body of men exercising the soldierly virtue of patience in this exposed situation, where there is much sun, and no water to speak of, while a town full of wine and feminine charms is ready to embrace you for the brave men you are. *Caballeros*, I have the honour to salute you. There will be much dancing tonight in Sulaco. Good-bye!'

But he reined in his horse and inclined his head sideways on seeing the old major step out, very tall and meagre, in a straight narrow coat coming down to his ankles as if it were the casing of the regimental colours rolled round their staff.

The intelligent old warrior, after enunciating in a dogmatic tone the general proposition that the 'world was full of traitors', went on pronouncing deliberately a panegyric upon Sotillo. He ascribed to him with leisurely emphasis every virtue under heaven, summing it all up in an absurd colloquialism current amongst the lower class of Occidentals (especially about Esmeralda). 'And,' he concluded, with a sudden rise in the voice, 'a man of many teeth – "*hombre de muchos dientes*". *Sí, señor*. As to us,' he pursued, portentous and impressive, 'your worship is beholding the finest body of officers in the Republic, men unequalled for valour and sagacity, "*y hombres de muchos dientes*".'

'What? All of them?' inquired the disreputable envoy of Señor Fuentes, with a faint, derisive smile.

'*Todos. Sí, señor*,' the major affirmed, gravely, with conviction. 'Men of many teeth.'

The other wheeled his horse to face the portal resembling the high gate of a dismal barn. He raised himself in his stirrups, extending one arm. He was a facetious scoundrel, entertaining for these stupid Occidentals a feeling of great scorn natural in a native from the central provinces. The folly of Esmeraldians especially aroused his amused contempt. He began an oration upon Pedro Montero, keeping a solemn countenance. He flourished his hand as if introducing him to their notice. And when he saw every face set, all the eyes fixed upon his lips, he began to shout a sort of catalogue of perfections: 'Generous, valorous, affable, profound' – he snatched off his hat enthusiastically – 'a statesman, an invincible chief of partisans—' He dropped his voice startingly to a deep, hollow note – 'and a dentist.'

He was off instantly at a smart walk; the rigid straddle of his legs, the turned-out feet, the stiff back, the rakish slant of the sombrero above the square, motionless set of the shoulders expressing an infinite, awe-inspiring impudence.

Upstairs, behind the jalousies, Sotillo did not move for a long time. The audacity of the fellow appalled him. What were his officers saying below? They were saying nothing. Complete silence. He quaked. It was not thus that he had imagined himself at that stage of the expedition. He had seen himself triumphant, unquestioned, appeared, the idol of the soldiers, weighing in secret complacency the agreeable alternatives of power and wealth open to his choice. Alas! How different! Distracted, restless, supine, burning with fury, or frozen with terror, he felt a dread as fathomless as the sea creep upon him from every side. That rogue of a doctor had to come out with his information. That was clear. It would be of no use to him – alone. He could do nothing with it. Malediction! The doctor would never come out. He was probably under arrest already, shut up together with Don Carlos. He laughed aloud insanely. Ha! ha! ha! ha! It was Pedrito Montero who would get the information. Ha! ha! ha! ha! – and the silver. Ha!

All at once, in the midst of the laugh, he became motionless and silent as if turned into stone. He, too, had a prisoner. A prisoner who must, must know the real truth. He would have to be made to speak. And Sotillo, who all that time had not quite forgotten Hirsch, felt an inexplicable reluctance at the notion of proceeding to extremities.

He felt a reluctance – part of that unfathomable dread that crept on all sides upon him. He remembered reluctantly, too, the dilated eyes of the hide merchant, his contortions, his loud sobs and protestations. It was not compassion or even mere nervous sensibility. The fact was that though Sotillo did never for a moment believe his story – he could not believe it; nobody could believe such nonsense – yet those accents of despairing truth impressed him disagreeably. They made him feel sick. And he suspected also that the man might have gone mad with fear. A lunatic is a hopeless subject. Bah! A pretence. Nothing but a pretence. He would know how to deal with that.

He was working himself up to the right pitch of ferocity. His fine eyes squinted slightly; he clapped his hands; a bare-footed orderly appeared noiselessly; a corporal, with his bayonet hanging on his thigh and a stick in his hand.

The colonel gave his orders, and presently the miserable Hirsch, pushed in by several soldiers, found him frowning awfully in a broad armchair, hat on head, knees wide apart, arms akimbo, masterful, imposing, irresistible, haughty, sublime, terrible.

Hirsch, with his arms tied behind his back, had been bundled violently into one of the smaller rooms. For many hours he remained apparently forgotten, stretched lifelessly on the floor. From that solitude, full of despair and terror, he was torn out brutally, with kicks and blows, passive, sunk in hebetude. He listened to threats and admonitions, and afterwards made his usual answers to questions, with his chin sunk on his breast, his hands tied behind his back, swaying a little in front of Sotillo, and never looking up. When he was forced to hold up his head, by means of a bayonet-point prodding him under the chin, his eyes had a vacant, trance-like stare, and drops of perspiration as big as peas were seen hailing down the dirt, bruises, and scratches of his white face. Then they stopped suddenly.

Sotillo looked at him in silence. 'Will you depart from your obstinacy, you rogue?' he asked. Already a rope, whose one end was fastened to Señor Hirsch's wrists, had been thrown over a beam, and three soldiers held the other end, waiting. He made no answer. His heavy lower lip hung stupidly. Sotillo made a sign. Hirsch was jerked up off his feet, and a yell of despair and agony burst out in the room, filled the passages of the great building, rent the air outside, caused every soldier of the camp along the shore to look up at the windows, started some of the officers in the hall babbling excitedly, with shining eyes; others, setting their lips, looked gloomily at the floor.

Sotillo, followed by the soldiers, had left the room. The sentry on the landing presented arms. Hirsch went on screaming all alone behind the half-closed jalousies while the sunshine, reflected from the water of the harbour, made an ever-running ripple of light high up on the wall. He screamed with uplifted eyebrows and a wide-open mouth – incredibly wide, black, enormous, full of teeth – comical.

In the still burning air of the windless afternoon he made the waves of his agony travel as far as the O.S.N. Company's offices. Captain Mitchell on the balcony, trying to make out what went on generally, had heard him faintly but distinctly, and the feeble and appalling sound lingered in his ears after he had retreated indoors with blanched cheeks. He had been driven off the balcony several times during that afternoon.

Sotillo, irritable, moody, walked restlessly about, held consultations with his officers, gave contradictory orders in this shrill clamour pervading the whole empty edifice. Sometimes there would be long and awful silences. Several times he had entered the torture-chamber where his sword, horsewhip, revolver, and field-glass were lying on the table, to ask with forced calmness, 'Will you speak the truth now? No? I can wait.' But he could not afford to wait much longer.

That was just it. Every time he went in and came out with a slam of the door, the sentry on the landing presented arms, and got in return a black, venomous, unsteady glance, which, in reality, saw nothing at all, being merely the reflection of the soul within – a soul of gloomy hatred, irresolution, avarice, and fury.

The sun had set when he went in once more. A soldier carried in two lighted candles and slunk out, shutting the door without noise.

'Speak, thou Jewish child of the devil! The silver! The silver, I say? Where is it? Where have you foreign rogues hidden it? Confess or—'

A slight quiver passed up the taut rope from the racked limbs, but the body of Señor Hirsch, enterprising businessman from Esmeralda, hung under the heavy beam perpendicular and silent, facing the colonel awfully. The inflow of the night air, cooled by the snows of the Sierra, spread gradually a delicious freshness through the close heat of the room.

'Speak – thief – scoundrel – *pícaro* – or—'

Sotillo had seized the riding-whip, and stood with his arm lifted up. For a word, for one little word, he felt he would have knelt, cringed, grovelled on the floor before the drowsy, conscious stare of those fixed eyeballs starting out of the grimy, dishevelled head that drooped very still with its mouth closed askew. The colonel ground his teeth with rage and struck. The rope vibrated leisurely to the blow, like the long string of a pendulum starting from a rest. But no swinging motion was imparted to the body of Señor Hirsch, the well-known hide merchant on the coast. With a convulsive effort of the twisted arms it leaped up a few inches, curling upon itself like a fish on the end of a line. Señor Hirsch's head was flung back on his straining throat; his chin trembled. For a moment the rattle of his chattering teeth pervaded the vast, shadowy room, where the candles made a patch of light round the two flames burning side by side. And as Sotillo, staying his raised hand, waited for him to speak, with the sudden flash of a grin and a straining forward of the wrenched shoulders, he spat violently into his face.

The uplifted whip fell, and the colonel sprang back with a low cry of dismay, as if aspersed by a jet of deadly venom. Quick as thought he snatched up his revolver, and fired twice. The report and the concussion of the shots seemed to throw him at once from ungovernable rage into idiotic stupor. He stood with drooping jaw and stony eyes. What had he done, *sangre de Dios!* What had he done? He was basely appalled at his impulsive act, sealing for ever these lips from which so much was to be extorted. What could he say? How could he explain? Ideas of headlong flight somewhere, anywhere, passed through his mind; even the craven and absurd notion of hiding under the table occurred to his cowardice. It was too late; his officers had rushed in tumultuously, in a great clatter of scabbards, clamouring, with astonishment and wonder. But since they did not immediately proceed to plunge their swords into his breast, the brazen side of his character asserted itself. Passing the sleeve of his uniform over his face he pulled himself together. His truculent glance turned slowly here and there, checked the noise where it fell; and the stiff body of the late Señor Hirsch, merchant, after swaying imperceptibly, made a half turn, and came to a rest in the midst of awed murmurs and uneasy shuffling.

A voice remarked loudly, 'Behold a man who will never speak again.' And another, from the back row of faces, timid and pressing, cried out:

'Why did you kill him, *mi coronel*?'

'Because he has confessed everything,' answered Sotillo, with the hardihood of desperation. He felt himself cornered. He brazened it out on the strength of his reputation with very fair success. His hearers thought him very capable of such an act. They were disposed to believe his flattering tale. There is no credulity so eager and blind as the credulity of covetousness, which, in its universal extent, measures the moral misery and the intellectual destitution of mankind. Ah! he had confessed everything, this fractious Jew, this *bribón*. Good! Then he was no longer wanted. A sudden dense guffaw was heard from the senior captain – a big-headed man, with little round eyes and monstrously fat cheeks which never moved. The old major, tall and fantastically ragged like a scarecrow, walked round the body of the late Señor Hirsch, muttering to himself with ineffable complacency that like this there was no need to guard against any future treacheries of that scoundrel. The others stared, shifting from foot to foot, and whispering short remarks to each other.

Sotillo buckled on his sword and gave curt, peremptory orders to hasten the retirement decided upon in the afternoon. Sinister, impressive, his sombrero pulled right down upon his eyebrows, he marched first through the door in such disorder of mind that he forgot utterly to provide for Dr Monygham's possible return. As the officers trooped out after him, one or two looked back hastily at the late Señor Hirsch, merchant from Esmeralda, left swinging rigidly at rest, alone with the two burning candles. In the emptiness of the room the burly shadow of head and shoulders on the wall had an air of life.

Below, the troops fell in silently and moved off by companies without drum or trumpet. The old scarecrow major commanded the rearguard; but the party he left behind with orders to fire the Custom House (and 'burn the carcass of the treacherous Jew where it hung') failed somehow in their haste to set the staircase properly alight. The body of the late Señor Hirsch dwelt alone for a time in the dismal solitude of the unfinished building, resounding weirdly with sudden slams and clicks of doors and latches, with rustling scurries of torn papers, and the tremulous sighs that at each gust of wind passed under the high roof. The light of the two candles burning before the perpendicular and breathless immobility of the late Señor Hirsch threw a gleam afar over land and water, like a signal in the night. He remained to startle Nostromo by his presence, and to puzzle Dr Monygham by the mystery of his atrocious end.

'But why shot?' the doctor again asked himself, audibly. This time he was answered by a dry laugh from Nostromo.

'You seem much concerned at a very natural thing. Señor Doctor. I wonder why? It is very likely that before long we shall all get shot one after another, if not by Sotillo, then by Pedrito, or Fuentes, or Gamacho. And we may even get the estrapade, too, or worse – *quién sabe?* – with your pretty tale of the silver you put into Sotillo's head.'

'It was in his head already,' the doctor protested. 'I only—'

'Yes. And you only nailed it there so that the devil himself—'

'That is precisely what I meant to do,' caught up the doctor.

'That is what you meant to do. *Bueno*. It is as I say. You are a dangerous man.'

Their voices, which without rising had been growing quarrelsome, ceased suddenly. The late Señor Hirsch, erect and shadowy against the stars, seemed to be waiting attentive, in impartial silence.

But Dr Monygham had no mind to quarrel with Nostromo. At this supremely critical point of Sulaco's fortunes it was borne upon him at last that this man was really indispensable, more indispensable than ever the infatuation of Captain Mitchell, his proud discoverer, could conceive; far beyond what Decoud's best dry raillery about 'my illustrious friend, the unique Capataz de Cargadores', had ever intended. The fellow was unique. He was not 'one in a thousand'. He was absolutely the only one. The doctor surrendered. There was something in the genius of that Genoese seaman which dominated in the destinies of great enterprises and of many people, the fortunes of Charles Gould, the fate of an admirable woman. At this last thought the doctor had to clear his throat before he could speak.

In a completely changed tone he pointed out to the Capataz that, to begin with, he personally ran no great risk. As far as everybody knew he was dead. It was an enormous advantage. He had only to keep out of sight in the Casa Viola, where the old Garibaldino was known to be alone – with his dead wife. The servants had all run away. No one would think of searching for him there, or anywhere else on earth, for that matter.

'That would be very true,' Nostromo spoke up, bitterly, 'if I had not met you.'

For a time the doctor kept silent. 'Do you mean to say that you think I may give you away?' he asked in an unsteady voice. 'Why? Why should I do that?'

'What do I know? Why not? To gain a day perhaps. It would take Sotillo a day to give me the estrapade, and try some other things perhaps, before he puts a bullet through my heart – as he did to that poor wretch here. Why not?'

The doctor swallowed with difficulty. His throat had gone dry in a moment. It was not from indignation. The doctor, pathetically enough, believed that he had forfeited the right to be indignant with anyone – for anything. It was simple dread. Had the fellow heard his story by some chance? If so, there was an end of his usefulness in that direction. The indispensable man escaped his influence, because of that indelible blot which made him fit for dirty work. A feeling as of sickness came upon the doctor. He would have given anything to know, but he dared not clear up the point. The fanaticism of his devotion, fed on the sense of his abasement, hardened his heart in sadness and scorn.

'Why not, indeed?' he re-echoed, sardonically. 'Then the safe thing for you is to kill me on the spot. I would defend myself. But you may just as well know I am going about unarmed.'

'*Por Dios!*' said the Capataz, passionately. 'You fine people are all alike. All dangerous. All betrayers of the poor who are your dogs.'

'You do not understand,' began the doctor, slowly.

'I understand you all!' cried the other with a violent movement, as shadowy to the doctor's eyes as the persistent immobility of the late Señor Hirsch. 'A poor man amongst you has got to look after himself. I say that you do not care for those that serve you. Look at me! After all these years, suddenly, here I find myself like one of these curs that bark outside the walls – without a kennel or a dry bone for my teeth. *Caramba!*' But he relented with a contemptuous fairness. 'Of course,' he went on, quietly, 'I do not suppose that you would hasten to give me up to Sotillo, for example. It is not that. It is that I am nothing! Suddenly he swung his arm downwards. 'Nothing to anyone,' he repeated.

The doctor breathed freely. 'Listen, Capataz,' he said, stretching out his arm almost affectionately towards Nostromo's shoulder. 'I am going to tell you a very simple thing. You are safe because you are needed. I would not give you away for any conceivable reason, because I want you.'

In the dark Nostromo bit his lip. He had heard enough of that. He knew what that meant. No more of that for him. But he had to look after himself now, he thought. And he thought, too, that it would not be prudent to part in anger from his companion. The doctor, admitted to be a great healer, had, amongst the populace of Sulaco, the reputation of being an evil sort of man. It was based solidly on his personal appearance, which was strange, and on his rough ironic manner – proofs visible, sensible, and incontrovertible of the doctor's malevolent disposition. And Nostromo was of the people. So he only grunted incredulously.

'You, to speak plainly, are the only man,' the doctor pursued. 'It is in your power to save this town and . . . everybody from the destructive rapacity of men who—'

'No, *señor*,' said Nostromo, sullenly. 'It is not in my power to get the treasure back for you to give up to Sotillo, or Pedrito, or Gamacho. What do I know?'

'Nobody expects the impossible,' was the answer.

'You have said it yourself – nobody,' muttered Nostromo, in a gloomy, threatening tone.

But Dr Monygham, full of hope, disregarded the enigmatic words and the threatening tone. To their eyes, accustomed to obscurity, the late Señor Hirsch, growing more distinct, seemed to have come nearer. And the doctor lowered his voice in exposing his scheme as though afraid of being overheard.

He was taking the indispensable man into his fullest confidence. Its implied flattery and suggestion of great risks came with a familiar sound to the Capataz. His mind, floating in irresolution and discontent, recognized it with bitterness. He understood well that the doctor was anxious to save the San Tomé mine from annihilation. He would be nothing without it. It was his interest. Just as it had been the interest of Señor Decoud, of the Blancos, and of the Europeans to get his Cargadores on their side. His thoughts became arrested upon Decoud. What would happen to him?

Nostromo's prolonged silence made the doctor uneasy. He pointed out, quite unnecessarily, that though for the present he was safe, he could not live concealed for ever. The choice was between accepting the mission to Barrios, with all its dangers and difficulties, and leaving Sulaco by stealth, ingloriously, in poverty.

'None of your friends could reward you and protect you just now, Capataz. Not even Don Carlos himself.'

'I would have none of your protection and none of your rewards. I only wish I could trust your courage and your sense. When I return in triumph, as you say, with Barrios, I may find you all destroyed. You have the knife at your throat now.'

It was the doctor's turn to remain silent in the contemplation of horrible contingencies.

'Well, we would trust your courage and your sense. And you, too, have a knife at your throat.'

'Ah! And whom am I to thank for that? What are your politics and your mines to me – your silver and your constitutions – your Don Carlos this, and Don José that—'

'I don't know,' burst out the exasperated doctor. 'There are innocent people in danger whose little finger is worth more than you or I and all the Ribierists together. I don't know. You should have asked yourself before you allowed Decoud to lead you into all this. It was your place to think like a man; but if you did not think, then try to act like a man now. Did you imagine Decoud cared very much for what would happen to you?'

'No more than you care for what will happen to me,' muttered the other.

'No; I care for what will happen to you as little as I care for what will happen to myself.'

'And all this because you are such a devoted Ribierist?' Nostromo said in an incredulous tone.

'All this because I am such a devoted Ribierist,' repeated Dr Monygham, grimly.

Again Nostromo, gazing abstractedly at the body of the late Señor Hirsch, remained silent, thinking that the doctor was a dangerous person in more than one sense. It was impossible to trust him.

'Do you speak in the name of Don Carlos?' he asked at last.

'Yes. I do,' the doctor said, loudly, without hesitation. 'He must come forward now. He must,' he added in a mutter, which Nostromo did not catch.

'What did you day, *señor*?'

The doctor started. 'I say that you must be true to yourself, Capataz. It would be worse than folly to fail now.'

'True to myself,' repeated Nostromo. 'How do you know that I would not be true to myself if I told you to go to the devil with your propositions?'

'I do not know. Maybe you would,' the doctor said, with a roughness of tone intended to hide the sinking of his heart and the faltering of his voice. 'All I know is that you had better get away from here. Some of Sotillo's men may turn up here looking for me.'

He slipped off the table, listening intently. The Capataz, too, stood up.

'Suppose I went to Cayta, what would you do meantime?' he asked.

'I would go to Sotillo directly you had left – in the way I am thinking of.'

'A very good way – if only that engineer-in-chief consents. Remind him, *señor*, that I looked after the old rich Englishman who pays for the railway, and that I saved the lives of some of his people that time when a gang of thieves came from the south to wreck one of his pay-trains. It was I who discovered it all at the risk of my life, by pretending to enter into their plans. Just as you are doing with Sotillo.'

'Yes. Yes, of course. But I can offer him better arguments,' the doctor said, hastily. 'Leave it to me.'

'Ah, yes! True. I am nothing.'

'Not at all. You are everything.'

They moved a few paces towards the door. Behind them the late Señor Hirsch preserved the immobility of a disregarded man.

'That will be all right. I know what to say to the engineer,' pursued the doctor, in a low tone. 'My difficulty will be with Sotillo.'

And Dr Monygham stopped short in the doorway as if intimidated by the difficulty. He had made the sacrifice of his life. He considered this a fitting opportunity. But he did not want to throw his life away too soon. In his quality of betrayer of Don Carlos's confidence, he would have ultimately to indicate the hiding-place of the treasure. That would be the end of his deception, and the end of himself as well, at the hands of the infuriated colonel. He wanted to delay him to the very last moment; and he had been racking his brains to invent some place of concealment at once plausible and difficult of access.

He imparted his trouble to Nostromo, and concluded:

'Do you know what, Capataz? I think that when the time comes and some information must be given, I shall indicate the Great Isabel. That is the best place I can think of. What is the matter?'

A low exclamation had escaped Nostromo. The doctor waited, surprised, and after a moment of profound silence, heard a thick voice stammer out 'Utter folly', and stop with a gasp.

'Why folly?'

'Ah! You do not see it,' began Nostromo, scathingly, gathering scorn as he went on. 'Three men in half an hour would see that no ground had been disturbed anywhere on that island. Do you think that such a treasure can be buried without leaving traces of the work – eh! Señor Doctor? Why, you would not gain half a day more before having your throat cut by Sotillo. The Isabel! What stupidity! What miserable invention! Ah! you are all alike, you fine men of intelligence. All you are fit for is to betray men of the people into undertaking deadly risks for objects that you are not even sure about. If it comes off you get the benefit. If not, then it does not matter. He is only a dog. Ah! *Madre de Dios*, I would—' He shook his fists above his head.

The doctor was overwhelmed at first by this fierce, hissing vehemence.

'Well! It seems to me on your own showing that the men of the people are no mean fools, too,' he said, sullenly. 'No, but come. You are so clever. Have you a better place?'

Nostromo had calmed down as quickly as he had flared up.

'I am clever enough for that,' he said, quietly, almost with indifference. 'You want to tell him of a hiding-place big enough to take days in ransacking – a place where a treasure of silver ingots can be buried without leaving a sign on the surface.'

'And close at hand,' the doctor put in.

'Just so, *señor*. Tell him it is sunk.'

'This has the merit of being the truth,' the doctor said, contemptuously. 'He will not believe it.'

'You tell him that it is sunk where he may hope to lay his hands on it, and he will believe you quick enough. Tell him it has been sunk in the harbour in order to be recovered afterwards by divers. Tell him you found out that I had orders from Don Carlos Gould to lower the cases quietly overboard somewhere in a line between the end of the jetty and the entrance. The depth is not too great there. He has no divers, but he has a ship, boats, ropes, chains, sailors – of a sort. Let him fish for the silver. Let him set his fools to drag backwards and forwards and crossways while he sits and watches till his eyes drop out of his head.'

'Really, this is an admirable idea,' muttered the doctor.

'*Sí*. You tell him that, and see whether he will not believe you! He will spend days in rage and torment – and still he will believe. He will have no thought for anything else. He will not give up till he is driven off – why, he may even forget to kill you. He will neither eat nor sleep. He—'

'They very thing! The very thing!' the doctor repeated in an excited whisper. 'Capataz, I begin to believe that you are a great genius in your way.'

Nostromo had paused; then began again in a changed tone, sombre, speaking to himself as though he had forgotten the doctor's existence.

'There is something in a treasure that fastens upon a man's mind. He will pray and blaspheme and still persevere, and will curse the day he ever heard of it, and will let his last hour come upon him unawares, still believing that he missed it only by a foot. He will see it every time he closes his eyes. He will never forget it till he is dead – and even then – Doctor, did you ever hear of the miserable *gringos* on Azuera, that cannot die? Ha! ha! Sailors like myself. There is no getting away from a treasure that once fastens upon your mind.'

'You are a devil of a man, Capataz. It is the most plausible thing.'

Nostromo pressed his arm.

'It will be worse for him than thirst at sea or hunger in a town full of people. Do you know what that is? He shall suffer greater torments than he inflicted upon that terrified wretch who had no invention. None! none! Not like me. I could have told Sotillo a deadly tale for very little pain.'

He laughed wildly and turned in the doorway towards the body of the late Señor Hirsch, an opaque long blotch in the semi-transparent obscurity of the room between the two tall parallelograms of the windows full of stars.

'You man of fear!' he cried. 'You shall be avenged by me – Nostromo. Out of my way, doctor! Stand aside – or, by the suffering soul of a woman dead without confession, I will strangle you with my two hands.'

He bounded downstairs into the black, smoky hall. With a grunt of astonishment, Dr Monygham threw himself recklessly into the pursuit. At the bottom of the charred stairs he had a fall, pitching forward on his face with a force that would have stunned a spirit less intent upon a task of love and devotion. He was up in a moment, jarred, shaken, with a queer impression of the terrestrial globe having been flung at his head in the dark. But it wanted more than that to stop Dr Monygham's body, possessed by the exaltation of self-sacrifice; a reasonable exaltation, determined not to lose whatever advantage chance put into its way. He ran with headlong, tottering swiftness, his arms going like a windmill in his effort to keep his balance on his crippled feet. He lost his hat; the tails of his open gaberdine flew behind him. He had no mind to lose sight of the indispensable man. But it was a long time, and a long way from the Custom House, before he managed to seize his arm from behind, roughly, out of breath.

'Stop! Are you mad?'

Already Nostromo was walking slowly, his head dropping, as if checked in his pace by the weariness of irresolution.

'What is that to you? Ah! I forgot you want me for something. Always. *Siempre Nostromo*.'

'What do you mean by talking of strangling me?' panted the doctor.

'What do I mean? I mean that the king of the devils himself has sent you out of this town of cowards and talkers to meet me tonight of all the nights of my life.'

Under the starry sky the Albergo d'Italia Una emerged, black and low, breaking the dark level of the plain. Nostromo stopped altogether.

'The priests say he is a tempter, do they not?' he added, through his clenched teeth.

'My good man, you drivel. The devil has nothing to do with this. Neither has the town, which you may call by what name you please. But Don Carlos Gould is neither a coward nor an empty talker. You will admit that?' He waited. 'Well?'

'Could I see Don Carlos?'

'Great heavens! No! Why? What for?' exclaimed the doctor in agitation. 'I tell you it is madness. I will not let you go into the town for anything.'

'I must.'

'You must not!' hissed the doctor, fiercely, almost beside himself with the fear of the man doing away with his usefulness for an imbecile whim of some sort. 'I tell you you shall not. I would rather—'

He stopped at a loss for words, feeling fagged out, powerless, holding on to Nostromo's sleeve, absolutely for support after his run.

'I am betrayed!' muttered the Capataz to himself; and the doctor, who overheard the last word, made an effort to speak calmly.

'That is exactly what would happen to you. You would be betrayed.'

He thought with a sickening dread that the man was so well known that he could not escape recognition. The house of the Señor Administrador was beset by spies, no doubt. And even the very servants of the *casa* were not to be trusted. 'Reflect, Capataz,' he said, impressively . . . 'What are you laughing at?'

'I am laughing to think that if somebody that did not approve of my presence in town, for instance – you understand, *señor doctor* – if somebody were to give me up to Pedrito, it would not be beyond my power to make friends even with him. It is true. What do you think of that?'

'You are a man of infinite resource, Capataz,' said Dr Monygham, dismally. 'I recognize that. But the town is full of talk about you; and those few *cargadores* that are not in hiding with the railway people have been shouting "*Viva Montero!*" on the Plaza all day.'

'My poor *cargadores*!' muttered Nostromo. 'Betrayed! Betrayed!'

'I understand that on the wharf you were pretty free in laying about you with a stick amongst your poor *cargadores*,' the doctor said in a grim tone, which showed that he was recovering from his exertions. 'Make no mistake. Pedrito is furious at Señor Ribiera's rescue, and at having lost the pleasure of shooting Decoud. Already there are rumours in the town of the treasure having been spirited away. To have missed that does not please Pedrito either; but let me tell you that if you had all the silver in your hand for your ransom it would not save you.'

Turning swiftly, and catching the doctor by the shoulders, Nostromo thrust his face close to his.

'*Maladetta!* You follow me speaking of the treasure. You have sworn my ruin. You were the last man who looked upon me before I went out with it. And Sidoni the engine-driver says you have an evil eye.'

'He ought to know. I saved his broken leg for him last year,' the doctor said, stoically. He felt on his shoulders the weight of these hands famed amongst the populace for snapping thick ropes and bending horseshoes. 'And to you I offer the best means of saving yourself – let me go – and of retrieving your great reputation. You boasted of making the Capataz de Cargadores famous from one end of America to the other about this wretched silver. But I bring you a better opportunity – let me go, *hombre*!'

Nostromo released him abruptly, and the doctor feared that the indispensable man would run off again. But he did not. He walked on slowly. The doctor hobbled by his side till, within a stone's throw from the Casa Viola, Nostromo stopped again.

Silent in inhospitable darkness, the Casa Viola seemed to have changed its nature; his home appeared to repel him with an air of hopeless and inimical mystery. The doctor said:

'You will be safe there. Go in, Capataz.'

'How can I go in?' Nostromo seemed to ask himself in a low, inward tone. 'She cannot unsay what she said, and I cannot undo what I have done.'

'I tell you it is all right. Viola is all alone in there. I looked in as I came out of the town. You will be perfectly safe in that house till you leave it to make your name famous on the Campo. I am going now to arrange for your departure with the engineer-in-chief, and I shall bring you news here long before daybreak.'

Dr Monygham, disregarding, or perhaps fearing to penetrate the meaning of Nostromo's silence, clapped him lightly on the shoulder, and starting off with his smart, lame walk, vanished utterly at the third or forth hop in the direction of the railway track. Arrested between the two wooden posts for people to fasten their horses to, Nostromo did not move, as if he, too, had been planted solidly in the ground. At the end of half an hour he lifted his head to the deep baying of the dogs at the railway yards, which had burst out suddenly, tumultuous and deadened as if coming out from under the plain. That lame doctor with the evil eye had got there pretty fast.

Step by step Nostromo approached the Albergo d'Italia Una, which he had never known so lightless, so silent, before. The door, all black in the pale wall, stood open as he had left it twenty-four hours before, when he had nothing to hide from the world. He remained before it irresolute, like a fugitive, like a man betrayed. Poverty, misery, starvation! Where had he heard these words? The anger of a dying woman had prophesied that fate for his folly. It looked as if it would come true very quickly. And the *leperos* would laugh – she had said. Yes, they would laugh if they knew that the Capataz de Cargadores was at the mercy of the mad doctor whom they could remember, only a few years ago, buying cooked food from a stall on the Plaza for a copper coin – like one of themselves.

At that moment the notion of seeking Captain Mitchell passed through his mind. He glanced in the direction of the jetty and saw a small gleam of light in the O.S.N. Company's building. The thought of lighted windows was not attractive. Two lighted windows had decoyed him into the empty Custom House, only to fall into the clutches of that doctor. No! He would not go near lighted windows again on that night. Captain Mitchell was there. And what could he be told? That doctor would worm it all out of him as if he were a child.

On the threshold he called out 'Giorgio!' in an undertone. Nobody answered. He stepped in. '*Olá! viejo!* Are you there? . . .' In the impenetrable darkness his head swam with the illusion that the obscurity of the kitchen was as vast as the Placid Gulf, and that the floor dipped forward like a sinking lighter. '*Olá! viejo!*' he repeated, falteringly, swaying where he stood. His hand, extended to steady himself, fell upon the table. Moving a step forward, he shifted it, and felt a box of matches under his fingers. He fancied he had heard a quiet sigh. He listened for a moment, holding his breath; then, with trembling hands, tried to strike a light.

The tiny piece of wood flamed up quite blindingly at the end of his fingers, raised above his blinking eyes. A concentrated glare fell upon the leonine white head of old Giorgio against the black fireplace – showed him leaning forward in a chair in staring immobility, surrounded, overhung, by great masses of shadow, his legs crossed, his cheek in his hand, and empty pipe in the corner of his mouth. It seemed hours before he attempted to turn his face; at the very moment the match went out, and he disappeared, overwhelmed by the shadows, as if the walls and roof of the desolate house had collapsed upon his white head in ghostly silence.

Nostromo heard him stir and utter dispassionately the words:

'It may have been a vision.'

'No,' he said, softly. 'It is no vision, old man.'

A strong chest voice asked in the dark:

'Is that you I hear, Giovann' Battista?'

'*Sí, viejo*. Steady. Not so loud.'

After his release by Sotillo, Giorgio Viola, attended to the very door by the good-natured engineer-in-chief, had re-entered his house, which he had been made to leave almost at the very moment of his wife's death. All was still. The lamp above was burning. He nearly called out to her by name; and the thought that no call from him would ever again evoke the answer of her voice, made him drop heavily into the chair with a loud groan, wrung out by the pain as of a keen blade piercing his breast.

The rest of the night he made no sound. The darkness turned to grey, and on the colourless, clear, glassy dawn the jagged sierra stood out flat and opaque, as if cut out of paper.

The enthusiastic and severe soul of Giorgio Viola, sailor, champion of oppressed humanity, enemy of kings, and, by the grace of Mrs Gould, hotel-keeper of the Sulaco harbour, had descended into the open abyss of desolation amongst the shattered vestiges of his past. He remembered his wooing between two campaigns a single short week in the season of gathering olives. Nothing approached the grave passion of that time but the deep, passionate sense of his bereavement. He discovered all the extent of his dependence upon the silenced voice of that woman. It was her voice that he missed. Abstracted, busy, lost in inward contemplation, he seldom looked at his wife in those later years. The thought of his girls was a matter of concern, not of consolation. It was her voice that he would miss. And he remembered the other child – the little boy who died at sea. Ah! a man would have been something to lean upon. And, alas! even Gian' Battista – he of whom, and of Linda, his wife had spoken to him so anxiously before she dropped off into her last sleep on earth, he on whom she had called aloud to save the children, just before she died – even he was dead!

And the old man, bent forward, his head in his hand, sat through the day in immobility and solitude. He never heard the brazen roar of the bells in town. When it ceased the earthenware filter in the corner of the kitchen kept on its swift musical drip, drip into the great porous jar below.

Towards sunset he got up, and with slow movements disappeared up the narrow staircase. His bulk filled it; and the rubbing of his shoulders made a small noise as of a mouse running behind the plaster of a wall. While he remained up there the house was as dumb as a grave. Then, with the same faint rubbing noise, he descended. He had to catch at the chairs and tables to regain his seat. He seized his pipe off the high mantel of the fireplace – but made no attempt to reach the tobacco – thrust it empty into the corner of his mouth, and sat down again in the same staring pose. The sun of Pedrito's entry into Sulaco, the last sun of Señor Hirsch's life, the first of Decoud's solitude on the Great Isabel, passed over the Albergo d'Italia Una on its way to the west. The tinkling drip, drip of the filter had ceased, the lamp upstairs had burnt itself out, and the night beset Giorgio Viola and his dead wife with its obscurity and silence that seemed invincible till the Capataz de Cargadores, returning from the dead, put them to flight with the splutter and flare of a match.

'*Sí, viejo*. It is me. Wait.'

Nostromo, after barricading the door and closing the shutters carefully, groped upon a shelf for a candle, and lit it.

Old Viola had risen. He followed with his eyes in the dark the sounds made by Nostromo. The light disclosed him standing without support, as if the mere presence of that man who was loyal, brave, incorruptible, who was all his son would have been, were enough for the support of his decaying strength.

He extended his hand grasping the briar-wood pipe, whose bowl was charred on the edge, and knitted his bushy eyebrows heavily at the light.

'You have returned,' he said, with shaky dignity. 'Ah! Very well! I—'

He broke off. Nostromo, leaning back against the table, his arms folded on his breast, nodded at him slightly.

'You thought I was drowned! No! The best dog of the rich, of the aristocrats, of these fine men who can only talk and betray the people, is not dead yet.'

The Garibaldino, motionless, seemed to drink in the sound of the well-known voice. His head moved slightly once as if in sign of approval; but Nostromo saw clearly that the old man understood nothing of the words. There was no one to understand; no one he could take into the confidence of Decoud's fate, of his own, into the secret of the silver. That doctor was an enemy of the people – a tempter . . .

Old Giorgio's heavy frame shook from head to foot with the effort to overcome his emotion at the sight of that man, who had shared the intimacies of his domestic life as though he had been a grown-up son.

'She believed you would return,' he said, solemnly.

Nostromo raised his head.

'She was a wise woman. How could I fail to come back—?'

He finished the thought mentally: 'Since she has prophesied for me an end of poverty, misery, and starvation.' These words of Teresa's anger, from the circumstances in which they had been uttered, like the cry of a soul prevented from making its peace with God, stirred the obscure superstition of personal fortune from which even the greatest genius amongst men of adventure and action is seldom free. They reigned over Nostromo's mind with the force of a potent malediction. And what a curse it was that which her words had laid upon him! He had been orphaned so young that he could remember no other woman whom he called mother. Henceforth there would be no enterprise in which he would not fail. The spell was working already. Death itself would elude him now . . . He said violently:

'Come, *viejo*! Get me something to eat. I am hungry! *Sangre de Dios!* The emptiness of my belly makes me light headed.'

With his chin dropped again upon his bare breast above his folded arms, barefooted, watching from under a gloomy brow the movements of old Viola foraging amongst the cupboards, he seemed as if indeed fallen under a curse – a ruined and sinister Capataz.

Old Viola walked out of a dark corner, and, without a word, emptied upon the table out of his hollowed palms a few dry crusts of bread and half a raw onion.

While the Capataz began to devour his beggar's fare, taking up with stony-eyed voracity piece after piece lying by his side, the Garibaldino went off, and squatting down in another corner filled an earthenware mug with red wine out of a wicker-covered demijohn. With a familiar gesture, as when serving customers in the café, he had thrust his pipe between his teeth to have his hands free.

The Capataz drank greedily. A slight flush deepened the bronze of his cheek. Before him, Viola, with a turn of his white and massive head towards the staircase, took his empty pipe out of his mouth, and pronounced slowly:

'After the shot was fired down here, which killed her as surely as if the bullet had struck her oppressed heart, she called upon you to save the children. Upon you, Gian' Battista.'

The Capataz looked up.

'Did she do that, Padrone? To save the children! They are with the English *señora*, their rich benefactress. Hey! old man of the people. Thy benefactress . . .'

'I am old,' muttered Giorgio Viola. 'An Englishwoman was allowed to give a bed to Garibaldi lying wounded in prison. The greatest man that ever lived. A man of the people, too – a sailor. I may let another keep a roof over my head. *Sí* . . . I am old. I may let her. Life lasts too long sometimes.'

'And she herself may not have a roof over her head before many days are out, unless I . . . What do you say? Am I to keep a roof over her head? Am I to try – and save all the Blancos together with her?'

'You shall do it,' said old Viola in a strong voice. 'You shall do it as my son would have . . .'

'Thy son, *viejo*! . . . There never has been a man like thy son. Ha, I must try . . . But what if it were only a part of the curse to lure me on? . . . And so she called upon me to save – and then –?'

'She spoke no more.' The heroic follower of Garibaldi, at the thought of the eternal stillness and silence fallen upon the shrouded form stretched out on the bed upstairs, averted his face and raised his hand to his furrowed brow. 'She was dead before I could seize her hands,' he stammered out, pitifully.

Before the wide eyes of the Capataz, staring at the doorway of the dark staircase, floated the shape of the Great Isabel, like a strange ship in distress, freighted with enormous wealth and the solitary life of a man. It was impossible for him to do anything. He could only hold his tongue, since there was no one to trust. The treasure would be lost, probably – unless Decoud . . . And his thought came abruptly to an end. He perceived that he could not imagine in the least what Decoud was likely to do.

Old Viola had not stirred. And the motionless Capataz dropped his long, soft eyelashes, which gave to the upper part of his fierce, black-whiskered face a touch of feminine ingenuousness. The silence had lasted for a long time.

'God rest her soul!' he murmured, gloomily.

Chapter X

The next day was quiet in the morning, except for the faint sound of firing to the northward, in the direction of Los Hatos. Captain Mitchell had listened to it from his balcony anxiously. The phrase, 'In my delicate position as the only consular agent then in the port, everything, sir, everything was a just cause for anxiety,' had its place in the more or less stereotyped relation of the 'historical events' which for the next few years was at the service of distinguished strangers visiting Sulaco. The mention of the dignity and neutrality of the flag, so difficult to preserve in his position, 'right in the thick of these events between the lawlessness of that piratical villain Sotillo and the more regularly established but scarcely less atrocious tyranny of his Excellency Don Pedro Montero', came next in order. Captain Mitchell was not the man to enlarge upon mere dangers much. But he insisted that it was a memorable day. On that day, towards dusk, he had seen 'that poor fellow of mine – Nostromo. The sailor whom I discovered, and, I may say, made, sir. The man of the famous ride to Cayta, sir. An historical event, sir!'

Regarded by the O.S.N. Company as an old and faithful servant, Captain Mitchell was allowed to attain the term of his usefulness in ease and dignity at the head of the enormously extended service. The augmentation of the establishment, with its crowds of clerks, an office in town, the old office in the harbour, the division into departments – passenger, cargo, lighterage, and so on – secured a greater leisure for his last years in the regenerated Sulaco, the capital of the Occidental Republic. Liked by the natives for his good nature and the formality of his manner, self-important and simple, known for years as a 'friend of our country', he felt himself a personality of mark in the town. Getting up early for a turn in the market-place while the gigantic shadow of Higuerota was still lying upon the fruit and flower stalls piled up with masses of gorgeous colouring, attending easily to current affairs, welcomed in houses, greeted by ladies on the Alameda, with his entry into all the clubs and a footing in the Casa Gould, he led his privileged old bachelor, man-about-town existence with great comfort and solemnity. But on mail-boat days he was down at the Harbour Office at an early hour, with his own gig, manned by a smart crew in white and blue, ready to dash off and board the ship directly she showed her bows between the harbour heads.

It would be into the Harbour Office that he would lead some privileged passenger he had brought off in his own boat, and invite him to take a seat for a moment while he signed a few papers. And Captain Mitchell, seating himself at his desk, would keep on talking hospitably:

'There isn't much time if you are to see everything in a day. We shall be off in a moment. We'll have lunch at the Amarilla Club – though I belong also to the Anglo-American – mining engineers and businessmen, don't you know – and to the Mirliflores as well, a new club – English, French, Italians, all sorts – lively young fellows mostly, who wanted to pay a compliment to an old resident, sir. But we'll lunch at the Amarilla. Interest you, I fancy. Real thing of the country. Men of the first families. The President of the Occidental Republic himself belongs to it, sir. Fine old bishop with a broken nose in the patio. Remarkable piece of statuary, I believe. Cavaliere Parrochetti – you know Parrochetti, the famous Italian sculptor – was working here for two years – thought very highly of our old bishop . . . There! I am very much at your service now.'

Proud of his experience, penetrated by the sense of historical importance of men, events, and buildings, he talked pompously in jerky periods, with slight sweeps of his short, thick arm, letting nothing 'escape the attention' of his privileged captive.

'Lot of building going on, as you observe. Before the Separation it was a plain of burnt grass smothered in clouds of dust, with an ox-cart track to our Jetty. Nothing more. This is the Harbour Gate. Picturesque, is it not? Formerly the town stopped short there. We enter now the Calle de la Constitución. Observe the old Spanish houses. Great dignity. Eh? I suppose it's just as it was in the time of the Viceroys, except for the pavement. Wood blocks now. Sulaco National Bank there, with the sentry boxes each side of the gate. Casa Avellanos this side, with all the ground-floor windows shuttered. A wonderful woman lives there – Miss Avellanos – the beautiful Antonia. A character, sir! A historical woman! Opposite – Casa Gould. Noble gateway. Yes, *the* Goulds of the original Gould Concession, that all the world knows of now. I hold seventeen of the thousand-dollar shares in the Consolidated San Tomé mines. All the poor savings of my lifetime, sir, and it will be enough to keep me in comfort to the end of my days at home when I retire. I got in on the ground floor, you see. Don Carlos, great friend of mine. Seventeen shares – quite a little fortune to leave behind one, too. I have a niece – married a parson – most worthy man, incumbent of a small parish in Sussex; no end of children. I was never married myself. A sailor should exercise self-denial. Standing under that very gateway, sir, with some young engineer-fellows, ready to defend that house where we had received so much kindness and hospitality, I saw the first and last charge of Pedrito's horsemen upon Barrios's troops, who had just taken the Harbour Gate. They could not stand the new rifles brought out by that poor Decoud. It was a murderous fire. In a moment the street became blocked with a mass of dead men and horses. They never came on again.'

And all day Captain Mitchell would talk like this to his more or less willing victim:

'The Plaza. I call it magnificent. Twice the area of Trafalgar Square.'

From the very centre, in the blazing sunshine, he pointed out the buildings:

'The Intendencia, now President's Palace – Cabildo, where the Lower Chamber of Parliament sits. You notice the new houses on that side of the Plaza? Compañia Anzani, a great general store, like those cooperative things at home. Old Anzani was murdered by the National Guards in front of his safe. It was even for that specific crime that the deputy Gamacho, commanding the Nationals, a bloodthirsty and savage brute, was executed publicly by garrotte upon the sentence of a courtmartial ordered by Barrios. Anzani's nephews converted the business into a company. All that side of the Plaza had been burnt; used to be colonnaded before. A terrible fire, by the light of which I saw the last of the fighting, the *llaneros* flying, the Nationals throwing their arms down, and the miners of San Tomé, all Indians from the Sierra, rolling by like a torrent to the sound of pipes and cymbals, green flags flying, a wild mass of men in white ponchos and green hats, on foot, on mules, on donkeys. Such a sight, sir, will never be seen again. The miners, sir, had marched upon the town, Don Pepe leading on his black horse, and their very wives in the rear on *burros*, screaming encouragement, sir, and beating tambourines. I remember one of these women had a green parrot seated on her shoulder, as calm as a bird of stone. They had just saved their Señor Administrador; for Barrios, though he ordered the assault at once, at night, too, would have been too late. Pedrito Montero had Don Carlos led out to be shot – like his uncle many years ago – and then, as Barrios said afterwards, 'Sulaco would not have been worth fighting for.' Sulaco without the Concession was nothing; and there were tons and tons of dynamite distributed all over the mountain with detonators arranged, and an old priest, Father Román, standing by to annihilate the San Tomé mine at the first news of failure. Don Carlos had made up his mind not to leave it behind, and he had the right men to see to it, too.'

Thus Captain Mitchell would talk in the middle of the Plaza, holding over his head a white umbrella with a green lining; but inside the cathedral, in the dim light, with a faint scent of incense floating in the cool atmosphere, and here and there a kneeling female figure, black or all white, with a veiled head, his lowered voice became solemn and impressive.

'Here,' he would say, pointing to a niche in the wall of the dusky aisle, 'you see the bust of Don José Avellanos, "Patriot and Statesman", as the inscription says, "Minister to Courts of England and Spain, etc., etc., died in the woods of Los Hatos worn out with his life-long struggle for Right and Justice at the dawn of the New Era." A fair likeness. Parrochetti's work from some old photographs and a pencil sketch by Mrs Gould. I was well acquainted with that distinguished Spanish-American of the old school, a true *hidalgo*, beloved by everybody who knew him. The marble medallion in the wall, in the antique style, representing a veiled woman seated with her hands clasped loosely over her knees, commemorates that unfortunate young gentleman who sailed out with Nostromo on that fatal night, sir. See, "To the memory of Martin Decoud, his betrothed Antonia Avellanos." Frank, simple, noble. There you have that lady, sir, as she is. An exceptional woman. Those who thought she would give way to despair were mistaken, sir. She has been blamed in many quarters for not having taken the veil. It was expected of her. But Doña Antonia is not the stuff they make nuns of. Bishop Corbelán, her uncle, lives with her in the Corbelán town house. He is a fierce sort of priest, everlastingly worrying the Government about the old Church lands and convents. I believe they think a lot of him in Rome. Now let us go to the Amarilla Club, just across the Plaza, to get some lunch.'

Directly outside the cathedral on the very top of the noble flight of steps, his voice rose pompously, his arm found again its sweeping gesture.

'*Porvenir*, over there on that first floor, above those French plate-glass shop-fronts; our biggest daily. Conservative, or, rather, I should say, Parliamentary. We have the Parliamentary party here on which the actual Chief of the State, Don Juste Lopez, is the head; a very sagacious man, I think. A first-rate intellect, sir. The Democratic party in opposition rests mostly, I am sorry to say, on these socialist Italians, sir, with their secret societies, *camorras*, and such-like. There are lots of Italians settled here on the railway lands, dismissed navvies, mechanics, and so on, all along the trunk line. There are whole villages of Italians on the Campo. And the natives, too, are being drawn into these ways . . . American bar? Yes. And over there you can see another. New Yorkers mostly frequent that one – Here we are at the Amarilla. Observe the bishop at the foot of the stairs to the right as we go in.'

And the lunch would begin and terminate its lavish and leisurely course at a little table in the gallery, Captain Mitchell nodding, bowing, getting up to speak for a moment to different officials in black clothes, merchants in jackets, officers in uniform, middle-aged *caballeros* from the Campo – sallow, little, nervous men, and fat, placid, swarthy men, and Europeans or North Americans of superior standing, whose faces looked very white amongst the majority of dark complexions and black, glistening eyes.

Captain Mitchell would lie back in the chair, casting around looks of satisfaction, and tender over the table a case full of thick cigars.

'Try a weed with your coffee. Local tobacco. The black coffee you get at the Amarilla, sir, you don't meet anywhere in the world. We get the bean from a famous cafeteria in the foot-hills, whose owner sends three sacks every year as a present to his fellow members in remembrance of the fight against Gamacho's Nationals, carried on from these very windows by the *caballeros*. He was in town at the time, and took part, sir, to the bitter end. It arrives on three mules – not in the common way, by rail; no fear! – right into the patio, escorted by mounted peons, in charge of the Mayoral of his estate, who walks upstairs, booted and spurred, and delivers it to our committee formally with the words, "For the sake of those fallen the third of May." We call it "Tres de Mayo" coffee. Taste it.'

Captain Mitchell, with an expression as though making ready to hear a sermon in a church, would lift the tiny cup to his lips. And the nectar would be sipped to the bottom during a restful silence in a cloud of cigar smoke.

'Look at this man in black just going out,' he would begin, leaning forward hastily. 'This is the famous Hernandez, Minister of War. *The Times*'s special correspondent, who wrote that striking series of letters calling the Occidental Republic the "Treasure House of the World", gave a whole article to him and the force he has organized – the renowned Carabineers of the Campo.'

'Captain Mitchell's guest, staring curiously, would see a figure in a long-tailed black coat walking gravely, with downcast eyelids in a long, composed face, a brow furrowed horizontally, a pointed head, whose grey hair, thin at the top, combed down carefully on all sides and rolled at the ends, fell low on the neck and shoulders. This, then, was the famous bandit of whom Europe had heard with interest. He put on a high-crowned sombrero with a wide flat brim; a rosary of wooden beads was twisted about his right wrist. And Captain Mitchell would proceed:

'The protector of the Sulaco refugees from the rage of Pedrito. As general of cavalry with Barrios he distinguished himself at the storming of Tonoro, where Señor Fuentes was killed with the last remnant of the Monterists. He is the friend and humble servant of Bishop Corbelán. Hears three Masses every day. I bet you he will step into the cathedral to say a prayer or two on his way home to his siesta.'

He took several puffs at his cigar in silence; then, in his best important manner, pronounced:

'The Spanish race, sir, is prolific of remarkable characters in every rank of life . . . I propose we go now into the billiard-room, which is cool, for a quiet chat. There's never anybody there till after five. I could tell you episodes of the Separationist revolution that would astonish you. When the great heat's over, we'll take a turn on the Alameda.'

The programme went on relentlessly, like a law of Nature. The turn on the Alameda was taken with slow steps and stately remarks.

'All the great world of Sulaco here, sir.' Captain Mitchell bowed right and left with no end of formality; then with animation, 'Doña Emilia, Mrs Gould's carriage. Look. Always white mules. The kindest, most gracious woman the sun ever shone upon. A great position, sir. A great position. First lady in Sulaco – far before the President's wife. And worthy of it.' He took off his hat; then, with a studied change of tone, added, negligently, that the man in black by her side, with a high white collar and a scarred, snarly face, was Dr Monygham, Inspector of State Hospitals, chief medical officer of the Consolidated San Tomé mines. 'A familiar of the house. Everlastingly there. No wonder. The Goulds made him. Very clever man and all that, but I never liked him. Nobody does. I can recollect him limping about the streets in a check shirt and native sandals with a water-melon under his arm – all he would get to eat for the day. A big-wig now, sir, and as nasty as ever. However . . . There's no doubt he played his part fairly well at the time. He saved us all from the deadly incubus of Sotillo, where a more particular man might have failed –'

His arm went up.

'The equestrial statue that used to stand on the pedestal over there has been removed. It was an anachronism,' Captain Mitchell commented, obscurely. 'There is some talk of replacing it by a marble shaft commemorative of Separation, with angels of peace at the four corners, and bronze Justice holding an even balance, all gilt, on the top. Cavaliere Parrochetti was asked to make a design, which you can see framed under glass in the Municipal Sala. Names are to be engraved all round the base. Well! They could do no better than begin with the name of Nostromo. He has done for Separation as much as anybody else, and,' added Captain Mitchell, 'has got less than many others by it – when it comes to that.' He dropped on to a stone seat under a tree, and tapped invitingly at the place by his side. 'He carried to Barrios the letters from Sulaco which decided the General to abandon Cayta for a time, and come back to our help here by sea. The transports were still in harbour fortunately. Sir, I did not even know that my Capataz de Cargadores was alive. I had no idea. It was Dr Monygham who came upon him, by chance, in the Custom House, evacuated an hour or two before by the wretched Sotillo. I was never told; never given a hint, nothing – as if I were unworthy of confidence. Monygham arranged it all. He went to the railway yards, and got admission to the engineer-in-chief, who, for the sake of the Goulds as much as for anything else, consented to let an engine make a dash down the line, one hundred and eighty miles, with Nostromo aboard. It was the only way to get him off. In the Construction Camp at the rail-head, he obtained a horse, arms, some clothing, and started alone on that marvellous ride – four hundred miles in six days, through a disturbed country, ending by the feat of passing through the Monterist lines outside Cayta. The history of that ride, sir, would make a most exciting book. He carried all our lives in his pocket. Devotion, courage, fidelity, intelligence were not enough. Of course, he was perfectly fearless and incorruptible. But a man was wanted that would know how to succeed. He was that man, sir. On the fifth of May, being practically a prisoner in the Harbour Office of my Company, I suddenly heard the whistle of an engine in the railway yards, a quarter of a mile away. I could not believe my ears. I made one jump on to the balcony, and beheld a locomotive under a great head of steam run out of the yard gates, screeching like mad, enveloped in a white cloud, and then, just abreast of old Viola's inn, check almost to a standstill. I made out, sir, a man – I couldn't tell who – dash out of the Albergo d'Italia Una, climb into the cab, and then, sir, that engine seemed positively to leap clear of the house, and was gone in the twinkling of an eye. As you blow a candle out, sir! There was a first-rate driver on the foot-plate, sir, I can tell you. They were fired heavily upon by the National Guards in Rincón and one other place. Fortunately the line had not been torn up. In four hours they reached the Construction Camp. Nostromo had his start . . . The rest you know. You've got only to look round you. There are people on this Alameda that ride in their carriages, or even are alive at all today, because years ago I engaged a runaway Italian sailor for a foreman of our wharf simply on the strength of his looks. And that's a fact. You can't get over it, sir. On the seventeenth of May, just twelve days after I saw the man from the Casa Viola get on the engine, and wondered what it meant, Barrios's transports were entering this harbour, and the "Treasure House of the World", as *The Times* man calls Sulaco in his book, was saved intact for civilization – for a great future, sir. Pedrito, with Hernandez on the west, and the San Tomé miners pressing on the land gate, was not able to oppose the landing. He had been sending messages to Sotillo for a week to join him. Had Sotillo done so there would have been massacres and proscription that would have left no man or woman of position alive. But that's where Dr Monygham comes in. Sotillo, blind and deaf to everything, stuck on board his steamer watching the dragging for silver, which he believed to be sunk at the bottom of the harbour. They say that for the last three days he was out of his mind raving and foaming with disappointment at getting nothing, flying about the deck, and yelling curses at the boats with the drags, ordering them in, and then suddenly stamping his foot and crying out, "And yet it is there! I see it! I feel it!"

'He was preparing to hang Dr Monygham (whom he had on board) at the end of the after-derrick, when the first of Barrios's transports, one of our own ships at that, steamed right in, and ranging close alongside opened a small-arm fire without as much preliminaries as a hail. It was the completest surprise in the world, sir. They were too astounded at first to bolt below. Men were falling right and left like ninepins. It's a miracle that Monygham, standing on the after-hatch with the rope already round his neck, escaped being riddled through and through like a sieve. He told me since that he had given himself up for lost, and kept on yelling with all the strength of his lungs: "Hoist a white flag! Hoist a white flag!" Suddenly an old major of the Esmeralda regiment, standing by, unsheathed his sword with a shriek: "Die, perjured traitor!" and ran Sotillo clean through the body, just before he fell himself shot through the head.'

Captain Mitchell stopped for a while.

'Begad, sir! I could spin you a yarn for hours. But it's time we started off to Rincón. It would not do for you to pass through Sulaco and not see the lights of the San Tomé mine, a whole mountain ablaze like a lighted palace above the dark Campo. It's a fashionable drive . . . But let me tell you one little anecdote, sir; just to show you. A fortnight or more later, when Barrios, declared Generalissimo, was gone in pursuit of Pedrito away south, when the Provisional Junta, with Don Juste Lopez at its head, had promulgated the new Constitution, and our Don Carlos Gould was packing up his trunk bound on a mission to San Francisco and Washington (the United States, sir, were the first great power to recognize the Occidental Republic) – a fortnight later, I say, when we were beginning to feel that our heads were safe on our shoulders, if I may express myself so, a prominent man, a large shipper by our line, came to see me on business, and, says he, the first thing: 'I say, Captain Mitchell, is that fellow" (meaning Nostromo) "still the Capataz of your *cargadores* or not?" "What's the matter?" says I. "Because, if he is, then I don't mind; I send and receive a good lot of cargo by your ships; but I have observed him several days loafing about the wharf, and just now he stopped me as cool as you please with a request for a cigar. Now, you know, my cigars are rather special, and I can't get them so easily as all that," "I hope you stretched a point," I said, very gently. "Why, yes. But it's a confounded nuisance. The fellow's everlastingly cadging for smokes." Sir, I turned my eyes away, and then asked, "Weren't you one of the prisoners in the *cabildo*?" "You know very well I was, and in chains, too," says he. "And under a fine of fifteen thousand dollars?" He coloured, sir, because it got about that he fainted from fright when they came to arrest him, and then behaved before Fuentes in a manner to make the very *policianos*, who had dragged him there by the hair of his head, smile at his cringing. "Yes," he says, in a sort of shy way. "Why?" "Oh, nothing. You stood to lose a tidy bit," says I, "even if you saved your life . . . But what can I do for you?" He never even saw the point. Not he. And that's how the world wags, sir.'

He rose a little stiffly, and the drive to Rincón would be taken with only one philosophical remark, uttered by the merciless *cicerone*, with his eyes fixed upon the lights of San Tomé that seemed suspended in the dark night between earth and heaven.

'A great power, this, for good and evil, sir. A great power.'

And the dinner of the Mirliflores would be eaten, excellent as to cooking, and leaving upon the traveller's mind an impression that there were in Sulaco many pleasant, able young men with salaries apparently too large for their discretion, and amongst them a few, mostly Anglo-Saxon, skilled in the art of, as the saying is, 'taking a rise' out of his kind host.

With a rapid, jingling drive to the harbour in a two-wheeled machine (which Captain Mitchell called a curricle) behind a fleet and scraggy mule beaten all the time by an obviously Neapolitan driver, the cycle would be nearly closed before the lighted-up offices of the O.S.N. Company, remaining open so late because of the steamer. Nearly – but not quite.

'Ten o'clock. Your ship won't be ready to leave till half past twelve, if by then. Come in for a brandy-and-soda and one more cigar.'

And in the superintendent's private room the privileged passenger by the *Ceres* or *Juno*, or *Pallas*, stunned and as it were annihilated mentally by a sudden surfeit of sights, sounds, names, facts, and complicated information imperfectly apprehended, would listen like a tired child to a fairy tale; would hear a voice, familiar and surprising in its pompousness, tell him, as if from another world, how there was 'in this very harbour' an international naval demonstration, which put an end to the Costaguana-Sulaco War. How the United States cruiser, *Powhattan*, was the first to salute the Occidental flag – white, with a wreath of green laurel in the middle encircling a yellow amarilla flower. Would hear how General Montero, in less than a month after proclaiming himself Emperor of Costaguana, was shot dead (during a solemn and public distribution of orders and crosses) by a young artillery officer, the brother of his then mistress.

'The abominable Pedrito, sir, fled the country,' the voice would say. And it would continue: 'A captain of one of our ships told me lately that he recognized Pedrito the Guerrillero, arrayed in purple slippers and a velvet smoking-cap with a gold tassel, keeping a disorderly house in one of the southern ports.'

'Abominable Pedrito! Who the devil was he?' would wonder the distinguished bird of passage hovering on the confines of waking and sleep with resolutely open eyes and a faint but amiable curl upon his lips, from between which stuck out the eighteenth or twentieth cigar of that memorable day.

'He appeared to me in this very room like a haunting ghost, sir' – Captain Mitchell was talking of his Nostromo with true warmth of feeling and a touch of wistful pride. 'You may imagine, sir, what an effect it produced on me. He had come round by sea with Barrios, of course. And the first thing he told me after I became fit to hear him was that he had picked up the lighter's boat floating in the gulf! He seemed quite overcome by the circumstance. And a remarkable enough circumstance it was, when you remember that it was then sixteen days since the sinking of the silver. At once I could see he was another man. He stared at the wall, sir, as if there had been a spider or something running about there. The loss of the silver preyed on his mind. The first thing he asked me about was whether Doña Antonia had heard yet of Decoud's death. His voice trembled. I had to tell him that Doña Antonia, as a matter of fact, was not then back in town yet. Poor girl! And just as I was making ready to ask him a thousand questions, with a sudden, "Pardon me, *señor*," he cleared out of the office altogether. I did not see him again for three days. I was terribly busy, you know. It seems that he wandered about in and out of the town, and on two nights he turned up to sleep in the baracoons of the railway people. He seemed absolutely indifferent to what went on. I asked him on the wharf, "When are you going to take hold again, Nostromo? There will be plenty of work for the *cargadores* presently."

' "*Señor*," says he, looking at me in a slow, inquisitive manner, "would it surprise you to hear that I am too tired to work just yet? And what work could I do now? How can I look my *cargadores* in the face after losing a lighter?"

'I begged him not to think any more about the silver, and he smiled. A smile that went to my heart, sir. "It was no mistake," I told him. "It was a fatality. A thing that could not be helped." "*Sí, sí*!" he said, and turned away. I thought it best to leave him alone for a bit to get over it. Sir, it took him years really, to get over it. I was present at his interview with Don Carlos. I must say that Gould is rather a cold man. He had to keep a tight hand on his feelings, dealing with thieves and rascals, in constant danger of ruin for himself and wife for so many years, that it had become a second nature. They looked at each other for a long time. Don Carlos asked what he could do for him, in his quiet, reserved way.

' "My name is known from one end of Sulaco to the other," he said, as quiet as the other. "What more can you do for me?" That was all that passed on that occasion. Later, however, there was a very fine coasting schooner for sale, and Mrs Gould and I put our heads together to get her bought and presented to him. It was done, but he paid all the price back within the next three years. Business was booming all along this seaboard, sir. Moreover, that man always succeeded in everything except in saving the silver. Poor Doña Antonia, fresh from her terrible experiences in the woods of Los Hatos, had an interview with him, too. Wanted to hear about Decoud: what they said, what they did, what they thought up to the last on that fatal night. Mrs Gould told me his manner was perfect for quietness and sympathy. Miss Avellanos burst into tears only when he told her how Decoud had happened to say that his plan would be a glorious success . . . And there's no doubt, sir, that it is. It is a success.'

The cycle was about to close at last. And while the privileged passenger, shivering with the pleasant anticipations of his berth, forgot to ask himself what on earth Decoud's plan could be, Captain Mitchell was saying, 'Sorry we must part so soon. Your intelligent interest made this a pleasant day to me. I shall see you now on board. You had a glimpse of the "Treasure House of the World". A very good name that.' And the Coxswain's voice at the door, announcing that the gig was ready, closed the cycle.

Nostromo had, indeed, found the lighter's boat, which he had left on the Great Isabel with Decoud, floating empty far out in the gulf. He was then on the bridge of the first of Barrios's transports, and within an hour's steaming from Sulaco. Barrios, always delighted with a feat of daring and a good judge of courage, had taken a great liking to the Capataz. During the passage round the coast the General kept Nostromo near his person, addressing him frequently in that abrupt and boisterous manner which was the sign of his high favour.

Nostromo's eyes were the first to catch, broad on the bow, the tiny, elusive dark speck, which, alone with the forms of the Three Isabels right ahead, appeared on the flat, shimmering emptiness of the gulf. There are times when no fact should be neglected as insignificant; a small boat so far from the land might have had some meaning worth finding out. At a nod of consent from Barrios the transport swept out of her course, passing near enough to ascertain that no one manned the little cockle-shell. It was merely a common small boat gone adrift with her oars in her. But Nostromo, to whose mind Decoud had been insistently present for days, had long before recognized with excitement the dinghy of the lighter.

There could be no question of stopping to pick up that thing. Every minute of time was momentous with the lives and futures of a whole town. The head of the leading ship, with the General on board, fell off to her course. Behind her, the fleet of transports, scattered haphazard over a mile or so in the offing, like the finish of an ocean race, pressed on, all black and smoking on the western sky.

'*Mi General*,' Nostromo's voice rang out loud, but quiet, from behind a group of officers, 'I should like to save that little boat. *Por Dios*, I know her. She belongs to my Company.'

'And, *por Dios*,' guffawed Barrios, in a noisy, good-humoured voice, 'you belong to me. I am going to make you a captain of cavalry directly we get within sight of a horse again.'

'I can swim far better than I can ride, *mi General*,' cried Nostromo, pushing through to the rail with a set stare in his eyes. 'Let me –'

'Let you? What a conceited fellow that is,' bantered the General, jovially, without even looking at him. 'Let him go! Ha! ha! ha! He wants me to admit that we cannot take Sulaco without him! Ha! ha! ha! Would you like to swim off to her, my son?'

A tremendous shout from one end of the ship to the other stopped his guffaw. Nostromo had leaped overboard; and his black head bobbed up far away already from the ship. The General muttered an appalled '*Cielo!* Sinner that I am!' in a thunderstruck tone. One anxious glance was enough to show him that Nostromo was swimming with perfect ease; and then he thundered terribly, 'No! no! We shall not stop to pick up this impertinent fellow. Let him drown – that mad Capataz.'

Nothing short of main force would have kept Nostromo from leaping overboard. That empty boat, coming out to meet him mysteriously, as if rowed by an invisible spectre, exercised the fascination of some sign, of some warning, seemed to answer in a startling and enigmatic way the persistent thought of a treasure and of a man's fate. He would have leaped if there had been death in that half mile of water. It was as smooth as a pond, and for some reason sharks are unknown in the Placid Gulf, though on the other side of the Punta Mala the coastline swarms with them.

The Capataz seized hold of the stern and blew with force. A queer, faint feeling had come over him while he swam. He had got rid of his boots and coat in the water. He hung on for a time, regaining his breath. In the distance the transports, more in a bunch now, held on straight for Sulaco, with their air of friendly contest, of nautical sport, of a regatta; and the united smoke of their funnels drove like a thin, sulphurous fogbank right over his head. It was his daring, his courage, his act that had set these ships in motion upon the sea, hurrying on to save the lives and fortunes of the Blancos, the taskmasters of the people; to save the San Tomé mine; to save the children.

With a vigorous and skilful effort he clambered over the stern. The very boat! No doubt of it; no doubt whatever. It was the dinghy of the lighter No. 3 – the dinghy left with Martin Decoud on the Great Isabel so that he should have some means to help himself if nothing could be done for him from the shore. And here she had come out to meet him empty and inexplicable. What had become of Decoud? The Capataz made a minute examination. He looked for some scratch, for some mark, for some sign. All he discovered was a brown stain on the gunwale abreast of the thwart. He bent his face over it and rubbed hard with his finger. Then he sat down in the stern sheets, passive, with his knees close together and legs aslant.

Streaming from head to foot, with his hair and whiskers hanging lank and dripping and a lustreless stare fixed upon the bottom boards, the Capataz of the Sulaco Cargadores resembled a drowned corpse come up from the bottom to idle away the sunset hour in a small boat. The excitement of his adventurous ride, the excitement of the return in time, of achievement, of success, all these excitements centred round the associated ideas of the great treasure and of the only other man who knew of its existence, had departed from him. To the very last moment he had been cudgelling his brains as to how he could manage to visit the Great Isabel without loss of time and undetected. For the idea of secrecy had come to be connected with the treasure so closely that even to Barrios himself he had refrained from mentioning the existence of Decoud and of the silver on the island. The letters he carried to the General, however, made brief mention of the loss of the lighter, as having its bearing upon the situation in Sulaco. In the circumstances, the one-eyed tiger-slayer, scenting battle from afar, had not wasted his time in making inquiries from the messenger. In fact, Barrios, talking with Nostromo, assumed that both Don Martin Decoud and the ingots of San Tomé were lost together, and Nostromo, not questioned directly, had kept silent, under the influence of some indefinable form of resentment and distrust. Let Don Martin speak of everything with his own lips – was what he told himself mentally.

And now, with the means of gaining the Great Isabel thrown thus in his way at the earliest possible moment, his excitement had departed, as when the soul takes flight leaving the body inert upon an earth it knows no more. Nostromo did not seem to know the gulf. For a long time even his eyelids did not flutter once upon the glazed emptiness of his stare. Then slowly, without a limb having stirred, without a twitch of muscle or quiver of an eyelash, an expression, a living expression came upon the still features, deep thought crept into the empty stare – as if an outcast soul, a quiet, brooding soul, finding that untenanted body in its way, had come in stealthily to take possession.

The Capataz frowned: and in the immense stillness of sea, islands, and coast, of cloud-forms on the sky and trails of light upon the water, the knitting of that brow had the emphasis of a powerful gesture. Nothing else budged for a long time; then the Capataz shook his head and again surrendered himself to the universal repose of all visible things. Suddenly he seized the oars, and with one movement made the dinghy spin round, head-on to the Great Isabel. But before he began to pull he bent once more over the brown stain on the gunwale.

'I know that thing,' he muttered to himself, with a sagacious jerk of the head. 'That's blood.'

His stroke was long, vigorous, and steady. Now and then he looked over his shoulder at the Great Isabel, presenting its low cliff to his anxious gaze like an impenetrable face. At last the stem touched the strand. He flung rather than dragged the boat up the little beach. At once, turning his back upon the sunset, he plunged with long strides into the ravine, making the water of the stream spurt and fly upwards at every step, as if spurning its shallow, clear, murmuring spirit with his feet. He wanted to save every moment of daylight.

A mass of earth, grass, and smashed bushes had fallen down very naturally from above upon the cavity under the leaning tree. Decoud had attended to the concealment of the silver as instructed, using the spade with some intelligence. But Nostromo's half-smile of approval changed into a scornful curl of the lip by the sight of the spade itself flung there in full view, as if in utter carelessness or sudden panic, giving away the whole thing. Ah! They were all alike in their folly, these *hombres finos* that invented laws and governments and barren tasks for the people.

The Capataz picked up the spade, and with the feel of the handle in his palm the desire to have a look at the horse-hide boxes of treasure came upon him suddenly. In a very few strokes he uncovered the edges and corners of several; then, clearing away more earth, became aware that one of them had been slashed with a knife.

He exclaimed at that discovery in a stifled voice, and dropped on his knees with a look of irrational apprehension over one shoulder, then over the other. The stiff hide had closed, and he hesitated before he pushed his hand through the long slit and felt the ingots inside. There they were. One, two, three. Yes, four gone. Taken away. Four ingots. But who? Decoud? Nobody else. And why? For what purpose? For what cursed fancy? Let him explain. Four ingots carried off in a boat, and – blood!

In the face of the open gulf, the sun, clear, unclouded, unaltered, plunged into the waters in a grave and untroubled mystery of self-immolation consummated far from all mortal eyes, with an infinite majesty of silence and peace. Four ingots short! – and blood!

The Capataz got up slowly.

'He might simply have cut his hand,' he muttered. 'But, then –'

He sat down on the soft earth, unresisting, as if he had been chained to the treasure, his drawn-up legs clasped in his hands with an air of hopeless submission, like a slave set on guard. Once only he lifted his head smartly: the rattle of hot musketry fire had reached his ears, like pouring from on high a stream of dry peas upon a drum. After listening for a while, he said, half aloud:

'He will never come back to explain.'

And he lowered his head again.

'Impossible!' he muttered gloomily.

The sounds of firing died out. The loom of a great conflagration in Sulaco flashed up red above the coast, played on the clouds at the head of the gulf, seemed to touch with a ruddy and sinister reflection the forms of the Three Isabels. He never saw it, though he raised his head.

'But, then, I cannot know,' he pronounced, distinctly, and remained silent and staring for hours.

He could not know. Nobody was to know. As might have been supposed, the end of Don Martin Decoud never became a subject of speculation for anyone except Nostromo. Had the truth of the facts been known, there would always have remained the question, Why? Whereas the version of his death at the sinking of the lighter had no uncertainty of motive. The young apostle of Separation had died striving for his idea by an ever-lamented accident. But the truth was that he died from solitude, the enemy known but to few on this earth, and whom only the simplest of us are fit to withstand. The brilliant Costaguanero of the boulevards had died from solitude and want of faith in himself and others.

For some good and valid reasons beyond mere human comprehension, the sea-birds of the gulf shun the Isabels. The rocky head of Azuera is their haunt, whose stony levels and chasms resound with their wild and tumultuous clamour as if they were for ever quarrelling over the legendary treasure.

At the end of his first day on the Great Isabel, Decoud, turning in his lair of coarse grass, under the shade of a tree, said to himself:

'I have not seen as much as one single bird all day.'

And he had not heard a sound, either, all day but that one now of his own muttering voice. It had been a day of absolute silence – the first he had known in his life. And he had not slept a wink. Not for all these wakeful nights and the days of fighting, planning, talking; not for all that last night of danger and hard physical toil upon the gulf, had he been able to close his eyes for a moment. And yet from sunrise to sunset he had been lying prone on the ground, either on his back or on his face.

He stretched himself, and with slow steps descended into the gully to spend the night by the side of the silver. If Nostromo returned – as he might have done at any moment – it was there that he would look first; and night would, of course, be the proper time for an attempt to communicate. He remembered with profound indifference that he had not eaten anything yet since he had been left alone on the island.

He spent the night open-eyed, and when the day broke he ate something with the same indifference. The brilliant 'Son Decoud', the spoiled darling of the family, the lover of Antonia and journalist of Sulaco, was not fit to grapple with himself single-handed. Solitude from mere outward condition of existence becomes very swiftly a state of soul in which the affectations of irony and scepticism have no place. It takes possession of the mind, and drives forth the thought into the exile of utter unbelief. After three days of waiting for the sight of some human face, Decoud caught himself entertaining a doubt of his own individuality. It had merged into the world of cloud and water, of natural forces and forms of nature. In our activity alone do we find the sustaining illusion of an independent existence as against the whole scheme of things of which we form a helpless part. Decoud lost all belief in the reality of his action past and to come. On the fifth day an immense melancholy descended upon him palpably. He resolved not to give himself up to these people in Sulaco, who had beset him, unreal and terrible, like jibbering and obscene spectres. He saw himself struggling feebly in their midst, and Antonia, gigantic and lovely like an allegorical statue, looking on with scornful eyes at his weakness.

Not a living being, not a speck of distant sail, appeared within the range of his vision; and, as if to escape from this solitude, he absorbed himself in his melancholy. The vague consciousness of a misdirected life given up to impulses whose memory left a bitter taste in his mouth was the first moral sentiment of his manhood. But at the same time he felt no remorse. What should he regret? He had recognized no other virtue than intelligence, and had erected passions into duties. Both his intelligence and his passion were swallowed up easily in this great unbroken solitude of waiting without faith. Sleeplessness had robbed his will of all energy, for he had not slept seven hours in the seven days. His sadness was the sadness of a sceptical mind. He beheld the universe as a succession of incomprehensible images. Nostromo was dead. Everything had failed ignominiously. He no longer dared to think of Antonia. She had not survived. But if she survived he could not face her. And all exertion seemed senseless.

On the tenth day, after a night spent without even dozing off once (it had occurred to him that Antonia could not possibly have ever loved a being so impalpable as himself), the solitude appeared like a great void, and the silence of the gulf like a tense, thin cord to which he hung suspended by both hands, without fear, without surprise, without any sort of emotion whatever. Only towards the evening, in the comparative relief of coolness, he began to wish that this cord would snap. He imagined it snapping with a report as of a pistol – a sharp, full crack. And that would be the end of him. He contemplated that eventuality with pleasure, because he dreaded the sleepless nights in which the silence, remaining unbroken in the shape of a cord to which he hung with both hands, vibrated with senseless phrases, always the same but utterly incomprehensible, about Nostromo, Antonia, Barrios, and proclamations mingled into an ironical and senseless buzzing. In the daytime he could look at the silence like a still cord stretched to breaking-point, with his life, his vain life, suspended from it like a weight.

'I wonder whether I would hear it snap before I fell,' he asked himself.

The sun was two hours above the horizon when he got up, gaunt, dirty, white-faced, and looked at it with his red-rimmed eyes. His limbs obeyed him slowly, as if full of lead, yet without tremor; and the effect of that physical condition gave to his movements an unhesitating, deliberate dignity. He acted as if accomplishing some sort of rite. He descended into the gully; for the fascination of all that silver, with its potential power, survived alone outside of himself. He picked up the belt with the revolver, that was lying there, and buckled it round his waist. The cord of silence could never snap on the island. It must let him fall and sink into the sea, he thought. And sink! He was looking at the loose earth covering the treasure. In the sea! His aspect was that of a somnambulist. He lowered himself down on his knees slowly and went on grubbing with his fingers with industrious patience till he uncovered one of the boxes. Without a pause, as if doing some work done many times before, he slit it open and took four ingots, which he put in his pockets. He covered up the exposed box again and step by step came out of the gully. The bushes closed after him with a swish.

It was on the third day of his solitude that he had dragged the dinghy near the water with an idea of rowing away somewhere, but had desisted partly at the whisper of lingering hope that Nostromo would return, partly from conviction of utter uselessness of all effort. Now she wanted only a slight shove to be set afloat. He had eaten a little every day after the first, and had some muscular strength left yet. Taking up the oars slowly, he pulled away from the cliff of the Great Isabel, that stood behind him warm with sunshine, as if with the heat of life bathed in a rich light from head to foot as if in a radiance of hope and joy. He pulled straight towards the setting sun. When the gulf had grown dark, he ceased rowing and flung the sculls in. The hollow clatter they made in falling was the loudest noise he had ever heard in his life. It was a revelation. It seemed to recall him from far away. Actually the thought, 'Perhaps I may sleep tonight,' passed through his mind. But he did not believe it. He believed in nothing; and he remained sitting on the thwart.

The dawn from behind the mountains put a gleam into his unwinking eyes. After a clear daybreak the sun appeared splendidly above the peaks of the range. The great gulf burst into a glitter all around the boat; and in this glory of merciless solitude the silence appeared again before him, stretched taut like a dark, thin string.

His eyes looked at it while, without haste, he shifted his seat from the thwart to the gunwhale. They looked at it fixedly, while his hand, feeling about his waist, unbuttoned the flap of the leather case, drew the revolver, cocked it, brought it forward pointing at his breast, pulled the trigger, and, with convulsive force, sent the still-smoking weapon hurtling through the air. His eyes looked at it while he fell forward and hung with his breast on the gunwhale and the fingers of his right hand hooked under the thwart. They looked –

'It is done,' he stammered out, in a sudden flow of blood. His last thought was: 'I wonder how that Capataz died.' The stiffness of the fingers relaxed, and the lover of Antonia Avellanos rolled overboard without having heard the cord of silence snap in the solitude of the Placid Gulf, whose glittering surface remained untroubled by the fall of his body.

A victim of the disillusioned weariness which is the retribution meted out to intellectual audacity, the brilliant Don Martin Decoud, weighted by the bars of San Tomé silver, disappeared without a trace, swallowed up in the immense indifference of things. His sleepless, crouching figure was gone from the side of the San Tomé silver; and for a time the spirits of good and evil that hover near every concealed treasure of the earth might have thought that this one had been forgotten by all mankind. Then, after a few days, another form appeared striding away from the setting sun to sit motionless and awake in the narrow black gully all through the night, in nearly the same pose, in the same place in which had sat that other sleepless man who had gone away for ever so quietly in a small boat, about the time of sunset. And the spirits of good and evil that hover about a forbidden treasure understood well that the silver of San Tomé was provided now with a faithful and lifelong slave.

The magnificent Capataz de Cargadores, victim of the disenchanted vanity which is the reward of audacious action, sat in the weary pose of a hunted outcast through a night of sleeplessness as tormenting as any known to Decoud, his companion in the most desperate affair of his life. And he wondered how Decoud had died. But he knew the part he had played himself. First a woman, then a man, abandoned each in their last extremity, for the sake of this accursed treasure. It was paid for by a soul lost and by a vanished life. The blank stillness of awe was succeeded by a gust of immense pride. There was no one in the world but Gian' Battista Fidanza, Capataz de Cargadores, the incorruptible and faithful Nostromo, to pay such a price.

He had made up his mind that nothing should be allowed now to rob him of his bargain. Nothing. Decoud had died. But how? That he was dead he had not a shadow of a doubt. But four ingots? . . . What for? Did he mean to come for more – some other time?

The treasure was putting forth its latent power. It troubled the clear mind of the man who had paid the price. He was sure that Decoud was dead. The island seemed full of that whisper. Dead? Gone! And he caught himself listening for the swish of bushes and the splash of footfalls in the bed of the brook. Dead! The talker, the *novio* of Doña Antonia!

'Ha!' he murmured, with his head on his knees, under the livid clouded dawn breaking over the liberated Sulaco and upon the gulf as grey as ashes. 'It is to her that he will fly. To her that he will fly!'

And four ingots! Did he take them in revenge, to cast a spell, like the angry woman who had prophesied remorse and failure, and yet had laid upon him the task of saving the children? Well, he had saved the children. He had defeated the spell of poverty and starvation. He had done it all alone – or perhaps helped by the devil. Who cared? He had done it, betrayed as he was, and saving by the same stroke the San Tomé mine, which appeared to him hateful and immense, lording it by its vast wealth over the valour, the toil, the fidelity of the poor, over war and peace, over the labours of the town, the sea, and the Campo.

The sun lit up the sky behind the peaks of the Cordillera. The Capataz looked down for a time upon the fall of loose earth, stones, and smashed bushes, concealing the hiding-place of the silver.

'I must grow rich very slowly,' he meditated, aloud.

Chapter XI

Sulaco outstripped Nostromo's prudence, growing rich swiftly on the hidden treasures of the earth, hovered over by the anxious spirits of good and evil, torn out by the labouring hands of the people. It was like a second youth, like a new life, full of promise, of unrest, of toil, scattering lavishly its wealth to the four corners of an excited world. Material changes swept along in the train of material interests. And other changes more subtle, outwardly unmarked, affected the minds and hearts of the workers. Captain Mitchell had gone home to live on his savings invested in the San Tomé mine; and Dr Monygham had grown older, with his head steel-grey and the unchanged expression of his face, living on the inexhaustible treasure of his devotion drawn upon in the secret of his heart like a store of unlawful wealth. The Inspector-General of State Hospitals (whose maintenance is a charge upon the Gould Concession), Official Adviser on Sanitation to the Municipality, Chief Medical Officer of the San Tomé Consolidated Mines (whose territory, containing gold, silver, copper, lead, cobalt, extends for miles along the foothills of the Cordillera), had felt poverty-stricken, miserable, and starved during the prolonged, second visit the Goulds paid to Europe and the United States of America. Intimate of the *casa*, proved friend, a bachelor without ties and without establishment (except of the professional sort), he had been asked to take up his quarters in the Gould house. In the eleven months of their absence the familiar rooms, recalling at every glance the woman to whom he had given all his loyalty, had grown intolerable. As the day approached for the arrival of the mail boat *Hermes* (the latest addition to the O.S.N. Company's splendid fleet), the doctor hobbled about more vivaciously, snapped more sardonically at simple and gentle out of sheer nervousness.

He packed up his modest trunk with speed, with fury, with enthusiasm, and saw it carried out past the old porter at the gate of the Casa Gould with delight, with intoxication; then, as the hour approached, sitting alone in the great landau behind the white mules, a little sideways, his drawn-in face positively venomous with effort of self-control, and holding a pair of new gloves in his left hand, he drove to the harbour.

His heart dilated within him so, when he saw the Goulds on the deck of the *Hermes*, that his greetings were reduced to a casual mutter. Driving back to town, all three were silent. And in the patio the doctor, in a more natural manner, said:

'I'll leave you now to yourselves. I'll call tomorrow if I may?'

'Come to lunch, dear Dr Monygham, and come early,' said Mrs Gould, in her travelling dress and her veil down, turning to look at him at the foot of the stairs; while at the top of the flight the Madonna, in blue robes and the Child on her arm, seemed to welcome her with an aspect of pitying tenderness.

'Don't expect to find me at home,' Charles Gould warned him. 'I'll be off early to the mine.'

After lunch, Doña Emilia and the Señor Doctor came slowly through the inner gateway of the patio. The large gardens of the Casa Gould, surrounded by high walls, and the red-tile slopes of neighbouring roofs, lay open before them, with masses of shade under the trees and level surfaces of sunlight upon the lawns. A triple row of old orange trees surrounded the whole. Barefooted, brown gardeners, in snowy white shirts and wide *calzoneras*, dotted the grounds, squatting over flowerbeds, passing between the trees, dragging slender india-rubber tubes across the gravel of the paths; and the fine jets of water crossed each other in graceful curves, sparkling in the sunshine with a slight pattering noise upon the bushes, and an effect of showered diamonds upon the grass.

Doña Emilia, holding up the train of a clear dress, walked by the side of Dr Monygham, in a longish black coat and severe black bow on an immaculate shirt-front. Under a shady clump of trees, where stood scattered little tables and wicker easy-chairs, Mrs Gould sat down in a low and ample seat.

'Don't go yet,' she said to Dr Monygham, who was unable to tear himself away from the spot. His chin nestling within the points of his collar, he devoured her stealthily with his eyes, which, luckily, were round and hard like clouded marbles, and incapable of disclosing his sentiments. His pitying emotion at the marks of time upon the face of that woman, the air of frailty and weary fatigue that had settled upon the eyes and temples of the 'Never-tired Señora' (as Don Pepe years ago used to call her with admiration), touched him almost to tears. 'Don't go yet. Today is all my own,' Mrs Gould urged, gently. 'We are not back yet officially. No one will come. It's only tomorrow that the windows of the Casa Gould are to be lit up for a reception.'

The doctor dropped into a chair.

'Giving a *tertulia*?' he said, with a detached air.

'A simple greeting for all the kind friends who care to come.'

'And only tomorrow?'

'Yes. Charles would be tired out after a day at the mine, and so I – It would be good to have him to myself for one evening on our return to this house I love. It has seen all my life.'

'Ah, yes!' snarled the doctor, suddenly. 'Women count time from the marriage feast. Didn't you live a little before?'

'Yes; but what is there to remember? There were no cares.'

Mrs Gould sighed. And as two friends, after a long separation, will revert to the most agitated period of their lives, they began to talk of the Sulaco Revolution. It seemed strange to Mrs Gould that people who had taken part in it seemed to forget its memory and its lesson.

'And yet,' struck in the doctor, 'we who played our part in it had our reward. Don Pepe, though superannuated, still can sit a horse. Barrios is drinking himself to death in jovial company away somewhere on his *fundación* beyond the Bolson de Tonoro. And the heroic Father Román – I imagine the old padre blowing up systematically the San Tomé mine, uttering a pious exclamation at every bang, and taking handfuls of snuff between the explosions – the heroic Padre Román says that he is not afraid of the harm Holroyd's missionaries can do to his flock, as long as *he* is alive.'

Mrs Gould shuddered a little at the allusion to the destruction that had come so near to the San Tomé mine.

'Ah, but you, dear friend?'

'I did the work I was fit for.'

'You faced the most cruel dangers of all. Something more than death.'

'No, Mrs Gould! Only death – by hanging. And I am rewarded beyond my deserts.'

Noticing Mrs Gould's gaze fixed upon him, he dropped his eyes.

'I've made my career – as you see,' said the Inspector-General of State Hospitals, taking up lightly the lapels of his superfine black coat. The doctor's self-respect, marked inwardly by the almost complete disappearance from his dreams of Father Berón, appeared visibly in what, by contrast with former carelessness, seemed an immoderate cult of personal appearance. Carried out within severe limits of form and colour, and in perpetual freshness, this change of apparel gave to Dr Monygham an air at the same time professional and festive; while his gait and the unchanged crabbed character of his face acquired from it a startling force of incongruity.

'Yes,' he went on. 'We all had our rewards – the engineer-in-chief, Captain Mitchell –'

'We saw him,' interrupted Mrs Gould, in her charming voice. 'The poor dear man came up from the country on purpose to call on us in our hotel in London. He comported himself with great dignity, but I fancy he regrets Sulaco. He rambled feebly about "historical events" till I felt I could have a cry.'

'H'm,' grunted the doctor; 'getting old, I suppose. Even Nostromo is getting older – though he is not changed. And, speaking of that fellow, I wanted to tell you something –'

For some time the house had been full of murmurs, of agitation. Suddenly the two gardeners, busy with rose trees at the side of the garden arch, fell upon their knees with bowed heads on the passage of Antonia Avellanos, who appeared walking beside her uncle.

Invested with the red hat after a short visit to Rome, where he had been invited by the Propaganda, Father Corbelán, missionary to the wild Indians, conspirator, friend and patron of Hernandez the robber, advanced with big, slow strides, gaunt and leaning forward, with his powerful hands clasped behind his back. The first Cardinal-Archbishop of Sulaco had preserved his fanatical and morose air; the aspect of a chaplain of bandits. It was believed that his unexpected elevation to the purple was a counter-move to the Protestant invasion of Sulaco organized by the Holroyd Missionary Fund. Antonia, the beauty of her face as if a little blurred, her figure slightly fuller, advanced with her light walk and her high serenity, smiling from a distance at Mrs Gould. She had brought her uncle over to see dear Emilia, without ceremony, just for a moment before the siesta.

When all were seated again, Dr Monygham, who had come to dislike heartily everybody who approached Mrs Gould with any intimacy, kept aside, pretending to be lost in profound meditation. A louder phrase of Antonia made him lift his head.

'How can we abandon, groaning under oppression, those who have been our countrymen only a few years ago, who *are* our countrymen now?' Miss Avellanos was saying. 'How can we remain blind, and deaf without pity to the cruel wrong suffered by our brothers? There is a remedy.'

'Annex the rest of Costaguana to the order and prosperity of Sulaco,' snapped the doctor. 'There is no other remedy.'

'I am convinced, Señor Doctor,' Antonia said, with the earnest calm of invincible resolution, 'that this was from the first poor Martin's intention.'

'Yes, but the material interests will not let you jeopardize their development for a mere idea of pity and justice,' the doctor muttered, grumpily. 'And it is just as well perhaps.'

The Cardinal-Archbishop straightened up his gaunt, bony frame.

'We have worked for them; we have made them, these material interests of the foreigners,' the last of the Corbeláns uttered in a deep, denunciatory tone.

'And without them you are nothing,' cried the doctor from the distance. 'They will not let you.'

'Let them beware, then, lest the people, prevented from their aspirations, should rise and claim their share of the wealth and their share of the power,' the popular Cardinal-Archbishop of Sulaco declared, significantly, menacingly.

A silence ensued, during which his Eminence stared, frowning at the ground, and Antonia, graceful and rigid in her chair, breathed calmly in the strength of her convictions. Then the conversation took a social turn, touching on the visit of the Goulds to Europe. The Cardinal-Archbishop, when in Rome, had suffered from neuralgia in the head all the time. It was the climate – the bad air.

When uncle and niece had gone away, with the servants again falling on their knees, and the old porter, who had known Henry Gould, almost totally blind and impotent now, creeping up to kiss his Eminence's extended hand, Dr Monygham, looking after them, pronounced the one word:

'Incorrigible!'

Mrs Gould, with a look upwards, dropped wearily on her lap her white hands flashing with the gold and stones of many rings.

'Conspiring. Yes!' said the doctor. 'The last of the Avellanos and the last of the Corbeláns are conspiring with the refugees from Sta Marta that flock here after every revolution. The Café Lambroso at the corner of the Plaza is full of them; you can hear their chatter across the street like the noise of a parrot-house. They are conspiring for the invasion of Costaguana. And do you know where they go for strength, for the necessary force? To the secret societies amongst immigrants and natives, where Nostromo – I should say Captain Fidanza – is the great man. What gives him that position? Who can say? Genius? He has genius. He is greater with the populace than ever he was before. It was as if he had some secret power; some mysterious means to keep up his influence. He holds conferences with the Archbishop, as in those old days which you and I remember. Barrios is useless. But for a military head they have the pious Hernandez. And they may raise the country with the new cry of wealth for the people.'

'Will there never be any peace? Will there be no rest?' Mrs Gould whispered. 'I thought that we –'

'No!' interrupted the doctor. 'There is no peace and no rest in the development of material interests. They have their law, and their justice. But it is founded on expediency, and is inhuman; it is without rectitude, without the continuity and the force that can be found only in a moral principle. Mrs Gould, the time approaches when all that the Gould Concession stands for shall weigh as heavily upon the people as the barbarism, cruelty, and misrule of a few years back.'

'How can you say that, Dr Monygham?' she cried out, as if hurt in the most sensitive place of her soul.

'I can say that is true,' the doctor insisted, obstinately. 'It'll weigh as heavily, and provoke resentment, bloodshed, and vengeance, because the men have grown different. Do you think that now the mine would march upon the town to save their Señor Administrador? Do you think that?'

She pressed the backs of her entwined hands on her eyes and murmured hopelessly:

'Is it this we have worked for, then?'

The doctor lowered his head. He could follow her silent thought. Was it for this that her life had been robbed of all the intimate felicities of daily affection which her tenderness needed as the human body needs air to breathe? And the doctor, indignant with Charles Gould's blindness, hastened to change the conversation.

'It is about Nostromo that I wanted to talk to you. Ah! that fellow has some continuity and force. Nothing will put an end to him. But never mind that. There's something inexplicable going on – or perhaps only too easy to explain. You know, Linda is practically the lighthouse keeper of the Great Isabel light. The Garibaldino is too old now. His part is to clean the lamps and to cook in the house; but he can't get up the stairs any longer. The black-eyed Linda sleeps all day and watches the light all night. Not all day, though. She is up towards five in the afternoon, when our Nostromo, whenever he is in harbour with his schooner, comes out on his courting visit, pulling in a small boat.'

'Aren't they married yet?' Mrs Gould asked. 'The mother wished it, as far as I can understand, while Linda was yet quite a child. When I had the girls with me for a year or so during the War of Separation, that extraordinary Linda used to declare quite simply that she was going to be Gian' Battista's wife.'

'They are not married yet,' said the doctor, curtly. 'I have looked after them a little.'

'Thank you, dear Dr Monygham,' said Mrs Gould; and under the shade of the big trees her little, even teeth gleamed in a youthful smile of her gentle malice. 'People don't know how really good you are. You will not let them know, as if on purpose to annoy me, who have put my faith in your good heart long ago.'

The doctor, with a lifting up of his upper lip, as though he were longing to bite, bowed stiffly in his chair. With the utter absorption of a man to whom love comes late, not as the most splendid of illusions, but like an enlightening and priceless misfortune, the sight of that woman (of whom he had been deprived for nearly a year) suggested ideas of adoration, of kissing the hem of her robe. And this excess of feeling translated itself naturally into an augmented grimness of speech.

'I am afraid of being overwhelmed by too much gratitude. However, these people interest me. I went out several times to the Great Isabel light to look after old Giorgio.'

He did not tell Mrs Gould that it was because he found there, in her absence, the relief of an atmosphere of congenial sentiment in old Giorgio's austere admiration for the 'English signora – the benefactress'; in black-eyed Linda's voluble, torrential, passionate affection for 'our Doña Emilia – that angel'; in the white-throated, fair Giselle's adoring upward turn of the eyes, which then glided towards him with a sidelong, half-arch, half-candid glance, which made the doctor exclaim to himself mentally, 'If I weren't what I am, old and ugly, I would think the minx is making eyes at me. And perhaps she is. I dare say she would make eyes at anybody.' Dr Monygham said nothing of this to Mrs Gould, the providence of the Viola family, but reverted to what he called 'our great Nostromo'.

'What I wanted to tell you is this: Our great Nostromo did not take much notice of the old man and the children for some years. It's true, too, that he was away on his coasting voyages certainly ten months out of the twelve. He was making his fortune, as he told Captain Mitchell once. He seems to have done uncommonly well. It was only to be expected. He is a man full of resource, full of confidence in himself, ready to take chances and risks of every sort. I remember being in Mitchell's office one day, when he came in with that calm, grave air he always carried everywhere. He had been away trading in the Gulf of California, he said, looking straight past us at the wall, as his manner is, and was glad to see on his return that a lighthouse was being built on the cliff of the Great Isabel. Very glad, he repeated. Mitchell explained that it was the O.S.N. Company who were building it, for the convenience of the mail service, on his own advice. Captain Fidanza was good enough to say that it was excellent advice. I remember him twisting up his moustaches and looking all round the cornice of the room before he proposed that old Giorgio should be made the keeper of that light.'

'I heard of this. I was consulted at the time,' Mrs Gould said. 'I doubted whether it would be good for these girls to be shut up on that island as if in a prison.'

'The proposal fell in with the Garibaldino's humour. As to Linda, any place was lovely and delightful enough for her as long as it was Nostromo's suggestion. She could wait for her Gian' Battista's good pleasure there as well as anywhere else. My opinion is that she was always in love with that incorruptible Capataz. Moreover, both father and sister were anxious to get Giselle away from the attentions of a certain Ramirez.'

'Ah!' said Mrs Gould, interested. 'Ramirez? What sort of man is that?'

'Just a *mozo* of the town. His father was a *cargador*. As a lanky boy he ran about the wharf in rags, till Nostromo took him up and made a man of him. When he got a little older, he put him into a lighter and very soon gave him charge of the No. 3 boat – the boat which took the silver away, Mrs Gould. Nostromo selected that lighter for the work because she was the best sailing and the strongest boat of all the Company's fleet. Young Ramirez was one of the five *cargadores* entrusted with the removal of the treasure from the Custom House on that famous night. As the boat he had charge of was sunk, Nostromo, on leaving the Company's service, recommended him to Captain Mitchell for his successor. He had trained him in the routine of work perfectly, and thus Mr Ramirez, from a starving waif, becomes a man and the Capataz of the Sulaco *cargadores*.'

'Thanks to Nostromo,' said Mrs Gould, with warm approval.

'Thanks to Nostromo,' repeated Dr Monygham. 'Upon my word, the fellow's power frightens me when I think of it. That our poor old Mitchell was only too glad to appoint somebody trained to work, who saved him trouble, is not surprising. What is wonderful is the fact that the Sulaco *cargadores* accepted Ramirez for their chief, simply because such was Nostromo's good pleasure. Of course, he is not a second Nostromo, as he fondly imagined he would be; but still, the position was brilliant enough. It emboldened him to make up to Giselle Viola, who, you know, is the recognized beauty of the town. The old Garibaldino, however, took a violent dislike to him. I don't know why. Perhaps because he was not a model of perfection like his Gian' Battista, the incarnation of the courage, the fidelity, the honour of "the people". Signor Viola does not think much of Sulaco natives. Both of them, the old Spartan and that white-faced Linda, with her red mouth and coal-black eyes, were looking rather fiercely after the fair one. Ramirez was warned off. Father Viola, I am told, threatened him with his gun once.'

'But what of Giselle herself?' asked Mrs Gould.

'She's a bit of a flirt, I believe,' said the doctor. 'I don't think she cared much one way or another. Of course, she likes men's attentions. Ramirez was not the only one, let me tell you, Mrs Gould. There was one engineer, at least, on the railway staff who got warned off with a gun, too. Old Viola does not allow any trifling with his honour. He has grown uneasy and suspicious since his wife died. He was very pleased to remove his youngest girl away from the town. But look what happens, Mrs Gould. Ramirez, the honest, lovelorn swain, is forbidden the island. Very well. He respects the prohibition. But naturally turns his eyes frequently towards the Great Isabel. It seems as though he had been in the habit of gazing late at night upon the light. And during these sentimental vigils, he discovers that Nostromo, Captain Fidanza that is, returns very late from his visits to the Violas. As late as midnight at times.'

The doctor paused and stared meaningly at Mrs Gould.

'Yes. But I don't understand,' she began, looking puzzled.

'Now comes the strange part,' went on Dr Monygham. 'Viola, who is king on his island, will allow no visitor on it after dark. Even Captain Fidanza has got to leave after sunset, when Linda has gone up to tend the light. And Nostromo goes away obediently. But what happens afterwards? What does he do in the gulf between half past six and midnight? He has been seen more than once at that late hour pulling quietly into the harbour. Ramirez is devoured by jealousy. He dare not approach old Viola; but he plucked up courage to rail Linda about it on Sunday morning as she came on the mainland to hear Mass and visit her mother's grave. There was a scene on the wharf, which, as a matter of fact, I witnessed. It was early morning. He must have been waiting for her on purpose. I was there by the merest chance, having been called to an urgent consultation by the doctor of the German gunboat in the harbour. She poured wrath, scorn, and flame upon Ramirez, who seemed out of his mind. It was a strange sight, Mrs Gould: the long jetty, with this raving *cargador* in his crimson sash and the girl all in black, at the end; the early Sunday-morning quiet of the harbour in the shade of the mountains; nothing but a canoe or two moving between the ships at anchor, and the German gunboat's gig coming to take me off. Linda passed me within a foot. I noticed her wild eyes. I called out to her. She never heard me. She never saw me. But I looked at her face. It was awful in its anger and wretchedness.'

Mrs Gould sat up, opening her eyes wide.

'What do you mean, Dr Monygham? Do you mean to say that you suspect the younger sister?'

'*Quién sabe!* Who can tell?' said the doctor, shrugging his shoulders like a born Costaguanero. 'Ramirez came up to me on the wharf. He reeled – he looked insane. He took his head into his hands. He had to talk to someone – simply had to. Of course for all his mad state he recognized me. People know me well here. I have lived too long amongst them to be anything else but the evil-eyed doctor, who can cure all the ills of the flesh, and bring bad luck by a glance. He came up to me. He tried to be calm. He tried to make it out that he wanted merely to warn me against Nostromo. It seems that Captain Fidanza at some secret meeting or other had mentioned me as the worst despiser of all the poor – of the people. It's very possible. He honours me with his undying dislike. And a word from the great Fidanza may be quite enough to send some fool's knife into my back. The Sanitary Commission I preside over is not in favour with the populace. "Beware of him, Señor Doctor. Destroy him, Señor Doctor," Ramirez hissed right into my face. And then he broke out, "That man," he spluttered, "has cast a spell upon both these girls." As to himself, he had said too much. He must run away now – run away and hide somewhere. He moaned tenderly about Giselle, and then called her names that cannot be repeated. If he thought she could be made to love him by any means, he would carry her off from the island. Off into the woods. But it was no good . . . He strode away, flourishing his arms above his head. Then I noticed an old Negro, who had been sitting behind a pile of cases, fishing from the wharf. He wound up his lines and slunk away at once. But he must have heard something, and must have talked, too, because some of the old Garibaldino's railway friends, I suppose, warned him against Ramirez. At any rate, the father had been warned. But Ramirez had disappeared from the town.'

'I feel I have a duty towards these girls,' said Mrs Gould, uneasily. 'Is Nostromo in Sulaco now?'

'He is, since last Sunday.'

'He ought to be spoken to – at once.'

'Who will dare speak to him? Even the love-mad Ramirez runs away from the mere shadow of Captain Fidanza.'

'I can. I will,' Mrs Gould declared. 'A word will be enough for a man like Nostromo.'

The doctor smiled sourly.

'He must end this situation which lends itself to – I can't believe it of that child,' pursued Mrs Gould.

'He's very attractive,' muttered the doctor, gloomily.

'He'll see it, I am sure. He must put an end to all this by marrying Linda at once,' pronounced the first lady of Sulaco with immense decision.

Through the garden gate emerged Basilio, grown fat and sleek, with an elderly hairless face, wrinkles at the corners of his eyes, and his jet-black, coarse hair plastered down smoothly. Stooping carefully behind an ornamental clump of bushes, he put down with precaution a small child he had been carrying on his shoulder – his own and Leonarda's last born. The pouting, spoiled *camerista* and the head *mozo* of the Casa Gould had been married for some years now.

He remained squatting on his heels for a time, gazing fondly at his offspring, which returned his stare with imperturbable gravity; then, solemn and respectable, walked down the path.

'What is it, Basilio?' asked Mrs Gould.

'A telephone call came through from the office of the mine. The master remains to sleep at the mountain tonight.'

Dr Monygham had got up and stood looking away. A profound silence reigned for a time under the shade of the biggest trees in the lovely gardens of the Casa Gould.

'Very well, Basilio,' said Mrs Gould. She watched him walk away along the path, step aside behind the flowering bush, and reappear with the child seated on his shoulder. He passed through the gateway between the garden and the patio with measured steps, careful of his light burden.

The doctor, with his back to Mrs Gould, contemplated a flower-bed away in the sunshine. People believed him scornful and soured. The truth of his nature consisted in his capacity for passion and in the sensitiveness of his temperament. What he lacked was the polished callousness of men of the world, the callousness from which springs an easy tolerance for oneself and others; the tolerance wide as poles asunder from the true sympathy and human compassion. This want of callousness accounted for his sardonic turn of mind and his biting speeches.

In profound silence, and glaring viciously at the brilliant flowerbed, Dr Monygham poured mental imprecations on Charles Gould's head. Behind him the immobility of Mrs Gould added to the grace of her seated figure the charm of art, of an attitude caught and interpreted for ever. Turning abruptly, the doctor took his leave.

Mrs Gould leaned back in the shade of the big trees planted in a circle. She leaned back with her eyes closed and her white hands lying idle on the arms of her seat. The half-light under the thick mass of leaves brought out the youthful prettiness of her face; made the clear, light fabrics and white lace of her dress appear luminous. Small and dainty, as if radiating a light of her own in the deep shade of the interlaced boughs, she resembled a good fairy, weary with a long career of well-doing, touched by the withering suspicion of the uselessness of her labours, the powerlessness of her magic.

Had anybody asked her of what she was thinking, along in the garden of the *casa*, with her husband at the mine and the house closed to the street like an empty dwelling, her frankness would have had to evade the question. It had come into her mind that for life to be large and full, it must contain the care of the past and of the future in every passing moment of the present. Our daily work must be done to the glory of the dead, and for the good of those who come after. She thought that, and sighed without opening her eyes – without moving at all. Mrs Gould's face became set and rigid for a second, as if to receive, without flinching, a great wave of loneliness that swept over her head. And it came into her mind, too, that no one would ever ask her with solicitude what she was thinking of. No one. No one, but perhaps the man who had just gone away. No; no one who could be answered with careless sincerity in the ideal perfection of confidence.

The word 'incorrigible' – a word lately pronounced by Dr Monygham – floated into her still and sad immobility. Incorrigible in his devotion to the great silver mine was the Señor Administrador! Incorrigible in his hard, determined service of the material interests to which he had pinned his faith in the triumph of order and justice. Poor boy! She had a clear vision of the great hairs on his temples. He was perfect – perfect. What more could she have expected? It was a colossal and lasting success; and love was only a short moment of forgetfulness, a short intoxication, whose delight one remembered with a sense of sadness, as if it had been a deep grief lived through. There was something inherent in the necessities of successful action which carried with it the moral degradation of the idea. She saw the San Tomé mountain hanging over the Campo, over the whole land, feared, hated, wealthy; more soulless than any tyrant, more pitiless and autocratic than the worst Government; ready to crush innumerable lives in the expansion of its greatness. He did not see it. He could not see it. It was not his fault. He was perfect, perfect; but she would never have him to herself. Never; not for one short hour altogether to herself in this old Spanish house she loved so well! Incorrigible, the last of the Corbeláns, the last of the Avellanos, the doctor had said; but she saw clearly the San Tomé mine possessing, consuming, burning up the life of the last of the Costaguana Goulds; mastering the energetic spirit of the son as it had mastered the lamentable weakness of the father. A terrible success for the last of the Goulds. The last! She had hoped for a long, long time that perhaps – But no! There were to be no more. An immense desolation, the dread of her own continued life, descended upon the first lady of Sulaco. With a prophetic vision she saw herself surviving alone the degradation of her young ideal life, of love, of work – all alone in the Treasure House of the World. The profound, blind, suffering expression of a painful dream settled on her face with its closed eyes. In the indistinct voice of an unlucky sleeper, lying passive in the grip of a merciless nightmare, she stammered out aimlessly the words:

'Material interest.'

Chapter XII

NOSTROMO HAD been growing rich very slowly. It was an effect of his prudence. He could command himself even when thrown off his balance. And to become the slave of a treasure with full self-knowledge is an occurrence rare and mentally disturbing. But it was also in a great part because of the difficulty of converting it into a form in which it could become available. The mere act of getting it away from the island piecemeal, little by little, was surrounded by difficulties, by the dangers of imminent detection. He had to visit the Great Isabel in secret, between his voyages along the coast, which were the ostensible source of his fortune. The crew of his own schooner were to be feared as if they had been spies upon their dreaded captain. He did not dare stay too long in port. When his coaster was unloaded, he hurried away on another trip, for he feared arousing suspicion even by a day's delay. Sometimes during a week's stay, or more, he could only manage one visit to the treasure. And that was all. A couple of ingots. He suffered through his fears as much as through his prudence. To do things by stealth humiliated him. And he suffered most from the concentration of his thought upon the treasure.

A transgression, a crime, entering a man's existence, eats it up like a malignant growth, consumes it like a fever. Nostromo had lost his peace; the genuineness of all his qualities was destroyed. He felt it himself, and often cursed the silver of San Tomé. His courage, his magnificence, his leisure, his work, everything was as before, only everything was a sham. But the treasure was real. He clung to it with a more tenacious, mental grip. But he hated the feel of the ingots. Sometimes, after putting away a couple of them in his cabin – the fruit of a secret night expedition to the Great Isabel – he would look fixedly at his fingers, as if surprised they had left no stain on his skin.

He had found means of disposing of the silver bars in distant ports. The necessity to go far afield made his coasting voyages long, and caused his visits to the Viola household to be rare and far between. He was fated to have his wife from there. He had said so once to Giorgio himself. But the Garibaldino had put the subject aside with a majestic wave of his hand, clutching a smouldering black briar-root pipe. There was plenty of time; he was not the man to force his girls upon anybody.

As time went on, Nostromo discovered his preference for the younger of the two. They had some profound similarities of nature, which must exist for complete confidence and understanding, no matter what outward differences of temperament there may be to exercise their own fascination of contrast. His wife would have to know his secret or else life would be impossible. He was attracted by Giselle, with her candid gaze and white throat, pliable, silent, fond of excitement under her quiet indolence; whereas Linda, with her intense, passionately pale face, energetic, all fire and words, touched with gloom and scorn, a chip off the old block, true daughter of the austere republican, but with Teresa's voice, inspired him with a deep-seated mistrust. Moreover, the poor girl could not conceal her love for Gian' Battista. He could see it would be violent, exacting, suspicious, uncompromising – like her soul. Giselle, by her fair but warm beauty, by the surface placidity of her nature holding a promise of submissiveness, by the charm of her girlish mysteriousness, excited his passion and allayed his fears as to the future.

His absences from Sulaco were long. On returning from the longest of them, he made out lighters loaded with blocks of stone lying under the cliff of the Great Isabel; cranes and scaffolding above; workmen's figures moving about, and a small lighthouse already rising from its foundations on the edge of the cliff.

At this unexpected, undreamt-of, startling sight, he thought himself lost irretrievably. What could save him from detection now? Nothing! He was struck with amazed dread at this turn of chance, that would kindle a far-reaching light upon the only secret spot of his life; that life whose very essence, value, reality, consisted in its reflection from the admiring eyes of men. All of it but that thing which was beyond common comprehension; which stood between him and the power that hears and gives effect to the evil intention of curses. It was dark. Not every man had such a darkness. And they were going to put a light there. A light! He saw it shining upon disgrace, poverty, contempt. Somebody was sure to . . . Perhaps somebody had already . . .

The incomparable Nostromo, the Capataz, the respected and feared Captain Fidanza, the unquestioned patron of secret societies, a republican like old Giorgio, and a revolutionist at heart (but in another manner), was on the point of jumping overboard from the deck of his own schooner. That man, subjective almost to insanity, looked suicide deliberately in the face. But he never lost his head. He was checked by the thought that this was no escape. He imagined himself dead, and the disgrace, the shame going on. Or, rather, properly speaking, he could not imagine himself dead. He was possessed too strongly by the sense of his own existence, a thing of infinite duration in its changes, to grasp the notion of finality. The earth goes on for ever.

And he was courageous. It was a corrupt courage, but it was as good for his purposes as the other kind. He sailed close to the cliff of the Great Isabel, throwing a penetrating glance from the deck at the mouth of the ravine, tangled in an undisturbed growth of bushes. He sailed close enough to exchange hails with the workmen, shading their eyes on the edge of the sheer drop of the cliff overhung by the jib-head of a powerful crane. He perceived that none of them had any occasion even to approach the ravine where the silver lay hidden; let alone to enter it. In the harbour he learned that no one slept on the island. The labouring gangs returned to port every evening, singing chorus songs in the empty lighters towed by a harbour tug. For the moment he had nothing to fear.

But afterwards? he asked himself. Later, when a keeper came to live in the cottage that was being built some hundred and fifty yards back from the low light-tower, and four hundred or so from the dark, shaded, jungly ravine, containing the secret of his safety, of his influence, of his magnificence, of his power over the future, of his defiance of ill-luck, of every possible betrayal from rich and poor alike – what then? He could never shake off the treasure. His audacity, greater than that of other men, had welded that vein of silver into his life. And the feeling of fearful and ardent subjection, the feeling of his slavery – so irremediable and profound that often, in his thoughts, he compared himself to the legendary *gringos*, neither dead nor alive, bound down to their conquest of unlawful wealth on Azuera – weighted heavily on the independent Captain Fidanza, owner and master of a coasting schooner, whose smart appearance (and fabulous good luck in trading) were so well known along the western seaboard of a vast continent.

Fiercely whiskered and grave, a shade less supple in his walk, the vigour and symmetry of his powerful limbs lost in the vulgarity of a brown tweed suit, made by Jews in the slums of London, and sold by the clothing department of the

Compañía Anzani, Captain Fidanza was seen in the streets of Sulaco attending to his business, as usual, that trip. And, as usual, he allowed it to get about that he had made a great profit on his cargo. It was a cargo of salt fish, and Lent was approaching. He was seen in tramcars going to and fro between the town and the harbour; he talked with people in a café or two in his measured steady voice. Captain Fidanza was *seen*. The generation that would know nothing of the famous ride to Cayta was not born yet.

Nostromo, the miscalled Capataz de Cargadores, had made for himself, under his rightful name, another public existence, but modified by the new conditions, less picturesque, more difficult to keep up in the increased size and varied population of Sulaco, the progressive capital of the Occidental Republic.

Captain Fidanza, unpicturesque, but always a little mysterious, was recognized quite sufficiently under the lofty glass and iron roof of the Sulaco railway station. He took a local train, and got out in Rincón, where he visited the widow of the *cargador* who had died of his wounds (at the dawn of the New Era, like Don José Avellanos) in the patio of the Casa Gould. He consented to sit down and drink a glass of cool lemonade in the hut, while the woman, standing up, poured a perfect torrent of words to which he did not listen. He left some money with her, as usual. The orphaned children, growing up and well schooled, calling him uncle, clamoured for his blessing. He gave that, too; and in the doorway paused for a moment to look at the flat face of the San Tomé mountain with a faint frown. This slight contraction of his bronzed brow casting a marked tinge of severity upon his usual unbending expression, was observed at the Lodge which he attended – but went away before the banquet. He wore it at the meeting of some good comrades, Italians and Occidentals, assembled in his honour under the presidency of an indigent, sickly, somewhat hunchbacked little photographer, with a white face and a magnanimous soul dyed crimson by a bloodthirsty hate of all capitalists, oppressors of the two hemispheres. The heroic Giorgio Viola, old revolutionist, would have understood nothing of this opening speech; and Captain Fidanza, lavishly generous as usual to some poor comrades, made no speech at all. He had listened, frowning with his mind far away, and walked off unapproachable, silent, like a man full of cares.

His frown deepened as, in the early morning, he watched the stone-masons go off to the Great Isabel, in lighters loaded with squared blocks of stone, enough to add another course to the squat light-tower. That was the rate of the work. One course per day.

And Captain Fidanza meditated. The presence of strangers on the island would cut him off completely from the treasure. It had been difficult and dangerous enough before. He was afraid, and he was angry. He thought with the resolution of a master and the cunning of a cowed slave. Then he went ashore.

He was a man of resource and ingenuity; and, as usual, the expedient he found at a critical moment was effective enough to alter the situation radically. He had the gift of evolving safety out of the very danger, this incomparable Nostromo, this 'fellow in a thousand'. With Giorgio established on the Great Isabel, there would be no need for concealment. He would be able to go openly, in daylight, to see his daughters – one of his daughters – and stay late talking to the old Garibaldino. Then in the dark . . . Night after night . . . He would dare to grow rich quicker now. He yearned to clasp, embrace, absorb, subjugate in unquestioned possession this treasure, whose tyranny had weighed upon his mind, his actions, his very sleep.

He went to see his friend Captain Mitchell – and the thing was done as Dr Monygham had related to Mrs Gould. When the project was mooted to the Garibaldino, something like the faint reflection, the dim ghost of a very ancient smile, stole under the white and enormous moustaches of the old hater of kings and ministers. His daughters were the object of his anxious care. The younger, especially. Linda, with her mother's voice, had taken more her mother's place. Her deep, vibrating 'Eh, Padre?' seemed, but for the change of the word, the very echo of the impassioned, remonstrating 'Eh, Giorgio?' of poor Signora Teresa. It was his fixed opinion that the town was no proper place for his girls. The infatuated but guileless Ramirez was the object of his profound aversion, as resuming the sins of the country whose people were blind, vile *esclavos*.

On his return from his next voyage, Captain Fidanza found the Violas settled in the light-keeper's cottage. His knowledge of Giorgio's idiosyncrasies had not played him false. The Garibaldino had refused to entertain the idea of any companion whatever, except his girls. And Captain Mitchell, anxious to please his poor Nostromo, with that felicity of inspiration which only true affection can give, had formally appointed Linda Viola as underkeeper of Isabel's Light.

'The light is private property,' he used to explain. 'It belongs to my Company. I've the power to nominate whom I like, and Viola it shall be. It's about the only thing Nostromo – a man worth his weight in gold, mind you – has ever asked me to do for him.'

Directly his schooner was anchored opposite the New Custom House, with its sham air of a Greek temple, flat-roofed, with a colonnade, Captain Fidanza went pulling his small boat out of the harbour, bound for the Great Isabel, openly in the light of a declining day, before all men's eyes, with a sense of having mastered the fates. He must establish a regular position. He would ask him for his daughter now. He thought of Giselle as he pulled. Linda loved him, perhaps, but the old man would be glad to keep the eldest, who had his wife's voice.

He did not pull for the narrow strand where he had landed with Decoud, and afterwards alone on his first visit to the treasure. He made for the beach at the other end, and walked up the regular and gentle slope of the wedge-shaped island. Giorgio Viola, whom he saw from afar, sitting on a bench under the front wall of the cottage, lifted his arm slightly to his loud hail. He walked up. Neither of the girls appeared.

'It is good here,' said the old man, in his austere, far-away manner.

Nostromo nodded; then, after a short silence:

'You saw my schooner pass in not two hours ago? Do you know why I am here before, so to speak, my anchor has fairly bitten into the ground of this port of Sulaco?'

'You are welcome like a son,' the old man declared, quietly, staring away upon the sea.

'Ah! thy son. I know. I am what thy son would have been. It is well, *viejo*. It is a very good welcome. Listen, I have come to ask you for –'

A sudden dread came upon the fearless and incorruptible Nostromo. He dared not utter the name in his mind. The slight pause only imparted a marked weight and solemnity to the changed end of the phrase.

'For my wife!' . . . His heart was beating fast. 'It is time you –'

The Garibaldino arrested him with an extended arm. 'That was left for you to judge.'

He got up slowly. His beard, unclipped since Teresa's death, thick, snow-white, covered his powerful chest. He turned his head to the door, and called out in his strong voice:

'Linda.'

Her answer came sharp and faint from within; and the appalled Nostromo stood up, too, but remained mute, gazing at the door. He was afraid. He was not afraid of being refused the girl he loved – no mere refusal could stand between him and a woman he desired – but the shining spectre of the treasure rose before him, claiming his allegiance in a silence that could not be gain-said. He was afraid, because, neither dead nor alive, like the *gringos* on Azuera, he belonged body and soul to the unlawfulness of his audacity. He was afraid of being forbidden the island. He was afraid, and said nothing.

Seeing the two men standing up side by side to await her. Linda stopped in the doorway. Nothing could alter the passionate dead whiteness of her face; but the black eyes seemed to catch and concentrate all the light of the low sun in a flaming spark within the black depths, covered at once by the slow descent of heavy eyelids.

'Behold thy husband, master, and benefactor.' Old Viola's voice resounded with a force that seemed to fill the whole gulf.

She stepped forward with her eyes nearly closed, like a sleepwalker in a beatific dream.

Nostromo made a superhuman effort. 'It is time, Linda, we two were betrothed,' he said, steadily, in his level, careless, unbending tone.

She put her hand into his offered palm, lowering her head, dark with bronze glints, upon which her father's hand rested for a moment.

'And so the soul of the dead is satisfied.'

This came from Giorgio Viola, who went on talking for a while of his dead wife; while the two, sitting side by side, never looked at each other. Then the old man ceased; and Linda, motionless, began to speak.

'Ever since I felt I lived in the world, I have lived for you alone, Gian' Battista. And that you knew! You knew it . . . Battistino.'

She pronounced the name exactly with her mother's intonation. A gloom as of the grave covered Nostromo's heart.

'Yes. I knew,' he said.

The heroic Garibaldino sat on the same bench bowing his hoary head, his old soul dwelling alone with its memories, tender and violent, terrible and dreary – solitary on the earth full of men.

And Linda, his best-loved daughter, was saying, 'I was yours ever since I can remember. I had only to think of you for the earth to become empty to my eyes. When you were there, I could see no one else. I was yours. Nothing is changed. The world belongs to you, and you let me live in it . . .' She dropped her low, vibrating voice to a still lower note, and found other things to say – torturing for the man at her side. Her murmur ran on ardent and voluble. She did not seem to see her sister, who came out with an altar-cloth she was embroidering in her hands, and passed in front of them, silent, fresh, fair, with a quick glance and a faint smile, to sit a little away on the other side of Nostromo.

The evening was still. The sun sank almost to the edge of a purple ocean; and the white lighthouse, livid against the background of clouds filling the head of the gulf, bore the lantern red and glowing, like a liver ember kindled by the fire of the sky. Giselle, indolent and demure, raised the altar-cloth from time to time to hide nervous yawns, as of a young panther.

Suddenly Linda rushed at her sister, and, seizing her head, covered her face with kisses. Nostromo's brain reeled. When she left her, as if stunned by the violent caresses, with her hands lying in her lap, the slave of the treasure felt as if he could shoot that woman. Old Giorgio lifted his leonine head.

'Where are you going, Linda?'

'To the light, *padre mio*.'

'*Sí, sâi* – to your duty.'

He got up, too, looked after his eldest daughter; then, in a tone whose festive note seemed the echo of a mood lost in the night of ages:

'I am going in to cook something. Aha! Son! The old man knows where to find a bottle of wine, too.'

He turned to Giselle, with a change to austere tenderness.

'And you, little one, pray not to the God of priests and slaves, but to the God of orphans, of the oppressed, of the poor, of little children, to give thee a man like this one for a husband.'

His hand rested heavily for a moment on Nostromo's shoulder; then he went in. The hopeless slave of the San Tomé silver felt at these words the venomous fangs of jealousy biting deep into his heart. He was appalled by the novelty of the experience, by its force, by its physical intimacy. A husband! A husband for her! And yet it was natural that Giselle should have a husband at some time or other. He had never realized that before. In discovering that her beauty could belong to another he felt as though he could kill this one of old Giorgio's daughters also. He muttered moodily:

'They say you love Ramirez.'

She shook her head without looking at him. Coppery glints rippled to and fro on the wealth of her gold hair. Her smooth forehead had the soft, pure sheen of a priceless pearl in the splendour of the sunset, mingling the gloom of starry spaces, the purple of the sea, and the crimson of the sky in a magnificent stillness.

'No,' she said, slowly. 'I never loved him. I think I never . . . He loves me – perhaps.'

The seduction of her slow voice died out of the air, and her raised eyes remained fixed on nothing, as if indifferent and without thought.

'Ramirez told you he loved you?' asked Nostromo, restraining himself.

'Ah! once – one evening . . .'

'The miserable . . . Ha!'

He had jumped up as if stung by a gad-fly, and stood before her mute with anger.

'*Misericordia Divina!* You, too, Gian' Battista! Poor wretch that I am!' she lamented in ingenuous tones. 'I told Linda, and she scolded – she scolded. Am I to live blind, dumb, and deaf in this world? And she told father, who took down his gun and cleaned it. Poor Ramirez! Then you came, and she told you.'

He looked at her. He fastened his eyes upon the hollow of her white throat, which had the invincible charm of things young, palpitating, delicate, and alive. Was this the child he had known? Was it possible? It dawned upon him that in these last years he had really seen very little – nothing – of her. Nothing. She had come into the world like a thing unknown. She had come upon him unawares. She was a danger. A frightful danger. The instinctive mood of fierce determination that had never failed him before the perils of this life added its steady force to the violence of his passion. She, in a voice that recalled to him the song of running water, the tinkling of a silver bell, continued:

'And between you three you have brought me here into this captivity to the sky and water. Nothing else. Sky and water. Oh, *Santissima Madre*. My hair shall turn grey on this tedious island. I could hate you, Gian' Battista!'

He laughed loudly. Her voice enveloped him like a caress. She bemoaned her fate, spreading unconsciously, like a flower with its perfume in the coolness of the evening, the indefinable seduction of her person. Was it her fault that nobody ever had admired Linda? Even when they were little, going out with their mother to Mass, she remembered that people took no notice of Linda, who was fearless, and chose instead to frighten her, who was timid, with their attention. It was her hair like gold, she supposed.

He broke out:

'Your hair like gold, and your eyes like violets, and your lips like the rose; your round arms, your white throat . . .'

Imperturbable in the indolence of her pose, she blushed deeply all over to the roots of her hair. She was not conceited. She was no more self-conscious than a flower. But she was pleased. And perhaps even a flower loves to hear itself praised. He glanced down, and added, impetuously:

'Your little feet!'

Leaning back against the rough stone wall of the cottage, she seemed to bask languidly in the warmth of the rosy flush. Only her lowered eyes glanced at her little feet.

'And so you are going at last to marry our Linda. She is terrible. Ah! now she will understand better since you have told her you love her. She will not be so fierce.'

'*Chica!*' said Nostromo, 'I have not told her anything.'

'Then make haste. Come tomorrow. Come and tell her, so that I may have some peace from her scolding and – perhaps – who knows . . .'

'Be allowed to listen to your Ramirez, eh? Is that it? You . . .'

'Mercy of God! How violent you are, Giovanni,' she said, unmoved. 'Who is Ramirez . . . Ramirez . . . Who is he?' she repeated, dreamily, in the dusk and gloom of the clouded gulf, with a low red streak in the west like a hot bar of glowing iron laid across the entrance of a world sombre as a cavern, where the magnificent Capataz de Cargadores had hidden his conquests of love and wealth.

'Listen, Giselle,' he said, in measured tones; 'I will tell no word of love to your sister. Do you want to know why?'

'Alas! I could not understand perhaps, Giovanni. Father says you are not like other men; that no one has ever understood you properly; that the rich will be surprised yet . . . Oh! saints in heaven! I am weary.'

She raised her embroidery to conceal the lower part of her face, then let it fall on her lap. The lantern was shaded on the land side, but slanting away from the dark column of the lighthouse they could see the long shaft of light, kindled by Linda, go out to strike the expiring glow in a horizon of purple and red.

Giselle Viola, with her head resting against the wall of the house, her eyes half closed, and her little feet, in white stockings and black slippers, crossed over each other, seemed to surrender herself, tranquil and fatal, to the gathering dusk. The charm of her body, the promising mysteriousness of her indolence, went out into the night of the Placid Gulf like a fresh and intoxicating fragrance spreading out in the shadows, impregnating the air. The incorruptible Nostromo breathed her ambient seduction in the tumultuous heaving of his breast. Before leaving the harbour he had thrown off the store clothing of Captain Fidanza, for greater ease in the long pull out to the islands. He stood before her in the red sash and check shirt as he used to appear on the Company's wharf – a Mediterranean sailor come ashore to try his luck in Costaguana. The dusk of purple and red enveloped him, too – close, soft, profound, as no more than fifty yards from that spot it had gathered evening after evening about the self-destructive passion of Don Martin Decoud's utter scepticism, flaming up to death in solitude.

'You have got to hear,' he began at last, with perfect self-control. 'I shall say no word of love to your sister, to whom I am betrothed from this evening, because it is you that I love. It is you! . . .'

The dusk let him see yet the tender and voluptuous smile that came instinctively upon her lips shaped for love and kisses, freeze hard in the drawn, haggard lines of terror. He could not restrain himself any longer. While she shrank from his approach, her arms went out to him, abandoned and regal in the dignity of her languid surrender. He held her head in his two hands, and showered rapid kisses upon the upturned face that gleamed in the purple dusk. Masterful and tender, he was entering slowly upon the fullness of his possession. And he perceived that she was crying. Then the incomparable Capataz, the man of careless loves, became gentle and caressing, like a woman to the grief of a child. He murmured to her fondly. He sat down by her and nursed her fair head on his breast. He called her his star and little flower.

It had grown dark. From the living-room of the light-keeper's cottage, where Giorgio, one of the Immortal Thousand, was bending his leonine and heroic head over a charcoal fire, there came the sound of sizzling and the aroma of an artistic *frittura*.

In the obscure disarray of that thing, happening like a cataclysm, it was in her feminine head that some gleam of reason survived. He was lost to the world in their embraced stillness. But she said, whispering into his ear:

'God of mercy! What will become of me – here – now – between this sky and this water I hate? Linda, Linda – I see her! . . .' She tried to get out of his arms, suddenly relaxed at the sound of that name. But there was no one approaching their black shapes, enlaced and struggling on the white background of the wall. 'Linda! Poor Linda! I tremble! I shall die of fear before my poor sister Linda, betrothed today to Giovanni – my lover! Giovanni, you must have been mad! I cannot understand you! You are not like other men! I will not give you up – never – only to God himself! But why have you done this blind, mad, cruel, frightful thing?'

Released, she hung her head, let fall her hands. The altar-cloth, as if tossed by a great wind, lay far away from them, gleaming white on the black ground.

'From fear of losing my hope of you,' said Nostromo.

'You knew that you had my soul! You know everything! It was made for you! But what could stand between you and me? What? Tell me!' she repeated, without impatience, in superb assurance.

'Your dead mother,' he said, very low.

'Ah! . . . Poor mother! She has always . . . She is a saint in heaven now, and I cannot give you up to her. No, Giovanni. Only to God alone. You were mad – but it is done. Oh! what have you done? Giovanni, my beloved, my life, my master, do not leave me here in this grave of clouds. You cannot leave me now. You must take me away – at once – this instant – in the little boat. Giovanni, carry me off tonight, from my fear of Linda's eyes, before I have to look at her again.'

She nestled closer to him. The slave of the San Tomé silver felt the weight as of chains upon his limbs, a pressure as of a cold hand upon his lips. He struggled against the spell.

'I cannot,' he said. 'Not yet. There is something that stands between us and the freedom of the world.'

She pressed her form closer to his side with a subtle and naïve instinct of seduction.

'You rave, Giovanni – my lover!' she whispered, engagingly. 'What can there be? Carry me off – in thy very hands – to Doña Emilia – away from here. I am not very heavy.'

It seemed as though she expected him to lift her up at once in his two palms. She had lost the notion of all impossibility. Anything could happen on this night of wonder. As he made no movement, she almost cried aloud:

'I tell you I am afraid of Linda!' And still he did not move. She became quiet and wily. 'What can there be?' she asked, coaxingly.

He felt her warm, breathing, alive, quivering in the hollow of his arm. In the exulting consciousness of his strength, and the triumphant excitement of his mind, he struck out for his freedom.

'A treasure,' he said. All was still. She did not understand. 'A treasure. A treasure of silver to buy a gold crown for thy brow.'

'A treasure?' she repeated in a faint voice, as if from the depths of a dream. 'What is it you say?'

She disengaged herself gently. He got up and looked down at her, aware of her face, of her hair, her lips, the dimples on her cheeks – seeing the fascination of her person in the night of the gulf as if in the blaze of noonday. Her nonchalant and seductive voice trembled with the excitement of admiring awe and ungovernable curiosity.

'A treasure of silver!' she stammered out. Then pressed on faster: 'What? Where? How did you get it, Giovanni?'

He wrestled with the spell of captivity. It was as if striking a heroic blow that he burst out:

'Like a thief!'

The densest blackness of the Placid Gulf seemed to fall upon his head. He could not see her now. She had vanished into a long, obscure, abysmal silence, whence her voice came back to him after a time with a faint glimmer, which was her face.

'I love you! I love you!'

These words gave him an unwonted sense of freedom; they cast a spell stronger than the accursed spell of the treasure; they changed his weary subjection to that dead thing into an exulting conviction of his power. He would cherish her, he said, in a splendour as great as Doña Emilia's. The rich lived on wealth stolen from the people, but he had taken from the rich nothing – nothing that was not lost to them already by their folly and their betrayal. For he had been betrayed – he said – deceived, tempted. She believed him . . . He had kept the treasure for purposes of revenge; but now he cared nothing for it. He cared only for her. He would put her beauty in a palace on a hill crowned with olive trees – a white palace above a blue sea. He would keep her there like a jewel in a casket. He would get land for her – her own land fertile with vines and corn – to set her little feet upon. He kissed them . . . He had already paid for it all with the soul of a woman and the life of a man . . . The Capataz de Cargadores tasted the supreme intoxication of his generosity. He flung the mastered treasure superbly at her feet in the impenetrable darkness of the gulf, in the darkness defying – as men said – the knowledge of God and the wit of the devil. But she must let him grow rich first – he warned her.

She listened as if in a trance. Her finger stirred in his hair. He got up from his knees reeling, weak, empty, as though he had flung his soul away.

'Make haste, then,' she said. 'Make haste, Giovanni, my lover, my master, for I will give thee up to no one but God. And I am afraid of Linda.'

He guessed at her shudder, and swore to do his best. He trusted the courage of her love. She promised to be brave in order to be loved always – far away in a white palace upon a hill above a blue sea. Then with a timid, tentative eagerness she murmured:

'Where is it? Where? Tell me that, Giovanni.'

He opened his mouth and remained silent – thunderstruck.

'Not that! Not that!' he gasped out, appalled at the spell of secrecy that had kept him dumb before so many people falling upon his lips again with unimpaired force. Not even to her. Not even to her. It was too dangerous. 'I forbid thee to ask,' he cried at her, deadening cautiously the anger of his voice.

He had not regained his freedom. The spectre of the unlawful treasure arose, standing by her side like a figure of silver, pitiless and secret, with a finger on its pale lips. His soul died within him at the vision of himself creeping in presently along the ravine, with the smell of earth, of damp foliage in his nostrils – creeping in, determined in a purpose that numbed his breast, and creeping out again loaded with silver, with his ears alert to every sound. It must be done on this very night – that work of a craven slave!

He stooped low, pressed the hem of her skirt to his lips, with a muttered command:

'Tell him I would not stay,' and was gone suddenly from her, silent, without as much as a footfall in the dark night.

She sat still, her head resting indolently against the wall, and her little feet in white stockings and black slippers crossed over each other. Old Giorgio, coming out, did not seem to be surprised at the intelligence as much as she had vaguely feared. For she was full of inexplicable fear now – fear of everything and everybody except of her Giovanni and his treasure. But that was incredible.

The heroic Garibaldino accepted Nostromo's abrupt departure with a sagacious indulgence. He remembered his own feelings, and exhibited a masculine penetration of the true state of the case.

'*Va bene*. Let him go. Ha! ha! No matter how fair the woman, it galls a little. Liberty, liberty. There's more than one kind! He had said the great word, and son Gian' Battista is not tame.' He seemed to be instructing the motionless and scared Giselle . . . 'A man should not be tame,' he added, dogmatically out of the doorway. Her stillness and silence seemed to displease him. 'Do not give way to the enviousness of your sister's lot,' he admonished her, very grave, in his deep voice.

Presently he had to come to the door again to call in his younger daughter. It was late. He shouted her name three times before she even moved her head. Left alone, she had become the helpless prey of astonishment. She walked into the bedroom she shared with Linda like a person profoundly asleep. That aspect was so marked that even old Giorgio, spectacled, raising his eyes from the Bible, shook his head as she shut the door behind her.

She walked right across the room without looking at anything, and sat down at once by the open window. Linda, stealing down from the tower in the exuberance of her happiness, found her with a lighted candle at her back, facing the black night full of sighing gusts of wind and the sound of distant showers – a true night of the gulf, too dense for the eye of God and the wiles of the devil. She did not turn her head at the opening of the door.

There was something in that immobility which reached Linda in the depths of her paradise. The elder sister guessed angrily: the child is thinking of that wretched Ramirez. Linda longed to talk. She said in her arbitrary voice, 'Giselle!' and was not answered by the slightest movement.

The girl that was going to live in a palace and walk on ground of her own was ready to die with terror. Not for anything in the world would she have turned her head to face her sister. Her heart was beating madly. She said with subdued haste:

'Do not speak to me. I am praying.'

Linda, disappointed, went out quietly; and Giselle sat on, unbelieving, lost, dazed, patient, as if waiting for the confirmation of the incredible. The hopeless blackness of the clouds seemed part of a dream, too. She waited.

She did not wait in vain. The man whose soul was dead within him, creeping out of the ravine, weighted with silver, had seen the gleam of the lighted window, and could not help retracing his steps from the beach.

On that impenetrable background, obliterating the lofty mountains by the seaboard, she saw the slave of the San Tomé silver, as if by an extraordinary power of a miracle. She accepted his return as if henceforth the world could hold no surprise for all eternity.

She rose, compelled and rigid, and began to speak long before the light from within fell upon the face of the approaching man.

'You have come back to carry me off. It is well! Open thy arms, Giovanni, my lover. I am coming.'

His prudent footsteps stopped, and with his eyes glistening wildly, he spoke in a harsh voice:

'Not yet. I must grow rich slowly.' . . . A threatening note came into his tone. 'Do not forget that you have a thief for your lover.'

'Yes! Yes!' she whispered, hastily. 'Come nearer! Listen! Do not give me up, Giovanni! Never, never! . . . I will be patient! . . .'

Her form drooped consolingly over the low casement towards the slave of the unlawful treasure. The light in the room went out, and weighted with silver, the magnificent Capataz clasped her round her white neck in the darkness of the gulf as a drowning man clutches at a straw.

Chapter XIII

On the day Mrs Gould was going, in Dr Monygham's words, to 'give a *tertulia*', Captain Fidanza went down the side of his schooner lying in Sulaco harbour, calm, unbending, deliberate in the way he sat down in his dinghy and took up his sculls. He was later than usual. The afternoon was well advanced before he landed on the beach of the Great Isabel, and with a steady pace climbed the slope of the island.

From a distance he made out Giselle sitting in a chair tilted back against the end of the house, under the window of the girl's room. She had her embroidery in her hands, and held it well up to her eyes. The tranquillity of that girlish figure exasperated the feeling of perpetual struggle and strife he carried in his breast. He became angry. It seemed to him that she ought to hear the clanking of his fetters – his silver fetters, from afar. And while ashore that day, he had met the doctor with the evil eye, who had looked at him very hard.

The raising of her eyes mollified him. They smiled in their flower-like freshness straight upon his heart. Then she frowned. It was a warning to be cautious. He stopped some distance away, and in a loud, indifferent tone, said:

'Good day, Giselle. Is Linda up yet?'

'Yes. She is in the big room with father.'

He approached then, and, looking through the window into the bedroom for fear of being detected by Linda returning there for some reason, he said, moving only his lips:

'You love me?'

'More than my life.' She went on with her embroidery under his contemplating gaze and continued to speak, looking at her work, 'Or I could not live. I could not, Giovanni. For this life is like death. Oh, Giovanni, I shall perish if you do not take me away.'

He smiled carelessly. 'I will come to the window when it's dark,' he said.

'No, don't, Giovanni. Not tonight, Linda and father have been talking together for a long time today.'

'What about?'

'Ramirez, I fancy I heard. I do not know. I am afraid. I am always afraid. It is like dying a thousand times a day. Your love is to me like your treasure to you. It is there, but I can never get enough of it.'

He looked at her very still. She was beautiful. His desire had grown within him. He had two masters now. But she was incapable of sustained emotion. She was sincere in what she said, but she slept placidly at night. When she saw him she flamed up always. Then only an increased taciturnity marked the change in her. She was afraid of betraying herself. She was afraid of pain, of bodily harm, of sharp words, of facing anger, and witnessing violence. For her soul was light and tender with a pagan sincerity in its impluses. She murmured:

'Give up the palazzo, Giovanni, and the vineyards on the hills, for which we are starving our love.'

She ceased, seeing Linda standing silent at the corner of the house.

Nostromo turned to his affianced wife with a greeting, and was amazed at her sunken eyes, at her hollow cheeks, at the air of illness and anguish in her face.

'Have you been ill?' he asked, trying to put some concern into this question.

Her black eyes blazed at him. 'Am I thinner?' she asked.

'Yes – perhaps – a little.'

'And older?'

'Every day counts – for all of us.'

'I shall go grey, I fear, before the ring is on my finger,' she said, slowly keeping her gaze fastened upon him.

She waited for what he would say, rolling down her turned-up sleeves.

'No fear of that,' he said, absently.

She turned away as if it had been something final, and busied herself with household cares while Nostromo talked with her father. Conversation with the old Garibaldino was not easy. Age had left his faculties unimpaired, only they seemed to have withdrawn somewhere deep within him. His answers were slow in coming, with an effect of august gravity. But that day he was more animated, quicker; there seemed to be more life in the old lion. He was uneasy for the integrity of his honour. He believed in Sidoni's warning as to Ramirez's designs upon his younger daughter. And he did not trust her. She was flighty. He said nothing of his cares to 'Son Gian' Battista'. It was a touch of senile vanity. He wanted to show that he was equal yet to the task of guarding alone the honour of his house.

Nostromo went away early. As soon as he had disappeared, walking towards the beach, Linda stepped over the threshold and, with a haggard smile, sat down by the side of her father.

Ever since that Sunday, when the infatuated and desperate Ramirez had waited for her on the wharf, she had no doubts whatever. The jealous ravings of that man were no revelation. They had only fixed with precision, as with a nail driven into her heart, that sense of unreality and deception which, instead of bliss and security, she had found in her intercourse with her promised husband. She had passed on, pouring indignation and scorn upon Ramirez; but, that Sunday, she nearly died of wretchedness and shame, lying on the carved and lettered stone of Teresa's grave, subscribed for by the engine-drivers and the fitters of the railway workshops, in sign of their respect for the hero of Italian Unity. Old Viola had not been able to carry out his desire of burying his wife in the sea; and Linda wept upon the stone.

The gratuitous outrage appalled her. If he wished to break her heart – well and good. Everything was permitted to Gian' Battista. But why trample upon the pieces; why seek to humiliate her spirit? Aha! He could not break that. She dried her tears. And Giselle! Giselle! The little one that, ever since she could toddle, had always clung to her skirt for protection. What duplicity! But she could not help it probably. When there was a man in the case the poor featherheaded wretch could not help herself.

Linda had a good share of the Viola stoicism. She resolved to say nothing. But woman-like she put passion into her stoicism. Giselle's short answers, prompted by fearful caution, drove her beside herself by their curtness that resembled disdain. One day she flung herself upon the chair in which her indolent sister was lying and impressed the mark of her teeth at the base of the whitest neck in Sulaco. Giselle cried out. But she had her share of the Viola heroism. Ready to faint with terror, she only said, in a lazy voice, '*Madre de Dios!* Are you going to eat me alive, Linda?' And this outburst passed off leaving no trace upon the situation. 'She knows nothing. She cannot know anything,' reflected Giselle. 'Perhaps it is not true. It cannot be true,' Linda tried to persuade herself.

But when she saw Captain Fidanza for the first time after her meeting with the distracted Ramirez, the certitude of her misfortune returned. She watched him from the doorway go away to his boat, asking herself stoically, 'Will they meet tonight?' She made up her mind not to leave the tower for a second. When he had disappeared she came out and sat down by her father.

The venerable Garibaldino felt, in his own words, 'a young man yet'. In one way or another a good deal of talk about Ramirez had reached him of late; and his contempt and dislike of that man who obviously was not what his son would have been, had made him restless. He slept very little now; but for several nights past instead of reading – or only sitting, with Mrs Gould's silver spectacles on his nose, before the open Bible – he had been prowling actively all about the island with his old gun, on watch over his honour.

Linda, laying her thin brown hand on his knee, tried to soothe his excitement. Ramirez was not in Sulaco. Nobody knew where he was. He was gone. His talk of what he would do meant nothing.

'No,' the old man interrupted. 'But son Gian' Battista told me – quite of himself – that the cowardly *esclavo* was drinking and gambling with the rascals of Zapiga, over there on the north side of the gulf. He may get some of the worst scoundrels of that scoundrelly town of Negroes to help him in his attempt upon the little one . . . But I am not so old. No!'

She argued earnestly against the probability of any attempt being made; and at last the old man fell silent, chewing his white moustache. Women had their obstinate notions which must be humoured – his poor wife was like that, and Linda resembled her mother. It was not seemly for a man to argue. 'Maybe. Maybe,' he mumbled.

She was by no means easy in her mind. She loved Nostromo. She turned her eyes upon Giselle, sitting at a distance, with something of maternal tenderness, and the jealous anguish of a rival outraged in her defeat. Then she rose and walked over to her.

'Listen – you,' she said, roughly.

The invincible candour of the gaze, raised up all violet and dew, excited her rage and admiration. She had beautiful eyes – the *chica* – this vile thing of white flesh and black deception. She did not know whether she wanted to tear them out with shouts of vengeance or cover up their mysterious and shameless innocence with kisses of pity and love. And suddenly they became empty, gazing blankly at her, except for a little fear not quite buried deep enough with all the other emotions in Giselle's heart.

Linda said, 'Ramirez is boasting in town that he will carry you off from the island.'

'What folly!' answered the other, and in a perversity born of long restraint, she added: 'He is not a man,' in a jesting tone with a resembling audacity.

'No?' said Linda, through her clenched teeth. 'Is he not? Well, then, look to it; because father has been walking about with a loaded gun at night.'

'It is not good for him. You must tell him not to, Linda. He will not listen to me.'

'I shall say nothing – never any more – to anybody,' cried Linda, passionately.

This could not last, thought Giselle. Giovanni must take her away soon – the very next time he came. She would not suffer these terrors for ever so much silver. To speak with her sister made her ill. But she was not uneasy at her father's watchfulness. She had begged Nostromo not to come to the window that night. He had promised to keep away for this once. And she did not know, could not guess or imagine, that he had another reason for coming on the island.

Linda had gone straight to the tower. It was time to light up. She unlocked the little door, and went heavily up the spiral staircase, carrying her love for the magnificent Capataz de Cargadores like an ever-increasing load of shameful fetters. No; she could not throw it off. No; let Heaven dispose of these two. And moving about the lantern, filled with twilight and the sheen of the moon, with careful movements she lighted the lamp. Then her arms fell along her body.

'And with our mother looking on,' she murmured. 'My own sister – the *chica*!'

The whole refracting apparatus, with its brass fittings and rings of prisms, glittered and sparkled like a dome-shaped shrine of diamonds, containing not a lamp, but some sacred flame, dominating the sea. And Linda, the keeper, in black, with a pale face, drooped low in a wooden chair, alone with her jealousy, far above the shames and passions of the earth. A strange, dragging pain, as if somebody were pulling her about brutally by her dark hair with bronze glints, made her put her hands up to her temples. They would meet. They would meet. And she knew where, too. At the window. The sweat of torture fell in drops on her cheeks, while the moonlight in the offing closed as if with a colossal bar of silver the entrance of the Placid Gulf – the sombre cavern of clouds and stillness in the surf-fretted seaboard.

Linda Viola stood up suddenly with a finger on her lip. He loved neither her nor her sister. The whole thing seemed so objectless as to frighten her, and also give her some hope. Why did he not carry her off? What prevented him? He was incomprehensible. What were they waiting for? For what end were these two lying and deceiving? Not for the ends of their love. There was no such thing. The hope of regaining him for herself made her break her vow of not leaving the tower that night. She must talk at once to her father, who was wise, and would understand. She ran down the spiral stairs. At the moment of opening the door at the bottom she heard the sound of the first shot ever fired on the Great Isabel.

She felt a shock, as though the bullet had struck her breast. She ran on without pausing. The cottage was dark. She cried at the door, 'Giselle! Giselle!' then dashed round the corner and screamed her sister's name at the open window, without getting an answer; but as she was rushing, distracted, round the house, Giselle came out of the door, and darted past her, running silently, her hair loose, and her eyes staring straight ahead. She seemed to skim along the grass as if on tiptoe, and vanished.

Linda walked on slowly, with her arms stretched out before her. All was still on the island; she did not know where she was going. The tree under which Martin Decoud spent his last days, beholding a life like a succession of senseless images, threw a large blotch of black shade upon the grass. Suddenly she saw her father, standing quietly all alone in the moonlight.

The Garibaldino – big, erect, with his snow-white hair and beard – had a monumental repose in his immobility, leaning upon a rifle. She put her hand upon his arm lightly. He never stirred.

'What have you done?' she asked, in her ordinary voice.

'I have shot Ramirez – *infame*!' he answered, with his eyes directed to where the shade was blackest. 'Like a thief he came, and like a thief he fell. The child had to be protected.'

He did not offer to move an inch, to advance a single step. He stood there, rugged and unstirring, like a statue of an old man guarding the honour of his house. Linda removed her trembling hand from his arm, firm and steady like an arm of stone, and, without a word, entered the blackness of the shade. She saw a stir of formless shapes on the ground, and stopped short. A murmur of despair and tears grew louder to her strained hearing.

'I entreated you not to come tonight. Oh, my Giovanni! And you promised. Oh! Why – why did you come, Giovanni?'

It was her sister's voice. It broke on a heartrending sob. And the voice of the resourceful Capataz de Cargadores, master and slave of the San Tomé treasure, who had been caught unawares by old Giorgio while stealing across the open towards the ravine to get some more silver, answered careless and cool, but sounding startlingly weak from the ground.

'It seemed as though I could not live through the night without seeing thee once more – my star, my little flower.'

The brilliant *tertulia* was just over, the last guests had departed, and the Señor Administrador had gone to his room already, when Dr Monygham, who had been expected in the evening but had not turned up, arrived driving along the wood-block pavement under the electric-lamps of the deserted Calle de la Constitución, and found the great gateway of the *casa* still open.

He limped in, stumped up the stairs, and found the fat and sleek Basilio on the point of turning off the lights on the *sala*. The prosperous majordomo remained open-mouthed at this late invasion.

'Don't put out the lights,' commanded the doctor. 'I want to see the *señora*.'

'The *señora* is in the Señora Administrador's *cancillaría*,' said Basilio, in an unctuous voice. 'The Señor Administrador starts for the mountain in an hour. There is some trouble with the workmen to be feared, it appears. A shameless people without reason and decency. And idle, *señor*. Idle.'

'You are shamelessly lazy and imbecile yourself,' said the doctor, with that faculty for exasperation which made him so generally beloved. 'Don't put the lights out.'

Basilio retired with dignity. Dr Monygham, waiting in the brilliantly lighted *sala*, heard presently a door close at the farther end of the house. A jingle of spurs died out. The Señor Administrador was off to the mountain.

With a measured swish of her long train, flashing with jewels and the shimmer of silk, her delicate head bowed as if under the weight of a mass of fair hair, in which the silver threads were lost, the 'first lady of Sulaco', as Captain Mitchell used to describe her, moved along the lighted corridor, wealthy beyond great dreams of wealth, considered, loved, respected, honoured, and as solitary as any human being had ever been, perhaps, on this earth.

The doctor's 'Mrs Gould! One minute!' stopped her with a start at the door of the lighted and empty *sala*. From the similarity of mood and circumstance, the sight of the doctor, standing there all alone amongst the groups of furniture, recalled to her emotional memory her unexpected meeting with Martin Decoud; she seemed to hear in the silence the voice of that man, dead miserably so many years ago, pronounce the words, 'Antonia left her fan here.' But it was the doctor's voice that spoke, a little altered by his excitement. She remarked his shining eyes.

'Mrs Gould, you are wanted. Do you know what has happened? You remember what I told you yesterday about Nostromo. Well, it seems that a *lancha*, a decked boat, coming from Zapiga, with four Negroes in her, passing close to the Great Isabel, was hailed from the cliff by a woman's voice – Linda's, as a matter of fact – commanding them (it's a moonlight night) to go round to the beach and take up a wounded man to the town. The *patron* (from whom I've heard all this), of course, did so at once. He told me that when they got round to the low side of the Great Isabel, they found Linda Viola waiting for them. They followed her: she led them under a tree not far from the cottage. There they found Nostromo lying on the ground with his head in the younger girl's lap, and father Viola standing some distance off leaning on his gun. Under Linda's direction they got a table out of the cottage for a stretcher, after breaking off the legs. They are here, Mrs Gould. I mean Nostromo and – and Giselle. The Negroes brought him in to the first-aid hospital near the harbour. He made the attendant send for me. But it is not me he wanted to see – it was you. Mrs Gould! It was you.'

'Me?' whispered Mrs Gould, shrinking a little.

'Yes, you!' the doctor burst out. 'He begged me – his enemy, as he thinks – to bring you to him at once. It seems he has something to say to you alone.'

'Impossible!' murmured Mrs Gould.

'He said to me, "Remind her that I have done something to keep a roof over her head." . . . Mrs Gould,' the doctor pursued, in the greatest excitement. 'Do you remember the silver? The silver in the lighter – that was lost!'

Mrs Gould remembered. But she did not say she hated the mere mention of that silver. Frankness personified, she remembered with an exaggerated horror that for the first time and last time of her life she had concealed the truth from her husband about that very silver. She had been corrupted by her fears at that time, and she had never forgiven herself. Moreover, that silver, which would never have come down if her husband had been made acquainted with the news brought by Decoud, had been in a roundabout way nearly the cause of Dr Monygham's death. And these things appeared to her very dreadful.

'Was it lost, though?' the doctor exclaimed. 'I've always felt that there was a mystery about our Nostromo ever since. I do believe he wants now, at the point of death –'

'The point of death,' repeated Mrs Gould.

'Yes. Yes . . . He wants perhaps to tell you something concerning that silver which –'

'Oh, no! No!' exclaimed Mrs Gould, in a low voice. 'Isn't it lost and done with? Isn't there enough treasure without it to make everybody in the world miserable?'

The doctor remained still, in a submissive, disappointed silence. At last he ventured, very low:

'And there is that Viola girl, Giselle. What are we to do? it looks as though father and sister had –'

Mrs Gould admitted that she felt in duty bound to do her best for these girls.

'I have a *volante* here,' the doctor said. 'If you don't mind getting into that –'

He waited, all impatience, till Mrs Gould reappeared, having thrown over her dress a grey cloak with a deep hood.

It was thus that, cloaked and monastically hooded over her evening costume, this woman, full of endurance and compassion, stood by the side of the bed on which the splendid Capataz de Cargadores lay stretched out motionless on his back. The whiteness of sheets and pillows gave a sombre and energetic relief to his bronzed face, to the dark, nervous hands, so good on a tiller, upon a bridle, and on a trigger, lying open and idle upon a white coverlet.

'She is innocent,' the Capataz was saying in a deep and level voice, as though afraid that a louder word would break the slender hold his spirit still kept upon his body. 'She is innocent. It is I alone. But no matter. For these things I would answer to no man or woman alive.'

He paused. Mrs Gould's face, very white within the shadow of the hood, bent over him with an invincible and dreary sadness. And the low sobs of Giselle

Viola, kneeling at the end of the bed, her gold hair with coppery gleams loose and scattered over the Capataz's feet, hardly troubled the silence of the room.

'Ha! Old Giorgio – the guardian of thine honour! Fancy the Vecchio coming upon me so light of foot, so steady of aim. I myself could have done no better. But the price of a charge of powder might have been saved. The honour was safe . . . *Señora*, she would have followed to the end of the world Nostromo the thief . . . I have said the word. The spell is broken!'

A low moan from the girl made him cast his eyes down.

'I cannot see her . . . No matter,' he went on, with the shadow of the old magnificent carelessness in his voice. 'One kiss is enough, if there is not time for more. An airy soul, *señora*! Bright and warm, like sunshine – soon clouded, and soon serene. They would crush it there between them. *Señora*, cast on her the eye of your compassion, as famed from one end of the land to the other as the courage and daring of the man who speaks to you. She will console herself in time. And even Ramirez is not a bad fellow. I am not angry. No! It is not Ramirez who overcame the Capataz of the Sulaco Cargadores.' He paused, made an effort, and in a louder voice, a little wildly, declared:

'I die betrayed – betrayed by –'

But he did not say by whom or by what he was dying betrayed.

'She would not have betrayed me,' he began again, opening eyes very wide. 'She was faithful. We were going very far – very soon. I could have torn myself away from that accursed treasure for her. For that child I would have left boxes and boxes of it – full. And Decoud took four. Four ingots. Why? *Picardia!* To betray me? How could I give back the treasure with four ingots missing? They would have said I had purloined them. The doctor would have said that. Alas! It holds me yet!'

Mrs Gould bent low, fascinated – cold with apprehension.

'What became of Don Martin on that night, Nostromo?'

'Who knows! I wondered what would become of me. Now I know. Death was to come upon me unawares. He went away! He betrayed me. And you think I have killed him! You are all alike, you fine people. The silver has killed me. It has held me. It holds me yet. Nobody knows where it is. But you are the wife of Don Carlos, who put it into my hands and said, 'Save it on your life.' And then I returned, and you all thought it was lost, what do I hear? It was nothing of importance. Let it go. Up, Nostromo, the faithful, and ride away to save us, for dear life!'

'Nostromo!' Mrs Gould whispered, bending very low. 'I, too, have hated the idea of that silver from the bottom of my heart.'

'Marvellous! – that one of you should hate the wealth that you know so well how to take from the hands of the poor. The world rests upon the poor, as old Giorgio says. You have been always good to the poor. But there is something accursed in wealth. *Señora*, shall I tell you where the treasure is? To you alone . . . Shining! Incorruptible!'

A pained, involuntary reluctance lingered in his tone, in his eyes, plain to the woman with the genius of sympathetic intuition. She averted her glance from the miserable subjection of the dying man appalled, wishing to hear no more of the silver.

'No Capataz,' she said. 'No one misses it now. Let it be lost for ever.'

After hearing these words, Nostromo closed his eyes, uttered no word, made no movement. Outside the door of the sick-room Dr Monygham, excited to the highest pitch, his eyes shining with eagerness, came up to the two women.

'Now, Mrs Gould,' he said, almost brutally in his impatience, 'tell me, was I right? There is a mystery. You have got the word of it, have you not? He told you –'

'He told me nothing,' said Mrs Gould steadily.

The light of his temperamental enmity to Nostromo went out of Dr Monygham's eyes. He stepped back submissively. He did not believe Mrs Gould. But her word was law. He accepted her denial like an inexplicable fatality affirming the victory of Nostromo's genius over his own. Even before that woman, whom he loved with secret devotion, he had been defeated by the magnificent Capataz de Cargadores, the man who had lived his own life on the assumption of unbroken fidelity, rectitude, and courage!

'Pray send at once somebody for my carriage,' spoke Mrs Gould from within her hood. Then, turning to Giselle Viola, 'Come nearer me, child; come closer. We will wait here.'

Giselle Viola, heartbroken and childlike, her face veiled in her falling hair, crept up to her side. Mrs Gould slipped her hand through the arm of the unworthy daughter of old Viola, the immaculate republican, the hero without a stain. Slowly, gradually, as a withered flower droops, the head of the girl, who would have followed a thief to the end of the world, rested on the shoulder of Doña Emilia, the first lady of Sulaco, the wife of the Señor Administrador of the San Tomé mine. And Mrs Gould, feeling her suppressed sobbing, nervous and excited, had the first and only moments of bitterness in her life. It was worthy of Dr Monygham himself.

'Console yourself, child. Very soon he would have forgotten you for his treasure.'

'*Señora*, he loved me. He loved me,' Giselle whispered, despairingly. 'He loved me as no one had ever been loved before.'

'I have been loved, too,' Mrs Gould said in a severe tone.

Giselle clung to her convulsively. 'Oh, *señora*, but you shall live adored to the end of your life,' she sobbed out.

Mrs Gould kept an unbroken silence till the carriage arrived. She helped in the half-fainting girl. After the doctor had shut the door of the landau, she leaned over to him.

'You can do nothing?' she whispered.

'No, Mrs Gould. Moreover, he won't let us touch him. It does not matter. I just had one look . . . Useless.'

But he promised to see old Viola and the other girl that very night. He could get the police-boat to take him off to the island. He remained in the street, looking after the landau rolling away slowly behind the white mules.

The rumour of some accident – an accident to Captain Fidanza – had been spreading along the new quays with their rows of lamps and the dark shapes of towering cranes. A knot of night-prowlers – the poorest of the poor – hung about the door of the first-aid hospital, whispering in the moonlight of the empty street.

There was no one with the wounded man but the pale photographer, small, frail, bloodthirsty, the hater of capitalists, perched on a high stool near the head of the bed with his knees up and his chin in his hands. He had been fetched by a comrade who, working late on the wharf, had heard from a Negro belonging to a *lancha* that Captain Fidanza had been brought ashore mortally wounded.

'Have you any dispositions to make, comrade?' he asked anxiously. 'Do not forget that we want money for our work. The rich must be fought with their own weapons.'

Nostromo made no answer. The other did not insist, remaining huddled up on the stool, shock-headed, wildly hairy, like a hunchbacked monkey. Then, after a long silence:

'Comrade Fidanza,' he began, solemnly, 'you have refused all aid from the doctor. Is he really a dangerous enemy of the people?'

In the dimly lit room Nostromo rolled his head slowly on the pillow and opened his eyes, directing at the weird figure perched by his bedside a glance of enigmatic and profound inquiry. Then his head rolled back, his eyelids fell, and the Capataz de Cargadores died without a word or moan after an hour of immobility, broken by short shudders testifying to the most atrocious sufferings.

Dr Monygham, going out in the police-galley to the islands, beheld the glitter of the moon upon the gulf and the high black shape of the Great Isabel sending a shaft of light afar, from under the the canopy of clouds.

'Pull easy,' he said, wondering what he would find there. He tried to imagine Linda and her father, and discovered a strange reluctance within himself. 'Pull easy,' he repeated.

From the moment he fired at the thief of his honour, Giorgio Viola had not stirred from the spot. He stood, his old gun grounded, his hand grasping the barrel near the muzzle. After the *lancha* carrying off Nostromo for ever from her had left the shore, Linda, coming up, stopped before him. He did not seem to be aware of her presence, but when, losing her forced calmness, she cried out: 'Do you know whom you have killed?' he answered: 'Ramirez the vagabond.'

White, and staring insanely at her father, Linda laughed in his face. After a time he joined her faintly in a deep-toned and distant echo of her peals. Then she stopped, and the old man spoke as if startled:

'He cried out in son Gian' Battista's voice.'

The gun fell from his opened hand, but the arm remained extended for a moment as if still supported. Linda seized it roughly.

'You are too old to understand. Come into the house.'

He let her lead him. On the threshold he stumbled heavily, nearly coming to the ground together with his daughter. His excitement, his activity of the last few days, had been like the flare of a dying lamp. He caught the back of his chair.

'In son Gian' Battista's voice,' he repeated in a severe tone. 'I heard him – Ramirez – the miserable –'

Linda helped him into the chair, and, bending low, hissed into his ear:

'You have killed Gian' Battista.'

The old man smiled under his thick moustache. Women had strange fancies.

'Where is the child,' he asked, surprised at the penetrating chilliness of the air and the unwonted dimness of the lamp by which he used to sit up half the night with the open Bible before him.

Linda hesitated a moment, then averted her eyes.

'She is asleep,' she said. 'We shall talk of her tomorrow.'

She could not bear to look at him. He filled her with terror and with an almost unbearable feeling of pity. She had observed the change that came over him. He would never understand what he had done; and even to her the whole thing remained incomprehensible. He said with difficulty.

'Give me the book.'

Linda laid on the table the closed volume in its worn leather cover, the Bible given him ages ago by an Englishman in Palermo.

'The child had to be protected,' he said, in a strange, mournful voice.

Behind his chair Linda wrung her hands, crying without noise. Suddenly she started for the door. He heard her move.

'Where are you going?' he asked.

'To the light,' she answered, turning round to look at him balefully.

'The light! *Sí* – duty.'

Very upright, white-haired, leonine, heroic in his absorbed quietness, he felt in the pocket of his red shirt for the spectacles given him by Doña Emilia. He put them on. After a long period of immobility he opened the book, and from on high looked through the glasses at the small print in double columns. A rigid, stern expression settled upon his features with a slight frown, as if in response to some gloomy thought or unpleasant sensation. But he never detached his eyes from the book while he swayed forward, gently, gradually, till his snow-white head rested upon the open pages. A wooden clock ticked methodically on the white-washed wall, and growing slowly cold the Garibaldino lay alone, rugged, undecayed, like an old oak uprooted by a treacherous gust of wind.

The light of the Great Isabel burned unfailing above the lost treasure of the San Tomé mine. Into the bluish sheen of a night without stars the lantern sent out a yellow beam towards the far horizon. Like a black speck upon the shining panes, Linda, crouching in the outer gallery, rested her head on the rail. The moon, drooping in the western board, looked at her radiantly.

Below, at the foot of the cliff, the regular splash of oars from a passing boat ceased, and Dr Monygham stood up in the stern sheets.

'Linda!' he shouted, throwing back his head. 'Linda!'

Linda stood up. She had recognized the voice.

'Is he dead?' she cried, bending over.

'Yes, my poor girl. I am coming round,' the doctor answered from below. 'Pull to the beach,' he said to the rowers.

Linda's black figure detached itself upright on the light of the lantern with her arms raised above her head as though she were going to throw herself over.

'It is I who loved you,' she whispered, with a face as set and white as marble in the moonlight. 'I! Only I! She will forget thee, killed miserably for her pretty face. I cannot understand. I cannot understand. But I shall never forget thee. Never!'

She stood silent and still, collecting her strength to throw all her fidelity, her pain, bewilderment, and despair into one great cry.

'Never! Gian' Battista!'

Dr Monygham, pulling round in the police-galley, heard the name pass over his head. It was another of Nostromo's triumphs, the greatest, the most enviable, the most sinister of all. In that true cry of undying passion that seemed to ring aloud from Punta Mala to Azuera and away to the bright line of the horizon, overhung by a big white cloud shining like a mass of solid silver, the genius of the magnificent Capataz de Cargadores dominated the dark gulf containing his conquests of treasure and love.

Under Western Eyes

I would take liberty from any hand
as a hungry man would snatch a piece of bread.

MISS HALDIN

To Agnes Tobin

who brought to our door her genius for friendship
from the uttermost shore of the west

Author's Note

It must be admitted that by the mere force of circumstances *Under Western Eyes* has become already a sort of historical novel dealing with the past.

This reflection bears entirely upon the events of the tale; but being as a whole an attempt to render not so much the political state as the psychology of Russia itself, I venture to hope that it has not lost all its interest. I am encouraged in this flattering belief by noticing that in many articles on Russian affairs of the present day reference is made to certain sayings and opinions uttered in the pages that follow, in a manner testifying to the clearness of my vision and the correctness of my judgement I need not say that in writing this novel I had no other object in view than to express imaginatively the general truth which underlies its action, together with my honest convictions as to the moral complexion of certain facts more or less known to the whole world.

As to the actual creation I may say that when I began to write I had a distinct conception of the first part only, with the three figures of Haldin, Razumov, and Councillor Mikulin defined exactly in my mind. It was only after I had finished writing the first part that the whole story revealed itself to me in its tragic character and in the march of its events as unavoidable and sufficiently ample in its outline to give free play to my creative instinct and to the dramatic possibilities of the subject.

The course of action need not be explained. It has suggested itself more as a matter of feeling than a matter of thinking. It is the result not of a special experience but of general knowledge, fortified by earnest meditation. My greatest anxiety was in being able to strike and sustain the note of scrupulous impartiality. The obligation of absolute fairness was imposed on me historically and hereditarily, by the peculiar experience of race and family, in addition to my primary conviction that truth alone is the justification of any fiction which makes the least claim to the quality of art or may hope to take its place in the culture of men and women of its time. I had never been called before to a greater effort of detachment: detachment from all passions, prejudices, and even from personal memories. *Under Western Eyes*, on its first appearance in England, was a failure with the public, perhaps because of that very detachment. I obtained my reward some six years later when I first heard that the book had found universal recognition in Russia and had been re-published there in many editions.

The various figures playing their part in the story also owe their existence to no special experience but to the general knowledge of the condition of Russia and of the moral and emotional reactions of the Russian temperament to the pressure of tyrannical lawlessness, which, in general human terms, could be reduced to the formula of senseless desperation provoked by senseless tyranny. What I was concerned with mainly was the aspect, the character, and the fate of the individuals as they appeared to the Western Eyes of the old teacher of languages. He himself has been much criticized; but I will not at this late hour undertake to justify his existence. He was useful to me and therefore I think that he must be useful to the reader both in the way of comment and by the part he plays in the development of the story. In my desire to produce the effect of actuality it seemed to me indispensable to have an eye-witness of the transactions in Geneva. I needed also a sympathetic friend for Miss Haldin, who otherwise would have been too much alone and unsupported to be perfectly credible. She would have had no one to whom she could give a glimpse of her idealistic faith, of her great heart, and of her simple emotions.

Razumov is treated sympathetically. Why should he not be? He is an ordinary young man, with a healthy capacity for work and sane ambitions. He has an average conscience. If he is slightly abnormal it is only in his sensitiveness to his position. Being nobody's child he feels rather more keenly than another would that he is a Russian – or he is nothing. He is perfectly right in looking on all Russia as his heritage. The sanguinary futility of the crimes and the sacrifices seething in that amorphous mass envelops and crushes him. But I don't think that in his distraction he is ever monstrous. Nobody is exhibited as a monster here – neither the simple-minded Tekla nor the wrong-headed Sophia Antonovna. Peter Ivanovitch and Madame de S. are fair game. They are the apes of a sinister jungle and are treated as their grimaces deserve. As to Nikita – nicknamed Necator – he is the perfect flower of the terroristic wilderness. What troubled me most in dealing with him was not his monstrosity but his banality. He has been exhibited to the public eye for years in so-called 'disclosures' in newspaper articles, in secret histories, in sensational novels.

The most terrifying reflection (I am speaking now for myself) is that all these people are not the product of the exceptional but of the general – of the normality of their place, and time, and race. The ferocity and imbecility of an autocratic rule rejecting all legality and in fact basing itself upon complete moral anarchism provokes the no less imbecile and atrocious answer of a purely Utopian revolutionism encompassing destruction by the first means to hand, in the strange conviction that a fundamental change of hearts must follow the downfall of any given human institutions. These people are unable to see that all they can effect is merely a change of names. The oppressors and the oppressed are all Russians together; and the world is brought once more face to face with the truth of the saying that the tiger cannot change his stripes nor the leopard his spots.

1920 J. C.

Part First

To begin with I wish to disclaim the possession of those high gifts of imagination and expression which would have enabled my pen to create for the reader the personality of the man who called himself, after the Russian custom, Cyril son of Isidor – Kirylo Sidorovitch – Razumov.

If I have ever had these gifts in any sort of living form they have been smothered out of existence a long time ago under a wilderness of words. Words, as is well known, are the great foes of reality. I have been for many years a teacher of languages. It is an occupation which at length becomes fatal to whatever share of imagination, observation, and insight an ordinary person may be heir to. To a teacher of languages there comes a time when the world is but a place of many words and man appears a mere talking animal not much more wonderful than a parrot.

This being so, I could not have observed Mr Razumov or guessed at his reality by the force of insight, much less have imagined him as he was. Even to invent the mere bald facts of his life would have been utterly beyond my powers. But I think that without this declaration the readers of these pages will be able to detect in the story the marks of documentary evidence. And that is perfectly correct. It is based on a document; all I have brought to it is my knowledge of the Russian language, which is sufficient for what is attempted here. The document, of course, is something in the nature of a journal, a diary, yet not exactly that in its actual form. For instance, most of it was not written up from day to day, though all the entries are dated. Some of these entries cover months of time and extend over dozens of pages. All the earlier part is a retrospect, in a narrative form, relating to an event which took place about a year before.

I must mention that I have lived for a long time in Geneva. A whole quarter of that town, on account of many Russians residing there, is called La Petite Russie – Little Russia. I had a rather extensive connection in Little Russia at that time. Yet I confess that I have no comprehension of the Russian character. The illogicality of their attitude, the arbitrariness of their conclusions, the frequency of the exceptional, should present no difficulty to a student of many grammars; but there must be something else in the way, some special human trait – one of those subtle differences that are beyond the ken of mere professors. What must remain striking to a teacher of languages is the Russians' extraordinary love of words. They gather them up; they cherish them, but they don't hoard them in their breasts; on the contrary, they are always ready to pour them out by the hour or by the night with an enthusiasm, a sweeping abundance, with such an aptness of application sometimes that, as in the case of very accomplished parrots, one can't defend oneself from the suspicion that they really understand what they say. There is a generosity in their ardour of speech which removes it as far as possible from common loquacity; and it is ever too disconnected to be classed as eloquence. . . . But I must apologize for this digression.

It would be idle to inquire why Mr Razumov has left this record behind him. It is inconceivable that he should have wished any human eye to see it. A mysterious impulse of human nature comes into play here. Putting aside Samuel Pepys, who has forced in this way the door of immortality, innumerable people, criminals, saints, philosophers, young girls, statesmen, and simple imbeciles, have kept self-revealing records from vanity no doubt, but also from other more inscrutable motives. There must be a wonderful soothing power in mere words since so many men have used them for self-communion. Being myself a quiet individual I take it that what all men are really after is some form or perhaps only some formula of peace. Certainly they are crying loud enough for it at the present day. What sort of peace Kirylo Sidorovitch Razumov expected to find in the writing up of his record it passeth my understanding to guess.

The fact remains that he had written it.

Mr Razumov was a tall, well-proportioned young man, quite unusually dark for a Russian from the Central Provinces. His good looks would have been unquestionable if it had not been for a peculiar lack of fineness in the features. It was as if a face modelled vigorously in wax (with some approach even to a classical correctness of type) had been held close to a fire till all sharpness of line had been lost in the softening of the material. But even thus he was sufficiently good-looking. His manner, too, was good. In discussion he was easily swayed by argument and authority. With his younger compatriots he took the attitude of an inscrutable listener, a listener of the kind that hears you out intelligently and then – just changes the subject.

This sort of trick, which may arise either from intellectual insufficiency or from an imperfect trust in one's own convictions, procured for Mr Razumov a reputation of profundity. Amongst a lot of exuberant talkers, in the habit of exhausting themselves daily by ardent discussion, a comparatively taciturn personality is naturally credited with reserve power. By his comrades at the St Petersburg University, Kirylo Sidorovitch Razumov, third year's student in philosophy, was looked upon as a strong nature – an altogether trustworthy man. This, in a country where an opinion may be a legal crime visited by death or sometimes by a fate worse than mere death, meant that he was worthy of being trusted with forbidden opinions. He was liked also for his amiability and for his quiet readiness to oblige his comrades even at the cost of personal inconvenience.

Mr Razumov was supposed to be the son of an Archpriest and to be protected by a distinguished nobleman – perhaps of his own distant province. But his outward appearance accorded badly with such humble origin. Such a descent was not credible. It was, indeed, suggested that Mr Razumov was the son of an Archpriest's pretty daughter – which, of course, would put a different complexion on the matter. This theory also rendered intelligible the protection of the distinguished nobleman. All this, however, had never been investigated maliciously or otherwise. No one knew or cared who the nobleman in question was. Razumov received a modest but very sufficient allowance from the hands of an obscure attorney, who seemed to act as his guardian in some measure. Now and then he appeared at some professor's informal reception. Apart from that Razumov was not known to have any social relations in the town. He attended the obligatory lectures regularly and was considered by the authorities as a very promising student. He worked at home in the manner of a man who means to get on, but did not shut himself up severely for that purpose. He was always accessible, and there was nothing secret or reserved in his life.

Chapter I

The origin of Mr Razumov's record is connected with an event characteristic of modern Russia in the actual fact: the assassination of a prominent statesman – and still more characteristic of the moral corruption of an oppressed society where the noblest aspirations of humanity, the desire of freedom, an ardent patriotism, the love of justice, the sense of pity, and even the fidelity of simple minds are prostituted to the lusts of hate and fear, the inseparable companions of an uneasy despotism.

The fact alluded to above is the successful attempt on the life of Mr de P—, the President of the notorious Repressive Commission of some years ago, the Minister of State invested with extraordinary powers. The newspapers made noise enough about that fanatical, narrow-chested figure in gold-laced uniform, with a face of crumpled parchment, insipid, bespectacled eyes, and the cross of the Order of St Procopius hung under the skinny throat. For a time, it may be remembered, not a month passed without his portrait appearing in some one of the illustrated papers of Europe. He served the monarchy by imprisoning, exiling, or sending to the gallows men and women, young and old, with an equable, unwearied industry. In his mystic acceptance of the principle of autocracy he was bent on extirpating from the land every vestige of anything that resembled freedom in public institutions; and in his ruthless persecution of the rising generation he seemed to aim at the destruction of the very hope of liberty itself.

It is said that this execrated personality had not enough imagination to be aware of the hate he inspired. It is hardly credible; but it is a fact that he took very few precautions for his safety. In the preamble of a certain famous State paper he had declared once that 'the thought of liberty has never existed in the Act of the Creator. From the multitude of men's counsel nothing could come but revolt and disorder; and revolt and disorder in a world created for obedience and stability is sin. It was not Reason but Authority which expressed the Divine Intention. God was the Autocrat of the Universe. . . .' It may be that the man who made this declaration believed that heaven itself was bound to protect him in his remorseless defence of Autocracy on this earth.

No doubt the vigilance of the police saved him many times; but, as a matter of fact, when his appointed fate overtook him, the competent authorities could not have given him any warning. They had no knowledge of any conspiracy against the Minister's life, had no hint of any plot through their usual channels of information, had seen no signs, were aware of no suspicious movements or dangerous persons.

Mr de P – was being driven towards the railway station in a two-horse uncovered sleigh with footman and coachman on the box. Snow had been falling all night, making the roadway, uncleared as yet at this early hour, very heavy for the horses. It was still falling thickly. But the sleigh must have been observed and marked down. As it drew over to the left before taking a turn, the footman noticed a peasant walking slowly on the edge of the pavement with his hands in the pockets of his sheepskin coat and his shoulders hunched up to his ears under the falling snow. On being overtaken this peasant suddenly faced about and swung his arm. In an instant there was a terrible shock, a detonation muffled in the multitude of snowflakes; both horses lay dead and mangled on the ground and the coachman, with a shrill cry, had fallen off the box mortally wounded. The footman (who survived) had no time to see the face of the man in the sheepskin coat. After throwing the bomb this last got away, but it is supposed that, seeing a lot of people surging up on all sides of him in the falling snow, and all running towards the scene of the explosion, he thought it safer to turn back with them.

In an incredibly short time an excited crowd assembled round the sledge. The Minister-President, getting out unhurt into the deep snow, stood near the groaning coachman and addressed the people repeatedly in his weak, colourless voice: 'I beg of you to keep off. For the love of God, I beg you good people to keep off.'

It was then that a tall young man who had remained standing perfectly still within a carriage gateway, two houses lower down, stepped out into the street and walking up rapidly flung another bomb over the heads of the crowd. It actually struck the Minister-President on the shoulder as he stooped over his dying servant, then falling between his feet exploded with a terrific concentrated violence, striking him dead to the ground, finishing the wounded man, and practically annihilating the empty sledge in the twinkling of an eye. With a yell of horror the crowd broke up and fled in all directions, except for those who fell dead or dying where they stood nearest to the Minister-President, and one or two others who did not fall till they had run a little way.

The first explosion had brought together a crowd as if by enchantment, the second made as swiftly a solitude in the streets for hundreds of yards in each direction. Through the falling snow people looked from afar at the small heap of deap bodies lying upon each other near the carcases of the two horses. Nobody dared to approach till some Cossacks of a street-patrol galloped up and, dismounting, began to turn over the dead. Amongst the innocent victims of the second explosion laid out on the pavement there was a body dressed in a peasant's sheepskin coat; but the face was unrecognizable, there was absolutely nothing found in the pockets of its poor clothing, and it was the only one whose identity was never established.

That day Mr Razumov got up at his usual hour and spent the morning within the University buildings listening to the lectures and working for some time in the library. He heard the first vague rumour of something in the way of bomb-throwing at the table of the students' ordinary, where he was accustomed to eat his two o'clock dinner. But this rumour was made up of mere whispers, and this was Russia, where it was not always safe, for a student especially, to appear too much interested in certain kinds of whispers. Razumov was one of those men who, living in a period of mental and political unrest, keep an instinctive hold on normal, practical, everyday life. He was aware of the emotional tension of his time; he even responded to it in an indefinite way. But his main concern was with his work, his studies, and with his own future.

Officially and in fact without a family (for the daughter of the Archpriest had long been dead), no home influences had shaped his opinions or his feelings. He was as lonely in the world as a man swimming in the deep sea. The word Rasumov was a mere label of a solitary individuality. There were no Rasumovs belonging to him anywhere. His closest parentage was defined in the statement that he was a Russian. Whatever good he expected from life would be given to or withheld from his hopes by that connection alone. This immense parentage suffered from the throes of internal dissensions, and he shrank mentally from the fray as a good-natured man may shrink from taking definite sides in a violent family quarrel.

Razumov, going home, reflected that having prepared all the matters of the forthcoming examination, he could now devote his time to the subject of the prize essay. He hankered after the silver medal. The prize was offered by the Ministry of Education; the names of the competitors would be submitted to the Minister himself. The mere fact of trying would be considered meritorious in the higher quarters; and the possessor of the prize would have a claim to an administrative appointment of the better sort after he had taken his degree. The student Razumov in an access of elation forgot the dangers menacing the stability of the institutions which give rewards and appointments. But remembering the medallist of the year before, Razumov, the young man of no parentage, was sobered. He and some others happened to be assembled in their comrade's room at the very time when that last received the official advice of his success. He was a quiet, unassuming young man: 'Forgive me,' he had said with a faint apologetic smile and taking up his cap, 'I am going out to order up some wine. But I must first send a telegram to my folk at home. I say! Won't the old people make it a festive time for the neighbours for twenty miles around our place.'

Razumov thought there was nothing of that sort for him in the world. His success would matter to no one. But he felt no bitterness against the nobleman his protector, who was not a provincial magnate as was generally supposed. He was in fact nobody less than Prince K—, once a great and splendid figure in the world and now, his day being over, a Senator and a gouty invalid, living in a still splendid but more domestic manner. He had some young children and a wife as aristocratic and proud as himself.

In all his life Razumov was allowed only once to come into personal contact with the Prince.

It had the air of a chance meeting in the little attorney's office. One day Razumov, coming in by appointment, found a stranger standing there – a tall, aristocratic-looking personage with silky, grey side-whiskers. The bald-headed, sly little lawyer-fellow called out, 'Come in – come in, Mr Razumov,' with a stort of ironic heartiness. Then turning deferentially to the stranger with the grand air, 'A ward of mine, your Excellency. One of the most promising students of his faculty in the St Petersburg University.'

To his intense surprise Razumov saw a white shapely hand extended to him. He took it in great confusion (it was soft and passive) and heard at the same time a condescending murmur in which he caught only the words 'Satisfactory' and

'Persevere'. But the most amazing thing of all was to feel suddenly a distinct pressure of the white shapely hand just before it was withdrawn: a light pressure like a secret sign. The emotion of it was terrible. Razumov's heart seemed to leap into his throat. When he raised his eyes the aristocratic personage, motioning the little lawyer aside, had opened the door and was going out.

The attorney rummaged amongst the papers on his desk for a time. 'Do you know who that was?' he asked suddenly.

Razumov, whose heart was thumping hard yet, shook his head in silence.

'That was Prince K—. You wonder what he could be doing in the hole of a poor legal rat like myself – eh? These awfully great people have their sentimental curiosities like common sinners. But if I were you, Kirylo Sidorovitch,' he continued, leering and laying a peculiar emphasis on the patronymic, 'I wouldn't boast at large of the introduction. It would not be prudent, Kirylo Sidorovitch. Oh dear no! It would be in fact dangerous for your future.'

The young man's ears burned like fire; his sight was dim. 'That man!' Razumov was saying to himself. 'He!'

Henceforth it was by this monosyllable that Mr Razumov got into the habit of referring mentally to the stranger with grey silky side-whiskers. From that time too, when walking in the more fashionable quarters, he noted with interest the magnificent horses and carriages with Prince K—'s liveries on the box. Once he saw the Princess get out – she was shopping – followed by two girls, of which one was nearly a head taller than the other. Their fair hair hung loose down their backs in the English style; they had merry eyes, their coats, muffs, and little fur caps were exactly alike, and their cheeks and noses were tinged a cheerful pink by the frost. They crossed the pavement in front of him, and Razumov went on his way smiling shyly to himself. 'His' daughters. They resembled 'Him'. The young man felt a glow of warm friendliness towards these girls who would never know of his existence. Presently they would marry Generals or Kammerherrs and have girls and boys of their own, who perhaps would be aware of him as a celebrated old professor, decorated, possibly a Privy Councillor, one of the glories of Russia – nothing more!

But a celebrated professor was a somebody. Distinction would convert the label Razumov into an honoured name. There was nothing strange in the student Razumov's wish for distinction. A man's real life is that accorded to him in the thoughts of other men by reason of respect or natural love. Returning home on the day of the attempt on Mr de P—'s life, Razumov resolved to have a good try for the silver medal.

Climbing slowly the four flights of the dark, dirty staircase in the house where he had his lodgings, he felt confident of success. The winner's name would be published in the papers on New Year's Day. And at the thought that 'He' would most probably read it there, Razumov stopped short on the stairs for an instant, then went on smiling faintly at his own emotion. 'This is but a shadow,' he said to himself, 'but the medal is a solid beginning.'

With those ideas of industry in his head the warmth of his room was agreeable and encouraging. 'I shall put in four hours of good work,' he thought. But no sooner had he closed the door than he was horribly startled. All black against the usual tall stove of white tiles gleaming in the dusk, stood a strange figure, wearing a skirted, close-fitting, brown cloth coat strapped round the waist, in long boots, and with a little Astrakhan cap on its head. It loomed lithe and martial. Razumov was utterly confounded. It was only when the figure advancing two paces asked in an untroubled, grave voice if the outer door was closed that he regained his power of speech.

'Haldin! . . . Victor Victorovitch! . . . Is that you? . . . Yes. The outer door is shut all right. But this is indeed unexpected.'

Victor Haldin, a student older than most of his contemporaries at the University, was not one of the industrious set. He was hardly ever seen at lectures; the authorities had marked him as 'restless' and 'unsound' – very bad notes. But he had a great personal prestige with his comrades and influenced their thoughts. Razumov had never been intimate with him. They had met from time to time at gatherings in other students' houses. They had even had a discussion together – one of those discussions on first principles dear to the sanguine minds of youth.

Razumov wished the man had chosen some other time to come for a chat. He felt in good trim to tackle the prize essay. But as Haldin could not be slightingly dismissed Razumov adopted the tone of hospitality, asking him to sit down and smoke.

'Kirylo Sidorovitch,' said the other, flinging off his cap, 'we are not perhaps in exactly the same camp. Your judgement is more philosophical. You are a man of few words, but I haven't met anybody who dared to doubt the generosity of your sentiments. There is a solidity about your character which cannot exist without courage.'

Razumov felt flattered and began to murmur shyly something about being very glad of his good opinion, when Haldin raised his hand.

'That is what I was saying to myself,' he continued, 'as I dodged in the woodyard down by the river-side. "He has a strong character, this young man," I said to myself. "He does not throw his soul to the winds." Your reserve has always fascinated me, Kirylo Sidorovitch. So I tried to remember your address. But look here – it was a piece of luck. Your dvornik was away from the gate talking to a sleigh-driver on the other side of the street. I met no one on the stairs, not a soul. As I came up to your floor I caught sight of your landlady coming out of your rooms. But she did not see me. She crossed the landing to her own side, and then I slipped in. I have been here two hours expecting you to come in every moment.'

Razumov had listened in astonishment; but before he could open his mouth Haldin added, speaking deliberately, 'It was I who removed de P— this morning.'

Razumov kept down a cry of dismay. The sentiment of his life being utterly ruined by this contact with such a crime expressed itself quaintly by a sort of half-derisive mental exclamation, 'There goes my silver medal!'

Haldin continued after waiting a while –

'You say nothing, Kirylo Sidorovitch! I understand your silence. To be sure, I cannot expect you with your frigid English manner to embrace me. But never mind your manners. You have enough heart to have heard the sound of weeping and gnashing of teeth this man raised in the land. That would be enough to get over any philosophical hopes. He was uprooting the tender plant. He had to be stopped. He was a dangerous man – a convinced man. Three more years of his work would have put us back fifty years into bondage – and look at all the lives wasted, at all the souls lost in that time.'

His curt, self-confident voice suddenly lost its ring and it was in a dull tone that he added, 'Yes, brother, I have killed him. It's weary work.'

Razumov had sunk into a chair. Every moment he expected a crowd of policemen to rush in. There must have been thousands of them out looking for that man walking up and down in his room. Haldin was talking again in a restrained, steady voice. Now and then he flourished an arm, slowly, without excitement.

He told Razumov how he had brooded for a year; how he had not slept properly for weeks. He and 'Another' had a warning of the Minister's movements from 'a certain person' late the evening before. He and that 'Another' prepared their 'engines' and resolved to have no sleep till 'the deed' was done. They walked the streets under the falling snow with the 'engines' on them, exchanging not a word the livelong night. When they happened to meet a police patrol they took each other by the arm and pretended to be a couple of peasants on the spree. They reeled and talked in drunken hoarse voices. Except for these strange outbreaks they kept silence, moving on ceaselessly. Their plans had been previously arranged. At daybreak they made their way to the spot which they knew the sledge must pass. When it appeared in sight they exchanged a muttered good-bye and separated. The 'other' remained at the corner. Haldin took up a position a little farther up the street. . . .

After throwing his 'engine' he ran off and in a moment was overtaken by the panic-struck people flying away from the spot after the second explosion. They were wild with terror. He was jostled once or twice. He slowed down for the rush to pass him and then turned to the left into a narrow street. There he was alone.

He marvelled at this immediate escape. The work was done. He could hardly believe it. He fought with an almost irresistible longing to lie down on the pavement and sleep. But this sort of faintness – a drowsy faintness – passed off quickly. He walked faster, making his way to one of the poorer parts of the town in order to look up Ziemianitch.

This Ziemianitch, Razumov understood, was a sort of town-peasant who had got on; owner of a small number of sledges and horses for hire. Haldin paused in his narrative to exclaim –

'A bright spirit! A hardy soul! The best driver in St Petersburg. He has a team of three horses there. . . . Ah! He's a fellow!'

This man had declared himself willing to take out safely, at any time, one or two persons to the second or third railway station on one of the southern lines. But there had been no time to warn him the night before. His usual haunt seemed to be a low-class eating-house on the outskirts of the town. When Haldin got there the man was not to be found. He was not expected to turn up again till the evening. Haldin wandered away restlessly.

He saw the gate of a woodyard open and went in to get out of the wind which swept the bleak broad thoroughfare. The great rectangular piles of cut wood loaded with snow resembled the huts of a village. At first the watchman who discovered him crouching amongst them talked in a friendly manner. He was a dried-up old man wearing two ragged army coats one over the other; his wizened little face, tied up under the jaw and over the ears in a dirty red handkerchief, looked comical. Presently he grew sulky, and then all at once without rhyme or reason began to shout furiously.

'Aren't you ever going to clear out of this, you loafer? We know all about factory hands of your sort. A big, strong, young chap! You aren't even drunk. What do you want here? You don't frighten us. Take yourself and your ugly eyes away.'

Haldin stopped before the sitting Razumov. His supple figure, with the white forehead above which the fair hair stood straight up, had an aspect of lofty daring.

'He did not like my eyes,' he said. 'And so . . . here I am.'

Razumov made an effort to speak calmly.

'But pardon me, Victor Victorovitch. We know each other so little. . . . I don't see why you . . .'

'Confidence,' said Haldin.

This word sealed Razumov's lips as if a hand had been clapped on his mouth. His brain seethed with arguments.

'And so – here you are,' he muttered through his teeth.

The other did not detect the tone of anger. Never suspected it.

'Yes. And nobody knows I am here. You are the last person that could be suspected – should I get caught. That's an advantage, you see. And then – speaking to a superior mind like yours I can well say all the truth. It occurred to me that you – you have no one belonging to you – no ties, no one to suffer for it if this came out by some means. There have been enough ruined Russian homes as it is. But I don't see how my passage through your rooms can be ever known. If I should be got hold of, I'll know how to keep silent – no matter what they may be pleased to do to me,' he added grimly.

He began to walk again while Razumov sat still, appalled.

'You thought that –' he faltered out almost sick with indignation.

'Yes, Razumov. Yes, brother. Some day you shall help to build. You suppose that I am a terrorist, now – a destructor of what is. But consider that the true destroyers are they who destroy the spirit of progress and truth, not the avengers who merely kill the bodies of the persecutors of human dignity. Men like me are necessary to make room for self-contained, thinking men like you. Well, we have made the sacrifice of our lives, but all the same I want to escape if it can be done. It is not my life I want to save, but my power to do. I won't live idle. Oh no! Don't make any mistake, Razumov. Men like me are rare. And, besides, an example like this is more awful to oppressors when the perpetrator vanishes without a trace. They sit in their offices and palaces and quake. All I want you to do is to help me to vanish. No great matter that. Only to go by and by and see Ziemianitch for me at that place where I went this morning. Just tell him, "He whom you know wants a well-horsed sledge to pull up half an hour after midnight at the seventh lamp-post on the left counting from the upper end of Karabelnaya. If nobody gets in, the sledge is to run round a block or two, so as to come back past the same spot in ten minutes' time." '

Razumov wondered why he had not cut short that talk and told this man to go away long before. Was it weakness or what?

He concluded that it was a sound instinct. Haldin must have been seen. It was impossible that some people should not have noticed the face and appearance of the man who threw the second bomb. Haldin was a noticeable person. The police in their thousands must have had his description within the hour. With every moment the danger grew. Sent out to wander in the streets he could not escape being caught in the end.

The police would very soon find out all about him. They would set about discovering a conspiracy. Everybody Haldin had ever known would be in the greatest danger. Unguarded expressions, little facts in themselves innocent would be counted for crimes. Razumov remembered certain words he said, the speeches he had listened to, the harmless gatherings he had attended – it was almost impossible for a student to keep out of that sort of thing, without becoming suspect to his comrades.

Razumov saw himself shut up in a fortress, worried, badgered, perhaps ill-used. He saw himself deported by an administrative order, his life broken, ruined, and robbed of all hope. He saw himself – at best – leading a miserable existence under police supervision, in some small, far-away provincial town, without friends to assist his necessities or even take any steps to alleviate his lot – as others had. Others had fathers, mothers, brothers, relations, connexions, to move heaven and earth on their behalf – he had no one. The very officials that sentenced him some morning would forget his existence before sunset.

He saw his youth pass away from him in misery and half-starvation – his strength give way, his mind become an abject thing. He saw himself creeping, broken down and shabby, about the streets – dying unattended in some filthy hole of a room, or on the sordid bed of a Government hospital.

He shuddered. Then the peace of bitter calmness came over him. It was best to keep this man out of the streets till he could be got rid of with some chance of escaping. That was the best that could be done. Razumov, of course, felt the safety of his lonely existence to be permanently endangered. This evening's doings could turn up against him at any time as long as this man lived and the present institutions endured. They appeared to him rational and indestructible at that moment. They had a force of harmony – in contrast with the horrible discord of this man's presence. He hated the man. He said quietly –

'Yes, of course, I will go. You must give me precise directions, and for the rest – depend on me.'

'Ah! You are a fellow! Collected – cool as a cucumber. A regular Englishman. Where did you get your soul from? There aren't many like you. Look here, brother! Men like me leave no posterity, but their souls are not lost. No man's soul is ever lost. It works for itself – or else where would be the sense of self-sacrifice, of martrydom, of conviction, of faith – the labours of the soul? What will become of my soul when I die in the way I must die – soon – very soon perhaps? It shall not perish. Don't make a mistake, Razumov. This is not murder – it is war, war. My spirit shall go on warring in some Russian body till all falsehood is swept out of the world. The modern civilization is false, but a new revelation shall come out of Russia. Ha! you say nothing. You are a sceptic. I respect your philosophical scepticism, Razumov, but don't touch the soul. The Russian soul that lives in all of us. It has a future. It has a mission, I tell you, or else why should I have been moved to do this – reckless – like a butcher – in the middle of all these innocent people – scattering death – I! I! . . . I wouldn't hurt a fly!'

'Not so loud,' warned Razumov harshly.

Haldin sat down abruptly, and leaning his head on his folded arms burst into tears. He wept for a long time. The dusk had deepened in the room. Razumov, motionless in sombre wonder, listened to the sobs.

The other raised his head, got up, and with an effort mastered his voice.

'Yes. Men like me leave no posterity,' he repeated in a subdued tone. 'I have a sister though. She's with my old mother – I persuaded them to go abroad this year – thank God. Not a bad little girl my sister. She has the most trustful eyes of any human being that ever walked this earth. She will marry well, I hope. She may have children – sons perhaps. Look at me. My father was a Government official in the provinces. He had a little land too. A simple servant of God – a true Russian in his way. His was the soul of obedience. But I am not like him. They say I resemble my mother's eldest brother, an officer. They shot him in '28. Under Nicholas, you know. Haven't I told you that this is war, war. . . . But God of Justice! This is weary work.'

Razumov, in his chair, leaning his head on his hand, spoke as if from the bottom of an abyss.

'You believe in God, Haldin?'

'There you go catching at words that are wrung from one. What does it matter? What was it the Englishman said: "There is a divine soul in things . . ." Devil take him – I don't remember now. But he spoke the truth. When the day of you thinkers comes don't you forget what's divine in the Russian soul – and that's resignation. Respect that in your intellectual restlessness and don't let your arrogant wisdom spoil its message to the world. I am speaking to you now like a man with a rope round his neck. What do you imagine I am? A being in revolt? No. It's you thinkers who are in everlasting revolt. I am one of the resigned. When the necessity of this heavy work came to me and I understood that it had to be done – what did I do? Did I exult? Did I take pride in my purpose? Did I try to weigh its worth and consequences? No! I was resigned. I thought "God's will be done." '

He threw himself full length on Razumov's bed and putting the backs of his hands over his eyes remained perfectly motionless and silent. Not even the sound of his breathing could be heard. The dead stillness of the room remained undisturbed till in the darkness Razumov said gloomily –

'Haldin.'

'Yes,' answered the other readily, quite invisible now on the bed and without the slightest stir.

'Isn't it time for me to start?'

'Yes, brother.' The other was heard, lying still in the darkness as though he were talking in his sleep. 'The time has come to put fate to the test.'

He paused, then gave a few lucid directions in the quiet impersonal voice of a man in a trance. Razumov made ready without a word of answer. As he was leaving the room the voice in the bed said after him –

'Go with God, thou silent soul.'

On the landing, moving softly, Razumov locked the door and put the key in his pocket.

Chapter II

The words and events of that evening must have been graven as if with a steel tool on Mr Razumov's brain since he was able to write his relation with such fullness and precision a good many months afterwards.

The record of the thoughts which assailed him in the street is even more minute and abundant. They seem to have rushed upon him with the greater freedom because his thinking powers were no longer crushed by Haldin's presence – the appalling presence of a great crime and the stunning force of a great fanaticism. On looking through the pages of Mr Razumov's diary I own that a 'rush of thoughts' is not an adequate image.

The more adequate description would be a tumult of thoughts – the faithful reflection of the state of his feelings. The thoughts in themselves were not numerous – they were like the thoughts of most human beings, few and simple – but they cannot be reproduced here in all their exclamatory repetitions which went on in an endless and weary turmoil – for the walk was long.

If to the Western reader they appear shocking, inappropriate, or even improper, it must be remembered that as to the first this may be the effect of my crude statement. For the rest I will only remark here that this is not a story of the West of Europe.

Nations it may be have fashioned their Governments, but the Governments have paid them back in the same coin. It is unthinkable that any young Englishman should find himself in Razumov's situation. This being so it would be a vain enterprise to imagine what he would think. The only safe surmise to make is that he would not think as Mr Razumov thought at this crisis of his fate. He would not have an hereditary and personal knowledge of the means by which a historical autocracy represses ideas, guards its power, and defends it existence. By an act of mental extravagance he might imagine himself arbitrarily thrown into prison, but it would never occur to him unless he were delirious (and perhaps not even then) that he could be beaten with whips as a practical measure either of investigation or of punishment.

This is but a crude and obvious example of the different conditions of Western thought. I don't know that this danger occurred specially to Mr Razumov. No doubt it entered unconsciously into the general dread and the general appallingness of this crisis. Razumov, as has been seen, was aware of more subtle ways in which an individual may be undone by the proceedings of a despotic Government. A simple expulsion from the University (the very least that could happen to him), with an impossibility to continue his studies anywhere, was enough to ruin utterly a young man depending entirely upon the development of his natural abilities for his place in the world. He was a Russian: and for him to be implicated meant simply sinking into the lowest social depths amongst the hopeless and the destitute – the night birds of the city.

The peculiar circumstances of Razumov's' parentage, or rather of his lack of parentage, should be taken into the account of his thoughts. And he remembered them too. He had been lately reminded of them in a peculiarly atrocious way by this fatal Haldin. 'Because I haven't that, must everything else be taken away from me?' he thought.

He nerved himself for another effort to go on. Along the roadway sledges glided phantom-like and jingling through a fluttering whiteness on the black face of the night. 'For it is a crime,' he was saying to himself. 'A murder is a murder. Though, of course, some sort of liberal institutions. . . .'

A feeling of horrible sickness came over him. 'I must be courageous,' he exhorted himself mentally. All his strength was suddenly gone as if taken out by a hand. Then by a mighty effort of will it came back because he was afraid of fainting in the street and being picked up by the police with the key of his lodgings in his pocket. They would find Haldin there, and then, indeed, he would be undone.

Strangely enough it was this fear which seems to have kept him up to the end. The passers-by were rare. They came upon him suddenly, looming up black in the snowflakes close by, then vanishing all at once – without footfalls.

It was the quarter of the very poor. Razumov noticed an elderly woman tied up in ragged shawls. Under the street lamp she seemed a beggar off duty. She walked leisurely in the blizzard as though she had no home to hurry to, she hugged under one arm a round loaf of black bread with an air of guarding a priceless booty; and Razumov averting his glance envied her the peace of her mind and the serenity of her fate.

To one reading Mr Razumov's narrative it is really a wonder how he managed to keep going as he did along one interminable street after another on pavements that were gradually becoming blocked with snow. It was the thought of Haldin locked up in his rooms and the desperate desire to get rid of his presence which drove him forward. No rational determination had any part in his exertions. Thus, when on arriving at the low eating-house he heard that the man of horses, Ziemianitch, was not there, he could only stare stupidly.

The waiter, a wild-haired youth in tarred boots and a pink shirt, exclaimed, uncovering his pale gums in a silly grin, that Ziemianitch had got his skinful early in the afternoon and had gone away with a bottle under each arm to keep it up amongst the horses – he supposed.

The owner of the vile den, a bony short man in a dirty cloth caftan coming down to his heels, stood by, his hands tucked into his belt, and nodded confirmation.

The reek of spirits, the greasy rancid steam of food got Razumov by the throat. He struck a table with his clenched hand and shouted violently –

'You lie.'

Bleary unwashed faces were turned to his direction. A mild-eyed ragged tramp drinking tea at the next table moved farther away. A murmur of wonder arose with an undertone of uneasiness. A laugh was heard too, and an exclamation, 'There! there!' jeering, soothing. The waiter looked all round and announced to the room –

'The gentleman won't believe that Ziemianitch is drunk.'

From a distant corner a hoarse voice belonging to a horrible, nondescript, shaggy being with a black face like the muzzle of a bear grunted angrily –

'The cursed driver of thieves. What do we want with this gentleman here? We are all honest folk in this place.'

Razumov, biting his lip till blood came to keep himself from bursting into imprecations, followed the owner of the den, who, whispering 'Come along, little father,' led him into a tiny hole of a place behind the wooden counter, whence proceeded a sound of splashing. A wet and bedraggled creature, a sort of sexless and shivering scarecrow, washed glasses in there, bending over a wooden tub by the light of a tallow dip.

'Yes, little father,' the man in the long caftan said plaintively. He had a brown, cunning little face, a thin greyish beard. Trying to light a tin lantern he hugged it to his breast and talked garrulously the while.

He would show Ziemianitch to the gentleman to prove there were no lies told. And he would show him drunk. His woman, it seems, ran away from him last night. 'Such a hag she was! Thin! Pfui!' He spat. They were always running away from that driver of the devil – and he sixty years old too; could never get used to it. But each heart knows sorrow after its own kind and Ziemianitch was a born fool all his days. And then he would fly to the bottle. ' "Who could bear life in our land without the bottle?" he says. A proper Russian man – the little pig. . . . Be pleased to follow me.'

Razumov crossed a quadrangle of deep snow enclosed between high walls with innumerable windows. Here and there a dim yellow light hung within the foursquare mass of darkness. The house was an enormous slum, a hive of human vermin, a monumental abode of misery towering on the verge of starvation and despair.

In a corner the ground sloped sharply down, and Razumov followed the light of the lantern through a small doorway into a long cavernous place like a neglected subterranean byre. Deep within, three shaggy little horses tied up to rings hung their heads together, motionless and shadowy in the dim light of the lantern. It must have been the famous team of Haldin's escape. Razumov peered fearfully into the gloom. His guide pawed in the straw with his foot.

'Here he is. Ah! the little pigeon. A true Russian man. "No heavy hearts for me," he says. "Bring out the bottle and take your ugly mug out of my sight." Ha! ha! ha! That's the fellow he is.'

He held the lantern over a prone form of a man, apparently fully dressed for outdoors. His head was lost in a pointed cloth hood. On the other side of a heap of straw protruded a pair of feet in monstrous thick boots.

'Always ready to drive,' commented the keeper of the eating-house. 'A proper Russian driver that. Saint or devil, night or day is all one to Ziemianich when his heart is free from sorrow. "I don't ask who you are, but where you want to go," he says. He would drive Satan himself to his own abode and come back chirruping to his horses. Many a one he has driven who is clanking his chains in the Nertchinsk mines by this time.'

Razumov shuddered.

'Call him, wake him up,' he faltered out.

The other set down his light, stepped back, and launched a kick at the prostrate sleeper. The man shook at the impact but did not move. At the third kick he grunted but remained inert as before.

The eating-house keeper desisted and fetched a deep sigh.

'You see for yourself how it is. We have done what we can for you.'

He picked up the lantern. The intense black spokes of shadow swung about in the circle of light. A terrible fury – the blind rage of self-preservation – possessed Razumov.

'Ah! The vile beast,' he bellowed out in an unearthly tone which made the lantern jump and tremble. 'I shall wake you! Give me . . . Give me . . .'

He looked round wildly, seized the handle of a stablefork and rushing forward struck at the prostrate body with inarticulate cries. After a time his cries ceased, and the rain of blows fell in the stillness and shadows of the cellar-like stable. Razumov belaboured Ziemianitch with an insatiable fury, in great volleys of sounding thwacks. Except for the violent movements of Razumov nothing stirred, neither the beaten man nor the spoke-like shadows on the walls. And only the sound of blows was heard. It was a weird scene.

Suddenly there was a sharp crack. The stick broke and half of it flew far away into the gloom beyond the light. At the same time Ziemianitch sat up. At this Razumov became as motionless as the man with the lantern – only his breast heaved for air as if ready to burst.

Some dull sensation of pain must have penetrated at last the consoling night of drunkenness enwrapping the 'bright Russian soul', of Haldin's enthusiastic praise. But Ziemianitch evidently saw nothing. His eyeballs blinked all white in the light once, twice – then the gleam went out. For a moment he sat in the straw with closed eyes with a strange air of weary meditation, then fell over slowly on his side without making the slightest sound. Only the straw rustled a little. Razumov stared wildly, fighting for his breath. After a second or two, he heard a light snore.

He flung from him the piece of stick remaining in his grasp, and went off with great hasty strides without looking back once.

After going heedlessly for some fifty yards along the street he walked into a snowdrift and was up to his knees before he stopped.

This recalled him to himself; and glancing about he discovered he had been going in the wrong direction. He retraced his steps, but now at a more moderate pace. When passing before the house he had just left he flourished his fist at the sombre refuge of misery and crime rearing its sinister bulk on the white ground. It had an air of brooding. He let his arm fall by his side – discouraged.

Ziemianitch's passionate surrender to sorrow and consolation had baffled him. That was the people. A true Russian man! Razumov was glad he had beaten that brute – the 'bright soul' of the other. Here they were: the people and the enthusiast.

Between the two he was done for. Between the drunkenness of the peasant incapable of action and the dream-intoxication of the idealist incapable of perceiving the reason of things, and the true character of men. It was a sort of terrible childishness. But children had their masters. 'Ah! the stick, the stick, the stern hand,' thought Razumov, longing for power to hurt and destroy.

He was glad he had thrashed that brute. The physical exertion had left his body in a comfortable glow. His mental agitation too was clarified as if all the feverishness had gone out of him in a fit of outward violence. Together with the persisting sense of terrible danger he was conscious now of a tranquil, unquenchable hate.

He walked slower and slower. And indeed, considering the guest he had in his rooms, it was no wonder he lingered on the way. It was like harbouring a pestilential disease that would not perhaps take your life, but would take from you all that made life worth living – a subtle pest that would convert earth into a hell.

What was he doing now? Lying on the bed as if dead, with the back of his hands over his eyes? Razumov had a morbidly vivid vision of Haldin on his bed – the white pillow hollowed by the head, the legs in long boots, the upturned feet. And in his abhorrence he said to himself, 'I'll kill him when I get home.' But he knew very well that that was of no use. The corpse hanging round his neck would be nearly as fatal as the living man. Nothing short of complete annihilation would do. And that was impossible. What then? Must one kill oneself to escape this visitation?

Razumov's despair was too profoundly tinged with hate to accept that issue.

And yet it was despair – nothing less – at the thought of having to live with Haldin for an indefinite number of days in mortal alarm at every sound. But perhaps when he heard that this 'bright soul' of Ziemianitch suffered from a drunken eclipse the fellow would take his infernal resignation somewhere else. And that was not likely on the face of it.

Razumov thought: 'I am being crushed – and I can't even run away.' Other men had somewhere a corner of the earth – some little house in the provinces where they had a right to take their troubles. A material refuge. He had nothing. He had not even a moral refuge – the refuge of confidence. To whom could he go with this tale – in all this great, great land?

Razumov stamped his foot – and under the soft carpet of snow felt the hard ground of Russia, inanimate, cold, inert, like a sullen and tragic mother hiding her face under a winding-sheet – his native soil! – his very own – without a fireside, without a hearth!

He cast his eyes upwards and stood amazed. The snow had ceased to fall, and now, as if by a miracle, he saw above his head the clear black sky of the northern winter, decorated with the sumptuous fires of the stars. It was a canopy fit for the resplendent purity of the snows.

Razumov received an almost physical impression of endless space and of countless millions.

He responded to it with the readiness of a Russian who is born to an inheritance of space and numbers. Under the sumptuous immensity of the sky, the snow covered the endless forests, the frozen rivers, the plains of an immense country, obliterating the landmarks, the accidents of the ground, levelling everything under its uniform whiteness, like a monstrous blank page awaiting the record of an inconceivable history. It covered the passive land with its lives of countless people like Ziemianitch and its handful of agitators like this Haldin – murdering foolishly.

It was a sort of sacred inertia. Razumov felt a respect for it. A voice seemed to cry within him, 'Don't touch it.' It was a guarantee of duration, of safety, while the travail of maturing destiny went on – a work not of revolutions with their passionate levity of action and their shifting impulses – but of peace. What it needed was not the conflicting aspirations of a people, but a will strong and one: it wanted not the babble of many voices, but a man – strong and one!

Razumov stood on the point of conversion. He was fascinated by its approach, by its overpowering logic. For a train of thought is never false. The falsehood lies deep in the necessities of existence, in secret fears and half-formed ambitions, in the secret confidence combined with a secret mistrust of ourselves, in the love of hope and the dread of uncertain days.

In Russia, the land of spectral ideas and disembodied aspirations, many brave minds have turned away at last from the vain and endless conflict to the one great historical fact of the land. They turned to autocracy for the peace of their patriotic conscience as a weary unbeliever, touched by grace, turns to the faith of his fathers for the blessing of spiritual rest. Like other Russians before him, Razumov, in conflict with himself, felt the touch of grace upon his forehead.

'Haldin means disruption,' he thought to himself, beginning to walk again. 'What is he with his indignation, with his talk of bondage – with his talk of God's justice? All that means disruption. Better that thousands should suffer than that a people should become a disintegrated mass, helpless like dust in the wind. Obscurantism is better than the light of incendiary torches. The seed germinates in the night. Out of the dark soil springs the perfect plant. But a volcanic eruption is sterile, the ruin of the fertile ground. And am I, who love my country – who have nothing but that to love and put my faith in – am I to have my future, perhaps my usefulness, ruined by this sanguinary fanatic?'

The grace entered into Razumov. He believed now in the man who would come at the appointed time.

What is a throne? A few pieces of wood upholstered in velvet. But a throne is a seat of power too. The form of government is the shape of a tool – an instrument. But twenty thousand bladders inflated by the noblest sentiments and jostling against each other in the air are a miserable encumbrance of space, holding no power, possessing no will, having nothing to give.

He went on thus, heedless of the way, holding a discourse with himself with extraordinary abundance and facility. Generally his phrases came to him slowly, after a conscious and painstaking wooing. Some superior power had inspired him with a flow of masterly argument as certain converted sinners become overwhelmingly loquacious.

He felt an austere exultation.

'What are the luridly smoky lucubrations of that fellow to the clear grasp of my intellect?' he thought. 'Is not this my country? Have I not got forty million brothers?' he asked himself, unanswerably victorious in the silence of his breast. And the fearful thrashing he had given the inanimate Ziemianitch seemed to him a sign of intimate union, a pathetically severe necessity of brotherly love.

'No! If I must suffer let me at least suffer for my convictions, not for a crime my reason – my cool superior reason – rejects.'

He ceased to think for a moment. The silence in his breast was complete. But he felt a suspicious uneasiness, such as we may experience when we enter an unlighted strange place – the irrational feeling that something may jump upon us in the dark – the absurd dread of the unseen.

Of course he was far from being a moss-grown reactionary. Everything was not for the best. Despotic bureaucracy . . . abuses . . . corruption . . . and so on. Capable men were wanted. Enlightened intelligences. Devoted hearts. But absolute power should be preserved – the tool ready for the man – for the great autocrat of the future. Razumov believed in him. The logic of history made him unavoidable. The state of the people demanded him. 'What else,' he asked himself ardently, 'could move all that mass in one direction? Nothing could. Nothing but a single will.'

He was persuaded that he was sacrificing his personal longings of liberalism – rejecting the attractive error for the stern Russian truth. 'That's patriotism,' he observed mentally, and added, 'There's no stopping midway on that road,' and then remarked to himself, 'I am not a coward.'

And again there was a dead silence in Razumov's breast. He walked with lowered head, making room for no one. He walked slowly and his thoughts returning spoke within him with solemn slowness.

'What is this Haldin? And what am I? Only two grains of sand. But a great mountain is made up of just such insignificant grains. And the death of a man or of many men is an insignificant thing. Yet we combat a contagious pestilence. Do I want his death? No! I would save him if I could – but no one can do that – he is the withered member which must be cut off. If I must perish through him, let me at least not perish with him, and associated against my will with his sombre folly that understands nothing either of men or things. Why should I leave a false memory?'

It passed through his mind that there was no one in the world who cared what sort of memory he left behind him. He exclaimed to himself instantly, 'Perish vainly for a falsehood! . . . What a miserable fate!'

He was now in a more animated part of the town. He did not remark the crash of two colliding sledges close to the kerb. The driver of one bellowed tearfully at his fellow –

'Oh, thou vile wretch!'

This hoarse yell, let out nearly in his ear, disturbed Razumov. He shook his head impatiently and went on looking straight before him. Suddenly on the snow, stretched on his back right across his path, he saw Haldin, solid, distinct, real, with his inverted hands over his eyes, clad in a brown close-fitting coat and long boots. He was lying out of the way a little, as though he had selected that place on purpose. The snow round him was untrodden.

This hallucination had such a solidity of aspect that the first movement of Razumov was to reach for his pocket to assure himself that the key of his rooms was there. But he checked the impulse with a disdainful curve of his lips. He understood. His thought, concentrated intensely on the figure left lying on his bed, had culminated in this extraordinary illusion of the sight. Razumov tackled the phenomenon calmly. With a stern face, without a check, and gazing far beyond the vision, he walked on, experiencing nothing but a slight tightening of the chest. After passing he turned his head for a glance, and saw only the unbroken track of his footsteps over the place where the breast of the phantom had been lying.

Razumov walked on and after a little time whispered his wonder to himself.

'Exactly as if alive! Seemed to breathe! And right in my way too! I have had an extraordinary experience.'

He made a few steps and muttered through his set teeth –

'I shall give him up.'

Then for some twenty yards or more all was blank. He wrapped his cloak closer round him. He pulled his cap well forward over his eyes.

'Betray. A great word. What is betrayal? They talk of a man betraying his country, his friends, his sweetheart. There must be a moral bond first. All a man can betray is his conscience. And how is my conscience engaged here; by what bond of common faith, of common conviction, am I obliged to let that fanatical idiot drag me down with him? On the contrary – every obligation of true courage is the other way.'

Razumov looked round from under his cap.

'What can the prejudice of the world reproach me with? Have I provoked his confidence? No! Have I by a single word, look, or gesture given him reason to suppose that I accepted his trust in me? No! It is true that I consented to go and see his Ziemianitch. Well, I have been to see him. And I broke a stick on his back too – the brute.'

Something seemed to turn over in his head bringing uppermost a singularly hard, clear facet of his brain.

'It would be better, however,' he reflected with a quite different mental accent, 'to keep that circumstance altogether to myself.'

He had passed beyond the turn leading to his lodgings, and had reached a wide and fashionable street. Some shops were still open, and all the restaurants. Lights fell on the pavement where men in expensive fur coats, with here and there the elegant figure of a woman, walked with an air of leisure. Razumov looked at them with the contempt of an austere believer for the frivolous crowd. It was the world – those officers, dignitaries, men of fashion, officials, members of the Yacht Club. The event of the morning affected them all. What would they say if they knew what this student in a cloak was going to do?

'Not one of them is capable of feeling and thinking as deeply as I can. How many of them could accomplish an act of conscience?

Razumov lingered in the well-lighted street. He was firmly decided. Indeed, it could hardly be called a decision. He had simply discovered what he had meant to do all along. And yet he felt the need of some other mind's sanction.

With something resembling anguish he said to himself –

'I want to be understood.' The universal aspiration with all its profound and melancholy meaning assailed heavily Razumov, who, amongst eighty millions of his kith and kin, had no heart to which he could open himself.

The attorney was not to be thought of. He despised the little agent of chicane too much. One could not go and lay one's conscience before the policeman at the corner. Neither was Razumov anxious to go to the chief of his district's police – common-looking person whom he used to see sometimes in the street in a shabby uniform and with a smouldering cigarette stuck to his lower lip. 'He would begin by locking me up most probably. At any rate, he is certain to get excited and create an awful commotion,' thought Razumov practically.

An act of conscience must be done with outward dignity.

Razumov longed desperately for a word of advice, for moral support. Who knows what true loneliness is – not the conventional word, but the naked terror? To the lonely themselves it wears a mask. The most miserable outcast hugs some memory or some illusion. Now and then a fatal conjunction of events may lift the veil for an instant. For an instant only. No human being could bear a steady view of moral solitude without going mad.

Razumov had reached that point of vision. To escape from it he embraced for a whole minute the delirious purpose of rushing to his lodgings and flinging himself on his knees by the side of the bed with the dark figure stretched on it; to pour out a full confession in passionate words that would stir the whole being of that man to its innermost depths; that would end in embraces and tears; in an incredible fellowship of souls – such as the world had never seen. It was sublime!

Inwardly he wept and trembled already. But to the casual eyes that were cast upon him he was aware that he appeared as a tranquil student in a cloak, out for a leisurely stroll. He noted, too, the sidelong, brilliant glance of a pretty woman – with a delicate head, and covered in the hairy skins of wild beasts down to her feet, like a frail and beautiful savage – which rested for a moment with a sort of mocking tenderness on the deep abstraction of that good-looking young man.

Suddenly Razumov stood still. The glimpse of a passing grey whisker, caught and lost in the same instant, had evoked the complete image of Prince K—, the man who once had pressed his hand as no other man had pressed it – a faint but lingering pressure like a secret sign, like a half-unwilling caress.

And Razumov marvelled at himself. Why did he not think of him before!

'A senator, a dignitary, a great personage, the very man – He!'

A strange softening emotion came over Razumov – made his knees shake a little. He repressed it with a new-born austerity. All that sentiment was pernicious nonsense. He couldn't be quick enough; and when he got into a sledge he shouted to the driver –

'To the K— Palace. Get on – you! Fly!'

The startled moujik, bearded up to the very whites of his eyes, answered obsequiously –

'I hear, your high Nobility.'

It was lucky for Razumov that Prince K— was not a man of timid character. On the day of Mr de P—'s murder an extreme alarm and despondency prevailed in the high official spheres.

Prince K—, sitting sadly alone in his study, was told by his alarmed servants that a mysterious young man had forced his way into the hall, refused to tell his name and the nature of his business, and would not move from there till he had seen his Excellency in private. Instead of locking himself up and telephoning for the police, as nine out of ten personages would have done that evening, the Prince gave way to curiosity and came quietly to the door of his study.

In the hall, the front door standing wide open, he recognized at once Razumov, pale as death, his eyes blazing, and surrounded by perplexed lackeys.

The Prince was vexed beyond measure, and even indignant. But his humane instincts and a subtle sense of self-respect could not allow him to let this young man be thrown out into the street by base menials. He retreated unseen into his room, and after a little rang his bell. Razumov heard in the hall an ominously raised harsh voice saying somewhere far away –

'Show the gentleman in here.'

Razumov walked in without a tremor. He felt himself invulnerable – raised far above the shallowness of common judgement. Though he saw the Prince looking at him with black displeasure, the lucidity of his mind, of which he was very conscious, gave him an extraordinary assurance. He was not asked to sit down.

Half an hour later they appeared in the hall together. The lackeys stood up, and the Prince, moving with difficulty on his gouty feet, was helped into his furs. The carriage had been ordered before. When the great double door was flung open with a crash, Razumov, who had been standing silent with a lost gaze but with every faculty intensely on the alert, heard the Prince's voice –

'Your arm, young man.'

The mobile, superficial mind of the ex-Guards officer, man of showy missions, experienced in nothing but the arts of gallant intrigue and worldly success, had been equally impressed by the more obvious difficulties of such a situation and by Razumov's quiet dignity in stating them.

He had said, 'No. Upon the whole I can't condemn the step you ventured to take by coming to me with your story. It is not an affair for police understrappers. The greatest importance is attached to . . . Set your mind at rest. I shall see you through this most extraordinary and difficult situation.'

Then the Prince rose to ring the bell, and Razumov, making a short bow, had said with deference –

'I have trusted my instinct. A young man having no claim upon anybody in the world has in an hour of trial involving his deepest political convictions turned to an illustrious Russian – that's all.'

The Prince had exclaimed hastily –

'You have done well.'

In the carriage – it was a small brougham on sleigh runners – Razumov broke the silence in a voice that trembled slightly.

'My gratitude surpasses the greatness of my presumption.'

He gasped, feeling unexpectedly in the dark a momentary pressure on his arm.

'You have done well,' repeated the Prince.

When the carriage stopped the Prince murmured to Razumov, who had never ventured a single question –

'The house of General T—.'

In the middle of the snow-covered roadway blazed a great bonfire. Some Cossacks, the bridles of their horses over the arm, were warming themselves around it. Two sentries stood at the door, several gendarmes lounged under the great carriage gateway, and on the first floor landing two orderlies rose and stood at attention. Razumov walked at the Prince's elbow.

A surprising quantity of hot-house plants in pots cumbered the floor of the ante-room. Servants came forward. A young man in civilian clothes arrived hurriedly, was whispered to, bowed low, and exclaiming zealously, 'Certainly – this minute,' fled within somewhere. The Prince signed to Razumov.

They passed through a suite of reception-rooms, all barely lit and one of them prepared for dancing. The wife of the General had put off her party. An atmosphere of consternation pervaded the place. But the General's own room, with heavy sombre hangings, two massive desks, and deep armchairs, had all the lights turned on. The footman shut the door behind them and they waited.

There was a coal fire in an English grate; Razumov had never before seen such a fire; and the silence of the room was like the silence of the grave; perfect, measureless, for even the clock on the mantelpiece made no sound. Filling a corner, on a black pedestal, stood a quarter-life-size smooth-limbed bronze of an adolescent figure, running. The Prince observed in an undertone –

'Spontini's. "Flight of Youth." Exquisite.'

'Admirable,' assented Razumov faintly.

They said nothing more after this, the Prince silent with his grand air, Razumov staring at the statue. He was worried by a sensation resembling the gnawing of hunger.

He did not turn when he heard an inner door fly open, and a quick footstep, muffled on the carpet.

The Prince's voice immediately exclaimed, thick with excitement –

'We have got him – *ce misérable*. A worthy young man came to me – No! It's incredible. . . .'

Razumov held his breath before the bronze as if expecting a crash. Behind his back a voice he had never heard before insisted politely –

'*Asseyez-vous donc*.'

The Prince almost shrieked, '*Mais comprenez-vous, mon cher! L'assassin!* the murderer – we have got him. . . .'

Razumov spun round. The General's smooth big cheeks rested on the stiff collar of his uniform. He must have been already looking at Razumov, because that last saw the pale blue eyes fastened on him coldly.

The Prince from a chair waved an impressive hand.

'This is a most honourable young man whom Providence itself . . . Mr Razumov.'

The General acknowledged the introduction by frowning at Razumov, who did not make the slightest movement.

Sitting down before his desk the General listened with compressed lips. It was impossible to detect any sign of emotion on his face.

Razumov watched the immobility of the fleshy profile. But it lasted only a moment, till the Prince had finished; and when the General turned to the providential young man, his florid complexion, the blue, unbelieving eyes, and the bright white flash of an automatic smile had an air of jovial, careless cruelty. He expressed no wonder at the extraordinary story – no pleasure or excitement – no incredulity either. He betrayed no sentiment whatever. Only with a politeness almost deferential suggested that 'the bird might have flown while Mr – Mr Razumov was running about the streets.'

Razumov advanced to the middle of the room and said, 'The door is locked and I have the key in my pocket.'

His loathing for the man was intense. It had come upon him so unawares that he felt he had not kept it out of his voice. The General looked up at him thoughtfully, and Razumov grinned.

All this went over the head of Prince K— seated in a deep armchair, very tired and impatient.

'A student called Haldin,' said the General thoughtfully.

Razumov ceased to grin.

'That is his name,' he said, unnecessarily loud. 'Victor Victorovitch Haldin – a student.'

The General shifted his position a little.

'How is he dressed? Would you have the goodness to tell me?'

Rasumov angrily described Haldin's clothing in a few jerky words. The General stared all the time, then addressing the Prince –

'We were not without some indications,' he said in French. 'A good woman who was in the street described to us somebody wearing a dress of the sort as the thrower of the second bomb. We have detained her at the Secretariat, and everyone in a Tcherkess coat we could lay our hands on has been brought to her to look at. She kept on crossing herself and shaking her head at them. It was exasperating. . . .'

He turned to Razumov, and in Russian, with friendly reproach –

'Take a chair, Mr Razumov – do. Why are you standing?'

Razumov sat down carelessly and looked at the General.

'This goggle-eyed imbecile understands nothing,' he thought.

The Prince began to speak loftily.

'Mr Razumov is a young man of conspicuous abilities. I have it at heart that his future should not. . . .'

'Certainly,' interrupted the General, with a movement of the hand. 'Has he any weapons on him, do you think, Mr Razumov?'

The general employed a gentle musical voice. Razumov answered with suppressed irritation –

'No. But my razors are lying about – you understand.'

The General lowered his head approvingly.

'Precisely.'

Then to the Prince, explaining courteously –

'We want that bird alive. It will be the devil if we can't make him sing a little before we are done with him.'

The grave-like silence of the room with its mute clock fell upon the polite modulations of this terrible phrase. The Prince, hidden in the chair, made no sound.

The General unexpectedly developed a thought.

'Fidelity to menaced institutions on which depend the safety of a throne and of a people is no child's play. We know that, *mon Prince*, and – *tenez* –' he went on with a sort of flattering harshness, 'Mr Razumov here begins to understand that too.'

His eyes which he turned upon Razumov seemed to be starting out of his head. This grotesqueness of aspect no longer shocked Razumov. He said with gloomy conviction –

'Haldin will never speak.'

'That remains to be seen,' muttered the General.

'I am certain,' insisted Razumov. 'A man like this never speaks. . . . Do you imagine that I am here from fear?' he added violently. He felt ready to stand by his opinion of Haldin to the last extremity.

'Certainly not,' protested the General, with great simplicity of tone. 'And I don't mind telling you, Mr Razumov, that if he had not come with his tale to such a staunch and loyal Russian as you, he would have disappeared like a stone in the water . . . which would have had a detestable effect,' he added, with a bright, cruel smile under his stony stare. 'So you see, there can be no suspicion of any fear here.'

The Prince intervened, looking at Razumov round the back of the armchair.

'Nobody doubts the moral soundness of your action. Be at ease in that respect, pray.'

He turned to the General uneasily.

'That's why I am here. You may be surprised why I should . . .'

The General hastened to interrupt.

'Not at all. Extremely natural. You saw the importance . . .'

'Yes,' broke in the Prince. 'And I venture to ask insistently that mine and Mr Razumov's intervention should not become public. He is a young man of promise – of remarkable aptitudes.'

'I haven't a doubt of it,' murmured the General. 'He inspires confidence.'

'All sorts of pernicious views are so widespread nowadays – they taint such unexpected quarters – that, monstrous as it seems, he might suffer. . . . His studies. . . . His . . .'

The General, with his elbows on the desk, took his head between his hands.

'Yes. Yes. I am thinking it out. . . . How long is it since you left him at your rooms, Mr Razumov?'

Razumov mentioned the hour which nearly corresponded with the time of his distracted flight from the big slum house. He had made up his mind to keep Ziemianitch out of the affair completely. To mention him at all would mean imprisonment for the 'bright soul', perhaps cruel floggings, and in the end a journey to Siberia in chains. Razumov, who had beaten Ziemianitch, felt for him now a vague, remorseful tenderness.

The General, giving way for the first time to his secret sentiments, exclaimed contemptuously –

'And you say he came in to make you this confidence like this – for nothing – *à propos des bottes*.'

Razumov felt danger in the air. The merciless suspicion of despotism had spoken openly at last. Sudden fear sealed Razumov's lips. The silence of the room resembled now the silence of a deep dungeon, where time does not count, and a suspect person is sometimes forgotten for ever. But the Prince came to the rescue.

'Providence itself has led the wretch in a moment of mental aberration to seek Mr Razumov on the strength of some old, utterly misinterpreted exchange of ideas – some sort of idle speculative conversation – months ago – I am told – and completely forgotten till now by Mr Razumov.'

'Mr Razumov,' queried the General meditatively, after a short silence, 'do you often indulge in speculative conversation?'

'No, Excellency,' answered Razumov, coolly, in a sudden access of self-confidence. 'I am a man of deep convictions. Crude opinions are in the air. They are not always worth combating. But even the silent contempt of a serious mind may be misinterpreted by headlong utopists.'

The General stared from between his hands. Prince K— murmured –

'A serious young man. *Un esprit supérieur*.'

'I see that, *mon cher Prince*,' said the General. 'Mr Razumov is quite safe with me. I am interested in him. He has, it seems, the great and useful quality of inspiring confidence. What I was wondering at is why the other should mention anything at all – I mean even the bare fact alone – if his object was only to obtain temporary shelter for a few hours. For, after all, nothing was easier than to say nothing about it unless, indeed, he were trying, under a crazy misapprehension of your true sentiments, to enlist your assistance – eh, Mr Razumov?'

It seemed to Razumov that the floor was moving slightly. This grotesque man in a tight uniform was terrible. It was right that he should be terrible.

'I can see what your Excellency has in your mind. But I can only answer that I don't know why.'

'I have nothing in my mind,' murmured the General with gentle surprise.

'I am his prey – his helpless prey,' thought Razumov. The fatigues and the disgusts of that afternoon, the need to forget, the fear which he could not keep off, reawakened his hate for Haldin.

'Then I can't help your Excellency. I don't know what he meant. I only know there was a moment when I wished to kill him. There was also a moment when I wished myself dead. I said nothing. I was overcome. I provoked no confidence – I asked for no explanations –'

Razumov seemed beside himself; but his mind was lucid. It was really a calculated outburst.

'It is rather a pity,' the General said, 'that you did not. Don't you know at all what he means to do?'

Razumov calmed down and saw an opening there.

'He told me he was in hopes that a sledge would meet him about half an hour after midnight at the seventh lamp-post on the left from the upper end of Karabelnaya. At any rate, he meant to be there at that time. He did not even ask me for a change of clothes.'

'*Ah voilà!*' said the General, turning to Prince K— with an air of satisfaction. 'There is a way to keep your *protégé*, Mr Razumov, quite clear of any connection with the actual arrest. We shall be ready for that gentleman in Karabelnaya.'

The Prince expressed his gratitude. There was real emotion in his voice.

Razumov, motionless, silent, sat staring at the carpet. The General turned to him.

'Half an hour after midnight. Till then we have to depend on you, Mr Razumov. You don't think he is likely to change his purpose?'

'How can I tell?' said Razumov. 'Those men are not of the sort that ever changes its purpose.'

'What men do you mean?'

'Fanatical lovers of liberty in general. Liberty with a capital L, Excellency. Liberty that means nothing precise. Liberty in whose name crimes are committed.'

The General murmured –

'I detest rebels of every kind. I can't help it. It's my nature!'

He clenched a fist and shook it, drawing back his arm. 'They shall be destroyed, then.'

'They have made a sacrifice of their lives beforehand,' said Razumov with malicious pleasure and looking the General straight in the face. 'If Haldin does change his purpose to-night, you may depend on it that it will not be to save his life by flight in some other way. He would have thought then of something else to attempt. But that is not likely.'

The General repeated as if to himself, 'They shall be destroyed.'

Razumov assumed an impenetrable expression.

The Prince exclaimed –

'What a terrible necessity!'

The General's arm was lowered slowly.

'One comfort there is. That brood leaves no posterity. I've always said it; one effort, pitiless, persistent, steady – and we are done with them for ever.'

Razumov thought to himself that this man entrusted with so much arbitrary power must have believed what he said or else he could not have gone on bearing the responsibility.

The General repeated again with extreme animosity –

'I detest rebels. These subversive minds! These intellectual *Débauchés*! My existence has been built on fidelity. It's a feeling. To defend it I am ready to lay down my life – and even my honour – if that were needed. But pray tell me what honour can there be as against rebels – against people that deny God Himself – perfect unbelievers! Brutes. It is horrible to think of.'

During this tirade Razumov, facing the General, had nodded slightly twice. Prince K—, standing on one side with his grand air, murmured, casting up his eyes –

'*Hélas!*'

Then lowering his glance and with great decision declared –

'This young man, General, is perfectly fit to apprehend the bearing of your memorable words.'

The General's whole expression changed from dull resentment to perfect urbanity.

'I would ask now, Mr Razumov,' he said, 'to return to his home. Note that I don't ask Mr Razumov whether he had justified his absence to his guest. No doubt he did this sufficiently. But I don't ask. Mr Razumov inspires confidence.

It is a great gift. I only suggest that a more prolonged absence might awaken the criminal's suspicions and induce him perhaps to change his plans.'

He rose and with a scrupulous courtesy escorted his visitors to the ante-room encumbered with flower-pots.

Razumov parted with the Prince at the corner of a street. In the carriage he had listened to speeches where natural sentiment struggled with caution. Evidently the Prince was afraid of encouraging any hopes of future intercourse. But there was a touch of tenderness in the voice uttering in the dark the guarded general phrases of goodwill. And the Prince too said –

'I have perfect confidence in you, Mr Razumov.'

'They all, it seems, have confidence in me,' thought Razumov dully. He had an indulgent contempt for the man sitting shoulder to shoulder with him in the confined space. Probably he was afraid of scenes with his wife. She was said to be proud and violent.

It seemed to him bizarre that secrecy should play such a large part in the comfort and safety of lives. But he wanted to put the Prince's mind at ease; and with a proper amount of emphasis he said that, being conscious of some small abilities and confident in his power of work, he trusted his future to his own exertion. He expressed his gratitude for the helping hand. Such dangerous situations did not occur twice in the course of one life – he added.

'And you have met this one with a firmness of mind and correctness of feeling which give me a high idea of your worth,' the Prince said solemnly. 'You have now only to persevere – to persevere.'

On getting out on the pavement Razumov saw an ungloved hand extended to him through the lowered window of the brougham. It detained his own in its grasp for a moment, while the light of a street lamp fell upon the Prince's long face and old-fashioned grey whiskers.

'I hope you are perfectly reassured now as to the consequences. . . .'

'After what your Excellency has condescended to do for me, I can only rely on my conscience.'

'*Adieu*,' said the whiskered head with feeling.

Razumov bowed. The brougham glided away with a slight swish in the snow – he was alone on the edge of the pavement.

He said to himself that there was nothing to think about, and began walking towards his home.

He walked quietly. It was a common experience to walk thus home to bed after an evening spent somewhere with his fellows or in the cheaper seats of a theatre. After he had gone a little way the familiarity of things got hold of him. Nothing was changed. There was the familiar corner; and when he turned it he saw the familiar dim light of the provision shop kept by a German woman. There were loaves of stale bread, bunches of onions, and strings of sausages behind the small window-panes. They were closing it. The sickly lame fellow whom he knew so well by sight staggered out into the snow embracing a large shutter.

Nothing would change. There was the familiar gateway yawning black with feeble glimmers marking the arches of the different staircases.

The sense of life's continuity depended on trifling bodily impressions. The trivialities of daily existence were an armour for the soul. And this thought reinforced the inward quietness of Razumov as he began to climb the stairs familiar to his feet in the dark, with his hand on the familiar clammy banister. The exceptional could not prevail against the material contacts which make one day resemble another. To-morrow would be like yesterday.

It was only on the stage that the unusual was outwardly acknowledged.

'I suppose,' thought Razumov, 'that if I had made up my mind to blow out my brains on the landing I would be going up these stairs as quietly as I am doing it now. What's a man to do? What must be must be. Extraordinary things do happen. But when they have happened they are done with. Thus, too, when the mind is made up. That question is done with. And the daily concerns, the familiarities of our thought swallow it up – and the life goes on as before with its mysterious and secret sides quite out of sight, as they should be. Life is a public thing.'

Razumov unlocked his door and took the key out; entered very quietly and bolted the door behind him carefully.

He thought, 'He hears me,' and after bolting the door he stood still holding his breath. There was not a sound. He crossed the bare outer room, stepping deliberately in the darkness. Entering the other, he felt all over his table for the matchbox. The silence, but for the groping of his hand, was profound. Could the fellow be sleeping so soundly?

He struck a light and looked at the bed. Haldin was lying on his back as before, only both his hands were under his head. His eyes were open. He stared at the ceiling.

Razumov held the match up. He saw the clear-cut features, the firm chin, the white forehead, and the top-knot of fair hair against the white pillow. There he was, lying flat on his back. Razumov thought suddenly, 'I have walked over his chest.'

He continued to stare till the match burnt itself out; then struck another and lit the lamp in silence without looking towards the bed any more. He had turned his back on it and was hanging his coat on a peg when he heard Haldin sigh profoundly, then ask in a tired voice –

'Well! And what have you arranged?'

The emotion was so great that Razumov was glad to put his hands against the wall. A diabolical impulse to say, 'I have given you up to the police,' frightened him exceedingly. But he did not say that. He said, without turning round, in a muffled voice –

'It's done.'

Again he heard Haldin sigh. He walked to the table, sat down with the lamp before him, and only then looked towards the bed.

In the distant corner of the large room far away from the lamp, which was small and provided with a very thick china shade, Haldin appeared like a dark and elongated shape – rigid with the immobility of death. This body seemed to have less substance than its own phantom walked over by Razumov in the street white with snow. It was more alarming in its shadowy, persistent reality than the distinct but vanishing illusion.

Haldin was heard again.

'You must have had a walk – such a walk . . .' he murmured deprecatingly. 'This weather . . .'

Razumov answered with energy –

'Horrible walk. . . . A nightmare of a walk.'

He shuddered audibly. Haldin sighed once more, then –

'And so you have seen Ziemianitch – brother?'

'I've seen him.'

Razumov, remembering the time he had spent with the Prince, thought it prudent to add, 'I had to wait some time.'

'A character – eh? It's extraordinary what a sense of the necessity of freedom there is in that man. And he had sayings too – simple, to the point, such as only the people can invent in their rough sagacity. A character that . . .'

'I, you understand, haven't had much opportunity . . .' Razumov muttered through his teeth.

Haldin continued to stare at the ceiling.

'You see, brother, I have been a good deal in that house of late. I used to take there books – leaflets. Not a few of the poor people who live there can read. And, you see, the guests for the feast of freedom must be sought for in byways and hedges. The truth is, I have almost lived in that house of late. I slept sometimes in the stable. There is a stable . . .'

'That's where I had my interview with Ziemianitch,' interrupted Razumov gently. A mocking spirit entered into him and he added, 'It was satisfactory in a sense. I came away from it much relieved.'

'Ah! he's a fellow,' went on Haldin, talking slowly at the ceiling. 'I came to know him in that way, you see. For some weeks now, ever since I resigned myself to do what had to be done, I tried to isolate myself. I gave up my rooms. What was the good of exposing a decent widow woman to the risk of being worried out of her mind by the police? I gave up seeing any of our comrades . . .'

Razumov drew to himself a half-sheet of paper and began to trace lines on it with a pencil.

'Upon my word,' he thought angrily, 'he seems to have thought of everybody's safety but mine.'

Haldin was talking on.

'This morning – ah! this morning – that was different. How can I explain to you? Before the deed was done I wandered at night and lay hid in the day, thinking it out, and I felt restful. Sleepless but restful. What was there for me to torment myself about? But this morning – after! Then it was that I became restless. I could not have stopped in that big house full of misery. The miserable of this world can't give you peace. Then when that silly caretaker began to shout, I said to myself, "There is a young man in this town head and shoulders above common prejudices." '

'Is he laughing at me?' Razumov asked himself, going on with his aimless drawing of triangles and squares. And suddenly he thought: 'My behaviour must appear to him strange. Should he take fright at my manner and rush off somewhere I shall be undone completely. That infernal General . . .'

He dropped the pencil and turned abruptly towards the bed with the shadowy figure extended full length on it – so much more indistinct than the one over whose breast he had walked without faltering. Was this, too, a phantom?

The silence had lasted a long time. 'He is no longer here,' was the thought against which Razumov struggled desperately, quite frightened at its absurdity. 'He is already gone and this . . . only . . .'

He could resist no longer. He sprang to his feet, saying aloud, 'I am intolerably anxious,' and in a few headlong strides stood by the side of the bed. His hand fell lightly on Haldin's shoulder, and directly he felt its reality he was beset by an insane temptation to grip that exposed throat and squeeze the breath out of that body, lest it should escape his custody, leaving only a phantom behind.

Haldin did not stir a limb, but his overshadowed eyes moving a little gazed upwards at Razumov with wistful gratitude for this manifestation of feeling.

Razumov turned away and strode up and down the room. 'It would have been possibly a kindness,' he muttered to himself, and was appalled by the nature of that apology for a murderous intention his mind had found somewhere within him. And all the same he could not give it up. He became lucid about it. 'What can he expect?' he thought. 'The halter – in the end. And I . . .'

This argument was interrupted by Haldin's voice.

'Why be anxious for me? They can kill my body, but they cannot exile my soul from this world. I tell you what – I believe in this world so much that I cannot conceive eternity otherwise than as a very long life. That is perhaps the reason I am so ready to die.'

'H'm,' muttered Razumov, and biting his lower lip he continued to walk up and down and to carry on his strange argument.

Yes, to a man in such a situation – of course it would be an act of kindness. The question, however, was not how to be kind, but how to be firm. He was a slippery customer . . .

'I too, Victor Victorovitch, believe in this world of ours,' he said with force. 'I too, while I live. . . . But you seem determined to haunt it. You can't seriously mean . . .'

The voice of the motionless Haldin began –

'Haunt it! Truly, the oppressors of thought which quickens the world, the destroyers of souls which aspire to perfection of human dignity, they shall be haunted. As to the destroyers of my mere body, I have forgiven them beforehand.'

Razumov had stopped apparently to listen, but at the same time he was observing his own sensations. He was vexed with himself for attaching so much importance to what Haldin said.

'The fellow's mad,' he thought firmly, but this opinion did not mollify him towards Haldin. It was a particularly impudent form of lunacy – and when it got loose in the sphere of public life of a country, it was obviously the duty of every good citizen . . .

This train of thought broke off short there and was succeeded by a paroxysm of silent hatred towards Haldin, so intense that Razumov hastened to speak at random.

'Yes. Eternity, of course. I, too, can't very well represent it to myself. . . . I imagine it, however, as something quiet and dull. There would be nothing unexpected – don't you see? The element of time would be wanting.'

He pulled out his watch and gazed at it. Haldin turned over on his side and looked on intently.

Razumov got frightened at this movement. A slippery customer this fellow with a phantom. It was not midnight yet. He hastened on –

'And unfathomable mysteries! Can you conceive secret places in Eternity? Impossible. Whereas life is full of them. There are secrets of birth, for instance. One carries them on to the grave. There is something comical . . . but never mind. And there are secret motives of conduct. A man's most open actions have a secret side to them. That is interesting and so unfathomable! For instance, a man goes out of a room for a walk. Nothing more trivial in appearance. And yet it may be momentous. He comes back – he has seen perhaps a drunken brute, taken particular notice of the snow on the ground – and behold he is no longer the same man. The most unlikely things have a secret power over one's thoughts – the grey whiskers of a particular person – the goggle eyes of another.'

Razumov's forehead was moist. He took a turn or two in the room, his head low and smiling to himself viciously.

'Have you ever reflected on the power of goggle eyes and grey whiskers? Excuse me. You seem to think I must be crazy to talk in this vein at such a time. But I am not talking lightly. I have seen instances. It has happened to me once to be talking to a man whose fate was affected by physical facts of that kind. And the man did not know it. Of course, it was a case of conscience, but the material facts such as these brought about the solution. . . . And you tell me, Victor Victorovitch, not to be anxious! Why! I am responsible for you,' Razumov almost shrieked.

He avoided with difficulty a burst of Mephistophelian laughter. Haldin, very pale, raised himself on his elbow.

'And the surprises of life,' went on Razumov, after glancing at the other uneasily. 'Just consider their astonishing nature. A mysterious impulse induces you to come here. I don't say you have done wrong. Indeed, from a certain point of view you could not have done better. You might have gone to a man with affections and family ties. You have such ties yourself. As to me, you know I have been brought up in an educational institute where they did not give us enough to eat. To talk of affection in such a connection – you perceive yourself. . . . As to ties, the only ties I have in the world are social. I must get acknowledged in some way before I can act at all. I sit here working. . . . And don't you think I am working for progress too? I've got to find my own ideas of the true way. . . . Pardon me,' continued Razumov, after drawing breath and with a short, throaty laugh, 'but I haven't inherited a revolutionary inspiration together with a resemblance from an uncle.'

He looked again at his watch and noticed with sickening disgust that there were yet a good many minutes to midnight. He tore watch and chain off his waistcoat and laid them on the table well in the circle of bright lamplight. Haldin, reclining on his elbow, did not stir. Razumov was made uneasy by this attitude. 'What move is he meditating over so quietly?' he thought. 'He must be prevented. I must keep on talking to him.'

He raised his voice.

'You are a son, a brother, a nephew, a cousin – I don't know what – to no end of people. I am just a man. Here I stand before you. A man with a mind. Did it ever occur to you how a man who had never heard a word of warm affection or praise in his life would think on matters on which you would think first with or against your class, your domestic tradition – your fireside prejudices? . . . Did you ever consider how a man like that would feel? I have no domestic tradition. I have nothing to think against. My tradition is historical. What have I to look back to but that national past from which you gentlemen want to wrench away your future? Am I to let my intelligence, my aspirations towards a better lot, be robbed of the only thing it has to go upon at the will of violent enthusiasts? You come from your province, but all this land is mine – or I have nothing. No doubt you shall be looked upon as a martyr some day – a sort of hero – a political saint. But I beg to be excused. I am content in fitting myself to be a worker. And what can you people do by scattering a few drops of blood on the snow? On this Immensity. On this unhappy Immensity! I tell you,' he cried, in a vibrating, subdued voice, and advancing one step nearer the bed, 'that what it needs is not a lot of haunting phantoms that I would walk through – but a man!'

Haldin threw his arms forward as if to keep him off in horror.

'I understand it all now,' he exclaimed, with awestruck dismay. 'I understand – at last.'

Razumov staggered back against the table. His forehead broke out in perspiration while a cold shudder ran down his spine.

'What have I been saying?' he asked himself. 'Have I let him slip through my fingers after all?'

He felt his lips go stiff like buckram, and instead of a reassuring smile only achieved an uncertain grimace.

'What will you have?' he began in a conciliating voice which got steady after the first trembling word or two. 'What will you have? Consider – a man of studious, retired habits – and suddenly like this. . . . I am not practised in talking delicately. But . . .'

He felt anger, a wicked anger, get hold of him again.

'What were we to do together till midnight? Sit here opposite each other and think of your – your – shambles?'

Haldin had a subdued, heartbroken attitude. He bowed his head; his hands hung between his knees. His voice was low and pained but calm.

'I see now how it is, Razumov – brother. You are a magnanimous soul, but my action is abhorrent to you – alas . . .'

Razumov stared. From fright he had set his teeth so hard that his whole face ached. It was impossible for him to make a sound.

'And even my person, too, is loathsome to you perhaps,' Haldin added mournfully, after a short pause, looking up for a moment, then fixing his gaze on the floor. 'For indeed, unless one . . .'

He broke off, evidently waiting for a word. Razumov remained silent. Haldin nodded is head dejectedly twice.

'Of course. Of course,' he murmured. . . . 'Ah! – weary work!'

He remained perfectly still for a moment, then made Razumov's leaden heart strike a ponderous blow by springing up briskly.

'So be it,' he cried sadly in a low, distinct tone. 'Farewell then.'

Razumov started forward, but the sight of Haldin's raised hand checked him before he could get away from the table. He leaned on it heavily, listening to the faint sounds of some town clock tolling the hour. Haldin, already at the door, tall and straight as an arrow, with his pale face and a hand raised attentively, might have posed for the statue of a daring youth listening to an inner voice. Razumov mechanically glanced down at his watch. When he looked towards the door again Haldin had vanished. There was a faint rustling in the outer room, the feeble click of a bolt drawn back lightly. He was gone – almost as noiseless as a vision.

Razumov ran forward unsteadily, with parted, voiceless lips. The outer door stood open. Staggering out on the landing, he leaned far over the banister. Gazing down into the deep black shaft with a tiny glimmering flame at the bottom, he traced by ear the rapid spiral descent of somebody running down the stairs on tiptoe. It was a light, swift, pattering sound, which sank away from him into the depths: a fleeting shadow passed over the glimmer – a wink of the tiny flame. Then stillness.

Razumov hung over, breathing the cold raw air tainted by the evil smells of the unclean staircase. All quiet.

He went back into his room slowly, shutting the doors after him. The peaceful steady light of his reading-lamp shone on the watch. Razumov stood looking down at the little white dial. It wanted yet three minutes to midnight. He took the watch into his hand fumblingly.

'Slow,' he muttered, and a strange fit of nervelessness came over him. His knees shook, the watch and chain slipped through his fingers in an instant and fell on the floor. He was so startled that he nearly fell himself. When at last he regained enough confidence in his limbs to stoop for it he held it to his ear at once. After a while he growled –

'Stopped,' and paused for quite a long time before he muttered sourly –

'It's done . . . And now to work.'

He sat down, reached haphazard for a book, opened it in the middle, and began to read; but after going conscientiously over two lines he lost his hold on the print completely and did not try to regain it. He thought –

'There was to a certainty a police agent of some sort watching the house across the street.'

He imagined him lurking in a dark gateway, goggle-eyed, muffled up in a cloak to the nose and with a General's plumed, cocked hat on his head. This absurdity made him start in the chair convulsively. He literally had to shake his head violently to get rid of it. The man would be disguised perhaps as a peasant . . . a beggar. . . . Perhaps he would be just buttoned up in a dark overcoat and carrying a loaded stick – a shifty-eyed rascal, smelling of raw onions and spirits.

This evocation brought on positive nausea. 'Why do I want to bother about this?' thought Razumov with disgust. 'Am I a gendarme? Moreover, it is done.'

He got up in great agitation. It was not done. Not yet. Not till half past twelve. And the watch had stopped. This reduced him to despair. Impossible to know the time! The landlady and all the people across the landing were asleep. How could he go and . . . God knows what they would imagine, or how much they would guess. He dared not go into the streets to find out. 'I am a suspect now. There's no use shirking that fact,' he said to himself bitterly. If Haldin from some cause or another gave them the slip and failed to turn up in the Karabelnaya the police would be invading his lodging. And if he were not in he could never clear himself. Razumov looked wildly about as if for some means of seizing upon time which seemed to have escaped him altogether. He had never, as far as he could remember, heard the striking of that town clock in his rooms before this night. And he was not even sure now whether he had heard it really on this night.

He went to the window and stood there with slightly bent head on the watch for the faint sound. 'I will stay here till I hear something,' he said to himself. He stood still, his ear turned to the panes. An atrocious aching numbness with shooting pains in his back and legs tortured him. He did not budge. His mind hovered on the borders of delirium. He heard himself suddenly saying, 'I confess,' as a person might do on the rack. 'I am on the rack,' he thought. He felt ready to swoon. The faint deep boom of the distant clock seemed to explode in his head – he heard it so clearly. . . . One!

If Haldin had not turned up the police would have been already here ransacking the house. No sound reached him. This time it was done.

He dragged himself painfully to the table and dropped into the chair. He flung the book away and took a square sheet of paper. It was like the pile of sheets covered with his neat minute handwriting, only blank. He took a pen brusquely and dipped it with a vague notion of going on with the writing of his essay – but his pen remained poised over the sheet. It hung there for some time before it came down and formed long scrawly letters.

Still-faced and his lips set hard. Razumov began to write. When he wrote a large hand his neat writing lost its character altogether – became unsteady, almost childish. He wrote five lines one under the other.

History not Theory.
Patriotism not Internationalism.
Evolution not Revolution.
Direction not Destruction.
Unity not Disruption.

He gazed at them dully. Then his eyes strayed to the bed and remained fixed there for a good many minutes, while his right hand groped all over the table for the penknife.

He rose at last, and walking up with measured steps stabbed the paper with the penknife to the lath and plaster wall at the head of the bed. This done he stepped back a pace and flourished his hand with a glance round the room.

After that he never looked again at the bed. He took his big cloak down from its peg and, wrapping himself up closely, went to lie down on the hard horse-hair sofa at the other side of his room. A leaden sleep closed his eyelids at once. Several times that night he woke up shivering from a dream of walking through drifts of snow in a Russia where he was as completely alone as any betrayed autocrat could be; an immense, wintry Russia which, somehow, his view could embrace in all its enormous expanse as if it were a map. But after each shuddering start his heavy eyelids fell over his glazed eyes and he slept again.

Chapter III

Approaching this part of Mr Razumov's story, my mind, the decent mind of an old teacher of languages, feels more and more the difficulty of the task.

The task is not in truth the writing in the narrative form a *précis* of a strange human document, but the rendering – I perceive it now clearly – of the moral conditions ruling over a large portion of this earth's surface; conditions not easily to be understood, much less discovered in the limits of a story, till some key-word is found; a word that could stand at the back of all the words covering the pages, a word which, if not truth itself, may perchance hold truth enough to help the moral discovery which should be the object of every tale.

I turn over for the hundredth time the leaves of Mr Razumov's record, I lay it aside, I take up the pen – and the pen being ready for its office of setting down black on white I hesitate. For the word that persists in creeping under its point is no other word than 'cynicism'.

For that is the mark of Russian autocracy and of Russian revolt. In its pride of numbers, in its strange pretensions of sanctity, and in the secret readiness to abase itself in suffering, the spirit of Russia is the spirit of cynicism. It informs the declarations of statesmen, the theories of her revolutionists, and the mystic vaticinations of prophets to the point of making freedom look like a form of debauch, and the Christian virtues themselves appear actually indecent . . . But I must apologize for the digression. It proceeds from the consideration of the course taken by the story of Mr Razumov after his conservative convictions, diluted in a vague liberalism natural to the ardour of his age, had become crystallized by the shock of his contact with Haldin.

Razumov woke up for the tenth time perhaps with a heavy shiver. Seeing the light of day in his window, he resisted the inclination to lay himself down again. He did not remember anything, but he did not think it strange to find himself on the sofa in his cloak and chilled to the bone. The light coming through the window seemed strangely cheerless, containing no promise as the light of each new day should for a young man. It was the awakening of a man mortally ill, or of a man ninety years old. He looked at the lamp which had burnt itself out. It stood there, the extinguished beacon of his labours, a cold object of brass and porcelain, amongst the scattered pages of his notes and small piles of books – a mere litter of blackened paper – dead matter – without significance or interest.

He got on his feet, and divesting himself of his cloak hung it on the peg, going through all the motions mechanically. An incredible dullness, a ditch-water stagnation was sensible to his perceptions as though life had withdrawn itself from all things and even from his own thoughts. There was not a sound in the house.

Turning away from the peg, he thought in that same lifeless manner that it must be very early yet; but when he looked at the watch on his table he saw both hands arrested at twelve o'clock.

'Ah! yes,' he mumbled to himself, and as if beginning to get roused a little he took a survey of his room. The paper stabbed to the wall arrested his attention. He eyed it from the distance without approval or perplexity; but when he heard the servant-girl beginning to bustle about in the outer room with the *samovar* for his morning tea, he walked up to it and took it down with an air of profound indifference.

While doing this he glanced down at the bed on which he had not slept that night. The hollow in the pillow made by the weight of Haldin's head was very noticeable.

Even his anger at this sign of the man's passage was dull. He did not try to nurse it into life. He did nothing all that day; he neglected even to brush his hair. The idea of going out never occurred to him – and if he did not start a connected train of thought it was not because he was unable to think. It was because he was not interested enough.

He yawned frequently. He drank large quantities of tea, he walked about aimlessly, and when he sat down he did not budge for a long time. He spent some time drumming on the window with his finger-tips quietly. In his listless wanderings round about the table he caught sight of his own face in the looking-glass and that arrested him. The eyes which returned his stare were the most unhappy eyes he had ever seen. And this was the first thing which disturbed the mental stagnation of that day.

He was not affected personally. He merely thought that life without happiness is impossible. What was happiness? He yawned and went on shuffling about and about between the walls of his room. Looking forward was happiness – that's all – nothing more. To look forward to the gratification of some desire, to the gratification of some passion, love, ambition, hate – hate too, indubitably. Love and hate. And to escape the dangers of existence, to live without fear, was also happiness. There was nothing else. Absence of fear – looking forward. 'Oh! the miserable lot of humanity!' he exclaimed mentally; and added at once in his thought, 'I ought to be happy enough as far as that goes.' But he was not excited by that assurance. On the contrary, he yawned again as he had been yawning all day. He was mildly surprised to discover himself being overtaken by night. The room grew dark swiftly though time had seemed to stand still. How was it that he had not noticed the passing of that day? Of course, it was the watch being stopped. . . .

He did not light his lamp, but went over to the bed and threw himself on it without any hesitation. Lying on his back, he put his hands under his head and stared upward. After a moment he thought, 'I am lying here like that man. I wonder if he slept while I was struggling with the blizzard in the streets. No, he did not sleep. But why should I not sleep?' and he felt the silence of the night press upon all his limbs like a weight.

In the calm of the hard frost outside, the clear-cut strokes of the town clock counting off midnight penetrated the quietness of his suspended animation.

Again he began to think. It was twenty-four hours since that man left his room. Razumov had a distinct feeling that Haldin in the fortress was sleeping that night. It was a certitude which made him angry because he did not want to think of Haldin, but he justified it to himself by physiological and psychological reasons. The fellow had hardly slept for weeks on his own confession, and now every incertitude was at an end for him. No doubt he was looking forward to the consummation of his martyrdom. A man who resigns himself to kill need not go very far for resignation to die. Haldin slept perhaps more soundly than General T—, whose task – weary work too – was not done, and over whose head hung the sword of revolutionary vengeance.

Razumov, remembering the thick-set man with his heavy jowl resting on the collar of his uniform, the champion of autocracy, who had let no sign of surprise, incredulity, or joy escape him, but whose goggle eyes could express a mortal hatred of all rebellion – Razumov moved uneasily on the bed.

'He suspected me,' he thought. 'I suppose he must suspect everybody. He would be capable of suspecting his own wife, if Haldin had gone to her boudoir with his confession.'

Razumov sat up in anguish. Was he to remain a political suspect all his days? Was he to go through life as a man not wholly to be trusted – with a bad secret police note tacked on to his record? What sort of future could he look forward to?

'I am now a suspect,' he thought again; but the habit of reflection and that desire of safety, of an ordered life, which was so strong in him came to his assistance as the night wore on. His quiet, steady, and laborious existence would vouch at length for his loyalty. There were many permitted ways to serve one's country. There was an activity that made for progress without being revolutionary. The field of influence was great and infinitely varied – once one had conquered a name.

His thought like a circling bird reverted after four-and-twenty hours to the silver medal, and as it were poised itself there.

When the day broke he had not slept, not for a moment, but he got up not very tired and quite sufficiently self-possessed for all practical purposes.

He went out and attended three lectures in the morning. But the work in the library was a mere dumb show of research. He sat with many volumes open before him trying to make notes and extracts. His new tranquillity was like a flimsy garment, and seemed to float at the mercy of a casual word. Betrayal! Why! the fellow had done all that was necessary to betray himself. Precious little had been needed to deceive him.

'I have said no word to him that was not strictly true. Not one word,' Razumov argued with himself.

Once engaged on this line of thought there could be no question of doing useful work. The same ideas went on passing through his mind, and he pronounced mentally the same words over and over again. He shut up all the books and rammed all his papers into his pocket with convulsive movements, raging inwardly against Haldin.

As he was leaving the library a long bony student in a threadbare overcoat joined him, stepping moodily by his side. Razumov answered his mumbled greeting without looking at him at all.

'What does he want with me?' he thought with a strange dread of the unexpected which he tried to shake off lest it should fasten itself upon his life for good and all. And the other, muttering cautiously with downcast eyes, supposed that his comrade had seen the news of de P—'s executioner – that was the expression he used – having been arrested the night before last. . . .

'I've been ill – shut up in my room,' Razumov mumbled through his teeth.

The tall student, raising his shoulders, shoved his hands deep into his pockets. He had a hairless, square, tallowy chin which trembled slightly as he spoke, and his nose nipped bright red by the sharp air looked like a false nose of painted cardboard between the sallow cheeks. His whole appearance was stamped with the mark of cold and hunger. He stalked deliberately at Razumov's elbow with his eyes on the ground.

'It's an official statement,' he continued in the same cautious mutter. 'It may be a lie. But there was somebody arrested between midnight and one in the morning on Tuesday. This is certain.'

And talking rapidly under the cover of his downcast air, he told Razumov that this was known through an inferior Government clerk employed at the Central Secretariat. That man belonged to one of the revolutionary circles. 'The same, in fact, I am affiliated to,' remarked the student.

They were crossing a wide quadrangle. An infinite distress possessed Razumov, annihilated his energy, and before his eyes everything appeared confused and as if evanescent. He dared not leave the fellow there. 'He may be affiliated to the police,' was the thought that passed through his mind. 'Who could tell?' But eyeing the miserable frost-nipped, famine-struck figure of his companion he perceived the absurdity of his suspicion.

'But I – you know – I don't belong to any circle. I . . .'

He dared not say any more. Neither dared he mend his pace. The other, raising and setting down his lamentably shod feet with exact deliberation, protested in a low tone that it was not necessary for everybody to belong to an organization. The most valuable personalities remained outside. Some of the best work was done outside the organization. Then very fast, with whispering, feverish lips –

'The man arrested in the street was Haldin.'

And accepting Razumov's dismayed silence as natural enough, he assured him that there was no mistake. That Government clerk was on night duty at the Secretariat. Hearing a great noise of footsteps in the hall and aware that political prisoners were brought over sometimes at night from the fortress, he opened the door of the room in which he was working, suddenly. Before the gendarme on duty could push him back and slam the door in his face, he had seen a prisoner being partly carried, partly dragged along the hall by a lot of policemen. He was being used very brutally. And the clerk had recognized Haldin perfectly. Less than half an hour afterwards General T— arrived at the Secretariat to examine the prisoner personally.

'Aren't you astonished?' concluded the gaunt student.

'No,' said Razumov roughly – and at once regretted his answer.

'Everybody supposed Haldin was in the provinces – with his people. Didn't you?'

The student turned his big hollow eyes upon Razumov, who said unguardedly—

'His people are abroad.'

He could have bitten his tongue out with vexation. The student pronounced in a tone of profound meaning –

'So! You alone were aware . . .' and stopped.

'They have sworn my ruin,' thought Razumov. 'Have you spoken of this to anyone else?' he asked with bitter curiosity.

The other shook his head.

'No, only to you. Our circle thought that as Haldin had been often heard expressing a warm appreciation of your character . . .'

Razumov could not restrain a gesture of angry despair which the other must have misunderstood in some way, because he ceased speaking and turned away his black, lack-lustre eyes.

They moved side by side in silence. Then the gaunt student began to whisper again, with averted gaze –

'As we have at present no one affiliated inside the fortress so as to make it possible to furnish him with a packet of poison, we have considered already some sort of retaliatory action – to follow very soon . . .'

Razumov trudging on interrupted –

'Were you acquainted with Haldin? Did he know where you live?'

'I had the happiness to hear him speak twice,' his companion answered in the feverish whisper contrasting with the gloomy apathy of his face and bearing. 'He did not know where I live. . . . I am lodging poorly . . . with an artisan family. . . . I have just a corner in a room. It is not very practicable to see me there but if you should need me for anything I am ready. . . .'

Razumov trembled with rage and fear. He was beside himself, but kept his voice low.

'You are not to come near me. You are not to speak to me. Never address a single word to me. I forbid you.'

'Very well,' said the other submissively, showing no surprise whatever at this abrupt prohibition. 'You don't wish for secret reasons . . . perfectly . . . I understand.'

He edged away at once, not looking up even; and Razumov saw his gaunt, shabby, famine-stricken figure cross the street obliquely with lowered head and that peculiar exact motion of the feet.

He watched him as one would watch a vision out of a nightmare, then he continued on his way, trying not to think. On his landing the landlady seemed to be waiting for him. She was a short, thick, shapeless woman with a large yellow face wrapped up everlastingly in a black woollen shawl. When she saw him come up the last flight of stairs she flung both her arms up excitedly, then clasped her hands before her face.

'Kirylo Sidorovitch – little father – what have you been doing? And such a quiet young man, too! The police are just gone this moment after searching your rooms.'

Razumov gazed down at her with silent, scrutinizing attention. Her puffy yellow countenance was working with emotion. She screwed up her eyes at him entreatingly.

'Such a sensible young man! Anybody can see you are sensible. And now – like this – all at once. . . . What is the good of mixing yourself up with these Nihilists? Do give over, little father. They are unlucky people.'

Razumov moved his shoulders slightly.

'Or is it that some secret enemy has been calumniating you, Kirylo Sidorovitch? The world is full of black hearts and false denunciations nowadays. There is much fear about.'

'Have you heard that I have been denounced by someone?' asked Razumov, without taking his eyes off her quivering face.

But she had not heard anything. She had tried to find out by asking the police captain while his men were turning the room upside down. The police captain of the district had known her for the last eleven years and was a humane person. But he said to her on the landing looking very black and vexed –

'My good woman, do not ask questions. I don't know anything myself. The order comes from higher quarters.'

And indeed there had appeared, shortly after the arrival of the policemen of the district, a very superior gentleman in a fur coat and a shiny hat, who sat down in the room and looked through all the papers himself. He came alone and went away by himself, taking nothing with him. She had been trying to put things straight a little since they left.

Razumov turned away brusquely and entered his rooms.

All his books had been shaken and thrown on the floor. His landlady followed him, and stooping painfully began to pick them up into her apron. His papers and notes which were kept always neatly sorted (they all related to his studies) had been shuffled up and heaped together in a ragged pile in the middle of the table.

This disorder affected him profoundly, unreasonably. He sat down and stared. He had a distinct sensation of his very existence being undermined in some mysterious manner, of his moral supports falling away from him one by one. He even experienced a slight physical giddiness and made a movement as if to reach for something to steady himself with.

The old woman, rising to her feet with a low groan, shot all the books she had collected in her apron on to the sofa and left the room muttering and sighing.

It was only then that he noticed that the sheet of paper which for one night had remained stabbed to the wall above his empty bed was lying on top of the pile.

When he had taken it down the day before he had folded it in four, absent-mindedly, before dropping it on the table. And now he saw it lying uppermost, spread out, smoothed out even and covering all the confused pile of pages, the record of his intellectual life for the last three years. It had n t been flung there. It had been placed there – smoothed out, too! He guessed in that an intention of profound meaning – or perhaps some inexplicable mockery.

He sat staring at the piece of paper till his eyes began to smart. He did not attempt to put his papers in order, either that evening or the next day – which he spent at home in a state of peculiar irresolution. This irresolution bore upon the question whether he should continue to live – neither more nor less. But its nature was very far removed from the hesitation of a man contemplating suicide. The idea of laying violent hands upon his body did not occur to Razumov. The unrelated organism bearing that label, walking, breathing, wearing these clothes, was of no importance to anyone, unless maybe to the landlady. The true Razumov had his being in the willed, in the determined future – in that future menaced by the lawlessness of autocracy – for autocracy knows no law – and the lawlessness of revolution. The feeling that his moral personality was at the mercy of these lawless forces was so strong that he asked himself seriously if it were worth while to go on accomplishing the mental functions of that existence which seemed no longer his own.

'What is the good of exerting my intelligence, of pursuing the systematic development of my faculties and all my plans of work?' he asked himself. 'I want to guide my conduct by reasonable convictions, but what security have I against something – some destructive horror – walking in upon me as I sit here? . . .'

Razumov looked apprehensively towards the door of the outer room as if expecting some shape of evil to turn the handle and appear before him silently.

'A common thief,' he said to himself, 'finds more guarantees in the law he is breaking, and even a brute like Ziemianitch has his consolation.' Razumov envied the materialism of the thief and the passion of the incorrigible lover. The consequences of their actions were always clear and their lives remained their own.

But he slept as soundly that night as though he had been consoling himself in the manner of Ziemianitch. He dropped off suddenly, lay like a log, remembered no dream on waking. But it was as if his soul had gone out in the night to gather the flowers of wrathful wisdom. He got up in a mood of grim determination and as if with a new knowledge of his own nature. He looked mockingly on the heap of papers on his table; and left his room to attend the lectures, muttering to himself, 'We shall see.'

He was in no humour to talk to anybody or hear himself questioned as to his absence from lectures the day before. But it was difficult to repulse rudely a very good comrade with a smooth pink face and fair hair, bearing the nickname amongst his fellow students of 'Madcap Kostia'. He was the idolized only son of a very wealthy and illiterate Government contractor, and attended the lectures only during the periodical fits of contrition following upon tearful paternal remonstrances. Noisily blundering like a retriever puppy, his elated voice and great gestures filled the bare academy corridors with the joy of thoughtless animal life, provoking indulgent smiles at a great distance. His usual discourses treated of trotting horses, wine-parties in expensive restaurants, and the merits of persons of easy virtue, with a disarming artlessness of outlook. He pounced upon Razumov about midday, somewhat less uproariously than his habit was, and led him aside.

'Just a moment, Kirylo Sidorovitch. A few words here in this quiet corner.'

He felt Razumov's reluctance, and insinuated his hand under his arm caressingly.

'No – pray do. I don't want to talk to you about any of my silly scrapes. What are my scrapes? Absolutely nothing. Mere childishness. The other night I flung a fellow out of a certain place where I has having a fairly good time. A tyrannical little beast of a quill-driver from the Treasury department. . . . He was bullying the people of the house. I rebuked him. "You are not behaving humanely to God's creatures that are a jolly sight more estimable than yourself," I said. I can't bear to see any tyranny, Kirylo Sidorovitch. Upon my word I can't. He didn't take it in good part at all. "Who's that impudent puppy?" he begins to shout. I was in excellent form as it happened, and he went through the closed window very suddenly. He flew quite a long way into the yard. I raged like – like a – minotaur. The women clung to me and screamed, the fiddlers got under the table. . . . Such fun! My dad had to put his hand pretty deep into his pocket, I can tell you.'

He chuckled.

'My dad is a very useful man. Jolly good thing it is for me, too. I do get into unholy scrapes.'

His elation fell. That was just it. What was his life? Insignificant; no good to anyone; a mere festivity. It would end some day in his getting his skull split with a champagne bottle in a drunken brawl. At such times, too, when men were sacrificing themselves to ideas. But he could never get any ideas into his head. His head wasn't worth anything better than to be split by a champagne bottle.

Razumov, protesting that he had no time, made an attempt to get away. The other's tone changed to confidential earnestness.

'For God's sake, Kirylo, my dear soul, let me make some sort of sacrifice. It would not be a sacrifice really. I have my rich dad behind me. There's positively no getting to the bottom of his pocket.'

And rejecting indignantly Razumov's suggestion that this was drunken raving, he offered to lend him some money to escape abroad with. He could always get money from his dad. He had only to say that he had lost it at cards or something of that sort, and at the same time promise solemnly not to miss a single lecture for three months on end. That would fetch the old man; and he, Kostia, was quite equal to the sacrifice. Though he really did not see what was the good for him to attend the lectures. It was perfectly hopeless.

'Won't you let me be of some use?' he pleaded to the silent Razumov, who with his eyes on the ground and utterly unable to penetrate the real drift of the other's intention, felt a strange reluctance to clear up the point.

'What makes you think I want to go abroad?' he asked at last very quietly.

Kostia lowered his voice.

'You had the police in your rooms yesterday. There are three or four of us who have heard of that. Never mind how we know. It is sufficient that we do. So we have been consulting together.'

'Ah! You got to know that so soon,' muttered Razumov negligently.

'Yes. We did. And it struck us that a man like you . . .'

'What sort of a man do you take me to be?' Razumov interrupted him.

'A man of ideas – and a man of action too. But you are very deep, Kirylo. There's no getting to the bottom of your mind. Not for fellows like me. But we all agreed that you must be preserved for our country. Of that we have no doubt whatever – I mean all of us who have heard Haldin speak of you on certain occasions. A man doesn't get the police ransacking his rooms without there being some devilry hanging over his head. . . . And so if you think that it would be better for you to bolt at once . . .'

Razumov tore himself away and walked down the corridor, leaving the other motionless with his mouth open. But almost at once he returned and stood before the amazed Kostia, who shut his mouth slowly. Razumov looked him straight in the eyes, before saying with marked deliberation and separating his words –

'I thank – you – very – much.'

He went away again rapidly. Kostia, recovering from his surprise at these manoeuvres, ran up behind him pressingly.

'No! Wait! Listen! I really mean it. It would be like giving your compassion to a starving fellow. Do you hear, Kirylo? And any disguise you may think of, that too I could procure from a costumier, a Jew I know. Let a fool be made serviceable according to his folly. Perhaps also a false beard or something of that kind may be needed.'

Razumov turned at bay.

'There are no false beards needed in this business, Kostia – you good-hearted lunatic, you. What do you know of my ideas? My ideas may be poison to you.'

The other began to shake his head in energetic protest.

'What have you got to do with ideas? Some of them would make an end of your dad's money-bags. Leave off meddling with what you don't understand. Go back to your trotting horses and your girls, and then you'll be sure at least of doing no harm to anybody, and hardly any to yourself.'

The enthusiastic youth was overcome by this disdain.

'You're sending me back to my pig's trough, Kirylo. That settles it. I am an unlucky beast – and I shall die like a beast too. But mind – it's your contempt that has done for me.'

Razumov went off with long strides. That this simple and grossly festive soul should have fallen too under the revolutionary curse affected him as an ominous symptom of the time. He reproached himself for feeling troubled. Personally he ought to have felt reassured. There was an obvious advantage in this conspiracy of mistaken judgement taking him for what he was not. But was it not strange?

Again he experienced that sensation of his conduct being taken out of his hands by Haldin's revolutionary tyranny. His solitary and laborious existence had been destroyed – the only thing he could call his own on this earth. By what right? he asked himself furiously. In what name?

What infuriated him most was to feel that the 'thinkers' of the University were evidently connecting him with Haldin – as a sort of confidant in the background apparently. A mysterious connection! Ha! ha! . . . He had been made a personage without knowing anything about it. How that wretch Haldin must have talked about him! Yet it was likely that Haldin had said very little. The fellow's casual utterances were caught up and treasured and pondered over by all these imbeciles. And was not all secret revolutionary action based upon folly, self-deception, and lies?

'Impossible to think of anything else,' muttered Razumov to himself. 'I'll become an idiot if this goes on. The scoundrels and the fools are murdering my intelligence.'

He lost all hope of saving his future, which depended on the free use of his intelligence.

He reached the doorway of his house in a state of mental discouragement which enabled him to receive with apparent indifference an official-looking envelope from the dirty hand of the dvornik.

'A gendarme brought it,' said the man. 'He asked if you were at home. I told him, "No, he's not at home." So he left it. "Give it into his own hands," says he. Now you've got it – eh?'

He went back to his sweeping, and Razumov climbed his stairs, envelope in hand. Once in his room he did not hasten to open it. Of course this official missive was from the superior direction of the police. A suspect! A suspect!

He stared in dreary astonishment at the absurdity of his position. He thought with a sort of dry, unemotional melancholy; three years of good work gone, the course of forty more perhaps jeopardized – turned from hope to terror, because events started by human folly link themselves into a sequence which no sagacity can foresee and no courage can break through. Fatality enters your rooms while your landlady's back is turned; you come home and find it in possession bearing a man's name, clothed in flesh – wearing a brown cloth coat and long boots – lounging against the stove. It asks you, 'Is the outer door closed?' – and you don't know enough to take it by the throat and fling it downstairs. You don't know. You welcome the crazy fate. 'Sit down,' you say. And it is all over. You cannot shake it off any more. It will cling to you for ever. Neither halter nor bullet can give you back the freedom of your life and the sanity of your thought. . . . It was enough to make one dash one's head against a wall.

Razumov looked slowly all round the walls as if to select a spot to dash his head against. Then he opened the letter. It directed the student Kirylo Sidorovitch Razumov to present himself without delay at the General Secretariat.

Razumov had a vision of General T—'s goggle eyes waiting for him – the embodied power of autocracy, grotesque and terrible. He embodied the whole power of autocracy because he was its guardian. He was the incarnate suspicion, the incarnate anger, the incarnate ruthlessness of a political and social régime on its defence. He loathed rebellion by instinct. And Razumov reflected that the man was simply unable to understand a reasonable adherence to the doctrine of absolutism.

'What can he want with me precisely – I wonder?' he asked himself.

As if that mental question had evoked the familiar phantom, Haldin stood suddenly before him in the room with extraordinary completeness of detail. Though the short winter day had passed already into the sinister twilight of a land buried in snow, Razumov saw plainly the narrow leather strap round the Tcherkess coat. The illusion of that hateful presence was so perfect that he half expected it to ask, 'Is the outer door closed?' He looked at it with hatred and contempt. Souls do not take a shape of clothing. Moreover, Haldin could not be dead yet. Razumov stepped forward menacingly; the vision vanished – and turning short on his heel he walked out of his room with infinite disdain.

But after going down the first flight of stairs it occurred to him that perhaps the superior authorities of the police meant to confront him with Haldin in the flesh. This thought struck him like a bullet, and had he not clung with both hands to the banister he would have rolled down to the next landing most likely. His legs were of no use for a considerable time. . . . But why? For what conceivable reason? To what end?

There could be no rational answer to these questions; but Razumov remembered the promise made by the General to Prince K—. His action was to remain unknown.

He got down to the bottom of the stairs, lowering himself as it were from step to step, by the banister. Under the gate he regained much of his firmness of thought and limb. He went out into the street without staggering visibly. Every moment he felt steadier mentally. And yet he was saying to himself that General T— was perfectly capable of shutting him up in the fortress for an indefinite time. His temperament fitted his remorseless task, and his omnipotence made him inaccessible to reasonable argument.

But when Razumov arrived at the Secretariat he discovered that he would have nothing to do with General T—. It is evident from Mr Razumov's diary that this dreaded personality was to remain in the background. A civilian of superior rank received him in a private room after a period of waiting in outer offices where a lot of scribbling went on at many tables in a heated and stuffy atmosphere.

The clerk in uniform who conducted him said in the corridor –

'You are going before Gregory Matvieitch Mikulin.'

There was nothing formidable about the man bearing that name. His mild, expectant glance was turned on the door already when Razumov entered. At once, with the penholder he was holding in his hand, he pointed to a deep sofa between two windows. He followed Razumov with his eyes while that last crossed the room and sat down. The mild gaze rested on him, not curious, not inquisitive – certainly not suspicious – almost without expression. In its passionless persistence there was something resembling sympathy.

Razumov, who had prepared his will and his intelligence to encounter General T— himself, was profoundly troubled. All the moral bracing up against the possible excesses of power and passion went for nothing before this sallow man, who wore a full unclipped beard. It was fair, thin and very fine. The light fell in coppery gleams on the protuberances of a high, rugged forehead. And the aspect of the broad, soft physiognomy was so homely and rustic that the careful middle parting of the hair seemed a pretentious affectation.

The diary of Mr Razumov testifies to some irritation on his part. I may remark here that the diary proper consisting of the more or less daily entries seems to have been begun on that very evening after Mr Razumov had returned home.

Mr Razumov, then, was irritated. His strung-up individuality had gone to pieces within him very suddenly.

'I must be very prudent with him,' he warned himself in the silence during which they sat gazing at each other. It lasted some little time, and was characterized (for silences have their character) by a sort of sadness imparted to it perhaps by the mild and thoughtful manner of the beaded official. Razumov learned later that he was the chief of a department in the General Secretariat, with a rank in the civil service equivalent to that of a colonel in the army.

Razumov's mistrust became acute. The main point was, not to be drawn into saying too much. He had been called there for some reason. What reason? To be given to understand that he was a suspect – and also no doubt to be pumped. As to what precisely? There was nothing. Or perhaps Haldin had been telling lies. . . . Every alarming uncertainty beset Razumov. He could bear the silence no longer, and cursing himself for his weakness spoke first, though he had promised himself not to do so on any account.

'I haven't lost a moment's time,' he began in a hoarse, provoking tone; and then the faculty of speech seemed to leave him and enter the body of Councillor Mikulin, who chimed in approvingly –

'Very proper. Very proper. Though as a matter of fact . . .'

But the spell was broken, and Razumov interrupted him boldly, under a sudden conviction that this was the safest attitude to take. With a great flow of words he complained of being totally misunderstood. Even as he talked with a perception of his own audacity he thought that the word 'misunderstood' was better than the word 'mistrusted', and he repeated it again with insistence. Suddenly he ceased, being seized with fright before the attentive immobility of the official. 'What am I talking about?' he thought, eyeing him with a vague gaze. Mistrusted – not misunderstood – was the right symbol of these people. Misunderstood was the other kind of curse. Both had been brought on his head by that fellow Haldin. And his head ached terribly. He passed his hand over his brow – an involuntary gesture of suffering, which he was too careless to restrain.

At that moment Razumov beheld his own brain suffering on the rack – a long, pale figure drawn asunder horizontally with terrific force in the darkness of a vault, whose face he failed to see. It was as though he had dreamed for an infinitesimal fraction of time of some dark print of the Inquisition. . . .

It is not to be seriously supposed that Razumov had actually dozed off and had dreamed, in the presence of Councillor Mikulin, of an old print of the Inquisition. He was indeed extremely exhausted, and he records a remarkably dream-like experience of anguish at the circumstance that there was no one whatever near the pale and extended figure. The solitude of the racked victim was particularly horrible to behold. The mysterious impossibility to see the face, he also notes, inspired a sort of terror. All these characteristics of an ugly dream were present. Yet he is certain that he never lost the consciousness of himself on the sofa, leaning forward with his hands between his knees and turning his cap round and round in his fingers. But everything vanished at the voice of Councillor Mikulin. Razumov felt profoundly grateful for the even simplicity of its tone.

'Yes. I have listened with interest. I comprehend in a measure your . . . But, indeed, you are mistaken in what you . . .' Councillor Mikulin uttered a series of broken sentences. Instead of finishing them he glanced down his beard. It was a deliberate curtailment which somehow made the phrases more impressive. But he could talk fluently enough as became apparent when changing his tone to persuasiveness he went on: 'By listening to you as I did, I think I have proved that I do not regard our intercourse as strictly official. In fact, I don't want it to have had that character at all. . . . Oh yes! I admit that the request for your presence here had an official form. But I put it to you whether it was a form which would have been used to secure the attendance of a . . .'

'Suspect,' exclaimed Razumov, looking straight into the official's eyes. They were big with heavy eyelids, and met his boldness with a dim, steadfast gaze. 'A suspect.' The open repetition of that word which had been haunting all his waking hours gave Razumov a strange sort of satisfaction. Councillor Mikulin shook his head slightly. 'Surely you do know that I've had my rooms searched by the police?'

'I was about to say a "misunderstood person", when you interrupted me,' insinuated quietly Councillor Mikulin.

Razumov smiled without bitterness. The renewed sense of his intellectual superiority sustained him in the hour of danger. He said a little disdainfully –

'I know I am but a reed. But I beg you to allow me the superiority of the thinking reed over the unthinking forces that are about to crush him out of existence. Practical thinking in the last instance is but criticism. I may perhaps be allowed to express my wonder at this action of the police being delayed for two full days during which, of course, I could have annihilated everything compromising by burning it – let us say – and getting rid of the very ashes, for that matter.'

'You are angry,' remarked the official, with an unutterable simplicity of tone and manner. 'Is that reasonable?'

Razumov felt himself colouring with annoyance.

'I am reasonable. I am even – permit me to say – a thinker, though to be sure, this name nowadays seems to be the monopoly of hawkers of revolutionary wares, the slaves of some French or German thought – devil knows what foreign notions. But I am not an intellectual mongrel. I think like a Russian. I think faithfully – and I take the liberty to call myself a thinker. It is not a forbidden word, as far as I know.'

'No. Why should it be a forbidden word?' Councillor Mikulin turned in his seat with crossed legs and resting his elbow on the table propped his head on the knuckles of a half-closed hand. Razumov noticed a thick forefinger clasped by a massive gold band set with a blood-red stone – a signet ring that, looking as if it could weigh half a pound, was an appropriate ornament for that ponderous man with the accurate middle-parting of glossy hair above a rugged Socratic forehead.

'Could it be a wig?' Razumov detected himself wondering with an unexpected detachment. His self-confidence was much shaken. He resolved to chatter no more. Reserve! Reserve! All he had to do was to keep the Ziemianitch episode secret with absolute determination, when the questions came. Keep Ziemianitch strictly out of all the answers.

Councillor Mikulin looked at him dimly. Razumov's self-confidence abandoned him completely. It seemed impossible to keep Ziemianitch out. Every question would lead to that, because, of course, there was nothing else. He made an effort to brace himself up. It was a failure. But Councillor Mikulin was surprisingly detached too.

'Why should it be forbidden?' he repeated. 'I too consider myself a thinking man, I assure you. The principal condition is to think correctly. I admit it is difficult sometimes at first for a young man abandoned to himself – with his generous impulses undisciplined, so to speak – at the mercy of every wild wind that blows. Religious belief, of course, is a great . . .'

Councillor Mikulin glanced down his beard, and Razumov, whose tension was relaxed by that unexpected and discursive turn, murmured with gloomy discontent –

'That man, Haldin, believed in God.'

'Ah! You are aware,' breathed out Councillor Mikulin, making the point softly, as if with discretion, but making it nevertheless plainly enough, as if he too were put off his guard by Razumov's remark. The young man preserved an impassive, moody countenance, though he reproached himself bitterly for a pernicious fool, to have given thus an utterly false impression of intimacy. He kept his eyes on the floor. 'I must positively hold my tongue unless I am obliged to speak,' he admonished himself. And at once against his will the question, 'Hadn't I better tell him everything?' presented itself with such force that he had to bite his lower lip. Councillor Mikulin could not, however, have nourished any hope of confession. He went on –

'You tell me more than his judges were able to get out of him. He was judged by a commission of three. He would tell them absolutely nothing. I have the report of the interrogatories here, by me. After every question there stands "Refuses to answer – refuses to answer". It's like that page after page. You see, I have been entrusted with some further investigations around and about this affair. He has left me nothing to begin my investigations on. A hardened miscreant. And so, you say, he believed in . . .'

Again Councillor Mikulin glanced down his beard with a faint grimace; but he did not pause for long. Remarking with a shade of scorn that blasphemers also had that sort of belief, he concluded by supposing that Mr Razumov had conversed frequently with Haldin on the subject.

'No,' said Razumov loudly, without looking up. 'He talked and I listened. That is not a conversation.'

'Listening is a great art,' observed Mikulin parenthetically.

'And getting people to talk is another,' mumbled Razumov.

'Well, no – that is not very difficult,' Mikulin said innocently, 'except, of course, in special cases. For instance, this Haldin. Nothing could induce him to talk. He was brought four times before the delegated judges. Four secret interrogatories – and even during the last, when your personality was put forward . . .'

'My personality put forward?' repeated Razumov, raising his head brusquely. 'I don't understand.'

Councillor Mikulin turned squarely to the table, and taking up some sheets of grey foolscap dropped them one after another, retaining only the last in his hand. He held it before his eyes while speaking.

'It was – you see – judged necessary. In a case of that gravity no means of action upon the culprit should be neglected. You understand that yourself, I am certain.'

Razumov stared with enormous wide eyes at the side view of Councillor Mikulin, who now was not looking at him at all.

'So it was decided (I was consulted by General T—) that a certain question should be put to the accused. But in deference to the earnest wishes of Prince K— your name has been kept out of the documents and even from the very knowledge of the judges themselves. Prince K— recognized the propriety, the necessity of what we proposed to do, but he was concerned for your safety. Things do leak out – that we can't deny. One cannot always answer for the discretion of inferior officials. There was, of course, the secretary of the special tribunal – one or two gendarmes in the room. Moreover, as I have said, in deference to Prince K— even the judges themselves were to be left in ignorance. The question ready framed was sent to them by General T— (I wrote it out with my own hand) with instructions to put it to the prisoner the very last of all. Here it is.'

Councillor Mikulin threw back his head into proper focus and went on reading monotonously: 'Question – Has the man well known to you, in whose rooms you remained for several hours on Monday and on whose information you have been arrested – has he had any previous knowledge of your intention to commit a political murder? . . . Prisoner refuses to reply.

'Question repeated. Prisoner preserves the same stubborn silence.

'The venerable Chaplain of the Fortress being then admitted and exhorting the prisoner to repentance, entreating him also to atone for his crime by an unreserved and full confession which should help to liberate from the sin of rebellion against the Divine laws and the sacred Majesty of the Ruler, our Christ-loving land – the prisoner opens his lips for the first time during this morning's audience and in a loud, clear voice rejects the venerable Chaplain's ministrations.

'At eleven o'clock the Court pronounces in summary form the death sentence.

'The execution is fixed for four o'clock in the afternoon, subject to further instructions from superior authorities.'

Councillor Mikulin dropped the page of foolscap, glanced down his beard, and turning to Razumov, added in an easy, explanatory tone –

'We saw no object in delaying the execution. The order to carry out the sentence was sent by telegraph at noon. I wrote out the telegram myself. He was hanged at four o'clock this afternoon.'

The definite information of Haldin's death gave Razumov the feeling of general lassitude which follows a great exertion or a great excitement. He kept very still on the sofa, but a murmur escaped him –

'He had a belief in a future existence.'

Councillor Mikulin shrugged his shoulders slightly, and Razumov got up with an effort. There was nothing now to stay for in that room. Haldin had been hanged at four o'clock. There could be no doubt of that. He had, it seemed, entered upon his future existence, long boots, Astrakhan fur cap and all, down to the very leather strap round his waist. A flickering, vanishing sort of existence. It was not his soul, it was his mere phantom he had left behind on this earth – thought Razumov, smiling caustically to himself while he crossed the room, utterly forgetful of where he was and of Councillor Mikulin's existence. The official could have set a lot of bells ringing all over the building without leaving his chair. He let Razumov go quite up to the door before he spoke.

'Come, Kirylo Sidorovitch – what are you doing?'

Razumov turned his head and looked at him in silence. He was not in the least disconcerted. Councillor Mikulin's arms were stretched out on the table before him and his body leaned forward a little with an effort of his dim gaze.

'Was I actually going to clear out like this?' Razumov wondered at himself with an impassive countenance. And he was aware of this impassiveness concealing a lucid astonishment.

'Evidently I was going out if he had not spoken,' he thought. 'What would he have done then? I must end this affair one way or another. I must make him show his hand.'

For a moment longer he reflected behind the mask as it were, then let go the door-handle and came back to the middle of the room.

'I'll tell you what you think,' he said explosively, but not raising his voice. 'You think that you are dealing with a secret accomplice of that unhappy man. No, I do not know that he was unhappy. He did not tell me. He was a wretch from my point of view, because to keep alive a false idea is a greater crime than to kill a man. I suppose you will not deny that? I hated him! Visionaries work everlasting evil on earth. Their Utopias inspire in the mass of mediocre minds a disgust of reality and a contempt for the secular logic of human development.'

Razumov shrugged his shoulders and stared. 'What a tirade!' he thought. The silence and immobility of Councillor Mikulin impressed him. The bearded bureaucrat sat at his post, mysteriously self-possessed like an idol with dim, unreadable eyes. Razumov's voice changed involuntarily.

'If you were to ask me where is the necessity of my hate for such as Haldin, I would answer you – there is nothing sentimental in it. I did not hate him because he had committed the crime of murder. Abhorrence is not hate. I hated him simply because I am sane. It is in that character that he outraged me. His death . . .'

Razumov felt his voice growing thick in his throat. The dimness of Councillor Mikulin's eyes seemed to spread all over his face and made it indistinct to Razumov's sight. He tried to disregard these phenomena.

'Indeed,' he pursued, pronouncing each word carefully, 'what is his death to me? If he were lying here on the floor I could walk over his breast. . . . The fellow is a mere phantom. . . .'

Razumov's voice died out very much against his will. Mikulin behind the table did not allow himself the slightest movement. The silence lasted for some little time before Razumov could go on again.

'He went about talking to me. . . . Those intellectual fellows sit in each other's rooms and get drunk on foreign ideas in the same way young Guards' officers treat each other with foreign wines. Merest debauchery. . . . Upon my word,' – Razumov, enraged by a sudden recollection of Ziemianitch, lowered his voice forcibly, – 'upon my word, we Russians are a drunken lot. Intoxication of some sort we must have: to get ourselves wild with sorrow or maudlin with resignation; to lie inert like a log or set fire to the house. What is a sober man to do, I should like to know? To cut oneself entirely from one's kind is impossible. To live in a desert one must be a saint. But if a drunken man runs out of the grog-shop, falls on your neck, and kisses you on both cheeks because something about your appearance has taken his fancy, what then – kindly tell me? You may break, perhaps, a cudgel on his back and yet not succeed in beating him off. . . .'

Councillor Mikulin raised his hand and passed it down his face deliberately.

'That's . . . of course,' he said in an undertone.

The quiet gravity of that gesture made Razumov pause. It was so unexpected, too. What did it mean? It had an alarming aloofness. Razumov remembered his intention of making him show his hand.

'I have said all this to Prince K—,' he began with assumed indifference, but lost it on seeing Councillor Mikulin's slow nod of assent. 'You know it? You've heard . . . Then why should I be called here to be told of Haldin's execution? Did you want to confront me with his silence now that the man is dead? What is his silence to me? This is incomprehensible. You want in some way to shake my moral balance.'

'No. Not that,' murmured Councillor Mikulin, just audibly. 'The service you have rendered is appreciated . . .'

'Is it?' interrupted Razumov ironically.

'. . . and your position too.' Councillor Mikulin did not raise his voice. 'But only think! You fall into Prince K—'s study as if from the sky with your startling information. . . . You are studying yet, Mr Razumov, but we are serving already – don't forget that. . . . And naturally some curiosity was bound to . . .'

Councillor Mikulin looked down his beard. Razumov's lips trembled.

'An occurrence of that sort marks a man,' the homely murmur went on. 'I admit I was curious to see you. General T— thought it would be useful, too. . . . Don't think I am incapable of understanding your sentiments. When I was young like you I studied . . .'

'Yes – you wished to see me,' said Razumov in a tone of profound distaste. 'Naturally you have the right – I mean the power. It all amounts to the same thing. But it is perfectly useless, if you were to look at me and listen to me for a year. I begin to think there is something about me which people don't seem able to make out. It's unfortunate. I imagine, however, that Prince K— understands. He seemed to.'

Councillor Mikulin moved slightly and spoke.

'Prince K— is aware of everything that is being done, and I don't mind informing you that he approved my intention of becoming personally acquainted with you.'

Razumov concealed an immense disappointment under the accents of railing surprise.

'So he is curious too! . . . Well – after all, Prince K— knows me very little. It is really very unfortunate for me, but – it is not exactly my fault.'

Councillor Mikulin raised a hasty deprecatory hand and inclined his head slightly over his shoulder.

'Now, Mr Razumov – is it necessary to take it in that way? Everybody I am sure can . . .'

He glanced rapidly down his beard, and when he looked up again there was for a moment an interested expression in his misty gaze. Razumov discouraged it with a cold, repellent smile.

'No. That's of no importance to be sure – except that in respect of all this curiosity being aroused by a very simple matter. . . . What is to be done with it? It is unappeasable. I mean to say there is nothing to appease it with. I happen to have been born a Russian with patriotic instincts – whether inherited or not I am not in a position to say.'

Razumov spoke consciously with elaborate steadiness.

'Yes, patriotic instincts developed by a faculty of independent thinking – of detached thinking. In that respect I am more free than any social democratic revolution could make me. It is more than probable that I don't think exactly as you are thinking. Indeed, how could it be? You would think most likely at this moment that I am elaborately lying to cover up the track of my repentance.'

Razumov stopped. His heart had grown too big for his breast. Councillor Mikulin did not flinch.

'Why so?' he said simply. 'I assisted personally at the search of your rooms. I looked through all the papers myself. I have been greatly impressed by a sort of political confession of faith. A very remarkable document. Now may I ask for what purpose . . .'

'To deceive the police naturally,' said Razumov savagely. . . . 'What is all this mockery? Of course, you can send me straight from this room to Siberia. That would be intelligible. To what is intelligible I can submit. But I protest against this comedy of persecution. The whole affair is becoming too comical altogether for my taste. A comedy of errors, phantoms, and suspicions. It's positively indecent . . .'

Councillor Mikulin turned an attentive ear.

'Did you say phantoms?' he murmured.

'I could walk over dozens of them.' Razumov, with an impatient wave of his hand, went on headlong. 'But, really, I must claim the right to be done once for all with that man. And in order to accomplish this I shall take the liberty . . .'

Razumov on his side of the table bowed slightly to the seated bureaucrat.

'. . . To retire – simply to retire,' he finished with great resolution.

He walked to the door, thinking, 'Now he must show his hand. He must ring and have me arrested before I am out of the building, or he must let me go. And either way . . .'

An unhurried voice said –

'Kirylo Sidorovitch.'

Razumov at the door turned his head.

'To retire,' he repeated.

'Where to?' asked Councillor Mikulin softly.

Part Second

Chapter I

In the conduct of an invented story there are, no doubt, certain proprieties to be observed for the sake of clearness and effect. A man of imagination, however inexperienced in the art of narrative, has his instinct to guide him in the choice of his words, and in the development of the action. A grain of talent excuses many mistakes. But this is not a work of imagination; I have no talent; my excuse for this undertaking lies not in its art, but in its artlessness. Aware of my limitations and strong in the sincerity of my purpose, I would not try (were I able) to invent anything. I push my scruples so far that I would not invent a transition.

Dropping then Mr Razumov's record at the point where Councillor Mikulin's question 'Where to?' comes in with the force of an insoluble problem, I shall simply say that I made the acquaintance of these ladies about six months before that time. By 'these ladies' I mean, of course, the mother and sister of the unfortunate Haldin.

By what arguments he had induced his mother to sell their little property and go abroad for an indefinite time, I cannot tell precisely. I have an idea that Mrs Haldin, at her son's wish, would have set fire to her house and emigrated to the moon without any sign of surprise or apprehension; and that Miss Haldin – Nathalie, caressingly Natalka – would have given her assent to the scheme.

Their proud devotion to that young man became clear to me in a very short time. Following his directions they went straight to Switzerland – to Zurich – where they remained the best part of a year. From Zurich, which they did not like, they came to Geneva. A friend of mine in Lausanne, a lecturer in history at the University (he had married a Russian lady, a distant connexion of Mrs Haldin's), wrote to me suggesting I should call on these ladies. It was a very kindly meant business suggestion. Miss Haldin wished to go through a course of reading the best English authors with a competent teacher.

Mrs Haldin received me very kindly. Her bad French, of which she was smilingly conscious, did away with the formality of the first interview. She was a tall woman in a black silk dress. A wide brow, regular features, and delicately cut lips, testified to her past beauty. She sat upright in an easy chair and in a rather weak, gentle voice told me that her Natalka simply thirsted after knowledge. Her thin hands were lying on her lap, her facial immobility had in it something monachal. 'In Russia,' she went on, 'all knowledge was tainted with falsehood. Not chemistry and all that, but education generally,' she explained. The Government corrupted the teaching for its own purposes. Both her children felt that. Her Natalka had obtained a diploma of a Superior School for Women and her son was a student at the St Petersburg University. He had a brilliant intellect, a most noble unselfish nature, and he was the oracle of his comrades. Early next year, she hoped he would join them and they would then go to Italy together. In any other country but their own she would have been certain of a great future for a man with the extraordinary abilities and the lofty character of her son – but in Russia . . .

The young lady sitting by the window turned her head and said—

'Come, mother. Even with us things change with years.'

Her voice was deep, almost harsh, and yet caressing in its harshness. She had a dark complexion, with red lips and a full figure. She gave the impression of strong vitality. The old lady sighed.

'You are both young – you two. It is easy for you to hope. But I, too, am not hopeless. Indeed, how could I be with a son like this.'

I addressed Miss Haldin, asking her what authors she wished to read. She directed upon me her grey eyes shaded by black eyelashes, and I became aware, notwithstanding my years, how attractive physically her personality could be to a man capable of appreciating in a woman something else than the mere grace of femininity. Her glance was as direct and trustful as that of a young man yet unspoiled by the world's wide lessons. And it was intrepid, but in this intrepedity there was nothing aggressive. A naïve yet thoughtful assurance is a better definition. She had reflected already (in Russia the young begin to think early), but she had never known deception as yet because obviously she had never yet fallen under the sway of passion. She was – to look at her was enough – very capable of being roused by an idea or simply by a person. At least, so I judged with I believed an unbiassed mind; for clearly my person could not be the person – and as to my idea! . . .

We became excellent friends in the course of our reading. It was very pleasant. Without fear of provoking a smile, I shall confess that I became very much attached to that young girl. At the end of four months I told her that now she could very well go on reading English by herself. It was time for the teacher to depart. My pupil looked unpleasantly surprised.

Mrs Haldin, with her immobility of feature and kindly expression of the eyes, uttered from her armchair in her uncertain French, '*Mais l'ami reviendra*.' And so it was settled. I returned – not four times a week as before, but pretty frequently. In the autumn we made some short excursions together in company with other Russians. My friendship with these ladies gave me a standing in the Russian colony which otherwise I could not have had.

The day I saw in the papers the news of Mr de P—'s assassination – it was a Sunday – I met the two ladies in the street and walked with them for some distance. Mrs Haldin wore a heavy grey cloak, I remember, over her black silk dress, and her fine eyes met mine with a very quiet expression.

'We have been to the late service,' she said. 'Natalka came with me. Her girl-friends, the students here, of course, don't. . . . With us in Russia the church is so identified with oppression, that it seems almost necessary when one wishes to be free in this life, to give up all hope of a future existence. But I cannot give up praying for my son.'

She added with a sort of stony grimness, colouring slightly, and in French, '*Ce n'est peut-être qu'une habitude*.' ('It may be only habit.')

Miss Haldin was carrying the prayer-book. She did not glance at her mother.

'You and Victor are both profound believers,' she said.

I communicated to them the news from their country which I had just read in a café. For a whole minute we walked together fairly briskly in silence. Then Mrs Haldin murmured—

'There will be more trouble, more persecutions for this. They may be even closing the University. There is neither peace nor rest in Russia for one but in the grave.'

'Yes. The way is hard,' came from the daughter, looking straight before her at the Chain of Jura covered with snow, like a white wall closing the end of the street. 'But concord is not so very far off.'

'That is what my children think,' observed Mrs Haldin to me.

I did not conceal my feeling that these were strange times to talk of concord. Nathalie Haldin surprised me by saying, as if she had thought very much on the subject, that the occidentals did not understand the situation. She was very calm and youthfully superior.

'You think it is a class conflict, or a conflict of interests, as social contests are with you in Europe. But it is not that at all. It is something quite different.'

'It is quite possible that I don't understand,' I admitted.

That propensity of lifting every problem from the plane of the understandable by means of some sort of mystic expression, is very Russian. I knew her well enough to have discovered her scorn for all the practical forms of political liberty known to the western world. I suppose one must be a Russian to understand Russian simplicity, a terrible corroding simplicity in which mystic phrases clothe a naïve and hopelsss cynicism. I think sometimes that the psychological secret of the profound difference of that people consists in this, that they detest life, the irremediable life of the earth as it is, whereas we westerners cherish it with perhaps an equal exaggeration of its sentimental value. But this is a digression indeed. . . .

I helped these ladies into the tramcar and they asked me to call in the afternoon. At least Mrs Haldin asked me as she climbed up, and her Natalka smiled down at the dense westerner indulgently from the rear platform of the moving car. The light of the clear wintry forenoon was softened in her grey eyes.

Mr Razumov's record, like the open book of fare, revives for me the memory of that day as something startlingly pitiless in its freedom from all forebodings. Victor Haldin was still with the living, but with the living whose only contact with life is the expectation of death. He must have been already referring to the last of his earthly affections, the hours of that obstinate silence, which for him was to be prolonged into eternity. That afternoon the ladies entertained a good many of their compatriots – more than was usual for them to receive at one time; and the drawing-room on the ground floor of a large house on the Boulevard des Philosophes was very much crowded.

I outstayed everybody; and when I rose Miss Haldin stood up too. I took her hand and was moved to revert to that morning's conversation in the street.

'Admitting that we occidentals do not understand the character of your people . . .' I began.

It was as if she had been prepared for me by some mysterious fore-knowledge. She checked me gently—

'Their impulses – their . . .' she sought the proper expression and found it, but in French . . . 'their *mouvements d'âme*.'

Her voice was not much above a whisper.

'Very well,' I said. 'But still we are looking at a conflict. You say it is not a conflict of classes and not a conflict of interests. Suppose I admitted that. Are antagonistic ideas then to be reconciled more easily – can they be cemented with blood and violence into that concord which you proclaim to be so near?'

She looked at me searchingly with her clear grey eyes, without answering my reasonable question – my obvious, my unanswerable question.

'It is inconceivable,' I added, with something like annoyance.

'Everything is inconceivable,' she said. 'The whole world is inconceivable to the strict logic of ideas. And yet the world exists to our senses, and we exist in it. There must be a necessity superior to our conceptions. It is a very miserable and a very false thing to belong to the majority. We Russians shall find some better form of national freedom than an artificial conflict of parties – which is wrong because it is a conflict and contemptible because it is artificial. It is left for us Russians to discover a better way.'

Mrs Haldin had been looking out of the window. She turned upon me the almost lifeless beauty of her face, and the living benign glance of her big dark eyes.

'That's what my children think,' she declared.

'I suppose,' I addressed Miss Haldin, 'that you will be shocked if I tell you that I haven't understood – I won't say a single word; I've understood all the words. . . . But what can be this era of disembodied concord you are looking forward to. Life is a thing of form. It has its plastic shape and a definite intellectual aspect. The most idealistic conceptions of love and forbearance must be clothed in flesh as it were before they can be made understandable.'

I took my leave of Mrs Haldin, whose beautiful lips never stirred. She smiled with her eyes only. Nathalie Haldin went with me as far as the door, very amiable.

'Mother imagines that I am the slavish echo of my brother Victor. It is not so. He understands me better than I can understand him. When he joins us and you come to know him you will see what an exceptional soul it is.' She paused. 'He is not a strong man in the conventional sense, you know,' she added. 'But his charrcter is without a flaw.'

'I believe that it will not be difficult for me to make friends with your brother Victor.'

'Don't expect to understand him quite,' she said, a little maliciously. 'He is not at all – at all – western at bottom.'

And on this unnecessary warning I left the room with another bow in the doorway to Mrs Haldin in her armchair by the window. The shadow of autocracy all unperceived by me had already fallen upon the Boulevard des Philosophes, in the free, independent and democratic city of Geneva, where there is a quarter called 'La Petite Russie'. Whenever two Russians come together, the shadow of autocracy is with them, tingeing their thoughts, their views, their most intimate feelings, their private life, their public utterances – haunting the secret of their silences.

What struck me next in the course of a week or so was the silence of these ladies. I used to meet them walking in the public garden near the University.

They greeted me with their usual friendliness, but I could not help noticing their taciturnity. By that time it was generally known that the assassin of Mr de P— had been caught, judged, and executed. So much had been declared officially to the news agencies. But for the world at large he remained anonymous. The official secrecy had withheld his name from the public. I really cannot imagine for what reason.

One day I saw Miss Haldin walking alone in the main valley of the Bastions under the naked trees.

'Mother is not very well,' she explained.

As Mrs Haldin had, it seemed, never had a day's illness in her life, this indisposition was disquieting. It was nothing definite, too.

'I think she is fretting because we have not heard from my brother for rather a long time.'

'No news – good news,' I said cheerfully, and we began to walk slowly side by side.

'Not in Russia,' she breathed out so low that I only just caught the words. I looked at her with more attention.

'You too are anxious?'

She admitted after a moment of hesitation that she was.

'It is really such a long time since we heard . . .'

And before I could offer the usual banal suggestions she confided in me.

'Oh! But it is much worse than that. I wrote to a family we know in Petersburg. They had not seen him for more than a month. They thought he was already with us. They were even offended a little that he should have left Petersburg without calling on them. The husband of the lady went at once to his lodgings. Victor had left there and they did not know his address.'

I remember her catching her breath rather pitifully. Her brother had not been seen at lectures for a very long time either. He only turned up now and then at the University gate to ask the porter for his letters. And the gentleman friend was told that the student Haldin did not come to claim the last two letters for him. But the police came to inquire if the student Haldin ever received any correspondence at the University and took them away.

'My two last letters,' she said.

We faced each other. A few snow-flakes fluttered under the naked boughs. The sky was dark.

'What do you think could have happened?' I asked.

Her shoulders moved slightly.

'One can never tell – in Russia.'

I saw then the shadow of autocracy lying upon Russian lives in their submission or their revolt. I saw it touch her handsome open face nestled in a fur collar and darken her clear eyes that shone upon me brilliantly grey in the murky light of a beclouded, inclement afternoon.

'Let us move on,' she said. 'It is cold standing today.'

She shuddered a little and stamped her little feet. We moved briskly to the end of the alley and back to the great gates of the garden.

'Have you told your mother?' I ventured to ask.

'No. Not yet. I came out to walk off the impression of this letter.'

I heard a rustle of paper somewhere. It came from her muff. She had the letter with her in there.

'What is it that you are afraid of?' I asked.

To us Europeans of the West, all ideas of political plots and conspiracies seem childish, crude inventions for the theatre or a novel. I did not like to be more definite in my inquiry.

'For us – for my mother specially, what I am afraid of is incertitude. People do disappear. Yes, they do disappear. I leave you to imagine what it is – the cruelty of the dumb weeks – months – years! This friend of ours has abandoned his inquiries when he heard of the police getting hold of the letters. I suppose he was afraid of compromising himself. He has a wife and children – and why should he, after all. . . . Moreover, he is without influential connections and not rich. What could he do? . . . Yes, I am afraid of silence – for my poor mother. She won't be able to bear it. For my brother I am afraid of . . .' she became almost indistinct, 'of anything.'

We were now near the gate opposite the theatre. She raised her voice.

'But lost people do turn up even in Russia. Do you know what my last hope is? Perhaps the next thing we know, we shall see him walking into our rooms.'

I raised my hat and she passed out of the gardens, graceful and strong, after a slight movement of the head to me, her hands in the muff, crumpling the cruel Petersburg letter.

On returning home I opened the newspaper I received from London, and glancing down the correspondence from Russia – not the telegrams but the correspondence – the first thing that caught my eye was the name of Haldin. Mr de P—'s death was no longer an actuality, but the enterprising correspondent was proud of having ferreted out some unofficial information about that fact of modern history. He had got hold of Haldin's name, and had picked up the story of the midnight arrest in the street. But the sensation from a journalistic point of view was already well in the past. He did not allot to it more than twenty lines out of a full column. It was quite enough to give me a sleepless night. I perceived that it would have been a sort of treason to let Miss Haldin come without preparation upon that journalistic discovery which would infallibly be reproduced on the morrow by French and Swiss newspapers. I had a very bad time of it till the morning, wakeful with nervous worry and nighmarish with the feeling of being mixed up with something theatrical and morbidly affected. The incongruity of such a complication in those two women's lives was sensible to me all night in the form of absolute anguish. It seemed due to their refined simplicity that it should remain concealed from them for ever. Arriving at an unconscionably early hour at the door of their apartment, I felt as if I were about to commit an act of vandalism.

The middle-aged servant woman led me into the drawing-room where there was a duster on a chair and a broom leaning against the centre table. The motes danced in the sunshine; I regretted I had not written a letter instead of coming myself, and was thankful for the brightness of the day. Miss Haldin in a plain black dress came lightly out of her mother's room with a fixed uncertain smile on her lips.

I pulled the paper out of my pocket. I did not imagine that a number of the

Standard could have the effect of Medusa's head. Her face went stony in a moment – her eyes – her limbs. The most terrible thing was that being stony she remained alive. One was conscious of her palpitating heart. I hope she forgave me the delay of my clumsy circumlocution. It was not very prolonged; she could not have kept so still from head to foot for more than a second or two; and then I heard her draw a breath. As if the shock had paralysed her moral resistance, and affected the firmness of her muscles, the contours of her face seemed to have given way. She was frightfully altered. She looked aged – ruined. But only for a moment. She said with decision—

'I am going to tell my mother at once.'

'Would that be safe in her state?' I objected.

'What can be worse than the state she has been in for the last month? We understand this in another way. The crime is not at his door. Don't imagine I am defending him before you.'

She went to the bedroom door, then came back to ask me in a low murmur not to go till she returned. For twenty interminable minutes not a sound reached me. At last Miss Haldin came out and walked across the room with her quick light step. When she reached the armchair she dropped into it heavily as if completely exhausted.

Mrs Haldin, she told me, had not shed a tear. She was sitting up in bed, and her immobility, her silence, were very alarming. At last she lay down gently and had motioned her daughter away.

'She will call me presently,' added Miss Haldin. 'I left a bell near the bed.'

I confess that my very real sympathy had no standpoint. The Western readers for whom this story is written will understand what I mean. It was, if I may say so, the want of experience. Death is a remorseless spoliator. The anguish of irreparable loss is familiar to us all. There is no life so lonely as to be safe against that experience. But the grief I had brought to those two ladies had gruesome associations. It had the associations of bombs and gallows – a lurid, Russian colouring which made the complexion of my sympathy uncertain.

I was grateful to Miss Haldin for not embarrassing me by an outward display of deep feeling. I admired her for that wonderful command over herself, even while I was a little frightened at it. It was the stillness of a great tension. What if it should suddenly snap? Even the door of Mrs Haldin's room, with the old mother alone in there, had a rather awful aspect.

Nathalie Haldin murmured sadly—

'I suppose you are wondering what my feelings are?'

Essentially that was true. It was that very wonder which unsettled my sympathy of a dense Occidental. I could get hold of nothing but of some commonplace phrases, those futile phrases that give the measure of our impotence before each other's trials. I mumbled something to the effect that, for the young, life held its hopes and compensations. It held duties too – but of that I was certain it was not necessary to remind her.

She had a handkerchief in her hands and pulled at it nervously.

'I am not likely to forget my mother,' she said. 'We used to be three. Now we are two – two women. She's not so very old. She may live quite a long time yet. What have we to look for in the future? For what hope and what consolation?'

'You must take a wider view,' I said resolutely, thinking that with this exceptional creature this was the right note to strike. She looked at me steadily for a moment, and then the tears she had been keeping down flowed unrestrained. She jumped up and stood in the window with her back to me.

I slipped away without attempting even to approach her. Next day I was told at the door that Mrs Haldin was better. The middle-aged servant remarked that a lot of people – Russians – had called that day, but Miss Haldin had not seen anybody. A fortnight later, when making my daily call, I was asked in and found Mrs Haldin sitting in her usual place by the window.

At first one would have thought that nothing was changed. I saw across the room the familiar profile, a little sharper in outline and overspread by a uniform pallor as might have been expected in an invalid. But no disease could have accounted for the change in her black eyes, smiling no longer with gentle irony. She raised them as she gave me her hand. I observed the three weeks' old number of the *Standard* folded with the correspondence from Russia uppermost, lying on a little table by the side of the armchair. Mrs Haldin's voice was startlingly weak and colourless. Her first words to me framed a question.

'Has there been anything more in your newspapers?'

I released her long emaciated hand, shook my head negatively, and sat down.

'The English press is wonderful. Nothing can be kept secret from it, and all the world must hear. Only our Russian news is not always easy to understand. Not always easy. . . . But English mothers do not look for news like that . . .'

She laid her hand on the newspaper and took it away again. I said—

'We too have had tragic times in our history.'

'A long time ago. A very long time ago.'

'Yes.'

'There are nations that have made their bargain with fate,' said Miss Haldin, who had approached us. 'We need not envy them.'

'Why this scorn?' I asked gently. 'It may be that our bargain was not a very lofty one. But the terms men and nations obtain from Fate are hallowed by the price.'

Mrs Haldin turned her head away and looked out of the windows for a time, with that new, sombre, extinct gaze of her sunken eyes which so completely made another woman of her.

'That Englishman, this correspondent,' she addressed me suddenly, 'do you think it is possible that he knew my son?'

To this strange question I could only say that it was possible of course. She saw my surprise.

'If one knew what sort of man he was one could perhaps write to him,' she murmured.

'Mother thinks,' explained Miss Haldin, standing between us, with one hand resting on the back of my chair, 'that my poor brother perhaps did not try to save himself.'

I looked up at Miss Haldin in sympathetic consternation, but Miss Haldin was looking down calmly at her mother. The latter said—

'We do not know the address of any of his friends. Indeed, we know nothing of his Petersburg comrades. He had a multitude of young friends, only he never spoke much of them. One could guess that they were his disciples and that they idolized him. But he was so modest. One would think that with so many devoted . . .'

She averted her head again and looked down the Boulevard des Philsophes, a singularly arid and dusty thoroughfare, where nothing could be seen at the moment but two dogs, a little girl in a pinafore hopping on one leg, and in the distance a workman wheeling a bicycle.

'Even amongst the Apostles of Christ there was found a Judas,' she whispered as if to herself, but with the evident intention to be heard by me.

The Russian visitors assembled in little knots, conversed amongst themselves meantime, in low murmurs, and with brief glances in our direction. It was a great contrast to the usual loud volubility of these gatherings. Miss Haldin followed me into the ante-room.

'People will come,' she said. 'We cannot shut the door in their faces.'

While I was putting on my overcoat she began to talk to me of her mother. Poor Mrs Haldin was fretting after more news. She wanted to go on hearing about her unfortunate son. She could not make up her mind to abandon him quietly to the dumb unknown. She would persist in pursuing him in there through the long days of motionless silence face to face with the empty Boulevard des Philosophes. She could not understand why he had not escaped – as so many other revolutionaries and conspirators had managed to escape in other instances of that kind. It was really inconceivable that the means of secret revolutionary organizations should have failed so inexcusably to preserve her son. But in reality the inconceivable that staggered her mind was nothing but the cruel audacity of Death passing over her head to strike at that young and precious heart.

Miss Haldin mechanically, with an absorbed look, handed me my hat. I understood from her that the poor woman was possessed by the sombre and simple idea that her son must have perished because he did not want to be saved. It could not have been that he despaired of his country's future. That was impossible. Was it possible that his mother and sister had not known how to merit his confidence; and that, after having done what he was compelled to do, his spirit became crushed by an intolerable doubt, his mind distracted by a sudden mistrust.

I was very much shocked by this piece of ingenuity.

'Our three lives were like that!' Miss Haldin twined the fingers of both her hands together in demonstration, then separated them slowly, looking straight into my face. 'That's what poor mother found to torment herself and me with, for all the years to come,' added the strange girl. At that moment her indefinable charm was revealed to me in the conjunction of passion and stoicism. I imagined what her life was likely to be by the side of Mrs Haldin's terrible immobility, inhabited by that fixed idea. But my concern was reduced to silence by my ignorance of her modes of feeling. Difference of nationality is a terrible obstacle for our complex Western natures. But Miss Haldin probably was too simple to suspect my embarrassment. She did not wait for me to say anything, but as if reading my thoughts on my face she went on courageously—

'At first poor mother went numb, as our peasants say; then she began to think and she will go on now thinking and thinking in that unfortunate strain. You see yourself how cruel that is. . . .'

I never spoke with greater sincerity than when I agreed with her that it would be deplorable in the highest degree. She took an anxious breath.

'But all these strange details in the English paper,' she exclaimed suddenly. 'What is the meaning of them? I suppose they are true? But is it not terrible that my poor brother should be caught wandering alone, as if in despair, about the streets at night. . . .'

We stood so close to each other in the dark ante-room that I could see her biting her lower lip to suppress a dry sob. After a short pause she said—

'I suggested to mother that he may have been betrayed by some false friend or simply by some cowardly creature. It may be easier for her to believe that.'

I understood now the poor woman's whispered allusion to Judas.

'It may be easier,' I admitted, admiring inwardly the directness and the subtlety of the girl's outlook. She was dealing with life as it was made for her by the political conditions of her country. She faced cruel realities, not morbid imaginings of her own making. I could not defend myself from a certain feeling of respect when she added simply—

'Time they say can soften every sort of bitterness. But I cannot believe that it has any power over remorse. It is better that mother should think of some person guilty of Victor's death, than that she should connect it with a weakness of her son or a shortcoming of her own.'

'But you, yourself, don't suppose that . . .' I began.

She compressed her lips and shook her head. She harboured no evil thoughts against anyone, she declared – and perhaps nothing that happened was unnecessary. On these words, pronounced low and sounding mysteries in the half obscurity of the ante-room, we parted with an expressive and warm handshake. The grip of her strong, shapely hand had a seductive frankness, a sort of exquisite virility. I do not know why she should have felt so friendly to me. It may be that she thought I understood her much better than I was able to do. The most precise of her sayings seemed always to me to have enigmatical prolongations vanishing somewhere beyond my reach. I am reduced to suppose that she appreciated my attention and my silence. The attention she could see was quite sincere, so that the silence could not be suspected of coldness. It seemed to satisfy her. And it is to be noted that if she confided in me it was clearly not with the expectation of receiving advice, for which, indeed, she never asked.

Chapter II

Our daily relations were interrupted at this period for something like a fortnight. I had to absent myself unexpectedly from Geneva. On my return I lost no time in directing my steps up the Boulevard des Philosophes.

Through the open door of the drawing-room I was annoyed to hear a visitor holding forth steadily in an unctuous deep voice.

Mrs Haldin's armchair by the window stood empty. On the sofa, Nathalie

Haldin raised her charming grey eyes in a glance of greeting accompanied by the merest hint of a welcoming smile. But she made no movement. With her strong white hands lying inverted in the lap of her mourning dress she faced a man who presented to me a robust back covered with black broadcloth, and well in keeping with the deep voice. He turned his head sharply over his shoulder, but only for a moment.

'Ah! your English friend. I know. I know. That's nothing.'

He wore spectacles with smoked glasses, a tall silk hat stood on the floor by the side of his chair. Flourishing slightly a big soft hand he went on with his discourse, precipitating his delivery a little more.

'I have never changed the faith I held while wandering in the forests and bogs of Siberia. It sustained me then – it sustains me now. The great Powers of Europe are bound to disappear – and the cause of their collapse will be very simple. They will exhaust themselves struggling against their proletariat. In Russia it is different. In Russia we have no classes to combat each other, one holding the power of wealth, and the other mighty with the strength of numbers. We have only an unclean bureaucracy in the face of a people as great and as incorruptible as the ocean. No, we have no classes. But we have the Russian woman. The admirable Russian woman! I receive most remarkable letters signed by women. So elevated in tone, so courageous, breathing such a noble ardour of service! The greatest part of our hopes rests on women. I behold their thirst for knowledge. It is admirable. Look how they absorb, how they are making it their own. It is miraculous. But what is knowledge? . . . I understand that you have not been studying anything especially – medicine for instance. No? That's right. Had I been honoured by being asked to advise you on the use of your time when you arrived here I would have been strongly opposed to such a course. Knowledge in itself is mere dross.'

He had one of those bearded Russian faces without shape, a mere appearance of flesh and hair with not a single feature having any sort of character. His eyes being hidden by the dark glasses there was an utter absence of all expression. I knew him by sight. He was a Russian refugee of mark. All Geneva knew his burly black-coated figure. At one time all Europe was aware of the story of his life written by himself and translated into seven or more languages. In his youth he had led an idle, dissolute life. Then a society girl he was about to marry died suddenly and thereupon he abandoned the world of fashion, and began to conspire in a spirit of repentance, and, after that, his native autocracy took good care that the usual things should happen to him. He was imprisoned in fortresses, beaten within an inch of his life, and condemned to work in mines, with common criminals. The great success of his book, however, was the chain.

I do not remember now the details of the weight and length of the fetters riveted on his limbs by an 'Administrative' order, but it was in the number of pounds and the thickness of links an appalling assertion of the divine right of autocracy. Appalling and futile too, because this big man managed to carry off that simple engine of government with him into the woods. The sensational clink of these fetters is heard all through the chapters describing his escape – a subject of wonder to two continents. He had begun by concealing himself successfully from his guard in a hole on a river bank. It was the end of the day; with infinite labour he managed to free one of his legs. Meantime night fell. He was going to begin on his other leg when he was overtaken by a terrible misfortune. He dropped his file.

All this is precise yet symbolic; and the file had its pathetic history. It was given to him unexpectedly one evening, by a quiet, pale-faced girl. The poor creature had come out to the mines to join one of his fellow convicts, a delicate young man, a mechanic and a social democrat, with broad cheekbones and large staring eyes. She had worked her way across half Russia and nearly the whole of Siberia to be near him, and, as it seems, with the hope of helping him to escape. But she arrived too late. Her lover had died only a week before.

Through that obscure episode, as he says, in the history of ideas in Russia, the file came into his hands, and inspired him with an ardent resolution to regain his liberty. When it slipped through his fingers it was as if it had gone straight into the earth. He could by no manner of means put his hand on it again in the dark. He groped systematically in the loose earth, in the mud, in the water; the night was passing meantime, the precious night on which he counted to get away into the forests, his only chance of escape. For a moment he was tempted by despair to give up; but recalling the quiet, sad face of the heroic girl, he felt profoundly ashamed of his weakness. She had selected him for the gift of liberty and he must show himself worthy of the favour conferred by her feminine, indomitable soul. It appeared to be a sacred trust. To fail would have been a sort of treason against the sacredness of self-sacrifice and womanly love.

There are in his book whole pages of self-analysis whence emerges like a white figure from a dark confused sea the conviction of woman's spiritual superiority – his new faith confessed since in several volumes. His first tribute to it, the great act of his conversion, was his extraordinary existence in the endless forests of the Okhotsk Province, with the loose end of the chain wound about his waist. A strip torn off his convict shirt secured the end firmly. Other strips fastened it at intervals up his left leg to deaden the clanking and to prevent the slack links from getting hooked in the bushes. He became very fierce. He developed an unsuspected genius for the arts of a wild and hunted existence. He learned to creep into villages without betraying his presence by anything more than an occasional faint jingle. He broke into outhouses with an axe he managed to purloin in a wood-cutters' camp. In the deserted tracts of country he lived on wild berries and hunted for honey. His clothing dropped off him gradually. His naked tawny figure glimpsed vaguely through the bushes with a cloud of mosquitoes and flies hovering about the shaggy head, spread tales of terror through whole districts. His temper grew savage as the days went by, and he was glad to discover that there was so much of a brute in him. He had nothing else to put his trust in. For it was as though there had been two human beings indissolubly joined in that enterprise. The civilized man, the enthusiast of advanced humanitarian ideals thirsting for the triumph of spiritual love and political liberty; and the stealthy, primeval savage, pitilessly cunning in the preservation of his freedom from day to day, like a tracked wild beast.

The wild beast was making its way instinctively eastward to the Pacific coast, and the civilized humanitarian in fearful anxious dependence watched the proceedings with awe. Through all these weeks he could never make up his mind to appeal to human compassion. In the wary primeval savage this shyness might have been natural, but the other too, the civilized creature, the thinker, the escaping 'political' had developed an absurd form of morbid pessimism, a form of temporary insanity, originating perhaps in the physical worry and discomfort of the chain. These links, he fancied, made him odious to the rest of mankind. It was a repugnant and suggestive load. Nobody could feel any pity at the disgusting sight of a man escaping with a broken chain. His imagination became affected by his fetters in a precise, matter-of-fact manner. It seemed to him impossible that people could resist the temptation of fastening the loose end to a staple in the wall while they went for the nearest police official. Crouching in holes or hidden in thickets, he had tried to read the faces of unsuspecting free settlers working in the clearings or passing along the paths within a foot or two of his eyes. His feeling was that no man on earth could be trusted with the temptation of the chain.

One day, however, he chanced to come upon a solitary woman. It was on an open slope of rough grass outside the forest. She sat on the bank of a narrow stream; she had a red handkerchief on her head and a small basket was lying on the ground near her hand. At a little distance could be seen a cluster of log cabins, with a water-mill over a damned pool shaded by birch trees and looking bright as glass in the twilight. He approached her silently; his hatchet stuck in his iron belt, a thick cudgel in his hand; there were leaves and bits of twigs in his tangled hair, in his matted beard; bunches of rags he had wound round the links fluttered from his waist. A faint clink of his fetters made the woman turn her head. Too terrified by this savage apparition to jump up or even to scream, she was yet too stout-hearted to faint. . . . Expecting nothing less than to be murdered on the spot she covered her eyes with her hands to avoid the sight of the descending axe. When at last she found courage to look again, she saw the shaggy wild man sitting on the bank six feet away from her. His thin, sinewy arms hugged his naked legs; the long beard covered the knees on which he rested his chin; all these clasped, folded limbs, the bare shoulders, the wild head with red staring eyes, shook and trembled violently while the bestial creature was making efforts to speak. It was six weeks since he had heard the sound of his own voice. It seemed as though he had lost the faculty of speech. He had become a dumb and despairing brute, till the woman's sudden, unexpected cry of profound pity, the insight of her feminine compassion discovering the complex misery of the man under the terrifying aspect of the monster, restored him to the ranks of humanity. This point of view is presented in his book, with a very effective eloquence. She ended, he says, by shedding tears over him, sacred, redeeming tears, while he also wept with joy in the manner of a converted sinner. Directing him to hide in the bushes and wait patiently (a police patrol was expected in the Settlement) she went away towards the houses, promising to return at night.

As if providentially appointed to be the newly wedded wife of the village blacksmith, the woman persuaded her husband to come out with her, bringing some tools of his trade, a hammer, a chisel, a small anvil. . . . 'My fetters' – the book says – 'were struck off on the banks of the stream, in the starlight of a calm night by an athletic, taciturn young man of the people, kneeling at my feet, while the woman like a liberating genius stood by with clasped hands.' Obviously a symbolic couple. At the same time they furnished his regained humanity with some decent clothing, and put heart into the new man by the information that the sea-coast of the Pacific was only a very few miles away. It could be seen, in fact, from the top of the next ridge. . . .

The rest of his escape does not lend itself to mystic treatment and symbolic interpretation. He ended by finding his way to the West by the Suez Canal route in the usual manner. Reaching the shores of South Europe he sat down to write his autobiography – the great literary success of its year. This book was followed by other books written with the declared purpose of elevating humanity. In these works he preached generally the cult of the woman. For his own part he practised it under the rites of special devotion to the transcendental merits of a certain Madame de S—, a lady of advanced views, no longer very young, once upon a time the intriguing wife of a now dead and forgotten diplomat. Her loud pretensions to be one of the leaders of modern thought and of modern sentiment, she sheltered (like Voltaire and Mme de Staël) on the republican territory of Geneva. Driving through the streets in her big landau she exhibited to the indifference of the natives and the stares of the tourists a long-waisted, youthful figure of hieratic stiffness, with a pair of big gleaming eyes, rolling restlessly behind a short veil of black lace, which, coming down no farther than her vividly red lips, resembled a mask. Usually the 'heroic fugitive' (this name was bestowed upon him in a review of the English edition of his book) – the 'heroic fugitive' accompanied her, sitting, portentously bearded and darkly bespectacled, not by her side, but opposite her, with his back to the horses. Thus, facing each other, with no one else in the roomy carriage, their airings suggested a conscious public manifestation. Or it may have been unconscious. Russian simplicity often marches innocently on the edge of cynicism for some lofty purpose. But it is a vain enterprise for sophisticated Europe to try and understand these doings. Considering the air of gravity extending even to the physiognomy of the coachman and the action of the showy horses, this quaint display might have possessed a mystic significance, but to the corrupt frivolity of a Western mind, like my own, it seemed hardly decent.

However it is not becoming for an obscure teacher of languages to criticize a 'heroic fugitive' of world-wide celebrity. I was aware from hearsay that he was an industrious busy-body, hunting up his compatriots in hotels, in private lodgings, and – I was told – conferring upon them the honour of his notice in public gardens when a suitable opening presented itself. I was under the impression that after a visit or two, several months before, he had given up the ladies Haldin – no doubt reluctantly, for there could be no question of his being a determined person. It was perhaps to be expected that he should reappear again on this terrible occasion as a Russian and a revolutionist, to say the right thing, to strike the true, perhaps a comforting, note. But I did not like to see him sitting there. I trust that an unbecoming jealousy of my privileged position had nothing to do with it. I made no claim to a special standing for my silent friendship. Removed by the difference of age and nationality as if into the sphere of another existence, I produced, even upon myself, the effect of a dumb helpless ghost, of an anxious immaterial thing that could only hover about without the power to protect or guide by as much as a whisper. Since Miss Haldin with her sure instinct had refrained from introducing me to the burly celebrity, I would have retired quietly and returned later on, had I not met a peculiar expression in her eyes which I interpreted as a request to stay, with the view, perhaps, of shortening an unwelcome visit.

He picked up his hat, but only to deposit it on his knees.

'We shall meet again, Natalia Victorovna. Today I have called only to mark those feelings towards your honoured mother and yourself, the nature of which you cannot doubt. I needed no urging, but Eleanor – Madame de S— herself has in a way sent me. She extends to you the hand of feminine fellowship. There is positively in all the range of human sentiments no joy and no sorrow that woman cannot understand, elevate, and spiritualize by her interpretation. That young man newly arrived from St Petersburg, I have mentioned to you, is already under the charm.'

At this point Miss Haldin got up abruptly. I was glad. He did not evidently expect anything so decisive and, at first, throwing his head back, he tilted up his dark glasses with bland curiosity. At last, recollecting himself, he stood up hastily, seizing his hat off his knees with great adroitness.

'How is it, Natalia Victorovna, that you have kept aloof so long, from what after all is – let disparaging tongues say what they like – a unique centre of intellectual freedom and of effort to shape a high conception of our future? In the case of your honoured mother I understand in a measure. At her age new ideas – new faces are not perhaps. . . . But you! Was it mistrust – or indifference? You must come out of your reserve. We Russians have no right to be reserved with each other. In our circumstances it is almost a crime against humanity. The luxury of private grief is not for us. Nowadays the devil is not combated by prayers and fasting. And what is fasting after all but starvation? You must not starve yourself, Natalia Victorovna. Strength is what we want. Spiritual strength, I mean. As to the other kind, what could withstand us Russians if we only put it forth? Sin is different in our day, and the way of salvation for pure souls is different too. It is no longer to be found in monasteries but in the world, in the . . .'

The deep sound seemed to rise from under the floor, and one felt steeped in it to the lips. Miss Haldin's interruption resembled the effort of a drowning person to keep above water. She struck in with an accent of impatience—

'But, Peter Ivanovitch, I don't mean to retire into a monastery. Who would look for salvation there?'

'I spoke figuratively,' he boomed.

'Well, then, I am speaking figuratively too. But sorrow is sorrow and pain is pain in the old way. They make their demands upon people. One has got to face them the best way one can. I know that the blow which has fallen upon us so unexpectedly is only an episode in the fate of a people. You may rest assured that I don't forget that. But just now I have to think of my mother. How can you expect me to leave her to herself . . .?'

'That is putting it in a very crude way,' he protested in his great effortless voice.

Miss Haldin did not wait for the vibration to die out.

'And run about visiting amongst a lot of strange people. The idea is distasteful for me; and I do not know what else you may mean?'

He towered before her, enormous, deferential, cropped as close as a convict; and this big pinkish poll evoked for me the vision of a wild head with matted locks peering through parted bushes, glimpses of naked, tawny limbs slinking behind the masses of sodden foliage under a cloud of flies and mosquitoes. It was an involuntary tribute to the vigour of his writing. Nobody could doubt that he had wandered in Siberian forests, naked and girt with a chain. The black broadcloth coat invested his person with a character of austere decency – something recalling a missionary.

'Do you know what I want, Natalia Victorovna?' he uttered solemnly. 'I want you to be a fanatic.'

'A fanatic?'

'Yes. Faith alone won't do.'

His voice dropped to a still lower tone. He raised for a moment one thick arm; the other remained hanging down against his thigh, with the fragile silk hat at the end.

'I shall tell you now something which I entreat you to ponder over carefully. Listen, we need a force that would move heaven and earth – nothing less.'

The profound, subterranean note of this 'nothing less' made one shudder, almost, like the deep mutterings of wind in the pipes of an organ.

'And are we to find that force in the salon of Madame de S—? Excuse me, Peter Ivanovitch, if I permit myself to doubt it. Is not that lady a woman of the great world, an aristocrat?'

'Prejudice!' he cried. 'You astonish me. And suppose she was all that! She is also a woman of flesh and blood. There is always something to weigh down the spiritual side in all of us. But to make of it a reproach is what I did not expect from you. No! I did not expect that. One would think you have listened to some malevolent scandal.'

'I have heard no gossip, I assure you. In our province how could we? But the world speaks of her. What can there be in common in a lady of that sort and an obscure country girl like me?'

'She is a perpetual manifestation of a noble and peerless spirit,' he broke in. 'Her charm – no, I shall not speak of her charm. But, of course, everybody who approaches her falls under the spell. . . . Contradictions vanish, trouble falls away from one. . . . Unless I am mistaken – but I never make a mistake in spiritual matters – you are troubled in your soul, Natalia Victorovna.'

Miss Haldin's clear eyes looked straight at his soft enormous face; I received the impression that behind these dark spectacles of his he could be as impudent as he chose.

'Only the other evening walking back to town from Château Borel with our latest interesting arrival from Petersburg, I could notice the powerful soothing influence – I must say reconciling influence. . . . There he was, all these kilometres along the shores of the lake, silent, like a man who has been shown the way of peace. I could feel the leaven working in his soul, you understand. For one thing he listened to me patiently. I myself was inspired that evening by the firm and exquisite genius of Eleanor – Madame de S—, you know. It was a full moon and I could observe his face. I cannot be deceived. . . .'

Miss Haldin, looking down, seemed to hesitate.

'Well! I will think of what you said, Peter Ivanovitch. I shall try to call as soon as I can leave mother for an hour or two safely.'

Coldly as these words were said I was amazed at the concession. He snatched her right hand with such fervour that I thought he was going to press it to his lips or his breast. But he only held it by the fingertips in his great paw and shook it a little up and down while he delivered his last volley of words.

'That's right. That's right. I haven't obtained your full confidence as yet, Natalia Victorovna, but that will come. All in good time. The sister of Victor Haldin cannot be without importance. . . . It's simply impossible. And no woman can remain sitting on the steps. Flowers, tears, applause – that has had its time; it's a medieval conception. The arena, the arena itself is the place for women!'

He relinquished her hand with a flourish, as if giving it to her for a gift, and remained still, his head bowed in dignified submission before her femininity.

'The arena . . . You must descend into the arena, Natalia.'

He made one step backwards, inclined his enormous body, and was gone swiftly. The door fell to behind him. But immediately the powerful resonance of his voice was heard addressing in the ante-room the middle-aged servant woman who was letting him out. Whether he exhorted her too to descend into the arena I cannot tell. The thing sounded like a lecture, and the slight crash of the outer door cut it short suddenly.

Chapter III

We remained looking at each other for a time.

'Do you know who he is?'

Miss Haldin, coming forward, put this question to me in English.

I took her offered hand.

'Everybody knows. He is a revolutionary feminist, a great writer, if you like, and – how shall I say it – the – the familiar guest of Madame de S—'s mystic revolutionary salon.'

Miss Haldin passed her hand over her forehead.

'You know, he was with me for more than an hour before you came in. I was so glad mother was lying down. She has many nights without sleep, and then sometimes in the middle of the day she gets a rest of several hours. It is sheer exhaustion – but still, I am thankful. . . . If it were not for these intervals. . . .'

She looked at me and, with that extraordinary penetration which used to disconcert me, shook her head.

'No. She would not go mad.'

'My dear young lady,' I cried, by way of protest, the more shocked because in my heart I was far from thinking Mrs Haldin quite sane.

'You don't know what a fine, lucid intellect mother had,' continued Nathalie

Haldin, with her calm, clear-eyed simplicity, which seemed to me always to have a quality of heroism.

'I am sure . . .' I murmured.

'I darkened mother's room and came out here. I've wanted for so long to think quietly.'

She paused, then, without giving any sign of distress, added, 'It's so difficult,' and looked at me with a strange fixity, as if watching for a sign of dissent or surprise.

I gave neither. I was irresistibly impelled to say—

'The visit from that gentleman has not made it any easier, I fear.'

Miss Haldin stood before me with a peculiar expression in her eyes.

'I don't pretend to understand Peter Ivanovitch completely. Some guide one must have, even if one does not wholly give up the direction of one's conduct to him. I am an inexperienced girl, but I am not slavish. There has been too much of that in Russia. Why should I not listen to him? There is no harm in having one's thoughts directed. But I don't mind confessing to you that I have not been completely candid with Peter Ivanovitch. I don't quite know what prevented me at the moment . . .'

She walked away suddenly from me to a distant part of the room; but it was only to open and shut a drawer in a bureau. She returned with a piece of paper in her hand. It was thin and blackened with close handwriting. It was obviously a letter.

'I wanted to read you the very words,' she said. 'This is one of my poor brother's letters. He never doubted. How could he doubt? They make only such a small handful, those miserable oppressors, before the unanimous will of our people.'

'Your brother believed in the power of a people's will to achieve anything?'

'It was his religion,' declared Miss Haldin.

I looked at her calm face and her animated eyes.

'Of course the will must be awakened, inspired, concentrated,' she went on. 'That is the true task of real agitators. One has got to give up one's life to it. The degradation of servitude, absolutist lies must be uprooted and swept out. Reform is impossible. There is nothing to reform. There is no legality, there are no institutions. There are only arbitrary decrees. There is only a handful of cruel – perhaps blind – officials against a nation.'

The letter rustled slightly in her hand. I glanced down at the flimsy blackened pages whose very handwriting seemed cabalistic, incomprehensible to the experience of Western Europe.

'Stated like this,' I confessed, 'the problem seems simple enough. But I fear I shall not see it solved. And if you go back to Russia I know that I shall not see you again. Yet once more I say: go back! Don't suppose that I am thinking of your preservation. No! I know that you will not be returning to personal safety. But I had much rather think of you in danger there than see you exposed to what may be met here.'

'I tell you what,' said Miss Haldin, after a moment of reflection. 'I believe that you hate revolution; you fancy it's not quite honest. You belong to a people which has made a bargain with fate and wouldn't like to be rude to it. But we have made no bargain. It was never offered to us – so much liberty for so much hard cash. You shrink from the idea of revolutionary action for those you think well of as if it were something – how shall I say it – not quite decent.'

I bowed my head.

'You are quite right,' I said. 'I think very highly of you.'

'Don't suppose I do not know it,' she began hurriedly. 'Your friendship has been very valuable.'

'I have done little else but look on.'

She was a little flushed under the eyes.

'There is a way of looking on which is valuable. I have felt less lonely because of it. It's difficult to explain.'

'Really? Well, I too have felt less lonely. That's easy to explain, though. But it won't go on much longer. The last thing I want to tell you is this: in a real revolution – not a simple dynastic change or a mere reform of institutions – in a real revolution the best characters do not come to the front. A violent revolution falls into the hands of narrow-minded fanatics and of tyrannical hypocrites at first. Afterwards comes the turn of all the pretentious intellectual failures of the time. Such are the chiefs and the leaders. You will notice that I have left out the mere rogues. The scrupulous and the just, the noble, humane, and devoted natures; the unselfish and the intelligent may begin a movement – but it passes away from them. They are not the leaders of a revolution. They are its victims: the victims of disgust, of disenchantment – often of remorse. Hopes grotesquely betrayed, ideals caricatured – that is the definition of revolutionary success. There have been in every revolution hearts broken by such successes. But enough of that. My meaning is that I don't want you to be a victim.'

'If I could believe all you have said I still wouldn't think of myself,' protested Miss Haldin. 'I would take liberty from any hand as a hungry man would snatch at a piece of bread. The true progress must begin after. And for that the right men shall be found. They are already amongst us. One comes upon them in their obscurity, unknown, preparing themselves. . . .'

She spread out the letter she had kept in her hand all the time, and looking down at it—

'Yes! One comes upon such men!' she repeated, and then read out the words, 'Unstained, lofty, and solitary existences.'

Folding up the letter, while I looked at her interrogatively, she explained—

'These are the words which my brother applies to a young man he came to know in St Petersburg. An intimate friend, I suppose. It must be. His is the only name my brother mentions in all his correspondence with me. Absolutely the only one, and – would you believe it? – the man is here. He arrived recently in Geneva.'

'Have you seen him?' I inquired. 'But, of course, you must have seen him.'

'No! No I haven't! I didn't know he was here. It's Peter Ivanovitch himself who told me. You have heard him yourself mentioning a new arrival from Petersburg. . . . Well, that is the man of 'unstained, lofty, and solitary existence.' My brother's friend!'

'Compromised politically, I suppose,' I remarked.

'I don't know. Yes. It must be so. Who knows! Perhaps it was this very friendship with my brother which . . . But no! It is scarcely possible. Really, I know nothing except what Peter Ivanovitch told me of him. He has brought a letter of introduction from Father Zosim – you know, the priest-democrat; you have heard of Father Zosim?'

'Oh yes. The famous Father Zosim was staying here in Geneva for some two months about a year ago,' I said. 'When he left here he seems to have disappeared from the world.'

'It appears that he is at work in Russia again. Somewhere in the centre,' Miss Haldin said, with animation. 'But please don't mention that to anyone – don't let it slip from you, because if it got into the papers it would be dangerous for him.'

'You are anxious, of course, to meet that friend of your brother?' I asked.

Miss Haldin put the letter into her pocket. Her eyes looked beyond my shoulder at the door of her mother's room.

'Not here,' she murmured. 'Not for the first time, at least.'

After a moment of silence I said good-bye, but Miss Haldin followed me into the ante-room, closing the door behind us carefully.

'I suppose you guess where I mean to go tomorrow?'

'You have made up your mind to call on Madame de S—.'

'Yes. I am going to the Château Borel. I must.'

'What do you expect to hear there?' I asked, in a low voice.

I wondered if she were not deluding herself with some impossible hope. It was not that, however.

'Only think – such a friend. The only man mentioned in his letters. He would have something to give me, if nothing more than a few poor words. It may be something said and thought in those last days. Would you want me to turn my back on what is left of my poor brother – a friend?'

'Certainly not,' I said. 'I quite understand your pious curiosity.'

'—Unstained, lofty, and solitary existences,' she murmured to herself. 'There are! There are! Well, let me question one of them about the loved dead.'

'How do you know, though, that you will meet him there? Is he staying in the Château as a guest – do you suppose?'

'I can't really tell,' she confessed. 'He brought a written introduction from Father Zosim – who, it seems, is a friend of Madame de S— too. She can't be such a worthless woman after all.'

'There were all sorts of rumours afloat about Father Zosim himself,' I observed.

She shrugged her shoulders.

'Calumny is a weapon of our government too. It's well known. Oh yes! It is a fact that Father Zosim had the protection of the Governor-General of a certain province. We talked on the subject with my brother two years ago, I remember. But his work was good. And now he is proscribed. What better proof can one require? But no matter what that priest was or is. All that cannot affect my brother's friend. If I don't meet him there I shall ask these people for his address. And, of course, mother must see him too, later on. There is no guessing what he may have to tell us. It would be a mercy if mamma could be soothed. You know what she imagines. Some explanation perhaps may be found, or – or even made up, perhaps. It would be no sin.'

'Certainly,' I said, 'it would be no sin. It may be a mistake, though.'

'I want her only to recover some of her old spirit. While she is like this I cannot think of anything calmly.'

'Do you mean to invent some sort of pious fraud for your mother's sake?' I asked.

'Why fraud? Such a friend is sure to know something of my brother in these last days. He could tell us. . . . There is something in the facts which will not let me rest. I am certain he meant to join us abroad – that he had some plans – some great patriotic action in view; not only for himself, but for both of us. I trusted in that. I looked forward to the time! Oh! with such hope and impatience. . . . I could have helped. And now suddenly this appearance of recklessness – as if he had not cared. . . .'

She remained silent for a time, then obstinately she concluded—

'I want to know . . .'

Thinking it over, later on, while I walked slowly away from the Boulevard des Philosophes, I asked myself critically, what precisely was it that she wanted to know? What I had heard of her history was enough to give me a clue. In the educational establishment for girls where Miss Haldin finished her studies she was looked upon rather unfavourably. She was suspected of holding independent views on matters settled by official teaching. Afterwards, when the two ladies returned to their country place, both mother and daughter, by speaking their minds openly on public events, had earned for themselves a reputation of liberalism. The three-horse trap of the district police-captain began to be seen frequently in their village. 'I must keep an eye on the peasants' – so he explained his visits up at the house. 'Two lonely ladies must be looked after a little.' He would inspect the walls as though he wanted to pierce them with his eyes, peer at the photographs, turn over the books in the drawing-room negligently, and after the usual refreshments, would depart. But the old priest of the village came one evening in the greatest distress and agitation, to confess that he – the priest – had been ordered to watch and ascertain in other ways (such as using his spiritual power with the servants) all that was going on in the house, and especially in respect of the visitors these ladies received, who they were, the length of their stay, whether any of them were strangers to that part of the country, and so on. The poor, simple old man was in an agony of humiliation and terror. 'I came to warn you. Be cautious in your conduct, for the love of God. I am burning with shame, but there is no getting out from under the net. I shall have to tell them what I see, because if I did not there is my deacon. He would make the worst of things to curry favour. And then my son-in-law, the husband of my Parasha, who is a writer in the Government Domain office, they would soon kick him out – and maybe send him away somewhere.' The old man lamented the necessities of the times – 'when people do not agree somehow' and wiped his eyes. He did not wish to spend the evening of his days with a shaven head in the penitent's cell of some monastery – 'and subjected to all the severities of ecclesiastical discipline; for they would show no mercy to an old man', he groaned. He became almost hysterical, and the two ladies, full of commiseration, soothed him the best they could before they let him go back to his cottage. But, as a matter of fact, they had very few visitors. The neighbours – some of them old friends – began to keep away; a few from timidity, others with marked disdain, being grand people that came only for the summer – Miss Haldin explained to me – aristocrats, reactionaries. It was a solitary existence for a young girl. Her relations with her mother were of the tenderest and most open kind; but Mrs Haldin had seen the experiences of her own generation, its sufferings, its deceptions, its apostasies too. Her affection for her children was expressed by the suppression of all signs of anxiety. She maintained a heroic reserve. To Nathalie Haldin, her brother with his Petersburg existence, not enigmatical in the least (there could be no doubt of what he felt or thought) but conducted a little mysteriously, was the only visible representative of a proscribed liberty. All the significance of freedom, its indefinite promises, lived in their long discussions, which breathed the loftiest hope of action and faith in success. Then, suddenly, the action, the hopes, came to an end with the details ferreted out by the English journalist. The concrete fact, the fact of his death remained but it remained obscure in its deeper causes. She felt herself abandoned without explanation. But she did not suspect him. What she wanted was to learn almost at any cost how she could remain faithful to his departed spirit.

Chapter IV

Several days elapsed before I met Nathalie Haldin again. I was crossing the place in front of the theatre when I made out her shapely figure in the very act of turning between the gate pillars of the unattractive public promenade of the Bastions. She walked away from me, but I knew we should meet as she returned down the main alley – unless, indeed, she were going home. In that case, I don't think I should have called on her yet. My desire to keep her away from these people was as strong as ever, but I had no illusions as to my power. I was but a Westerner, and it was clear that Miss Haldin would not, could not listen to my wisdom; and as to my desire of listening to her voice, it were better, I thought, not to indulge overmuch in that pleasure. No, I should not have gone to the Boulevard des Philosophes; but when at about the middle of the principal alley I saw Miss Haldin coming towards me, I was too curious, and too honest, perhaps, to run away.

There was something of the spring harshness in the air. The blue sky was hard, but the young leaves clung like soft mist about the uninteresting range of trees; and the clear sun put little points of gold into the grey of Miss Haldin's frank eyes, turned to me with a friendly greeting.

I inquired after the health of her mother.

She gave a slight movement of the shoulders and a little sad sigh.

'But, you see, I did come out for a walk . . . for exercise, as you English say.'

I smiled approvingly, and she added an unexpected remark –

'It is a glorious day.'

Her voice, slightly harsh, but fascinating with its masculine and bird-like quality, had the accent of spontaneous conviction. I was glad of it. It was as though she had become aware of her youth – for there was but little of spring-like glory in the rectangular railed space of grass and trees, framed visibly by the orderly roof-slopes of that town, comely without grace, and hospitable without sympathy. In the very air through which she moved there was but little warmth; and the sky, the sky of a land without horizons, swept and washed clean by the April showers, extended a cold cruel blue, without elevation, narrowed suddenly by the ugly, dark wall of the Jura where, here and there, lingered yet a few miserable trails and patches of snow. All the glory of the season must have been within herself – and I was glad this feeling had come into her life, if only for a little time.

'I am pleased to hear you say these words.'

She gave me a quick look. Quick, not stealthy. If there was one thing of which she was absolutely incapable, it was stealthiness. Her sincerity was expressed in the very rhythm of her walk. It was I who was looking at her covertly – if I may say so. I knew where she had been, but I did not know what she had seen and heard in that nest of aristocratic conspiracies. I use the word aristocratic, for want of a better term. The Château Borel, embowered in the trees and thickets of its neglected grounds, had its fame in our day, like the residences of that other dangerous and exiled woman, Madame de Staël, in the Napoleonic era. Only the Napoleonic despotism, the booted heir of the Revolution, which counted that intellectual woman for an enemy worthy to be watched, was something quite unlike the autocracy in mystic vestments, engendered by the slavery of a Tartar conquest. And Madame de S— was very far from resembling the gifted author of *Corinne*. She made a great noise about being persecuted. I don't know if she were regarded in certain circles as dangerous. As to being watched, I imagine that the Château Borel could be subjected only to a most distant observation. It was in its exclusiveness an ideal abode for hatching superior plots – whether serious or futile. But all this did not interest me. I wanted to know the effect its extraordinary inhabitants and its special atmosphere had produced on a girl like Miss Haldin, so true, so honest, but so dangerously inexperienced! Her unconsciously lofty ignorance of the baser instincts of mankind left her disarmed before her own impulses. And there was also that friend of her brother, the significant new arrival from Russia. . . . I wondered whether she had managed to meet him.

We walked for some time, slowly and in silence.

'You know,' I attacked her suddenly, 'if you don't intend telling me anything, you must say so distinctly, and then, of course, it shall be final. But I won't play at delicacy. I ask you pointblank for all the details.'

She smiled faintly at my threatening tone.

'You are as curious as a child.'

'No. I am only an anxious old man,' I replied earnestly.

She rested her glance on me as if to ascertain the degreee of my anxiety or the number of my years. My physiognomy has never been expressive, I believe, and as to my years I am not ancient enough as yet to be strikingly decrepit. I have no long beard like the good hermit of a romantic ballad; my footsteps are not tottering, my aspect not that of a slow, venerable sage. Those picturesque advantages are not mine. I am old, alas, in a brisk, commonplace way. And it seemed to me as though there were some pity for me in Miss Haldin's prolonged glance. She stepped out a little quicker.

'You ask for all the details. Let me see. I ought to remember them. It was novel enough for a – a village girl like me.'

After a moment of silence she began by saying that the Château Borel was almost as neglected inside as outside. It was nothing to wonder at. A Hamburg banker, I believe, retired from business, had it built to cheer his remaining days by the view of that lake whose precise, orderly, and well-to-do beauty must have been attractive to the unromantic imagination of a business man. But he died soon. His wife departed too (but only to Italy), and this house of moneyed ease, presumably unsaleable, had stood empty for several years. One went to it up a gravel drive, round a large, coarse grass-plot, with plenty of time to observe the degradation of its stuccoed front. Miss Haldin said that the impression was unpleasant. It grew more depressing as one came nearer.

She observed green stains of moss on the steps of the terrace. The front door stood wide open. There was no one about. She found herself in a wide, lofty, and absolutely empty hall, with a good many doors. These doors were all shut. A broad, bare stone staircase faced her, and the effect of the whole was of an untenanted house. She stood still, disconcerted by the solitude, but after a while she became aware of a voice speaking continuously somewhere.

'You were probably being observed all the time,' I suggested. 'There must have been eyes.'

'I don't see how that could be,' she retorted. 'I haven't seen even a bird in the grounds. I don't remember hearing a single twitter in the trees. The whole place appeared utterly deserted except for the voice.'

She could not make out the language – Russian, French, or German. No one seemed to answer it. It was as though the voice had been left behind by the departed inhabitants to talk to the bare walls. It went on volubly, with a pause now and then. It was lonely and sad. The time seemed very long to Miss Haldin. An invincible repugnance prevented her from opening one of the doors in the hall. It was so hopeless. No one would come, the voice would never stop. She confessed to me that she had to resist an impulse to turn round and go away unseen, as she had come.

'Really? You had that impulse?' I cried, full of regret. 'What a pity you did not obey it.'

She shook her head.

'What a strange memory it would have been for one. Those deserted grounds, that empty hall, that impersonal, voluble voice, and – nobody, nothing, not a soul.'

The memory would have been unique and harmless. But she was not a girl to run away from an intimidating impression of solitude and mystery. 'No, I did not run away,' she said. 'I stayed where I was – and I did see a soul. Such a strange soul.'

As she was gazing up the broad staircase, and had concluded that the voice came from somewhere above, a rustle of dress attracted her attention. She looked down and saw a woman crossing the hall, having issued apparently through one of the many doors. Her face was averted, so that at first she was not aware of Miss Haldin.

On turning her head and seeing a stranger, she appeared very much startled. From her slender figure Miss Haldin had taken her for a young girl; but if her face was almost childishly round, it was also sallow and wrinkled, with dark rings under the eyes. A thick crop of dusty brown hair was parted boyishly on the side with a lateral wave above the dry, furrowed forehead. After a moment of dumb blinking, she suddenly squatted down on the floor.

'What do you mean by squatted down?' I asked, astonished. 'This is a very strange detail.'

Miss Haldin explained the reason. This person when first seen was carrying a small bowl in her hand. She had squatted down to put it on the floor for the benefit of a large cat, which appeared then from behind her skirts, and hid its head into the bowl greedily. She got up, and approaching Miss Haldin asked with nervous bluntness –

'What do you want? Who are you?'

Miss Haldin mentioned her name and also the name of Peter Ivanovich. The girlish, elderly woman nodded and puckered her face into a momentary expression of sympathy. Her black silk blouse was old and even frayed in places; the black serge skirt was short and shabby. She continued to blink at close quarters, and her eyelashes and eyebrows seemed shabby too. Miss Haldin, speaking gently to her, as if to an unhappy and sensitive person, explained how it was that her visit could not be an altogether unexpected event to Madame de S—.

'Ah! Peter Ivanovitch brought you an invitation. How was I to know? A *dame de compagnie* is not consulted, as you may imagine.'

The shabby woman laughed a little. Her teeth, splendidly white and admirably even, looked absurdly out of place, like a string of pearls on the neck of a ragged tramp. 'Peter Ivanovitch is the greatest genius of the century perhaps, but he is the most inconsiderate man living. So if you have an appointment with him you must not be surprised to hear that he is not here.'

Miss Haldin explained that she had no appointment with Peter Ivanovitch. She became interested at once in that bizarre person.

'Why should he put himself out for you or any one else? Oh! these geniuses. If you only knew! Yes! And their books – I mean, of course, the books that the world admires, the inspired books. But you have not been behind the scenes. Wait till you have to sit at a table for a half a day with a pen in your hand. He can walk up and down his rooms for hours and hours. I used to get so stiff and numb that I was afraid I would lose my balance and fall off the chair all at once.'

She kept her hands folded in front of her, and her eyes, fixed on Miss Haldin's face, betrayed no animation whatever. Miss Haldin, gathering that the lady who called herself a *dame de compagnie* was proud of having acted as secretary to Peter Ivanovich, made an amiable remark.

'You could not imagine a more trying experience,' declared the lady. 'There is an Anglo-American journalist interviewing Madame de S— now, or I would take you up,' she continued in a changed tone and glancing towards the staircase. 'I act as master of ceremonies.'

It appeared that Madame de S— could not bear Swiss servants about her person; and, indeed, servants would not stay for very long in the Château Borel. There were always difficulties. Miss Haldin had already noticed that the hall was like a dusty barn of marble and stucco with cobwebs in the corners and faint tracks of mud on the black and white tessellated floor.

'I look also after this animal,' continued the *dame de compagnie*, keeping her hands folded quietly in front of her; and she bent her worn gaze upon the cat. 'I don't mind a bit. Animals have their right; though, strictly speaking, I see no reason why they should not suffer as well as human beings. Do you? But of course they never suffer so much. That is impossible. Only, in their case it is more pitiful because they cannot make a revolution. I used to be a Republican. I suppose you are a Republican?'

Miss Haldin confessed to me that she did not know what to say. But she nodded slightly, and asked in her turn –

'And are you no longer a Republican?'

'After taking down Peter Ivanovitch from dictation for two years, it is difficult for me to be anything. First of all, you have to sit perfectly motionless. The slightest movements you make puts to flight the ideas of Peter Ivanovitch. You hardly dare to breathe. And as to coughing – God forbid. Peter Ivanovitch changed the position of the table to the wall because at first I could not help raising my eyes to look out of the window, while waiting for him to go on with his dictation. That was not allowed. He said I stared so stupidly. I was likewise not permitted to look at him over my shoulder. Instantly Peter Ivanovitch stamped his foot, and would roar, "Look down on the paper!" It seems my expression, my face, put him off. Well, I know that I am not beautiful, and that my expression is not hopeful either. He said that my air of unintelligent expectation irritated him. These are his own words.'

Miss Haldin was shocked, but admitted to me that she was not altogether surprised.

'Is it possible that Peter Ivanovitch could treat any woman so rudely?' she cried.

The *dame de compagnie* nodded several times with an air of discretion, then assured Miss Haldin that she did not mind in the least. The trying part of it was to have the secret of the composition laid bare before her; to see the great author of the revolutionary gospels grope for words as if he were in the dark as to what he meant to say.

'I am quite willing to be the blind instrument of higher ends. To give one's life for the cause is nothing. But to have one's illusions destroyed – that is really almost more than one can bear. I really don't exaggerate,' she insisted. 'It seemed to freeze my very beliefs in me – the more so that when we worked in winter Peter Ivanovitch, walking up and down the room, required no artificial heat to keep himself warm. Even when we move to the South of France there are bitterly cold days, especially when you have to sit still for six hours at a stretch. The walls of these villas on the Riviera are so flimsy. Peter Ivanovitch did not seem to be aware of anything. It is true that I kept down my shivers from fear of putting him out. I used to set my teeth till my jaws felt absolutely locked. In the moments when Peter Ivanovitch interrupted his dictation, and sometimes these intervals were very long – often twenty minutes, no less, while he walked to and fro behind my back muttering to himself – I felt I was dying by inches, I assure you. Perhaps if I had let my teeth rattle Peter Ivanovitch might have noticed my distress, but I don't think it would have had any practical effect. He's very miserly in such matters.'

The *dame de compagnie* glanced up the staircase. The big cat had finished the milk and was rubbing its whiskered cheek sinuously against her skirt. She dived to snatch it up from the floor.

'Miserliness is rather a quality than otherwise, you know,' she continued, holding the cat in her folded arms. 'With us it is misers who can spare money for worthy objects – not the so-called generous natures. But pray don't think I am a sybarite. My father was a clerk in the Ministry of Finances with no position at all. You may guess by this that our home was far from luxurious, though of course we did not actually suffer from cold. I ran away from my parents, you know, directly I began to think by myself. It is not very easy, such thinking. One has got to be put in the way of it, awakened to the truth. I am indebted for my salvation to an old apple-woman, who had her stall under the gateway of the house we lived in. She had a kind wrinkled face, and the most friendly voice imaginable. One day, casually, we began to talk about a child, a ragged little girl we had seen begging from men in the streets at dusk; and from one thing to another my eyes began to open gradually to the horrors from which innocent people are made to suffer in this world, only in order that governments might exist. After I once understood the crime of the upper classes, I could not go on living with my parents. Not a single charitable word was to be heard in our home from year's end to year's end; there was nothing but the talk of vile office intrigues, and of promotion and of salaries, and of courting the favour of the chiefs. The mere idea of marrying one day such another man as my father made me shudder. I don't mean that there was any one wanting to marry me. There was not the slightest prospect of anything of the kind. But was it not sin enough to live on a Government salary while half Russia was dying of hunger? The Ministry of Finances! What a grotesque horror it is! What does the starving, ignorant people want with a Ministry of Finances? I kissed my old folks on both cheeks, and went away from them to live in cellars, with the proletariat. I tried to make myself useful to the utterly hopeless. I suppose you understand what I mean? I mean the people who have nowhere to go and nothing to look forward to in this life. Do you understand how frightful that is – nothing to look forward to! Sometimes I think that it is only in Russia that there are such people and such a depth of misery can be reached. Well, I plunged into it, and – do you know – there isn't much that one can do in there. No, indeed – at least as long as there are Ministries of Finances and such like grotesque horrors to stand in the way. I suppose I would have gone mad there just trying to fight the vermin, if it had not been for a man. It was my old friend and teacher, the poor saintly apple-woman, who discovered him for me, quite accidentally. She came to fetch me late one evening in her quiet way. I followed her where she would lead; that part of my life was in her hand altogether, and without her my spirit would have perished miserably. The man was a young workman, a lithographer by trade, and he had got into trouble in connection with that affair of temperance tracts –

you remember. There was a lot of people put in prison for that. The Ministry of Finances again! What would become of it if the poor folk ceased making beasts of themselves with drink? Upon my word, I would think that finances and all the rest of it are an invention of the devil; only that a belief in a supernatural source of evil is not necessary; men alone are quite capable of every wickedness. Finances indeed!'

Hatred and contempt hissed in her utterance of the word 'finances', but at the very moment she gently stroked the cat reposing in her arms. She even raised them slightly, and inclining her head rubbed her cheek against the fur of the animal, which received this caress with the complete detachment so characteristic of its kind. Then looking at Miss Haldin she excused herself once more for not taking her upstairs to Madame de S—. The interview could not be interrupted. Presently the journalist would be seen coming down the stairs. The best thing was to remain in the hall; and besides, all these rooms (she glanced all round at the many doors), all these rooms on the ground floor were unfurnished.

'Positively there is no chair down here to offer you,' she continued. 'But if you prefer your own thoughts to my chatter, I will sit down on the bottom step here and keep silent.'

Miss Haldin hastened to assure her that, on the contrary, she was very much interested in the story of the journeyman lithographer. He was a revolutionist, of course.

'A martyr, a simple man,' said the *dame de compagnie* with a faint sigh, and gazing through the open front door dreamily. She turned her misty brown eyes on Miss Haldin.

'I lived with him for four months. It was like a nightmare.'

As Miss Haldin looked at her inquisitively she began to describe the emaciated face of the man, his fleshless limbs, his destitution. The room into which the apple-woman had led her was a tiny garret, a miserable den under the roof of a sordid house. The plaster fallen off the walls covered the floor, and when the door was opened a horrible tapestry of black cobwebs waved in the draught. He had been liberated a few days before – flung out of prison into the streets. And Miss Haldin seemed to see for the first time, a name and a face upon the body of that suffering people whose hard fate had been the subject of so many conversations, between her and her brother, in the garden of their country house.

He had been arrested with scores and scores of other people in that affair of the lithographed temperance tracts. Unluckily, having got hold of a great many suspected persons, the police thought they could extract from some of them other information relating to the revolutionist propaganda.

'They beat him so cruelly in the course of investigation,' went on the *dame de compagnie*, 'that they injured him internally. When they had done with him he was doomed. He could do nothing for himself. I beheld him lying on a wooden bedstead without any bedding, with his head on a bundle of dirty rags, lent to him out of charity by an old rag-picker, who happened to live in the basement of the house. There he was, uncovered, burning with fever, and there was not even a jug in the room for the water to quench his thirst with. There was nothing whatever – just that bedstead and the bare floor.'

'Was there no one in all that great town amongst the liberals and revolutionaries, to extend a helping hand to a brother?' asked Miss Haldin indignantly.

'Yes. But you do not know the most terrible part of that man's misery. Listen. It seems that they ill-used him so atrociously that, at last, his firmness gave way, and he did let out some information. Poor soul, the flesh is weak, you know. What it was he did not tell me. There was a crushed spirit in that mangled body. Nothing I found to say could make him whole. When they let him out, he crept into that hole, and bore his remorse stoically. He would not go near any one he knew. I would have sought assistance for him, but, indeed, where could I have gone looking for it? Where was I to look for any one who had anything to spare or any power to help? The people living round us were all starving and drunken. They were the victims of the Ministry of Finances. Don't ask me how we lived. I couldn't tell you. It was like a miracle of wretchedness. I had nothing to sell, and I assure you my clothes were in such a state that it was impossible for me to go out in the daytime. I was indecent. I had to wait till it was dark before I ventured into the streets to beg for a crust of bread, or whatever I could get, to keep him and me alive. Often I got nothing, and then I would crawl back and lie on the floor by the side of his couch. Oh yes, I can sleep quite soundly on bare boards. That is nothing, and I am only mentioning it to you so that you should not think I am a sybarite. It was infinitely less killing than the task of sitting for hours at a table in a cold study to take the books of Peter Ivanovitch from dictation. But you shall see yourself what that is like, so I needn't say any more about it.'

'It is by no means certain that I will ever take Peter Ivanovitch from dictation,' said Miss Haldin.

'No!' cried the other incredulously. 'Not certain? You mean to say that you have not made up your mind?'

When Miss Haldin assured her that there never had been any question of that between her and Peter Ivanovitch, the woman with the cat compressed her lips tightly for a moment.

'Oh, you will find yourself settled at the table before you know that you have made up your mind. Don't make a mistake, it is disenchanting to hear Peter Ivanovitch dictate, but at the same time there is a fascination about it. He is a man of genius. Your face is certain not to irritate him; you may perhaps even help his inspiration, make it easier for him to deliver his message. As I look at you, I feel certain that you are the kind of woman who is not likely to check the flow of his inspiration.'

Miss Haldin thought it useless to protest against all these assumptions.

'But this man – this workman – did he die under your care?' she said, after a short silence.

The *dame de compagnie*, listening up the stairs where now two voices were alternating with some animation, made no answer for a time. When the loud sounds of the discussion had sunk into an almost inaudible murmur, she turned to Miss Haldin.

'Yes, he died, but not, literally speaking, in my arms, as you might suppose. As a matter of fact, I was asleep when he breathed his last. So even now I cannot say I have seen anybody die. A few days before the end, some young men found us out in our extremity. They were revolutionists, as you might guess. He ought to have trusted in his political friends when he came out of prison. He had been liked and respected before, and nobody would have dreamed of reproaching him with his indiscretion before the police. Everybody knows how they go to work, and the strongest man has his moments of weakness before pain. Why, even hunger alone is enough to give one queer ideas as to what may be done. A doctor came, our lot was alleviated as far as physical comforts go, but otherwise he could not be consoled – poor man. I assure you, Miss Haldin, that he was very lovable, but I had not the strength to weep. I was nearly dead myself. But there were kind hearts to take care of me. A dress was found to clothe my nakedness. I tell you, I was not decent – and after a time the revolutionists placed me with a Jewish family going abroad, as governess. Of course I could teach the children, I finished the sixth class of the Lyceum; but the real object was, that I should carry some important papers across the frontier. I was entrusted with a packet which I carried next my heart. The gendarmes at the station did not suspect the governess of a Jewish family, busy looking after three children. I don't suppose those Hebrews knew what I had on me, for I had been introduced to them in a very roundabout way by persons who did not belong to the revolutionary movement, and naturally I had been instructed to accept a very small salary. When we reached Germany I left that family and delivered my papers to a revolutionist in Stuttgart; after this I was employed in various ways. But you do not want to hear all that. I have never felt that I was very useful, but I live in hopes of seeing all the Ministries destroyed, finances and all. The greatest joy of my life has been to hear what your brother has done.'

She directed her round eyes again to the sunshine outside, while the cat reposed within her folded arms in lordly beatitude and sphinx-like meditation.

'Yes! I rejoiced,' she began again. 'For me there is a heroic ring about the very name of Haldin. They must have been trembling with fear in their Ministries – all those men with fiendish hearts. Here I stand talking to you, and when I think of all the cruelties, oppressions, and injustices that are going on at this very moment, my head begins to swim. I have looked closely at what would seem inconceivable if one's own eyes had not to be trusted. I have looked at things that made me hate myself for my helplessness. I hated my hands that had no power, my voice that could not be heard, my very mind that would not become unhinged. Ah! I have seen things. And you?'

Miss Haldin was moved. She shook her head slightly.

'No, I have seen nothing for myself as yet,' she murmured. 'We have always lived in the country. It was my brother's wish.'

'It is a curious meeting – this – between you and me,' continued the other. 'Do you believe in chance, Miss Haldin? How could I have expected to see you, his sister, with my own eyes? Do you know that when the news came the revolutionaries here were as much surprised as pleased, every bit? No one seemed to know anything about your brother. Peter Ivanovitch himself had not foreseen that such a blow was going to be struck. I suppose your brother was simply inspired. I myself think that such deeds should be done by inspiration. It is a great privilege to have the inspiration and the opportunity. Did he resemble you at all? Don't you rejoice, Miss Haldin?'

'You must not expect too much from me,' said Miss Haldin, repressing an inclination to cry which came over her suddenly. She succeeded, then added calmly, 'I am not a heroic person!'

'You think you couldn't have done such a thing yourself, perhaps?'

'I don't know. I must not even ask myself till I have lived a little longer, seen more. . . .'

The other moved her head appreciatively. The purring of the cat had a loud complacency in the empty hall. No sounds of voices came from upstairs. Miss Haldin broke the silence.

'What is it precisely that you heard people say about my brother? You said that they were surprised. Yes, I supposed they were. Did it not seem strange to them that my brother should have failed to save himself after the most difficult part – that is, getting away from the spot – was over? Conspirators should understand these things well. There are reasons why I am very anxious to know how it is he failed to escape.'

The *dame de compagnie* had advanced to the open hall-door. She glanced rapidly over her shoulder at Miss Haldin, who remained within the hall.

'Failed to escape,' she repeated absently. 'Didn't he make the sacrifice of his life? Wasn't he just simply inspired? Wasn't it an act of abnegation? Aren't you certain?'

'What I am certain of,' said Miss Haldin, 'is that it was not an act of despair. Have you not heard some opinion expressed here upon his miserable capture?'

The *dame de compagnie* mused for a while in the doorway.

'Did I hear? Of course, everything is discussed here. Has not all the world been speaking about your brother? For my part, the mere mention of his achievement plunges me into an envious ecstasy. Why should a man certain of immortality think of his life at all?'

She kept her back turned to Miss Haldin. Upstairs from behind a great dingy white and gold door, visible behind the balustrade of the first floor landing, a deep voice began to drone formally, as if reading over notes or something of the sort. It paused frequently, and then ceased altogether.

'I don't think I can stay any longer now,' said Miss Haldin. 'I may return another day.'

She waited for the *dame de compagnie* to make room for her exit; but the woman appeared lost in the contemplation of sunshine and shadows, sharing between themselves the stillness of the deserted grounds. She concealed the view of the drive from Miss Haldin. Suddenly she said –

'It will not be necessary; here is Peter Ivanovitch himself coming up. But he is not alone. He is seldom alone now.'

Hearing that Peter Ivanovitch was approaching, Miss Haldin was not so pleased as she might have been expected to be. Somehow she had lost the desire to see either the heroic captive or Madame de S—, and the reason of that shrinking which came upon her at the very last minute is accounted for by the feeling that those two people had not been treating the woman with the cat kindly.

'Would you please let me pass?' said Miss Haldin at last, touching lightly the shoulder of the *dame de compagnie*.

But the other, pressing the cat to her breast, did not budge.

'I know who is with him,' she said, without even looking back.

More unaccountably than ever Miss Haldin felt a strong impulse to leave the house.

'Madame de S— may be engaged for some time yet, and what I have got to say to Peter Invanovitch is just a simple question which I might put to him when I meet him in the grounds on my way down. I really think I must go. I have been some time here, and I am anxious to get back to my mother. Will you let me pass, please?'

The *dame de compagnie* turned her head at last.

'I never supposed that you really wanted to see Madame de S—,' she said, with unexpected insight. 'Not for a moment.' There was something confidential and mysterious in her tone. She passed through the door, with Miss Haldin following her, on to the terrace, and they descended side by side the moss-grown stone steps. There was no one to be seen on the part of the drive visible from the front of the house.

'They are hidden by the trees over there,' explained Miss Haldin's new acquaintance, 'but you shall see them directly. I don't know who that young man is to whom Peter Ivanovitch has taken such a fancy. He must be one of us, or he would not be admitted here when the others come. You know what I mean by the others. But I must say that he is not at all mystically inclined. I don't know that I have made him out yet. Naturally I am never for very long in the drawing room. There is always something to do for me, though the establishment here is not so extensive as the villa on the Riviera. But still there are plenty of opportunities for me to make myself useful.'

To the left, passing by the ivy-grown end of the stables, appeared Peter Ivanovitch and his companion. They walked very slowly, conversing with some animation. They stopped for a moment, and Peter Ivanovitch was seen to gesticulate, while the young man listened motionless, with his arms hanging down and his head bowed a little. He was dressed in a dark brown suit and a black hat. The round eyes of the *dame de compagnie* remained fixed on the two figures, which had resumed their leisurely approach.

'An extremely polite young man,' she said. 'You shall see what a bow he will make; and it won't altogether be so exceptional either. He bows in the same way when he meets me alone in the hall.'

She moved on a few steps, with Miss Haldin by her side, and things happened just as she had foretold. The young man took off his hat, bowed, and fell back, while Peter Ivanovitch advanced quicker, his black, thick arms extended heartily, and seized hold of both Miss Haldin's hands, shook them, and peered at her through his dark glasses.

'That's right, that's right!' he exclaimed twice, approvingly. 'And so you have been looked after by . . .' He frowned slightly at the *dame de compagnie*, who was still nursing the cat. 'I conclude Eleanor – Madame de S— is engaged. I know she expected somebody today. So the newspaper man did turn up, eh? She is engaged?'

For all answer the *dame de compagnie* turned away her head.

'It is very unfortunate – very unfortunate indeed. I very much regret that you should have been . . .' He lowered suddenly his voice. 'But what is it – surely you are not departing, Natalia Victorovna? You got bored waiting, didn't you?'

'Not in the least,' Miss Haldin protested. 'Only I have been here some time, and I am anxious to get back to my mother.'

'The time seemed long, eh? I am afraid our worthy friend here' (Peter Ivanovitch suddenly jerked his head sideways towards his right shoulder and jerked it up again), – 'our worthy friend here has not the art of shortening the moments of waiting. No, distinctly she has not the art; and in that respect good intentions alone count for nothing.'

The *dame de compagnie* dropped her arms, and the cat found itself suddenly on the ground. It remained quite still after alighting, one hind leg stretched backwards. Miss Haldin was extremely indignant on behalf of the lady companion.

'Believe me, Peter Ivanovitch, that the moments I have passed in the hall of this house have been not a little interesting, and very instructive too. They are memorable. I do not regret the waiting, but I see that the object of my call here can be attained without taking up Madame de S—'s time.'

At this point I interrupted Miss Haldin. The above relation is founded on her narrative, which I have not so much dramatized as might be supposed. She had rendered, with extraordinary feeling and animation, the very accent almost of the disciple of the old apple-woman, the irreconcilable hater of Ministries, the voluntary servant of the poor. Miss Haldin's true and delicate humanity had been extremely shocked by the uncongenial fate of her new acquaintance, that lady companion, secretary, whatever she was. For my own part, I was pleased to discover in it one more obstacle to intimacy with Madame de S—. I had a positive abhorrence for the painted, bedizened, dead-faced, glassy-eyed Egeria of Peter Ivanovitch. I do not know what was her attitude to the unseen, but I know that in the affairs of this world she was avaricious, greedy, and unscrupulous. It was within my knowledge that she had been worsted in a sordid and desperate quarrel about money matters with the family of her late husband, the diplomatist. Some very august personages indeed (whom in her fury she had insisted upon scandalously involving in her affairs) had incurred her animosity. I find it perfectly easy to believe that she had come to within an ace of being spirited away, for reasons of state, into some discreet *maison de santé* – a madhouse of sorts, to be plain. It appears, however, that certain high-placed personages opposed it for reasons which . . .

But it's no use to go into details.

Wonder may be expressed at a man in the position of a teacher of languages knowing all this with such definiteness. A novelist says this and that of his personages, and if only he knows how to say it earnestly enough he may not be questioned upon the inventions of his brain in which his own belief is made sufficiently manifest by a telling phrase, a poetic image, the accent of emotion. Art is great! But I have no art, and not having invented Madame de S—, I feel bound to explain how I came to know so much about her.

My informant was the Russian wife of a friend of mine already mentioned, the professor of Lausanne University. It was from her that I learned the last fact of Madame de S—'s history, with which I intend to trouble my readers. She told me, speaking positively, as a person who trusts her sources, of the cause of Madame de S—'s flight from Russia, some years before. It was neither more or less than this: that she became suspect to the police in connection with the assassination of the Emperor Alexander. The ground of this suspicion was either some unguarded expressions that escaped her in public, or some talk overheard in her *salon*. Overheard, we must believe, by some guest, perhaps a friend, who hastened to play the informer, I suppose. At any rate, the overheard matter seemed to imply her foreknowledge of that event, and I think she was wise in not waiting for the investigation of such a charge. Some of my readers may remember a little book from her pen, published in Paris, a mystically bad-tempered, declamatory, and frightfully disconnected piece of writing, in which she all but admits the foreknowledge, more than hints at its supernatural origin, and plainly suggests in venomous innuendoes that the guilt of the act was not with the terrorists, but with a palace intrigue. When I observed to my friend, the professor's wife, that the life of Madame de S—, with its unofficial diplomacy, its intrigues, lawsuits, favours, disgrace, expulsions, its atmosphere of scandal, occultism, and charlatanism, was more fit for the eighteenth century than for the conditions of our own time, she assented with a smile, but a moment after went on in a reflective tone: 'Charlatanism? – yes, in a certain measure. Still, times are changed. There are forces now which were non-existent in the eighteenth century. I should not be surprised if she were more dangerous than an Englishman would be willing to believe. And what's more, she is looked upon as really dangerous by certain people – *chez nous*.'

Chez nous in this connection meant Russia in general, and the Russian political police in particular. The object of my digression from the straight course of Miss Haldin's relation (in my own words) of her visit to the Château Borel, was to bring forward that statement of my friend, the professor's wife. I wanted to bring it forward simply to make what I have to say presently of Mr Razumov's presence in Geneva, a little more credible – for this is a Russian story for Western ears, which, as I have observed already, are not attuned to certain tones of cynicism and cruelty, of moral negation, and even of moral distress already silenced at our end of Europe. And this I state as my excuse for having left Miss Haldin standing, one of the little group of two women and two men who had come together below the terrace of the Château Borel.

The knowledge which I have just stated was in my mind when, as I have said, I interrupted Miss Haldin. I interrupted her with the cry of profound satisfaction –

'So you never saw Madame S—, after all?'

Miss Haldin shook her head. It was very satisfactory to me. She had not seen Madame de S—! That was excellent, excellent! I welcomed the conviction that she would never know Madame de S— now. I could not explain the reason of the conviction but by the knowledge that Miss Haldin was standing face to face with her brother's wonderful friend. I preferred him to Madame de S— as the companion and guide of that young girl abandoned to her inexperience by the miserable end of her brother. But, at any rate, that life now ended had been sincere, and perhaps its thoughts might have been lofty, its moral sufferings profound, its last act a true sacrifice. It is not for us, the staid lovers calmed by the possession of a conquered liberty, to condemn without appeal the fierceness of thwarted desire.

I am not ashamed of the warmth of my regard for Miss Haldin. It was, it must be admitted, an unselfish sentiment, being its own reward. The late Victor Haldin – in the light of that sentiment – appeared to me not as a sinister conspirator, but as a pure enthusiast. I did not wish indeed to judge him, but the very fact that he did not escape, that fact which brought so much trouble to both his mother and his sister, spoke to me in his favour. Meantime, in my fear of seeing the girl surrender to the influence of the Château Borel revolutionary feminism, I was more than willing to put my trust in that friend of the late Victor Haldin. He was nothing but a name, you will say. Exactly! A name! And what's more, the only name; the only name to be found in the correspondence between brother and sister. The young man had turned up; they had come face to face, and, fortunately, without the direct interference of Madame de S—. What will come of it? what will she tell me presently? I was asking myself.

It was only natural that my thought should turn to the young man, the bearer of the only name uttered in all the dream-talk of a future to be brought about by a revolution. And my thought took the shape of asking myself why this young man had not called upon these ladies. He had been in Geneva for some days before Miss Haldin heard of him first in my presence from Peter Ivanovitch. I regretted that last's presence at their meeting. I would rather have had it happen somewhere out of his spectacled sight. But I supposed that, having both these young people there, he introduced them to each other.

I broke the silence by beginning a question on that point –

'I suppose Peter Ivanovitch . . .'

Miss Haldin gave vent to her indignation. Peter Ivanovitch directly he had got his answer from her had turned upon the *dame de compagnie* in a shameful manner.

'Turned upon her?' I wondered. 'What about? For what reason?'

'It was unheard of; it was shameful,' Miss Haldin pursued, with angry eyes. '*Il lui a fait une scène* – like this, before strangers. And for what? You would never guess. For some eggs. . . . Oh!'

I was astonished. 'Eggs, did you say?'

'For Madame de S—. That lady observes a special diet, or something of the sort. It seems she complained the day before to Peter Ivanovitch that the eggs were not rightly prepared. Peter Ivanovitch suddenly remembered this against the poor woman, and flew out at her. It was most astonishing. I stood as if rooted.'

'Do you mean to say that the great feminist allowed himself to be abusive to a woman?' I asked.

'Oh, not that! It was something you have no conception of. It was an odious performance. Imagine, he raised his hat to begin with. He made his voice soft and deprecatory. "Ah! you are not kind to us – you will not deign to remember . . ." This sort of phrases, that sort of tone. The poor creature was terribly upset. Her eyes ran full of tears. She did not know where to look. I shouldn't wonder if she would have preferred abuse, or even a blow.'

I did not remark that very possibly she was familiar with both on occasions when no one was by. Miss Haldin walked by my side, her head up in scornful and angry silence.

'Great men have their surprising peculiarities,' I observed inanely. 'Exactly like men who are not great. But that sort of thing cannot be kept up for ever. How did the great feminist wind up this very characteristic episode?'

Miss Haldin, without turning her face my way, told me that the end was brought about by the appearance of the interviewer, who had been closeted with Madame de S—.

He came up rapidly, unnoticed, lifted his hat slightly, and paused to say in French: 'The Baroness has asked me, in case I met a lady on my way out, to desire her to come in at once.'

After delivering this message, he hurried down the drive. The *dame de compagnie* flew towards the house, and Peter Ivanovitch followed her hastily, looking uneasy. In a moment Miss Haldin found herself alone with the young man, who undoubtedly must have been the new arrival from Russia. She wondered whether her brother's friend had not already guessed who she was.

I am in a position to say that, as a matter of fact, he had guessed. It is clear to me that Peter Ivanovitch, for some reason or other, had refrained from alluding to these ladies' presence in Geneva. But Razumov had guessed. The trustful girl! Every word uttered by Haldin lived in Razumov's memory. They were like haunting shapes; they could not be exorcized. The most vivid amongst them was the mention of the sister. The girl had existed for him ever since. But he did not recognize her at once. Coming up with Peter Ivanovitch, he did observe her; their eyes had met, even. He had responded, as no one could help responding, to the harmonious charm of her whole person, its strength, its grace, its tranquil frankness – and then he had turned his gaze away. He said to himself that all this was not for him; the beauty of women and the friendship of men were not for him. He accepted that feeling with a purposeful sternness, and tried to pass on. It was only her outstretched hand which brought about the recognition. It stands recorded in the pages of his self-confession, that it nearly suffocated him physically with an emotional reaction of hate and dismay, as though her appearance had been a piece of accomplished treachery.

He faced about. The considerable elevation of the terrace concealed them from anyone lingering in the doorway of the house; and even from the upstairs windows they could not have been seen. Through the thickets run wild, and the trees of the gently sloping grounds, he had cold, placid glimpses of the lake. A moment of perfect privacy had been vouchsafed to them at this juncture. I wondered to myself what use they had made of that fortunate circumstance.

'Did you have time for more than a few words?' I asked.

That animation with which she had related to me the incidents of her visit to the Château Borel had left her completely. Strolling by my side, she looked straight before her; but I noticed a little colour on her cheek. She did not answer me.

After some little time I observed that they could not have hoped to remain forgotten for very long, unless the other two had discovered Madame de S— swooning with fatigue, perhaps, or in a state of morbid exaltation after the long interview. Either would require their devoted ministrations. I could depict to myself Peter Ivanovitch rushing busily out of the house again, bareheaded, perhaps, and on across the terrace with his swinging gait, the black skirts of the frock-coat floating clear of his stout light grey legs. I confess to having looked upon these young people as the quarry of the 'heroic fugitive'. I had the notion that they would not be allowed to escape capture. But of that I said nothing to Miss Haldin, only as she still remained uncommunicative, I pressed her a little.

'Well – but you can tell me at least your impression.'

She turned her head to look at me, and turned away again.

'Impression?' she repeated slowly, almost dreamily; then in a quicker tone –

'He seems to be a man who has suffered more from his thoughts than from evil fortune.'

'From his thoughts, you say?'

'And that is natural enough in a Russian,' she took me up. 'In a young Russian; so many of them are unfit for action, and yet unable to rest.'

'And you think he is that sort of man?'

'No, I do not judge him. How could I, so suddenly? You asked for my impression – I explain my impression. I – I don't know the world, nor yet the people in it; I have been too solitary – I am too young to trust my own opinions.'

'Trust your instinct,' I advised her. 'Most women trust to that, and make no worse mistakes than men. In this case you have your brother's letter to help you.'

She drew a deep breath like a light sigh.

'Unstained, lofty, and solitary existences,' she quoted as if to herself. But I caught the wistful murmur distinctly.

'High praise,' I whispered to her.

'The highest possible.'

'So high that, like the award of happiness, it is more fit to come only at the end of a life. But still no common or altogether unworthy personality could have suggested such a confident exaggeration of praise and . . .'

'Ah!' She interrupted me ardently. 'And if you had only known the heart from which that judgement has come!'

She ceased on that note, and for a space I reflected on the character of the words which I perceived very well must tip the scale of the girl's feeling in that young man's favour. They had not the sound of a casual utterance. Vague they were to my Western mind and to my Western sentiment, but I could not forget that, standing by Miss Haldin's side, I was like a traveller in a strange country. It had also become clear to me that Miss Haldin was unwilling to enter into the details of the only material part of their visit to the Château Borel. But I was not hurt. Somehow I didn't feel it to be a want of confidence. It was some other difficulty – a difficulty I could not resent. And it was without the slightest resentment that I said –

'Very well. But on that high ground, which I will not dispute, you, like anyone else in such circumstances, you must have made for yourself a representation of that exceptional friend, a mental image of him, and – please tell me – you were not disappointed?'

'What do you mean? His personal appearance?'

'I don't mean precisely his good looks, or otherwise.'

We turned at the end of the alley and made a few steps without looking at each other.

'His appearance is not ordinary,' said Miss Haldin at last.

'No, I should have thought not – from the little you've said of your first impression. After all, one has to fall back on that word. Impression! What I mean is that something indescribable which is likely to mark a "not ordinary" person.'

I perceived that she was not listening. There was no mistaking her expression; and once more I had the sense of being out of it – not because of my age, which at any rate could draw inferences – but altogether out of it, on another plane whence I could only watch her from afar. And so ceasing to speak I watched her stepping out by my side.

'No,' she exclaimed suddenly, 'I could not have been disappointed with a man of such strong feeling.'

'Aha! Strong feeling,' I muttered, thinking to myself censoriously: like this, at once, all in a moment!

'What did you say?' inquired Miss Haldin innocently.

'Oh, nothing. I beg your pardon. Strong feeling. I am not surprised.'

'And you don't know how abruptly I behaved to him!' she cried remorsefully.

I suppose I must have appeared surprised, for, looking at me with a still more heightened colour, she said she was ashamed to admit that she had not been sufficiently collected; she had failed to control her words and actions as the situation demanded. She lost the fortitude worthy of both the men, the dead and the living; the fortitude which should have been the note of the meeting of Victor Haldin's sister with Victor Haldin's only known friend. He was looking at her keenly, but said nothing, and she was – she confessed – painfully affected by his want of comprehension. All she could say was: 'You are Mr Razumov.' A slight frown passed over his forehead. After a short, watchful pause, he made a little bow of assent, and waited.

At the thought that she had before her the man so highly regarded by her brother, the man who had known his value, spoken to him, understood him, had listened to his confidences, perhaps had encouraged him – her lips trembled, her eyes ran full of tears; she put out her hand, made a step towards him impulsively, saying with an effort to restrain her emotions, 'Can't you guess who I am?' He did not take the proffered hand. He even recoiled a pace, and Miss Haldin imagined that he was unpleasantly affected. Miss Haldin excused him, directing her displeasure at herself. She had behaved unworthily, like an emotional French girl. A manifestation of that kind could not be welcomed by a man of stern, self-contained character.

He must have been stern indeed, or perhaps very timid with women, not to respond in a more human way to the advances of a girl like Nathalie Haldin – I thought to myself. Those lofty and solitary existences (I remembered the words suddenly) make a young man shy and an old man savage – often.

'Well,' I encouraged Miss Haldin to proceed.

She was still very dissatisfied with herself.

'I went from bad to worse,' she said, with an air of discouragement very foreign to her. 'I did everything foolish except actually bursting into tears. I am thankful to say I did not do that. But I was unable to speak for quite a long time.'

She had stood before him speechless, swallowing her sobs, and when she managed at last to utter something, it was only her brother's name – 'Victor – Victor Haldin!' she gasped out, and again her voice failed her.

'Of course,' she commented to me, 'this distressed him. He was quite overcome. I have told you my opinion that he is a man of deep feeling – it is impossible to doubt it. You should have seen his face. He positively reeled. He leaned against the wall of the terrace. Their friendship must have been the very brotherhood of souls! I was grateful to him for that emotion, which made me feel less ashamed of my own lack of self-control. Of course I had regained the power of speech at once, almost. All this lasted not more than a few seconds. "I am his sister," I said. "Maybe you have heard of me." '

'And had he?' I interrupted.

'I don't know. How could it have been otherwise? And yet . . . But what does that matter? I stood there before him, near enough to be touched and surely not looking like an impostor. All I know is, that he put out both his hands then to me, I may say flung them out at me, with the greatest readiness and warmth, and that I seized and pressed them, feeling that I was finding again a little of what I thought was lost to me for ever, with the loss of my brother – some of that hope, inspiration, and support which I used to get from my dear dead . . .'

I understood quite well what she meant. We strolled on slowly. I refrained from looking at her. And it was as if answering my own thoughts that I murmured –

'No doubt it was a great friendship – as you say. And that young man ended by welcoming your name, so to speak, with both hands. After that, of course, you would understand each other. Yes, you would understand each other quickly.'

It was a moment before I heard her voice.

'Mr Razumov seems to be a man of few words. A reserved man – even when he is strongly moved.'

Unable to forget – or even to forgive – the bass-toned expansiveness of Peter Ivanovitch, the Arch-Patron of revolutionary parties, I said that I took this for a favourable trait of character. It was associated with sincerity – in my mind.

'And, besides, we had not much time,' she added.

'No, you would not have, of course.' My suspicion and even dread of the feminist and his Egeria was so ineradicable that I could not help asking with real anxiety, which I made smiling –

'But you escaped all right?'

She understood me, and smiled, too, at my uneasiness.

'Oh yes! I escaped, if you like to call it that. I walked away quickly. There was no need to run. I am neither frightened nor yet fascinated, like that poor woman who received me so strangely.'

'And Mr – Mr Razumov . . . ?'

'He remained there, of course. I suppose he went into the house after I left him. You remember that he came here strongly recommended to Peter Ivanovitch – possibly entrusted with important messages for him.'

'Ah yes! From that priest who . . .'

'Father Zosim – yes. Or from others, perhaps.'

'You left him, then. But have you seen him since, may I ask?'

For some time Miss Haldin made no answer to this very direct question, then –

'I have been expecting to see him here today,' she said quietly.

'You have! Do you meet him, then, in this garden? In that case I had better leave you at once.'

'No, why leave me? And we don't meet in this garden. I have not seen Mr Razumov since that first time. Not once. But I have been expecting him . . .'

She paused. I wondered to myself why that young revolutionist should show so little alacrity.

'Before we parted I told Mr Razumov that I walked here for an hour every day at this time. I could not explain to him then why I did not ask him to come and see us at once. Mother must be prepared for such a visit. And then, you see, I do not know myself what Mr Razumov has to tell us. He, too, must be told first how it is with poor mother. All these thoughts flashed through my mind at once. So I told him hurriedly that there was a reason why I could not ask him to see us at home, but that I was in the habit of walking here. . . . This is a public place, but there are never many people about at this hour. I thought it would do very well. And it is so near our apartments. I don't like to be very far away from mother. Our servant knows where I am in case I should be wanted suddenly.'

'Yes. It is very convenient from that point of view,' I agreed.

In fact, I thought the Bastions a very convenient place since the girl did not think it prudent as yet to introduce that young man to her mother. It was here, then, I thought, looking round at that plot of ground of deplorable banality, that their acquaintance will begin and go on in the exchange of generous indignations and of extreme sentiments, too poignant, perhaps, for a non-Russian mind to conceive. I saw these two, escaped out of four score of millions of human beings ground between the upper and nether millstone, walking under these trees, their young heads close together. Yes, an excellent place to stroll and talk in. It even occurred to me, while we turned once more away from the wide iron gates, that when tired they would have plenty of accommodation to rest themselves. There was a quantity of tables and chairs displayed between the restaurant chalet and the bandstand, a whole raft of painted deals spread out under the trees. In the very middle of it I observed a solitary Swiss couple, whose fate was made secure from the cradle to the grave by the perfected mechanism of democratic institutions in a republic that could almost be held in the palm of one's hand. The man, colourlessly uncouth, was drinking beer out of a glittering glass; the woman, rustic and placid, leaning back in the rough chair, gazed idly around.

There is little logic to be expected on this earth, not only in the matter of thought, but also of sentiment. I was surprised to discover myself displeased with that unknown young man. A week had gone by since they met. Was he callous, or shy, or very stupid? I could not make it out.

'Do you think,' I asked Miss Haldin, after we have gone some distance up the great alley, 'that Mr Razumov understood your intention?'

'Understood what I meant?' she wondered. 'He was greatly moved. That I know! In my own agitation I could see it. But I spoke distinctly. He heard me; he seemed, indeed, to hang on my words . . .'

Unconsciously she had hastened her pace. Her utterance, too, became quicker.

I waited a little before I observed thoughtfully –

'And yet he allowed all these days to pass.'

'How can we tell what work he may have to do here? He is not an idler travelling for his pleasure. His time may not be his own – nor yet his thoughts, perhaps.'

She slowed her pace suddenly, and in a lowered voice added –

'Or his very life' – then paused and stood still. 'For all I know, he may have had to leave Geneva the very day he saw me.'

'Without telling you!' I exclaimed incredulously.

'I did not give him time. I left him quite abruptly. I behaved emotionally to the end. I am sorry for it. Even if I had given him the opportunity he would have been justified in taking me for a person not to be trusted. An emotional, tearful girl is not a person to confide in. But even if he has left Geneva for a time, I am confident that we shall meet again.'

'Ah! you are confident. . . . I dare say. But on what ground?'

'Because I've told him that I was in great need of someone, a fellow-countryman, a felow-believer, to whom I could give my confidence in a certain matter.'

'I see. I don't ask you what answer he made. I confess that this is good ground for your belief in Mr Razumov's appearance before long. But he has not turned up today?'

'No,' she said quietly, 'not today'; and we stood for a time in silence, like people that have nothing more to say to each other and let their thoughts run widely asunder before their bodies go off their different ways. Miss Haldin glanced at the watch on her wrist and made a brusque movement. She had already overstayed her time, it seemed.

'I don't like to be away from mother,' she murmured, shaking her head. 'It is not that she is very ill now. But somehow when I am not with her I am more uneasy than ever.'

Mrs Haldin had not made the slightest allusion to her son for the last week or more. She sat, as usual, in the armchair by the window, looking out silently on that hopeless stretch of the Boulevard des Philosophes. When she spoke, a few lifeless words, it was of indifferent, trivial things.

'For any one who knows what the poor soul is thinking of, that sort of talk is more painful than her silence. But that is bad too; I can hardly endure it, and I dare not break it.'

Miss Haldin sighed, refastening a button of her glove which had come undone. I knew well enough what a hard time of it she must be having. The stress, its causes, its nature, would have undermined the health of an Occidental girl; but Russian natures have a singular power of resistance against the unfair strains of life. Straight and supple, with a short jacket open on her black dress, which made her figure appear more slender and her fresh but colourless face more pale, she compelled my wonder and admiration.

'I can't stay a moment longer. You ought to come soon to see mother. You know she calls you "*L'ami*". It is an excellent name and she really means it. And now *au revoir*, I must run.'

She glanced vaguely down the broad walk – the hand she put out to me eluded my grasp by an unexpected upward movement, and rested upon my shoulder. Her red lips were slightly parted, not in a smile, however, but expressing a sort of startled pleasure. She gazed towards the gates and said quickly, with a gasp –

'There! I knew it. Here he comes!'

I understood that she must mean Mr Razumov. A young man was walking up the alley, without haste. His clothes were some dull shade of brown, and he carried a stick. When my eyes first fell on him, his head was hanging on his breast as if in deep thought. While I was looking at him he raised it sharply, and at once stopped. I am certain he did, but that pause was nothing more perceptible than a faltering check in his gait, instantaneously overcome. Then he continued his approach, looking at us steadily. Miss Haldin signed to me to remain, and advanced a step or two to meet him.

I turned my head away from that meeting, and did not look at them again till I heard Miss Haldin's voice uttering his name in the way of introduction. Mr Razumov was informed, in a warm, low tone, that, besides being a wonderful teacher, I was a great support 'in our sorrow and distress'.

Of course I was described also as an Englishman. Miss Haldin spoke rapidly, faster than I have ever heard her speak, and that by contrast made the quietness of her eyes more expressive.

'I have given him my confidence,' she added, looking all the time at Mr Razumov. That young man did, indeed, rest his gaze on Miss Haldin, but certainly did not look into her eyes which were so ready for him. Afterwards he glanced backwards and forwards at us both, while the faint commencement of a forced smile, followed by the suspicion of a frown, vanished one after another; I detected them, though neither could have been noticed by a person less intensely bent upon divining him than myself. I don't know what Nathalie Haldin had observed, but my attention seized the very shades of these movements. The attempted smile was given up, the incipient frown was checked, and smoothed so that there should be no sign; but I imagined him exclaiming inwardly –

'Her confidence! To this elderly person – this foreigner!'

I imagined this because he looked foreign enough to me. I was upon the whole favourably impressed. He had an air of intelligence and even some distinction quite above the average of the students and other inhabitants of the *Petite Russie*. His features were more decided than in the generality of Russian faces; he had a line of the jaw, a clean-shaven, sallow cheek; his nose was a ridge, and not a mere protuberance. He wore the hat well down over his eyes, his dark hair curled low on the nape of his neck; in the ill-fitting brown clothes there were sturdy limbs; a slight stoop brought out a satisfactory breadth of shoulders. Upon the whole I was not disappointed. Studious – robust – shy. . . .

Before Miss Haldin had ceased speaking I felt the grip of his hand on mine, a muscular, firm grip, but unexpectedly hot and dry. Not a word or even a mutter assisted this short and arid handshake.

I intended to leave them to themselves, but Miss Haldin touched me lightly on the forearm with a significant contact, conveying a distant wish. Let him smile who likes, but I was only too ready to stay near Nathalie Haldin, and I am not ashamed to say that it was no smiling matter to me. I stayed, not as a youth would have stayed, uplifted, as it were poised in the air, but soberly, with my feet on the ground and my mind trying to penetrate her intention. She had turned to Razumov.

'Well. This is the place. Yes, it is here that I meant you to come. I have been walking every day. . . . Don't excuse yourself – I understand. I am grateful to you for coming to-day, but all the same I cannot stay now. It is impossible. I must hurry off home. Yes, even with you standing before me, I must run off. I have been too long away. . . . You know how it is?'

These last words were addressed to me. I noticed that Mr Razumov passed the tip of his tongue over his lips just as a parched, feverish man might do. He took her hand in its black glove, which closed on his, and held it – detained it quite visibly to me against a drawing-back movement.

'Thank you once more for – for understanding me,' she went on warmly. He interrupted her with a certain effect of roughness. I didn't like him speaking to this frank creature so much from under the brim of his hat, as it were. And he produced a faint, rasping voice quite like a man with a parched throat.

'What is there to thank me for? Understand you? . . . How did I understand you? . . . You had better know that I understand nothing. I was aware that you wanted to see me in this garden. I could not come before. I was hindered. And even to-day, you see . . . late.'

She still held his hand.

'I can, at any rate, thank you for not dismissing me from your mind as a weak, emotional girl. No doubt I want sustaining. I am very ignorant. But I can be trusted. Indeed I can!'

'You are ignorant,' he repeated thoughtfully. He had raised his head, and was looking straight into her face now, while she held his hand. They stood like this for a long moment. She released his hand.

'Yes. You did come late. It was good of you to come on the chance of me having loitered beyond my time. I was talking with this good friend here. I was talking of you. Yes, Kirylo Sidorovitch, of you. He was with me when I first heard of your being here in Geneva. He can tell you what comfort it was to my bewildered spirit to hear that news. He knew I meant to seek you out. It was the only object of my accepting the invitation of Peter Ivanovitch. . . .'

'Peter Ivanovitch talked to you of me,' he interrupted, in that wavering, hoarse voice which suggested a horribly dry throat.

'Very little. Just told me your name, and that you had arrived here. Why should I have asked for more? What could he have told me that I did not know already from my brother's letter? Three lines! And how much they meant to me! I will show them to you one day, Kirylo Sidorovitch. But now I must go. The first talk between us cannot be a matter of five minutes, so we had better not begin. . . .'

I had been standing a little aside, seeing them both in profile. At that moment it occurred to me that Mr Razumov's face was older than his age.

'If mother' – the girl had turned suddenly to me – 'were to wake up in my absence (so much longer than usual) she would perhaps question me. She seems to miss me more, you know, of late. She would want to know what delayed me – and, you see, it would be painful for me to dissemble before her.'

I understood the point very well. For the same reason she checked what seemed to be on Mr Razumov's part a movement to accompany her.

'No! No! I go alone, but meet me here as soon as possible.' Then to me in a lower, significant tone –

'Mother may be sitting at the window at this moment, looking down the street. She must not know anything of Mr Razumov's presence here till – till something is arranged.' She paused before she added a little louder, but still speaking to me, 'Mr Razumov does not quite understand my difficulty, but you know what it is.'

CHAPTER V

WITH A quick inclination of the head for us both, and an earnest, friendly glance at the young man, Miss Haldin left us covering our heads and looking after her straight, supple figure receding rapidly. Her walk was not that hybrid and uncertain gliding affected by some women, but a frank, strong, healthy movement forward. Rapidly she increased the distance – disappeared with suddenness at last. I discovered only then that Mr Razumov, after ramming his hat well over his brow, was looking me over from head to foot. I daresay I was a very unexpected fact for that young Russian to stumble upon. I caught in his physiognomy, in his whole bearing, an expression compounded of curiosity and scorn, tempered by alarm – as though he had been holding his breath while I was not looking. But his eyes met mine with a gaze direct enough. I saw then for the first time that they were of a clear brown colour and fringed with thick black eyelashes. They were the youngest feature of his face. Not at all unpleasant eyes. He swayed slightly, leaning on his stick and generally hung in the wind. It flashed upon me that in leaving us together Miss Haldin had an intention – that something was entrusted to me, since, by a mere accident I had been found at hand. On this assumed ground I put all possible friendliness into my manner. I cast about for some right thing to say, and suddenly in Miss Haldin's last words I perceived the clue to the nature of my mission.

'No,' I said gravely, if with a smile, 'you cannot be expected to understand.'

His clean-shaven lip quivered ever so little before he said, as if wickedly amused –

'But haven't you heard just now? I was thanked by that young lady for understanding so well.'

I looked at him rather hard. Was there a hidden and inexplicable sneer in this retort? No. It was not that. It might have been resentment. Yes. But what had he to resent? He looked as though he had not slept very well of late. I could almost feel on me the weight of his unrefreshed, motionless stare, the stare of a man who lies unwinking in the dark, angrily passive in the toils of disastrous thoughts.

Now, when I know how true it was, I can honestly affirm that this *was* the effect produced on me. It was painful in a curiously indefinite way – for, of course, the definition comes to me now while I sit writing in the fullness of my knowledge. But this is what the effect was at that time of absolute ignorance. This new sort of uneasiness which he seemed to be forcing upon me I attempted to put down by assuming a conversational, easy familiarity.

'That extremely charming and essentially admirable young girl (I am – as you see – old enough to be frank in my expressions) was referring to her own feelings. Surely you must have understood that much?'

He made such a brusque movement that he even tottered a little.

'Must understand this! Not expected to understand that! I may have other things to do. And the girl is charming and admirable. Well – and if she is! I suppose I can see that for myself.'

This sally would have been insulting if his voice had not been practically extinct, dried up in his throat; and the rustling effort of his speech too painful to give real offence.

I remained silent, checked between the obvious fact and the subtle impression. It was open to me to leave him there and then; but the sense of having been entrusted with a mission, the suggestion of Miss Haldin's last glance was strong upon me. After a moment of reflection I said –

'Shall we walk together a little?'

He shrugged his shoulders so violently that he tottered again. I saw it out of the corner of my eye as I moved on, with him at my elbow. He had fallen back a little and was practically out of my sight, unless I turned my head to look at him. I did not wish to indispose him still further by an appearance of marked curiosity. It might have been distasteful to such a young and secret refugee from under the pestilential shadow hiding the true, kindly face of his land. And the shadow, the attendant of his countrymen, stretching across the middle of Europe, was lying on him too, darkening his figure to my mental vision. 'Without doubt,' I said to myself, 'he seems a sombre, even a desperate revolutionist; but he is young, he may be unselfish and humane, capable of compassion, of . . .'

I heard him clear gratingly his parched throat, and became all attention.

'This is beyond everything,' were his first words. 'It is beyond everything! I find you here, for no reason that I can understand, in possession of something I cannot be expected to understand! A confidant! A foreigner! Talking about an admirable Russian girl. Is the admirable girl a fool, I begin to wonder? What are you at? What is your object?'

He was barely audible, as if his throat had no more resonance than a dry rag, a piece of tinder. It was so pitiful that I found it extremely easy to control my indignation.

'When you have lived a little longer, Mr Razumov, you will discover that no woman is an absolute fool. I am not a feminist, like that illustrious author, Peter Ivanovitch, who, to say the truth, is not a little suspect to me. . . .'

He interrupted me, in a surprising note of whispering astonishment.

'Suspect to you! Peter Ivanovitch suspect to you! To you! . . .'

'Yes, in a certin aspect he is,' I said, dismissing my remark lightly. 'As I was saying, Mr Razumov, when you have lived long enough, you will learn to discriminate between the noble trustfulness of a nature foreign to every meanness and the flattered credulity of some women; though even the credulous, silly as they may be, unhappy as they are sure to be, are never absolute fools. It is my belief that no woman is ever completely deceived. Those that are lost leap into the abyss with their eyes open, if all the truth were known.'

'Upon my word,' he cried at my elbow, 'what is it to me whether women are fools or lunatics? I really don't care what you think of them. I – I am not interested in them. I let them be. I am not a young man in a novel. How do you know that I want to learn anything about women? . . . What is the meaning of all this?'

'The object, you mean, of this conversation, which I admit I have forced upon you in a measure.'

'Forced! Object!' he repeated, still keeping half a pace or so behind me. 'You wanted to talk about women, apparently. That's a subject. But I don't care for it. I have never . . . In fact, I have had other subjects to think about.'

'I am concerned here with one woman only – a young girl – the sister of your dead friend – Miss Haldin. Surely you can think a little of her. What I meant from the first was that there is a situation which you cannot be expected to understand.'

I listened to his unsteady footfalls by my side for the space of several strides.

'I think that it may prepare the ground for your next interview with Miss Haldin if I tell you of it. I imagine that she might have had something of the kind in her mind when she left us together. I believe myself authorized to speak. The peculiar situation I have alluded to has arisen in the first grief and distress of Victor Haldin's execution. There was something peculiar in the circumstances of his arrest. You no doubt know the whole truth. . . .'

I felt my arm seized above the elbow, and next instant found myself swung so as to face Mr Razumov.

'You spring up from the ground before me with this talk. Who the devil are you? This is not to be borne! Why! What for? What do you know of what is or is not peculiar? What have you to do with any confounded circumstances, or with anything that happens in Russia, anyway?'

He leaned on his stick with his other hand, heavily; and when he let go of my arm, I was certain in my mind that he was hardly able to keep on his feet.

'Let us sit down at one of these vacant tables,' I proposed, disregarding this display of unexpectedly profound emotion. It was not without its effect on me, I confess. I was sorry for him.

'What tables? What are you talking about? Oh – the empty tables? The tables there. Certainly. I will sit at one of the empty tables.'

I led him away from the path to the very centre of the raft of deals before the *châlet*. The Swiss couple were gone by that time. We were alone on the raft, so to speak. Mr Razumov dropped into a chair, let fall his stick, and propped on his elbows, his head between his hands, stared at me persistently, openly, and continuously, while I signalled the waiter and ordered some beer. I could not quarrel with this silent inspection very well, because, truth to tell, I felt somewhat guilty of having been sprung on him with some abruptness – of having 'sprung from the ground', as he expressed it.

While waiting to be served I mentioned that, born from parents settled in St Petersburg, I had acquired the language as a child. The town I did not remember, having left it for good as a boy of nine, but in later years I had renewed my acquaintance with the language. He listened, without as much as moving his eyes the least little bit. He had to change his position when the beer came, and the instant draining of his glass revived him. He leaned back in his chair and, folding his arms across his chest, continued to stare at me squarely. It occurred to me that his clean-shaven, almost swarthy face was really of the very mobile sort, and that the absolute stillness of it was the acquired habit of a revolutionist, of a conspirator everlastingly on his guard against self-betrayal in a world of secret spies.

'But you are an Englishman – a teacher of English literature,' he murmured, in a voice that was no longer issuing from a parched throat. 'I have heard of you. People told me you have lived here for years.'

'Quite true. More than twenty years. And I have been assisting Miss Haldin with her English studies.'

'You have been reading English poetry with her,' he said, immovable now, like another man altogether, a complete stranger to the man of the heavy and uncertain footfalls a little while ago – at my elbow.

'Yes, English poetry,' I said. 'But the trouble of which I speak was caused by an English newspaper.'

He continued to stare at me. I don't think he was aware that the story of the midnight arrest had been ferreted out by an English journalist and given to the world. When I explained this to him he muttered contemptuously, 'It may have been altogether a lie.'

'I should think you are the best judge of that,' I retorted, a little disconcerted. 'I must confess that to me it looks to be true in the main.'

'How can you tell truth from lies?' he queried in his new, immovable manner.

'I don't know how you do it in Russia,' I began, rather nettled by his attitude. He interrupted me.

'In Russia, and in general everywhere – in a newspaper, for instance. The colour of the ink and the shapes of the letters are the same.'

'Well, there are other trifles one can go by. The character of the publication, the general verisimilitude of the news, the consideration of the motive, and so on. I don't trust blindly the accuracy of special correspondents – but why should this one have gone to the trouble of concocting a circumstantial falsehood on a matter of no importance to the world?'

'That's what it is,' he grumbled. 'What's going on with us is of no importance – a mere sensational story to amuse the readers of the papers – the superior contemptuous Europe. It is hateful to think of. But let them wait a bit!'

He broke off on this sort of threat addressed to the Western world. Disregarding the anger in his stare, I pointed out that whether the journalist was well- or ill-informed, the concern of the friends of these ladies was with the effect the few lines of print in question had produced – the effect alone. And surely he must be counted as one of the friends – if only for the sake of his late comrade and intimate fellow-revolutionist. At that point I thought he was going to speak vehemently; but he only astounded me by the convulsive start of his whole body. He restrained himself, folded his loosened arms tighter across his chest, and sat back with a smile in which there was a twitch of scorn and malice.

'Yes, a comrade and an intimate. . . . Very well,' he said.

'I ventured to speak to you on that assumption. And I cannot be mistaken. I was present when Peter Ivanovitch announced your arrival here to Miss Haldin, and I saw her relief and thankfulness when your name was mentioned. Afterwards she showed me her brother's letter, and read out the few words in which he alludes to you. What else but a friend could you have been?'

'Obviously. That's perfectly well known. A friend. Quite correct. . . . Go on. You were talking of some effect.'

I said to myself: 'He puts on the callousness of a stern revolutionist, the insensibility to common emotions of a man devoted to a destructive idea. He is young, and his sincerity assumes a pose before a stranger, a foreigner, an old man. Youth must assert itself. . . .' As concisely as possible I exposed to him the state of mind poor Mrs Haldin had been thrown into by the news of her son's untimely end.

He listened – I felt it – with profound attention. His level stare deflected gradually downwards, left my face, and rested at last on the ground at his feet.

'You can enter into the sister's feelings. As you said, I have only read a little English poetry with her, and I won't make myself ridiculous in your eyes by trying to speak of her. But you have seen her. She is one of these rare human beings that do not want explaining. At least I think so. They had only that son, that brother, for a link with the wider world, with the future. The very groundwork of active existence for Nathalie Haldin is gone with him. Can you wonder then that she turns with eagerness to the only man her brother mentions in his letters. Your name is a sort of legacy.'

'What could he have written of me?' he cried, in a low, exasperated tone.

'Only a few words. It is not for me to repeat them to you, Mr Razumov; but you may believe my assertion that these words are forcible enough to make both his mother and his sister believe implicitly in the worth of your judgement and in the truth of anything you may have to say to them. It's impossible for you now to pass them by like strangers.'

I paused, and for a moment sat listening to the footsteps of the few people passing up and down the broad central walk. While I was speaking his head had sunk upon his breast above his folded arms. He raised it sharply.

'Must I go then and lie to that old woman!'

It was not anger; it was something else, something more poignant, and not so simple. I was aware of it sympathetically, while I was profoundly concerned at the nature of that exclamation.

'Dear me! Won't the truth do, then? I hoped you could have told me something consoling. I am thinking of the poor mother now. Your Russia *is* a cruel country.'

He moved a little in his chair.

'Yes,' I repeated. 'I thought you would have had something authentic to tell.'

The twitching of his lips before he spoke was curious.

'What if it is not worth telling?'

'Not worth – from what point of view? I don't understand.'

'From every point of view.'

I spoke with some asperity.

'I should think that anything which could explain the circumstances of that midnight arrest. . . .'

'Reported by a journalist for the amusement of the civilized Europe,' he broke in scornfully.

'Yes, reported. . . . But aren't they true? I can't make out your attitude in this. Either the man is a hero to you, or . . .'

He approached his face with fiercely distended nostrils close to mine so suddenly that I had the greatest difficulty in not starting back.

'You ask me! I suppose it amuses you, all this. Look here! I am a worker. I studied. Yes, I studied very hard. There is intelligence here.' (He tapped his forehead with his finger-tips.) 'Don't you think a Russian may have sane ambitions? Yes – I had even prospects. Certainly! I had. And now you see me here, abroad, everything gone, lost, sacrificed. You see me here – and you ask! You see me, don't you? – sitting before you.'

He threw himself back violently. I kept outwardly calm.

'Yes, I see you here; and I assume you are here on account of the Haldin affair?'

His manner changed.

'You call it the Haldin affair – do you?' he observed indifferently.

'I have no right to ask you anything,' I said. 'I wouldn't presume. But in that case the mother and the sister of him who must be a hero in your eyes cannot be indifferent to you. The girl is a frank and generous creature, having the noblest – well – illusions. You will tell her nothing – or you will tell her everything. But speaking now of the object with which I've approached you: first, we have to deal with the morbid state of the mother. Perhaps something could be invented under your authority as a cure for a distracted and suffering soul filled with maternal affection.'

His air of weary indifference was accentuated, I could not help thinking, wilfully.

'Oh yes. Something might,' he mumbled carelessly.

He put his hands over his mouth to conceal a yawn. When he uncovered his lips they were smiling faintly.

'Pardon me. This has been a long conversation, and I have not had much sleep the last two nights.'

This unexpected, somewhat insolent sort of apology had the merit of being perfectly true. He had had no nightly rest to speak of since that day when, in the grounds of the Château Borel, the sister of Victor Haldin had appeared before him. The perplexities and the complex terrors – I may say – of this sleeplessness are recorded in the document I was to see later – the document which is the main source of this narrative. At the moment he looked to me convincingly tired, gone slack all over, like a man who has passed through some sort of crisis

'I have had a lot of urgent writing to do,' he added.

I rose from my chair at once, and he followed my example, without haste, a little heavily.

'I must apologize for detaining you so long,' I said.

'Why apologize? One can't very well go to bed before night. And you did not detain me. I could have left you at any time.'

I had not stayed with him to be offended.

'I am glad you have been sufficiently interested,' I said calmly. 'No merit of mine, though – the commonest sort of regard for the mother of your friend was enough. . . . As to Miss Haldin herself, she at one time was disposed to think that her brother had been betrayed to the police in some way.'

To my great surprise Mr Razumov sat down again suddenly. I stared at him, and I must say that he returned my stare without winking for quite a considerable time.

'In some way,' he mumbled, as if he had not understood or could not believe his ears.

'Some unforeseen event, a sheer accident might have done that,' I went on. 'Or, as she characteristically put it to me, the folly or weakness of some unhappy fellow-revolutionist.'

'Folly or weakness,' he repeated bitterly.

'She is a very generous creature,' I observed after a time. The man admired by Victor Haldin fixed his eyes on the ground. I turned away and moved off, apparently unnoticed by him. I nourished no resentment of the moody brusqueness with which he had treated me. The sentiment I was carrying away from that conversation was that of hopelessness. Before I had got fairly clear of the raft of chairs and tables he had rejoined me.

'H'm, yes!' I heard him at my elbow again. 'But what do you think?'

I did not look round even.

'I think that you people are under a curse.'

He made no sound. It was only on the pavement outside the gate that I heard him again.

'I should like to walk with you a little.'

After all, I preferred this enigmatical young man to his celebrated compatriot, the great Peter Ivanovitch. But I saw no reason for being particularly gracious.

'I am going now to the railway station, by the shortest way from here, to meet a friend from England,' I said, for all answer to his unexpected proposal. I hoped that something informing could come of it. As we stood on the kerbstone waiting for a tramcar to pass, he remarked gloomily –

'I like what you said just now.'

'Do you?'

We stepped off the pavement together.

'The great problem,' he went on, 'is to understand thoroughly the nature of the curse.'

'That's not very difficult, I think.'

'I think so too,' he agreed with me, and his readiness, strangely enough, did not make him less enigmatical in the least.

'A curse is an evil spell,' I tried him again. 'And the important, the great problem, is to find the means to break it.'

'Yes. To find the means.'

That was also an assent, but he seemed to be thinking of something else. We had crossed diagonally the open space before the theatre, and began to descend a broad, sparsely frequented street in the direction of one of the smaller bridges. He kept on by my side without speaking for a long time.

'You are not thinking of leaving Geneva soon?' I asked.

He was silent for so long that I began to think I had been indiscreet, and should get no answer at all. Yet on looking at him I almost believed that my question had caused him something in the nature of positive anguish. I detected it mainly in the clasping of his hands, in which he put a great force stealthily. Once, however, he had overcome that sort of agonizing hesitation sufficiently to tell me that he had no such intention, he became rather communicative – at least relatively to the former off-hand curtness of his speeches. The tone, too, was more amiable. He informed me that he intended to study and also to write. He went even so far as to tell me he had been to Stuttgart. Stuttgart, I was aware, was one of the revolutionary centres. The directing committee of one of the Russian parties (I can't tell now which) was located in that town. It was there that he got into touch with the active work of the revolutionists outside Russia.

'I have never been abroad before,' he explained, in a rather inanimate voice now. Then, after a slight hesitation, altogether different from the agonizing irresolution my first simple question 'whether he meant to stay in Geneva' had aroused, he made me an unexpected confidence –

'The fact is, I have received a sort of mission from them.'

'Which will keep you here in Geneva?'

'Yes. Here. In this odious . . .'

I was satisfied with my faculty for putting two and two together when I drew the inference that the mission had something to do with the person of the great Peter Ivanovitch. But I kept that surmise to myself naturally, and Mr Razumov said nothing more for some considerable time. It was only when we were nearly on the bridge we had been making for that he opened his lips again, abruptly –

'Could I see that precious article anywhere?'

I had to think for a moment before I saw what he was referring to.

'It has been reproduced in parts by the Press here. There are files to be seen in various places. My copy of the English newspaper I have left with Miss Haldin, I remember, on the day after it reached me. I was sufficiently worried by seeing it lying on a table by the side of the poor mother's chair for weeks. Then it disappeared. It was a relief, I assure you.'

He had stopped short.

'I trust,' I continued, 'that you will find time to see these ladies fairly often – that you will make time.'

He stared at me so queerly that I hardly know how to define his aspect. I could not understand it in this connection at all. What ailed him? I asked myself. What strange thought had come into his head? What vision of all the horrors that can be seen in his hopeless country had come suddenly to haunt his brain? If it were anything connected with the fate of Victor Haldin, then I hoped earnestly he would keep it to himself for ever. I was, to speak plainly, so shocked that I tried to conceal my impression by – Heaven forgive me – a smile and the assumption of a light manner.

'Surely,' I exclaimed, 'that needn't cost you a great effort.'

He turned away from me and leaned over the parapet of the bridge. For a moment I waited, looking at his back. And yet, I assure you, I was not anxious just then to look at his face again. He did not move at all. He did not mean to move. I walked on slowly on my way towards the station, and at the end of the bridge I glanced over my shoulder. No, he had not moved. He hung well over the parapet, as if captivated by the smooth rush of the blue water under the arch. The current there is swift, extremely swift; it makes some people dizzy; I myself can never look at it for any length of time without experiencing a dread of being suddenly snatched away by its destructive force. Some brains cannot resist the suggestion of irresistible power and of headlong motion.

It apparently had a charm for Mr Razumov. I left him hanging far over the parapet of the bridge. The way he had behaved to me could not be put down to mere boorishness. There was something else under his scorn and impatience. Perhaps, I thought, with sudden approach to hidden truth, it was the same thing which had kept him over a week, nearly ten days indeed, from coming near Miss Haldin. But what it was I could not tell.

Part Third

Chapter I

The water under the bridge ran violent and deep. Its slightly undulating rush seemed capable of scouring out a channel for itself through solid granite while you looked. But had it flowed through Razumov's breast, it could not have washed away the accumulated bitterness the wrecking of his life had deposited there.

'What is the meaning of all this?' he thought, staring downwards at the headlong flow so smooth and clean that only the passage of a faint air-bubble, or a thin vanishing streak of foam like a white hair, disclosed its vertiginous rapidity, its terrible force. 'Why has that meddlesome old Englishman blundered against me? And what is this silly tale of a crazy old woman?'

He was trying to think brutally on purpose, but he avoided any mental reference to the young girl. 'A crazy old woman,' he repeated to himself. 'It is a fatality! Or ought I to despise all this as absurd? But no! I am wrong! I can't afford to despise anything. An absurdity may be the starting-point of the most dangerous complications. How is one to guard against it? It puts to rout one's intelligence. The more intelligent one is the less one suspects an absurdity.'

A wave of wrath choked his thoughts for a moment. It even made his body leaning over the parapet quiver; then he resumed his silent thinking, like a secret dialogue with himself. And even in that privacy, his thought had some reservations of which he was vaguely conscious.

'After all, this is not absurd. It is insignificant. It is absolutely insignificant – absolutely. The craze of an old woman – the fussy officiousness of a blundering elderly Englishman. What devil put him in the way? Haven't I treated him cavalierly enough? Haven't I just? That's the way to treat these meddlesome persons. Is it possible that he still stands behind my back, waiting?'

Razumov felt a faint chill run down his spine. It was not fear. He was certain that it was not fear – not fear for himself – but it was, all the same, a sort of apprehension as if for another, for someone he knew without being able to put a name to the personality. But the recollection that the officious Englishman had a train to meet tranquillized him for a time. It was too stupid to suppose that he should be wasting his time in waiting. It was unnecessary to look round and make sure.

But what did the man mean by his extraordinary rigmarole about the newspaper, and that crazy old woman? he thought suddenly. It was a damnable presumption, anyhow, something that only an Englishman could be capable of. All this was a sort of sport for him – the sport of revolution – a game to look at from the height of his superiority. And what on earth did he mean by his exclamation, 'Won't the truth do?'

Razumov pressed his folded arms to the stone coping over which he was leaning with force. 'Won't the truth do? The truth for the crazy old mother of the –'

The young man shuddered again. Yes. The truth would do! Apparently it would do. Exactly. And receive thanks, he thought, formulating the unspoken words cynically. 'Fall on my neck in gratitude, no doubt,' he jeered mentally. But this mood abandoned him at once. He felt sad, as if his heart had become empty suddenly. 'Well, I must be cautious,' he concluded, coming to himself as though his brain had been awakened from a trance. 'There is nothing, no one, too insignificant, too absurd to be disregarded,' he thought wearily. 'I must be cautious.'

Razumov pushed himself with his hand away from the balustrade and, retracing his steps along the bridge, walked straight to his lodgings, where, for a few days, he led a solitary and retired existence. He neglected Peter Ivanovitch, to whom he was accredited by the Stuttgart group; he never went near the refugee revolutionists, to whom he had been introduced on his arrival. He kept out of that world altogether. And he felt that such conduct, causing surprise and arousing suspicion, contained an element of danger for himself.

This is not to say that during these few days he never went out. I met him several times in the streets, but he gave me no recognition. Once, going home after an evening call on the ladies Haldin, I saw him crossing the dark road of the Boulevard des Philosophes. He had a broad-brimmed soft hat, and the collar of his coat turned up. I watched him make straight for the house, but, instead of going in, he stopped opposite the still lighted windows, and after a time went away down a side-street.

I knew that he had not been to see Mrs Haldin yet. Miss Haldin told me he was reluctant; moreover, the mental condition of Mrs Haldin had changed. She seemed to think now that her son was living, and she perhaps awaited his arrival. Her immobility in the great armchair in front of the window had an air of expectancy, even when the blind was down and the lamps lighted.

For my part, I was convinced that she had received her deathstroke; Miss Haldin, to whom, of course, I said nothing of my forebodings, thought that no good would come from introducing Mr Razumov just then, an opinion which I shared fully. I knew that she met the young man on the Bastions. Once or twice I saw them strolling slowly up the main alley. They met every day for weeks. I avoided passing that way during the hour when Miss Haldin took her exercise there. One day, however, in a fit of absent-mindedness, I entered the gates and came upon her walking alone. I stopped to exchange a few words. Mr Razumov failed to turn up, and we began to talk about him – naturally.

'Did he tell you anything definite about your brother's activities – his end?' I ventured to ask.

'No,' admitted Miss Haldin, with some hesitation. 'Nothing definite.'

I understood well enough that all their conversations must have been referred mentally to that dead man who had brought them together. That was unavoidable. But it was in the living man that she was interested. That was unavoidable too, I suppose. And as I pushed my inquiries I discovered that he had disclosed himself to her as a by no means conventional revolutionist, contemptuous of catchwords, of theories of men too. I was rather pleased at that – but I was a little puzzled.

'His mind goes forward, far ahead of the struggle,' Miss Haldin explained. 'Of course, he is an actual worker too,' she added.

'And do you understand him?' I inquired point-blank.

She hesitated again. 'Not altogether,' she murmured.

I perceived that he had fascinated her by an assumption of mysterious reserve.

'Do you know what I think?' she went on, breaking through her reserved, almost reluctant attitude: 'I think that he is observing, studying me, to discover whether I am worthy of his trust . . .'

'And that pleases you?'

She kept mysteriously silent for a moment. Then with energy, but in a confidential tone –

'I am convinced,' she declared, 'that this extraordinary man is meditating some vast plan, some great undertaking; he is possessed by it – he suffers from it – and from being alone in the world.'

'And so he's looking for helpers?' I commented, turning away my head.

Again there was a silence.

'Why not?' she said at last.

The dead brother, the dying mother, the foreign friend, had fallen into a distant background. But, at the same time, Peter Ivanovitch was absolutely nowhere now. And this thought consoled me. Yet I saw the gigantic shadow of Russian life deepening around her like the darkness of an advancing night. It would devour her presently. I inquired after Mrs Haldin – that other victim of the deadly shade.

A remorseful uneasiness appeared in her frank eyes. Mother seemed no worse, but if I only knew what strange fancies she had sometimes! Then Miss Haldin, glancing at her watch, declared that she could not stay a moment longer, and with a hasty hand-shake ran off lightly.

Decidedly, Mr Razumov was not to turn up that day. Incomprehensible youth!

But less than an hour afterwards, while crossing the Place Mollard, I caught sight of him boarding a South Shore tramcar.

'He's going to the Château Borel,' I thought.

After depositing Razumov at the gates of the Château Borel, some half a mile or so from the town, the car continued its journey between two straight lines of shady trees. Across the roadway in the sunshine a short wooden pier jutted into the shallow pale water, which farther out had an intense blue tint contrasting unpleasantly with the green orderly slopes on the opposite shore. The whole view, with the harbour jetties of white stone underlining lividly the dark front of the town to the left, and the expanding space of water to the right with jutting promontories of no particular character, had the uninspiring, glittering quality of a very fresh oleograph. Razumov turned his back on it with contempt. He thought it odious – oppressively odious – in its unsuggestive finish: the very perfection of mediocrity attained at last after centuries of toil and culture. And turning his back on it, he faced the entrance to the grounds of the Château Borel.

The bars of the central way and the wrought-iron arch between the dark weather-stained stone piers were very rusty; and, though fresh tracks of wheels ran under it, the gate looked as if it had not been opened for a very long time. But close against the lodge, built of the same grey stone as the piers (its windows were all boarded up), there was a small side entrance. The bars of that were rusty too; it stood ajar and looked as though it had not been closed for a long time. In fact, Razumov, trying to push it open a little wider, discovered it was immovable.

'Democratic virtue. There are no thieves here, apparently,' he muttered to himself, with displeasure. Before advancing into the grounds he looked back sourly at an idle working man lounging on a bench in the clean, broad avenue. The fellow had thrown his feet up; one of his arms hung over the low back of the public seat; he was taking a day off in lordly repose, as if everything in sight belonged to him.

'Elector! Eligible! Enlightened!' Razumov muttered to himself. 'A brute, all the same.'

Razumov entered the grounds and walked fast up the wide sweep of the drive, trying to think of nothing – to rest his head, to rest his emotions too. But arriving at the foot of the terrace before the house he faltered, affected physically by some invisible interference. The mysteriousness of his quickened heart-beats startled him. He stopped short and looked at the brick wall of the terrace, faced with shallow arches, meagrely clothed by a few unthriving creepers, with an ill-kept narrow flower-bed along its foot.

'It is here' he thought, with a sort of awe. 'It is here – on this very spot . . .'

He was tempted to flight at the mere recollection of his first meeting with Nathalie Haldin. He confessed it to himself; but he did not move, and that not because he wished to resist an unworthy weakness, but because he knew that he had no place to fly to. Moreover, he could not leave Geneva. He recognized, even without thinking, that it was impossible. It would have been a fatal admission, an act of moral suicide. It would have been also physically dangerous. Slowly he ascended the stairs of the terrace, flanked by two stained greenish stone urns of funereal aspect.

Across the broad platform, where a few blades of grass sprouted on the discoloured gravel, the door of the house, with its ground-floor windows shuttered, faced him, wide open. He believed that his approach had been noted, because, framed in the doorway, without his tall hat, Peter Ivanovitch seemed to be waiting for his approach.

The ceremonious black frock-coat and the bared head of Europe's greatest feminist accentuated the dubiousness of his status in the house rented by Madame de S—, his Egeria. His aspect combined the formality of the caller with the freedom of the proprietor. Florid and bearded and masked by the dark blue glasses, he met the visitor, and at once took him familiarly under the arm.

Razumov suppressed every sign of repugnance by an effort which the constant necessity of prudence had rendered almost mechanical. And this necessity had settled his expression in a cast of austere, almost fanatical, aloofness. The 'heroic fugitive', impressed afresh by the severe detachment of this new arrival from revolutionary Russia, took a conciliatory, even a confidential tone. Madame de S— was resting after a bad night. She often had bad nights. He had left his hat upstairs on the landing and had come down to suggest to his young friend a stroll and a good open-hearted talk in one of the shady alleys behind the house. After voicing this proposal, the great man glanced at the unmoved face by his side, and could not restrain himself from exclaiming –

'On my word, young man, you are an extraordinary person.'

'I fancy you are mistaken, Peter Ivanovitch. If I were really an extraordinary person, I would not be here, walking with you in a garden of Switzerland, Canton of Geneva, Commune of – what's the name of the Commune this place belongs to? . . . Never mind – the heart of democracy, anyhow. A fit heart for it; no bigger than a parched pea and about as much value. I am no more extraordinary than the rest of us Russians, wandering abroad.'

But Peter Ivanovitch dissented emphatically –

'No! No! You are not ordinary. I have some experience of Russians who are – well – living abroad. You appear to me, and to others too, a marked personality.'

'What does he mean by this?' Razumov asked himself, turning his eyes fully on his companion. The face of Peter Ivanovitch expressed a meditative seriousness.

'You don't suppose, Kirylo Sidorovitch, that I have not heard of you from various points where you made yourself known on your way here? I have had letters.'

'Oh, we are great in talking about each other,' interjected Razumov, who had listened with great attention. 'Gossip, tales, suspicions, and all that sort of thing, we know how to deal in to perfection. Calumny, even.'

In indulging in this sally, Razumov managed very well to conceal the feeling of anxiety which had come over him. At the same time he was saying to himself that there could be no earthly reason for anxiety. He was relieved by the evident sincerity of the protesting voice.

'Heavens!' cried Peter Ivanovitch. 'What are you talking about? What reasons can *you* have to . . .?'

The great exile flung up his arms as if words had failed him in sober truth. Razumov was satisfied. Yet he was moved to continue in the same vein.

'I am talking of the poisonous plants which flourish in the world of conspirators, like evil mushrooms in a dark cellar.'

'You are casting aspersions,' remonstrated Peter Ivanovitch, 'which as far as you are concerned –'

'No!' Razumov interrupted without heat. 'Indeed, I don't want to cast aspersions, but it's just as well to have no illusions.'

Peter Ivanovitch gave him an inscrutable glance of his dark spectacles, accompanied by a faint smile.

'The man who says that he has no illusions has at least that one,' he said, in a very friendly tone. 'But I see how it is, Kirylo Sidorovitch. You aim at stoicism.'

'Stoicism! That's a pose of the Greeks and the Romans. Let's leave it to them. We are Russians, that is – children; that is – sincere; that is – cynical, if you like. But that's not a pose.'

A long silence ensued. They strolled slowly under the lime-trees. Peter Ivanovitch had put his hands behind his back. Razumov felt the ungravelled ground of the deeply shaded walk damp and as if slippery under his feet. He asked himself, with uneasiness, if he were saying the right things. The direction of the conversation ought to have been more under his control, he reflected. The great man appeared to be reflecting on his side too. He cleared his throat slightly, and Razumov felt at once a painful reawakening of scorn and fear.

'I am astonished,' began Peter Ivanovitch gently. 'Supposing you are right in your indictment, how can you raise any question of calumny or gossip, in your case? It is unreasonable. The fact is, Kirylo Sidorovitch, there is not enough known of you to give hold to gossip or even calumny. Just now you are a man associated with a great deed, which had been hoped for, and tried for too, without success. People have perished for attempting that which you and Haldin have done at last. You come to us out of Russia, with that prestige. But you cannot deny that you have not been communicative, Kirylo Sidorovitch. People you have met imparted their impressions to me; one wrote this, another that, but I form my own opinions. I waited to see you first. You are a man out of the common. That's positively so. You are close, very close. This taciturnity, this severe brow, this something inflexible and secret in you, inspires hopes and a little wonder as to what you may mean. There is something of a Brutus . . .'

'Pray spare me those classical allusions!' burst out Razumov nervously. 'What comes Junius Brutus to do here? It is ridiculous! Do you mean to say,' he added sarcastically, but lowering his voice, 'that the Russian revolutionists are all patricians and that I am an aristocrat?'

Peter Ivanovitch, who had been helping himself with a few gestures, clasped his hands again behind his back, and made a few steps, pondering.

'Not *all* patricians,' he muttered at last. 'But you, at any rate, are one of *us*.'

Razumov smiled bitterly.

'To be sure my name is not Gugenheimer,' he said in a sneering tone. 'I am not a democratic Jew. How can I help it? Not everybody has such luck. I have no name, I have no . . .'

The European celebrity showed a great concern. He stepped back a pace and his arms flew in front of his person, extended, deprecatory, almost entreating. His deep bass voice was full of pain.

'But, my dear young friend!' he cried. 'My dear Kirylo Sidorovitch . . .'

Razumov shook his head.

'The very patronymic you are so civil as to use when addressing me I have no legal right to – but what of that? I don't wish to claim it. I have no father. So much the better. But I will tell you what: my mother's grandfather was a peasant – a serf. See how much I am one of *you*. I don't want anyone to claim me. But Russia *can't* disown me. She cannot!'

Razumov struck his breast with his fist.

'I am *it*!'

Peter Ivanovitch walked on slowly, his head lowered. Razumov followed, vexed with himself. That was not the right sort of talk. All sincerity was an imprudence. Yet one could not renounce truth altogether, he thought, with despair. Peter Ivanovitch, meditating behind his dark glasses, became to him suddenly so odious that if he had had a knife, he fancied he could have stabbed him not only without compunction, but with a horrible triumphant satisfaction.

His imagination dwelt on that atrocity in spite of himself. It was as if he were becoming light-headed. 'It is not what is expected of me,' he repeated to himself. 'It is not what is – I could get away by breaking the fastening on the little gate I see there in the back wall. It is a flimsy lock. Nobody in the house seems to know he is here with me. Oh yes. The hat! These women would discover presently that hat he has left on the landing. They would come upon him, lying dead in this damp, gloomy shade – but I would be gone and no one could ever . . . Lord! Am I going mad?' he asked himself in a fright.

The great man was heard – musing in an undertone.

'H'm, yes! That – no doubt – in a certain sense . . .' He raised his voice. 'There is a deal of pride about you . . .'

The intonation of Peter Ivanovitch took on a homely, familiar ring, acknowledging, in a way, Razumov's claim to peasant descent.

'A great deal of pride, brother Kirylo. And I don't say that you have no justification for it. I have admitted you had. I have ventured to allude to the facts of your birth simple because I attach no means importance to it. You are one of us – *un des nôtres*. I reflect on that with satisfaction.'

'I attach some importance to it also,' and Razumov quietly. 'I won't even deny that it may have some importance for you too,' he continued, after a slight pause and with a touch of grimness of which he was himself aware, with some annoyance. He hoped it had escaped the perception of Peter Ivanovitch. 'But suppose we talk no more about it?'

'Well, we shall not – not after this one time, Kirylo Sidorovitch,' persisted the noble arch-priest of Revolution. 'This shall be the last occasion. You cannot believe for a moment that I had the slightest idea of wounding your feelings. You are clearly a superior nature – that's how I read you. Quite above the common – h'm – susceptibilities. But the fact is, Kirylo Sidorovitch, I don't know your susceptibilities. Nobody, out of Russia, knows much of you – as yet!'

'You have been watching me?' suggested Razumov.

'Yes.'

The great man had spoken in a tone of perfect frankness, but as they turned their faces to each other Razumov felt baffled by the dark spectacles. Under their cover, Peter Ivanovitch hinted that he had felt for some time the need of meeting a man of energy and character, in view of a certain point. He said nothing more precise, however; and after some critical remarks upon the personalities of the various members of the committee of revolutionary action in Stuttgart, he let the conversation lapse for quite a long while. They paced the alley from end to end. Razumov, silent too, raised his eyes from time to time to cast a glance at the back of the house. It offered no sign of being inhabited. With its grimy, weather-stained walls and all the windows shuttered from top to bottom, it looked damp and gloomy and deserted. It might very well have been haunted in traditional style by some doleful, groaning, futile ghost of a middleclass order. The shades evoked, as worldly rumour had it, by Madame de S— to meet statesmen, diplomats, deputies of various European Parliaments, must have been of another sort. Razumov had never seen Madame de S— but in the carriage.

Peter Ivanovitch came out of his abstraction.

'Two things I may say to you at once. I believe, first, that neither a leader nor any decisive action can come out of the dregs of a people. Now, if you ask me what are the dregs of a people – h'm – it would take too long to tell. You would be surprised at the variety of ingredients that for me go to the making up of these dregs – of that which ought, *must* remain at the bottom. Moreover, such a statement might be subject to discussion. But I can tell you what is *not* the dregs. On that it is impossible for us to disagree. The peasantry of a people is not the dregs; neither is its highest class – well – the nobility. Reflect on that, Kirylo Sidorovitch! I believe you are well fitted for reflection. Everything in a people that is not genuine, not its own by origin or development, is – well – dirt! Intelligence in the wrong place is that. Foreign-bred doctrines are that. Dirt! Dregs! The second thing I would offer to your meditation is this: that for us at this moment there yawns a chasm between the past and the future. It can never be bridged by foreign liberalism. All attempts at it are either folly or cheating. Bridged it can never be! It has to be filled up.'

A sort of sinister jocularity had crept into the tones of the burly feminist. He seized Razumov's arm above the elbow, and gave it a slight shake.

'Do you understand, enigmatical young man? It has got to be just filled up.'

Razumov kept an unmoved countenance.

'Don't you think that I have already gone beyond meditation on that subject?' he said, freeing his arm by a quiet movement which increased the distance a little between himself and Peter Ivanovitch, as they went on strolling abreast. And he added that surely whole cartloads of words and theories could never fill that chasm. No meditation was necessary. A sacrifice of many lives could alone – He fell silent without finishing the phrase.

Peter Ivanovitch inclined his big hairy head slowly. After a moment he proposed that they should go and see if Madame de S— was now visible.

'We shall get some tea,' he said, turning out of the shaded gloomy walk with a brisker step.

The lady companion had been on the look-out. Her dark skirt whisked into the doorway as the two men came in sight round the corner. She ran off somewhere altogether, and had disappeared when they entered the hall. In the crude light falling from the dusty glass skylight upon the black and white tessellated floor, covered with muddy tracks, their footsteps echoed faintly. The great feminist led the way up the stairs. On the balustrade of the first-floor landing a shiny tall hat reposed, rim upwards, opposite the double door of the drawing-room, haunted, it was said, by evoked ghosts, and frequented, it was to be supposed, by fugitive revolutionists. The cracked white paint of the panels, the tarnished gilt of the mouldings, permitted one to imagine nothing but dust and emptiness within. Before turning the massive brass handle, Peter Ivanovitch gave his young companion a sharp, partly critical, partly preparatory glance.

'No one is perfect,' he murmured discreetly. Thus the possessor of a rare jewel might, before the casket, warn the profane that no gem perhaps is flawless.

He remained with his hand on the door-handle so long that Razumov assented by a moody 'No.'

'Perfection itself would not produce that effect,' pursued Peter Ivanovitch, 'in a world not meant for it. But you shall find there a mind – no! – the quintessence of feminine intuition which will understand any perplexity you may be suffering from by the irresistible, enlightening force of sympathy. Nothing can remain obscure before that – that – inspired, yes, inspired penetration, this true light of femininity.'

The gaze of the dark spectacles in its glossy steadfastness gave his face an air of absolute conviction. Razumov felt a momentary shrinking before that closed door.

'Penetration? Light,' he stammered out. 'Do you mean some sort of thought-reading?'

Peter Ivanovitch seemed shocked.

'I mean something utterly different,' he retorted, with a faint, pitying smile.

Razumov began to feel angry, very much against his wish.

'This is very mysterious,' he muttered through his teeth.

'You don't object to being understood, to being guided?' queried the great feminist.

Razumov exploded in a fierce whisper.

'In what sense? Be pleased to understand that I am a serious person. Who do you take me for?'

They looked at each other very closely. Razumov's temper was cooled by the impenetrable earnestness of the blue glasses meeting his stare. Peter Ivanovitch turned the handle at last.

'You shall know directly,' he said, pushing the door open.

A low-pitched grating voice was heard within the room.

'*Enfin vous voilà.*'

In the doorway, his black-coated bulk blocking the view, Peter Ivanovitch boomed in a hearty tone with something boastful in it:

'Yes. Here I am!'

He glanced over his shoulder at Razumov, who waited for him to move on.

'And I am bringing you a proved conspirator – a real one this time. *Un vrai celui-là.*'

This pause in the doorway gave the 'proved conspirator' time to make sure that his face did not betray his angry curiosity and his mental disgust.

These sentiments stand confessed in Mr Razumov's memorandum of his first interview with Madame de S—. The very words I use in my narrative are written where their sincerity cannot be suspected. The record, which could not have been meant for anyone's eyes but his own, was not, I think, the outcome of that strange impulse of indiscretion common to men who lead secret lives, and account for the invariable existence of 'compromising documents' in all the plots and conspiracies of history. Mr Razumov looked at it, I suppose, as a man looks at himself in a mirror, with wonder, perhaps with anguish, with anger or despair. Yes, as a threatened man may look fearfully at his own face in the glass, formulating to himself reassuring excuses for his appearance marked by the taint of some insidious hereditary disease.

Chapter II

The Egeria of the 'Russian Mazzini' produced, at first view, a strong effect by the death-like immobility of an obviously painted face. The eyes appeared extraordinarily brilliant. The figure, in a close-fitting dress, admirably made, but by no means fresh, had an elegant stiffness. The rasping voice inviting him to sit down, the rigidity of the upright attitude with one arm extended along the back of the sofa, the white gleam of the big eyeballs setting off the black, fathomless stare of the enlarged pupils, impressed Razumov more than anything he had seen since his hasty and secret departure from St Petersburg. A witch in Parisian clothes, he thought. A portent! He actually hesitated in his advance, and did not even comprehend, at first, what the rasping voice was saying.

'Sit down. Draw your chair nearer me. There –'

He sat down. At close quarters the rouged cheek-bones, the wrinkles, the fine lines on each side of the vivid lips, astounded him. He was being received graciously, with a smile which made him think of a grinning skull.

'We have been hearing about you for some time.'

He did not know what to say, and murmured some disconnected words. The grinning skull effect vanished.

'And do you know that the general complaint is that you have shown yourself very reserved everywhere?'

Razumov remained silent for a time, thinking of his answer.

'I, don't you see, am a man of action,' he said huskily, glancing upwards.

Peter Ivanovitch stood in portentous expectant silence by the side of his chair. A slight feeling of nausea came over Razumov. What could be the relations of these two people to each other? She like a galvanized corpse out of some Hoffmann's Tale – he the preacher of feminist gospel for all the world, and a super-revolutionist besides! This ancient, painted mummy with unfathomable eyes, and this burly, bull-necked, deferential . . . what was it? Witchcraft, fascination. . . . 'It's for her money,' he thought. 'She has millions!'

The walls, the floor of the room were bare like a barn. The few pieces of furniture had been discovered in the garrets and dragged down into service without having been properly dusted, even. It was the refuse the banker's widow had left behind her. The windows without curtains had an indigent, sleepless look. In two of them the dirty yellowy-white blinds had been pulled down. All this spoke, not of poverty, but of sordid penuriousness.

The hoarse voice on the sofa uttered angrily –

'You are looking round, Kirylo Sidorovitch. I have been shamefully robbed, positively ruined.'

A rattling laugh, which seemed beyond her control, interrupted her for a moment.

'A slavish nature would find consolation in the fact that the principal robber was an exalted and almost a sacrosanct person – a Grand Duke, in fact. Do you understand, Mr Razumov? A Grand Duke – No! You have no idea what thieves those people are! Downright thieves!'

Her bosom heaved, but her left arm remained rigidly extended along the back of the couch.

'You will only upset yourself,' breathed out a deep voice, which, to Razumov's startled glance, seemed to proceed from under the steady spectacles of Peter Ivanovitch, rather than from his lips, which had hardly moved.

'What of that? I say thieves! *Voleurs! Voleurs!*'

Razumov was quite confounded by this unexpected clamour, which had in it something of wailing and croaking, and more than a suspicion of hysteria.

'*Voleurs! Voleurs! Vol . .*'

'No power on earth can rob you of your genius,' shouted Peter Ivanovitch in an overpowering bass, but without stirring, without a gesture of any kind. A profound silence fell.

Razumov remained outwardly impassive. 'What is the meaning of this performance? he was asking himself. But with a preliminary sound of bumping outside some door behind him, the lady companion, in a threadbare black skirt and frayed blouse, came in rapidly, walking on her heels, and carrying in both hands a big Russian samovar, obviously too heavy for her. Razumov made an instinctive movement to help which startled her so much that she nearly dropped her hissing burden. She managed, however to land it on the table, and looked so frightened that Razumov hastened to sit down. She produced then, from an adjacent room, four glass tumblers, a teapot, and a sugar-basin, on a black iron tray.

The rasping voice asked from the sofa abruptly –

'*Les gâteaux*? Have you remembered to bring the cakes?'

Peter Ivanovitch, without a word, marched out on to the landing, and returned instantly with a parcel wrapped up in white glazed paper, which he must have extracted from the interior of his hat. With imperturbable gravity he undid the string and smoothed the paper open on a part of the table within reach of Madame de S—'s hand. The lady companion poured out the tea, then retired into a distant corner out of everybody's sight. From time to time Madame de S— extended a claw-like hand, glittering with costly rings, towards the paper of cakes, took up one and devoured it, displaying her big false teeth ghoulishly. Meantime she talked in a hoarse tone of the political situation in the Balkans. She built great hopes on some complication in the peninsula for arousing a great movement of national indignation in Russia against 'these thieves – thieves – thieves'.

'You will only upset yourself,' Peter Ivanovitch interposed, raising his glassy gaze. He smoked cigarettes and drank tea in silence, continuously. When he had finished a glass, he flourished his hand above his shoulder. At that signal the lady companion, ensconced in her corner, with round eyes like a watchful animal, would dart out to the table and pour him out another tumblerful.

Razumov looked at her once or twice. She was anxious, tremulous, though neither Madame de S— nor Peter Ivanovitch paid the slightest attention to her. 'What have they done between them to that forlorn creature?' Razumov asked himself. 'Have they terrified her out of her senses with ghosts, or have they only been beating her?' When she gave him his second glass of tea, he noticed that her lips trembled in the manner of a scared person about to burst into speech. But of course she said nothing, and retired into her corner, as if hugging to herself the smile of thanks he gave her.

'She may be worth cultivating,' thought Razumov suddenly.

He was calming down, getting hold of the actuality into which he had been thrown – for the first time perhaps since Victor Haldin had entered his room . . . and had gone out again. He was distinctly aware of being the object of the famous – or notorious – Madame de S—'s ghastly graciousness.

Madame de S— was pleased to discover that this young man was different from the other types of revolutionist members of committees, secret emissaries, vulgar and unmannerly fugitive professors, rough students, ex-cobblers with apostolic faces, consumptive and ragged enthusiasts. Hebrew youths, common fellows of all sorts that used to come and go around Peter Ivanovitch – fanatics, pedants, proletarians all. It was pleasant to talk to this young man of notably good appearance – for Madame de S— was not always in a mystical state of mind. Razumov's taciturnity only excited her to a quicker, more voluble utterance. It still dealt with the Balkans. She knew all the statesmen of that region, Turks, Bulgarians, Montenegrins, Roumanians, Greeks, Armenians, and nondescripts young and old, the living and the dead. With some money an intrigue could be started which would set the Peninsula in a blaze and outrage the sentiment of the Russian people. A cry of abandoned brothers could be raised, and then, with the nation seething with indignation, a couple of regiments or so would be enough to begin a military revolution in St Petersburg and make an end of these thieves. . . .

'Apparently I've got only to sit still and listen,' the silent Razumov thought to himself. 'As to that hairy and obscene brute' (in such terms did Mr Razumov refer mentally to the popular expounder of a feministic conception of social state), 'as to him, for all his cunning he too shall speak out some day.'

Razumov ceased to think for a moment. Then a sombre-toned reflection formulated itself in his mind, ironical and bitter. 'I have the gift of inspiring confidence.' He heard himself laughing aloud. It was like a goad to the painted, shiny-eyed harridan on the sofa.

'You may well laugh,' she cried hoarsely. 'What else can one do! Perfect swindlers – and what base swindlers at that! Cheap Germans – Holstein-Gottorps! Though, indeed, it's hardly safe to say who and what they are. A family that counts a creature like Catherine the Great in its ancestry – you understand!'

'You are only upsetting yourself,' said Peter Ivanovitch, patiently but in a firm tone. This admonition had its usual effect on the Egeria. She dropped her thick, discoloured eyelids and changed her position on the sofa. All her angular and lifeless movements seemed completely automatic now that her eyes were closed. Presently she opened them very full. Peter Ivanovitch drank tea steadily, without haste.

'Well, I declare!' She addressed Razumov directly. 'The people who have seen you on your way here are right. You are very reserved. You haven't said twenty words altogether since you came in. You let nothing of your thoughts be seen in your face either.'

'I have been listening, Madame,' said Razumov, using French for the first time, hesitatingly, not being certain of his accent. But it seemed to produce an excellent impression. Madame de S— looked meaningly into Peter Ivanovitch's spectacles, as if to convey her conviction of this young man's merit. She even nodded the least bit in his direction, and Razumov heard her murmur under her breath the words, 'Later on in the diplomatic service,' which could not but refer to the favourable impression he had made. The fantastic absurdity of it revolted him because it seemed to outrage his ruined hopes with the vision of a mock-career. Peter Ivanovitch, impassive as though he were deaf, drank some more tea. Razumov felt that he must say something.

'Yes,' he began deliberately, as if uttering a meditated opinion. 'Clearly. Even in planning a purely military revolution the temper of the people should be taken into account.'

'You have understood me perfectly. The discontent should be spiritualized. That is what the ordinary heads of revolutionary committees will not understand. They aren't capable of it. For instance, Mordatiev was in Geneva last month. Peter Ivanovitch brought him here. You know Mordatiev? Well, yes – you have heard of him. They call him an eagle – a hero! He has never done half as much as you have. Never attempted – not half . . .'

Madame de S— agitated herself angularly on the sofa.

'We, of course, talked to him. And do you know what he said to me? "What have we to do with Balkan intrigues? We must simply extirpate the scoundrels." Extirpate is all very well – but what then? The imbecile! I screamed at him, "But you must spiritualize – don't you understand? – spiritualize the discontent" . . .'

She felt nervously in her pocket for a handkerchief; she pressed it to her lips.

'Spiritualize?' said Razumov interrogatively, watching her heaving breast. The long ends of an old black lace scarf she wore over her head slipped off her shoulders and hung down on each side of her ghastly rosy cheeks.

'An odious creature,' she burst out again. 'Imagine a man who takes five lumps of sugar in his tea. . . . Yes, I said spiritualize! How else can you make discontent effective and universal?'

'Listen to this, young man,' Peter Ivanovitch made himself heard solemnly. 'Effective and universal.'

Razumov looked at him suspiciously.

'Some say hunger will do that,' he remarked.

'Yes. I know. Our people are starving in heaps. But you can't make famine universal. And it is not despair that we want to create. There is no moral support to be got out of that. It is indignation. . . .'

Madame de S— let her thin, extended arm sink on her knees.

'I am not a Mordatiev,' began Razumov.

'*Bien sûr*!' murmured Madame de S—.

'Though I too am ready to say extirpate, extirpate! But in my ignorance of political work, permit me to ask: A Balkan – well – intrigue, wouldn't that take a very long time?'

Peter Ivanovitch got up and moved off quietly, to stand with his face to the window. Razumov heard a door close; he turned his head and perceived that the lady companion had scuttled out of the room.

'In matters of politics I am a supernaturalist.' Madame de S— broke the silence harshly.

Peter Ivanovitch moved away from the window and struck Razumov lightly on the shoulder. This was a signal for leaving, but at the same time he addressed Madame de S— in a peculiar reminding tone –

'Eleanor!'

Whatever it meant, she did not seem to hear him. She leaned back in the corner of the sofa like a wooden figure. The immovable peevishness of the face, framed in the limp, rusty lace, had a character of cruelty.

'As to extirpating,' she croaked at the attentive Razumov, 'there is only one class in Russia which must be extirpated. Only one. And that class consists of only one family. You understand me? That one family must be extirpated.'

Her rigidity was frightful, like the rigour of a corpse galvanized into harsh speech and glittering stare by the force of murderous hate. The sight fascinated Razumov – yet he felt more self-possessed than at any other time since he had entered this weirdly bare room. He was interested. But the great feminist by his side again uttered his appeal –

'Eleanor.'

She disregarded it. Her carmine lips vaticinated with an extraordinary rapidity. The liberating spirit would use arms before which rivers would part like Jordan, and ramparts fall down like the walls of Jericho. The deliverance from bondage would be effected by plagues and by signs, by wonders and by war. The women . . .

'Eleanor!'

She ceased; she had heard him at last. She pressed her hand to her forehead.

'What is it? Ah yes! That girl – the sister of . . .'

It was Miss Haldin that she meant. That young girl and her mother had been leading a very retired life. They were provincial ladies – were they not? The mother had been very beautiful – traces were left yet. Peter Ivanovitch, when he called there for the first time, was greatly struck. . . . But the cold way they received him was really surprising.

'He is one of our national glories,' Madame de S— cried out, with sudden vehemence. 'All the world listens to him.'

'I don't know these ladies,' said Razumov loudly, rising from his chair.

'What are you saying, Kirylo Sidorovitch? I understand that she was talking to you here, in the garden, the other day.'

'Yes, in the garden,' said Razumov gloomily. Then, with an effort, 'She made herself known to me.'

'And then ran away from us all,' Madame de S— continued, with ghastly vivacity. 'After coming to the very door! What a peculiar proceeding! Well, I have been a shy little provincial girl at one time. Yes, Razumov' (she fell into this familiarity intentionally, with an appalling grimace of graciousness. Razumov gave a perceptible start), 'yes, that's my origin. A simple provincial family.'

'You are a marvel,' Peter Ivanovitch uttered in his deepest voice.

But it was to Razumov that she gave her death's-head smile. Her tone was quite imperious.

'You must bring the wild young thing here. She is wanted. I reckon upon your success – mind!'

'She is not a wild young thing,' muttered Razumov, in a surly voice.

'Well, then – that's all the same. She may be one of these young conceited democrats. Do you know what I think? I think she is very much like you in character. There is a smouldering fire of scorn in you. You are darkly self-sufficient, but I can see your very soul.'

Her shiny eyes had a dry, intense stare, which, missing Razumov, gave him an absurd notion that she was looking at something which was visible to her behind him. He cursed himself for an impressionable fool, and asked with forced calmness –

'What is it you see? Anything resembling me?'

She moved her rigidly set face from left to right, negatively.

'Some sort of phantom in my image?' pursued Razumov slowly. 'For, I suppose, a soul when it is seen is just that. A vain thing. There are phantoms of the living as well as of the dead.'

The tenseness of Madame de S—'s stare had relaxed, and now she looked at Razumov in a silence that became disconcerting.

'I myself have had an experience,' he stammered out, as if compelled. 'I've seen a phantom once.'

The unnaturally red lips moved to frame a question harshly.

'Of a dead person?'

'No. Living.'

'A friend?'

'No.'

'An enemy?'

'I hated him.'

'Ah! It was not a woman, then?'

'A woman!' repeated Razumov, his eyes looking straight into the eyes of Madame de S—. 'Why should it have been a woman? And why this conclusion? Why should I not have been able to hate a woman?'

As a matter of fact, the idea of hating a woman was new to him. At that moment he hated Madame de S—. But it was not exactly hate. It was more like the abhorrence that may be caused by a wooden or plaster figure of a repulsive kind. She moved no more than if she were such a figure; even her eyes, whose unwinking stare plunged into his own, though shining, were lifeless, as though they were as artificial as her teeth. For the first time Razumov became aware of a faint perfume, but faint as it was it nauseated him exceedingly. Again Peter Ivanovitch tapped him slightly on the shoulder. Thereupon he bowed, and was about to turn away when he received the unexpected favour of a bony, inanimate hand extended to him, with the two words in hoarse French –

'*Au revoir!*'

He bowed over the skeleton hand and left the room, escorted by the great man, who made him go out first. The voice from the sofa cried after them –

'You remain here, *Pierre*.'

'Certainly, *ma chère amie*.'

But he left the room with Razumov, shutting the door behind him. The landing was prolonged into a bare corridor, right and left, desolate perspectives of white and gold decoration without a strip of carpet. The very light, pouring through a large window at the end, seemed dusty; and a solitary speck reposing on the balustrade of white marble – the silk top-hat of the great feminist – asserted itself extremely, black and glossy in all that crude whiteness.

Peter Ivanovitch escorted the visitor without opening his lips. Even when they had reached the head of the stairs Peter Ivanovitch did not break the silence. Razumov's impulse to continue down the flight and out of the house without as much as a nod abandoned him suddenly. He stopped on the first step and leaned his back against the wall. Below him the great hall with its chequered floor of black and white seemed absurdly large and like some public place where a great power of resonance awaits the provocation of footfalls and voices. As if afraid of awakening the loud echoes of that empty house, Razumov adopted a low tone.

'I really have no mind to turn into a dilettante spiritualist.'

Peter Ivanovitch shook his head slightly, very serious.

'Or spend my time in spiritual ecstasies or sublime meditations upon the gospel of feminism,' continued Razumov. 'I made my way here for my share of action – action, most respected Peter Ivanovitch! It was not the great European writer who attracted me, here, to this odious town of liberty. It was somebody much greater. It was the idea of the chief which attracted me. There are starving young men in Russia who believe in you so much that it seems the only thing that keeps them alive in their misery. Think of that, Peter Ivanovitch! No! But only think of that!'

The great man, thus entreated, perfectly motionless and silent, was the very image of patient, placid respectability.

'Of course I don't speak of the people. They are brutes,' added Razumov, in the same subdued but forcible tone. At this, a protesting murmur issued from the 'heroic fugitive's' beard. A murmur of authority.

'Say – children.'

'No! Brutes.' Razumov insisted bluntly.

'But they are sound, they are innocent,' the great man pleaded in a whisper.

'As far as that goes, a brute is sound enough.' Razumov raised his voice at last. 'And you can't deny the natural innocence of a brute. But what's the use of disputing about names? You just try to give these children the power and stature of men and see what they will be like. You just give it to them and see. . . . But never mind. I tell you, Peter Ivanovitch, that half a dozen young men do not come together nowadays in a shabby student's room without your name being whispered, not as a leader of thought, but as a centre of revolutionary energies – the centre of action. What else has drawn me near you, do you think? It is not what all the world knows of you surely. It's precisely what the world at large does not know. I was irresistibly drawn – let us say impelled, yes, impelled; or, rather, compelled, driven – driven,' repeated Razumov loudly, and ceased, as if startled by the hollow reverberation of the word 'driven' along two bare corridors and in the great empty hall.

Peter Ivanovitch did not seem startled in the least. The young man could not control a dry, uneasy laugh. The great revolutionist remained unmoved with an effect of commonplace, homely superiority.

'Curse him,' said Razumov to himself, 'he is waiting behind his spectacles for me to give myself away.' Then aloud, with a satanic enjoyment of the scorn prompting him to play with the greatness of the great man –

'Ah, Peter Ivanovitch, if you only knew the force which drew – no, which *drove* me towards you! The irresistible force.'

He did not feel any desire to laugh now. This time Peter Ivanovitch moved his head sideways, knowingly, as much as to say, 'Don't I?' This expressive movement was almost imperceptible. Razumov went on in secret derision –

'All these days you have been trying to read me, Peter Ivanovitch. That is natural. I have perceived it and I have been frank. Perhaps you may think I have not been very expansive? But with a man like you it was not needed; it would have looked like an impertinence, perhaps. And besides, we Russians are prone to talk too much as a rule. I have always felt that. And yet, as a nation, we are dumb. I assure you that I am not likely to talk to you so much again – ha! ha! –'

Razumov, still keeping on the lower step, came a little nearer to the great man.

'You have been condescending enough. I quite understood it was to lead me on. You must render me the justice that I have not tried to please. I have been impelled, compelled, or rather sent – let us say sent – towards you for a work that no one but myself can do. You would call it a harmless delusion: a ridiculous delusion at which you don't even smile. It is absurd of me to talk like this, yet some day you will remember these words, I hope. Enough of this. Here I stand before you – confessed! But one thing more I must add to complete it: a mere blind tool I can never consent to be.'

Whatever acknowledgement Razumov was prepared for, he was not prepared to have both his hands seized in the great man's grasp. The swiftness of the movement was aggressive enough to startle. The burly feminist could not have been quicker had his purpose been to jerk Razumov treacherously up on the landing and bundle him behind one of the numerous closed doors near by. This idea actually occurred to Razumov; his hands being released after a darkly eloquent squeeze, he smiled, with a beating heart, straight at the beard and the spectacles hiding that impenetrable man.

He thought to himself (it stands confessed in his hand-writing), 'I won't move from here till he either speaks or turns away. This is a duel.' Many seconds passed without a sign or sound.

'Yes, yes,' the great man said hurriedly, in subdued tones, as if the whole thing had been a stolen, breathless interview. 'Exactly. Come to see us here in a few days. This must be gone into deeply – deeply, between you and me. Quite to the bottom. To the . . . And, by the by, you must bring along Natalia Victorovna – you know, the Haldin girl . . .'

'Am I to take this as my first instruction from you?' inquired Razumov stiffly.

Peter Ivanovitch seemed perplexed by this new attitude.

'Ah! h'm! You are naturally the proper person – *la personne indiquée*. Everyone shall be wanted presently. Everyone.'

He bent down from the landing over Razumov, who had lowered his eyes.

'The moment of action approaches,' he murmured.

Razumov did not look up. He did not move till he heard the door of the drawing-room close behind the greatest of feminists returning to his painted Egeria. Then he walked down slowly into the hall. The door stood open, and the shadow of the house was lying aslant over the greatest part of the terrace. While crossing it slowly, he lifted his hat and wiped his damp forehead, expelling his breath with force to get rid of the last vestiges of the air he had been breathing inside. He looked at the palms of his hands, and rubbed them gently against his thighs.

He felt, bizarre as it may seem, as though another self, an independent sharer of his mind, had been able to view his whole person very distinctly indeed. 'This is curious,' he thought. After a while he formulated his opinion of it in the mental ejaculation: 'Beastly!' This disgust vanished before a marked uneasiness. 'This is an effect of nervous exhaustion,' he reflected with weary sagacity. 'How am I to go on day after day if I have no more power of resistance – moral resistance?'

He followed the path at the foot of the terrace. 'Moral resistance. Moral resistance'. he kept on repeating these words mentally. Moral endurance. Yes, that was the necessity of the situation. An immense longing to make his way out of these grounds and to the other end of the town, of throwing himself on his bed and going to sleep for hours, swept everything clean out of his mind for a moment. 'Is it possible that I am but a weak creature after all?' he asked himself in sudden alarm. 'Eh! What's that?'

He gave a start as if awakened from a dream. He even swayed a little before recovering himself.

'Ah! You stole away from us quietly to walk about here,' he said.

The lady companion stood before him, but how she came there he had not the slightest idea. Her folded arms were closely cherishing the cat.

'I have been unconscious as I walked, it's a positive fact,' said Razumov to himself in wonder. He raised his hat with marked civility.

The sallow woman blushed duskily. She had her invariably scared expression, as if somebody had just disclosed to her some terrible news. But she held her ground, Razumov noticed, without timidity. 'She is incredibly shabby,' he thought. In the sunlight her black costume looked greenish, with here and there threadbare patches where the stuff seemed decomposed by age into a velvety, black, furry state. Her very hair and eyebrows looked shabby. Razumov wondered whether she were sixty years old. Her figure, though, was young enough. He observed that she did not appear starved, but rather as if she had been fed on unwholesome scraps and leavings of plates.

Razumov smiled amiably and moved out of her way. She turned her head to keep her scared eyes on him.

'I know what you have been told in there,' she affirmed, without preliminaries. Her tone, in contrast with her manner, had an unexpectedly assured character which put Razumov at his ease.

'Do you? You must have heard all sorts of talk on many occasions in there.'

She varied her phrase, with the same incongruous effect of positiveness.

'I know to a certainty what you have been told to do.'

'Really?' Razumov shrugged his shoulders a little. He was about to pass on with a bow, when a sudden thought struck him. 'Yes. To be sure! In your confidential position you are aware of many things,' he murmured, looking at the cat.

That animal got a momentary convulsive hug from the lady companion.

'Everything was disclosed to me a long time ago,' she said.

'Everything,' Razumov repeated absently.

'Peter Ivanovitch is an awful despot,' she jerked out.

Razumov went on studying the stripes on the grey fur of the cat.

'An iron will is an integral part of such a temperament. How else could he be a leader? And I think that you are mistaken in –'

'There!' she cried. 'You tell me that I am mistaken. But I tell you all the same that he cares for no one.' She jerked her head up. 'Don't you bring that girl here. That's what you have been told to do – to bring that girl here. Listen to me; you had better tie a stone round her neck and throw her into the lake.'

Razumov had a sensation of chill and gloom, as if a heavy cloud had passed over the sun.

'The girl?' he said. 'What have I to do with her?'

'But you have been told to bring Nathalie Haldin here. Am I not right? Of course I am right. I was not in the room, but I know. I know Peter Ivanovitch sufficiently well. He is a great man. Great men are horrible. Well, that's it. Have nothing to do with her. That's the best you can do, unless you want her to become like me – disillusioned! Disillusioned!'

'Like you,' repeated Razumov, glaring at her face, as devoid of all comeliness of feature and complexion as the most miserable beggar is of money. He smiled, still feeling chilly: a peculiar sensation which annoyed him. 'Disillusioned as to Peter Ivanovitch! Is that all you have lost?'

She declared, looking frightened, but with immense conviction, 'Peter Ivanovitch stands for everything.' Then she added, in another tone, 'Keep the girl away from this house.'

'And are you absolutely inciting me to disobey Peter Ivanovitch just because – because you are disillusioned?'

She began to blink.

'Directly I saw you for the first time I was comforted. You took your hat off to me. You looked as if one could trust you. Oh!'

She shrank before Razumov's savage snarl of, 'I have heard something like this before.'

She was so confounded that she could do nothing but blink for a long time.

'It was your humane manner,' she explained plaintively. 'I have been starving for, I won't say kindness, but just for a little civility, for I don't know how long. And now you are angry . . .'

'But no, on the contrary,' he protested. 'I am very glad you trust me. It's possible that later on I may . . .'

'Yes, if you were to get ill,' she interrupted eagerly, 'or meet some bitter trouble, you would find I am not a useless fool. You have only to let me know.

I will come to you. I will indeed. And I will stick to you. Misery and I are old acquaintances – but this life here is worse than starving.'

She paused anxiously, then in a voice for the first time sounding really timid, she added –

'Or if you were engaged in some dangerous work. Sometimes a humble companion – I would not want to know anything. I would follow you with joy. I could carry out orders. I have the courage.'

Razumov looked attentively at the scared round eyes, at the withered, sallow, round cheeks. They were quivering about the corners of the mouth.

'She wants to escape from here,' he thought.

'Suppose I were to tell you that I am engaged in dangerous work?' he uttered slowly.

She pressed the cat to her threadbare bosom with a breathless exclamation. 'Ah!' Then not much above a whisper: 'Under Peter Ivanovitch?'

'No, not under Peter Ivanovitch.'

He read admiration in her eyes, and made an effort to smile.

'Then – alone?'

He held up his closed hand with the index raised.

'Like this finger,' he said.

She was trembling slightly. But it occurred to Razumov that they might have been observed from the house, and he became anxious to be gone. She blinked, raising up to him her puckered face, and seemed to beg mutely to be told something more, to be given a word of encouragement for her starving, grotesque, and pathetic devotion.

'Can we be seen from the house?' asked Razumov confidentially.

She answered, without showing the slightest surprise at the question –

'No, we can't, on account of this end of the stables.' And she added, with an acuteness which surprised Razumov, 'But anybody looking out of an upstairs window would know that you have not passed through the gates yet.'

'Who's likely to spy out of the window?' queried Razumov. 'Peter Ivanovitch?'

She nodded.

'Why should he trouble his head?'

'He expects somebody this afternoon.'

'You know the person?'

'There's more than one.'

She had lowered her eyelids. Razumov looked at her curiously.

'Of course. You hear everything they say.'

She murmured without any animosity –

'So do the tables and chairs.'

He understood that the bitterness accumulated in the heart of that helpless creature had got into her veins and, like some subtle poison, had decomposed her fidelity to that hateful pair. It was a great piece of luck for him, he reflected; because women are seldom venal after the manner of men, who can be bought for material considerations. She would be a good ally, though it was not likely that she was allowed to hear as much as the tables and chairs of the Château Borel. That could not be expected. But still . . . And, at any rate, she could be made to talk.

When she looked up her eyes met the fixed stare of Razumov, who began to speak at once.

'Well, well, dear . . . but upon my word, I haven't the pleasure of knowing your name yet. Isn't it strange?'

For the first time she made a movement of the shoulders.

'Is it strange? No one is told my name. No one cares. No one talks to me, no one writes to me. My parents don't even know if I'm alive. I have no use for a name, and I have almost forgotten it myself.'

Razumov murmured gravely, 'Yes, but still . . .'

She went on much slower, with indifference –

'You may call me Tekla, then. My poor Andrei called me so. I was devoted to him. He lived in wretchedness and suffering, and died in misery. That is the lot of all us Russians, nameless Russians. There is nothing else for us, and no hope anywhere, unless . . .'

'Unless what?'

'Unless all these people with names are done away with,' she finished, blinking and pursing up her lips.

'It will be easier to call you Tekla, as you direct me,' said Razumov, 'if you consent to call me Kirylo, when we are talking like this – quietly – only you and me.'

And he said to himself, 'Here's a being who must be terribly afraid of the world, else she would have run away from this situation before.' Then he reflected that the mere fact of leaving the great man abruptly would make her a suspect. She could expect no support or countenance from anyone This revolutionist was not fit for an independent existence.

She moved with him a few steps, blinking and nursing the cat with a small balancing movement of her arms.

'Yes – only you and I. That's how I was with my poor Andrei, only he was dying, killed by these official brutes – while you! You are strong. You kill the monsters. You have done a great deed. Peter Ivanovitch himself must consider you. Well – don't forget me – especially if you are going back to work in Russia. I could follow you, carrying anything that was wanted – at a distance, you know. Or I could watch for hours at the corner of a street if necessary – in wet or snow – yes, I could – all day long. Or I could write for you dangerous documents, lists of names or instructions, so that in case of mischance the handwriting could not compromise you. And you need not be afraid if they were to catch me. I would know how to keep dumb. We women are not so easily daunted by pain. I heard Peter Ivanovitch say it is our blunt nerves or something. We can stand it better. And it's true; I would just as soon bite my tongue out and throw it at them as not. What's the good of speech to me? Who would ever want to hear what I could say? Ever since I closed the eyes of my poor Andrei I haven't met a man who seemed to care for the sound of my voice. I should never have spoken to you if the very first time you appeared here you had not taken notice of me so nicely. I could not help speaking of you to that charming dear girl. Oh, the sweet creature! And strong! One can see that at once. If you have a heart don't let her set her foot in here. Good-bye!'

Razumov caught her by the arm. Her emotion at being thus seized manifested itself by a short struggle, after which she stood still, not looking at him.

'But you can tell me,' he spoke in her ear, 'why they – these people in that house there – are so anxious to get hold of her?'

She freed herself to turn upon him, as if made angry by the question.

'Don't you understand that Peter Ivanovitch must direct, inspire, influence? It is the breath of his life. There can never be too many disciples. He can't bear thinking of anyone escaping him. And a woman, too! There is nothing to be done without women, he says. He has written it. He –'

The young man was staring at her passion when she broke off suddenly and ran away behind the stable.

Chapter III

Razumov, thus left to himself, took the direction of the gate. But on this day of many conversations, he discovered that very probably he could not leave the grounds without having to hold another one.

Stepping in view from beyond the lodge appeared the expected visitors of Peter Ivanovitch: a small party composed of two men and a woman. They noticed him too, immediately, and stopped short as if to consult. But in a moment the woman, moving aside, motioned with her arm to the two men, who, leaving the drive at once, struck across the large neglected lawn, or rather grass-plot, and made directly for the house. The woman remained on the path waiting for Razumov's approach. She had recognized him. He, too, had recognized her at the first glance. He had been made known to her at Zürich, where he had broken his journey while on his way from Dresden. They had been much together for the two days of his stay.

She was wearing the very same costume in which he had seen her first. A blouse of crimson silk made her noticeable at a distance. With that she wore a short brown skirt and a leather belt. Her complexion was the colour of coffee and milk, but very clear; her eyes black and glittering, her figure erect. A lot of thick hair, nearly white, was done up loosely under a dusty Tyrolese hat of dark cloth, which seemed to have lost some of its trimmings.

The expression of her face was grave, intent; so grave that Razumov, after approaching her close, felt obliged to smile. She greeted him with a manly hand-grasp.

'What! Are you going away?' she exclaimed. 'How is that, Razumov?'

'I am going away because I haven't been asked to stay,' Razumov answered, returning the pressure of her hand with much less force than she had put into it.

She jerked her head sideways like one who understands. Meantime Razumov's eyes had strayed after the two men. They were crossing the grass-plot obliquely, without haste. The shorter of the two was buttoned up in a narrow overcoat of some thin grey material, which came nearly to his heels. His companion, much taller and broader, wore a short, close-fitting jacket and tight trousers tucked into shabby top-boots.

The woman, who had sent them out of Razumov's way apparently, spoke in a businesslike voice.

'I had to come rushing from Zürich on purpose to meet the train and take these two along here to see Peter Ivanovitch. I've just managed it.'

'Ah! indeed,' Razumov said perfunctorily, and very vexed at her staying behind to talk to him. 'From Zürich – yes, of course. And these two, they come from . . .'

She interrupted, without emphasis –

'From quite another direction. From a distance, too. A considerable distance.'

Razumov shrugged his shoulders. The two men from a distance, after having reached the wall of the terrace, disappeared suddenly at its foot as if the earth had opened to swallow them up.

'Oh, well, they have just come from America.' The woman in the crimson blouse shrugged her shoulders too a little before making that statement. 'The time is drawing near,' she interjected, as if speaking to herself. 'I did not tell them who you were. Yakovlitch would have wanted to embrace you.'

'Is that he with the wisp of hair hanging from his chin, in the long coat?'

'You've guessed aright. That's Yakovlitch.'

'And they could not find their way here from the station without you coming on purpose from Zürich to show it to them? Verily, without women we can do nothing. So it stands written, and apparently so it is.'

He was conscious of an immense lassitude under his effort to be sarcastic. And he could see that she had detected it with those steady, brilliant black eyes.

'What is the matter with you?'

'I don't know. Nothing. I've had a devil of a day.'

She waited, with her black eyes fixed on his face. Then –

'What of that? You men are so impressionable and self-conscious. One day is like another, hard, hard – and there's an end of it, till the great day comes. I came over for a very good reason. They wrote to warn Peter Ivanovitch of their arrival. But where from? Only from Cherbourg on a bit of ship's notepaper. Anybody could have done that. Yakovlitch has lived for years and years in America. I am the only one at hand who had known him well in the old days. I knew him very well indeed. So Peter Ivanovitch telegraphed, asking me to come. It's natural enough, is it not?'

'You came to vouch for his identity?' inquired Razumov.

'Yes. Something of the kind. Fifteen years of a life like his make changes in a man. Lonely, like a crow in a strange country. When I think of Yakovlitch before he went to America –'

The softness of the low tone caused Razumov to glance at her sideways. She sighed; her black eyes were looking away; she had plunged the fingers of her right hand deep into the mass of nearly white hair, and stirred them there absently. When she withdrew her hand the little hat perched on the top of her head remained slightly tilted, with a queer inquisitive effect, contrasting strongly with the reminiscent murmur that escaped her.

'We were not in our first youth even then. But a man is a child always.'

Razumov thought suddenly, 'They have been living together.' Then aloud –

'Why didn't you follow him to America?' he asked point-blank.

She looked up at him with a perturbed air.

'Don't you remember what was going on fifteen years ago? It was a time of activity. The Revolution has its history by this time. You are in it and yet you don't seem to know it. Yakovlitch went away then on a mission; I went back to Russia. It had to be so. Afterwards there was nothing for him to come back to.'

'Ah! indeed,' muttered Razumov, with affected surprise. 'Nothing!'

'What are you trying to insinuate?' she exclaimed quickly. 'Well, and what then if he did get discouraged a little . . .'

'He looks like a Yankee, with that goatee hanging from his chin. A regular Uncle Sam,' growled Razumov. 'Well, and you? You who went to Russia? You did not get discouraged.'

'Never mind. Yakovlitch is a man who cannot be doubted. He, at any rate, is the right sort.'

Her black, penetrating gaze remained fixed upon Razumov while she spoke, and for a moment afterwards.

'Pardon me,' Razumov inquired coldly, 'but does it mean that you, for instance, think that I am not the right sort?'

She made no protest, gave no sign of having heard the question; she continued looking at him in a manner which he judged not to be absolutely unfriendly. In Zürich when he passed through she had taken him under her charge, in a way, and was with him from morning till night during his stay of two days. She took him round to see several people. At first she talked to him a great deal and rather unreservedly, but always avoiding all reference to herself; towards the middle of the second day she fell silent, attending him zealously as before, and even seeing him off at the railway station, where she pressed his hand firmly through the lowered carriage window, and, stepping back without a word, waited till the train moved. He had noticed that she was treated with quiet regard. He knew nothing of her parentage, nothing of her private history or political record; he judged her from his own private point of view, as being a distinct danger in his path. 'Judged' is not perhaps the right word. It was more of a feeling, the summing up of slight impressions aided by the discovery that he could not despise her as he despised all the others. He had not expected to see her again so soon.

No, decidedly; her expression was not unfriendly. Yet he perceived an acceleration in the beat of his heart. The conversation could not be abandoned at that point. He went on in accents of scrupulous inquiry –

'Is it perhaps because I don't seem to accept blindly every development of the general doctrine – such for instance as the feminism of our great Peter Ivanovitch? If that is what makes me suspect, then I can only say I would scorn to be a slave even to an idea.'

She had been looking at him all the time, not as a listener looks at one, but as if the words he chose to say were only of secondary interest. When he finished she slipped her hand, by a sudden and decided movement, under his arm and impelled him gently towards the gate of the grounds. He felt her firmness and obeyed the impulsion at once, just as the other two men had, a moment before, obeyed unquestioningly the wave of her hand.

They made a few steps like this.

'No, Razumov, your ideas are probably all right,' she said. 'You may be valuable – very valuable. What's the matter with you is that you don't like us.'

She released him. He met her with a frosty smile.

'Am I expected then to have love as well as convictions?'

She shrugged her shoulders.

'You know very well what I mean. People have been thinking you not quite whole-hearted. I have heard that opinion from one side and another. But I have understood you at the end of the first day . . .'

Razumov interrupted her, speaking steadily.

'I assure you that your perspicacity is at fault here.'

'What phrases he uses!' she exclaimed parenthetically. 'Ah! Kirylo Sidorovitch, you like other men are fastidious, full of self-love and afraid of trifles. Moreover, you had no training. What you want is to be taken in hand by some woman. I am sorry I am not staying here a few days. I am going back to Zürich tomorrow, and shall take Yakovlitch with me most likely.'

This information relieved Razumov.

'I am sorry too,' he said. 'But, all the same, I don't think you understand me.'

He breathed more freely; she did not protest, but asked, 'And how did you get on with Peter Ivanovitch? You have seen a good deal of each other. How is it between you two?'

Not knowing what answer to make, the young man inclined his head slowly.

Her lips had been parted in expectation. She pressed them together, and seemed to reflect.

'That's all right.'

This had a sound of finality, but she did not leave him. It was impossible to guess what she had in her mind. Razumov muttered –

'It is not of me that you should have asked that question. In a moment you shall see Peter Ivanovitch himself, and the subject will come up naturally. He will be curious to know what has delayed you so long in this garden.'

'No doubt Peter Ivanovitch will have something to say to me. Several things. He may even speak of you – question me. Peter Ivanovitch is inclined to trust me generally.'

'Question you? That's very likely.'

She smiled, half serious.

'Well – and what shall I say to him?'

'I don't know. You may tell him of your discovery.'

'What's that?'

'Why – my lack of love for . . .'

'Oh! That's between ourselves,' she interrupted, it was hard to say whether in jest or earnest.

'I see that you want to tell Peter Ivanovitch something in my favour,' said Razumov, with grim playfulness. 'Well, then, you can tell him that I am very much in earnest about my mission. I mean to succeed.'

'You have been given a mission!' she exclaimed quickly.

'It amounts to that. I have been told to bring about a certain event.'

She looked at him searchingly.

'A mission,' she repeated, very grave and interested all at once. 'What sort of mission?'

'Something in the nature of propaganda work.'

'Ah! Far away from here?'

'No. Not very far,' said Razumov, restraining a sudden desire to laugh, though he did not feel joyous in the least.

'So!' she said thoughtfully. 'Well, I am not asking questions. It's sufficient that Peter Ivanovitch should know what each of us is doing. Everything is bound to come right in the end.'

'You think so?'

'I don't think, young man. I just simply believe it.'

'And is it to Peter Ivanovitch that you owe that faith?'

She did not answer the question, and they stood idle, silent, as if reluctant to part with each other.

'That's just like a man,' she murmured at last. 'As if it were possible to tell how a belief comes to one.' Her thin Mephistophelian eyebrows moved a little. 'Truly there are millions of people in Russia who would envy the life of dogs in this country. It is a horror and a shame to confess this even between ourselves. One must believe for very pity. This can't go on. No! It can't go on. For twenty years I have been coming and going, looking neither to the left nor to the right. . . . What are you smiling to yourself for? You are only at the beginning. You have begun well, but you just wait till you have trodden every particle of yourself under your feet in your comings and goings. For that is what it comes to. You've got to trample down every particle of your own feelings; for stop you cannot, you must not. I have been young, too – but perhaps you think that I am complaining – eh?'

'I don't think anything of the sort,' protested Razumov indifferently.

'I dare say you don't, you dear superior creature. You don't care.'

She plunged her fingers into the bunch of hair on the left side, and that brusque movement had the effect of setting the Tyrolese hat straight on her head. She frowned under it without animosity, in the manner of an investigator. Razumov averted his face carelessly.

'You men are all alike. You mistake luck for merit. You do it in good faith too! I would not be too hard on you. It's masculine nature. You men are ridiculously pitiful in your aptitude to cherish childish illusions down to the very grave. There are a lot of us who have been at work for fifteen years – I mean constantly – trying one way after another, underground and above ground, looking neither to the right nor to the left! I can talk about it. I have been one of these that never rested. . . . There! What's the use of talking. . . . Look at my grey hairs! And here two babies come along – I mean you and Haldin – you come along and manage to strike a blow at the very first try.'

At the name of Haldin falling from the rapid and energetic lips of the woman revolutionist, Razumov had the usual brusque consciousness of the irrevocable. But in all the months which had passed over his head he had become hardened to the experience. The consciousness was no longer accompanied by the blank dismay and the blind anger of the early days. He had argued himself into new beliefs; and he had made for himself a mental atmosphere of gloomy and sardonic reverie, a sort of murky medium through which the event appeared like a featureless shadow having vaguely the shape of a man; a shape extremely familiar, yet utterly inexpressive, except for its air of discreet waiting in the dusk. It was not alarming.

'What was *he* like?' the woman revolutionist asked unexpectedly.

'What was he like?' echoed Razumov, making a painful effort not to turn upon her savagely. But he relieved himself by laughing a little while he stole a glance at her out of the corners of his eyes. This reception of her inquiry disturbed her.

'How like a woman,' he went on. 'What is the good of concerning yourself with his appearance? Whatever it was, he is removed beyond all feminine influences now.'

A frown, making three folds at the root of her nose, accentuated the Mephistophelian slant of her eyebrows.

'You suffer, Razumov,' she suggested, in her low, confident voice.

'What nonsense!' Razumov faced the woman fairly. 'But now I think of it, I am not sure that he is beyond the influence of one woman at least; the one over there – Madame de S—, you know. Formerly the dead were allowed to rest, but now it seems they are at the beck and call of a crazy old harridan. We revolutionists make wonderful discoveries. It is true that they are not exactly our own. We have nothing of our own. But couldn't the friend of Peter Ivanovitch satisfy your feminine curiosity? Couldn't she conjure him up for you?' – he jested like a man in pain.

Her concentrated frowning expression relaxed, and she said, a little wearily, 'Let us hope she will make an effort and conjure up some tea for us. But that is by no means certain. I am tired, Razumov.'

'You tired! What a confession! Well, there has been tea up there. I had some. If you hurry on after Yakovlitch, instead of wasting your time with such an unsatisfactory sceptical person as myself, you may find the ghost of it – the cold ghost of it – still lingering in the temple. But as to your being tired I can hardly believe it. We are not supposed to be. We mustn't. We can't. The other day I read in some paper or other an alarmist article on the tireless activity of the revolutionary parties. It impresses the world. It's our prestige.'

'He flings out continually these flouts and sneers,' the woman in the crimson blouse spoke as if appealing quietly to a third person, but her black eyes never left Razumov's face. 'And what for, pray? Simply because some of his conventional notions are shocked, some of his petty masculine standards. You might think he was one of these nervous sensitives that come to a bad end. And yet.' she went on, after a short, reflective pause and changing the mode of her address, 'and yet I have just learned something which makes me think that you are a man of character, Kirylo Sidorovitch. Yes! indeed – you are.'

The mysterious positiveness of this assertion startled Razumov. Their eyes met. He looked away and, through the bars of the rusty gate, stared at the clean, wide road shaded by the leafy trees. An electric tramcar, quite empty, ran along the avenue with a metallic rustle. It seemed to him he would have given anything to be sitting inside all alone. He was inexpressibly weary, weary in every fibre of his body, but he had a reason for not being the first to break off the conversation.

At any instant, in the visionary and criminal babble of revolutionists, some momentous words might fall on his ear; from her lips, from anybody's lips. As long as he managed to preserve a clear mind and to keep down his irritability there was nothing to fear. The only condition of success and safety was indomitable will-power, he reminded himself.

He longed to be on the other side of the bars, as though he were actually a prisoner within the grounds of this centre of revolutionary plots, of this house of folly, of blindness, of villainy and crime. Silently he indulged his wounded spirit in a feeling of immense moral and mental remoteness. He did not even smile when he heard her repeat the words –

'Yes! A strong character.'

He continued to gaze through the bars like a moody prisoner, not thinking of escape, but merely pondering upon the faded memories of freedom.

'If you don't look out,' he mumbled, still looking away, 'you will certainly miss seeing as much as the mere ghost of that tea.'

She was not to be shaken off in such a way. As a matter of fact he had not expected to succeed.

'Never mind, it will be no great loss. I mean the missing of her tea and only the ghost of it at that. As to the lady, you must understand that she has her positive uses. See *that*, Razumov.'

He turned his head at this imperative appeal and saw the woman revolutionist making the motions of counting money into the palm of her hand.

'That's what it is. You see?'

Razumov uttered a slow 'I see,' and returned to his prisoner-like gazing upon the neat and shady road.

'Material means must be obtained in some way, and this is easier than breaking into banks. More certain too. There! I am joking . . . What is he muttering to himself now?' she cried under her breath.

'My admiration of Peter Ivanovitch's devoted self-sacrifice, that's all. It's enough to make one sick.'

'Oh, you squeamish, masculine creature. Sick! Makes him sick! And what do you know of the truth of it? There's no looking into the secrets of the heart. Peter Ivanovitch knew her years ago, in his worldly days, when he was a young officer in the Guards. It is not for us to judge an inspired person. That's where you men have an advantage. You are inspired sometimes both in thought and action. I have always admitted that when you *are* inspired, when you manage to throw off your masculine cowardice and prudishness you are not to be equalled by us. Only, how seldom . . . Whereas the silliest woman can always be made of use. And why? Because we have passion, unappeasable passion . . . I should like to know what he is smiling at?'

'I am not smiling,' protested Razumov gloomily.

'Well! How is one to call it? You made some sort of face. Yes, I know! You men can love here and hate there and desire something or other – and you make a great to-do about it, and you call it passion! Yes! While it lasts. But we women are in love with love, and with hate, with these very things I tell you, and with desire itself. That's why we can't be bribed off so easily as you men. In life, you see, there is not much choice. You have either to rot or to burn. And there is not one of us, painted or unpainted, that would not rather burn than rot.'

She spoke with energy, but in a matter-of-fact tone. Razumov's attention had wandered away on a track of its own – outside the bars of the gate – but not out of earshot. He stuck his hands into the pockets of his coat.

'Rot or burn! Powerfully stated. Painted or unpainted. Very vigorous. Painted or . . . Do tell me – she would be infernally jealous of him, wouldn't she?'

'Who? What? The Baroness? Eleanor Maximovna? Jealous of Peter Ivanovitch? Heavens! Are these the questions the man's mind is running on? Such a thing is not to be thought of.'

'Why? Can't a wealthy old woman be jealous? Or, are they all pure spirits together?'

'But what put it into your head to ask such a question?' she wondered.

'Nothing. I just asked. Masculine frivolity, if you like.'

'I don't like,' she retorted at once. 'It is not the time to be frivolous. What are you flinging your very heart against? Or, perhaps, you are only playing a part.'

Razumov had felt that woman's observation of him like a physical contact, like a hand resting lightly on his shoulder. At that moment he received the mysterious impression of her having made up her mind for a closer grip. He stiffened himself inwardly to bear it without betraying himself.

'Playing a part,' he repeated, presenting to her an unmoved profile. 'It must be done very badly since you see through the assumption.'

She watched him, her forehead drawn into perpendicular folds, the thin black eyebrows diverging upwards like the antennae of an insect. He added hardly audibly –

'You are mistaken. I am doing it no more than the rest of us.'

'Who is doing it?' she snapped out.

'Who? Everybody,' he said impatiently. 'You are a materialist, aren't you?'

'Eh! My dear soul, I have outlived all that nonsense.'

'But you must remember the definition of Cabanis: "Man is a digestive tube." I imagine now . . .'

'I spit on him.'

'What? On Cabanis? All right. But you can't ignore the importance of a good digestion. The joy of life – you know the joy of life? – depends on a sound stomach, whereas a bad digestion inclines one to scepticism, breeds black fancies and thoughts of death. These are facts ascertained by physiologists. Well, I assure you that ever since I came over from Russia I have been stuffed with indigestible foreign concoctions of the most nauseating kind – pah!'

'You are joking,' she murmured incredulously. He assented in a detached way.

'Yes. It is all a joke. It's hardly worth while talking to a man like me. Yet for that very reason men have been known to take their own life.'

'On the contrary, I think it *is* worth while talking to you.'

He kept her in the corner of his eye. She seemed to be thinking out some scathing retort, but ended by only shrugging her shoulders slightly.

'Shallow talk! I suppose one must pardon this weakness in you,' she said, putting a special accent on the last word. There was something anxious in her indulgent conclusion.

Razumov noted the slightest shades in this conversation, which he had not expected, for which he was not prepared. That was it. 'I was not prepared,' he said to himself. 'It has taken me unawares.' It seemed to him that if he only could allow himself to pant openly like a dog for a time this oppression would pass away. 'I shall never be found prepared,' he thought, with despair. He laughed a little, saying as lightly as he could –

'Thanks. I don't ask for mercy.' Then affecting a playful uneasiness, 'But aren't you afraid Peter Ivanovitch might suspect us of plotting something unauthorized together by the gate here?'

'No, I am not afraid. You are quite safe from suspicions while you are with me, my dear young man.' The humorous gleam in her black eyes went out. 'Peter Ivanovitch trusts me,' she went on, quite austerely. 'He takes my advice. I am his right hand, as it were, in certain most important things. . . . That amuses you – what? Do you think I am boasting?'

'God forbid. I was just only saying to myself that Peter Ivanovitch seems to have solved the woman question pretty completely.'

Even as he spoke he reproached himself for his words, for his tone. All day long he had been saying the wrong things. It was folly, worse than folly. It was weakness; it was this disease of perversity overcoming his will. Was this the way to meet speeches which certainly contained the promise of future confidences from that woman who apparently had a great store of secret knowledge and so much influence? Why give her this puzzling impression? But she did not seem inimical. There was no anger in her voice. It was strangely speculative.

'One does not know what to think, Razumov. You must have bitten something bitter in your cradle.'

Razumov gave her a sidelong glance.

'H'm! Something bitter? That's an explanation,' he muttered. 'Only it was much later. And don't you think, Sophia Antonovna, that you and I come from the same cradle?'

The woman, whose name he had forced himself at last to pronounce (he had experienced a strong repugnance in letting it pass his lips), the woman revolutionist murmured, after a pause –

'You mean – Russia?'

He disdained even to nod. She seemed softened, her black eyes very still, as though she were pursuing the smile in her thoughts to all its tender associations. But suddenly she knitted her brows in a Mephistophelian frown.

'Yes. Perhaps no wonder, then. Yes. One lies there lapped up in evils, watched over by beings that are worse than ogres, ghouls, and vampires. They must be driven away, destroyed utterly. In regard of that task nothing else matters if men and women are determined and faithful. That's how I came to feel in the end. The great thing is not to quarrel amongst ourselves about all sorts of conventional trifles. Remember that, Razumov.'

Razumov was not listening. He had even lost the sense of being watched in a sort of heavy tranquillity. His uneasiness, his exasperation, his scorn were blunted at last by all these trying hours. It seemed to him that now they were blunted for ever. 'I am a match for them all,' he thought, with a conviction too firm to be exulting. The woman revolutionist had ceased speaking; he was not looking at her; there was no one passing along the road. He almost forgot that he was not alone. He heard her voice again, curt, businesslike, and yet betraying the hesitation which had been the real reason of her prolonged silence.

'I say, Razumov!'

Razumov, whose face was turned away from her, made a grimace like a man who hears a false note.

'Tell me: is it true that on the very morning of the deed you actually attended the lectures at the University?'

An appreciable fraction of a second elapsed before the real import of the question reached him, like a bullet which strikes some time after the flash of the fired shot. Luckily his disengaged hand was ready to grip a bar of the gate. He held it with a terrible force, but his presence of mind was gone. He could make only a sort of gurgling, grumpy sound.

'Come, Kirylo Sidorovitch!' she urged him. 'I know you are not a boastful man. *That* one must say for you. You are a silent man. Too silent, perhaps. You are feeding on some bitterness of your own. You are not an enthusiast. You are, perhaps, all the stronger for that. But you might tell me. One would like to understand you a little more. I was so immensely struck . . . Have you really done it?'

He got his voice back. The shot had missed him. It had been fired at random, altogether, more like a signal for coming to close quarters. It was to be a plain struggle for self-preservation. And she was a dangerous adversary too. But he was ready for battle; he was so ready that when he turned towards her not a muscle of his face moved.

'Certainly,' he said, without animation, secretly strung up but perfectly sure of himself. 'Lectures – certainly. But what makes you ask?'

It was she who was animated.

'I had it in a letter, written by a young man in Petersburg; one of us, of course. You were seen – you were observed with your notebook, impassible, taking notes . . .'

He enveloped her with his fixed stare.

'What of that?'

'I call such coolness superb – that's all. It is a proof of uncommon strength of character. The young man writes that nobody could have guessed from your face and manner the part you had played only some two hours before – the great, momentous, glorious part . . .'

'Oh no. Nobody could have guessed,' assented Razumov gravely, 'because, don't you see, nobody at that time . . .'

'Yes, yes. But all the same you are a man of exceptional fortitude, it seems. You looked exactly as usual. It was remembered afterwards with wonder . . .'

'It cost me no effort,' Razumov declared, with the same staring gravity.

'Then it's almost more wonderful still!' she exclaimed, and fell silent while Razumov asked himself whether he had not said there something utterly unnecessary – or even worse.

She raised her head eagerly.

'Your intention was to stay in Russia? You had planned . . .'

'No,' interrupted Razumov without haste. 'I had made no plans of any sort.'

'You just simply walked away?' she struck in.

He bowed his head in slow assent. 'Simply – yes.' He had gradually released his hold on the bar of the gate, as though he had acquired the conviction that no random shot could knock him over now. And suddenly he was inspired to add. 'The snow was coming down very thick, you know.'

She had a slight appreciative movement of the head, like an expert in such enterprises, very interested, capable of taking every point professionally. Razumov remembered something he had heard.

'I turned into a narrow side street, you understand,' he went on negligently, and paused as if it were not worth talking about. Then he remembered another detail and dropped it before her, like a disdainful dole to her curiosity.

'I felt inclined to lie down and go to sleep there.'

She clicked her tongue at that symptom, very struck indeed. Then –

'But the notebook! The amazing notebook, man. You don't mean to say you had it in your pocket beforehand!' she cried.

Razumov gave a start. It might have been a sign of impatience.

'I went home. Straight home to my rooms,' he said distinctly.

'The coolness of the man! You dared?'

'Why not? I assure you I was perfectly calm. Ha! Calmer than I am now perhaps.'

'I like you much better as you are now than when you indulge that bitter vein of yours, Razumov. And nobody in the house saw you return – eh? That might have appeared queer.'

'No one,' Razumov said firmly. 'Dvornik, landlady, girl, all out of the way. I went up like a shadow. It was a murky morning. The stairs were dark. I glided up like a phantom. Fate? Luck? What do you think?'

'I just see it!' The eyes of the woman revolutionist snapped darkly. 'Well – and you considered . . .'

Razumov had it all ready in his head.

'No. I looked at my watch, since you want to know. There was just time. I took that notebook, and ran down the stairs on tiptoe. Have you ever listened to the pit-pat of a man running round and round the shaft of a deep staircase? They have a gaslight at the bottom burning night and day. I suppose it's gleaming down there now . . . The sound dies out – the flame winks . . .'

He noticed the vacillation of surprise passing over the steady curiosity of the black eyes fastened on his face as if the woman revolutionist received the sound of his voice into her pupils instead of her ears. He checked himself, passed his hand over his forehead, confused, like a man who has been dreaming aloud.

'Where could a student be running if not to his lectures in the morning? At night it's another matter. I did not care if all the house had been there to look at me. But I don't suppose there was anyone. It's best not to be seen or heard. Aha! The people that are neither seen nor heard are the lucky ones – in Russia. Don't you admire my luck?'

'Astonishing,' she said. 'If you have luck as well as determination, then indeed you are likely to turn out an invaluable acquisition for the work in hand.'

Her tone was earnest; and it seemed to Razumov that it was speculative, even as though she were already apportioning him, in her mind, his share of the work. Her eyes were cast down. He waited, not very alert now, but with the grip of the ever-present danger giving him an air of attentive gravity. Who could have written about him in that letter from Petersburg? A fellow-student, surely – some imbecile victim of revolutionary propaganda, some foolish slave of foreign, subversive ideals. A long, famine-striken red-nosed figure presented itself to his mental search. That must have been the fellow!

He smiled inwardly at the absolute wrong-headedness of the whole thing, the self-deception of a criminal idealist shattering his existence like a thunder-clap out of a clear sky, and re-echoing amongst the wreckage in the false assumptions of those other fools. Fancy that hungry and piteous imbecile furnishing to the curiosity of the revolutionist refugees this utterly fantastic detail! He appreciated it as by no means constituting a danger. On the contrary. As things stood it was for his advantage rather, a piece of sinister luck which had only to be accepted with proper caution.

'And yet, Razumov,' he heard the musing voice of the woman, 'you have not the face of a lucky man.' She raised her eyes with renewed interest. 'And so that was the way of it. After doing your work you simply walked off and made for your rooms. That sort of thing succeeds sometimes. I suppose it was agreed beforehand that, once the business over, each of you would go his own way?'

Razumov preserved the seriousness of his expression and the deliberate, if cautious, manner of speaking.

'Was not that the best thing to do?' he asked, in a dispassionate tone. 'And anyway, he added, after waiting a moment, 'we did not give much thought to what would come after. We never discussed formally any line of conduct. It was understood, I think.'

She approved his statement with slight nods.

'You, of course, wished to remain in Russia?'

'In St Petersburg itself,' emphasized Razumov. 'It was the only safe course for me. And, moreover, I had nowhere else to go.'

'Yes! Yes! I know. Clearly. And the other – this wonderful Haldin appearing only to be regretted – you don't know what he intended?'

Razumov had foreseen that such a question would certainly come to meet him sooner or later. He raised his hands a little and let them fall helplessly by his side – nothing more.

It was the white-haired woman conspirator who was the first to break the silence.

'Very curious,' she pronounced slowly. 'And you did not think, Kirylo Sidorovitch, that he might perhaps wish to get in touch with you again?'

Razumov discovered that he could not suppress the trembling of his lips. But he thought that he owed it to himself to speak. A negative sign would not do again. Speak he must, if only to get at the bottom of what that St Petersburg letter might have contained.

'I stayed at home next day,' he said, bending down a little and plunging his glance into the black eyes of the woman so that she should not observe the trembling of his lips. 'Yes, I stayed at home. As my actions are remembered and written about, then perhaps you are aware that I was *not* seen at the lectures next day. Eh? You didn't know? Well, I stopped at home – the livelong day.'

As if moved by his agitated tone, she murmured a sympathetic 'I see! It must have been trying enough.'

'You seem to understand one's feeling,' said Razumov steadily. 'It was trying. It was horrible; it was an atrocious day. It was not the last.'

'Yes, I understand. Afterwards, when you heard they had got him. Don't I know how one feels after losing a comrade in the good fight? One's ashamed of being left. And I can remember so many. Never mind. They shall be avenged before long. And what is death? At any rate, it is not a shameful thing like some kinds of life.'

Razumov felt something stir in his breast, a sort of feeble and unpleasant tremor.

'Some kinds of life?' he repeated, looking at her searchingly.

'The subservient, submissive life. Life? No! Vegetation on the filthy heap of inquity which the world is. Life. Razumov, not to be vile must be a revolt – a pitiless protest – all the time.'

She calmed down, the gleam of suffused tears in her eyes dried out instantly by the heat of her passion, and it was in her capable, businesslike manner that she went on –

'You understand me, Razumov. You are not an enthusiast, but there is an immense force of revolt in you. I felt it from the first, directly I set my eyes on you – you remember – in Zürich. Oh! You are full of bitter revolt. That is good. Indignation flags sometimes, revenge itself may become a weariness, but that uncompromising sense of necessity and justice which armed your and Haldin's hands to strike down that fanatical brute . . . for it was that – nothing but that! I have been thinking it out. It could have been nothing else but that.'

Razumov made a slight bow, the irony of which was concealed by an almost sinister immobility of feature.

'I can't speak for the dead. As for myself, I can assure you that my conduct was dictated by necessity and by the sense of – well – retributive justice.'

'Good, that,' he said to himself, while her eyes rested upon him, black and impenetrable like the mental caverns where revolutionary thought should sit plotting the violent way of its dream of changes. As if anything could be changed! In this world of men nothing can be changed – neither happiness nor misery. They can only be displaced at the cost of corrupted consciences and broken lives – a futile game for arrogant philosophers and sanguinary triflers. Those thoughts darted through Razumov's head while he stood facing the old revolutionary hand, the respected, trusted, and influential Sophia Antonovna, whose word had such a weight in the 'active' section of every party. She was much more representative than the great Peter Ivanovitch. Stripped of rhetoric, mysticism, and theories, she was the true spirit of destructive revolution. And she was the personal adversary he had to meet. It gave him a feeling of triumphant pleasure to deceive her out of her own mouth. The epigrammatic saying that speech has been given to us for the purpose of concealing our thoughts came into his mind. Of that cynical theory this was a very subtle and a very scornful application, flouting in its own words the very spirit of ruthless revolution, embodied in that woman with her white hair and black eyebrows, like slightly sinuous lines of Indian ink, drawn together by the perpendicular folds of a thoughtful frown.

'That's it. Retributive. No pity' was the conclusion of her silence. And this once broken, she went on impulsively in short, vibrating sentences –

'Listen to my story, Razumov! . . .' Her father was a clever but unlucky artisan. No joy had lighted up his laborious days. He died at fifty; all the years of his life he had panted under the thumb of masters whose rapacity exacted from him the price of the water, of the salt, of the very air he breathed; taxed the sweat of his brow and claimed the blood of his sons. No protection, no guidance! What had society to say to him? Be submissive and be honest. If you rebel I shall kill you. If you steal I shall imprison you. But if you suffer I have nothing for you – nothing except perhaps a beggarly dole of bread – but no consolation for your trouble, no respect for your manhood, no pity for the sorrows of your miserable life.

And so he laboured, he suffered, and he died. He died in the hospital. Standing by the common grave she thought of his tormented existence – she saw it whole. She reckoned the simple joys of life, the birthright of the humblest, of which his gentle heart had been robbed by the crime of a society which nothing can absolve.

'Yes, Razumov,' she continued, in an impressive, lowered voice, 'it was like a lurid light in which I stood, still almost a child, and cursed not the toil, not the misery which had been his lot, but the great social iniquity of the system resting on unrequired toil and unpitied sufferings. From that moment I was a revolutionist.'

Razumov, trying to raise himself above the dangerous weaknesses of contempt or compassion, had preserved an impassive countenance. She, with an unaffected touch of mere bitterness, the first he could notice since he had come in contact with the woman, went on –

'As I could not go to the Church where the priests of the system exhorted such unconsidered vermin as I to resignation, I went to the secret society as soon as I knew how to find my way. I was sixteen years old – no more, Razumov! And – look at my white hair.'

In these last words there was neither pride nor sadness. The bitterness too was gone.

'There is a lot of it. I had always magnificent hair, even as a chit of a girl. Only at that time we were cutting it short and thinking that there was the first step towards crushing the social infamy. Crush the Infamy! A fine watchword! I would placard it on the walls of prisons and palaces, carve it on hard rocks, hang it out in letters of fire on that empty sky for a sign of hope and terror – a portent of the end . . .'

'You are eloquent, Sophia Antonovna,' Razumov interrupted suddenly. 'Only, so far you seem to have been writing it in water . . .'

She was checked but not offended. 'Who knows? Very soon it may become a fact written all over that great land of ours,' she hinted meaningly. 'And then one would have lived long enough. White hair won't matter.'

Razumov looked at her white hair: and this mark of so many uneasy years seemed nothing but a testimony to the invincible vigour of revolt. It threw out into an astonishing relief the unwrinkled face, the brilliant black glance, the upright compact figure, the simple, brisk self-possession of the mature personality – as though in her revolutionary pilgrimage she had discovered the secret, not of everlasting youth, but of everlasting endurance.

How un-Russian she looked, thought Razumov. Her mother might have been a Jewess or an Armenian or – devil knew what. He reflected that a revolutionist is seldom true to the settled type. All revolt is the expression of strong individualism – ran his thought vaguely. One can tell them a mile off in any society, in any surroundings. It was astonishing that the police . . .

'We shall not meet again very soon, I think,' she was saying. 'I am leaving to-morrow.'

'For Zürich?' Razumov asked casually, but feeling relieved, not from any distinct apprehension, but from a feeling of stress as if after a wrestling match.

'Yes, Zürich – and farther on, perhaps, much farther. Another journey. When I think of all my journeys! The last must come some day. Never mind, Razumov. We had to have a good long talk. I would have certainly tried to see you if we had not met. Peter Ivanovitch knows where you live? Yes. I meant to have asked him – but it's better like this. You see, we expect two more men; and I had much rather wait here talking with you than up there at the house with . . .'

Having cast a glance beyond the gate, she interrupted herself. 'Here they are,' she said rapidly. 'Well, Kirylo Sidorovitch, we shall have to say good-bye presently.'

Chapter IV

In his incertitude of the ground on which he stood Razumov felt perturbed. Turning his head quickly, he saw two men on the opposite side of the road. Seeing themselves noticed by Sophia Antonovna, they crossed over at once, and passed one after another through the little gate by the side of the empty lodge. They looked hard at the stranger, but without mistrust, the crimson blouse being a flaring safety signal. The first, great white hairless face, double chin, prominent stomach, which he seemed to carry forward consciously within a strongly distended overcoat, only nodded and averted his eyes peevishly; his companion – lean, flushed cheekbones, a military red moustache below a sharp, salient nose – approached Sophia Antonovna at once, greeting her warmly. His voice was very strong but inarticulate. It sounded like a deep buzzing. The woman revolutionist was quietly cordial. . . .

'This is Razumov,' she announced in a clear voice.

The lean new-comer made an eager half-turn. 'He will want to embrace me,' thought our young man with a deep recoil of all his being, while his limbs seemed too heavy to move. But it was a groundless alarm. He had to do now with a generation of conspirators who did not kiss each other on both cheeks; and raising an arm that felt like lead he dropped his hand into a largely outstretched palm, fleshless and hot as if dried up by fever, giving a bony pressure, expressive, seeming to say, 'Between us there's no need of words.'

The man had big, wide-open eyes. Razumov fancied he could see a smile behind their sadness.

'This is Razumov,' Sophia Antonovna repeated loudly for the benefit of the fat man, who at some distance displayed the profile of his stomach.

No one moved. Everything, sounds, attitudes, movements, and immobility seemed to be part of an experiment, the result of which was a thin voice piping with comic peevishness –

'Oh yes! Razumov. We have been hearing of nothing but Mr Razumov for months. For my part, I confess I would rather have seen Haldin on this spot instead of Mr Razumov.'

The squeaky stress put on the name 'Razumov – Mr Razumov' pierced the ear ridiculously, like the falsetto of a circus clown beginning an elaborate joke. Astonishment was Razumov's first response, followed by sudden indignation.

'What's the meaning of this?' he asked in a stern tone.

'Tut! Silliness. He's always like that.' Sophia Antonovna was obviously vexed. But she dropped the information, 'Necator', from her lips just loud enough to be heard by Razumov. The abrupt squeaks of the fat man seemed to proceed from that thing like a balloon he carried under his overcoat. The stolidity of his attitude, the big feet, the lifeless, hanging hands, the enormous bloodless cheek, the thin wisps of hair straggling down the fat nape of the neck, fascinated Razumov into a stare on the verge of horror and laughter.

Nikita, nicknamed Necator, with a sinister aptness of alliteration! Razumov had heard of him. He had heard so much since crossing the frontier of these celebrities of the militant revolution; the legends, the stories, the authentic chronicle, which now and then peeps out before a half-incredulous world. Razumov had heard of him. He was supposed to have killed more gendarmes and police agents than any revolutionist living. He had been entrusted with executions.

The paper with the letters N.N., the very pseudonym of murder, found pinned on the stabbed breast of a certain notorious spy (this picturesque detail of a sensational murder case had got into the newspapers), was the mark of his handiwork. 'By order of the Committee. – N.N.' A corner of the curtain lifted to strike the imagination of the gaping world. He was said to have been innumerable times in and out of Russia, the Necator of bureaucrats, of provincial governors, of obscure informers. He lived between whiles, Razumov had heard, on the shores of the Lake of Como, with a charming wife, devoted to the cause, and two young children. But how could that creature, so grotesque as to set town dogs barking at its mere sight, go about on those deadly errands and slip through the meshes of the police?

'What now? what now?' the voice squeaked. 'I am only sincere. It's not denied that the other was the leading spirit. Well, it would have been better if he had been the one spared to us. More useful. I am not a sentimentalist. Say what I think . . . only natural.'

Squeak, squeak, squeak, without a gesture, without a stir – the horrible squeaky burlesque of professional jealousy – this man of a sinister alliterative nickname, this executioner of revolutionary verdicts, the terryifying N.N. exasperated like a fashionable tenor by the attention attracted to the performance of an obscure amateur. Sophia Antonovna shrugged her shoulders. The comrade with the martial moustache hurried towards Razumov full of conciliatory intentions in his strong buzzing voice.

'Devil take it! And in this place, too, in the public street, so to speak. But you can see yourself how it is. One of his fantastic sallies. Absolutely of no consequence.'

'Pray don't concern yourself,' cried Razumov, going off into a long fit of laughter. 'Don't mention it.'

The other, his hectic flush like a pair of burns on his cheekbones, stared for a moment and burst out laughing too. Razumov, whose hilarity died out all at once, made a step forward.

'Enough of this,' he began in a clear, incisive voice, though he could hardly control the trembling of his legs. 'I will have no more of it. I shall not permit any one. . . . I can see very well what you are at with those allusions. . . . Inquire, investigate! I defy you but I will not be played with.'

He had spoken such words before. He had been driven to cry them out in the face of other suspicions. It was an infernal cycle bringing round that protest like a fatal necessity of his existence. But it was no use. He would be always played with. Luckily life docs not last for ever.

'I won't have it,' he shouted, striking his fist into the palm of his other hand.

'Kirylo Sidorovitch – what has come to you?' The woman revolutionist interfered with authority. They were all looking at Razumov now; the slayer of spies and gendarmes had turned about, presenting his enormous stomach in full, like a shield.

'Don't shout. There are people passing.' Sophia Antonovna was apprehensive of another outburst. A steam-launch from Monrepos had come to the landing-stage opposite the gate, its hoarse whistle and the churning noise alongside all unnoticed, had landed a small bunch of local passengers who were dispersing their several ways. Only a specimen of early tourist in knickerbockers, conspicuous by a brand-new yellow leather glass-case, hung about for a moment, scenting something unusual about these four people within the rusty iron gates of what looked like the grounds run wild of an unoccupied private house. Ah! If he had only known what the chance of common-place travelling had suddenly put in his way! But he was a well-bred person; he averted his gaze and moved off with short steps along the avenue, on the watch for a tramcar.

A gesture from Sophia Antonovna, 'Leave him to me,' had sent the two men away – the buzzing of the inarticulate voice growing fainter and fainter, and the thin pipe of 'What now? what's the matter?' reduced to the proportions of a squeaking toy by the distance. They had left him to her. So many things could be left safely to the experience of Sophia Antonovna. And at once, her black eyes turned to Razumov, her mind tried to get at the heart of that outburst. It had some meaning. No one is born an active revolutionist. The change comes disturbingly, with the force of a sudden vocation, bringing in its train agonizing doubts, assertive violences, an unstable state of the soul, till the final appeasement of the convert in the perfect fierceness of conviction. She had seen – often had only divined – scores of these young men and young women going through an emotional crisis. This young man looked like a moody egotist. And besides, it was a special – a unique case. She had never met an individuality which interested and puzzled her so much.

'Take care, Razumov, my good friend. If you carry on like this you will go mad. You are angry with everybody and bitter with yourself, and on the look out for something to torment yourself with.'

'It's intolerable!' Razumov could only speak in gasps. 'You must admit that I can have no illusions on the attitude which . . . it isn't clear . . . or rather . . . only too clear.'

He made a gesture of despair. It was not his courage that failed him. The choking fumes of falsehood had taken him by the throat – the thought of being condemned to struggle on and on in that tainted atmosphere without the hope of ever renewing his strength by a breath of fresh air.

'A glass of cold water is what you want.' Sophia Antonovna glanced up the grounds at the house and shook her head, then out of the gate at the brimful placidity of the lake. With a half-comical shrug of the shoulders, she gave the remedy up in the face of that abundance.

'It is you, my dear soul, who are flinging yourself at something which does not exist. What is it? Self-reproach or what? It's absurd. You couldn't have gone and given yourself up because your comrade was taken.'

She remonstrated with him reasonably, at some length too. He had nothing to complain of in his reception. Every newcomer was discussed more or less. Everybody had to be thoroughly understood before being accepted. No one that she could remember had been shown from the first so much confidence. Soon, very soon, perhaps sooner than he expected, he would be given an opportunity of showing his devotion to the sacred task of crushing the Infamy.

Razumov, listening quietly, thought: 'It may be that she is trying to lull my suspicions to sleep. On the other hand, it is obvious that most of them are fools.' He moved aside a couple of paces and folding his arms on his breasts, leaned back against the stone pillar of the gate.

'As to what remains obscure in the fate of that poor Haldin,' Sophia Antonovna dropped into a slowness of utterance which was to Razumov like the falling of molten lead drop by drop; 'as to that – though no one ever hinted that either from fear or neglect your conduct has not been what it should have been – well, I have a bit of intelligence . . .'

Razumov could not prevent himself from raising his head, and Sophia Antonovna nodded slightly.

'I have. You remember that letter from St Petersburg I mentioned to you a moment ago?'

'The letter? Perfectly. Some busybody has been reporting my conduct on a certain day. It's rather sickening. I suppose our police are greatly edified when they open these interesting and – and – superfluous letters.'

'Oh dear no! The police do not get hold of our letters as easily as you imagine. The letter in question did not leave St Petersburg till the ice broke up. It went by the first English steamer which left the Neva this spring. They have a fireman on board – one of us, in fact. It has reached me from Hull . . .'

She paused as if she were surprised at the sullen fixity of Razumov's gaze, but went on at once, and much faster.

'We have some of our people there who . . . but never mind. The writer of the letter relates an incident which he thinks may possibly be connected with Haldin's arrest. I was just going to tell you when those two men came along.'

'That also was an incident,' muttered Razumov, 'of a very charming kind – for me.'

'Leave off that!' cried Sophia Antonovna. 'Nobody cares for Nikita's barking. There's no malice in him. Listen to what I have to say. You may be able to throw a light. There was in St Petersburg a sort of town peasant – a man who owned horses. He came to town years ago to work for some relation as a driver and ended by owning a cab or two.'

She might well have spared herself the slight effort of the gesture: 'Wait!' Razumov did not mean to speak; he could not have interrupted her now, not to save his life. The contraction of his facial muscles had been involuntary, a mere surface stir, leaving him sullenly attentive as before.

'He was not a quite ordinary man of his class – it seems,' she went on. 'The people of the house – my informant talked with many of them – you know, one of those enormous houses of shame and misery . . .'

Sophia Antonovna need not have enlarged on the character of the house. Razumov saw clearly, towering at her back, a dark mass of masonry veiled in snowflakes, with the long row of windows of the eating-shop shining greasily very near the ground. The ghost of that night pursued him. He stood up to it with rage and with weariness.

'Did the late Haldin ever by chance speak to you of that house?' Sophia Antonovna was anxious to know.

'Yes.' Razumov, making that answer, wondered whether he were falling into a trap. It was so humiliating to lie to these people that he probably could not have said no. 'He mentioned to me once,' he added, as if making an effort of memory, 'a house of that sort. He used to visit some workmen there.'

'Exactly.'

Sophia Antonovna triumphed. Her correspondent had discovered that fact quite accidentally from the talk of the people of the house, having made friends with a workman who occupied a room there. They described Haldin's appearance perfectly. He brought comforting words of hope into their misery. He came irregularly, but he came very often, and – her correspondent wrote – sometimes he spent a night in the house, sleeping, they thought, in a stable which opened upon the inner yard.

'Note that, Razumov. In a stable.'

Razumov had listened with a sort of ferocious but amused acquiescence.

'Yes. In the straw. It was probably the cleanest spot in the whole house.'

'No doubt,' assented the woman with that deep frown which seemed to draw closer together her black eyes in a sinister fashion. No four-footed beast could stand the filth and wretchedness so many human beings were condemned to suffer from in Russia. The point of this discovery was that it proved Haldin to have been familiar with that horse-owning peasant – a reckless, independent, free-living fellow not much liked by the other inhabitants of the house. He was believed to have been the associate of a band of housebreakers. Some of these got captured. Not while he was driving them, however, but still there was a suspicion against the fellow of having given a hint to the police and . . .

The woman revolutionist checked herself suddenly.

'And you? Have you ever heard your friend refer to a certain Ziemianitch?'

Razumov was ready for the name. He had been looking out for the question. 'When it comes I shall own up,' he had said to himself. But he took his time.

'To be sure!' he began slowly. 'Ziemianitch, a peasant owning a team of horses. Yes. On one occasion. Ziemianitch! Certainly! Ziemianitch of the horses. . . . How could it have slipped my memory like this? One of the last conversations we had together.'

'That means,' – Sophia Antonovna looked very grave, – 'that means, Razumov, it was very shortly before – eh?'

'Before what?' shouted Razumov, advancing at the woman, who looked astonished but stood her ground. 'Before . . . Oh! Of course, it was before! How could it have been after? Only a few hours before.'

'And he spoke of him favourably?'

'With enthusiasm! The horses of Ziemianitch! The free soul of Ziemianitch!'

Razumov took a savage delight in the loud utterance of that name, which had never before crossed his lips audibly. He fixed his blazing eyes on the woman till at last her fascinated expression recalled him to himself.

'The late Haldin,' he said, holding himself in, with downcast eyes, 'was inclined to take sudden fancies to people, on – on – what shall I say – insufficient grounds.'

'There!' Sophia Antonovna clapped her hands. 'That, to my mind, settles it. The suspicions of my correspondent were aroused . . .'

'Aha! Your correspondent,' Razumov said in an almost openly mocking tone. 'What suspicions? How aroused? By this Ziemianitch? Probably some drunken, gabbling, plausible . . .'

'You talk as if you had known him.'

Razumov looked up.

'No. But I knew Haldin.'

Sophia Antonovna nodded gravely.

'I see. Every word you say confirms to my mind the suspicion communicated to me in that very interesting letter. This Ziemianitch was found one morning hanging from a hook in the stable – dead.'

Razumov felt a profound trouble. It was visible, because Sophia Antonovna was moved to observe vivaciously –

'Aha! You begin to see.'

He saw it clearly enough – in the light of a lantern casting spokes of shadow in a cellar-like stable, the body in a sheepskin coat and long boots hanging against the wall. A pointed hood, with the ends wound about up to the eyes, hid the face. 'But that does not concern me,' he reflected. 'It does not affect my position at all. He never knew who had thrashed him. He could not have known.' Razumov felt sorry for the old lover of the bottle and women.

'Yes. Some of them end like that,' he muttered. 'What is your idea, Sophia Antonovna?'

It was really the idea of her correspondent, but Sophia Antonovna had adopted it fully. She stated it in one word – 'Remorse.' Razumov opened his eyes very wide at that. Sophia Antonovna's informant, by listening to the talk of the house, by putting this and that together, had managed to come very near to the truth of Haldin's relation to Ziemianitch.

'It is I who can tell you what you were not certain of – that your friend had some plan for saving himself afterwards, for getting out of St Petersburg, at any rate. Perhaps that and no more, trusting to luck for the rest. And that fellow's horses were part of the plan.'

'They have actually got at the truth,' Razumov marvelled to himself, while he nodded judicially. 'Yes, that's possible, very possible.' But the woman revolutionist was very positive that it was so. First of all, a conversation about horses between Haldin and Ziemianitch had been partly overheard. Then there were the suspicions of the people in the house when their 'young gentleman' (they did not know Haldin by his name) ceased to call at the house. Some of them used to charge Ziemianitch with knowing something of this absence. He denied it with exasperation; but the fact was that ever since Haldin's disappearance he was not himself, growing moody and thin. Finally, during a quarrel with some woman (to whom he was making up), in which most of the inmates of the house took part apparently, he was openly abused by his chief enemy, an athletic pedlar, for an informer, and for having driven 'our young gentleman to Siberia, the same as you did those young fellows who broke into houses'. In consequence of this there was a fight, and Ziemianitch got flung down a flight of stairs. Thereupon he drank and moped for a week, and then hanged himself.

Sophia Antonovna drew her conclusions from the tale. She charged Ziemianitch either with drunken indiscretion as to a driving job on a certain date, overheard by some spy in some low grog-shop – perhaps in the very eating-shop on the ground floor of the house – or, maybe, a downright denunciation, followed by remorse. A man like that would be capable of anything. People said he was a flighty old chap. And if he had been once before mixed up with the police – as seemed certain, though he always denied it – in connection with these thieves, he would be sure to be acquainted with some police underlings, always on the look-out for something to report. Possibly at first his tale was not made anything of till the day that scoundrel de P— got his deserts. Ah! But then every bit and scrap of hint and information would be acted on, and fatally they were bound to get Haldin.

Sophia Antonovna spread out her hands – 'Fatally.'

Fatality – chance! Razumov meditated in silent astonishment upon the queer verisimilitude of these inferences. They were obviously to his advantage.

'It is right now to make this conclusive evidence known generally.' Sophia Antonovna was very calm and deliberate again. She had received the letter three days ago, but did not write at once to Peter Ivanovitch. She knew then that she would have the opportunity presently of meeting several men of action assembled for an important purpose.

'I thought it would be more effective if I could show the letter itself at large. I have it in my pocket now. You understand how pleased I was to come upon you.'

Razumov was saying to himself, 'She won't offer to show the letter to me.

Not likely. Has she told me everything that correspondent of hers has found out?' He longed to see the letter, but he felt he must not ask.

'Tell me, please, was this an investigation ordered, as it were?'

'No, no,' she protested. 'There you are again with your sensitiveness. It makes you stupid. Don't you see, there was no starting-point for an investigation even if anyone had thought of it. A perfect blank! That's exactly what some people were pointing out as the reason for receiving you cautiously. It was all perfectly accidental, arising from my informant striking an acquaintance with an intelligent skindresser lodging in that particular slum-house. A wonderful coincidence!'

'A pious person,' suggested Razumov, with a pale smile, 'would say that the hand of God has done it all.'

'My poor father would have said that.' Sophia Antonovna did not smile. She dropped her eyes. 'Not that his God ever helped him. It's a long time since God has done anything for the people. Anyway, it's done.'

'All this would be quite final,' said Razumov, with every appearance of reflective impartiality, 'if there was any certitude that the "our young gentleman" of these people was Victor Haldin. Have we got that?'

'Yes. There's no mistake. My correspondent was as familiar with Haldin's personal appearance as with your own,' the woman affirmed decisively.

'It's the red-nosed fellow beyond a doubt,' Razumov said to himself, with reawakened uneasiness. Had his own visit to that accursed house passed unnoticed? It was barely possible. Yet it was hardly probable. It was just the right sort of food for the popular gossip that gaunt busybody had been picking up. But the letter did not seem to contain any allusion to that. Unless she had suppressed it. And, if so, why? If it had really escaped the prying of that hunger-stricken democrat with a confounded genius for recognizing people from description, it could only be for a time. He would come upon it presently and hasten to write another letter – and then!

For all the envenomed recklessness of his temper, fed on hate and disdain, Razumov shuddered inwardly. It guarded him from common fear, but it could not defend him from disgust at being dealt with in any way by these people. It was a sort of superstitious dread. Now, since his position had been made more secure by their own folly at the cost of Ziemianitch, he felt the need of perfect safety, with its freedom from direct lying, with its power of moving amongst them silent, unquestioning, listening, impenetrable, like the very fate of their crimes and their folly. Was this advantage his already? Or not yet? Or never would be?

'Well, Sophia Antonovna,' his air of reluctant concession was genuine in so far that he was really loath to part with her without testing her sincerity by a question it was impossible to bring about in any way; 'well, Sophia Antonovna, if that is so, then –'

'The creature has done justice to himself,' the woman observed, as if thinking aloud.

'What? Ah yes! Remorse,' Razumov muttered with equivocal contempt.

'Don't be harsh, Kirylo Sidorovitch, if you have lost a friend.' There was no hint of softness in her tone, only the black glitter of her eyes seemed detached for an instant from vengeful visions. 'He was a man of the people. The simple Russian soul is never wholly impenitent. It's something to know that.'

'Consoling?' insinuated Razumov, in a stone of inquiry.

'Leave off railing,' she checked him explosively. 'Remember, Razumov, that women, children, and revolutionists hate irony, which is the negation of all saving instincts, of all faith, of all devotion, of all action. Don't rail! Leave off. . . . I don't know how it is, but there are moments when you are abhorrent to me. . . .'

She averted her face. A languid silence, as if all the electricity of the situation had been discharged in this flash of passion, lasted for some time. Razumov had not flinched. Suddenly she laid the tips of her fingers on his sleeve.

'Don't mind.'

'I don't mind,' he said very quietly.

He was proud to feel that she could read nothing on his face. He was really mollified, relieved, if only for a moment, from an obscure oppression. And suddenly he asked himself, 'Why the devil did I go to that house? It was an imbecile thing to do.'

A profound disgust came over him. Sophia Antonovna lingered, talking in a friendly manner with an evident conciliatory intention. And it was still about the famous letter, referring to various minute details given by her informant, who had never seen Ziemianitch. The 'victim of remorse' had been buried several weeks before her correspondent began frequenting the house. It – the house – contained very good revolutionary material. The spirit of the heroic Haldin had passed through these dens of black wretchedness with a promise of universal redemption from all the miseries that oppress mankind. Razumov listened without hearing, gnawing by the newborn desire of safety with its independence from that degrading method of direct lying which at times he found it almost impossible to practice.

No. The point he wanted to hear about could never come into this conversation. There was no way of bringing it forward. He regretted not having composed a perfect story for use abroad, in which his fatal connexion with the house might have been owned up to. But when he left Russia he did not know that Ziemianitch had hanged himself. And, anyway, who could have foreseen this woman's 'informant' stumbling upon that particular slum of all the slums awaiting destruction in the purifying flame of social revolution? Who could have foreseen? Nobody! 'It's a perfect, diabolic surprise,' thought Razumov, calm-faced in his attitude of inscrutable superiority, nodding assent to Sophia Antonovna's remarks upon the psychology of 'the people', 'Oh yes – certainly,' rather coldly, but with a nervous longing in his fingers to tear some sort of confession out of her throat.

Then, at the very last, on the point of separating, the feeling of relaxed tension already upon him he heard Sophia Antonovna allude to the subject of his uneasiness. How it came about he could only guess, his mind being absent at the moment, but it must have sprung from Sophia Antonovna's complaints of the illogical absurdity of the people. For instance – that Ziemianitch was notoriously irreligious, and yet, in the last weeks of his life, he suffered from the notion that he had been beaten by the devil.

'The devil,' repeated Razumov, as though he had not heard aright.

'The actual devil. The devil in person. You may well look astonished, Kirylo Sidorovitch. Early on the very night poor Haldin was taken, a complete stranger turned up and gave Ziemianitch a most fearful thrashing while he was lying dead-drunk in the stable. The wretched creature's body was one mass of bruises. He showed them to the people in the house.'

'But you, Sophia Antonovna, you don't believe in the actual devil?'

'Do you?' retorted the woman curtly. 'Not but that there are plenty of men worse than devils to make a hell of this earth,' she muttered to herself.

Razumov watched her, vigorous and white-haired, with the deep fold between her thin eyebrows, and her black glance turned idly away. It was obvious that she did not make much of the story – unless, indeed, this was the perfection of duplicity. 'A dark young man,' she explained further. 'Never seen there before, never seen afterwards. Why are you smiling, Razumov?'

'At the devil being still younger after all these ages,' he answered composedly. 'But who was able to describe him, since the victim, you say, was dead-drunk at the time?'

'Oh! The eating-house keeper has described him. An over-bearing, swarthy young man in a student's cloak, who came rushing in, demanded Ziemianitch, beat him furiously, and rushed away without a word, leaving the eating-house keeper paralysed with astonishment.'

'Does he, too, believe it was the devil?'

'That I can't say. I am told he's very reserved on the matter. Those sellers of spirits are great scoundrels generally. I should think he knows more of it than anybody.'

'Well, and you, Sophia Antonovna, what's your theory?' asked Razumov in a tone of great interest. 'Yours and your informant's, who is on the spot.'

'I agree with him. Some police-hound in disguise. Who else could beat a helpless man so unmercifully? As for the rest, if they were out that day on every trail, old and new, it is probable enough that they might have thought it just as well to have Ziemianitch at hand for more information, or for identification, or what not. Some scoundrelly detective was sent to fetch him along, and being vexed at finding him so drunk broke a stable fork over his ribs. Later on, after they had the big game safe in the net, they troubled their heads no more about that peasant.'

Such were the last words of the woman revolutionist in this conversation, keeping so close to the truth, departing from it so far in the verisimilitude of thoughts and conclusions as to give one the notion of the invincible nature of human error, a glimpse into the utmost depths of self-deception. Razumov, after shaking hands with Sophia Antonovna, left the grounds, crossed the road, and walking out on the little steam-boat pier leaned over the rail.

His mind was at ease; ease such as he had not known for many days, ever since that night . . . the night. The conversation with the woman revolutionist had given him the view of his danger vanished, characteristically enough. 'I ought to have foreseen the doubts that would arise in those people's minds,' he thought. Then his attention being attracted by a stone of peculiar shape, which he could see clearly lying at the bottom, he began to speculate as to the depth of water in that spot. But very soon, with a start of wonder at this extraordinary instance of ill-timed detachment, he returned to his train of thought. 'I ought to have told very circumstantial lies from the first,' he said to himself, with a mortal distaste of the mere idea which silenced his mental utterance for quite a perceptible interval. 'Luckily, that's all right now,' he reflected, and after a time spoke to himself, half aloud, 'Thanks to the devil,' and laughed a little.

The end of Ziemianitch then arrested his wandering thoughts. He was not exactly amused at the interpretation, but he could not help detecting in it a certain piquancy. He owned to himself that, had he known of that suicide before leaving Russia, he would have been incapable of making such excellent use of it for his own purposes. He ought to be infinitely obliged to the fellow with the red nose for his patience and ingenuity, 'A wonderful psychologist apparently,' he said to himself sarcastically. Remorse, indeed! It was a striking example of your true conspirator's blindness, of the stupid subtlety of people with one idea. This was a drama of love, not of conscience, Razumov continued to himself mockingly. A woman the old fellow was making up to! A robust pedlar, clearly a rival, throwing him down a flight of stairs. . . . And at sixty, for a lifelong lover, it was not an easy matter to get over. That was a feminist of a different stamp from Peter Ivanovitch. Even the comfort of the bottle might conceivably fail him in this supreme crisis. At such an age nothing but a halter could cure the pangs of an unquenchable passion. And, besides, there was the wild exasperation aroused by the unjust aspersions and the contumely of the house, with the maddening impossibility to account for that mysterious thrashing, added to these simple and bitter sorrows. 'Devil, eh?' Razumov exclaimed, with mental excitement, as if he had made an interesting discovery. 'Ziemianitch ended by falling into mysticism. So many of our true Russian souls end in that way! Very characteristic.' He felt pity for Ziemianitch, a large neutral pity, such as one may feel for an unconscious multitude, a great people seen from above – like a community of crawling ants working out its destiny. It was as if this Ziemianitch could not possibly have done anything else. And Sophia Antonovna's cocksure and contemptuous 'some police-hound' was characteristically Russian in another way. But there was no tragedy there. This was a comedy of errors. It was as if the devil himself were playing a game with all of them in turn. First with him, then with Ziemianitch, then with those revolutionists. The devil's own game this. . . . He interrupted his earnest mental soliloquy with a jocular thought at his own expense. 'Hallo! I am falling into mysticism too.'

His mind was more at ease than ever. Turning about he put his back against the rail comfortably. 'All this fits with marvellous aptness,' he continued to think. 'The brilliance of my reputed exploit is no longer darkened by the fate of my supposed colleague. The mystic Ziemianitch accounts for that. An incredible chance has served me. No more need of lies. I shall have only to listen and to keep my scorn from getting the upper hand of my caution.'

He sighed, folded his arms, his chin dropped on his breast, and it was a long time before he started forward from that pose, with the recollection that he had made up his mind to do something important that day. What it was he could not immediately recall, yet he made no effort of memory, for he was uneasily certain that he would remember presently.

He had not gone more than a hundred yards towards the town when he slowed down, almost faltered in his walk, at the sight of a figure walking in the contrary direction, draped in a cloak, under a soft, broad-brimmed hat, picturesque but diminutive, as if seen through the big end of an opera-glass. It was impossible to avoid that tiny man, for there was no issue for retreat.

'Another one going to that mysterious meeting,' thought Razumov. He was right in his surmise, only *this* one, unlike the others who came from a distance, was known to him personally. Still, he hoped to pass on with a mere bow, but it was impossible to ignore the little thin hand with hairy wrist and knuckles protruded in a friendly wave from under the folds of the cloak, worn Spanish-wise, in disregard of a fairly warm day, a corner flung over the shoulder.

'And how is Herr Razumov?' sounded the greeting in German, by that alone made more odious to the object of the affable recognition. At closer quarters the diminutive personage looked like a reduction of an ordinary-sized man, with a lofty brow bared for a moment by the raising of the hat, the great pepper-and-salt full beard spread over the proportionally broad chest. A fine bold nose jutted over a thin mouth hidden in the mass of fine hair. All this, accented features, strong limbs in their relative smallness, appeared delicate without the slightest sign of debility. The eyes alone, almond-shaped and brown, were too big, with the whites slightly bloodshot by much pen labour under a lamp. The obscure celebrity of the tiny man was well known to Razumov. Polyglot, of unknown parentage, of indefinite nationality, anarchist, with a pedantic and ferocious temperament, and an amazingly inflammatory capacity for invective, he was a power in the background, this violent pamphleteer clamouring for revolutionary justice, this Julius Laspara, editor of the *Living Word*, confidant of conspirators, inditer of sanguinary menaces and manifestos, suspected of being in the secret of every plot. Laspara lived in the old town in a sombre, narrow house presented to him by a naïve middle-class admirer of his humanitarian eloquence. With him lived his two daughters, who overtopped him head and shoulders, and a pasty-faced, lean boy of six, languishing in the dark rooms in blue cotton overalls and clumsy boots, who might have belonged to either one of them or to neither. No stranger could tell. Julius Laspara no doubt knew which of his girls it was who, after casually vanishing for a few years, had as casually returned to him possessed of that child; but, with admirable pedantry, he had refrained from asking her for details – no, not so much as the name of his father, because maternity should be an anarchist function. Razumov had been admitted twice to that suite of several small dark rooms on the top floor: dusty windowpanes, litter of all sorts of sweepings all over the place, half-full glasses of tea forgotten on every table, the two Laspara daughters prowling about enigmatically silent, sleepy-eyed, corsetless, and generally, in their want of shape and the disorder of their rumpled attire, resembling old dolls; the great but obscure Julius, his feet twisted round his three-legged stool, always ready to receive the visitors, the pen instantly dropped, the body screwed round with a striking display of the lofty brow and of the great austere beard. When he got down from his stool it was as though he had descended from the heights of Olympus. He was dwarfed by his daughters, by the furniture, by any caller of ordinary stature. But he very seldom left it, and still more rarely was seen walking in broad daylight.

It must have been some matter of serious importance which had driven him out in that direction that afternoon. Evidently he wished to be amiable to that young man whose arrival had made some sensation in the world of political refugees. In Russian now, which he spoke, as he spoke and wrote four or five other European languages, without distinction and without force (other than that of invective), he inquired if Razumov had taken his inscriptions at the University as yet. And the young man, shaking his head negatively –

'There's plenty of time for that. But, meantime, are you not going to write something for us?'

He could not understand how anyone could refrain from writing on anything, social, economic, historical – anything. Any subject could be treated in the right spirit, and for the ends of social revolution. And, as it happened, a friend of his in London had got in touch with a review of advanced ideas. 'We must educate, educate everybody – develop the great thought of absolute liberty and of revolutionary justice.'

Razumov muttered rather surlily that he did not even know English.

'Write in Russian. We'll have it translated. There can be no difficulty. Why, without seeking further, there is Miss Haldin. My daughters go to see her sometimes.' He nodded significantly. 'She does nothing, has never done anything in her life. She would be quite competent, with a little assistance. Only write. You know you must. And so good-bye for the present.'

He raised his arm and went on. Razumov backed against the low wall, looked after him, spat violently, and went on his way with an angry mutter –

'Cursed Jew!'

He did not know anything about it. Julius Laspara might have been a Transylvanian, a Turk, an Andalusian, or a citizen of one of the Hanse towns for anything he could tell to the contrary. But this is not a story of the West, and this exclamation must be recorded, accompanied by the comment that it was merely an expression of hate and contempt, best adapted to the nature of the feelings Razumov suffered from at the time. He was boiling with rage, as though he had been grossly insulted. He walked as if blind, following instinctively the shore of the diminutive harbour along the quay, through a pretty, dull garden, where dull people sat on chairs under the trees, till, his fury abandoning him, he discovered himself in the middle of a long, broad bridge. He slowed down at once. To his right, beyond the toy-like jetties, he saw the green slopes framing the Petit Lac in all the marvellous banality of the picturesque made of painted cardboard, with the more distant stretch of water inanimate and shining like a piece of tin.

He turned his head away from that view for the tourists, and walked on slowly, his eyes fixed on the ground. One or two persons had to get out of his way, and then turned round to give a surprised stare to his profound absorption. The insistence of the celebrated subversive journalist rankled in his mind strangely. Write. Must write! He! Write! A sudden light flashed upon him. To write was the very thing he had made up his mind to do that day. He had made up his mind irrevocably to that step and then had forgotten all about it. That incorrigible tendency to escape from the grip of the situation was fraught with serious danger. He was ready to despise himself for it. What was it? Levity, or deep-seated weakness? Or an unconscious dread?

'Is it that I am shrinking? It can't be! It's impossible. To shrink now would be worse than moral suicide; it would be nothing less than moral damnation,' he thought. 'Is it possible that I have a conventional conscience?'

He rejected that hypothesis with scorn, and, checked on the edge of the pavement, made ready to cross the road and proceed up the wide street facing the head of the bridge; and that for no other reason except that it was there before him. But at the moment a couple of carriages and a slow-moving cart interposed, and suddenly he turned sharp to the left, following the quay again, but away from the lake.

'It may be just my health,' he thought, allowing himself a very unusual doubt of his soundness; for, with the exception of a childish ailment or two, he had never been ill in his life. But that was a danger, too. Only, it seemed as though he were being looked after in a specially remarkable way. 'If I believed in an active Providence,' Razumov said to himself, amused grimly, 'I would see here the working of an ironical finger. To have a Julius Laspara put in my way as if expressly to remind me of my purpose is – Write, he had said. I must write – I must, indeed! I shall write – never fear. Certainly. That's why I am here. And for the future I shall have something to write about.'

He was exciting himself by this mental soliloquy. But the idea of writing evoked the thought of a place to write in, of shelter, of privacy, and naturally of his lodgings, mingled with a distaste for the necessary exertion of getting there, with a mistrust as of some hostile influence awaiting him within those odious four walls.

'Suppose one of these revolutionists,' he asked himself, 'were to take a fancy to call on me while I am writing?' The mere prospect of such an interruption made him shudder. One could lock one's door, or ask the tobacconist downstairs (some sort of refugee himself) to tell inquirers that one was not in. Not very good precautions those. The manner of his life, he felt, must be kept clear of every cause for suspicion or even occasion for wonder, down to such trifling occurrences as a delay in opening a locked door. 'I wish I were in the middle of some field miles away from everywhere,' he thought.

He had unconsciously turned to the left once more and now was aware of being on a bridge again. This one was much narrower than the other, and instead of being straight, made a sort of elbow or angle. At the point of that angle a short arm joined it to a hexagonal islet with a soil of gravel and its shores faced with dressed stone, a perfection of puerile neatness. A couple of tall poplars and a few other trees stood grouped on the clean, dark gravel, and under them a few garden benches and a bronze effigy of Jean Jacques Rousseau seated on its pedestal.

On setting his foot on it Razumov became aware that, except for the woman in charge of the refreshment chalet, he would be alone on the island. There was something of naïve, odious, and inane simplicity about that unfrequented tiny crumb of earth named after Jean Jacques Rousseau. Something pretentious and shabby, too. He asked for a glass of milk, which he drank standing, at one draught (nothing but tea had passed his lips since the morning), and was going away with a weary, lagging step when a thought stopped him short. He had found precisely what he needed. If solitude could ever be secured in the open air in the middle of a town, he would have it there on this absurd island, together with the faculty of watching the only approach.

He went back heavily to a garden seat, dropped into it. This was the place for making a beginning of that writing which had to be done. The materials he had on him. 'I shall always come here,' he said to himself, and afterwards sat for quite a long time motionless, without thought and sight and hearing, almost without life. He sat long enough for the declining sun to dip behind the roofs of the town at his back, and throw the shadow of the houses on the lake front over the islet, before he pulled out of his pocket a fountain pen, opened a small notebook on his knee, and began to write quickly, raising his eyes now and then at the connecting arm of the bridge. These glances were needless; the people crossing over in the distance seemed unwilling even to look at the islet where the exiled effigy of the author of the *Social Contract* sat enthroned above the bowed head of Razumov in the sombre immobility of bronze. After finishing his scribbling, Razumov, with a sort of feverish haste, put away the pen, then rammed the notebook into his pocket, first tearing out the written pages with an almost convulsive brusqueness. But the folding of the flimsy batch on his knee was executed with thoughtful nicety. That done, he leaned back in his seat and remained motionless holding the papers in his left hand. The twilight had deepened. He got up and began to pace to and fro slowly under the trees.

'There can be no doubt that now I am safe,' he thought. His fine ear could detect the faintly accentuated murmurs of the current breaking against the point of the island, and he forgot himself in listening to them with interest. But even to his acute sense of hearing the sound was too elusive.

'Extraordinary occupation I am giving myself up to,' he murmured. And it occurred to him that this was about the only sound he could listen to innocently, and for his own pleasure, as it were. Yes, the sound of water, the voice of the wind – completely foreign to human passions. All the other sounds of this earth brought contamination to the solitude of a soul.

This was Mr Razumov's feeling, the soul, of course, being his own, and the word being used not in the theological sense, but standing, as far as I can understand it, for that part of Mr Razumov which was not his body, and more especially in danger from the fires of this earth. And it must be admitted that in Mr Razumov's case the bitterness of solitude from which he suffered was not an altogether morbid phenomenon.

PART FOURTH

CHAPTER I

THAT I should, at the beginning of this retrospect, mention again that Mr Razumov's youth had no one in the world, as literally no one as it can be honestly affirmed of any human being, is but a statement of fact from a man who believes in the psychological value of facts. There is also, perhaps, a desire of punctilious fairness. Unidentified with anyone in this narrative where the aspects of honour and shame are remote from the ideas of the Western world, and taking my stand on the ground of common humanity, it is for that very reason that I feel a strange reluctance to state baldly here what every reader has more likely already discovered himself. Such reluctance may appear absurd if it were not for the thought that because of the imperfection of language there is always something ungracious (and even disgraceful) in the exhibition of naked truth. But the time has come when Councillor of State Mikulin can no longer be ignored. His simple question 'Where to?' on which we left Mr Razumov in St Petersburg, throws a light on the general meaning of this individual case.

'Where to?' was the answer in the form of a gentle question to what we may call Mr Razumov's declaration of independence. The question was not menacing in the least and, indeed, had the ring of innocent inquiry. Had it been taken in a merely topographical sense, the only answer to it would have appeared sufficiently appalling to Mr Razumov. Where to? Back to his rooms, where the Revolution had sought him out to put to a sudden test his dormant instincts, his half-conscious thoughts and almost wholly unconscious ambitions, by the touch as of some furious and dogmatic religion, with its calls to frantic sacrifices, its tender resignations, its dreams and hopes uplifting the soul by the side of the most sombre moods of despair. And Mr Razumov had let go the door-handle and had come back to the middle of the room, asking Councillor Milkulin angrily, 'What do you mean by it?'

As far as I can tell, Councillor Mikulin did not answer that question. He drew Mr Razumov into familiar conversation. It is the peculiarity of Russian natures, that, however strongly engaged in the drama of action, they are still turning their ear to the murmur of abstract ideas. This conversation (and others later on) need not be recorded. Suffice it to say that it brought Mr Razumov as we know him to the test of another faith. There was nothing official in its expression, and Mr Razumov was led to defend his attitude of detachment. But Councillor Mikulin would have none of his arguments. 'For a man like you,' were his last weighty words in the discussion, 'such a position is impossible. Don't forget that I have seen that interesting piece of paper. I understand your liberalism. I have an intellect of that kind myself. Reform for me is mainly a question of method. But the principle of revolt is a physical intoxication, a sort of hysteria which must be kept away from the masses. You agree to this without reserve, don't you? Because, you see, Kirylo Sidorovitch, abstention, reserve, in certain situations, come very near to political crime. The ancient Greeks understood that very well.'

Mr Razumov, listening with a faint smile, asked Councillor Mikulin point-blank if this meant that he was going to have him watched.

The high official took no offence at the cynical inquiry.

'No, Kirylo Sidorovitch,' he answered gravely. 'I don't mean to have you watched.'

Razumov, suspecting a lie, affected yet the greatest liberty of mind during the short remainder of that interview. The older man expressed himself throughout in familiar terms, and with a sort of shrewd simplicity. Razumov concluded that to get to the bottom of that mind was an impossible feat. A great disquiet made his heart beat quicker. The high official, issuing from behind the desk, was actually offering to shake hands with him.

'Good-bye, Mr Razumov. An understanding between intelligent men is always a satisfactory occurrence. Is it not? And, of course, these rebel gentlemen have not the monopoly of intelligence.'

'I presume that I shall not be wanted any more?' Razumov brought out that question while his hand was still being grasped. Councillor Mikulin released it slowly.

'That, Mr Razumov,' he said with great earnestness, 'is as it may be. God alone knows the future. But you may rest assured that I never thought of having you watched. You are a young man of great independence. Yes. You are going away free as air, but you shall end by coming back to us.'

'I! I!' Razumov exclaimed in an appalled murmur of protest. 'What for?' he added feebly.

'Yes! You yourself, Kirylo Sidorovitch,' the high police functionary insisted in a low, severe tone of conviction. 'You shall be coming back to us. Some of our greatest minds had to do that in the end.'

'Our greatest minds,' repeated Razumov in a dazed voice.

'Yes, indeed. Our greatest minds. . . . Good-bye.'

Razumov, shown out of the room, walked away from the door. But before he got to the end of the passage he heard heavy footsteps, and a voice calling upon him to stop. He turned his head and was startled to see Councillor Mikulin pursuing him in person. The high functionary hurried up, very simple, slightly out of breath.

'One minute. As to what we were talking about just now, it shall be as God wills it. But I may have occasion to require you again. You look surprised, Kirylo Sidorovitch. Yes, again . . . to clear up any further point that may turn up.'

'But I don't know anything,' stammered out Razumov. 'I couldn't possibly know anything.'

'Who can tell? Things are ordered in a wonderful manner. Who can tell what *may* become disclosed to you before this day is out? You have been already the instrument of Providence. You smile, Kirylo Sidorovitch; you are an *esprit fort*.' (Razumov was not conscious of having smiled.) 'But I believe firmly in Providence. Such a confession on the lips of an old hardened official like me may sound to you funny. But you yourself yet some day shall recognize . . . Or else what happened to you cannot be accounted for at all. Yes, decidedly I shall have occasion to see you again, but not here. This wouldn't be quite – h'm . . . Some convenient place shall be made known to you. And even the written communications between us in *that* respect or in any other had better pass through the intermediacy of our – if I may express myself so – common friend, Prince K—. Now I beg you, Kirylo Sidorovitch – don't. I am certain he'll consent. You must give me the credit of being aware of what I am saying. You have no better friend than Prince K—, and as to myself it is a long time now since I've been honoured by his . . .'

He glanced down his beard.

'I won't detain you any longer. We live in difficult times, in times of monstrous chimeras and evil dreams and criminal follies. We shall certainly meet once more. It may be some little time, though, before we do. Till then may Heaven send you fruitful reflections!'

Once in the street, Razumov started off rapidly, without caring for the direction. At first he thought of nothing; but in a little while the consciousness of his position presented itself to him as something so ugly, dangerous, and absurd, the difficulty of ever freeing himself from the toils of that complication so insoluble, that the idea of going back and, as he termed it to himself, *confessing* to Councillor Mikulin flashed through his mind.

Go back! What for? Confess! To what? 'I have been speaking to him with the greatest openness,' he said to himself with perfect truth. 'What else could I tell him? That I have undertaken to carry a message to that brute Ziemianitch? Establish a false complicity and destroy what chance of safety I have won for nothing – what folly!'

Yet he could not defend himself from fancying that Councillor Mikulin was, perhaps, the only man in the world able to understand his conduct. To be understood appeared extremely fascinating.

On the way home he had to stop several times; all his strength seemed to run out of his limbs; and in the movement of the busy streets, isolated as if in a desert, he remained suddenly motionless for a minute or so before he could proceed on his way. He reached his rooms at last.

Then came an illness, something in the nature of a low fever, which all at once removed him to a great distance from the perplexing actualities, from his very room, even. He never lost consciousness; he only seemed to himself to be existing languidly somewhere very far away from everything that had ever happened to him. He came out of this state slowly, with an effect, that is to say, of extreme slowness, though the actual number of days was not very great. And when he had got back into the middle of things they were all changed, subtly and provokingly in their nature: inanimate objects, human faces, the landlady, the rustic servant-girl, the staircase, the streets, the very air. He tackled these changed conditions in a spirit of severity. He walked to and fro to the University, ascended stairs, paced the passages, listened to lectures, took notes, crossed courtyards in angry aloofness, his teeth set hard till his jaws ached.

He was perfectly aware of madcap Kostia gazing like a young retriever from a distance, of the famished student with the red drooping nose, keeping scrupulously away as desired; of twenty others, perhaps, he knew well enough to speak to. And they all had an air of curiosity and concern as if they expected something to happen. 'This can't last much longer,' thought Razumov more than once. On certain days he was afraid that anyone addressing him suddenly in a certain way would make him scream out insanely a lot of filthy abuse. Often, after returning home, he would drop into a chair in his cap and cloak and remain still for hours holding some book he had got from the library in his hand; or he would pick up the little penknife and sit there scraping his nails endlessly and feeling furious all the time – simply furious. 'This is impossible,' he would mutter suddenly to the empty room.

Fact to be noted: this room might conceivably have become physically repugnant to him, emotionally intolerable, morally uninhabitable. But no. Nothing of the sort (and he had himself dreaded it at first), nothing of the sort happened. On the contrary, he liked his lodgings better than any other shelter he, who had never known a home, had ever hired before. He liked his lodgings so well that often, on that very account, he found a certain difficulty in making up his mind to go out. It resembled a physical seduction such as, for instance, makes a man reluctant to leave the neighbourhood of a fire on a cold day.

For as, at that time, he seldom stirred except to go to the University (what else was there to do?) it followed that whenever he went abroad he felt himself at once closely involved in the moral consequences of his act. It was there that the dark prestige of the Haldin mystery fell on him, clung to him like a poisoned robe it was impossible to fling off. He suffered from it exceedingly, as well as from the conversational, commonplace, unavoidable intercourse with the other kind of students. 'They must be wondering at the change in me,' he reflected anxiously. He had an uneasy recollection of having savagely told one or two innocent, nice enough fellows to go to the devil. Once a married professor he used to call upon formerly addressed him in passing: 'How is it we never see you at our Wednesdays now, Kirylo Sidorovitch?' Razumov was conscious of meeting this advance with odious, muttering boorishness. The professor was obviously too astonished to be offended. All this was bad. And all this was Haldin, always Haldin – nothing but Haldin – everywhere Haldin: a moral spectre infinitely more effective than any visible apparition of the dead. It was only the room through which that man had blundered on his way from crime to death that his spectre did not seem to be able to haunt. Not, to be exact, that he was ever completely absent from it, but that there he had no sort of power. There it was Razumov who had the upper hand, in a composed sense of his own superiority. A vanquished phantom – nothing more. Often in the evening, his repaired watch faintly ticking on the table by the side of the lighted lamp, Razumov would look up from his writing and stare at the bed with an expectant, dispassionate attention. Nothing was to be seen there. He never really supposed that anything ever could be seen there. After a while he would shrug his shoulders slightly and bend again over his work. For he had gone to work and, at first, with some success. His unwillingness to leave that place where he was safe from Haldin grew so strong that at last he ceased to go out at all. From early morning till far into the night he wrote, he wrote for nearly a week; never looking at the time, and only throwing himself on the bed when he could keep his eyes open no longer. Then, one afternoon, quite casually, he happened to glance at his watch. He laid down his pen slowly.

'At this very hour,' was his thought, 'the fellow stole unseen into this room while I was out. And there he sat quiet as a mouse – perhaps in this very chair.'

Razumov got up and began to pace the floor steadily, glancing at the watch now and then. 'This is the time when I returned and found him standing against the stove,' he observed to himself. When it grew dark he lit his lamp. Later on he interrupted his tramping once more, only to wave away angrily the girl who attempted to enter the room with tea and something to eat on a tray. And presently he noted the watch pointing at the hour of his own going forth into the falling snow on that terrible errand.

'Complicity,' he muttered faintly, and resumed his pacing, keeping his eye on the hands as they crept on slowly to the time of his return.

'And, after all,' he thought suddenly, 'I might have been the chosen instrument of Providence. This is a manner of speaking, but there may be truth in every manner of speaking. What if that absurd saying were true in its essence?'

He meditated for a while, then sat down, his legs stretched out, with stony eyes, and with his arms hanging down on each side of the chair like a man totally abandoned by Providence – desolate.

He noted the time of Haldin's departure and continued to sit still for another half-hour; then muttering, 'And now to work,' drew up to the table, seized the pen and instantly dropped it under the influence of a profoundly disquieting reflection: 'There's three weeks gone by and no word from Mikulin.'

What did it mean? Was he forgotten? Possibly. Then why not remain forgotten – creep in somewhere? Hide. But where? How? With whom? In what hole? And was it to be for ever, or what?

But a retreat was big with shadowy dangers. The eye of the social revolution was on him, and Razumov for a moment felt an unnamed and despairing dread, mingled with an odious sense of humiliation. Was it possible that he no longer belonged to himself? This was damnable. But why not simply keep on as before? Study. Advance. Work hard as if nothing had happened (and first of all win the Silver Medal), acquire distinction, become a great reforming servant of the greatest of States. Servant, too, of the mightiest homogeneous mass of mankind with a capability for logical, guided development in a brotherly solidarity of force and aim such as the world had never dreamt of . . . the Russian nation! . . .

Calm, resolved, steady in his great purpose, he was stretching his hand towards the pen when he happened to glance towards the bed. He rushed at it, enraged, with a mental scream: 'It's you, crazy fanatic, who stands in the way!' He flung the pillow on the floor violently, tore the blankets aside. . . . Nothing there. And, turning away, he caught for an instant in the air, like a vivid detail in a dissolving view of two heads, the eyes of General T— and of Privy-Councillor Mikulin side by side fixed upon him, quite different in character, but with the same unflinching and weary and yet purposeful expression . . . servants of the nation!

Razumov tottered to the washstand very alarmed about himself, drank some water and bathed his forehead. 'This will pass and leave no trace,' he thought confidently. 'I am all right.' But as to supposing that he had been forgotten it was perfect nonsense. He was a marked man on that side. And that was nothing. It was what that miserable phantom stood for which had to be got out of the way . . . 'If one only could go and spit it all out at some of them – and take the consequences.'

He imagined himself accosting the red-nosed student and suddenly shaking his fist in his face. 'From that one, though,' he reflected, 'there's nothing to be got, because he has no mind of his own. He's living in a red democratic trance. Ah! you want to smash your way into universal happiness, my boy. I will give you universal happiness, you silly, hypnotized ghoul, you! And what about my own happiness, eh? Haven't I got any right to it, just because I can think for myself? . . .'

And again, but with a different mental accent, Razumov said to himself, 'I am young. Everything can be lived down.' At that moment he was crossing the room slowly, intending to sit down on the sofa and try to compose his thoughts. But before he had got so far everything abandoned him – hope, courage, belief in himself, trust in men. His heart had, as it were, suddenly emptied itself. It was no use struggling on. Rest, work, solitude, and the frankness of intercourse with his kind were alike forbidden to him. Everything was gone. His existence was a great cold blank, something like the enormous plain of the whole of Russia levelled with snow and fading gradually on all sides into shadows and mists.

He sat down, with swimming head, closed his eyes, and remained like that, sitting bolt upright on the sofa and perfectly awake for the rest of the night; till the girl bustling into the outer room with the samovar thumped with her fist on the door calling out 'Kirylo Sidorovitch, please! It is time for you to get up!'

Then, pale like a corpse obeying the dread summons of judgement, Razumov opened his eyes and got up.

Nobody will be surprised to hear, I suppose, that when the summons came he went to see Councillor Mikulin. It came that very morning, while, looking white and shaky, like an invalid just out of bed, he was trying to shave himself. The envelope was addressed in the little attorney's handwriting. That envelope contained another, superscribed to Razumov, in Prince K—'s hand, with the request 'Please forward under cover at once' in a corner. The note inside was an autograph of Councillor Mikulin. The writer stated candidly that nothing had arisen which needed clearing up, but nevertheless appointed a meeting with Mr Razumov at a certain address in town which seemed to be that of an oculist.

Razumov read it, finished shaving, dressed, looked at the note again, and muttered gloomily, 'Oculist.' He pondered over it for a time, lit a match, and burned the two envelopes and the enclosure carefully. Afterwards he waited, sitting perfectly idle and not even looking at anything in particular till the appointed hour drew near – and then went out.

Whether, looking at the unofficial character of the summons, he might have refrained from attending to it is hard to say. Probably not. At any rate, he went; but, what's more, he went with a certain eagerness, which may appear incredible till it is remembered that Councillor Mikulin was the only person on earth with whom Razumov could talk, taking the Haldin adventure for granted. And Haldin, when once taken for granted, was no longer a haunting, falsehood-breeding spectre. Whatever troubling power he exercised in all the other places of the earth, Razumov knew very well that at this oculist's address he would be merely the hanged murderer of M. de P— and nothing more. For the dead can live only with the exact intensity and quality of the life imparted to them by the living. So Mr Razumov, certain of relief, went to meet Councillor Mikulin with the eagerness of a pursued person welcoming any sort of shelter.

This much said, there is no need to tell anything more of that first interview and of the several others. To the morality of a Western reader an account of these meetings would wear perhaps the sinister character of old legendary tales where the Enemy of Mankind is represented holding subtly mendacious dialogues with some tempted soul. It is not my part to protest. Let me but remark that the Evil One, with his single passion of satanic pride for the only motive, is yet, on a larger, modern view, allowed to be not quite so black as he used to be painted. With what greater latitude, then, should we appraise the exact shade of mere mortal man, with his many passions and his miserable ingenuity in error, always dazzled by the base glitter of mixed motives, everlastingly betrayed by a short-sighted wisdom.

Councillor Mikulin was one of those powerful officials who, in a position not obscure, not occult, but simply inconspicuous, exercise a great influence over the methods rather than over the conduct of affairs. A devotion to Church and Throne is not in itself a criminal sentiment; to prefer the will of one to the will of many does not argue the possession of a black heart or prove congenital idiocy. Councillor Mikulin was not only a clever but also a faithful official. Privately he was a bachelor with a love of comfort, living alone in an apartment of five rooms luxuriously furnished; and was known by his intimates to be an enlightened patron of the art of female dancing. Later on the larger world first heard of him in the very hour of his downfall, during one of those State trials which astonish and puzzle the average plain man who reads the newspapers, by a glimpse of unsuspected intrigues. And in the stir of vaguely seen monstrosities, in that momentary, mysterious disturbance of muddy waters, Councillor Mikulin went under, dignified, with only a calm, emphatic protest of his innocence – nothing more. No disclosures damaging to a harassed autocracy, complete fidelity to the secrets of the miserable *arcana imperii* deposited in his patriotic breast, a display of bureaucratic stoicism in a Russian official's ineradicable, almost sublime contempt for truth; stoicism of silence understood only by the very few of the initiated, and not without a certain cynical grandeur of self-sacrifice on the part of a sybarite. For the terribly heavy sentence turned Councillor Mikulin civilly into a corpse, and actually into something very much like a common convict.

It seems that the savage autocracy, no more than the divine democracy, does not limit its diet exclusively to the bodies of its enemies. It devours its friends and servants as well. The downfall of His Excellency Gregory Gregorievitch Mikulin (which did not occur till some years later) completes all that is known of the man. But at the time of M. de P—'s murder (or execution) Councillor Mikulin, under the modest style of Head of Department at the General Secretariat, exercised a wide influence as the confidant and right-hand man of his former schoolfellow and lifelong friend, General T—. One can imagine them talking over the case of Mr Razumov, with the full sense of their unbounded power over all the lives in Russia, with cursory disdain, like two Olympians glancing at a worm. The relationship with Prince K— was enough to save Razumov from some carelessly arbitrary proceeding, and it is also very probable that after the interview at the Secretariat he would have been left alone. Councillor Mikulin would not have forgotten him (he forgot no one who ever fell under his observation), but would have simply dropped him for ever. Councilor Mikulin was a good-natured man and wished no harm to anyone. Besides (with his own reforming tendencies) he was favourably impressed by that young student, the son of Prince K—, and apparently no fool.

But as fate would have it, while Mr Razumov was finding that no way of life was possible to him, Councillor Mikulin's discreet abilities were rewarded by a very responsible post – nothing less than the direction of the general police supervision over Europe. And it was then, and then only, when taking in hand the perfecting of the service which watches the revolutionist activities abroad, that he thought again of Mr Razumov. He saw great possibilities of special usefulness in that uncommon young man on whom he had a hold already, with his peculiar temperament, his unsettled mind and shaken conscience, a struggling in the toils of a false position. . . . It was as if the revolutionists themselves had put into his hand that tool so much finer than the common base instruments, so perfectly fitted, if only vested with sufficient credit, to penetrate into places inaccessible to common informers. Providential! Providential! And Prince K—, taken into the secret, was ready enough to adopt that mystical view too. 'It will be necessary, though, to make a career for him afterwards,' he had stipulated anxiously. 'Oh! absolutely. We shall make that our affair,' Mikulin had agreed. Prince K—'s mysticism was of an artless kind; but Councillor Mikulin was astute enough for two.

Things and men have always a certain sense, a certain side by which they must be got hold of if one wants to obtain a solid grasp and a perfect command. The power of Councillor Mikulin consisted in the ability to seize upon that sense, that side in the men he used. It did not matter to him what it was – vanity, despair, love, hate, greed, intelligent pride, or stupid conceit, it was all one to him as long as the man could be made to serve. The obscure, unrelated young student Razumov, in the moment of great moral loneliness, was allowed to feel that he was an object of interest to a small group of people of high position. Prince K— was persuaded to intervene personally, and on a certain occasion gave way to a manly emotion which, all unexpected as it was, quite upset Mr Razumov. The sudden embrace of that man, agitated by his loyalty to a throne and by suppressed paternal affection, was a revelation to Mr Razumov of something within his own breast.

'So that was it!' he exclaimed to himself. A sort of contemptuous tenderness softened the young man's grim view of his position as he reflected upon that agitated interview with Prince K—. This simple-minded, worldly ex-Guardsman and senator whose soft grey official whiskers had brushed against his cheek, his aristocratic and convinced father, was he a whit less estimable or more absurd than that famine-stricken, fanatical revolutionist, the red-nosed student?

And there was some pressure, too, besides the persuasiveness. Mr Razumov was always being made to feel that he had committed himself. There was no getting away from that feeling, from that soft, unanswerable, 'Where to?' of Councillor Mikulin. But no susceptibilities were ever hurt. It was to be a dangerous mission to Geneva for obtaining, at a critical moment, absolutely reliable information from a very inaccessible quarter of the inner revolutionary circle. There were indications that a very serious plot was being matured. . . . The repose indispensable to a great country was at stake. . . . A great scheme of orderly reforms would be endangered. . . . The highest personages in the land were patriotically uneasy, and so on. In short, Councillor Mikulin knew what to say. This skill is to be inferred clearly from the mental and psychological self-confession, self-analysis of Mr Razumov's written journal – the pitiful resource of a young man who had near him no trusted intimacy, no natural affection to turn to.

How all this preliminary work was concealed from observation need not be recorded. The expedient of the oculist gives a sufficient instance. Councillor

Mikulin was resourceful, and the task not very difficult. Any fellow-student, even the red-nosed one, was perfectly welcome to see Mr Razumov entering a private house to consult an oculist. Ultimate success depended solely on the revolutionary self-delusion which credited Razumov with a mysterious complicity in the Haldin affair. To be compromised in it was credit enough – and it was their own doing. It was precisely *that* which stamped Mr Razumov as a providential man, wide as poles apart from the usual type of agent for 'European supervision'.

And it was *that* which the Secretariat set itself the task to foster by a course of calculated and false indiscretions.

It came at last to this, that one evening, Mr Razumov was unexpectedly called upon by one of the 'thinking' students whom formerly, before the Haldin affair, he used to meet at various private gatherings; a big fellow with a quiet, unassuming manner and a pleasant voice.

Recognizing his voice raised in the ante-room, 'May one come in?' Razumov, lounging idly on his couch, jumped up. 'Suppose he were coming to stab me?' he thought sardonically, and, assuming a green shade over his left eye, said in a severe tone, 'Come in.'

The other was embarrassed; hoped he was not intruding.

'You haven't been seen for several days, and I've wondered.' He coughed a little. 'Eye better?'

'Nearly well now.'

'Good. I won't stop a minute; but you see I, that is, we – anyway, I have undertaken the duty to warn you, Kirylo Sidorovitch, that you are living in false security maybe.'

Razumov sat still with his head leaning on his hand, which nearly concealed the unshaded eye.

'I have that idea, too.'

'That's all right, then. Everything seems quiet now, but those people are preparing some move of general repression. That's of course. But it isn't that I came to tell you.' He hitched his chair closer, dropped his voice. 'You will be arrested before long – we fear.'

An obscure scribe in the Secretariat had overheard a few words of a certain conversation, and had caught a glimpse of a certain report. This intelligence was not to be neglected.

Razumov laughed a little, and his visitor became very anxious.

'Ah! Kirylo Sidorovitch, this is no laughing matter. They have left you alone for a while, but . . .! Indeed, you had better try to leave the country, Kirylo Sidorovitch, while there's yet time.'

Razumov jumped up and began to thank him for the advice with mocking effusiveness, so that the other, colouring up, took himself off with the notion that this mysterious Razumov was not a person to be warned or advised by inferior mortals.

Councillor Mikulin, informed the next day of the incident, expressed his satisfaction. 'H'm. Ha! Exactly what was wanted to . . .' and glanced down his beard.

'I conclude,' said Razumov, 'that the moment has come for me to start on my mission.'

'The psychological moment,' Councillor Mikulin insisted softly – very gravely – as if awed.

All the arrangements to give verisimilitude to the appearance of a difficult escape were made. Councillor Mikulin did not expect to see Mr Razumov again before his departure. These meetings were a risk, and there was nothing more to settle.

'We have said everything to each other by now, Kirylo Sidorovitch,' said the high official feelingly, pressing Razumov's hand with that unreserved heartiness a Russian can convey in his manner. 'There is nothing obscure between us. And I will tell you that I consider myself fortunate in having – h'm – your . . .'

He glanced down his beard, and, after a moment of thoughtful silence, handed to Razumov a half-sheet of notepaper – an abbreviated note of matters already discussed, certain points of inquiry, the line of conduct agreed on, a few hints as to personalities, and so on. It was the only compromising document in the case, but, as Councillor Mikulin observed, it could be easily destroyed. Mr Razumov had better not see anyone now – till on the other side of the frontier, when, of course, it will be just that . . . See and hear and . . .'

He glanced down his beard; but when Razumov declared his intention to see one person at least before leaving St Petersburg, Councillor Mikulin failed to conceal a sudden uneasiness. The young man's studious, solitary, and austere existence was well known to him. It was the great guarantee of fitness. He became deprecatory. Had his dear Kirylo Sidorovitch considered whether, in view of such a momentous enterprise, it wasn't really advisable to sacrifice every sentiment . . .

Razumov interrupted the remonstrance scornfully. It was not a young woman, it was a young fool he wished to see for a certain purpose. Councillor Mikulin was relieved, but surprised.

'Ah! And what for – precisely?'

'For the sake of improving the aspect of verisimilitude,' said Razumov curtly, in a desire to affirm his independence. 'I must be trusted in what I do.'

Councillor Mikulin gave way tactfully, murmuring, 'Oh, certainly, certainly. Your judgement . . .'

And with another handshake they parted.

The fool of whom Mr Razumov had thought was the rich and festive student known as madcap Kostia. Feather-headed, loquacious, excitable, one could make certain of his utter and complete indiscretion. But that riotous youth, when reminded by Razumov of his offers of service some time ago, passed from his usual elation into boundless dismay.

'Oh, Kirylo Sidorovitch, my dearest friend – my saviour – what shall I do? I've blown last night every rouble I had from my dad the other day. Can't you give me till Thursday? I shall rush round to all the usurers I know . . . No, of course, you can't! Don't look at me like that. What shall I do? No use asking the old man. I tell you he's given me a fistful of big notes three days ago. Miserable wretch that I am.'

He wrung his hands in despair. Impossible to confide in the old man. 'They' had given him a decoration, a cross on the neck only last year, and he had been cursing the modern tendencies ever since. Just then he would see all the intellectuals in Russia hanged in a row rather than part with a single rouble.

'Kirylo Sidorovitch, wait a moment. Don't despise me. I have it. I'll, yes – I'll do it – I'll break into his desk. There's no help for it. I know the drawer where he keeps his plunder, and I can buy a chisel on my way home. He will be terribly upset, but, you know, the dear old duffer really loves me. He'll have to get over it – and I, too. Kirylo, my dear soul, if you can only wait for a few hours – till this evening – I shall steal all the blessed lot I can lay my hands on! You doubt me! Why? You've only to say the word.'

'Steal, by all means,' said Razumov, fixing him stonily.

'To the devil with the ten commandments!' cried the other, with the greatest animation. 'It's the new future now.'

But when he entered Razumov's room late in the evening it was with an unaccustomed soberness of manner, almost solemnly.

'It's done,' he said.

Razumov sitting bowed, his clasped hands hanging between his knees, shuddered at the familiar sound of these words. Kostia deposited slowly in the circle of lamplight a small brown-paper parcel tied with a piece of string.

'As I've said – all I could lay my hands on. The old boy'll think the end of the world has come.'

Razumov nodded from the couch, and contemplated the hare-brained fellow's gravity with a feeling of malicious pleasure.

'I've made my little sacrifice,' sighed mad Kostia. 'And I've to thank you, Kirylo Sidorovitch, for the opportunity.'

'It has cost you something?'

'Yes, it has. You see, the dear old duffer really loves me. He'll be hurt.'

'And you believe all they tell you of the new future and the sacred will of the people?'

'Implicitly. I would give my life . . . Only you see I am like a pig at a trough. I am no good. It's my nature.'

Razumov, lost in thought, had forgotten his existence till the youth's voice, entreating him to fly without loss of time, roused him unpleasantly.

'All right. Well – good-bye.'

'I am not going to leave you till I've seen you out of St Petersburg,' declared Kostia unexpectedly, with calm determination. 'You can't refuse me that now. For God's sake, Kirylo, my soul, the police may be here any moment, and when they get you they'll immure you somewhere for ages – till your hair turns grey. I have down there the best trotter of dad's stables and light sledge. We shall do thirty miles before the moon sets, and find some roadside station . . .'

Razumov looked up amazed. The journey was decided – unavoidable. He had fixed the next day for his departure on the mission. And now he discovered suddenly that he had not believed in it. He had gone about listening, speaking, thinking, planning his simulated flight, with the growing conviction that all this was preposterous. As if anybody ever did such things! It was like a game of make-believe. And now he was amazed! Here was somebody who believed in it with desperate earnestness. 'If I don't go now, at once,' thought Razumov, with a start of fear, 'I shall never go.' He rose without a word, and the anxious Kostia thrust his cap on him, helped him into his cloak, or else he would have left the room bareheaded as he stood. He was walking out silently when a sharp cry arrested him.

'Kirylo!'

'What?' He turned reluctantly in the doorway. Upright, with a stiffly extended arm, Kostia, his face set and white, was pointing an eloquent forefinger at the brown little packet lying forgotten in the circle of bright light on the table. Razumov hesitated, came back for it under the severe eyes of his companion, at whom he tried to smile. But the boyish, mad youth was frowning. 'It's a dream,' thought Razumov, putting the little parcel into his pocket and descending the stairs; 'nobody does such things.' The other held him under the arm, whispering of dangers ahead, and of what he meant to do in certain contingencies. 'Preposterous,' murmured Razumov, as he was being tucked up in the sledge. He gave himself up to watching the development of the dream with extreme attention. It continued on foreseen lines, inexorably logical – the long drive, the wait at the small station sitting by a stove. They did not exchange half a dozen words altogether. Kostia, gloomy himself, did not care to break the silence. At parting they embraced twice – it had to be done; and then Kostia vanished out of the dream.

When dawn broke, Razumov, very still in a hot, stuffy railway-car full of bedding and of sleeping people in all its dimly lighted length, rose quietly, lowered the glass a few inches, and flung out on the great plain of snow a small brown-paper parcel. Then he sat down again muffled up and motionless. 'For the people,' he thought, staring out of the window. The great white desert of frozen, hard earth glided past his eyes without a sign of human habitation.

That had been a waking act; and then the dream had him again: Prussia, Saxony, Württemberg, faces, sights, words – all a dream, observed with an angry, compelled attention. Zürich, Geneva – still a dream, minutely followed, wearing one into harsh laughter, to fury, to death – with the fear of awakening at the end. . . .

CHAPTER II

'PERHAPS LIFE is just that,' reflected Razumov, pacing to and fro under the trees of the little island, all alone with the bronze statue of Rousseau. 'A dream and a fear.' The dusk deepened. The pages written over and torn out of his notebook were the first-fruit of his 'mission'. No dream that. They contained the assurance that he was on the eve of real discoveries. 'I think there is no longer anything in the way of my being completely accepted.'

He had resumed his impressions in those pages, some of the conversations. He even went so far as to write: 'By the by, I have discovered the personality of that terrible N.N. A horrible, paunchy brute. If I hear anything of his future movements I shall send a warning.'

The futility of all this overcame him like a curse. Even then he could not believe in the reality of his mission. He looked round desparingly, as if for some way to redeem his existence from that unconquerable feeling. He crushed angrily in his hand the pages of the notebook. 'This must be posted,' he thought.

He gained the bridge and returned to the north shore, where he remembered having seen in one of the narrower streets a little obscure shop stocked with cheap wood carvings, its walls lined with extremely dirty cardboard-bound volumes of a small circulating library. They sold stationery there, too. A morose, shabby old man dozed behind the counter. A thin woman in black, with a sickly face, produced the envelope he had asked for without even looking at him. Razumov thought that these people were safe to deal with because they no longer cared for anything in the world. He addressed the envelope on the counter with the German name of a certain person living in Vienna. But Razumov knew that this, his first communication for Councillor Mikulin, would find its way to the Embassy there, be copied in cipher by somebody trustworthy, and sent on to its destination, all safe, along with the diplomatic correspondence. That was the arrangement contrived to cover up the track of the information from all unfaithful eyes, from all indiscretions, from all mishaps and treacheries. It was to make him safe – absolutely safe.

He wandered out of the wretched shop and made for the post office. It was then that I saw him for the second time that day. He was crossing the Rue Mont Blanc with every appearance of an aimless stroller. He did not recognize me, but I made him out at some distance. He was very good-looking, I thought, this remarkable friend of Miss Haldin's brother. I watched him go up to the letter-box and then retrace his steps. Again he passed me very close, but I am certain he did not see me that time, either. He carried his head well up, but he had the expression of a somnambulist struggling with the very dream which drives him forth to wander in dangerous places. My thoughts reverted to Natalia Haldin, to her mother. He was all that was left to them of their son and brother.

The Westerner in me was discomposed. There was something shocking in the expression of that face. Had I been myself a conspirator, a Russian political refugee, I could have perhaps been able to draw some practical conclusion from this chance glimpse. As it was, it only discomposed me strongly, even to the extent of awakening an indefinite apprehension in regard to Natalia Haldin. All this is rather inexplicable, but such was the origin of the purpose I formed there and then to call on these ladies in the evening, after my solitary dinner. It was true that I had met Miss Haldin only a few hours before, but Mrs Haldin herself I had not seen for some considerable time. The truth is, I had shirked calling of late.

Poor Mrs Haldin! I confess she frightened me a little. She was one of those natures, rare enough, luckily, in which one cannot help being interested, because they provoke both terror and pity. One dreads their contact for oneself, and still more for those one cares for, so clear it is that they are born to suffer and to make others suffer, too. It is strange to think that, I won't say liberty, but the mere liberalism of outlook which for us is a matter of words, of ambitions, of votes (and if of feeling at all, then of the sort of feeling which leaves our deepest affections untouched) may be for other beings very much like ourselves and living under the same sky, a heavy trial of fortitude, a matter of tears and anguish and blood. Mrs Haldin had felt the pangs of her own generation. There was that enthusiast brother of hers – the officer they shot under Nicholas. A faintly ironic resignation is no armour for a vulnerable heart. Mrs Haldin, struck at through her children, was bound to suffer afresh from the past, and to feel the anguish of the future. She was of those who do not know how to heal themselves, of those who are too much aware of their heart, who, neither cowardly nor selfish, look passionately at its wounds – and count the cost.

Such thoughts as these seasoned my modest, lonely bachelor's meal. If anybody wishes to remark that this was a roundabout way of thinking of Natalia Haldin, I can only retort that she was well worth some concern. She had all her life before her. Let it be admitted, then, that I was thinking of Natalia Haldin's life in terms of her mother's character, a manner of thinking about a girl permissible for an old man, not too old yet to have become a stranger to pity. There was almost all her youth before her; a youth robbed arbitrarily of its natural lightness and joy, overshadowed by an un-European despotism; a terribly sombre youth given over to the hazards of a furious strife between equally ferocious antagonisms.

I lingered over my thoughts more than I should have done. One felt so helpless, and even worse – so unrelated, in a way. At the last moment I hesitated as to going there at all. What was the good?

The evening was already advanced when, turning into the Boulevard des Philosophes, I saw the light in the window at the corner. The blind was down, but I could imagine behind it Mrs Haldin seated in the chair, in her usual attitude, looking out for someone, which had lately acquired the poignant quality of mad expectation.

I thought that I was sufficiently authorized by the light to knock at the door. The ladies had not retired as yet. I only hoped they would not have any visitors of their own nationality. A broken-down, retired Russian official was to be found there sometimes in the evening. He was infinitely forlorn and wearisome by mere dismal presence. I think these ladies tolerated his frequent visits because of an ancient friendship with Mr Haldin, the father, or something of that sort. I made up my mind that if I found him prosing away there in his feeble voice I should remain but a very few minutes.

The door surprised me by swinging open before I could ring the bell. I was confronted by Miss Haldin, in hat and jacket, obviously on the point of going out. At that hour! For the doctor, perhaps?

Her exclamation of welcome reassured me. It sounded as if I had been the very man she wanted to see. My curiosity was awakened. She drew me in, and the faithful Anna, the elderly German maid, closed the door, but did not go away afterwards. She remained near it as if in readiness to let me out presently. It appeared that Miss Haldin had been on the point of going out to find me.

She spoke in a hurried manner very unusual with her. She would have gone straight and rung at Mrs Ziegler's door, late as it was, for Mrs Ziegler's habits . . .

Mrs Ziegler, the widow of a distinguished professor who was an intimate friend of mine, lets me have three rooms out of her very large and fine apartment, which she didn't give up after her husband's death; but I have my own entrance opening on the same landing. It was an arrangement of at least ten years' standing. I said that I was very glad that I had the idea to . . .

Miss Haldin made no motion to take off her outdoor things. I observed her heightened colour, something pronouncedly resolute in her tone. Did I know where Mr Razumov lived?

Where Mr Razumov lived? Mr Razumov? At this hour – so urgently? I threw my arms up in sign of utter ignorance. I had not the slightest idea where he lived. If I could have foreseen her question only three hours ago, I might have ventured to ask him on the pavement before the new post office building, and possibly he would have told me, but very possibly, too, he would have dismissed me rudely to mind my own business. And possibly, I thought, remembering that extraordinary hallucinated, anguished, and absent expression, he might have fallen down in a fit from the shock of being spoken to. I said nothing of all this to Miss Haldin, not even mentioning that I had a glimse of the young man so recently. The impression had been so extremely unpleasant that I would have been glad to forget it myself.

'I don't see where I could make inquiries,' I murmured helplessly. I would have been glad to be of use in any way, and would have set off to fetch any man, young or old, for I had the greatest confidence in her common sense. 'What made you think of coming to me for that information?' I asked.

'It wasn't exactly for that,' she said, in a low voice. She had the air of someone confronted by an unpleasant task.

'Am I to understand that you must communicate with Mr Razumov this evening?'

Natalia Haldin moved her head affirmatively; then after a glance at the door of the drawing-room, said in French –

'*C'est maman*,' and remained perplexed for a moment. Always serious, not a girl to put out by any imaginary difficulties, my curiosity was suspended on her lips, which remained closed for a moment. What was Mr Razumov's connexion with this mention of her mother? Mrs Haldin had not been informed of her son's friend's arrival in Geneva.

'May I hope to see your mother this evening?' I inquired.

Miss Haldin extended her hand as if to bar the way.

'She is in a terrible state of agitation. Oh, you would not be able to detect. . . . It's inward, but I who know mother, I am appalled. I haven't the courage to face it any longer. It's all my fault; I suppose I cannot play a part; I've never before hidden anything from mother. There has never been an occasion for anything of that sort between us. But you know yourself the reason why I refrained from telling her at once of Mr Razumov's arrival here. You understand, don't you? Owing to her unhappy state. And – there – I am no actress. My own feelings being strongly engaged, I somehow . . . I don't know. She noticed something in my manner. She thought I was concealing something from her. She noticed my longer absences, and, in fact, as I have been meeting Mr Razumov daily, I used to stay away longer than usual when I went out. Goodness knows what suspicions arose in her mind. You know that she has not been herself ever since. . . . So this evening she – who has been so awfully silent for weeks – began to talk all at once. She said that she did not want to reproach me; that I had my character as she had her own; that she did not want to pry into my affairs or even into my thoughts; for her part, she had never had anything to conceal from her children . . . cruel things to listen to. And all this in her quiet voice, with that poor, wasted face as calm as a stone. It was unbearable.'

Miss Haldin talked in an undertone and more rapidly than I had ever heard her speak before. That in itself was disturbing. The ante-room being strongly lighted, I could see under the veil the heightened colour of her face. She stood erect, her left hand was resting lightly on a small table. The other hung by her side without stirring. Now and then she caught her breath slightly.

'It was too startling. Just fancy! She thought that I was making preparations to leave her without saying anything. I knelt by the side of her chair and entreated her to think of what she was saying! She put her hand on my head, but she persists in her delusion all the same. She had always thought that she was worthy of her children's confidence, but apparently it was not so. Her son could not trust her love nor yet her understanding – and now I was planning to abandon her in the same cruel and unjust manner, and so on, and so on. Nothing I could say. . . . It is morbid obstinacy. . . . She said that she felt there was something, some change in me. . . . If my convictions were calling me away, why this secrecy, as though she had been a coward or a weakling not safe to trust? "As if my heart could play traitor to my children," she said. . . . It was hardly to be borne. And she was smoothing my head all the time. . . . It was perfectly useless to protest. She is ill. Her very soul is . . .'

I did not venture to break the silence which fell between us. I looked into her eyes, glistening through the veil.

'I! Changed!' she exclaimed in the same low tone. 'My convictions calling me away! It was cruel to hear this, because my trouble is that I am weak and cannot see what I ought to do. You know that. And to end it all I did a selfish thing. To remove her suspicions of myself I told her of Mr Razumov. It was selfish of me. You know we were completely right in agreeing to keep the knowledge away from her. Perfectly right. Directly I told her of our poor Victor's friend being here I saw how right we have been. She ought to have been prepared; but in my distress I just blurted it out. Mother got terribly excited at once. How long has he been here? What did he know, and why did he not come to see us at once, this friend of her Victor? What did that mean? Was she not to be trusted even with such memories as there were left of her son? . . . Just think how I felt seeing her, white as a sheet, perfectly motionless, with her thin hands gripping the arms of the chair. I told her it was all my fault.'

I could imagine the motionless dumb figure of the mother in her chair, there, behind the door, near which the daughter was talking to me. The silence in there seemed to call aloud for vengeance against an historical fact and the modern instances of its working. That view flashed through my mind, but I could not doubt that Miss Haldin had had an atrocious time of it. I quite understood when she said that she could not face the night upon the impression of that scene. Mrs Haldin had given way to most awful imaginings, to most fantastic and cruel suspicions. All this had to be lulled at all costs and without loss of time. It was no shock to me to learn that Miss Haldin had said to her, 'I will go and bring him here at once.' There was nothing absurd in that cry, no exaggeration of sentiment. I was not even doubtful in my 'Very well, but how?'

It was perfectly right that she should think of me, but what could I do in my ignorance of Mr Razumov's quarters?

'And to think he may be living near by, within a stone's-throw, perhaps!' she exclaimed.

I doubted it; but I would have gone off cheerfully to fetch him from the other end of Geneva. I suppose she was certain of my readiness, since her first thought was to come to me. But the service she meant to ask of me really was to accompany her to the Château Borel.

I had an unpleasant mental vision of the dark road, of the sombre grounds, and the desolately suspicious aspect of that home of necromancy and intrigue and feminist adoration. I objected that Madame de S— most likely would know nothing of what we wanted to find out. Neither did I think it likely that the young man would be found there. I remembered my glimpse of his face, and somehow gained the conviction that a man who looked worse than if he had seen the dead would want to shut himself up somewhere where he could be alone. I felt a strange certitude that Mr Razumov was going home when I saw him.

'It is really of Peter Ivanovitch that I was thinking,' said Miss Haldin quietly.

Ah! He, of course, would know. I looked at my watch. It was twenty minutes past nine only. . . . Still.

'I would try his hotel, then,' I advised. 'He has rooms at the Cosmopolitan, somewhere on the top floor.'

I did not offer to go by myself, simply from mistrust of the reception I should meet with. But I suggested the faithful Anna, with a note asking for the information.

Anna was still waiting by the door at the other end of the room, and we two discussed the matter in whispers. Miss Haldin thought she must go herself. Anna was timid and slow. Time would be lost in bringing back the answer, and from that point of view it was getting late, for it was by no means certain that Mr Razumov lived near by.

'If I go myself,' Miss Haldin argued, 'I can go straight to him from the hotel. And in any case I should have to go out, because I must explain to Mr Razumov personally – prepare him in a way. You have no idea of mother's state of mind.'

Her colour came and went. She even thought that both for her mother's sake and for her own it was better that they should not be together for a little time. Anna, whom her mother liked, would be at hand.

'She could take her sewing into the room,' Miss Haldin continued, leading the way to the door. Then, addressing in German the maid who opened it before us. 'You may tell my mother that this gentleman called and is gone with me to find Mr Razumov. She must not be uneasy if I am away for some length of time.'

We passed out quickly into the street, and she took deep breaths of the cool night air. 'I did not even ask you,' she murmured.

'I should think not,' I said, with a laugh. The manner of my reception by the great feminist could not be considered now. That he would be annoyed to see me, and probably treat me to some solemn insolence, I had no doubt, but I supposed that he would not absolutely dare to throw me out. And that was all I cared for. 'Won't you take my arm?' I asked.

She did so in silence, and neither of us said anything worth recording till I let her go first into the great hall of the hotel. It was brilliantly lighted, and with a good many people lounging about.

'I could very well go up there without you,' I suggested.

'I don't like to be left waiting in this place,' she said in a low voice. 'I will come too.'

I led her straight to the lift then. At the top floor the attendant directed us to the right: 'End of the corridor.'

The walls were white, the carpet red, electric lights blazed in profusion, and the emptiness, the silence, the closed doors all alike and numbered, made me think of the perfect order of some severely luxurious model penitentiary on the solitary confinement principle. Up there under the roof of that enormous pile for housing travellers no sound of any kind reached us, the thick crimson felt muffled our footsteps completely. We hastened on, looking at each other till we found ourselves before the very last door of that long passage. Then our eyes met, and we stood thus for a moment lending ear to a faint murmur of voices inside.

'I suppose this is it,' I whispered unnecessarily. I saw Miss Haldin's lips move without a sound, and after my sharp knock the murmur of voices inside ceased. A profound stillness lasted for a few seconds, and then the door was brusquely opened by a short, black-eyed woman in a red blouse, with a great lot of nearly white hair, done up negligently in an untidy and unpicturesque manner. Her thin, jetty eyebrows were drawn together. I learned afterwards with interest that she was the famous – or the notorious – Sophia Antonovna, but I was struck then by the quaint Mephistophelian character of her inquiring glance, because it was so curiously evil-less, so – I may say – undevillish. It got softened still more as she looked up at Miss Haldin, who stated, in her rich, even voice, her wish to see Peter Ivanovitch for a moment.

'I am Miss Haldin,' she added.

At this, with her brow completely smoothed out now, but without a word in answer, the woman in the red blouse walked away to a sofa and sat down, leaving the door wide open.

And from the sofa, her hands lying on her lap, she watched us enter, with her black glittering eyes.

Miss Haldin advanced into the middle of the room; I, faithful to my part of mere attendant, remained by the door after closing it behind me. The room, quite a large one, but with a low ceiling, was scantily furnished, and an electric bulb with a porcelain shade pulled low down over a big table (with a very large map spread on it) left its distant parts in a dim, artificial twilight. Peter Ivanovitch was not to be seen, neither was Mr Razumov present. But, on the sofa, near Sophia Antonovna, a bony-faced man with a goatee beard leaned forward with his hands on his knees, staring hard with a kindly expression. In a remote corner a broad, pale face and a bulky shape could be made out, uncouth, and as if insecure on the low seat on which it rested. The only person known to me was little Julius Laspara, who seemed to have been poring over the map, his feet twined tightly round the chair-legs. He got down briskly and bowed to Miss Haldin, looking absurdly like a hook-nosed boy with a beautiful false pepper-and-salt beard. He advanced, offering his seat, which Miss Haldin declined. She had only come in for a moment to say a few words to Peter Ivanovitch.

His high-pitched voice became painfully audible in the room.

'Strangely enough, I was thinking of you this very afternoon, Natalia Victorovna. I met Mr Razumov. I asked him to write me an article on anything he liked. You could translate it into English – with such a teacher.'

He nodded complimentarily in my direction. At the name of Razumov an indescribable sound, a sort of feeble squeak, as of some angry small animal, was heard in the corner occupied by the man who seemed much too large for the chair on which he sat. I did not hear what Miss Haldin said. Laspara spoke again.

'It's time to do something, Natalia Victorovna. But I suppose you have your own ideas. Why not write something yourself? Suppose you came to see us soon? We could talk it over. Any advice . . .'

Again I did not catch Miss Haldin's words. It was Laspara's voice once more.

'Peter Ivanovitch? He's retired for a moment into the other room. We are all waiting for him.'

The great man, entering at that moment, looked bigger, taller, quite imposing in a long dressing-gown of some dark stuff. It descended in straight lines down to his feet. He suggested a monk or a prophet, a robust figure of some desert-dweller – something Asiatic; and the dark glasses in conjunction with this costume made him more mysterious than ever in the subdued light.

Little Laspara went back to his chair to look at the map, the only brilliantly lit object in the room. Even from my distant position by the door I could make out, by the shape of the blue part representing the water, that it was a map of the Baltic provinces. Peter Ivanovitch exclaimed slightly, advancing towards Miss Haldin, checked himself on perceiving me, very vaguely no doubt, and peered with his dark, bespectacled stare. He must have recognized me by my grey hair, because, with a marked shrug of his broad shoulders, he turned to Miss Haldin in benevolent indulgence. He seized her hand in his thick cushioned palm, and put his other big paw over it like a lid.

While those two standing in the middle of the floor were exchanging a few inaudible phrases no one else moved in the room: Laspara, with his back to us, kneeling on the chair, his elbows propped on the big-scale map, the shadowy enormity in the corner, the frankly staring man with the goatee on the sofa, the woman in the red blouse by his side – not one of them stirred. I suppose that really they had no time, for Miss Haldin withdrew her hand immediately from Peter Ivanovitch and before I was ready for her was moving to the door. A disregarded Westerner, I threw it open hurriedly and followed her out, my last glance leaving them all motionless in their varied poses: Peter Ivanovitch alone standing up, with his dark glasses like an enormous blind teacher, and behind him the vivid patch of light on the coloured map, pored over by the diminutive Laspara.

Later on, much later on, at the time of the newspaper rumours (they were vague and soon died out) of an abortive military conspiracy in Russia, I remembered the glimpse I had of that motionless group with its central figure. No details ever came out, but it was known that the revolutionary parties abroad had given their assistance, had sent emissaries in advance, that even money was found to dispatch a steamer with a cargo of arms and conspirators to invade the Baltic provinces. And while my eyes scanned the imperfect disclosures (in which the world was not much interested) I thought that the old, settled Europe had been given in my person attending that Russian girl something like a glimpse behind the scenes. A short, strange glimpse on the top floor of a great hotel of all places in the world: the great man himself; the motionless great bulk in the corner of the slayer of spies and gendarmes; Yakovlitch the veteran of ancient terrorist campaigns; the woman with her hair as white as mine and the lively black eyes, all in a mysterious half-light, with the strongly lighted map of Russia on the table. The woman I had the opportunity to see again. As we were waiting for the lift she came hurrying along the corridor, with her eyes fastened on Miss Haldin's face, and drew her aside as if for a confidential communication. It was not long. A few words only.

Going down in the lift, Natalia Haldin did not break the silence. It was only when out of the hotel and as we moved along the quay in the fresh darkness spangled by the quay lights, reflected in the black water of the little port on our left hand, and with lofty piles of hotels on our right, that she spoke.

'That was Sophia Antonovna – you know the woman? . . .'

'Yes, I know – the famous . . .'

'The same. It appears that after we went out Peter Ivanovitch told them why I had come. That was the reason she ran out after us. She named herself to me, and then she said, "You are the sister of a brave man who shall be remembered. You may see better times." I told her I hoped to see the time when all this would be forgotten, even if the name of my brother were to be forgotten too. Something moved me to say that, but you understand?'

'Yes,' I said. 'You think of the era of concord and justice.'

'Yes. There is too much hate and revenge in that work. It must be done. It is a sacrifice – and so let it be all the greater. Destruction is the work of anger. Let the tyrants and the slayers be forgotten together, and only the reconstructors be remembered.'

'And did Sophia Antonovna agree with you?' I asked sceptically.

'She did not say anything except, "It is good for you to believe in love." I should think she understood me. Then she asked me if I hoped to see Mr Razumov presently. I said I trusted I could manage to bring him to see my mother this evening, as my mother had learned of his being here and was morbidly impatient to learn if he could tell us something of Victor. He was the only friend of my brother we knew of, and a great intimate. She said, "Oh! Your brother – yes. Please tell Mr Razumov that I have made public the story which came to me from St Petersburg. It concerns your brother's arrest," she added. "He was betrayed by a man of the people who has since hanged himself. Mr Razumov will explain it all to you. I gave him the full information this afternoon. And please tell Mr Razumov that Sophia Antonovna sends him her greetings. I am going away early in the morning – far away." '

And Miss Haldin added, after a moment of silence –

'I was so moved by what I heard so unexpectedly that I simply could not speak to you before. . . . A man of the people! Oh, our poor people!'

She walked slowly, as if tired out suddenly. Her head drooped; from the windows of a building with terraces and balconies came the banal sound of hotel music; before the low mean portals of the Casino two red posters blazed under the electric lamps, with a cheap provincial effect – and the emptiness of the quays, the desert aspect of the streets, had an air of hypocritical respectability and of inexpressible dreariness.

I had taken for granted she had obtained the address, and let myself be guided by her. On the Mont Blanc bridge, where a few dark figures seemed lost in the wide and long perspective defined by the lights, she said –

'It isn't very far from our house. I somehow thought it couldn't be. The address is Rue de Carouge. I think it must be one of those big new houses for artisans.'

She took my arm confidingly, familiarly, and accelerated her pace. There was something primitive in our proceedings. We did not think of the resources of civilization. A late tramcar overtook us; a row of *fiacres* stood by the railing of the gardens. It never entered our heads to make use of these conveyances. She was too hurried, perhaps, and as to myself – well, she had taken my arm confidingly. As we were ascending the easy incline of the Corraterie, all the shops shuttered and no light in any of the windows (as if all the mercenary population had fled at the end of the day), she said tentatively –

'I could run in for a moment to have a look at mother. It would not be much out of the way.'

I dissuaded her. If Mrs Haldin really expected to see Razumov that night it would have been unwise to show herself without him. The sooner we got hold of the young man and brought him along to calm her mother's agitation, the better. She assented to my reasoning, and we crossed diagonally the Place du Théâtre, bluish grey with its floor of slabs of stone, under the electric light, and the lonely equestrian statue all black in the middle. In the Rue de Carouge we were in the poorer quarters and approaching the outskirts of the town. Vacant building plots alternated with high, new houses. At the corner of a side street the crude light of a whitewashed shop fell into the night, fan-like, through a wide doorway. One could see from a distance the inner wall with its scantily furnished shelves, and the deal counter painted brown. That was the house. Approaching it along the dark stretch of a fence of tarred planks, we saw the narrow pallid face of the cut angle, five single windows high, without a gleam in them, and crowned by the heavy shadow of a jutting roof slope.

'We must inquire in the shop,' Miss Haldin directed me.

A sallow, thinly whiskered man, wearing a dingy white collar and a frayed tie, laid down a newspaper, and, leaning familiarly on both elbows far over the bare counter, answered that the person I was inquiring for was indeed his *locataire* on the third floor, but that for the moment he was out.

'For the moment,' I repeated, after a glance at Miss Haldin. 'Does this mean that you expect him back at once?'

He was very gentle, with ingratiating eyes and soft lips. He smiled faintly as though he knew all about everything. Mr Razumov, after being absent all day, had returned early in the evening. He was very surprised about half an hour or a little more ago to see him come down again. Mr Razumov left his key, and in the course of some words which passed between them had remarked that he was going out because he needed air.

From behind the bare counter he went on smiling at us, his head held between his hands. Air. Air. But whether that meant a long or a short absence it was difficult to say. The night was very close, certainly.

After a pause, his ingratiating eyes turned to the door, he added –

'The storm will drive him in.'

'There's going to be a storm?' I asked.

'Why, yes!'

As if to confirm his words we heard a very distant, deep rumbling noise.

Consulting Miss Haldin by a glance, I saw her so reluctant to give up her quest that I asked the shopkeeper, in case Mr Razumov came home within half an hour, to beg him to remain downstairs in the shop. We would look in again presently.

For all answer he moved his head imperceptibly. The approval of Miss Haldin was expressed by her silence. We walked slowly down the street, away from the town; the low garden walls of the modest villas doomed to demolition were overhung by the boughs of trees and masses of foliage, lighted from below by gas lamps. The violent and monotonous noise of the icy waters of the Arve falling over a low dam swept towards us with a chilly draught of air across a great open space, where a double line of lamp-lights outlined a street as yet without houses. But on the other shore, overhung by the awful blackness of the thundercloud, a solitary dim light seemed to watch us with a weary stare. When we had strolled as far as the bridge, I said –

'We had better get back. . . .'

In the shop the sickly man was studying his smudgy newspaper, now spread out largely on the counter. He just raised his head when I looked in and shook it negatively, pursing up his lips. I rejoined Miss Haldin outside at once, and we moved off at a brisk pace. She remarked that she would send Anna with a note the first thing in the morning. I respected her taciturnity, silence being perhaps the best way to show my concern.

The semi-rural street we followed on our return changed gradually to the usual town thoroughfare, broad and deserted. We did not meet four people altogether, and the way seemed interminable, because my companion's natural anxiety had communicated itself sympathetically to me. At last we turned into the Boulevard des Philosophes, more wide, more empty, more dead – the very desolation of slumbering respectability. At the sight of the two lighted windows, very conspicuous from afar, I had the mental vision of Mrs Haldin in her armchair keeping a dreadful, tormenting vigil under the evil spell of an arbitrary rule: a victim of tyranny and revolution, a sight at once cruel and absurd.

Chapter III

'You will come in for a moment?' said Natalia Haldin.

I demurred on account of the late hour. 'You know mother likes you so much,' she insisted.

'I will just come in to hear how your mother is.'

She said, as if to herself, 'I don't even know whether she will believe that I could not find Mr Razumov, since she has taken it into her head that I am concealing something from her. You may be able to persuade her. . . .'

'Your mother may mistrust me too,' I observed.

'You? Why? What could you have to conceal from her? You are not a Russian nor a conspirator.'

I felt profoundly my European remoteness, and said nothing, but I made up my mind to play my part of helpless spectator to the end. The distant rolling of thunder in the valley of the Rhône was coming nearer to the sleeping town of prosaic virtues and universal hospitality. We crossed the street opposite the great dark gateway, and Miss Haldin rang at the door of the apartment. It was opened almost instantly, as if the elderly maid had been waiting in the ante-room for our return. Her flat physiognomy had an air of satisfaction. The gentleman was there, she declared, while closing the door.

Neither of us understood. Miss Haldin turned round brusquely to her. 'Who?'

'Herr Razumov,' she explained.

She had heard enough of our conversation before we left to know why her young mistress was going out. Therefore, when the gentleman gave his name at the door, she admitted him at once.

'No one could have foreseen that,' Miss Haldin murmured, with her serious grey eyes fixed upon mine. And, remembering the expression of the young man's face seen not much more than four hours ago, the look of a haunted somnambulist, I wondered with a sort of awe.

'You asked my mother first?' Miss Haldin inquired of the maid.

'No. I announced the gentleman,' she answered, surprised at our troubled faces.

'Still,' I said in an undertone, 'your mother was prepared.'

'Yes. But he has no idea . . .'

It seemed to me she doubted his tact. To her question how long the gentleman had been with her mother, the maid told us that *der Herr* had been in the drawing-room no more than a short quarter of an hour.

She waited a moment, then withdrew, looking a little scared. Miss Haldin gazed at me in silence.

'As things have turned out,' I said, 'you happen to know exactly what your brother's friend has to tell your mother. And surely after that . . .'

'Yes,' said Natalia Haldin slowly. 'I only wonder, as I was not here when he came, if it wouldn't be better not to interrupt now.'

We remained silent, and I suppose we both strained our ears, but no sound reached us through the closed door. The features of Miss Haldin expressed a painful irresolution; she made a movement as if to go in, but checked herself. She had heard footsteps on the other side of the door. It came open, and Razumov, without pausing, stepped out into the ante-room. The fatigue of that day and the struggle with himself had changed him so much that I would have hesitated to recognize that face which, only a few hours before, when he brushed against me in front of the post office, had been startling enough but quite different. It had been not so livid then, and its eyes not so sombre. They certainly looked more sane now, but there was upon them the shadow of something consciously evil.

I speak of that, because, at first, their glance fell on me, though without any sort of recognition or even comprehension. I was simply in the line of his stare. I don't know if he had heard the bell or expected to see anybody. He was going out, I believe, and I do not think that he saw Miss Haldin till she advanced towards him a step or two. He disregarded the hand she put out.

'It's you, Natalia Victorovna. . . . Perhaps you are surprised . . . at this late hour. But, you see, I remembered our conversations in that garden. I thought really it was your wish that I should – without loss of time . . . so I came. No other reason. Simply to tell . . .'

He spoke with difficulty. I noticed that, and remembered his declaration to the man in the shop that he was going out because he 'needed air'. If that was his object, then it was clear that he had miserably failed. With downcast eyes and lowered head he made an effort to pick up the strangled phrase.

'To tell what I have heard myself only today – today . . .'

Through the door he had not closed I had a view of the drawing-room. It was lighted only by a shaded lamp – Mrs Haldin's eyes could not support either gas or electricity. It was a comparatively big room, and in contrast with the strongly lighted ante-room its length was lost in semi-transparent gloom backed by heavy shadows; and on that ground I saw the motionless figure of Mrs Haldin, inclined slightly forward, with a pale hand resting on the arm of the chair.

She did not move. With the window before her she had no longer that attitude suggesting expectation. The blind was down; and outside there was only the night sky harbouring a thundercloud, and the town indifferent and hospitable in its cold, almost scornful, toleration – a respectable town of refuge to which all these sorrows and hopes were nothing. Her white head was bowed.

The thought that the real drama of autocracy is not played on the great stage of politics came to me as, fated to be a spectator, I had this other glimpse behind the scenes, something more profound than the words and gestures of the public play. I had the certitude that this mother refused in her heart to give her son up after all. It was more than Rachel's inconsolable mourning, it was something deeper, more inaccessible in its frightful tranquillity. Lost in the ill-defined mass of the high-backed chair, her white, inclined profile suggested the contemplation of something in her lap, as though a beloved head were resting there.

I had this glimpse behind the scenes, and then Miss Haldin, passing by the young man, shut the door. It was not done without hesitation. For a moment I thought that she would go to her mother, but she sent in only an anxious glance. Perhaps if Mrs Haldin had moved . . . but no. There was in the immobility of that bloodless face the dreadful aloofness of suffering without remedy.

Meantime the young man kept his eyes fixed on the floor. The thought that he would have to repeat the story he had told already was intolerable to him. He had expected to find the two women together. And then, he had said to himself, it would be over for all time – for all time. 'It's lucky I don't believe in another world,' he had thought cynically.

Alone in his room after having posted his secret letter, he had regained a certain measure of composure by writing in his secret diary. He was aware of the danger of that strange self-indulgence. He alludes to it himself, but he could not refrain. It calmed him – it reconciled him to his existence. He sat there scribbling by the light of a solitary candle, till it occurred to him that having heard the explanation of Haldin's arrest, as put forward by Sophia Antonovna, it behoved him to tell these ladies himself. They were certain to hear the tale through some other channel, and then his abstention would look strange, not only to the mother and sister of Haldin, but to other people also. Having come to this conclusion, he did not discover in himself any marked reluctance to face the necessity, and very soon an anxiety to be done with it began to torment him. He looked at his watch. No; it was not absolutely too late.

The fifteen minutes with Mrs Haldin were like the revenge of the unknown: that white face, that weak, distinct voice; that head, at first turned to him eagerly, then, after a while, bowed again and motionless – in the dim, still light of the room in which his words which he tried to subdue resounded so loudly – had troubled him like some strange discovery. And there seemed to be a secret obstinacy in that sorrow, something he could not understand; at any rate, something he had not expected. Was it hostile? But it did not matter. Nothing could touch him now; in the eyes of the revolutionists there was now no shadow on his past. The phantom of Haldin had been indeed walked over, was left behind lying powerless and passive on the pavement covered with snow. And this was the phantom's mother consumed with grief and white as a ghost. He had felt a pitying surprise. But that, of course, was of no importance. Mothers did not matter. He could not shake off the poignant impression of that silent, quiet, white-haired woman, but a sort of sternness crept into his thoughts. These were the consequences. Well, what of it? 'Am I then on a bed of roses?' he had exclaimed to himself, sitting at some distance with his eyes fixed upon that figure of sorrow. He had said all he had to say to her, and when he had finished she had not uttered a word. She had turned away her head while he was speaking. The silence which had fallen on his last words had lasted for five minutes or more. What did it mean? Before its incomprehensible character he became conscious of anger in his stern mood, the old anger against Haldin reawakened by the contemplation of Haldin's mother. And was it not something like enviousness which gripped his heart, as if of a privilege denied to him alone of all the men that had ever passed through this world? It was the other who had attained to repose and yet continued to exist in the affection of that mourning old woman, in the thoughts of all these people posing as lovers of humanity. It was impossible to get rid of him. 'It's myself whom I have given up to destruction,' thought Razumov. 'He has induced me to do it. I can't shake him off.'

Alarmed by that discovery, he got up and strode out of the silent, dim room with its silent old woman in the chair, that mother! He never looked back. It was frankly a flight. But on opening the door he saw his retreat cut off. There was the sister. He had never forgotten the sister, only he had not expected to see her then – or ever any more, perhaps. Her presence in the ante-room was as unforeseen as the apparition of her brother had been. Razumov gave a start as though he had discovered himself cleverly trapped. He tried to smile, but could not manage it, and lowered his eyes. 'Must I repeat that silly story now?' he asked himself, and felt a sinking sensation. Nothing solid had passed his lips since the day before, but he was not in a state to analyse the origins of his weakness. He meant to take up his hat and depart with as few words as possible, but Miss Haldin's swift movement to shut the door took him by surprise. He half turned after her, but without raising his eyes, passively, just as a feather might stir in the disturbed air. The next moment she was back in the place she had started from, with another half-turn on his part, so that they came again into the same relative positions.

'Yes, yes,' she said hurriedly. 'I am very grateful to you, Kirylo Sidorovitch, for coming at once – like this. . . . Only, I wish I had . . . Did mother tell you?'

'I wonder what she could have told me that I did not know before,' he said, obviously to himself, but perfectly audible. 'Because I always *did* know it,' he added louder, as if in despair.

He hung his head. He had such a strong sense of Natalia Haldin's presence that to look at her he felt would be a relief. It was she who had been haunting him now. He had suffered that persecution ever since she had suddenly appeared before him in the garden of the Villa Borel with an extended hand and the name of her brother on her lips. . . . The ante-room had a row of books on the wall nearest to the outer door, while against the wall opposite there stood a small dark table and one chair. The paper, bearing a very faint design, was all but white. The light of an electric bulb high up under the ceiling searched that clear square box into its four bare corners, crudely, without shadows – a strange stage for an obscure drama.

'What do you mean?' asked Miss Haldin. 'What is it that you knew always?'

He raised his face, pale, full of unexpressed suffering. But that look in his eyes of dull, absent obstinacy, which struck, and surprised everybody he was talking to, began to pass away. It was as though he were coming to himself in the awakened consciousness of that marvellous harmony of feature, of lines, of glances, of voice, which made of the girl before him a being so rare, outside, and, as it were, above the common notion of beauty. He looked at her so long that she coloured slightly.

'What is it that you knew?' she repeated vaguely.

That time he managed to smile.

'Indeed, if it had not been for a word of greeting or two, I would doubt whether your mother was aware at all of my existence. You understand?'

Natalia Haldin nodded; her hands moved slightly by her side.

'Yes. Is it not heart-breaking? She has not shed a tear yet – not a single tear.'

'Not a tear! And you, Natalia Victorovna? You have been able to cry?'

'I have. And then I am young enough, Kirylo Sidorovitch, to believe in the future. But when I see my mother so terribly distracted, I almost forget everything. I ask myself whether one should feel proud – or only resigned. We had such a lot of people coming to see us. There were utter strangers who wrote asking for permission to call to present their respects. It was impossible to keep our door shut for ever. You know that Peter Ivanovitch himself . . . Oh yes, there was much sympathy, but there were persons who exulted openly at that death. Then, when I was left alone with poor mother, all this seemed so wrong in spirit, something not worth the price she is paying for it. But directly I heard you were here in Geneva, Kirylo Sidorovitch, I felt that you were the only person who could assist me . . .'

'In comforting a bereaved mother? Yes!' he broke in in a manner which made her open her clear unsuspecting eyes. 'But there is a question of fitness. Has this occurred to you?'

There was a breathlessness in his utterance which contrasted with the monstrous hint of mockery in his intention.

'Why!' whispered Natalia Haldin with feeling. 'Who more fit than you?'

He had a convulsive movement of exasperation, but controlled himself.

'Indeed! Directly you heard that I was in Geneva, before even seeing me? It is another proof of that confidence which . . .'

All at once his tone changed, became more incisive and more detached.

'Men are poor creatures, Natalia Victorovna. They have no intuition of sentiment. In order to speak fittingly to a mother of her lost son one must have had some experience of the filial relation. It is not the case with me – if you must know the whole truth. Your hopes have to deal here with "a breast unwarmed by any affection," as the poet says. . . . That does not mean it is insensible,' he added in a lower tone.

'I am certain your heart is not unfeeling,' said Miss Haldin softly.

'No. It is not as hard as a stone,' he went on in the same introspective voice, and looking as if his heart were lying as heavy as a stone in that unwarmed breast of which he spoke. 'No, not so hard. But how to prove what you give me credit for – ah! that's another question. No one has ever expected such a thing from me before. No one whom my tenderness would have been of any use to. And now you come. You! Now! No, Natalia Victorovna. It's too late. You come too late. You must expect nothing from me.'

She recoiled from him a little, though he had made no movement, as if she had seen some change in his face, charging his words with the significance of some hidden sentiment they shared together. To me, the silent spectator, they looked like two people becoming conscious of a spell which had been lying on them ever since they first set eyes on each other. Had either of them cast a glance then in my direction, I would have opened the door quietly and gone out. But neither did; and I remained, every fear of indiscretion lost in the sense of my enormous remoteness from their captivity within the sombre horizon of Russian problems, the boundary of their eyes, of their feelings – the prison of their souls.

Frank, courageous, Miss Haldin controlled her voice in the midst of her trouble.

'What can this mean?' she asked, as if speaking to herself.

'It may mean that you have given yourself up to vain imaginings while I have managed to remain amongst the truth of things and the realities of life – our Russian life – such as they are.'

'They are cruel,' she murmured.

'And ugly. Don't forget that – and ugly. Look where you like. Look near you, here abroad where you are, and then look back at home, whence you came.'

'One must look beyond the present.' Her tone had an ardent conviction.

'The blind can do that best. I have had the misfortune to be born clear-eyed. And if you only knew what strange things I have seen! What amazing and unexpected apparitions! . . . But why talk of all this?'

'On the contrary, I want to talk of all this with you,' she protested with earnest serenity. The sombre humours of her brother's friend left her unaffected, as though that bitterness, that suppressed anger, were the signs of an indignant rectitude. She saw that he was not an ordinary person, and perhaps she did not want him to be other than he appeared to her trustful eyes. 'Yes, with you especially,' she insisted. 'With you of all the Russian people in the world. . . .' A faint smile dwelt for a moment on her lips. 'I am like poor mother in a way. I too seem unable to give up our beloved dead, who, don't forget, was all in all to us. I don't want to abuse your sympathy, but you must understand that it is in you that we can find all that is left of his generous soul.'

I was looking at him; not a muscle of his face moved in the least. And yet, even at the time, I did not suspect him of insensibility. It was a sort of rapt thoughtfulness. Then he stirred slightly.

'You are going, Kirylo Sidorovitch?' she asked.

'I! Going? Where? Oh yes, but I must tell you first . . .' His voice was muffled and he forced himself to produce it with visible repugnance, as if speech were something disgusting or deadly. 'That story, you know – the story I heard this afternoon. . . .'

'I know the story already,' she said sadly.

'You know it! Have you correspondents in St Petersburg too?'

'No. It's Sophia Antonovna. I have seen her just now. She sends you her greetings. She is going away tomorrow.'

He had lowered at last his fascinated glance; she too was looking down, and standing thus before each other in the glaring light, between the four bare walls, they seemed brought out from the confused immensity of the Eastern borders to be exposed cruelly to the observation of my Western eyes. And I observed them. There was nothing else to do. My existence seemed so utterly forgotten by these two that I dared not now make a movement. And I thought to myself that, of course, they had to come together, the sister and the friend of that dead man. The ideas, the hopes, the aspirations, the cause of Freedom, expressed in their common affection for Victor Haldin, the moral victim of autocracy, – all this must draw them to each other fatally. Her very ignorance and his loneliness to which he had alluded so strangely must work to that end. And, indeed, I saw that the work was done already. Of course. It was manifest that they must have been thinking of each other for a long time before they met. She had the letter from that beloved brother kindling her imagination by the severe praise attached to that one name; and for him to see that exceptional girl was enough. The only cause for surprise was his gloomy aloofness before her clearly expressed welcome. But he was young, and however austere and devoted to his revolutionary ideals, he was not blind. The period of reserve was over; he was coming forward in his own way. I could not mistake the significance of this late visit, for in what he had to say there was nothing urgent. The true cause dawned upon me: he had discovered that he needed her – and she was moved by the same feeling. It was the second time that I saw them together, and I knew that next time they met I would not be there, either remembered or forgotten. I would have virtually ceased to exist for both these young people.

I made this discovery in a very few moments. Meantime, Natalia Haldin was telling Razumov briefly of our peregrinations from one end of Geneva to the other. While speaking she raised her hands above her head to untie her veil, and that movement displayed for an instant the seductive grace of her youthful figure, clad in the simplest of mourning. In the transparent shadow the hat rim threw on her face her grey eyes had an enticing lustre. Her voice, with its unfeminine yet exquisite timbre, was steady, and she spoke quickly, frankly, unembarrassed. As she justified her action by the mental state of her mother, a spasm of pain marred the generously confiding harmony of her features. I perceived that with his downcast eyes he had the air of a man who is listening to a strain of music rather than to articulated speech. And in the same way, after she had ceased, he seemed to listen yet, motionless, as if under the spell of suggestive sound. He came to himself, muttering –

'Yes, yes. She has not shed a tear. She did not seem to hear what I was saying. I might have told her anything. She looked as if no longer belonging to this world.'

Miss Haldin gave signs of profound distress. Her voice faltered. 'You don't know how bad it has come to be. She expects now to *see him*!' The veil dropped from her fingers and she clasped her hands in anguish. 'It shall end by her seeing him,' she cried.

Razumov raised his head sharply and attached on her a prolonged thoughtful glance.

'H'm. That's very possible,' he muttered in a peculiar tone, as if giving his opinion on a matter of fact. 'I wonder what . . .' He checked himself.

'That would be the end. Her mind will be gone then, and her spirit will follow.'

Miss Haldin unclasped her hands and let them fall by her side.

'You think so?' he queried profoundly. Miss Haldin's lips were slightly parted. Something unexpected and unfathomable in that young man's character had fascinated her from the first. 'No. There's neither truth nor consolation to be got from the phantoms of the dead,' he added after a weighty pause. 'I might have told her something true; for instance, that your brother meant to save his life – to escape. There can be no doubt of that. But I did not.'

'You did not! But why?'

'I don't know. Other thoughts came into my head,' he answered. He seemed to me to be watching himself inwardly, as though he were trying to count his own heart-beats, while his eyes never for a moment left the face of the girl. 'You were not there,' he continued. 'I had made up my mind never to see you again.'

This seemed to take her breath away for a moment.

'You . . . How is it possible?'

'You may well ask. . . . However, I think that I refrained from telling your mother from prudence. I might have assured her that in the last conversation he held as a free man he mentioned you both . . .'

'That last conversation was with you,' she struck in her deep, moving voice. 'Some day you must. . . .'

'It was with me. Of you he said that you had trustful eyes. And why I have not been able to forget that phrase I don't know. It meant that there is in you no guile, no deception, no falsehood, no suspicion – nothing in your heart that could give you a conception of a living, acting, speaking lie, if ever it came in your way. That you are a predestined victim . . . Ha! what a devilish suggestion!'

The convulsive, uncontrolled tone of the last words disclosed the precarious hold he had over himself. He was like a man defying his own dizziness in high places and tottering suddenly on the very edge of the precipice. Miss Haldin pressed her hand to her breast. The dropped black veil lay on the floor between them. Her movement steadied him. He looked intently on that hand till it descended slowly, and then raised again his eyes to her face. But he did not give her time to speak.

'No? You don't understand? Very well.' He had recovered his calm by a miracle of will. 'So you talked with Sophia Antonovna?'

'Yes. Sophia Antonovna told me. . . .' Miss Haldin stopped, wonder growing in her wide eyes.

'H'm. That's the respectable enemy,' he muttered, as though he were alone.

'The tone of her references to you was extremely friendly,' remarked Miss Haldin, after waiting for a while.

'Is that your impression? And she the most intelligent of the lot, too. Things then are going as well as possible. Everything conspires to. . . . Ah! these conspirators,' he said slowly, with an accent of scorn; 'they would get hold of you in no time! You know, Natalia Victorovna, I have the greatest difficulty in saving myself from the superstition of an active Providence. It's irresistible. . . . The alternative, of course, would be the personal Devil of our simple ancestors. But, if so, he has overdone it altogether – the old Father of Lies – our national patron – our domestic god, whom we take with us when we go abroad. He has overdone it. It seems that

I am not simple enough. . . . That's it, I ought to have known. . . . And I did know it,' he added in a tone of poignant distress which overcame my astonishment.

'This man is deranged,' I said to myself, very much frightened.

The next moment he gave me a very special impression beyond the range of commonplace definitions. It was as though he had stabbed himself outside and had come in there to show it; and more than that – as though he were turning the knife in the wound and watching the effect. That was the impression, rendered in physical terms. One could not defend oneself from a certain amount of pity. But it was for Miss Haldin, already so tried in her deepest affections, that I felt a serious concern. Her attitude, her face, expressed compassion struggling with doubt on the verge of terror.

'What is it, Kirylo Sidorovitch?' There was a hint of tenderness in that cry. He only stared at her in that complete surrender of all his faculties which in a happy lover would have had the name of ecstasy.

'Why are you looking at me, like this, Kirylo Sidorovitch? I have approached you frankly. I need at this time to see clearly in myself. . . .' She ceased for a moment as if to give him an opportunity to utter at last some word worthy of her exalted trust in her brother's friend. His silence became impressive, like a sign of a momentous resolution.

In the end Miss Haldin went on, appealingly –

'I have waited for you anxiously. But now that you have been moved to come to us in your kindness, you alarm me. You speak obscurely. It seems as if you were keeping back something from me.'

'Tell me, Natalia Victorovna,' he was heard at last in a strange unringing voice, 'whom did you see in that place?'

She was startled, and as if deceived in her expectations.

'Where? In Peter Ivanovitch's rooms? There was Mr Laspara and three other people.'

'Ha! The vanguard – the forlorn hope of the great plot,' he commented to himself. 'Bearers of the spark to start an explosion which is meant to change fundamentally the lives of so many millions in order that Peter Ivanovitch should be the head of a State.'

'You are teasing me,' she said. 'Our dear one told me once to remember that men serve always something greater than themselves – the idea.'

'Our dear one,' he repeated slowly. The effort he made to appear unmoved absorbed all the force of his soul. He stood before her like a being with hardly a breath of life. His eyes, even as under great physical suffering, had lost all their fire. 'Ah! your brother. . . . But on your lips, in your voice, it sounds . . . and indeed in you everything is divine. . . . I wish I could know the innermost depths of your thoughts, of your feelings.'

'But why, Kirylo Sidorovitch?' she cried, alarmed by these words coming out of strangely lifeless lips.

'Have no fear. It is not to betray you. So you went there? . . . And Sophia Antonovna, what did she tell you, then?'

'She said very little, really. She knew that I should hear everything from you. She had no time for more than a few words.' Miss Haldin's voice dropped and she became silent for a moment. 'The man, it appears, has taken his life,' she said sadly.

'Tell me, Natalia Victorovna,' he asked after a pause, 'do you believe in remorse?'

'What a question!'

'What can *you* know of it?' he muttered thickly. 'It is not for such as you . . . What I meant to ask was whether you believed in the efficacy of remorse?'

She hesitated as though she had not understood, then her face lighted up.

'Yes,' she said firmly.

'So he is absolved. Moreover, that Ziemianitch was a brute, a drunken brute.'

A shudder passed through Natalia Haldin.

'But a man of the people,' Razumov went on, 'to whom they, the revolutionists, tell a tale of sublime hopes. Well, the people must be forgiven. . . . And you must not believe all you've heard from that source, either,' he added, with a sort of sinister reluctance.

'You are concealing something for me,' she exclaimed.

'Do you, Natalia Victorovna, believe in the duty of revenge?'

'Listen, Kirylo Sidorovitch. I believe that the future will be merciful to us all. Revolutionist and reactionary, victim and executioner, betrayer and betrayer, they shall all be pitied together when the light breaks on our black sky at last. Pitied and forgotten; for without that there can be no union and no love.'

'I hear. No revenge for you, then? Never? Not the least bit?' He smiled bitterly with his colourless lips. 'You yourself are like the very spirit of that merciful future. Strange that it does not make it easier. . . . No! But suppose that the real betrayer of your brother – Ziemianitch had a part in it too, but insignificant and quite involuntary – suppose that he was a young man, educated, an intellectual worker, thoughtful, a man your brother might have trusted lightly, perhaps, but still – suppose. . . . But there's a whole story there.'

'And you know the story! But why, then –'

'I have heard it. There is a staircase in it, and even phantoms, but that does not matter if a man always serves something greater than himself – the idea. I wonder who is the greatest victim in that tale?'

'In that tale!' Miss Haldin repeated. She seemed turned into stone.

'Do you know why I came to you? It is simply because there is no one anywhere in the whole great world I could go to. Do you understand what I say? No one to go to. Do you conceive the desolation of the thought – no one – to – go – to?'

Utterly misled by her own enthusiastic interpretation of two lines in the letter of a visionary, under the spell of her own dread of lonely days, in their overshadowed world of angry strife, she was unable to see the truth struggling on his lips. What she was conscious of was the obscure form of his suffering. She was on the point of extending her hand to him impulsively when he spoke again.

'An hour after I saw you first I knew how it would be. The terrors of remorse, revenge, confession, anger, hate, fear, are like nothing to the atrocious temptation which you put in my way the day you appeared before me with your voice, with your face, in the garden of that accursed villa.'

She looked utterly bewildered for a moment; then, with a sort of despairing insight went straight to the point.

'The story, Kirylo Sidorovitch, the story!'

'There is no more to tell!' He made a movement forward, and she actually put her hand on his shoulder to push him away; but her strength failed her, and he kept his ground, though trembling in every limb. 'It ends here – on this very spot.' He pressed a denunciatory finger to his breast with force, and became perfectly still.

I ran forward, snatching up the chair, and was in time to catch hold of Miss Haldin and lower her down. As she sank into it she swung half round on my arm, and remained averted from us both, drooping over the back. He looked at her with an appalling expressionless tranquillity. Incredulity, struggling with astonishment, anger, and disgust, deprived me for a time of the power of speech. Then I turned on him, whispering from very rage –

'This is monstrous. What are you staying for? Don't let her catch sight of you again. Go away! . . .' He did not budge. 'Don't you understand that your presence is intolerable – even to me? If there's any sense of shame in you. . . .'

Slowly his sullen eyes moved in my direction. 'How did this old man come here?' he muttered, astounded.

Suddenly Miss Haldin sprang up from the chair, made a few steps, and tottered. Forgetting my indignation, and even the man himself, I hurried to her assistance. I took her by the arm, and she let me lead her into the drawing-room. Away from the lamp, in the deeper dusk of the distant end, the profile of Mrs Haldin, her hands, her whole figure had the stillness of a sombre painting. Miss Haldin stopped, and pointed mournfully at the tragic immobility of her mother, who seemed to watch a beloved head lying in her lap.

That gesture had an unequalled force of expression, so far-reaching in its human distress that one could not believe that it pointed out merely the ruthless working of political institutions. After assisting Miss Haldin to the sofa, I turned round to go back and shut the door. Framed in the opening, in the searching glare of the white ante-room, my eyes fell on Razumov, still there, standing before the empty chair, as if rooted for ever to the spot of his atrocious confession. A wonder came over me that the mysterious force which had torn it out of him had failed to destroy his life, to shatter his body. It was there unscathed. I stared at the broad line of his shoulders, his dark head, the amazing immobility of his limbs. At his feet the veil dropped by Miss Haldin looked intensely black in the white crudity of the light. He was gazing at it spellbound. Next moment, stooping with an incredible, savage swiftness, he snatched it up and pressed it to his face with both hands. Something, extreme astonishment perhaps, dimmed my eyes, so that he seemed to vanish before he moved.

The slamming of the outer door restored my sight, and I went on contemplating the empty chair in the empty ante-room. The meaning of what I had seen reached my mind with a staggering shock. I seized Natalia Haldin by the shoulder.

'That miserable wretch has carried off your veil!' I cried, in the scared, deadened voice of an awful discovery. 'He . . .'

The rest remained unspoken. I stepped back and looked down at her, in silent horror. Her hands were lying lifelessly, palms upwards, on her lap. She raised her grey eyes slowly. Shadows seemed to come and go in them as if the steady flame of her soul had been made to vacillate at last in the cross-currents of poisoned air from the corrupted dark immensity claiming her for its own, where virtues themselves fester into crimes in the cynicism of oppression and revolt.

'It is impossible to be more unhappy. . . .' The languid whisper of her voice struck me with dismay. 'It is impossible. . . . I feel my heart becoming like ice.'

Chapter IV

Razumov walked straight home on the wet glistening pavement. A heavy shower passed over him; distant lightning played faintly against the fronts of the dumb houses with the shuttered shops all along the Rue de Carouge; and now and then, after the faint flash, there was a faint, sleepy rumble; but the main forces of the thunderstorm remained massed down the Rhone valley as if loath to attack the respectable and passionless abode of democratic liberty, the serious-minded town of dreary hotels, tendering the same indifferent hospitality to tourists of all nations and to international conspirators of every shade.

The owner of the shop was making ready to close when Razumov entered and without a word extended his hand for the key of his room. On reaching it for him, from a shelf, the man was about to pass a small joke as to taking the air in a thunderstorm, but, after looking at the face of his lodger, he only observed, just say something –

'You've got very wet.'

'Yes, I am washed clean,' muttered Razumov, who was dripping from head to foot, and passed through the inner door towards the staircase leading to his room.

He did not change his clothes, but, after lighting the candle, took off his watch and chain, laid them on the table, and sat down at once to write. The book of his compromising record was kept in a locked drawer, which he pulled out violently, and did not even trouble to push back afterwards.

In his queer pedanticism of a man who had read, thought, lived, pen in hand, there is the sincerity of the attempt to grapple by the same means with another profounder knowledge. After some passages which have been already made use of in the building up of this narrative, or add nothing new to the psychological side of this disclosure (there is even one more allusion to the silver medal in this last entry), comes a page and a half of incoherent writing where his expression is baffled by the novelty and the mysteriousness of that side of our emotional life to which his solitary existence had been a stranger. Then only he begins to address directly the reader he had in his mind, trying to express in broken sentences, full of wonder and awe, the sovereign (he uses that very word) power of her person over his imagination, in which lay the dormant seed of her brother's words.

'. . . The most trustful eyes in the world – your brother said of you when he was as well as a dead man already. And when you stood before me with your hand extended, I remembered the very sound of his voice, and I looked into your eyes – and that was enough. I knew that something had happened, but I did not know then what. . . . But don't be deceived, Natalia Victorovna. I believed that I had in my breast nothing but an inexhaustible fund of anger and hate for you both. I remembered that he had looked to you for the perpetuation of his visionary soul. He, this man who had robbed me of my hard-working, purposeful existence. I, too, had my guiding idea; and remember that, amongst us, it is more difficult to lead a life of toil and self-denial than to go out in the street and kill from conviction. But enough of that. Hate or no hate, I felt at once that, while shunning the sight of you, I could never succeed in driving away your image. I would say, addressing the dead man, "Is this the way you are going to haunt me?" It is only later on that I understood – only today, only a few hours ago. What could I have known of what was tearing me to pieces and dragging the secret for ever to my lips? You were appointed to undo the evil by making me betray myself back into truth and peace. You! And you have done it in the same way, too, in which he ruined me: by forcing upon me your confidence. Only what I detested him for, in you ended by appearing noble and exalted. But, I repeat, be not deceived. I was given up to evil. I exulted in having induced that silly innocent fool to steal his father's money. He was a fool, but not a thief. I made him one. It was necessary. I had to confirm myself in my contempt and hate for what I betrayed. I have suffered from as many vipers in my heart, as any social democrat of them all – vanity, ambitions, jealousies, shameful desires, evil passions of envy and revenge. I had my security stolen from me, years of good work, my best hopes. Listen – now comes the true confession. The other was nothing. To save me, your trustful eyes had to entice my thought to the very edge of the blackest treachery. I could see them constantly looking at me with the confidence of your pure heart which had not been touched by evil things. Victor Haldin had stolen the truth of my life from me, who had nothing else in the world, and he boasted of living on through you on this earth where I had no place to lay my head. She will marry some day, he had said – and your eyes were trustful. And do you know what I said to myself? I shall steal his sister's soul from her. When we met that first morning in the gardens, and you spoke to me confidingly in the generosity of your spirit, I was thinking, "Yes, he himself by talking of her trustful eyes has delivered her into my hands!" If you could have looked then into my heart, you would have cried out aloud with terror and disgust.

'Perhaps no one will believe the baseness of such an intention to be possible. It's certain that, when we parted that morning, I gloated over it. I brooded upon the best way. The old man you introduced me to insisted on walking with me. I don't know who he is. He talked of you, of your lonely, helpless state, and every word of that friend of yours was egging me on to the unpardonable sin of stealing a soul. Could he have been the devil himself in the shape of an old Englishman? Natalia Victorovna, I was possessed! I returned to look at you every day, and drank in your presence the poison of my infamous intention. But I foresaw difficulties. Then Sophia Antonovna, of whom I was not thinking – had forgotten her existence – appears suddenly with that tale from St Petersburg. . . . The only thing needed to make me safe – a trusted revolutionist for ever.

'It was as if Ziemianitch had hanged himself to help me on to further crime. The strength of falsehood seemed irresistible. These people stood doomed by the folly and the illusion that was in them – they being themselves the slaves of lies. Natalia Victorovna, I embraced the might of falsehood, I exulted in it – I gave myself up to it for a time. Who could have resisted! You yourself were the prize of it. I sat alone in my room, planning a life, the very thought of which makes me shudder now, like a believer who had been tempted to an atrocious sacrilege. But I brooded ardently over its images. The only thing was that there seemed to be no air in it. And also I was afraid of your mother. I never knew mine. I've never known any kind of love. There is something in the mere word. . . . Of you, I was not afraid – forgive me for telling you this. No, not of you. You were truth itself. You could not suspect me. As to your mother, you yourself feared already that her mind had given way from grief. Who could believe anything against me? Had not Ziemianitch hanged himself from remorse? I said to myself, "Let's put it to the test, and be done with it once for all." I trembled when I went in; but your mother hardly listened to what I was saying to her, and, in a little while, seemed to have forgotten my very existence. I sat looking at her. There was no longer anything between you and me. You were defenceless – and soon, very soon, you would be alone. . . . I thought of you. Defenceless. For days you have talked with me – opening your heart. I remembered the shadow of your eyelashes over your grey trustful eyes. And your pure forehead! It is low like the forehead of statues – calm, unstained. It was as if your pure brow bore a light which fell on me, searched my heart and saved me from ignominy, from ultimate undoing. And it saved you too. Pardon my presumption. But there was that in your glances which seemed to tell me that you . . . Your light! your truth! I felt that I must tell you that I had ended by loving you. And to tell you that I must first confess. Confess, go out – and perish.

'Suddenly you stood before me! You alone in all the world to whom I must confess. You fascinated me – you have freed me from the blindness of anger and hate – the truth shining in you drew the truth out of me. Now I have done it; and as I write here, I am in the depths of anguish, but there is air to breathe at last – air! And, by the by, the old man sprang up from somewhere as I was speaking to you, and raged at me like a disappointed devil. I suffer horribly, but I am not in despair. There is only one more thing to do for me. After that – if they let me – I shall go away and bury myself in obscure misery. In giving Victor Haldin up, it was myself, after all, whom I have betrayed most basely. You must believe what I say now, you can't refuse to believe this. Most basely. It is through you that I came to feel this so deeply. After all, it is they and not I who have the right on their side! – theirs is the strength of invisible powers. So be it. Only don't be deceived, Natalia Victorovna, I am not converted. Have I then the soul of a slave? No! I am independent – and therefore perdition is my lot.'

On these words, he stopped writing, shut the book, and wrapped it in the black veil he had carried off. He then ransacked the drawers for paper and string, made up a parcel which he addressed to Miss Haldin, Boulevard des Philosophes, and then flung the pen away from him into a distant corner.

This done, he sat down with the watch before him. He could have gone out at once, but the hour had not struck yet. The hour would be midnight. There was no reason for that choice except that the facts and the words of a certain evening in his past were timing his conduct in the present. The sudden power Natalia Haldin had gained over him he ascribed to the same cause. 'You don't walk with impunity over a phantom's breast,' he heard himself mutter. 'Thus he saves me,' he thought suddenly. 'He himself, the betrayed man.' The vivid image of Miss Haldin seemed to stand by him, watching him relentlessly. She was not disturbing. He had done with life, and his thought even in her presence tried to take an impartial survey. Now his scorn extended to himself. 'I had neither the simplicity nor the courage nor the self-possession to be a scoundrel, or an exceptionally able man. For who, with us in Russia, is to tell a scoundrel from an exceptionally able man? . . .'

He was the puppet of his past, because at the very stroke of midnight he jumped up and ran swiftly downstairs as if confident that, by the power of destiny, the house door would fly open before the absolute necessity of his errand. And as a matter of fact, just as he got to the bottom of the stairs, it was opened for him by some people of the house coming home late – two men and a woman. He slipped out through them into the street, swept then by a fitful gust of wind. They were, of course, very much startled. A flash of lightning enabled them to observe him walking away quickly. One of the men shouted, and was starting in pursuit but the woman had recognized him. 'It's all right. It's only that young Russian from the third floor.' The darkness returned with a single clap of thunder, like a gun fired for a warning of his escape from the prison of lies.

He must have heard at some time or other and now remembered unconsciously that there was to be a gathering of revolutionists at the house of Julius Laspara that evening. At any rate, he made straight for the Laspara house, and found himself without surprise ringing at its street door, which, of course, was closed. By that time the thunderstorm had attacked in earnest. The steep incline of the street ran with water, the thick fall of rain enveloped him like a luminous veil in the play of lightning. He was perfectly calm, and, between the crashes, listened attentively to the delicate tinkling of the doorbell somewhere within the house.

There was some difficulty before he was admitted. His person was not known to that one of the guests who had volunteered to go downstairs and see what was the matter. Razumov argued with him patiently. There could be no harm in admitting a caller. He had something to communicate to the company upstairs.

'Something of importance?'

'That'll be for the hearers to judge.'

'Urgent?'

'Without a moment's delay.'

Meantime, one of the Laspara daughters descended the stairs, small lamp in hand, in a grimy and crumpled gown, which seemed to hang on her by a miracle, and looking more than ever like an old doll with a dusty brown wig, dragged from under a sofa. She recognized Razumov at once.

'How do you do? Of course you may come in.'

Following her light Razumov climbed two flights of stairs from the lower darkness. Leaving the lamp on a bracket on the landing, she opened a door, and went in, accompanied by the sceptical guest. Razumov entered last. He closed the door behind him, and stepping on one side, put his back against the wall.

The three little rooms *en suite*, with low, smoky ceilings and lit by paraffin lamps were crammed with people. Loud talking was going on in all three, and tea-glasses, full, half-full, and empty, stood everywhere, even on the floor. The other Laspara girl sat, dishevelled and languid, behind an enormous samovar. In the inner doorway Razumov had a glimpse of the protuberance of a large stomach, which he recognized. Only a few feet from him Julius Laspara was getting down hurriedly from his high stool.

The appearance of the midnight visitor caused no small sensation. Laspara is very summary in his version of that night's happenings. After some words of greeting, disregarded by Razumov, Laspara (ignoring purposely his guest's soaked condition and his extraordinary manner of presenting himself) mentioned something about writing an article. He was growing uneasy, and Razumov appeared absent-minded. 'I have written already all I shall ever write,' he said at last, with a little laugh.

The whole company's attention was riveted on the newcomer, dripping with water, deadly pale, and keeping his position against the wall. Razumov put Laspara gently aside, as though he wished to be seen from head to foot by everybody. By then the buzz of conversations had died down completely, even in the most distant of the three rooms. The doorway facing Razumov became blocked by men and women, who craned their necks and certainly seemed to expect something startling to happen.

A squeaky, insolent declaration was heard from that group.

'I know this ridiculously conceited individual.'

'What individual?' asked Razumov, raising his bowed head, and searching with his eyes all the eyes fixed upon him. An intense surprised silence lasted for a time. 'If it's me. . . .'

He stopped, thinking over the form of his confession, and found it suddenly, unavoidably suggested by the fateful evening of his life.

'I am come here,' he began, in a clear voice, 'to talk of an individual called Ziemianitch. Sophia Antonovna has informed me that she would make public a certain letter from St Petersburg. . . .'

'Sophia Antonovna has left us early in the evening,' said Laspara. 'It's quite correct. Everybody here has heard. . . .'

'Very well,' Razumov interrupted, with a shade of impatience, for his heart was beating strongly. Then mastering his voice so far that there was even a touch of irony in his clear, forcible enunciation –

'In justice to that individual, the much ill-used peasant, Ziemianitch, I now declare solemnly that the conclusions of that letter calumniate a man of the people – a bright Russian soul. Ziemianitch had nothing to do with the actual arrest of Victor Haldin.'

Razumov dwelt on the name heavily, and then waited till the faint, mournful murmur which greeted it had died out.

'Victor Victorovitch Haldin,' he began again, 'acting with, no doubt, noble-minded imprudence, took refuge with a certain student of whose opinions he knew nothing but what his own illusions suggested to his generous heart. It was an unwise display of confidence. But I am not here to appreciate the actions of Victor Haldin. Am I to tell you of the feelings of that student, sought out in his obscure solitude, and menaced by the complicity forced upon him? Am I to tell you what he did? It's a rather complicated story. In the end the student went to General T— himself, and said, "I have the man who killed de P— locked up in my room, Victor Haldin – a student like myself." '

A great buzz arose, in which Razumov raised his voice.

'Observe – that man had certain honest ideals in view. But I didn't come here to explain him.'

'No. But you must explain how you know all this,' came in grave tones from somebody.

'A vile coward!' This simple cry vibrated with indignation. 'Name him!' shouted other voices.

'What are you clamouring for?' said Razumov disdainfully, in the profound silence which fell on the raising of his hand. 'Haven't you all understood that I am that man?'

Laspara went away brusquely from his side and climbed upon his stool. In the first forward surge of people towards him, Razumov expected to be torn to pieces, but they fell back without touching him, and nothing came of it but noise. It was bewildering. His head ached terribly. In the confused uproar he made out several times the name of Peter Ivanovitch, the word 'judgement', and the phrase, 'But this is a confession', uttered by somebody in a desperate shriek. In the midst of the tumult, a young man, younger than himself, approached him with blazing eyes.

'I must beg you,' he said, with venomous politeness, 'to be good enough not to move from this spot till you are told what you are to do.'

Razumov shrugged his shoulders.

'I came in voluntarily.'

'Maybe. But you won't go out till you are permitted,' retorted the other.

He beckoned with his hand, calling out, 'Louisa! Louisa! come here, please'; and, presently, one of the Laspara girls (they had been staring at Razumov from behind the samovar) came along, trailing a bedraggled tail of dirty flounces, and dragging with her a chair, which she set against the door, and, sitting down on it, crossed her legs. The young man thanked her effusively, and rejoined a group carrying on an animated discussion in low tones. Razumov lost himself for a moment.

A squeaky voice screamed, 'Confession or no confession, you are a police spy!'

The revolutinist Nikita had pushed his way in front of Razumov, and faced him with his big, livid cheeks, his heavy paunch, bull neck, and enormous hands. Razumov looked at the famous slayer of gendarmes in silent disgust.

'And what are you?' he said, very low, then shut his eyes, and rested the back of his head against the wall.

'It would be better for you to depart now.' Razumov heart a mild, sad voice, and opened his eyes. The gentle speaker was an elderly man, with a great brush of fine hair making a silvery halo all round his keen, intelligent face. 'Peter Ivanovitch shall be informed of your confession – and you shall be directed . . .'

Then, turning to Nikita, nicknamed Necator, standing by, he appealed to him in a murmur –

'What else can we do? After this piece of sincerity he cannot be dangerous any longer.'

The other muttered, 'Better make sure of that before we let him go. Leave that to me. I know how to deal with such gentlemen.'

He exchanged meaning glances with two or three men, who nodded slightly, then turning roughly to Razumov, 'You have heard? You are not wanted here. Why don't you get out?'

The Laspara girl on guard rose, and pulled the chair out of the way unemotionally. She gave a sleepy stare to Razumov, who started, looked round the room and passed slowly by her as if struck by some sudden thought.

'I beg you to observe,' he said, already on the landing, 'that I had only to hold my tongue. Today, of all days since I came amongst you, I was made safe, and today I made myself free from falsehood, from remorse – independent of every single human being on this earth.'

He turned his back on the room, and walked towards the stairs, but, at the violent crash of the door behind him, he looked over his shoulder and saw that Nikita, with three others, had followed him out. 'They are going to kill me, after all,' he thought.

Before he had time to turn round and confront them fairly, they set on him with a rush. He was driven headlong against the wall. 'I wonder how,' he completed his thought. Nikita cried, with a shrill laugh right in his face, 'We shall make you harmless. You wait a bit.'

Razumov did not struggle. The three men held him pinned against the wall, while Nikita, taking up a position a little on one side, deliberately swung off his enormous arm. Razumov, looking for a knife in his hand, saw it come at him open, unarmed, and received a tremendous blow on the side of his head over his ear. At the same time he heard a faint, dull detonating sound, as if someone had fired a pistol on the other side of the wall. A raging fury awoke in him at this outrage. The people in Laspara's rooms, holding their breath, listened to the desperate scuffling of four men all over the landing; thuds against the walls, a terrible crash against the very door, then all of them went down together with a violence which seemed to shake the whole house. Razumov, overpowered, breathless, crushed under the weight of his assailants, saw the monstrous Nikita squatting on his heels near his head, while the others held him down, kneeling on his chest, gripping his throat, lying across his legs.

'Turn his face the other way,' the paunchy terrorist directed, in an excited, gleeful squeak.

Razumov could struggle no longer. He was exhausted; he had to watch passively the heavy open hand of the brute descend again in a degrading blow over his other ear. It seemed to split his head in two, and all at once the men holding him became perfectly silent – soundless as shadows. In silence they pulled him brutally to his feet, rushed with him noiselessly down the staircase, and, opening the door, flung him out into the street.

He fell forward, and at once rolled over and over helplessly, going down the short slope together with the rush of running rain water. He came to rest in the roadway of the street at the bottom, lying on his back, with a great flash of lightning over his face – a vivid, silent flash of lightning which blinded him utterly. He picked himself up, and put his arm over his eyes to recover his sight. Not a sound reached him from anywhere, and he began to walk, staggering, down a long, empty street. The lightning waved and darted round him its silent flames, the water of the deluge fell, ran, leaped, drove – noiseless like the drift of mist. In this unearthly stillness his footsteps fell silent on the pavement, while a dumb wind drove him on and on, like a lost mortal in a phantom world ravaged by a soundless thunderstorm. God only knows where his noiseless feet took him to that night, here and there, and back again without pause or rest. Of one place, at least, where they did lead him, we heard afterwards; and, in the morning, the driver of the first south-shore tram-car, clanging his bell desperately, saw a bedraggled, soaked man without a hat, and walking in the roadway unsteadily with his head down, step right in front of his car, and go under.

When they picked him up, with two broken limbs and a crushed side, Razumov had not lost consciousness. It was as though he had tumbled, smashing himself, into a world of mutes. Silent men, moving unheard, lifted him up, laid him on the sidewalk, gesticulating and grimacing round him their alarm, horror, and compassion. A red face with moustaches stooped close over him, lips moving, eyes rolling. Razumov tried hard to understand the reason of this dumb show. To those who stood around him, the features of that stranger, so grievously hurt, seemed composed in meditation. Afterwards his eyes sent out at them a look of fear and closed slowly. They stared at him. Razumov made an effort to remember some French words.

'*Je suis sourd*,' he had time to utter feebly, before he fainted.

'He is deaf,' they exclaimed to each other. 'That's why he did not hear the car.'

They carried him off in that same car. Before it started on its journey, a woman in a shabby black dress, who had run out of the iron gate of some private grounds up the road, clambered on to the rear platform and would not be put off.

'I am a relation,' she insisted, in bad French. 'This young man is a Russian, and I am his relation.'

On this plea they let her have her way. She sat down calmly, and took his head on her lap; her scared faded eyes avoided looking at his deathlike face. At the corner of a street, on the other side of the town, a stretcher met the car. She followed it to the door of the hospital, where they let her come in and see him laid on a bed. Razumov's new-found relation never shed a tear, but the officials had some difficulty in inducing her to go away. The porter observed her lingering on the opposite pavement for a long time. Suddenly, as though she had remembered something, she ran off.

The ardent hater of all Finance ministers, the slave of Madame de S—, had made up her mind to offer her resignation as lady companion to the Egeria of Peter Ivanovitch. She had found work to do after her own heart.

But hours before, while the thunderstorm still raged in the night, there had been in the rooms of Julius Laspara a great sensation. The terrible Nikita, coming in from the landing, uplifted his squeaky voice in horrible glee before all the company –

'Razumov, Mr Razumov! The wonderful Razumov! He shall never be any use as a spy on anyone. He won't talk, because he will never hear anything in his life – not a thing! I have burst the drums of his ears for him. Oh, you may trust me. I know the trick. Ha! Ha! Ha! I know the trick.'

Chapter V

It was nearly a fortnight after her mother's funeral that I saw Natalia Haldin for the last time.

In those silent, sombre days the doors of the *appartement* on the Boulevard des Philosophes were closed to everyone but myself. I believe I was of some use, if only in this, that I alone was aware of the incredible part of the situation. Miss Haldin nursed her mother alone to the last moment. If Razumov's visit had anything to do with Mrs Haldin's end (and I cannot help thinking that it hastened it considerably), it is because the man, trusted impulsively by the ill-fated Victor Haldin, had failed to gain the confidence of Victor Haldin's mother. What tale, precisely, he told her cannot be known – at any rate, I do not know it – but to me she seemed to die from the shock of an ultimate disappointment borne in silence. She had not believed him. Perhaps she could no longer believe anyone, and consequently had nothing to say to anyone – not even to her daughter. I suspect that Miss Haldin lived the heaviest hours of her life by that silent death-bed. I confess I was angry with the broken-hearted old woman passing away in the obstinacy of her mute distrust of her daughter.

When it was all over I stood aside. Miss Haldin had her compatriots round her then. A great number of them attended the funeral. I was there too, but afterwards managed to keep away from Miss Haldin, till I received a short note rewarding my self-denial. 'It is as you would have it. I am going back to Russia at once. My mind is made up. Come and see me.'

Verily, it was a reward of discretion. I went without delay to receive it. The *appartement* of the Boulevard des Philosophes presented the dreary signs of impending abandonment. It looked desolate and as if already empty to my eyes.

Standing, we exchanged a few words about her health, mine, remarks as to some people of the Russian colony, and then Natalia Haldin, establishing me on the sofa, began to talk openly of her future work, of her plans. It was all to be as I had wished it. And it was to be for life. We should never see each other again. Never!

I gathered this success to my breast. Natalia Haldin looked matured by her open and secret experiences. With her arms folded she walked up and down the whole length of the room, talking slowly, smooth-browed, with a resolute profile. She gave me a new view of herself, and I marvelled at that something grave and measured in her voice, in her movements, in her manner. It was the perfection of collected independence. The strength of her nature had come to the surface because the obscure depths had been stirred.

'We two can talk of it now,' she observed, after a silence and stopping short before me. 'Have you been to inquire at the hospital lately?'

'Yes, I have.' And as she looked at me fixedly, 'He will live, the doctors say. But I thought that Tekla . . .'

'Tekla has not been near me for several days,' explained Miss Haldin quickly. 'As I never offered to go to the hospital with her, she thinks that I have no heart. She is disillusioned about me.'

And Miss Haldin smiled faintly.

'Yes. She sits with him as long and as often as they will let her,' I said. 'She says she must never abandon him – never as long as she lives. He'll need somebody – a hopeless cripple, and stone deaf with that.'

'Stone deaf? I didn't know,' murmured Natalia Haldin.

'He is. It seems strange. I am told there were no apparent injuries to the head. They say, too, that it is not very likely that he will live so very long for Tekla to take care of him.'

Miss Haldin shook her head.

'While there are travellers ready to fall by the way our Tekla will never be idle.

She is a good Samaritan by an irresistible vocation. The revolutionists didn't understand her. Fancy a devoted creature like that being employed to carry about documents sewn in her dress, or made to write from dictation.'

'There is not much perspicacity in the world.'

No sooner uttered, I regretted that observation. Natalia Haldin, looking me straight in the face, assented by a slight movement of her head. She was not offended, but turning away began to pace the room again. To my Western eyes she seemed to be getting farther and farther from me, quite beyond my reach now, but undiminished in the increasing distance. I remained silent as though it were hopeless to raise my voice. The sound of hers, so close to me, made me start a little.

'Tekla saw him picked up after the accident. The good soul never explained to me really how it came about. She affirms that there was some understanding between them – some sort of compact – that in any sore need, in misfortune, or difficulty, or pain, he was to come to her.'

'Was there?' I said. 'It is lucky for him that there was, then. He'll need all the devotion of the good Samaritan.'

It was a fact that Tekla, looking out of her window at five in the morning, for some reason or other, had beheld Razumov in the grounds of the Château Borel, standing stockstill, bareheaded in the rain, at the foot of the terrace. She had screamed out to him, by name, to know what was the matter. He never even raised his head. By the time she had dressed herself sufficiently to run downstairs he was gone. She started in pursuit, and rushing out into the road, came almost directly upon the arrested tramcar and the small knot of people picking up Razumov. That much Tekla had told me herself one afternoon we happened to meet at the door of the hospital, and without any kind of comment. But I did not want to meditate very long on the inwardness of this peculiar episode.

'Yes, Natalia Victorovna, he will need somebody when they dismiss him, on crutches and stone deaf from the hospital. But I do not think that when he rushed like an escaped madman into the grounds of the Château Borel it was to seek the help of that good Tekla.'

'No,' said Natalia, stopping short before me, 'perhaps not.' She sat down and leaned her head on her hand thoughtfully. The silence lasted for several minutes. During that time I remembered the evening of his atrocious confession – the plaint she seemed to have hardly enough life left in her to utter, 'It is impossible to be more unhappy. . . .' The recollection would have given me a shudder if I had not been lost in wonder at her force and her tranquillity. There was no longer any Natalia Haldin, because she had completely ceased to think of herself. It was a great victory, a characteristically Russian exploit in self-suppression.

She recalled me to myself by getting up suddenly like a person who has come to a decision. She walked to the writing-table, now stripped of all the small objects associated with her by daily use – a mere piece of dead furniture; but it contained something living, still, since she took from a recess a flat parcel which she brought to me.

'It's a book,' she said rather abruptly. 'It was sent to me wrapped up in my veil. I told you nothing at the time, but now I've decided to leave it with you. I have the right to do that. It was sent to me. It is mine. You may preserve it, or destroy it after you have read it. And while you read it, please remember that I *was* defenceless. And that he . . .'

'Defenceless!' I repeated, surprised, looking hard at her.

'You'll find the very word written there,' she whispered. 'Well, it's true! I *was* defenceless – but, perhaps you were able to see that for yourself.' Her face coloured, then went deadly pale. 'In justice to the man, I want you to remember that I was. Oh, I was, I was!'

I rose, a little shakily.

'I am not likely to forget anything you say at this our last parting.'

Her hand fell into mine.

'It's difficult to believe that it must be good-bye with us.'

She returned my pressure and our hands separated.

'Yes. I am leaving here tomorrow. My eyes are open at last and my hands are free now. As for the rest – which of us can fail to hear the stifled cry of our great distress? It may be nothing to the world.'

'The world is more conscious of your discordant voices,' I said. 'It is the way of the world.'

'Yes.' She bowed her head in assent, and hesitated for a moment. 'I must own to you that I shall never give up looking forward to the day when all discord shall be silenced. Try to imagine its dawn! The tempest of blows and of execrations is over; all is still; the new sun is rising, and the weary men united at last, taking count in their conscience of the ended contest, feel saddened by their victory, because so many ideas have perished for the triumph of one, so many beliefs have abandoned them without support. They feel alone on the earth and gather close together. Yes, there must be many bitter hours! But at last the anguish of hearts shall be extinguished in love.'

And on this last word of wisdom, a word so sweet, so bitter, so cruel sometimes, I said good-bye to Natalia Haldin. It is hard to think I shall never look any more into the trustful eyes of that girl – wedded to an invincible belief in the advent of loving concord springing like a heavenly flower from the soil of men's earth, soaked in blood, torn by struggles, watered with tears.

It must be understood that at that time I didn't know anything of Mr Razumov's confession to the assembled revolutionists. Natalia Haldin might have guessed what was the 'one thing more' which remained for him to do; but this my Western eyes had failed to see.

Tekla, the ex-lady-companion of Madame de S—, haunted his bedside at the hospital. We met once or twice at the door of that establishment, but on these occasions she was not communicative. She gave me news of Mr Razumov as concisely as possible. He was making a slow recovery, but would remain a hopeless cripple all his life. Personally, I never went near him: I never saw him again, after the awful evening when I stood by, a watchful but ignored spectator of his scene with Miss Haldin. He was in due course discharged from the hospital, and his 'relative' – so I was told – had carried him off somewhere.

My information was completed nearly two years later. The opportunity, certainly, was not of my seeking; it was quite accidentally that I met a much-trusted woman revolutionist at the house of a distinguished Russian gentleman of liberal convictions, who came to live in Geneva for a time.

He was quite a different sort of celebrity from Peter Ivanovitch – a dark-haired man with kind eyes, high-shouldered, courteous, and with something hushed and circumspect in his manner. He approached me, choosing the moment when there was no one near, followed by a grey-haired, alert lady in a crimson blouse.

'Our Sophia Antonovna wishes to be made known to you,' he addressed me, in his guarded voice. 'And so I leave you two to have a talk together.'

'I would never have intruded myself upon your notice,' the grey-haired lady began at once, 'if I had not been charged with a message for you.'

It was a message of a few friendly words from Natalia Haldin. Sophia Antonovna had just returned from a secret excursion into Russia, and had seen Miss Haldin. She lived in a town in the centre, sharing her compassionate labours between the horrors of overcrowded jails, and the heartrending misery of bereaved homes. She did not spare herself in good service, Sophia Antonovna assured me.

'She has a faithful soul, an undaunted spirit, and an indefatigable body,' the woman revolutionist summed it all up, with a touch of enthusiasm.

A conversation thus engaged was not likely to drop from want of interest on my side. We went to sit apart in a corner where no one interrupted us. In the course of our talk about Miss Haldin, Sophia Antonovna remarked suddenly –

'I suppose you remember seeing me before? That evening when Natalia came to ask Peter Ivanovitch for the address of a certain Razumov, that young man who . . .'

'I remember perfectly,' I said. When Sophia Antonovna learned that I had in my possession that young man's journal given me by Miss Haldin she became intensely interested. She did not conceal her curiosity to see the document.

I offered to show it to her, and she at once volunteered to call on me next day for that purpose.

She turned over the pages greedily for an hour or more, and then handed me the book with a faint sigh. While moving about Russia, she had seen Razumov too. He lived, not 'in the centre', but 'in the south'. She described to me a little two-roomed wooden house, in the suburb of some very small town, hiding within the high plank-fence of a yard overgrown with nettles. He was crippled, ill, getting weaker every day, and Tekla the Samaritan tended him unweariedly with the pure joy of unselfish devotion. There was nothing in that task to become disillusioned about.

I did not hide from Sophia Antonovna my surprise that she should have visited Mr Razumov. I did not even understand the motive. But she informed me that she was not the only one.

'Some of *us* always go to see him when passing through. He is intelligent. He has ideas. . . . He talks well, too.'

Presently I heard for the first time of Razumov's public confession in Laspara's house. Sophia Antonovna gave me a detailed relation of what had occurred there. Razumov himself had told her all about it, most minutely.

Then, looking hard at me with her brilliant black eyes –

'There are evil moments in every life. A false suggestion enters one's brain, and then fear is born – fear of oneself, fear for oneself. Or else a false courage –

who knows? Well, call it what you like; but tell me, how many of them would deliver themselves up deliberately to perdition (as he himself says in that book) rather than go on living, secretly debased in their own eyes? How many? . . . And please mark this – he was safe when he did it. It was just when he believed himself safe and more – infinitely more – when the possibility of being loved by that admirable girl first dawned upon him, that he discovered that his bitterest railings, the worst wickedness, the devil work of his hate and pride, could never cover up the ignominy of the existence before him. There's character in such a discovery.'

I accepted her conclusion in silence. Who would care to question the grounds of forgiveness or compassion? However, it appeared later on, that there was some compunction, too, in the charity extended by the revolutionary world to Razumov the betrayer. Sophia Antonovna continued uneasily –

'And then, you know, he was the victim of an outrage. It was not authorized. Nothing was decided as to what was to be done with him. He had confessed voluntarily. And that Nikita who burst the drums of his ears purposely, out on the landing, you know, as if carried away by indignation – well, he has turned out to be a scoundrel of the worst kind – a traitor himself, a betrayer – a spy. Razumov told me he had charged him with it by a sort of inspiration . . .'

'I had a glimpse of that brute,' I said. 'How any of you could have been deceived for half a day passes my comprehension!'

She interrupted me.

'There! There! Don't talk of it. The first time I saw him, I, too, was appalled. They cried me down. We were always telling each other, "Oh! you mustn't mind his appearance." And then he was always ready to kill. There was no doubt of it. He killed – yes, in both camps. The fiend . . .'

Then Sophia Antonovna, after mastering the angry trembling of her lips, told me a very queer tale. It went that Councillor Mikulin, travelling in Germany (shortly after Razumov's disappearance from Geneva), happened to meet Peter Ivanovitch in a railway carriage. Being alone in the compartment, these two talked together half the night, and it was then that Mikulin the Police Chief gave a hint to the Arch-Revolutionist as to the true character of the arch-slayer of gendarmes. It looks as though Mikulin had wanted to get rid of that particular agent of his own! He might have grown tired of him, or frightened of him. It must also be said that Mikulin had inherited the sinister Nikita from his predecessor in office.

And this story, too, I received without comment in my character of a mute witness of things Russian, unrolling their Eastern logic under my Western eyes. But I permitted myself a question –

'Tell me, please, Sophia Antonovna, did Madame de S— leave all her fortune to Peter Ivanovitch?'

'Not a bit of it.' The woman revolutionist shrugged her shoulders in disgust. 'She died without making a will. A lot of nephews and nieces came down from St Petersburg, like a flock of vultures, and fought for her money amongst themselves. All beastly Kammerherrs and Maids of Honour – abominable court flunkeys. Tfui!'

'One does not hear much of Peter Ivanovitch now,' I remarked, after a pause.

'Peter Ivanovitch,' said Sophia Antonovna gravely, 'has united himself to a peasant girl.'

I was truly astonished.

'What! On the Riviera?'

'What nonsense! Of course not.'

Sophia Antonovna's tone was slightly tart.

'Is he, then, living actually in Russia? It's a tremendous risk – isn't it?' I cried. 'And all for the sake of a peasant girl. Don't you think it's very wrong of him?'

Sophia Antonovna preserved a mysterious silence for a while, then made a statement.

'He just simply adores her.'

'Does he? Well, then, I hope that she won't hesitate to beat him.'

Sophia Antonovna got up and wished me good-bye, as though she had not heard a word of my impious hope; but, in the very doorway, where I attended her, she turned round for an instant, and declared in a firm voice –

'Peter Ivanovitch is an inspired man.'

The Secret Sharer

An Episode from the Coast

Chapter I

On my right hand there were lines of fishing-stakes resembling a mysterious system of half-submerged bamboo fences, incomprehensible in its division of the domain of tropical fishes, and crazy of aspect as if abandoned for ever by some nomad tribe of fishermen now gone to the other end of the ocean; for there was no sign of human habitation as far as the eye could reach. To the left a group of barren islets, suggesting ruins of stone walls, towers, and blockhouses, had its foundations set in a blue sea that itself looked solid, so still and stable did it lie below my feet; even the track of light from the westering sun shone smoothly, without that animated glitter which tells of an imperceptible ripple. And when I turned my head to take a parting glance at the tug which had just left us anchored outside the bar, I saw the straight line of the flat shore joined to the stable sea, edge to edge, with a perfect and unmarked closeness, in one levelled floor half brown, half blue under the enormous dome of the sky. Corresponding in their insignificance to the islets of the sea, two small clumps of trees, one on each side of the only fault in the impeccable joint, marked the mouth of the river Meinam we had just left on the first preparatory stage of our homeward journey; and, far back on the inland level, a larger and loftier mass, the grove surrounding the great Paknam pagoda, was the only thing on which the eye could rest from the vain task of exploring the monotonous sweep of the horizon. Here and there gleams as of a few scattered pieces of silver marked the windings of the great river; and on the nearest of them, just within the bar, the tug steaming right into the land became lost to my sight, hull and funnel and masts, as though the impassive earth had swallowed her up without an effort, without a tremor. My eye followed the light cloud of her smoke, now here, now there, above the plain, according to the devious curves of the stream, but always fainter and farther away, till I lost it at last behind the mitre-shaped hill of the great pagoda. And then I was left alone with my ship, anchored at the head of the Gulf of Siam.

She floated at the starting-point of a long journey, very still in an immense stillness, the shadows of her spars flung far to the eastward by the setting sun. At that moment I was alone on her decks. There was not a sound in her – and around us nothing moved, nothing lived, not a canoe on the water, not a bird in the air, not a cloud in the sky. In this breathless pause at the threshold of a long passage we seemed to be measuring our fitness for a long and arduous enterprise, the appointed task of both our existences to be carried out, far from all human eyes, with only sky and sea for spectators and for judges.

There must have been some glare in the air to interfere with one's sight, because it was only just before the sun left us that my roaming eyes made out beyond the highest ridge of the principal islet of the group something which did away with the solemnity of perfect solitude. The tide of darkness flowed on swiftly; and with tropical suddenness a swarm of stars came out above the shadowy earth, while I lingered yet, my hand resting lightly on my ship's rail as if on the shoulder of a trusted friend. But, with all that multitude of celestial bodies staring down at one, the comfort of quiet communion with her was gone for good. And there were also disturbing sounds by this time – voices, footsteps forward; the steward flitted along the maindeck, a busily ministering spirit; a handbell tinkled urgently under the poop-deck . . .

I found my two officers waiting for me near the supper table, in the lighted cuddy. We sat down at once, and as I helped the chief mate, I said:

'Are you aware that there is a ship anchored inside the islands? I saw her mastheads above the ridge as the sun went down.'

He raised sharply his simple face, overcharged by a terrible growth of whisker, and emitted his usual ejaculations: 'Bless my soul, sir! You don't say say so!'

My second mate was a round-cheeked, silent young man, grave beyond his years, I thought; but as our eyes happened to meet I detected a slight quiver on his lips. I looked down at once. It was not my part to encourage sneering on board my ship. It must be said, too, that I knew very little of my officers. In consequence of certain events of no particular significance, except to myself, I had been appointed to the command only a fortnight before. Neither did I know much of the hands forward. All these people had been together for eighteen months or so, and my position was that of the only stranger on board. I mention this because it has some bearing on what is to follow. But what I felt most was my being a stranger to the ship; and if all the truth must be told, I was somewhat of a stranger to myself. The youngest man on board (barring the second mate), and untried as yet by a position of the fullest responsibility, I was willing to take the adequacy of the others for granted. They had simply to be equal to their tasks; but I wondered how far I should turn out faithful to that ideal conception of one's own personality every man sets up for himself secretly.

Meantime the chief mate, with an almost visible effect of collaboration on the part of his round eyes and frightful whiskers, was trying to evolve a theory of the anchored ship. His dominant trait was to take all things into earnest consideration. He was of a painstaking turn of mind. As he used to say, he 'liked to account to himself' for practically everything that came in his way, down to a miserable scorpion he had found in his cabin a week before. The why and the wherefore of that scorpion – how it got on board and came to select his room rather than the pantry (which was a dark place and more what a scorpion would be partial to), and how on earth it managed to drown itself in the inkwell of his writing-desk – had exercised him infinitely. The ship within the islands was much more easily accounted for; and just as we were about to rise from table he made his pronouncement. She was, he doubted not, a ship from home lately arrived. Probably she drew too much water to cross the bar except at the top of spring tides. Therefore she went into that natural harbour to wait for a few days in preference to remaining in an open roadstead.

'That's so,' confirmed the second mate, suddenly, in his slightly hoarse voice. 'She draws over twenty feet. She's the Liverpool ship *Sephora* with a cargo of coal. Hundred and twenty-three days from Cardiff.'

We looked at him in surprise.

'The tugboat skipper told me when he came on board for your letters, sir,' explained the young man. 'He expects to take her up the river the day after tomorrow.'

After thus overwhelming us with the extent of his information he slipped out of the cabin. The mate observed regretfully that he 'could not account for that young fellow's whims'. What prevented him telling us all about it at once, he wanted to know.

I detained him as he was making a move. For the last two days the crew had had plenty of hard work, and the night before they had very little sleep. I felt painfully that I – a stranger – was doing something unusual when I directed him to let all hands turn in without setting an anchor-watch. I proposed to keep on deck myself till one o'clock or thereabouts. I would get the second mate to relieve me at that hour.

'He will turn out the cook and the steward at four,' I concluded, 'and then give you a call. Of course at the slightest sign of any sort of wind we'll have the hands up and make a start at once.'

He concealed his astonishment. 'Very well, sir.' Outside the cuddy he put his head in the second mate's door to inform him of my unheard-of caprice to take a five hours' anchor-watch on myself. I heard the other raise his voice incredulously – 'What? The Captain himself?' Then a few more murmurs, a door closed, then another. A few moments later I went on deck.

My strangeness, which had made me sleepless, had prompted that unconventional arrangement, as if I had expected in those solitary hours of the night to get on terms with the ship of which I knew nothing, manned by men of whom I knew very little more. Fast alongside a wharf, littered like any ship in port with a tangle of unrelated things, invaded by unrelated shore people, I had hardly seen her properly yet. Now, as she lay cleared for sea, the stretch of her main-deck seemed to me very fine under the stars. Very fine, very roomy for her size, and very inviting. I descended the poop and paced the waist, my mind picturing to myself the coming passage through the Malay Archipelago, down the Indian Ocean, and up the Atlantic. All its phases were familiar enough to me, every characteristic, all the alternatives which were likely to face me on the high seas – everything! . . . except the novel responsibility of command. But I took heart from the reasonable thought that the ship was like other ships, the men like other men, and that the sea was not likely to keep any special surprises expressly for my discomfiture.

Arrived at that comforting conclusion, I bethought myself of a cigar and went below to get it. All was still down there. Everybody at the after end of the ship was sleeping profoundly. I came out again on the quarter-deck, agreeably at ease in my sleeping-suit on that warm breathless night, bare-footed, a glowing cigar in my teeth, and, going forward, I was met by the profound silence of the fore end of the ship. Only as I passed the door of the forecastle I heard a deep, quiet, trustful sigh of some sleeper inside. And suddenly I rejoiced in the great security of the sea as compared with the unrest of the land, in my choice of that untempted life presenting no disquieting problems, invested with an elementary moral beauty by the absolute straightforwardness of its appeal and by the singleness of its purpose.

The riding-light in the fore-rigging burned with a clear, untroubled, as if symbolic, flame, confident and bright in the mysterious shades of the night. Passing on my way aft along the other side of the ship, I observed that the rope side-ladder, put over, no doubt, for the master of the tug when he came to fetch away our letters, had not been hauled in as it should have been. I became annoyed at this, for exactitude in small matters is the very soul of discipline. Then I reflected that I had myself peremptorily dismissed my officers from duty, and by my own act had prevented the anchor-watch being formally set and things properly attended to. I asked myself whether it was wise ever to interfere with the established routine of duties even from the kindest of motives. My action might have made me appear eccentric. Goodness only knew how that absurdly whiskered mate would 'account' for my conduct, and what the whole ship thought of the informality of their new captain. I was vexed with myself.

Not from compunction certainly, but, as it were mechanically, I proceeded to get the ladder in myself. Now a sideladder of that sort is a light affair and comes in easily, yet my vigorous tug, which should have brought it flying on board, merely recoiled upon my body in a totally unexpected jerk. What the devil! . . . I was so astounded by the immovableness of that ladder that I remained stock-still, trying to account for it to myself like that imbecile mate of mine. In the end, of course, I put my head over the rail.

The side of the ship made an opaque belt of shadow on the darkling glassy shimmer of the sea. But I saw at once something elongated and pale floating very close to the ladder. Before I could form a guess a faint flash of phosphorescent light, which seemed to issue suddenly from the naked body of a man, flickered in the sleeping water with the elusive, silent play of summer lightning in a night sky. With a gasp I saw revealed to my stare a pair of feet, the long legs, a broad livid back immersed right up to the neck in a greenish cadaverous glow. One hand, awash, clutched the bottom rung of the ladder. He was complete but for the head. A headless corpse! The cigar dropped out of my gaping mouth with a tiny plop and a short hiss quite audible in the absolute stillness of all things under heaven. At that I suppose he raised up his face, a dimly pale oval in the shadow of the ship's side. But even then I could only barely make out down there the shape of his black-haired head. However, it was enough for the horrid, frost-bound sensation which had gripped me about the chest to pass off. The moment of vain exclamations was past, too. I only climbed on the spare spar and leaned over the rail as far as I could, to bring my eyes nearer to that mystery floating alongside.

As he hung by the ladder, like a resting swimmer, the sea-lightning played about his limbs at every stir; and he appeared in it ghastly, silvery, fish-like. He remained as mute as a fish, too. He made no motion to get out of the water, either. It was inconceivable that he should not attempt to come on board, and strangely troubling to suspect that perhaps he did not want to. And my first words were prompted by just that troubled incertitude.

'What's the matter?' I asked in my ordinary tone, speaking down to the face upturned exactly under mine.

'Cramp,' it answered, no louder. Then slightly anxious, 'I say, no need to call anyone.'

'I was not going to,' I said.

'Are you alone on deck?'

'Yes.'

I had somehow the impression that he was on the point of letting go the ladder to swim away beyond my ken – mysterious as he came. But, for the moment, this being appearing as if he had risen from the bottom of the sea (it was certainly the nearest land to the ship) wanted only to know the time. I told him. And he, down there, said tentatively:

'I suppose your captain's turned in?'

'I am sure he hasn't,' I said.

He seemed to struggle with himself, for I heard something like the low, bitter murmur of doubt. 'What's the good?' His next words came out with a hesitating effort.

'Look here, my man. Could you call him out quietly?'

I thought the time had come to declare myself.

'*I* am the captain.'

I heard a 'By Jove!' whispered at the level of the water. The phosphorescence flashed in the swirl of the water all about his limbs, his other hand seized the ladder.

'My name's Leggatt.'

The voice was calm and resolute. A good voice. The self-possession of that man had somehow induced a corresponding state in myself. It was very quietly that I remarked:

'You must be a good swimmer.'

'Yes. I've been in the water practically since nine o'clock. The question for me now is whether I am to let go this ladder and go on swimming till I sink from exhaustion, or – to come on board here.'

I felt this was no mere formula of desperate speech, but a real alternative in the view of a strong soul. I should have gathered from this that he was young; indeed, it is only the young who are ever confronted by such clear issues. But at the time it was pure intuition on my part. A mysterious communication was established already between us two – in the face of that silent, darkened tropical sea. I was young, too; young enough to make no comment. The man in the water began suddenly to climb up the ladder, and I hastened away from the rail to fetch some clothes.

Before entering the cabin I stood still, listening in the lobby at the foot of the stairs. A faint snore came through the closed door of the chief mate's room. The second mate's door was on the hook, but the darkness in there was absolutely soundless. He, too, was young and could sleep like a stone. There remained the steward, but he was not likely to wake up before he was called. I got a sleeping-suit out of my room and, coming back on deck, saw the naked man from the sea sitting on the main-hatch, glimmering white in the darkness, his elbows on his knees and his head in his hands. In a moment he had concealed his damp body in a sleeping-suit of the same grey-stripe pattern as the one I was wearing and followed me like my double on the poop. Together we moved right aft, barefooted, silent.

'What is it?' I asked in a deadened voice, taking the lighted lamp out of the binnacle, and raising it to his face.

'An ugly business.'

He had rather regular features; a good mouth; light eyes under somewhat heavy, dark eyebrows; a smooth, square forehead; no growth on his cheeks; a small, brown moustache, and a well-shaped, round chin. His expression was concentrated, meditative, under the inspecting light of the lamp I held up to his face; such as a man thinking hard in solitude might wear. My sleeping-suit was just right for his size. A well-knit young fellow of twenty-five at most. He caught his lower lip with the edge of white, even teeth.

'Yes,' I said, replacing the lamp in the binnacle. The warm, heavy tropical night closed upon his head again.

'There's a ship over there,' he murmured.

'Yes, I know. The *Sephora*. Did you know of us?'

'Hadn't the slightest idea. I am the mate of her –' He paused and corrected himself. 'I should say I *was*.'

'Aha! Something wrong?'

'Yes. Very wrong indeed. I've killed a man.'

'What do you mean? Just now?'

'No, on the passage. Weeks ago. Thirty-nine south. When I say a man –'

'Fit of temper,' I suggested, confidently.

The shadowy, dark head, like mine, seemed to nod imperceptibly above the ghostly grey of my sleeping-suit. It was, in the night, as though I had been faced by my own reflection in the depths of a sombre and immense mirror.

'A pretty thing to have to own up to for a Conway boy,' murmured my double, distinctly.

'You're a Conway boy?'

'I am,' he said, as if startled. Then, slowly . . . 'Perhaps you too –'

It was so; but being a couple of years older I had left before he joined. After a quick interchange of dates a silence fell; and I thought suddenly of my absurd mate with his terrific whiskers and the 'Bless my soul – you don't say so' type of intellect. My double gave me an inkling of his thoughts by saying: 'My father's a parson in Norfolk. Do you see me before a judge and jury on that charge? For myself I can't see the necessity. There are fellows that an angel from heaven – And I am not that. He was one of those creatures that are just simmering all the time with a silly sort of wickedness. Miserable devils that have no business to live at all. He wouldn't do his duty and wouldn't let anybody else do theirs. But what's the good of talking! You know well enough the sort of ill-conditioned, snarling cur –'

He appealed to me as if our experiences had been as identical as our clothes. And I knew well enough the pestiferous danger of such a character where there are no means of legal repression. And I knew well enough also that my double there was no homicidal ruffian. I did not think of asking him for details, and he told me the story roughly in brusque, disconnected sentences. I needed no more. I saw it all going on as though I were myself inside that other sleeping-suit.

'It happened while we were setting a reefed foresail, at dusk. Reefed foresail! You understand the sort of weather. The only sail we had left to keep the ship running; so you may guess what it had been like for days. Anxious sort of job, that. He gave me some of his cursed insolence at the sheet. I tell you I was overdone with this terrific weather that seemed to have no end to it. Terrific, I tell you – and a deep ship. I believe the fellow himself was half crazed with funk. It was no time for gentlemanly reproof, so I turned round and felled him like an ox. He up and at me. We closed just as an awful sea made for the ship. All hands saw it coming and took to the rigging, but I had him by the throat, and went on shaking him like a rat, the men above us yelling, "Look out! look out!" Then a crash as if the sky had fallen on my head. They say that for over ten minutes hardly anything was to be seen of the ship – just the three masts and a bit of the forecastle head and of the poop all awash driving along in a smother of foam. It was a miracle that they found us, jammed together behind the forebits. It's clear that I meant business, because I was holding him by the throat still when they picked us up. He was black in the face. It was too much for them. It seems they rushed us aft together, gripped as we were, screaming "Murder!" like a lot of lunatics, and broke into the cuddy. And the ship running for her life, touch and go all the time, any minute her last in a sea fit to turn your hair grey only a-looking at it. I understand that the skipper, too, started raving like the rest of them. The man had been deprived of sleep for more than a week, and to have this sprung on him at the height of a furious gale nearly drove him out of his mind. I wonder they didn't fling me overboard after getting the carcass of their precious ship-mate out of my fingers. They had rather a job to separate us, I've been told. A sufficiently fierce story to make an old judge and a respectable jury sit up a bit. The first thing I heard when I came to myself was the maddening howling of that endless gale, and on that the voice of the old man. He was hanging on to my bunk staring into my face out of his sou'wester.

' "Mr Leggatt, you have killed a man. You can act no longer as chief mate of this ship." '

His care to subdue his voice made it sound monotonous. He rested a hand on the end of the skylight to steady himself with, and all that time did not stir a limb, so far as I could see. 'Nice little tale for a quiet tea-party,' he concluded in the same tone.

One of my hands, too, rested on the end of the skylight; neither did I stir a limb, so far as I knew. We stood less than a foot from each other. It occurred to me that if old 'Bless my soul – you don't say so' were to put his head up the companion and catch sight of us, he would think he was seeing double, or imagine himself coming upon a scene of weird witchcraft; the strange captain having a quiet confabulation by the wheel with his own grey ghost. I became very much concerned to prevent anything of the sort. I heard the other's soothing undertone.

'My father's a parson in Norfolk,' it said. Evidently he had forgotten he had told me this important fact before. Truly a nice little tale.

'You had better slip down into my stateroom now,' I said, moving off stealthily. My double followed my movements; our bare feet made no sound; I let him in, closed the door with care, and, after giving a call to the second mate, returned on deck for my relief.

'Not much sign of any wind yet,' I remarked when he approached.

'No, sir. Not much,' he assented, sleepily, in his hoarse voice, with just enough deference, no more, and barely suppressing a yawn.

'Well, that's all you have to look out for. You have got your orders.'

'Yes, sir.'

I paced a turn or two on the poop and saw him take up his position face forward with his elbow in the ratlines of the mizzen-rigging before I went below. The mate's faint snoring was still going on peacefully. The cuddy lamp was burning over the table on which stood a vase with flowers, a polite attention from the ship's provision merchant – the last flowers we should see for the next three months at the very least. Two bunches of bananas hung from the beam symmetrically, one on each side of the rudder-casing. Everything was as before in the ship – except that two of her captain's sleeping-suits were simultaneously in use, one motionless in the cuddy, the other keeping very still in the captain's stateroom.

It must be explained here that my cabin had the form of the capital letter L, the door being within the angle and opening into the short part of the letter. A couch was to the left, the bed-place to the right; my writing-desk and the chronometers' table faced the door. But anyone opening it, unless he stepped right inside, had no view of what I call the long (or vertical) part of the letter. It contained some lockers surmounted by a bookcase; and a few clothes, a thick jacket or two, caps, oilskin coat, and such like, hung on hooks. There was at the bottom of that part a door opening into my bathroom, which could be entered also directly from the saloon. But that way was never used.

The mysterious arrival had discovered the advantage of this particular shape. Entering my room, lighted strongly by a big bulkhead lamp swung on gimbals above my writing-desk, I did not see him anywhere till he stepped out quietly from behind the coats hung in the recessed part.

'I heard somebody moving about, and went in there at once,' he whispered.

I, too, spoke under my breath.

'Nobody is likely to come in here without knocking and getting permission.'

He nodded. His face was thin and the sunburn faded, as though he had been ill. And no wonder. He had been, I heard presently, kept under arrest in his cabin for nearly seven weeks. But there was nothing sickly in his eyes or in his expression. He was not a bit like me, really; yet, as we stood leaning over my bed-place, whispering side by side, with our dark heads together and our backs to the door, anybody bold enough to open it stealthily would have been treated to the uncanny sight of a double captain busy talking in whispers with his other self.

'But all this doesn't tell me how you came to hang on to our side-ladder,' I inquired, in the hardly audible murmurs we used, after he had told me something more of the proceedings on board the *Sephora* once the bad weather was over.

'When we sighted Java Head I had had time to think all those matters out several times over. I had six weeks of doing nothing else, and with only an hour or so every evening for a tramp on the quarter-deck.'

He whispered, his arms folded on the side of my bed-place, staring through the open port. And I could imagine perfectly the manner of this thinking out – a stubborn if not a steadfast operation; something of which I should have been perfectly incapable.

'I reckoned it would be dark before we closed with the land,' he continued, so low that I had to strain my hearing, near as we were to each other, shoulder touching shoulder almost. 'So I asked to speak to the old man. He always seemed very sick when he came to see me – as if he could not look me in the face. You know, that foresail saved the ship. She was too deep to have run long under bare poles. And it was I that managed to set it for him. Anyway, he came. When I had him in my cabin – he stood by the door looking at me as if I had the halter round my neck already – I asked him right away to leave my cabin door unlocked at night while the ship was going through Sunda Straits. There would be the Java coast within two or three miles, off Angier Point. I wanted nothing more. I've had a prize for swimming my second year in the Conway.'

'I can believe it,' I breathed out.

'God only knows why they locked me in every night. To see some of their faces you'd have thought they were afraid I'd go about at night strangling people. Am I a murdering brute? Do I look it? By Jove! if I had been he wouldn't have trusted himself like that into my room. You'll say I might have chucked him aside and bolted out, there and then – it was dark already. Well, no. And for the same reason I wouldn't think of trying to smash the door. There would have been a rush to stop me at the noise, and I did not mean to get into a confounded scrimmage. Somebody else might have got killed – for I would not have broken out only to get chucked back, and I did not want any more of that work. He refused, looking more sick than ever. He was afraid of the men, and also of that old second mate of his who had been sailing with him for years – a grey-headed old humbug; and his steward, too, had been with him devil knows how long – seventeen years or more – a dogmatic sort of loafer who hated me like poison, just because I was the chief mate. No chief mate ever made more than one voyage in the *Sephora*, you know. Those two old chaps ran the ship. Devil only knows what the skipper wasn't afraid of (all his nerve went to pieces altogether in that hellish spell of bad weather we had) – of what the law would do to him – or his wife, perhaps. Oh, yes! she's on board. Though I don't think she would have meddled. She would have been only too glad to have me out of the ship in any case. The "brand of Cain" business, don't you see. That's all right. I was ready enough to go off wandering on the face of the earth – and that was price enough to pay for an Abel of that sort. Anyhow, he wouldn't listen to me. "This thing must take its course. I represent the law here." He was shaking like a leaf. "So you won't?" "No!" "Then I hope you will be able to sleep on that," I said, and turned my back on him. "I wonder that *you* can," cries he, and locks the door.

'Well, after that, I couldn't. Not very well. That was three weeks ago. We have had a slow passage through the Java Sea; drifted about Carimata for ten days. When we anchored here they thought, I suppose, it was all right. The nearest land (and that's five miles) is the ship's destination; the consul would soon set about catching me; and there would have been no object in bolting to these islets there. I don't suppose there's a drop of water on them. I don't know how it was, but tonight that steward, after bringing me my supper, went out to let me eat it, and left the door unlocked. And I ate it – all there was, too. After I had finished I strolled out on the quarter-deck. I don't know that I meant to do anything. A breath of fresh air was all I wanted, I believe. Then a sudden temptation came over me. I kicked off my slippers and was in the water before I had made up my mind fairly. Somebody heard the splash and they raised an awful hullabaloo. "He's gone! Lower the boats! He's committed suicide! No, he's swimming." Certainly I was swimming. It's not so easy for a swimmer like me to commit suicide by drowning. I landed on the nearest islet before the boat left the ship's side. I heard them pulling about in the dark, hailing, and so on, but after a bit they gave up. Everything quietened down and the anchorage became as still as death. I sat down on a stone and began to think. I felt certain they would start searching for me at daylight. There was no place to hide on those stony things – and if there had been, what would have been the good? But now I was clear of that ship, I was not going back. So after a while I took off all my clothes, tied them up in a bundle with a stone inside, and dropped them in the deep water on the outer side of that islet. That was suicide enough for me. Let them think what they liked, but I didn't mean to drown myself. I meant to swim till I sank – but that's not the same thing. I struck out for another of these little islands, and it was from that one that I first saw your riding-light. Something to swim for. I went on easily, and on the way I came upon a flat rock a foot or two above water. In the daytime, I dare say, you might make it out with a glass from your poop. I scrambled up on it and rested myself for a bit. Then I made another start. That last spell must have been over a mile.'

His whisper was getting fainter and fainter, and all the time he stared straight out through the port-hole, in which there was not even a star to be seen. I had not interrupted him. There was something that made comment impossible in his narrative, or perhaps in himself; a sort of feeling, a quality, which I can't find a name for. And when he ceased, all I found was a futile whisper: 'So you swam for our light?'

'Yes – straight for it. It was something to swim for. I couldn't see any stars low down because the coast was in the way, and I couldn't see the land, either. The water was like glass. One might have been swimming in a confounded thousand-feet deep cistern with no place for scrambling out anywhere; but what I didn't like was the notion of swimming round and round like a crazed bullock before I gave out; and as I didn't mean to go back . . . No. Do you see me being hauled back, stark naked, off one of these little islands by the scruff of the neck and fighting like a wild beast? Somebody would have got killed for certain, and I did not want any of that. So I went on. Then your ladder –'

'Why didn't you hail the ship?' I asked, a little louder.

He touched my shoulder lightly. Lazy footsteps came right over our heads and stopped. The second mate had crossed from the other side of the poop and might have been hanging over the rail, for all we knew.

'He couldn't hear us talking – could he?' My double breathed into my very ear, anxiously.

His anxiety was an answer, a sufficient answer, to the question I had put to him. An answer containing all the difficulty of that situation. I closed the port-hole quietly, to make sure. A louder word might have been overheard.

'Who's that?' he whispered then.

'My second mate. But I don't know much more of the fellow than you do.'

And I told him a little about myself. I had been appointed to take charge while I least expected anything of the sort, not quite a fortnight ago. I didn't know either the ship or the people. Hadn't had the time in port to look about me or size anybody up. And as to the crew, all they knew was that I was appointed to take the ship home. For the rest, I was almost as much of a stranger on board as himself, I said. And at the moment I felt it most acutely. I felt that it would take very little to make me a suspect person in the eyes of the ship's company.

He had turned about meantime; and we, the two strangers in the ship, faced each other in identical attitudes.

'Your ladder –' he murmured, after a silence. 'Who'd have thought of finding a ladder hanging over at night in a ship anchored out here! I felt just then a very unpleasant faintness. After the life I've been leading for nine weeks, anybody would have got out of condition. I wasn't capable of swimming round as far as your rudder-chains. And, lo and behold! there was a ladder to get hold of. After I gripped it I said to myself, "What's the good?" When I saw a man's head looking over I thought I would swim away presently and leave him shouting – in whatever language it was. I didn't mind being looked at. I – I liked it. And then you speaking to me so quietly – as if you had expected me – made me hold on a little longer. It had been a confounded lonely time – I don't mean while swimming. I was glad to talk a little to somebody that didn't belong to the *Sephora*. As to asking for the captain, that was a mere impulse. It could have been no use, with all the ship knowing about me and the other people pretty certain to be round here in the morning. I don't know – I wanted to be seen, to talk with somebody, before I went on, I don't know what I would have said . . . "Fine night, isn't it?" or something of the sort.'

'Do you think they will be round here presently?' I asked with some incredulity.

'Quite likely,' he said, faintly.

He looked extremely haggard all of a sudden. His head rolled on his shoulders.

'H'm. We shall see then. Meantime get into that bed,' I whispered. 'Want help? There.'

It was a rather high bed-place with a set of drawers underneath. This amazing swimmer really needed the lift I gave him by seizing his leg. He tumbled in, rolled over on his back, and flung one arm across his eyes. And then, with his face nearly hidden, he must have looked exactly as I used to look in that bed. I gazed upon my other self for a while before drawing across carefully the two green serge curtains which ran on a brass rod. I thought for a moment of pinning them together for greater safety, but I sat down on the couch, and once there I felt unwilling to rise and hunt for a pin. I would do it in a moment. I was extremely tired, in a peculiarly intimate way, by the strain of stealthiness, by the effort of whispering and the general secrecy of this excitement. It was three o'clock by now and I had been on my feet since nine, but I was not sleepy; I could not have gone to sleep. I sat there, fagged out, looking at the curtains, trying to clear my mind of the confused sensation of being in two places at once, and greatly bothered by an exasperating knocking in my head. It was a relief to discover suddenly that it was not in my head at all, but on the outside of the door. Before I could collect myself the words 'Come in' were out of my mouth, and the steward entered with a tray, bringing in my morning coffee. I had slept, after all, and I was so frightened that I shouted, 'This way! I am here, steward,' as though he had been miles away. He put down the tray on the table next to the couch and only then said, very quietly, 'I can see you are here, sir.' I felt him give me a keen look, but I dared not meet his eyes just then. He must have wondered why I had drawn the curtains of my bed before going to sleep on the couch. He went out, hooking the door open as usual.

I heard the crew washing decks above me. I knew I would have been told at once if there had been any wind. Calm, I thought, and I was doubly vexed. Indeed, I felt dual more than ever. The steward reappeared suddenly in the doorway. I jumped up from the couch so quickly that he gave a start.

'What do you want here?'

'Close your port, sir – they are washing decks.'

'It is closed,' I said, reddening.

'Very well, sir.' But he did not move from the doorway and returned my stare in an extraordinary, equivocal manner for a time. Then his eyes wavered, all his expression changed, and in a voice unusually gentle, almost coaxingly:

'May I come in to take the empty cup away, sir?'

'Of course!' I turned my back on him while he popped in and out. Then I unhooked and closed the door and even pushed the bolt. This sort of thing could not go on very long. The cabin was as hot as an oven, too. I took a peep at my double, and discovered that he had not moved, his arm was still over his eyes; but his chest heaved; his hair was wet; his chin glistened with perspiration. I reached over him and opened the port.

'I must show myself on deck,' I reflected.

Of course, theoretically, I could do what I liked, with no one to say nay to me within the whole circle of the horizon; but to lock my cabin door and take the key away I did not dare. Directly I put my head out of the companion I saw the group of my two officers, the second mate barefooted, the chief mate in long india-rubber boots, near the break of the poop, and the steward half-way down the poop-ladder talking to them eagerly. He happened to catch sight of me and dived, the second ran down on the maindeck shouting some order or other, and the chief mate came to meet me, touching his cap.

There was a sort of curiosity in his eye that I did not like. I don't know whether the steward had told them that I was 'queer' only, or downright drunk, but I know the man meant to have a good look at me. I watched him coming with a smile which, as he got into point-blank range, took effect and froze his very whiskers. I did not give him time to open his lips.

'Square the yards by lifts and braces before the hands go to breakfast.'

It was the first particular order I had given on board that ship; and I stayed on deck to see it executed, too. I had felt the need of asserting myself without loss of time. That sneering young cub got taken down a peg or two on that occasion, and I also seized the opportunity of having a good look at the face of every foremast man as they filed past me to go to the after braces. At breakfast time, eating nothing myself, I presided with such frigid dignity that the two mates were only too glad to escape from the cabin as soon as decency permitted; and all the time the dual working of my mind distracted me almost to the point of insanity. I was constantly watching myself, my secret self, as dependent on my actions as my own personality, sleeping in that bed, behind that door which faced me as I sat at the head of the table. It was very much like being mad, only it was worse because one was aware of it.

I had to shake him for a solid minute, but when at last he opened his eyes it was in the full possession of his senses, with an inquiring look.

'All's well so far,' I whispered. 'Now you must vanish into the bath-room.'

He did so, as noiseless as a ghost, and then I rang for the steward, and facing him boldly, directed him to tidy up my stateroom while I was having my bath – 'and be quick about it'. As my tone admitted of no excuses, he said, 'Yes, sir,' and ran off to fetch his dust-pan and brushes. I took a bath and did most of my dressing, splashing, and whistling softly for the steward's edification, while the secret sharer of my life stood drawn up bolt upright in that little space, his face looking very sunken in daylight, his eyelids lowered under the stern, dark line of his eyebrows drawn together by a slight frown.

When I left him there to go back to my room the steward was finishing dusting. I sent for the mate and engaged him in some insignificant conversation. It was, as it were, trifling with the terrific character of his whiskers; but my object was to give him an opportunity for a good look at my cabin. And then I could at last shut, with a clear conscience, the door of my stateroom and get my double back into the recessed part. There was nothing else for it. He had to sit still on a small folding stool, half smothered by the heavy coats hanging there. We listened to the steward going into the bath-room out of the saloon, filling the water-bottles there, scrubbing the bath, setting things to rights, whisk, bang, clatter – out again into the saloon – turn the key – click. Such was my scheme for keeping my second self invisible. Nothing better could be contrived under the circumstances. And there we sat; I at my writing-desk ready to appear busy with some papers, he behind me out of sight of the door. It would not have been prudent to talk in daytime; and I could not have stood the excitement of that queer sense of whispering to myself. Now and then, glancing over my shoulder, I saw him far back there, sitting rigidly on the low stool, his bare feet close together, his arms folded, his head hanging on his breast – and perfectly still. Anybody would have taken him for me.

I was fascinated by it myself. Every moment I had to glance over my shoulder. I was looking at him when a voice outside the door said:

'Beg pardon, sir.'

'Well' . . . I kept my eyes on him, and so when the voice outside the door announced. 'There's a ship's boat coming our way, sir,' I saw him give a start – the first movement he had made for hours. But he did not raise his bowed head.

'All right. Get the ladder over.'

I hesitated. Should I whisper something to him? But what? His immobility seemed to have been never disturbed. What could I tell him he did not know already? . . . Finally I went on deck.

Chapter II

The skipper of the *Sephora* had a thin red whisker all round his face, and the sort of complexion that goes with hair of that colour; also the particular, rather smeary shade of blue in the eyes. He was not exactly a showy figure; his shoulders were high, his stature but middling – one leg slightly more bandy than the other. He shook hands, looking vaguely around. A spiritless tenacity was his main characteristic, I judged. I behaved with a politeness which seemed to disconcert him. Perhaps he was shy. He mumbled to me as if he were ashamed of what he was saying; gave his name (it was something like Archbold – but at this distance of years I hardly am sure), his ship's name, and a few other particulars of that sort, in the manner of a criminal making a reluctant and doleful confession. He had had terrible weather on the passage out – terrible – terrible – wife aboard, too.

'By this time we were seated in the cabin and the steward brought in a tray with a bottle and glasses. 'Thanks! No.' Never took liquor. Would have some water, though. He drank two tumblerfuls. Terrible thirsty work. Ever since daylight had been exploring the islands round his ship.

'What was that for – fun?' I asked, with an appearance of polite interest.

'No!' He sighed. 'Painful duty.'

As he persisted in his mumbling and I wanted my double to hear every word, I hit upon the notion of informing him that I regretted to say I was hard of hearing.

'Such a young man, too!' he nodded, keeping his smeary blue, unintelligent eyes fastened upon me. What was the cause of it – some disease? he inquired, without the least sympathy and as if he thought that, if so, I'd got no more than I deserved.

'Yes; disease,' I admitted in a cheerful tone which seemed to shock him. But my point was gained, because he had to raise his voice to give me his tale. It is not worth while to record that version. It was just over two months since all this had happened, and he had thought so much about it that he seemed completely muddled as to its bearings, but still immensely impressed.

'What would you think of such a thing happening on board your own ship? I've had the *Sephora* for these fifteen years. I am a well-known shipmaster.'

He was densely distressed – and perhaps I should have sympathized with him if I had been able to detach my mental vision from the unsuspected sharer of my cabin as though he were my second self. There he was on the other side of the bulkhead, four or five feet from us, no more, as we sat in the saloon. I looked politely at Captain Archbold (if that was his name), but it was the other I saw, in a grey sleeping-suit, seated on a low stool, his bare feet close together, his arms folded, and every word said between us falling into the ears of his dark head bowed on his chest.

'I have been at sea now, man and boy, for seven-and-thirty years, and I've never heard of such a thing happening in an English ship. And that it should be my ship. Wife on board, too.'

I was hardly listening to him.

'Don't you think,' I said, 'that the heavy sea which, you told me, came aboard just then might have killed the man? I have seen the sheer weight of a sea kill a man very neatly, by simply breaking his neck.'

'Good God!' he uttered, impressively, fixing his smeary blue eyes on me. 'The sea! No man killed by the sea ever looked like that.' He seemed positively scandalized at my suggestion. And as I gazed at him, certainly not prepared for anything original on his part, he advanced his head close to mine and thrust his tongue out at me so suddenly that I couldn't help starting back.

After scoring over my calmness in this graphic way he nodded wisely. If I had seen the sight, he assured me, I would never forget it as long as I lived. The weather was too bad to give the corpse a proper sea burial. So next day at dawn they took it up on the poop, covering its face with a bit of bunting; he read a short prayer, and then, just as it was, in its oilskins and long boots, they launched it among those mountainous seas that seemed ready every moment to swallow up the ship herself and the terrified lives on board of her.

'That reefed foresail saved you,' I threw in.

'Under God – it did,' he exclaimed fervently. 'It was by a special mercy, I firmly believe, that it stood some of those hurricane squalls.'

'It was the setting of that sail which –' I began.

'God's own hand in it,' he interrupted me. 'Nothing less could have done it. I don't mind telling you that I hardly dared give the order. It seemed impossible that we could touch anything without losing it, and then our last hope would have been gone.'

The terror of that gale was on him yet. I let him go on for a bit, then said, casually – as if returning to a minor subject:

'You were very anxious to give up your mate to the shore people, I believe?'

He was. To the law. His obscure tenacity on that point had in it something incomprehensible and a little awful; something, as it were, mystical, quite apart from his anxiety that he should not be suspected of 'countenancing any doings of that sort'. Seven-and-thirty virtuous years at sea, of which over twenty of immaculate command, and the last fifteen in the *Sephora*, seemed to have laid him under some pitiless obligation.

'And you know,' he went on, groping shamefacedly among his feelings, 'I did not engage that young fellow. His people had some interest with my owners. I was in a way forced to take him on. He looked very smart, very gentlemanly, and all that. But do you know – I never liked him, somehow. I am a plain man. You see, he wasn't exactly the sort for the chief mate of a ship like the *Sephora*.'

I had become so connected in thoughts and impressions with the secret sharer of my cabin that I felt as if I, personally, were being given to understand that I, too, was not the sort that would have done for the chief mate of a ship like the *Sephora*. I had no doubt of it in my mind.

'Not at all the style of man. You understand,' he insisted, superfluously, looking hard at me.

I smiled urbanely. He seemed at a loss for a while.

'I suppose I must report a suicide.'

'Beg pardon?'

'Sui-cide! That's what I'll have to write to my owners directly I get in.'

'Unless you manage to recover him before tomorrow,' I assented, dispassionately . . . 'I mean, alive.'

He mumbled something which I really did not catch, and I turned my ear to him in a puzzled manner. He fairly bawled:

'The land – I say, the mainland is at least seven miles off my anchorage.'

'About that.'

My lack of excitement, of curiosity, of surprise, of any sort of pronounced interest, began to arouse his distrust. But except for the felicitous pretence of deafness I had not tried to pretend anything. I had felt utterly incapable of playing the part of ignorance properly, and therefore was afraid to try. It is also certain that he had brought some ready-made suspicions with him, and that he viewed my politeness as a strange and unnatural phenomenon. And yet how else could I have received him? Not heartily! That was impossible for psychological reasons, which I need not state here. My only object was to keep off his inquiries. Surlily? Yes, but surliness might have provoked a point-blank question. From its novelty to him and from its nature, punctilious courtesy was the manner best calculated to restrain the man. But there was the danger of his breaking through my defence bluntly. I could not, I think, have met him by a direct lie, also for psychological (not moral) reasons. If he had only known how afraid I was of his putting my feeling of identity with the other to the test! But, strangely enough – (I thought of it only afterwards) – I believe that he was not a little disconcerted by the reverse side of that weird situation, by something in me that reminded him of the man he was seeking – suggested a mysterious similitude to the young fellow he had distrusted and disliked from the first.

However that might have been, the silence was not very prolonged. He took another oblique step.

'I reckon I had no more than a two-mile pull to your ship. Not a bit more.'

'And quite enough, too, in this awful heat,' I said.

Another pause full of mistrust followed. Necessity, they say, is mother of invention, but fear, too, is not barren of ingenious suggestions. And I was afraid he would ask me point-blank for news of my other self.

'Nice little saloon, isn't it?' I remarked, as if noticing for the first time the way his eyes roamed from one closed door to the other. 'And very well fitted out, too. Here, for instance,' I continued, reaching over the back of my seat negligently and flinging the door open, 'is my bath-room.'

He made an eager movement, but hardly gave it a glance. I got up, shut the door of the bath-room, and invited him to have a look round, as if I were very proud of my accommodation. He had to rise and be shown round, but he went through the business without any raptures whatever.

'And now we'll have a look at my stateroom,' I declared, in a voice as loud as I dared to make it, crossing the cabin to the starboard side with purposely heavy steps.

He followed me in and gazed around. My intelligent double had vanished. I played my part.

'Very convenient – isn't it?'

'Very nice. Very comf . . .' He didn't finish and went out brusquely as if to escape from some unrighteous wiles of mine. But it was not to be. I had been too frightened not to feel vengeful; I felt I had him on the run, and I meant to keep him on the run. My polite insistence must have had something menacing in it, because he gave in suddenly. And I did not let him off a single item; mate's room, pantry, storerooms, the very sail-locker which was also under the poop – he had to look into them all. When at last I showed him out on the quarter-deck he drew a long, spiritless sigh, and mumbled dismally that he must really be going back to his ship now. I desired my mate, who had joined us, to see to the captain's boat.

The man of whiskers gave a blast on the whistle which he used to wear hanging round his neck, and yelled, '*Sephora*'s away!' My double down there in my cabin must have heard, and certainly could not feel more relieved than I. Four fellows came running out from somewhere forward and went over the side, while my own men, appearing on deck too, lined the rail. I escorted my visitor to the gangway ceremoniously, and nearly overdid it. He was a tenacious beast. On the very ladder he lingered, and in that unique, guiltily conscientious manner of sticking to the point:

'I say . . . you . . . you don't think that –'

I covered his voice loudly:

'Certainly not . . . I am delighted. Good-bye.'

I had an idea of what he meant to say, and just saved myself by the privilege of defective hearing. He was too shaken generally to insist, but my mate, close witness of that parting, looked mystified and his face took on a thoughtful cast. As I did not want to appear as if I wished to avoid all communication with my officers, he had the opportunity to address me.

'Seems a very nice man. His boat's crew told our chaps a very extraordinary story, if what I am told by the steward is true. I suppose you had it from the captain, sir?'

'Yes. I had a story from the captain.'

'A very horrible affair – isn't it, sir?'

'It is.'

'Beats all these tales we hear about murders in Yankee ships.'

'I don't think it beats them. I don't think it resembles them in the least.'

'Bless my soul – you don't say so! But of course I've no acquaintance whatever with American ships, not I, so I couldn't go against your knowledge. It's horrible enough for me . . . But the queerest part is that those fellows seemed to have some idea the man was hidden aboard here. They had really. Did you ever hear of such a thing?'

'Preposterous – isn't it?'

We were walking to and fro athwart the quarter-deck. No one of the crew forward could be seen (the day was Sunday), and the mate pursued:

'There was some little dispute about it. Our chaps took offence. "As if we would harbour a thing like that," they said. "Wouldn't you like to look for him in our coal-hole?" Quite a tiff. But they made it up in the end. I suppose he did drown himself. Don't you, sir?'

'I don't suppose anything.'

'You have no doubt in the matter, sir?'

'None whatever.'

I left him suddenly. I felt I was producing a bad impression, but with my double down there it was most trying to be on deck. And it was almost as trying to be below. Altogether a nerve-trying situation. But on the whole I felt less torn in two when I was with him. There was no one in the whole ship whom I dared take into my confidence. Since the hands had got to know his story, it would have been impossible to pass him off for anyone else, and an accidental discovery was to be dreaded now more than ever . . .

The steward being engaged in laying the table for dinner, we could talk only with our eyes when I first went down. Later in the afternoon we had a cautious try at whispering. The Sunday quietness of the ship was against us; the stillness of air and water around her was against us; the elements, the men were against us – everything was against us in our secret partnership; time itself – for this could not go on for ever. The very trust in Providence was, I suppose, denied to his guilt. Shall I confess that this thought cast me down very much? And as to the chapter of accidents which counts for so much in the book of success, I could only hope that it was closed. For what favourable accident could be expected?

'Did you hear everything?' were my first words as soon as we took up our position side by side, leaning over my bed-place.

He had. And the proof of it was his earnest whisper, 'The man told you he hardly dared to give the order.'

I understood the reference to be to that saving foresail.

'Yes. He was afraid of it being lost in the setting.'

'I assure you he never gave the order. He may think he did, but he never gave it. He stood there with me on the break of the poop after the maintopsail blew away, and whimpered about our last hope – positively whimpered about it and nothing else – and the night coming on! To hear one's skipper go on like that in such weather was enough to drive any fellow out of his mind. It worked me up into a sort of desperation. I just took it into my own hands and went away from him, boiling, and – But what's the use telling you? *You* know! . . . Do you think that if I had not been pretty fierce with them I should have got the men to do anything? Not it! The bo's'n perhaps! It wasn't a heavy sea – it was a sea gone mad! I suppose the end of the world will be something like that; and a man may have the heart to see it coming once and be done with it – but to have to face it day after day – I don't blame anybody. I was precious little better than the rest. Only – I was an officer of that old coal-wagon, anyhow –'

'I quite understand,' I conveyed that sincere assurance into his ear. He was out of breath with whispering; I could hear him pant slightly. It was all very simple. The same strung-up force which had given twenty-four men a chance, at least, for their lives, had, in a sort of recoil, crushed an unworthy mutinous existence.

But I had no leisure to weigh the merits of the matter – footsteps in the saloon, a heavy knock. 'There's enough wind to get under way with, sir.' Here was the call of a new claim upon my thoughts and even upon my feelings.

'Turn the hands up,' I cried through the door. 'I'll be on deck directly.'

I was going out to make the acquaintance of my ship. Before I left the cabin our eyes met – the eyes of the only two strangers on board. I pointed to the recessed part where the little camp-stool awaited him and laid my finger on my lips. He made a gesture – somewhat vague – a little mysterious, accompanied by a faint smile, as if of regret.

This is not the place to enlarge upon the sensations of a man who feels for the first time a ship move under his feet to his own independent word. In my case they were not unalloyed. I was not wholly alone with my command; for there was that stranger in my cabin. Or rather, I was not completely and wholly with her. Part of me was absent. That mental feeling of being in two places at once affected me physically as if the mood of secrecy had penetrated my very soul. Before an hour had elapsed since the ship had begun to move, having occasion to ask the mate (he stood by my side) to take a compass bearing of the Pagoda, I caught myself reaching up to his ear in whispers. I say I caught myself, but enough had escaped to startle the man. I can't describe it otherwise than by saying that he shied. A grave, preoccupied manner, as though he were in possession of some perplexing intelligence, did not leave him henceforth. A little later I moved away from the rail to look at the compass with such a stealthy gait that the helmsman noticed it – and I could not help noticing the unusual roundness of his eyes. These are trifling instances, though it's to no commander's advantage to be suspected of ludicrous eccentricities. But I was also more seriously affected. There are to a seaman certain words, gestures, that should in given conditions come as naturally, as instinctively as the winking of a menaced eye. A certain order should spring on to his lips without thinking; a certain sign should get itself made, so to speak, without reflection. But all unconscious alertness had abandoned me. I had to make an effort of will to recall myself back (from the cabin) to the conditions of the moment. I felt that I was appearing an irresolute commander to those people who were watching me more or less critically.

And, besides, there were the scares. On the second day out, for instance, coming off the deck in the afternoon (I had straw slippers on my bare feet) I stopped at the open pantry door and spoke to the steward. He was doing something there with his back to me. At the sound of my voice he nearly jumped out of his skin, as the saying is, and incidentally broke a cup.

'What on earth's the matter with you?' I asked, astonished.

He was extremely confused. 'Beg pardon, sir. I made sure you were in your cabin.'

'You see I wasn't.'

'No, sir. I could have sworn I had heard you moving in there not a moment ago. It's most extraordinary . . . very sorry, sir.'

I passed on with an inward shudder. I was so identified with my secret double that I did not even mention the fact in those scanty, fearful whispers we exchanged. I suppose he had made some slight noise of some kind or other. It would have been miraculous if he hadn't at one time or another. And yet, haggard as he appeared, he looked always perfectly self-controlled, more than calm – almost invulnerable. On my suggestion he remained almost entirely in the bath-room, which, upon the whole, was the safest place. There could be really no shadow of an excuse for anyone ever wanting to go in there, once the steward had done with it. It was a very tiny place. Sometimes he reclined on the floor, his legs bent, his head sustained on one elbow. At others I would find him on the camp-stool, sitting in his grey sleeping-suit and with his cropped dark hair like a patient, unmoved convict. At night I would smuggle him into my bed-place, and we would whisper together, with the regular footfalls of the officer of the watch passing and repassing over our heads. It was an infinitely miserable time. It was lucky that some tins of fine preserves were stowed in a locker in my stateroom; hard bread I could always get hold of; and so he lived on stewed chicken, pâté de foie gras, asparagus, cooked oysters, sardines – on all sorts of abominable sham delicacies out of tins. My early morning coffee he always drank; and it was all I dared do for him in that respect.

Every day there was the horrible manoeuvring to go through so that my room and then the bath-room should be done in the usual way. I came to hate the sight of the steward, to abhor the voice of that harmless man. I felt that it was he who would bring on the disaster of discovery. It hung like a sword over our heads.

The fourth day out, I think (we were then working down the east side of the Gulf of Siam, tack for tack, in light winds and smooth water) – the fourth day, I say, of this miserable juggling with the unavoidable, as we sat at our evening meal, that man, whose slightest movement I dreaded, after putting down the dishes ran up on deck busily. This could not be dangerous. Presently he came down again; and then it appeared that he had remembered a coat of mine which I had thrown over a rail to dry after having been wetted in a shower which had passed over the ship in the afternoon. Sitting stolidly at the head of the table I became terrified at the sight of the garment on his arm. Of course he made for my door. There was no time to lose.

'Steward,' I thundered. My nerves were so shaken that I could not govern my voice and conceal my agitation. This was the sort of thing that made my terrifically whiskered mate tap his forehead with his forefinger. I had detected him using that gesture while talking on deck with a confidential air to the carpenter. It was too far to hear a word, but I had no doubt that this pantomime could only refer to the strange new captain.

'Yes, sir,' the pale-faced steward turned resignedly to me. It was this maddening course of being shouted at, checked without rhyme or reason, arbitrarily chased out of my cabin, suddenly called into it, sent flying out of his pantry on incomprehensible errands, that accounted for the growing wretchedness of his expression.

'Where are you going with that coat?'

'To your room, sir.'

'Is there another shower coming?'

'I'm sure I don't know, sir. Shall I go up again and see, sir?'

'No! never mind.'

My object was attained, as of course my other self in there would have heard everything that passed. During this interlude my two officers never raised their eyes off their respective plates; but the lip of that confounded cub, the second mate, quivered visibly.

I expected the steward to hook my coat on and come out at once. He was very slow about it; but I dominated my nervousness sufficiently not to shout after him. Suddenly I became aware (it could be heard plainly enough) that the fellow for some reason or other was opening the door of the bath-room. It was the end. The place was literally not big enough to swing a cat in. My voice died in my throat and I went stony all over. I expected to hear a yell of surprise and terror, and made a movement, but had not the strength to get on my legs. Everything remained still. Had my second self taken the poor wretch by the throat? I don't know what I could have done next moment if I had not seen the steward come out of my room, close the door, and then stand quietly by the sideboard.

'Saved,' I thought. 'But, no! Lost! Gone! He was gone!'

I laid my knife and fork down and leaned back in my chair. My head swam. After a while, when sufficiently recovered to speak in a steady voice, I instructed my mate to put the ship round at eight o'clock himself.

'I won't come on deck,' I went on. 'I think I'll turn in, and unless the wind shifts I don't want to be disturbed before midnight. I feel a bit seedy.'

'You did look middling bad a little while ago,' the chief mate remarked without showing any great concern.

They both went out, and I stared at the steward clearing the table. There was nothing to be read on that wretched man's face. But why did he avoid my eyes, I asked myself. Then I thought I should like to hear the sound of his voice.

'Steward!'

'Sir!' Startled as usual.

'Where did you hang up that coat?'

'In the bath-room, sir.' The usual anxious tone. 'It's not quite dry yet, sir.'

For some time longer I sat in the cuddy. Had my double vanished as he had come? But of his coming there was an explanation, whereas his disappearance would be inexplicable . . . I went slowly into my dark room, shut the door, lighted the lamp, and for a time dared not turn round. When at last I did I saw him standing bolt-upright in the narrow recessed part. It would not be true to say I had a shock, but an irresistible doubt of his bodily existence flitted through my mind. Can it be, I asked myself, that he is not visible to other eyes than mine? It was like being haunted. Motionless, with a grave face, he raised his hands slightly at me in a gesture which meant clearly, 'Heavens! what a narrow escape!' Narrow indeed. I think I had come creeping quietly as near insanity as any man who has not actually gone over the border. That gesture restrained me, so to speak.

The mate with the terrific whiskers was now putting the ship on the other tack. In the moment of profound silence which follows upon the hands going to their stations I heard on the poop his raised voice: 'Hard alee!' and the distant shout of the order repeated on the maindeck. The sails, in that light breeze, made but a faint fluttering noise. It ceased. The ship was coming round slowly; I held my breath in the renewed stillness of expectation; one wouldn't have thought that there was a single living soul on her decks. A sudden brisk shout, 'Mainsail haul!' broke the spell, and in the noisy cries and rush overhead of the men running away with the main-brace we two, down in my cabin, came together in our usual position by the bed-place.

He did not wait for my question. 'I heard him fumbling here and just managed to squat myself down in the bath,' he whispered to me. 'The fellow only opened the door and put his arm in to hang the coat up. All the same –'

'I never thought of that,' I whispered back, even more appalled than before at the closeness of the shave, and marvelling at that something unyielding in his character which was carrying him through so finely. There was no agitation in his whisper. Whoever was being driven distracted, it was not he. He was sane. And the proof of his sanity was continued when he took up the whispering again.

'It would never do for me to come to life again.'

It was something that a ghost might have said. But what he was alluding to was his old captain's reluctant admission of the theory of suicide. It would obviously serve his turn – if I had understood at all the view which seemed to govern the unalterable purpose of his action.

'You must maroon me as soon as ever you can get among these islands off the Cambodje shore,' he went on.

'Maroon you! We are not living in a boy's adventure tale,' I protested. His scornful whispering took me up.

'We aren't indeed! There's nothing of a boy's tale in this. But there's nothing else for it. I want no more. You don't suppose I am afraid of what can be done to me? Prison or gallows or whatever they may please. But you don't see me coming back to explain such things to an old fellow in a wig and twelve respectable tradesmen, do you? What can they know whether I am guilty or not – or of *what* I am guilty, either? That's my affair. What does the Bible say? "Driven off the face of the earth." Very well. I am off the face of the earth now. As I came at night so I shall go.'

'Impossible!' I murmured. 'You can't.'

'Can't? . . . Not naked like a soul on the Day of Judgement. I shall freeze on to this sleeping-suit. The Last Day is not yet – and . . . and you have understood thoroughly. Didn't you?'

I felt suddenly ashamed of myself. I may say truly that I understood – and my hesitation in letting that man swim away from my ship's side had been a mere sham sentiment, a sort of cowardice.

'It can't be done now till next night,' I breathed out. 'The ship is on the off-shore tack and the wind may fail us.'

'As long as I know that you understand,' he whispered. 'But of course you do. It's a great satisfaction to have got somebody to understand. You seem to have been there on purpose.' And in the same whisper, as if we two whenever we talked had to say things to each other which were not fit for the world to hear, he added, 'It's very wonderful.'

We remained side by side talking in our secret way – but sometimes silent or just exchanging a whispered word or two at long intervals. And as usual he stared through the port. A breath of wind came now and again into our faces. The ship might have been moored in dock, so gently and on an even keel she slipped through the water, that did not murmur even at our passage, shadowy and silent like a phantom sea.

At midnight I went on deck, and to my mate's great surprise put the ship round on the other tack. His terrible whiskers flitted round me in silent criticism. I certainly should not have done it if it had been only a question of getting out of that sleepy gulf as quickly as possible. I believe he told the second mate, who relieved him, that it was a great want of judgement. The other only yawned. That intolerable cub shuffled about so sleepily and lolled against the rails in such a slack, improper fashion that I came down on him sharply.

'Aren't you properly awake yet?'

'Yes, sir! I am awake.'

'Well, then, be good enough to hold yourself as if you were. And keep a look-out. If there's any current we'll be closing with some islands before daylight.'

The east side of the gulf is fringed with islands, some solitary, others in groups. On the blue background of the high coast they seem to float on silvery patches of calm water, arid and grey, or dark green and rounded like clumps of evergreen bushes, with the larger ones, a mile or two long, showing the outlines of ridges, ribs of grey rock under the dank mantle of matted leafage. Unknown to trade, to travel, almost to geography, the manner of life they harbour is an unsolved secret. There must be villages – settlements of fishermen at least – on the largest of them, and some communication with the world is probably kept up by native craft. But all that forenoon, as we headed for them, fanned along by the faintest of breezes, I saw no sign of man or canoe in the field of the telescope I kept on pointing at the scattered group.

At noon I gave no orders for a change of course, and the mate's whiskers became much concerned and seemed to be offering themselves unduly to my notice. At last I said:

'I am going to stand right in. Quite in – as far as I can take her.'

The stare of extreme surprise imparted an air of ferocity also to his eyes, and he looked truly terrific for a moment.

'We're not doing well in the middle of the gulf,' I continued, casually. 'I am going to look for the land breezes tonight.'

'Bless my soul! Do you mean, sir, in the dark among the lot of all them islands and reefs and shoals?'

'Well – if there are any regular land breezes at all on this coast one must get close inshore to find them, mustn't one?'

'Bless my soul!' he exclaimed again under his breath. All that afternoon he wore a dreamy, contemplative appearance which in him was a mark of perplexity. After dinner I went into my stateroom as if I meant to take some rest. There we two bent our dark heads over a half-unrolled chart lying on my bed.

'There,' I said. 'It's got to be Koh-ring. I've been looking at it ever since sunrise. It has got two hills and a low point. It must be inhabited. And on the coast opposite there is what looks like the mouth of a biggish river – with some town, no doubt, not far up. It's the best chance for you that I can see.'

'Anything. Koh-ring let it be.'

He looked thoughtfully at the chart as if surveying chances and distances from a lofty height – and following with his eyes his own figure wandering on the blank land of Cochin China, and then passing off that piece of paper clean out of sight into uncharted regions. And it was as if the ship had two captains to plan her course for her. I had been so worried and restless running up and down that

I had not had the patience to dress that day. I had remained in my sleeping-suit, with straw slippers and soft floppy hat. The closeness of the heat in the gulf had been most oppressive, and the crew were used to see me wandering in that airy attire.

'She will clear the south point as she heads now,' I whispered into his ear. 'Goodness only knows when, though, but certainly after dark. I'll edge her into half a mile, as far as I may be able to judge in the dark –'

'Be careful,' he murmured, warningly – and I realized suddenly that all my future, the only future for which I was fit, would perhaps go irretrievably to pieces in any mishap to my first command.

I could not stop a moment longer in the room. I motioned him to get out of sight and made my way on the poop. That unplayful cub had the watch. I walked up and down for a while thinking things out, then beckoned him over.

'Send a couple of hands to open the two quarter-deck ports,' I said, mildly.

He actually had the impudence, or else so forgot himself in his wonder at such an incomprehensible order, as to repeat:

'Open the quarter-deck ports! What for, sir?'

'The only reason you need concern yourself about is because I tell you to do so. Have them open wide and fastened properly.'

He reddened and went off, but I believe made some jeering remark to the carpenter as to the sensible practice of ventilating in a ship's quarter-deck. I know he popped into the mate's cabin to impart the fact to him because the whiskers came on deck, as it were by chance, and stole glances at me from below – for signs of lunacy or drunkenness, I suppose.

A little before supper, feeling more restless than ever, I rejoined, for a moment, my second self. And to find him sitting so quietly was surprising, like something against nature, inhuman.

I developed my plan in a hurried whisper.

'I shall stand in as close as I dare and then put her round. I will presently find means to smuggle you out of here into the sail-locker, which communicates with the lobby. But there is an opening, a sort of square for hauling the sails out, which gives straight on the quarter-deck and which is never closed in fine weather, so as to give air to the sails. When the ship's way is deadened in stays and all the hands are aft at the main-braces you will have a clear road to slip out and get overboard through the open quarter-deck port. I've had them both fastened up. Use a rope's end to lower yourself into the water so as to avoid a splash – you know. It could be heard and cause some beastly complication.'

He kept silent for a while, then whispered, 'I understand.'

'I won't be there to see you go,' I began with an effort. 'The rest . . . I only hope I have understood, too.'

'You have. From first to last' – and for the first time there seemed to be a faltering, something strained in his whisper. He caught hold of my arm, but the ringing of the supper bell made me start. He didn't, though; he only released his grip.

After supper I didn't come below again till well past eight o'clock. The faint, steady breeze was loaded with dew; and the wet, darkened sails held all there was of propelling power in it. The night, clear and starry, sparkled darkly, and the opaque, lightless patches shifting slowly against the low stars were the drifting islets. On the port bow there was a big one more distant and shadowily imposing by the great space of sky it eclipsed.

On opening the door I had a back view of my very own self looking at a chart. He had come out of the recess and was standing near the table.

'Quite dark enough,' I whispered.

He stepped back and leaned against my bed with a level, quiet glance. I sat on the couch. We had nothing to say to each other. Over our heads the officer of the watch moved here and there. Then I heard him move quickly. I knew what that meant. He was making for the companion; and presently his voice was outside my door.

'We are drawing in pretty fast, sir. Land looks rather close.'

'Very well,' I answered. 'I am coming on deck directly.'

I waited till he was gone out of the cuddy, then rose. My double moved too. The time had come to exchange our last whispers, for neither of us was ever to hear each other's natural voice.

'Look here!' I opened a drawer and took out three sovereigns. 'Take this anyhow. I've got six and I'd give you the lot, only I must keep a little money to buy some fruit and vegetables for the crew from native boats as we go through Sunda Straits.'

He shook his head.

'Take it,' I urged him, whispering desperately. 'No one can tell what –'

He smiled and slapped meaningly the only pocket of the sleeping-jacket. It was not safe, certainly. But I produced a large old silk handkerchief of mine, and tying the three pieces of gold in a corner, pressed it on him. He was touched, I suppose, because he took it at last and tied it quickly round his waist under the jacket, on his bare skin.

Our eyes met; several seconds elapsed, till, our glances still mingled, I extended my hand and turned the lamp out. Then I passed through the cuddy, leaving the door of my room wide open . . . 'Steward!'

He was still lingering in the pantry in the greatness of his zeal, giving a rub-up to a plated cruet stand the last thing before going to bed. Being careful not to wake up the mate, whose room was opposite, I spoke in an undertone.

He looked round anxiously. 'Sir!'

'Can you get me a little hot water from the galley?'

'I am afraid, sir, the galley fire's been out for some time now.'

'Go and see.'

He flew up the stairs.

'Now,' I whispered, loudly, into the saloon – too loudly, perhaps, but I was afraid I couldn't make a sound. He was by my side in an instant – the double captain slipped past the stairs – through a tiny dark passage . . . a sliding door. We were in the sail-locker, scrambling on our knees over the sails. A sudden thought struck me. I saw myself wandering bare-footed, bareheaded, the sun beating on my dark poll. I snatched off my floppy hat and tried hurriedly in the dark to ram it on my other self. He dodged and fended off silently. I wonder what he thought had come to me before he understood and suddenly desisted. Our hands met gropingly, lingered united in a steady, motionless clasp for a second . . . No word was breathed by either of us when they separated.

I was standing quietly by the pantry door when the steward returned.

'Sorry, sir. Kettle barely warm. Shall I light the spirit-lamp?'

'Never mind.'

I came out on deck slowly. It was now a matter of conscience to shave the land as close as possible – for now he must go overboard whenever the ship was put in stays. Must! There could be no going back for him. After a moment I walked over to leeward and my heart flew into my mouth at the nearness of the land on the bow. Under any other circumstances I would not have held on a minute longer. The second mate had followed me anxiously.

I looked on till I felt I could command my voice.

'She may weather,' I said then in a quiet tone.

'Are you going to try that, sir?' he stammered out incredulously.

I took no notice of him and raised my tone just enough to be heard by the helmsman.

'Keep her good full.'

'Good full, sir.'

The wind fanned my cheek, the sails slept, the world was silent. The strain of watching the dark loom of the land grow bigger and denser was too much for me. I had shut my eyes – because the ship must go closer. She must! The stillness was intolerable. Were we standing still?

When I opened my eyes the second view started my heart with a thump. The black southern hull of Koh-ring seemed to hang right over the ship like a towering fragment of the everlasting night. On that enormous mass of blackness there was not a gleam to be seen, not a sound to be heard. It was gliding irresistibly towards us and yet seemed already within reach of the hand. I saw the vague figures of the watch grouped in the waist, gazing in awed silence.

'Are you going on, sir?' inquired an unsteady voice at my elbow.

I ignored it. I had to go on.

'Keep her full. Don't check her way. That won't do now,' I said, warningly.

'I can't see the sails very well,' the helmsman answered me, in strange, quavering tones.

Was she close enough? Already she was, I won't say in the shadow of the land, but in the very blackness of it, already swallowed up as it were, gone too close to be recalled, gone from me altogether.

'Give the mate a call,' I said to the young man who stood at my elbow as still as death. 'And turn all hands up.'

My tone had a borrowed loudness reverberated from the height of the land. Several voices cried out together: 'We are all on deck, sir.'

Then stillness again, with the great shadow gliding closer, towering higher, without light, without a sound. Such a hush had fallen on the ship that she might have been a bark of the dead floating in slowly under the very gate of Erebus.

'My God! Where are we?'

It was the mate moaning at my elbow. He was thunderstruck, and as it were deprived of the moral support of his whiskers. He clapped his hands and absolutely cried out, 'Lost!'

'Be quiet,' I said, sternly.

He lowered his tone, but I saw the shadowy gesture of his despair. 'What are we doing here?'

'Looking for the land wind.'

He made as if to tear his hair, and addressed me recklessly.

'She will never get out. You have done it, sir. I knew it'd end in something like this. She will never weather, and you are too close now to stay. She'll drift ashore before she's round. O my God!'

I caught his arm as he was raising it to batter his poor devoted head, and shook it violently.

'She's ashore already,' he wailed, trying to tear himself away.

'Is she? . . . Keep good full there!'

'Good full, sir,' cried the helmsman in a frightened, thin, child-like voice.

I hadn't let go the mate's arm and went on shaking it. 'Ready about, do you hear? You go forward' – shake – 'and stop there' – shake – 'and hold your noise' – shake – 'and see these head-sheets properly overhauled' – shake, shake – shake.

And all the time I dared not look towards the land lest my heart should fail me. I released my grip at last and he ran forward as if fleeing for dear life.

I wondered what my double there in the sail-locker thought of this commotion. He was able to hear everything – and perhaps he was able to understand why, on my conscience, it had to be thus close – no less. My first order 'Hard alee!' re-echoed ominously under the towering shadow of Koh-ring as if I had shouted in a mountain gorge. And then I watched the land intently. In that smooth water and light wind it was impossible to feel the ship coming-to. No! I could not feel her. And my second self was making now ready to slip out and lower himself overboard. Perhaps he was gone already . . .?

The great black mass brooding over our very mastheads began to pivot away from the ship's side silently. And now I forgot the secret stranger ready to depart, and remembered only that I was a total stranger to the ship. I did not know her. Would she do it? How was she to be handled?

I swung the mainyard and waited helplessly. She was perhaps stopped, and her very fate hung in the balance, with the black mass of Koh-ring like the gate of the everlasting night towering over her taffrail. What would she do now? Had she way on her yet? I stepped to the side swiftly, and on the shadowy water I could see nothing except a faint phosphorescent flash revealing the glassy smoothness of the sleeping surface. It was impossible to tell – and I had not learned yet the feel of my ship. Was she moving? What I needed was something easily seen, a piece of paper, which I could throw overboard and watch. I had nothing on me. To run down for it I didn't dare. There was no time. All at once my strained, yearning stare distinguished a white object floating within a yard of the ship's side. White on the black water. A phosphorescent flash passed under it. What was that thing? . . . I recognized my own floppy hat. It must have fallen off his head . . . and he didn't bother. Now I had what I wanted – the saving mark for my eyes. But I hardly thought of my other self, now gone from the ship, to be hidden for ever from all friendly faces, to be a fugitive and a vagabond on the earth, with no brand of the curse on his sane forehead to stay a slaying hand . . . too proud to explain.

And I watched the hat – the expression of my sudden pity for his mere flesh. It had been meant to save his homeless head from the dangers of the sun. And now – behold – it was saving the ship, by serving me for a mark to help out the ignorance of my strangeness. Ha! It was drifting forward, warning me just in time that the ship had gathered sternway.

'Shift the helm,' I said in a low voice to the seaman standing still like a statue.

The man's eyes glistened wildly in the binnacle light as he jumped round to the other side and spun round the wheel.

I walked to the break of the poop. On the overshadowed deck all hands stood by the forebraces waiting for my order. The stars ahead seemed to be gliding from right to left. And all was so still in the world that I heard the quiet remark 'She's round', passed in a tone of intense relief between two seamen.

'Let go and haul.'

The foreyards ran round with a great noise, amidst cheery cries. And now the frightful whiskers made themselves heard giving various orders. Already the ship was drawing ahead. And I was alone with her. Nothing! no one in the world should stand now between us, throwing a shadow on the way of silent knowledge and mute affection, the perfect communion of a seaman with his first command.

Walking to the taffrail, I was in time to make out, on the very edge of a darkness thrown by a towering black mass like the very gateway of Erebus – yes, I was in time to catch an evanescent glimpse of my white hat left behind to mark the spot where the secret sharer of my cabin and of my thoughts, as though he were my second self, had lowered himself into the water to take his punishment: a free man, a proud swimmer striking out for a new destiny.

Freya of the Seven Isles

A Story of Shallow Waters

CHAPTER I

ONE DAY – and that day was many years ago now – I received a long, chatty letter from one of my old chums and fellow-wanderers in Eastern waters. He was still out there, but settled down, and middle-aged; I imagined him grown portly in figure and domestic in his habits; in short, overtaken by the fate common to all except to those who, being specially beloved by the gods, get knocked on the head early. The letter was of the reminiscent 'do you remember' kind – a wistful letter of backward glances. And, among other things, 'surely you remember old Nelson', she wrote.

Remember old Nelson! Certainly. And to begin with, his name was not Nelson. The Englishmen in the Archipelago called him Nelson because it was more convenient, I suppose, and he never protested. It would have been mere pedantry. The true form of his name was Nielsen. He had come out East long before the advent of telegraph cables, had served English firms, had married an English girl, had been one of us for years, trading and sailing in all directions through the Eastern Archipelago, across and around, transversely, diagonally, perpendicularly, in semicircles, and zigzags, and figures of eights, for years and years.

There was no nook or cranny of these tropical waters that the enterprise of old Nelson (or Nielsen) had not penetrated in an eminently pacific way. His tracks, if plotted out, would have covered the map of the Archipelago like a cobweb – all of it, with the sole exception of the Philippines. He would never approach that part, from a strange dread of Spaniards, or, to be exact, of the Spanish authorities. What he imagined they could do to him it is impossible to say. Perhaps at some time in his life he had read some stories of the Inquisition.

But he was in general afraid of what he called 'authorities'; not the English authorities, which he trusted and respected, but the other two of that part of the world. He was not so horrified at the Dutch as he was at the Spaniards, but he was even more mistrustful of them. Very mistrustful indeed. The Dutch, in his view, were capable of 'playing any ugly trick on a man' who had the misfortune to displease them. There were their laws and regulations, but they had no notion of fair play in applying them. It was really pitiable to see the anxious circumspection of his dealings with some official or other, and remember that this man had been known to stroll up to a village of cannibals in New Guinea in a quiet, fearless manner (and note that he was always fleshy all his life, and, if I may say so, an appetising morsel) on some matter of barter that did not amount perhaps to fifty pounds in the end.

Remember old Nelson! Rather! Truly, none of us in my generation had known him in his active days. He was 'retired' in our time. He had bought, or else leased, part of a small island from the sultan of a little group called the Seven Isles, not far north from Banka. It was, I suppose, a legitimate transaction, but I have no doubt that had he been an Englishman the Dutch would have discovered a reason to fire him out without ceremony. In this connection the real form of his name stood him in good stead. In the character of an unassuming Dane whose conduct was most correct, they let him be. With all his money engaged in cultivation he was naturally careful not to give even the shadow of offence, and it was mostly for prudential reasons of that sort that he did not look with a favourable eye on Jasper Allen. But of that later. Yes! One remembered well enough old Nelson's big, hospitable bungalow erected on a shelving point of land, his portly form, costumed generally in a white shirt and trousers (he had a confirmed habit of taking off his alpaca jacket on the slightest provocation), his round blue eyes, his straggly, sandy-white moustache sticking out all ways like the quills of the fretful porcupine, his propensity to sit down suddenly and fan himself with his hat. But there's no use concealing the fact that what one remembered really was his daughter, who at that time came out to live with him – and be a sort of Lady of the Isles.

Freya Nelson (or Nielsen) was the kind of a girl one remembers. The oval of her face was perfect; and within that fascinating frame the most happy disposition of line and feature, with an admirable complexion, gave an impression of health, strength, and what I might call unconscious self-confidence – a most pleasant and, as it were, whimsical determination. I will not compare her eyes to violets, because the real shade of their colour was peculiar, not so dark and most lustrous. They were of the wide-open kind, and looked at one frankly in every mood. I never did see the long, dark eyelashes lowered – I dare say Jasper Allen did, being a privileged person – but I have no doubt that the expression must have been charming in a complex way. She could – Jasper told me once with a touchingly imbecile exultation – sit on her hair. I dare say, I dare say. It was not for me to behold these wonders; I was content to admire the neat and becoming way she used to do it up so as not to conceal the good shape of her head. And this wealth of hair was so glossy that when the screens of the west verandah were down, making a pleasant twilight there, or in the shade of the grove of fruit-trees near the house, it seemed to give out a golden light of its own.

She dressed generally in a white frock, with a skirt of walking length, showing her neat, laced, brown boots. If there was any colour about her costume it was just a bit of blue perhaps. No exertion seemed to distress her. I have seen her land from the dinghy after a long pull in the sun (she rowed herself about a good deal) with no quickened breath and not a single hair out of its place. In the morning when she came out on the verandah for the first look westward, Sumatra way, over the sea, she seemed as fresh and sparkling as a dewdrop. But a dewdrop is evanescent, and there was nothing evanescent about Freya. I remember her round, solid arms with the fine wrists, and her broad, capable hands with tapering fingers.

I don't know whether she was actually born at sea, but I do know that up to twelve years of age she sailed about with her parents in various ships. After old Nelson lost his wife it became a matter of serious concern for him what to do with the girl. A kind lady in Singapore, touched by his dumb grief and deplorable perplexity, offered to take charge of Freya. This arrangement lasted some six years, during which old Nelson (or Nielsen) 'retired' and established himself on his island and then it was settled (the kind lady going away to Europe) that his daughter should join him.

As the first and most important preparation for that event the old fellow ordered from his Singapore agent a Steyn and Ebhart's 'upright grand'. I was then commanding a little steamer in the island trade, and it fell to my lot to take it out to him, so I know something of Freya's 'upright grand'. We landed the enormous packing-case with difficulty on a flat piece of rock among some bushes, nearly knocking the bottom out of one of my boats in the course of that nautical operation. Then, all my crew assisting, engineers and firemen included, by the exercise of much anxious ingenuity, and by means of rollers, levers, tackles, and inclined planes of soaped planks, toiling in the sun like ancient Egyptians at the building of a pyramid, we got it as far as the house and up on to the edge of the west verandah – which was the actual drawing-room of the bungalow. There, the case being ripped off cautiously, the beautiful rosewood monster stood revealed at last. In reverent excitement we coaxed it against the wall and drew the first free breath of the day. It was certainly the heaviest movable object on that islet since the creation of the world. The volume of sound it gave out in that bungalow (which acted as a sounding-board) was really astonishing. It thundered sweetly right over the sea. Jasper Allen told me that early of a morning on the deck of the *Bonito* (his wonderfully fast and pretty brig) he could hear Freya playing her scales quite distinctly. But the fellow always anchored foolishly close to the point, as I told him more than once. Of course, these seas are almost uniformly serene, and the Seven Isles is a particularly calm and cloudless spot as a rule. But still, now and again, an afternoon thunderstorm over Banka, or even one of these vicious thick squalls, from the distant Sumatra coast, would make a sudden sally upon the group, enveloping it for a couple of hours in whirlwinds and bluish-black murk of a particularly sinister aspect. Then, with the lowered rattan-screens rattling desperately in the wind and the bungalow shaking all over, Freya would sit down to the piano and play fierce Wagner music in the flicker of blinding flashes, with thunderbolts falling all round, enough to make your hair stand on end; and Jasper would remain stock still on the verandah, adoring the back view of her supple, swaying figure, the miraculous sheen of her fair head, the rapid hands on the keys, the white nape of her neck – while the brig, down at the point there, surged at her cables within a hundred yards of nasty, shiny, black rock-heads. Ugh!

And this, if you please, for no reason but that, when he went on board at night and laid his head on the pillow, he should feel that he was as near as he could conveniently get to his Freya slumbering in the bungalow. Did you ever! And, mind, this brig was the home to be – their home – the floating paradise which he was gradually fitting out like a yacht to sail his life blissfully away in with Freya. Imbecile! But the fellow was always taking chances.

One day, I remembered I watched with Freya on the verandah the brig approaching the point from the northward. I suppose Jasper made the girl out with his long glass. What does he do? Instead of standing on for another mile and a half along the shoals and then tacking for the anchorage in a proper and seaman-like manner, he spies a gap between two disgusting old jagged reefs, puts the helm down suddenly, and shoots the brig through, with all her sails shaking and rattling, so that we could hear the racket on the verandah. I drew my breath through my teeth, I can tell you, and Freya swore. Yes! She clenched her capable fists and stamped with her pretty brown boot and said 'Damn!' Then, looking at me with a little heightened colour – not much – she remarked, 'I forgot you were there,' and laughed. To be sure, to be sure. When Jasper was in sight she was not likely to remember that anybody else in the world was there. In my concern at this mad trick I couldn't help appealing to her sympathetic common sense.

'Isn't he a fool!' I said with feeling.

'Perfect idiot,' she agreed warmly, looking at me straight with her wide-open, earnest eyes and the dimple of a smile on her cheek.

'And that,' I pointed out to her, 'just to save twenty minutes or so in meeting you.'

We heard the anchor go down, and then she became very resolute and threatening.

'Wait a bit. I'll teach him.'

She went into her own room and shut the door, leaving me alone on the verandah with my instructions. Long before the brig's sails were furled, Jasper came up three steps at a time, forgetting to say how d'ye do, and looking right and left eagerly.

'Where's Freya? Wasn't she here just now?'

When I explained to him that he was to be deprived of Miss Freya's presence for a whole hour, 'just to teach him', he said I had put her up to it, no doubt, and that he feared he would have yet to shoot me some day. She and I were getting too thick together. Then he flung himself into a chair, and tried to talk to me about his trip. But the funny thing was that the fellow actually suffered. I could see it. His voice failed him, and he sat there dumb, looking at the door with the face of a man in pain. Fact . . . And the next still funnier thing was that the girl calmly walked out of her room in less than ten minutes. And then I left. I mean to say that I went away to seek old Nelson (or Nielsen) on the back verandah, which was his own special nook in the distribution of that house, with the kind purpose of engaging him in conversation lest he should start roaming about and intrude unwittingly where he was not wanted just then.

He knew that the brig had arrived, though he did not know that Jasper was already with his daughter. I suppose he didn't think it was possible in the time. A father naturally wouldn't. He suspected that Allen was sweet on his girl; the fowls of the air and the fishes of the sea, most of the traders in the Archipelago, and all sorts and conditions of men in the town of Singapore were aware of it. But he was not capable of appreciating how far the girl was gone on the fellow. He had an idea that Freya was too sensible to ever be gone on anybody – I mean to an unmanageable extent. No; it was not that which made him sit on the back verandah and worry himself in his unassuming manner during Jasper's visits. What he worried about were the Dutch 'authorities'. For it is a fact that the Dutch looked askance at the doings of Jasper Allen, owner and master of the brig *Bonito*. They considered him much too enterprising in his trading. I don't know that he ever did anything illegal; but it seems to me that his immense activity was repulsive to their stolid character and slow-going methods. Anyway, in old Nelson's opinion, the captain of the *Bonito* was a smart sailor, and a nice young man, but not a desirable acquaintance upon the whole. Somewhat compromising, you understand. On the other hand, he did not like to tell Jasper in so many words to keep away. Poor old Nelson himself was a nice fellow. I believe he would have shrunk from hurting the feelings even of a mop-headed cannibal, unless, perhaps, under very strong provocation. I mean the feelings, not the bodies. As against spears, knives, hatchets, clubs, or arrows, old Nelson had proved himself capable of taking his own part. In every other respect he had a timorous soul. So he sat on the back verandah with a concerned expression, and whenever the voices of his daughter and Jasper Allen reached him, he would blow out his cheeks and let the air escape with a dismal sound, like a much tried man.

Naturally I derided his fears which he, more or less, confided to me. He had a certain regard for my judgement, and a certain respect, not for my moral qualities, however, but for the good terms I was supposed to be on with the Dutch 'authorities'. I knew for a fact that his greatest bugbear, the Governor of Banka – charming, peppery, hearty, retired rear-admiral – had a distinct liking for him. This consoling assurance, which I used always to put forward, made old Nelson (or Nielsen) brighten up for a moment; but in the end he would shake his head doubtfully, as much as to say that this was all very well, but that there were depths in the Dutch official nature which no one but himself had ever fathomed. Perfectly ridiculous.

On this occasion I am speaking of, old Nelson was even fretty; for while I was trying to entertain him with a very funny and somewhat scandalous adventure which happened to a certain acquaintance of ours in Saigon, he exclaimed suddenly:

'What the devil he wants to turn up here for!'

Clearly he had not heard a word of the anecdote. And this annoyed me, because the anecdote was really good. I stared at him.

'Come, come!' I cried. 'Don't you know what Jasper Allen is turning up here for?'

This was the first open allusion I had ever made to the true state of affairs between Jasper and his daughter. He took it very calmly.

'Oh, Freya is a sensible girl!' he murmured absently, his mind's eyes obviously fixed on the 'authorities'. No; Freya was no fool. He was not concerned about that. He didn't mind it in the least. The fellow was just company for her; he amused the girl; nothing more.

When the perspicacious old chap left off mumbling, all was still in the house. The other two were amusing themselves very quietly, and no doubt very heartily. What more absorbing and less noisy amusement could they have found than to plan their future? Side by side on the verandah they must have been looking at the brig, the third party in that fascinating game. Without her there would have been no future. She was the fortune and the home, and the great free world for them. Who was it that likened a ship to a prison? May I be ignominiously hanged at a yardarm if that's true. The white sails of that craft were the white wings – pinions, I believe, would be the more poetical style – well, the white pinions, of their soaring love. Soaring as regards Jasper. Freya, being a woman, kept a better hold of the mundane connections of this affair.

But Jasper was elevated in the true sense of the word ever since the day when, after they had been gazing at the brig in one of those decisive silences that alone establish a perfect communion between creatures gifted with speech, he proposed that she should share the ownership of that treasure with him. Indeed, he presented the brig to her altogether. But then his heart was in the brig since the day he bought her in Manila from a certain middle-aged Peruvian, in a sober suit of black broadcloth, enigmatic and sententious, who, for all I know, might have stolen her on the South American coast, whence he said he had come over to the Philippines 'for family reasons'. This 'for family reasons' was distinctly good. No true *caballero* would care to push on inquiries after such a statement.

Indeed, Jasper was quite the *caballero*. The brig herself was then all black and enigmatical, and very dirty; a tarnished gem of the sea, or, rather a neglected work of art. For he must have been an artist, the obscure builder who had put her body together on lovely lines out of the hardest tropical timber fastened with the purest copper. Goodness only knows in what part of the world she was built. Jasper himself had not been able to ascertain much of her history from his sententious, saturnine Peruvian – if the fellow was a Peruvian, and not the devil himself in disguise, as Jasper jocularly pretended to believe. My opinion is that she was old enough to have been one of the last pirates, a slaver perhaps, or else an opium clipper of the early days, if not an opium smuggler.

However that may be, she was as sound as on the day she first took the water, sailed like a witch, steered like a little boat, and, like some fair women of adventurous life famous in history, seemed to have the secret of perpetual youth; so that there was nothing unnatural in Jasper Allen treating her like a lover. And that treatment restored the lustre of her beauty. He clothed her in many coats of the very best white paint so skilfully, carefully, artistically put on and kept clean by his badgered crew of picked Malays, that no costly enamel such as jewellers use for their work could have looked better and felt smoother to the touch. A narrow gilt moulding defined her elegant sheer as she sat on the water, eclipsing easily the professional good looks of any pleasure yacht that ever came to the East in those days. For myself, I must say I prefer a moulding of deep crimson colour on a white hull. It gives a stronger relief besides being less expensive; and I told Jasper so. But no, nothing less than the best gold-leaf would do, because no decoration could be gorgeous enough for the future abode of his Freya.

His feelings for the brig and for the girl were as indissolubly united in his heart as you may fuse two precious metals together in one crucible. And the flame was pretty hot, I can assure you. It induced in him a fierce inward restlessness both of activity and desire. Too fine in face, with a lateral wave in his chestnut hair, spare, long-limbed, with an eager glint in his steely eyes and quick, brusque movements, he made me think sometimes of a flashing sword-blade perpetually leaping out of the scabbard. It was only when he was near the girl, when he had her there to look at, that this peculiarly tense attitude was replaced by a grave devout watchfulness of her slightest movements and utterances. Her cool, resolute, capable, good-humoured self-possession seemed to steady his heart. Was it the magic of her face, of her voice, of her glances which calmed him so? Yet these were the very things one must believe which had set his imagination ablaze – if love begins in imagination. But I am no man to discuss such mysteries, and it strikes me that we have neglected poor old Nelson inflating his cheeks in a state of worry on the back verandah.

I pointed out to him that, after all, Jasper was not a very frequent visitor. He and his brig worked hard all over the Archipelago. But all old Nelson said, and he said it uneasily, was:

'I hope Heemskirk won't turn up here while the brig's about.'

Getting up a scare about Heemskirk now! Heemskirk! . . . Really, one hadn't the patience –.

Chapter II

For, pray, who was Heemskirk? You shall see at once how unreasonable was this dread of Heemskirk . . . Certainly, his nature was malevolent enough. That was obvious, directly you heard him laugh. Nothing gives away more a man's secret disposition than the unguarded ring of his laugh. But, bless my soul! if we were to start at every evil guffaw like a hare at every sound, we shouldn't be fit for anything but the solitude of a desert, or the seclusion of a hermitage. And even there we should have to put up with the unavoidable company of the devil.

However, the devil is a considerable personage, who has known better days and has moved high up in the hierarchy of Celestial Host; but in the hierarchy of mere earthly Dutchmen, Heemskirk, whose early days could not have been very splendid, was merely a naval officer forty years of age, of no particular connections or ability to boast of. He was commanding the *Neptun*, a little gunboat employed on dreary patrol duty up and down the Archipelago, to look after the traders. Not a very exalted position truly. I tell you, just a common middle-aged lieutenant of some twenty-five years' service and sure to be retired before long – that's all.

He never bothered his head very much as to what was going on in the Seven Isles group till he learned from some talk in Mintok or Palembang, I suppose, that there was a pretty girl living there. Curiosity, I presume, caused him to go poking around that way and then, after he had once seen Freya, he made a practice of calling at the group whenever he found himself within half a day's steaming from it.

I don't mean to say that Heemskirk was a typical Dutch naval officer. I have seen enough of them not to fall into that absurd mistake. He had a big, clean-shaven face; great flat, brown cheeks, with a thin, hooked nose and a small, pursy mouth squeezed in between. There were a few silver threads in his black hair, and his unpleasant eyes were nearly black, too. He had a surly way of casting side glances without moving his head, which was set low on a short, round neck. A thick, round trunk in a dark undress jacket with gold shoulder-straps, was sustained by a straddly pair of thick, round legs, in white drill trousers. His round skull under a white cap looked as if it were immensely thick too, but there were brains enough in it to discover and take advantage maliciously of poor old Nelson's nervousness before everything that was invested with the merest shred of authority.

Heemskirk would land on the point and perambulate silently every part of the plantation as if the whole place belonged to him, before he went to the house. On the verandah he would take the best chair, and would stay for tiffin or dinner, just simply stay on, without taking the trouble to invite himself by so much as a word.

He ought to have been kicked, if only for his manner to Miss Freya. Had he been a naked savage, armed with spears and poisoned arrows, old Nelson (or Nielsen) would have gone for him with his bare fists. But these gold shoulder-straps – Dutch shoulder-straps at that – were enough to terrify the old fellow; so he let the beggar treat him with heavy contempt, devour his daughter with his eyes, and drink the best part of his little stock of wine.

I saw something of this, and on one occasion I tried to pass a remark on the subject. It was pitiable to see the trouble in old Nelson's round eyes. At first he cried out that the lieutenant was a good friend of his; a very good fellow. I went on staring at him pretty hard, so that at last he faltered, and had to own that, of course, Heemskirk was not a very genial person outwardly, but all the same at bottom . . .

'I haven't yet met a genial Dutchman out here,' I interrupted. 'Geniality, after all, is not of much consequence, but don't you see –'

Nelson looked suddenly so frightened at what I was going to say that I hadn't the heart to go on. Of course, I was going to tell him that the fellow was after his girl. That just describes it exactly. What Heemskirk might have expected or what he thought he could do, I don't know. For all I can tell, he might have imagined himself irresistible, or have taken Freya for what she was not, on account of her lively, assured, unconstrained manner. But there it is. He was after that girl. Nelson could see it well enough. Only he preferred to ignore it. He did not want to be told of it.

'All I want is to live in peace and quietness with the Dutch authorities,' he mumbled shamefacedly.

He was incurable. I was sorry for him, and I really think Miss Freya was sorry for her father, too. She restrained herself for his sake, and like everything she did she did it simply, unaffectedly, and even good humouredly. No small effort that, because in Heemskirk's attentions there was an insolent touch of scorn, hard to put up with. Dutchmen of that sort are overbearing to their inferiors, and that officer of the king looked upon old Nelson and Freya as quite beneath him in every way.

I can't say I felt sorry for Freya. She was not the sort of girl to take anything tragically. One could feel for her and sympathize with her difficulty, but she seemed equal to any situation. It was rather admiration she extorted by her competent serenity. It was only when Jasper and Heemskirk were together at the bungalow, as it happened now and then, that she felt the strain, and even then it was not for everybody to see. My eyes alone could detect a faint shadow on the radiance of her personality. Once I could not help saying to her appreciatively:

'Upon my word you are wonderful.'

She let it pass with a faint smile.

'The great thing is to prevent Jasper becoming unreasonable,' she said; and

I could see real concern lurking in the quiet depths of her frank eyes gazing straight at me. 'You will help to keep him quiet, won't you?'

'Of course, we must keep him quiet,' I declared, understanding very well the nature of her anxiety.

'He's such a lunatic, too, when he's roused.'

'He is!' she assented, in a soft tone; for it was our joke to speak of Jasper abusively. 'But I have tamed him a bit. He's quite a good boy now.'

'He would squash Heemskirk like a black beetle all the same,' I remarked.

'Rather!' she murmured. 'And that wouldn't do,' she added quickly. 'Imagine the state poor papa would get into. Besides, I mean to be mistress of the dear brig and sail about these seas, not go off wandering ten thousand miles away from here.'

'The sooner you are on board to look after the man and the brig the better,' I said seriously. 'They need you to steady them both a bit. I don't think Jasper will ever get sobered down till he has carried you off from this island. You don't see him when he is away from you, as I do. He's in a state of perpetual elation which almost frightens me.'

At this she smiled again, and then looked serious. For it could not be unpleasant to her to be told of her power, and she had some sense of her responsibility. She slipped away from me suddenly, because Heemskirk, with old Nelson in attendance at his elbow, was coming up the steps of the verandah. Directly his head came above the level of the floor his ill-natured black eyes shot glances here and there.

'Where's your girl, Nelson?' he asked, in a tone as if every soul in the world belonged to him. And then to me: 'The goddess has flown, eh?'

Nelson's Cove – as we used to call it – was crowded with shipping that day. There was first my steamer, then the *Neptun* gunboat further out, and the *Bonito* brig, anchored as usual so close inshore that it looked as if, with a little skill and judgement, one could shy a hat from the verandah on to her scrupulously holystoned quarter-deck. Her brasses flashed like gold, her white body-paint had a sheen like a satin robe. The rake of her varnished spars and the big yards, squared to a hair, gave her a sort of martial elegance. She was a beauty. No wonder that in possession of a craft like that and the promise of a girl like Freya, Jasper lived in a state of perpetual elation fit, perhaps, for the seventh heaven, but not exactly safe in a world like ours.

I remarked politely to Heemskirk that, with three guests in the house, Miss Freya had no doubt domestic matters to attend to. I knew, of course, that she had gone to meet Jasper at a certain cleared spot on the banks of the only stream on Nelson's little island. The commander of the *Neptun* gave me a dubious black look, and began to make himself at home, flinging his thick, cylindrical carcass into a rocking-chair, and unbuttoning his coat. Old Nelson sat down opposite him in a most unassuming manner, staring anxiously with his round eyes and fanning himself with his hat. I tried to make conversation to while the time away; not an easy task with a morose, enamoured Dutchman constantly looking from one door to another and answering one's advances either with a jeer or a grunt.

However, the evening passed off all right. Luckily there is a degree of bliss too intense for elation. Jasper was quiet and concentrated silently in watching Freya. As we went on board our respective ships I offered to give his brig a tow out next morning. I did it on purpose to get him away at the earliest possible moment. So in the first cold light of the dawn we passed by the gunboat lying black and still without a sound in her at the mouth of the glassy cove. But with tropical swiftness the sun had climbed twice its diameter above the horizon before we had rounded the reef and got abreast of the point. On the biggest boulder there stood Freya, all in white and, in her helmet, like a feminine and martial statue with a rosy face, as I could see very well with my glasses. She fluttered an expressive handkerchief, and Jasper, running up the main rigging of the white and warlike brig, waved his hat in response. Shortly afterwards we parted, I to the northward, and Jasper heading east with a light wind on the quarter, for Banjermassin and two other ports, I believe it was, that trip.

This peaceful occasion was the last on which I saw all these people assembled together; the charmingly fresh and resolute Freya, the innocently round-eyed old Nelson, Jasper, keen, long limbed, lean faced, admirably self-contained in his manner, because inconceivably happy under the eyes of his Freya; all three tall, fair, and blue-eyed in varied shades, and among them the swarthy, arrogant, black-haired Dutchman, shorter nearly by a head, and so much thicker than any of them that he seemed to be a creature capable of inflating itself, a grotesque specimen of mankind from some other planet.

The contrast struck me all at once as we stood in the lighted verandah, after rising from the dinner-table. I was fascinated by it for the rest of the evening, and I remember the impression of something funny and ill-omened at the same time in it to this day.

Chapter III

A few weeks later, coming early one morning into Singapore, from a journey to the southward, I saw the brig lying at anchor in all her usual symmetry and splendour of aspect as though she had been taken out of a glass case and put delicately into the water that very moment.

She was well out in the roadstead, but I steamed in and took up my habitual berth close in front of the town. Before we had finished breakfast a quartermaster came to tell me that Captain Allen's boat was coming our way.

His smart gig dashed alongside, and in two bounds he was up our accommodation-ladder and shaking me by the hand with his nervous grip, his eyes snapping inquisitively, for he supposed I had called at the Seven Isles group on my way. I reached into my pocket for a nicely folded little note, which he grabbed out of my hand without ceremony and carried off on the bridge to read by himself. After a decent interval I followed him up there, and found him pacing to and fro; for the nature of his emotions made him restless even in his most thoughtful moments.

He shook his head at me triumphantly.

'Well, my dear boy,' he said, 'I shall be counting the days now.'

I understood what he meant. I knew that those young people had settled already on a runaway match without official preliminaries. This was really a logical decision. Old Nelson (or Nielsen) would never have agreed to give up Freya peaceably to this compromising Jasper. Heavens! What would the Dutch authorities say to such a match! It sounds too ridiculous for words. But there's nothing in the world more selfishly hard than a timorous man in a fright about his 'little estate', as old Nelson used to call it in apologetic accents. A heart permeated by a particular sort of funk is proof against sense, feeling, and ridicule. It's a flint.

Jasper would have made his request all the same and then taken his own way; but it was Freya who decided that nothing should be said, on the ground that, 'Papa would only worry himself to distraction.' He was capable of making himself ill, and then she wouldn't have the heart to leave him. Here you have the sanity of feminine outlook and the frankness of feminine reasoning. And for the rest, Miss Freya could read 'poor dear papa' in the way a woman reads a man – like an open book. His daughter once gone, old Nelson would not worry himself. He would raise a great outcry, and make no end of lamentable fuss, but that's not the same thing. The real agonies of indecision, the anguish of conflicting feelings would be spared to him. And as he was too unassuming to rage, he would, after a period of lamentation, devote himself to his 'little estate', and to keeping on good terms with the authorities.

Time would do the rest. And Freya thought she could afford to wait, while ruling over her own home in the beautiful brig and over the man who loved her. This was the life for her who had learned to walk on a ship's deck. She was a ship-child, a sea-girl if ever there was one. And of course she loved Jasper and trusted him; but there was a shade of anxiety in her pride. It is very fine and romantic to possess for your very own a finely tempered and trusty sword-blade, but whether it is the best weapon to counter with the common cudgel-play of Fate – that's another question.

She knew that she had the more substance of the two – you needn't try any cheap jokes, I am not talking of their weights. She was just a little anxious while he was away, and she had me who, being a tried confidant, took the liberty to whisper frequently 'The sooner the better'. But there was a peculiar vein of obstinacy in Miss Freya, and her reason for delay was characteristic. 'Not before my twenty-first birthday; so that there shall be no mistake in people's minds as to me being old enough to know what I am doing.'

Jasper's feelings were in such subjection that he had never even remonstrated against the decree. She was just splendid, whatever she did or said, and there was an end of it for him. I believe that he was subtle enough to be even flattered at bottom – at times. And then to console him he had the brig, which seemed pervaded by the spirit of Freya, since whatever he did on board was always done under the supreme sanction of his love.

'Yes. I'll soon begin to count the days,' he repeated. 'Eleven months more. I'll have to crowd three trips into that.'

'Mind you don't come to grief trying to do too much,' I admonished him. But he dismissed my caution with a laugh and an elated gesture. Pooh! Nothing, nothing could happen to the brig, he cried, as if the flame of his heart could light up the dark nights of uncharted seas, and the image of Freya serve for an unerring beacon among hidden shoals; as if the winds had to wait on his future, the stars fight for it in their courses; as if the magic of his passion had the power to float a ship on a drop of dew or sail her through the eye of a needle – simply because it was her magnificent lot to be the servant of a love so full of grace as to make all the ways of the earth safe, resplendent, and easy.

'I suppose,' I said, after he had finished laughing at my innocent enough remark, 'I suppose you will be off today.'

That was what he meant to do. He had not gone at daylight only because he expected me to come in.

'And only fancy what has happened yesterday,' he went on. 'My mate left me suddenly. Had to. And as there's nobody to be found at a short notice I am going to take Schultz with me. The notorious Schultz! Why don't you jump out of your skin? I tell you I went and unearthed Schultz late last evening, after no end of trouble. "I am your man, Captain," he says, in that wonderful voice of his, "but I am sorry to confess I have practically no clothes to my back. I have had to sell all my wardrobe to get a little food from day to day." What a voice that man has got. Talk about moving stones! But people seem to get used to it. I had never seen him before, and, upon my word, I felt suddenly tears rising to my eyes. Luckily it was dusk. He was sitting very quiet under a tree in a native compound as thin as a lath, and when I peered down at him all he had on was an old cotton singlet and a pair of ragged pyjamas. I bought him six white suits and two pairs of canvas shoes. Can't clear the ship without a mate. Must have somebody. I am going on shore presently to sign him on, and I shall take him with me as I go back on board to get under way. Now, I am a lunatic – am I not? Mad, of course. Come on! Lay it on thick. Let yourself go. I like to see you get excited.'

He so evidently expected me to scold that I took especial pleasure in exaggerating the calmness of my attitude.

'The worst that can be brought up against Schultz,' I began, folding my arms and speaking dispassionately, 'is an awkward habit of stealing the stores of every ship he has ever been in. He will do it. That's really all that's wrong. I don't credit absolutely that story Captain Robinson tells of Schultz conspiring in Chantabun with some ruffians in a Chinese junk to steal the anchor off the starboard bow of the *Bohemian Girl* schooner. Robinson's story is too ingenious altogether. That other tale of the engineers of the *Nan-Shan* finding Schultz at midnight in the engine-room busy hammering at the brass bearings to carry them off for sale on shore seems to me more authentic. Apart from this little weakness, let me tell you that Schultz is a smarter sailor than many who never took a drop of drink in their lives, and perhaps no worse morally than some men you and I know who have never stolen the value of a penny. He may not be a desirable person to have on board one's ship, but since you have no choice he may be made to do, I believe. The important thing is to understand his psychology. Don't give him any money till you have done with him. Not a cent, if he begs you ever so. For as sure as Fate the moment you give him any money he will begin to steal. Just remember that.'

I enjoyed Jasper's incredulous surprise.

'The devil he will!' he cried. 'What on earth for? Aren't you trying to pull my leg, old boy?'

'No. I'm not. You must understand Schultz's psychology. He's neither a loafer nor a cadger. He's not likely to wander about looking for somebody to stand him drinks. But suppose he goes on shore with five dollars, or fifty for that matter, in his pocket? After the third or fourth glass he becomes fuddled and charitable. He either drops his money all over the place, or else distributes the lot around; gives it to anyone who will take it. Then it occurs to him that the night is young yet, and that he may require a good many more drinks for himself and his friends before morning. So he starts off cheerfully for his ship. His legs never get affected nor his head either in the usual way. He gets aboard and simply grabs the first thing that seems to him suitable – the cabin lamp, a coil of rope, a bag of biscuits, a drum of oil – and converts it into money without thinking twice about it. This is the process and no other. You have only to look out that he doesn't get a start. That's all.'

'Confound his psychology,' muttered Jasper. 'But a man with a voice like his is fit to talk to the angels. Is he incurable do you think?'

I said that I thought so. Nobody had prosecuted him yet, but no one would employ him any longer. His end would be, I feared, to starve in some hole or other.

'Ah, well,' reflected Jasper. 'The *Bonito* isn't trading to any ports of civilization. That'll make it easier for him to keep straight.'

That was true. The brig's business was on uncivilized coasts, with obscure rajahs dwelling in nearly unknown bays; with native settlements up mysterious rivers opening their sombre, forest-lined estuaries among a welter of pale green reefs and dazzling sandbanks, in lonely straits of calm blue water all aglitter with sunshine. Alone, far from the beaten tracks, she glided, all white, round dark, frowning headlands, stole out, silent like a ghost, from behind points of land stretching out all black in the moonlight; or lay hove-to, like a sleeping sea-bird, under the shadow of some nameless mountain waiting for a signal. She would be glimpsed suddenly on misty, squally days dashing disdainfully aside the short aggressive waves of the Java Sea; or be seen far, far away, a tiny dazzling white speck flying across the brooding purple masses of thunderclouds piled up on the horizon. Sometimes, on the rare mail tracks, where civilization brushes against wild mystery, when the naïve passengers crowding along the rail exclaimed, pointing at her with interest: 'Oh, here's a yacht!' the Dutch captain, with a hostile glance, would grunt contemptuously: 'Yacht! No! That's only English Jasper. A pedlar –'

'A good seaman you say,' ejaculated Jasper, still in the matter of the hopeless Schultz with the wonderfully touching voice.

'First rate. Ask any one. Quite worth having – only impossible,' I declared.

'He shall have his chance to reform in the brig,' said Jasper, with a laugh. 'There will be no temptations either to drink or steal where I am going to this time.'

I didn't press him for anything more definite on that point. In fact, intimate as we were, I had a pretty clear notion of the general run of his business.

But as we are going ashore in his gig he asked suddenly: 'By the way, do you know where Heemskirk is?'

I eyed him covertly, and was reassured. He had asked the question, not as a lover, but as a trader. I told him that I had heard in Palembang that the *Neptun* was on duty down about Flores and Sumbawa. Quite out of his way. He expressed his satisfaction.

'You know,' he went on, 'that fellow, when he gets on the Borneo coast, amuses himself by knocking down my beacons. I have had to put up a few to help me in and out of the rivers. Early this year a Celebes trader becalmed in a prau was watching him at it. He steamed the gunboat fult tilt at two of them, one after another, smashing them to pieces, and then lowered a boat on purpose to pull out a third, which I had a lot of trouble six months ago to stick up in the middle of a mudflat for a tide mark. Did you ever hear of anything more provoking – eh?'

'I wouldn't quarrel with the beggar,' I observed casually, yet disliking that piece of news strongly. 'It isn't worth while.'

'I quarrel?' cried Jasper. 'I don't want to quarrel. I don't want to hurt a single hair of his ugly head. My dear fellow, when I think of Freya's twenty-first birthday, all the world's my friend, Heemskirk included. It's a nasty, spiteful amusement, all the same.'

We parted rather hurriedly on the quay, each of us having his own pressing business to attend to. I would have been very much cut up had I known that this hurried grasp of the hand with 'So long, old boy. Good luck to you!' was the last of our partings.

On his return to the Straits I was away, and he was gone again before I got back. He was trying to achieve three trips before Freya's twenty-first birthday. At Nelson's Cove I missed him again by only a couple of days. Freya and I talked of 'that lunatic' and 'perfect idiot' with great delight and infinite appreciation. She was very radiant, with a more pronounced gaiety, notwithstanding that she had just parted from Jasper. But this was to be their last separation.

'Do get aboard as soon as you can, Miss Freya,' I entreated.

She looked me straight in the face, her colour a little heightened and with a sort of solemn ardour – if there was a little catch in her voice.

'The very next day.'

Ah, yes! The very next day after her twenty-first birthday. I was pleased at this hint of deep feeling. It was as if she had grown impatient at last of the self-imposed delay. I supposed that Jasper's recent visit had told heavily.

'That's right,' I said approvingly. 'I shall be much easier in my mind when I know you have taken charge of that lunatic. Don't you lose a minute. He, of course, will be on time – unless heavens fall.'

'Yes. Unless –' she repeated in a thoughtful whisper, raising her eyes to the evening sky without a speck of cloud anywhere. Silent for a time, we let our eyes wander over the waters below, looking mysteriously still in the twilight, as if trustfully composed for a long, long dream in the warm, tropical night. And the peace all round us seemed without limits and without end.

And then we began to talk Jasper over in our usual strain. We agreed that he was too reckless in many ways. Luckily, the brig was equal to the situation.

Nothing apparently was too much for her. A perfect darling of a ship, said Miss Freya. She and her father had spent an afternoon on board. Jasper had given them some tea. Papa was grumpy . . . I had a vision of old Nelson under the brig's snowy awnings, nursing his unassuming vexation, and fanning himself with his hat. A comedy father . . . As a new instance of Jasper's lunacy, I was told that he was distressed at his inability to have solid silver handles fitted to all the cabin doors. 'As if I would have let him!' commented Miss Freya, with amused indignation. Incidentally, I learned also that Schultz, the nautical kleptomaniac with the pathetic voice, was still hanging on to his job, with Miss Freya's approval. Jasper had confided to the lady of his heart his purpose of straightening out the fellow's psychology. Yes, indeed. All the world was his friend because it breathed the same air with Freya.

Somehow or other, I brought Heemskirk's name into conversation, and, to my great surprise, startled Miss Freya. Her eyes expressed something like distress, while she bit her lip as if to contain an explosion of laughter. Oh! Yes. Heemskirk was at the bungalow at the same time with Jasper, but he arrived the day after. He left the same day as the brig, but a few hours later.

'What a nuisance he must have been to you two,' I said feelingly.

Her eyes flashed at me a sort of frightened merriment, and suddenly she exploded into a clear burst of laughter. 'Ha, ha, ha!'

I echoed it heartily, but not with the same charming tone: 'Ha, ha, ha! . . . Isn't he grotesque? Ha, ha ha!' And the ludicrousness of old Nelson's inanely fierce round eyes in association with his conciliatory manner to the lieutenant presenting itself to my mind brought on another fit.

'He looks,' I spluttered, 'he looks – Ha, ha ha! – among you three . . . like an unhappy blackbeetle. Ha, ha ha!'

She gave out another ringing peal, ran off into her own room, and slammed the door behind her, leaving me profoundly astounded. I stopped laughing at once.

'What's the joke?' asked old Nelson's voice, half way down the steps.

He came up, sat down, and blew out his cheeks, looking inexpressibly fatuous. But I didn't want to laugh any more. And what on earth, I asked myself, have we been laughing at in this uncontrollable fashion. I felt suddenly depressed.

Oh, yes. Freya had started it. The girl's overwrought, I thought. And really one couldn't wonder at it.

I had no answer to old Nelson's question, but he was too aggrieved at Jasper's visit to think of anything else. He as good as asked me whether I wouldn't undertake to hint to Jasper that he was not wanted at the Seven Isles group. I declared that it was not necessary. From certain circumstances which had come to my knowledge lately, I had reason to think that he would not be much troubled by Jasper Allen in the future.

He emitted an earnest 'Thank God!' which nearly set me laughing again, but he did not brighten up proportionately. It seemed Heemskirk had taken special pains to make himself disagreeable. The lieutenant had frightened old Nelson very much by expressing a sinister wonder at the Government permitting a white man to settle down in that part at all. 'It is against our declared policy,' he had remarked. He had also charged him with being in reality no better than an

Englishman. He had even tried to pick a quarrel with him for not learning to speak Dutch.

'I told him I was too old to learn now,' sighed out old Nelson (or Nielsen) dismally. 'He said I ought to have learned Dutch long before. I had been making my living in Dutch dependencies. It was disgraceful of me not to speak Dutch, he said. He was as savage with me as if I had been a Chinaman.'

It was plain he had been viciously badgered. He did not mention how many bottles of his best claret he had offered up on the altar of conciliation. It must have been a generous libation. But old Nelson (or Nielsen) was really hospitable. He didn't mind that; and I only regretted that this virtue should be lavished on the lieutenant-commander of the *Neptun*. I longed to tell him that in all probability he would be relieved from Heemskirk's visitations also. I did not do so only from the fear (absurd, I admit) of arousing some sort of suspicion in his mind. As if with this guileless comedy father such a thing were possible!

Strangely enough, the last words on the subject of Heemskirk were spoken by Freya, and in that very sense. The lieutenant was turning up persistently in old Nelson's conversation at dinner. At last I muttered a half audible 'Damn the lieutenant'. I could see that the girl was getting exasperated, too.

'And he wasn't well at all – was he, Freya?' old Nelson went on moaning. 'Perhaps it was that which made him so snappish, hey, Freya? He looked very bad when he left us so suddenly. His liver must be in a bad state, too.'

'Oh, he will end by getting over it,' said Freya impatiently. 'And do leave off worrying about him, papa. Very likely you won't see much of him for a long time to come.'

The look she gave me in exchange for my discreet smile had no hidden mirth in it. Her eyes seemed hollowed, her face gone wan in a couple of hours. We had been laughing too much. Overwrought! Overwrought by the approach of the decisive moment. After all, sincere, courageous, and self-reliant as she was, she must have felt both the passion and the compunction of her resolve. The very strength of love which had carried her up to that point must have put her under a great moral strain, in which there might have been a little simple remorse, too. For she was honest – and there, across the table, sat poor old Nelson (or Nielsen) staring at her, round-eyed and so pathetically comic in his fierce aspect as to touch the most lightsome heart.

He retired early to his room to soothe himself for a night's rest by perusing his account-books. We two remained on the verandah for another hour or so, but we exchanged only languid phrases on things without importance, as though we had been emotionally jaded by our long day's talk on the only momentous subject. And yet there was something she might have told a friend. But she didn't. We parted silently. She distrusted my masculine lack of common sense, perhaps . . . O! Freya!

Going down the precipitous path to the landing-stage, I was confronted in the shadows of boulders and bushes by a draped feminine figure whose appearance startled me at first. It glided into my way suddenly from behind a piece of rock. But in a moment it occurred to me that it could be no one else but Freya's maid, a half-caste Malacca Portuguese. One caught fleeting glimpses of her olive face and dazzling white teeth about the house. I had also observed her at times from a distance, as she sat within call under the shade of some fruit-trees, brushing and plaiting her long raven locks. It seemed to be the principal occupation of her leisure hours. We had often exchanged nods and smiles – and a few words, too. She was a pretty creature. And once I had watched her approvingly make funny and expressive grimaces behind Heemskirk's back. I understood (from Jasper) that she was in the secret, like a comedy camerista. She was to accompany Freya on her irregular way to matrimony and 'ever after' happiness. Why should she be roaming by night near the cove – unless on some love affair of her own – I asked myself. But there was nobody suitable within the Seven Isles group, as far as I knew. It flashed upon me that it was myself she had been lying in wait for.

She hesitated, muffled from head to foot, shadowy and bashful. I advanced another pace, and how I felt is nobody's business.

'What is it?' I asked, very low.

'Nobody knows I am here,' she whispered.

'And nobody can see us,' I whispered back.

The murmur of words 'I've been so frightened' reached me. Just then forty feet above our head, from the yet lighted verandah, unexpected and startling, Freya's voice rang out in a clear, imperious call:

'Antonia!'

With a stifled exclamation, the hesitating girl vanished out of the path. A bush near by rustled; then silence. I waited wondering. The lights on the verandah went out. I waited a while longer then continued down the path to my boat, wondering more than ever.

I remember the occurrences of that visit especially, because this was the last time I saw the Nelson bungalow. On arriving at the Straits I found cable messages which made it necessary for me to throw up my employment at a moment's notice and go home at once. I had a desperate scramble to catch the mailboat which was due to leave next day, but I found time to write two short notes, one to Freya, the other to Jasper. Later on I wrote at length, this time to Allen alone. I got no answer. I hunted up then his brother, or, rather, half-brother, a solicitor in the city, a sallow, calm, little man who looked at me over his spectacles thoughtfully.

Jasper was the only child of his father's second marriage, a transaction which had failed to commend itself to the first grown-up family.

'You haven't heard for ages,' I repeated, with secret annoyance. 'May I ask what "for ages" means in this connection?'

'It means that I don't care whether I ever hear from him or not,' retorted the little man of law, turning nasty suddenly.

I could not blame Jasper for not wasting his time in correspondence with such an outrageous relative. But why didn't he write to me – a decent sort of friend, after all; enough of a friend to find for his silence the excuse of forgetfulness natural to a state of transcendental bliss? I waited indulgently, but nothing ever came. And the East seemed to drop out of my life without an echo, like a stone falling into a well of prodigious depth.

Chapter IV

I SUPPOSE praiseworthy motives are a sufficient justification almost for anything. What could be more commendable in the abstract than a girl's determination that 'poor papa' should not be worried, and her anxiety that the man of her choice should be kept by any means from every occasion of doing something rash, something which might endanger the whole scheme of their happiness?

Nothing could be more tender and more prudent. We must also remember the girl's self-reliant temperament, and the general unwillingness of women – I mean women of sense – to make a fuss over matters of that sort.

As has been said already, Heemskirk turned up some time after Jasper's arrival at Nelson's Cove. The sight of the brig lying right under the bungalow was very offensive to him. He did not fly ashore before his anchor touched the ground as Jasper used to do. On the contrary, he hung about his quarter-deck mumbling to himself; and when he ordered his boat to be manned it was in an angry voice. Freya's existence, which lifted Jasper out of himself into a blissful elation, was for Heemskirk a cause of secret torment, of hours of exasperated brooding.

While passing the brig he hailed her harshly and asked if the master was on board. Schultz, smart and neat in a spotless white suit, leaned over the taffrail, finding the question somewhat amusing. He looked humorously down into Heemskirk's boat, and answered, in the most amiable modulations of his beautiful voice: 'Captain Allen is up at the house, sir.' But his expression changed suddenly at the savage growl: 'What the devil are you grinning at?' which acknowledged that information.

He watched Heemskirk land and, instead of going to the house, stride away by another path into the grounds.

The desire-tormented Dutchman found old Nelson (or Nielsen) at his drying-sheds, very busy superintending the manipulation of his tobacco crop, which, though small, was of excellent quality, and enjoying himself thoroughly. But Heemskirk soon put a stop to this simple happiness. He sat down by the old chap, and by the sort of talk which he knew was best calculated for the purpose, reduced him before long to a state of concealed and perspiring nervousness. It was a horrid talk of 'authorities', and old Nelson tried to defend himself. If he dealt with English traders it was because he had to dispose of his produce somehow. He was as conciliatory as he knew how to be, and this very thing seemed to excite Heemskirk, who had worked himself up into a heavily breathing state of passion.

'And the worst of them all is that Allen,' he growled. 'Your particular friend – eh? You have let in a lot of these Englishmen into this part. You ought never to have been allowed to settle here. Never. What's he doing here now?'

Old Nelson (or Nielsen), becoming very agitated, declared that Jasper Allen was no particular friend of his. No friend at all – at all. He had bought three tons of rice from him to feed his workpeople on. What sort of evidence of friendship was that? Heemskirk burst out at last with the thought that had been gnawing at his vitals:

'Yes. Sell three tons of rice and flirt three days with that girl of yours. I am speaking to you as a friend, Nielsen. This won't do. You are only on sufferance here.'

Old Nelson was taken aback at first, but recovered pretty quickly. Won't do! Certainly! Of course, it wouldn't do! The last man in the world. But his girl didn't care for the fellow, and was too sensible to fall in love with anyone. He was very earnest in impressing on Heemskirk his own feeling of absolute security. And the lieutenant, casting doubting glances sideways, was yet willing to believe him.

'Much you know about it,' he grunted nevertheless.

'But I do know,' insisted old Nelson, with the greater desperation because he wanted to resist the doubts arising in his own mind. 'My own daughter! In my own house, and I not to know! Come! It would be a good joke, lieutenant.'

'They seem to be carrying on considerably,' remarked Heemskirk moodily. 'I suppose they are together now,' he added, feeling a pang which changed what he meant for a mocking smile into a strange grimace.

The harassed Nelson shook his hand at him. He was at bottom shocked at this insistence, and was even beginning to feel annoyed at the absurdity of it.

'Pooh! Pooh! I'll tell you what, lieutenant: you go to the house and have a drop of gin-and-bitters before dinner. Ask for Freya. I must see the last of this tobacco put away for the night, but I'll be along presently.'

Heemskirk was not insensible to this suggestion. It answered to his secret longing, which was not a longing for drink, however. Old Nelson shouted solicitously after his broad back a recommendation to make himself comfortable, and that there was a box of cheroots on the verandah.

It was the west verandah that old Nelson meant, the one which was the living-room of the house, and had split-rattan screens of the very finest quality. The east verandah, sacred to his own privacy, puffing out of cheeks, and other signs of perplexed thinking, was fitted with stout blinds of sailcloth. The north verandah was not a verandah at all, really. It was more like a long balcony. It did not communicate with the other two, and could only be approached by a passage inside the house. Thus it had a privacy which made it a convenient place for a maiden's meditations without words, and also for the discourses, apparently without sense, which, passing between a young man and a maid, become pregnant with a diversity of transcendental meanings.

This north verandah was embowered with climbing plants. Freya, whose room opened out on it, had furnished it as a sort of boudoir for herself, with a few cane chairs and a sofa of the same kind. On this sofa she and Jasper sat as close together as is possible in this imperfect world where neither can a body be in two places at once nor yet two bodies can be in one place at the same time. They had been sitting together all the afternoon, and I won't say that their talk had been without sense. Loving him with a little judicious anxiety lest in his elation he should break his heart over some mishap, Freya naturally would talk to him soberly. He, nervous and brusque when away from her, appeared always as if overcome by her visibility, by the great wonder of being palpably loved. An old man's child, having lost his mother early, thrown out to sea out of the way while very young, he had not much experience of tenderness of any kind.

In this private, foliage-embowered verandah, and at this late hour of the afternoon, he bent down a little, and, possessing himself of Freya's hands, was kissing them one after another, while she smiled and looked down at his head with the eyes of approving compassion. At that same moment Heemskirk was approaching the house from the north.

Antonia was on the watch on that side. But she did not keep a very good watch. The sun was setting; she knew that her young mistress and the captain of the *Bonito* were about to separate. She was walking to and fro in the dusky grove with a flower in her hair, and singing softly to herself, when suddenly, within a foot of her, the lieutenant appeared from behind a tree. She bounded aside like a startled fawn, but Heemskirk, with a lucid comprehension of what she was there for, pounced upon her, and, catching her arm, clapped his other thick hand over her mouth.

'If you try to make a noise I'll twist your neck!'

This ferocious figure of speech terrified the girl sufficiently. Heemskirk had seen plainly enough on the verandah Freya's golden head with another head very close to it. He dragged the unresisting maid with him by a circuitous way into the compound, where he dismissed her with a vicious push in the direction of the cluster of bamboo huts for the servants.

She was very much like the faithful camerista of Italian comedy, but in her terror she bolted away without a sound from that thick, short, black-eyed man with a cruel grip of fingers like a vice. Quaking all over at a distance, extremely scared and half inclined to laugh, she saw him enter the house at the back.

The interior of the bungalow was divided by two passages crossing each other in the middle. At that point Heemskirk, by turning his head slightly to the left as he passed, secured the evidence of 'carrying on' so irreconcilable with old Nelson's assurances that it made him stagger, with a rush of blood to his head. Two white figures, distinct against the light, stood in an unmistakable attitude. Freya's arms were round Jasper's neck. Their faces were characteristically superimposed on each other, and Heemskirk went on, his throat choked with a sudden rising of curses, till on the west verandah he stumbled blindly against a chair and then dropped into another as though his legs had been swept from under him. He had indulged too long in the habit of appropriating Freya to himself in his thoughts. 'Is that how you entertain your visitors – you . . .' he thought, so outraged that he could not find a sufficiently degrading epithet.

Freya struggled a little and threw her head back.

'Somebody has come in,' she whispered. Jasper, holding her clasped closely to his breast, and looking down into her face, suggested casually:

'Your father.'

Freya tried to disengage herself, but she had not the heart absolutely to push him away with her hands.

'I believe it's Heemskirk,' she breathed out at him.

He, plunging into her eyes in a quiet rapture, was provoked to a vague smile by the sound of the name.

'The ass is always knocking down my beacons outside the river,' he murmured. He attached no other meaning to Heemskirk's existence; but Freya was asking herself whether the lieutenant had seen them.

'Let me go, kid,' she ordered in a peremptory whisper. Jasper obeyed, and, stepping back at once, continued his contemplation of her face under another angle. 'I must go and see,' she said to herself anxiously.

She instructed him hurriedly to wait a moment after she was gone and then to slip on to the back verandah and get a quiet smoke before he showed himself.

'Don't stay late this evening,' was her last recommendation before she left him.

Then Freya came out on the west verandah with her light, rapid step. While going through the doorway she managed to shake down the folds of the looped-up curtains at the end of the passage so as to cover Jasper's retreat from the bower. Directly she appeared Heemskirk jumped up as if to fly at her. She paused and he made her an exaggerated low bow.

It irritated Freya.

'Oh! It's you, Mr Heemskirk. How do you do?'

She spoke in her usual tone. Her face was not plainly visible to him in the dusk of the deep verandah. He dared not trust himself to speak, his rage at what he had seen was so great. And when she added with serenity: 'Papa will be coming in before long,' he called her horrid names silently, to himself, before he spoke with contorted lips.

'I have seen your father already. We had a talk in the sheds. He told me some very interesting things. Oh, very –'

Freya sat down. She thought: 'He has seen us, for certain.' She was not ashamed. What she was afraid of was some foolish or awkward complication. But she could not conceive how much her person had been appropriated by Heemskirk (in his thoughts). She tried to be conversational.

'You are coming now from Palembang, I suppose?'

'Eh? What? Oh, yes! I come from Palembang. Ha, ha, ha! You know what your father said? He said he was afraid you were having a very dull time of it here.'

'And I suppose you are going to cruise in the Moluccas,' continued Freya, who wanted to impart some useful information to Jasper if possible. At the same time she was always glad to know that those two men were a few hundred miles apart when not under her eye.

Heemskirk growled angrily.

'Yes. Moluccas,' glaring in the direction of her shadowy figure. 'Your father thinks it's very quiet for you here. I tell you what, Miss Freya. There isn't such a quiet spot on earth that a woman can't find an opportunity of making a fool of somebody.'

Freya thought: 'I mustn't let him provoke me.' Presently the Tamil boy, who was Nelson's head servant, came in with the lights. She addressed him at once with voluble directions where to put the lamps, told him to bring the tray with the gin-and-bitters, and to send Antonia into the house.

'I will have to leave you to yourself, Mr Heemskirk, for a while,' she said.

And she went to her room to put on another frock. She made a quick change of it because she wished to be on the verandah before her father and the lieutenant met again. She relied on herself to regulate that evening's intercourse between these two. But Antonia, still scared and hysterical, exhibited a bruise on her arm which roused Freya's indignation.

'He jumped on me out of the bush like a tiger,' said the girl, laughing nervously with frightened eyes.

'The brute!' thought Freya. 'He meant to spy on us, then.' She was enraged, but the recollection of the thick Dutchman in white trousers wide at the hips and narrow at the ankles, with his shoulder-straps and black bullet head, glaring at her in the light of the lamps, was so repulsively comical that she could not help a smiling grimace. Then she became anxious. The absurdities of three men were forcing this anxiety upon her: Jasper's impetuosity, her father's fears, Heemskirk's infatuation. She was very tender to the first two, and she made up her mind to display all her feminine diplomacy. All this, she said to herself, will be over and done with before very long now.

Heemskirk on the verandah, lolling in a chair, his legs extended and his white cap reposing on his stomach, was lashing himself into a fury of an atrocious character altogether incomprehensible to a girl like Freya. His chin was resting on his chest, his eyes gazed stonily at his shoes. Freya examined him from behind the curtain. He didn't stir. He was ridiculous. But this absolute stillness was impressive. She stole back along the passage to the east verandah, where Jasper was sitting quietly in the dark, doing what he was told, like a good boy.

'Psst,' she hissed. He was by her side in a moment.

'Yes. What is it?' he murmured.

'It's that beetle,' she whispered uneasily. Under the impression of Heemskirk's sinister immobility she had half a mind to let Jasper know that they had been seen. But she was by no means certain that Heemskirk would tell her father – and at any rate not that evening. She concluded rapidly that the safest thing would be to get Jasper out of the way as soon as possible.

'What has he been doing?' asked Jasper in a calm undertone.

'Oh, nothing! Nothing. He sits there looking cross. But you know how he's always worrying papa.'

'Your father's quite unreasonable,' pronounced Jasper judicially.

'I don't know,' she said in a doubtful tone. Something of old Nelson's dread of the authorities had rubbed off on the girl since she had to live with it day after day. 'I don't know. Papa's afraid of being reduced to beggary, as he says, in his old days. Look here, kid, you had better clear out tomorrow, first thing.'

Jasper had hoped for another afternoon with Freya, an afternoon of quiet felicity with the girl by his side and his eyes on his brig, anticipating a blissful future. His silence was eloquent with disappointment, and Freya understood it very well. She, too, was disappointed. But it was her business to be sensible.

'We shan't have a moment to ourselves with that beetle creeping round the house,' she argued in a low, hurried voice. 'So what's the good of your staying? And he won't go while the brig's here. You know he won't.'

'He ought to be reported for loitering,' murmured Jasper with a vexed little laugh.

'Mind you get under way at daylight,' recommended Freya under her breath.

He detained her after the manner of lovers. She expostulated without struggling because it was hard for her to repulse him. He whispered into her ear while he put his arms round her.

'Next time we two meet, next time I hold you like this, it shall be on board. You and I, in the brig – all the world, all the life –' And then he flashed out: 'I wonder I can wait! I feel as if I must carry you off now, at once. I could run with you in my hands – down the path – without stumbling – without touching the earth –'

She was still. She listened to the passion in his voice. She was saying to herself that if she were to whisper the faintest yes, if she were but to sigh lightly her consent, he would do it. He was capable of doing it – without touching the earth. She closed her eyes and smiled in the dark, abandoning herself in a delightful giddiness, for an instant, to his encircling arm. But before he could be tempted to tighten his grasp she was out of it, a foot away from him and in full possession of herself.

That was the steady Freya. She was touched by the deep sigh which floated up to her from the white figure of Jasper, who did not stir.

'You are a mad kid,' she said tremulously. Then with a change of tone: 'No one could carry me off. Not even you. I am not the sort of girl that gets carried off.' His white form seemed to shrink a little before the force of that assertion and she relented. 'Isn't it enough for you to know that you have – that you have carried me away?' she added in a tender tone.

He murmured an endearing word, and she continued:

'I've promised you – I've said I would come – and I shall come of my own free will. You shall wait for me on board. I shall get up the side – by myself, and walk up to you on the deck and say: "Here I am, kid." And then – and then I shall be carried off. But it will be no man who will carry me off – it will be the brig, your brig – our brig . . . I love the beauty!'

She heard an inarticulate sound, something like a moan wrung out by pain or delight, and glided away. There was that other man on the other verandah, that dark, surly Dutchman who could make trouble between Jasper and her father, bring about a quarrel, ugly words, and perhaps a physical collision. What a horrible situation! But, even putting aside that awful extremity, she shrank from having to live for some three months with a wretched, tormented, angry, distracted, absurd man. And when the day came, the day and the hour, what should she do if her father tried to detain her by main force – as was, after all, possible? Could she actually struggle with him hand to hand? But it was of lamentations and entreaties that she was really afraid. Could she withstand them? What an odious, cruel, ridiculous position would that be!

'But it won't be. He'll say nothing,' she thought as she came out quickly on the west verandah, and, seeing that Heemskirk did not move, sat down on a chair near the doorway and kept her eyes on him. The outraged lieutenant had not changed his attitude; only his cap had fallen off his stomach and was lying on the floor. His thick black eyebrows were knitted by a frown, while he looked at her out of the corners of his eyes. And their sideways glance in conjunction with the hooked nose, the whole bulky, ungainly, sprawling person, struck Freya as so comically moody that, inwardly discomposed as she was, she could not help smiling. She did her best to give that smile a conciliatory character. She did not want to provoke Heemskirk needlessly.

And the lieutenant, perceiving that smile, was mollified. It never entered his head that his outward appearance, a naval officer, in uniform, could appear ridiculous to that girl of no position – the daughter of old Nielsen. The recollection of her arms round Jasper's neck still irritated and excited him. 'The hussy!' he thought. 'Smiling – eh? That's how you are amusing yourself. Fooling your father finely, aren't you? You have a taste for that sort of fun – have you? Well, we shall see –' He did not alter his position, but on his pursed-up lips there also appeared a smile of surly and ill-omened amusement, while his eyes returned to the contemplation of his boots.

Freya felt hot with indignation. She sat radiantly fair in the lamplight, her strong, well-shaped hands lying one on top of the other in her lap . . . 'Odious creature,' she thought. Her face coloured with sudden anger. 'You have scared my maid out of her senses,' she said aloud. 'What possessed you?'

He was thinking so deeply of her that the sound of her voice, pronouncing these unexpected words, startled him extremely. He jerked up his head and looked so bewildered that Freya insisted impatiently:

'I mean Antonia. You have bruised her arm. What did you do it for?'

'Do you want to quarrel with me?' he asked thickly, with a sort of amazement. He blinked like an owl. He was funny. Freya, like all women, had a keen sense of the ridiculous in outward appearance.

'Well, no; I don't think I do.' She could not help herself. She laughed outright, a clear, nervous laugh in which Heemskirk joined suddenly with a harsh 'Ha, ha, ha!'

Voices and footsteps were heard in the passage, and Jasper, with old Nelson, came out. Old Nelson looked at his daughter approvingly, for he liked the lieutenant to be kept in good humour. And he also joined sympathetically in the laugh. 'Now, lieutenant, we shall have some dinner,' he said, rubbing his hands cheerily. Jasper had gone straight to the balustrade. The sky was full of stars, and in the blue velvety night the cove below had a denser blackness, in which the riding-lights of the brig and of the gunboat glimmered redly, like suspended sparks. 'Next time this riding-light glimmers down there, I'll be waiting for her on the quarter-deck to come and say "Here I am",' Jasper thought; and his heart seemed to grow bigger in his chest, dilated by an oppressive happiness that nearly wrung out a cry from him. There was no wind. Not a leaf below him stirred, and even the sea was but a still uncomplaining shadow. Far away on the unclouded sky the pale lightning, the heat-lightning of the tropics, played tremulously among the low stars in short, faint, mysteriously consecutive flashes, like incomprehensible signals from some distant planet.

The dinner passed off quietly. Freya sat facing her father, calm but pale. Heemskirk affected to talk only to old Nelson. Jasper's behaviour was exemplary. He kept his eyes under control, basking in the sense of Freya's nearness, as people bask in the sun without looking up to heaven. And very soon after dinner was over, mindful of his instructions, he declared that it was time for him to go on board his ship.

Heemskirk did not look up. Ensconced in the rocking-chair, and puffing at a cheroot, he had the air of meditating surlily over some odious outbreak. So at least it seemed to Freya. Old Nelson said at once, 'I'll stroll down with you.' He had begun a professional conversation about the dangers of the New Guinea coast, and wanted to relate to Jasper some experience of his own 'over there'. Jasper was such a good listener! Freya made as if to accompany them but her father frowned, shook his head, and nodded significantly towards the immovable Heemskirk blowing out smoke with half-closed eyes and protruded lips. The lieutenant must not be left alone. Take offence, perhaps.

Freya obeyed these signs. 'Perhaps it is better for me to stay,' she thought. Women are not generally prone to review their own conduct, still less to condemn it. The embarrassing masculine absurdities are in the main responsible for its ethics. But, looking at Heemskirk, Freya felt regret and even remorse. His thick bulk in repose suggested the idea of repletion, but as a matter of fact he had eaten very little. He had drunk a great deal, however. The fleshy lobes of his unpleasant big ears with deeply folded rims were crimson. They quite flamed in the neighbourhood of the flat, sallow cheeks. For a considerable time he did not raise his heavy brown eyelids. To be at the mercy of such a creature was humiliating; and Freya, who always ended by being frank with herself, thought regretfully: 'If only I had been open with papa from the first! But then what an impossible life he would have led me!' Yes. Men were absurd in many ways; lovably like Jasper, impracticably like her father, odiously like that grotesquely supine creature in the chair. Was it possible to talk him over? Perhaps it was not necessary? 'Oh! I can't talk to him,' she thought. And when Heemskirk, still without looking at her, began resolutely to crush his half-smoked cheroot on the coffee-tray, she took alarm, glided towards the piano, opened it in tremendous haste, and struck the keys before she sat down.

In an instant the verandah, the whole carpetless wooden bungalow raised on piles, became filled with an uproarious, confused resonance. But through it all she heard, she felt on the floor the heavy, prowling footsteps of the lieutenant moving to and fro at her back. He was not exactly drunk, but he was sufficiently primed to make the suggestions of his excited imagination seem perfectly feasible and even clever; beautifully, unscrupulously clever. Freya, aware that he had stopped just behind her, went on playing without turning her head. She played with spirit, brilliantly, a fierce piece of music, but when his voice reached her she went cold all over. It was the voice, not the words. The insolent familiarity of tone dismayed her to such an extent that she could not understand at first what he was saying. His utterance was thick, too.

'I suspected . . . Of course I suspected something of your little goings on. I am not a child. But from suspecting to seeing – seeing, you understand – there's an enormous difference. That sort of thing . . . Come! One isn't made of stone. And when a man has been worried by a girl as I have been worried by you, Miss Freya – sleeping and waking, then, of course . . . But I am a man of the world. It must be dull for you here . . . I say, won't you leave off this confounded playing . . .?'

This last was the only sentence really which she made out. She shook her head negatively, and in desperation put on the loud pedal, but she could not make the sound of the piano cover his raised voice.

'Only, I am surprised that you should . . . An English trading skipper, a common fellow. Low, cheeky lot, infesting these islands. I would make short work of such trash! While you have here a good friend, a gentleman ready to worship at your feet – your pretty feet – an officer, a man of family. Strange, isn't it? But what of that! You are fit for a prince.'

Freya did not turn her head. Her face went stiff with horror and indignation. This adventure was altogether beyond her conception of what was possible. It was not in her character to jump up and run away. It seemed to her, too, that if she did move there was no saying what might happen. Presently her father would be back, and then the other would have to leave off. It was best to ignore – to ignore. She went on playing loudly and correctly as though she were alone, as if Heemskirk did not exist. That proceeding irritated him.

'Come! You may deceive your father,' he bawled angrily, 'but I am not to be made a fool of! Stop this infernal noise . . . Freya . . . Hey! You Scandinavian Goddess of Love! Stop! Do you hear? That's what you are – of love. But the heathen gods are only devils in disguise, and that's what you are, too – a deep little devil. Stop it, I say, or I will lift you off that stool!'

Standing behind her, he devoured her with his eyes, from the golden crown of her rigidly motionless head to the heels of her shoes, the line of her shapely shoulders, the curves of her fine figure swaying a little before the keyboard. She had on a light dress; the sleeves stopped short at the elbows in an edging of lace. A satin ribbon encircled her waist. In an access of irresistible, reckless hopefulness he clapped both his hands on that waist – and then the irritating music stopped at last. But, quick as she was in springing away from the contact (the round music-stool going over with a crash), Heemskirk's lips, aiming at her neck, landed a hungry, smacking kiss just under her ear. A deep silence reigned for a time. And then he laughed rather feebly.

He was disconcerted somewhat by her white, still face, the big light violet eyes resting on him stonily. She had not uttered a sound. She faced him, steadying herself on the corner of the piano with one extended hand. The other went on rubbing with mechanical persistency the place his lips had touched.

'What's the trouble?' he said, offended. 'Startled you? Look here: don't let us have any of that nonsense. You don't mean to say a kiss frightens you so much as all that . . . I know better . . . I don't mean to be left out in the cold.'

He had been gazing into her face with such strained intentness that he could no longer see it distinctly. Everything round him was rather misty. He forgot the overturned stool, caught his foot against it, and lurched forward slightly, saying in an ingratiating tone:

'I'm not bad fun, really. You try a few kisses to begin with –'

He said no more, because his head received a terrific concussion, accompanied by an explosive sound. Freya had swung her round, strong arm with such force that the impact of her open palm on his flat cheek turned him half round. Uttering a faint, hoarse yell, the lieutenant clapped both his hands to the left side of his face, which had taken on suddenly a dusky brick-red tinge. Freya, very erect, her violet eyes darkened, her palm still tingling from the blow, a sort of restrained, determined smile showing a tiny gleam of her white teeth, heard her father's rapid, heavy tread on the path below the verandah. Her expression lost its pugnacity and became sincerely concerned. She was sorry for her father. She stooped quickly to pick up the music-stool, as if anxious to obliterate the traces . . . But that was no good. She had resumed her attitude, one hand resting lightly on the piano, before old Nelson got up to the top of the stairs.

Poor father! How furious he will be – how upset! And afterwards, what tremors, what unhappiness! Why had she not been open with him from the first? His round, innocent state of amazement cut her to the quick. But he was not looking at her. His stare was directed to Heemskirk, who, with his back to him and with his hands still up to his face, was hissing curses through his teeth, and (she saw him in profile) glaring at her balefully with one black, evil eye.

'What's the matter?' asked old Nelson, very much bewildered.

She did not answer him. She thought of Jasper on the deck of the brig, gazing up at the lighted bungalow, and she felt frightened. It was a mercy that one of them at least was on board out of the way. She only wished he were a hundred miles off. And yet she was not certain that she did. Had Jasper been mysteriously moved that moment to reappear on the verandah she would have thrown her consistency, her firmness, her self-possession, to the winds, and flown into his arms.

'What is it? What is it?' insisted the unsuspecting Nelson, getting quite excited. 'Only this minute you were playing a tune, and –'

Freya, unable to speak in her apprehension of what was coming (she was also fascinated by that black, evil, glaring eye), only nodded slightly at the lieutenant, as much as to say: 'Just look at him!'

'Why, yes!' exclaimed old Nelson. 'I see. What on earth –'

Meantime he had cautiously approached Heemskirk, who, bursting into coherent imprecations, was stamping with both feet where he stood. The indignity of the blow, the rage of baffled purpose, the ridicule of the exposure, and the impossibility of revenge maddened him to a point when he simply felt he must howl with fury.

'Oh, oh, oh!' he howled, stamping across the verandah as though he meant to drive his foot through the floor at every step.

'Why, is his face hurt?' asked the astounded old Nelson. The truth dawned suddenly upon his innocent mind. 'Dear me!' he cried, enlightened. 'Get some brandy, quick, Freya . . . You are subject to it, lieutenant? Fiendish, eh? I know, I know! Used to go crazy all of a sudden myself at the time . . . And the little bottle of laudanum from the medicine-chest, too, Freya. Look sharp . . . Don't you see he's got a toothache?'

And, indeed, what other explanation could have presented itself to the guileless old Nelson, beholding this cheek nursed with both hands, these wild glances, these stampings, this distracted swaying of the body? It would have demanded a preternatural acuteness to hit upon the true cause. Freya had not moved. She watched Heemskirk's savagely inquiring, black stare directed stealthily upon herself. 'Aha, you would like to be let off!' she said to herself. She looked at him unflinchingly, thinking it out. The temptation of making an end of it all without further trouble was irresistible. She gave an almost imperceptible nod of assent, and glided away.

'Hurry up that brandy!' old Nelson shouted, as she disappeared in the passage.

Heemskirk relieved his deeper feelings by a sudden string of curses in Dutch and English which he sent after her. He raved to his heart's content, flinging to and fro the verandah and kicking chairs out of his way; while Nelson (or Nielsen), whose sympathy was profoundly stirred by these evidences of agonizing pain, hovered round this dear (and dreaded) lieutenant, fussing like an old hen.

'Dear me, dear me! Is it so bad? I know well what it is. I used to frighten my poor wife sometimes. Do you get it often like this, lieutenant?'

Heemskirk shouldered him viciously out of his way, with a short, insane laugh. But his staggering host took it in good part; a man beside himself with excruciating toothache is not responsible.

'Go into my room, lieutenant,' he suggested urgently. 'Throw yourself on my bed. We will get something to ease you in a minute.'

He seized the poor sufferer by the arm and forced him gently onwards to the very bed, on which Heemskirk, in a renewed access of rage, flung himself down with such force that he rebounded from the mattress to the height of quite a foot.

'Dear me!' exclaimed the scared Nelson, and incontinently ran off to hurry up the brandy and the laudanum, very angry that so little alacrity was shown in relieving the tortures of his precious guest. In the end he got these things himself.

Half an hour later he stood in the inner passage of the house, surprised by faint, spasmodic sounds of a mysterious nature, between laughter and sobs. He frowned; then went straight towards his daughter's room and knocked at the door.

Freya, her glorious fair hair framing her white face and rippling down a dark-blue dressing-gown, opened it partly.

The light in the room was dim. Antonia, crouching in a corner, rocked herself backwards and forwards, uttering feeble moans. Old Nelson had not much experience in various kinds of feminine laughter, but he was certain there had been laughter there.

'Very unfeeling, very unfeeling!' he said, with weighty displeasure. 'What is there so amusing in a man being in pain? I should have thought a woman – a young girl –'

'He was so funny,' murmured Freya, whose eyes glistened strangely in the semi-obscurity of the passage. 'And then, you know, I don't like him,' she added, in an unsteady voice.

'Funny!' repeated old Nelson, amazed at this evidence of callousness in one so young. 'You don't like him! Do you mean to say that, because you don't like him, you – Why, it's simply cruel! Don't you know it's about the worst sort of pain there is? Dogs have been known to go mad with it.'

'He certainly seemed to have gone mad,' Freya said with an effort, as if she were struggling with some hidden feeling.

But her father was launched.

'And you know how he is. He notices everything. He is a fellow to take offence for the least little thing – regular Dutchman – and I want to keep friendly with him. 'It's like this, my girl: if that rajah of ours were to do something silly

– and you know he is a sulky, rebellious beggar – and the authorities took into their heads that my influence over him wasn't good, you would find yourself without a roof over your head –'

She cried: 'What nonsense, father!' in a not very assured tone, and discovered that he was angry, angry enough to achieve irony; yes, old Nelson (or Nielsen), irony! Just a gleam of it.

'Oh, of course, if you have means of your own – a mansion, a plantation that I know nothing of –' But he was not capable of sustained irony. 'I tell you they would bundle me out of here,' he whispered forcibly; 'without compensation, of course. I know these Dutch. And the lieutenant's just the fellow to start the trouble going. He has the ear of influential officials. I wouldn't offend him for anything – for anything – on no consideration whatever . . . What did you say?'

It was only an inarticulate exclamation. If she ever had a half-formed intention of telling him everything she had given it up now. It was impossible, both out of regard for his dignity and for the peace of his poor mind.

'I don't care for him myself very much,' old Nelson's subdued undertone confessed in a sigh. 'He's easier now,' he went on, after a silence. 'I've given him up my bed for the night. I shall sleep on my verandah, in the hammock. No; I can't say I like him either, but from that to laugh at a man because he's driven crazy with pain is a long way. You've surprised me, Freya. That side of his face is quite flushed.'

Her shoulders shook convulsively under his hands, which he laid on her paternally. His straggly, wiry moustache brushed her forehead in a good-night kiss. She closed the door, and went away from it to the middle of the room before she allowed herself a tired-out sort of laugh, without buoyancy.

'Flushed! A little flushed!' she repeated to herself. 'I hope so, indeed! A little –'

Her eyelashes were wet. Antonia, in her corner, moaned and giggled, and it was impossible to tell where the moans ended and the giggles began.

The mistress and the maid had been somewhat hysterical, for Freya, on fleeing into her room, had found Antonia there, and had told her everything.

'I have avenged you, my girl,' she exclaimed.

And then they had laughingly cried and cryingly laughed with admonitions – 'Ssh, not so loud! Be quiet!' on one part, and interludes of 'I am so frightened . . . He's an evil man,' on the other.

Antonia was very much afraid of Heemskirk. She was afraid of him because of his personal appearance: because of his eyes and his eyebrows, and his mouth and his nose and his limbs. Nothing could be more rational. And she thought him an evil man, because, to her eyes, he looked evil. No ground for an opinion could be sounder. In the dimness of the room, with only a nightlight burning at the head of Freya's bed, the camerista crept out of her corner to crouch at the feet of her mistress, supplicating in whispers:

'There's the brig. Captain Allen. Let us run away at once – oh, let us run away! I am so frightened. Let us! Let us!'

'I! Run away!' thought Freya to herself, without looking down at the scared girl. 'Never.'

Both the resolute mistress under the mosquito-net and the frightened maid lying curled up on a mat at the foot of the bed did not sleep very well that night. The person that did not sleep at all was Lieutenant Heemskirk. He lay on his back staring vindictively in the darkness. Inflaming images and humiliating reflections succeeded each other in his mind, keeping up, augmenting his anger. A pretty tale this to get about! But it must not be allowed to get about. The outrage had to be swallowed in silence. A pretty affair! Fooled, led on, and struck by the girl – and probably fooled by the father, too. But no. Nielsen was but another victim of that shameless hussy, that brazen minx, that sly, laughing, kissing, lying . . .

'No; he did not deceive me on purpose,' thought the tormented lieutenant. 'But I should like to pay him off, all the same, for being such an imbecile –'

Well, some day, perhaps. One thing he was firmly resolved on: he had made up his mind to steal early out of his house. He did not think he could face the girl without going out of his mind with fury.

'Fire and perdition! Ten thousand devils! I shall choke here before the morning!' he muttered to himself, lying rigid on his back on old Nelson's bed, his breast heaving for air.

He arose at daylight and started cautiously to open the door. Faint sounds in the passage alarmed him, and remaining concealed he saw Freya coming out. This unexpected sight deprived him of all power to move away from the crack of the door. It was the narrowest crack possible, but commanding the view of the end of the verandah. Freya made for that end hastily to watch the brig passing the point. She wore her dark dressing-gown; her feet were bare, because, having fallen asleep towards the morning, she ran out headlong in her fear of being too late. Heemskirk had never seen her looking like this, with her hair drawn back smoothly to the shape of her head, and hanging in one heavy, fair tress down her back, and with that air of extreme youth, intensity, and eagerness. And at first he was amazed, and then he gnashed his teeth. He could not face her at all. He muttered a curse, and kept still behind the door.

With a low, deep-breathed 'Ah!' when she first saw the brig already under way, she reached for Nelson's long glass reposing on brackets high up the wall. The wide sleeve of the dressing-gown slipped back, uncovering her white arm as far as the shoulder. Heemskirk, gripping the door-handle, as if to crush it, felt like a man just risen to his feet from a drinking bout.

And Freya knew that he was watching her. She knew. She had seen the door move as she came out of the passage. She was aware of his eyes being on her, with scornful bitterness, with triumphant contempt.

'You are there,' she thought, levelling the long glass. 'Oh, well, look on, then!'

The green islets appeared like black shadows, the ashen sea was smooth as glass, the clear robe of the colourless dawn, in which even the brig appeared shadowy, had a hem of light in the east. Directly Freya had made out Jasper on deck with his own long glass directed to the bungalow, she laid hers down and raised both her beautiful white arms above her head. In that attitude of supreme cry she stood still, glowing with the consciousness of Jasper's adoration going out to her figure held in the field of his glass away there, and warmed too, by the feeling of evil passion, the burning, covetous eyes of the other, fastened on her back. In the fervour of her love, in the caprice of her mind, and with that mysterious knowledge of masculine nature women seem to be born to, she thought:

'You are looking on – you will – you must! Then you shall see something.'

She brought both her hands to her lips, then flung them out, sending a kiss over the sea, as if she wanted to throw her heart along with it on the deck of the brig. Her face was rosy, her eyes shone. Her repeated, passionate gesture seemed to fling kisses by the hundred again and again and again, while the slowly ascending sun brought the glory of colour to the world, turning the islets green, the sea blue, the brig below her white – dazzlingly white in the spread of her wings – with the red ensign streaming like a tiny flame from the peak. And each time she murmured with a rising inflexion: 'Take this – and this – and this –' till suddenly her arms fell. She had seen the ensign dipped in response, and next moment the point below hid the hull of the brig from her view. Then she turned away from the balustrade, and, passing slowly before the door of her father's room with her eyelids lowered, and an enigmatic expression on her face, she disappeared behind the curtain.

But instead of going along the passage, she remained concealed and very still on the other side to watch what would happen. For some time the broad, furnished verandah remained empty. Then the door of old Nelson's room came open suddenly, and Heemskirk staggered out. His hair was rumpled, his eyes bloodshot, his unshaven face looked very dark. He gazed wildly about, saw his cap on a table, snatched it up, and made for the stairs quietly, but with a strange, tottering gait, like the last effort of waning strength.

Shortly after his head had sunk below the level of the floor, Freya came out from behind the curtain, with compressed, scheming lips, and no softness at all in her luminous eyes. He could not be allowed to sneak off scot free. Never – never! She was excited, she tingled all over, she had tasted blood! He must be made to understand that she had been aware of having been watched; he must know that he had been seen slinking off shamefully. But to run to the front rail and shout after him would have been childish, crude – undignified. And to shout – what? What word? What phrase? No; it was impossible. Then how? . . . She frowned, discovered it, dashed at the piano, which had stood open all night, and made the rosewood monster growl savagely in an irritated bass. She struck chords as if firing shots after that straddling, broad figure in ample white trousers and a dark uniform jacket with gold shoulder-straps, and then she pursued him with the same thing she had played the evening before – a modern, fierce piece of love music which had been tried more than once against the thunderstorms of the group. She accentuated its rhythm with triumphant malice, so absorbed in her purpose that she did not notice the presence of her father, who, wearing an old threadbare ulster of a check pattern over his sleeping-suit, had run out from the back verandah to inquire the reason for this untimely performance. He stared at her.

'What on earth? . . . Freya! . . . His voice was nearly drowned by the piano. 'What's become of the lieutenant?' he shouted.

She looked up at him as if her soul were lost in her music, with unseeing eyes. 'Gone.'

'Wha-a-t? . . . Where?'

She shook her head slightly, and went on playing louder than before. Old Nelson's innocently anxious gaze, starting from the open door of his room, explored the whole place high and low, as if the lieutenant were something small which might have been crawling on the floor or clinging to a wall. But a shrill whistle coming somewhere from below pierced the ample volume of sound rolling out of the piano in great, vibrating waves. The lieutenant was down at the cove, whistling for the boat to come and take him off to his ship. And he seemed to be in a terrific hurry, too, for he whistled again almost directly, waited for a moment, and then sent out a long, interminable, shrill call as distressful to hear as though he had shrieked without drawing breath. Freya ceased playing suddenly.

'Going on board,' said old Nelson, perturbed by the event. 'What could have made him clear out so early? Queer chap. Devilishly touchy, too! I shouldn't wonder if it was your conduct last night that hurt his feelings? I noticed you, Freya. You as well as laughed in his face, while he was suffering agonies from neuralgia. It isn't the way to get yourself liked. He's offended with you.'

Freya's hand now reposed passive on the keys; she bowed her fair head, feeling a sudden discontent, a nervous lassitude, as though she had passed through some exhausting crisis. Old Nelson (or Nielsen), looking aggrieved, was resolving matters of policy in his bald head.

'I think it would be right for me to go on board just to inquire, some time this morning,' he declared fussily. 'Why don't they bring me my morning tea? Do you hear, Freya? You have astonished me, I must say. I didn't think a young girl could be so unfeeling. And the lieutenant thinks himself a friend of ours, too! What? No? Well, he calls himself a friend, and that's something to a person in my position. Certainly! Oh, yes, I must go on board.'

'Must you?' murmured Freya listlessly; then added in her thought: 'Poor man!'

Chapter V

In respect of the next seven weeks, all that is necessary to say is, first, that old Nelson (or Nielsen) failed in paying his politic call. The *Neptun* gunboat of H.M. the King of the Netherlands, commanded by an outraged and infuriated lieutenant, left the cove at an unexpectedly early hour. When Freya's father came down to the shore, after seeing his precious crop of tobacco spread out properly in the sun, she was already steaming round the point. Old Nelson regretted the circumstance for many days.

'Now, I don't know in what disposition the man went away,' he lamented to his hard daughter. He was amazed at her hardness. He was almost frightened by her indifference.

Next, it must be recorded that the same day the gunboat *Neptun*, steering east, passed the big *Bonito* becalmed in sight of Carimata, with her head to the eastward, too. Her captain, Jasper Allen, giving himself up consciously to a tender, possessive reverie of his Freya, did not get out of his long chair on the poop to look at the *Neptun*, which passed so close that the smoke belching out suddenly from her short black funnel rolled between the masts of the *Bonito*, obscuring for a moment the sunlit whiteness of her sails, consecrated to the service of love. Jasper did not even turn his head for a glance. But Heemskirk, on the bridge, had gazed long and earnestly at the brig from the distance, gripping hard the brass rail in front of him, till, the two ships closing, he lost all confidence in himself, and retreating to the chartroom, pulled the door to with a crash. There, his brows knitted, his mouth drawn on one side in sardonic meditation, he sat through many still hours – a sort of Prometheus in the bonds of unholy desire, having his very vitals torn by the beak and claws of humiliated passion.

That species of fowl is not to be shooed off as easily as a chicken. Fooled, cheated, deceived, led on, outraged, mocked at – beak and claws! A sinister bird! The lieutenant had no mind to become the talk of the Archipelago, as the naval officer who had had his face slapped by a girl. Was it possible that she really loved that rascally trader? He tried not to think, but worse than thoughts, definite impressions beset him in his retreat. He saw her – a vision plain, close to, detailed, plastic, coloured, lighted up – he saw her hanging round the neck of that fellow. And he shut his eyes, only to discover that this was no remedy. Then a piano began to play near by, very plainly; and he put his fingers to his ears with no better effect. It was not to be borne – not in solitude. He bolted out of the chartroom, and talked of indifferent things somewhat wildly with the officer of the watch on the bridge, to the mocking accompaniment of a ghostly piano.

The last thing to be recorded is that Lieutenant Heemskirk, instead of pursuing his course towards Ternate, where he was expected, went out of his way to call at Makasser, where no one was looking for his arrival. Once there, he gave certain explanations and laid a certain proposal before the governor, or some other authority, and obtained permission to do what he thought fit in these matters. Thereupon the *Neptun*, giving up Ternate altogether, steamed north in view of the mountainous coast of Celebes, and then crossing the broad straits took up her station on the low coast of virgin forests, inviolate and mute, in waters phosphorescent at night, deep blue in daytime with gleaming green patches over the submerged reefs. For days the *Neptun* could be seen moving smoothly up and down the sombre face of the shore, or hanging about with a watchful air near the silver breaks of broad estuaries, under the great luminous sky never softened, never veiled, and flooding the earth with the everlasting sunshine of the tropics – that sunshine which, in its unbroken splendour, oppresses the soul with an inexpressible melancholy more intimate, more penetrating, more profound than the grey sadness of the northern mists.

The trading brig *Bonito* appeared gliding round a sombre forest-clad point of land on the silvery estuary of a great river. The breath of air that gave her motion would not have fluttered the flame of a torch. She stole out into the open from behind a veil of unstirring leaves, mysteriously silent, ghostly white, and solemnly stealthy in her imperceptible progress; and Jasper, his elbow in the main rigging, and his head leaning against his hand, thought of Freya. Everything in the world reminded him of her. The beauty of the loved woman exists in the beauties of Nature. The swelling outlines of the hills, the curves of a coast, the free sinuosities of a river are less suave than the harmonious lines of her body, and when she moves, gliding lightly, the grace of her progress suggests the power of occult forces which rule the fascinating aspects of the visible world.

Dependent on things as all men are, Jasper loved his vessel – the house of his dreams. He lent to her something of Freya's soul. Her deck was the foothold of their love. The possession of his brig appeased his passion in a soothing certitude of happiness already conquered.

The full moon was some way up, perfect and serene, floating in air as calm and limpid as the glance of Freya's eyes. There was not a sound in the brig.

'Here she will stand, by my side, on evenings like this,' he thought, with rapture.

And it was at that moment, in this peace, in this serenity, under the full, benign gaze of the moon propitious to lovers, on a sea without a wrinkle, under a sky without a cloud, as if all Nature had assumed its most clement mood in a spirit of mockery, that the gunboat *Neptun*, detaching herself from the dark coast under which she had been lying invisible, steamed out to intercept the trading brig *Bonito* standing out to sea.

Directly the gunboat had been made out emerging from her ambush, Schultz, of the fascinating voice, had given signs of strange agitation. All that day, ever since leaving the Malay town up the river, he had shown a haggard face, going about his duties like a man with something weighing on his mind. Jasper had noticed it, but the mate, turning away, as though he had not liked being looked at, had muttered shamefacedly of a headache and a touch of fever. He must have had it very badly when, dodging behind his captain, he wondered aloud: 'What can that fellow want with us?' . . . A naked man standing in a freezing blast and trying not to shiver could not have spoken with a more harshly uncertain intonation. But it might have been fever – a cold fit.

'He wants to make himself disagreeable, simply,' said Jasper, with perfect good humour. 'He has tried it on me before. However, we shall soon see.'

And, indeed, before long the two vessels lay abreast within easy hail. The brig, with her fine lines and her white sails, looked vaporous and sylph-like in the moonlight. The gunboat, short, squat, with her stumpy dark spars naked like dead trees, raised against the luminous sky of that resplendent night, threw a heavy shadow on the lane of water between the two ships.

Freya haunted them both like a ubiquitous spirit, and as if she were the only woman in the world. Jasper remembered her earnest recommendation to be guarded and cautious in all his acts and words while he was away from her. In this quite unforeseen encounter he felt on his ear the very breath of these hurried admonitions customary to the last moment of their partings, heard the half-jesting final whisper of the 'Mind, kid, I'd never forgive you!' with a quick pressure on his arm, which he answered by a quiet, confident smile. Heemskirk was haunted in another fashion. There were no whispers in it; it was more like visions. He saw that girl hanging round the neck of a low vagabond – *that* vagabond, the vagabond who had just answered his hail. He saw her stealing barefooted across a verandah with great, clear wide-open, eager eyes to look at a brig – *that* brig. If she had shrieked, scolded, called names! . . . But she had simply triumphed over him. That was all. Led on (he firmly believed it), fooled, deceived, outraged, struck, mocked at . . . Beak and claws! The two men, so differently haunted by Freya of the Seven Isles, were not equally matched.

In the intense stillness, as of sleep, which had fallen upon the two vessels, in a world that itself seemed but a delicate dream, a boat pulled by Javanese sailors crossing the dark lane of water came alongside the brig. The white warrant officer in her, perhaps the gunner, climbed abroad. He was a short man, with a rotund stomach and a wheezy voice. His immovable fat face looked lifeless in the moonlight, and he walked with his thick arms hanging away from his body as though he had been stuffed. His cunning little eyes glittered like bits of mica. He conveyed to Jasper, in broken English, a request to come on board the *Neptun*.

Jasper had not expected anything so unusual. But after a short reflection he decided to show neither annoyance, nor even surprise. The river from which he had come had been politically disturbed for a couple of years, and he was aware that his visits there were looked upon with some suspicion. But he did not mind much the displeasure of the authorities, so terrifying to old Nelson. He prepared to leave the brig, and Schultz followed him to the rail as if to say something, but in the end stood by in silence. Jasper, getting over the side, noticed his ghastly face. The eyes of the man who had found salvation in the brig from the effects of his peculiar psychology looked at him with a dumb, beseeching expression.

'What's the matter?' Jasper asked.

'I wonder how this will end?' said he of the beautiful voice, which had even fascinated the steady Freya herself. But where was its charming timbre now? These words had sounded like a raven's croak.

'You are ill,' said Jasper positively.

'I wish I were dead!' was the startling statement uttered by Schultz talking to himself in the extremity of some mysterious trouble. Jasper gave him a keen glance, but this was not the time to investigate the morbid outbreak of a feverish man. He did not look as though he were actually delirious, and that for the moment must suffice. Schultz made a dart forward.

'That fellow means harm!' he said desperately. 'He means harm to you, Captain Allen. I feel it, and I –'

He choked with inexplicable emotion.

'All right, Schultz. I won't give him an opening.' Jasper cut him short and swung himself into the boat.

On board the *Neptun* Heemskirk, standing straddle-legs in the flood of moonlight, his inky shadow falling right across the quarter-deck, made no sign at his approach, but secretly he felt something like the heave of the sea in his chest at the sight of that man. Jasper waited before him in silence.

Brought face to face in direct personal contact, they fell at once into the manner of their casual meetings in old Nelson's bungalow. They ignored each other's existence – Heemskirk moodily; Jasper, with a perfectly colourless quietness.

'What's going on in that river you've just come out of?' asked the lieutenant straight away.

'I know nothing of the troubles, if you mean that,' Jasper answered. 'I've landed there half a cargo of rice, for which I got nothing in exchange, and went away. There's no trade there now, but they would have been starving in another week if I hadn't turned up.'

'Meddling! English meddling! And suppose the rascals don't deserve anything better than to starve, eh?'

'There are women and children there, you know,' observed Jasper, in his even tone.

'Oh, yes! When an Englishman talks of women and children, you may be sure there's something fishy about the business. Your doings will have to be investigated.'

They spoke in turn, as though they had been disembodied spirits – mere voices in empty air; for they looked at each other as if there had been nothing there, or, at most, with as much recognition as one gives to an inanimate object, and no more. But now a silence fell. Heemskirk had thought, all at once: 'She will tell him all about it. She will tell him while she hangs round his neck laughing.' And the sudden desire to annihilate Jasper on the spot almost deprived him of his senses by its vehemence. He lost the power of speech, of vision. For a moment he absolutely couldn't see Jasper. But he heard him inquiring, as of the world at large:

'Am I, then, to conclude that the brig is detained?'

Heemskirk made a recovery in a flush of malignant satisfaction.

'She is. I am going to take her to Makassar in tow.'

'The courts will have to decide on the legality of this,' said Jasper, aware that the matter was becoming serious, but with assumed indifference.

'Oh, yes the courts! Certainly. And as to you, I shall keep you on board here.'

Jasper's dismay at being parted from his ship was betrayed by a stony immobility. It lasted but an instant. Then he turned away and hailed the brig. Mr Schultz answered:

'Yes, sir.'

'Get ready to receive a tow-rope from the gunboat! We are going to be taken to Makassar.'

'Good God! What's that for, sir?' came an anxious cry faintly.

'Kindness, I suppose,' Jasper, ironical, shouted with great deliberation. 'We might have been – becalmed in here – for days. And hospitality. I am invited to stay – on board here.'

The answer to this information was a loud ejaculation of distress. Jasper thought anxiously: 'Why, the fellow's nerve's gone to pieces'; and with an awkward uneasiness of a new sort, looked intently at the brig. The thought that he was parted from her – for the first time since they came together – shook the apparently careless fortitude of his character to its very foundations, which were deep. All that time neither Heemskirk nor even his inky shadow had stirred in the least.

'I am going to send a boat's crew and an officer on board your vessel,' he announced to no one in particular. Jasper, tearing himself away from the absorbed contemplation of the brig, turned round, and, without passion, almost without expression in his voice, entered his protest against the whole of the proceedings. What he was thinking of was the delay. He counted the days. Makassar was actually on his way; and to be towed there really saved time. On the other hand, there would be some vexing formalities to go through. But the thing was too absurd. 'The beetle's gone mad,' he thought. 'I'll be released at once. And if not, Mesman must enter into a bond for me.' Mesman was a Dutch merchant with whom Jasper had had many dealings, a considerable person in Makassar.

'You protest? H'm!' Heemskirk muttered, and for a little longer remained motionless, his legs planted well apart, and his head lowered as though he were studying his own comical, deeply split shadow. Then he made a sign to the rotund gunner, who had kept at hand, motionless, like a vilely stuffed specimen of a fat man, with a lifeless face and glittering little eyes. The fellow approached, and stood at attention.

'You will board the brig with a boat's crew!'

'Ya, mynherr!'

'You will have one of your men to steer her all the time,' went on Heemskirk, giving his orders in English, apparently for Jasper's edification. 'You hear?'

'Ya, mynherr.'

'You will remain on deck and in charge all the time.'

'Ya mynherr.'

Jasper felt as if, together with the command of the brig, his very heart were being taken out of his breast. Heemskirk asked, with a change of tone:

'What weapons have you on board?'

At one time all the ships trading in the China Seas had a licence to carry a certain quantity of firearms for purposes of defence. Jasper answered:

'Eighteen rifles with their bayonets, which were on board when I bought her, four years ago. They have been declared.'

'Where are they kept?'

'Fore-cabin. Mate has the key.'

'You will take possession of them,' said Heemskirk to the gunner.

'Ya, mynherr.'

'What is this for? What do you mean to imply?' cried out Jasper; then bit his lip. 'It's monstrous!' he muttered.

Heemskirk raised for a moment a heavy, as if suffering, glance.

'You may go,' he said to his gunner. The fat man saluted, and departed.

During the next thirty hours the steady towing was interrupted once. At a signal from the brig, made by waving a flag on the forecastle, the gunboat was stopped. The badly stuffed specimen of a warrant-officer, getting into his boat, arrived on board the *Neptun* and hurried straight into his commander's cabin, his excitement at something he had to communicate being betrayed by the blinking of his small eyes. These two were closeted together for some time, while Jasper at the taffrail tried to make out if anything out of the common had occurred on board the brig. But nothing seemed to be amiss on board. However, he kept a look-out for the gunner; and, though he had avoided speaking to anybody since he had finished with Heemskirk, he stopped that man when he came out on deck again to ask how his mate was.

'He was feeling not very well when I left,' he explained.

The fat warrant-officer, holding himself as though the effort of carrying his big stomach in front of him demanded a rigid carriage, understood with difficulty. Not a single one of his features showed the slightest animation, but his little eyes blinked rapidly at last.

'Oh, ya! The mate. Ya, ya! He is very well. But, mein Gott, he is one very funny man!'

Jasper could get no explanation of that remark, because the Dutchman got into the boat hurriedly, and went back on board the brig. But he consoled himself with the thought that very soon all this unpleasant and rather absurd experience would be over. The roadstead of Makassar was in sight already. Heemskirk passed by him going on the bridge. For the first time the lieutenant looked at Jasper with marked intention; and the strange roll of his eyes was so funny – it had been long agreed by Jasper and Freya that the lieutenant was funny – so ecstatically gratified, as though he were rolling a tasty morsel on his tongue, that Jasper could not help a broad smile. And then he turned to his brig again.

To see her, his cherished possession, animated by something of his Freya's soul, the only foothold of two lives on the wide earth, the security of his passion, the companion of adventure, the power to snatch the calm, adorable Freya to his breast, and carry her off to the end of the world; to see this beautiful thing embodying worthily his pride and his love, to see her captive at the end of a tow-rope was not indeed a pleasant experience. It had something nightmarish in it, as, for instance, the dream of a wild sea-bird loaded with chains.

Yet what else could he want to look at? Her beauty would sometimes come to his heart with the force of a spell, so that he would forget where he was. And, besides, that sense of superiority which the certitude of being loved gives to a young man, that illusion of being set above the Fates by a tender look in a woman's eyes, helped him, the first shock over, to go through these experiences with an amused self-confidence. For what evil could touch the elect of Freya?

It was now afternoon, the sun being behind the two vessels as they headed for the harbour. 'The beetle's little joke will soon be over,' thought Jasper, without any great animosity. As a seaman well acquainted with that part of the world, a casual glance was enough to tell him what was being done. 'Hallo,' he thought, 'he is going through Spermonde Passage. We shall be rounding Tamissa reef presently.' And again he returned to the contemplation of his brig, that mainstay of his material and emotional existence which would be soon in his hands again. On a sea, calm as a millpond, a heavy smooth ripple undulated and streamed away from her bows, for the powerful *Neptun* was towing at great speed, as if for a wager. The Dutch gunner appeared on the forecastle of the *Bonito*, and with him a couple of men. They stood looking at the coast, and Jasper lost himself in a loverlike trance.

The deep-toned blast of the gunboat's steam-whistle made him shudder by its unexpectedness. Slowly he looked about. Swift as lightning he leaped from where he stood, bounding forward along the deck.

'You will be on Tamissa reef!' he yelled.

High up on the bridge Heemskirk looked back over his shoulder heavily; two seamen were spinning the wheel round, and the *Neptun* was already swinging rapidly away from the edge of the pale water over the danger. Ha! Just in time. Jasper turned about instantly to watch his brig; and, even before he realized that – in obedience, it appears, to Heemskirk's orders given beforehand to the gunner – the tow-rope had been let go at the blast of the whistle, before he had time to cry out or to move a limb, he saw her cast adrift and shooting across the gunboat's stern with the impetus of her speed. He followed her fine, gliding form with eyes growing big with incredulity, wild with horror. The cries on board of her came to him only as a dreadful and confused murmur through the loud thumping of blood in his ears, while she held on. She ran upright in a terrible display of her gift of speed, with an incomparable air of life and grace. She ran on till the smooth level of water in front of her bows seemed to sink down suddenly as if sucked away; and, with a strange, violent tremor of her mastheads she stopped, inclined her lofty spars a little, and lay still. She lay still on the reef, while the *Neptun*, fetching a wide circle, continued at full speed up Spermonde Passage, heading for the town. She lay still, perfectly still, with something ill-omened and unnatural in her attitude. In an instant the subtle melancholy of things touched by decay had fallen on her in the sunshine; she was but a speck in the brilliant emptiness of space, already lonely, already desolate.

'Hold him!' yelled a voice from the bridge.

Jasper had started to run to his brig with a headlong impulse, as a man dashes forward to pull away with his hands a living, breathing, loved creature from the brink of destruction. 'Hold him! Stick to him!' vociferated the lieutenant at the top of the bridge-ladder, while Jasper struggled madly without a word, only his head emerging from the heaving crowd of the *Neptun*'s seamen, who had flung themselves upon him obediently. 'Hold – I would not have that fellow drown himself for anything now!'

Jasper ceased struggling.

One by one they let go of him; they fell back gradually farther and farther, in attentive silence, leaving him standing unsupported in a widened, clear space, as if to give him plenty of room to fall after the struggle. He did not even sway perceptibly. Half an hour later, when the *Neptun* anchored in front of the town, he had not stirred yet, had moved neither head nor limb as much as a hair's breadth. Directly the rumble of the gunboat's cable had ceased, Heemskirk came down heavily from the bridge.

'Call a sampan,' he said, in a gloomy tone, as he passed the sentry at the gangway, and then moved on slowly towards the spot where Jasper, the object of many awed glances, stood looking at the deck, as if lost in a brown study. Heemskirk came up close, and stared at him thoughtfully, with his fingers over his lips. Here he was, the favoured vagabond, the only man to whom that infernal girl was likely to tell the story. But he would not find it funny. The story how Lieutenant Heemskirk – No, he would not laugh at it. He looked as though he would never laugh at anything in his life.

Suddenly Jasper looked up. His eyes, without any other expression but bewilderment, met those of Heemskirk, observant and sombre.

'Gone on the reef!' he said, in a low, astounded tone. 'On – the – reef!' he repeated still lower and as if attending inwardly to the birth of some awful and amazing sensation.

'On the very top of high-water, spring tides,' Heemskirk struck in, with a vindictive, exulting violence which flashed and expired. He paused, as if weary, fixing upon Jasper his arrogant eyes, over which secret disenchantment, the unavoidable shadow of all passion, seemed to pass like a saddening cloud. 'On the very top,' he repeated, rousing himself in fierce reaction to snatch his laced cap off his head with a horizontal, derisive flourish towards the gangway. 'And now you may go ashore to the courts, you damned Englishman!' he said.

CHAPTER VI

THE AFFAIR of the brig *Bonito* was bound to cause a sensation in Makassar, the prettiest, and perhaps the cleanest-looking of all the towns in the Islands; which however knows few occasions for excitement. The 'front', with its special population, was soon aware that something had happened. A steamer towing a sailing vessel had been observed far out to sea for some time, and when the steamer came in alone, leaving the other outside, attention was aroused. Why was that? Her masts only could be seen – with furled sails – remaining in the same place to the southward. And soon the rumour ran all along the crowded seashore street that there was a ship on Tamissa reef. That crowd interpreted the appearance correctly. Its cause was beyond their penetration, for who could associate a girl nine hundred miles away with the stranding of a ship on Tamissa reef, or look for the remote filiation of that event in the psychology of at least three people, even if one of them, Lieutenant Heemskirk, was at that very moment passing among them on his way to make his verbal report?

No; the minds on the 'front' were not competent for that sort of investigation, but many hands there – brown hands, yellow hands, white hands – were raised to shade the eyes gazing out to sea. The rumour spread quickly. Chinese shopkeepers came to their doors, more than one white merchant, even, rose from his desk to go to the window. After all, a ship on Tamissa was not an everyday occurrence. And presently the rumour took a more definite shape. An English trader – detained on suspicion at sea by the *Neptun* – Heemskirk was towing him in to test a case, and by some strange accident –

Later on the name came out. 'The *Bonito* – what! Impossible! Yes – yes, the *Bonito*. Look! You can see from here; only two masts. It's a brig. Didn't think that man would ever let himself be caught. Heemskirk's pretty smart, too. They say she's fitted out in her cabin like a gentleman's yacht. That Allen is a sort of gentleman too. An extravagant beggar.'

A young man entered smartly Messrs. Mesman Brothers' office on the 'front', bubbling with some further information.

'Oh, yes; that's the *Bonito* for certain! But you don't know the story I've heard just now. The fellow must have been feeding that river with firearms for the last year or two. Well, it seems he has grown so reckless from long impunity that he has actually dared to sell the very ship's rifles this time. It's a fact. The rifles are not on board. What impudence! Only, he didn't know that there was one of our warships on the coast. But those Englishmen are so impudent that perhaps he thought that nothing would be done to him for it. Our courts do let off these fellows too often, on some miserable excuse or other. But, at any rate, there's an end of the famous *Bonito*. I have just heard in the harbour-office that she must have gone on at the very top of high-water; and she is in ballast, too. No human power, they think, can move her from where she is. I only hope it is so. It would be fine to have the notorious *Bonito* stuck up there as a warning to others.'

Mr J. Mesman, a colonial-born Dutchman, a kind, paternal old fellow, with a clean-shaven, quiet, handsome face, and a head of fine iron-grey hair curling a little on his collar, did not say a word in defence of Jasper and the *Bonito*. He rose from his arm-chair suddenly. His face was visibly troubled. It had so happened that once, from a business talk of ways and means, island trade, money matters, and so on, Jasper had been led to open himself to him on the subject of Freya; and the excellent man, who had known old Nelson years before and even remembered something of Freya, was much astonished and amused by the unfolding of the tale.

'Well, well, well! Nelson! Yes; of course. A very honest sort of man. And a little child with very fair hair. Oh, yes! I have a distinct recollection. And so she has grown into such a fine girl, so very determined, so very –' And he laughed almost boisterously. 'Mind, when you have happily eloped with your future wife, Captain Allen, you must come along this way, and we shall welcome her here. A little fair-headed child! I remember. I remember.'

It was that knowledge which brought trouble to his face at the first news of the wreck. He took up his hat.

'Where are you going, Mr Mesman?'

'I am going to look for Allen. I think he must be ashore. Does anybody know?'

No one of those present knew. And Mr Mesman went out on the 'front' to make inquiries.

The other part of the town, the part near the church and the fort, got its information in another way. The first thing disclosed to it was Jasper himself walking rapidly, as though he were pursued. And, as a matter of fact, a Chinaman, obviously a sampan man, was following him at the same headlong pace. Suddenly, while passing Orange House, Jasper swerved and went in, or, rather, rushed in, startling Gomez, the hotel clerk, very much. But a Chinaman beginning to make an unseemly noise at the door claimed the immediate attention of Gomez. His grievance was that the white man whom he had brought on shore from the gunboat had not paid him his boat-fare. He had pursued him so far, asking for it all the way. But the white man had taken no notice whatever of his just claim. Gomez satisfied the coolie with a few coppers, and then went to look for Jasper, whom he knew very well. He found him standing stiffly by a little round table. At the other end of the verandah a few men sitting there had stopped talking, and were looking at him in silence. Two billiard-players, with cues in their hands, had come to the door of the billiard-room and stared, too.

On Gomez coming up to him, Jasper raised one hand to point at his own throat. Gomez noted the somewhat soiled state of his white clothes, then took one look at his face, and fled away to order the drink for which Jasper seemed to be asking.

Where he wanted to go – for what purpose – where he, perhaps, only imagined himself to be going, when a sudden impulse or the sight of a familiar place had made him turn into Orange House – it is impossible to say. He was steadying himself lightly with the tips of his fingers on the little table. There were on that verandah two men whom he knew well personally, but his gaze, roaming incessantly as though he were looking for a way of escape, passed and repassed over them without a sign of recognition. They, on their side, looking at him, doubted the evidence of their own eyes. It was not that his face was distorted. On the contrary, it was still, it was set. But its expression, somehow, was unrecognizable. Can that be him? they wondered with awe.

In his head there was a wild chaos of clear thoughts. Perfectly clear. It was this clearness which was so terrible in conjunction with the utter inability to lay hold of any single one of them all. He was saying to himself, or to them: 'Steady, steady.' A China boy appeared before him with a glass on a tray. He poured the drink down his throat, and rushed out. His disappearance removed the spell of wonder from the beholders. One of the men jumped up and moved quickly to that side of the verandah from which almost the whole of the roadstead could be seen. At the very moment when Jasper, issuing from the door of the Orange House, was passing under him in the street below, he cried to the others excitedly:

'That was Allen right enough! But where is his brig?'

Jasper heard these words with extraordinary loudness. The heavens rang with them as if calling him to account; for those were the very words Freya would have to use. It was an annihilating question; it struck his consciousness like a thunderbolt and brought a sudden night upon the chaos of his thoughts even as he walked. He did not check his pace. He went on in the darkness for another three strides, and then fell.

The good Mesman had to push on as far as the hospital before he found him. The doctor there talked of a slight heartstroke. Nothing very much. Out in three days . . . It must be admitted that the doctor was right. In three days, Jasper Allen came out of the hospital and became visible to the town – very visible indeed – and remained so for quite a long time; long enough to become almost one of the sights of the place; long enough to become disregarded at last; long enough for the tale of his haunting visibility to be remembered in the islands to this day.

The talk on the 'front' and Jasper's appearance in the Orange House stand at the beginning of the famous *Bonito* case, and give a view of its two aspects – the practical and the psychological. The case for the courts and the case for compassion; that last terribly evident and yet obscure.

It has, you must understand, remained obscure even for that friend of mine who wrote me the letter mentioned in the very first lines of this narrative. He was one of those in Mr Mesman's office, and accompanied that gentleman in his search for Jasper. His letter described to me the two aspects and some of the episodes of the case. Heemskirk's attitude was that of deep thankfulness for not having lost his own ship, and that was all. Haze over the land was his explanation of having got so close to Tamissa reef. He saved his ship, and for the rest he did not care. As to the fat gunner, he deposed simply that he thought at the time that he was acting for the best by letting go the tow-rope, but admitted that he was greatly confused by the suddenness of the emergency.

As a matter of fact, he had acted on very precise instructions from Heemskirk, to whom through several years' service together in the East he had become a sort of devoted henchman. What was most amazing in the detention of the *Bonito* was his story how, proceeding to take possession of the firearms as ordered, he discovered that there were no firearms on board. All he found in the fore-cabin was an empty rack for the proper number of eighteen rifles, but of the rifles themselves never a single one anywhere in the ship. The mate of the brig, who looked rather ill and behaved excitedly, as though he were perhaps a lunatic, wanted him to believe that Captain Allen knew nothing of this; that it was he, the mate, who had recently sold these rifles in the dead of night to a certain person up the river. In proof of this story he produced a bag of silver dollars and pressed it on his, the gunner's, acceptance. Then, suddenly flinging it down on the deck, he beat his own head with both his fists and started heaping shocking curses upon his own soul for an ungrateful wretch not fit to live.

All this the gunner reported at once to his commanding officer.

What Heemskirk intended by taking upon himself to detain the *Bonito* it is difficult to say, except that he meant to bring some trouble into the life of the man favoured by Freya. He had been looking at Jasper with a desire to strike that man of kisses and embraces to the earth. The question was: How could he do it without giving himself away? But the report of the gunner created a serious case enough. Yet Allen had friends – and who could tell whether he wouldn't somehow succeed in wriggling out of it? The idea of simply towing the brig so much compromised on to the reef came to him while he was listening to the fat gunner in his cabin. There was but little risk of being disapproved now. And it should be made to appear an accident.

Going out on deck he had gloated upon his unconscious victim with such a sinister roll of his eyes, such a queerly pursed mouth, that Jasper could not help smiling. And the lieutenant had gone on the bridge, saying to himself:

'You wait! I shall spoil the taste of those sweet kisses for you. When you hear of Lieutenant Heemskirk in the future that name won't bring a smile on your lips, I swear. You are delivered into my hands.'

And this possibility had come about without any planning, one could almost say naturally, as if events had mysteriously shaped themselves to fit the purposes of a dark passion. The most astute scheming could not have served Heemskirk better. It was given to him to taste a transcendental, an incredible perfection of vengeance; to strike a deadly blow into that hated person's heart, and to watch him afterwards walking about with the dagger in his breast.

For that is what the state of Jasper amounted to. He moved, acted, weary-eyed, keen-faced, lank and restless, with brusque movements and fierce gestures; he talked incessantly in a frenzied and fatigued voice, but within himself he knew that nothing would ever give him back the brig, just as nothing can heal a pierced heart. His soul, kept quiet in the stress of love by the unflinching Freya's influence, was like a still but overwound string. The shock had started it vibrating, and the string had snapped. He had waited for two years in a perfectly intoxicated confidence for a day that now would never come to a man disarmed for life by the loss of the brig, and, it seemed to him, made unfit for love to which he had no foothold to offer.

Day after day he would traverse the length of the town, follow the coast, and, reaching the point of land opposite that part of the reef on which his brig lay stranded, look steadily across the water at her beloved form, once the home of an exulting hope, and now, in her inclined, desolated immobility, towering above the lonely sea-horizon, a symbol of despair.

The crew had left her in due course in her own boats, which directly they reached the town were sequestrated by the harbour authorities. The vessel, too, was sequestrated pending proceedings; but these same authorities did not take the trouble to set a guard on board. For, indeed, what could move her from there? Nothing, unless a miracle; nothing, unless Jasper's eyes, fastened on her tensely for hours together, as though he hoped by the mere power of vision to draw her to his breast.

All this story, read in my friend's very chatty letters, dismayed me not a little. But it was really appalling to read his relation of how Schultz, the mate, went about everywhere affirming with desperate pertinacity that it was he alone who had sold the rifles. 'I stole them,' he protested. Of course, no one would believe him. My friend himself did not believe him, though he, of course, admired this self-sacrifice. But a good many people thought it was going too far to make oneself out a thief for the sake of a friend. Only, it was such an obvious lie, too, that it did not matter, perhaps.

I, who, in view of Schultz's psychology, knew how true that must be, admit that I was appalled. So this was how a perfidious destiny took advantage of a generous impulse! And I felt as though I were an accomplice in this perfidy, since I did to a certain extent encourage Jasper. Yet I had warned him as well.

'The man seemed to have gone crazy on this point,' wrote my friend. 'He went to Mesman with his story. He says that some rascally white man living among the natives up that river made him drunk with some gin one evening, and then jeered at him for never having any money. Then he, protesting to us that he was an honest man and must be believed, described himself as being a thief whenever he took a drop too much, and told us that he went on board and passed the rifles one by one without the slightest compunction to a canoe which came alongside that night, receiving ten dollars apiece for them.

'Next day he was ill with shame and grief, but had not the courage to confess his lapse to his benefactor. When the gunboat stopped the brig he felt ready to die with the apprehension of the consequences, and would have died happily, if he could have been able to bring the rifles back by the sacrifice of his life. He said nothing to Jasper, hoping that the brig would be released presently. When it turned out otherwise and his captain was detained on board the gunboat, he was ready to commit suicide from despair; only he thought it his duty to live in order to let the truth be known. "I am an honest man! I am an honest man!" he repeated, in a voice that brought tears to our eyes. "You must believe me when I tell you that I am a thief – a vile, low, cunning, sneaking thief as soon as I've had a glass or two. Take me somewhere where I may tell the truth on oath."

'When we had at last convinced him that his story could be of no use to Jasper – for what Dutch court, having once got hold of an English trader, would accept such an explanation; and, indeed, how, when, where could one hope to find proofs of such a tale? – he made as if to tear his hair in handfuls, but, calming down, said: "Good-bye, then, gentlemen," and went out of the room so crushed that he seemed hardly able to put one foot before the other. That very night he committed suicide by cutting his throat in the house of a half-caste with whom he had been lodging since he came ashore from the wreck.'

That throat, I thought with a shudder, which could produce the tender, persuasive, manly, but fascinating voice which had aroused Jasper's ready compassion and had secured Freya's sympathy! Who could ever have supposed such an end in store for the impossible, gentle Schultz, with his idiosyncrasy of naïve pilfering, so absurdly straightforward that, even in the people who had suffered from it, it aroused nothing more than a sort of amused exasperation? He was really impossible. His lot evidently should have been a half-starved, mysterious, but by no means tragic existence as a mild-eyed, inoffensive beachcomber on the fringe of native life. There are occasions when the irony of fate, which some people profess to discover in the working out of our lives, wears the aspect of crude and savage jesting.

I shook my head over the manes of Schultz, and went on with my friend's letter. It told me how the brig on the reef, looted by the natives from the coast villages, acquired gradually the lamentable aspect, the grey ghostliness of a wreck; while Jasper, fading daily into a mere shadow of a man, strode brusquely all along the 'front' with horribly lively eyes and a faint, fixed smile on his lips, to spend the day on a lonely spit of sand looking eagerly at her, as though he had expected some shape on board to rise up and make some sort of sign to him over the decaying bulwarks. The Mesmans were taking care of him as far as it was possible. The *Bonito* case had been referred to Batavia, where no doubt it would fade away in a fog of official papers . . . It was heartrending to read all this. That active and zealous officer, Lieutenant Heemskirk, his air of sullen, darkly pained self-importance not lightened by the approval of his action conveyed to him unofficially, had gone on to take up his station in the Moluccas . . .

Then, at the end of the bulky, kindly meant epistle, dealing with the island news of half a year at least, my friend wrote: 'A couple of months ago old Nelson turned up here, arriving by the mail-boat from Java. Came to see Mesman, it seems. A rather mysterious visit, and extraordinarily short, after coming all that way. He stayed just four days at the Orange House with apparently nothing in particular to do, and then caught the south-going steamer for the Straits. I remember people saying at one time that Allen was rather sweet on old Nelson's daughter, the girl that was brought up by Mrs Harley and then went to live with him at the Seven Isles group. Surely you remember old Nelson –'

Remember old Nelson! Rather!

The letter went on to inform me further that old Nelson, at least, remembered me, since some time after his flying visit to Makassar he had written to the Mesmans asking for my address in London.

That old Nelson (or Nielsen), the note of whose personality was a profound, echoless irresponsiveness to everything around him, should wish to write, or find anything to write about to anybody, was in itself a cause for no small wonder. And to me, of all people? I waited with uneasy impatience for whatever disclosure could come from that naturally benighted intelligence, but my impatience had time to wear out before my eyes beheld old Nelson's trembling, painfully formed handwriting, senile and childish at the same time, on an envelope bearing a penny stamp and the postal mark of the Notting Hill office. I delayed opening it in order to pay the tribute of astonishment due to the event by flinging my hands above my head. So he had come home to England, to be definitely Nelson; or else was on his way home to Denmark, where he would revert for ever to his original Nielsen! But old Nelson (or Nielsen) out of the tropics seemed unthinkable. And yet he was there, asking me to call.

His address was at a boarding-house in one of those Bayswater Squares, once of leisure, which nowadays are reduced to earning their living. Somebody had recommended him there. I started to call on him on one of those January days in London, one of those wintry days composed of the four devilish elements, cold, wet, mud, and grime, combined with a particular stickiness of atmosphere that clings like an unclean garment to one's very soul. Yet on approaching his abode I saw, like a flicker far behind the soiled veil of the four elements, the wearisome and splendid glitter of a blue sea with the Seven Islets like minute specks swimming in my eye, the high red roof of the bungalow crowning the very smallest of them all. The visual reminiscence was profoundly disturbing. I knocked at the door with a faltering hand.

Old Nelson (or Nielsen) got up from the table at which he was sitting with a shabby pocket-book full of papers before him. He took off his spectacles before shaking hands. For a moment neither of us said a word; then, noticing me looking round somewhat expectantly, he murmured some words, of which I caught only 'daughter' and 'Hong Kong', cast his eyes down and sighed.

His moustache, sticking all ways out, as of yore, was quite white now. His old cheeks were softly rounded, with some colour in them; strangely enough, that something childlike always noticeable in the general contour of his physiognomy had become much more marked. Like his handwriting, he looked childish and senile. He showed his age most in his unintelligently furrowed, anxious forehead and in his round, innocent eyes, which appeared to me weak and blinking and watery; or was it that they were full of tears? . . .

To discover old Nelson fully informed upon any matter whatever was a new experience. And after the first awkwardness had worn off he talked freely, with, now and then, a question to start him going whenever he lapsed into silence, which he would do suddenly, clasping his hands on his waistcoat in an attitude which would recall to me the east verandah, where he used to sit talking quietly and puffing out his cheeks in what seemed now old, very old days. He talked in a reasonable, somewhat anxious tone.

'No, no. We did not know anything for weeks. Out of the way like that, we couldn't, of course. No mail service to the Seven Isles. But one day I ran over to Banka in my big sailing-boat to see whether there were any letters, and saw a Dutch paper. But it looked only like a bit of marine news: English brig *Bonito* gone ashore outside Makassar roads. That was all. I took the paper home with me and showed it to her. "I will never forgive him!" she cries with her old spirit.

"My dear," I said, "you are a sensible girl. The best man may lose a ship. But what about your health?" I was beginning to be frightened at her looks. She would not let me talk even of going to Singapore before. But, really, such a sensible girl couldn't keep on objecting for ever. "Do what you like, papa," she says. Rather a job, that. Had to catch a steamer at sea, but I got her over all right. There, doctors, of course. Fever. Anaemia. Put her to bed. Two or three women very kind to her. Naturally in our papers the whole story came out before long. She reads it to the end, lying on the couch; then hands the newspaper back to me, whispers "Heemskirk", and goes off into a faint.'

He blinked at me for quite a long time, his eyes running full of tears again.

'Next day,' he began, without any emotion in his voice, 'she felt stronger, and we had a long talk. She told me everything.'

Here old Nelson, with his eyes cast down, gave me the whole story of the Heemskirk episode in Freya's words; then went on in his rather jerky utterance, and looking up innocently:

' "My dear," I said, "you have behaved in the main like a sensible girl." "I have been horrid," she cries, "and he is breaking his heart over there." Well, she was too sensible not to see she wasn't in a state to travel. But I went. She told me to go. She was being looked after very well. Anaemia. Getting better, they said.'

He paused.

'You did see him?' I murmured.

'Oh, yes; I did see him,' he started again, talking in that reasonable voice as though he were arguing a point. 'I did see him. I came upon him. Eyes sunk an inch into his head; nothing but skin on the bones of his face, a skeleton in dirty white clothes. That's what he looked like. How Freya . . . But she never did – not really. He was sitting there, the only live thing for miles along that coast, on a drift-log washed up on the shore. They had clipped his hair in the hospital, and it had not grown again. He stared, holding his chin in his hand, and with nothing on the sea between him and the sky but that wreck. When I came up to him he just moved his head a bit. "Is that you, old man?" says he – like that.

'If you had seen him you would have understood at once how impossible it was for Freya to have ever loved that man. Well, well. I don't say. She might have – something. She was lonely, you know. But really to go away with him! Never! Madness. She was too sensible . . . I began to reproach him gently. And by and by he turns on me. "Write to you! What about? Come to her? What with? If I had been a man I would have carried her off, but she made a child, a happy child, of me. Tell her that the day the only thing I had belonging to me in the world perished on this reef I discovered that I had no power over her . . . Has she come here with you?" he shouts, blazing at me suddenly with his hollow eyes. I shook my head. Come with me, indeed! Anaemia! "Aha! You see? Go away, then, old man, and leave me alone here with that ghost," he says, jerking his head at the wreck of his brig.

'Mad! It was getting dusk. I did not care to stop any longer all by myself with that man in that lonely place. I was not going to tell him of Freya's illness. Anaemia! What was the good? Mad! And what sort of husband would he have made, anyhow, for a sensible girl like Freya? Why, even my little property I could not have left them. The Dutch authorities would never have allowed an

Englishman to settle there. It was not sold then. My man Mahmat, you know, was looking after it for me. Later on I let it go for a tenth of its value to a Dutch half-caste. But never mind. It was nothing to me then. Yes; I went away from him. I caught the return mail-boat. I told everything to Freya. "He's mad," I said; "and, my dear, the only thing he loved was his brig."

' "Perhaps," she says to herself, looking straight away – her eyes were nearly as hollow as his – "perhaps it is true. Yes! I would never allow him any power over me." '

Old Nelson paused. I sat fascinated, and feeling a little cold in that room with a blazing fire.

'So you see,' he continued, 'she never really cared for him. Much too sensible. I took her away to Hong Kong. Change of climate, they said. Oh, these doctors! My God! Winter time! There came ten days of cold mists and wind and rain. Pneumonia. But look here! We talked a lot together. Days and evenings. Who else had she? . . . She talked a lot to me, my own girl. Sometimes she would laugh a little. Look at me and laugh a little –'

I shuddered. He looked up vaguely, with a childish, puzzled moodiness.

'She would say: "I did not really mean to be a bad daughter to you, papa." And I would say: "Of course, my dear. You could not have meant it." She would lie quiet and then say: "I wonder?" And sometimes, "I've been really a coward," she would tell me. You know, sick people they say things. And so she would say too: "I've been conceited, headstrong, capricious. I sought my own gratification. I was selfish or afraid." . . . But sick people, you know, they say anything. And once, after lying silent almost all day, she said: "Yes; perhaps, when the day came I would not have gone. Perhaps! I don't know," she cried. "Draw the curtain, papa. Shut the sea out. It reproaches me with my folly." ' He gasped and paused.

'So you see,' he went on in a murmur. 'Very ill, very ill indeed. Pneumonia. Very sudden.' He pointed his finger at the carpet, while the thought of the poor girl, vanquished in her struggle with three men's absurdities, and coming at last to doubt her own self, held me in a very anguish of pity.

'You see yourself,' he began again in a downcast manner. 'She could not have really . . . She mentioned you several times. Good friend. Sensible man. So I wanted to tell you myself – let you know the truth. A fellow like that! How could it be? She was lonely. And perhaps for a while . . . Mere nothing. There could never have been a question of love for my Freya – such a sensible girl –'

'Man!' I cried, rising upon him wrathfully, 'don't you see that she died of it?'

He got up too. 'No! no!' he stammered, as if angry. 'The doctors! Pneumonia. Low state. The inflammation of the . . . They told me. Pneu –'

He did not finish the word. It ended in a sob. He flung his arms out in a gesture of despair, giving up his ghastly pretence with a low, heartrending cry:

'And I thought that she was so sensible!'

Victory

An Island Tale

Of calling shapes, and beckoning shadows dire,
And airy tongues that syllable men's names
On sands and shores and desert wilderness.

MILTON: *Comus*

TO PERCEVAL AND MAISIE GIBBON

Contents

Note to the First Edition

THE LAST word of this novel was written on 29 May 1914. And that last word was the single word of the title.

Those were the times of peace. Now that the moment of publication approaches I have been considering the discretion of altering the title-page. The word 'Victory', the shining and tragic goal of noble effort, appeared too great, too august, to stand at the head of a mere novel. There was also the possibility of falling under the suspicion of commercial astuteness deceiving the public into the belief that the book had something to do with war.

Of that, however, I was not afraid very much. What influenced my decision most were the obscure promptings of that pagan residuum of awe and wonder which lurks still at the bottom of our old humanity. 'Victory' was the last word I had written in peace-time. It was the last literary thought which had occurred to me before the doors of the Temple of Janus flying open with a crash shook the minds, the hearts, the consciences of men all over the world. Such coincidence could not be treated lightly. And I made up my mind to let the word stand, in the same hopeful spirit in which some simple citizen of Old Rome would have 'accepted the Omen'.

The second point on which I wish to offer a remark is the existence (in the novel) of a person named Schomberg.

That I believe him to be true goes without saying. I am not likely to offer pinchbeck wares to my public consciously. Schomberg is an old member of my company. A very subordinate personage in *Lord Jim* as far back as the year 1899, he became notably active in a certain short story of mine published in 1902. Here he appears in a still larger part, true to life (I hope), but also true to himself. Only, in this instance, his deeper passions come into play, and thus his grotesque psychology is completed at last.

I don't pretend to say that this is the entire Teutonic psychology; but it is indubitably the psychology of a Teuton. My object in mentioning him here is to bring out the fact that, far from being the incarnation of recent animosities, he is the creature of my old, deep-seated, and, as it were, impartial conviction.

J. C.

AUTHOR'S NOTE

ON APPROACHING the task of writing this Note for *Victory*, the first thing I am conscious of is the actual nearness of the book, its nearness to me personally, to the vanished mood in which it was written, and to the mixed feelings aroused by the critical notices the book obtained when first published almost exactly a year after the beginning of the war. The writing of it was finished in 1914 long before the murder of an Austrian Archduke sounded the first note of warning for a world already full of doubts and fears.

The contemporaneous very short Author's Note which is preserved in this edition bears sufficient witness to the feelings with which I consented to the publication of the book. The fact of the book having been published in the United States early in the year made it difficult to delay its appearance in England any longer. It came out in the thirteenth month of the war, and my conscience was troubled by the awful incongruity of throwing this bit of imagined drama into the welter of reality, tragic enough in all conscience but even more cruel than tragic and more inspiring than cruel. It seemed awfully presumptuous to think there would be eyes to spare for those pages in a community which in the crash of the big guns and in the din of brave words expressing the truth of an indomitable faith could not but feel the edge of a sharp knife at its throat.

The unchanging Man of history is wonderfully adaptable both by his power of endurance and in his capacity for detachment. The fact seems to be that the play of his destiny is too great for his fears and too mysterious for his understanding. Were the trump of the Last Judgement to sound suddenly on a working day the musician at his piano would go on with his performance of Beethoven's sonata and the cobbler at his stall stick to his last in undisturbed confidence in the virtues of the leather. And with perfect propriety. For what are we to let ourselves be disturbed by an angel's vengeful music too mighty for our ears and too awful for our terrors? Thus it happens to us to be struck suddenly by the lightning of wrath. The reader will go on reading if the book pleases him and the critic will go on criticizing with that faculty of detachment born perhaps from a sense of infinite littleness and which is yet the only faculty that seems to assimilate man to the immortal gods.

It is only when the catastrophe matches the natural obscurity of our fate that even the best representative of the race is liable to lose his detachment. It is very obvious that on the arrival of the gentlemanly Mr Jones, the single-minded Ricardo, and the faithful Pedro, Heyst, the man of universal detachment, loses his mental self-possession, that fine attitude before the university irremediable which wears the name of stoicism. It is all a matter of proportion. There should have been a remedy for that sort of thing. And yet there is no remedy. Behind this minute instance of life's hazards Heyst sees the power of blind destiny. Besides, Heyst in his fine detachment had lost the habit of asserting himself. I don't mean the courage of self-assertion, either moral or physical, but the mere way of it, the trick of the thing, the readiness of mind and the turn of the hand that come without reflection and lead the man to excellence in life, in art, in crime, in virtue, and, for the matter of that, even in love. Thinking is the great enemy of perfection. The habit of profound reflection, I am compelled to say, is the most pernicious of all the habits formed by the civilized man.

But I wouldn't be suspected even remotely of making fun of Axel Heyst. I have always liked him. The flesh-and-blood individual who stands behind the infinitely more familiar figure of the book I remember as a mysterious Swede right enough. Whether he was a baron, too, I am not so certain. He himself never laid claim to that distinction. His detachment was too great to make any claims, big or small, on one's credulity. I will not say where I met him because I fear to give my readers a wrong impression, since a marked incongruity between a man and his surroundings is often a very misleading circumstance. We became very friendly for a time, and I would not like to expose him to unpleasant suspicions though, personally, I am sure he would have been indifferent to suspicions as he was indifferent to all the other disadvantages of life. He was not the whole Heyst of course; he is only the physical and moral foundation of my Heyst laid on the ground of a short acquaintance. That it was short was certainly not my fault for he had charmed me by the mere amenity of his detachment which, in this case, I cannot help thinking he had carried to excess. He went away from his rooms without leaving a trace. I wondered where he had gone to – but now I know. He vanished from my ken only to drift into this adventure that, unavoidably, waited for him in a world which he persisted in looking upon as a malevolent shadow spinning in the sunlight. Often in the course of years an expressed sentiment, the particular sense of a phrase heard casually, would recall him to my mind so that I have fastened on to him many words heard on other men's lips and belonging to other men's less perfect, less pathetic moods.

The same observation will apply *mutatis mutandis* to Mr Jones, who is built on a much slenderer connection. Mr Jones (or whatever his name was) did not drift away from me. He turned his back on me and walked out of the room. It was in a little hotel on the island of St Thomas in the West Indies (in the year '75) where we found him one hot afternoon extended on three chairs, all alone in the loud buzzing of flies to which his immobility and his cadaverous aspect gave a most gruesome significance. Our invasion must have displeased him because he got off the chairs brusquely and walked out, leaving with me an indelibly weird impression of his thin shanks. One of the men with me said that the fellow was the most desperate gambler he had ever come across. I said: 'A professional sharper?' and got for an answer: 'He's a terror; but I must say that up to a certain point he will play fair . . .' I wonder what the point was. I never saw him again because I believe he went straight on board a mail-boat which left within the hour for other ports of call in the direction of Aspinall. Mr Jones's characteristic insolence belongs to another man of a quite different type. I will say nothing as to the origins of his mentality because I don't intend to make any damaging admissions.

It so happened that the very same year Ricardo – the physical Ricardo – was a fellow passenger of mine on board an extremely small and extremely dirty little schooner, during a four days' passage between two places in the Gulf of Mexico whose names don't matter. For the most part he lay on deck aft as it were at my feet, and raising himself from time to time on his elbow would talk about himself and go on talking, not exactly to me or even at me (he would not even look up but kept his eyes fixed on the deck) but more as if communing in a low voice with his familiar devil. Now and then he would give me a glance and make the hairs of his stiff little moustache stir quaintly. His eyes were green and every cat I see to this day reminds me of the exact contour of his face. What he was travelling for or what was his business in life he never confided to me. Truth to say, the only passenger on board that schooner who could have talked openly about his activities and purposes was a very snuffly and conversationally delightful friar, the superior of a convent, attended by a very young lay brother, of a particularly ferocious countenance. We had with us also, lying prostrate in the dark and unspeakable cuddy of that schooner, an old Spanish gentleman, owner of much luggage and, as Ricardo assured me, very ill indeed. Ricardo seemed to be either a servant or the confidant of that aged and distinguished-looking invalid, who early on the passage held a long murmured conversation with the friar, and after that did nothing but groan feebly, smoke cigarettes, and now and then call for Martin in a voice full of pain. Then he who had become Ricardo in the book would go below into that beastly and noisome hole, remain there mysteriously, and coming up on deck again with a face on which nothing could be read, would as likely as not resume for my edification the exposition of his moral attitude toward life illustrated by striking particular instances of the most atrocious complexion. Did he mean to frighten me? Or seduce me? Or astonish me? Or arouse my admiration? All he did was to arouse my amused incredulity. As scoundrels go he was far from being a bore. For the rest my innocence was so great then that I could not take his philosophy seriously. All the time he kept one ear turned to the cuddy in the manner of a devoted servant, but I had the idea that in some way or other he had imposed the connection on the invalid for some end of his own. The reader, therefore, won't be surprised to hear that one morning I was told without any particular emotion by the *padrone* of the schooner that the 'rich man' down there was dead: He had died in the night. I don't remember ever being so moved by the desolate end of a complete stranger. I looked down the skylight, and there was the devoted Martin busy cording cowhide trunks belonging to the deceased whose white beard and hooked nose were the only parts I could make out in the dark depths of a horrible stuffy bunk.

As it fell calm in the course of the afternoon and continued calm during all that night and the terrible, flaming day, the late 'rich man' had to be thrown overboard at sunset, though as a matter of fact we were in sight of the low pestilential mangrove-lined coast of our destination. The excellent Father Superior mentioned to me with an air of immense commiseration: 'The poor man has left a young daughter.' Who was to look after her I don't know, but I saw the devoted Martin taking the trunks ashore with great care just before I landed myself. I would perhaps have tracked the ways of that man of immense sincerity for a little while, but I had some of my own very pressing business to attend to, which in the end got mixed up with an earthquake and so I had no time to give to Ricardo. The reader need not be told that I have not forgotten him, though.

My contact with the faithful Pedro was much shorter and my observation of him was less complete but incomparably more anxious. It ended in a sudden inspiration to get out of his way. It was in a hovel of sticks and mats by the side of a path. As I went in there only to ask for a bottle of lemonade I have not to this day the slightest idea what in my appearance or actions could have roused his terrible ire. It became manifest to me less than two minutes after I had set eyes on him for the first time, and though immensely surprised of course I didn't stop to think it out. I took the nearest short cut – through the wall. This bestial apparition and a certain enormous buck nigger encountered in Haiti only a couple of months afterwards, have fixed my conception of blind, furious, unreasoning rage, as manifested in the human animal, to the end of my days. Of the nigger I used to dream for years afterwards. Of Pedro never. The impression was less vivid. I got away from him too quickly.

It seems to me but natural that those three buried in a corner of my memory should suddenly get out into the light of the world – so natural that I offer no excuse for their existence. They were there, they had to come out; and this is a sufficient excuse for a writer of tales who had taken to his trade without preparation, or premeditation, and without any moral intention but that which pervades the whole scheme of this world of senses.

Since this Note is mostly concerned with personal contacts and the origins of the persons in the tale, I am bound also to speak of Lena, because if I were to leave her out it would look like a slight; and nothing would be further from my thoughts than putting a slight on Lena. If of all the personages involved in the 'mystery of Samburan' I have lived longest with Heyst (or with him I call Heyst) it was at her, whom I call Lena, that I have looked the longest and with a most sustained attention. This attention originated in idleness for which I have a natural talent. One evening I wandered into a café, in a town not of the tropics but of the South of France. It was filled with tobacco smoke, the hum of voices, the rattling of dominoes, and the sounds of strident music. The orchestra was rather smaller than the one that performed at Schomberg's hotel, had the air more of a family party than of an enlisted band, and, I must confess, seemed rather more respectable than the Zangiacomo musical enterprise. It was less pretentious also, more homely and familiar, so to speak, insomuch that in the intervals when all the performers left the platform one of them went amongst the marble tables collecting offerings of sous and francs in a battered tin receptacle recalling the shape of a sauceboat. It was a girl. Her detachment from her task seems to me now to have equalled or even surpassed Heyst's aloofness from all the mental degradations to which a man's intelligence is exposed in its way through life. Silent and wide-eyed she went from table to table with the air of a sleep-walker and with no other sound but the slight rattle of the coins to attract attention. It was long after the sea-chapter of my life had been closed but it is difficult to discard completely the characteristics of half a lifetime, and it was in something of the Jack-ashore spirit that I dropped a five-franc piece into the sauceboat; whereupon the sleep-walker turned her head to gaze at me and said '*Merci, Monsieur*' in a tone in which there was no gratitude but only surprise. I must have been idle indeed to take the trouble to remark on such slight evidence that the voice was very charming and when the performers resumed their seats I shifted my position slightly in order not to have that particular performer hidden from me by the little man with the beard who conducted, and who might for all I know have been her father, but whose real mission in life was to be a model for the Zangiacomo of *Victory*. Having got a clear line of sight I naturally (being idle) continued to look at the girl through all the second part of the programme. The shape of her dark head inclined over the violin was fascinating, and, while resting between the pieces of that interminable programme she was, in her white dress and with her brown hands reposing in her lap, the very image of dreamy innocence. The mature, bad-tempered woman at the piano might have been her mother, though there was not the slightest resemblance between them. All I am certain of in their personal relation to each other is that cruel pinch on the upper part of the arm. That I am sure I have seen! There could be no mistake. I was in too idle a mood to imagine such a gratuitous barbarity. It may have been playfulness, yet the girl jumped up as if she had been stung by a wasp. It may have been playfulness. Yet I saw plainly poor 'dreamy innocence' rub gently the affected place as she filed off with the other performers down the middle aisle between the marble tables in the uproar of voices, the rattling of dominoes, through a blue atmosphere of tobacco smoke. I believe that those people left the town next day.

Or perhaps they had only migrated to the other big café, on the other side of the Place de la Comédie. It is very possible. I did not go across to find out. It was my perfect idleness that had invested the girl with a peculiar charm, and I did not want to destroy it by any superfluous exertion. The receptivity of my indolence made the impression so permanent that when the moment came for her meeting with Heyst I felt that she would be heroically equal to every demand of the risky and uncertain future. I was so convinced of it that I let her go with Heyst, I won't say without a pang but certainly without misgivings. And in view of her triumphant end what more could I have done for her rehabilitation and her happiness?

1920 J.C.

Part One

Chapter I

There is, as every schoolboy knows in this scientific age, a very close chemical relation between coal and diamonds. It is the reason, I believe, why some people allude to coal as 'black diamonds'. Both these commodities represent wealth; but coal is a much less portable form of property. There is, from that point of view, a deplorable lack of concentration in coal. Now, if a coal-mine could be put into one's waistcoat pocket – but it can't! At the same time, there is a fascination in coal, the supreme commodity of the age in which we are camped like bewildered travellers in a garish, unrestful hotel. And I suppose those two considerations, the practical and the mystical, prevented Heyst – Axel Heyst – from going away.

The Tropical Belt Coal Company went into liquidation. The world of finance is a mysterious world in which, incredible as the fact may appear, evaporation precedes liquidation. First the capital evaporates, and then the company goes into liquidation. These are very unnatural physics, but they account for the persistent inertia of Heyst, at which we 'out there' used to laugh among ourselves – not inimically. An inert body can do no harm to anyone, provokes no hostility, is scarcely worth derision. It may, indeed, be in the way sometimes; but this could not be said of Axel Heyst. He was out of everybody's way, as if he were perched on the highest peak of the Himalayas, and in a sense as conspicuous. Everyone in that part of the world knew of him, dwelling on his little island. An island is but the top of a mountain. Axel Heyst, perched on it immovably, was surrounded, instead of the imponderable stormy and transparent ocean of air merging into infinity, by a tepid, shallow sea; a passionless offshoot of the great waters which embrace the continents of this globe. His most frequent visitors were shadows, the shadows of clouds, relieving the monotony of the inanimate, brooding sunshine of the tropics. His nearest neighbour – I am speaking now of things showing some sort of animation – was an indolent volcano which smoked faintly all day with its head just above the northern horizon, and at night levelled at him, from amongst the clear stars, a dull red glow, expanding and collapsing spasmodically like the end of a gigantic cigar puffed at intermittently in the dark. Axel Heyst was also a smoker; and when he lounged out on his veranda with his cheroot, the last thing before going to bed, he made in the night the same sort of glow and of the same size as that other one so many miles away.

In a sense, the volcano was company to him in the shades of the night – which were often too thick, one would think, to let a breath of air through. There was seldom enough wind to blow a feather along. On most evenings of the year Heyst could have sat outside with a naked candle to read one of the books left him by his late father. It was not a mean store. But he never did that. Afraid of mosquitoes, very likely. Neither was he ever tempted by the silence to address any casual remarks to the companion glow of the volcano. He was not mad.

Queer chap – yes, that may have been said, and in fact was said; but there is a tremendous difference between the two, you will allow.

On the nights of full moon the silence around Samburan – the 'Round Island' of the charts – was dazzling; and in the flood of cold light Heyst could see his immediate surroundings, which had the aspect of an abandoned settlement invaded by the jungle: vague roofs above low vegetation, broken shadows of bamboo fences in the sheen of long grass, something like an overgrown bit of road slanting among ragged thickets towards the shore only a couple of hundred yards away, with a black jetty and a mound of some sort, quite inky on its unlighted side. But the most conspicuous object was a gigantic blackboard raised on two posts and presenting to Heyst, when the moon got over that side, the white letters 'T.B.C.Co.' in a row at least two feet high. These were the initials of the Tropical Belt Coal Company, his employers – his late employers, to be precise.

According to the unnatural mysteries of the financial world, the T.B.C. Company's capital having evaporated in the course of two years, the company went into liquidation – forced, I believe, not voluntary. There was nothing forcible in the process, however. It was slow; and while the liquidation – in London and Amsterdam – pursued its languid course, Axel Heyst, styled in the prospectus 'manager in the tropics', remained at his post on Samburan, the No. 1 coaling-station of the company.

And it was not merely a coaling-station. There was a coalmine there, with an outcrop in the hillside less than five hundred yards from the rickety wharf and the imposing blackboard. The company's object had been to get hold of all the outcrops on tropical islands and exploit them locally. And, Lord knows, there were any amount of outcrops. It was Heyst who had located most of them in this part of the tropical belt during his rather aimless wanderings, and being a ready letter-writer had written pages and pages about them to his friends in Europe. At least, so it was said.

We doubted whether he had any visions of wealth – for himself, at any rate. What he seemed mostly concerned for was the 'stride forward', as he expressed it, in the general organization of the universe, apparently. He was heard by more than a hundred persons in the islands talking of a 'great stride forward for these regions'. The convinced wave of the hand which accompanied the phrase suggested tropical distances being impelled onward. In connection with the finished courtesy of his manner, it was persuasive, or at any rate silencing – for a time, at least. Nobody cared to argue with him when he talked in this strain. His earnestness could do no harm to anybody. There was no danger of anyone taking seriously his dream of tropical coal, so what was the use of hurting his feelings?

Thus reasoned men in reputable business offices where he had his entrée as a person who came out East with letters of introduction – and modest letters of credit, too – some years before these coal outcrops began to crop up in his playfully courteous talk. From the first there was some difficulty in making him out. He was not a traveller. A traveller arrives and departs, goes on somewhere. Heyst did not depart. I met a man once – the manager of the branch of the

Oriental Banking Corporation in Malacca – to whom Heyst exclaimed, in no connection with anything in particular (it was in the billiard-room of the club):

'I am enchanted with these islands!'

He shot it out suddenly, *à propos des bottes*, as the French say, and while chalking his cue. And perhaps it was some sort of enchantment. There are more spells than your commonplace magicians ever dreamed of.

Roughly speaking, a circle with a radius of eight hundred miles drawn round a point in North Borneo was in Heyst's case a magic circle. It just touched Manila, and he had been seen there. It just touched Saigon, and he was likewise seen there once. Perhaps these were his attempts to break out. If so, they were failures. The enchantment must have been an unbreakable one. The manager – the man who heard the exclamation – had been so impressed by the tone, fervour, rapture, what you will, or perhaps by the incongruity of it that he had related the experience to more than one person.

'Queer chap, that Swede,' was his only comment; but this is the origin of the name 'Enchanted Heyst' which some fellows fastened on our man.

He also had other names. In his early years, long before he got so becomingly bald on the top, he went to present a letter of introduction to Mr Tesman of Tesman Brothers, a Sourabaya firm – tip-top house. Well, Mr Tesman was a kindly, benevolent old gentleman. He did not know what to make of that caller. After telling him that they wished to render his stay among the islands as pleasant as possible, and that they were ready to assist him in his plans, and so on, and after receiving Heyst's thanks – you know the usual kind of conversation – he proceeded to query in a slow, paternal tone:

'And you are interested in –?'

'Facts,' broke in Heyst in his courtly voice. 'There's nothing worth knowing but facts. Hard facts! Facts alone, Mr Tesman.'

I don't know if old Tesman agreed with him or not, but he must have spoken about it, because, for a time, our man got the name of 'Hard Facts'. He had the singular good fortune that his sayings stuck to him and became part of his name. Thereafter he mooned about the Java Sea in some of the Tesmans' trading schooners, and then vanished, on board an Arab ship, in the direction of New Guinea. He remained so long in that outlying part of his enchanted circle that he was nearly forgotten before he swam into view again in a native proa full of Goram vagabonds, burnt black by the sun, very lean, his hair much thinned, and a portfolio of sketches under his arm. He showed these willingly, but was very reserved as to anything else. He had had an 'amusing time', he said. A man who will go to New Guinea for fun – well!

Later, years afterward, when the last vestiges of youth had gone off his face and all the hair off the top of his head, and his red-gold pair of horizontal moustaches had grown to really noble proportions, a certain disreputable white man fastened upon him an epithet. Putting down with a shaking hand a long glass emptied of its contents – paid for by Heyst – he said, with that deliberate sagacity which no mere water-drinker ever attained:

'Heyst's a puffect g'n'lman. Puffect! But he's a ut-uto-utopist.'

Heyst had just come out of the place of public refreshment where this pronouncement was voiced. Utopist, eh? Upon my word, the only thing I heard him say which might have had a bearing on the point was his invitation to old McNab himself. Turning with that finished courtesy of attitude, movement, voice, which was his obvious characteristic, he had said with delicate playfulness:

'Come along and quench your thirst with us, Mr McNab!'

Perhaps that was it. A man who could propose, even playfully, to quench old McNab's thirst must have been a utopist, a pursuer of chimeras; for of downright irony Heyst was not prodigal. And, may be, this was the reason why he was generally liked. At that epoch in his life, in the fulness of his physical development, of a broad, martial presence, with his bald head and long moustaches, he resembled the portraits of Charles XII, of adventurous memory. However, there was no reason to think that Heyst was in any way a fighting man.

CHAPTER II

IT WAS about this time that Heyst became associated with Morrison on terms about which people were in doubt. Some said he was a partner, others said he was a sort of paying guest, but the real truth of the matter was more complex. One day Heyst turned up in Timor. Why in Timor, of all places in the world, no one knows. Well, he was mooning about Delli, that highly pestilential place, possibly in search of some undiscovered facts, when he came in the street upon Morrison, who, in his way, was also an 'enchanted' man. When you spoke to Morrison of going home – he was from Dorsetshire – he shuddered. He said it was dark and wet there; that it was like living with your head and shoulders in a moist gunny-bag. That was only his exaggerated style of talking. Morrison was 'one of us'. He was owner and master of the *Capricorn*, trading brig, and was understood to be doing well with her, except for the drawback of too much altruism. He was the dearly beloved friend of a quantity of God-forsaken villages up dark creeks and obscure bays, where he traded for 'produce'. He would often sail through awfully dangerous channels up to some miserable settlement, only to find a very hungry population clamorous for rice, and without so much 'produce' between them as would have filled Morrison's suitcase. Amid general rejoicings, he would land the rice all the same, explain to the people that it was an advance, that they were in debt to him now; would preach to them energy and industry, and make an elaborate note in a pocket-diary which he always carried; and this would be the end of that transaction. I don't know if Morrison thought so, but the villagers had no doubt whatever about it. Whenever a coast village sighted the brig it would begin to beat all its gongs and hoist all its streamers, and all its girls would put flowers in their hair and the crowd would line the river bank, and Morrison would beam and glitter at all this excitement through his single eyeglass with an air of intense gratification. He was tall and lantern-jawed, and clean-shaven, and looked like a barrister who had thrown his wig to the dogs.

We used to remonstrate with him:

'You will never see any of your advances if you go on like this, Morrison.'

He would put on a knowing air.

'I shall squeeze them yet some day – never you fear. And that reminds me' – pulling out his inseparable pocketbook – 'there's that So-and-So village. They are pretty well off again; I may just as well squeeze them to begin with.'

He would make a ferocious entry in the pocketbook.

Memo: Squeeze the So-and-So village at the first time of calling. Then he would stick the pencil back and snap the elastic on with inflexible finality; but he never began the squeezing. Some men grumbled at him. He was spoiling the trade. Well, perhaps to a certain extent; not much. Most of the places he traded with were unknown not only to geography but also to the traders' special lore which is transmitted by word of mouth, without ostentation, and forms the stock of mysterious local knowledge. It was hinted also that Morrison had a wife in each and every one of them, but the majority of us repulsed these innuendoes with indignation. He was a true humanitarian and rather ascetic than otherwise.

When Heyst met him in Delli, Morrison was walking along the street, his eyeglass tossed over his shoulder, his head down, with the hopeless aspect of those hardened tramps one sees on our roads trudging from workhouse to workhouse. Being hailed across the street he looked up with a wild worried expression. He was really in trouble. He had come the week before into Delli, and the Portuguese authorities, on some pretence of irregularity in his papers, had inflicted a fine upon him and had arrested his brig.

Morrison never had any spare cash in hand. With his system of trading it would have been strange if he had; and all these debts entered in the pocketbook weren't good enough to raise a *millrei* on – let alone a shilling. The Portuguese officials begged him not to distress himself. They gave him a week's grace, and then proposed to sell the brig at auction. This meant ruin for Morrison; and when Heyst hailed him across the street in his usual courtly tone, the week was nearly out.

Heyst crossed over, and said with a slight bow, and in the manner of a prince addressing another prince on a private occasion:

'What an unexpected pleasure. Would you have any objection to drink something with me in that infamous wine-shop over there? The sun is really too strong to talk in the street.'

The haggard Morrison followed obediently into a sombre, cool hovel which he would have disdained to enter at any other time. He was distracted. He did not know what he was doing. You could have led him over the edge of a precipice just as easily as into that wine-shop. He sat down like an automaton. He was speechless, but he saw a glass full of rough red wine before him, and emptied it. Heyst meantime, politely watchful, had taken a seat opposite.

'You are in for a bout of fever, I fear,' he said sympathetically.

Poor Morrison's tongue was loosened at that.

'Fever!' he cried. 'Give me fever. Give me plague. They are diseases. One gets over them. But I am being murdered. I am being murdered by the Portuguese. The gang here downed me at last among them. I am to have my throat cut the day after tomorrow.'

In the face of this passion Heyst made, with his eyebrows, a slight motion of surprise which would not have been misplaced in a drawing-room. Morrison's despairing reserve had broken down. He had been wandering with a dry throat all over that miserable town of mud hovels, silent, with no soul to turn to in his distress, and positively maddened by his thoughts; and suddenly he had stumbled on a white man, figuratively and actually white – for Morrison refused to accept the racial whiteness of the Portuguese officials. He let himself go for the mere relief of violent speech, his elbows planted on the table, his eyes bloodshot, his voice nearly gone, the brim of his round pith hat shading an unshaven, livid face. His white clothes, which he had not taken off for three days, were dingy. He had already gone to the bad, past redemption. The sight was shocking to Heyst; but he let nothing of it appear in his bearing, concealing his impression under that consummate good-society manner of his. Polite attention, what's due from one gentleman listening to another, was what he showed; and, as usual, it was catching; so that Morrison pulled himself together and finished his narrative in a conversational tone, with a man-of-the-world air.

'It's a villainous plot. Unluckily, one is helpless. That scoundrel Cousinho – Andreas, you know – has been coveting the brig for years. Naturally, I would never sell. She is not only my livelihood; she's my life. So he has hatched this pretty little plot with the chief of the customs. The sale, of course, will be a farce. There's no one here to bid. He will get the brig for a song – no, not even that – a line of a song. You have been some years now in the island, Heyst. You know us all; you have seen how we live. Now you shall have the opportunity to see how some of us end; for it is the end, for me. I can't deceive myself any longer. You see it – don't you?'

Morrison had pulled himself together, but one felt the snapping strain on his recovered self-possession. Heyst was beginning to say that he 'could very well see all the bearings of this unfortunate –' when Morrison interrupted him jerkily.

'Upon my word, I don't know why I have been telling you all this. I suppose seeing a thoroughly white man made it impossible to keep my trouble to myself. Words can't do it justice; but since I've told you so much I may as well tell you more. Listen. This morning on board, in my cabin I went down on my knees and prayed for help. I went down on my knees!'

'You are a believer, Morrison?' asked Heyst with a distinct note of respect.

'Surely I am not an infidel.'

Morrison was swiftly reproachful in his answer, and there came a pause, Morrison perhaps interrogating his conscience, and Heyst preserving a mien of unperturbed, polite interest.

'I prayed like a child, of course. I believe in children praying – well, women, too, but I rather think God expects men to be more self-reliant. I don't hold with a man everlastingly bothering the Almighty with his silly troubles. It seems such cheek. Anyhow, this morning I – I have never done any harm to any God's creature knowingly – I prayed. A sudden impulse – I went flop on my knees; so you may judge –'

They were gazing earnestly into each other's eyes. Poor Morrison added, as a discouraging afterthought:

'Only this is such a God-forsaken spot.'

Heyst inquired with a delicate intonation whether he might know the amount for which the brig was seized.

Morrison suppressed an oath, and named curtly a sum which was in itself so insignificant that any other person than Heyst would have exclaimed at it. And even Heyst could hardly keep incredulity out of his politely modulated voice as he asked if it was a fact that Morrison had not that amount in hand.

Morrison hadn't. He had only a little English gold, a few sovereigns, on board. He had left all his spare cash with the Tesmans, in Samarang, to meet certain bills which would fall due while he was away on his cruise. Anyhow, that money would not have been any more good to him than if it had been in the innermost depths of the infernal regions. He said all this brusquely. He looked with sudden disfavour at that noble forehead, at those great martial moustaches, at the tired eyes of the man sitting opposite him. Who the devil was he? What was he, Morrison, doing there, talking like this? Morrison knew no more of Heyst than the rest of us trading in the Archipelago did. Had the Swede suddenly risen and hit him on the nose, he could not have been taken more aback than when this stranger, this nondescript wanderer, said with a little bow across the table:

'Oh! If that's the case I would be very happy if you'd allow me to be of use!'

Morrison didn't understand. This was one of those things that don't happen – unheard of things. He had no real inkling of what it meant, till Heyst said definitely:

'I can lend you the amount.'

'You have the money?' whispered Morrison. 'Do you mean here, in your pocket?'

'Yes, on me. Glad to be of use.'

Morrison, staring open-mouthed, groped over his shoulder for the cord of the eyeglass hanging down his back. When he found it, he stuck it in his eye hastily. It was as if he expected Heyst's usual white suit of the tropics to change into a shining garment flowing down to his toes, and a pair of great dazzling wings to sprout on the Swede's shoulders – and didn't want to miss a single detail of the transformation. But if Heyst was an angel from on high, sent in answer to prayer, he did not betray his heavenly origin by outward signs. So, instead of going on his knees, as he felt inclined to do, Morrison stretched out his hand, which Heyst grasped with formal alacrity and a polite murmur in which 'Trifle – delighted – of service,' could just be distinguished.

'Miracles do happen,' thought the awestruck Morrison. To him, as to all of us in the islands, this wandering Heyst, who didn't toil or spin visibly, seemed the very last person to be the agent of Providence in an affair concerned with money. The fact of his turning up in Timor or anywhere else was no more wonderful than the settling of a sparrow on one's window-sill at any given moment. But that he should carry a sum of money in his pocket seemed somehow inconceivable.

So inconceivable that as they were trudging together through the sand of the roadway to the custom-house – another mud hovel – to pay the fine, Morrison broke into a cold sweat, stopped short, and exclaimed in faltering accents:

'I say! You aren't joking, Heyst?'

'Joking!' Heyst's blue eyes went hard as he turned them on the discomposed Morrison. 'In what way, may I ask?' he continued with austere politeness.

Morrison was abashed.

'Forgive me, Heyst. You must have been sent by God in answer to my prayer. But I have been nearly off my chump for three days with worry; and it suddenly struck me: "What if it's the Devil who has sent him?" '

'I have no connection with the supernatural,' said Heyst graciously, moving on. 'Nobody has sent me. I just happened along.'

'I know better,' contradicted Morrison. 'I may be unworthy, but I have been heard. I know it. I feel it. For why should you offer –'

Heyst inclined his head, as from respect for a conviction in which he could not share. But he stuck to his point by muttering that in the presence of an odious fact like this, it was natural –

Later in the day, the fine paid, and the two of them on board the brig, from which the guard had been removed, Morrison – who, besides being a gentleman, was also an honest fellow – began to talk about repayment. He knew very well his inability to lay by any sum of money. It was partly the fault of circumstances and partly of his temperament; and it would have been very difficult to apportion the responsibility between the two. Even Morrison himself could not say, while confessing to the fact. With a worried air he ascribed it to fatality.

'I don't know how it is that I've never been able to save. It's some sort of curse. There's always a bill or two to meet.'

He plunged his hand into his pocket for the famous notebook so well known in the islands, the fetish of his hopes, and fluttered the pages feverishly.

'And yet – look,' he went on. 'There it is – more than five thousand dollars owing. Surely that's something.'

He ceased suddenly. Heyst, who had been all the time trying to look as unconcerned as he could, made reassuring noises in his throat. But Morrison was not only honest. He was honourable, too; and on this stressful day, before this amazing emissary of Providence and in the revulsion of his feelings, he made his great renunciation. He cast off the abiding illusion of his existence.

'No. No. They are no good. I'll never be able to squeeze them. Never. I've been saying for years I would; but I give it up. I never really believed I could. Don't reckon on that, Heyst. I have robbed you.'

Poor Morrison actually laid his head on the cabin table, and remained in that crushed attitude while Heyst talked to him soothingly with the utmost courtesy. The Swede was as much distressed as Morrison; for he understood the other's feelings perfectly. No decent feeling was ever scorned by Heyst. But he was incapable of outward cordiality of manner, and he felt acutely his defect. Consummate politeness is not the right tonic for an emotional collapse. They must have had, both of them, a fairly painful time of it in the cabin of the brig. In the end Morrison, casting desperately for an idea in the blackness of his despondency, hit upon the notion of inviting Heyst to travel with him in his brig and have a share in his trading ventures up to the amount of his loan.

It is characteristic of Heyst's unattached, floating existence that he was in a position to accept that proposal. There is no reason to think that he wanted particularly just then to go poking aboard the brig into all the holes and corners of the Archipelago where Morrison picked up most of his trade. Far from it; but he would have consented to almost any arrangement in order to put an end to the harrowing scene in the cabin. There was at once a great transformation act: Morrison raising his diminished head and sticking the glass in his eye to look affectionately at Heyst, a bottle being uncorked, and so on. It was agreed that nothing should be said to anyone of this transaction. Morrison, you understand, was not proud of the episode, and he was afraid of being unmercifully chaffed.

'An old bird like me! To let myself be trapped by those damned Portuguese rascals! I should never hear the last of it. We must keep it dark.'

From quite other motives, among which his native delicacy was the principal, Heyst was even more anxious to bind himself to silence. A gentleman would naturally shrink from the part of heavenly messenger that Morrison would force upon him. It made Heyst uncomfortable, as it was. And perhaps he did not care that it should be known that he had some means, whatever they might have been – sufficient, at any rate, to enable him to lend money to people. These two had a duet down there, like conspirators in a comic opera, of 'Sh – ssh, shssh! Secrecy! Secrecy!' It must have been funny, because they were very serious about it.

And for a time the conspiracy was successful in so far that we all concluded that Heyst was boarding with the good-natured – some said: sponging on the imbecile – Morrison, in his brig. But you know how it is with all such mysteries. There is always a leak somewhere. Morrison himself, not a perfect vessel by any means, was bursting with gratitude, and under the stress he must have let out something vague – enough to give the island gossip a chance. And you know how kindly the world is in its comments on what it does not understand. A rumour sprang out that Heyst, having obtained some mysterious hold on Morrison, had fastened himself on him and was sucking him dry. Those who had traced these mutters back to their origin were very careful not to believe them. The originator, it seems, was a certain Schomberg, a big, manly, bearded creature of the Teutonic persuasion, with an ungovernable tongue which surely must have worked on a pivot. Whether he was a Lieutenant of the Reserve, as he declared, I don't know. Out there he was by profession a hotel-keeper, first in Bangkok, then somewhere else, and ultimately in Sourabaya. He dragged after him up and down that section of the tropical belt a silent, frightened, little woman with long ringlets, who smiled at one stupidly, showing a blue tooth. I don't know why so many of us patronized his various establishments. He was a noxious ass, and he satisfied his lust for silly gossip at the cost of his customers. It was he who, one evening, as Morrison and Heyst went past the hotel – they were not his regular patrons – whispered mysteriously to the mixed company assembled on the veranda:

'The spider and the fly just gone by, gentlemen.' Then, very important and confidential, his thick paw at the side of his mouth: 'We are among ourselves; well, gentlemen, all I can say is, don't you ever get mixed up with that Swede. Don't you ever get caught in his web.'

Chapter III

Human nature being what it is, having a silly side to it as well as a mean side, there were not a few who pretended to be indignant on no better authority than a general propensity to believe every evil report; and a good many others who found it simply funny to call Heyst the Spider – behind his back, of course. He was as serenely unconscious of this as of his several other nicknames. But soon people found other things to say of Heyst; not long afterward he came very much to the fore in larger affairs. He blossomed out into something definite. He filled the public eye as the manager on the spot of the Tropical Belt Coal Company with offices in London and Amsterdam, and other things about it that sounded and looked grandiose. The offices in the two capitals may have consisted – and probably did – of one room in each; but at that distance, out East there, all this had an air. We were more puzzled than dazzled, it is true; but even the most sober-minded among us began to think that there was something in it. The Tesmans appointed agents, a contract for government mail-boats secured, the era of steam beginning for the islands – a great stride forward – Heyst's stride!

And all this sprang from the meeting of the concerned Morrison and of the wandering Heyst, which may or may not have been the direct outcome of a prayer. Morrison was not an imbecile, but he seemed to have got himself into a state of remarkable haziness as to his exact position towards Heyst. For, if Heyst had been sent with money in his pocket by a direct decree of the Almighty in answer to Morrison's prayer then there was no reason for special gratitude, since obviously he could not help himself. But Morrison believed both in the efficacy of prayer and in the infinite goodness of Heyst. He thanked God with awed sincerity for His mercy, and could not thank Heyst enough for the service rendered as between man and man. In this (highly creditable) tangle of strong feelings Morrison's gratitude insisted on Heyst's partnership in the great discovery. Ultimately we heard that Morrison had gone home through the Suez Canal in order to push the magnificent coal idea personally in London. He parted from his brig and disappeared from our ken; but we heard that he had written a letter or letters to Heyst, saying that London was cold and gloomy; that he did not like either the men or things, that he was 'as lonely as a crow in a strange country'. In truth, he pined after the *Capricorn* – I don't mean only the tropic; I mean the ship too. Finally he went into Dorsetshire to see his people, caught a bad cold, and died with extraordinary precipitation in the bosom of his appalled family. Whether his exertions in the City of London had enfeebled his vitality I don't know; but I believe it was this visit which put life into the coal idea. Be it as it may, the Tropical Belt Coal Company was born very shortly after Morrison, the victim of gratitude and his native climate, had gone to join his forefathers in a Dorsetshire churchyard.

Heyst was immensely shocked. He got the news in the Moluccas through the Tesmans, and then disappeared for a time. It appears that he stayed with a Dutch government doctor in Amboyna, a friend of his who looked after him for a bit in his bungalow. He became visible again rather suddenly, his eyes sunk in his head, and with a sort of guarded attitude, as if afraid someone would reproach him with the death of Morrison.

Naïve Heyst! As if anybody would. . . . Nobody amongst us had any interest in men who went home. They were all right; they did not count any more. Going to Europe was nearly as final as going to Heaven. It removed a man from the world of hazard and adventure.

As a matter of fact, many of us did not hear of this death till months afterward – from Schomberg, who disliked Heyst gratuitously and made up a piece of sinister whispered gossip:

'That's what comes of having anything to do with that fellow. He squeezes you dry like a lemon, then chucks you out – sends you home to die. Take warning by Morrison.'

Of course, we laughed at the innkeeper's suggestions of black mystery. Several of us heard that Heyst was prepared to go to Europe himself, to push on his coal enterprise personally; but he never went. It wasn't necessary. The company was formed without him, and his nomination of manager in the tropics came out to him by post.

From the first he had selected Samburan, or Round Island, for the central station. Some copies of the prospectus issued in Europe, having found their way out East, were passed from hand to hand. We greatly admired the map which accompanied them for the edification of the shareholders. On it Samburan was represented as the central spot of the Eastern Hemisphere with its name engraved in enormous capitals. Heavy lines radiated from it in all directions through the tropics, figuring a mysterious and effective star – lines of influence or lines of distance, or something of that sort. Company promoters have an imagination of their own. There's no more romantic temperament on earth than the temperament of a company promoter. Engineers came out, coolies were imported, bungalows were put up on Samburan, a gallery driven into the hillside, and actually some coal got out.

These manifestations shook the soberest minds. For a time everybody in the islands was talking of the Tropical Belt Coal, and even those who smiled quietly to themselves were only hiding their uneasiness. Oh, yes; it had come, and anybody could see what would be the consequences – the end of the individual trader, smothered under a great invasion of steamers. We could not afford to buy steamers. Not we. And Heyst was the manager.

'You know, Heyst, enchanted Heyst.'

'Oh, come! He has been no better than a loafer around here as far back as any of us can remember.'

'Yes, he said he was looking for facts. Well, he's got hold of one that will do for all of us,' commented a bitter voice.

'That's what they call development – and be hanged to it!' muttered another.

Never was Heyst talked about so much in the tropical belt before.

'Isn't he a Swedish baron or something?'

'He, a baron? Get along with you!'

For my part I haven't the slightest doubt that he was. While he was still drifting amongst the islands, enigmatical and disregarded like an insignificant ghost, he told me so himself on a certain occasion. It was a long time before he materialized in this alarming way into the destroyer of our little industry – Heyst the Enemy.

It became the fashion with a good many to speak of Heyst as the Enemy. He was very concrete, very visible now. He was rushing all over the Archipelago, jumping in and out of local mail-packets as if they had been tram-cars, here, there, and everywhere – organizing with all his might. This was no mooning about. This was business. And this sudden display of purposeful energy shook the incredulity of the most sceptical more than any scientific demonstration of the value of these coal-outcrops could have done. It was impressive. Schomberg was the only one who resisted the infection. Big, manly in a portly style, and profusely bearded, with a glass of beer in his thick paw, he would approach some table where the topic of the hour was being discussed, would listen for a moment, and then come out with his invariable declaration:

'All this is very well, gentlemen; but he can't throw any of his coal-dust in my eyes. There's nothing in it. Why, there can't be anything in it. A fellow like that for manager? Phoo!'

Was it the clairvoyance of imbecile hatred, or mere stupid tenacity of opinion, which ends sometimes by scoring against the world in a most astonishing manner? Most of us can remember instances of triumphant folly; and that ass Schomberg triumphed. The T.B.C. Company went into liquidation, as I began by telling you. The Tesmans washed their hands of it. The Government cancelled those famous contracts, the talk died out, and presently it was remarked here and there that Heyst had faded completely away. He had become invisible, as in those early days when he used to make a bolt clear out of sight in his attempts to break away from the enchantment of 'these isles', either in the direction of New Guinea or in the direction of Saigon – to cannibals or to cafés. The enchanted Heyst! Had he at last broken the spell? Had he died? We were too indifferent to wonder over-much. You see we had on the whole liked him well enough. And liking is not sufficient to keep going the interest one takes in a human being. With hatred, apparently, it is otherwise. Schomberg couldn't forget Heyst. The keen, manly Teutonic creature was a good hater. A fool often is.

'Good evening, gentlemen. Have you got everything you want? So! Good! You see? What was I always telling you? Aha! There was nothing in it. I knew it. But what I would like to know is what became of that – Swede.'

He put a stress on the word Swede as if it meant scoundrel. He detested Scandinavians generally. Why? Goodness only knows. A fool like that is unfathomable. He continued:

'It's five months or more since I have spoken to anybody who has seen him.'

As I have said, we were not much interested; but Schomberg, of course, could not understand that. He was grotesquely dense. Whenever three people came together in his hotel, he took good care that Heyst should be with them.

'I hope the fellow did not go and drown himself,' he would add with a comical earnestness that ought to have made us shudder; only our crowd was superficial, and did not apprehend the psychology of this pious hope.

'Why? Heyst isn't in debt to you for drinks, is he?' somebody asked him once with shallow scorn.

'Drinks! Oh, dear no!'

The innkeeper was not mercenary. Teutonic temperament seldom is. But he put on a sinister expression to tell us that Heyst had not paid perhaps three visits altogether to his 'establishment'. This was Heyst's crime, for which Schomberg wished him nothing less than a long and tormented existence. Observe the Teutonic sense of proportion and nice forgiving temper.

At last, one afternoon, Schomberg was seen approaching a group of his customers. He was obviously in high glee. He squared his manly chest with great importance.

'Gentlemen, I have news of him. Who? Why, that Swede. He is still on Samburan. He's never been away from it. The company is gone, the engineers are gone, the clerks are gone, the coolies are gone, everything's gone; but there he sticks. Captain Davidson, coming by from the westward, saw him with his own eyes. Something white on the wharf; so he steamed in and went ashore in a small boat. Heyst, right enough. Put a book into his pocket, always very polite. Been strolling on the wharf and reading. "I remain in possession here," he told Captain Davidson. What I want to know is what he gets to eat there. A piece of dried fish now and then – what? That's coming down pretty low for a man who turned up his nose at my table d'hôte!'

He winked with immense malice. A bell started ringing, and he led the way to the dining-room as if into a temple, very grave, with the air of a benefactor of mankind. His ambition was to feed it at a profitable price, and his delight was to talk of it behind its back. It was very characteristic of him to gloat over the idea of Heyst having nothing decent to eat.

Chapter IV

A few of us who were sufficiently interested went to Davidson for details. These were not many. He told us that he passed to the north of Samburan on purpose to see what was going on. At first, it looked as if that side of the island had been altogether abandoned. This was what he expected. Presently, above the dense mass of vegetation that Samburan presents to view, he saw the head of the flagstaff without a flag. Then, while steaming across the slight indentation which for a time was known officially as Black Diamond Bay, he made out with his glass the white figure on the coaling-wharf. It could be no one but Heyst.

'I thought for certain he wanted to be taken off, so I steamed in. He made no signs. However, I lowered a boat. I could not see another living being anywhere. Yes. He had a book in his hand. He looked exactly as we have always seen him – very neat, white shoes, cork helmet. He explained to me that he had always had a taste for solitude. It was the first I ever heard of it, I told him. He only smiled. What could I say? He isn't the sort of man one can speak familiarly to. There's something in him. One doesn't care to.

' "But what's the object? Are you thinking of keeping possession of the mine?" I asked him.

' "Something of the sort," he says. "I am keeping hold."

‘ “But all this is as dead as Julius Caesar,” I cried. “In fact, you have nothing worth holding on to, Heyst.”

‘ “Oh, I am done with facts,” says he, putting his hand to his helmet sharply with one of his short bows.’

Thus dismissed, Davidson went on board his ship, swung her out, and as he was steaming away he watched from the bridge Heyst walking shoreward along the wharf. He marched into the long grass and vanished – all but the top of his white cork helmet, which seemed to swim in a green sea. Then that too disappeared, as if it had sunk into the living depths of the tropical vegetation, which is more jealous of men’s conquests than the ocean, and which was about to close over the last vestiges of the liquidated Tropical Belt Coal Company – A. Heyst, manager in the East.

Davidson, a good, simple fellow in his way, was strangely affected. It is to be noted that he knew very little of Heyst. He was one of those whom Heyst’s finished courtesy of attitude and intonation most strongly disconcerted. He himself was a fellow of fine feeling, I think, though of course he had no more polish than the rest of us. We were naturally a hail-fellow-well-met crowd, with standards of our own – no worse, I daresay, than other people’s; but polish was not one of them. Davidson’s fineness was real enough to alter the course of the steamer he commanded. Instead of passing to the south of Samburan, he made it his practice to take the passage along the north shore, within about a mile of the wharf.

‘He can see us if he likes to see us,’ remarked Davidson. Then he had an afterthought: ‘I say! I hope he won’t think I am intruding, eh?’

We reassured him on the point of correct behaviour. The sea is open to all.

This slight deviation added some ten miles to Davidson’s round trip, but as that was sixteen hundred miles it did not matter much.

‘I have told my owner of it,’ said the conscientious commander of the *Sissie*.

His owner had a face like an ancient lemon. He was small and wizened – which was strange, because generally a Chinaman, as he grows in prosperity, puts on inches of girth and stature. To serve a Chinese firm is not so bad. Once they become convinced you deal straight by them, their confidence becomes unlimited. You can do no wrong. So Davidson’s old Chinaman squeaked hurriedly:

‘All right, all right, all right. You do what you like, captain.’

And there was an end of the matter; not altogether, though. From time to time the Chinaman used to ask Davidson about the white man. He was still there, eh?

‘I never see him,’ Davidson had to confess to his owner, who would peer at him silently through round, horn-rimmed spectacles, several sizes too large for his little old face. ‘I never see him.’

To me, on occasions, he would say:

‘I haven’t a doubt he’s there. He hides. It’s very unpleasant.’ Davidson was a little vexed with Heyst. ‘Funny thing,’ he went on. ‘Of all the people I speak to, nobody ever asks after him but that Chinaman of mine – and Schomberg,’ he added after a while.

Yes, Schomberg, of course. He was asking everybody about everything, and arranging the information into the most scandalous shape his imagination could invent. From time to time he would step up, his blinking, cushioned eyes, his thick lips, his very chestnut beard, looking full of malice.

' 'Evening, gentlemen. Have you got all you want? So! Good! Well, I am told the jungle has choked the very sheds in Black Diamond Bay. Fact. He's a hermit in the wilderness now. But what can this manager get to eat there? It beats me.'

Sometimes a stranger would inquire with natural curiosity:

'Who? What manager?'

'Oh, a certain Swede,' – with a sinister emphasis, as if he were saying 'a certain brigand'. 'Well known here. He's turned hermit from shame. That's what the devil does when he's found out.'

Hermit. This was the latest of the more or less witty labels applied to Heyst during his aimless pilgrimage in this section of the tropical belt, where the inane clacking of Schomberg's tongue vexed our ears.

But apparently Heyst was not a hermit by temperament. The sight of his kind was not invincibly odious to him. We must believe this, since for some reason or other he did come out from his retreat for a while. Perhaps it was only to see whether there were any letters for him at the Tesmans. I don't know. No one knows. But this reappearance shows that his detachment from the world was not complete. And incompleteness of any sort leads to trouble. Axel Heyst ought not to have cared for his letters – or whatever it was that brought him out after something more than a year and a half in Samburan. But it was of no use. He had not the hermit's vocation! That was the trouble, it seems.

Be this as it may, he suddenly reappeared in the world, broad chest, bald forehead, long moustaches, polite manner, and all – the complete Heyst, even to the kindly sunken eyes on which there still rested the shadow of Morrison's death. Naturally, it was Davidson who had given him a lift out of his forsaken island. There were no other opportunities, unless some native craft were passing by – a very remote and unsatisfactory chance to wait for. Yes, he came out with Davidson, to whom he volunteered the statement that it was only for a short time – a few days, no more. He meant to go back to Samburan.

Davidson expressing his horror and incredulity of such foolishness, Heyst explained that when the company came into being he had his few belongings sent out from Europe.

To Davidson as to any of us, the idea of Heyst, the wandering, drifting, unattached Heyst, having any belongings of the sort that can furnish a house was startlingly novel. It was grotesquely fantastic. It was like a bird owning real property.

'Belongings? Do you mean chairs and tables?' Davidson asked with unconcealed astonishment.

Heyst did mean that. 'My poor father died in London. It has been all stored there ever since,' he explained.

'For all these years?' exclaimed Davidson, thinking how long we all had known Heyst flitting from tree to tree in a wilderness.

'Even longer,' said Heyst, who had understood very well.

This seemed to imply that he had been wandering before he came under our observation. In what regions? At what early age? Mystery. Perhaps he was a bird that had never had a nest.

'I left school early,' he remarked once to Davidson, on the passage. 'It was in England. A very good school. I was not a shining success there.'

The confessions of Heyst. Not one of us – with the probable exception of Morrison, who was dead – had ever heard so much of his history. It looks as if the experience of hermit life had the power to loosen one's tongue, doesn't it?

During that memorable passage, in the *Sissie*, which took about two days, he volunteered other hints – for you could not call it information – about his history. And Davidson was interested. He was interested not because the hints were exciting but because of that innate curiosity about our fellows which is a trait of human nature. Davidson's existence, too, running the *Sissie* along the Java Sea and back again, was distinctly monotonous and, in a sense, lonely. He never had any sort of company on board. Native deck-passengers in plenty, of course, but never a white man, so the presence of Heyst for two days must have been a godsend. Davidson was telling us all about it afterward. Heyst said that his father had written a lot of books. He was a philosopher.

'Seems to me he must have been something of a crank, too,' was Davidson's comment. 'Apparently he had quarrelled with his people in Sweden. Just the sort of father you would expect Heyst to have. Isn't he a bit of a crank himself? He told me that directly his father died he lit out into the wide world on his own, and had been on the move till he fetched up against this famous coal business. Fits the son of the father somehow, don't you think?'

For the rest, Heyst was as polite as ever. He offered to pay for his passage; but when Davidson refused to hear of it he seized him heartily by the hand, gave one of his courtly bows, and declared that he was touched by his friendly proceedings.

'I am not alluding to this trifling amount which you decline to take,' he went on, giving a shake to Davidson's hand. 'But I am touched by your humanity.' Another shake. 'Believe me, I am profoundly aware of having been an object of it.' Final shake of the hand. All this meant that Heyst understood in a proper sense the little *Sissie's* periodic appearance in sight of his hermitage.

'He's a genuine gentleman,' Davidson said to us. 'I was really sorry when he went ashore.'

We asked him where he had left Heyst.

'Why, in Sourabaya – where else?'

The Tesmans had their principal counting-house in Sourabaya. There had long existed a connection between Heyst and the Tesmans. The incongruity of a hermit having agents did not strike us, nor yet the absurdity of a forgotten cast-off, derelict manager of a wrecked, collapsed, vanished enterprise, having business to attend to. We said Sourabaya, of course, and took it for granted that he would stay with one of the Tesmans. One of us even wondered what sort of reception he would get; for it was known that Julius Tesman was unreasonably bitter about the Tropical Belt Coal fiasco. But Davidson set us right. It was nothing of the kind. Heyst went to stay in Schomberg's hotel, going ashore in the hotel launch. Not that Schomberg would think of sending his launch alongside a mere trader like the *Sissie*. But she had been meeting a coastal mail-packet, and had been signalled to. Schomberg himself was steering her.

'You should have seen Schomberg's eyes bulge out when Heyst jumped in with an ancient brown leather bag!' said Davidson. 'He pretended not to know who it was – at first, anyway. I didn't go ashore with them. We didn't stay more than a couple of hours altogether. Landed two thousand coconuts and cleared out. I have agreed to pick him up again on my next trip in twenty days' time.'

CHAPTER V

DAVIDSON HAPPENED to be two days late on his return trip; no great matter, certainly, but he made a point of going ashore at once, during the hottest hour of the afternoon, to look for Heyst. Schomberg's hotel stood back in an extensive enclosure containing a garden, some large trees, and, under their spreading boughs, a detached 'hall available for concerts and other performances', as Schomberg worded it in his advertisements. Torn and fluttering bills, intimating in heavy red capitals CONCERTS EVERY NIGHT, were stuck on the brick pillars on each side of the gateway.

The walk had been long and confoundedly sunny. Davidson stood wiping his wet neck and face on what Schomberg called 'the piazza'. Several doors opened on to it, but all the screens were down. Not a soul was in sight, not even a China boy – nothing but a lot of painted iron chairs and tables. Solitude, shade, and gloomy silence – and a faint, treacherous breeze which came from under the trees and quite unexpectedly caused the melting Davidson to shiver slightly – the little shiver of the tropics which in Sourabaya, especially, often means fever and the hospital to the incautious white man.

The prudent Davidson sought shelter in the nearest darkened room. In the artificial dusk, beyond the levels of shrouded billiard-tables, a white form heaved up from two chairs on which it had been extended. The middle of the day, table d'hôte tiffin once over, was Schomberg's easy time. He lounged out, portly, deliberate, on the defensive, the great fair beard like a cuirass over his manly chest. He did not like Davidson, never a very faithful client of his. He hit a bell on one of the tables as he went by, and asked in a distant, Office-in-Reserve manner:

'You desire?'

The good Davidson, still sponging his wet neck, declared with simplicity that he had come to fetch away Heyst, as agreed.

'Not here!'

A Chinaman appeared in response to the bell. Schomberg turned to him very severely:

'Take the gentleman's order.'

Davidson had to be going. Couldn't wait – only begged that Heyst should be informed that the *Sissie* would leave at midnight.

'Not – here, I am telling you!'

Davidson slapped his thigh in concern.

'Dear me! Hospital, I suppose.' A natural enough surmise in a very feverish locality.

The Lieutenant of the Reserve only pursed up his mouth and raised his eyebrows without looking at him. It might have meant anything, but Davidson dismissed the hospital idea with confidence. However, he had to get hold of Heyst between this and midnight.

'He has been staying here?' he asked.

'Yes, he was staying here.'

'Can you tell me where he is now?' Davidson went on placidly. Within himself he was beginning to grow anxious, having developed the affection of a self-appointed protector towards Heyst. The answer he got was:

'Can't tell. It's none of my business,' accompanied by majestic oscillations of the hotel-keeper's head, hinting at some awful mystery.

Davidson was placidity itself. It was his nature. He did not betray his sentiments, which were not favourable to Schomberg.

'I am sure to find out at the Tesman's office,' he thought. But it was a very hot hour, and if Heyst was down at the port he would have learned already that the *Sissie* was in. It was even possible that Heyst had already gone on board, where he could enjoy a coolness denied to the town. Davidson, being stout, was much preoccupied with coolness and inclined to immobility. He lingered awhile, as if irresolute. Schomberg, at the door, looking out, affected perfect indifference. He could not keep it up, though. Suddenly he turned inward and asked with brusque rage:

'You wanted to see him?'

'Why, yes,' said Davidson. 'We agreed to meet –'

'Don't you bother. He doesn't care about that now.'

'Doesn't he?'

'Well, you can judge for yourself. He isn't here, is he? You take my word for it. Don't you bother about him. I am advising you as a friend.'

'Thank you,' said Davidson, inwardly startled at the savage tone. 'I think I will sit down for a moment and have a drink, after all.'

This was not what Schomberg had expected to hear. He called brutally:

'Boy!'

The Chinaman approached, and after referring him to the white man by a nod the hotel-keeper departed, muttering to himself. Davidson heard him gnash his teeth as he went.

Davidson sat alone with the billiard-tables as if there had been not a soul staying in the hotel. His placidity was so genuine that he was not unduly fretting himself over the absence of Heyst or the mysterious manners Schomberg had treated him to. He was considering these things in his own fairly shrewd way. Something had happened; and he was loath to go away to investigate, being restrained by a presentiment that somehow enlightenment would come to him there. A poster of CONCERTS EVERY EVENING, like those on the gate, but in a good state of preservation, hung on the wall fronting him. He looked at it idly and was struck by the fact – then not so very common – that it was a ladies' orchestra; 'Zangiacomo's eastern tour – eighteen performers'. The poster stated that they had had the honour of playing their select repertoire before various colonial excellencies, also before pashas, sheiks, chiefs, H. H. the Sultan of Mascate, etc., etc.

Davidson felt sorry for the eighteen lady-performers. He knew what that sort of life was like, the sordid conditions and brutal incidents of such tours led by such Zangiacomos who often were anything but musicians by profession. While he was staring at the poster, a door somewhere at his back opened, and a woman came in who was looked upon as Schomberg's wife, no doubt with truth. As somebody remarked cynically once, she was too unattractive to be anything else. The opinion that he treated her abominably was based on her frightened expression. Davidson lifted his hat to her. Mrs Schomberg gave him an inclination of her sallow head and incontinently sat down behind a sort of raised counter, facing the door, with a mirror and rows of bottles at her back. Her hair was very elaborately done with two ringlets on the left side of her scraggy neck; her dress was of silk, and she had come on duty for the afternoon. For some reason or other Schomberg exacted this from her, though she added nothing to the fascinations of the place. She sat there in the smoke and noise, like an enthroned idol, smiling stupidly over the billiards from time to time, speaking to no one, and no one speaking to her. Schomberg himself took no more interest in her than may be implied in a sudden and totally unmotived scowl. Otherwise the very Chinamen ignored her existence.

She had interrupted Davidson in his reflections. Being alone with her, her silence and open-mouthed immobility made him uncomfortable. He was easily sorry for people. It seemed rude not to take any notice of her. He said, in allusion to the poster: 'Are you having these people in the house?'

She was so unused to being addressed by customers that at the sound of his voice she jumped in her seat. Davidson was telling us afterward that she jumped exactly like a figure made of wood, without losing her rigid immobility. She did not even move her eyes; but she answered him freely, though her very lips seemed made of wood.

'They stayed here over a month. They are gone now. They played every evening.'

'Pretty good, were they?'

To this she said nothing; and as she kept on staring fixedly in front of her, her silence disconcerted Davidson. It looked as if she had not heard him – which was impossible. Perhaps she drew the line of speech at the expression of opinions. Schomberg might have trained her, for domestic reasons, to keep them to herself. But Davidson felt in honour obliged to converse; so he said, putting his own interpretation on this surprising silence:

'I see – not much account. Such bands hardly ever are. An Italian lot, Mrs Schomberg, to judge by the name of the boss?'

She shook her head negatively.

'No. He is a German really; only he dyes his hair and beard black for business. Zangiacomo is his business name.'

'That's a curious fact,' said Davidson. His head being full of Heyst, it occurred to him that she might be aware of other facts. This was a very amazing discovery to anyone who looked at Mrs Schomberg. Nobody had ever suspected her of having a mind. I mean even a little of it, I mean any at all. One was inclined to think of her as an It – an automaton, a very plain dummy, with an arrangement for bowing the head at times and smiling stupidly now and then. Davidson viewed her profile with a flattened nose, a hollow cheek, and one staring, unwinking, goggle eye. He asked himself: Did that speak just now? Will it speak again? It was as exciting, for the mere wonder of it, as trying to converse with a mechanism. A smile played about the fat features of Davidson; the smile of a man making an amusing experiment. He spoke again to her:

'But the other members of that orchestra were real Italians, were they not?'

Of course, he didn't care. He wanted to see whether the mechanism would work again. It did. It said they were not. They were of all sorts, apparently. It paused, with the one goggle eye immovably gazing down the whole length of the room and through the door opening on to the 'piazza'. It paused, then went on in the same low pitch:

'There was even one English girl.'

'Poor devil!' said Davidson. 'I suppose these women are not much better than slaves really. Was that fellow with the dyed beard decent in his way?'

The mechanism remained silent. The sympathetic soul of Davidson drew its own conclusions.

'Beastly life for these women!' he said. 'When you say an English girl, Mrs Schomberg, do you really mean a young girl? Some of these orchestra girls are no chicks.'

'Young enough,' came the low voice out of Mrs Schomberg's unmoved physiognomy.

Davidson, encouraged, remarked that he was sorry for her. He was easily sorry for people.

'Where did they go to from here?' he asked.

'She did not go with them. She ran away.'

This was the pronouncement Davidson obtained next. It introduced a new sort of interest.

'Well! Well!' he exclaimed placidly; and then, with the air of a man who knows life: 'Who with?' he inquired with assurance.

Mrs Schomberg's immobility gave her an appearance of listening intently. Perhaps she was really listening; but Schomberg must have been finishing his sleep in some distant part of the house. The silence was profound, and lasted long enough to become startling. Then, enthroned above Davidson, she whispered at last:

'That friend of yours.'

'Oh, you know I am here looking for a friend,' said Davidson hopefully. 'Won't you tell me –'

'I've told you.'

'Eh?'

A mist seemed to roll away from before Davidson's eyes, disclosing something he could not believe.

'You can't mean it!' he cried. 'He's not the man for it.' But the last words came out in a faint voice. Mrs Schomberg never moved her head the least bit. Davidson, after the shock which made him sit up, went slack all over.

'Heyst! Such a perfect gentleman!' he exclaimed weakly.

Mrs Schomberg did not seem to have heard him. This startling fact did not tally somehow with the idea Davidson had of Heyst. He never talked of women, he never seemed to think of them, or to remember that they existed; and then all at once – like this! Running off with a casual orchestra girl!

'You might have knocked me down with a feather,' Davidson told us some time afterward.

By then he was taking an indulgent view of both the parties to that amazing transaction. First of all, on reflection, he was by no means certain that it prevented Heyst from being a perfect gentleman, as before. He confronted our open grins or quiet smiles with a serious round face. Heyst had taken the girl away to Samburan; and that was no joking matter. The loneliness, the ruins of the spot, had impressed Davidson's simple soul. They were incompatible with the frivolous comments of people who had not seen it. That black jetty, sticking out of the jungle into the empty sea; these roof-ridges of deserted houses peeping dismally above the long grass! Ough! The gigantic and funeral blackboard sign of the Tropical Belt Coal Company, still emerging from a wild growth of bushes like an inscription stuck above a grave figured by the tall heap of unsold coal at the shore end of the wharf, added to the general desolation.

Thus the sensitive Davidson. The girl must have been miserable indeed to follow such a strange man to such a spot. Heyst had, no doubt, told her the truth. He was a gentleman. But no words could do justice to the conditions of life on Samburan. A desert island was nothing to it. Moreover, when you were cast away on a desert island – why, you could not help yourself; but to expect a fiddle-playing girl out of an ambulant ladies' orchestra to remain content there for a day, for one single day, was inconceivable. She would be frightened at the first sight of it. She would scream.

The capacity for sympathy in these stout, placid men! Davidson was stirred to the depths; and it was easy to see that it was about Heyst that he was concerned. We asked him if he had passed that way lately.

'Oh, yes. I always do – about half a mile off.'

Seen anybody about?'

'No, not a soul. Not a shadow.'

'Did you blow your whistle?'

'Blow the whistle? You think I would do such a thing?'

He rejected the mere possibility of such an unwarrantable intrusion. Wonderfully delicate fellow, Davidson!

'Well, but how do you know that they are there?' he was naturally asked.

Heyst had entrusted Mrs Schomberg with a message for Davidson – a few lines in pencil on a scrap of crumpled paper. It was to the effect that an unforeseen necessity was driving him away before the appointed time. He begged Davidson's indulgence for the apparent discourtesy. The woman of the house – meaning Mrs Schomberg – would give him the facts, though unable to explain them, of course.

'What was there to explain?' wondered Davidson dubiously. 'He took a fancy to that fiddle-playing girl, and –'

'And she to him, apparently,' I suggested.

'Wonderfully quick work,' reflected Davidson. 'What do you think will come of it?'

'Repentance, I should say. But how is it that Mrs Schomberg has been selected for a confidante?'

For indeed a waxwork figure would have seemed more useful than that woman whom we all were accustomed to see sitting elevated above the two billiard-tables – without expression, without movement, without voice, without sight.

'Why, she helped the girl to bolt,' said Davidson turning at me his innocent eyes, rounded by the state of constant amazement in which this affair had left him, like those shocks of terror or sorrow which sometimes leave their victim afflicted by nervous trembling. It looked as though he would never get over it.

'Mrs Schomberg jerked Heyst's note, twisted like a pipe-light, into my lap while I sat there unsuspecting,' Davidson went on. 'Directly I had recovered my senses, I asked her what on earth she had to do with it that Heyst should leave it with her. And then, behaving like a painted image rather than a live woman, she whispered, just loud enough for me to hear:

' "I helped them. I got her things together, tied them up in my own shawl, and threw them into the compound out of a back window. I did it."

'That woman that you would say hadn't the pluck to lift her little finger!' marvelled Davidson in his quiet, slightly panting voice. 'What do you think of that?'

I thought she must have had some interest of her own to serve. She was too lifeless to be suspected of impulsive compassion. It was impossible to think that Heyst had bribed her. Whatever means he had, he had not the means to do that. Or could it be that she was moved by that disinterested passion for delivering a woman to a man which in respectable spheres is called matchmaking? – a highly irregular example of it!

'It must have been a very small bundle,' remarked Davidson further.

'I imagine the girl must have been specially attractive,' I said.

'I don't know. She was miserable. I don't suppose it was more than a little linen and a couple of these white frocks they wear on the platform.'

Davidson pursued his own train of thought. He supposed that such a thing had never been heard of in the history of the tropics. For where could you find anyone to steal a girl out of an orchestra? No doubt fellows here and there took a fancy to some pretty one – but it was not for running away with her. Oh dear no! It needed a lunatic like Heyst.

'Only think what it means,' wheezed Davidson, imaginative under his invincible placidity. 'Just only try to think! Brooding alone on Samburan has upset his brain. He never stopped to consider, or he couldn't have done it. No sane man . . . How is a thing like that to go on? What's he going to do with her in the end? It's madness.'

'You say that he's mad. Schomberg tells us that he must be starving on his island; so he may end yet by eating her,' I suggested.

Mrs Schomberg had had no time to enter into details, Davidson told us. Indeed, the wonder was that they had been left alone so long. The drowsy afternoon was slipping by. Footsteps and voices resounded on the veranda – I beg pardon, the piazza; the scraping of chairs, the ping of a smitten bell. Customers were turning up. Mrs Schomberg was begging Davidson hurriedly, but without looking at him, to say nothing to anyone, when on a half-uttered word her nervous whisper was cut short. Through a small inner door Schomberg came in, his hair brushed, his beard combed neatly, but his eyelids still heavy from his nap. He looked with suspicion at Davidson, and even glanced at his wife; but he was baffled by the natural placidity of the one and the acquired habit of immobility in the other.

'Have you sent out the drinks?' he asked surlily.

She did not open her lips, because just then the head boy appeared with a loaded tray, on his way out. Schomberg went to the door and greeted the customers outside, but did not join them. He remained blocking half the doorway, with his back to the room, and was still there when Davidson, after sitting still for a while, rose to go. At the noise he made Schomberg turned his head, watched him lift his hat to Mrs Schomberg and receive her wooden bow accompanied by a stupid grin, and then looked away. He was loftily dignified. Davidson stopped at the door, deep in his simplicity.

'I am sorry you won't tell me anything about my friend's absence,' he said. 'My friend Heyst, you know. I suppose the only course for me now is to make inquiries down at the port. I shall hear something there, I don't doubt.'

'Make inquiries of the devil!' replied Schomberg in a hoarse mutter.

Davidson's purpose in addressing the hotel-keeper had been mainly to make Mrs Schomberg safe from suspicion; but he would fain have heard something more of Heyst's exploit from another point of view. It was a shrewd try. It was successful in a rather startling way, because the hotel-keeper's point of view was horribly abusive. All of a sudden, in the same hoarse sinister tone, he proceeded to call Heyst many names, of which 'pigdog' was not the worst, with such vehemence that he actually choked himself. Profiting from the pause, Davidson, whose temperament could withstand worse shocks, remonstrated in an undertone:

'It's unreasonable to get so angry as that. Even if he had run off with your cash-box –'

The big hotel-keeper bent down and put his infuriated face close to Davidson's.

'My cash-box! My – he – look here, Captain Davidson! He ran off with a girl. What do I care for the girl? The girl is nothing to me.'.

He shot out an infamous word which made Davidson start. That's what the girl was; and he reiterated the assertion that she was nothing to him. What he was concerned for was the good name of his house. Wherever he had been established, he had always had 'artist parties' staying in his house. One recommended him to the others; but what would happen now, when it got about that leaders ran the risk in his house – his house – of losing members of their troupe? And just now, when he had spent seven hundred and thirty-four guilders in building a concert-hall in his compound. Was that a thing to do in a respectable hotel? The cheek, the indecency, the impudence, the atrocity! Vagabond, imposter, swindler, ruffian, *schweinhund*!

He had seized Davidson by a button of his coat, detaining him in the doorway, and exactly in the line of Mrs Schomberg's stony gaze. Davidson stole a glance in that direction and thought of making some sort of reassuring sign to her, but she looked so bereft of senses, and almost of life, perched up there, that it seemed not worth while. He disengaged his button with firm placidity. Thereupon, with a last stifled curse, Schomberg vanished somewhere within, to try and compose his spirits in solitude. Davidson stepped out on the veranda. The party of customers there had become aware of the explosive interlude in the doorway. Davidson knew one of these men, and nodded to him in passing; but his acquaintance called out:

'Isn't he in a filthy temper? He's been like that ever since.'

The speaker laughed aloud, while all the others sat smiling. Davidson stopped.

'Yes, rather.' His feelings were, he told us, those of bewildered resignation; but of course that was no more visible to the others than the emotions of a turtle when it withdraws into its shell.

'It seems unreasonable,' he murmured thoughtfully.

'Oh, but they had a scrap!' the other said.

'What do you mean? Was there a fight! – a fight with Heyst?' asked Davidson, much perturbed, if somewhat incredulous.

'Heyst? No, these two – the bandmaster, the fellow who's taking these women about and our Schomberg. Signor Zangiacomo ran amuck in the morning, and went for our worthy friend. I tell you, they were rolling on the floor together on this very veranda, after chasing each other all over the house, doors slamming, women screaming, seventeen of them, in the dining-room; Chinamen up the trees – Hey, John? You climb tree to see the fight, eh?'

The boy, almond-eyed and impassive, emitted a scornful grunt, finished wiping the table, and withdrew.

'That's what it was – a real, go-as-you-please scrap. And Zangiacomo began it. Oh, here's Schomberg. Say, Schomberg, didn't he fly at you, when the girl was missed, because it was you who insisted that the artists should go about the audience during the interval?'

Schomberg had reappeared in the doorway. He advanced. His bearing was stately, but his nostrils were extraordinarily expanded, and he controlled his voice with apparent effort.

'Certainly. That was only business. I quoted him special terms and all for your sake, gentlemen. I was thinking of my regular customers. There's nothing to do in the evenings in this town. I think, gentlemen, you were all pleased at the opportunity of hearing a little good music; and where's the harm of offering a grenadine, or what not, to a lady artist? But that fellow – that Swede – he got round the girl. He got round all the people out here. I've been watching him for years. You remember how he got round Morrison.'

He changed front abruptly, as if on parade, and marched off. The customers at the table exchanged glances silently. Davidson's attitude was that of a spectator. Schomberg's moody pacing of the billiard-room could be heard on the veranda.

'And the funniest part is,' resumed the man who had been speaking before – an English clerk in a Dutch house – 'the funniest part is that before nine o'clock that same morning those two were driving together in a gharry down to the port, to look for Heyst and the girl. I saw them rushing around making inquiries. I don't know what they would have done to the girl, but they seemed quite ready to fall upon your Heyst, Davidson, and kill him on the quay.'

He had never, he said, seen anything so queer. Those two investigators working feverishly to the same end were glaring at each other with surprising ferocity. In hatred and mistrust they entered a steam-launch, and went flying from ship to ship all over the harbour, causing no end of sensation. The captains of vessels, coming on shore later in the day, brought tales of a strange invasion, and wanted to know who were the two offensive lunatics in a steam-launch, apparently after a man and a girl, and telling a story of which one could make neither head nor tail. Their reception by the roadstead was generally unsympathetic, even to the point of the mate of an American ship bundling them out over the rail with unseemly precipitation.

Meantime Heyst and the girl were a good few miles away, having gone in the night on board one of the Tesman schooners bound to the eastward. This was known afterward from the Javanese boatmen whom Heyst hired for the purpose at three o'clock in the morning. The Tesman schooner had sailed at daylight with the usual land breeze, and was probably still in sight in the offing at the time. However, the two pursuers after their experience with the American mate made for the shore. On landing, they had another violent row in the German language. But there was no second fight; and finally, with looks of fierce animosity, they got together into a gharry – obviously with the frugal view of sharing expenses – and drove away, leaving an astonished little crowd of Europeans and natives on the quay.

After hearing this wondrous tale, Davidson went away from the hotel veranda, which was filling with Schomberg's regular customers. Heyst's escapade was the general topic of conversation. Never before had that unaccountable individual been the cause of so much gossip, he judged. No! Not even in the beginnings of the Tropical Belt Coal Company when, becoming for a moment a public character, he was the object of silly criticism and unintelligent envy for every vagabond and adventurer in the islands. Davidson concluded that people liked to discuss that sort of scandal better than any other.

I asked him if he believed that this was such a great scandal after all.

'Heavens, no!' said that excellent man who, himself, was incapable of any impropriety of conduct. 'But it isn't a thing I would have done myself; I mean even if I had not been married.'

There was no implied condemnation in the statement; rather something like regret. Davidson shared my suspicion that this was in its essence the rescue of a distressed human being. Not that we were two romantics, tingeing the world to the hue of our temperament, but that both of us had been acute enough to discover a long time ago that Heyst was.

'I shouldn't have had the pluck,' he continued. 'I see a thing all round, as it were; but Heyst doesn't, or else he would have been scared. You don't take a woman into a desert jungle without being made sorry for it sooner or later, in one way or another; and Heyst being a gentleman only makes it worse.'

Chapter VI

We said no more about Heyst on that occasion, and it so happened that I did not meet Davidson again for some three months. When we did come together, almost the first thing he said to me was:

'I've seen him.'

Before I could exclaim, he assured me that he had taken no liberty, that he had not intruded. He was called in. Otherwise he would not have dreamed of breaking in upon Heyst's privacy.

'I am certain you wouldn't,' I assured him, concealing my amusement at his wonderful delicacy. He was the most delicate man that ever took a small steamer to and fro among the islands. But his humanity, which was not less strong and praiseworthy, had induced him to take his steamer past Samburan wharf (at an average distance of a mile) every twenty-three days – exactly. Davidson was delicate, humane, and regular.

'Heyst called you in?' I asked, interested.

Yes, Heyst had called him in as he was going by on his usual date. Davidson was examining the shore through his glasses with his unwearied and punctual humanity as he steamed past Samburan.

'I saw a man in white. It could only have been Heyst. He had fastened some sort of enormous flag to a bamboo pole, and was waving it at the end of the old wharf.'

Davidson didn't like to take his steamer alongside – for fear of being indiscreet, I suppose; but he steered close inshore, stopped his engines, and lowered a boat. He went himself in that boat, which was manned, of course, by his Malay seamen.

Heyst, when he saw the boat pulling towards him, dropped his signalling-pole; and when Davidson arrived, he was kneeling down engaged busily in unfastening the flag from it.

'Was there anything wrong?' I inquired, Davidson having paused in his narrative and my curiosity being naturally aroused. You must remember that Heyst as the Archipelago knew him was not – what shall I say – was not a signalling sort of man.

'The very words that came out of my mouth,' said Davidson, 'before I laid the boat against the piles. I could not help it.'

Heyst got up from his knees and began carefully folding up the flag thing, which struck Davidson as having the dimensions of a blanket.

'No, nothing wrong,' he cried. His white teeth flashed agreeably below the coppery horizontal bar of his long moustaches.

I don't know whether it was his delicacy or his obesity which prevented Davidson from clambering upon the wharf. He stood up in the boat, and, above him, Heyst stooped low with urbane smiles, thanking him and apologizing for the liberty, exactly in his usual manner. Davidson had expected some change in the man, but there was none. Nothing in him betrayed the momentous fact that within that jungle there was a girl, a performer in a ladies' orchestra, whom he had carried straight off the concert platform into the wilderness. He was not ashamed or defiant or abashed about it. He might have been a shade confidential when addressing Davidson. And his words were enigmatical.

'I took this course of signalling to you,' he said to Davidson, 'because to preserve appearances might be of the utmost importance. Not to me, of course. I don't care what people may say, and of course no one can hurt me. I suppose I have done a certain amount of harm, since I allowed myself to be tempted into action. It seemed innocent enough, but all action is bound to be harmful. It is devilish. That is why this world is evil upon the whole. But I have done with it! I shall never lift a little finger again. At one time I thought that intelligent observation of facts was the best way of cheating the time which is allotted to us whether we want it or not; but now I have done with observation, too.'

Imagine poor, simple Davidson being addressed in such terms alongside an abandoned, decaying wharf jutting out of tropical bush. He had never heard anybody speak like this before; certainly not Heyst, whose conversation was concise, polite, with a faint ring of playfulness in the cultivated tones of his voice.

'He's gone mad,' Davidson thought to himself.

But, looking at the physiognomy above him on the wharf, he was obliged to dismiss the notion of common, crude lunacy. It was truly most unusual talk. Then he remembered – in his surprise he had lost sight of it – that Heyst now had a girl there. This bizarre discourse was probably the effect of the girl. Davidson shook off the absurd feeling, and asked, wishing to make clear his friendliness, and not knowing what else to say:

'You haven't run short of stores or anything like that?'

Heyst smiled and shook his head.

'No, no. Nothing of the kind. We are fairly well off here. Thanks, all the same. If I have taken the liberty to detain you, it is not from any uneasiness for myself and my – companion. The person I was thinking of when I made up my mind to invoke your assistance is Mrs Schomberg.'

'I have talked with her,' interjected Davidson.

'Oh! You? Yes, I hoped she would find means to –'

'But she didn't tell me much,' interrupted Davidson, who was not averse from hearing something – he hardly knew what.

'H'm – yes. But that note of mine? Yes? She found an opportunity to give it to you? That's good, very good. She's more resourceful than one would give her credit for.'

'Women often are,' remarked Davidson. The strangeness from which he had suffered, merely because his interlocutor had carried off a girl, wore off as the minutes went by. 'There's a lot of unexpectedness about women,' he generalized with a didactic aim which seemed to miss its mark; for the next thing Heyst said was:

'This is Mrs Schomberg's shawl.' He touched the stuff hanging over his arm. 'An Indian thing, I believe,' he added, glancing at his arm sideways.

'It isn't of particular value,' said Davidson truthfully.

'Very likely. The point is that it belongs to Schomberg's wife. That Schomberg seems to be an unconscionable ruffian – don't you think so?'

Davidson smiled faintly.

'We out here have got used to him,' he said, as if excusing a universal and guilty toleration of a manifest nuisance. 'I'd hardly call him that. I only know him as a hotel-keeper.'

'I never knew him even at that – not till this time, when you were so obliging as to take me to Sourabaya, I went to stay there from economy. The Netherlands House is very expensive, and they expect you to bring your own servant with you. It's a nuisance.'

'Of course, of course,' protested Davidson hastily.

After a short silence Heyst returned to the matter of the shawl. He wanted to send it back to Mrs Schomberg. He said that it might be very awkward for her if she were unable, if asked, to produce it. This had given him, Heyst, much uneasiness. She was terrified of Schomberg. Apparently she had reason to be.

Davidson had remarked that, too. Which did not prevent her, he pointed out, from making a fool of him, in a way, for the sake of a stranger.

'Oh! You know!' said Heyst. 'Yes, she helped me – us.'

'She told me so. I had quite a talk with her,' Davidson informed him. 'Fancy anyone having a talk with Mrs Schomberg! If I were to tell the fellows they wouldn't believe me. How did you get round her, Heyst? How did you think of it? Why, she looks too stupid to understand human speech and too scared to shoo a chicken away. Oh, the women, the women! You don't know what there may be in the quietest of them.'

'She was engaged in the task of defending her position in life,' said Heyst. 'It's a very respectable task.'

'Is that it? I had some idea it was that,' confessed Davidson.

He then imparted to Heyst the story of the violent proceedings following on the discovery of his flight. Heyst's polite attention to the tale took on a sombre cast; but he manifested no surprise, and offered no comment. When Davidson had finished he handed down the shawl into the boat, and Davidson promised to do his best to return it to Mrs Schomberg in some secret fashion. Heyst expressed his thanks in a few simple words, set off by his manner of finished courtesy. Davidson prepared to depart. They were not looking at each other. Suddenly Heyst spoke:

'You understand that this was a case of odious persecution, don't you? I became aware of it and –'

It was a view which the sympathetic Davidson was capable of appreciating.

'I am not surprised to hear it,' he said placidly. 'Odious enough, I dare say. And you, of course – not being a married man – were free to step in. Ah, well!'

He sat down in the stern-sheets, and already had the steering lines in his hands when Heyst observed abruptly:

'The world is a bad dog. It will bite you if you give it a chance; but I think that here we can safely defy the fates.'

When relating all this to me, Davidson's only comment was:

'Funny notion of defying the fates – to take a woman in tow!'

Chapter VII

Some considerable time afterward – we did not meet very often – I asked Davidson how he had managed about the shawl and heard that he had tackled his mission in a direct way, and had found it easy enough. At the very first call he made in Samarang he rolled the shawl as tightly as he could into the smallest possible brown-paper parcel, which he carried ashore with him. His business in the town being transacted, he got into a gharry with the parcel and drove to the hotel. With his precious experience, he timed his arrival accurately for the hour of Schomberg's siesta. Finding the place empty as on the former occasion, he marched into the billiard-room, took a seat at the back, near the sort of dais which Mrs Schomberg would in due course come to occupy, and broke the slumbering silence of the house by thumping a bell vigorously. Of course a Chinaman appeared promptly. Davidson ordered a drink and sat tight.

'I would have ordered twenty drinks one after another, if necessary,' he said – Davidson's a very abstemious man – 'rather than take that parcel out of the house again. Couldn't leave it in a corner without letting the woman know it was there. It might have turned out worse for her than not bringing the thing back at all.'

And so he waited, ringing the bell again and again, and swallowing two or three iced drinks which he did not want. Presently, as he hoped it would happen, Mrs Schomberg came in, silk dress, long neck, ringlets, scared eyes, and silly grin – all complete. Probably that lazy beast had sent her out to see who was the thirsty customer waking up the echoes of the house at this quiet hour. Bow, nod – and she clambered up to her post behind the raised counter, looking so helpless, so inane, as she sat there, that if it hadn't been for the parcel, Davidson declared, he would have thought he had merely dreamed all that had passed between them. He ordered another drink, to get the Chinaman out of the room, and then seized the parcel, which was reposing on a chair near him, and with no more than a mutter – 'This is something of yours' – he rammed it swiftly into a recess in the counter, at her feet. There! The rest was her affair. And just in time, too. Schomberg turned up, yawning affectedly, almost before Davidson had regained his seat. He cast about suspicious and irate glances. An invincible placidity of expression helped Davidson wonderfully at the moment, and the other, of course, could have no grounds for the slightest suspicion of any sort of understanding between his wife and this customer.

As to Mrs Schomberg, she sat there like a joss. Davidson was lost in admiration. He believed, now, that the woman had been putting it on for years. She never even winked. It was immense! The insight he had obtained almost frightened him; he couldn't get over his wonder at knowing more of the real Mrs Schomberg than anybody in the Islands, including Schomberg himself. She was a miracle of dissimulation. No wonder Heyst got the girl away from under two men's noses, if he had her to help with the job!

The greatest wonder, after all, was Heyst getting mixed up with petticoats.

The fellow's life had been open to us for years and nothing could have been more detached from feminine associations. Except that he stood drinks to people on suitable occasions, like any other man, this observer of facts seemed to have no connection with earthly affairs and passions. The very courtesy of his manner, the flavour of playfulness in the voice set him apart. He was like a feather floating lightly in the workaday atmosphere which was the breath of our nostrils. For this reason whenever this looker-on took contact with things he attracted attention. First, it was the Morrison partnership of mystery; then came the great sensation of the Tropical Belt Coal where indeed varied interests were involved: a real business matter. And then came this elopement, this incongruous phenomenon of self-assertion, the greatest wonder of all, astonishing and amusing.

Davidson admitted to me that the hubbub was subsiding; and the affair would have been already forgotten, perhaps, if that ass Schomberg had not kept on gnashing his teeth publicly about it. It was really provoking that Davidson should not be able to give one some idea of the girl. Was she pretty? He didn't know. He had stayed the whole afternoon in Schomberg's hotel, mainly for the purpose of finding out something about her. But the story was growing stale. The parties at the tables on the veranda had other, fresher, events to talk about and Davidson shrank from making direct inquiries. He sat placidly there, content to be disregarded and hoping for some chance word to turn up. I shouldn't wonder if the good fellow hadn't been dozing. It's difficult to give you an adequate idea of Davidson's placidity.

Presently Schomberg, wandering about, joined a party that had taken the table next to Davidson's.

'A man like that Swede, gentlemen, is a public danger,' he began. 'I remember him for years. I won't say anything of his spying – well, he used to say himself he was looking for out-of-the-way facts and what is that if not spying? He was spying into everybody's business. He got hold of Captain Morrison, squeezed him dry, like you would an orange, and scared him off to Europe to die there. Everybody knows that Captain Morrison had a weak chest. Robbed first and murdered afterward! I don't mince words – not I. Next he gets up that swindle of the Belt Coal. You know all about it. And now, after lining his pockets with other people's money, he kidnaps a white girl belonging to an orchestra which is performing in my public room for the benefit of my patrons, and goes off to live like a prince on that island, where nobody can get at him. A damn silly girl . . . It's disgusting – tfui!'

He spat. He choked with rage – for he saw visions, no doubt. He jumped up from his chair, and went away to flee from them – perhaps. He went into the room where Mrs Schomberg sat. Her aspect could not have been very soothing to the sort of torment from which he was suffering.

Davidson did not feel called upon to defend Heyst. His proceeding was to enter into conversation with one and another, casually, and showing no particular knowledge of the affair, in order to discover something about the girl. Was she anything out of the way? Was she pretty? She couldn't have been markedly so. She had not attracted special notice. She was young – on that everybody agreed. The English clerk of Tesmans remembered that she had a sallow face. He was respectable and highly proper. He was not the sort to associate with such people.

Most of these women were fairly battered specimens. Schomberg had them housed in what he called the Pavilion, in the grounds, where they were hard at it mending and washing their white dresses, and could be seen hanging them out to dry between the trees, like a lot of washerwomen. They looked very much like middle-aged washerwomen on the platform, too. But the girl had been living in the main building along with the boss, the director, the fellow with the black beard, and a hard-bitten, oldish woman who took the piano and was understood to be the fellow's wife.

This was not a very satisfactory result. Davidson stayed on, and even joined the table d'hôte dinner, without gleaning any more information. He was resigned.

'I suppose,' he wheezed placidly, 'I am bound to see her some day.'

He meant to take the Samburan channel every trip, as before, of course.

'Yes,' I said. 'No doubt you will. Some day Heyst will be signalling to you again; and I wonder what it will be for.'

Davidson made no reply. He had his own ideas about that, and his silence concealed a good deal of thought. We spoke no more of Heyst's girl. Before we separated, he gave me a piece of unrelated observation.

'It's funny,' he said, 'but I fancy there's some gambling going on in the evening at Schomberg's place, on the quiet. I've noticed men strolling away in twos and threes towards that hall where the orchestra used to play. The windows must be specially well shuttered, because I could not spy the smallest gleam of light from that direction; but I can't believe that those beggars would go in there only to sit and think of their sins in the dark.'

'That's strange. It's incredible that Schomberg should risk that sort of thing,' I said.

Part Two

Chapter I

As we know, Heyst had gone to stay in Schomberg's hotel in complete ignorance that his person was odious to that worthy. When he arrived, Zangiacomo's Ladies' Orchestra had been established there for some time.

The business which had called him out from his seclusion in his lost corner of the Eastern seas was with the Tesmans, and it had something to do with money. He transacted it quickly, and then found himself with nothing to do while he awaited Davidson, who was to take him back to his solitude; for back to his solitude Heyst meant to go. He whom we used to refer to as the Enchanted Heyst was suffering from thorough disenchantment. Not with the islands, however. The Archipelago has lasting fascination. It is not easy to shake off the spell of island life. Heyst was disenchanted with life as a whole. His scornful temperament, beguiled into action, suffered from failure in a subtle way unknown to men accustomed to grapple with the realities of common human enterprise. It was like the gnawing pain of useless apostasy, a sort of shame before his own betrayed nature; and, in addition, he also suffered from plain, downright remorse. He deemed himself guilty of Morrison's death. A rather absurd feeling, since no one could possibly have foreseen the horrors of the cold, wet summer lying in wait for poor Morrison at home.

It was not in Heyst's character to turn morose; but his mental state was not compatible with a sociable mood. He spent his evenings sitting apart on the veranda of Schomberg's hotel. The lamentations of string instruments issued from the building in the hotel compound, the approaches to which were decorated with Japanese paper lanterns strung up between the trunks of several big trees. Scraps of tunes more or less plaintive reached his ears. They pursued him even into his bedroom, which opened into an upstairs veranda. The fragmentary and rasping character of these sounds made their intrusion inexpressibly tedious in the long run. Like most dreamers, to whom it is given sometimes to hear the music of the spheres, Heyst, the wanderer of the Archipelago, had a taste for silence which he had been able to gratify for years. The islands are very quiet. One sees them lying about, clothed in their dark garments of leaves, in a great hush of silver and azure, where the sea without murmurs meets the sky in a ring of magic stillness. A sort of smiling somnolence broods over them; the very voices of their people are soft and subdued, as if afraid to break some protecting spell.

Perhaps this was the very spell which had enchanted Heyst in the early days. For him, however, that was broken. He was no longer enchanted, though he was still a captive of the islands. He had no intention to leave them ever. Where could he have gone to, after all these years? Not a single soul belonging to him lived anywhere on earth. Of this fact – not such a remote one, after all – he had only lately become aware; for it is failure that makes a man enter into himself and reckon up his resources. And though he had made up his mind to retire from the world in hermit fashion, yet he was irrationally moved by this sense of loneliness which had come to him in the hour of renunciation. It hurt him. Nothing is more painful than the shock of sharp contradictions that lacerate our intelligence and our feelings.

Meantime Schomberg watched Heyst out of the corner of his eye. Towards the unconscious object of his enmity he preserved a distant Lieutenant-of-the-Reserve demeanour. Nudging certain of his customers with his elbow, he begged them to observe what airs 'that Swede' was giving himself.

'I really don't know why he has come to stay in my house. This place isn't good enough for him. I wish to goodness he had gone somewhere else to show off his superiority. Here I have got up this series of concerts for you gentlemen, just to make things a little brighter generally; and do you think he'll condescend to step in and listen to a piece or two of an evening? Not he. I know him of old. There he sits at the dark end of the piazza, all the evening long – planning some new swindle, no doubt. For twopence I would ask him to go and look for quarters somewhere else; only one doesn't like to treat a white man like that out in the tropics. I don't know how long he means to stay, but I'm willing to bet a trifle that he'll never work himself up to the point of spending the fifty cents of entrance money for the sake of a little good music.'

Nobody cared to bet, or the hotel-keeper would have lost. One evening Heyst was driven to desperation by the rasped, squeaked, scraped snatches of tunes pursuing him even to his hard couch, with a mattress as thin as a pancake and a diaphanous mosquito net. He descended among the trees, where the soft glow of Japanese lanterns picked out parts of their great rugged trunks, here and there, in the great mass of darkness under the lofty foliage. More lanterns, of the shape of cylindrical concertinas, hanging in a row from a slack string, decorated the doorway of what Schomberg called grandiloquently 'my concert-hall'. In his desperate mood Heyst ascended three steps, lifted a calico curtain, and went in.

The uproar in that small, barn-like structure, built of imported pine boards, and raised clear of the ground, was simply stunning. An instrumental uproar, screaming, grunting, whining, sobbing, scraping, squeaking some kind of lively air; while a grand piano, operated upon by a bony, red-faced woman with bad-tempered nostrils, rained hard notes like hail through the tempest of fiddles. The small platform was filled with white muslin dresses and crimson sashes slanting from shoulders provided with bare arms, which sawed away without respite. Zangiacomo conducted. He wore a white mess-jacket, a black dress waistcoat, and white trousers. His longish, tousled hair and his great beard were purple-black. He was horrible. The heat was terrific. There were perhaps thirty people having drinks at several little tables. Heyst, quite overcome by the volume of noise, dropped into a chair. In the quick time of that music, in the varied, piercing clamour of the strings, in the movements of the bare arms, in the low dresses, the coarse faces, the stony eyes of the executants, there was a suggestion of brutality – something cruel, sensual, and repulsive.

'This is awful!' Heyst murmured to himself.

But there is an unholy fascination in systematic noise. He did not flee from it incontinently, as one might have expected him to do. He remained, astonished at himself for remaining, since nothing could have been more repulsive to his tastes, more painful to his senses, and, so to speak, more contrary to his genius, than this rude exhibition of vigour. The Zangiacomo band was not making music; it was simply murdering silence with a vulgar, ferocious energy. One felt as if witnessing a deed of violence; and that impression was so strong that it seemed marvellous to see the people sitting so quietly on their chairs, drinking so calmly out of their glasses, and giving no signs of distress, anger, or fear. Heyst averted his gaze from the unnatural spectacle of their indifference.

When the piece of music came to an end, the relief was so great that he felt slightly dizzy, as if a chasm of silence had yawned at his feet. When he raised his eyes, the audience, most perversely, was exhibiting signs of animation and interest in their faces, and the women in white muslin dresses were coming down in pairs from the platform into the body of Schomberg's 'concert-hall'. They dispersed themselves all over the place. The male creature with the hooked nose and purple-black beard disappeared somewhere. This was the interval during which, as the astute Schomberg had stipulated, the members of the orchestra were encouraged to favour the members of the audience with their company – that is, such members as seemed inclined to fraternize with the arts in a familiar and generous manner; the symbol of familiarity and generosity consisting in offers of refreshment.

The procedure struck Heyst as highly incorrect. However, the impropriety of Schomberg's ingenious scheme was defeated by the circumstance that most of the women were no longer young, and that none of them had ever been beautiful. Their more or less worn cheeks were slightly roughed; but apart from that fact, which might have been simply a matter of routine, they did not seem to take the success of the scheme unduly to heart. The impulse to fraternize with the arts being obviously weak in the audience, some of the musicians sat down listlessly at unoccupied tables, while others went on perambulating the central passage arm in arm, glad enough, no doubt, to stretch their legs while resting their arms. Their crimson sashes gave a factitious touch of gaiety to the smoky atmosphere of the concert-hall; and Heyst felt a sudden pity for these beings, exploited, hopeless, devoid of charm and grace, whose fate of cheerless dependence invested their coarse and joyless features with a touch of pathos.

Heyst was temperamentally sympathetic. To have them passing and repassing close to his little table was painful to him. He was preparing to rise and go out when he noticed that two white muslin dresses and crimson sashes had not yet left the platform. One of these dresses concealed the raw-boned frame of the woman with the bad-tempered curve to her nostrils. She was no less a personage than Mrs Zangiacomo. She had left the piano, and, with her back to the hall, was preparing the parts for the second half of the concert, with a brusque, impatient action of her ugly elbows. This task done, she turned, and, perceiving the other white muslin dress motionless on a chair in the second row, she strode towards it between the music-stands with an aggressive and masterful gait. On the lap of that dress there lay, unclasped and idle, a pair of small hands, not very white, attached to well-formed arms. The next detail Heyst was led to observe was the arrangement of the hair – two thick brown tresses rolled round an attractively shaped head.

'A girl, by Jove!' he exclaimed mentally.

It was evident that she was a girl. It was evident in the outline of the shoulders, in the slender white bust springing up, barred slantwise by the crimson sash, from the bell-shaped spread of muslin skirt hiding the chair on which she sat averted a little from the body of the hall. Her feet, in low white shoes, were crossed prettily.

She had captured Heyst's awakened faculty of observation; he had the sensation of a new experience. That was because his faculty of observation had never before been captured by any feminine creature in that marked and exclusive fashion. He looked at her anxiously, as no man ever looks at another man; and he positively forgot where he was. He had lost touch with his surroundings. The big woman, advancing, concealed the girl from his sight for a moment. She bent over the seated youthful figure, in passing it very close, as if to drop a word into its ear. Her lips did certainly move. But what sort of word could it have been to make the girl jump up so swiftly? Heyst, at his table, was surprised into a sympathetic start. He glanced quickly round. Nobody was looking towards the platform; and when his eyes swept back there again, the girl, with the big woman treading at her heels, was coming down the three steps from the platform to the floor of the hall. There she paused, stumbled one pace forward, and stood still again, while the other – the escort, the dragoon, the coarse big woman of the piano – passed her roughly, and, marching truculently down the centre aisle between the chairs and tables, went out to rejoin the hook-nosed Zangiacomo somewhere outside. During her extraordinary transit, as if everything in the hall were dirt under her feet, her scornful eyes met the upward glance of Heyst, who looked away at once towards the girl. She had not moved. Her arms hung down; her eyelids were lowered.

Heyst laid down his half-smoked cigar and compressed his lips. Then he got up. It was the same sort of impulse which years ago had made him cross the sandy street of the abominable town of Delli in the island of Timor and accost Morrison, practically a stranger to him then, a man in trouble, expressively harassed, dejected, lonely.

It was the same impulse. But he did not recognize it. He was not thinking of Morrison then. It may be said that, for the first time since the final abandonment of the Samburan coal mine, he had completely forgotten the late Morrison. It is true that to a certain extent he had forgotten also where he was. Thus, unchecked by any sort of self-consciousness, Heyst walked up the central passage.

Several of the women, by this time, had found anchorage here and there among the occupied tables. They talked to the men, leaning on their elbows, and suggesting funnily – if it hadn't been for the crimson sashes – in their white dresses an assembly of middle-aged brides with free and easy manners and hoarse voices. The murmuring noise of conversations carried on with some spirit filled Schomberg's concert-room. Nobody remarked Heyst's movements; for indeed he was not the only man on his legs there. He had been confronting the girl for some time before she became aware of his presence. She was looking down, very still, without colour, without glances, without voice, without movement. It was only when Heyst addressed her in his courteous tone that she raised her eyes.

'Excuse me,' he said in English, 'but that horrible female has done something to you. She has pinched you, hasn't she? I am sure she pinched you just now, when she stood by your chair.'

The girl received this overture with the wide, motionless stare of profound astonishment. Heyst, vexed with himself, suspected that she did not understand what he said. One could not tell what nationality these women were, except that they were of all sorts. But she was astonished almost more by the near presence of the man himself, by his largely bald head, by the white brow, the sunburnt cheeks, the long, horizontal moustaches of crinkly bronze hair, by the kindly expression of the man's blue eyes looking into her own. He saw the stony amazement in hers give way to a momentary alarm, which was succeeded by an expression of resignation.

'I am sure she pinched your arm most cruelly,' he murmured, rather disconcerted now at what he had done.

It was a great comfort to hear her say:

'It wouldn't have been the first time. And suppose she did – what are you going to do about it?'

'I don't know,' he said with a faint, remote playfulness in his tone which had not been heard in it lately, and which seemed to catch her ear pleasantly. 'I am grieved to say that I don't know. But can I do anything? What would you wish me to do? Pray command me.'

Again the greatest astonishment became visible in her face; for she now perceived how different he was from the other men in the room. He was as different from them as she was different from the other members of the ladies' orchestra.

'Command you?' she breathed, after a time, in a bewildered tone. 'Who are you?' she asked a little louder.

'I am staying in this hotel for a few days. I just dropped in casually here. This outrage –'

'Don't you try to interfere,' she said so earnestly that Heyst asked, in his faintly playful tone:

'Is it your wish that I should leave you?'

'I haven't said that,' the girl answered. 'She pinched me because I didn't get down here quick enough.'

'I can't tell you how indignant I am,' said Heyst. 'But since you are down here now,' he went on, with the ease of a man of the world speaking to a young lady in a drawing-room, 'hadn't we better sit down?'

She obeyed his inviting gesture, and they sat down on the nearest chairs. They looked at each other across a little round table with a surprised, open gaze, self-consciousness growing on them so slowly that it was a long time before they averted their eyes; and very soon they met again, temporarily, only to rebound, as it were. At last they steadied in contact, but by that time, say some fifteen minutes from the moment when they sat down, the 'interval' came to an end.

So much for their eyes. As to the conversation, it had been perfectly insignificant, because naturally they had nothing to say to each other. Heyst had been interested by the girl's physiognomy. Its expression was neither simple nor yet very clear. It was not distinguished – that could not be expected – but the features had more fineness than those of any other feminine countenance he had ever had the opportunity to observe so closely. There was in it something indefinably audacious and infinitely miserable – because the temperament and the existence of that girl were reflected in it. But her voice! It seduced Heyst by its amazing quality. It was a voice fit to utter the most exquisite things, a voice which would have made silly chatter supportable and the roughest talk fascinating. Heyst drank in its charm as one listens to the tone of some instrument without heeding the tune.

'Do you sing as well as play?' he asked her abruptly.

'Never sang a note in my life,' she said, obviously surprised by the irrelevant question; for they had not been discoursing of sweet sounds. She was clearly unaware of her voice. 'I don't remember that I ever had much reason to sing since I was little,' she added.

That inelegant phrase, by the mere vibrating, warm nobility of the sound, found its way into Heyst's heart. His mind, cool, alert, watched it sink there with a sort of vague concern at the absurdity of the occupation, till it rested at the bottom, deep down, where our unexpressed longings lie.

'You are English, of course?' he said.

'What do you think?' she answered in the most charming accents. Then, as if thinking that it was her turn to place a question: 'Why do you always smile when you speak?'

It was enough to make anyone look grave; but her good faith was so evident that Heyst recovered himself at once.

'It's my unfortunate manner,' he said with his delicate, polished playfulness. 'It is very objectionable to you?'

She was very serious.

'No. I only noticed it. I haven't come across so many pleasant people as all that, in my life.'

'It's certain that this woman who plays the piano is infinitely more disagreeable than any cannibal I have ever had to do with.'

'I believe you!' She shuddered. 'How did you come to have anything to do with cannibals?'

'It would be too long a tale,' said Heyst, with a faint smile. Heyst's smiles were rather melancholy, and accorded badly with his great moustaches, under which his mere playfulness lurked as comfortably as a shy bird in its native thicket. 'Much too long. How did you get amongst this lot here?'

'Bad luck,' she answered briefly.

'No doubt, no doubt,' Heyst assented with slight nods. Then, still indignant at the pinch which he had divined rather than actually seen inflicted: 'I say, couldn't you defend yourself somehow?'

She had risen already. The ladies of the orchestra were slowly regaining their places. Some were already seated, idle, stoney-eyed, before the music-stands. Heyst was standing up, too.

'They are too many for me,' she said.

These few words came out of the common experience of mankind; yet by virtue of her voice, they thrilled Heyst like a revelation. His feelings were in a state of confusion, but his mind was clear.

'That's bad. But it isn't actual ill-usage that this girl is complaining of,' he thought lucidly after she left him.

Chapter II

That was how it began. How it was that it ended, as we know it did end, is not so easy to state precisely. It is very clear that Heyst was not indifferent. I won't say to the girl, but to the girl's fate. He was the same man who had plunged after the submerged Morrison whom he hardly knew otherwise than by sight and through the usual gossip of the islands. But this was another sort of plunge altogether, and likely to lead to a very different kind of partnership.

Did he reflect at all? Probably. He was sufficiently reflective. But if he did, it was with insufficient knowledge. For there is no evidence that he paused at any time between the date of that evening and the morning of the flight. Truth to say, Heyst was not one of those men who pause much. Those dreamy spectators of the world's agitation are terrible once the desire to act gets hold of them. They lower their heads and charge a wall with an amazing serenity which nothing but an indisciplined imagination can give.

He was not a fool. I suppose he knew – or at least he felt – where this was leading him. But his complete inexperience gave him the necessary audacity. The girl's voice was charming when she spoke to him of her miserable past, in simple terms, with a sort of unconscious cynicism inherent in the truth of the ugly conditions of poverty. And whether because he was humane or because her voice included all the modulations of pathos, cheerfulness, and courage in its compass, it was not disgust that the tale awakened in him, but the sense of an immense sadness.

On a later evening, during the interval between the two parts of the concert, the girl told Heyst about herself. She was almost a child of the streets. Her father was a musician in the orchestras of small theatres. Her mother ran away from him while she was little, and the landladies of various poor lodging-houses had attended casually to her abandoned childhood. It was never positive starvation and absolute rags, but it was the hopeless grip of poverty all the time. It was her father who taught her to play the violin. It seemed that he used to get drunk sometimes, but without pleasure, and only because he was unable to forget his fugitive wife. After he had a paralytic stroke, falling over with a crash in the well of a music-hall orchestra during the performance, she had joined the Zangiacomo company. He was now in a home for incurables.

'And I am here,' she finished, 'with no one to care if I make a hole in the water the next chance I get or not.'

Heyst told her that he thought she could do a little better than that, if it was only a question of getting out of the world. She looked at him with special attention, and with a puzzled expression which gave to her face an air of innocence.

This was during one of the 'intervals' between the two parts of the concert. She had come down that time without being incited thereto by a pinch from the awful Zangiacomo woman. It is difficult to suppose that she was seduced by the uncovered intellectual forehead and the long reddish moustaches of her new friend. New is not the right word. She had never had a friend before; and the sensation of this friendliness going out to her was exciting by its novelty alone. Besides, any man who did not resemble Schomberg appeared for that very reason attractive. She was afraid of the hotel-keeper, who, in the daytime, taking advantage of the fact that she lived in the hotel itself, and not in the Pavilion with the other 'artists', prowled round her, mute, hungry, portentous behind his great beard, or else assailed her in quiet corners and empty passages with deep, mysterious murmurs from behind, which, notwithstanding their clear import, sounded horribly insane somehow.

The contrast of Heyst's quiet, polished manner gave her special delight and filled her with admiration. She had never seen anything like that before. If she had, perhaps, known kindness in her life, she had never met the forms of simple courtesy. She was interested by it as a very novel experience, not very intelligible, but distinctly pleasurable.

'I tell you there are too many for me,' she repeated, sometimes recklessly, but more often shaking her head with ominous dejection.

She had, of course, no money at all. The quantities of 'black men' all about frightened her. She really had no definite idea where she was on the surface of the globe. The orchestra was generally taken from the steamer to some hotel, and kept shut up there till it was time to go on board another steamer. She could not remember the names she heard.

'How do you call this place again?' she used to ask Heyst.

'Sourabaya,' he would say distinctly, and would watch the discouragement at the outlandish sound coming into her eyes, which were fastened on his face.

He could not defend himself from compassion. He suggested that she might go to the consul, but it was his conscience that dictated this advice, not his conviction. She had never heard of the animal or of its uses. A consul! What was it? Who was he? What could he do? And when she learned that perhaps he could be induced to send her home, her head dropped on her breast.

'What am I to do when I get there?' she murmured with an intonation so just, with an accent so penetrating – the charm of her voice did not fail her even in whispering – that Heyst seemed to see the illusion of human fellowship on earth vanish before the naked truth of her existence, and leave them both face to face in a moral desert as arid as the sands of Sahara, without restful shade, without refreshing water.

She leaned slightly over the little table, the same little table at which they had sat when they first met each other; and with no other memories but of the stones in the streets her childhood had known, in the distress of the incoherent, confused, rudimentary impressions of her travels inspiring her with a vague terror of the world, she said rapidly, as one speaks in desperation:

'*You* do something! You are a gentleman. It wasn't I who spoke to you first, was it? I didn't begin, did I? It was you who came along and spoke to me when I was standing over there. What did you want to speak to me for? I don't care what it is, but you must do something.'

Her attitude was fierce and entreating at the same time – clamorous, in fact, though her voice had hardly risen above a breath. It was clamorous enough to be noticed. Heyst, on purpose, laughed aloud. She nearly choked with indignation at this brutal heartlessness.

'What did you mean, then, by saying "command me"?' she almost hissed.

Something hard in his mirthless stare, and a quiet final 'All right', steadied her.

'I am not rich enough to buy you out,' he went on, speaking with an extraordinary detached grin, 'even if it were to be done; but I can always steal you.'

She looked at him profoundly, as though these words had a hidden and very complicated meaning.

'Get away now,' he said rapidly, 'and try to smile as you go.'

She obeyed with unexpected readiness; and as she had a set of very good white teeth, the effect of the mechanical, ordered smile was joyous, radiant. It astonished Heyst. No wonder, it flashed through his mind, women can deceive men so completely. The faculty was inherent in them; they seemed to be created with a special aptitude. Here was a smile the origin of which was well known to him; and yet it had conveyed a sensation of warmth, had given him a sort of ardour to live which was very new to his experience.

By this time she was gone from the table, and had joined the other 'ladies of the orchestra'. They trooped towards the platform, driven in truculently by the haughty mate of Zangiacomo, who looked as though she were restraining herself with difficulty from punching their backs. Zangiacomo followed, with his great, pendulous dyed beard and short mess-jacket, with an aspect of hang-dog concentration imparted by his drooping head and the uneasiness of his eyes, which were set very close together. He climbed the steps last of all, turned about, displaying his purple beard to the hall, and tapped with his bow. Heyst winced in anticipation of the horrible racket. It burst out immediately unabashed and awful. At the end of the platform the woman at the piano, presenting her cruel profile, her head tilted back, banged the keys without looking at the music.

Heyst could not stand the uproar for more than a minute. He went out, his brain racked by the rhythm of some more or less Hungarian dance music. The forests inhabited by the New Guinea cannibals where he had encountered the most exciting of his earlier futile adventures were silent. And this adventure, not in its execution, perhaps, but in its nature, required even more nerve than anything he had faced before. Walking among the paper lanterns suspended to trees he remembered with regret the gloom and the dead stillness of the forests at the back of Geelvink Bay, perhaps the wildest, the unsafest, the most deadly spot on earth from which the sea can be seen. Oppressed by his thoughts, he sought the obscurity and peace of his bedroom; but they were not complete. The distant sounds of the concert reached his ear, faint indeed but still disturbing. Neither did he feel very safe in there; for that sentiment depends not on extraneous circumstances but on our inward conviction. He did not attempt to go to sleep; he did not even unbutton the top button of his tunic. He sat in a chair and mused. Formerly, in solitude and in silence, he had been used to thinking clearly and sometimes even profoundly, seeing life outside the flattering optical delusion of everlasting hope, of conventional self-deceptions, of an ever-expected happiness. But now he was troubled; a light veil seemed to hang before his mental vision; the awakening of a tenderness, indistinct and confused as yet, towards an unknown woman.

Gradually silence, a real silence, had established itself round him. The concert was over; the audience had gone, the concert-hall was dark; and even the Pavilion, where the ladies' orchestra slept after its noisy labours, showed not a gleam of light. Heyst suddenly felt restless in all his limbs. As this reaction from the long immobility would not be denied, he humoured it by passing quietly along the back veranda and out into the grounds at the side of the house, into the black shadows under the trees, where the extinguished paper lanterns were gently swinging their globes like withered fruit.

He paced there to and fro for a long time, a calm, meditative ghost in his white drill-suit, revolving in his head thoughts absolutely novel, disquieting, and seductive; accustoming his mind to the contemplation of his purpose, in order that by being faced steadily it should appear praiseworthy and wise. For the use of reason is to justify the obscure desires that move our conduct, impulses, passions, prejudices, and follies, and also our fears.

He felt that he had engaged himself by a rash promise to an action big with incalculable consequences. And then he asked himself if the girl had understood what he meant. Who could tell? He was assailed by all sorts of doubts. Raising his head, he perceived something white flitting between the trees. It vanished almost at once; but there could be no mistake. He was vexed at being detected roaming like this in the middle of the night. Who could that be? It never occurred to him that perhaps the girl, too, would not be able to sleep. He advanced prudently. Then he saw the white, phantom-like apparition again; and the next moment all his doubts as to the state of her mind were laid at rest, because he felt her clinging to him after the manner of supplicants all the world over. Her whispers were so incoherent that he could not understand anything; but this did not prevent him from being profoundly moved. He had no illusions about her; but his sceptical mind was dominated by the fulness of his heart.

'Calm yourself, calm yourself,' he murmured in her ear, returning her clasp at first mechanically, and afterward with a growing appreciation of her distressed humanity. The heaving of her breast and the trembling of all her limbs, in the closeness of his embrace, seemed to enter his body, to infect his very heart. While she was growing quieter in his arms, he was becoming more agitated, as if there were only a fixed quantity of violent emotion on this earth. The very night seemed more dumb, more still, and the immobility of the vague, black shapes, surrounding him more perfect.

'It will be all right,' he tried to reassure her, with a tone of conviction, speaking into her ear, and of necessity clasping her more closely than before.

Either the words or the action had a very good effect. He heard a light sigh of relief. She spoke with a calmed ardour.

'Oh, I knew it would be all right from the first time you spoke to me! Yes, indeed, I knew directly you came up to me that evening. I knew it would be all right, if you only cared to make it so; but of course I could not tell if you meant it. "Command me," you said. Funny thing for a man like you to say. Did you really mean it? You weren't making fun of me?'

He protested that he had been a serious person all his life.

'I believe you,' she said ardently. He was touched by this declaration. 'It's the way you have of speaking as if you were amused with people,' she went on. 'But I wasn't deceived. I could see you were angry with that beast of a woman. And you are clever. You spotted something at once. You saw it in my face, eh? It isn't a bad face – say? You'll never be sorry. Listen – I'm not twenty yet. It's the truth, and I can't be so bad looking, or else – I will tell you straight that I have been worried and pestered by fellows like this before. I don't know what comes to them –'

She was speaking hurriedly. She choked, and then exclaimed, with an accent of despair:

'What is it? What's the matter?'

Heyst had removed his arms from her suddenly, and had recoiled a little. 'Is it my fault? I didn't even look at them, I tell you straight. Never! Have I looked at you? Tell me. It was you that began it.'

In truth, Heyst had shrunk from the idea of competition with fellows unknown, with Schomberg the hotel-keeper. The vaporous white figure before him swayed pitifully in the darkness. He felt ashamed of his fastidiousness.

'I am afraid we have been detected,' he murmured. 'I think I saw somebody on the path between the house and the bushes behind you.'

He had seen no one. It was a compassionate lie, if there ever was one. His compassion was as genuine as his shrinking had been, and in his judgement more honourable.

She didn't turn her head. She was obviously relieved.

'Would it be that brute?' she breathed out, meaning Schomberg, of course. 'He's getting too forward with me now. What can you expect? Only this evening, after supper, he – but I slipped away. You don't mind him, do you? Why, I could face him myself now that I know you care for me. A girl can always put up a fight. You believe me? Only it isn't easy to stand up for yourself when you feel there's nothing and nobody at your back. There's nothing so lonely in the world as a girl who has got to look after herself. When I left poor dad in that home – it was in the country, near a village – I came out of the gates with seven shillings and threepence in my old purse, and my railway ticket. I tramped a mile, and got into a train –'

She broke off, and was silent for a moment.

'Don't you throw me over now,' she went on. 'If you did, what should I do? I should have to live, to be sure, because I'd be afraid to kill myself; but you would have done a thousand times worse than killing a body. You told me you had been always alone, you had never had a dog, even. Well, then, I won't be in anybody's way if I live with you – not even a dog's. And what else did you mean when you came up and looked at me so close?'

'Close? Did I?' he murmured unstirring before her in the profound darkness. 'So close as that?'

She had an outbreak of anger and despair in subdued tones.

'Have you forgotten, then? What did you expect to find? I know what sort of girl I am; but all the same I am not the sort that men turn their backs on – and you ought to know it, unless you aren't made like the others. Oh, forgive me!

You aren't like the others; you are like no one in the world I ever spoke to. Don't you care for me? Don't you see –?'

What he saw was that, white and spectral, she was putting out her arms to him out of the black shadows like an appealing ghost. He took her hands, and was affected, almost surprised, to find them so warm, so real, so firm, so living in his grasp. He drew her to him, and she dropped her head on his shoulder with a deep sigh.

'I am dead tired,' she whispered plaintively.

He put his arms around her, and only by the convulsive movements of her body became aware that she was sobbing without a sound. Sustaining her, he lost himself in the profound silence of the night. After a while she became still, and cried quietly. Then, suddenly, as if waking up, she asked:

'You haven't seen any more of that somebody you thought was spying about?'

He started at her quick, sharp whisper, and answered that very likely he had been mistaken.

'If it was anybody at all,' she reflected aloud, 'it wouldn't have been anyone but that hotel woman – the landlord's wife.'

'Mrs Schomberg,' Heyst said, surprised.

'Yes. Another one that can't sleep o' nights. Why? Don't you see why? Because, of course, she sees what's going on. That beast doesn't even try to keep it from her. If she had only the least bit of spirit! She knows how I feel, too, only she's too frightened even to look him in the face, let alone open her mouth. He would tell her to go hang herself.'

For some time Heyst said nothing. A public, active contest with the hotel-keeper was not to be thought of. The idea was horrible. Whispering gently to the girl, he tried to explain to her that as things stood, an open withdrawal from the company would be probably opposed. She listened to his explanation anxiously, from time to time pressing the hand she had sought and got hold of in the dark.

'As I told you, I am not rich enough to buy you out; so I shall steal you as soon as I can arrange some means of getting away from here. Meantime it would be fatal to be seen together at night. We mustn't give ourselves away. We had better part at once. I think I was mistaken just now; but if, as you say, that poor Mrs Schomberg can't sleep of nights, we must be more careful. She would tell the fellow.'

The girl had disengaged herself from his loose hold while he talked, and now stood free of him, but still clasping his hand firmly.

'Oh, no,' she said with perfect assurance. 'I tell you she daren't open her mouth to him. And she isn't as silly as she looks. She wouldn't give us away. She knows a trick worth two of that. She'll help – that's what she'll do, if she dares do anything at all.'

'You seem to have a very clear view of the situation,' said Heyst, and received a warm, lingering kiss for this commendation.

He discovered that to part from her was not such an easy matter as he had supposed it would be.

'Upon my word,' he said before they separated, 'I don't even know your name.'

'Don't you? They call me Alma. I don't know why. Silly name! Magdalen too. It doesn't matter; you can call me by whatever name you choose. Yes, you give me a name. Think of one you would like the sound of – something quite new. How I should like to forget everything that has gone before, as one forgets a dream that's done with, fright and all! I would try.'

'Would you really?' he asked in a murmur. 'But that's not forbidden. I understand that women easily forget whatever in their past diminishes them in their eyes.'

'It's your eyes that I was thinking of, for I'm sure I've never wished to forget anything till you came up to me that night and looked me through and through. I know I'm not much account; but I know how to stand by a man. I stood by Father ever since I could understand. He wasn't a bad chap. Now that I can't be of any use to him, I would just as soon forget all that and make a fresh start. But these aren't things that I could talk to you about. What could I ever talk to you about?'

'Don't let it trouble you,' Heyst said. 'Your voice is enough. I am in love with it, whatever it says.'

She remained silent for a while, as if rendered breathless by this quiet statement.

'Oh! I wanted to ask you –'

He remembered that she probably did not know his name, and expected the question to be put to him now; but after a moment of hesitation she went on:

'Why was it that you told me to smile this evening in the concert-room there – you remember?'

'I thought we were being observed. A smile is the best of masks. Schomberg was at a table next but one to us, drinking with some Dutch clerks from the town. No doubt he was watching us – watching you, at least. That's why I asked you to smile.'

'Ah, that's why. It never came into my head.'

'And you did it very well, too – very readily, as if you had understood my intention.'

'Readily!' she repeated. 'Oh, I was ready enough to smile then. That's the truth. It was the first time for years I may say that I felt disposed to smile. I've not had many chances to smile in my life, I can tell you; especially of late.'

'But you do it most charmingly – in a perfectly fascinating way.'

He paused. She stood still, waiting for more with the stillness of extreme delight, wishing to prolong the sensation.

'It astonished me,' he added. 'It went as straight to my heart as though you had smiled for the purpose of dazzling me. I felt as if I had never seen a smile before in my life. I thought of it after I left you. It made me restless.'

'It did all that?' came her voice, unsteady, gentle, and incredulous.

'If you had not smiled as you did, perhaps I should not have come out here tonight,' he said, with his playful earnestness of tone. 'It was your triumph.'

He felt her lips touch his lightly, and the next moment she was gone. Her white dress gleamed in the distance, and then the opaque darkness of the house seemed to swallow it. Heyst waited a little before he went the same way, round the corner, up the steps of the veranda, and into his room, where he lay down at last – not to sleep, but to go over in his mind all that had been said at their meeting.

'It's exactly true about that smile,' he thought. There he had spoken the truth to her; and about her voice, too. For the rest – what must be must be.

A great wave of heat passed over him. He turned on his back, flung his arms crosswise on the broad, hard bed, and lay still, open-eyed under the mosquito net, till daylight entered his room, brightened swiftly, and turned to unfailing sunlight. He got up then, went to a small looking-glass hanging on the wall, and stared at himself steadily. It was not a new-born vanity which induced this long survey. He felt so strange that he could not resist the suspicion of his personal appearance having changed during the night. What he saw in the glass, however, was the man he knew before. It was almost a disappointment – a belittling of his recent experience. And then he smiled at his naïveness; for, being over five and thirty years of age, he ought to have known that in most cases the body is the unalterable mask of the soul, which even death itself changes but little, till it is put out of sight where no changes matter any more, either to our friends or to our enemies.

Heyst was not conscious of either friends or of enemies. It was the very essence of his life to be a solitary achievement, accomplished not by hermit-like withdrawal with its silence and immobility, but by a system of restless wandering, by the detachment of an impermanent dweller amongst changing scenes. In this scheme he had perceived the means of passing through life without suffering and almost without a single care in the world – invulnerable because elusive.

Chapter III

For fifteen years Heyst had wandered, invariably courteous and unapproachable, and in return was generally considered a 'queer chap'. He had started off on these travels of his after the death of his father, an expatriated Swede who died in London, dissatisfied with his country and angry with all the world, which had instinctively rejected his wisdom.

Thinker, stylist, and man of the world in his time, the elder Heyst had begun by coveting all the joys, those of the great and those of the humble, those of the fools and those of the sages. For more than sixty years he had dragged on this painful earth of ours the most weary, the most uneasy soul that civilization had ever fashioned to its end of disillusion and regret. One could not refuse him a measure of greatness, for he was unhappy in a way unknown to mediocre souls. His mother Heyst had never known, but he kept his father's pale, distinguished face in affectionate memory. He remembered him mainly in an ample blue dressing-gown in a large house of a quiet London suburb. For three years, after leaving school at the age of eighteen, he had lived with the elder Heyst, who was then writing his last book. In this work, at the end of his life, he claimed for mankind that right to absolute moral and intellectual liberty of which he no longer believed them worthy.

Three years of such companionship at that plastic and impressionable age were bound to leave in the boy a profound mistrust of life. The young man learned to reflect, which is a destructive process, a reckoning of the cost. It is not the clearsighted who lead the world. Great achievements are accomplished in a blessed, warm mental fog, which the pitiless cold blasts of the father's analysis had blown away from the son.

'I'll drift,' Heyst had said to himself deliberately.

He did not mean intellectually or sentimentally or morally. He meant to drift altogether and literally, body and soul, like a detached leaf drifting in the wind-currents under the immovable trees of a forest glade; to drift without ever catching on to anything.

'This shall be my defence against life,' he had said to himself with a sort of inward consciousness that for the son of his father there was no other worthy alternative.

He became a waif and stray, austerely, from conviction, as others do through drink, from vice, from some weakness of character – with deliberation, as others do in despair. This, stripped of its facts, had been Heyst's life up to that disturbing night. Next day, when he saw the girl called Alma, she managed to give him a glance of frank tenderness, quick as lightning and leaving a profound impression, a secret touch on the heart. It was in the grounds of the hotel, about tiffin time, while the ladies of the orchestra were strolling back to their pavilion after rehearsal, or practice, or whatever they called their morning musical exercises in the hall. Heyst, returning from the town, where he had discovered that there would be difficulties in the way of getting away at once, was crossing the compound, disappointed and worried. He had walked almost unwittingly into the straggling group of Zangiacomo's performers. It was a shock to him, on coming out of his brown study, to find the girl so near to him, as if one waking suddenly should see the figure of his dream turned into flesh and blood. She did not raise her shapely head, but her glance was no dream thing. It was real, the most real impression of his detached existence – so far.

Heyst had not acknowledged it in any way, though it seemed to him impossible that its effect on him should not be visible to anyone who happened to be looking on. And there were several men on the veranda, steady customers of Schomberg's table d'hôte, gazing in his direction – at the ladies of the orchestra, in fact. Heyst's dread arose, not out of shame or timidity, but from his fastidiousness. On getting amongst them, however, he noticed no signs of interest or astonishment on their faces, any more than if they had been blind men. Even Schomberg himself, who had to make way for him at the top of the stairs, was completely unperturbed, and continued the conversation he was carrying on with a client.

Schomberg, indeed, had observed 'that Swede' talking with the girl in the intervals. A crony of his had nudged him; and he had thought that it was so much the better; the silly fellow would keep everybody else off. He was rather pleased than otherwise and watched them out of the corner of his eye with a malicious enjoyment of the situation – a sort of Satanic glee. For he had little doubt of his personal fascination, and still less of his power to get hold of the girl, who seemed too ignorant to know how to help herself, and who was worse than friendless, since she had for some reason incurred the animosity of Mrs

Zangiacomo, a woman with no conscience. The aversion she showed him as far as she dared (for it is not always safe for the helpless to display the delicacy of their sentiments), Schomberg pardoned on the score of feminine conventional silliness. He had told Alma, as an argument, that she was a clever enough girl to see that she could do no better than to put her trust in a man of substance, in the prime of life, who knew his way about. But for the excited trembling of his voice, and the extraordinary way in which his eyes seemed to be starting out of his crimson, hirsute countenance, such speeches had every character of calm, unselfish advice – which, after the manner of lovers, passed easily into sanguine plans for the future.

'We'll soon get rid of the old woman,' he whispered to her hurriedly, with panting ferocity. 'Hang her! I've never cared for her. The climate doesn't suit her; I shall tell her to go to her people in Europe. She will have to go, too! I will see to it. *Eins, zwei*, march! And then we shall sell this hotel and start another somewhere else.'

He assured her that he didn't care what he did for her sake; and it was true. Forty-five is the age of recklessness for many men, as if in defiance of the decay and death waiting with open arms in the sinister valley at the bottom of the inevitable hill. Her shrinking form, her downcast eyes, when she had to listen to him, cornered at the end of any empty corridor, he regarded as signs of submission to the overpowering force of his will, the recognition of his personal fascinations. For every age is fed on illusions, lest men should renounce life early and the human race come to an end.

It's easy to imagine Schomberg's humiliation, his shocked fury, when he discovered that the girl who had for weeks resisted his attacks, his prayers, and his fiercest protestations, had been snatched from under his nose by 'that Swede', apparently without any trouble worth speaking of. He refused to believe the fact. He would have it, at first, that the Zangiacomos, for some unfathomable reason, had played him a scurvy trick, but when no further doubt was possible, he changed his view of Heyst. The despised Swede became for Schomberg the deepest, the most dangerous, the most hateful of scoundrels. He could not believe that the creature he had coveted with so much force and with so little effect, was in reality tender, docile to her impulse, and had almost offered herself to Heyst without a sense of guilt, in a desire of safety, and from a profound need of placing her trust where her woman's instinct guided her ignorance. Nothing would serve Schomberg but that she must have been circumvented by some occult exercise of force or craft, by the laying of some subtle trap. His wounded vanity wondered ceaselessly at the means 'that Swede' had employed to seduce her away from a man like him – Schomberg – as though those means were bound to have been extraordinary, unheard of, inconceivable. He slapped his forehead openly before his customers; he would sit brooding in silence or else would burst out unexpectedly declaiming against Heyst without measure, discretion, or prudence, with swollen features and an affectation of outraged virtue which could not have deceived the most childlike of moralists for a moment – and greatly amused his audience.

It became a recognized entertainment to go and hear his abuse of Heyst, while sipping iced drinks on the veranda of the hotel. It was, in a manner, a more successful draw than the Zangiacomo concerts had ever been – intervals and all. There was never any difficulty in starting the performer off. Anybody could do it, by almost any distant allusion. As likely as not he would start his endless denunciations in the very billiard-room where Mrs Schomberg sat enthroned as usual, swallowing her sobs, concealing her tortures of abject humiliation and terror under her stupid, set, everlasting grin, which, having been provided for her by nature, was an excellent mask, inasmuch as nothing – not even death itself, perhaps – could tear it away.

But nothing lasts in this world, at least without changing its physiognomy. So, after a few weeks, Schomberg regained his outward calm, as if his indignation had dried up within him. And it was time. He was becoming a bore with his inability to talk of anything else but Heyst's unfitness to be at large, Heyst's wickedness, his wiles, his astuteness, and his criminality. Schomberg no longer pretended to despise him. He could not have done it. After what had happened he could not pretend, even to himself. But his bottled-up indignation was fermenting venomously. At the time of his immoderate loquacity one of his customers, an elderly man, had remarked one evening:

'If that ass keeps on like this, he will end by going crazy.'

And this belief was less than half wrong. Schomberg had Heyst on the brain. Even the unsatisfactory state of his affairs, which had never been so unpromising since he came out East directly after the Franco-Prussian War, he referred to some subtly noxious influence of Heyst. It seemed to him that he could never be himself again till he had got even with that artful Swede. He was ready to swear that Heyst had ruined his life. The girl so unfairly, craftily, basely decoyed away would have inspired him to success in a new start. Obviously Mrs Schomberg, whom he terrified by savagely silent moods combined with underhand, poisoned glances, could give him no inspiration. He had grown generally neglectful, but with a partiality for reckless expedients, as if he did not care when and how his career as a hotel-keeper was to be brought to an end. This demoralized state accounted for what Davidson had observed on his last visit to the Schomberg establishment, some two months after Heyst's secret departure with the girl to the solitude of Samburan.

The Schomberg of a few years ago – the Schomberg of the Bangkok days, for instance, when he started the first of his famed table d'hôte dinners – would never have risked anything of the sort. His genius ran to catering, 'white man for white men', and to the inventing, elaborating, and retailing of scandalous gossip with asinine unction and impudent delight. But now his mind was perverted by the pangs of wounded vanity and of thwarted passion. In this state of moral weakness Schomberg allowed himself to be corrupted.

Chapter IV

The business was done by a guest who arrived one fine morning by mail-boat – immediately from Celebes, having boarded her in Macassar, but generally, Schomberg understood, from up China Sea way; a wanderer clearly, even as Heyst was, but not alone and of quite another kind.

Schomberg, looking up from the stern-sheets of his steam-launch, which he used for boarding passenger ships on arrival, discovered a dark, sunken stare plunging down on him over the rail of the first-class part of the deck. He was no great judge of physiognomy. Human beings, for him, were either the objects of scandalous gossip or else the recipients of narrow strips of paper, with proper bill-heads stating the name of his hotel – 'W. Schomberg, proprietor; accounts settled weekly.'

So in the clean-shaven, extremely thin face hanging over the mail-boat's rail Schomberg saw only the face of a possible 'account'. The steam-launches of other hotels were also alongside, but he obtained the preference.

'You are Mr Schomberg, aren't you?' the face asked quite unexpectedly.

'I am, at your service,' he answered from below; for business is business, and its forms and formulas must be observed, even if one's manly bosom is tortured by that dull rage which succeeds the fury of baffled passion, like the glow of embers after a fierce blaze.

Presently the possessor of the handsome but emaciated face was seated beside Schomberg in the stern-sheets of the launch. His body was long and loose-jointed; his slender fingers, intertwined, clasped the leg resting on the knee, as he lolled back in a careless yet tense attitude. On the other side of Schomberg sat another passenger, who was introduced by the clean-shaven man as –

'My secretary. He must have the room next to mine.'

'We can manage that easily for you.'

Schomberg steered with dignity, staring straight ahead, but very much interested by these two promising 'accounts'. Their belongings, a couple of large leather trunks browned by age and a few smaller packages, were piled up in the bows. A third individual – a nondescript, hairy creature – had modestly made his way forward and had perched himself on the luggage. The lower part of his physiognomy was over-developed; his narrow and low forehead, unintelligently furrowed by horizontal wrinkles, surmounted wildly hirsute cheeks and a flat nose with wide, baboon-like nostrils. There was something equivocal in the appearance of his shaggy, hair-smothered humanity. He, too, seemed to be a follower of the clean-shaven man, and apparently had travelled on deck with native passengers, sleeping under the awnings. His broad, squat frame denoted great strength. Grasping the gunwales of the launch, he displayed a pair of remarkably long arms, terminating in thick, brown hairy paws of simian aspect.

'What shall we do with that fellow of mine?' the chief of the party asked Schomberg. 'There must be a boarding-house somewhere near the port – some grog-shop where they could let him have a mat to sleep on?'

Schomberg said there was a place kept by a Portuguese half-caste.

'A servant of yours?' he asked.

'Well, he hangs on to me. He is an alligator-hunter. I picked him up in Colombia, you know. Ever been in Colombia?'

'No,' said Schomberg, very much surprised. 'An alligator-hunter? Funny trade! Are you coming from Colombia, then?'

'Yes, but I have been coming for a long time. I come from a good many places. I am travelling west, you see.'

'For sport, perhaps?' suggested Schomberg.

'Yes. Sort of sport. What do you say to chasing the sun?'

'I see – a gentleman at large,' said Schomberg, watching a sailing canoe about to cross his bow, and ready to clear it by a touch of the helm.

The other passenger made himself heard suddenly.

'Hang these native craft! They always get in the way.'

He was a muscular, short man with eyes that gleamed and blinked, a harsh voice, and a round, toneless, pock-marked face ornamented by a thin, dishevelled moustache, sticking out quaintly under the tip of a rigid nose. Schomberg made the reflection that there was nothing secretarial about him. Both he and his long, lank principal wore the usual white suit of the tropics, cork helmets, pipe-clayed white shoes – all correct. The hairy nondescript creature perched on their luggage in the bow had a check shirt and blue dungaree trousers. He gazed in their direction from forward in an expectant, trained-animal manner.

'You spoke to me first,' said Schomberg in his manly tones. 'You were acquainted with my name. Where did you hear of me, gentlemen, may I ask?'

'In Manila,' answered the gentleman at large, readily. 'From a man with whom I had a game of cards one evening in the Hotel Castille.'

'What man? I've no friends in Manila that I know of,' wondered Schomberg with a severe frown.

'I can't tell you his name. I've clean forgotten it; but don't you worry. He was anything but a friend of yours. He called you all the names he could think of. He said you set a lot of scandal going about him once, somewhere – in Bangkok, I think. Yes, that's it. You were running a table d'hôte in Bangkok at one time, weren't you?'

Schomberg, astounded by the turn of the information, could only thow out his chest more and exaggerate his austere Lieutenant-of-the-Reserve manner. A table d'hôte? Yes, certainly. He always – for the sake of white men. And here in this place, too? Yes, in this place, too.

'That's all right, then.' The stranger turned his black, cavernous, mesmerizing glance away from the bearded Schomberg, who sat gripping the brass tiller in a sweating palm. 'Many people in the evening at your place?'

Schomberg had recovered somewhat.

'Twenty covers or so, take one day with another,' he answered feelingly, as befitted a subject on which he was sensitive. 'Ought to be more, if only people would see that it's for their own good. Precious little profit I get out of it. You are partial to tables d'hôte, gentlemen?'

The new guest made answer that he liked a hotel where one could find some local people in the evening. It was infernally dull otherwise. The secretary, in sign of approval, emitted a grunt of astonishing ferocity, as if proposing to himself to eat the local people. All this sounded like a longish stay, thought Schomberg, satisfied under his grave air; till, remembering the girl snatched away from him by the last guest who had made a prolonged stay in his hotel, he ground his teeth so audibly that the other two looked at him in wonder. The momentary convulsion of his florid physiognomy seemed to strike them dumb. They exchanged a quick glance. Presently the clean-shaven man fired out another question in his curt, unceremonious manner:

'You have no women in your hotel, eh?'

'Women!' Schomberg exclaimed indignantly, but also as if a little frightened. 'What on earth do you mean by women? What women? There's Mrs Schomberg, of course,' he added, suddenly appeased, with lofty indifference.

'If she knows how to keep her place, then it will do. I can't stand women near me. They give me the horrors,' declared the other. 'They are a perfect curse!'

During this outburst the secretary wore a savage grin. The chief guest closed his sunken eyes, as if exhausted, and leaned the back of his head against the stanchion of the awning. In this pose, his long, feminine eyelashes were very noticeable, and his regular features, sharp line of the jaw, and well-cut chin were brought into prominence, giving him a used-up, weary, depraved distinction. He did not open his eyes till the steam-launch touched the quay. Then he and the other man got ashore quickly, entered a carriage, and drove away to the hotel, leaving Schomberg to look after their luggage and take care of their strange companion. The latter, looking more like a performing bear abandoned by his showmen than a human being, followed all Schomberg's movements step by step, close behind his back, muttering to himself in a language that sounded like some sort of uncouth Spanish. The hotel-keeper felt uncomfortable till at last he got rid of him at an obscure den where a very clean, portly Portuguese half-caste, standing serenely in the doorway, seemed to understand exactly how to deal with clients of every kind. He took from the creature the strapped bundle it had been hugging closely through all its peregrinations in that strange town, and cut short Schomberg's attempts at explanation by a most confident –

'I comprehend very well, sir.'

'It's more than I do,' thought Schomberg, going away thankful at being relieved of the alligator-hunter's company. He wondered what these fellows were, without being able to form a guess of sufficient probability. Their names he learned that very day by direct inquiry – 'to enter in my books', he explained in his formal military manner, chest thrown out, beard very much in evidence.

The shaven man, sprawling in a long chair, with his air of withered youth, raised his eyes languidly.

'My name? Oh, plain Mr Jones – put that down – a gentleman at large. And this is Ricardo.' The pock-marked man, lying prostrate in another long chair, made a grimace, as if something had tickled the end of his nose, but did not come out of his supineness. 'Martin Ricardo, secretary. You don't want any more of our history, do you? Eh, what? Occupation? Put down, well – tourists. We've been called harder names before now; it won't hurt our feelings. And that fellow of mine – where did you tuck him away? Oh, he will be all right. When he wants anything he'll take it. He's Peter. Citizen of Colombia. Peter, Pedro –

I don't know that he ever had any other name. Pedro, alligator-hunter. Oh, yes – I'll pay his board with the half-caste. Can't help myself. He's so confoundedly devoted to me that if I were to give him the sack he would fly at my throat. Shall I tell you how I killed his brother in the wilds of Colombia? Well, perhaps some other time – it's a rather long story. What I shall always regret is that I didn't kill him, too. I could have done it without any extra trouble then; now it's too late. Great nuisance; but he's useful sometimes. I hope you are not going to put all this in your book?'

The offhand, hard manner and the contemptuous tone of 'plain Mr Jones' disconcerted Schomberg utterly. He had never been spoken to like this in his life. He shook his head in silence and withdrew, not exactly scared – though he was in reality of a timid disposition under his manly exterior – but distinctly mystified and impressed.

Chapter V

Three weeks later, after putting his cash-box in the safe which filled with its iron bulk a corner of their bedroom, Schomberg turned towards his wife, but without looking at her exactly, and said:

'I must get rid of these two. It won't do!'

Mrs Schomberg had entertained that very opinion from the first; but she had been broken years ago into keeping her opinions to herself. Sitting in her night attire in the light of a single candle, she was careful not to make a sound, knowing from experience that her very assent would be resented. With her eyes she followed the figure of Schomberg, clad in his sleeping suit, and moving restlessly about the room.

He never glanced her way, for the reason that Mrs Schomberg, in her night attire, looked the most unattractive object in existence – miserable, insignificant, faded, crushed, old. And the contrast with the feminine form he had ever in his mind's eye made his wife's appearance painful to his aesthetic sense.

Schomberg walked about swearing and fuming for the purpose of screwing his courage up to the sticking point.

'Hang me if I ought not to go now, at once, this minute, into his bedroom, and tell him to be off – him and that secretary of his – early in the morning. I don't mind a round game of cards, but to make a decoy of my table d'hôte – my blood boils! He came here because some lying rascal in Manila told him I kept a table d'hôte.'

He said these things, not for Mrs Schomberg's information, but simply thinking aloud, and trying to work his fury up to a point where it would give him courage enough to face 'plain Mr Jones'.

'Impudent, overbearing, swindling sharper,' he went on. 'I have a good mind to –'

He was beside himself in his lurid, heavy, Teutonic manner, so unlike the picturesque, lively rage of the Latin races; and though his eyes strayed about irresolutely, yet his swollen, angry features awakened in the miserable woman over whom he had been tyrannizing for years a fear for his precious carcass, since the poor creature had nothing else but that to hold on to in the world. She knew him well; but she did not know him altogether. The last thing a woman will consent to discover in a man whom she loves, or on whom she simply depends, is want of courage. And, timid in her corner, she ventured to say pressingly:

'Be careful, Wilhelm! Remember the knives and revolvers in their trunks.'

In guise of thanks for that anxious reminder, he swore horribly in the direction of her shrinking person. In her scanty nightdress, and barefooted, she recalled a mediaeval penitent being reproved for her sins in blasphemous terms. Those lethal weapons were always present to Schomberg's mind. Personally, he had never seen them. His part, ten days after his guests' arrival, had been to lounge in manly, careless attitudes on the veranda – keeping watch – while Mrs Schomberg, provided with a bunch of assorted keys, her discoloured teeth chattering and her globular eyes absolutely idiotic with fright, was 'going through' the luggage of these strange clients. Her terrible Wilhelm had insisted on it.

'I'll be on the look-out, I tell you,' he said. 'I shall give you a whistle when I see them coming back. You couldn't whistle. And if he were to catch you at it, and chuck you out by the scruff of the neck, it wouldn't hurt you much; but he won't touch a woman. Not he! He has told me so. Affected beast. I must find out something about their little game, and so there's an end of it. Go in! Go now! Quick march!'

It had been an awful job; but she did go in, because she was much more afraid of Schomberg than of any possible consequences of the act. Her greatest concern was lest no key of the bunch he had provided her with should fit the locks. It would have been such a disappointment for Wilhelm. However, the trunks, she found, had been left open; but her investigation did not last long. She was frightened of firearms, and generally of all weapons, not from personal cowardice, but as some women are, almost superstitiously, from an abstract horror of violence and murder. She was out again on the veranda long before Wilhelm had any occasion for a warning whistle. The instinctive, motiveless fear being the most difficult to overcome, nothing could induce her to return to her investigations, neither threatening growls nor ferocious hisses, nor yet a poke or two in the ribs.

'Stupid female!' muttered the hotel-keeper, perturbed by the notion of that armoury in one of his bedrooms. This was from no abstract sentiment; with him it was constitutional. 'Get out of my sight!' he snarled. 'Go and dress yourself for the table d'hôte.'

Left to himself, Schomberg had meditated. What the devil did this mean? His thinking processes were sluggish and spasmodic; but suddenly the truth came to him.

'By heavens, they are desperadoes!' he thought.

Just then he beheld 'plain Mr Jones' and his secretary with the ambiguous name of Ricardo entering the grounds of the hotel. They had been down to the port on some business, and now were returning; Mr Jones lank, spare, opening his long legs with angular regularity like a pair of compasses, the other stepping out briskly by his side. Conviction entered Schomberg's heart. They *were* two desperadoes – no doubt about it. But as the funk which he experienced was merely a general sensation, he managed to put on his most severe Officer-of-the-Reserve manner, long before they had closed with him.

'Good morning, gentlemen.'

Being answered with derisive civility, he became confirmed in his sudden conviction of their desperate character. The way Mr Jones turned his hollow eyes on one, like an incurious spectre, and the way the other, when addressed, suddenly retracted his lips and exhibited his teeth without looking round – here was evidence enough to settle that point. Desperadoes! They passed through the billiard-room, inscrutably mysterious, to the back of the house, to join their violated trunks.

'Tiffin bell will ring in five minutes, gentlemen,' Schomberg called after them, exaggerating the deep manliness of his tone.

He had managed to upset himself very much. He expected to see them come back infuriated and begin to bully him with an odious lack of restraint. Desperadoes! However they didn't; they had not noticed anything unusual about their trunks and Schomberg recovered his composure and said to himself that he must get rid of this deadly incubus as soon as practicable. They couldn't possibly want to stay very long; this was not the town – the colony – for desperate characters. He shrank from action. He dreaded any kind of disturbance – 'fracas', he called it – in his hotel. Such things were not good for business. Of course, sometimes one had to have a 'fracas'; but it had been a comparatively trifling task to seize the frail Zangiacomo – whose bones were no larger than a chicken's – round the ribs, lift him up bodily, dash him to the ground, and fall on him. It had been easy. The wretched, hook-nosed creature lay without movement, buried under its purple beard.

Suddenly, remembering the occasion of that 'fracas', Schomberg groaned with the pain as of a hot coal under his breastbone, and gave himself up to desolation. Ah, if he only had that girl with him he would have been masterful and resolute and fearless – fight twenty desperadoes – care for nobody on earth! Whereas the possession of Mrs Schomberg was no incitement to a display of manly virtues. Instead of caring for no one, he felt that he cared for nothing. Life was a hollow sham; he wasn't going to risk a shot through his lungs or his liver in order to preserve its integrity. It had no savour – damn it!

In his state of moral decomposition, Schomberg, master as he was of the art of hotel-keeping, and careful of giving no occasion for criticism to the powers regulating that branch of human activities, let things take their course; though he saw very well where that course was tending. It began first with a game or two after dinner – for the drinks, apparently – with some lingering customer, at one of the little tables ranged against the walls of the billiard-room. Schomberg detected the meaning of it at once. That's what it was! This was what they were! And, moving about restlessly (at that time his morose silent period had set in), he cast sidelong looks at the game; but he said nothing. It was not worth while having a row with men who were so overbearing. Even when money appeared in connection with these postprandial games, into which more and more people were being drawn, he still refrained from raising the question; he was reluctant to draw unduly the attention of 'plain Mr Jones' and of the equivocal Ricardo, to his person. One evening, however, after the public rooms of the hotel had become empty, Schomberg made an attempt to grapple with the problem in an indirect way.

In a distant corner the tired China boy dozed on his heels, his back against the wall. Mrs Schomberg had disappeared, as usual, between ten and eleven. Schomberg walked about slowly, in and out of the room and the veranda, thoughtful, waiting for his two guests to go to bed. Then suddenly he approached them, militarily, his chest thrown out, his voice curt and soldierly.

'Hot night, gentlemen.'

Mr Jones, lolling back idly in a chair, looked up. Ricardo, as idle, but more upright, made no sign.

'Won't you have a drink with me before retiring?' went on Schomberg, sitting down by the little table.

'By all means,' said Mr Jones lazily.

Ricardo showed his teeth in a strange, quick grin. Schomberg felt painfully how difficult it was to get in touch with these men, both so quiet, so deliberate, so menacingly unceremonious. He ordered the Chinaman to bring in the drinks. His purpose was to discover how long these guests intended to stay. Ricardo displayed no conversational vein, but Mr Jones appeared communicative enough. His voice somehow matched his sunken eyes. It was hollow without being in the least mournful; it sounded distant, uninterested, as though he were speaking from the bottom of a well. Schomberg learned that he would have the privilege of lodging and boarding these gentlemen for at least a month more. He could not conceal his discomfiture at this piece of news.

'What's the matter? Don't you like to have people in your house?' asked plain Mr Jones languidly. 'I should have thought the owner of a hotel would be pleased.'

He lifted his delicate and beautifully pencilled eyebrows. Schomberg muttered something about the locality being dull and uninteresting to travellers – nothing going on – too quiet altogether; but he only provoked the declaration that quiet had its charms sometimes, and even dullness was welcome as a change.

'We haven't had time to be dull for the last three years,' added plain Mr Jones, his eyes fixed darkly on Schomberg, whom he furthermore invited to have another drink, this time with him, and not to worry himself about things he did not understand; and especially not to be inhospitable – which in a hotel-keeper is highly unprofessional.

'I don't understand,' grumbled Schomberg. 'Oh, yes, I understand perfectly well. I –'

'You are frightened,' interrupted Mr Jones. 'What *is* the matter?'

'I don't want any scandal in my place. That's what's the matter.'

Schomberg tried to face the situation bravely, but that steady, black stare affected him. And when he glanced aside uncomfortably, he met Ricardo's grin uncovering a lot of teeth, though the man seemed absorbed in his thoughts all the time.

'And, moreover,' went on Mr Jones in that distant tone of his, 'you can't help yourself. Here we are and here we stay. Would you try to put us out? I dare say you could do it; but you couldn't do it without getting hurt – very badly hurt. We can promise him that, can't we, Martin?'

The secretary retracted his lips and looked up sharply at Schomberg, as if only too anxious to leap upon him with teeth and claws.

Schomberg managed to produce a deep laugh.

'Ha! Ha! Ha!'

Mr Jones closed his eyes wearily, as if the light hurt them, and looked remarkably like a corpse for a moment. This was bad enough; but when he opened them again, it was almost a worse trial for Schomberg's nerves. The spectral intensity of that glance, fixed on the hotel-keeper (and this was most frightful), without any definite expression, seemed to dissolve the last grain of resolution in his character.

'You don't think, by any chance, that you have to do with ordinary people, do you?' inquired Mr Jones, in his lifeless manner, which seemed to imply some sort of menace from beyond the grave.

'He's a gentleman,' testified Martin Ricardo with a sudden snap of the lips, after which his moustaches stirred by themselves in an odd, feline manner.

'Oh, I wasn't thinking of that,' said plain Mr Jones, while Schomberg, dumb and planted heavily in his chair, looked from one to the other, leaning forward a little. 'Of course I am that; but Ricardo attaches too much importance to a social advantage. What I mean, for instance, is that he, quiet and inoffensive as you see him sitting here, would think nothing of setting fire to this house of entertainment of yours. It would blaze like a box of matches. Think of that! It wouldn't advance your affairs much, would it? – whatever happened to us.'

'Come, come gentlemen,' remonstrated Schomberg, in a murmur. 'This is very wild talk!'

'And you have been used to deal with tame people, haven't you? But we aren't tame. We once kept a whole angry town at bay for two days, and then we got away with our plunder. It was in Venezuela. Ask Martin here – he can tell you.'

Instinctively Schomberg looked at Ricardo, who only passed the tip of his tongue over his lips with an uncanny sort of gusto, but did not offer to begin.

'Well, perhaps it would be a rather long story,' Mr Jones conceded after a short silence.

'I have no desire to hear it, I am sure,' said Schomberg. 'This isn't Venezuela. You wouldn't get away from here like that. But all this is silly talk of the worst sort. Do you mean to say you would make deadly trouble for the sake of a few guilders that you and that other' – eyeing Ricardo suspiciously, as one would look at a strange animal – 'gentleman can win of an evening? 'Tisn't as if my customers were a lot of rich men with pockets full of cash. I wonder you take so much trouble and risk for so little money.'

Schomberg's argument was met by Mr Jones's statement that one must do something to kill time. Killing time was not forbidden. For the rest, being in a communicative mood, Mr Jones said languidly and in a voice indifferent, as if issuing from a tomb, that he depended on himself, as if the world were still one great, wild jungle without law. Martin was something like that too – for reasons of his own.

All these statements Ricardo confirmed by short, inhuman grins. Schomberg lowered his eyes, for the sight of these two men intimidated him; but he was losing patience.

'Of course, I could see at once that you were two desperate characters – something like what you say. But what would you think if I told you that I am pretty near as desperate as you two gentlemen? "Here's that Schomberg has an easy time running his hotel," people think; and yet it seems to me I would just as soon let you rip me open and burn the whole show as not. There!'

A low whistle was heard. It came from Ricardo, and was derisive. Schomberg, breathing heavily, looked on the floor. He was really desperate. Mr Jones remained languidly sceptical.

'Tut, tut! You have a tolerable business. You are perfectly tame; you –' He paused, then added in a tone of disgust: 'You have a wife.'

Schomberg tapped the floor angrily with his foot and uttered an indistinct, laughing curse.

'What do you mean by flinging that damned trouble at my head?' he cried. 'I wish you would carry her off with you somewhere to the devil! I wouldn't run after you.'

The unexpected outburst affected Mr Jones strangely. He had a horrified recoil, chair and all, as if Schomberg had thrust a wriggling viper in his face.

'What's this infernal nonsense?' he muttered thickly. 'What do you mean? How dare you?'

Ricardo chuckled audibly.

'I tell you I am desperate,' Schomberg repeated. 'I am as desperate as any man ever was. I don't care a hang what happens to me!'

'Well, then' – Mr Jones began to speak with a quietly threatening effect, as if the common words of daily use had some other deadly meaning to his mind – 'well, then, why should you make yourself ridiculously disagreeable to us? If you don't care, as you say, you might just as well let us have the key of that music-shed of yours for a quiet game; a modest bank – a dozen candles or so. It would be greatly appreciated by your clients, as far as I can judge from the way they betted on a game of écarté I had with that fair, baby-faced man – what's his name? They just yearn for a modest bank. And I am afraid Martin here would take it badly if you objected; but of course you won't. Think of the calls for drinks!'

Schomberg, raising his eyes, at last met the gleams in two dark caverns under Mr Jones's devilish eyebrows, directed upon him impenetrably. He shuddered as if horrors worse than murder had been lurking there, and said, nodding towards Ricardo:

'I dare say he wouldn't think twice about sticking me, if he had you at his back! I wish I had sunk my launch, and gone to the bottom myself in her, before I boarded the steamer you came by. Ah, well, I've been already living in hell for weeks, so you don't make much difference. I'll let you have the concert-room – and hang the consequences. But what about the boy on late duty? If he sees the cards and actual money passing, he will be sure to blab, and it will be all over the town in no time.'

A ghastly smile stirred the lips of Mr Jones.

'Ah, I see you want to make a success of it. Very good. That's the way to get on. Don't let it disturb you. You chase all the Chinamen to bed early, and we'll get Pedro here every evening. He isn't the conventional waiter's cut, but he will do to run to and fro with the tray, while you sit here from nine to eleven serving out drinks and gathering the money.'

'There will be three of them now,' thought the unlucky Schomberg.

But Pedro, at any rate, was just a simple, straightforward brute, if a murderous one. There was no mystery about him, nothing uncanny, no suggestion of a stealthy, deliberate wildcat turned into a man, or of an insolent spectre on leave from Hades, endowed with skin and bones and a subtle power of terror. Pedro with his fangs, his tangled beard, and queer stare of his little bear's eyes was, by comparison, delightfully natural. Besides, Schomberg could no longer help himself.

'That will do very well,' he asserted mournfully. 'But mind, gentlemen, if you had turned up here only three months ago – ay, less than three months ago – you would have found somebody very different from what I am now to talk to you. It's true. What do you think of that?'

'I scarcely know what to think. I should think it was a lie. You were probably as tame three months ago as you are now. You were born tame, like most people in the world.'

Mr Jones got up spectrally, and Ricardo imitated him with a snarl and a stretch. Schomberg, in a brown study, went on, as if to himself:

'There has been an orchestra here – eighteen women.'

Mr Jones let out an exclamation of dismay, and looked about as if the walls around him and the whole house had been infected with plague. Then he became very angry, and swore violently at Schomberg for daring to bring up such subjects. The hotel-keeper was too much surprised to get up. He gazed from his chair at Mr Jones's anger, which had nothing spectral in it, but was not the more comprehensible for that.

'What's the matter?' he stammered out. 'What subject? Didn't you hear me say it was an orchestra? There's nothing wrong in that. Well, there was a girl amongst them –' Schomberg's eyes went stony; he clasped his hands in front of his breast with such force that his knuckles came out white. 'Such a girl! Tame, am I? I would have kicked everything to pieces about me for her. And she, of course . . . I am in the prime of life. . . . Then a fellow bewitched her – a vagabond, a false, lying, swindling, underhand, stick-at-nothing brute. Ah!'

His entwined fingers cracked as he tore his hands apart, flung out his arms, and leaned his forehead on them in a passion of fury. The other two looked at his shaking back – the attenuated Mr Jones with mingled scorn and a sort of fear, Ricardo with the expression of a cat which sees a piece of fish in the pantry out of reach. Schomberg flung himself backwards. He was dry-eyed, but he gulped as if swallowing sobs.

'No wonder you can do with me what you like. You have no idea – just let me tell you of my trouble –'

'I don't want to know anything of your beastly trouble,' said Mr Jones, in his most lifelessly positive voice.

He stretched forth an arresting hand, and, as Schomberg remained open-mouthed, he walked out of the billiard-room in all the uncanniness of his thin shanks. Ricardo followed at his leader's heels; but he showed his teeth to Schomberg over his shoulder.

CHAPTER VI

FROM THAT evening dated those mysterious but significant phenomena in Schomberg's establishment which attracted Captain Davidson's casual notice when he dropped in, placid yet astute, in order to return Mrs Schomberg's Indian shawl. And, strangely enough, they lasted some considerable time. It argued either honesty and bad luck or extraordinary restraint on the part of 'plain Mr Jones and Co.' in their discreet operations with cards.

It was a curious and impressive sight, the inside of Schomberg's concert-hall, encumbered at one end by a great stack of chairs piled up on and about the musicians' platform, and lighted at the other by two dozen candles disposed about a long trestle table covered with green cloth. In the middle, Mr Jones, a starved spectre turned into a banker, faced Ricardo, a rather nasty, slow-moving cat turned into a croupier. By contrast, the other faces round that table, anything between twenty and thirty, must have looked like collected samples of intensely artless, helpless humanity – pathetic in their innocent watch for the small turns of luck which indeed might have been serious enough for them. They had no notice to spare for the hairy Pedro, carrying a tray with the clumsiness of a creature caught in the woods and taught to walk on its hind legs.

As to Schomberg, he kept out of the way. He remained in the billiard-room, serving out drinks to the unspeakable Pedro with an air of not seeing the growling monster, of not knowing where the drinks went, of ignoring that there was such a thing as a music-room over there under the trees within fifty yards of the hotel. He submitted himself to the situation with a low-spirited stoicism compounded of fear and resignation. Directly the party had broken up (he could see dark shapes of the men drifting singly and in knots through the gate of the compound), he would withdraw out of sight behind a door not quite closed, in order to avoid meeting his two extraordinary guests; but he would watch through the crack their contrasted forms pass through the billiard-room and disappear on their way to bed. Then he would hear doors being slammed upstairs; and a profound silence would fall upon the whole house, upon his hotel appropriated, haunted by those insolently outspoken men provided with a whole armoury of weapons in their trunks. A profound silence. Schomberg sometimes could not resist the notion that he must be dreaming. Shuddering, he would pull himself together, and creep out, with movements strangely inappropriate to the Lieutenant-of-the-Reserve bearing by which he tried to keep up his self-respect before the world.

A great loneliness oppressed him. One after another he would extinguish the lamps, and move softly towards his bedroom, where Mrs Schomberg waited for him – no fit companion for a man of his ability and 'in the prime of life'. But that life, alas, was blighted. He felt it; and never with such force as when on opening the door he perceived that woman sitting patiently in a chair, her toes peeping out under the edge of her night-dress, an amazingly small amount of hair on her head drooping on the long stalk of scraggy neck, with that everlasting scared grin showing a blue tooth and meaning nothing – not even real fear. For she was used to him.

Sometimes he was tempted to screw the head off the stalk. He imagined himself doing it – with one hand, a twisting movement. Not seriously, of course. Just a simple indulgence for his exasperated feelings. He wasn't capable of murder. He was certain of that. And, remembering suddenly the plain speeches of Mr Jones, he would think: 'I suppose I *am* too tame for that' – quite unaware that he had murdered the poor woman morally years ago. He was too unintelligent to have the notion of such a crime. Her bodily presence was bitterly offensive, because of its contrast with a very different feminine image. And it was no use getting rid of her. She was a habit of years, and there would be nothing to put in her place. At any rate, he could talk to that idiot half the night if he chose.

That night he had been vapouring before her as to his intention to face his two guests and, instead of that inspiration he needed, had merely received the usual warning: 'Be careful, Wilhelm.' He did not want to be told to be careful by an imbecile female. What he needed was a pair of woman's arms which, flung round his neck, would brace him up for the encounter. Inspire him, he called it to himself.

He lay awake a long time; and his slumbers, when they came, were unsatisfactory and short. The morning light had no joy for his eyes. He listened dismally to the movements in the house. The Chinamen were unlocking and flinging wide the doors of the public rooms which opened on the veranda. Horrors! Another poisoned day to get through somehow! The recollection of his resolve made him feel actually sick for a moment. First of all the lordly, abandoned attitudes of Mr Jones disconcerted him. Then there was his contemptuous silence. Mr Jones never addressed himself to Schomberg with any general remarks, never opened his lips to him unless to say 'Good morning' – two simple words which, uttered by that man, seemed a mockery of a threatening character. And, lastly, it was not a frank physical fear he inspired – for, as to that, even a cornered rat will fight – but a superstitious shrinking awe, something like an invincible repugnance to seek speech with a wicked ghost. That it was a daylight ghost, surprisingly angular in his attitudes, and for the most part spread out on three chairs, did not make it any easier. Daylight only made him a more weird, a more disturbing and unlawful apparition. Strangely enough in the evening, when he came out of his mute supineness, this unearthly side of him was less obtrusive. At the gaming-table, when actually handling the cards, it was probably sunk quite out of sight; but Schomberg, having made up his mind in ostrich-like fashion to ignore what was going on, never entered the desecrated music-room. He had never seen Mr Jones in the exercise of his vocation – or perhaps it was only his trade.

'I will speak to him tonight,' Schomberg said to himself, while he drank his morning tea, in pyjamas, on the veranda, before the rising sun had topped the trees of the compound, and while the undried dew still lay silvery on the grass, sparkled on the blossoms of the central flower-bed, and darkened the yellow gravel of the drive. 'That's what I'll do. I won't keep out of sight tonight. I shall come out and catch him as he goes to bed carrying the cash-box.'

After all, what was the fellow but a common desperado? Murderous? Oh, yes; murderous enough, perhaps – and the muscles of Schomberg's stomach had a quivering contraction under his airy attire. But even a common desperado would think twice or, more likely, a hundred times, before openly murdering an inoffensive citizen in a civilized, European-ruled town. He jerked his shoulders. Of course! He shuddered again, and paddled back to his room to dress himself. His mind was made up, and he would think no more about it; but still he had his doubts. They grew and unfolded themselves with the progress of the day, as some plants do. At times they made him perspire more than usual, and they did away with the possibility of his afternoon siesta. After turning over on his couch more than a dozen times, he gave up this mockery of repose, got up, and went downstairs.

It was between three and four o'clock, the hour of profound peace. The very flowers seemed to doze on their stalks set with sleepy leaves. Not even the air stirred, for the sea-breeze was not due till later. The servants were out of sight, catching naps in the shade somewhere behind the house. Mrs Schomberg, in a dim upstairs room with closed jalousies, was elaborating those two long pendant ringlets which were such a feature of her hairdressing for her afternoon duties. At that time no customers ever troubled the repose of the establishment. Wandering about his premises in profound solitude, Schomberg recoiled at the door of the billiard room, as if he had seen a snake in his path. All alone with the billiards, the bare little tables, and a lot of untenanted chairs, Mr Secretary Ricardo sat near the wall, performing with lightning rapidity something that looked like tricks with his own personal pack of cards, which he always carried about in his pocket. Schomberg would have backed out quietly if Ricardo had not turned his head. Having been seen, the hotel-keeper elected to walk in as the lesser risk of the two. The consciousness of his inwardly abject attitude towards these men caused him always to throw his chest out and assume a severe expression. Ricardo watched his approach, clasping the pack of cards in both hands.

'You want something, perhaps?' suggested Schomberg in his Lieutenant-of-the-Reserve voice.

Ricardo shook his head in silence and looked expectant. With him Schomberg exchanged at least twenty words every day. He was infinitely more communicative than his patron. At times he looked very much like an ordinary human being of his class; and he seemed to be in an amiable mood at that moment. Suddenly spreading some ten cards face downward in the form of a fan, he thrust them towards Schomberg.

'Come, man, take one quick!'

Schomberg was so surprised that he took one hurriedly, after a very perceptible start. The eyes of Martin Ricardo gleamed phosphorescent in the half-light of the room screened from the heat and glare of the tropics.

'That's the king of hearts you've got,' he chuckled, showing his teeth in a quick flash.

Schomberg, after looking at the card, admitted that it was, and laid it down on the table.

'I can make you take any card I like nine times out of ten,' exulted the secretary, with a strange curl of his lips and a green flicker in his raised eyes.

Schomberg looked down at him dumbly. For a few seconds neither of them stirred; then Ricardo lowered his glance, and, opening his fingers, let the whole pack fall on the table. Schomberg sat down. He sat down because of the faintness in his legs, and for no other reason. His mouth was dry. Having sat down, he felt that he must speak. He squared his shoulders in parade style.

'You are pretty good at that sort of thing,' he said.

'Practice makes perfect,' replied the secretary.

His precarious amiability made it impossible for Schomberg to get away. Thus, from his very timidity, the hotel-keeper found himself engaged in a conversation the thought of which filled him with apprehension. It must be said, in justice to Schomberg, that he concealed his funk very creditably. The habit of throwing out his chest and speaking in a severe voice stood him in good stead. With him, too, practice made perfect; and he would probably have kept it up to the end, to the very last moment, to the ultimate instant of breaking strain which would leave him grovelling on the floor. To add to his secret trouble, he was at a loss what to say. He found nothing else but the remark:

'I suppose you are fond of cards.'

'What would you expect?' asked Ricardo in a simple, philosophical tone. 'It is likely I should not be?' Then, with sudden fire: 'Fond of cards? Ay, passionately!'

The effect of this outburst was augmented by the quiet lowering of the eyelids, by a reserved pause as though this had been a confession of another kind of love. Schomberg cudgelled his brains for a new topic, but he could not find one. His usual scandalous gossip would not serve this turn. That desperado did not know anyone anywhere within a thousand miles. Schomberg was almost compelled to keep to the subject.

'I suppose you've always been so – from your early youth.'

Ricardo's eyes remained cast down. His fingers toyed absently with the pack on the table.

'I don't know that it was so early. I first got in the way of it playing for tobacco – in forecastles of ships, you know – common sailor games. We used to spend whole watches below at it, round a chest, under a slush lamp. We would hardly spare the time to get a bite of salt horse – neither eat nor sleep. We could hardly stand when the watches were mustered on deck. Talk of gambling!' He dropped the reminiscent tone to add the information, 'I was bred to the sea from a boy, you know.'

Schomberg had fallen into a reverie, but without losing the sense of impending calamity. The next words he heard were:

'I got on all right at sea, too. Worked up to be mate. I was mate of a schooner – yacht, you might call her – a special good berth too, in the Gulf of Mexico, a soft job that you don't run across more than once in a lifetime. Yes, I was mate of her when I left the sea to follow him.'

Ricardo tossed up his chin to indicate the room above; from which

Schomberg, his wits painfully aroused by this reminder of Mr Jones's existence, concluded that the latter had withdrawn into his bedroom. Ricardo, observing him from under lowered eyelids went on:

'It so happened that we were shipmates.'

'Mr Jones, you mean? Is he a sailor too?'

Ricardo raised his eyelids at that.

'He's no more Mr Jones than you are,' he said with obvious pride. 'He's a sailor! That just shows your ignorance. But there! A foreigner can't be expected to know any better. I am an Englishman, and I know a gentleman at sight. I should know one drunk, in the gutter, in jail, under the gallows. There's a something – it isn't exactly the appearance, it's a – no use me trying to tell you. You ain't an Englishman; and if you were, you wouldn't need to be told.'

An unsuspected stream of loquacity had broken its dam somewhere deep within the man, had diluted his fiery blood and softened his pitiless fibre. Schomberg experienced mingled relief and apprehension, as if suddenly an enormous savage cat had begun to wind itself about his legs in inexplicable friendliness. No prudent man under such circumstances would dare to stir. Schomberg didn't stir. Ricardo assumed an easy attitude, with an elbow on the table. Schomberg squared his shoulders afresh.

'I was employed, in that there yacht – schooner, whatever you call it – by ten gentlemen at once. That surprises you, eh? Yes, yes, ten. Leastwise there were nine of them gents good enough in their way, and one downright gentleman, and that was . . .'

Ricardo gave another upward jerk of his chin as much as to say: He! The only one.

'And no mistake,' he went on. 'I spotted him from the first day. How? Why? Ay, you may ask. Hadn't seen that many gentlemen in my life. Well, somehow I did. If you were an Englishman, you would –'

'What was your yacht?' Schomberg interrupted as impatiently as he dared; for this harping on nationality jarred on his already tried nerves. 'What was the game?'

'You have a headpiece on you! Game! 'Xactly. That's what it was – the sort of silliness gentlemen will get up among themselves to play at adventure. A treasure-hunting expedition. Each of them put down so much money, you understand, to buy the schooner. Their agent in the city engaged me and the skipper. The greatest secrecy and all that. I reckon he had a twinkle in his eye all the time – and no mistake. But that wasn't our business. Let them bust their money as they like. The pity of it was that so little of it came our way. Just fair pay and no more. And damn any pay, much or little, anyhow – that's what I say!'

He blinked his eyes greenishly in the dim light. The heat seemed to have stilled everything in the world but his voice. He swore at large, abundantly, in snarling undertones, it was impossible to say why; then calmed down as inexplicably and went on, as a sailor yarns.

'At first there were only nine of them adventurous sparks; then, just a day or two before the sailing date, *he* turned up. Heard of it somehow, somewhere – I would say from some woman, if I didn't know him as I do. He would give any woman a ten-mile berth. He can't stand them. Or maybe in a flash bar. Or maybe in one of them grand clubs in Pall Mall. Anyway the agent netted him in all right – cash down, and only about four and twenty hours for him to get ready; but he didn't miss his ship. Not he! You might have called it a pier-head jump – for a gentleman. I saw him come along. Know the West India Docks, eh?'

Schomberg did not know the West India Docks. Ricardo looked at him pensively for a while, and then continued, as if such ignorance had to be disregarded.

'Our tug was already alongside. Two loafers were carrying his dunnage behind him. I told the dockman at our moorings to keep all fast for a minute. The gangway was down already; but he made nothing of it. Up he jumps, one leap, swings his long legs over the rail, and there he is on board. They pass up his swell dunnage, and he puts his hand in his trousers' pocket and throws all his small change on the wharf for them chaps to pick up. They were still promenading that wharf on all fours when we cast off. It was only then that he looked at me – quietly, you know; in a slow way. He wasn't so thin then as he is now; but I noticed he wasn't so young as he looked – not by a long chalk. He seemed to touch me inside somewhere. I went away pretty quick from there; I was wanted forward anyhow. I wasn't frightened. What should I be frightened for? I only felt touched – on the very spot. But Jee-miny, if anybody had told me we should be partners before the year was out – well, I would have –'

He swore a variety of strange oaths, some common, others quaintly horrible to Schomberg's ears, and all mere innocent exclamations of wonder at the shifts and changes of human fortune. Schomberg moved slightly in his chair. But the admirer and partner of 'plain Mr Jones' seemed to have forgotten Schomberg's existence for the moment. The stream of ingenuous blasphemy – some of it in bad Spanish – had run dry, and Martin Ricardo, connoisseur in gentlemen, sat dumb with a stony gaze as if still marvelling inwardly at the amazing elections, conjunctions, and associations of events which influence man's pilgrimage on this earth.

At last Schomberg spoke tentatively:

'And so the – the gentleman, up there, talked you over into leaving a good berth?'

Ricardo started.

'Talked me over! Didn't need to talk me over. Just beckoned to me, and that was enough. By that time we were in the Gulf of Mexico. One night we were lying at anchor, close to a dry sandbank – to this day I am not sure where it was – off the Colombian coast or thereabouts. We were to start digging the next morning, and all hands had turned in early, expecting a hard day with the shovels. Up he comes, and in his quiet, tired way of speaking – you can tell a gentleman by that as much as by anything else almost – up he comes behind me and says, just like that into my ear, in a manner: "Well, what do you think of our treasure hunt now?"

'I didn't even turn my head; 'xactly as I stood, I remained, and I spoke no louder than himself:

' "If you want to know, sir, it's nothing but just damned tomfoolery."

'We had, of course, been having short talks together at one time or another during the passage. I dare say he had read me like a book. There ain't much to me, except that I have never been tame, even when walking the pavement and cracking jokes and standing drinks to chums – ay, and to strangers, too. I would watch them lifting their elbows at my expense, or splitting their sides at my fun – I *can* be funny when I like, you bet!'

A pause for self-complacent contemplation of his own fun and generosity checked the flow of Ricardo's speech. Schomberg was concerned to keep within bounds the enlargement of his eyes, which he seemed to feel growing bigger in his head.

'Yes, yes,' he whispered hastily.

'I would watch them and think: "You boys don't know who I am. If you did –!" With girls, too. Once I was courting a girl. I used to kiss her behind the ear and say to myself: "If you only knew who's kissing you, my dear, you would scream and bolt!" Ha! ha! Not that I wanted to do them any harm; but I felt the power in myself. Now, here we sit, friendly like, and that's all right. You aren't in my way. But I am not friendly to you. I just don't care. Some men do say that; but I really don't. You are no more to me one way or another than that fly there. Just so. I'd squash you or leave you alone. I don't care what I do.'

If real force of character consists in overcoming our sudden weaknesses, Schomberg displayed plenty of that quality. At the mention of the fly, he re-enforced the severe dignity of his attitude as one inflates a collapsing toy balloon with a great effort of breath. The easygoing, relaxed attitude of Ricardo was really appalling.

'That's so,' he went on. 'I am that sort of fellow. You wouldn't think it, would you? No. You have to be told. So I am telling you, and I dare say you only half believe it. But you can't say to yourself that I am drunk, stare at me as you may. I haven't had anything stronger than a glass of iced water all day. Takes a real gentleman to see through a fellow. Oh, yes – he spotted me. I told you we had a few talks at sea about one thing or another. And I used to watch him down the skylight, playing cards in the cuddy with the others. They had to pass the time away somehow. By the same token he caught me at it once, and it was then that I told him I was fond of cards – and generally lucky in gambling, too. Yes, he had sized me up. Why not? A gentleman's just like any other man – and something more.'

It flashed through Schomberg's mind that these two were indeed well matched in their enormous dissimilarity, identical souls in different disguises.

'Says he to me' – Ricardo started again in a gossiping manner – ' "I'm packed up. It's about time to go, Martin."

'It was the first time he called me Martin. Says I:

' "Is that it, sir?"

' "You didn't think I was after that sort of treasure, did you? I wanted to clear out from home quietly. It's a pretty expensive way of getting a passage across, but it has served my turn."

'I let him know very soon that I was game for anything, from pitch and toss to wilful murder, in his company.

' "Wilful murder?" says he in his quiet way. "What the deuce is that? What are you talking about? People do get killed sometimes when they get in one's way, but that's self-defence – you understand?"

'I told him I did. And then I said I would run below for a minute, to ram a few of my things into a sailor's bag I had. I've never cared for a lot of dunnage; I believed in going about flying light when I was at sea. I came back and found him strolling up and down the deck, as if he were taking a breath of fresh air before turning in, like on any other evening.

' "Ready?"

' "Yes, sir."

'He didn't even look at me. We had had a boat in the water astern ever since we came to anchor in the afternoon. He throws the stump of his cigar overboard.

' "Can you get the captain out on deck?" he asks.

'That was the last thing in the world I should have thought of doing. I lost my tongue for a moment.

' "I can try," says I.

' "Well, then, I am going below. You get him up and keep him with you till I come back on deck. Mind! Don't let him go below till I return."

'I could not help asking why he told me to rouse a sleeping man, when we wanted everybody on board to sleep sweetly till we got clear of the schooner. He laughs a little and says that I didn't see all the bearings of this business.

' "Mind," he says, "don't let him leave you till you see me come up again." He puts his eyes close to mine. "Keep him with you at all costs."

' "And that means?" says I.

' "All costs to him – by every possible or impossible means. I don't want to be interrupted in my business down below. He would give me lots of trouble. I take you with me to save myself trouble in various circumstances; and you've got to enter on your work right away."

' "Just so, sir," says I; and he slips down the companion.

'With a gentleman you know at once where you are; but it was a ticklish job. The skipper was nothing to me one way or another, any more than you are at this moment, Mr Schomberg. You may light your cigar or blow your brains out this minute, and I don't care a hang which you do, both or neither. To bring the skipper up was easy enough. I had only to stamp on the deck a few times over his head. I stamped hard. But how to keep him up when he got there?

' "Anything the matter, Mr Ricardo?" I heard his voice behind me.

'There he was, and I hadn't thought of anything to say to him; so I didn't turn round. The moonlight was brighter than many a day I could remember in the North Sea.

' "Why did you call me? What are you staring at out there, Mr Ricardo?"

'He was deceived by my keeping my back to him. I wasn't staring at anything, but his mistake gave me a notion.

' "I am staring at something that looks like a canoe over there,' I said very slowly.

'The skipper got concerned at once. It wasn't any danger from the inhabitants, whoever they were.

' "Oh, hang it!" says he. "That's very unfortunate." He had hoped that the schooner being on the coast would not get known so very soon. "Dashed awkward, with the business we've got in hand, to have a lot of niggers watching operations. But are you certain this is a canoe?"

' "It may be a drift-log," I said; "but I thought you had better have a look with your own eyes. You may make it out better than I can."

'His eyes weren't anything as good as mine. But he says:

' "Certainly. Certainly. You did quite right."

'And it's a fact I had seen some drift-logs at sunset. I saw what they were then and didn't trouble my head about them, forgot all about it till that very moment. Nothing strange in seeing drift-logs off a coast like that; and I'm hanged if the skipper didn't make one out in the wake of the moon. Strange what a little thing a man's life hangs on sometimes – a single word! Here you are, sitting unsuspicious before me, and you may let out something unbeknown to you that would settle your hash. Not that I have any ill-feeling. I have no feelings. If the skipper had said, "O, bosh!" and had turned his back on me, he would not have gone three steps towards his bed; but he stood there and stared. And now the job was to get him off the deck when he was no longer wanted there.

' "We are just trying to make out if that object there is a canoe or a log," says he to Mr Jones.

'Mr Jones had come up, lounging as carelessly as when he went below. While the skipper was jawing about boats and drifting logs, I asked by signs, from behind, if I hadn't better knock him on the head and drop him quietly overboard. The night was slipping by, and we had to go. It couldn't be put off till next night no more. No. No more. And do you know why?'

Schomberg made a slight negative sign with his head. This direct appeal annoyed him, jarred on the induced quietude of a great talker forced into the part of a listener and sunk in it as a man sinks into slumber. Mr Ricardo struck a note of scorn.

'Don't know why? Can't you guess? No? Because the boss had got hold of the skipper's cash-box by then. See?'

Chapter VII

'A common thief!'

Schomberg bit his tongue just too late, and woke up completely as he saw Ricardo retract his lips in a cat-like grin; but the companion of 'plain Mr Jones' didn't alter his comfortable, gossiping attitude.

'Garn! What if he did want to see his money back, like any tame shopkeeper, hash-seller, gin-slinger, or ink-spewer does? Fancy a mud turtle like you trying to pass an opinion on a gentleman! A gentleman isn't to be sized up so easily. Even I ain't up to it sometimes. For instance, that night, all he did was to waggle his finger at me. The skipper stops his silly chatter, surprised.

' "Eh? What's the matter?" asks he.

'The matter! It was his reprieve – that's what was the matter.

' "O, nothing, nothing," says my gentleman. "You are perfectly right. A log – nothing but a log."

'Ha, ha! Reprieve, I call it, because if the skipper had gone on with his silly argument much longer he would have had to be knocked out of the way. I could hardly hold myself in on account of the precious minutes. However, his guardian angel put it into his head to shut up and go back to his bed. I was ramping mad about the lost time.

' "Why didn't you let me give him one on his silly coconut, sir?" I asks.

' "No ferocity, no ferocity," he says, raising his finger at me as calm as you please.

'You can't tell how a gentleman takes that sort of thing. They don't lose their temper. It's bad form. You'll never see him lose his temper – not for anybody to see, anyhow. Ferocity ain't good form, either – that much I've learned by this time, and more, too. I've had that schooling that you couldn't tell by my face if I meant to rip you up the next minute – as of course I could do in less than a jiffy. I have a knife up the leg of my trousers.'

'You haven't?' exclaimed Schomberg incredulously.

Mr Ricardo was as quick as lightning in changing his lounging, idle attitude for a stooping position, and exhibiting the weapon with one jerk at the left leg of his trousers. Schomberg had just a view of it, strapped to a very hairy limb, when Mr Ricardo, jumping up, stamped his foot to get the trouser-leg down, and resumed his careless pose with one elbow on the table.

'It's a more handy way to carry a tool than you would think,' he went on, gazing abstractedly into Schomberg's wide-open eyes. 'Suppose some little difference comes up during a game. Well, you stoop to pick up a dropped card, and when you come up – there you are ready to strike, or with the thing up your sleeve ready to throw. Or you just dodge under the table when there's some shooting coming. You wouldn't believe the damage a fellow with a knife under the table can do to ill-conditioned skunks that want to raise trouble, before they begin to understand what the screaming's about, and make a bolt – those that can, that is.'

The roses of Schomberg's cheek at the root of his chestnut beard faded perceptibly. Ricardo chuckled faintly.

'But no ferocity – no ferocity! A gentleman knows. What's the good of getting yourself into a state? And no shirking necessity, either. No gentleman ever shirks. What I learn I don't forget. Why! We gambled on the plains, with a damn lot of cattlemen in ranches; played fair, mind – and then had to fight for our winnings afterwards as often as not. We've gambled on the hills and in the valleys and on the sea-shore, and out of sight of land – mostly fair. Generally it's good enough. We began in Nicaragua first, after we left that schooner and her fool errand. There were one hundred and twenty-seven sovereigns and some Mexican dollars in that skipper's cash-box. Hardly enough to knock a man on the head for from behind, I must confess; but that the skipper had a narrow escape the governor himself could not deny afterwards.'

' "Do you want me to understand, sir, that you mind there being one life more or less on this earth?" I asked him, a few hours after we got away.

' "Certainly not," says he.

' "Well, then, why did you stop me?"

' "There's a proper way of doing things. You'll have to learn to be correct. There's also unnecessary exertion. That must be avoided, too – if only for the look of the thing." A gentleman's way of putting things to you – and no mistake!

'At sunrise we got into a creek, to lie hidden in case the treasure-hunt party had a mind to take a spell hunting for us. And dash me if they didn't! We saw the schooner away out, running to leeward, with ten pairs of binoculars sweeping the sea, no doubt, on all sides. I advised the governor to give her time to beat back again before we made a start. So we stayed up that creek something like ten days, as snug as can be. On the seventh day we had to kill a man, though – the brother of this Pedro here. They were alligator-hunters, right enough. We got our lodgings in their hut. Neither the boss nor I could *habla español* – speak Spanish, you know – much then. Dry bank, nice shade, jolly hammocks, fresh fish, good game, everything lovely. The governor chucked them a few dollars to begin with; but it was like boarding with a pair of savage apes, anyhow. By and by we noticed them talking a lot together. They had twigged the cash-box, and the leather portmanteaus, and my bag – a jolly lot of plunder to look at. They must have been saying to each other:

' "No one's ever likely to come looking for these two fellows, who seem to have fallen from the moon. Let's cut their throats."

'Why, of course! Clear as daylight. I didn't need to spy one of them sharpening a devilish long knife behind some bushes, while glancing right and left with his wild eyes, to know what was in the wind. Pedro was standing by, trying the edge of another long knife. They thought we were away on our look-out at the mouth of the river, as was usual with us during the day. Not that we expected to see much of the schooner, but it was just as well to make certain, if possible; and then it was cooler out of the woods, in the breeze. Well, the governor was there right enough, lying comfortable on a rug, where he could watch the offing, but I had gone back to the hut to get a chew of tobacco out of my bag. I had not broken myself of the habit then, and I couldn't be happy unless I had a lump as big as a baby's fist in my cheek.'

At the cannibalistic comparison, Schomberg muttered a faint, sickly 'don't'. Ricardo hitched himself up in his seat and glanced down his outstretched legs complacently.

'I am tolerably light on my feet, as a general thing,' he went on. 'Dash me if I don't think I could drop a pinch of salt on a sparrow's tail, if I tried. Anyhow, they didn't hear me. I watched them two brown, hairy brutes not ten yards off. All they had on was white linen drawers rolled up on their thighs. Not a word they said to each other. Antonio was down on his thick hams, busy rubbing the knife on a flat stone; Pedro was leaning against a small tree and passing his thumb along the edge of his blade. I got away quieter than a mouse, you bet.

'I didn't say anything to the boss then. He was leaning on his elbow on his rug, and didn't seem to want to be spoken to. He's like that – sometimes that familiar you might think he would eat out of your hand, and at others he would snub you sharper than a devil – but always quiet. Perfect gentleman, I tell you. I didn't bother him then; but I wasn't likely to forget them two fellows, so businesslike with their knives. At that time we had only one revolver between us two – the governor's six-shooter, but loaded only in five chambers; and we had no more cartridges. He had left the box behind in a drawer in his cabin. Awkward! I had nothing but an old clasp-knife – no good at all for anything serious.

'In the evening we four sat round a bit of fire outside the sleeping-shed, eating broiled fish off plantain leaves, with roast yams for bread – the usual thing. The governor and I were on one side, and these two beauties cross-legged on the other, grunting a word or two to each other now and then, hardly human speech at all, and their eyes down, fast on the ground. For the last three days we couldn't get them to look us in the face. Presently I began to talk to the boss quietly, just as I am talking to you now, careless like, and I told him all I had observed. He goes on picking up pieces of fish and putting them into his mouth as calm as anything. It's a pleasure to have anything to do with a gentleman. Never looked across at them once.

' "And now," says I, yawning on purpose, "we've got to stand watch at night, turn about, and keep our eyes skinned all day, too, and mind we don't get jumped upon suddenly."

' "It's perfectly intolerable," says the governor. "And you with no weapon of any sort!"

' "I mean to stick pretty close to you, sir, from this on, if you don't mind," says I.

'He just nods the least bit, wipes his fingers on the plantain leaf, puts his hand behind his back, as if to help himself to rise from the ground, snatches his revolver from under his jacket, and plugs a bullet plumb centre into Mr Antonio's chest. See what it is to have to do with a gentleman. No confounded fuss, and things done out of hand. But he might have tipped me a wink or something. I nearly jumped out of my skin. Scared ain't in it! I didn't even know who had fired. Everything had been so still just before that the bang of the shot seemed the loudest noise I had ever heard. The honourable Antonio pitches forward – they always do, towards the shot; you must have noticed that yourself – yes, he pitches forward on to the embers, and all that lot of hair on his face and head flashes up like a pinch of gunpowder, Greasy, I expect; always scraping the fat off them alligators' hides –'

'Look here,' exclaimed Schomberg violently, as if trying to burst some invisible bonds, 'do you mean to say that all this happened?'

'No,' said Ricardo coolly. 'I am making it all up as I go along, just to help you through the hottest part of the afternoon. So down he pitches, his nose on the red embers, and up jumps our handsome Pedro and I at the same time, like two Jacks-in-the box. He starts to bolt away, with his head over his shoulder, and I, hardly knowing what I was doing, spring on his back. I had the sense to get my hands round his neck at once, and it's about all I could do to lock my fingers tight under his jaw. You saw the beauty's neck, didn't you? Hard as iron, too. Down we both went. Seeing this the governor puts his revolver in his pocket.

' "Tie his legs together, sir," I yell. "I'm trying to strangle him."

'There was a lot of their fibre-lines lying about. I gave him a last squeeze and then got up.

' "I might have shot you," says the governor, quite concerned.

' "But you are glad to have saved a cartridge, sir," I tell him.

'My jump did save it. It wouldn't have done to let him get away in the dark like that, and have the beauty dodging around in the bushes, perhaps, with the rusty flint-lock gun they had. The governor owned up that the jump was the correct thing.

' "But he isn't dead," says he, bending over him.

'Might as well hope to strangle an ox. We made haste to tie his elbows back, and then, before he came to himself, we dragged him to a small tree, sat him up, and bound him to it, not by the waist but by the neck – some twenty turns of small line round his throat and the trunk, finished off with a reef-knot under his ear. Next thing we did was to attend to the honourable Antonio, who was making a great smell frizzling his face on the red coals. We pushed and rolled him into the creek, and left the rest to the alligators.

'I was tired. That little scrap took it out of me something awful. The governor hadn't turned a hair. That's where a gentleman has the pull of you. He don't get excited. No gentleman does – or hardly ever. I fell asleep all of a sudden and left him smoking by the fire I had made up, his railway rug round his legs, as calm as if he were sitting in a first-class carriage. We hardly spoke ten words to each other after it was over, and from that day to this we have never talked of the business. I wouldn't have known he remembered it if he hadn't alluded to it when talking with you the other day – you know, with regard to Pedro.

'It surprised you, didn't it? That's why I am giving you this yarn of how he came to be with us, like a sort of dog – dashed sight more useful, though. You know how he can trot around with trays? Well, he could bring down an ox with his fist, at a word from the boss, just as cleverly. And fond of the governor! Oh, my word! More than any dog is of any man.'

Schomberg squared his chest.

'Oh, and that's one of the things I wanted to mention to Mr Jones,' he said. 'It's unpleasant to have that fellow round the house so early. He sits on the stairs at the back for hours before he is needed here, and frightens people so that the service suffers. The Chinamen –'

Ricardo nodded and raised his hand.

'When I first saw him he was fit to frighten a grizzly bear, let alone a Chinaman. He's become civilized now to what he once was. Well, that morning, first thing on opening my eyes, I saw him sitting there, tied up by the neck to the tree. He was blinking. We spent the day watching the sea, and we actually made out the schooner working to windward, which showed that she had given us up. Good! When the sun rose again, I took a squint at our Pedro. He wasn't blinking. He was rolling his eyes, all white one minute and black the next, and his tongue was hanging out a yard. Being tied up short by the neck like this would daunt the arch devil himself – in time – in time, mind! I don't know but that even a real gentleman would find it difficult to keep a stiff lip to the end. Presently we went to work getting our boat ready. I was busying myself setting up the mast, when the governor passes the remark:

' "I think he wants to say something."

'I had heard a sort of croaking going on for some time, only I wouldn't take any notice; but then I got out of the boat and went up to him, with some water.

His eyes were red – red and black and half out of his head. He drank all the water I gave him, but he hadn't much to say for himself. I walked back to the governor.

' "He asks for a bullet in his head before we go," I said. I wasn't at all pleased.

' "Oh, that's out of the question altogether," says the governor.

'He was right there. Only four shots left, and ninety miles of wild coast to put behind us before coming to the first place where you could expect to buy revolver cartridges.

' "Anyhow," I tells him, "he wants to be killed some way or other, as a favour."

'And then I go on setting up the boat's mast. I didn't care much for the notion of butchering a man bound hand and foot and fastened by the neck besides. I had a knife then – the honourable Antonio's knife; and that knife is this knife.'

Ricardo gave his leg a resounding slap.

'First spoil in my new life,' he went on with harsh joviality. 'The dodge of carrying it down there I learned later. I carried it stuck in my belt that day. No, I hadn't much stomach for the job; but when you work with a gentleman of the real right sort you may depend on your feelings being seen through your skin. Says the governor suddenly:

' "It may even be looked upon as his right" – you hear a gentleman speaking there? – "but what do you think of taking him with us in the boat?"

'And the governor starts arguing that the beggar would be useful in working our way along the coast. We could get rid of him before coming to the first place that was a little civilized. I didn't want much talking over. Out I scrambled from the boat.

' "Ay, but will he be manageable, sir?"

' "Oh, yes. He's daunted. Go on, cut him loose – I take the responsibility."

' "Right you are, sir."

'He sees me come along smartly with his brother's knife in my hand – I wasn't thinking how it looked from his side of the fence, you know – and jiminy, it nearly killed him! He stared like a crazed bullock and began to sweat and twitch all over, something amazing. I was so surprised that I stopped to look at him. The drops were pouring over his eyebrows, down his beard, off his nose and he gurgled. Then it struck me that he couldn't see what was in my mind. By favour or by right he didn't like to die when it came to it; not in that way, anyhow. When I stepped round to get at the lashing, he let out a sort of soft bellow. Thought I was going to stick him from behind, I guess. I cut all the turns with one slash, and he went over on his side, flop, and started kicking with his tied legs. Laugh! I don't know what there was so funny about it, but I fairly shouted. What between my laughing and his wriggling, I had a job in cutting him free. As soon as he could feel his limbs he makes for the bank, where the governor was standing, crawls up to him on his hands and knees, and embraces his legs. Gratitude, eh? You could see that being allowed to live suited that chap down to the ground. The governor gets his legs away from him gently and just mutters to me:

"Let's be off. Get him into the boat."

'It was not difficult,' continued Ricardo, after eyeing Schomberg fixedly for a moment. 'He was ready enough to get into the boat, and – here he is. He would let himself be chopped into small pieces – with a smile, mind; with a smile! – for the governor. I don't know about him doing that much for me; but pretty near, pretty near. I did the tying up and the untying, but he could see who was the boss. And then he knows a gentleman. A dog knows a gentleman – any dog. It's only some foreigners that don't know; and nothing can teach them, either.'

'And you mean to say,' asked Schomberg, disregarding what might have been annoying for himself in the emphasis of the final remark, 'you mean to say that you left steady employment and good wages for a life like this?'

'There!' began Ricardo quietly. 'That's just what a man like you would say. You are that tame! I follow a gentleman. That ain't the same thing as to serve an employer. They give you wages as they'd fling a bone to a dog, and they expect you to be grateful. It's worse than slavery. You don't expect a slave that's bought for money to be grateful. And if you sell your work – what is it but selling your own self? You've got so many days to live and you sell them one after another. Hey? Who can pay me enough for my life? Ay! But they throw at you your week's money and expect you to say "thank you" before you pick it up.'

He mumbled some curses, directed at employers generally, as it seemed, then blazed out:

'Work be damned! I ain't a dog walking on its hind legs for a bone; I am a man who's following a gentleman. There's a difference which you will never understand, Mr Tame Schomberg.'

He yawned slightly. Schomberg, preserving a military stiffness reinforced by a slight frown, had allowed his thoughts to stray away. They were busy detailing the image of a young girl – absent – gone – stolen from him. He became enraged. There was that rascal looking at him insolently. If the girl had not been shamefully decoyed away from him, he would not have allowed anyone to look at him insolently. He would have made nothing of hitting that rogue between the eyes. Afterwards he would have kicked the other without hesitation. He saw himself doing it; and in sympathy with this glorious vision Schomberg's right foot and arm moved convulsively.

At this moment he came out of his sudden reverie to note with alarm the wide-awake curiosity of Mr Ricardo's stare.

'And so you go like this about the world, gambling,' he remarked inanely, to cover his confusion. But Ricardo's stare did not change its character, and he continued vaguely:

'Here and there and everywhere.' He pulled himself together, squared his shoulders. 'Isn't it very precarious?' he said firmly.

The word precarious seemed to be effective, because Ricardo's eyes lost their dangerously interested expression.

'No, not so bad,' Ricardo said, with indifference. 'It's my opinion that men will gamble as long as they have anything to put on a card. Gamble? That's nature. What's life itself? You never know what may turn up. The worst of it is that you never can tell exactly what sort of cards you are holding yourself.

What's trumps? – that is the question. See? Any man will gamble if only he's given a chance, for anything or everything. You too –'

'I haven't touched a card now for twenty years,' said Schomberg in an austere tone.

'Well, if you got your living that way you would be no worse than you are now, selling drinks to people – beastly beer and spirits, rotten stuff fit to make an old he-goat yell if you poured it down its throat. Pooh! I can't stand the confounded liquor. Never could. A whiff of neat brandy in a glass makes me feel sick. Always did. If everybody was like me, liquor would be going a-begging. You think it's funny in a man, don't you?'

Schomberg made a vague gesture of toleration. Ricardo hitched up in his chair and settled his elbow afresh on the table.

'French *sirops* I must say I do like. Saigon's the place for them. I see you have *sirops* in the bar. Hang me if I ain't getting dry, conversing like this with you. Come Mr Schomberg, be hospitable, as the governor says.'

Schomberg rose and walked with dignity to the counter. His footsteps echoed loudly on the floor of polished boards. He took down a bottle labelled 'Sirop de Groseille'. The little sounds he made, the clink of glass, the gurgling of the liquid, the pop of the soda-water cork had a preternatural sharpness. He came back carrying a pink and glistening tumbler. Mr Ricardo had followed his movements with oblique, coyly expectant yellow eyes, like a cat watching the preparation of a saucer of milk; and the satisfied sound after he had drunk might have been a slightly modified form of purring, very soft and deep in his throat. It affected Schomberg unpleasantly as another example of something inhuman in those men wherein lay the difficulty of dealing with them. A spectre, a cat, an ape – there was a pretty association for a mere man to remonstrate with, he reflected with an inward shudder; for Schomberg had been over-powered, as it were, by his imagination, and his reason could not react against that fanciful view of his guests. And it was not only their appearance. The morals of Mr Ricardo seemed to him to be pretty much the morals of a cat. Too much. What sort of argument could a mere man offer to a . . . or to a spectre, either! What the morals of a spectre could be, Schomberg had no idea. Something dreadful, no doubt. Compassion certainly had no place in them. As to the ape – well, everybody knew what an ape was. It had no morals. Nothing could be more hopeless.

Outwardly, however, having picked up the cigar which he had laid aside to get the drink, with his thick fingers, one of them ornamented by a gold ring, Schomberg smoked with moody composure. Facing him, Ricardo blinked slowly for a time, then closed his eyes altogether, with the placidity of the domestic cat dozing on the hearth-rug. In another moment he opened them very wide, and seemed surprised to see Schomberg there.

'You're having a very slack time today, aren't you?' he observed. 'But then this whole town is confoundedly slack, anyhow; and I've never faced such a slack party at a table before. Come eleven o'clock, they begin to talk of breaking up. What's the matter with them? Want to go to bed so early, or what?'

'I reckon you don't lose a fortune by their wanting to go to bed,' said Schomberg, with sombre sarcasm.

'No,' admitted Ricardo, with a grin that stretched his thin mouth from ear to ear, giving a sudden glimpse of his white teeth. 'Only, you see, when I once start, I would play for nuts, for parched peas, for any rubbish. I would play for them for their souls. But these Dutchmen aren't any good. They never seem to get warmed up properly, win or lose. I've tried them both ways, too. Hang them for a beggarly, bloodless lot of animated cucumbers!'

'And if anything out of the way were to happen, they would be just as cool in locking you and your gentleman up,' Schomberg snarled unpleasantly.

'Indeed!' said Ricardo slowly, taking Schomberg's measure with his eyes. 'And what about you?'

'You talk mighty big,' burst out the hotel-keeper. 'You talk of ranging all over the world, and doing great things, and taking fortune by the scruff of the neck, but here you stick at this miserable business!'

'It isn't much of a lay – that's a fact,' admitted Ricardo unexpectedly.

Schomberg was red in the face with audacity.

'I call it paltry,' he spluttered.

'That's how it looks. Can't call it anything else.' Ricardo seemed to be in an accommodating mood. 'I should be ashamed of it myself, only you see the governor is subject to fits –'

'Fits!' Schomberg cried out, but in a low tone. 'You don't say so!' He exulted inwardly, as if this disclosure had in some way diminished the difficulty of the situation. 'Fits! That's a serious thing, isn't it? You ought to take him to the civil hospital – a lovely place.'

Ricardo nodded slightly, with a faint grin.

'Serious enough. Regular fits of laziness, I call them. Now and then he lays down on me like this, and there's no moving him. If you think I like it, you're a long way out. Generally speaking, I can talk him over. I know how to deal with a gentleman. I am no daily-bread slave. But when he has said, "Martin, I am bored", then look out! There's nothing to do but to shut up, confound it!'

Schomberg, very much cast down, had listened open-mouthed.

'What's the cause of it?' he asked. 'Why is he like this? I don't understand.'

'I think I do,' said Ricardo. 'A gentleman, you know, is not such a simple person as you or I; and not so easy to manage, either. If only I had something to lever him out with!'

'What do you mean, to lever him out with?' muttered Schomberg hopelessly.

Ricardo was impatient with this denseness.

'Don't you understand English? Look here! I couldn't make this billiard table move an inch if I talked to it from now till the end of days – could I? Well, the governor is like that, too, when the fits are on him. He's bored. Nothing's worth while, nothing's good enough, that's mere sense. But if I saw a capstan bar lying about here, I would soon manage to shift that billiard table of yours a good many inches. And that's all there is to it.'

He rose noiselessly, stretched himself, supple and stealthy, with curious sideways movements of his head and unexpected elongations of his thick body, glanced out of the corners of his eyes in the direction of the door and finally leaned back against the table, folding his arms on his breast comfortably, in a completely human attitude.

'That's another thing you can tell a gentleman by – his freakishness. A gentleman ain't accountable to nobody, any more than a tramp on the roads. He ain't got to keep time. The governor got like this once in a one-horse Mexican *pueblo* on the uplands, away from everywhere. He lay all day long in a dark room –'

'Drunk?' This word escaped Schomberg by inadvertence, at which he became frightened. But the devoted secretary seemed to find it natural.

'No, that never comes on together with this kind of fit. He just lay there full length on a mat, while a ragged, bare-legged boy that he had picked up in the street sat in the *patio*, between two oleanders near the open door of his room, strumming on a guitar and singing *tristes* to him from morning to night. You know *tristes* – twang, twang, twang, aouh, hoo! Chroo, yah!'

Schomberg uplifted his hands in distress. This tribute seemed to flatter Ricardo. His mouth twitched grimly.

'Like that – enough to give colic to an ostrich, eh? Awful. Well, there was a cook there who loved me – an old fat, Negro woman with spectacles. I used to hide in the kitchen and turn her to, to make me *dulces* – sweet things, you know, mostly eggs and sugar – to pass the time away. I am like a kid for sweet things. And, by the way, why don't you ever have a pudding at your tablydott, Mr Schomberg? Nothing but fruit, morning, noon, and night. Sickening! What do you think a fellow is – a wasp?'

Schomberg disregarded the injured tone.

'And how long did that fit, as you call it, last?' he asked anxiously.

'Weeks, months, years, centuries, it seemed to me,' returned Mr Ricardo with feeling. 'Of an evening the governor would stroll out into the *sala* and fritter his life away playing cards with the *juez* of the place – a little Dago with a pair of black whiskers – ekarty, you know, a quick French game, for small change. And the *commandante*, a one-eyed, half-Indian, flat-nosed ruffian, and I, we had to stand around and bet on their hands. It was awful!'

'Awful,' echoed Schomberg, in a Teutonic throaty tone of despair. 'Look here, I need your rooms.'

'To be sure. I have been thinking that for some time past,' said Ricardo indifferently.

'I was mad when I listened to you. This must end!'

'I think you are mad yet,' said Ricardo, not even unfolding his arms or shifting his attitude an inch. He lowered his voice to add: 'And if I thought you had been to the police, I would tell Pedro to catch you round the waist and break your fat neck by jerking your head backward – *snap*! I saw him do it to a big buck nigger who was flourishing a razor in front of the governor. It can be done. You hear a low crack, that's all – and the man drops down like a limp rag.'

Not even Ricardo's head, slightly inclined on the left shoulder, had moved; but when he ceased the greenish irises which had been staring out of doors glided into the corners of his eyes nearest to Schomberg and stayed there with a coyly voluptuous expression.

CHAPTER VIII

SCHOMBERG FELT desperation, that lamentable substitute for courage, ooze out of him. It was not so much the threat of death as the weirdly circumstantial manner of its declaration which affected him. A mere 'I'll murder you,' however ferocious in tone and earnest in purpose, he could have faced; but before this novel mode of speech and procedure, his imagination being very sensitive to the unusual, he collapsed as if indeed his moral neck had been broken – snap!

'Go to the police? Of course not. Never dreamed of it. Too late now. I've let myself be mixed up in this. You got my consent while I wasn't myself. I explained it to you at the time.'

Ricardo's eye glided gently off Schomberg to stare far away.

'Ay! Some trouble with a girl. But that's nothing to us.'

'Naturally. What I say is, what's the good of all that savage talk to me?' A bright argument occurred to him. 'It's out of proportion; for even if I were fool enough to go to the police now, there's nothing serious to complain about. It would only mean deportation for you. They would put you on board the first west-bound steamer to Singapore.' He had become animated. 'Out of this to the devil,' he added between his teeth for his own private satisfaction.

Ricardo made no comment, and gave no sign of having heard a single word. This discouraged Schomberg, who had looked up hopefully.

'Why do you want to stick here?' he cried. 'It can't pay you people to fool around like this. Didn't you worry just now about moving your governor? Well, the police would move him for you; and from Singapore you can go on to the east coast of Africa.'

'I'll be hanged if the fellow isn't up to that silly trick!' was Ricardo's comment, spoken in an ominous tone which recalled Schomberg to the realities of his position.

'No! No!' he protested. 'It's a manner of speaking. Of course I wouldn't.'

'I think that trouble about the girl has really muddled your brains, Mr Schomberg. Believe me, you had better part friends with us; for, deportation or no deportation, you'll be seeing one of us turning up before long to pay you off for any nasty dodge you may be hatching in that fat head of yours.'

'*Gott im Himmel!*' groaned Schomberg. 'Will nothing move him out? Will he stop here *immer* – I mean always? Suppose I were to make it worth your while, couldn't you –'

'No,' Ricardo interrupted. 'I couldn't, unless I had something to lever him out with. I've told you that before.'

'An inducement?' muttered Schomberg.

'Ay. The east coast of Africa isn't good enough. He told me the other day that it will have to wait till he is ready for it; and he may not be ready for a long time, because the east coast can't run away, and no one is likely to run off with it.'

These remarks, whether considered as truisms or as depiciting Mr Jones's mental state, were distinctly discouraging to the long-suffering Schomberg; but there is truth in the well-known saying that places the darkest hour before the dawn. The sound of words, apart from the context, has its power; and these two words, 'run off', had a special affinity to the hotel-keeper's haunting idea. It was always present in his brain, and now it came forward evoked by a purely fortuitous expression. No, nobody could run off with a continent; but Heyst had run off with the girl!

Ricardo could have had no conception of the cause of Schomberg's changed expression. Yet it was noticeable enough to interest him so much that he stopped the careless swinging of his leg and said, looking at the hotel-keeper:

'There's not much use arguing against that sort of talk – is there?'

Schomberg was not listening.

'I could put you on another track,' he said slowly, and stopped, as if suddenly choked by an unholy emotion of intense eagerness combined with fear of failure. Ricardo waited, attentive, yet not without a certain contempt.

'On the track of a man!' Schomberg uttered convulsively, and paused again, consulting his rage and his conscience.

'The man in the moon, eh?' suggested Ricardo, in a jeering murmur.

Schomberg shook his head.

'It would be nearly as safe to rook him as if he were the man in the moon. You go and try. It isn't so very far.'

He reflected. These men were thieves and murderers as well as gamblers. Their fitness for purposes of vengeance was appallingly complete. But he preferred not to think of it in detail. He put it to himself summarily that he would be paying Heyst out and would, at the same time, relieve himself of these men's oppression. He had only to let loose his natural gift for talking scandalously about his fellow creatures. And in this case his great practice in it was assisted by hate, which, like love, has an eloquence of its own. With the utmost ease he portrayed for Ricardo, now seriously attentive, a Heyst fattened by years of private and public rapines, the murderer of Morrison, the swindler of many shareholders, a wonderful mixture of craft and impudence, of deep purposes and simple wiles, of mystery and futility. In this exercise of his natural function Schomberg revived, the colour coming back to his face, loquacious, florid, eager, his manliness set off by the military bearing.

'That's the exact story. He was seen hanging about this part of the world for years, spying into everybody's business: but I am the only one who has seen through him from the first – contemptible, double-faced, stick-at-nothing, dangerous fellow.'

'Dangerous, is he?'

Schomberg came to himself at the sound of Ricardo's voice.

'Well, you know what I mean,' he said uneasily. 'A lying, circumventing, soft-spoken, polite, stuck-up rascal. Nothing open about him.'

Mr Ricardo had slipped off the table, and was prowling about the room in an oblique, noiseless manner. He flashed a grin at Schomberg in passing, and a snarling:

'Ah! H'm!'

'Well, what more dangerous do you want?' argued Schomberg. 'He's in no way a fighting man, I believe,' he added negligently.

'And you say he has been living alone there?'

'Like the man in the moon,' answered Schomberg readily. 'There's no one that cares a rap what becomes of him. He has been lying low, you understand, after bagging all that plunder.'

'Plunder, eh? Why didn't he go home with it?' inquired Ricardo.

The henchman of 'plain Mr Jones' was beginning to think that this was something worth looking into. And he was pursuing truth in the manner of men of sounder morality and purer intentions than his own; that is, he pursued it in the light of his own experience and prejudices. For facts, whatever their origin (and God only knows where they come from), can be only tested by our own particular suspicions. Ricardo was suspicious all round. Schomberg, such is the tonic of recovered self-esteem, retorted fearlessly:

'Go home? Why don't *you* go home? To hear you talk, you must have made a pretty considerable pile going round winning people's money. You ought to be ready by this time.'

Ricardo stopped to look at Schomberg with surprise.

'You think yourself very clever, don't you?' he said.

Schomberg just then was so conscious of being clever that the snarling irony left him unmoved. There was positively a smile in his noble Teutonic beard, the first smile for weeks. He was in a felicitous vein.

'How do you know that he wasn't thinking of going home? As a matter of fact, he was on his way home.'

'And how do I know that you are not amusing yourself by spinning out a blamed fairy tale?' interrupted Ricardo roughly. 'I wonder at myself listening to the silly rot!'

Schomberg received this turn of temper unmoved. He did not require to be very subtly observant to notice that he had managed to arouse some sort of feeling, perhaps of greed, in Ricardo's breast.

'You won't believe me? Well! You can ask anybody that comes here if that – that Swede hadn't got as far as this house on his way home. Why should he turn up here if not for that? You ask anybody.'

'Ask, indeed!' returned the other. 'Catch me asking at large about a man I mean to drop on! Such jobs must be done on the quiet – or not at all.'

The peculiar intonation of the last phrase touched the nape of Schomberg's neck with a chill. He cleared his throat slightly and looked away as though he had heard something indelicate. Then, with a jump as it were:

'Of course he didn't tell me. Is it likely? But haven't I got eyes? Haven't I got my common sense to tell me? I can see through people. By the same token, he called on the Tesmans. Why did he call on the Tesmans two days running, eh? You don't know? You can't tell?'

He waited complacently till Ricardo had finished swearing quite openly at him for a confounded chatterer, and then went on:

'A fellow doesn't go to a counting-house in business hours for a chat about the weather, two days running. Then why? To close his account with them one day, and to get his money out the next! Clear, what?'

Ricardo, with his trick of looking one way and moving another approached Schomberg slowly.

'To get his money?'

'*Gewiss*,' snapped Schomberg with impatient superiority. 'What else? That is, only the money he had with the Tesmans. What he has buried or put away on the island, devil only knows. When you think of the lot of hard cash that passed through that man's hands, for wages and stores and all that – and he's just a cunning thief, I tell you.' Ricardo's hard stare discomposed the hotel-keeper, and he added in an embarrassed tone: 'I mean a common, sneaking thief – no account at all. And he calls himself a Swedish baron, too! Tfui!'

'He's a baron, is he? That foreign nobility ain't much,' commented Ricardo seriously. 'And then what? He hung about here.'

'Yes, he hung about,' said Schomberg, making a wry mouth. 'He – hung about. That's it. Hung –'

His voice died out. Curiosity was depicted in Ricardo's countenance.

'Just like that; nothing? And then turned about and went back to that island again?'

'And went back to that island again,' Schomberg echoed lifelessly, fixing his gaze on the floor.

'What's the matter with you?' asked Ricardo with genuine surprise. 'What is it?'

Schomberg, without looking up, made an impatient gesture. His face was crimson, and he kept it lowered. Ricardo went back to the point.

'Well, but how do you account for it? What was his reason? What did he go back to the island for?'

'Honeymoon!' spat out Schomberg viciously.

Perfectly still, his eyes downcast, he suddenly, with no preliminary stir, hit the table with his fist a blow which caused the utterly unprepared Ricardo to leap aside. And only then did Schomberg look up with a dull, resentful expression.

Ricardo stared hard for a moment, spun on his heel, walked to the end of the room, came back smartly, and muttered a profound 'Ay! Ay!' above Schomberg's rigid head. That the hotel-keeper was capable of a great moral effort was proved by a gradual return of his severe, Lieutenant-of-the-Reserve manner.

'Ay, ay!' repeated Ricardo more deliberately than before, and as if after a further survey of the circumstances, 'I wish I hadn't asked you, or that you had told me a lie. It don't suit me to know that there's a woman mixed up in this affair. What's she like? It's the girl you –'

'Leave off!' muttered Schomberg, utterly pitiful behind his stiff military front.

'Ay, ay!' Ricardo ejaculated for the third time, more and more enlightened and perplexed. 'Can't bear to talk about it – so bad as that? And yet I would bet she isn't a miracle to look at.'

Schomberg made a gesture as if he didn't know, as if he didn't care. Then he squared his shoulders and frowned at vacancy.

'Swedish baron – h'm!' Ricardo continued meditatively. 'I believe the governor would think that business quite worth looking up, if I put it to him properly. The governor likes a duel, if you will call it so; but I don't know a man that can stand up to him on the square. Have you ever seen a cat play with a mouse? It's a pretty sight.'

Ricardo, with his voluptuously gleaming eyes and the coy expression, looked so much like a cat that Schomberg would have felt all the alarm of a mouse if other feelings had not had complete possession of his breast.

'There are no lies between you and me,' he said, more steadily than he thought he could speak.

'What's the good now? He funks women. In that Mexican *pueblo* where we lay grounded on our beef-bones, so to speak, I used to go to dances of an evening. The girls there would ask me if the English *caballero* in the *posada* was a monk in disguise, or if he had taken a vow to the *sanctissima madre* not to speak to a woman, or whether – You can imagine what fairly free-spoken girls will ask when they come to the point of not caring what they say; and it used to vex me. Yes, the governor funks facing women.'

'One woman?' interjected Schomberg in guttural tones.

'One may be more awkward to deal with than two, or two hundred, for that matter. In a place that's full of women you needn't look at them unless you like; but if you go into a room where there is only one woman, young or old, pretty or ugly, you have got to face her. And, unless you are after her, then – the governor is right enough – she's in the way.'

'Why notice them?' muttered Schomberg. 'What can they do?'

'Make a noise, if nothing else,' opined Mr Ricardo curtly, with the distaste of a man whose path is a path of silence; for indeed, nothing is more odious than a noise when one is engaged in a weighty and absorbing card game. 'Noise, noise, my friend,' he went on forcibly; 'confounded screeching about something or other, and I like it no more than the governor does. But with the governor there's something else besides. He can't stand them at all.'

He paused to reflect on this psychological phenomenon, and as no philosopher was at hand to tell him that there is no strong sentiment without some terror, as there is no real religion without a little fetishism, he emitted his own conclusion, which surely could not go to the root of the matter.

'I'm hanged if I don't think they are to him what liquor is to me. Brandy – pah!'

He made a disgusted face, and produced a genuine shudder. Schomberg listened to him in wonder. It looked as if the very scoundrelism of that – that Swede would protect him; the spoil of his iniquity standing between the thief and the retribution.

'That's so, old buck.' Ricardo broke the silence after contemplating Schomberg's mute dejection with a sort of sympathy. 'I don't think this trick will work.'

'But that's silly,' whispered the man deprived of the vengeance which he had seemed already to hold in his hand, by a mysterious and exasperating idiosyncrasy.

'Don't you set yourself to judge a gentleman.' Ricardo, without anger, administered a moody rebuke. 'Even I can't understand the governor thoroughly. And I am an Englishman and his follower. No; I don't think I care to put it before him, sick as I am of staying here.'

Ricardo could not be more sick of staying than Schomberg was of seeing him stay. Schomberg believed so firmly in the reality of Heyst as created by his own power of false inferences, of his hate, of his love of scandal, that he could not contain a stifled cry of conviction as sincere as most of our convictions, the disguised servants of our passions, can appear at a supreme moment.

'It would have been like going to pick up a nugget of a thousand pounds, or two or three times as much, for all I know. No trouble, no –'

'The petticoat's the trouble,' Ricardo struck in.

He had resumed his noiseless, feline, oblique prowling, in which an observer would have detected a new character of excitement, such as a wild animal of the cat species, anxious to make a spring, might betray. Schomberg saw nothing. It would probably have cheered his drooping spirits; but in a general way he preferred not to look at Ricardo. Ricardo, however, with one of his slanting, gliding, restless glances, observed the bitter smile on Schomberg's bearded lips – the unmistakable smile of ruined hopes.

'You are a pretty unforgiving sort of chap,' he said, stopping for a moment with an air of interest. 'Hang me if I ever saw anybody look so disappointed! I bet you would send black plague to that island if you only knew how – eh, what? Plague too good for them? Ha, ha, ha!'

He bent down to stare at Schomberg who sat unstirring with stony eyes and set features, and apparently deaf to the rasping derision of that laughter so close to his red fleshy ear.

'Black plague too good for them, ha, ha!' Ricardo pressed the point on the tormented hotel-keeper. Schomberg kept his eyes down obstinately.

'I don't wish any harm to the girl,' he muttered.

'But did she bolt from you? A fair bilk? Come!'

'Devil only knows what that villainous Swede had done to her – what he promised her, how he frightened her. She couldn't have cared for him, I know.' Schomberg's vanity clung to the belief in some atrocious, extraordinary means of seduction employed by Heyst. 'Look how he bewitched that poor Morrison,' he murmured.

'Ah, Morrison – got all his money, what?'

'Yes – and his life.'

'Terrible fellow, that Swedish baron! How is one to get at him?'

Schomberg exploded.

'Three against one! Are you shy? Do you want me to give you a letter of introduction?'

'You ought to look at yourself in a glass,' Ricardo said quietly. 'Dash me if you don't get a stroke of some kind presently. And this is the fellow who says women can do nothing! That one will do for you, unless you manage to forget her.'

'I wish I could,' Schomberg admitted earnestly. 'And it's all the doing of that Swede. I don't get enough sleep, Mr Ricardo. And then, to finish me off, you gentlemen turn up . . . as if I hadn't enough worry.'

'That's done you good,' suggested the secretary with ironic seriousness. 'Takes your mind off that silly trouble. At your age too.'

He checked himself, as if in pity, and changing his tone:

'I would really like to oblige you while doing a stroke of business at the same time.'

'A good stroke,' insisted Schomberg, as if it were mechanically. In his simplicity he was not able to give up the idea which had entered his head. An idea must be driven out by another idea, and with Schomberg ideas were rare and therefore tenacious. 'Minted gold,' he murmured with a sort of anguish.

Such an expressive combination of words was not without effect upon Ricardo. Both these men were amenable to the influence of verbal suggestions. The secretary of 'plain Mr Jones' sighed and murmured:

'Yes. But how is one to get at it?'

'Being three to one,' said Schomberg, 'I suppose you could get it for the asking.'

'One would think the fellow lived next door,' Ricardo growled impatiently. 'Hang it all, can't you understand a plain question? I have asked you the way.'

Schomberg seemed to revive.

'The way?'

The torpor of deceived hopes underlying his superficial changes of mood had been pricked by these words which seemed pointed with purpose.

'The way is over the water, of course,' said the hotel-keeper. 'For people like you, three days in a good, big boat is nothing. It's no more than a little outing, a bit of a change. At this season the Java Sea is a pond. I have an excellent, safe boat – a ship's life-boat – carry thirty, let alone three, and a child could handle her. You wouldn't get a wet face at this time of the year. You might call it a pleasure-trip.'

'And yet, having this boat, you didn't go after her yourself – or after him? Well, you are a fine fellow for a disappointed lover.'

Schomberg gave a start at the suggestion.

'I am not three men,' he said sulkily, as the shortest answer of the several he could have given.

'Oh, I know your sort,' Ricardo let fall negligently. 'You are like most people – or perhaps just a little more peaceable than the rest of the buying and selling gang that bosses this rotten show. Well, well, you respectable citizen,' he went on, 'let us go thoroughly into the matter.'

When Schomberg had been made to understand that Mr Jones's henchman was ready to discuss, in his own words, 'this boat of yours, with courses and distances', and such concrete matters of no good augury to that villainous Swede, he recovered his soldierly bearing, squared his shoulders, and asked in his military manner:

'You wish, then, to proceed with the business?'

Ricardo nodded. He had a great mind to, he said. A gentleman had to be humoured as much as possible; but he must be managed, too, on occasions, for his own good. And it was the business of the right sort of 'follower' to know the proper time and the proper methods of that delicate part of his duty. Having exposed this theory Ricardo proceeded to the application.

'I've never actually lied to him,' he said, 'and I ain't going to now. I shall just say nothing about the girl. He will have to get over the shock the best he can. Hang it all! Too much humouring won't do here.'

'Funny thing,' Schomberg observed crisply.

'Is it? Ay, you wouldn't mind taking a woman by the throat in some dark corner and nobody by, I bet!'

Ricardo's dreadful, vicious, cat-like readiness to get his claws out at any moment startled Schomberg as usual. But it was provoking too.

'And you?' he defended himself. 'Don't you want me to believe you are up to anything?'

'I, my boy? Oh, yes, I am not that gentleman; neither are you. Take 'em by the throat or chuck 'em under the chin is all one to me – almost,' affirmed Ricardo, with something obscurely ironical in his complacency. 'Now, as to this business. A three days' jaunt in a good boat isn't a thing to frighten people like us. You are right, so far; but there are other details.'

Schomberg was ready enough to enter into details. He explained that he had a small plantation, with a fairly habitable hut on it, on Madura. He proposed that his guest should start from town in his boat, as if going for an excursion to that rural spot. The custom-house people on the quay were used to see his boat go off on such trips.

From Madura, after some repose and on a convenient day, Mr Jones and party would make the real start. It would all be plain sailing. Schomberg undertook to provision the boat. The greatest hardship the voyagers need apprehend would be a mild shower of rain. At that season of the year there were no serious thunderstorms.

Schomberg's heart began to thump as he saw himself nearing his vengeance. His speech was thick but persuasive.

'No risk at all – none whatever.'

Ricardo dismissed these assurances of safety with an impatient gesture. He was thinking of other risks.

'The getting away from here is all right; but we may be sighted at sea, and that may bring awkwardness later on. A ship's boat with three white men in her, knocking about out of sight of land, is bound to make talk. Are we likely to be seen on our way?'

'No, unless by native craft,' said Schomberg.

Ricardo nodded, satisfied. Both these white men looked on native life as a mere play of shadows. A play of shadows the dominant race could walk through unaffected and disregarded in the pursuit of its incomprehensible aims and needs. No. Native craft did not count, of course. It was an empty, solitary part of the sea, Schomberg expounded further. Only the Ternate mail-boat crossed that region about the eighth of every month, regularly – nowhere near the island, though. Rigid, his voice hoarse, his heart thumping, his mind concentrated on the success of his plan, the hotel-keeper multiplied words, as if to keep as many of them as possible between himself and the murderous aspect of his purpose.

'So, if you gentlemen depart from my plantation quietly at sunset on the eighth – always best to make a start at night, with a land breeze – it's a hundred to one – what am I saying? – it's a thousand to one that no human eye will see you on the passage. All you've got to do is keep her heading north-east for, say, fifty hours; perhaps not quite so long. There will always be draught enough to keep a boat moving; you may reckon on that; and then –'

The muscles about his waist quivered under his clothes with eagerness, with impatience, and with something like apprehension, the true nature of which was not clear to him. And he did not want to investigate it. Ricardo regarded him steadily, with those dry eyes of his shining more like polished stones than living tissue.

'And then what?' he asked.

'And then – why, you will astonish *der Herr Baron* – ha, ha!'

Schomberg seemed to force the words and the laugh out of himself in a hoarse bass.

'And you believe he has all that plunder by him?' asked Ricardo, rather perfunctorily, because the fact seemed to him extremely probable when looked at all round by his acute mind.

Schomberg raised his hands and lowered them slowly.

'How can it be otherwise? He was going home, he was on his way, in this hotel. Ask people. Was it likely he would leave it behind him?'

Ricardo was thoughtful. Then, suddenly raising his head, he remarked:

'Steer north-east for fifty hours, eh? That's not much of a sailing direction. I've heard of a port being missed before on better information. Can't you say what sort of landfall a fellow may expect? But I suppose you have never seen that island yourself?'

Schomberg admitted that he had not seen it, in a tone in which a man congratulates himself on having escaped the contamination of an unsavoury experience. No, certainly not. He had never had any business to call him there. But what of that? He could give Mr Ricardo as good a sea-mark as anybody need wish for. He laughed nervously. Miss it! He defied anyone that came within forty miles of it to miss the retreat of that villainous Swede.

'What do you think of a pillar of smoke by day and a loom of fire at night? There's a volcano in full blast near that island – enough to guide almost a blind man. What more do you want? An active volcano to steer by!'

These last words he roared out exultingly, then jumped up and glared. The door to the left of the bar had swung open, and Mrs Schomberg, dressed for duty, stood facing him down the whole length of the room. She clung to the handle for a moment, then came in and glided to her place, where she sat down to stare straight before her, as usual.

Part Three

Chapter I

Tropical nature had been kind to the failure of the commercial enterprise. The desolation of the headquarters of the Tropical Belt Coal Company had been screened from the side of the sea; from the side where prying eyes – if any were sufficiently interested, either in malice or in sorrow – could have noted the decaying bones of that once sanguine enterprise.

Heyst had been sitting among the bones buried so kindly in the grass of two wet seasons' growth. The silence of his surroundings, broken only by such sounds as a distant roll of thunder, the lash of rain through the foliage of some big trees, the noise of the wind tossing the leaves of the forest, and of the short seas breaking against the shore, favoured rather than hindered his solitary meditation.

A meditation is always – in a white man, at least – more or less an interrogative exercise. Heyst meditated in simple terms on the mystery of his actions; and he answered himself with the honest reflection:

'There must be a lot of the original Adam in me, after all.'

He reflected, too, with the sense of making a discovery, that his primeval ancestor is not easily suppressed. The oldest voice in the world is just the one that never ceases to speak. If anybody could have silenced its imperative echoes, it should have been Heyst's father, with his contemptuous inflexible negation of all effort; but apparently he could not. There was in the son a lot of that first ancestor who, as soon as he could uplift his muddy frame from the celestial mould, started inspecting and naming the animals of that paradise which he was so soon to lose.

Action – the first thought, or perhaps the first impulse, on earth! The barbed hook, baited with the illusion of progress, to bring out of the lightless void the shoals of unnumbered generations!

'And I, the son of my father, have been caught too, like the silliest fish of them all,' Heyst said to himself.

He suffered. He was hurt by the sight of his own life, which ought have been a masterpiece of aloofness. He remembered always his last evening with his father. He remembered the thin features, the great mass of white hair, and the ivory complexion. A five-branched candlestick stood on a little table by the side of the easy chair. They had been talking a long time. The noises of the street had died out one by one, till at last, in the moonlight, the London houses began to look like the tombs of an unvisited, unhonoured, cemetery of hopes.

He had listened. Then, after a silence, he had asked – for he was really young then:

'Is there no guidance?'

His father was in an unexpectedly soft mood on that night, when the moon swam in a cloudless sky over the begrimed shadows of the town.

'You still believe in something, then?' he said in a clear voice, which had been growing feeble of late. 'You believe in flesh and blood, perhaps? A full and equable contempt would soon do away with that, too. But since you have not attained to it, I advise you to cultivate that form of contempt which is called pity. It is perhaps the least difficult – always remembering that you, too, if you are anything, are as pitiful as the rest, yet never expecting any pity for yourself.'

'What is one to do, then?' sighed the young man, regarding his father, rigid in the high-backed chair.

'Look on – make no sound,' were the last words of the man who had spent his life in blowing blasts upon a terrible trumpet which filled heaven and earth with ruins, while mankind went on its way unheeding.

That very night he died in his bed, so quietly that they found him in his usual attitude of sleep, lying on his side, one hand under his cheek, and his knees slightly bent. He had not even straightened his legs.

His son buried the silenced destroyer of systems, of hopes, of beliefs. He observed that the death of that bitter contemner of life did not trouble the flow of life's stream, where men and women go by thick as dust, revolving and jostling one another like figures cut out of cork and weighted with lead just sufficiently to keep them in their proudly upright posture.

After the funeral, Heyst sat alone, in the dusk, and his meditation took the form of a definite vision of the stream, of the fatuously jostling, nodding, spinning figures hurried irresistibly along, and giving no sign of being aware that the voice on the bank had been suddenly silenced. . . . Yes. A few obituary notices generally insignificant and some grossly abusive. The son had read them all with mournful detachment.

'This is the hate and rage of their fear,' he thought to himself, 'and also of wounded vanity. They shriek their little shriek as they fly past. I suppose I ought to hate him too. . . .'

He became aware of his eyes being wet. It was not that the man was his father. For him it was purely a matter of hearsay which could not in itself cause this emotion. No! It was because he had looked at him so long that he missed him so much. The dead man had kept him on the bank by his side. And now Heyst felt acutely that he was alone on the bank of the stream. In his pride he determined not to enter it.

A few slow tears rolled down his face. The rooms, filling with shadows, seemed haunted by a melancholy, uneasy presence which could not express itself. The young man got up with a strange sense of making way for something impalpable that claimed possession, went out of the house, and locked the door. A fortnight later he started on his travels – to 'look on and never make a sound'.

The elder Heyst had left behind him a little money and a certain quantity of movable objects, such as books, tables, chairs, and pictures, which might have complained of heartless desertion after many years of faithful service; for there is a soul in things. Heyst, our Heyst, had often thought of them, reproachful and mute, shrouded and locked up in those rooms, far away in London with the sounds of the street reaching them faintly, and sometimes a little sunshine, when the blinds were pulled up and the windows opened from time to time in pursuance of his original instructions and later reminders. It seemed as if in his conception of a world not worth touching, and perhaps not substantial enough to grasp, these objects familiar to his childhood and his youth, and associated with the memory of an old man, were the only realities, something having an absolute existence. He would never have them sold, or even moved from the places they occupied when he looked upon them last. When he was advised from London that his lease had expired, and that the house, with some others as like it as two peas, was to be demolished, he was surprisingly distressed.

He had entered by then the broad, human path of inconsistencies. Already the Tropical Belt Coal Company was in existence. He sent instructions to have some of the things sent out to him at Samburan, just as any ordinary, credulous person would have done. They came, torn out from their long repose – a lot of books, some chairs and tables, his father's portrait in oils, which surprised Heyst by its air of youth, because he remembered his father as a much older man; a lot of small objects, such as candlesticks, inkstands, and statuettes from his father's study, which surprised him because they looked so old and so much worn.

The manager of the Tropical Belt Coal Company, unpacking them on the veranda in the shade besieged by a fierce sunshine, must have felt like a remorseful apostate before these relics. He handled them tenderly; and it was perhaps their presence there which attached him to the island when he woke up to the failure of his apostasy. Whatever the decisive reason, Heyst had remained where another would have been glad to be off. The excellent Davidson had discovered the fact without discovering the reason, and took a human interest in Heyst's strange existence, while at the same time his native delicacy kept him from intruding on the other's whim of solitude. He could not possibly guess that Heyst, alone on the island, felt neither more nor less lonely than in any other place, desert or populous. Davidson's concern was, if one may express it so, the danger of spiritual starvation; but this was a spirit which had renounced all outside nourishment, and was sustaining itself proudly on its own contempt of the usual coarse ailments which life offers to the common appetites of men.

Neither was Heyst's body in danger of starvation, as Schomberg had so confidently asserted. At the beginning of the company's operations the island had been provisioned in a manner which had outlasted the need. Heyst did not need to fear hunger; and his very loneliness had not been without some alleviation. Of the crowd of imported Chinese labourers, one at least had remained in Samburan, solitary and strange, like a swallow left behind at the migrating season of his tribe.

Wang was not a common coolie. He had been a servant to white men before. The agreement between him and Heyst consisted in the exchange of a few words on the day when the last batch of the mine coolies was leaving Samburan. Heyst, leaning over the balustrade of the veranda, was looking on, as calm in appearance as though he had never departed from the doctrine that this world, for the wise, is nothing but an amusing spectacle. Wang came round the house, and standing below, raised up his yellow, thin face.

'All finish?' he asked.

Heyst nodded slightly from above, glancing towards the jetty. A crowd of blue-clad figures with yellow faces and calves was being hustled down into the boats of the chartered steamer lying well out, like a painted ship on a painted sea; painted in crude colours, without shadows, without feeling, with brutal precision.

'You had better hurry up if you don't want to be left behind.'

But the Chinaman did not move.

'Me stop,' he declared. Heyst looked down at him for the first time.

'You want to stop here?'

'Yes.'

'What were you? What was your work here?'

'Mess-loom boy.'

'Do you want to stay with me here as my boy?' inquired Heyst, surprised.

The Chinaman unexpectedly put on a deprecatory expression, and said, after a marked pause:

'Can do.'

'You needn't,' said Heyst, 'unless you like. I propose to stay on here – it may be for a very long time. I have no power to make you go if you wish to remain, but I don't see why you should.'

'Catchee one piecee wife,' remarked Wang unemotionally, and marched off, turning his back on the wharf and the great world beyond, represented by the steamer waiting for her boats.

Heyst learned presently that Wang had persuaded one of the women of Alfuro village, on the west shore of the island, beyond the central ridge, to come over to live with him in a remote part of the company's clearing. It was a curious case, inasmuch as the Alfuros, having been frightened by the sudden invasion of Chinamen, had blocked the path over the ridge by felling a few trees, and had kept strictly on their own side. The coolies, as a body, mistrusting the manifest mildness of these harmless fisher-folk, had kept to their lines, without attempting to cross the island. Wang was the brilliant exception. He must have been uncommonly fascinating, in a way that was not apparent to Heyst, or else uncommonly persuasive. The woman's services to Heyst were limited to the fact that she had anchored Wang to the spot by her charms, which remained unknown to the white man, because she never came near the houses. The couple lived at the edge of the forest, and she could sometimes be seen gazing towards the bungalow shading her eyes with her hand. Even from a distance she appeared to be a shy, wild creature, and Heyst, anxious not to try her primitive nerves unduly, scrupulously avoided that side of the clearing in his strolls.

The day – or rather the first night – after his hermit life began, he was aware of vague sounds of revelry in that direction. Emboldened by the departure of the invading strangers, some Alfuros, the woman's friends and relations, had ventured over the ridge to attend something in the nature of a wedding feast. Wang had invited them. But this was the only occasion when any sound louder than the buzzing of insects had troubled the profound silence of the clearing. The natives were never invited again. Wang not only knew how to live according to conventional proprieties, but had strong personal views as to the manner of arranging his domestic existence. After a time Heyst perceived that Wang had annexed all the keys. Any keys left lying about vanished after Wang had passed that way. Subsequently some of them – those that did not belong to the storerooms and empty bungalows, and could not be regarded as the common property of this community of two – were returned to Heyst, tied in a bunch with a piece of string. He found them one morning lying by the side of his plate. He had not been inconvenienced by their absence, because he never locked up anything in the way of drawers and boxes. Heyst said nothing. Wang also said nothing. Perhaps he had always been a taciturn man; perhaps he was influenced by the genius of the locality, which was certainly that of silence. Till Heyst and Morrison had landed in Black Diamond Bay, and named it, that side of Samburan had hardly ever heard the sound of human speech. It was easy to be taciturn with Heyst, who had plunged himself into an abyss of meditation over books, and remained in it till the shadow of Wang falling across the page, and the sound of a rough, low voice uttering the Malay word *makan*, would force him to climb out to a meal.

Wang in this native province in China might have been an aggressively, sensitively genial person; but in Samburan he had clothed himself in a mysterious stolidity and did not seem to resent not being spoken to except in single words, at a rate which did not average half a dozen per day. And he gave no more than he got. It is to be presumed that if he suffered constraint, he made up for it with the Alfuro woman. He always went back to her at the first fall of dusk, vanishing from the bungalow suddenly at this hour, like a sort of topsy-turvy, day-hunting Chinese ghost with a white jacket and a pigtail. Presently, giving way to a Chinaman's ruling passion, he could be observed breaking the ground near his hut, between the mighty stumps of felled trees, with a miner's pickaxe. After a time, he discovered a rusty but serviceable spade in one of the empty store-rooms, and it is to be supposed that he got on famously; but nothing of it could be seen, because he went to the trouble of pulling to pieces one of the company's sheds in order to get materials for making a high and very close fence round his patch, as if the growing of vegetables were a patented process, or an awful and holy mystery entrusted to the keeping of his race.

Heyst, following from a distance the progress of Wang's gardening and of these precautions – there was nothing else to look at – was amused at the thought that he, in his own person, represented the market for its produce. The Chinaman had found several packets of seeds in the store-rooms, and had surrendered to an irresistible impulse to put them into the ground. He would make his master pay for the vegetables which he was raising to satisfy his instinct. And, looking silently at the silent. Wang going about his work in the bungalow in his unhasty, steady way, Heyst envied the Chinaman's obedience to his instincts, the powerful simplicity of purpose which made his existence appear almost automatic in the mysterious precision of its facts.

Chapter II

During his master's absence at Sourabaya, Wang had busied himself with the ground immediately in front of the principal bungalow. Emerging from the fringe of grass growing across the shore end of the coal-jetty, Heyst beheld a broad, clear space, black and level, with only one or two clumps of charred twigs, where the flame had swept from the front of his house to the nearest trees of the forest.

'You took the risk of firing the grass?' Heyst asked.

Wang nodded. Hanging on the arm of the white man before whom he stood was the girl called Alma; but neither from the Chinaman's eyes nor from his expression could anyone have guessed that he was in the slightest degree aware of the fact.

'He has been tidying the place in this labour-saving way,' explained Heyst, without looking at the girl, whose hand rested on his forearm. 'He's the whole establishment, you see. I told you I hadn't even a dog to keep me company here.'

Wang had marched off towards the wharf.

'He's like those waiters in that place,' she said. That place was Schomberg's hotel.

'One Chinaman looks very much like another,' Heyst remarked. 'We shall find it useful to have him here. This is the house.'

They faced, at some distance, the six shallow steps leading up to the veranda. The girl had abandoned Heyst's arm.

'This is the house,' he repeated.

She did not offer to budge away from his side, but stood staring fixedly at the steps, as if they had been something unique and impracticable. He waited a little, but she did not move.

'Don't you want to go in?' he asked, without turning his head to look at her. 'The sun's too heavy to stand about here.' He tried to overcome a sort of fear, a sort of impatient faintness, and his voice sounded rough. 'You had better go in,' he concluded.

They both moved then, but at the foot of the stairs Heyst stopped, while the girl went on rapidly, as if nothing could stop her now. She crossed the veranda swiftly, and entered the twilight of the big central room opening upon it, and then the deeper twilight of the room beyond. She stood still in the dusk, in which her dazzled eyes could scarcely make out the forms of objects, and sighed a sigh of relief. The impression of the sunlight, of sea and sky, remained with her like a memory of a painful trial gone through – done with at last!

Meanwhile Heyst had walked back slowly towards the jetty; but he did not get so far as that. The practical and automatic Wang had got hold of one of the little trucks that had been used for running baskets of coal alongside ships. He appeared pushing it before him, loaded lightly with Heyst's bag and the bundle of the girl's belongings, wrapped in Mrs Schomberg's shawl. Heyst turned about and walked by the side of the rusty rails on which the truck ran. Opposite the house Wang stopped, lifted the bag to his shoulder, balanced it carefully, and then took the bundle in his hand.

'Leave those things on the table in the big room – understand?'

'Me savee,' grunted Wang, moving off.

Heyst watched the Chinaman disappear from the veranda. It was not till he had seen Wang come out that he himself entered the twilight of the big room. By that time Wang was out of sight at the back of the house, but by no means out of hearing. The Chinaman could hear the voice of him who, when there were many people there, was generally referred to as 'Number One'. Wang was not able to understand the words, but the tone interested him.

'Where are you?' cried Number One.

Then Wang heard, much more faint, a voice he had never heard before – a novel impression which he acknowledged by cocking his head slightly to one side.

'I am here – out of the sun.'

The new voice sounded remote and uncertain. Wang heard nothing more, though he waited for some time, very still, the top of his shaven poll exactly level with the floor of the back veranda. His face meanwhile preserved an inscrutable immobility. Suddenly he stooped to pick up the lid of a deal candle-box which was lying on the ground by his foot. Breaking it up with his fingers, he directed his steps towards the cookshed, where, squatting on his heels, he proceeded to kindle a small fire under a very sooty kettle, possibly to make tea. Wang had some knowledge of the more superficial rites and ceremonies of white men's existence, otherwise so enigmatically remote to his mind, and containing unexpected possibilities of good and evil, which had to be watched for with prudence and care.

Chapter III

That morning, as on all the others of the full tale of mornings since his return with the girl to Samburan, Heyst came out on the veranda and spread his elbows on the railing, in an easy attitude of proprietorship. The bulk of the central ridge of the island cut off the bungalow from sunrises, whether glorious or cloudy, angry or serene. The dwellers therein were debarred from reading early the fortune of the new-born day. It sprang upon them in its fulness with a swift retreat of the great shadow when the sun, clearing the ridge, looked down, hot and dry, with a devouring glare like the eye of an enemy. But Heyst, once the Number One of this locality, while it was comparatively teeming with mankind, appreciated the prolongation of early coolness, the subdued, lingering half-light, the faint ghost of the departed night, the fragrance of its dewy, dark soul captured for a moment longer between the great glow of the sky and the intense blaze of the uncovered sea.

It was naturally difficult for Heyst to keep his mind from dwelling on the nature and consequences of this, his latest departure from the part of an unconcerned spectator. Yet he had retained enough of his wrecked philosophy to prevent him from asking himself consciously how it would end. But at the same time he could not help being temperamentally, from long habit and from set purpose, a spectator still, perhaps a little less naïve but (as he discovered with some surprise) not much more far-sighted than the common run of men. Like the rest of us who act, all he could say to himself, with a somewhat affected grimness, was:

'We shall see!'

This mood of grim doubt intruded on him only when he was alone. There were not many such moments in this day now; and he did not like them when they came. On this morning he had no time to grow uneasy. Alma came out to join him long before the sun, rising above the Samburan ridge, swept the cool shadow of the early morning and the remnant of the night's coolness clear off the roof under which they had dwelt for more than three months already. She came out as on other mornings. He had heard her light footsteps in the big room – the room where he had unpacked the cases from London; the room now lined with the backs of books half-way up on its three sides. Above the cases the fine matting met the ceiling of tightly stretched white calico. In the dusk and coolness nothing gleamed except the gilt frame of the portrait of Heyst's father, signed by a famous painter, lonely in the middle of a wall.

Heyst did not turn round.

'Do you know what I was thinking of?' he asked.

'No,' she said. Her tone betrayed always a shade of anxiety, as though she were never certain how a conversation with him would end. She leaned on the guard-rail by his side.

'No,' she repeated. 'What was it?' She waited. Then, rather with reluctance than shyness, she asked:

'Were you thinking of me?'

'I was wondering when you would come out,' said Heyst, still without looking at the girl – to whom, after several experimental essays in combining detached letters and loose syllables, he had given the name of Lena.

She remarked after a pause:

'I was not very far from you.'

'Apparently you were not near enough for me.'

'You could have called if you wanted me,' she said. 'And I wasn't so long doing my hair.'

'Apparently it was too long for me.'

'Well, you were thinking of me, anyhow. I am glad of it. Do you know, it seems to me, somehow, that if you were to stop thinking of me I shouldn't be in the world at all!'

He turned round and looked at her. She often said things which surprised him. A vague smile faded away on her lips before his scrutiny.

'What is it?' he asked. 'It is a reproach?'

'A reproach! Why, how could it be?' she defended herself.

'Well, what did it mean?' he insisted.

'What I said – just what I said. Why aren't you fair?'

'Ah, this is at least a reproach!'

She coloured to the roots of her hair.

'It looks as if you were trying to make out that I am disagreeable,' she murmured. 'Am I? You will make me afraid to open my mouth presently. I shall end by believing I am no good.'

Her head drooped a little. He looked at her smooth, low brow, the faintly coloured cheeks, and the red lips parted slightly, with the gleam of her teeth within.

'And then I *won't* be any good,' she added with conviction. 'That I won't! I can only be what you think I am.'

He made a slight movement. She put her hand on his arm, without raising her head, and went on, her voice animated in the stillness of her body:

'It is so. It couldn't be any other way with a girl like me and a man like you. Here we are, we two alone, and I can't even tell where we are.'

'A very well-known spot of the globe,' Heyst uttered gently. 'There must have been at least fifty thousand circulars issued at the time – a hundred and fifty thousand, more likely. My friend was looking after that, and his ideas were large and his belief very strong. Of us two it was he who had the faith. A hundred and fifty thousand, certainly.'

'What is it you mean?' she asked in a low tone.

'What should I find fault with you for?' Heyst went on. 'For being amiable, good, gracious – and pretty?'

A silence fell. Then she said:

'It's all right that you should think that of me. There's no one here to think anything of us, good or bad.'

The rare timbre of her voice gave a special value to what she uttered. The indefinable emotion which certain intonations gave him, he was aware, was more physical than moral. Every time she spoke to him she seemed to abandon to him something of herself – something excessively subtle and inexpressible, to which he was infinitely sensible, which he would have missed horribly if she were to go away. While he was looking into her eyes she raised her bare forearm, out of the short sleeve, and held it in the air till he noticed it and hastened to pose his great bronze moustaches on the whiteness of the skin. Then they went in.

Wang immediately appeared in front, and, squatting on his heels, began to potter mysteriously about some plants at the foot of the veranda. When Heyst and the girl came out again, the Chinaman had gone in his peculiar manner, which suggested vanishing out of existence rather than out of sight, a process of evaporation rather than of movement. They descended the steps, looking at each other, and started off smartly across the cleared ground; but they were not ten yards away when, without perceptible stir or sound, Wang materialized inside the empty room. The Chinaman stood still with roaming eyes, examining the walls as if for signs, for inscriptions; exploring the floor as if for pitfalls, for dropped coins. Then he cocked his head slightly at the profile of Heyst's father, pen in hand above a white sheet of paper on a crimson tablecloth; and, moving forward noiselessly, began to clear away the breakfast things.

Though he proceeded without haste, the unerring precision of his movements, the absolute soundlessness of the operation, gave it something of the quality of a conjuring trick. And, the trick having been performed, Wang vanished from the scene, to materialize presently in front of the house. He materialized walking away from it, with no visible or guessable intention; but at the end of some ten paces he stopped, made a half turn, and put his hand up to shade his eyes. The sun had topped the grey ridge of Samburan. The great morning shadow was gone; and far away in the devouring sunshine Wang was in time to see Number One, and the woman, two remote white specks against the sombre line of the forest. In a moment they vanished. With the smallest display of action. Wang also vanished from the sunlight of the clearing.

Heyst and Lena entered the shade of the forest path which crossed the island, and which, near its highest point, had been blocked by felled trees. But their intention was not to go so far. After keeping to the path for some distance, they left it at a point where the forest was bare of undergrowth, and the trees, festooned with creepers, stood clear of one another in the gloom of their own making. Here and there great splashes of light lay on the ground. They moved, silent in the great stillness, breathing the calmness, the infinite isolation, the repose of a slumber without dreams. They emerged at the upper limit of vegetation, among some rocks; and in a depression of the sharp slope, like a small platform, they turned about and looked from on high over the sea, lonely, its colour effaced by sunshine, its horizon a heat mist, a mere unsubstantial shimmer in the pale and blinding infinity overhung by the darker blaze of the sky.

'It makes my head swim,' the girl murmured, shutting her eyes and putting her hand on his shoulder.

Heyst, gazing fixedly to the southward, exclaimed:

'Sail ho!'

A moment of silence ensued.

'It must be very far away,' he went on. 'I don't think you could see it. Some native craft making for the Moluccas, probably. Come, we mustn't stay here.'

With his arm round her waist, he led her down a little distance, and they settled themselves in the shade; she, seated on the ground, he a little lower, reclining at her feet.

'You don't like to look at the sea from up there?' he said after a time.

She shook her head. That empty space was to her the abomination of desolation. But she only said again:

'It makes my head swim.'

'Too big?' he inquired.

'Too lonely. It makes my heart sink, too,' she added in a low voice, as if confessing a secret.

'I am afraid,' said Heyst, 'that you would be justified in reproaching me for these sensations. But what would you have?'

His tone was playful, but his eyes, directed at her face, were serious. She protested.

'I am not feeling lonely with you – not a bit. It is only when we come up to that place, and I look at all that water and all that light –'

'We will never come here again, then,' he interrupted her.

She remained silent for a while, returning his gaze till he removed it.

'It seems as if everything that there is had gone under,' she said.

'Reminds you of the story of the deluge,' muttered the man, stretched at her feet and looking at them. 'Are you frightened at it?'

'I should be rather frightened to be left behind alone. When I say, *I*, of course I mean we.'

'Do you?' . . . Heyst remained silent for a while. 'The vision of a world destroyed,' he mused aloud. 'Would you be sorry for it?'

'I should be sorry for the happy people in it,' she said simply.

His gaze travelled up her figure and reached her face, where he seemed to detect the veiled glow of intelligence, as one gets a glimpse of the sun through the clouds.

'I should have thought it's they specially who ought to have been congratulated. Don't you?'

'Oh, yes – I understand what you mean; but there were forty days before it was all over.'

'You seem to be in possession of all the details.'

Heyst spoke just to say something rather than to gaze at her in silence. She was not looking at him.

'Sunday school,' she murmured. 'I went regularly from the time I was eight till I was thirteen. We lodged in the north of London, off Kingsland Road. It wasn't a bad time. Father was earning good money then. The woman of the house used to pack me off in the afternoon with her own girls. She was a good woman. Her husband was in the post office. Sorter or something. Such a quiet man. He used to go off after supper for night duty, sometimes. Then one day they had a row, and broke up the home. I remember I cried when we had to pack up all of a sudden and go into other lodgings. I never knew what it was, though –'

'The deluge,' muttered Heyst absently.

He felt intensely aware of her personality, as if this were the first moment of leisure he had found to look at her since they had come together. The peculiar timbre of her voice, with its modulations of audacity and sadness, would have given interest to the most inane chatter. But she was no chatterer. She was rather silent, with a capacity for immobility, an upright stillness, as when resting on the concert platform between the musical numbers, her feet crossed, her hands reposing on her lap. But in the intimacy of their life her grey, unabashed gaze forced upon him the sensation of something inexplicable reposing within her; stupidity or inspiration, weakness or force – or simply an abysmal emptiness, reserving itself even in the moments of complete surrender.

During a long pause she did not look at him. Then suddenly, as if the word 'deluge' had stuck in her mind, she asked, looking up at the cloudless sky:

'Does it ever rain here?'

'There is a season when it rains almost every day,' said Heyst, surprised. 'There are also thunderstorms. We once had a mud-shower.'

'Mud-shower?'

'Our neighbour there was shooting up ashes. He sometimes clears his red-hot gullet like that; and a thunderstorm came along at the same time. It was very messy; but our neighbour is generally well behaved – just smokes quietly, as he did that day when I first showed you the smudge in the sky from the schooner's deck. He's a good-natured, lazy fellow of a volcano.'

'I saw a mountain smoking like that before,' she said, staring at the slender stem of a tree-fern some dozen feet in front of her. 'It wasn't very long after we left England – some few days, though. I was so ill at first that I lost count of days. A smoking mountain – I can't think how they called it.'

'Vesuvius, perhaps,' suggested Heyst.

'That's the name.'

'I saw it, too, years, ages ago,' said Heyst.

'On your way here?'

'No, long before I ever thought of coming into this part of the world. I was yet a boy.'

She turned and looked at him attentively, as if seeking to discover some trace of that boyhood in the mature face of the man with the hair thin at the top and the long, thick moustaches. Heyst stood the frank examination with a playful smile, hiding the profound effect these veiled grey eyes produced – whether on his heart or on his nerves, whether sensuous or spiritual, tender or irritating, he was unable to say.

'Well, princess of Samburan,' he said at last, 'have I found favour in your sight?'

She seemed to wake up, and shook her head.

'I was thinking,' she murmured very low.

'Thought, action – so many snares! If you begin to think you will be unhappy.'

'I wasn't thinking of myself,' she declared with a simplicity which took Heyst aback somewhat.

'On the lips of a moralist this would sound like a rebuke,' he said, half seriously; 'but I won't suspect you of being one. Moralists and I haven't been friends for many years.'

She had listened with an air of attention.

'I understood you had no friends,' she said. 'I am pleased that there's nobody to find fault with you for what you have done. I like to think that I am in no one's way.'

Heyst would have said something, but she did not give him time. Unconscious of the movement he made she went on:

'What I was thinking to myself was, why are you here?'

Heyst let himself sink on his elbow again.

'If by "you" you mean "we" – well, you know why we are here.'

She bent her gaze down at him.

'No, it isn't that. I meant before – all that time before you came across me and guessed at once that I was in trouble, with no one to turn to. And you know it was desperate trouble too.'

Her voice fell on the last words, as if she would end there; but there was something so expectant in Heyst's attitude as he sat at her feet, looking up at her steadily, that she continued, after drawing a short, quick breath:

'It was, really, I told you I had been worried before by bad fellows. It made me unhappy, disturbed – angry, too. But oh, how I hated, hated, *hated* that man!'

'That man' was the florid Schomberg with the military bearing, benefactor of white men ('decent food to eat in decent company') – mature victim of belated passion. The girl shuddered. The characteristic harmoniousness of her face became, as it were, decomposed for an instant. Heyst was startled.

'Why think of it now?' he cried.

'It's because I was cornered that time. It wasn't as before. It was worse, ever so much. I wished I could die of my fright – and yet it's only now that I begin to understand what a horror it might have been. Yes, only now, since we –'

Heyst stirred a little.

'Came here,' he finished.

Her tenseness relaxed, her flushed face went gradually back to its normal tint.

'Yes,' she said indifferently, but at the same time she gave him a stealthy glance of passionate appreciation; and then her face took on a melancholy cast, her whole figure drooped imperceptibly. 'But you were coming back here anyhow?' she asked.

'Yes. I was only waiting for Davidson. Yes, I was coming back here, to these ruins – to Wang, who perhaps did not expect to see me again. It's impossible to guess at the way that Chinaman draws his conclusions, and how he looks upon one.'

'Don't talk about him. He makes me feel uncomfortable. Talk about yourself.'

'About myself? I see you are still busy with the mystery of my existence here; but it isn't at all mysterious. Primarily the man with the quill pen in his hand in that picture you so often look at is responsible for my existence. He is also responsible for what my existence is, or rather has been. He was a great man in his way. I don't know much of his history. I suppose he began like other people; took fine words for good, ringing coin and noble ideals for valuable banknotes. He was a great master of both, himself, by the way. Later he discovered – how am I to explain it to you? Suppose the world were a factory and all mankind workmen in it. Well, he discovered that the wages were not good enough. That they were paid in counterfeit money.'

'I see!' the girl said slowly.

'Do you?'

Heyst, who had been speaking as if to himself, looked up curiously.

'It wasn't a new discovery, but he brought his capacity for scorn to bear on it. It was immense. It ought to have withered this globe. I don't know how many minds he convinced. But my mind was very young then, and youth I suppose can be easily seduced – even by a negation. He was very ruthless, and yet he was not without pity. He dominated me without difficulty. A heartless man could not have done so. Even to fools he was not utterly merciless. He could be indignant, but he was too great for flouts and jeers. What he said was not meant for the crowd; it could not be; and I was flattered to find myself among the elect. They read his books, but I have heard his living word. It was irresistible. It was as if that mind were taking me into its confidence, giving me a special insight into its mastery of despair. Mistake, no doubt. There is something of my father in every man who lives long enough. But they don't say anything. They can't. They wouldn't know how, or perhaps they wouldn't speak if they could. Man on this earth is an unforeseen accident which does not stand close investigation. However, that particular man died as quietly as a child goes to sleep. But, after listening to him, I could not take my soul down into the street to fight there. I started off to wander about, an independent spectator – if that is possible.'

For a long time the girl's grey eyes had been watching his face. She discovered that, addressing her, he was really talking to himself. Heyst looked up, caught sight of her as it were, and caught himself up, with a low laugh and a change of tone.

'All this does not tell you why I ever came here. Why, indeed? It's like prying into inscrutable mysteries which are not worth scrutinizing. A man drifts. The most successful men have drifted into their successes. I don't want to tell you that this is a success. You wouldn't believe me if I did. It isn't; neither is it the ruinous failure it looks. It proves nothing, unless perhaps some hidden weakness in my character – and even that is not certain.'

He looked fixedly at her, and with such grave eyes that she felt obliged to smile faintly at him, since she did not understand what he meant. Her smile was reflected, still fainter, on his lips.

'This does not advance you much in your inquiry,' he went on. 'And in truth your question is unanswerable; but facts have a certain positive value, and I will tell you a fact. One day I met a cornered man. I use the word because it expresses the man's situation exactly, and because you just used it yourself. You know what that means?'

'What do you say?' she whispered, astounded. 'A man!'

Heyst laughed at her wondering eyes.

'No! No! I mean in his own way.'

'I knew very well it couldn't be anything like that,' she observed under her breath.

'I won't bother you with the story. It was a custom-house affair, strange as it may sound to you. He would have preferred to be killed outright – that is, to have his soul dispatched to another world, rather than to be robbed of his substance, his very insignificant substance, in this. I saw that he believed in another world because, being cornered, as I have told you, he went down on his knees and prayed. What do you think of that?'

Heyst paused. She looked at him earnestly.

'You didn't make fun of him for that?' she said.

Heyst made a brusque movement of protest.

'My dear girl, I am not a ruffian,' he cried. Then, returning to his usual tone: 'I didn't even have to conceal a smile. Somehow it didn't look a smiling matter. No, it was not funny; it was rather pathetic; he was so representative of all the past victims of the Great Joke. But it is by folly alone that the world moves, and so it is a respectable thing upon the whole. And besides, he was what one could call a good man. I don't mean especially because he had offered up a prayer. No! He was really a decent fellow, he was quite unfitted for this world, he was a failure, a good man cornered – a sight for the gods; for no decent mortal cares to look at that sort.' A thought seemed to occur to him. He turned his face to the girl. 'And you, who have been cornered too – did you think of offering a prayer?'

Neither her eyes nor a single one of her features moved the least bit. She only let fall the words:

'I am not what they call a good girl.'

'That sounds evasive,' said Heyst after a short silence. 'Well, the good fellow did pray and after he had confessed to it I was struck by the comicality of the situation. No, don't misunderstand me – I am not alluding to his act, of course. And even the idea of Eternity, Infinity, Omnipotence, being called upon to defeat the conspiracy of two miserable Portuguese half-castes did not move my mirth. From the point of view of the supplicant, the danger to be conjured was something like the end of the world, or worse. No! What captivated my fancy was that I, Axel Heyst, the most detached of creatures in this earthly captivity, the veriest tramp on this earth, an indifferent stroller going through the world's bustle – that I should have been there to step into the situation of an agent of Providence. *I*, a man of universal scorn and unbelief. . . .'

'You are putting it on,' she interrupted in her seductive voice, with a coaxing intonation.

'No. I am not like that, born or fashioned, or both. I am not for nothing the son of my father, of that man in the painting. I am he, all but the genius. And there is even less in me than I make out, because the very scorn is falling away from me year after year. I have never been so amused as by that episode in which I was suddenly called to act such an incredible part. For a moment I enjoyed it greatly. It got him out of his corner, you know.'

'You saved a man for fun – is that what you mean? Just for fun?'

'Why this tone of suspicion?' remonstrated Heyst. 'I suppose the sight of this particular distress was disagreeable to me. What you call fun came afterward, when it dawned on me that I was for him a walking, breathing, incarnate proof of the efficacy of prayer. I was a little fascinated by it – and then, could I have argued with him? You don't argue against such evidence, and besides it would have looked as if I had wanted to claim all the merit. Already his gratitude was simply frightful. Funny position, wasn't it? The boredom came later, when we lived together on board his ship. I had, in a moment of inadvertence, created for myself a tie. How to define it precisely I don't know. One gets attached in a way to people one has done something for. But is that friendship? I am not sure what it was. I only know that he who forms a tie is lost. The germ of corruption has entered into his soul.'

Heyst's tone was light, with the flavour of playfulness which seasoned all his speeches and seemed to be of the very essence of this thoughts. The girl he had come across, of whom he had possessed himself, to whose presence he was not yet accustomed, with whom he did not yet know how to live; that human being so near and still so strange, gave him a greater sense of his own reality than he had ever known in all his life.

Chapter IV

With her knees drawn up, Lena rested her elbows on them and held her head in both her hands.

'Are you tired of sitting here?' Heyst asked.

An almost imperceptible negative movement of the head was all the answer she made.

'Why are you looking so serious?' he pursued, and immediately thought that habitual seriousness, in the long run, was much more bearable than constant gaiety. 'However, this expression suits you exceedingly,' he added, not diplomatically, but because, by the tendency of his taste, it was a true statement. 'And as long as I can be certain that it is not boredom which gives you this severe air, I am willing to sit here and look at you till you are ready to go.'

And this was true. He was still under the fresh sortilege of their common life, the surprise of novelty, the flattered vanity of his possession of this woman; for a man must feel that, unless he has ceased to be masculine. Her eyes moved in his direction, rested on him, then returned to their stare into the deeper gloom at the foot of the straight tree-trunks, whose spreading crowns were slowly withdrawing their shade. The warm air stirred slightly about her motionless head. She would not look at him, from some obscure fear of betraying herself. She felt in her innermost depths an irresistible desire to give herself up to him more completely, by some act of absolute sacrifice. This was something of which he did not seem to have an idea. He was a strange being without needs. She felt his eyes fixed upon her; and as he kept silent, she said uneasily – for she didn't know what his silences might mean:

'And so you lived with that friend – that good man?'

'Excellent fellow,' Heyst responded, with a readiness that she did not expect. 'But it was a weakness on my part. I really didn't want to, only he wouldn't let me off, and I couldn't explain. He was the sort of man to whom you can't explain anything. He was extremely sensitive, and it would have been a tigerish thing to do to mangle his delicate feelings by the sort of plain speaking that would have been necessary. His mind was like a white-walled, pure chamber, furnished with, say, six straw-bottomed chairs, and he was always placing and displacing them in various combinations. But they were always the same chairs. He was extremely easy to live with; but then he got hold of this coal idea – or, rather, the idea got hold of him. It entered into that scantily furnished chamber of which I have just spoken, and sat on all the chairs. There was no dislodging it, you know! It was going to make his fortune, my fortune, everybody's fortune. In past years, in moments of doubt that will come to a man determined to remain free from absurdities of existence, I often asked myself, with a momentary dread, in what way would life try to get hold of me? And this was the way! He got it into his head that he could do nothing without me. And was I now, he asked me, to spurn and ruin him? Well, one morning – I wonder if he had gone down on his knees to pray that night! – one morning I gave in.'

Heyst tugged violently at a tuft of dried grass, and cast it away from him with a nervous gesture.

'I gave in,' he repeated.

Looking towards him with a movement of her eyes only, the girl noticed the strong feeling on his face with that intense interest which his person awakened in her mind and in her heart. But it soon passed away, leaving only a moody expression.

'It's difficult to resist where nothing matters,' he observed. 'And perhaps there is a grain of freakishness in my nature. It amused me to go about uttering silly, commonplace phrases. I was never so well thought of in the islands till I began to jabber commercial gibberish like the veriest idiot. Upon my word, I believe that I was actually respected for a time. I was as grave as an owl over it; I had to be loyal to the man. I have been, from first to last, completely, utterly loyal to the best of my ability. I thought he understood something about coal. And if I had been aware that he knew nothing of it, as in fact he didn't, well – I don't know what I could have done to stop him. In one way or another I should have had to be loyal. Truth, work, ambition, love itself, may be only counters in the lamentable or despicable game of life, but when one takes a hand one must play the game. No, the shade of Morrison needn't haunt me. What's the matter? I say, Lena, why are you staring like that? Do you feel ill?'

Heyst made as if to get on his feet. The girl extended her arm to arrest him, and he remained staring in a sitting posture, propped on one arm, observing her indefinable expression of anxiety, as if she were unable to draw breath.

'What has come to you?' he insisted, feeling strangely unwilling to move, to touch her.

'Nothing.' She swallowed painfully. 'Of course it can't be. What name did you say? I didn't hear it properly.'

'Name?' repeated Heyst dazedly. 'I only mentioned Morrison. It's the name of that man of whom I've been speaking. What of it?'

'And you mean to say that he was your friend?'

'You have heard enough to judge for yourself. You know as much of our connection as I know myself. The people in this part of the world went by appearances, and called us friends, as far as I can remember. Appearances – what more, what better can you ask for? In fact you can't have better. You can't have anything else.'

'You are trying to confuse me with your talk,' she cried. 'You can't make fun of this.'

'Can't? Well, no I can't. It's a pity. Perhaps it would have been the best way,' said Heyst, in a tone which for him could be called gloomy. 'Unless one could forget the silly business altogether.' His faint playfulness of manner and speech returned, like a habit one has schooled oneself into, even before his forehead had cleared completely. 'But why are you looking so hard at me? Oh, I don't object, and I shall try not to flinch. Your eyes –'

He was looking straight into them, and as a matter of fact had forgotten all about the late Morrison at that moment.

'No,' he exclaimed suddenly. 'What an impenetrable girl you are Lena, with those grey eyes of yours! Windows of the soul, as some poet has said. The fellow must have been a glazier by vocation. Well, nature has provided excellently for the shyness of your soul.'

When he ceased speaking, the girl came to herself with a catch of her breath. He heard her voice, the varied charm of which he thought he knew so well, saying with an unfamiliar intonation:

'And that partner of yours is dead?'

'Morrison? Oh, yes, as I've told you, he –'

'You never told me.'

'Didn't I? I Thought I did; or, rather, I thought you must know. It seems impossible that anybody with whom I speak should not know that Morrison is dead.'

She lowered her eyelids, and Heyst was startled by something like an expression of horror on her face.

'Morrison!' she whispered in an appalled tone. 'Morrison!' Her head drooped. Unable to see her features, Heyst could tell from her voice that for some reason or other she was profoundly moved by the syllables of that unromantic name. A thought flashed through his head – could she have known Morrison? But the mere difference of their origins made it wildly improbable.

'This is very extraordinary!' he said. 'Have you ever heard the name before?'

Her head moved quickly several times in tiny affirmative nods, as if she could not trust herself to speak, or even to look at him. She was biting her lower lip.

'Did you ever know anybody of that name?' he asked.

The girl answered by a negative sign; and then at last she spoke, jerkily, as if forcing herself against some doubt or fear. She had heard of that very man, she told Heyst.

'Impossible!' he said positively. 'You are mistaken. You couldn't have heard of him. It's –'

He stopped short, with the thought that to talk like this was perfectly useless; that one doesn't argue against thin air.

'But I did hear of him; only I didn't know then, I couldn't guess, that it was your partner they were talking about.'

'Talking about my partner?' repeated Heyst slowly.

'No.' Her mind seemed almost as bewildered, as full of incredulity, as his. 'No. They were talking of you really; only I didn't know it.'

'Who were they?' Heyst raised his voice. 'Who was talking of me? Talking where?'

With the first question he had lifted himself from his reclining position; at the last he was on his knees before her, their heads on a level.

'Why, in that town, in that hotel. Where else could it have been?' she said.

The idea of being talked about was always novel to Heyst's simplified conception of himself. For a moment he was as much surprised as if he had believed himself to be a mere gliding shadow among men. Besides, he had in him a half-unconscious notion that he was above the level of island gossip.

'But you said first that it was of Morrison they talked,' he remarked to the girl, sinking on his heels, and no longer much interested. 'Strange that you should have the opportunity to hear any talk at all! I was rather under the impression that you never saw anybody belonging to the town except from the platform.'

'You forget that I was not living with the other girls,' she said. 'After meals they used to go back to the Pavilion, but I had to stay in the hotel and do my sewing, or what not, in the room where they talked.'

'I didn't think of that. By the by, you never told me who *they* were.'

'Why, that horrible red-faced beast,' she said, with all the energy of disgust which the mere thought of the hotel-keeper provoked in her.

'Oh, Schomberg!' Heyst murmured carelessly.

'He talked to the boss – to Zangiacomo, I mean. I had to sit there. That devil-woman sometimes wouldn't let me go away. I mean Mrs Zangiacomo.'

'I guessed,' murmured Heyst. 'She liked to torment you in a variety of ways. But it is really strange that the hotel-keeper should talk of Morrison to Zangiacomo. As far as I can remember he saw very little of Morrison professionally. He knew many others much better.'

The girl shuddered slightly.

'That was the only name I ever overheard. I would get as far away from them as I could, to the other end of the room; but when that beast started shouting I could not help hearing. I wish I had never heard anything. If I had got up and gone out of the room I don't suppose the woman would have killed me for it; but she would have rowed me in a nasty way. She would have threatened me and called me names. That sort, when they know you are helpless, there's nothing to stop them. I don't know how it is, but bad people, real bad people that you can see are bad, they get over me somehow. It's the way they set about downing one. I am afraid of wickedness.'

Heyst watched the changing expressions of her face. He encouraged her, profoundly sympathetic, a little amused.

'I quite understand. You needn't apologize for your great delicacy in the perception of inhuman evil. I am a little like you.'

'I am not very plucky,' she said.

'Well! I don't know myself what I would do, what countenance I would have before a creature which would strike me as being evil incarnate. Don't you be ashamed.'

She sighed, looked up with her pale, candid gaze and a timid expression on her face, and murmured:

'You don't seem to want to know what he was saying.'

'About poor Morrison? It couldn't have been anything bad, for the poor fellow was innocence itself. And then, you know, he is dead, and nothing can possibly matter to him now.'

'But I tell you that it was of *you* he was talking!' she cried. 'He was saying that Morrison's partner first got all there was to get out of him, and then, and then – well, as good as murdered him – sent him out to die somewhere!'

'You believe that of me?' said Heyst, after a moment of perfect silence.

'I didn't know it had anything to do with you. Schomberg was talking of some Swede. How was I to know? It was only when you began telling me about how you came here –'

'And now you have my version.' Heyst forced himself to speak quietly. 'So that's how the business looked from outside!' he muttered.

'I remember him saying that everybody in these parts knew the story,' the girl added breathlessly.

'Strange that it should hurt me!' mused Heyst to himself; 'yet it does. I seem to be as much of a fool as those everybodies who know the story – and no doubt believe it. Can you remember any more?' he addressed the girl in a grimly polite tone. 'I've often heard of the moral advantages of seeing oneself as others see one. Let us investigate further. Can't you recall something else that everybody knows?'

'Oh! Don't laugh!' she cried.

'Did I laugh? I assure you I was not aware of it. I won't ask you whether you believe the hotel-keeper's version. Surely you must know the value of human judgement.'

She unclasped her hands, moved them slightly, and twined her fingers as before. Protest? Assent? Was there to be nothing more? He was relieved when she spoke in that warm and wonderful voice which in itself comforted and fascinated one's heart, which made her lovable.

'I heard this before you and I ever spoke to each other. It went out of my memory afterwards. Everything went out of my memory then; and I was glad of it. It was a fresh start for me, with you – and you know it. I wish I had forgotten who I was – that would have been best; and I very nearly did forget.'

He was moved by the vibrating quality of the last words. She seemed to be talking low of some wonderful enchantment, in mysterious terms of special significance. He thought that if she only could talk to him in some unknown tongue, she would enslave him altogether by the sheer beauty of the sound, suggesting infinite depths of wisdom and feeling.

'But,' she went on, 'the name stuck in my head, it seems; and when you mentioned it –'

'It broke the spell,' muttered Heyst in angry disappointment, as if he had been deceived in some hope.

The girl, from her position a little above him, surveyed with still eyes the abstracted silence of the man on whom she now depended with a completeness of which she had not been vividly conscious before, because, till then, she had never felt herself swinging between the abysses of earth and heaven in the hollow of his arm. What if he should grow weary of the burden?

'And, moreover, nobody had ever believed that tale!'

Heyst came out with an abrupt burst of sound which made her open her steady eyes wider, with an effect of immense surprise. It was a purely mechanical effect, because she was neither surprised nor puzzled. In fact, she could understand him better then than at any moment since she first set eyes on him.

He laughed scornfully.

'What am I thinking of?' he cried. 'As if it could matter to me what anybody had ever said or believed, from the beginning of the world till the crack of doom!'

'I never heard you laugh till today,' she observed. 'This is the second time.'

He scrambled to his feet and towered above her.

'That's because, when one's heart has been broken into in the way you have broken into mine, all sorts of weaknesses are free to enter – shame, anger, stupid indignations, stupid fears – stupid laughter, too. I wonder what interpretation you are putting on it?'

'It wasn't gay, certainly,' she said. 'But why are you angry with me? Are you sorry you took me away from those beasts? I told you who I was. You could see it.'

'Heavens!' he muttered. He had regained his command of himself. 'I assure you I could see much more than you could tell me. I could see quite a lot that you don't even suspect yet; but you can't be seen quite through.'

He sank to the ground by her side and took her hand. She asked gently:

'What more do you want from me?'

He made no sound for a time.

'The impossible, I suppose,' he said very low, as one makes a confidence, and pressing the hand he grasped.

It did not return the pressure. He shook his head as if to drive away the thought of this, and added in a louder, light tone:

'Nothing less. And it isn't because I think little of what I've got already. Oh, no! It is because I think so much of this possession of mine that I can't have it complete enough. I know it's unreasonable. You can't hold back anything – now.'

'Indeed I couldn't,' she whispered, letting her hand lie passive in his tight grasp. 'I only wish I could give you something more, or better, or whatever it is you want.'

He was touched by the sincere accent of these simple words.

'I tell you what you can do – you can tell me whether you would have gone with me like this if you had known of whom that abominable idiot of a hotel-keeper was speaking. A murderer – no less!'

'But I didn't know you at all then,' she cried. 'And I had the sense to understand what he was saying. It wasn't murder, really. I never thought it was.'

'What made him invent such an atrocity?' Heyst exclaimed. 'He seems a stupid animal. He *is* stupid. How did he manage to hatch that pretty tale? Have I a particularly vile countenance? Is black selfishness written all over my face? Or is that sort of thing so universally human that it might be said of anybody?'

'It wasn't murder,' she insisted earnestly.

'I know. I understand. It was worse. As to killing a man, which would be a comparatively decent thing to do, well – I have never done that.'

'Why should you do it?' she asked in a frightened voice.

'My dear girl, you don't know the sort of life I have been leading in unexplored countries, in the wilds; it's difficult to give you an idea. There are men who haven't been in such tight places as I have found myself in who have had to – to shed blood, as the saying is. Even the wilds hold prizes which tempt some people; but I had no schemes, no plans – and not even great firmness of mind to make me unduly obstinate. I was simply moving on, while the others, perhaps, were going somewhere. An indifference as to roads and purposes makes one meeker, as it were. And I may say truly, too, that I never did care, I won't say for life – I had scorned what people called by that name from the first – but for being alive. I don't know if that is what men call courage, but I doubt it very much.'

'You! You have no courage?' she protested.

'I really don't know. Not the sort that always itches for a weapon, for I have never been anxious to use one in the quarrels that a man gets into in the most innocent way, sometimes. The differences for which men murder each other are, like everything else they do, the most contemptible, the most pitiful things to look back upon. No, I've never killed a man or loved a woman – not even in my thoughts, not even in my dreams.'

He raised her hand to his lips, and let them rest on it for a space, during which she moved a little closer to him. After the lingering kiss he did not relinquish his hold.

'To slay, to love – the greatest enterprises of life upon a man! And I have no experience of either. You must forgive me anything that may have appeared to you awkward in my behaviour, inexpressive in my speeches, untimely in my silences.'

He moved uneasily, a little disappointed by her attitude, but indulgent to it, and feeling, in this moment of perfect quietness, that in holding her surrendered hand he had found a closer communion than they had ever achieved before. But even then there still lingered in him a sense of incompleteness not altogether overcome – which, it seemed, nothing ever would overcome – the fatal imperfection of all the gifts of life, which makes of them a delusion and a snare.

All of a sudden he squeezed her hand angrily. His delicately playful equanimity, the product of kindness and scorn, had perished with the loss of his bitter liberty.

'Not murder, you say! I should think not. But when you led me to talk just now, when the name turned up, when you understood that it was of me that these things had been said, you showed a strange emotion. I could see it.'

'I was a bit startled,' she said.

'At the baseness of my conduct?' he asked.

'I wouldn't judge you; not for anything.'

'Really?'

'It would be as if I dared to judge everything that there is.' With her other hand she made a gesture that seemed to embrace in one movement the earth and the heaven. 'I wouldn't do such a thing.'

Then came a silence, broken at last by Heyst:

'I! I! do a deadly wrong to my poor Morrison!' he cried. 'I, who could not bear to hurt his feelings. I, who respected his very madness! Yes, this madness, the wreck of which you can see lying about the jetty of Diamond Bay. What else could I do? He insisted on regarding me as his saviour; he was always restraining the eternal obligation on the tip of his tongue, till I was burning with shame at his gratitude. What could I do? He was going to repay me with this infernal coal, and I had to join him as one joins a child's game in a nursery. One would no more have thought of humiliating him than one would think of humiliating a child. What's the use of talking of all this! Of course, the people here could not understand the truth of our relation to each other. But what business of theirs was it? Kill old Morrison! Well, it is less criminal, less base – I am not saying it is less difficult – to kill a man than to cheat him in that way. You understand that?'

She nodded slightly, but more than once and with evident conviction. His eyes rested on her, inquisitive, ready for tenderness.

'But it was neither one nor the other,' he went on. 'Then, why your emotion? All you confess is that you wouldn't judge me.'

She turned upon him her veiled, unseeing grey eyes in which nothing of her wonder could be read.

'I said I couldn't,' she whispered.

'But you thought that there was no smoke without fire!' The playfulness of tone hardly concealed his irritation. 'What power there must be in words, only imperfectly heard – for you did not listen with particular care, did you? What were they? What evil effort of invention drove them into that idiot's mouth out of his lying throat? If you were to try to remember, they would perhaps convince me, too.'

'I didn't listen,' she protested. 'What was it to me what they said of anybody? He was saying that there never were such loving friends to look at as you two; then, when you got all you wanted out of him and got thoroughly tired of him, too, you kicked him out to go home and die.'

Indignation, with an undercurrent of some other feeling, rang in these quoted words, uttered in her pure and enchanting voice. She ceased abruptly and lowered her long, dark lashes, as if mortally weary, sick at heart.

'Of course, why shouldn't you get tired of that or any other – company? You aren't like anyone else and – and the thought of it made me unhappy suddenly; but indeed, I did not believe anything bad of you. I –'

A brusque movement of his arm, flinging her hand away, stopped her short. Heyst had again lost control of himself. He would have shouted, if shouting had been in his character.

'No, this earth must be the appointed hatching planet of calumny enough to furnish the whole universe. I feel a disgust at my own person, as if I had tumbled into some filthy hole. Pah! And you – all you can say is that you won't judge me; that you –'

She raised her head at this attack, though indeed he had not turned to her.

'I don't believe anything bad of you,' she repeated. 'I couldn't.'

He made a gesture as if to say:

'That's sufficient.'

In his soul and in his body he experienced a nervous reaction from tenderness. All at once, without transition, he detested her. But only for a moment. He remembered that she was pretty, and, more, that she had a special grace in the intimacy of life. She had the secret of individuality which excites – and escapes.

He jumped up and began to walk to and fro. Presently his hidden fury fell into dust within him, like a crazy structure, leaving behind emptiness, desolation, regret. His resentment was not against the girl, but against life itself – that commonest of snares, in which he felt himself caught, seeing clearly the plot of plots and unconsoled by the lucidity of his mind.

He swerved and, stepping up to her, sank to the ground by her side. Before she could make a movement, or even turn her head his way, he took her in his arms and kissed her lips. He tasted on them the bitterness of a tear fallen there. He had never seen her cry. It was like another appeal to his tenderness – a new seduction. The girl glanced round, moved suddenly away, and averted her face. With her hand she signed imperiously to him to leave her alone – a command which Heyst did not obey.

Chapter V

When she opened her eyes at last and sat up, Heyst scrambled quickly to his feet and went to pick up her cork helmet, which had rolled a little way off. Meanwhile she busied herself in doing up her hair, plaited on the top of her head in two heavy, dark tresses, which had come loose. He tendered her the helmet in silence, and waited as if unwilling to hear the sound of his own voice.

'We had better go down now,' he suggested in a low tone.

He extended his hand to help her up. He had the intention to smile, but abandoned it at the nearer sight of her still face, in which was depicted the infinite lassitude of her soul. On their way to regain the forest path they had to pass through the spot from which the view of the sea could be obtained. The flaming abyss of emptiness, the liquid, undulating glare, the tragic brutality of the light, made her long for the friendly night, with its stars stilled by an austere spell; for the velvety dark sky and the mysterious great shadow of the sea, conveying peace to the day-weary heart. She put her hand to her eyes. Behind her back Heyst spoke gently.

'Let us get on, Lena.'

She walked ahead in silence. Heyst remarked that they had never been out before during the hottest hours. It would do her no good, he feared. This solicitude pleased and soothed her. She felt more and more like herself – a poor London girl playing in an orchestra, and snatched out from the humiliations, the squalid dangers of a miserable existence, by a man like whom there was not, there could not be, another in this world. She felt this with elation, with uneasiness, with an intimate pride – and with a peculiar sinking of the heart.

'I am not easily knocked out by any such thing as heat,' she said decisively.

'Yes, but I don't forget that you're not a tropical bird.'

'You weren't born in these parts, either,' she returned.

'No, and perhaps I haven't even your physique. I am a transplanted being. Transplanted! I ought to call myself uprooted – an unnatural state of existence; but a man is supposed to stand anything.'

She looked back at him and received a smile. He told her to keep in the shelter of the forest path, which was very still and close, full of heat if free from glare. Now and then they had glimpses of the company's old clearing blazing with light, in which the black stumps of trees stood charred, without shadows, miserable and sinister. They crossed the open in a direct line for the bungalow. On the veranda they fancied they had a glimpse of the vanishing Wang, though the girl was not at all sure that she had seen anything move. Heyst had no doubts.

'Wang has been looking out for us. We are late.'

'Was he? I thought I saw something white for a moment, and then I did not see it any more.'

'That's it – he vanishes. It's a very remarkable gift in that Chinaman.'

'Are they all like that?' she asked with naïve curiosity and uneasiness.

'Not in such perfection,' said Heyst, amused.

He noticed with approval that she was not heated by the walk. The drops of perspiration on her forehead were like dew on the cool, white petal of a flower. He looked at her figure of grace and strength, solid and supple, with an ever-growing appreciation.

'Go in and rest yourself for a quarter of an hour; and then Mr Wang will give us something to eat,' he said.

They had found the table laid. When they came together again and sat down to it, Wang materialized without a sound, unheard, uncalled, and did his office. Which being accomplished, at a given moment he was not.

A great silence brooded over Samburan – the silence of the great heat that seems pregnant with fatal issues, like the silence of ardent thought. Heyst remained alone in the big room. The girl seeing him take up a book, had retreated to her chamber. Heyst sat down under his father's portrait; and the abominable calumny crept back into his recollection. The taste of it came on his lips, nauseating and corrosive like some kinds of poison. He was tempted to spit on the floor, naïvely, in sheer unsophisticated disgust of the physical sensation. He shook his head, surprised at himself. He was not used to receive his intellectual impressions in that way – reflected in movements of carnal emotion. He stirred impatiently in his chair, and raised the book to his eyes with both hands. It was one of his father's. He opened it haphazard, and his eyes fell on the middle of the page. The elder Heyst had written of everything in many books – of space and of time, of animals and of stars; analysing ideas and actions, the laughter and the frowns of men, and the grimaces of their agony. The son read, shrinking into himself, composing his face as if under the author's eye, with a vivid consciousness of the portrait on his right hand, a little above his head; a wonderful presence in its heavy frame on the flimsy wall of mats, looking exiled and at home, out of place and masterful, in the painted immobility of profile.

And Heyst, the son, read:

> Of the stratagems of life the most cruel is the consolation of love – the most subtle, too; for the desire is the bed of dreams.

He turned the pages of the little volume, *Storm and Dust*, glancing here and there at the broken text of reflections, maxims, short phrases, enigmatical sometimes and sometimes eloquent. It seemed to him that he was hearing his father's voice, speaking and ceasing to speak again. Startled at first, he ended by finding a charm in the illusion. He abandoned himself to the half-belief that something of his father dwelt yet on earth – a ghostly voice, audible to the ear of his own flesh and blood. With what strange serenity, mingled with terrors, had that man considered the universal nothingness! He had plunged into it headlong, perhaps to render death, the answer that faced one at every inquiry, more supportable.

Heyst stirred, and the ghostly voice ceased; but his eyes followed the words on the last page of the book:

> Men of tormented conscience, or of a criminal imagination, are aware of much that minds of a peaceful, resigned cast do not even suspect. It is not poets alone who dare descend into the abyss of infernal regions, or even who dream of such a descent. The most inexpressive of human beings must have said to himself, at one time or another: 'Anything but this!' . . .
>
> We all have our instants of clairvoyance. They are not very helpful. The character of the scheme does not permit that or anything else to be helpful. Properly speaking its character, judged by the standards established by its victims, is infamous. It excuses every violence of protest and at the same time never fails to crush it, just as it crushes the blindest assent. The so-called wickedness must be, like the so-called virtue, its own reward – to be anything at all . . .
>
> Clairvoyance or no clairvoyance, men love their captivity. To the unknown force of negation they prefer the miserably tumbled bed of their servitude. Man alone can give one the disgust of pity; yet I find it easier to believe in the misfortune of mankind than in its wickedness.

These were the last words. Heyst lowered the book to his knees. Lena's voice spoke above his drooping head:

'You sit there as if you were unhappy.'

'I thought you were asleep,' he said.

'I was lying down right enough, but I never closed my eyes.'

'The rest would have done you good after our walk. Didn't you try?'

'I was lying down, I tell you, but sleep I couldn't.'

'And you made no sound! What want of sincerity. Or did you want to be alone for a time?'

'I – alone!' she murmured.

He noticed her eyeing the book, and got up to put it back in the bookcase. When he turned round, he saw that she had dropped into the chair – it was the one she always used – and looked as if her strength had suddenly gone from her, leaving her only her youth, which seemed very pathetic, very much at his mercy. He moved quickly towards the chair.

'Tired, are you? It's my fault, taking you up so high and keeping you out so long. Such a windless day, too!'

She watched his concern, her pose languid, her eyes raised to him, but as unreadable as ever. He avoided looking into them for that very reason. He forgot himself in the contemplation of those passive arms, of these defenceless lips, and – yes, one had to go back to them – of these wide-open eyes. Something wild in their grey stare made him think of sea-birds in the cold murkiness of high latitudes. He started when she spoke, all the charm of physical intimacy revealed suddenly in that voice.

'You should try to love me!' she said.

He made a movement of astonishment.

'Try,' he muttered. 'But it seems to me –' He broke off, saying to himself that if he loved her, he had never told her so in so many words. Simple words! They died on his lips. 'What makes you say that?' he asked.

She lowered her eyelids and turned her head a little.

'I have done nothing,' she said in a low voice. 'It's you who have been good, helpful, and tender to me. Perhaps you love me for that – just for that; or perhaps you love me for company, and because – well! But sometimes it seems to me that you can never love me for myself, only for myself, as people do love each other when it is to be for ever.' Her head drooped. 'For ever,' she breathed out again; then, still more faintly, she added an entreating: 'Do try!'

These last words went straight to his heart – the sound of them more than the sense. He did not know what to say, either from want of practice in dealing with women or simply from his innate honesty of thought. All his defences were broken now. Life had him fairly by the throat. But he managed a smile, though she was not looking at him; yes, he did manage it – the well-known Heyst smile of playful courtesy, so familiar to all sorts and conditions of men in the islands.

'My dear Lena,' he said, 'it looks as if you were trying to pick a very unnecessary quarrel with me – of all people!'

She made no movement. With his elbows spread out he was twisting the ends of his long moustaches, very masculine and perplexed, enveloped in the atmosphere of femininity as in a cloud, suspecting pitfalls, and as if afraid to move.

'I must admit, though,' he added, 'that there is no one else; and I suppose a certain amount of quarrelling is necessary for existence in this world.'

That girl, seated in her chair in graceful quietude, was to him like a script in an unknown language, or even more simply mysterious; like any writing to the illiterate. As far as women went, he was altogether uninstructed and he had not the gift of intuition which is fostered in the days of youth by dreams and visions, exercises of the heart fitting it for the encounters of a world in which love itself rests as much on antagonism as on attraction. His mental attitude was that of a man looking this way and that on a piece of writing which he is unable to decipher, but which may be big with some revelation. He didn't know what to say. All he found to add was:

'I don't even understand what I have done or left undone to distress you like this.'

He stopped, struck afresh by the physical and moral sense of the imperfections of their relations – a sense which made him desire her constant nearness, before his eyes, under his hand, and which, when she was out of his sight, made her so vague, so elusive and illusory, a promise that could not be embraced and held.

'No! I don't see clearly what you mean. Is your mind turned towards the future?' he interpellated her with marked playfulness, because he was ashamed to let such a word pass his lips. But all his cherished negations were falling off him one by one.

'Because if it is so there is nothing easier than to dismiss it. In our future, as in what people call the other life, there is nothing to be frightened of.'

She raised her eyes to him; and if nature had formed them to express anything else but blank candour he would have learned how terrified she was by his talk and the fact that her sinking heart loved him more desperately than ever. He smiled at her.

'Dismiss all thought of it,' he insisted. 'Surely you don't suspect after what I have heard from you, that I am anxious to return to mankind. I! I! murder my poor Morrison! It's possible that I may be really capable of that which they say I have done. The point is that I haven't done it. But it is an unpleasant subject to me. I ought to be ashamed to confess it – but it is! Let us forget it. There's that in you, Lena, which can console me for worse things, for uglier passages. And if we forget, there are no voices here to remind us.'

She had raised her head before he paused.

'Nothing can break in on us here,' he went on and, as if there had been an appeal or a provocation in her upward glance, he bent down and took her under the arms, raising her straight out of the chair into a sudden and close embrace. Her alacrity to respond, which made her seem as light as a feather, warmed his heart at that moment more than closer caresses had done before. He had not expected that ready impulse towards himself which had been dormant in her passive attitude. He had just felt the clasp of her arms round his neck, when, with a slight exclamation – 'He's here!' – she disengaged herself and bolted away into her room.

Chapter VI

Heyst was astounded. Looking all round, as if to take the whole room to witness of this outrage, he became aware of Wang materialized in the doorway. The intrusion was as surprising as anything could be, in view of the strict regularity with which Wang made himself visible. Heyst was tempted to laugh at first. This practical comment on his affirmation that nothing could break in on them relieved the strain of his feelings. He was a little vexed, too. The Chinaman preserved a profound silence.

'What do you want?' asked Heyst sternly.

'Boat out there,' said the Chinaman.

'Where? What do you mean? Boat adrift in the straits?'

Some subtle change in Wang's bearing suggested his being out of breath; but he did not pant, and his voice was steady.

'No – row.'

It was Heyst now who was startled and raised his voice.

'Malay man, eh?'

Wang made a slight negative movement with his head.

'Do you hear, Lena?' Heyst called out. 'Wang says there is a boat in sight – somewhere near, apparently. Where's that boat, Wang?'

'Round the point,' said Wang, leaping into Malay unexpectedly, and in a loud voice. 'White men – three.'

'So close as that?' exclaimed Heyst, moving out on the veranda followed by Wang. 'White men? Impossible!'

Over the clearing the shadows were already lengthening. The sun hung low; a ruddy glare lay on the burnt black patch in front of the bungalow, and slanted on the ground between the straight, tall, mast-like trees soaring a hundred feet or more without a branch. The growth of bushes cut off all view of the jetty from the veranda. Far away to the right Wang's hut, or rather its dark roof of mats, could be seen above the bamboo fence which ensured the privacy of the Alfuro woman. The Chinaman looked that way swiftly. Heyst paused, and then stepped back a pace into the room.

'White men, Lena, apparently. What are you doing?'

'I am just bathing my eyes a little,' the girl's voice said from the inner room.

'Oh, yes; all right!'

'Do you want me?'

'No. You had better – I am going down to the jetty. Yes, you had better stay in. What an extraordinary thing!'

It was so extraordinary that nobody could possibly appreciate how extraordinary it was but himself. His mind was full of mere exclamations, while his feet were carrying him in the direction of the jetty. He followed the line of the rails, escorted by Wang.

'Where were you when you first saw the boat?' he asked over his shoulder.

Wang explained in Malay that he had gone to the shore end of the wharf, to get a few lumps of coal from the big heap, when, happening to raise his eyes from the ground, he saw the boat – a white man boat, not a canoe. He had good eyes. He had seen the boat, with the men at the oars; and here Wang made a particular gesture over his eyes, as if his vision had received a blow. He had turned at once and run to the house to report.

'No mistake, eh?' said Heyst, moving on. At the very outer edge of the belt he stopped short. Wang halted behind him on the path, till the voice of Number One called him sharply forward into the open. He obeyed.

'Where's that boat?' asked Heyst forcibly. 'I say – where is it?'

Nothing whatever was to be seen between the point and the jetty. The stretch of Diamond Bay was like a piece of purple shadow, lustrous and empty, while beyond the land, the open sea lay blue and opaque under the sun. Heyst's eyes swept all over the offing till they met, far off, the dark cone of the volcano, with its faint plume of smoke broadening and vanishing everlastingly, at the top, without altering its shape in the glowing transparency of the evening.

'The fellow has been dreaming,' he muttered to himself.

He looked hard at the Chinaman. Wang seemed turned into stone. Suddenly, as if he had received a shock, he started, flung his arm out with a pointing forefinger, and made guttural noises to the effect that there, there, there, he had seen a boat.

It was very uncanny. Heyst thought of some strange hallucination. Unlikely enough; but that a boat with three men in it should have sunk between the point and the jetty, suddenly, like a stone, without leaving as much on the surface as a floating oar, was still more unlikely. The theory of a phantom boat would have been more credible than that.

'Confound it!' he muttered to himself.

He was unpleasantly affected by this mystery; but now a simple explanation occurred to him. He stepped hastily out on the wharf. The boat, if it had existed and had retreated, could perhaps be seen from the far end of the long jetty.

Nothing was to be seen. Heyst let his eyes roam idly over the sea. He was so absorbed in his perplexity that a hollow sound, as of somebody tumbling about in a boat, with a clatter of oars and spars, failed to make him move for a moment. When his mind seized its meaning, he had no difficulty in locating the sound. It had come from below – under the jetty.

He ran back for a dozen yards or so, and then looked over. His sight plunged straight into the stern-sheets of a big boat, the greater part of which was hidden from him by the planking of the jetty. His eyes fell on the thin back of a man doubled up over the tiller in a queer, uncomfortable attitude of drooping sorrow. Another man, more directly below Heyst, sprawled on his back from gunwale to gunwale, half off the after thwart, his head lower than his feet. This second man glared wildly upward, and struggled to raise himself, but to all appearance was much too drunk to succeed. The visible part of the boat contained also a flat, leather trunk, on which the first man's long legs were tucked up nervelessly. A large earthenware jug, with its wide mouth uncorked, rolled out on the bottom-boards from under the sprawling man.

Heyst had never been so much astonished in his life. He stared dumbly at the strange boat's crew. From the first he was positive that these men were no sailors.

They wore the white drill-suit of tropical civilization; but their apparition in a boat Heyst could not connect with anything plausible. The civilization of the tropics could have had nothing to do with it. It was more like those myths, current in Polynesia, of amazing strangers, who arrive at an island, gods or demons, bringing good or evil to the innocence of the inhabitants – gifts of unknown things, words never heard before.

Heyst noticed a cork helmet floating alongside the boat, evidently fallen from the head of the man doubled over the tiller, who displayed a dark, bony poll. An oar, too, had been knocked overboard, probably by the sprawling man, who was still struggling between the thwarts. By this time Heyst regarded the visitation no longer with surprise, but with the sustained attention demanded by a difficult problem. With one foot posed on the string-piece, and leaning on his raised knee, he was taking in everything. The sprawling man rolled off the thwart, collapsed, and, most unexpectedly, got on his feet. He swayed dizzily, spreading his arms out, and uttered faintly a hoarse, dreamy 'Hallo!' His upturned face was swollen, red, peeling all over the nose and cheeks. His stare was irrational. Heyst perceived stains of dried blood all over the front of his dirty white coat, and also on one sleeve.

'What's the matter? Are you wounded?'

The other glanced down, reeled – one of his feet was inside a large pith hat – and, recovering himself, let out a dismal, grating sound in the manner of a grim laugh.

'Blood – not mine. Thirst's the matter. Exhausted's the matter. Done up. Drink, man! Give us water!'

Thirst was in the very tone of his words, alternating a broken croak and a faint, throaty rustle which just reached Heyst's ears. The man in the boat raised his hands to be helped up on the jetty, whispering:

'I tried. I am too weak. I tumbled down.'

Wang was coming along the jetty slowly, with intent, straining eyes.

'Run back and bring a crowbar here. There's one lying by the coal-heap,' Heyst shouted to him.

The man standing in the boat sat down on the thwart behind him. A horrible coughing laugh came through his swollen lips.

'Crowbar? What's that for?' he mumbled, and his head dropped on his chest mournfully.

Meantime Heyst, as if he had forgotten the boat, started kicking hard at a large brass tap projecting above the planks. To accommodate ships that came for coal and happened to need water as well, a stream had been tapped in the interior and an iron pipe led along the jetty. It terminated with a curved end almost exactly where the strangers' boat had been driven between the piles; but the tap was set fast.

'Hurry up!' Heyst yelled to the Chinaman, who was running with the crowbar in his hand.

Heyst snatched it from him and, obtaining a leverage against the string-piece, wrung the stiff tap round with a mighty jerk.

'I hope that pipe hasn't got choked!' he muttered to himself anxiously.

It hadn't; but it did not yield a strong gush. The sound of a thin stream, partly breaking on the gunwale of the boat and partly splashing alongside, became at once audible. It was greeted by a cry of inarticulate and savage joy. Heyst knelt on the string-piece and peered down. The man who had spoken was already holding his open mouth under the bright trickle. Water ran over his eyelids and over his nose, gurgled down his throat, flowed over his chin. Then some obstruction in the pipe gave way, and a sudden thick jet broke on his face. In a moment his shoulders were soaked, the front of his coat inundated; he streamed and dripped; water ran into his pockets, down his legs, into his shoes; but he had clutched the end of the pipe, and, hanging on with both hands, swallowed, spluttered, choked, snorted with the noises of a swimmer. Suddenly a curious dull roar reached Heyst's ears. Something hairy and black flew from under the jetty. A dishevelled head, coming on like a cannon-ball, took the man at the pipe in flank, with enough force to tear his grip loose and fling him headlong into the stern-sheets. He fell upon the folded legs of the man at the tiller, who, roused by the commotion in the boat, was sitting up, silent, rigid, and very much like a corpse. His eyes were but two black patches, and his teeth glistened with a death's-head grin between his retracted lips, no thicker than blackish parchment glued over the gums.

From him Heyst's eyes wandered to the creature who had replaced the first man at the end of the water-pipe. Enormous brown paws clutched it savagely; the wild, big head hung back, and in a face covered with a wet mass of hair there gaped crookedly a wide mouth full of fangs. The water filled it, welled up in hoarse coughs, ran down on each side of the jaws and down the hairy throat, soaked the black pelt of the enormous chest, naked under a torn check shirt, heaving convulsively with a play of massive muscles carved in red mahogany.

As soon as the first man had recovered the breath knocked out of him by the irresistible charge, a scream of mad cursing issued from the stern-sheets. With a rigid, angular crooking of the elbow, the man at the tiller put his hand back to his hip.

'Don't shoot him, sir!' yelled the first man. 'Wait! Let me have that tiller. I will teach him to shove himself in front of a *caballero*!'

Martin Ricardo flourished the heavy piece of wood, leaped forward with astonishing vigour, and brought it down on Pedro's head with a crash that resounded all over the quiet sweep of Black Diamond Bay. A crimson patch appeared on the matted hair; red veins appeared in the water flowing all over his face, and it dripped in rosy drops off his head. But the man hung on. Not till a second furious blow descended did the hairy paws let go their grip and the squirming body sink limply. Before it could touch the bottom-boards, a tremendous kick in the ribs from Ricardo's foot shifted it forward out of sight, whence came the noise of a heavy thud, a clatter of spars, and a pitiful grunt. Ricardo stooped to look under the jetty.

'Aha, dog! This will teach you to keep back where you belong, you murdering brute, you slaughtering savage, you! You infidel, you robber of churches! Next time I will rip you open from neck to heel, you carrion-eater! *Esclavo!*'

He backed a little and straightened himself up.

'I don't mean it really,' he remarked to Heyst, whose steady eyes met his from above. He ran aft briskly.

'Come along, sir. It's your turn. I oughtn't to have drunk first. 'S truth, I forgot myself! A gentleman like you will overlook that, I know.' As he made these apologies, Ricardo extended his hand. 'Let me steady you, sir.'

Slowly Mr Jones unfolded himself in all his slenderness, rocked, staggered, and caught Ricardo's shoulder. His henchman assisted him to the pipe, which went on gushing a clear stream of water, sparkling exceedingly against the black piles and the gloom under the jetty.

'Catch hold, sir,' Ricardo advised solicitously. 'All right?'

He stepped back, and, while Mr Jones revelled in the abundance of water, he addressed himself to Heyst with a sort of justificatory speech, the tone of which, reflecting his feelings, partook of purring and spitting. They had been thirty hours tugging at the oars, he explained, and they had been more than forty hours without water, except that the night before they had licked the dew off the gunwales.

Ricardo did not explain to Heyst how it happened. At that precise moment he had no explanation ready for the man on the wharf, who, he guessed, must be wondering much more at the presence of his visitors than at their plight.

Chapter VII

The explanation lay in the two simple facts that the light winds and strong currents of the Java Sea had drifted the boat about until they partly lost their bearings; and that by some extraordinary mistake one of the two jars put into the boat by Schomberg's man contained salt water. Ricardo tried to put some pathos into his tones. Pulling for thirty hours with eighteen foot oars! And the sun! Ricardo relieved his feelings by cursing the sun. They had felt their hearts and lungs shrivel within them. And then, as if all that hadn't been trouble enough, he complained bitterly, he had had to waste his fainting strength in beating their servant about the head with a stretcher. The fool had wanted to drink sea water, and wouldn't listen to reason. There was no stopping him otherwise. It was better to beat him into insensibility than to have him go crazy in the boat, and to be obliged to shoot him. The preventive, administered with enough force to brain an elephant, boasted Ricardo, had to be applied on two occasions – the second time all but in sight of the jetty.

'You have seen the beauty,' Ricardo went on expansively, hiding his lack of some sort of probable story under this loquacity. 'I had to hammer him away from the spout. Opened afresh all the old broken spots on his head. You saw how hard I had to hit. He has no restraint, no restraint at all. If it wasn't that he can be made useful in one way or another, I would just as soon have let the governor shoot him.'

He smiled up at Heyst in his peculiar lip-retracting manner, and added by way of afterthought:

'That's what will happen to him in the end, if he doesn't learn to restrain himself. But I've taught him to mind his manners for a while, anyhow!'

And again he addressed his quick grin up to the man on the wharf. His round eyes had never left Heyst's face ever since he began to deliver his account of the voyage.

'So that's how he looks!' Ricardo was saying to himself.

He had not expected Heyst to be like this. He had formed for himself a conception containing the helpful suggestion of a vulnerable point. These solitary men were often tipplers. But no! – this was not a drinking man's face; nor could he detect the weakness of alarm, or even the weakness of surprise, on these features, in those steady eyes.

'We were too far gone to climb out,' Ricardo went on. 'I heard you walking along though. I thought I shouted; I tried to. You didn't hear me shout?'

Heyst made an almost imperceptible negative sign, which the greedy eyes of Ricardo – greedy for all signs – did not miss.

'Throat too parched. We didn't even care to whisper to each other lately. Thirst chokes one. We might have died there under this wharf before you found us.'

'I couldn't think where you had gone to.' Heyst was heard at last, addressing directly the newcomers from the sea. 'You were seen as soon as you cleared that point.'

'We were seen, eh?' grunted Mr Ricardo. 'We pulled like machines – daren't stop. The governor sat at the tiller, but he couldn't speak to us. She drove in between the piles till she hit something, and we all tumbled off the thwarts as if we had been drunk. Drunk – ha, ha! Too dry, by George! We fetched in here with the very last of our strength, and no mistake. Another mile would have done for us. When I heard your footsteps above, I tried to get up, and I fell down.'

'That was the first sound I heard,' said Heyst.

Mr Jones, the front of his soiled white tunic soaked and plastered against his breast-bone, staggered away from the waterpipe. Steadying himself on Ricardo's shoulder, he drew a long breath, raised his dripping head, and produced a smile of ghastly amiability, which was lost upon the thoughtful Heyst. Behind his back the sun, touching the water, was like a disc of iron cooled to a dull red glow, ready to start rolling round the circular steel plate of the sea, which, under the darkening sky, looked more solid than the high ridge of Samburan; more solid than the point, whose long outlined slope melted into its own unfathomable shadow blurring the dim sheen on the bay. The forceful stream from the pipe broke like shattered glass on the boat's gunwale. Its loud, fitful, and persistent splashing revealed the depths of the world's silence.

'Great notion, to lead the water out here,' pronounced Ricardo appreciatively.

Water was life. He felt now as if he could run a mile, scale a ten-foot wall, sing a song. Only a few minutes ago he was next door to a corpse, done up, unable to stand, to lift a hand; unable to groan. A drop of water had done that miracle.

'Didn't you feel life itself running and soaking into you, sir?' he asked his principal, with deferential but forced vivacity.

Without a word, Mr Jones stepped off the thwart and sat down in the stern-sheets.

'Isn't that man of yours bleeding to death in the bows under there?' inquired Heyst.

Ricardo ceased his ecstacies over the life-giving water and answered in a tone of innocence:

'He? You may call him a man, but his hide is a jolly sight tougher than the toughest alligator he ever skinned in the good old days. You don't know how much he can stand: I do. We have tried him a long time ago. *Olá*, there! Pedro! Pedro!' he yelled, with a force of lung testifying to the regenerative virtues of water.

A weak '*Señor?*' came from under the wharf.

'What did I tell you?' said Ricardo triumphantly. 'Nothing can hurt him. He's all right. But, I say, the boat's getting swamped. Can't you turn this water off before you sink her under us? She's half full already.'

At a sigh from Heyst, Wang hammered at the brass tap on the wharf, then stood behind Number One, crowbar in hand, motionless as before. Ricardo was perhaps not so certain of Pedro's toughness as he affirmed; for he stooped, peering under the wharf, then moved forward out of sight. The gush of water, ceasing suddenly, made a silence which became complete when the after-trickle stopped. Afar, the sun was reduced to a red spark, glowing very low in the breathless immensity of twilight. Purple gleams lingered on the water all round the boat. The spectral figure in the stern-sheets spoke in a languid tone:

'That – er – companion – er – secretary of mine is a queer chap. I am afraid we aren't presenting ourselves in a very favourable light.'

Heyst listened. It was the conventional voice of an educated man, only strangely lifeless. But more strange yet was this concern for appearances, expressed, he did not know, whether in jest or in earnest. Earnestness was hardly to be supposed under the circumstances, and no one had ever jested in such dead tones. It was something which could not be answered, and Heyst said nothing. The other went on:

'Travelling as I do, I find a man of his sort extremely useful. He has his little weaknesses, no doubt.'

'Indeed!' Heyst was provoked into speaking. 'Weakness of the arm is not one of them; neither is an exaggerated humanity, as far as I can judge.'

'Defects of temper,' explained Mr Jones from the stern-sheets.

The subject of this dialogue, coming out just then from under the wharf into the visible part of the boat, made himself heard in his own defence, in a voice full of life, and with nothing languid in his manner. On the contrary, it was brisk, almost jocose. He begged pardon for contradicting. He was never out of temper with 'our Pedro'. The fellow was a Dago of immense strength and of no sense whatever. This combination made him dangerous, and he had to be treated accordingly, in a manner which he could understand. Reasoning was beyond him.

'And so' – Ricardo addressed Heyst with animation – 'you mustn't be surprised if –'

'I assure you,' Heyst interrupted, 'that my wonder at your arrival in your boat here is so great that it leaves no room for minor astonishments. But hadn't you better land?'

'That's the talk, sir!' Ricardo began to bustle about the boat, talking all the time. Finding himself unable to 'size up' this man, he was inclined to credit him with extraordinary powers of penetration, which, it seemed to him, would be favoured by silence. Also, he feared some pointblank question. He had no ready-made story to tell. He and his patron had put off considering that rather important detail too long. For the last two days, the horrors of thirst, coming on them unexpectedly, had prevented consultation. They had had to pull for dear life. But the man on the wharf, were he in league with the devil himself, would pay for all their sufferings, thought Ricardo with an unholy joy.

Meantime, splashing in the water which covered the bottom-boards, Ricardo congratulated himself aloud on the luggage being out of the way of the wet. He had piled it up forward. He had roughly tied up Pedro's head. Pedro had nothing to grumble about. On the contrary, he ought to be mighty thankful to him, Ricardo, for being alive at all.

'Well, now, let me give you a leg up, sir,' he said cheerily to his motionless principal in the stern-sheets. 'All our troubles are over – for a time, anyhow. Ain't it luck to find a white man on this island? I would have just as soon expected to meet an angel from heaven – eh, Mr Jones? Now then – ready, sir? One, two, three, up you go!'

Helped from below by Ricardo, and from above by the man more unexpected than an angel, Mr Jones scrambled up and stood on the wharf by the side of Heyst. He swayed like a reed. The night descending on Samburan turned into dense shadow the point of land and the wharf itself, and gave a dark solidity to the unshimmering water extending to the last faint trace of light away to the west. Heyst stared at the guests whom the renounced world had sent him thus at the end of the day. The only other vestige of light left on earth lurked in the hollows of the thin man's eyes. They gleamed, mobile and languidly evasive. The eyelids fluttered.

'You are feeling weak,' said Heyst.

'For the moment, a little,' confessed the other.

With loud panting, Ricardo scrambled on his hands and knees upon the wharf, energetic and unaided. He rose up at Heyst's elbow and stamped his foot on the planks, with a sharp, provocative, double beat, such as is heard sometimes in fencing-schools before the adversaries engage their foils. Not that the renegade seaman Ricardo knew anything of fencing. What he called 'shooting-irons' were his weapons, or the still less aristocratic knife, such as was even then ingeniously strapped to his leg. He thought of it, at that moment. A swift stooping motion, then, on the recovery, a ripping blow, a shove off the wharf, and no noise except a splash in the water that would scarcely disturb the silence. Heyst would have no time for a cry. It would be quick and neat, and immensely in accord with Ricardo's humour. But he repressed this gust of savagery. The job was not such a simple one. This piece had to be played to another tune, and in much slower time. He returned to his note of talkative simplicity.

'Ay; and I too don't feel as strong as I thought I was when the first drink set me up. Great wonder-worker water is! And to get it right here on the spot! It was heaven – hey, sir?'

Mr Jones, being directly addressed, took up his part in the concerted piece:

'Really, when I saw a wharf on what might have been an uninhabited island, I couldn't believe my eyes. I doubted its existence. I thought it was a delusion, till the boat actually drove between the piles, as you see her lying now.'

While he was speaking faintly, in a voice which did not seem to belong to the earth, his henchman, in extremely loud and terrestrial accents, was fussing about their belongings in the boat, addressing himself to Pedro:

'Come, now – pass up the dunnage there! Move yourself, *hombre*, or I'll have to get down again and give you a tap on those bandages of yours, you growling bear, you!'

'Ah! You didn't believe in the reality of the wharf?' Heyst was saying to Mr Jones.

'You ought to kiss my hands!'

Ricardo caught hold of an ancient Gladstone bag and swung it on the wharf with a thump.

'Yes! You ought to burn a candle before me as they do before the saints in your country. No saint has ever done so much for you as I have, you ungrateful vagabond. Now then! Up you get.'

Helped by the talkative Ricardo, Pedro scrambled up on the wharf, where he remained for some time on all fours, swinging to and fro his shaggy head tied up in white rags. Then he got up clumsily, like a bulky animal in the dusk, balancing itself on its hind legs.

Mr Jones began to explain languidly to Heyst that they were in a pretty bad state that morning, when they caught sight of the smoke of the volcano. It nerved them to make an effort for their lives. Soon afterwards they made out the island.

'I had just wits enough left in my baked brain to alter the direction of the boat,' the ghostly voice went on. 'As to finding assistance, a wharf, a white man – nobody would have dreamed of it. Simply preposterous!'

'That's what I thought when my Chinaman came and told me he had seen a boat with white men pulling up,' said Heyst.

'Most extraordinary luck,' interjected Ricardo, standing by anxiously attentive to every word. 'Seems a dream,' he added. 'A lovely dream!'

A silence fell on that group of three, as if everyone had become afraid to speak, in an obscure sense of an impending crisis. Pedro on one side of them and Wang on the other had the air of watchful spectators. A few stars had come out pursuing the ebbing twilight. A light draught of air, tepid enough in the thickening twilight after the scorching day, struck a chill into Mr Jones in his soaked clothes.

'I may infer, then, that there is a settlement of white people here?' he murmured, shivering visibly.

Heyst roused himself.

'Oh, abandoned, abandoned. I am alone here – practically alone; but several empty houses are still standing. No lack of accommodation. We may just as well – here, Wang, go back to the shore and run the trolley out here.'

The last words having been spoken in Malay, he explained courteously that he had given directions for the transport of the luggage. Wang had melted into the night in his soundless manner.

'My word! Rails laid down and all,' exclaimed Ricardo softly, in a tone of admiration. 'Well, I never!'

'We were working a coal-mine here,' said the late manager of the Tropical Belt Coal Company. 'These are only the ghosts of things that have been.'

Mr Jones's teeth were suddenly started chattering by another faint puff of wind, a mere sigh from the west, where Venus cast her rays on the dark edge of the horizon, like a bright lamp hung above the grave of the sun.

'We might be moving on,' proposed Heyst. 'The Chinaman and that – ah –

ungrateful servant of yours, with the broken head, can load the things and come along after us.'

The suggestion was accepted without words. Moving towards the shore, the three men met the trolley, a mere metallic rustle which whisked past them, the shadowy Wang running noiselessly behind. Only the sound of their footsteps accompanied them. It was a long time since so many footsteps had rung together on that jetty. Before they stepped on to the path trodden through the grass, Heyst said:

'I am prevented from offering you a share of my own quarters.' The distant courtliness of this beginning arrested the other two suddenly, as if amazed by some manifest incongruity. 'I should regret it more,' he went on, 'if I were not in a position to give you the choice of those empty bungalows for a temporary home.'

He turned round and plunged into the narrow track, the two others following in single file.

'Queer start!' Ricardo took the opportunity for whispering, as he fell behind Mr Jones, who swayed in the gloom, enclosed by the stalks of tropical grass, almost as slender as a stalk of grass himself.

In this order they emerged into the open space kept clear of vegetation by Wang's judicious system of periodic firing. The shapes of buildings, unlighted, high-roofed, looked mysteriously extensive and featureless against the increasing glitter of the stars. Heyst was pleased at the absence of light in his bungalow. It looked as uninhabited as the others. He continued to lead the way, inclining to the right. His equable voice was heard:

'This one would be the best. It was our counting-house. There is some furniture in it yet. I am pretty certain that you'll find a couple of camp bedsteads in one of the rooms.'

The high-pitched roof of the bungalow towered up very close, eclipsing the sky.

'Here we are. Three steps. As you see, there's a wide veranda. Sorry to keep you waiting for a moment; the door is locked, I think.'

He was heard trying it. Then he leaned against the rail, saying:

'Wang will get the keys.'

The others waited, two vague shapes nearly mingled together in the darkness of the veranda, from which issued a sudden chattering of Mr Jones's teeth, directly suppressed, and a slight shuffle of Ricardo's feet. Their guide and host, his back against the rail, seemed to have forgotten their existence. Suddenly he moved, and murmured:

'Ah, here's the trolley.'

Then he raised his voice in Malay, and was answered, '*Ya tuan*,' from an indistinct group that could be made out in the direction of the track.

'I have sent Wang for the key and a light,' he said, in a voice that came out without any particular direction – a peculiarity which disconcerted Ricardo.

Wang did not tarry long on his mission. Very soon from the distant recesses of obscurity appeared the swinging lantern he carried. It cast a fugitive ray on the arrested trolley with the uncouth figure of the wild Pedro drooping over the load; then it moved towards the bungalow and ascended the stairs. After working at the stiff lock, Wang applied his shoulder to the door. It came open with explosive suddenness, as if in a passion at being thus disturbed after two years' repose. From the dark slope of a tall stand-up writing-desk a forgotten, solitary sheet of paper flew up and settled gracefully on the floor.

Wang and Pedro came and went through the offended door, bringing the things off the trolley, one flitting swiftly in and out, the other staggering heavily. Later, directed by a few quiet words from Number One, Wang made several journeys with the lantern to the store-rooms, bringing in blankets, provisions in tins, coffee, sugar, and a packet of candles. He lighted one, and stuck it on the ledge of the stand-up desk. Meantime Pedro, being introduced to some kindling-wood and a bundle of dry sticks, had busied himself outside in lighting a fire, on which he placed a ready-filled kettle handed to him by Wang impassively, at arm's length, as if across a chasm. Having received the thanks of his guests, Heyst wished them good night and withdrew, leaving them to their repose.

Chapter VIII

Heyst walked away slowly. There was still no light in his bungalow, and he thought that perhaps it was just as well. By this time he was much less perturbed. Wang had preceded him with the lantern, as if in a hurry to get away from the two white men and their hairy attendant. The light was not dancing along any more; it was standing perfectly still by the steps of the veranda.

Heyst, glancing back casually, saw behind him still another light – the light of the strangers' open fire. A black, uncouth form, stooping over it monstrously, staggered away into the outlying shadows. The kettle had boiled, probably.

With that weird vision of something questionably human impressed upon his senses, Heyst moved on a pace or two. What could the people be who had such a creature for their familiar attendant? He stopped. The vague apprehension of a distant future, in which he saw Lena unavoidably separated from him by profound and subtle differences; the sceptical carelessness which had accompanied every one of his attempts at action, like a secret reserve of his soul, fell away from him. He no longer belonged to himself. There was a call far more imperious and august. He came up to the bungalow, and, at the very limit of the lantern's light, on the top step, he saw her feet and the bottom part of her dress. The rest of her person was suggested dimly as high as her waist. She sat on a chair, and the gloom of the low eaves descended upon her head and shoulders. She didn't stir.

'You haven't gone to sleep here?' he asked.

'Oh, no! I was waiting for you – in the dark.'

Heyst, on the top step, leaned against a wooden pillar, after moving the lantern to one side.

'I have been thinking that it is just as well you had no light. But wasn't it dull for you to sit in the dark?'

'I don't need a light to think of you.' Her charming voice gave a value to this banal answer, which had also the merit of truth. Heyst laughed a little, and said that he had had a curious experience. She made no remark. He tried to figure to himself the outlines of her easy pose. A spot of dim light here and there hinted at the unfailing grace of attitude which was one of her natural possessions.

She had thought of him, but not in connection with the strangers. She had admired him from the first; she had been attracted by his warm voice, his gentle eye, but she had felt him too wonderfully difficult to know. He had given to life a savour, a movement, a promise mingled with menaces, which she had not suspected were to be found in it – or, at any rate, not by a girl wedded to misery as she was. She said to herself that she must not be irritated because he seemed too self-contained, and as if shut up in a world of his own. When he took her in his arms, she felt that his embrace had a great and compelling force, that he was moved deeply, and that perhaps he would not get tired of her so very soon. She thought that he had opened to her the feelings of delicate joy, that the very uneasiness he caused her was delicious in its sadness, and that she would try to hold him as long as she could – till her fainting arms, her sinking soul, could cling to him no more.

'Wang's not here, of course?' Heyst said suddenly. She answered as if in her sleep.

'He put this light down here without stopping, and ran.'

'Ran, did he? H'm! Well, it's considerably later than his usual time to go home to his Alfuro wife; but to be seen running is a sort of degradation for Wang, who has mastered the art of vanishing. Do you think he was startled out of his perfection by something?'

'Why should he be startled?'

Her voice remained dreamy, a little uncertain.

'I have been startled,' Heyst said.

She was not listening to him. The lantern at their feet threw the shadows of her face upward. Her eyes glistened, as if frightened and attentive, above a lighted chin and a very white throat.

'Upon my word,' mused Heyst, 'now that I don't see them, I can hardly believe that those fellows exist!'

'And what about me?' she asked, so swiftly that he made a movement like somebody pounced upon from an ambush. 'When you don't see me, do you believe that I exist?'

'Exist? Most charmingly! My dear Lena, you don't know your own advantages. Why, your voice alone would be enough to make you unforgettable!'

'Oh, I didn't mean forgetting in that way. I dare say if I were to die you would remember me right enough. And what good would that be to anybody? It's while I am alive that I want –'

Heyst stood by her chair, a stalwart figure imperfectly lighted. The broad shoulders, the martial face that was like a disguise of his disarmed soul, were lost in the gloom above the plane of light in which his feet were planted. He suffered from a trouble with which she had nothing to do. She had no general conception of the conditions of the existence he had offered to her. Drawn into its peculiar stagnation she remained unrelated to it because of her ignorance.

For instance, she could never perceive the prodigious improbability of the arrival of that boat. She did not seem to be thinking of it. Perhaps she had already forgotten the fact herself. And Heyst resolved suddenly to say nothing more of it. It was not that he shrank from alarming her. Not feeling anything definite himself he could not imagine a precise effect being produced on her by any amount of explanation. There is a quality in events which is apprehended differently by different minds or even by the same mind at different times. Any man living at all consciously knows that embarrassing truth. Heyst was aware that this visit could bode nothing pleasant. In his present soured temper towards all mankind he looked upon it as a visitation of a particularly offensive kind.

He glanced along the veranda in the direction of the other bungalow. The fire of sticks in front of it had gone out. No faint glow of embers, not the slightest thread of light in that direction, hinted at the presence of strangers. The darker shapes in the obscurity, the dead silence, betrayed nothing of that strange intrusion. The peace of Samburan asserted itself as on any other night. Everything was as before, except – Heyst became aware of it suddenly – that for a whole minute, perhaps, with his hand on the back of the girl's chair and within a foot of her person, he had lost the sense of her existence, for the first time since he had brought her over to share this invincible, this undefiled peace. He picked up the lantern, and the act made a silent stir all along the veranda. A spoke of shadow swung swiftly across her face, and the strong light rested on the immobility of her features, as of a woman looking at a vision. Her eyes were still, her lips serious. Her dress, open at the neck, stirred slightly to her even breathing.

'We had better go in, Lena,' suggested Heyst, very low, as if breaking a spell cautiously.

She rose without a word. Heyst followed her indoors. As they passed through the living-room, he left the lantern burning on the centre table.

Chapter IX

THAT NIGHT the girl woke up, for the first time in her new experience, with the sensation of having been abandoned to her own devices. She woke up from a painful dream of separation brought about in a way which she could not understand, and missed the relief of the waking instant. The desolate feeling of being alone persisted. She was really alone. A night-light made it plain enough in the dim, mysterious manner of a dream; but this was reality. It startled her exceedingly.

In a moment she was at the curtain that hung in the doorway, and raised it with a steady hand. The conditions of their life in Samburan would have made peeping absurd; nor was such a thing in her character. This was not a movement of curiosity, but of downright alarm – the continued distress and fear of the dream. The night could not have been very far advanced. The light in the lantern was burning strongly, striping the floor and walls of the room with thick black bands. She hardly knew whether she expected to see Heyst or not; but she saw him at once, standing by the table in his sleeping-suit, his back to the doorway. She stepped in noiselessly with her bare feet, and let the curtain fall behind her. Something characteristic in Heyst's attitude made her say, almost in a whisper:

'You are looking for something.'

He could not have heard her before; but he didn't start at the unexpected whisper. He only pushed the drawer of the table in and, without even looking over his shoulder, asked quietly, accepting her presence as if he had been aware of all her movements:

'I say, are you certain that Wang didn't go through this room this evening?'

'Wang? When?'

'After leaving the lantern, I mean.'

'Oh, no. He ran on. I watched him.'

'Or before, perhaps – while I was with these boat people? Do you know? Can you tell?'

'I hardly think so. I came out as the sun went down, and sat outside till you came back to me.'

'He could have popped in for an instant through the back veranda.'

'I heard nothing in here,' she said. 'What is the matter?'

'Naturally you wouldn't hear. He can be as quiet as a shadow, when he likes. I believe he could steal the pillows from under our heads. He might have been here ten minutes ago.'

'What woke you up? Was it a noise?'

'Can't say that. Generally one can't tell; but is it likely, Lena? You are, I believe, the lighter sleeper of us two. A noise loud enough to wake me up would have awakened you, too. I tried to be as quiet as I could. What roused you?'

'I don't know – a dream, perhaps. I woke up crying.'

'What was the dream?'

Heyst, with one hand resting on the table, had turned in her direction, his round, uncovered head set on a fighter's muscular neck. She left his question unanswered, as if she had not heard it.

'What is it you have missed?' she asked in her turn, very grave.

Her dark hair, drawn smoothly back, was done in two thick tresses for the night. Heyst noticed the good form of her brow, the dignity of its width, its unshining whiteness. It was a sculptural forehead. He had a moment of acute appreciation intruding upon another order of thoughts. It was as if there could be no end of his discoveries about that girl, at the most incongruous moments.

She had on nothing but a hand-woven cotton sarong – one of Heyst's few purchases, years ago, in Celebes, where they are made. He had forgotten all about it till she came, and then had found it at the bottom of an old sandalwood trunk dating back to pre-Morrison days. She had quickly learned to wind it up under her armpits with a safe twist, as Malay village girls do when going to bathe in a river. Her shoulders and arms were bare; one of her tresses, hanging forward, looked almost black against the white skin. As she was taller than the average Malay woman, the sarong ended a good way above her ankles. She stood poised firmly, half-way between the table and the curtained doorway, the insteps of her bare feet gleaming like marble on the overshadowed matting of the floor. The fall of her lighted shoulders, the strong and fine modelling of her arms hanging down her sides, her immobility, too, had something statuesque, the charm of art tense with life. She was not very big – Heyst used to think of her, at first, as 'that poor little girl' – but revealed free from the shabby banality of a white platform dress, in the simple drapery of the sarong, there was that in her form and in the proportions of her body which suggested a reduction from a heroic size.

She moved forward a step.

'What is it you have missed?' she asked again.

Heyst turned his back altogether on the table. The black spokes of darkness over the floor and the walls, joining up on the ceiling in a path of shadow, were like the bars of a cage about them. It was his turn to ignore a question.

'You woke up in a fright, you say?' he said.

She walked up to him, exotic yet familiar, with her white woman's face and shoulders above the Malay sarong, as if it were an airy disguise; but her expression was serious.

'No!' she replied. 'It was distress, rather. You see, you weren't there, and I couldn't tell why you had gone away from me. A nasty dream – the first I've had, too, since –'

'You don't believe in dreams, do you?' asked Heyst.

'I once knew a woman who did. Leastwise, she used to tell people what dreams mean, for a shilling.'

'Would you go now and ask her what this dream means?' inquired Heyst jocularly.

'She lived in Camberwell. She was a nasty old thing!'

Heyst laughed a little uneasily.

'Dreams are madness, my dear. It's things that happen in the waking world, while one is asleep, that one would be glad to know the meaning of.'

'You have missed something out of this drawer,' she said positively.

'This or some other. I have looked into every single one of them and come back to this again, as people do. It's difficult to believe the evidence of my own senses; but it isn't there. Now, Lena, are you sure that you didn't –'

'I have touched nothing in the house but what you have given me.'

'Lena!' he cried.

He was painfully affected by this disclaimer of a charge which he had not made. It was what a servant might have said – an inferior open to suspicion – or, at any rate, a stranger. He was angry at being so wretchedly misunderstood; disenchanted at her not being instinctively aware of the place he had secretly given her in his thoughts.

'After all,' he said to himself, 'we are strangers to each other.'

And then he felt sorry for her. He spoke calmly:

'I was about to say, are you sure you have no reason to think that the Chinaman has been in this room tonight?'

'You suspect him?' she asked, knitting her eyebrows.

'There is no one else to suspect. You may call it a certitude.'

'You don't want to tell me what it is?' she inquired, in the equable tone in which one takes a fact into account.

Heyst only smiled faintly.

'Nothing very precious, as far as value goes,' he replied.

'I thought it might have been money,' she said.

'Money!' exclaimed Heyst, as if the suggestion had been altogether preposterous. She was so visibly surprised that he hastened to add: 'Of course, there is some money in the house – there, in that writing-desk, the drawer on the left. It's not locked. You can pull it right out. There is a recess, and the board at the back pivots; a very simple hiding-place, when you know the way to it. I discovered it by accident, and I keep our store of sovereigns in there. The treasure, my dear, is not big enough to require a cavern.'

He paused, laughed very low, and returned her steady stare.

'The loose silver, some guilders and dollars, I have always kept in that unlocked left drawer. I have no doubt Wang knows what there is in it; but he isn't a thief, and that's why I – no, Lena, what I've missed is not gold or jewels; and that's what makes the fact interesting – which the theft of money cannot be.'

She took a long breath, relieved to hear that it was not money. A great curiosity was depicted on her face, but she refrained from pressing him with questions. She only gave him one of her deep-gleaming smiles.

'It isn't me, so it must be Wang. You ought to make him give it back to you.'

Heyst said nothing to that naïve and practical suggestion, for the object that he missed from the drawer was his revolver.

It was a heavy weapon which he had owned for many years and had never used in his life. Ever since the London furniture had arrived in Samburan, it had been reposing in the drawer of the table. The real dangers of life, for him, were not those which could be repelled by swords or bullets. On the other hand, neither his manner nor his appearance looked sufficiently inoffensive to expose him to light-minded aggression.

He could not have explained what had induced him to go to the drawer in the middle of the night. He had started up suddenly – which was very unusual with him. He had found himself sitting up and extremely wide awake all at once, with the girl reposing by his side, lying with her face away from him, a vague, characteristically feminine form in the dim light. She was perfectly still.

At that season of the year there were no mosquitoes in Samburan, and the sides of the mosquito net were looped up. Heyst swung his feet to the floor, and found himself standing there, almost before he had become aware of his intention to get up. Why he did this he did not know. He didn't wish to wake her up, and the slight creak of the broad bedstead had sounded very loud to him. He turned round apprehensively and waited for her to move, but she did not stir. While he looked at her, he had a vision of himself lying there too, also fast asleep, and – it occurred to him for the first time in his life – very defenceless. This quite novel impression of the dangers of slumber made him think suddenly of his revolver. He left the bedroom with noiseless footsteps. The lightness of the curtain he had to lift as he passed out, and the outer door, wide open on the blackness of the veranda – for the roof eaves came down low, shutting out the starlight – gave him a sense of having been dangerously exposed, he could not have said to what. He pulled the drawer open. Its emptiness cut his train of self-communion short. He murmured to the assertive fact:

'Impossible! Somewhere else!'

He tried to remember where he had put the thing; but those provoked whispers of memory were not encouraging. Foraging in every receptacle and nook big enough to contain a revolver, he came slowly to the conclusion that it was not in that room. Neither was it in the other. The whole bungalow consisted of the two rooms and a profuse allowance of veranda all round. Heyst stepped out on the veranda.

'It's Wang, beyond a doubt,' he thought, staring into the night. 'He has got hold of it for some reason.'

There was nothing to prevent that ghostly Chinaman from materializing suddenly at the foot of the stairs, or anywhere, at any moment, and toppling him over with a dead sure shot. The danger was so irremediable that it was not worth worrying about, any more than the general precariousness of human life. Heyst speculated on this added risk. How long had he been at the mercy of a slender yellow finger on the trigger? That is, if that was the fellow's reason for purloining the revolver.

'Shoot and inherit,' thought Heyst. 'Very simple!' Yet there was in his mind a marked reluctance to regard the domesticated grower of vegetables in the light of a murderer.

'No, it wasn't that. For Wang could have done it any time this last twelve months or more.'

Heyst's mind had worked on the assumption that Wang had possessed himself of the revolver during his own absence from Samburan; but at that period of his speculation his point of view changed. It struck him with the force of manifest certitude that the revolver had been taken only late in the day, or on that very night. Wang, of course – But why? So there had been no danger in the past. It was all ahead.

'He has me at his mercy now,' thought Heyst, without particular excitement.

The sentiment he experienced was curiosity. He forgot himself in it: it was as if he were considering somebody else's strange predicament. But even that sort of interest was dying out when, looking to his left, he saw the accustomed shapes of the other bungalows looming in the night, and remembered the arrival of the thirsty company in the boat. Wang would hardly risk such a crime in the presence of other white men. It was a peculiar instance of the 'safety in numbers' principle, which somehow was not much to Heyst's taste.

He went in gloomily, and stood over the empty drawer in deep and unsatisfactory thought. He had just made up his mind that he must breathe nothing of this to the girl, when he heard her voice behind him. She had taken him by surprise, but he resisted the impulse to turn round at once under the impression that she might read his trouble in his face. Yes, she had taken him by surprise; and for that reason the conversation which began was not exactly as he would have conducted it if he had been prepared for her pointblank question. He ought to have said at once: 'I've missed nothing.' It was a deplorable thing that he should have let it come so far as to have her ask what it was he missed. He closed the conversation by saying lightly:

'It's an object of very small value. Don't worry about it – it isn't worth while. The best you can do is to go and lie down again, Lena.'

Reluctant she turned away, and only in the doorway asked:

'And you?'

'I think I shall smoke a cheroot on the veranda. I don't feel sleepy for the moment.'

'Well, don't be long.'

He made no answer. She saw him standing there, very still, with a frown on his brow, and slowly dropped the curtain.

Heyst did really light a cheroot before going out again on the veranda. He glanced up from under the low eaves, to see by the stars how the night went on. It was going very slowly. Why it should have irked him he did not know; for he had nothing to expect from the dawn; but everything round him had become unreasonable, unsettled, and vaguely urgent, laying him under an obligation, but giving him no line of action. He felt contemptuously irritated with the situation. The outer world had broken upon him; and he did not know what wrong he had done to bring this on himself, any more than he knew what he had done to provoke the horrible calumny about his treatment of poor Morrison. For he could not forget this. It had reached the ears of one who needed to have the most perfect confidence in the rectitude of his conduct.

'And she only half disbelieves it,' he thought, with hopeless humiliation.

This moral stab in the back seemed to have taken some of his strength from him, as a physical wound would have done. He hed no desire to do anything – neither to bring Wang to terms in the matter of the revolver nor to find out from the strangers who they were, and how their predicament had come about. He flung his glowing cigar away into the night. But Samburan was no longer a solitude wherein he could indulge in all his moods. The fiery parabolic trail the cast-out stump traced in the air was seen from another veranda at a distance of some twenty yards. It was noted as a symptom of importance by an observer with his faculties greedy for signs, and in a state of alertness tense enough almost to hear the grass grow.

Chapter X

The observer was Martin Ricardo. To him life was not a matter of passive renunciation, but of a particularly active warfare. He was not mistrustful of it, he was not disgusted with it, still less was he inclined to be suspicious of its disenchantments; but he was vividly aware that it held many possibilities of failure. Though very far from being a pessimist, he was not a man of foolish illusions. He did not like failure; not only because of its unpleasant and dangerous consequences, but also because of its damaging effect upon his own appreciation of Martin Ricardo. And this was a special job, of his own contriving, and of considerable novelty. It was not, so to speak, in his usual line of business – except, perhaps, from a moral standpoint, about which he was not likely to trouble his head. For these reasons Martin Ricardo was unable to sleep.

Mr Jones, after repeated shivering fits, and after drinking much hot tea, had apparently fallen into deep slumber. He had very peremptorily discouraged attempts at conversation on the part of his faithful follower. Ricardo listened to his regular breathing. It was all very well for the governor. He looked upon it as a sort of sport. A gentleman naturally would. But this ticklish and important job had to be pulled off at all costs, both for honour and for safety. Ricardo rose quietly, and made his way on the veranda. He could not lie still. He wanted to go out for air; and he had a feeling that by the force of his eagerness even the darkness and the silence could be made to yield something to his eyes and ears.

He noted the stars, and stepped back again into the dense darkness. He resisted the growing impulse to go out and steal toward the other bungalow. It would have been madness to start prowling in the dark on unknown ground. And for what end? Unless to relieve the oppression. Immobility lay on his limbs like a leaden garment. And yet he was unwilling to give up. He persisted in his objectless vigil. The man of the island was keeping quiet.

It was at that moment that Ricardo's eyes caught the vanishing red trail of light made by the cigar – a startling revelation of the man's wakefulness. He could not suppress a low 'Hallo!' and began to sidle along towards the door, with his shoulders rubbing the wall. For all he knew, the man might have been out in front by this time, observing the veranda. As a matter of fact, after flinging away the cheroot, Heyst had gone indoors with the feeling of a man who gives up an unprofitable occupation. But Ricardo fancied he could hear faint footfalls on the open ground, and dodged quickly into the room. There he drew breath, and meditated for a while. His next step was to feel for the matches on the tall desk, and to light the candle. He had to communicate to his governor views and reflections of such importance that it was absolutely necessary for him to watch their effect on the very countenance of the hearer. At first he had thought that these matters could have waited till daylight; but Heyst's wakefulness, disclosed in that startling way, made him feel suddenly certain that there could no sleep for him that night.

He said as much to his governor. When the little dagger-like flame had done its best to dispel the darkness, Mr Jones was to be seen reposing on a camp bedstead, in a distant part of the room. A railway rug concealed his spare form up to his very head, which rested on the other railway rug rolled up for a pillow. Ricardo plumped himself down cross-legged on the floor, very close to the low bedstead; so that Mr Jones – who perhaps had not been so very profoundly asleep – on opening his eyes found them conveniently levelled at the face of his secretary.

'Eh? What is it you say? No sleep for you tonight? But why can't you let *me* sleep? Confound your fussiness!'

'Because that there fellow can't sleep – that's why. Dash me if he hasn't been doing a think just now! What business has he to think in the middle of the night?'

'How do you know?'

'He was out, sir – up in the middle of the night. My own eyes saw it.'

'But how do you know that he was up to think?' inquired Mr Jones. 'It might have been anything – toothache, for instance. And you may have dreamed it for all I know. Didn't you try to sleep?'

'No, sir. I didn't even try to go to sleep.'

Ricardo informed his patron of his vigil on the veranda, and of the revelation which put an end to it. He concluded that a man up with a cigar in the middle of the night must be doing a think.

Mr Jones raised himself on his elbow. This sign of interest comforted his faithful henchman.

'Seems to me it's time we did a little think ourselves,' added Ricardo, with more assurance. Long as they had been together the moods of his governor were still a source of anxiety to his simple soul.

'You are always making a fuss,' remarked Mr Jones, in a tolerant tone.

'Ay, but not for nothing, am I? You can't say that sir. Mine may not be a gentleman's way of looking round a thing, but it isn't a fool's way, either. You've admitted that much yourself at odd times.'

Ricardo was growing warmly argumentative. Mr Jones interrupted him without heat.

'You haven't roused me to talk about yourself, I presume.'

'No, sir.' Ricardo remained silent for a minute, with the tip of his tongue caught between his teeth. 'I don't think I could tell you anything about myself that you don't know,' he continued. There was a sort of amused satisfaction in his tone which changed completely as he went on. 'It's that man, over there, that's got to be talked over. I don't like him!'

He failed to observe the flicker of a ghastly smile on his governor's lips.

'Don't you?' murmured Mr Jones, whose face, as he reclined on his elbow, was on a level with the top of his follower's head.

'No, sir,' said Ricardo emphatically. The candle from the other side of the room threw his monstrous black shadow on the wall. 'He – I don't know how to say it – he isn't hearty-like.'

Mr Jones agreed languidly in his own manner:

'He seems to be a very self-possessed man.'

'Ah, that's it. Self –' Ricardo choked with indignation. 'I would soon let out some of his self-possession through a hole between his ribs, if this weren't a special job!'

Mr Jones had been making his own reflections, for he asked:

'Do you think he is suspicious?'

'I don't see very well what he can be suspicious of,' pondered Ricardo. 'Yet there he was, doing a think. And what could be the object of it? What made him get out of his bed in the middle of the night. 'Tain't fleas, surely.'

'Bad conscience, perhaps,' suggested Mr Jones jocularly.

His faithful secretary suffered from irritation, and did not see the joke. In a fretful tone he declared that there was no such thing as conscience. There was such a thing as funk; but there was nothing to make that fellow funky in any special way. He admitted, however, that the man might have been uneasy at the arrival of strangers, because of all that plunder of his put away somewhere.

Ricardo glanced here and there, as if he were afraid of being overheard by the heavy shadows cast by the dim light all over the room. His patron, very quiet, spoke in a calm whisper:

'And perhaps that hotel-keeper has been lying to you about him. He may be a very poor devil indeed.'

Ricardo shook his head slightly. The Schombergian theory of Heyst had become in him a profound conviction, which he had absorbed as naturally as a sponge takes up water. His patron's doubts were a wanton denying of what was self-evident; but Ricardo's voice remained as before, a soft purring with a snarling undertone.

'I am sup-prised at you, sir! It's the very way them tame ones – the common 'yporcrits of the world – get on. When it comes to plunder drifting under one's very nose, there's not one of them that would keep his hands off. And I don't blame them. It's the way they do it that sets my back up. Just look at the story of how he got rid of that pal of his! Send a man home to croak of a cold on the chest – that's one of your tame tricks. And d'you mean to say, sir, that a man that's up to it wouldn't bag whatever he could lay his hands on in his 'yporcritical way? What was all that coal business? Tame citizen dodge; 'yporcrisy – nothing else. No, no, sir! The thing is to 'xtract it from him as neatly as possible. That's the job; and it isn't so simple as it looks. I reckon you have looked at it all round, sir, before you took up the notion of this trip.'

'No.' Mr Jones was hardly audible, staring far away from his couch. 'I didn't think about it much. I was bored.'

'Ay, that you were – bad. I was feeling pretty desperate that afternoon when that bearded softy of a landlord got talking to me about this fellow here. Quite accidentally, it was. Well, sir, here we are after a mighty narrow squeak. I feel all limp yet; but never mind – his swag will pay for the lot!'

'He's all alone here,' remarked Mr Jones in a hollow murmur.

'Ye-es, in a way. Yes, alone enough. Yes, you may say he is.'

'There's that Chinaman, though.'

'Ah, there's the Chink,' assented Ricardo rather absentmindedly.

He was debating in his mind the advisability of making a clean breast of his knowledge of the girl's existence. Finally he concluded he wouldn't. The enterprise was difficult enough without complicating it with an upset to the sensibilities of the gentleman with whom he had the honour of being associated. Let the discovery come of itself, he thought, and then he could swear that he had known nothing of that offensive presence.

He did not need to lie. He had only to hold his tongue.

'Yes,' he muttered reflectively, 'there's that Chink, certainly.'

At bottom, he felt a certain ambiguous respect for his governor's exaggerated dislike of women, as if that horror of feminine presence were a sort of depraved morality; but still morality, since he counted it as an advantage. It prevented many undesirable complications. He did not pretend to understand it. He did not even try to investigate this idiosyncrasy of his chief. All he knew was that he himself was differently inclined, and that it did not make him any happier or safer. He did not know how he would have acted if he had been knocking about the world on his own. Luckily he was a subordinate, not a wage-slave but a follower – which was a restraint. Yes! The other sort of disposition simplified matters in general; it wasn't to be gainsaid. But it was clear that it could also complicate them – as in this most important and, in Ricardo's view, already sufficiently delicate case. And the worst of it was that one could not tell exactly in what precise manner it would act.

It was unnatural, he thought somewhat peevishly. How was one to reckon up the unnatural? There were no rules for that. The faithful henchman of plain Mr Jones, foreseeing many difficulties of a material order, decided to keep the girl out of the governor's knowledge; out of his sight, too, for as long a time as it could be managed. That, alas, seemed to be at most a matter of a few hours; whereas Ricardo feared that to get the affair properly going would take some days. Once well started, he was not afraid of his gentleman failing him. As is often the case with lawless natures, Ricardo's faith in any given individual was of a simple, unquestioning character. For man must have some support in life.

Cross-legged, his head drooping a little and perfectly still, he might have been meditating in a bonze-like attitude upon the sacred syllable 'Om'. It was a striking illustration of the untruth of appearances, for his contempt for the world was of a severely practical kind. There was nothing oriental about Ricardo but the amazing quietness of his pose. Mr Jones was also very quiet. He had let his head sink on the rolled-up rug, and lay stretched out on his side with his back to the light. In that position the shadows gathered in the cavities of his eyes made them look perfectly empty. When he spoke, his ghostly voice had only to travel a few inches straight into Ricardo's left ear.

'Why don't you say something, now that you've got me awake?'

'I wonder if you were sleeping as sound as you are trying to make out, sir,' said the unmoved Ricardo.

'I wonder,' repeated Mr Jones. 'At any rate, I was resting quietly.'

'Come, sir!' Ricardo's whisper was alarmed. 'You don't mean to say you're going to be bored?'

'No.'

'Quite right!' The secretary was very much relieved. 'There's no occasion to be, I can tell you, sir,' he whispered earnestly. 'Anything but that! If I didn't say anything for a bit, it ain't because there isn't plenty to talk about. Ay, more than enough.'

'What's the matter with you?' breathed out his patron. 'Are you going to turn pessimist?'

'Me turn? No, sir! I ain't of those that turn. You may call me hard names, if you like, but you know very well that I ain't a croaker.' Ricardo changed his tone. 'If I said nothing for a while, it was because I was meditating over the Chink, sir.'

'You were? Waste of time, my Martin. A Chinaman is unfathomable.'

Ricardo admitted that this might be so. Anyhow, a Chink was neither here nor there, as a general thing, unfathomable as he might be; but a Swedish baron wasn't – couldn't be! The woods were full of such barons.

'I don't know that he is so tame,' was Mr Jones's remark, in a sepulchral undertone.

'How do you mean, sir? He ain't a rabbit, of course. You couldn't hypnotize him, as I saw you do to more than one Dago, and other kinds of tame citizens, when it came to the point of holding them down to a game.'

'Don't you reckon on that,' murmured plain Mr Jones seriously.

'No, sir, I don't: though you have a wonderful power of the eye. It's a fact.'

'I have a wonderful patience,' remarked Mr Jones drily.

A dim smile flitted over the lips of the faithful Ricardo who never raised his head.

'I don't want to try you too much, sir; but this is like no other job we ever turned our minds to.'

'Perhaps not. At any rate let us think so.'

A weariness with the monotony of life was reflected in the tone of this qualified assent. It jarred on the nerves of the sanguine Ricardo.

'Let us think of the way to go to work,' he retorted a little impatiently. 'He's a deep one. Just look at the way he treated that chum of his. Did you ever hear of anything so low? And the artfulness of the beast – the dirty, tame artfulness!'

'Don't you start moralizing, Martin,' said Mr Jones warningly. 'As far as I can make out the story that German hotel-keeper told you, it seems to show a certain amount of character; and independence from common feelings which is not usual. It's very remarkable, if true.'

'Ay, ay! Very remarkable. It's mighty low down, all the same,' muttered Ricardo obstinately. 'I must say I am glad to think he will be paid off for it in a way that'll surprise him!'

The tip of his tongue appeared lively for an instant, as if trying for the taste of that ferocious retribution on his compressed lips. For Ricardo was sincere in his indignation before the elementary principle of loyalty to a chum violated in cold blood, slowly, in a patient duplicity of years. There are standards in villainy as in virtue, and the act as he pictured it to himself acquired an additional horror from the slow pace of that treachery so atrocious and so tame. But he understood too the educated judgement of his governor, a gentleman looking on all this with the privileged detachment of a cultivated mind, of an elevated personality.

'Ay, he's deep – he's artful,' he mumbled between his sharp teeth.

'Confound you!' Mr Jones's calm whisper crept into his ear. 'Come to the point.'

Obedient, the secretary shook off his thoughtfulness. There was a similarity of mind between these two – one the outcast of his vices, the other inspired by a spirit of scornful defiance, the aggressiveness of a beast of prey looking upon all the tame creatures of the earth as its natural victims. Both were astute enough, however, and both were aware that they had plunged into this adventure without sufficient scrutiny of detail. The figure of a lonely man far from all assistance had loomed up largely, fascinating and defenceless in the middle of the sea, filling the whole field of their vision. There had not seemed to be any need for thinking. As Schomberg had been saying: 'Three to one.'

But it did not look so simple now in the face of that solitude which was like an armour for this man. The feeling voiced by the henchman in his own way – 'We don't seem much forwarder now we are here' – was acknowledged by the silence of the patron. It was easy enough to rip a fellow up or drill a hole in him, whether he was alone or not, Ricardo reflected in low, confidential tones, but –

'He isn't alone,' Mr Jones said faintly, in his attitude of a man composed for sleep. 'Don't forget that Chinaman.' Ricardo started slightly.

'Oh, ay – the Chink!'

Ricardo had been on the point of confessing about the girl; but no! He wanted his governor to be unperturbed and steady. Vague thoughts, which he hardly dared to look in the face, were stirring his brain in connection with that girl. She couldn't be of much account, he thought. She could be frightened. And there were also other possibilities. The Chink, however, could be considered openly.

'What I was thinking about it, sir,' he went on earnestly, 'is this – here we've got a man. He's nothing. If he won't be good, he can be made quiet. That's easy. But then there's his plunder. He doesn't carry it in his pocket.'

'I hope not,' breathed Mr Jones.

'Same here. It's too big, we know; but if he were alone, he would not feel worried about it overmuch – I mean the safety of the pieces. He would just put the lot into any box or drawer that was handy.'

'Would he?'

'Yes, sir. He would keep it under his eye, as it were. Why not? It is natural. A fellow doesn't put his swag underground, unless there's a very good reason for it.'

'A very good reason, eh?'

'Yes, sir. What do you think a fellow is – a mole?'

From this experience, Ricardo declared that man was not a burrowing beast. Even the misers very seldom buried their hoard, unless for exceptional reasons. In the given situation of a man alone on an island, the company of a Chink was a very good reason. Drawers would not be safe, nor boxes, either, from a prying, slant-eyed Chink. No, sir; unless a safe – a proper office safe. But the safe was there in the room.

'Is there a safe in this room? I didn't notice it,' whispered Mr Jones.

That was because the thing was painted white, like the walls of the room; and besides, it was tucked away in the shadows of a corner. Mr Jones had been too tired to observe anything on his first coming ashore; but Ricardo had very soon spotted the characteristic form. He only wished he could believe that the plunder of treachery, duplicity, and all the moral abominations of Heyst had been there. But no; the blamed thing was open.

'It might have been there at one time or another,' he commented gloomily, 'but it isn't there now.'

'The man did not elect to live in this house,' remarked Mr Jones. 'And by the by, what could he have meant by speaking of circumstances which prevented him lodging us in the other bungalow? You remember what he said, Martin? Sounded cryptic.'

Martin, who remembered and understood the phrase as directly motived by the existence of the girl, waited a little before saying:

'Some of his artfulness, sir; and not the worst of it either. That manner of his to us, this asking no questions, is some more of his artfulness. A man's bound to be curious, and he is; yet he goes on as if he didn't care. He does care – or else what was he doing up with a cigar in the middle of the night, doing a think? I don't like it!'

'He may be outside, observing the light here, and saying the very same thing to himself of our own wakefulness,' gravely suggested Ricardo's governor.

'He may be, sir; but this is too important to be talked over in the dark. And the night is all right. It can be accounted for. There's a light in this bungalow in the middle of the night because – why, because you are not well. Not well, sir – that's what's the matter; and you will have to act up to it.'

The consideration had suddenly occurred to the faithful henchman, in the light of a felicitous expedient to keep his governor and the girl apart as long as possible. Mr Jones received the suggestion without the slightest stir, even in the deep sockets of his eyes, where a steady, faint gleam was the only thing telling of life and attention in his attenuated body. But Ricardo, as soon as he had enunciated his happy thought, perceived in it other possibilities more to the point and of greater practical advantage.

'With your looks, sir, it will be easy enough,' he went on evenly, as if no silence had intervened, always respectful, but frank, with perfect simplicity of purpose. 'All you've got to do is just to lie down quietly. I noticed him looking sort of surprised at you on the wharf, sir.'

At these words, a naïve tribute to the aspect of his physique, even more suggestive of the grave than of the sick-bed, a fold appeared on that side of the governor's face which was exposed to the dim light – a deep, shadowy, semicircular fold from the side of the nose to bottom of the chin – a silent smile. By a side-glance Ricardo had noted this play of features. He smiled, too, appreciative, encouraged.

'And you as hard as nails all the time,' he went on. 'Hang me if anybody would believe you aren't sick, if I were to swear myself black in the face! Give us a day or two to look into matters and size up that 'yporcrit.'

Ricardo's eyes remained fixed on his crossed shins. The chief, in his lifeless accents, approved.

'Perhaps it would be a good idea.'

'The Chink, he's nothing. He can be made quiet any time.'

One of Ricardo's hands, reposing palm upwards on his folded legs, made a swift thrusting gesture, repeated by the enormous darting shadow of an arm very low on the wall. It broke the spell of perfect stillness in the room. The secretary eyed moodily the wall from which the shadow had gone. Anybody could be made quiet, he pointed out. It was not anything that the Chink could do; no, it was the effect that his company must have produced on the conduct of the doomed man. A man! What was a man? A Swedish baron could be ripped up, or else holed by a shot, as easily as any other creature; but that was exactly what was to be avoided, till one knew where he had hidden his plunder.

'I shouldn't think it would be some sort of hole in his bungalow,' argued Ricardo with real anxiety.

No. A house can be burnt – set on fire accidentally, or on purpose, while a man's asleep. Under the house – or in some crack, cranny, or crevice? Something told him it wasn't that. The anguish of mental effort contracted Ricardo's brow. The skin of his head seemed to move in this travail of vain and tormenting suppositions.

'What did you think a fellow is, sir – a baby?' he said, in answer to Mr Jones's objections. 'I am trying to find out what I would do myself. He wouldn't be likely to be cleverer than I am.'

'And what do you know about yourself?'

Mr Jones seemed to watch his follower's perplexities with amusement concealed in a death-like composure.

Ricardo disregarded the question. The material vision of the spoil absorbed all his faculties. A great vision! He seemed to see it. A few small canvas bags tied up with thin cord, their distended rotundity showing the inside pressure of the disk-like forms of coins – gold, solid, heavy, eminently portable. Perhaps steel cash-boxes with a chased design on the covers; or perhaps a black and brass box with a handle on the top, and full of goodness knows what. Bank notes? Why not? The fellow had been going home; so it was surely something worth going home with.

'And he may have put it anywhere outside – anywhere!' cried Ricardo in a deadened voice. 'In the forest –'

That was it! A temporary darkness replaced the dim light of the room. The darkness of the forest at night, and in it the gleam of a lantern, by which a figure is digging at the foot of a tree-trunk. As likely as not, another figure holding that lantern – ha, feminine! The girl!

The prudent Ricardo stifled a picturesque and profane exclamation, partly joy, partly dismay. Had the girl been trusted or mistrusted by that man? Whatever it was, it was bound to be wholly! With women there could be no half-measures. He could not imagine a fellow half-trusting a woman in that intimate relation to himself, and in those particular circumstances of conquest and loneliness where no confidences could appear dangerous since, apparently, there could be no one she could give him away to. Moreover, in nine cases out of ten the woman would be trusted. But, trusted or mistrusted, was her presence a favourable or unfavourable condition of the problem? That was the question!

The temptation to consult his chief, to talk over the weighty fact and get his opinion on it, was great indeed. Ricardo resisted it; but the agony of his solitary mental conflict was extremely sharp. A woman in a problem is an incalculable quantity, even if you have something to go upon in forming your guess. How much more so when you haven't even once caught sight of her.

Swift as were his mental processes, he felt that a longer silence was inadvisable. He hastened to speak:

'And do you see us, sir, you and I, with a couple of spades having to tackle this whole confounded island?'

He allowed himself a slight movement of the arm. The shadow enlarged it into a sweeping gesture.

'This seems rather discouraging, Martin,' murmured the unmoved governor.

'We mustn't be discouraged – that's all,' retorted his henchman. 'And after what we had to go through in that boat too! Why it would be –'

He couldn't find the qualifying words. Very calm, faithful, and yet astute, he expressed his new-born hopes darkly.

'Something's sure to turn up to give us a hint; only this job can't be rushed. You may depend on me to pick up the least little bit of a hint; but you, sir – you've got to play him very gently. For the rest you can trust me.'

'Yes; but I ask myself what *you* are trusting to.'

'Our luck,' said the faithful Ricardo. 'Don't say a word against that. It might spoil the run of it.'

'You are a superstitious beggar. No, I won't say anything against it.'

'That's right, sir. Don't you even think lightly of it. Luck's not to be played with.'

'Yes, luck's a delicate thing,' assented Mr Jones in a dreamy whisper.

A short silence ensued, which Ricardo ended in a discreet and tentative voice.

'Talking of luck, I suppose he could be made to take a hand with you, sir – two-handed picket or ekarty, you being seedy and keeping indoors – just to pass the time. For all we know, he may be one of them hot ones once they start –'

'Is it likely?' came coldly from the principal. 'Considering what we know of his history – say with his partner.'

'True, sir. He's a cold-blooded beast; a cold-blooded, inhuman –'

'And I'll tell you another thing that isn't likely. He would not be likely to let himself be stripped bare. We haven't to do with a young fool that can be led on by chaff or flattery, and in the end simply overawed. This is a calculating man.'

Ricardo recognized that clearly. What he had in his mind was something on a small scale, just to keep the enemy busy while he, Ricardo, had time to nose around a bit.

'You could even lose a little money to him, sir,' he suggested.

'I could.'

Ricardo was thoughtful for a moment.

'He strikes me, too, as the sort of man to start prancing when one didn't expect it. What do you think, sir? Is he a man that would prance? That is, if something startled him. More likely to prance than to run – what?'

The answer came at once, because Mr Jones understood the peculiar idiom of his faithful follower.

'Oh, without doubt! Without doubt!'

'It does me good to hear that you think so. He's a prancing beast, and so we mustn't startle him – not till I have located the stuff. Afterwards –'

Ricardo paused, sinister in the stillness of his pose. Suddenly he got up with a swift movement and gazed down at his chief in moody abstraction. Mr Jones did not stir.

'There's one thing that's worrying me', began Ricardo in a subdued voice.

'Only one?' was the faint comment from the motionless body on the bedstead.

'I mean more than all the others put together.'

'That's grave news.'

'Ay, grave enough. It's this – how do you feel in yourself, sir? Are you likely to get bored? I know them fits come on you suddenly; but surely you can tell –'

'Martin, you are an ass.'

The moody face of the secretary brightened up.

'Really, sir? Well, I am quite content to be on these terms – I mean as long as you don't get bored. It wouldn't do, sir.'

For coolness, Ricardo had thrown open his shirt and rolled up his sleeves. He moved stealthily across the room, bare-footed, towards the candle, the shadow of his head and shoulders growing bigger behind him on the opposite wall, to which the face of plain Mr Jones was turned. With a feline movement, Ricardo glanced over his shoulder at the thin back of the spectre reposing on the bed, and then blew out the candle.

'In fact, I am rather amused, Martin,' Mr Jones said in the dark.

He heard the sound of a slapped thigh and the jubilant exclamation of his henchman:

'Good! That's the way to talk, sir!'

PART FOUR

CHAPTER I

RICARDO ADVANCED prudently by short darts from one tree-trunk to another, more in the manner of a squirrel than a cat. The sun had risen some time before. Already the sparkle of open sea was encroaching rapidly on the dark, cool, early-morning blue of Diamond Bay; but the deep dusk lingered yet under the mighty pillars of the forest, between which the secretary dodged.

He was watching Number One's bungalow with an animal-like patience, if with a very human complexity of purpose. This was the second morning of such watching. The first one had not been rewarded by success. Well, strictly speaking, there was no hurry.

The sun, swinging above the ridge all at once, inundated with light the space of burnt grass in front of Ricardo and the face of the bungalow, on which his eyes were fixed, leaving only the one dark spot of the doorway. To his right, to his left, and behind him, splashes of gold appeared in the deep shade of the forest, thinning the gloom under the ragged roof of leaves.

This was not a very favourable circumstance for Ricardo's purpose. He did not wish to be detected in his patient occupation. For what he was watching for was a sight of the girl – that girl! Just a glimpse across the burnt patch to see what she was like. He had excellent eyes, and the distance was not so great. He would be able to distinguish her face quite easily if she only came out on the veranda; and she was bound to do that sooner or later. He was confident that he could form some opinion about her – which, he felt, was very necessary, before venturing on some steps to get in touch with her behind that Swedish baron's back. His theoretical view of the girl was such that he was quite prepared, on the strength of that distant examination, to show himself discreetly – perhaps even make a sign. It all depended on his reading of the face. She couldn't be much. He knew that sort!

By protruding his head a little he commanded, through the foliage of a festooning creeper, a view of the three bungalows, irregularly disposed along a flat curve. Over the veranda rail of the farthermost one hung a dark rug of a tartan pattern, amazingly conspicuous. Ricardo could see the very checks. A brisk fire of sticks was burning on the ground in front of the steps, and in the sunlight the thin, fluttering flame had paled almost to invisibility – a mere rosy stir under a faint wreath of smoke. He could see the white bandage on the head of Pedro bending over it, and the wisps of black hair standing up weirdly. He had wound that bandage himself, after breaking that shaggy and enormous head. The creature balanced it like a load, staggering towards the steps. Ricardo could see a small, long-handled saucepan at the end of a great hairy paw.

Yes, he could see all that there was to be seen, far and near. Excellent eyes! The only thing they could not penetrate was the dark oblong of the doorway on the veranda under the low eaves of the bungalow's roof. And that was vexing. It was an outrage. Ricardo was easily outraged. Surely she would come out presently! Why didn't she? Surely the fellow did not tie her up to the bedpost before leaving the house!

Nothing appeared. Ricardo was as still as the leafy cables of creepers depending in a convenient curtain from the mighty limb sixty feet above his head. His very eyelids were still, and this unblinking watchfulness gave him the dreamy air of a cat posed on a hearth-rug contemplating the fire. Was he dreaming? There, in plain sight, he had before him a white, blouse-like jacket, short blue trousers, a pair of bare yellow calves, a pigtail, long and slender –

'The confounded Chink!' he muttered, astounded.

He was not conscious of having looked away; and yet right there, in the middle of the picture, without having come round the right-hand corner or the left-hand corner of the house, without falling from the sky or surging up from the ground, Wang had become visible, large as life, and engaged in the young-ladyish occupation of picking flowers. Step by step, stooping repeatedly over the flower-beds at the foot of the veranda, the startlingly materialized Chinaman passed off the scene in a very commonplace manner, by going up the steps and disappearing in the darkness of the doorway.

Only then the yellow eyes of Martin Ricardo lost their intent fixity. He understood that it was time for him to be moving. That bunch of flowers going into the house in the hand of a Chinaman was for the breakfast-table. What else could it be for?

'I'll give you flowers!' he muttered threateningly. 'You wait!'

Another moment, just for a glance towards the Jones bungalow, whence he expected Heyst to issue on his way to that breakfast so offensively decorated, and Ricardo began his retreat. His impulse, his desire, was for a rush into the open, face to face with the appointed victim, for what he called a 'ripping up', visualized greedily, and always with the swift preliminary stooping movement on his part – the forerunner of certain death to his adversary. This was his impulse; and it was, so to speak, constitutional, it was extremely difficult to resist when his blood was up. What could be more trying than to have a skulk and dodge and restrain oneself, mentally and physically, when one's blood was up? Mr Secretary Ricardo began his retreat from his post of observation behind a tree opposite Heyst's bungalow, using great care to remain unseen. His proceedings were made easier by the declivity of the ground, which sloped sharply down to the water's edge. There, his feet feeling the warmth of the island's rocky foundation already heated by the sun, through the thin soles of his straw slippers he was, as it were, sunk out of sight of the houses. A short scramble of some twenty feet brought him up again to the upper level, at the place where the jetty had its root in the shore. He leaned his back against one of the lofty uprights which still held up the company's signboard above the mound of derelict coal. Nobody could have guessed how much his blood was up. To contain himself he folded his arms tightly on his breast.

Ricardo was not used to a prolonged effort of self-control. His craft, his artfulness, felt themselves always at the mercy of his nature, which was truly feral and only held in subjection by the influence of the 'governor', the prestige of a gentleman. It had its cunning too, but it was being almost too severely tried since the feral solution of a growl and a spring was forbidden by the problem. Ricardo dared not venture out on the cleared ground. He dared not.

'If I meet the beggar,' he thought. 'I don't know what I mayn't do. I daren't trust myself.'

What exasperated him just now was his inability to understand Heyst. Ricardo was human enough to suffer from the discovery of his limitations. No, he couldn't size Heyst up. He could kill him with extreme ease – a growl and a spring – but that was forbidden! However, he could not remain indefinitely under the funereal blackboard.

'I must make a move,' he thought.

He moved on, his head swimming a little with the repressed desire of violence, and came out openly in front of the bungalows, as if he had just been down to the jetty to look at the boat. The sunshine enveloped him, very brilliant, very still, very hot. The three buildings faced him. The one with the rug on the balustrade was the most distant; next to it was the empty bungalow; the nearest, with the flower-beds at the foot of its veranda, contained that bothersome girl, who had managed so provokingly to keep herself invisible. That was why Ricardo's eyes lingered on that building. The girl would surely be easier to 'size up' than Heyst. A sight of her, a mere glimpse, would have been something to go by, a step nearer to the goal – the first real move, in fact. Ricardo saw no other move. And any time she might appear on that veranda!

She did not appear; but, like a concealed magnet, she exercised her attraction. As he went on, he deviated towards the bungalow. Though his movements were deliberate, his feral instincts had such sway that if he had met Heyst walking towards him, he would have had to satisfy his need of violence. But he saw nobody. Wang was at the back of the house, keeping the coffee hot against Number One's return for breakfast. Even the simian Pedro was out of sight, no doubt crouching on the doorstep, his red little eyes fastened with animal-like devotion on Mr Jones, who was in discourse with Heyst in the other bungalow – the conversation of an evil spectre with a disarmed man, watched by an ape.

His will having very little to do with it, Ricardo, darting swift glances in all directions, found himself at the steps of the Heyst bungalow. Once there, falling under an uncontrollable force of attraction, he mounted them with a savage and stealthy action of his limbs, and paused for a moment under the eaves to listen to the silence. Presently he advanced over the threshold one leg – it seemed to stretch itself, like a limb of india-rubber – planted his foot within, brought up the other swiftly, and stood inside the room, turning his head from side to side. To his eyes, brought in there from the dazzling sunshine, all was gloom for a moment. His pupils, like a cat's, dilating swiftly, he distinguished an enormous quantity of books. He was amazed; and he was put off, too. He was vexed in his astonishment. He had meant to note the aspect and nature of things, and hoped to draw some useful inference, some hint as to the man. But what guess could one make out of a multitude of books? He didn't know what to think; and he formulated his bewilderment in the mental exclamation:

'What the devil has this fellow been trying to set up here – a school?'

He gave a prolonged stare to the portrait of Heyst's father, that severe profile ignoring the vanities of this earth. His eyes gleamed sideways at the heavy silver candlesticks – signs of opulence. He prowled as a stray cat entering a strange place might have done; for if Ricardo had not Wang's miraculous gift of materializing and vanishing, rather than coming and going, he could be nearly as noiseless in his less elusive movements. He noted the back door standing just ajar; and all the time his slightly pointed ears, at the utmost stretch of watchfulness, kept in touch with the profound silence outside enveloping the absolute stillness of the house.

He had not been in the room two minutes when it occurred to him that he must be alone in the bungalow. The woman, most likely, had sneaked out, and was walking about somewhere in the grounds at the back. She had been probably ordered to keep out of sight. Why? Because the fellow mistrusted his guests; or was it because he mistrusted *her*?

Ricardo reflected that from a certain point of view it amounted nearly to the same thing. He remembered Schomberg's story. He felt that running away with somebody only to get clear of that beastly, tame, hotel-keeper's attention was no proof of hopeless infatuation. She could be got in touch with.

His moustaches stirred. For some time he had been looking at a closed door. He would peep into that other room, and perhaps see something more informing than a confounded lot of books. As he crossed over, he thought recklessly:

'If the beggar comes in suddenly, and starts to prance, I'll rip him up and be done with it!'

He laid his hand on the handle, and felt the door come unlatched. Before he pulled it open, he listened again to the silence. He felt it all about him, complete, without a flaw.

The necessity of prudence had exasperated his self-restraint. A mood of ferocity woke up in him, and, as always at such times, he became physically aware of the sheeted knife strapped to his leg. He pulled at the door with fierce curiosity. It came open without a squeak of hinge, without a rustle, with no sound at all; and he found himself glaring at the opaque surface of some rough blue stuff, like serge. A curtain was fitted inside, heavy enough and long enough not to stir.

A curtain! This unforeseen veil, baffling his curiosity, checked his brusqueness. He did not fling it aside with an impatient movement; he only looked at it closely, as if its texture had to be examined before his hand could touch such stuff. In this interval of hesitation, he seemed to detect a flaw in the perfection of the silence, the faintest possible rustle, which his ears caught and instantly, in the effort of conscious listening, lost again. No! Everything was still inside and outside the house, only he had no longer the sense of being alone there.

When he put out his hand towards the motionless folds it was with extreme caution, and merely to push the stuff aside a little, advancing his head at the same time to peep within. A moment of complete immobility ensued. Then, without anything else of him stirring, Ricardo's head shrank back on his shoulders, his arm descended slowly to his side. There was a woman in there. The very woman! Lighted dimly by the reflection of the outer glare, she loomed up strangely big and shadowy at the other end of the long, narrow room. With her back to the door, she was doing her hair with bare arms uplifted. One of them gleamed pearly white; the other detached its perfect form in black against the unshuttered, uncurtained window-hole. She was there, her fingers busy with her dark hair, utterly unconscious, exposed and defenceless – and tempting.

Ricardo drew back one foot and pressed his elbows close to his sides; his chest started heaving convulsively as if he were wrestling or running a race; his body began to sway gently back and forth. The self-restraint was at an end: his psychology must have its way. The instinct for the feral spring could no longer be denied. Ravish or kill – it was all one to him, as long as by the act he liberated the suffering soul of savagery repressed for so long. After a quick glance over his shoulder, which hunters of big game tell us no lion or tiger omits to give before charging home, Ricardo charged, head down, straight at the curtain. The stuff, tossed up violently by his rush, settled itself with a slow, floating descent into vertical folds, motionless, without a shudder even, in the still, warm air.

Chapter II

The clock – which once upon a time had measured the hours of philosophic meditation – could not have ticked away more than five seconds when Wang materialized within the living-room. His concern primarily was with the delayed breakfast, but at once his slanting eyes became immovably fixed upon the unstirring curtain. For it was behind it that he had located the strange, deadened scuffling sounds which filled the empty room. The slanting eyes of his race could not achieve a round, amazed stare, but they remained still, dead still, and his impassive yellow face grew all at once careworn and lean with the sudden strain of intense, doubtful, frightened watchfulness. Contrary impulses swayed his body, rooted to the floor-mats. He even went so far as to extend his hand towards the curtain. He could not reach it, and he didn't make the necessary step forward.

The mysterious struggle was going on with confused thuds of bare feet, in a mute wrestling match, no human sound, hiss, groan, murmur, or exclamation coming through the curtain. A chair fell over, not with a crash but lightly, as if just grazed, and a faint metallic ring of the tin bath succeeded. Finally the tense silence, as of two adversaries locked in a deadly grip, was ended by the heavy, dull thump of a soft body flung against the inner partition of planks. It seemed to shake the whole bungalow. By that time, walking backward, his eyes, his very throat, strained with fearful excitement, his extended arm still pointing at the curtain, Wang had disappeared through the back door. Once out in the compound, he bolted round the end of the house. Emerging innocently between the two bungalows he lingered and lounged in the open, where anybody issuing from any of the dwellings was bound to see him – a self-possessed Chinaman idling there, with nothing but perhaps an unserved breakfast on his mind.

It was at this time that Wang made up his mind to give up all connection with Number One, a man not only disarmed but already half vanquished. Till that morning he had had doubts as to his course of action, but this overheard scuffle decided the question. Number One was a doomed man – one of those beings whom it is unlucky to help. Even as he walked in the open with a fine air of unconcern, Wang wondered that no sound of any sort was to be heard inside the house. For all he knew, the white woman might have been scuffling in there with an evil spirit, which had of course killed her. Nothing visible came out of the house, for he watched out of the slanting corner of his eye. The sunshine and the silence outside the bungalow reigned undisturbed.

But in the house the silence of the big room would not have struck an acute ear as perfect. It was troubled by a stir so faint that it could hardly be called a ghost of whispering from behind the curtain.

Ricardo, feeling his throat with tender care, breathed out admiringly:

'You have fingers like steel. Jimminy! You have muscles like a giant!'

Luckily for Lena, Ricardo's onset had been so sudden – she was winding her two heavy tresses round her head – that she had no time to lower her arms. This, which saved them from being pinned to her sides, gave her a better chance to resist. His spring had nearly thrown her down. Luckily, again, she was standing so near the wall that, though she was driven against it headlong, yet the shock was not heavy enough to knock all the breath out of her body. On the contrary, it helped her first instinctive attempt to drive her assailant backward.

After the first gasp of a surprise that was really too overpowering for a cry, she was never in doubt of the nature of her danger. She defended herself in the full, clear knowledge of it, from the force of instinct which is the true source of every great display of energy, and with a determination which could hardly have been expected from a girl who, cornered in a dim corridor by the red-faced, stammering Schomberg, had trembled with shame, disgust, and fear; had drooped, terrified, before mere words spluttered out odiously by a man who had never in his life laid his big paw on her.

This new enemy's attack was simple, straightforward violence. It was not the slimy, underhand plotting to deliver her up like a slave, which had sickened her heart and had made her feel in her loneliness that her oppressors were too many for her. She was no longer alone in the world now. She resisted without a moment of faltering, because she was no longer deprived of moral support; because she was a human being who counted; because she was no longer defending herself for herself alone; because of the faith that had been born in her – the faith in the man of her destiny, and perhaps in the Heaven which had sent him so wonderfully to cross her path.

She had defended herself principally by maintaining a desperate, murderous clutch on Ricardo's windpipe, till she felt a sudden relaxation of the terrific hug in which he stupidly and ineffectually persisted to hold her. Then with a supreme effort of her arms and of her suddenly raised knee, she sent him flying against the partition. The cedar-wood chest stood in the way, and Ricardo, with a thump which boomed hollow through the whole bungalow, fell on it in a sitting posture, half strangled, and exhausted not so much by the efforts as by the emotions of the struggle.

With the recoil of her exerted strength, she too reeled, staggered back, and sat on the edge of the bed. Out of breath, but calm and unabashed, she busied herself in readjusting under her arms the brown and yellow figured Celebes sarong, the tuck of which had come undone during the fight. Then, folding her bare arms tightly on her breast, she leaned forward on her crossed legs, determined and without fear.

Ricardo, leaning forward too, his nervous force gone, crestfallen like a beast of prey that has missed its spring, met her big grey eyes looking at him – wide open, observing, mysterious – from under the dark arches of her courageous eyebrows. Their faces were not a foot apart. He ceased feeling about his aching throat and dropped the palms of his hands heavily on his knees. He was not looking at her bare shoulders, at her strong arms; he was looking down at the floor. He had lost one of his straw slippers. A chair with a white dress on it had been overturned. These, with splashes of water on the floor out of a brusquely misplaced sponge-bath, were the only traces of the struggle.

Ricardo swallowed twice consciously, as if to make sure of his throat, before he spoke again:

'All right. I never meant to hurt you – though I am no joker when it comes to it.'

He pulled up the leg of his pyjamas to exhibit the strapped knife. She glanced at it without moving her head, and murmured, with scornful bitterness:

'Ah, yes – with that thing stuck in my side. In no other way.'

He shook his head with a shamefaced smile.

'Listen! I am quiet now. Straight – I am. I don't need to explain why – you know how it is. And I can see, now, this wasn't the way with you.'

She made no sound. Her still, upward gaze had a patient mournfulness which troubled him like a suggestion of an inconceivable depth. He added thoughtfully:

'You are not going to make a noise about this silly try of mine?'

She moved her head the least bit.

'Jee-miny! You are a wonder,' he murmured earnestly, relieved more than she could have guessed.

Of course, if she had attempted to run out, he would have stuck the knife between her shoulders, to stop her screaming; but all the fat would have been in the fire, the business utterly spoiled, and the rage of the governor – especially when he learned the cause – boundless. A woman that does not make a noise after an attempt of that kind has tacitly condoned the offence. Ricardo had no small vanities. But clearly, if she would pass it over like this, then he could not be so utterly repugnant to her. He felt flattered. And she didn't seem afraid of him either. He already felt almost tender towards the girl – that plucky, fine girl who had not tried to run screaming from him.

'We shall be friends yet. I don't give you up. Don't think it. Friends as friends can be!' he whispered confidently. 'Jee-miny! You aren't a tame one. Neither am I. You will find that out before long.'

He could not know that if she had not run out, it was because that morning, under the stress of growing uneasiness at the presence of the incomprehensible visitors, Heyst had confessed to her that it was his revolver he had been looking for in the night; that it was gone; that he was a disarmed, defenceless man. She had hardly comprehended the meaning of his confession. Now she understood better what it meant. The effort of her self-control, her stillness, impressed Ricardo. Suddenly she spoke:

'What are you after?'

He did not raise his eyes. His hands reposing on his knees, his drooping head, something reflective in his pose, suggested the weariness of a simple soul, the fatigue of a mental rather than physical contest. He answered the direct question by a direct statement, as if he were too tired to dissemble:

'After the swag.'

The word was strange to her. The veiled ardour of her grey gaze from under the dark eyebrows never left Ricardo's face.

'A swag?' she murmured quietly. 'What's that?'

'Why, swag, plunder – what your gentleman has been pinching right and left for years – the pieces. Don't you know? This!'

Without looking up, he made the motion of counting money into the palm of his hand. She lowered her eyes slightly to observe this bit of pantomime, but returned them to his face at once. Then, in a mere breath:

'How do you know anything about him?' she asked, concealing her puzzled alarm. 'What has it got to do with you?'

'Everything,' was Ricardo's concise answer, in a low, emphatic whisper. He reflected that this girl was really his best hope. Out of the unfaded impression of past violence there was growing the sort of sentiment which prevents a man from being indifferent to a woman he has once held in his arms – if even against her will – and still more so if she has pardoned the outrage. It becomes then a sort of bond. He felt positively the need to confide in her – a subtle trait of masculinity, this almost physical need of trust which can exist side by side with the most brutal readiness of suspicion.

'It's a game of grab – see?' he went on, with a new inflection of intimacy in his murmur. He was looking straight at her now. 'That fat, tame slug of a gin-slinger, Schomberg, put us up to it.'

So strong is the impression of helpless and persecuted misery, that the girl who had fought down a savage assault without faltering could not completely repress a shudder at the mere sound of the abhorred name.

Ricardo became more rapid and confidential:

'He wants to pay him off – pay both of you, at that; so he told me. He was hot after you. He would have given all he had into those hands of yours that have nearly strangled me. But you couldn't, eh? Nohow – what?' He paused. 'So, rather than – you followed a gentleman?'

He noticed a slight movement of her head and spoke quickly.

'Same here – rather than be a wage-slave. Only these foreigners aren't to be trusted. You're too good for him. A man that will rob his best chum!' She raised her head. He went on, well pleased with his progress, whispering hurriedly: 'Yes. I know all about him. So you may guess how he's likely to treat a woman after a bit!'

He did not know that he was striking terror into her breast now. Still the grey eyes remained fixed on him unmovably watchful, as if sleepy, under the white forehead. She was beginning to understand. His words conveyed a definite, dreadful meaning to her mind, which he proceeded to enlighten further in a convinced murmur.

'You and I are made to understand each other. Born alike, bred alike, I guess. You are not tame. Same here! You have been chucked out into this rotten world of 'yporcrits. Same here!'

Her stillness, her appalled stillness, wore to him an air of fascinated attention. He asked abruptly:

'Where is it?'

She made an effort to breathe out:

'Where's what?'

His tone expressed excited secrecy.

'The swag – plunder – pieces. It's a game of grab. We must have it; but it isn't easy, and so you will have to lend a hand. Come! Is it kept in the house?'

As often with women, her wits were sharpened by the very terror of the glimpsed menace. She shook her head negatively.

'No.'

'Sure?'

'Sure,' she said.

'Ay! Thought so. Does your gentleman trust you?'

Again she shook her head.

'Blamed 'yporcrit,' he said feelingly, and then reflected: 'He's one of the tame ones, ain't he?'

'You had better find out for yourself,' she said.

'You trust me. I don't want to die before you and I have made friends.' This was said with a strange air of feline gallantry. Then, tentatively: 'But he could be brought to trust you, couldn't he?'

'Trust me?' she said, in a tone which bordered on despair, but which he mistook for derision.

'Stand in with us,' he urged. 'Give the chuck to all this blamed 'yporcrisy. Perhaps, without being trusted, you have managed to find out something already, eh?'

'Perhaps I have,' she uttered with lips that seemed to her to be freezing fast.

Ricardo now looked at her calm face with something like respect. He was even a little awed by her stillness, by her economy of words. Womanlike, she felt the effect she had produced, the effect of knowing much and of keeping all her knowledge in reserve. So far, somehow, this had come about of itself. Thus encouraged, directed in the way of duplicity, the refuge of the weak, she made a heroically conscious effort and forced her stiff, cold lips into a smile.

Duplicity – the refuge of the weak and the cowardly, but of the disarmed, too! Nothing stood between the enchanted dream of her existence and a cruel catastrophe but her duplicity. It seemed to her that the man sitting there before her was an unavoidable presence, which had attended all her life. He was the embodied evil of the world. She was not ashamed of her duplicity. With a woman's frank courage, as soon as she saw that opening she threw herself into it without reserve, with only one doubt – that of her own strength. She was appalled by the situation; but already all her aroused feminity, understanding that whether Heyst loved her or not she loved him, and feeling that she had brought this on his head, faced the danger with a passionate desire to defend her own.

Chapter III

To Ricardo the girl had been so unforeseen that he was unable to bring upon her the light of his critical faculties. Her smile appeared to him full of promise. He had not expected her to be what she was. Who, from the talk he had heard, could expect to meet a girl like this? She was a blooming miracle, he said to himself, familiarly, yet with a tinge of respect. She was no meat for the likes of that tame, respectable gin-slinger. Ricardo grew hot with indignation. Her courage, her physical strength, demonstrated at the cost of his discomfiture, commanded his sympathy. He felt himself drawn to her by the proofs of her amazing spirit. Such a girl! She had a strong soul; and her reflective disposition to throw over her connection proved that she was no hypocrite.

'Is your gentleman a good shot?' he said, looking down on the floor again, as if indifferent.

She hardly understood the phrase; but in its form it suggested some accomplishment. It was safe to whisper an affirmative.

'Yes.'

'Mine, too – and better than good,' Ricardo murmured, and then, in a confidential burst: 'I am not so good at it, but I carry a pretty deadly thing about me, all the same!'

He tapped his leg. She was past the stage of shudders now. Stiff all over, unable even to move her eyes, she felt an awful mental tension which was like blank forgetfulness. Ricardo tried to influence her in his own way.

'And my gentleman is not the sort that would drop me. He ain't no foreigner; whereas you, with your baron, you don't know what's before you – or, rather, being a woman, you know only too well. Much better not to wait for the chuck. Pile in with us and get your share – of the plunder, I mean. You have some notion about it already.'

She felt that if she as much as hinted by word or sign that there was no such thing on the island, Heyst's life wouldn't be worth half an hour's purchase; but all power of combining words had vanished in the tension of her mind. Words themselves were too difficult to think of – all except the word 'yes'. The saving word! She whispered it with not a feature of her face moving. To Ricardo the faint and concise sound proved a cool, reserved assent, more worth having from that amazing mistress of herself than a thousand words from any other woman. He thought with exultation that he had come upon one in a million – in ten millions! His whisper became frankly entreating.

'That's good! Now all you've got to do is to make sure where he keeps his swag. Only do be quick about it! I can't stand much longer this crawling-on-the-stomach business so as not to scare your gentleman. What do you think a fellow is – a reptile?'

She stared without seeing anyone, as a person in the night sits staring and listening to deadly sounds, to evil incantations. And always in her head there was that tension of the mind trying to get hold of something, of a saving idea which seemed to be so near and could not be captured. Suddenly she seized it. Yes – she had to get that man out of the house. At that very moment, raised outside, not very near, but heard distinctly, Heyst's voice uttered the words:

'Have you been looking out for me, Wang?'

It was for her like a flash of lightning framed in the darkness which had beset her on all sides, showing a deadly precipice right under her feet. With a convulsive movement she sat up straight, but had no power to rise. Ricardo, on the contrary, was on his feet on the instant, as noiseless as a cat. His yellow eyes gleamed, gliding here and there; but he, too, seemed unable to make another movement. Only his moustaches stirred visibly, like the feelers of some animal.

Wang's answer, '*Ya tuan*,' was heard by the two in the room, but more faintly. Then Heyst again:

'All right! You may bring the coffee in. Mem Putih out in the room yet?'

To this question Wang made no answer.

Ricardo's and the girl's eyes met, utterly without expression, all their faculties being absorbed in listening for the first sound of Heyst's footsteps, for any sound outside which would mean that Ricardo's retreat was cut off. Both understood perfectly well that Wang must have gone round the house, and that he was now at the back, making it impossible for Ricardo to slip out unseen that way before Heyst came in at the front.

A darkling shade settled on the face of the devoted secretary. Here was the business utterly spoiled! It was the gloom of anger, and even of apprehension. He would perhaps have made a dash for it through the back door, if Heyst had not been heard ascending the front steps. He climbed them slowly, very slowly, like a man who is discouraged or weary – or simply thoughtful; and Ricardo had a mental vision of his face, with its martial moustaches, the lofty forehead, the impassive features, and the quiet, meditative eyes. Trapped! Confound it! After all, perhaps the governor was right. Women had to be shunned. Fooling with this one had apparently ruined the whole business. For, trapped as he was, he might just as well kill, since, anyhow, to be seen was to be unmasked. But he was too fair-minded to be angry with the girl.

Heyst had paused on the veranda, or in the very doorway.

'I shall be shot down like a dog if I ain't quick,' Ricardo muttered excitedly to the girl.

He stooped to get hold of his knife; and the next moment would have hurled himself out through the curtain, nearly as prompt and fully as deadly to Heyst as an unexpected thunderbolt. The feel more than the strength of the girl's hand, clutching at his shoulder, checked him. He swung round, crouching with a yellow upward glare. Ah! Was she turning against him?

He would have stuck his knife into the hollow of her bare throat if he had not seen her other hand pointing to the window. It was a long opening, high up, close under the ceiling almost, with a single pivoting shutter.

While he was still looking at it, she moved noiselessly away, picking up the overturned chair, and placed it under the wall. Then she looked round; but he didn't need to be beckoned to. In two long, tiptoeing strides he was at her side.

'Be quick!' she gasped.

He seized her hand and wrung it with all the force of his dumb gratitude, as a man does to a chum when there is no time for words. Then he mounted the chair. Ricardo was short – too short to get over without a noisy scramble. He hesitated an instant; she, watchful, bore rigidly on the seat with her beautiful bare arms, while, light and sure, he used the back of the chair as a ladder. The masses of her brown hair fell all about her face.

Footsteps resounded in the next room, and Heyst's voice, not very loud, called her by name.

'Lena!'

'Yes! In a minute,' she answered with a particular intonation which she knew would prevent Heyst from coming in at once.

When she looked up, Ricardo had vanished, letting himself down outside so lightly that she had not heard the slightest noise. She stood up then, bewildered, frightened, as if awakened from a drugged sleep, with heavy, downcast, unseeing eyes, her fortitude tired out, her imagination as if dead within her and unable to keep her fear alive.

Heyst moved about aimlessly in the other room. This sound roused her exhausted wits. At once she began to think, hear, see; and what she saw – or rather recognized, for her eyes had been resting on it all the time – was Ricardo's straw slipper, lost in the scuffle, lying near the bath. She had just time to step forward and plant her foot on it when the curtains shook, and, pushed aside, disclosed Heyst in the doorway.

Out of the appeased enchantment of the senses she had found with him, like a sort of bewitched state, his danger brought a sensation of warmth to her breast. She felt something stir in there, something profound, like a new sort of life.

The room was in partial darkness, Ricardo having accidentally swung the pivoted shutter as he went out of the window. Heyst peered from the doorway.

'Why, you haven't done your hair yet,' he said.

'I won't stop to do it now. I shan't be long,' she replied steadily, and remained still, feeling Ricardo's slipper under the sole of her foot.

Heyst, with a movement of retreat, let the curtain drop slowly. On the instant she stooped for the slipper, and, with it in her hand, spun round wildly, looking for some hiding-place; but there was no such spot in the bare room. The chest, the leather trunk, a dress or two of hers hanging on pegs – there was no place where the merest hazard might not guide Heyst's hand at any moment. Her wildly roaming eyes were caught by the half-closed window. She ran to it, and by raising herself on her toes was able to reach the shutter with her fingertips. She pushed it square, stole back to the middle of the room, and, turning about, swung her arm, regulating the force of the throw so as not to let the slipper fly too far out and hit the edge of the overhanging eaves. It was a task of the nicest judgement for the muscles of those round arms, still quivering from the deadly wrestle with a man, for that brain, tense with the excitement of the situation and for the unstrung nerves flickering darkness before her eyes. At last the slipper left her hand. As soon as it passed the opening, it was out of her sight. She listened. She did not hear it strike anything; it just vanished, as if it had wings to fly on through the air. Not a sound! It had gone clear.

Her valiant arms hanging close against her side, she stood as if turned into stone. A faint whistle reached her ears. The forgetful Ricardo, becoming very much aware of his loss, had been hanging about in great anxiety, which was relieved by the appearance of the slipper flying from under the eaves; and now, thoughtfully, he had ventured a whistle to put her mind at ease.

Suddenly the girl reeled forward. She saved herself from a fall only by embracing with both arms one of the tall, roughly carved posts holding the mosquito net above the bed. For a long time she clung to it, with her forehead leaning against the wood. One side of her loosened sarong had slipped down as low as her hip. The long brown tresses of her hair fell in lank wisps, as if wet, almost black against her white body. Her uncovered flank, damp with the sweat of anguish and fatigue, gleamed coldly with the immobility of polished marble in the hot, diffused light falling through the window above her head – a dim reflection of the consuming, passionate blaze of sunshine outside, all aquiver with the effort to set the earth on fire, to burn it to ashes.

Chapter IV

HEYST, SEATED at the table with his chin on his breast, raised his head at the faint rustle of Lena's dress. He was startled by the dead pallor of her cheeks, by something lifeless in her eyes, which looked at him strangely, without recognition. But to his anxious inquiries she answered reassuringly that there was nothing the matter with her, really. She had felt giddy on rising. She had even had a moment of faintness, after her bath. She had to sit down to wait for it to pass. This had made her late dressing.

'I didn't try to do my hair. I didn't want to keep you waiting any longer,' she said.

He was unwilling to press her with questions about her health, since she seemed to make light of this indisposition. She had not done her hair, but she had brushed it, and had tied it with a ribbon behind. With her forehead uncovered, she looked very young, almost a child, a careworn child; a child with something on its mind.

What surprised Heyst was the non-appearance of Wang. The Chinaman had always materialized at the precise moment of his service, neither too soon nor too late. This time the usual miracle failed. What was the meaning of this?

Heyst raised his voice – a thing he disliked doing. It was promptly answered from the compound:

'*Ada tuan!*'

Lena, leaning on her elbow, with her eyes on her plate, did not seem to hear anything. When Wang entered with a tray, his narrow eyes, tilted inward by the prominence of salient cheekbones, kept her under stealthy observation all the time. Neither the one nor the other of that white couple paid the slightest attention to him and he withdrew without having heard them exchange a single word. He squatted on his heels on the back veranda. His Chinaman's mind, very clear but not far-reaching, was made up according to the plain reason of things, such as it appeared to him in the light of his simple feeling for self-preservation, untrammelled by any notions of romantic honour or tender conscience. His yellow hands, lightly clasped, hung idly between his knees. The graves of Wang's ancestors were far away, his parents were dead, his elder brother was a soldier in the yamen of some Mandarin away in Formosa. No one near by had a claim on his veneration or his obedience. He had been for years a labouring, restless vagabond. His only tie in the world was the Alfuro woman, in exchange for whom he had given away some considerable part of his hard-earned substance; and his duty, in reason, could be to no one but himself.

The scuffle behind the curtain was a thing of bad augury for that Number One for whom the Chinaman had neither love nor dislike. He had been awed enough by that development to hang back with the coffee-pot till at last the white man was induced to call him in. Wang went in with curiosity. Certainly, the white woman looked as if she had been wrestling with a spirit, which had managed to tear half her blood out of her before letting her go. As to the man, Wang had long looked upon him as being in some sort bewitched; and now he was doomed. He heard their voices in the room. Heyst was urging the girl to go and lie down again. He was extremely concerned. She had eaten nothing

'The best thing for you. You really must!'

She sat listless, shaking her head from time to time negatively, as if nothing could be any good. But he insisted; she saw the beginning of wonder in his eyes, and suddenly gave way.

'Perhaps I had better.'

She did not want to arouse his wonder, which would lead him straight to suspicion. He must not suspect!

Already, with the consciousness of her love for this man, of that something rapturous and profound going beyond the mere embrace, there was born in her a woman's innate mistrust of masculinity, of that seductive strength allied to an absurd, delicate shrinking from the recognition of the naked necessity of facts, which never yet frightened a woman worthy of the name. She had no plan; but her mind, quieted down somewhat by the very effort to preserve outward composure for his sake, perceived that her behaviour had secured, at any rate, a short period of safety. Perhaps because of the similarity of their miserable origin in the dregs of mankind, she had understood Ricardo perfectly. He would keep quiet for a time now. In this momentarily soothing certitude her bodily fatigue asserted itself, the more overpoweringly since its cause was not so much the demand on her strength as the awful suddenness of the stress she had had to meet. She would have tried to overcome it from the mere instinct of resistance, if it had not been for Heyst's alternate pleadings and commands. Before this eminently masculine fussing she felt the woman's need to give way, the sweetness of surrender.

'I will do anything you like,' she said.

Getting up, she was surprised by a wave of languid weakness that came over her, embracing and enveloping her like warm water, with a noise in her ears as of a breaking sea.

'You must help me along,' she added quickly.

While he put his arm round her waist – not by any means an uncommon thing for him to do – she found a special satisfaction in the feeling of being thus sustained. She abandoned all her weight to that encircling and protecting pressure, while a thrill went through her at the sudden thought that it was she who would have to protect him, to be the defender of a man who was strong enough to lift her bodily, as he was doing even then in his two arms. For Heyst had done this as soon as they had crept through the doorway of the room. He thought it was quicker and simpler to carry her the last step or two. He had grown really too anxious to be aware of the effort. He lifted her high and deposited her on the bed, as one lays a child on its side in a cot. Then he sat down on the edge, masking his concern with a smile which obtained no response from the dreamy immobility of her eyes. But she sought his hand, seized it eagerly; and while she was pressing it with all the force of which she was capable, the sleep she needed overtook her suddenly, overwhelmingly, as it overtakes a child in a cot, with her lips parted for a safe, endearing word which she had thought of but had no time to utter.

The usual flaming silence brooded over Samburan.

'What in the world is this new mystery?' murmured Heyst to himself, contemplating her deep slumber.

It was so deep, this enchanted sleep, that when some time afterward he gently tried to open her fingers and free his hand, he succeeded without provoking the slightest stir.

'There is some very simple explanation, no doubt,' he thought, as he stole out into the living-room.

Absent-mindedly he pulled a book out of the top shelf, and sat down with it; but even after he had opened it on his knee, and had been staring at the pages for a time, he had not the slightest idea of what it was about. He stared and stared at the crowded, parallel lines. It was only when, raising his eyes for no particular reason, he saw Wang standing motionless on the other side of the table, that he regained complete control of his faculties.

'Oh, yes,' he said, as if suddenly reminded of a forgotten appointment of a not particularly welcome sort.

He waited a little, and then, with reluctant curiosity, forced himself to ask the silent Wang what he had to say. He had some idea that the matter of the vanished revolver would come up at last; but the guttural sounds which proceeded from the Chinaman did not refer to that delicate subject. His speech was concerned with cups, saucers, plates, forks, and knives. All these things had been put away in the cupboards on the back veranda, where they belonged, perfectly clean, 'all plopel'. Heyst wondered at the scrupulosity of a man who was about to abandon him; for he was not surprised to hear Wang conclude the account of his stewardship with the words:

'Me go now.'

'Oh! You go now?' said Heyst, leaning back, his book on his knees.

'Yes. Me no likee. One man, two man, thlee man – no can do! Me go now.'

'What's frightening you away like this?' asked Heyst, while through his mind flashed the hope that something enlightening might come from that being so unlike himself, taking contact with the world with a simplicity and directness of which his own mind was not capable. 'Why?' he went on. 'You are used to white men. You know them well.'

'Yes. Me savee them,' assented Wang inscrutably. 'Me savee plenty.'

All that he really knew was his own mind. He had made it up to withdraw himself and the Alfuro woman from the uncertainties of the relations which were going to establish themselves between those white men. It was Pedro who had been the first cause of Wang's suspicion and fear. The Chinaman had seen wild men. He had penetrated, in the train of a Chinese pedlar, up one or two of the Bornean rivers into the country of the Dyaks. He had also been in the interior of Mindanao, where there are people who live in trees – savages, no better than animals; but a hairy brute like Pedro, with his great fangs and ferocious growls, was altogether beyond his conception of anything that could be looked upon as human. The strong impression made on him by Pedro was the prime inducement which had led Wang to purloin the revolver. Reflection on the general situation, and on the insecurity of Number One, came later, after he had obtained possession of the revolver and of the box of cartridges out of the table drawer in the living-room.

'Oh, you savee plenty about white men,' Heyst went on in a slightly bantering tone, after a moment of silent reflection in which he had confessed to himself that the recovery of the revolver was not to be thought of, either by persuasion or by some more forcible means. 'You speak in that fashion, but you are frightened of those white men over there.'

'Me no flightened,' protested Wang raucously, throwing up his head – which gave to his throat a more strained, anxious appearance than ever. 'Me no likee,' he added in a quieter tone. 'Me velly sick.'

He put his hand over the region under the breast-bone.

'That,' said Heyst, serenely positive, 'belong one piecee lie. That isn't proper man-talk at all. And after stealing my revolver, too!'

He had suddenly decided to speak about it, because this frankness could not make the situation much worse than it was. He did not suppose for a moment that Wang had the revolver anywhere about his person; and after having thought the matter over, he had arrived at the conclusion that the Chinaman never meant to use the weapon against him. After a slight start, because the direct charge had taken him unawares, Wang tore open the front of his jacket with a convulsive show of indignation.

'No hab got. Look see!' he mouthed in pretended anger.

He slapped his bare chest violently; he uncovered his very ribs, all astir with the panting of outraged virtue; his smooth stomach heaved with indignation. He started his wide blue breeches flapping about his yellow calves. Heyst watched him quietly.

'I never said you had it on you,' he observed, without raising his voice; 'but the revolver is gone from where I kept it.'

'Me no savee levolvel,' Wang said obstinately.

The book lying open on Heyst's knee slipped suddenly and he made a sharp movement to catch it up. Wang was unable to see the reason of this because of the table, and leaped away from what seemed to him a threatening symptom. When Heyst looked up, the Chinaman was already at the door facing the room, not frightened, but alert.

'What's the matter?' asked Heyst.

Wang nodded his shaven head significantly at the curtain closing the doorway of the bedroom.

'Me no likee,' he repeated.

'What the devil do you mean?' Heyst was genuinely amazed. 'Don't like what?'

Wang pointed a long, lemon-coloured finger at the motionless folds.

'Two,' he said.

'Two what? I don't understand.'

'Suppose you savee, you no like that fashion. Me savee plenty. Me go now.'

Heyst had risen from his chair, but Wang kept his ground in the doorway for a little longer. His almond-shaped eyes imparted to his face an expression of soft and sentimental melancholy. The muscles of his throat moved visibly while he uttered a distinct and guttural 'Good-bye', and vanished from Number One's sight.

The Chinaman's departure altered the situation. Heyst reflected on what would be best to do in view of that fact. For a long time he hesitated; then, shrugging his shoulders wearily, he walked out on the veranda, down the steps, and continued at a steady gait, with a thoughtful mien, in the direction of his guests' bungalow. He wanted to make an important communication to them, and he had no other object – least of all to give them the shock of a surprise call. Nevertheless, their brutish henchman not being on watch, it was Heyst's fate to startle Mr Jones and his secretary by his sudden appearance in the doorway. Their conversation must have been very interesting to prevent them from hearing the visitor's approach. In the dim room – the shutters were kept constantly closed against the heat – Heyst saw them start apart. It was Mr Jones who spoke:

'Ah, here you are again! Come in, come in!'

Heyst, taking his hat off in the doorway, entered the room.

Chapter V

Waking up suddenly, Lena looked, without raising her head from the pillow, at the room in which she was alone. She got up quickly, as if to counteract the awful sinking of her heart by the vigorous use of her limbs. But this sinking was only momentary. Mistress of herself from pride, from love, from necessity, and also because of a woman's vanity in self-sacrifice, she met Heyst, returning from the strangers' bungalow, with a clear glance and a smile.

The smile he managed to answer; but, noticing that he avoided her eyes, she composed her lips and lowered her gaze. For the same reason she hastened to speak to him in a tone of indifference, which she put on without effort, as if she had grown adept in duplicity since sunrise.

'You have been over there again?'

'I have. I thought – but you had better know first that we have lost Wang for good.'

She repeated 'For good?' as if she had not understood.

'For good or evil – I shouldn't know which if you were to ask me. He has dismissed himself. He's gone.'

'You expected him to go, though, didn't you?'

Heyst sat down on the other side of the table.

'Yes. I expected it as soon as I discovered that he had annexed my revolver. He says he hasn't taken it. That's untrue of course. A Chinaman would not see the sense of confessing under any circumstances. To deny any charge is a principle of right conduct; but he hardly expected to be believed. He was a little enigmatic at the last, Lena. He startled me.'

Heyst paused. The girl seemed absorbed in her own thoughts.

'He startled me,' repeated Heyst. She noted the anxiety in his tone, and turned her head slightly to look at him across the table.

'It must have been something – to startle *you*,' she said. In the depth of her parted lips, like a ripe pomegranate, there was a gleam of white teeth.

'It was only a single word – and some of his gestures. He had been making a good deal of noise. I wonder we didn't wake you up. How soundly you can sleep! I say, do you feel all right now?'

'As fresh as can be,' she said, treating him to another deep gleam of a smile. 'I heard no noise, and I'm glad of it. The way he talks in his harsh voice frightens me. I don't like all these foreign people.'

'It was just before he went away – bolted out, I should say. He nodded and pointed at the curtain to our room. He knew you were there, of course. He seemed to think – he seemed to try to give me to understand that you were in special – well, danger. You know how he talks.'

She said nothing; she made no sound, only a faint tinge of colour ebbed out of her cheek.

'Yes,' Heyst went on. 'He seemed to try to warn me. That must have been it. Did he imagine I had forgotten your existence? The only word he said was "two". It sounded so, at least. Yes, "two" – and that he didn't like it.'

'What does that mean?' she whispered.

'We know what the word two means, don't we, Lena? We are two. Never were such a lonely two out of the world, my dear! He might have tried to remind me that he himself has a woman to look after. Why are you so pale, Lena?'

'Am I pale?' she asked negligently.

'You are.' Heyst was really anxious.

'Well, it isn't from fright,' she protested truthfully.

Indeed, what she felt was a sort of horror which left her absolutely in the full possession of all her faculties; more difficult to bear, perhaps, for that reason, but not paralysing to her fortitude.

Heyst in his turn smiled at her.

'I really don't know that there is any reason to be frightened.'

'I mean I am not frightened for myself.'

'I believe you are very plucky,' he said. The colour had returned to her face. 'I,' continued Heyst, 'am so rebellious to outward impressions that I can't say that much about myself. I don't react with sufficient distinctness.' He changed his tone. 'You know I went to see those men first thing this morning.'

'I know. Be careful!' she murmured.

'I wonder how one can be careful! I had a long talk with – but I don't believe you have seen them. One of them is a fantastically thin, long person, apparently ailing; I shouldn't wonder if he were really so. He makes rather a point of it in a mysterious manner. I imagine he must have suffered from tropical fevers, but not so much as he tries to make out. He's what people would call a gentleman. He seemed on the point of volunteering a tale of his adventures – for which I didn't ask him – but remarked that it was a long story; some other time, perhaps.

' "I suppose you would like to know who I am?" he asked me. 'I told him I would leave it to him, in a tone which, between gentlemen, could have left no doubt in his mind. He raised himself on his elbow – he was lying down on the camp-bed – and said:

' "I am he who is –" '

Lena seemed not to be listening; but when Heyst paused, she turned her head quickly to him. He took it for a movement of inquiry, but in this he was wrong. A great vagueness enveloped her impressions, but all her energy was concentrated on the struggle that she wanted to take upon herself, in a great exaltation of love and self-sacrifice, which is woman's sublime faculty; altogether on herself, every bit of it, leaving him nothing, not even the knowledge of what she did, if that were possible. She would have liked to lock him up by some stratagem. Had she known of some means to put him to sleep for days she would have used incantations or philtres without misgivings. He seemed to her too good for such contacts, and not sufficiently equipped. This last feeling had nothing to do with the material fact of the revolver being stolen. She could hardly appreciate that fact at its full value.

Observing her eyes fixed and as if sightless – for the concentration on her purpose took all expression out of them – Heyst imagined it to be the effect of a great mental effort.

'No use asking me what he meant, Lena; I don't know, and I did not ask him. The gentleman, as I have told you before, seems devoted to mystification. I said nothing, and he laid down his head again on the bundle of rugs he uses for a pillow. He affects a state of great weakness, but I suspect that he's perfectly capable of leaping to his feet if he likes. Having been ejected, he said, from his proper social sphere because he had refused to conform to certain usual conventions, he was a rebel now, and was coming and going up and down the earth. As I really did not want to listen to all this nonsense, I told him that I had heard that sort of story about somebody else before. His grin is really ghastly. He confessed that I was very far from the sort of man he expected to meet. Then he said:

' "As to me, I am no blacker than the gentleman you are thinking of, and I have neither more nor less determination." '

Heyst looked across the table at Lena. Propped on her elbows, and holding her head in both hands, she moved it a little with an air of understanding.

'Nothing could be plainer, eh?' said Heyst grimly. 'Unless, indeed, this is his idea of a pleasant joke; for, when he finished speaking, he burst into a loud, long laugh. I didn't join him!'

'I wish you had,' she breathed out.

'I didn't join him. It did not occur to me. I am not much of a diplomatist. It would probably have been wise; for, indeed, I believe he had said more than he meant to say, and was trying to take it back by this affected jocularity. Yet, when one thinks of it, diplomacy without force in the background is but a rotten reed to lean upon. And I don't know whether I could have done it if I had thought of it. I don't know. It would have been against the grain. Could I have done it? I have lived too long within myself, watching the mere shadows and shades of life. To deceive a man on some issue which could be decided quicker by his destruction while one is disarmed, helpless, without even the power to run away – no! *That* seems to me too degrading. And yet I have you here. I have your very existence in my keeping. What do you say, Lena? Would I be capable of throwing you to the lions to save my dignity?'

She got up, walked quickly round the table, posed herself on his knees lightly, throwing one arm round his neck, and whispered in his ear:

'You may if you like. And may be that's the only way I would consent to leave you. For something like that. If it were something no bigger than your little finger.'

She gave him a light kiss on the lips and was gone before he could detain her. She regained her seat and propped her elbows again on the table. It was hard to believe that she had moved from the spot at all. The fleeting weight of her body on his knees, the hug round his neck, the whisper in his ear, the kiss on his lips, might have been the unsubstantial sensations of a dream invading the reality of waking life; a sort of charming mirage in the barren aridity of his thoughts. He hesitated to speak till she said, businesslike:

'Well. And what then?'

Heyst gave a start.

'Oh, yes. I didn't join him. I let him have his laugh out by himself. He was shaking all over, like a merry skeleton, under a cotton sheet he was covered with – I believe in order to conceal the revolver that he had in his right hand. I didn't see it, but I have a distinct impression it was there in his fist. As he had not been looking at me for some time, but staring into a certain part of the room, I turned my head and saw a hairy, wild sort of creature which they take about with them, squatting on its heels in the angle of the walls behind me. He wasn't there when I came in. I didn't like the notion of that watchful monster behind my back. If I had been less at their mercy, I should certainly have changed my position. As things are now, to move would have been a mere weakness. So I remained where I was. The gentleman on the bed said he could assure me of one thing; and that was that his presence here was no more morally reprehensible than mine.

' "We pursue the same ends," he said, "only perhaps I pursue them with more openness than you – with more simplicity."

'That's what he said,' Heyst went on, after looking at Lena in a sort of inquiring silence. 'I asked him if he knew beforehand that I was living here; but he only gave me a ghastly grin. I didn't press him for an answer, Lena. I thought I had better not.'

On her smooth forehead a ray of light always seemed to rest. Her loose hair, parted in the middle, covered the hands sustaining her head. She seemed spellbound by the interest of the narrative. Heyst did not pause long. He managed to continue his relation smoothly enough, beginning afresh with a piece of comment.

'He would have lied impudently – and I detest being told a lie. It makes me uncomfortable. It's pretty clear that I am not fitted for the affairs of the wide world. But I did not want him to think that I accepted his presence too meekly; so I said that his comings or goings on the earth were none of my business, of course, except that I had a natural curiosity to know when he would find it convenient to resume them.

'He asked me to look at the state he was in. Had I been all alone here, as they think I am, I should have laughed at him. But not being alone– I say, Lena, you are sure you haven't shown yourself where you could be seen?'

'Certain,' she said promptly.

He looked relieved.

'You understand, Lena, that when I ask you to keep so strictly out of sight, it is because you are not for them to look at – to talk about. My poor Lena! I can't help that feeling. Do you understand it?'

She moved her head slightly in a manner that was neither affirmative nor negative.

'People will have to see me some day,' she said.

'I wonder how long it will be possible for you to keep out of sight!' murmured Heyst thoughtfully. He bent over the table. 'Let me finish telling you. I asked him pointblank what it was he wanted with me; he appeared extremely unwilling to come to the point. It was not really so pressing as all that, he said. His secretary, who was in fact his partner, was not present, having gone down to the wharf to look at their boat. Finally the fellow proposed that he should put off a certain communication he had to make till the day after tomorrow. I agreed; but I also told him that I was not at all anxious to hear it. I had no conception in what way his affairs could concern me.

' "Ah, Mr Heyst," he said, "you and I have much more in common than you think." '

Heyst struck the table with his fist unexpectedly.

'It was a jeer; I am sure it was!'

He seemed ashamed of this outburst and smiled faintly into the motionless eyes of the girl.

'What could I have done – even if I had had my pockets full of revolvers?'

She made an appreciative sign.

'Killing's a sin, sure enough,' she murmured.

'I went away,' Heyst continued. 'I left him there, lying on his side with his eyes shut. When I got back here, I found you looking ill. What was it, Lena? You did give me a scare! Then I had the interview with Wang while you rested. You were sleeping quietly. I sat here to consider all these things calmly, to try to penetrate their inner meaning and their outward bearing. It struck me that the two days we have before us have the character of a sort of truce. The more I thought of it, the more I felt that this was tacitly understood between Jones and myself. It was to our advantage, if anything can be of advantage to people caught so completely unawares as we are. Wang was gone. He, at any rate, had declared himself, but as I did not know what he might take it into his head to do,

I thought I had better warn these people that I was no longer responsible for the Chinaman. I did not want Mr Wang making some move which would precipitate the action against us. Do you see my point of view?'

She made a sign that she did. All her soul was wrapped in her passionate determination, in an exalted belief in herself – in the contemplation of her amazing opportunity to win the certitude, the eternity, of that man's love.

'I never saw two men,' Heyst was saying, 'more affected by a piece of information than Jones and his secretary, who was back in the bungalow by then. They had not heard me come up. I told them I was sorry to intrude.

' "Not at all! Not at all," said Jones.

'The secretary backed away into a corner and watched me like a wary cat. In fact, they both were visibly on their guard.

' "I am come," I told them, "to let you know that my servant has deserted – gone off.'

'At first they looked at each other as if they had not understood what I was saying; but very soon they seemed quite concerned.

' "You mean to say your Chink's cleared out?" said Ricardo, coming forward from his corner. "Like this – all at once? What did he do it for?"

'I said that a Chinaman had always a simple and precise reason for what he did, but that to get such a reason out of him was not so easy. All he told me, I said, was that he "didn't like".

'They were extremely disturbed at this. Didn't like what, they wanted to know.

' "The looks of you and your party,' I told Jones.

' "Nonsense!' he cried out; and immediately Ricardo, the short man, struck in.

' "Told you *that*? What did he take you for, sir – an infant? Or do you take us for kids? – meaning no offence. Come, I bet you will tell us next that you've missed something.'

' "I didn't mean to tell you anything of the sort," I said, "but as a matter of fact it is so."

'He slapped his thigh.

' "Thought so. What do you think of this trick, governor?"

'Jones made some sort of sign to him, and then that extraordinary cat-faced associate proposed that he and their servant should come out and help me catch or kill the Chink.

'My object, I said, was not to get assistance. I did not intend to chase the Chinaman. I had come only to warn them that he was armed, and that he really objected to their presence on the island. I wanted them to understand that I was not responsible for anything that might happen.

' "Do you mean to tell us," asked Ricardo, 'that there is a crazy Chink with a six-shooter broke loose on this island, and that you don't care?"

'Strangely enough, they did not seem to believe my story. They were exchanging significant looks all the time. Ricardo stole up close to his principal; they had a confabulation together, and then something happened which I did not expect. It's rather awkward, too.

'Since I would not have their assistance to get hold of the Chink and recover my property, the least they could do was to send me their servant. It was Jones who said that, and Ricardo backed up the idea.

' "Yes, yes – let our Pedro cook for all hands in your compound! He isn't so bad as he looks. That's what we will do!"

'He bustled out of the room to the veranda, and let out an ear-splitting whistle for their Pedro. Having heard the brute's answering howl, Ricardo ran back into the room.

' "Yes, Mr Heyst. This will do capitally, Mr Heyst. You just direct him to do whatever you are accustomed to have done for you in the way of attendance. See?'

'Lena, I confess to you that I was taken completely by surprise. I had not expected anything of the sort. I don't know what I expected. I am so anxious about you that I can't keep away from these infernal scoundrels. And only two months ago I would not have cared. I would have defied their scoundrelism as much as I have scorned all the other intrusions of life. But now I have you! You stole into my life, and –'

Heyst drew a deep breath. The girl gave him a quick, wide-eyed glance.

'Ah! That's what you are thinking of – that you have me!'

It was impossible to read the thoughts veiled by her steady grey eyes, to penetrate the meaning of her silences, her words, and even her embraces. He used to come out of her very arms with the feeling of a baffled man.

'If I haven't you, if you are not here, then where are you?' cried Heyst. 'You understand me very well.'

She shook her head a little. Her red lips, at which he looked now, her lips as fascinating as the voice that came out of them, uttered the words:

'I hear what you say; but what does it mean?'

'It means that I could lie and perhaps cringe for your sake.'

'No! No! Don't you ever do that,' she said in haste, while her eyes glistened suddenly. 'You would hate me for it afterwards!'

'Hate you?' repeated Heyst, who had recalled his polite manner. 'No! You needn't consider the extremity of the improbable – as yet. But I will confess to you that I – how shall I call it? – that I dissembled. First I dissembled my dismay at the unforeseen result of my idiotic diplomacy. Do you understand, my dear girl?'

It was evident that she did not understand the word. Heyst produced his playful smile, which contrasted oddly with the worried character of his whole expression. His temples seemed to have sunk in, his face looked a little leaner.

'A diplomatic statement, Lena, is a statement of which everything is true but the sentiment which seems to prompt it. I have never been diplomatic in my relation with mankind – not from regard for its feelings, but from a certain regard for my own. Diplomacy doesn't go well with consistent contempt. I cared little for life and still less for death.'

'Don't talk like that!'

'I dissembled my extreme longing to take these wandering scoundrels by their throats,' he went on. 'I have only two hands – I wish I had a hundred to defend you – and there were three throats. By that time their Pedro was in the room too. Had he seen me engaged with their two throats, he would have been at mine like a fierce dog, or any other savage and faithful brute. I had no difficulty in dissembling my longing for the vulgar, stupid, and hopeless argument of fight. I remarked that I really did not want a servant. I couldn't think of depriving them of their man's services; but they would not hear me. They had made up their minds.

' "We shall send him over at once," Ricardo said, "to start cooking dinner for everybody. I hope you won't mind me coming to eat it with you in your bungalow; and we will send the governor's dinner over to him here."

'I could do nothing but hold my tongue or bring on a quarrel – some manifestation of their dark purpose, which we have no means to resist. Of course, you may remain invisible this evening; but with that atrocious brute prowling all the time at the back of the house, how long can your presence be concealed from these men?'

Heyst's distress could be felt in his silence. The girl's head, sustained by her hands buried in the thick masses of her hair, had a perfect immobility.

'You are certain you have not been seen so far?' he asked suddenly.

The motionless head spoke.

'How can I be certain? You told me you wanted me to keep out of the way. I kept out of the way. I didn't ask your reason. I thought you didn't want people to know that you had a girl like me about you.'

'What? Ashamed?' cried Heyst.

'It isn't what's right, perhaps – I mean for you – is it?'

Heyst lifted his hands, reproachfully courteous.

'I look upon it as so very much right that I couldn't bear the idea of any other than sympathetic, respectful eyes resting on you. I disliked and mistrusted these fellows from the first. Didn't you understand?'

'Yes; I did keep out of sight,' she said.

A silence fell. At last Heyst stirred slightly.

'All this is of very little importance now,' he said with a sigh. 'This is a question of something infinitely worse than mere looks and thoughts, however base and contemptible. As I have told you, I met Ricardo's suggestions by silence. As I was turning away he said:

' "If you happen to have the key of that store-room of yours on you, Mr Heyst, you may just as well let me have it; I will give it to our Pedro."

'I had it on me, and I tendered it to him without speaking. The hairy creature was at the door by then, and caught the key, which Ricardo threw to him, better than any trained ape could have done. I came away. All the time I had been thinking anxiously of you, whom I had left asleep, alone here, and apparently ill.'

Heyst interrupted himself, with a listening turn of his head. He had heard the faint sound of sticks being snapped in the compound. He rose and crossed the room to look out of the back door.

'And here the creature is,' he said, returning to the table. 'Here he is, already attending to the fire. Oh, my dear Lena!'

She had followed him with her eyes. She watched him go out on the front veranda cautiously. He lowered stealthily a couple of screens that hung between the columns, and remained outside very still, as if interested by something on the open ground. Meantime she had risen in her turn, to take a peep into the compound. Heyst, glancing over his shoulder, saw her returning to her seat. He beckoned to her, and she continued to move, crossing the shady room, pure and bright in her white dress, her hair loose, with something of a sleep-walker in her unhurried motion, in her extended hand, in the sightless effect of her grey eyes luminous in the half-light. He had never seen such an expression in her face before. It had dreaminess in it, intense attention, and something like sternness. Arrested in the doorway by Heyst's extended arm, she seemed to wake up, flushed faintly – and this flush, passing off, carried away with it the strange transfiguring mood. With a courageous gesture she pushed back the heavy masses of her hair. The light clung to her forehead. Her delicate nostrils quivered. Heyst seized her arm and whispered excitedly:

'Slip out here, quickly! The screens will conceal you. Only you must mind the stair-space. They are actually out – I mean the other two. You had better see them before you –'

She made a barely perceptible movement of recoil, checked at once, and stood still. Heyst released her arm.

'Yes, perhaps I had better,' she said with unnatural deliberation, and stepped out on the veranda to stand close by his side.

Together, one on each side of the screen, they peeped between the edge of the canvas and the veranda-post entwined with creepers. A great heat ascended from the sun-smitten ground, in an ever-rising wave, as if from some secret store of earth's fiery heart; for the sky was growing cooler already, and the sun had declined sufficiently for the shadows of Mr Jones and his henchman to be projected towards the bungalow side by side – one infinitely slender, the other short and broad.

The two visitors stood still and gazed. To keep up the fiction of his invalidism, Mr Jones, the gentleman, leaned on the arm of Ricardo, the secretary, the top of whose hat just came up to his governor's shoulder.

'Do you see them?' Heyst whispered into the girl's ear. 'Here they are, the envoys of the outer world. Here they are before you – evil intelligence, instinctive savagery, arm in arm. The brute force is at the back. A trio of fitting envoys perhaps – but what about the welcome? Suppose I were armed, could I shoot these two down where they stand? Could I?'

Without moving her head, the girl felt for Heyst's hand, pressed it, and thereafter did not let it go. He continued, bitterly playful:

'I don't know. I don't think so. There is a strain in me which lays me under an insensate obligation to avoid even the appearance of murder. I have never pulled a trigger or lifted my hand on a man, even in self-defence.'

The suddenly tightened grip of her hand checked him.

'They are making a move,' she murmured.

'Can they be thinking of coming here?' Heyst wondered anxiously.

'No, they aren't coming this way,' she said; and there was another pause. 'They are going back to their house,' she reported finally.

After watching them a little longer, she let go Heyst's hand and moved away from the screen. He followed her into the room.

'You have seen them now,' he began. 'Think what it was to me to see them land in the dusk, fantasms from the sea – apparitions, chimeras! And they persist. That's the worst of it – they persist. They have no right to be – but they are. They ought to have aroused my fury. But I have refined everything away by this time – anger, indignation, scorn itself. Nothing's left but disgust. Since you have told me of that abominable calumny, it has become immense – it extends even to myself.' He looked up at her.

'But luckily I have you. And if only Wang had not carried off that miserable revolver – yes, Lena, here we are, we two!'

She put both her hands on his shoulders and looked straight into his eyes. He returned her penetrating gaze. It baffled him. He could not pierce the grey veil of her eyes; but the sadness of her voice thrilled him profoundly.

'You are not reproaching me?' she asked slowly.

'Reproach? What a word between us! It could only be myself – but the mention of Wang has given me an idea. I have been, not exactly cringing, not exactly lying, but still dissembling. You have been hiding yourself, to please me, but still you have been hiding. All this is very dignified. Why shouldn't we try begging now? A noble art? Yes, Lena, we must go out together. I couldn't think of leaving you alone, and I must – yes, I must speak to Wang. We shall go and seek that man, who knows what he wants and how to secure what he wants. We will go at once!'

'Wait till I put my hair up,' she agreed instantly, and vanished behind the curtain.

When the curtain had fallen behind her, she turned her head back with an expression of infinite and tender concern for him – for him whom she could never hope to understand, and whom she was afraid she could never satisfy; as if her passion were of a hopelessly lower quality, unable to appease some exalted and delicate desire of his superior soul. In a couple of minutes she reappeared. They left the house by the door of the compound, and passed within three feet of the thunderstruck Pedro, without even looking in his direction. He rose from stooping over a fire of sticks, and, balancing himself clumsily, uncovered his enormous fangs in gaping astonishment. Then suddenly he set off rolling on his bandy legs to impart to his masters the astonishing discovery of a woman.

Chapter VI

As luck would have it, Ricardo was lounging alone on the veranda of the former counting-house. He scented some new development at once, and ran down to meet the trotting, bear-like figure. The deep, growling noises it made, though they had only a very remote resemblance to the Spanish language, or indeed to any sort of human speech, were from long practice quite intelligible to Mr Jones's secretary. Ricardo was rather surprised! He had imagined that the girl would continue to keep out of sight. That line apparently was given up. He did not mistrust her. How could he? Indeed, he could not think of her existence calmly.

He tried to keep her image out of his mind so that he should be able to use its powers with some approach to that coolness which the complex nature of the situation demanded from him, both for his own sake and as the faithful follower of plain Mr Jones, gentleman.

He collected his wits and thought. This was a change of policy, probably on the part of Heyst. If so, what could it mean? A deep fellow! Unless it was her doing; in which case – h'm – all right. Must be. She would know what she was doing. Before him Pedro, lifting his feet alternately, swayed to and fro sideways – his usual attitude of expectation. His little red eyes, lost in the mass of hair, were motionless. Ricardo stared into them with calculated contempt and said in a rough, angry voice:

'Woman! Of course there is. We know that without you!' He gave the tame monster a push. 'Git! *Vamos!* Waddle! Get back and cook the dinner. Which way did they go, then?'

Pedro extended a huge, hairy forearm to show the direction, and went off on his bandy legs. Advancing a few steps, Ricardo was just in time to see, above some bushes, two white helmets moving side by side in the clearing. They disappeared. Now that he had managed to keep Pedro from informing the governor that there was a woman on the island, he could indulge in speculation as to the movements of these people. His attitude towards Mr Jones had undergone a spiritual change, of which he himself was not yet fully aware.

That morning, before tiffin, after his escape from the Heyst bungalow, completed in such an inspiring way by the recovery of the slipper, Ricardo had made his way to their allotted house, reeling as he ran, his head in a whirl. He was wildly excited by visions of inconceivable promise. He waited to compose himself before he dared to meet the governor. On entering the room, he found Mr Jones sitting on the camp bedstead like a tailor on his board, cross-legged, his long back against the wall.

'I say, sir! You aren't going to tell me you are bored?'

'Bored? No! Where the devil have you been all this time?'

'Observing – watching – nosing around. What else? I knew you had company. Have you talked freely, sir?'

'Yes, I have,' muttered Mr Jones.

'Not downright plain, sir?'

'No. I wished you had been here. You loaf all the morning, and now you come in out of breath. What's the matter?'

'I haven't been wasting my time out there,' said Ricardo. 'Nothing's the matter. I – I – might have hurried a bit.' He was in truth still panting; only it was not with running, but with the tumult of thoughts and sensations long repressed, which had been set free by the adventure of the morning. He was almost distracted by them now. He forgot himself in the maze of possibilities threatening and inspiring. 'And so you had a long talk?' he said, to gain time.

'Confound you! The sun hasn't affected your head, has it? Why are you staring at me like a basilisk?'

'Beg pardon, sir. Wasn't aware I stared,' Ricardo apologized good-humouredly. 'The sun might well affect a thicker skull than mine. It blazes. Phew! What do you think a fellow is, sir – a salamander?'

'You ought to have been here,' observed Mr Jones.

'Did the beast give any signs of wanting to prance?' asked Ricardo quickly, with absolutely genuine anxiety. 'It wouldn't do, sir. You must play him easy for at least a couple of days, sir. I have a plan. I have a notion that I can find out a lot in a couple of days.'

'You have? In what way?'

'Why, by watching,' Ricardo answered slowly.

Mr Jones grunted.

'Nothing new, that. Watch, eh? Why not pray a little, too?'

'Ha, ha, ha! That's a good one,' burst out the secretary, fixing Mr Jones with mirthless eyes.

The latter dropped the subject indolently.

'Oh, you may be certain of at least two days,' he said.

Ricardo recovered himself. His eyes gleamed voluptuously.

'We'll pull this off yet – clean – whole – right through, if you will only trust me, sir.'

'I am trusting you right enough,' said Mr Jones. 'It's your interest, too.'

And, indeed, Ricardo was truthful enough in his statement. He did absolutely believe in success now. But he couldn't tell his governor that he had intelligences in the enemy's camp. It wouldn't do to tell him of the girl. Devil only knew what he would do if he learned there was a woman about. And how could he begin to tell of it? He couldn't confess his sudden escapade.

'We'll pull it off, sir,' he said, with perfectly acted cheerfulness. He experienced gusts of awful joy expanding in his heart and hot like a fanned flame.

'We must,' pronounced Mr Jones. 'This thing, Martin, is not like our other tries. I have a peculiar feeling about this. It's a different thing. It's a sort of test.'

Ricardo was impressed by the governor's manner; for the first time a hint of passion could be detected in him. But also a word he used, the word 'test', had struck him as particularly significant somehow. It was the last word uttered during that morning's conversation. Immediately afterwards Ricardo went out of the room. It was impossible for him to keep still. An elation in which an extraordinary softness mingled with savage triumph would not allow it. It prevented his thinking, also. He walked up and down the veranda far into the afternoon, eyeing the bungalow at every turn. It gave no sign of being inhabited. Once or twice he stopped dead short and looked down at his left slipper. Each time he chuckled audibly. His restlessness kept on increasing till at last it frightened him. He caught hold of the balustrade of the veranda and stood still, smiling not at his thought but at the strong sense of life within him. He abandoned himself to it carelessly, even recklessly. He cared for no one, friend or enemy. At that moment Mr Jones called him by name from within. A shadow fell on the secretary's face.

'Here, sir,' he answered; but it was a moment before he could make up his mind to go in.

He found the governor on his feet. Mr Jones was tired of lying down when there was no necessity for it. His slender form, gliding about the room, came to a standstill.

'I've been thinking, Martin, of something you suggested. At the time it did not strike me as practical; but on reflection it seems to me that to propose a game is as good a way as any to let him understand that the time has come to disgorge. It's less – how should I say? – vulgar. He will know what it means. It's not a bad form to give to the business – which in itself is crude, Martin, crude.'

'Want to spare his feelings?' jeered the secretary in such a bitter tone that Mr Jones was really surprised.

'Why, it was your own notion, confound you!!'

'Who says it wasn't?' retorted Ricardo sulkily. 'But I am fairly sick of this crawling. No! No! Get the exact bearings of his swag and then a rip up. That's plenty good enough for him.'

His passions being thoroughly aroused, a thirst for blood was allied in him with a thirst for tenderness – yes, tenderness. A sort of anxious, melting sensation pervaded and softened his heart when he thought of that girl – one of his own sort. And at the same time jealousy started gnawing at his breast as the image of Heyst intruded itself on his fierce anticipation of bliss.

'The crudeness of your ferocity is positively gross, Martin,' Mr Jones said disdainfully. 'You don't even understand my purpose. I mean to have some sport out of him. Just try to imagine the atmosphere of the game – the fellow handling the cards – the agonizing mockery of it! Oh, I shall appreciate this greatly. Yes, let him lose his money instead of being forced to hand it over. You, of course, would shoot him at once, but I shall enjoy the refinement and the jest of it. He's a man of the best society. I've been hounded out of my sphere by people very much like that fellow. How enraged and humiliated he will be! I promise myself some exquisite moments while watching his play.'

'Ay, and suppose he suddenly starts prancing. He may not appreciate the fun.'

'I mean you to be present,' Mr Jones remarked calmly.

'Well, as long as I am free to plug him or rip him up whenever I think the time has come, you are welcome to your bit of sport, sir. I shan't spoil it.'

Chapter VII

It was at this precise moment of their conversation that Heyst had intruded on Mr Jones and his secretary with his warning about Wang, as he had related to Lena. When he left them, the two looked at each other in wondering silence. Mr Jones was the first to break it.

'I say, Martin!'

'Yes, sir.'

'What does this mean?'

'It's some move. Blame me if I can understand.'

'Too deep for you?' Mr Jones inquired drily.

'It's nothing but some of his infernal impudence,' growled the secretary. 'You don't believe all that about the Chink, do you, sir? 'Taint true.'

'It isn't necessary for it to be true to have meaning for us. It's the why of his coming to tell us this tale that's important.'

'Do you think he made it up to frighten us?' asked Ricardo.

Mr Jones scowled at him thoughtfully.

'The man looked worried,' he muttered, as if to himself. 'Suppose that Chinaman has really stolen his money! The man looked very worried.'

'Nothing but his artfulness, sir,' protested Ricardo earnestly, for the idea was too disconcerting to entertain. 'Is it likely that he would have trusted a Chink with enough knowledge to make it possible?' he argued warmly. 'Why, it's the very thing that he would keep close about. There's something else there. Ay, but what?'

'Ho, ha, ha!' Mr Jones let out a ghostly, squeaky laugh. 'I've never been placed in such a ridiculous position before,' he went on, with a sepulchral equanimity of tone. 'It's you, Martin, who dragged me into it. However, it's my own fault too. I ought to – but I was really too bored to use my brain, and yours is not to be trusted. You are a hothead!'

A blasphemous exclamation of grief escaped from Ricardo. Not to be trusted! Hothead! He was almost tearful.

'Haven't I heard you, sir, saying more than twenty times since we got fired out from Manila that we should want a lot of capital to work the East Coast with? You were always telling me that to prime properly all them officials and Portuguese scallywags we should have to lose heavily at first. Weren't you always worrying about some means of getting hold of a good lot of cash? It wasn't to be got hold of by allowing yourself to become bored in that rotten Dutch town and playing a two-penny game with confounded beggarly bank clerks and such like. Well, I've brought you here, where there is cash to be got – and a big lot, to a moral,' he added through his set teeth.

Silence fell. Each of them was staring into a different corner of the room. Suddenly, with a slight stamp of his foot, Mr Jones made for the door. Ricardo caught him up outside.

'Put an arm through mine, sir,' he begged him gently but firmly. 'No use giving the game away. An invalid may well come out for a breath of fresh air after the sun's gone down a bit. That's it, sir. But where do you want to go? Why did you come out, sir?'

Mr Jones stopped short.

'I hardly know myself,' he confessed in a hollow mutter, staring intently at the Number One bungalow. 'It's quite irrational,' he declared in a still lower tone.

'Better go in, sir,' suggested Ricardo. 'What's that? Those screens weren't down before. He's spying from behind them now, I bet – the dodging, artful plotting beast!'

'Why not go over there and see if we can't get to the bottom of this game?' was the unexpected proposal uttered by Mr Jones. 'He will have to talk to us.'

Ricardo repressed a start of dismay, but for a moment could not speak. He only pressed the governor's hand to his side instinctively.

'No, sir. What could you say? Do you expect to get to the bottom of his lies? How could you make him talk? It isn't time yet to come to grips with that gent. You don't think I would hang back, do you? His Chink, of course, I'll shoot like a dog the moment I catch sight of him; but as to that Mr Blasted Heyst, the time isn't yet. My head's cooler just now than yours. Let's go in again. Why, we are exposed here. Suppose he took it into his head to let off a gun on us! He's an unaccountable, 'yporcritical skunk.'

Allowing himself to be persuaded, Mr Jones returned to his seclusion. The secretary, however, remained on the veranda – for the purpose, he said, of seeing whether that Chink wasn't sneaking around; in which case he proposed to take a long shot at the galoot and chance the consequences. His real reason was that he wanted to be alone, away from the governor's deep-sunk eyes. He felt a sentimental desire to indulge his fancies in solitude. A great change had come over Mr Ricardo since that morning. A whole side of him which from prudence, from necessity, from loyalty, had been kept dormant, was aroused now, colouring his thoughts and disturbing his mental poise by the vision of such staggering consequences as, for instance, the possibility of an active conflict with the governor. The appearance of the monstrous Pedro with his news drew Ricardo out of a feeling of dreaminess wrapped up in a sense of impending trouble. A woman? Yes, there was one; and it made all the difference. After driving away Pedro, and watching the white helmets of Heyst and Lena vanish among the bushes he stood lost in meditation.

'Where could they be off to like this?' he mentally asked himself.

The answer found by his speculative faculties on their utmost stretch was – to meet that Chink. For in the desertion of Wang Ricardo did not believe. It was a lying yarn, the organic part of a dangerous plot. Heyst had gone to combine some fresh move. But then Ricardo felt sure that the girl was with him – the girl full of pluck, full of sense, full of understanding; an ally of his own kind!

He went indoors briskly. Mr Jones had resumed his cross-legged pose at the head of the bed, with his back against the wall.

'Anything new?'

'No, sir.'

Ricardo walked about the room as if he had no care in the world. He hummed snatches of song. Mr Jones raised his waspish eyebrows at the sound. The secretary got down on his knees before an old leather trunk, and, rummaging in there, brought out a small looking-glass. He fell to examining his physiognomy in it with silent absorption.

'I think I'll shave,' he decided, getting up.

He gave a sidelong glance to the governor, and repeated it several times during the operation, which did not take long, and even afterwards, when after putting away the implements, he resumed his walking, humming more snatches of unknown songs. Mr Jones preserved a complete immobility, his thin lips compressed, his eyes veiled. His face was like a carving.

'So you would like to try your hand at cards with that skunk, sir?' said Ricardo, stopping suddenly and rubbing his hands.

Mr Jones gave no sign of having heard anything.

'Well, why not? Why shouldn't he have the experience? You remember in that Mexican town – what's its name? – the robber fellow they caught in the mountains and condemned to be shot? He played cards half the night with the jailer and the sheriff. Well, this fellow is condemned, too. He must give you your game. Hang it all, a gentleman ought to have some little relaxation! And you have been uncommonly patient, sir.'

'You are uncommonly volatile all of a sudden,' Mr Jones remarked in a bored voice. 'What's come to you?'

The secretary hummed for a while, and then said:

'I'll try to get him over here for you tonight, after dinner. If I ain't here myself, don't you worry, sir. I shall be doing a bit of nosing around – see?'

'I see,' sneered Mr Jones languidly. 'But what do *you* expect to see in the dark?'

Ricardo made no answer, and after another turn or two slipped out of the room. He no longer felt comfortable alone with the governor.

Chapter VIII

Meantime Heyst and Lena, walking rather fast, approached Wang's hut. Asking the girl to wait, Heyst ascended the little ladder of bamboos giving access to the door. It was as he had expected. The smoky interior was empty, except for a big chest of sandalwood too heavy for hurried removal. Its lid was thrown up, but whatever it might have contained was no longer there. All Wang's possessions were gone. Without tarrying in the hut, Heyst came back to the girl, who asked no questions, with her strange air of knowing or understanding everything.

'Let us push on,' he said.

He went ahead, the rustle of her white skirt following him into the shades of the forest, along the path of their usual walk. Though the air lay heavy between straight denuded trunks, the sunlit patches moved on the ground, and raising her eyes Lena saw far above her head the flutter of the leaves, the surface shudder on the mighty limbs extended horizontally in the perfect immobility of patience. Twice Heyst looked over his shoulder at her. Behind the readiness of her answering smile there was a fund of devoted, concentrated passion, burning with the hope of a more perfect satisfaction. They passed the spot where it was their practice to turn towards the barren summit of the central hill. Heyst held steadily on his way towards the upper limit of the forest. The moment they left its shelter, a breeze enveloped them, and a great cloud, racing over the sun, threw a peculiar sombre tint over everything. Heyst pointed up a precipitous, rugged path clinging to the side of the hill. It ended in a barricade of felled trees, a primitively conceived obstacle which must have cost much labour to erect at just that spot.

'This,' Heyst explained in his urbane tone, 'is a barrier against the march of civilization. The poor folk over there did not like it, as it appeared to them in the shape of my company – a great step forward, as some people used to call it with mistaken confidence. The advanced foot has been drawn back, but the barricade remains.'

They went on climbing slowly. The cloud had driven over, leaving an added brightness on the face of the world.

'It's a very ridiculous thing,' Heyst went on; 'but then it is the product of honest fear – fear of the unknown, of the incomprehensible. It's pathetic, too, in a way. And I heartily wish, Lena, that we were on the other side of it.'

'Oh, stop, stop!' she cried, seizing his arm.

The face of the barricade they were approaching had been piled up with a lot of fresh-cut branches. The leaves were still green. A gentle breeze, sweeping over the top, stirred them a little; but what had startled the girl was the discovery of several spear-blades protruding from the mass of foliage. She had made them out suddenly. They did not gleam, but she saw them with extreme distinctness, very still, very vicious to look at.

'You had better let me go forward alone, Lena,' said Heyst.

She tugged persistently at his arm, but after a time, during which he never ceased to look smilingly into her terrified eyes, he ended by disengaging himself.

'It's a sign rather than a demonstration,' he argued persuasively. 'Just wait here a moment. I promise not to approach near enough to be stabbed.'

As in a nightmare she watched Heyst go up the few yards of the path as if he never meant to stop; and she heard his voice, like voices heard in dreams, shouting unknown words in an unearthly tone. Heyst was only demanding to see Wang. He was not kept waiting very long. Recovering from the first flurrying of her fright, Lena noticed a commotion in the green top-dressing of the barricade. She exhaled a sigh of relief when the spear-blades retreated out of sight, sliding inward – the horrible things! In a spot facing Heyst a pair of yellow hands parted the leaves, and a face filled the small opening – a face with very noticeable eyes. It was Wang's face, of course, with no suggestion of a body belonging to it, like those cardboard faces at which she remembered gazing as a child in the window of a certain dim shop kept by a mysterious little man in Kingsland Road. Only this face, instead of mere holes, had eyes which blinked. She could see the beating of the eyelids. The hands on each side of the face, keeping the boughs apart, also did not look as if they belonged to any real body. One of them was holding a revolver – a weapon which she recognized merely by intuition, never having seen such an object before.

She leaned her shoulders against the rock of the perpendicular hillside and kept her eyes on Heyst, with comparative composure, since the spears were not menacing him any longer. Beyond the rigid and motionless back he presented to her, she saw Wang's unreal cardboard face moving its thin lips and grimacing artificially. She was too far down the path to hear the dialogue, carried on in an ordinary voice. She waited patiently for its end. Her shoulders felt the warmth of the rock; now and then a whiff of cooler air seemed to slip down upon her head from above; the ravine at her feet, choked full of vegetation, emitted the faint, drowsy hum of insect life. Everything was very quiet. She failed to notice the exact moment when Wang's head vanished from the foliage, taking the unreal hands away with it. To her horror, the spear-blades came gliding slowly out. The very hair on her head stirred; but before she had time to cry out, Heyst, who seemed rooted to the ground, turned round abruptly and began to move towards her. His great moustaches did not quite hide an ugly but irresolute smile; and when he had come down near enough to touch her, he burst out into a harsh laugh:

'Ha, ha, ha!'

She looked at him, uncomprehending. He cut short his laugh and said curtly:

'We had better go down as we came.'

She followed him into the forest. The advance of the afternoon had filled it with gloom. Far away a slant of light between the trees closed the view. All was dark beyond. Heyst stopped.

'No reason to hurry, Lena,' he said in his ordinary, serenely polite tones. 'We return unsuccessful. I suppose you know, or at least can guess, what was my object in coming up there?'

'No, I can't guess, dear,' she said, and smiled, noticing with emotion that his breast was heaving as if he had been out of breath. Nevertheless, he tried to command his speech, pausing only a little between the words.

'No? I went up to find Wang. I went up' – he gasped again here, but this was for the last time – 'I made you come with me because I didn't like to leave you unprotected in the proximity of those fellows.' Suddenly he snatched his cork helmet off his head and dashed it on the ground. 'No!' he cried roughly. 'All this is too unreal altogether. It isn't to be borne! I can't protect you! I haven't the power.'

He glared at her for a moment, then hastened after his hat, which had bounded away to some distance. He came back looking at her face, which was very white.

'I ought to beg your pardon for these antics,' he said, adjusting his hat. 'A moment of childish petulance! Indeed, I feel very much like a child in my ignorance, in my powerlessness, in my want of resource, in everything except in the dreadful consciousness of some evil hanging over your head – yours!'

'It's you they are after,' she murmured.

'No doubt, but unfortunately –'

'Unfortunately – what?'

'Unfortunately, I have not succeeded with Wang,' he said. 'I failed to move his Celestial heart – that is, if there is such a thing. He told me with horrible Chinese reasonableness that he could not let us pass the barrier, because we should be pursued. He doesn't like fights. He gave me to understand that he would shoot me with my own revolver without any sort of compunction, rather than risk a rude and distasteful contest with the strange barbarians for my sake. He has preached to the villagers. They respect him. He is the most remarkable man they have ever seen, and their kinsman by marriage. They understand his policy. And anyway only women and children and a few old fellows are left in the village. This is the season when the men are away in trading vessels. But it would have been all the same. None of them have a taste for fighting – and with white men too! They are peaceable, kindly folk and would have seen me shot with extreme satisfaction. Wang seemed to think my insistence – for I insisted, you know – very stupid and tactless. But a drowning man clutches at straws. We were talking in such Malay as we are both equal to.

' "Your fears are foolish," I said to him.

' "Foolish? Of course I am foolish," he replied. "If I were a wise man, I would be a merchant with a big hong in Singapore, instead of being a mine coolie turned houseboy. But if you don't go away in time, I will shoot you before it grows too dark to take aim. Not till then, Number One, but I will do it then. Now – finish!"

' "All right," I said. "Finish as far as I am concerned; but you can have no objections to the *mem putih* coming over to stay with the Orang Kaya's woman for a few days. I will make a present in silver for it." Orang Kaya is the head man of the village, Lena,' added Heyst.

She looked at him in astonishment.

'You wanted me to go to that village of savages?' she gasped. 'You wanted me to leave you?'

'It would have given me a freer hand.'

Heyst stretched out his hands and looked at them for a moment, then let them fall by his side. Indignation was expressed more in the curve of her lips than in her clear eyes, which never wavered.

'I believe Wang laughed,' he went on. 'He made a noise like a turkey-cock.'

' "That would be worse than anything," he told me.

'I was taken aback. I pointed out to him that he was talking nonsense. It could not make any difference to his security where you were, because the evil men, as he calls them, did not know of your existence. I did not lie exactly, Lena, though I did stretch the truth till it cracked; but the fellow seems to have an uncanny insight. He shook his head. He assured me they knew all about you. He made a horrible grimace at me.'

'It doesn't matter,' said the girl. 'I didn't want – I would not have gone.'

Heyst raised his eyes.

'Wonderful intuition! As I continued to press him, Wang made that very remark about you. When he smiles, his face looks like a conceited death's head. It was his very last remark – that you wouldn't want to. I went away then.'

She leaned back against a tree. Heyst faced her in the same attitude of leisure, as if they had done with time and all the other concerns of the earth. Suddenly, high above their heads the roof of leaves whispered at them tumultuously and then ceased.

'That was a strange notion of yours, to send me away,' she said, 'Send me away? What for? Yes, what for?'

'You seem indignant,' he remarked listlessly.

'To these savages, too!' she pursued. 'And you think I would have gone? You can do what you like with me – but not that, not that!'

Heyst looked into the dim aisles of the forest. Everything was so still now that the very ground on which they stood seemed to exhale silence into the shade.

'Why be indignant?' he remonstrated. 'It has not happened. I gave up pleading with Wang. Here we are, repulsed! Not only without power to resist the evil, but unable to make terms for ourselves with the worthy envoys, the envoys extraordinary of the world we thought we had done with for years and years. And that's bad, Lena, very bad.'

'It's funny,' she said thoughtfully. 'Bad? I suppose it is. I don't know that it is. But do you? Do you? You talk as if you didn't believe in it.'

She gazed at him earnestly.

'Do I? Ah! That's it. I don't know how to talk. I have managed to refine everything away. I've said to the Earth that bore me: "I am I and you are a shadow." And, by Jove, it is so! But it appears that such words cannot be uttered with impunity. Here I am on a Shadow inhabited by Shades. How helpless a man is against the Shades! How is one to intimidate, persuade, resist, assert oneself against them? I have lost all belief in realities. . . . Lena, give me your hand.'

She looked at him surprised, uncomprehending.

'Your hand,' he cried.

She obeyed; he seized it with avidity as if eager to raise it to his lips, but halfway up released his grasp. They looked at each other for a time.

'What's the matter, dear?' she whispered timidly.

'Neither force nor conviction,' Heyst muttered wearily to himself. 'How am I to meet this charmingly simple problem?'

'I am sorry,' she murmured.

'And so am I,' he confessed quickly. 'And the bitterest of this humiliation is its complete uselessness – which I feel, I feel!'

She had never before seen him give such signs of feeling. Across his ghastly face the long moustaches flamed in the shade. He spoke suddenly:

'I wonder if I could find enough courage to creep among them in the night, with a knife, and cut their throats one after another, as they slept! I wonder –'

She was frightened by his unwonted appearance more than by the words in his mouth, and said earnestly:

'Don't you try to do such a thing! Don't you think of it!'

'I don't possess anything bigger than a penknife. As to thinking of it, Lena, there's no saying what one may think of. I don't think. Something in me thinks – something foreign to my nature. What is the matter?'

He noticed her parted lips, and the peculiar stare in her eyes, which had wandered from his face.

'There's somebody after us. I saw something white moving,' she cried.

Heyst did not turn his head; he only glanced at her outstretched arm.

'No doubt we are followed; we are watched.'

'I don't see anything now,' she said.

'And it does not matter,' Heyst went on in his ordinary voice. 'Here we are in the forest. I have neither strength nor persuasion. Indeed, it's extremely difficult to be eloquent before a Chinaman's head stuck at one out of a lot of brushwood. But can we wander among these big trees indefinitely? Is this a refuge? No! What else is left to us? I did think for a moment of the mine; but even there we could not remain very long. And then the gallery is not safe. The props were too weak to begin with. Ants have been at work there – ants after the men. A death-trap, at best. One can die but once, but there are many manners of death.'

The girl glanced about fearfully, in search of the watcher or follower whom she had glimpsed once among the trees; but if he existed, he had concealed himself. Nothing met her eyes but the deepening shadows of the short vistas between the living columns of the still roof of leaves. She looked at the man beside her expectantly, tenderly, with suppressed affright and a sort of awed wonder.

'I have also thought of these people's boat,' Heyst went on. 'We could get into that, and – only they have taken everything out of her. I have seen her oars and mast in a corner of their room. To shove off in an empty boat would be nothing but a desperate expedition, supposing even that she would drift out a good distance between the islands before the morning. It would only be a complicated manner of committing suicide – to be found dead in a boat, dead from sun and thirst. A sea mystery. I wonder who would find us! Davidson, perhaps; but Davidson passed westward ten days ago. I watched him steaming past one early morning, from the jetty.'

'You never told me,' she said.

'He must have been looking at me through his big binoculars. Perhaps, if I had raised my arm – but what did we want with Davidson then, you and I? He won't be back this way for three weeks or more, Lena. I wish I had raised my arm that morning.'

'What would have been the good of it?' she sighed out.

'What good? No good, of course. We had no forebodings. This seemed to be an inexpugnable refuge, where we could live untroubled and learn to know each other.'

'It's perhaps in trouble that people get to know each other,' she suggested.

'Perhaps,' he said indifferently. 'At any rate, we would not have gone away from here with him; though I believe he would have come in eagerly enough, and ready for any service he could render. It's that fat man's nature – a delightful fellow. You would not come on the wharf that time I sent the shawl back to Mrs Schomberg through him. He has never seen you.'

'I didn't know that you wanted anybody ever to see me,' she said.

He had folded his arms on his breast and hung his head.

'And I did not know that you cared to be seen as yet. A misunderstanding evidently. An honourable misunderstanding. But it does not matter now.'

He raised his head after a silence.

'How gloomy this forest has grown! Yet surely the sun cannot have set already.'

She looked round; and as if her eyes had just been opened, she perceived the shades of the forest surrounding her, not so much with gloom, but with a sullen, dumb, menacing hostility. Her heart sank in the engulfing stillness, at that moment she felt the nearness of death breathing on her and on the man with her. If there had been a sudden stir of leaves, the crack of a dry branch, the faintest rustle, she would have screamed aloud. But she shook off the unworthy weakness. Such as she was, a fiddle-scraping girl picked up on the very threshold of infamy, she would try to rise above herself, triumphant and humble; and then happiness would burst on her like a torrent, flinging at her feet the man whom she loved.

Heyst stirred slightly.

'We had better be getting back, Lena, since we can't stay all night in the woods – or anywhere else, for that matter. We are the slaves of this infernal surprise which has been sprung on us by – shall I say fate? – your fate, or mine.'

It was the man who had broken the silence, but it was the woman who led the way. At the very edge of the forest she stopped, concealed by a tree. He joined her cautiously.

'What is it? What do you see, Lena?' he whispered.

She said that it was only a thought that had come into her head. She hesitated for a moment, giving him over her shoulder a shining gleam in her grey eyes. She wanted to know whether this trouble, this danger, this evil, whatever it was, finding them out in their retreat, was not a sort of punishment.

'Punishment?' repeated Heyst. He could not understand what she meant. When she explained, he was still more surprised. 'A sort of retribution from an angry Heaven?' he said in wonder. 'On us? What on earth for?'

He saw her pale face darken in the dusk. She had blushed. Her whispering flowed very fast. It was the way they lived together – that wasn't right, was it? It was a guilty life. For she had not been forced into it, driven, scared into it. No, no – she had come to him of her own free will, with her whole soul yearning unlawfully.

He was so profoundly touched that he could not speak for a moment. To conceal his trouble, he assumed his best Heystian manner.

'What? Are our visitors then messengers of morality, avengers of righteousness, agents of Providence? That's certainly an original view. How flattered they would be if they could hear you!'

'Now you are making fun of me,' she said in subdued voice which broke suddenly.

'Are you conscious of sin?' Heyst asked gravely. She made no answer. 'For I am not,' he added; 'before Heaven, I am not!'

'You! You are different. Woman is the tempter. You took me up from pity. I threw myself at you.'

'Oh, you exaggerate, you exaggerate. It was not so bad as that,' he said playfully, keeping his voice steady with an effort.

He considered himself a dead man already, yet forced to pretend that he was alive for her sake, for her defence. He regretted that he had no Heaven to which he could recommend this fair, palpitating handful of ashes and dust – warm, living, sentient, his own – and exposed helplessly to insult, outrage, degradation, and infinite misery of the body.

She had averted her face from him and was still. He suddenly seized her passive hand.

'You will have it so?' he said. 'Yes? Well, let us then hope for mercy together.'

She shook her head without looking at him, like an abashed child.

'Remember,' he went on incorrigible with his delicate raillery, 'that hope is a Christian virtue, and surely you can't want all the mercy for yourself.'

Before their eyes the bungalow across the cleared ground stood bathed in a sinister light. An unexpected chill gust of wind made a noise in the tree-tops. She snatched her hand away and stepped out into the open; but before she had advanced more than three yards, she stood still and pointed to the west.

'Oh, look there!' she exclaimed.

Beyond the headland of Diamond Bay, lying black on a purple sea, great masses of cloud stood piled up and bathed in a mist of blood. A crimson crack like an open wound zigzagged between them, with a piece of dark red sun showing at the bottom. Heyst cast an indifferent glace at the ill-omened chaos of the sky.

'Thunderstorm making up. We shall hear it all night, but it won't visit us, probably. The clouds generally gather round the volcano.'

She was not listening to him. Her eyes reflected the sombre and violent hues of the sunset.

'That does not look much like a sign of mercy,' she said slowly, as if to herself, and hurried on, followed by Heyst. Suddenly she stopped. 'I don't care. I would do more yet! And some day you'll forgive me. You'll have to forgive me!'

Chapter IX

Stumbling up the steps, as if suddenly exhausted, Lena entered the room and let herself fall on the nearest chair. Before following her, Heyst took a survey of the surroundings from the veranda. It was a complete solitude. There was nothing in the aspect of this familiar scene to tell him that he and the girl were not completely alone as they had been in the early days of their common life on this abandoned spot, with only Wang discreetly materializing from time to time and the uncomplaining memory of Morrison to keep them company.

After the cold gust of wind there was an absolute stillness of the air. The thunder-charged mass hung unbroken beyond the low, ink-black headland, darkening the twilight. By contrast, the sky at the zenith displayed pellucid clearness, the sheen of a delicate glass bubble which the merest movement of air might shatter. A little to the left, between the black masses of the headland and of the forest, the volcano, a feather of smoke by day and a cigar-glow at night, took its first fiery expanding breath of the evening. Above it a reddish star came out like an expelled spark from the fiery bosom of the earth, enchanted into permanency by the mysterious spell of frozen spaces.

In front of Heyst the forest, already full of the deepest shades, stood like a wall. But he lingered, watching its edge, especially where it ended at the line of bushes, masking the land end of the jetty. Since the girl had spoken of catching a glimpse of something white among the trees, he believed pretty firmly that they had been followed in their excursion up the mountain by Mr Jones's secretary. No doubt the fellow had watched them out of the forest, and now, unless he took the trouble to go back some distance and fetch a considerable circuit inland over the clearing, he was bound to walk out into the open space before the bungalows. Heyst did, indeed, imagine at one time some movement between the trees, lost as soon as perceived. He stared patiently, but nothing more happened. After all, why should he trouble about these people's actions? Why this stupid concern for the preliminaries, since, when the issue was joined, it would find him disarmed and shrinking from the ugliness and degradation of it?

He turned and entered the room. Deep dusk reigned in there already. Lena, near the door, did not move or speak. The sheen of the white tablecloth was very obtrusive. The brute these two vagabonds had tamed had entered on its service while Heyst and Lena were away. The table was laid. Heyst walked up and down the room several times. The girl remained without sound or movement on the chair. But when Heyst, placing the two silver candelabra on the table, struck a match to light the candles, she got up suddenly and went into the bedroom. She came out again almost immediately, having taken off her hat. Heyst looked at her over his shoulder.

'What's the good of shirking the evil hour? I've lighted these candles for a sign of our return. After all, we might not have been watched – while returning, I mean. Of course we were seen leaving the house.'

The girl sat down again. The great wealth of her hair looked very dark above her colourless face. She raised her eyes, glistening softly in the light with a sort of unreadable appeal, with a strange effect of unseeing innocence.

'Yes,' said Heyst across the table, the fingertips of one hand resting on the immaculate cloth. 'A creature with an antediluvian lower jaw, hairy like a mastodon, and formed like a prehistoric ape, has laid this table. Are you awake, Lena? Am I? I would pinch myself, only I know that nothing would do away with this dream. Three covers. You know it is the shorter of the two who's coming – the gentleman who, in the play of his shoulders as he walks, and in his facial structure, recalls a jaguar. Ah, you don't know what a jaguar is? But you have had a good look at these two. It's the short one, you know, who's to be our guest.'

She made a sign with her head that she knew. Heyst's insistence brought Ricardo vividly before her mental vision. A sudden languor, like the physical echo of her struggle with the man, paralysed all her limbs. She lay still in the chair, feeling very frightened at this phenomenon – ready to pray aloud for strength.

Heyst had started to pace the room.

'Our guest! There is a proverb – in Russia, I believe – that when a guest enters the house, God enters the house. The sacred virtue of hospitality! But it leads one into trouble as well as any other.'

The girl unexpectedly got up from the chair, swaying her supple figure and stretching her arms above her head. He stopped to look at her curiously, paused, and then went on:

'I venture to think that God has nothing to do with such a hospitality and with such a guest!'

She had jumped to her feet to react against the numbness, to discover whether her body would obey her will. It did. She could stand up, and she could move her arms freely. Though no physiologist, she concluded that all that sudden numbness was in her head, not in her limbs. Her fears assuaged, she thanked God for it mentally, and to Heyst murmured a protest:

'Oh, yes! He's got to do with everything – every little thing. Nothing can happen –'

'Yes,' he said hastily, 'one of the two sparrows can't be struck to the ground – you are thinking of that.' The habitual playful smile faded on the kindly lips under the martial moustache. 'Ah, you remember what you have been told – as a child – on Sundays.'

'Yes, I do remember.' She sank into the chair again. 'It was the only decent bit of time I ever had when I was a kid, with our landlady's two girls, you know.'

'I wonder, Lena,' Heyst said, with a return to his urbane playfulness, 'whether you are just a little child, or whether you represent something as old as the world.'

She surprised Heyst by saying dreamily:

'Well – and what about you?'

'I? I date later – much later. I can't call myself a child, but I am so recent that I may call myself a man of the last hour – or is it the hour before last? I have been out of it so long that I am not certain how far the hands of the clock have moved since – since –'

He glanced at the portrait of his father, exactly above the head of the girl, as if it were ignoring her in its painted austerity of feeling. He did not finish the sentence; but he did not remain silent for long.

'Only what must be avoided are fallacious inferences, my dear Lena – especially at this hour.'

'Now you are making fun of me again,' she said without looking up.

'Am I?' he cried. 'Making fun? No, giving warning. Hang it all, whatever truth people told you in the old days, there is also this one – that sparrows do fall to the ground, that they are brought to the ground. This is no vain assertion, but a fact. That's why' – again his tone changed, while he picked up the table knife and let it fall disdainfully – 'that's why I wish these wretched round knives had some edge on them. Absolute rubbish – neither edge, point, nor substance. I believe one of these forks would make a better weapon at a pinch. But can I go about with a fork in my pocket?' He gnashed his teeth with a rage very real, and yet comic.

'There used to be a carver here, but it was broken and thrown away a long time ago. Nothing much to carve here. It would have made a noble weapon, no doubt; but –'

He stopped. The girl sat very quiet, with downcast eyes. As he kept silent for some time, she looked up and said thoughtfully:

'Yes, a knife – it's a knife that you would want, wouldn't you, in case, in case –'

He shrugged his shoulders.

'There must be a crowbar or two in the sheds; but I have given up all the keys together. And then, do you see me walking about with a crowbar in my hand? Ha, ha! And besides, that edifying sight alone might start the trouble for all I know. In truth, why has it not started yet?'

'Perhaps they are afraid of you,' she whispered, looking down again.

'By Jove, it looks like it,' he assented meditatively. 'They do seem to hang back for some reason. Is that reason prudence, or downright fear, or perhaps the leisurely method of certitude?'

Out in the black night, not very far from the bungalow, resounded a loud and prolonged whistle. Lena's hands grasped the sides of the chair, but she made no movement. Heyst started, and turned his face away from the door.

The startling sound had died away.

'Whistles, yells, omens, signals, portents – what do they matter?' he said. 'But what about the crowbar? Suppose I had it! Could I stand in ambush at the side of the door – this door – and smash the first protruding head, scatter blood and brains over the floor, over these walls, and then run stealthily to the other door to do the same thing – and repeat the performance for a third time, perhaps? Could I? On suspicion, without compunction, with a calm and determined purpose? No, it is not in me. I date too late. Would you like to see me attempt this thing while that mysterious prestige of mine lasts – or their not less mysterious hesitation?'

'No, no!' she whispered ardently, as if compelled to speak by his eyes fixed on her face. 'No, it's a knife you want to defend yourself with – to defend – there will be time –'

'And who knows if it isn't really my duty?' he began again, as if he had not heard her disjointed words at all. 'It may be – my duty to you, to myself. For why should I put up with the humiliation of their secret menaces? Do you know what the world would say?'

He emitted a low laugh, which struck her with terror. She would have got up, but he stooped so low over her that she could not move without first pushing him away.

'It would say, Lena, that I – the Swede – after luring my friend and partner to his death from mere greed of money, have murdered these unoffending shipwrecked strangers from sheer funk. That would be the story whispered – perhaps shouted – certainly spread out, and believed – and *believed*, my dear Lena!'

'Who would believe such awful things?'

'Perhaps you wouldn't – not at first, at any rate; but the power of calumny grows with time. It's insidious and penetrating. It can even destroy one's faith in oneself – dry-rot the soul.'

All at once her eyes leaped to the door and remained fixed, stony, a little enlarged. Turning his head, Heyst beheld the figure of Ricardo framed in the doorway. For a moment none of the three moved; then, looking from the newcomer to the girl in the chair, Heyst formulated a sardonic introduction.

'Mr Ricardo, my dear.'

Her head drooped a little. Ricardo's hand went up to his moustache. His voice exploded in the room.

'At your service, ma'am!'

He stepped in, taking his hat off with a flourish, and dropping it carelessly on a chair near the door.

'At your service,' he repeated, in quite another tone. 'I was made aware there was a lady about, by that Pedro of ours; only I didn't know I should have the privilege of seeing you tonight, ma'am.'

Lena and Heyst looked at him covertly, but he, with a vague gaze avoiding them both, looked at nothing, seeming to pursue some point in space.

'Had a pleasant walk?' he asked suddenly.

'Yes. And you?' returned Heyst, who had managed to catch his glance.

'I? I haven't been a yard away from the governor this afternoon till I started for here.' The genuineness of the accent surprised Heyst, without convincing him of the truth of the words. 'Why do you ask?' pursued Ricardo with every inflexion of perfect candour.

'You might have wished to explore the island a little,' said Heyst, studying the man, who, to render him justice, did not try to free his captured gaze. 'I may remind you that it wouldn't be a perfectly safe proceeding.'

Ricardo presented a picture of innocence.

'Oh, yes – meaning that Chink that has run away from you. He ain't much!'

'He has a revolver,' observed Heyst meaningly.

'Well, and you have a revolver, too,' Mr Ricardo argued unexpectedly. 'I don't worry myself about that.'

'I? That's different. I am not afraid of you,' Heyst made answer after a short pause.

'Of me?'

'Of all of you.'

'You have a queer way of putting things,' began Ricardo.

At that moment the door on the compound side of the house came open with some noise, and Pedro entered, pressing the edge of a loaded tray to his breast. His big, hairy head rolled a little, his feet fell in front of each other with a short, hard thump on the floor. The arrival changed the current of Ricardo's thought, perhaps, but certainly of his speech.

'You heard me whistling a little while ago outside? That was to give him a hint, as I came along, that it was time to bring in the dinner; and here it is.'

Lena rose and passed to the right of Ricardo, who lowered his glance for a moment. They sat down at the table. The enormous gorilla back of Pedro swayed out through the door.

'Extraordinary strong brute, ma'am,' said Ricardo. He had a propensity to talk about 'his Pedro', as some men will talk of their dog. 'He ain't pretty, though. No, he ain't pretty. And he has got to be kept under. I am his keeper, as it might be. The governor don't trouble his head much about dee-tails. All that's left to Martin. Martin, that's me, ma'am.'

Heyst saw the girl's eyes turn towards Mr Jones's secretary and rest blankly on his face. Ricardo, however, looked vaguely into space, and, with faint flickers of a smile about his lips, made conversation indefatigably against the silence of his entertainers. He boasted largely of his long association with Mr Jones – over four years now, he said. Then, glancing rapidly at Heyst:

'You can see at once he's a gentleman, can't you?'

'You people,' Heyst said, his habitual playful intonation tinged with gloom, 'are divorced from all reality in my eyes.'

Ricardo received this speech as if he had been expecting to hear those very words, or else did not mind at all what Heyst might say. He muttered an absentminded 'Ay, ay', played with a bit of biscuit, sighed, and said, with a peculiar stare which did not seem to carry any distance, but to stop short at a point in the air very near his face:

'Anybody can see at once *you* are one. You and the governor ought to understand each other. He expects to see you tonight. The governor isn't well, and we've got to think of getting away from here.'

'While saying these words he turned himself full towards Lena, but without any marked expression. Leaning back with folded arms, the girl stared before her as if she had been alone in the room. But under that aspect of almost vacant unconcern the perils and emotion that had entered into her life warmed her heart, exalted her mind with a sense of an inconceivable intensity of existence.

'Really? Thinking of going away from here?' Heyst murmured.

'The best of friends must part,' Ricardo pronounced slowly. 'And, as long as they part friends, there's no harm done. We two are used to be on the move. You, I understand, prefer to stick in one place.'

It was obvious that all this was being said merely for the sake of talking, and that Ricardo's mind was concentrated on some purpose unconnected with the words that were coming out of his mouth.

'I should like to know,' Heyst asked with incisive politeness, 'how you have come to understand this or anything else about me? As far as I can remember, I've made you no confidences.'

Ricardo, gazing comfortably into space out of the back of his chair – for some time all three had given up any pretence of eating – answered abstractedly:

'Any fellow might have guessed it.' He sat up suddenly, and uncovered all his teeth in a grin of extraordinary ferocity, which was belied by the persistent amiability of his tone. 'The governor will be the man to tell you something about that. I wish you would say you would see my governor. He's the one who does all our talking. Let me take you to him this evening. He ain't at all well; and he can't make up his mind to go away without having a talk with you.'

Heyst, looking up, met Lena's eyes. Their expression of candour seemed to hide some struggling intention. Her head, he fancied, had made an imperceptible affirmative movement. Why? What reason could she have? Was it the prompting of some obscure instinct? Or was it simply a delusion of his own senses? But in this strange complication invading the quietude of his life, in his state of doubt and disdain and almost of despair with which he looked at himself, he would let even a delusive appearance guide him through a darkness so dense that it made for indifference.

'Well, suppose I *do* say so.'

Ricardo did not conceal his satisfaction, which for a moment interested Heyst.

'It can't be my life they are after,' he said to himself. 'What good could it be to them?'

He looked across the table at the girl. What did it matter whether she had nodded or not? As always when looking into her unconscious eyes, he tasted something like the dregs of tender pity. He had decided to go. Her nod, imaginary or not imaginary, advice or illusion, had tipped the scale. He reflected that Ricardo's invitation could scarcely be anything in the nature of a trap. It would have been too absurd. Why carry subtly into a trap someone bound hand and foot, as it were?

All this time he had been looking fixedly at the girl he called Lena. In the submissive quietness of her being, which had been her attitude ever since they had begun their life on the island, she remained as secret as ever. Heyst got up abruptly, with a smile of such enigmatic and despairing character that Mr Secretary Ricardo, whose abstract gaze had an all-round efficiency, made a slight crouching start, as if to dive under the table for his leg-knife – a start that was repressed as soon as begun. He had expected Heyst to spring on him or draw a revolver, because he created for himself a vision of him in his own image. Instead of doing either of these obvious things, Heyst walked across the room, opened the door, and put his head through it to look out into the compound.

As soon as his back was turned, Ricardo's hand sought the girl's arm under the table. He was not looking at her, but she felt the groping, nervous touch of his search, felt suddenly the grip of his fingers above her wrist. He leaned forward a little; still he dared not look at her. His hard stare remained fastened on Heyst's back. In an extremely low hiss, his fixed idea of argument found expression scathingly:

'See! He's no good. He's not the man for you!'

He glanced at her at last. Her lips moved a little, and he was awed by that movement without a sound. Next instant the hard grasp of his fingers vanished from her arm. Heyst had shut the door. On his way back to the table, he crossed the path of the girl they had called Alma – she didn't know why – also Magdalen, whose mind had remained so long in doubt as to the reason of her own existence. She no longer wondered at that bitter riddle, since her heart found its solution in a blinding, hot glow of passionate pride.

Chapter X

She passed by Heyst as if she had indeed been blinded by some secret, lurid, and consuming glare into which she was about to enter. The curtain of the bedroom door fell behind her into rigid folds. Ricardo's vacant gaze seemed to be watching the dancing flight of a fly in mid air.

'Extra dark outside, ain't it?' he muttered.

'Not so dark but that I could see that man of yours prowling about there,' said Heyst in measured tones.

'What – Pedro? He's scarcely a man you know; or else I wouldn't be so fond of him as I am.'

'Very well. Let's call him your worthy associate.'

'Ay! Worthy enough for what we want of him. A great stand-by is Peter in a scrimmage. A growl and a bite – oh, my! And you don't want him about?'

'I don't.'

'You want him out of the way?' insisted Ricardo with an affectation of incredulity which Heyst accepted calmly, though the air in the room seemed to grow more oppressive with every word spoken.

'That's it. I do want him out of the way.' He forced himself to speak equably.

'Lor'! That's no great matter. Pedro's not much use here. The business my governor's after can be settled by ten minutes' rational talk with – with another gentleman. Quiet talk!'

He looked up suddenly with hard, phosphorescent eyes. Heyst didn't move a muscle. Ricardo congratulated himself on having left his revolver behind. He was so exasperated that he didn't know what he might have done. He said at last:

'You want poor, harmless Peter out of the way before you let me take you to see the governor – is that it?'

'Yes, that is it.'

'H'm! One can see,' Ricardo said with hidden venom, 'that you are a gentleman; but all that gentlemanly fancifulness is apt to turn sour on a plain man's stomach. However – you'll have to pardon me.'

He put his fingers into his mouth and let out a whistle which seemed to drive a thin, sharp shaft of air solidly against one's nearest ear-drum. Though he greatly enjoyed Heyst's involuntary grimace, he sat perfectly stolid waiting for the effect of the call.

It brought Pedro in with an extraordinary, uncouth, primeval impetuosity. the door flew open with a clatter, and the wild figure it disclosed seemed anxious to devastate the room in leaps and bounds; but Ricardo raised his open palm, and the creature came in quietly. His enormous half-closed paws swung to and fro a little in front of his bowed trunk as he walked. Ricardo looked on truculently.

'You go to the boat – understand? Go now!'

The little red eyes of the tame monster blinked with painful attention in the mass of hair.

'Well? Why don't you get? Forgot human speech, eh? Don't you know any longer what a boat is?'

'*Sí* – boat,' the creature stammered out doubtfully.

Well, go there – the boat at the jetty. March off to it and sit there, lie down there, do anything but go to sleep there – till you hear my call, and then fly here. Them's your orders. March! Get, *vamos*! No, not that way – out through the front door. No sulks!'

Pedro obeyed with uncouth alacrity. When he had gone, the gleam of pitiless savagery went out of Ricardo's yellow eyes, and his physiognomy took on, for the first time that evening, the expression of a domestic cat which is being noticed.

'You can watch him right into the bushes, if you like. Too dark, eh? Why not go with him to the very spot, then?'

Heyst made a gesture of vague protest.

'There's nothing to assure me that he will stay there. I have do doubt of his going; but it's an act without guarantee.'

'There you are!' Ricardo shrugged his shoulders philosophically. 'Can't be helped. Short of shooting our Pedro, nobody can make absolutely sure of his staying in the same place longer than he has a mind to; but I tell you, he lives in holy terror of my temper. That's why I put on my sudden-death air when I talk to him. And yet I wouldn't shoot him – not I, unless in such a fit of rage as would make a man shoot his favourite dog. Look here, sir! This deal is on the square. I didn't tip him a wink to do anything else. He won't budge from the jetty. Are you coming along now, sir?'

A short silence ensued. Ricardo's jaws were working ominously under his skin. His eyes glided voluptuously here and there, cruel and dreamy. Heyst checked a sudden movement, reflected for a while, then said:

'You must wait a little.'

'Wait a little! Wait a little! What does he think a fellow is – a graven image?' grumbled Ricardo half audibly.

Heyst went into the bedroom, and shut the door after him with a bang. Coming from the light, he could not see a thing in there at first; yet he received the impression of the girl getting up from the floor. On the less opaque darkness of the shutter-hole, her head detached itself suddenly, very faint, a mere hint of a round, dark shape without a face.

'I am going, Lena. I am going to confront these scroundrels.' He was surprised to feel two arms falling on his shoulders. 'I thought that you –' he began.

'Yes, yes!' the girl whispered hastily.

She neither clung to him, nor yet did she try to draw him to her. Her hands grasped his shoulders, and she seemed to him to be staring into his face in the dark. And now he could see something of her face, too – an oval without features – and faintly distinguish her person, in the blackness, a form without definite lines.

'You have a black dress here, haven't you, Lena?' he asked, speaking rapidly, and so low that she could just hear him.

'Yes – an old thing.'

'Very good. Put it on at once.'

'But why?'

'Not for mourning!' There was something peremptory in the slightly ironic murmur. 'Can you find it and get into it in the dark?'

She could. She would try. He waited, very still. He could imagine her movements over there at the far end of the room; but his eyes, accustomed now to the darkness, had lost her completely. When she spoke, her voice surprised him by its nearness. She had done what he had told her to do, and had approached him, invisible.

'Good! Where's that piece of purple veil I've seen lying about?' he asked.

There was no answer, only a slight rustle.

'Where is it?' he repeated impatiently.

Her unexpected breath was on his cheek.

'In my hands.'

'Capital! Listen, Lena. As soon as I leave the bunagalow with that horrible scoundrel, you slip out at the back – instantly, lose no time! – and run round into the forest. That will be your time, while we are walking away, and I am sure he won't give me the slip. Run into the forest behind the fringe of bushes between the big trees. You will know, surely, how to find a place in full view of the front door. I fear for you; but in this black dress, with most of your face muffled up in that dark veil, I defy anybody to find you there before daylight. Wait in the forest till the table is pushed into full view of the doorway, and you see three candles out of four blown out and one relighted – or, should the lights be put out here while you watch them, wait till three candles are lighted and then two put out. At either of these signals run back as hard as you can, for it will mean that I am waiting for you here.'

While he was speaking, the girl had sought and seized one of his hands. She did not press it; she held it loosely, as it were timidly, caressingly. It was no grasp; it was a mere contact, as if only to make sure that he was there, that he was real and no mere darker shadow in the obscurity. The warmth of her hand gave Heyst a strange, intimate sensation of all her person. He had to fight down a new sort of emotion, which almost unmanned him. He went on, whispering sternly:

'But if you see no such signals, don't let anything – fear, curiosity, despair, or hope – entice you back to this house; and with the first sign of dawn steal away along the edge of the clearing till you strike the path. Wait no longer, because I shall probably be dead.'

The murmur of the word 'Never!' floated into his ear as if it formed itself in the air.

'You know the path,' he continued. 'Make your way to the barricade. Go to Wang – yes, to Wang. Let nothing stop you!' It seemed to him that the girl's hand trembled a little. 'The worst he can do to you is to shoot you; but he won't. I really think he won't, if I am not there. Stay with the villagers, with the wild people, and fear nothing. They will be more awed by you than you can be frightened of them. Davidson's bound to turn up before very long. Keep a look-out for a passing steamer. Think of some sort of signal to call him.'

She made no answer. The sense of the heavy, brooding silence in the outside world seemed to enter and fill the room – the oppressive infinity of it, without breath, without light. It was as if the heart of hearts had ceased to beat and the end of all things had come.

'Have you understood? You are to run out of the house at once,' Heyst whispered urgently.

She lifted his hand to her lips and let it go. He was startled.

'Lena!' he cried out under his breath.

She was gone from his side. He dared not trust himself – no, not even to the extent of a tender word.

Turning to go out, he heard a thud somewhere in the house. To open the door, he had first to lift the curtain; he did so with his face over his shoulder. The merest trickle of light, coming through the keyhole and one or two cracks, was enough for his eyes to see her plainly, all black, down on her knees, with her head and arms flung on the foot of the bed – all black in the desolation of a mourning sinner. What was this? A suspicion that there were everywhere more things than he could understand crossed Heyst's mind. Her arm, detached from the bed, motioned him away. He obeyed, and went out, full of disquiet.

The curtain behind him had not ceased to tremble when she was up on her feet, close against it, listening for sounds, for words, in a a stooping, tragic attitude of stealthy attention, one hand clutching at her breast as if to compress, to make less loud the beating of her heart. Heyst had caught Mr Jones's secretary in the contemplation of his closed writing-desk. Ricardo might have been meditating how to break into it; but when he turned about suddenly, he showed so distorted a face that it made Heyst pause in wonder at the upturned whites of the eyes, which were blinking horribly, as if the man were inwardly convulsed.

'I thought you were never coming,' Ricardo mumbled.

'I didn't know you were pressed for time. Even if your going away depends on this conversation, as you say, I doubt if you are the men to put to sea on such a night as this,' said Heyst, motioning Ricardo to precede him out of the house.

With feline undulations of hip and shoulder, the secretary left the room at once. There was something cruel in the absolute dumbness of the night. The great cloud covering half the sky hung right against one, like an enormous curtain hiding menacing preparations of violence. As the feet of the two men touched the ground, a rumble came from behind it, preceded by a swift, mysterious gleam of light on the waters of the bay.

'Ha!' said Ricardo. 'It begins.'

'It may be nothing in the end,' observed Heyst, stepping along steadily.

'No! Let it come!' Ricardo said viciously. 'I am in the humour for it!'

By the time the two men had reached the other bungalow, the far-off modulated rumble growled incessantly, while pale lightning in waves of cold fire flooded and ran off the island in rapid succession. Ricardo, unexpectedly, dashed ahead up the steps and put his head through the doorway.

'Here he is, governor! Keep him with you as long as you can – till you hear me whistle. I am on the track.'

He flung these words into the room with inconceivable speed, and stood aside to let the visitor pass through the doorway; but he had to wait an appreciable moment, because Heyst, seeing his purpose, had scornfully slowed his pace. When Heyst entered the room it was with a smile, the Heyst smile, lurking under his martial moustache.

Chapter XI

Two candles were burning on the stand-up desk. Mr Jones, tightly enfolded in an old but gorgeous blue silk dressing-gown, kept his elbows close against his sides and his hands deeply plunged into the extraordinarily deep pockets of the garment. The costume accentuated his emaciation. He resembled a painted pole leaning against the edge of the desk, with a dried head of dubious distinction stuck on the top of it. Ricardo lounged in the doorway. Indifferent, in appearance, to what was going on, he was biding his time. At a given moment, between two flickers of lightning, he melted out of his frame into the outer air. His disappearance was observed on the instant by Mr Jones, who abandoned his nonchalant immobility against the desk, and made a few steps calculated to put him between Heyst and the doorway.

'It's awfully close,' he remarked.

Heyst, in the middle of the room, had made up his mind to speak plainly.

'We haven't met to talk about the weather. You favoured me earlier in the day with a rather cryptic phrase about yourself. "I am he that is," you said. What does that mean?'

Mr Jones, without looking at Heyst, continued his absentminded movements till, attaining the desired position, he brought his shoulders with a thump against the wall near the door, and raised his head. In the emotion of the decisive moment his haggard face glistened with perspiration. Drops ran down his hollow cheeks and almost blinded the spectral eyes in their bony caverns.

'It means that I am a person to be reckoned with. No – stop! Don't put your hand into your pocket – don't.'

His voice had a wild, unexpected shrillness. Heyst started, and there ensued a moment of suspended animation, during which the thunder's deep bass muttered distantly and the doorway to the right of Mr Jones flickered with bluish light. At last Heyst shrugged his shoulders; he even looked at his hand. He didn't put it in his pocket, however. Mr Jones, glued against the wall, watched him raise both his hands to the ends of his horizontal moustaches, and answered the note of interrogation in his steady eyes.

'A matter of prudence,' said Mr Jones in his natural hollow tones, and with a face of deathlike composure. 'A man of your free life has surely perceived that. You are a much talked-about man, Mr Heyst – and though, as far as I understand, you are accustomed to employ the subtler weapons of intelligence, still I can't afford to take any risks of the – er – grosser methods. I am not unscrupulous enough to be a match for you in the use of intelligence; but I assure you, Mr Heyst, that in the other way you are no match for me. I have you covered at this very moment. You have been covered ever since you entered this room. Yes – from my pocket.'

During this harangue Heyst looked deliberately over his shoulder, stepped back a pace, and sat down on the end of the camp bedstead. Leaning his elbow on one knee, he laid his cheek in the palm of his hand and seemed to meditate on what he should say next. Mr Jones, planted against the wall, was obviously waiting for some sort of overture. As nothing came, he resolved to speak himself; but he hesitated. For, though he considered that the most difficult step had been taken, he said to himself that every stage of progess required great caution, lest the man, in Ricardo's phraseology, should 'start to prance' – which would be most inconvenient. He fell back on a previous statement:

'And I am a person to be reckoned with.'

The other man went on looking at the floor, as if he were alone in the room. There was a pause.

'You have heard of me, then?' Heyst said at length, looking up.

'I should think so! We have been staying at Schomberg's hotel.'

'Schom –' Heyst choked on the word.

'What's the matter, Mr Heyst?'

'Nothing. Nausea,' Heyst said resignedly. He resumed his former attitude of meditative indifference. 'What is this reckoning you are talking about?' he asked after a time, in the quietest possible tone. 'I don't know you.'

'It's obvious that we belong to the same – social sphere,' began Mr Jones with languid irony. Inwardly he was as watchful as he could be. 'Something has driven you out – the originality of your ideas, perhaps. Or your tastes.'

Mr Jones indulged in one of his ghastly smiles. In repose his features had a curious character of evil, exhausted austerity; but when he smiled, the whole mask took on an unpleasantly infantile expression. A recrudescence of the rolling thunder invaded the room loudly, and passed into silence.

'You are not taking this very well,' observed Mr Jones. This was what he said, but as a matter of fact he thought that the business was shaping quite satisfactorily. The man, he said to himself, had no stomach for a fight. Aloud he continued: 'Come! You can't expect to have it always your own way. You are a man of the world.'

'And you?' Heyst interrupted him unexpectedly. 'How do you define yourself?'

'I, my dear sir? In one way I am – yes, I am the world itself, come to pay you a visit. In another sense I am an outcast – almost an outlaw. If you prefer a less materialistic view, I am a sort of fate – the retribution that waits its time.'

'I wish to goodness you were the commonest sort of ruffian!' said Heyst, raising his equable gaze to Mr Jones. 'One would be able to talk to you straight, then, and hope for some humanity. As it is –'

'I dislike violence and ferocity of every sort as much as you do,' Mr Jones declared, looking very languid as he leaned against the wall, but speaking fairly loud. 'You can ask my Martin if it is not so. This, Mr Heyst, is a soft age. It is also an age without prejudices. I've heard that you are free from them yourself. You mustn't be shocked if I tell you plainly that we are after your money – or I am, if you prefer to make me alone responsible. Pedro, of course, knows no more of it than any other animal would. Ricardo is of the faithful-retainer class – absolutely identified with all my ideas, wishes, and even whims.'

Mr Jones pulled his left hand out of his pocket, got a handkerchief out of another, and began to wipe the perspiration from his forehead, neck, and chin. The excitement from which he suffered made his breathing visible. In his long dressing-gown he had the air of a convalescent invalid who had imprudently overtaxed his strength. Heyst, broad-shouldered, robust, watched the operation from the end of the camp bedstead, very calm, his hands on his knees.

'And by the by,' he asked, 'where is he now, that henchman of yours? Breaking into my desk?'

'That would be crude. Still, crudeness is one of life's conditions.' There was the slightest flavour of banter in the tone of Ricardo's governor. 'Conceivable, but unlikely. Martin is a little crude; but you are not, Mr Heyst. To tell you the truth, I don't know precisely where he is. He has been a little mysterious of late; but he has my confidence. No, don't get up, Mr Heyst!'

The viciousness of his spectral face was indescribable. Heyst, who had moved a little, was surprised by the disclosure.

'It was not my intention,' he said.

'Pray remain seated,' Mr Jones insisted in a languid voice, but with a very determined glitter in his black eye-caverns.

'If you were more observant,' said Heyst with dispassionate contempt, 'you would have known before I had been five minutes in the room that I had no weapon of any sort on me.'

'Possibly; but pray keep your hands still. They are very well where they are. This is too big an affair for me to take any risks.'

'Big? Too big?' Heyst repeated with genuine surprise. 'Good Heavens! Whatever you are looking for, there's very little of it here – very little of anything.'

'You would naturally say so, but that's not what we have heard,' retorted Mr Jones quickly, with a grin so ghastly that it was impossible to think it voluntary.

Heyst's face had grown very gloomy. He knitted his brows.

'What have you heard?' he asked.

'A lot, Mr Heyst – a lot,' affirmed Mr Jones. He was trying to recover his manner of languid superiority. 'We have heard, for instance, of a certain Mr Morrison, once your partner.'

Heyst could not repress a slight movement.

'Aha!' said Mr Jones, with a sort of ghostly glee on his face.

The muffled thunder resembled the echo of a distant canonade below the horizon, and the two men seemed to be listening to it in sullen silence.

'This diabolical calumny will end in actually and literally taking my life from me,' thought Heyst.

Then, suddenly, he laughed. Portentously spectral, Mr Jones frowned at the sound.

'Laugh as much as you please,' he said. 'I, who have been hounded out from society by a lot of highly moral souls, can't see anything funny in that story. But here we are, and you will now have to pay for your fun, Mr Heyst.'

'You have heard a lot of ugly lies,' observed Heyst. 'Take my word for it.'

'You would say so, of course – very natural. As a matter of fact, I haven't heard very much. Strictly speaking, it was Martin. He collects information, and so on. You don't suppose I would talk to that Schomberg animal more than I could help? It was Martin whom he took into his confidence.'

'The stupidity of that creature is so great that it becomes formidable,' Heyst said, as if speaking to himself.

Involuntarily, his mind turned to the girl, wandering in the forest, alone and terrified. Would he ever see her again? At that thought he nearly lost his self-possession. But the idea that if she followed his instructions those men were not likely to find her steadied him a little. They did not know that the island had any inhabitants; and he himself once disposed of, they would be too anxious to get away to waste time hunting for a vanished girl.

All this passed through Heyst's mind in a flash, as men think in moments of danger. He looked speculatively at Mr Jones, who, of course, had never for a moment taken his eyes from his intended victim. And the conviction came to Heyst that this outlaw from the higher spheres was an absolutely hard and pitiless scoundrel.

Mr Jones's voice made him start.

'It would be useless, for instance, to tell me that your Chinaman has run off with your money. A man living alone with a Chinaman on an island takes care to conceal property of that kind so well that the devil himself –'

'Certainly,' Heyst muttered.

Again, with his left hand, Mr Jones mopped his frontal bone, his stalk-like neck, his razor jaws, his fleshless chin. Again his voice faltered and his aspect became still more gruesomely malevolent, as of a wicked and pitiless corpse.

'I see what you mean,' he cried, 'but you mustn't put too much trust in your ingenuity. You don't strike me as a very ingenious person, Mr Heyst. Neither am I. My talents lie another way. But Martin –'

'Who is now engaged in rifling my desk,' interjected Heyst.

'I don't think so. What I was going to say is that Martin is much cleverer than a Chinaman. Do you believe in racial superiority, Mr Heyst? I do, firmly. Martin is great at ferreting out such secrets as yours, for instance.'

'Secrets like mine!' repeated Heyst bitterly. 'Well, I wish him joy of all he can ferret out!'

'That's very kind of you,' remarked Mr Jones. He was beginning to be anxious for Martin's return. Of iron self-possession at the gaming-table, fearless in a sudden affray, he found that this rather special kind of work was telling on his nerves. 'Keep still as you are!' he cried sharply.

'I've told you I am not armed,' said Heyst, folding his arms on his breast.

'I am really inclined to believe that you are not,' admitted Mr Jones seriously. 'Strange!' he mused aloud, the caverns of his eyes turned upon Heyst. Then briskly: 'But my object is to keep you in this room. Don't provoke me, by some unguarded movement, to smash your knee or do something definite of that sort.' He passed his tongue over his lips, which were dry and black, while his forehead glistened with moisture. 'I don't know if it wouldn't be better to do it at once!'

'He who deliberates is lost,' said Heyst with grave mockery.

Mr Jones disregarded the remark. He had the air of communing with himself.

'Physically I am no match for you,' he said slowly, his black gaze fixed upon the man sitting on the end of the bed. 'You could spring –'

'Are you trying to frighten yourself?' asked Heyst abruptly. 'You don't seem to have quite enough pluck for your business. Why don't you do it at once?'

Mr Jones, taking violent offence, snorted like a savage skeleton.

'Strange as it may seem to you, it is because of my origin, my breeding, my traditions, my early associations, and such-like trifles. Not everybody can divest himself of the prejudices of a gentleman as easily as you have done, Mr Heyst. But don't worry about my pluck. If you were to make a clean spring at me, you would receive in mid air, so to speak, something that would make you perfectly harmless by the time you landed. No, don't misapprehend us, Mr Heyst. We are – er – adequate bandits; and we are after the fruit of your labours as a – er – successful swindler. It's the way of the world – gorge and disgorge!'

He leaned the back of his head wearily against the wall. His vitality seemed exhausted. Even his sunken eyelids drooped within the bony sockets. Only his thin, waspish, beautifully pencilled eyebrows, drawn together a little, suggested the will and the power to sting – something vicious, unconquerable, and deadly.

'Fruits! Swindler!' repeated Heyst, without heat, almost without contempt. 'You are giving yourself no end of trouble, you and your faithful henchman, to crack an empty nut. There are no fruits here, as you imagine. There are a few sovereigns, which you may have if you like, and since you have called yourself a bandit –'

'Yaas!' drawled Mr Jones. 'That, rather than a swindler. Open warfare at least!'

'Very good! Only let me tell you that there were never in the world two more deluded bandits – never!'

Heyst uttered these words with such energy that Mr Jones, stiffening up, seemed to become thinner and taller in his metallic blue dressing-gown against the whitewashed wall.

'Fooled by a silly, rascally innkeeper!' Heyst went on. 'Talked over like a pair of children with a promise of sweets!'

'I didn't talk with that disgusting animal,' muttered Mr Jones sullenly; 'but he convinced Martin, who is no fool.'

'I should think he wanted very much to be convinced,' said Heyst, with the courteous intonation so well known in the islands. 'I don't want to disturb your touching trust in your – your follower, but he must be the most credulous brigand in existence. What do you imagine? If the story of my riches were ever so true, do you think Schomberg would have imparted it to you from sheer altruism? Is that the way of the world, Mr Jones?'

For a moment the lower jaw of Ricardo's gentleman dropped; but it came up with a snap of scorn, and he said with spectral intensity:

'The beast is cowardly! He was frightened, and wanted to get rid of us, if you want to know, Mr Heyst. I don't know that the material inducement was so very great, but I was bored, and we decided to accept the bribe. I don't regret it. All my life I have been seeking new impressions, and you have turned out to be something quite out of the common. Martin, of course, looks to the material results. He's simple – and faithful – and wonderfully acute.'

'Ah, yes! He's on the track –' and now Heyst's speech had the character of politely grim raillery – 'but not sufficiently on the track, as yet, to make it quite convenient to shoot me without more ado. Didn't Schomberg tell you precisely where I conceal the fruit of my rapines? Pah! Don't you know he would have told you anything, true or false, from a very clear motive? Revenge! Mad hate – the unclean idiot!'

Mr Jones did not seem very much moved. On his right hand the doorway incessantly flickered with distant lightning, and the continuous rumble of thunder went on irritatingly, like the growl of an inarticulate giant muttering fatuously.

Heyst overcame his immense repugnance to allude to her whose image, cowering in the forest, was constantly before his eyes, with all the pathos and force of its appeal, august, pitiful, and almost holy to him. It was in a hurried, embarrassed manner that he went on:

'If it had not been for that girl whom he persecuted with his insane and odious passion, and who threw herself on my protection, he would never have – but you know well enough!'

'I *don't* know!' burst out Mr Jones with amazing heat. 'That hotel-keeper tried to talk to me once of some girl he had lost, but I told him I didn't want to hear any of his beastly women stories. It had something to do with you, had it?'

Heyst looked on serenely at this outburst, then lost his patience a little.

'What sort of comedy is this? You don't mean to say that you didn't know that I had – that there was a girl living with me here?'

One could see that the eyes of Mr Jones had become fixed in the depths of their black holes by the gleam of white becoming steady there. The whole man seemed frozen still.

'Here! Here!' he screamed out twice. There was no mistaking his astonishment, his shocked incredulity – something like frightened disgust.

Heyst was disgusted also, but in another way. He too was incredulous. He regretted having mentioned the girl; but the thing was done, his repugnance had been overcome in the heat of his argument against the absurd bandit.

'It is possible that you didn't know of that significant fact?' he inquired. 'Of the only effective truth in the welter of silly lies that deceived you so easily?'

'No, I didn't!' Mr Jones shouted. 'But Martin did!' he added in a faint whisper, which Heyst's ears just caught and no more.

'I kept her out of sight as long as I could,' said Heyst. 'Perhaps, with your bringing up, traditions, and so on, you will understand my reason for it.'

'He knew. He knew before!' Mr Jones mourned in a hollow voice. 'He knew of her from the first!'

Backed hard against the wall, he no longer watched Heyst. He had the air of a man who had seen an abyss yawning under his feet.

'If I want to kill him, this is my time,' thought Heyst; but he did not move.

Next moment Mr Jones jerked his head up, glaring with sardonic fury.

'I have a good mind to shoot you, you woman-ridden hermit, you man in the moon, that can't exist without – no, it won't be you that I'll shoot. It's the other woman-lover – the prevaricating, sly, low-class, amorous cuss! And he shaved – shaved under my very nose. I'll shoot him!'

'He's gone mad,' thought Heyst, startled by the spectre's sudden fury.

He felt himself more in danger, nearer death, than ever since he had entered that room. An insane bandit is a deadly combination. He did not, could not know that Mr Jones was quick-minded enough to see already the end of his reign over his excellent secretary's thoughts and feelings; the coming failure of Ricardo's fidelity. A woman had intervened! A woman, a girl, who apparently possessed the power to awaken men's disgusting folly. Her power had been proved in two instances already – the beastly innkeeper, and that man with moustaches, upon whom Mr Jones, his deadly right hand twitching in his pocket, glared more in repulsion than in anger. The very object of the expedition was lost from view in his sudden and overwhelming sense of utter insecurity. And this made Mr Jones feel very savage; but not against the man with the moustaches. Thus, while Heyst was really feeling that his life was not worth two minutes' purchase, he heard himself addressed with no affectation of languid impertinence, but with a burst of feverish determination.

'Here! Let's call a truce!' said Mr Jones.

Heyst's heart was too sick to allow him to smile.

'Have I been making war on you?' he asked wearily. 'How do you expect me to attach any meaning to your words?' he went on. 'You seem to be a morbid, senseless sort of bandit. We don't speak the same language. If I were to tell you why I am here, talking to you, you wouldn't believe me, because you would not understand me. It certainly isn't the love of life, from which I have divorced myself long ago – not sufficiently, perhaps; but if you are thinking of yours, then I repeat to you that it has never been in danger from me. I am unarmed.'

Mr Jones was biting his lower lip, in a deep meditation. It was only towards the last that he looked at Heyst.

'Unarmed, eh?' Then he burst out violently: 'I tell you, a gentleman is no match for the common herd. And yet one must make use of the brutes. Unarmed, eh? And I suppose that creature is of the commonest sort. You could hardly have got her out of a drawing-room. Though they're all alike, for that matter. Unarmed! It's a pity. I am in much greater danger than you are, or were – or I am much mistaken. But I am not – I know my man!'

He lost his air of mental vacancy and broke out into shrill exclamations. To Heyst they seemed madder than anything that had gone before.

'On the track! On the scent!' he cried, forgetting himself to the point of executing a dance of rage in the middle of the floor.

Heyst looked on, fascinated by this skeleton in a gay dressing-gown, jerkily agitated like a grotesque toy on the end of an invisible string. It became quiet suddenly.

'I might have smelt a rat! I always knew that this would be the danger.' He changed suddenly to a confidential tone, fixing his sepulchral stare on Heyst. 'And yet here I am, taken in by the fellow, like the veriest fool. I've been always on the watch for some beastly influence, but here I am, fairly caught. He shaved himself right in front of me – and I never guessed!'

The shrill laugh, following on the low tone of secrecy, sounded so convincingly insane that Heyst got up as if moved by a spring. Mr Jones stepped back two paces, but displayed no uneasiness.

'It's as clear as daylight!' he uttered mournfully, and fell silent.

Behind him the doorway flickered lividly, and the sound as of a naval action somewhere away on the horizon filled the breathless pause. Mr Jones inclined his head on his shoulder. His mood had completely changed.

'What do you say, unarmed man? Shall we go and see what is detaining my trusted Martin so long? He asked me to keep you engaged in friendly conversation till he made a further examination of that track. Ha, ha, ha!'

'He is no doubt ransacking my house,' said Heyst.

He was so bewildered. It seemed to him that all this was an incomprehensible dream, or perhaps an elaborate other-world joke, contrived by that spectre in a gorgeous dressing-gown.

Mr Jones looked at him with a horrible, cadaverous smile of inscrutable mockery, and pointed to the door. Heyst passed through it first. His feelings had become so blunted that he did not care how soon he was shot in the back.

'How oppressive the air is!' the voice of Mr Jones said at his elbow. 'This stupid storm gets on my nerves. I would welcome some rain, though it would be unpleasant to get wet. On the other hand, this exasperating thunder has the advantage of covering the sound of our approach. The lightning's not so convenient. Ah, your house is fully illuminated! My clever Martin is punishing your stock of candles. He belongs to the unceremonious classes, which are also unlovely, untrustworthy, and so on.'

'I left the candles burning,' said Heyst, 'to save him trouble.'

'You really believed he would go to your house?' asked Mr Jones with genuine interest.

'I had that notion, strongly. I do believe he is there now.'

'And you don't mind?'

'No!'

'You don't!' Mr Jones stopped to wonder. 'You are an extraordinary man,' he said suspiciously, and moved on, touching elbows with Heyst.

In the latter's breast dwelt a deep silence, the complete silence of unused faculties. At this moment, by simply shouldering Mr Jones, he could have thrown him down and put himself, by a couple of leaps, beyond the certain aim of the revolver; but he did not even think of that. His very will seemed dead of weariness. He moved automatically, his head low, like a prisoner captured by the evil power of a masquerading skeleton out of a grave. Mr Jones took charge of the direction. They fetched a wide sweep. The echoes of distant thunder seemed to dog their footsteps.

'By the by,' said Mr Jones, as if unable to restrain his curiosity. 'aren't you anxious about that – ouch! – that fascinating creature to whom you owe whatever pleasure you can find in our visit?'

'I have placed her in safety,' said Heyst. 'I – I took good care of that.'

Mr Jones laid a hand on his arm.

'You have? Look! Is that what you mean?'

Heyst raised his head. In the flicker of lightning the desolation of the cleared ground on his left leaped out and sank into the night, together with the elusive forms of things distant, pale, unearthly. But in the brilliant square of the door he saw the girl – the woman he had longed to see once more – as if enthroned, with her hands on the arms of the chair. She was in black; her face was white, her head dreamily inclined on her breast. He saw her only as low as her knees. He saw her – there, in the room, alive with a sombre reality. It was no mocking vision. She was not in the forest – but there! She sat there in the chair, seemingly without strength, yet without fear, tenderly stooping.

'Can you understand their power?' whispered the hot breath of Mr Jones into his ear. 'Can there be a more disgusting spectacle? It's enough to make the earth detestable. She seems to have found her affinity. Move on closer. If I have to shoot you in the end, then perhaps you will die cured.'

Heyst obeyed the pushing pressure of a revolver barrel between his shoulders. He felt it distinctly, but he did not feel the ground under his feet. They found the steps, without his being aware that he was ascending them – slowly, one by one. Doubt entered into him – a doubt of a new kind, formless, hideous. It seemed to spread itself all over him, enter his limbs, and lodge in his entrails. He stopped suddenly, with a thought that he who experienced such a feeling had no business to live – or perhaps was no longer living.

Everything – the bungalow, the forest, the open ground – trembled incessantly; the earth, the sky itself shivered all the time, and the only thing immovable in the shuddering universe was the interior of the lighted room and the woman in black sitting in the light of the eight candle-flames. They flung around her an intolerable brilliance which hurt his eyes, seemed to sear his very brain with the radiation of infernal heat. It was some time before his scorched eyes made out Ricardo seated on the floor at some little distance, his back to the doorway, but only partly so; one side of his upturned face showing the absorbed, all-forgetful rapture of his contemplation.

The grip of Mr Jones's hard claw drew Heyst back a little. In the roll of thunder, swelling and subsiding, he whispered in his ear a sarcastic: 'Of course!'

A great shame descended upon Heyst – the shame of guilt, absurd and maddening. Mr Jones drew him still farther back into the darkness of the veranda.

'This is serious,' he went on, distilling his ghostly venom into Heyst's very ear. 'I had to shut my eyes many times to his little flings; but this is serious. He has found his soul-mate. Mud souls, obscene and cunning! Mud bodies, too – the mud of the gutter! I tell you, we are no match for the vile populace. I, even I, have been nearly caught. He asked me to detain you till he gave me the signal. It won't be you that I'll have to shoot, but him. I wouldn't trust him near me for five minutes after this!'

He shook Heyst's arm a little.

'If you had not happened to mention the creature, we should both have been dead before morning. He would have stabbed you as you came down the steps after leaving me, and then he would have walked up to me and planted the same knife between my ribs. He has no prejudices. The viler the origin, the greater the freedom of these simple souls!'

He drew a cautious, hissing breath and added in an agitated murmur: 'I can see right into his mind; I have been nearly caught napping by his cunning.'

He stretched his neck to peer into the room from the side. Heyst, too, made a step forward, under the slight impulse of that slender hand clasping his hand with a thin, bony grasp.

'Behold!' the skeleton of the crazy bandit jabbered thinly into his ear in spectral fellowship. 'Behold the simple Acis kissing the sandals of the nymph, on the way to her lips, all forgetful, while the menacing life of Polyphemus already sounds close at hand – if he could only hear it! Stoop a little.'

Chapter XII

On returning to the Heyst bungalow, rapid as if on wings, Ricardo found Lena waiting for him. She was dressed in black; and at once his uplifting exultation was replaced by an awed and quivering patience before her white face, before the immobility of her restful pose, the more amazing to him who had encountered the strength of her limbs and the indomitable spirit in her body. She had come out after Heyst's departure, and had sat down under the portrait to wait for the return of the man of violence and death. While lifting the curtain, she felt the anguish of her disobedience to her lover, which was soothed by a feeling she had known before – a gentle flood of penetrating sweetness. She was not automatically obeying a momentary suggestion; she was under influences more deliberate, more vague, and of greater potency. She had been prompted, not by her will, but by a force that was outside of her and more worthy. She reckoned upon nothing definite; she had calculated nothing. She saw only her purpose of capturing death – savage, sudden, irresponsible death, prowling round the man who possessed her; death embodied in the knife ready to strike into his heart. No doubt it had been a sin to throw herself into his arms. With that inspiration that descends at times from above for the good or evil of our common mediocrity, she had a sense of having been for him only a violent and sincere choice of curiosity and pity – a thing that passes. She did not know him. If he were to go away from her and disappear, she would utter no reproach, she would not resent it; for she would hold in herself the impress of something most rare and precious – his embraces made her own by her courage in saving his life.

All she thought of – the essence of her tremors, her flushes of heat, and her shudders of cold – was the question of how to get hold of that knife, the mark and sign of stalking death. A tremor of impatience to clutch the frightful thing, glimpsed once and unforgettable, agitated her hands.

The instinctive flinging forward of these hands stopped Ricardo dead short between the door and her chair, with the ready obedience of a conquered man who can bide his time. Her success disconcerted her. She listened to the man's impassioned transports of terrible eulogy and even more awful declarations of love. She was even able to meet his eyes, oblique, apt to glide away, throwing feral gleams of desire.

'No!' he was saying, after a fiery outpouring of words in which the most ferocious phrases of love were mingled with wooing accents of entreaty. 'I will have no more of it! Don't you mistrust me. I am sober in my talk. Feel how quietly my heart beats. Ten times today when you, you, you, swam in my eye, I thought it would burst one of my ribs or leap out of my throat. It has knocked itself dead tired, waiting for this evening, for this very minute. And now it can do no more. Feel how quiet it is!'

He made a step forward, but she raised her clear voice commandingly:

'No nearer!'

He stopped with a smile of imbecile worship on his lips, and with the delighted obedience of a man who could at any moment seize her in his hands and dash her to the ground.

'Ah! If I had taken you by the throat this morning and had my way with you, I should never have known what you are. And now I do. You are a wonder! And so am I, in my way. I have nerve, and I have brains, too. We should have been lost many times but for me. I plan – I plot for my gentleman. Gentleman – pah! I am sick of him. And you are sick of yours, eh? You, you!'

He shook all over; he cooed at her a string of endearing names, obscene and tender, and then asked abruptly:

'Why don't you speak to me?'

'It's my part to listen,' she said, giving him an inscrutable smile, with a flush in her cheek and her lips cold as ice.

'But you will answer me?'

'Yes,' she said, her eyes dilated as if with sudden interest.

'Where's that plunder? Do you know?'

'No! Not yet.'

'But there is plunder stowed somewhere that's worth having?'

'Yes, I think so. But who knows?' she added after a pause.

'And who cares?' he retorted recklessly. 'I've had enough of this crawling on my belly. It's you who are my treasure. It's I who found you out where a gentleman had buried you to rot for his accursed pleasure!'

He looked behind him and all around for a seat, then turned to her his troubled eyes and dim smile.

'I am dog-tired,' he said, and sat down on the floor. 'I went tired this morning, since I came in here and started talking to you – as tired as if I had been pouring my life-blood here on these planks for you to dabble your white feet in.'

Unmoved, she nodded at him thoughtfully. Woman-like, all her faculties remained concentrated on her heart's desire – on the knife – while the man went on babbling insanely at her feet, ingratiating and savage, almost crazy with elation. But he, too, was holding on to his purpose.

'For you! For you I will throw away money, lives – all the lives but mine! What you want is a man, a master that will let you put the heel of your shoe on his neck; not that skulker, who will get tired of you in a year – and you of him. And then what? You are not the one to sit still; neither am I. I live for myself, and you shall live for yourself, too – not for a Swedish baron. They make a convenience of people like you and me. A gentleman is better than an employer, but an equal partnership against all the 'yporcrits is the thing for you and me. We'll go on wandering the world over, you and I, both free and both true. You are no cage bird. We'll rove together, for we are of them that have no homes. We are born rovers!'

She listened to him with the utmost attention, as if any unexpected word might give her some sort of opening to get that dagger, that awful knife – to disarm murder itself, pleading for her love at her feet. Again she nodded at him thoughtfully, rousing a gleam in his yellow eyes, yearning devotedly upon her face. When he hitched himself a little closer, her soul had no movement of recoil. This had to be. Anything had to be which would bring the knife within her reach. He talked more confidentially now.

'We have met, and their time has come,' he began, looking up into her eyes. 'The partnership between me and my gentleman has to be ripped up. There's no room for him where we two are. Why, he would shoot me like a dog! Don't you worry. This will settle it not later than tonight!'

He tapped his folded leg below the knee, and was surprised, flattered, by the lighting up of her face, which stooped towards him eagerly and remained expectant, the lips girlishly parted, red in the pale face, and quivering in the quickened drawing of her breath.

'You marvel, you miracle, you man's luck and joy – one in a million! No, the only one. You have found your man in me,' he whispered tremulously. 'Listen! They are having their last talk together; for I'll do for your gentleman, too, by midnight.'

Without the slightest tremor she murmured, as soon as the tightening of her breast had eased off and the words would come:

'I wouldn't be in too much of a hurry – with him.'

The pause, the tone, had all the value of meditated advice.

'Good, thrifty girl!' he laughed low, with a strange feline gaiety, expressed by the undulating movement of his shoulders and the sparkling snap of his oblique eyes. 'You are still thinking about the chance of that swag. You'll make a good partner, that you will! And, I say, what a decoy you will make! Jeeminy!'

He was carried away for a moment, but his face darkened swiftly.

'No! No reprieve. What do you think a fellow is – a scarecrow? All hat and clothes and no feeling, no inside, no brain to make fancies for himself! No!' he went on violently. 'Never in his life will he go again into that room of yours – never any more!'

A silence fell. He was gloomy with the torment of his jealousy, and did not even look at her. She sat up and slowly, gradually, bent lower and lower over him, as if ready to fall into his arms. He looked up at last, and checked this droop unwittingly.

'Say! You, who are up to fighting a man with your bare hands, could you – eh? – could you manage to stick one with a thing like that knife of mine?'

She opened her eyes very wide and gave him a wild smile.

'How can I tell?' she whispered enchantingly. 'Will you let me have a look at it?'

Without taking his eyes from her face, he pulled the knife out of its sheath – a short, broad, cruel, double-edged blade with a bone handle – and only then looked down at it.

'A good friend,' he said simply. 'Take it in your hand and feel the balance,' he suggested.

At the moment when she bent forward to receive it from him, there was a flash of fire in her mysterious eyes – a red gleam in the white mist which wrapped the promptings and longings of her soul. She had done it! The very sting of death was in her hands; the venom of the viper in her paradise, extracted, safe in her possession – and the viper's head all but lying under her heel. Ricardo, stretched on the mats of the floor, crept closer and closer to the chair in which she sat.

All her thoughts were busy planning how to keep possession of that weapon which had seemed to have drawn into itself every danger and menace on the death-ridden earth. She said with a low laugh, the exultation in which he failed to recognize:

'I didn't think that you would ever trust me with that thing!'

'Why not?'

'For fear I should suddenly strike you with it.'

'What for? For this morning's work? Oh, no! There's no spite in you for that. You forgave me. You saved me. You got the better of me, too. And anyhow, what good would it be?'

'No, no good,' she admitted.

In her heart she felt that she would not know how to do it; that if it came to a struggle, she would have to drop the dagger and fight with her hands.

'Listen. When we are going about the world together, you shall always call me husband. Do you hear?'

'Yes,' she said bracing herself for the contest, in whatever shape it was coming.

The knife was lying in her lap. She let it slip into the fold of her dress, and laid her forearms with clasped fingers over her knees, which she pressed desperately together. The dreaded thing was out of sight at last. She felt a dampness break out all over her.

'I am not going to hide you, like that good-for-nothing, finicky, sneery gentleman. You shall be my pride and my chum. Isn't that better than rotting on an island for the pleasure of a gentleman, till he gives you the chuck?'

'I'll be anything you like,' she said.

In his intoxication he crept closer with every word she uttered, with every movement she made.

'Give your foot,' he begged in a timid murmur, and in the full consciousness of his power.

Anything! Anything to keep murder quiet and disarmed till strength had returned to her limbs and she could make up her mind what to do. Her fortitude had been shaken by the very facility of success that had come to her. She advanced her foot forward a little from under the hem of her skirt; and he threw himself on it greedily. She was not even aware of him. She had thought of the forest, to which she had been told to run. Yes, the forest – that was the place for her to carry off the terrible spoil, the sting of vanquished death. Ricardo, clasping her ankle, pressed his lips time after time to the instep, muttering gasping words that were like sobs, making little noises that resembled the sounds of grief and distress. Unheard by them both, the thunder growled distantly with angry modulations of its tremendous voice, while the world outside shuddered incessantly around the dead stillness of the room where the framed profile of Heyst's father looked severely into space.

Suddenly Ricardo felt himself spurned by the foot he had been cherishing – spurned with a push of such violence into the very hollow of his throat that it swung him back instantly into an upright position on his knees. He read his danger in the stony eyes of the girl; and in the very act of leaping to his feet he heard sharply, detached on the comminatory voice of the storm, the brief report of a shot which half stunned him, in the manner of a blow. He turned his burning head, and saw Heyst towering in the doorway. The thought that the beggar had started to prance darted through his mind. For a fraction of a second his distracted eyes sought for his weapon all over the floor. He couldn't see it.

'Stick him, you!' he called hoarsely to the girl, and dashed headlong for the door of the compound.

While he thus obeyed the instinct of self-preservation, his reason was telling him that he could not possibly reach it alive. It flew open, however, with a crash, before his launched weight, and instantly he swung it to behind him. There, his shoulder leaning against it, his hands clinging to the handle, dazed and alone in the night full of shudders and muttered menaces, he tried to pull himself together. He asked himself if he had been shot at more than once. His shoulder was wet with the blood trickling from his head. Feeling above his ear, he ascertained that it was only a graze, but the shock of the surprise had unmanned him for the moment.

What the deuce was the governor about, to let the beggar break loose like this? Or – was the governor dead, perhaps?

The silence within the room awed him. Of going back there could be no question.

'But she knows how to take care of herself,' he muttered.

She had his knife. It was she now who was deadly, while he was disarmed, no good for the moment. He stole away from the door, staggering, the warm trickle running down his neck, to find out what had become of the governor and to provide himself with a firearm from the armoury in the trunks.

Chapter XIII

Mr Jones, after firing his shot over Heyst's shoulder, had thought it proper to dodge away. Like the spectre he was, he noiselessly vanished from the veranda. Heyst stumbled into the room and looked around. All the objects in there – the books, the gleam of old silver familiar to him from boyhood, the very portrait on the wall – seemed shadowy, unsubstantial, the dumb accomplices of an amazing dream-plot ending in an illusory effect of awakening and the impossibility of ever closing his eyes again. With dread he forced himself to look at the girl. Still in the chair, she was leaning forward far over her knees, and had hidden her face in her hands. Heyst remembered Wang suddenly. How clear all this was – and how extremely amusing! Very.

She sat up a little, then leaned back, and taking her hands from her face, pressed both of them to her breast, as if moved to the heart by seeing him there looking at her with a black, horror-struck curiosity. He would have pitied her, if the triumphant expression of her face had not given him a shock which destroyed the balance of his feelings. She spoke with an accent of wild joy:

'I knew you would come back in time! You are safe now. I have done it! I would never, never have let him –' Her voice died out, while her eyes shone at him as when the sun breaks through a mist. 'Never get it back. Oh, my beloved!'

He bowed his head gravely, and said in his polite, Heystian tone:

'No doubt you acted from instinct. Women have been provided with their own weapon. I was a disarmed man, I have been a disarmed man all my life as I see it now. You may glory in your resourcefulness and your profound knowledge of yourself; but I may say that the other attitude, suggestive of shame, had its charm. For you are full of charm!'

The exultation vanished from her face.

'You mustn't make fun of me now. I know no shame. I was thanking God with all my sinful heart for having been able to do it – for giving you to me in that way – oh, my beloved – all my own at last!'

He stared as if mad. Timidly she tried to excuse herself for disobeying his directions for her safety. Every modulation of her enchanting voice cut deep into his very breast, so that he could hardly understand the words for the sheer pain of it. He turned his back on her; but a sudden drop, an extraordinary faltering of her tone, made him spin around. On her white neck her pale head dropped as in a cruel drought a withered flower droops on its stalk. He caught his breath, looked at her closely, and seemed to read some awful intelligence in her eyes. At the moment when her eyelids fell as if smitten from above by an invisible power, he snatched her up bodily out of the chair, and disregarding an unexpected metallic clatter on the floor, carried her off into the other room. The limpness of her body frightened him. Laying her down on the bed, he ran out again, seized a four-branched candlestick on the table, and ran back, tearing down with a furious jerk the curtain that swung stupidly in his way; but after putting the candlestick on the table by the bed, he remained absolutely idle.

There did not seem anything more for him to do. Holding his chin in his hand, he looked down intently at her still face.

'Has she been stabbed with this thing?' asked Davidson, whom suddenly he saw standing by his side and holding up Ricardo's dagger to his sight. Heyst uttered no word of recognition or surprise. He gave Davidson only a dumb look of unutterable awe; then, as if possessed with a sudden fury, started tearing open the front of the girl's dress. She remained insensible under his hands, and Heyst let out a groan which made Davidson shudder inwardly – the heavy plaint of a man who falls clubbed in the dark.

They stood side by side, looking mournfully at the little black hole made by Mr Jones's bullet under the swelling breast of a dazzling and as it were sacred whiteness. It rose and fell slightly – so slightly that only the eyes of the lover could detect the faint stir of life. Heyst, calm and utterly unlike himself in the face, moving about noiselessly, prepared a wet cloth, and laid it on the insignificant wound, round which there was hardly a trace of blood to mar the charm, the fascination, of that mortal flesh.

Her eyelids fluttered. She looked drowsily about, serene, as if fatigued only by the exertions of her tremendous victory, capturing the very sting of death in the service of love. But her eyes became very wide awake when they caught sight of Ricardo's dagger, the spoil of vanquished death, which Davidson was still holding unconsciously.

'Give it to me!' she said. 'It's mine.'

Davidson put the symbol of her victory into her feeble hands extended to him with the innocent gesture of a child reaching eagerly for a toy.

'For you,' she gasped, turning her eyes to Heyst. 'Kill nobody.'

'No,' said Heyst, taking the dagger and laying it gently on her breast, while her hands fell powerless by her side.

The faint smile on her deep-cut lips waned, and her head sank deep into the pillow, taking on the majestic pallor and immobility of marble. But over the muscles, which seemed set in their transfigured beauty for ever, passed a slight and awful tremor. With an amazing strength she asked loudly:

'What's the matter with me?'

'You have been shot, dear Lena,' Heyst said in a steady voice, while Davidson, at the question, turned away and leaned his forehead against the post of the foot of the bed.

'Shot? I did think too, that something had struck me.'

Over Samburan the thunder had ceased to growl at last, and the world of material forms shuddered no more under the emerging stars. The spirit of the girl which was passing away from under them clung to her triumph convinced of the reality of her victory over death.

'No more,' she muttered. 'There will be no more! Oh, my beloved,' she cried weakly, 'I've saved you! Why don't you take me into your arms and carry me out of this lonely place?'

Heyst bent low over her, cursing his fastidious soul, which even at that moment kept the true cry of love from his lips in its infernal mistrust of all life. He dared not touch her, and she had no longer the strength to throw her arms about his neck.

'Who else could have done this for you?' she whispered gloriously.

'No one in the world,' he answered her in a murmur of unconcealed despair.

She tried to raise herself, but all she could do was to lift her head a little from the pillow. With a terrified and gentle movement, Heyst hastened to slip his arm under her neck. She felt relieved at once of an intolerable weight, and was content to surrender to him the infinite weariness of her tremendous achievement. Exulting, she saw herself extended on the bed, in a black dress, and profoundly at peace; while, stooping over her with a kindly, playful smile, he was ready to lift her up in his firm arms and take her into the sanctuary of his innermost heart – for ever! The flush of rapture flooding her whole being broke out in a smile of innocent, girlish happiness; and with that divine radiance on her lips she breathed her last, triumphant, seeking for his glance in the shades of death.

CHAPTER XIV

'YES, EXCELLENCY,' said Davidson in his placid voice; 'there are more dead in this affair – more white people, I mean – than have been killed in many of the battles in the last Achin war.'

Davidson was talking with an Excellency, because what was alluded to in conversation as 'the mystery of Samburan' had caused such a sensation in the Archipelago that even those in the highest spheres were anxious to hear something at first hand. Davidson had been summoned to an audience. It was a high official on his tour.

'You knew the late Baron Heyst well?'

'The truth is that nobody out here can boast of having known him well,' said Davidson. 'He was a queer chap. I doubt if he himself knew how queer he was. But everybody was aware that I was keeping my eye on him in a friendly way. And that's how I got the warning which made me turn round in my tracks in the middle of my trip and steam back to Samburan, where, I am grieved to say, I arrived too late.'

Without enlarging very much, Davidson explained to the attentive Excellency how a woman, the wife of a certain hotel-keeper named Schomberg, had overheard two card-sharping rascals making inquiries from her husband as to the exact position of the island. She caught only a few words referring to the neighbouring volcano, but there were enough to arouse her suspicions – 'which', went on Davidson, 'she imparted to me, your Excellency. They were only too well founded!'

'That was very clever of her,' remarked the great man.

'She's much cleverer than people have any conception of,' said Davidson.

But he refrained from disclosing to the Excellency the real cause which had sharpened Mrs Schomberg's wits. The poor woman was in mortal terror of the girl being brought back within reach of her infatuated Wilhelm. Davidson only said that her agitation had impressed him; but he confessed that while going back, he began to have his doubts as to there being anything in it.

'I steamed into one of those silly thunderstorms that hang about the volcano, and had some trouble in making the island,' narrated Davidson. 'I had to grope my way dead slow into Diamond Bay. I don't suppose that anybody, even if looking out for me, could have heard me let go the anchor.'

He admitted that he ought to have gone ashore at once; but everything was perfectly dark and absolutely quiet. He felt ashamed of his impulsiveness. What a fool he would have looked, waking up a man in the middle of the night just to ask him if he was all right! And then, the girl being there, he feared that Heyst would look upon his visit as an unwarrantable intrusion.

The first intimation he had of there being anything wrong was a big white boat, adrift, with the dead body of a very hairy man inside, bumping against the bows of his steamer. Then indeed he lost no time in going ashore – alone, of course, from motives of delicacy.

'I arrived in time to see that poor girl die, as I have told your Excellency,' pursued Davidson. 'I won't tell you what a time I had with him afterwards. He talked to me. His father seems to have been a crank, and to have upset his head when he was young. He was a queer chap. Practically the last words he said to me, as we came out on the veranda, were:

' "Ah, Davidson, woe to the man whose heart has not learned while young to hope, to love – and to put its trust in life!"

'As we stood there, just before I left him, for he said he wanted to be alone with his dead for a time, we heard a snarly sort of voice near the bushes by the shore calling out:

' "Is that you, governor?"

' "Yes, it's me."

' "Jeeminy! I thought the beggar had done for you. He has started prancing and nearly had me. I have been dodging around, looking for you ever since."

' "Well, here I am," suddenly screamed the other voice, and then a shot rang out.

' "This time he has not missed him," Heyst said to me bitterly, and went back into the house.

'I returned on board as he had insisted I should do. I didn't want to intrude on his grief. Later, about five in the morning, some of my calashes came running to me, yelling that there was a fire ashore. I landed at once, of course. The principal bungalow was blazing. The heat drove us back. The other two houses caught one after another like kindling-wood. There was no going beyond the shore end of the jetty till the afternoon.'

Davidson sighed placidly.

'I suppose you are certain that Baron Heyst is dead?'

'He is – ashes, your Excellency,' said Davidson, wheezing a little; 'he and the girl together. I suppose he couldn't stand his thoughts before her dead body – and fire purifies everything. That Chinaman of whom I told your Excellency helped me to investigate next day, when the embers got cooled a little. We found enough to be sure. He's not a bad Chinaman. He told me that he had followed Heyst and the girl through the forest from pity, and partly out of curiosity. He watched the house till he saw Heyst go out, after dinner, and Ricardo come back alone. While he was dodging there, it occurred to him that he had better cast the boat adrift, for fear those scoundrels should come round by water and bombard the village from the sea with their revolvers and Winchesters. He judged that they were devils enough for anything. So he walked down the wharf quietly; and as he got into the boat, to cast her off, that hairy man who, it seems, was dozing in her, jumped up growling, and Wang shot him dead. Then he shoved the boat off as far as he could and went away.

There was a pause. Presently Davidson went on, in his tranquil manner:

'Let Heaven look after what has been purified. The wind and rain will take care of the ashes. The carcass of that follower, secretary, or whatever the unclean ruffian called himself, I left where it lay, to swell and rot in the sun. His principal had shot him neatly through the heart. Then, apparently, this Jones went down to the wharf to look for the boat and for the hairy man. I suppose he tumbled into the water by accident – or perhaps not by accident. The boat and the man were gone, and the scoundrel saw himself alone, his game clearly up, and fairly trapped. Who knows? The water's very clear there, and I could see him huddled up on the bottom between two piles, like a heap of bones in a blue silk bag, with only the head and feet sticking out. Wang was very pleased when he discovered him. That made everything safe, he said, and he went at once over the hill to fetch his Alfuro woman back to the hut.'

Davidson took out his handkerchief to wipe the perspiration off his forehead.

'And then, your Excellency, I went away. There was nothing to be done there.'

'Clearly,' assented the Excellency.

Davidson, thoughtful, seemed to weigh the matter in his mind, and then murmured with placid sadness:

'Nothing!'

October 1912–May 1914.